I0766998

Red Jade Omnibus
Books 1-4

Journeys in Kallisor
The Shattered Shards
The Assembly
The Forgotten Tribe

Stephen J. Wolf

To Mom, for always being on my side.
To Jared, for his music.
To Kevin, the Randler to my Dariak.
To Kim, without whom there could be no Kitalla.

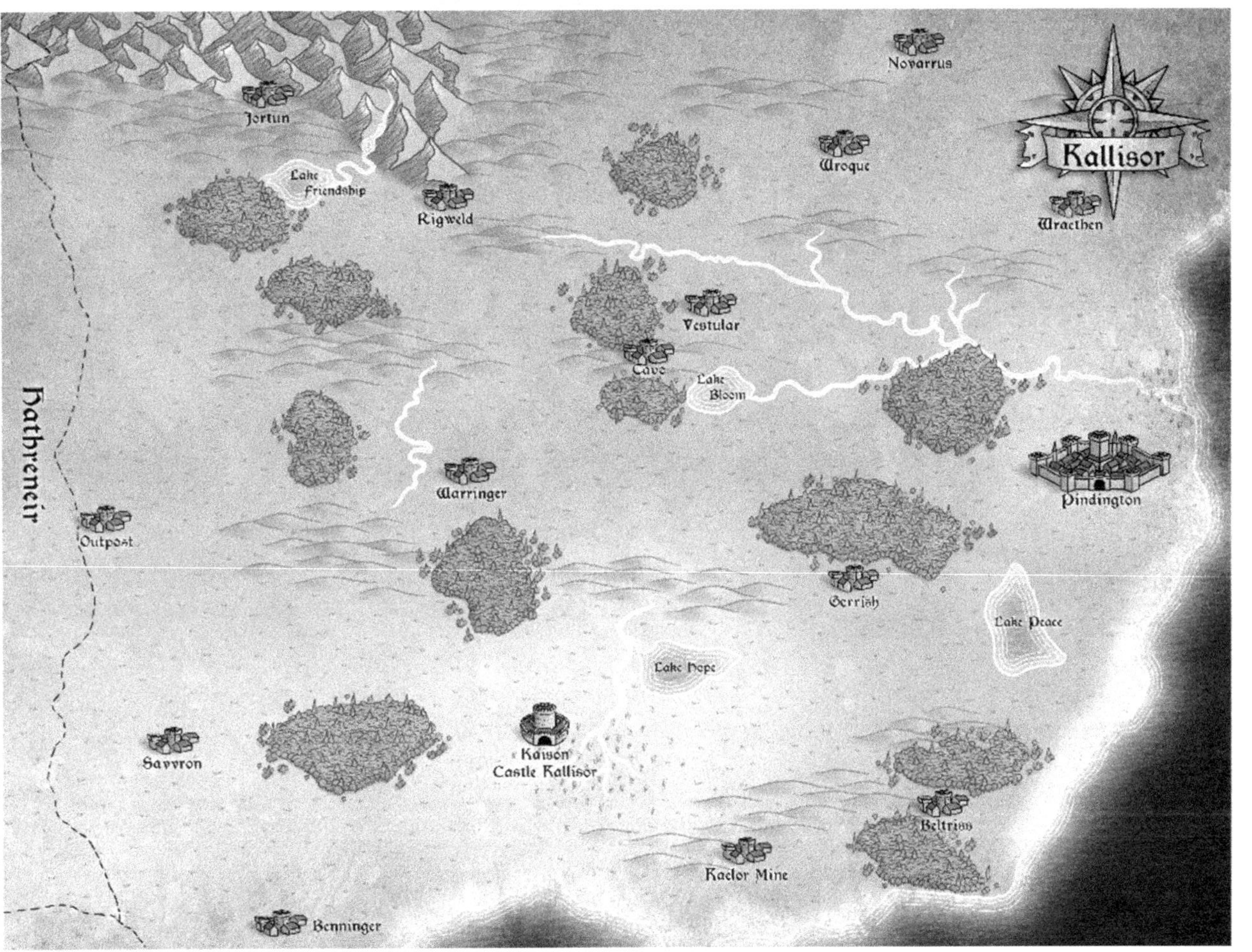

Kallisor
Hathreneir
Jortun
Novarrus
Wroque
Wracthen
Lake Friendship
Rigweld
Vestular
Cave
Lake Bloom
Pindington
Warringer
Outpost
Gerrish
Lake Peace
Lake Hope
Savvron
Kaison Castle Kallisor
Beltrion
Kaelor Mine
Benninger

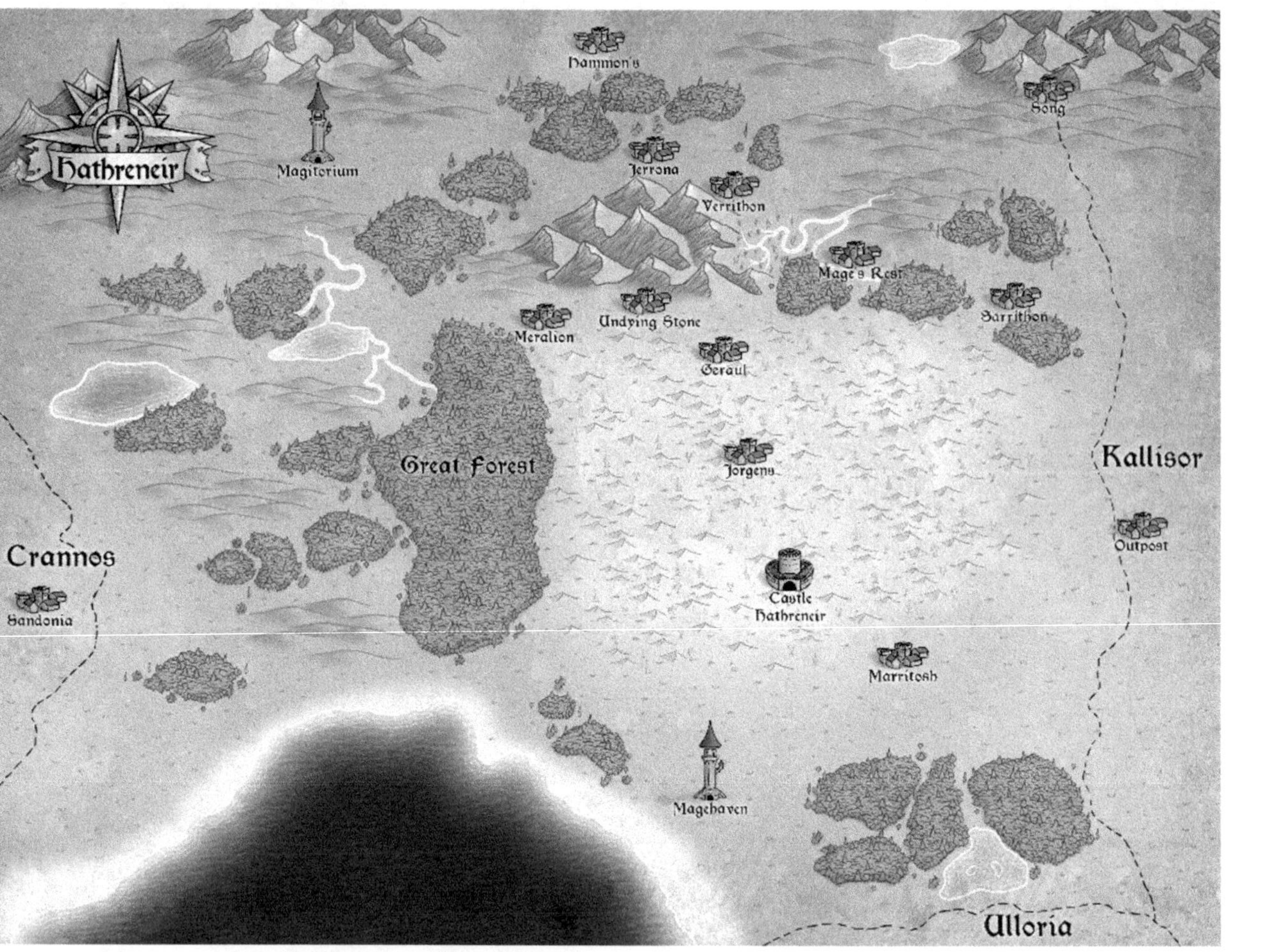

Hathreneir
Magiterium
Hammon's
Song
Jerrona
Verrithon
Mage's Rest
Sarrithon
Undying Stone
Meralion
Geraul
Great Forest
Jorgeny
Kallisor
Outpost
Crannos
Sandonia
Castle Hathreneir
Marritosh
Magehaven
Ulloria

TABLE OF CONTENTS

Foreword

THE STORY OF the Red Jade started in 2013 while I was on the elliptical machine with my personal trainer cheering me on from the side. We discussed magical artifacts that were imbued with unique powers, and from there, the concept of the individual jades came to be.

While writing the initial drafts, my trainer read the chapters and shared with me music he was composing. We developed a symbiotic creative relationship at that point. I wrote chapters inspired by his music and he crafted music inspired by my chapters. I listened to the playlist on repeat as the saga progressed, ever keeping the inspiration flowing.

My husband supported my writing endeavors, even before we were married. He pooled funds from friends and family so I could bring my work through CreateSpace's editing process. Journeys in Kallisor underwent three major edits, bringing the story to its current state.

I wanted a particular style of cover art for the book, but CreateSpace was unable to produce it, so I sought an artist of my own. Fyodor Ananiev took my sketches and brought them to life for all four books in the main series, which are included in this omnibus. He also designed the Red Jade symbol that unites the series.

Journeys in Kallisor was released in 2015 near the end of the first quarter of classes. The Shattered Shards, The Assembly, and The Forgotten Tribe were already written and needed editing. I found Rochelle Deans, who did an amazing job of diving in to the motivations of the characters and helping me improve each book. I released each of the other books throughout the school year, one per quarter. And so, during my fifteenth year of teaching, I shared the main saga with the world.

The story of the Red Jade didn't stop there. Fans wanted to know more about Delminor. So for NaNoWriMo 2018, I crafted Delminor's tale as a prequel to the series. Delminor's Trials released in 2019. As it is not part of the main series, it is not included in this omnibus.

Beyond that, I received requests for a story about Dariak's childhood. What really motivated him to partake his journey? Was it really just to end the war? I wanted to share his teenage life and the events that shaped him, so I wrote Dariak's Shadow. As it is also a prequel to the main series, it is not included in this omnibus.

If you would like to read the entire Red Jade collection in chronological order, start with Delminor's Trials, continue to Dariak's Shadow, and finish with this omnibus.

While working on the prequels, I needed to find a new cover artist. Giovanni Panarello stepped up and created amazing scenes for the two new books. He also drew full-body character sketches, which blew me away. I asked him to sketch all the main characters in the series and he did an amazing job. I gathered all the artwork of the Red Jade series and put together an art collection book just to showcase the creativity.

All six books of the Red Jade series have been recorded and are available on Audible. Dylan White brought each character to life in a way I couldn't imagine possible.

I have also always wanted to create a video game. I love the original Dragon Quest and Final Fantasy games and they have been an inspiration to me. After learning to code in JavaScript, I started working on a video game in the Red Jade world. The story follows Krazzick, a Hathren mage, who doubts the motivations of his brother, Malris, and seeks to stop his actions. The story takes place during the time of Dariak's journey in Kallisor.

To organize all the information of the Red Jade world, I created a website at RedJade.com. There you can find excerpts from all the stories, animated covers, character sketches, and maps. You can also discover my other works, including Garinor's Adventure and Of Ages Past, to name but two.

For now, kick back and indulge yourself in this saga, following Dariak's journey as he finds new companions, faces numerous challenges, battles fearsome beasts, and quests to unite the pieces of the Red Jade.

Journeys in Kallisor

War of the Colossus

"TELL ME AGAIN, Gran-mama!"

Meriad smiled down at the child and rustled his hair. "Very well. But I must say that by now, you could tell it better than I."

"Nuh-uh," the eleven-year-old boy insisted as he pulled the blanket up to his chin and hunkered down into his pillow.

"I'm ready." He beamed.

Meriad doused the nearby lantern, allowing the full glow of the moonlight to illuminate the room. She watched her smiling grandson's face as she gathered the threads of the story, ready to embark upon the tale. It was a familiar tale, told to many children, for it entertained them and held an important lesson. But she thought perhaps after this telling, she would finally reveal the events that happened after. A shadow weighed heavily on her heart, for it meant the truth would at last be revealed. Nonetheless, it was her penance, and for the good of this child and all the land, she had to follow through.

It would take her a while to tell the whole of it, but she cherished these moments with him. He was all the family she had left, and she was determined to fill their time together as completely as possible. Meriad knew guards were posted outside the room, listening to their conversation in full, ensuring she didn't stray from her task. However, she wouldn't repeat the mistakes of her past—they had cost her everything—so they need not have bothered. The boy had no idea that his grandmother was a barely-tolerated guest or that her visits were purposely scripted. Meriad reminded herself that none of that mattered now.

With a weighted sigh, she pushed her darkening thoughts aside and focused on Perrios, who was eagerly awaiting the tale. "Many years ago," she began, "before you were even born, there was a war between two big countries."

"Our land of Hathreneir and next door's Kallisor." He scowled at the second name.

"Now, now," Meriad admonished gently with a raised eyebrow. "First, we are friendly with Kallisor. Second, I thought you wanted me to tell the tale."

He giggled and nodded his head, then zigzagged his finger across his lips as if he were sewing them together.

Meriad cleared her throat and continued…

* * *

"Vetrimon, get moving. If we don't get this done now, we're lost." The rogue pulled a dark shroud over her head, neatly concealing herself in the dark night.

"King Kannilon will have our heads for this," the man complained.

Another from the group of five piped in. "This war's been going on long enough. If we're successful here, then we may be able to turn the tide. His Majesty would thank us."

"Besides," Freth noted grimly, her voice barely heard, "we're not likely to make it back anyway."

"Thanks for the reminder," Vetrimon groaned. A moment later, he shuddered. "What if we encounter any mages?"

Freth spat on the ground. "Curse those nature-mangling fools. That's the whole reason we're here, to stop them from destroying the natural order of things."

A white-haired thief jabbed Vetrimon in the arm. "If you're not with us on this venture, then stay behind here and be lost on the field tomorrow. I've heard enough complaints. Freth, are we doing this?"

The five rogues reached their hands together and whispered tightly, "For Kallisor!" Each took a pouch from Freth and tucked it away. They shared a last solemn look of commitment and darted off into the night.

The band of rogues kept their movements as still as possible, skirting around their allies as they made their way to the forces of Hathreneir. Neither friend nor foe could spot them, or everything would be ruined.

The hatred between the two kingdoms was deep and stretched back for centuries. They were ever at war, and in the brief respites between major battles, each kingdom worked to build a stronger force for the next incursion. The Hathrens employed their mages, and the Kallisorians defended against them with swords, shields, and greater numbers.

The kings had agreed to this one last grand battle in an attempt to put an end to the wars that tore their lands apart. The winner would rule both kingdoms unchallenged. Too much depended on victory this time, and though the rogues were set to break the code of war, they had to give their liege his best chance at success.

Vetrimon pulled his cloak tighter, both excited and scared that his life would end this night. He tucked himself into the brush and waited until he was sure he would be unseen. Then, with a low scamper, he made his way, one hiding place at a time, until he approached his designated camp among the Hathren forces.

Avoiding sentries was easy, for few men were posted around the camp at all. No one expected a move like this, and though he hoped his actions wouldn't curse him in the histories, if he helped to end the war in Kallisor's favor, then it would all be worthwhile. Not that he would be around to enjoy it, he reminded himself with a roll of his eyes.

Torchlight flickered. Vetrimon took a breath and let it out slowly, his eyes on the ground, searching for movement among the shadows. A slight creak of boots crunched on gritty dirt, and he knew someone was close by. He resisted the urge to budge away from his hiding place. He had to rely on his training and his nerve. One breath at a time.

The meager footsteps turned and paced the other way, signaling that he had not been spotted. With a grin, he made his way around the sleeping camp, searching for his target. No one would be guarding it, per se, but it would probably be attended. He kept his eyes scanning left and right, watching for movement and hoping for none.

Sometime later, he found the tent that housed the food and water. He absent-mindedly tapped the pouch tied to his waist, hoping Freth had swiped the correct herb from the healers, though why they would carry poison among their wares eluded him.

Two water barrels stood at the western edge of the tent, so Vetrimon snaked his way closer. As expected, three men were sitting near the barrels, chatting idly, but what irked Vetrimon the most was that one was a mage. The last thing he needed was some pagan nature-warper flinging rampant energy at him and tearing a rip in the fabric of the world just to put him down. Or whatever mages did. It didn't matter. He had a job to do, and he would get it done.

Vetrimon lifted the nearest edge of the tent and reached blindly underneath, fumbling until he grasped something he could remove. An apple became his ally as he grasped it in his hand and then hurled it over the tent, taking care not to throw it so far away the trio would miss it.

"What's that, a rodia?" one warrior asked. "I'll find out."

Though only the one man left, the other two were distracted, which allowed Vetrimon to slink his way to the barrels, where he upended the wolfsbane quickly. He backed into the shadows and made his way around the tent again.

Now it was time for the ruse.

The dire plan called for this action, and though he hadn't originally cared for it, he realized its necessity. The others had all committed to it as well, and he would do his part for his king. He made his way through the camp and sought out the lieutenant's quarters. The area would be well protected, he knew, but he could still achieve his goal. He kept to the shadows, hiding beside the makeshift waste bins that reeked enough to make him gag. Skirting around those, he found a darker corner of the lit tent. Drawing his dagger, Vetrimon sliced into the fabric when he heard voices speaking from within, trying to match his cuts with their words. He followed with a second long slit, then gently lifted the flap.

The shadow along the tent's wall was due to a chair and a pair of legs that tapped furiously on the ground in front of it. Vetrimon watched for a moment and realized the legs belonged to some subordinate listening to the lieutenant's tirade as he paced about the tent. The rogue could just see the steps the commander was taking on the other side of the chamber, but he couldn't wait forever; a sentry would likely come around the outside perimeter and discover him any time now.

Once the lieutenant's feet turned the other way, Vetrimon slipped into the tent, behind the chair, and slammed his hand against the unsuspecting soldier's mouth and slit his throat. The lieutenant was so engrossed in his ranting he didn't hear the brief struggle. Vetrimon dodged off to the side, seeking shelter behind a crate, but the tent was too small, and when the other man turned, he screamed aloud, "Intruder! Guards!"

"You will die, Hathren scum," Vetrimon vowed. He bounced from his perch, dagger leading the way. The guards rushed in, but he ignored them, his eyes focused on the leader.

The lieutenant's eyes widened with surprise, but his battle prowess was greater, and he smacked the assassin with a gauntleted fist. Vetrimon couldn't see, but he didn't need to survive this fight. Like a cornered lupino, he growled with feral rage and snapped his jaws, pressing toward his target relentlessly.

His dagger struck, and a mad howl burned in his ears. "Guards!" the man gasped desperately. "Healer!" Vetrimon stabbed again and again, even as fire erupted along his body with each sword thrust and magic spell that pierced his leathers.

"Guar—" With a final gasp, the lieutenant and his assassin perished within seconds of each other.

The Hathren camps erupted in turmoil as all five lieutenants were slaughtered in similar fashion. News was sent immediately to their king, who was roused ungracefully from slumber. Grumbling, King Pennithor of Hathreneir called to his head mage and advisor. "There is little time left. How go your preparations, Delminor?"

The mage bit his lip, but his gaze was firm. "Perhaps a few hours is all."

"Perhaps?" the king echoed angrily. "We will defeat the Kallisorians this day, and that is all. You will be ready."

"I will begin immediately." Delminor bowed his head and swept from the king's tent.

Pennithor called out to his commanders to assemble the troops into one large fighting contingent. It wouldn't be as organized as he liked, but with the lieutenants gone, it couldn't be helped. Each set of fighters was bolstered by the efforts of mages skilled in various schools of magic. Fire, water, and lightning made up the majority of his forces, but a few nature, healing, and other mages were scattered about as well.

It seemed unfair, he laughed to himself, to pit his foe against his mages, for Kannilon, like all his ancestors before him, was a fool of a king who refused to see the benefits of magic. Yet still, he growled, they always held back his own attempts at victory, and he could never determine why. Despite that, he would play by the rules of war and not resort to the underhanded slaughter his men had faced last night.

"Move out!" he shouted once the army was assembled.

The morning sun lifted into the sky as the two armies approached each other, facing off for one last rout. Pennithor bellowed over the din, "It is with foul treachery that you attempt to win this war, fool."

The Kallisorian army responded by shaking their swords and shields. Their king turned to silence them, making a strange gesture with his hand. Kannilon shook his head and looked at his foe. "The rogues acted without my knowledge or consent. It was never my intent to—"

"I care little for your excuses, King of Kallisor. If you cannot maintain control over your troops, then you are not fit to rule one kingdom, never mind two." Pennithor's army cheered as the others raised their swords again in denial.

"You will see just how well I control my troops, little Pennithor."

"No!" the Hathren king shouted. "You will lay down your weapons in forfeit."

Kannilon scoffed. "Forfeit?"

"Your army's actions last night violated the rules of war. You will—"

Kannilon raised his hand and lowered it swiftly; in response, arrows filled the sky, pelting down upon the Hathren forces. "Attack!" he ordered, sending his troops forward with anger and haste.

"Again?" Pennithor spat. "Very well." He waved his arms about, but his mages had already erected fire shields to burn away the incoming projectiles. Earth and nature mages jogged to the front line and bolstered the fighters' defenses with spells of their own.

The battle was on, and soldiers fell on both sides. Throughout, Pennithor gritted his teeth, defending when he had to but shouting orders the rest of the time. He grabbed one wounded man and yanked him from the battle, ordering, "Find Delminor and tell him to arrive now!"

Kannilon watched as the Hathren mages supported their fighters, but his warriors were trained to dispatch the spellcasters. Wave after wave raced forward, fending off Hathren swords but seeking the mages as their top priority. Pennithor's tactic had changed, however, and the mages were using their skills primarily for defense now, which made them harder, though not impossible, to target.

"Healers!" Kannilon summoned.

"Are you injured, sire?"

"No. I have a task for you, and you will not fail."

Immediately, the tone set the healers on edge. Among all the mages in their combined lands, the Kallisorian king only tolerated those who specialized in the healing arts. They kept his fighters on the battlefield longer and with more vigor than they could ever have had without healer support. The special mages knew their opportunity was unique, and when the king laid out his plan, they blanched, but they could not refute him.

Their liege bade them to erect a protective shield that would deflect attacks and spells alike. Alone, no healer could succeed in this task, but together they might.

Fifteen healers, arms linked awkwardly together in a line, strode forth in sharply marched steps. Much the way they would shield a body from infection, the team now deflected larger influences, turning that skill outward, but they had to act as a single unit in order for the energies to support this bizarre use of their ability.

Ahead went the healers, followed closely by archers, soldiers, and the Kallisorian king himself. They pierced through the Hathren forces, seeking and ending the mages. Yet as they went, the healers, whose lives were typically spent off the actual field of battle, fell one by one, until the protective shield was useless. When it collapsed and only a few healers remained, Kannilon gave them their next command.

Grudgingly, the healers anointed the archers' arrows with various poisons, using their magic to increase the toxicity. The deadly projectiles struck one man down after another, but a second factor was affecting the Hathren troops as well.

The Hathren fighters had been drinking poisoned water throughout the day, and it weakened them further and further, until whole contingents of Hathren warriors fell to their knees in massive, unexplained pain, soiling the land as they vomited or were slain effortlessly.

Pennithor demanded an answer, and a nature mage brought the explanation moments before being pierced by an arrow and dropping to the ground.

"The murder of my lieutenants was a decoy?" Pennithor marveled with glorious rage. "Their murders were not even the lowest your men sank? You resorted to poison?" He bellowed aloud and hurled his sword angrily through the air, even as three arrows plummeted into his chest, piercing his armor and crashing him to the ground.

Kannilon hurried over to the fallen liege and ensured his doom by piercing the man's chest with his own sword. "The Hathren king is dead!" Kannilon announced in glee. "Lay down your swords, Hathren fools, for you are now mine!" He brought his three remaining healers around himself to erect another shield, despite their exhaustion, and he called aloud his victory once more. "The Hathren king is—" Despite himself, his jaw dropped.

From the horizon, a fiery, flickering giant rose up into the sky. It wasn't a wild creature from the south but an abomination of pure magic. Fully erect, the giant was at least the height of six men, and its power was remarkable. Blasts of lightning flickered across its surface with each swing. Every impact cracked the ground and exploded in fiery rage, flinging friend and foe alike into the air.

Outraged, Kannilon drew his forces together and commanded them to eliminate the mages creating and controlling the monster. Yet wherever they struck, they found no one. The apparent strength of the spell suggested that the mages would have to be very close to the creature, but it was as if the colossus propelled itself. At a loss, the king commanded his forces to attack the construct directly. Arrows passed through the colossus as its massive arms and hands crashed down and decimated the Kallisorian troops below.

Kannilon panicked and screamed his fury. "Foul betrayers of nature! Face us man to man. Enough of this treachery!"

"Treachery?" a voice rumbled from the glowing colossus. "You surely speak of yourself, invading our camps, poisoning our troops, slaying our lieutenants, magically fortifying your arrows, using your healers as a shield, to name your acts within only the past few hours. Who is it that excels in treachery, I ask?"

Kannilon looked all around for the source of the voice, but the mages were somehow projecting their voices from every part of the enormous being. Confused, Kannilon waved his hand to direct his archers once more, targeting the center of the colossus as it continued to rampage.

The monster shouted, its voice shaking the air. "You have killed our liege, you poor excuse for a monarch. There are rules for war, but now I will rewrite one to counteract your own revisions."

With that, lightning sizzled and lashed out in all directions. Everyone in the blast radius collapsed to the ground, dead or unconscious. The thundercrack that followed deafened all those beyond the immediate blast range. The king clutched his ears in agony, and he could hear nothing but a painful inner ringing.

But with the release of such a concentrated blast of energy, the defenses of the giant were significantly reduced, if only for a moment. Volleys of arrows already in flight found their mark, striking deep within the light and bringing down the beast. The light flickered and then raveled inward, until it vanished with a pop.

The Kallisorian king staggered forward, enraged. So many of his men and women had died in this altercation. Even with the losses on the other side, including the death of the Hathren king, he vowed the Hathrens would pay for this day. He made his way to the center of the colossus, certain now that the cloak concealing the team of mages would at last be gone.

And so it was, but to his shock, he saw only one mage, pierced with several arrows, breathing raggedly, his body wrapped tightly around a strange crimson figurine.

"Now it ends," the king spat, drawing a short sword, eyeing the figurine closely. "Was it this device that summoned your creation, mage?"

"You'll never be able to harness it," Delminor gasped, tightening his grip as if to keep the statue away from the king.

"This power is mine alone."

His ears still damaged, Kannilon couldn't hear what the mage said. He pressed the tip of his sword against the mage's throat. "I suppose your trinket did affect this battle, but your king is dead, and now you follow. My sword is the power here."

The mage opened his mouth to speak, but the king pressed his blade through the man's throat. At once, the red figurine in the mage's grasp started to glow. The radiance brightened until the king had to shield his eyes, and then it exploded with a bang, breaking into a handful of pieces and impaling the king in the process.

The few remaining combatants rushed over to the explosion. The king gasped in pain as one healer turned him over. "The Red Jade," he breathed, pulling a chunk of it from his chest, its color fading to a pale blue. "Claim it. For…Kallisor."

There was one last scramble to gather the shards of the Red Jade figurine. Survivors from both sides of the battle claimed a few pieces, then fled before the other side could retaliate.

So ended the horrific war, with both kings dead and pieces of the Red Jade scattered to both kingdoms, where mages from each side would seek the hidden powers within.

* * *

The boy looked up. "Gran-mama?"

"Yes, dear?"

"Do you think it's real? The Red Jade?"

"I do. And I pray no one messes with its power again. But that isn't the point of this story, and you know it." Meriad smiled.

"I know," he said. "The good king and the evil king wouldn't work together, and so a lot of people died in the end. No matter how strong one side is, the other side can always be stronger. So there really isn't any point to war."

Meriad nodded and sighed. "If only more people saw it that way, indeed."

"But Gran-mama?" he asked hesitantly. "If both kings died, what happened to the kingdoms then? I mean, we still live in Hathreneir, and Kallisor still has a king, so where did they come from?"

"With all the times I have told you this story, you've never asked me that before," she noted proudly. "So I think I was right. You're ready to find out what happened after that war."

"There's more?" he asked in awe, his whole face lighting up with excitement.

"Oh yes, indeed, there is. It will take some time to tell it to you properly, so let me finish with one little bit for tonight, and then we will continue tomorrow. Deal?"

"Oh, only one little bit?"

She ruffled his hair and laughed. "Yes, little one. You asked how we still have kingdoms if the kings died, and the answer is easy enough. The kings had sons, like you. Those sons became the kings, but they were very young, so they had help at first. Times were tough, and there was still tension between the two kingdoms. However, their resources were severely depleted because of the wars, and it took years for everyone to rebuild their homes. So, things were quiet for years to come.

"But," she added mysteriously as she stepped toward the door to leave, "not everyone forgot about the Red Jade."

CHAPTER 1

Gabrion's Promotion

GABRION BREATHED IN the warm spring air and stretched deeply into the dawn. A bright smile lit his face, for this was a day that would change his life. He rose from his bed, and as he tended to his morning routine, he sang merrily, making up an impromptu song as he went.

> *It must be perfect, for my lady waits.*
> *I have to hurry, for I can't be late.*
> *A golden sun shines in the sky,*
> *With a deep-set blue to match her eyes.*
>
> *Do I wear the green or go with white?*
> *Everything has to be just right.*
> *Ready for the picnic, my heart does sing,*
> *So don't you forget to bring the ring!*

He chuckled to himself and gathered his belongings, then bounced from his home and nearly skipped the way to hers, tipping his head to other villagers and whistling his tune as he went.

Savvron was a quiet Kallisorian town, far from the woes of the big cities. It was founded centuries ago, according to town legend, when a traveler who was walking across the countryside saw a beautiful patch of orange flowers, set himself down among them, and decided that it would be a perfect place to live. The brilliantly colored flowers still covered the hillock, and tall trees surrounded them in a warm embrace. It was a meadow where many lovestruck couples went to simply drink in the glorious view. It was there that Gabrion would officially seek Mira's hand.

He laughed aloud at the sight he conjured in his mind of the two of them celebrating their union among friends, enjoying years of fulfillment, complete with a small pack of children. It was an image they had constructed together as kids and one that he could finally put forth in earnest.

He arrived at her door, rapping gently. It didn't take long for her to respond. She wore a soft yellow dress with white flowers scattered across it. It made her dark hair and azure eyes glow in contrast.

"You do look lovely today, Mira," he said with a bow.

"Well thank you, Gabe." She laughed. "You seem lively this morning."

He nodded. "We have a nice day ahead of us. But first…" He opened one side of the basket and pulled out a deep-yellow ribbon. "I think this would match your hair quite well today."

Mira chuckled. "You always seem to know what I'm going to wear." She took the ribbon and tied a tidy bow in her hair. "You're either magical, or you have a spy watching me." He winked merrily and closed the basket before she could see the other ribbons he had waiting there. A simple secret, but it amused them both. He drew his arm around her, and they started on the trek to the meadow.

It was a quiet journey at first, and then Gabrion released a soft sigh. "You know, Mira, I was thinking of getting you something."

She looked at him and raised an eyebrow. "Not another wooden sword so we can practice together, I hope."

"No," he answered with a laugh. "Even better. I thought about getting you a dog."

She stopped short and gave him a quizzical look. "Gabe, you know I'm terrified of dogs."

He smiled and tugged her along. "I know. But it would be a tree dog. You'd be fine with that."

"A what?"

"A tree dog." He paused for just a moment and then said, "You know, the kind of dog that barks and leaves!"

It took her a second, but then she laughed while simultaneously slapping his arm. "You're an idiot," she accused. A strange look came over her face, and her eyes cast down to the ground as she pursed her lips for a moment before quietly adding, "But…you do make me laugh."

"It is only fair," he retorted lightly, "because you do make me smile."

They walked past a few houses and eventually toward the path that would lead them to the meadow. It would be at least an hour's journey, more with a leisurely stroll, but this day was not about schedules.

"Gabrion?"

"Hmm?"

"What do you think is going to happen?" she asked tentatively.

He didn't need her to clarify the question. The whole village was abuzz with stories of Hathren troops gathering along the nearby borders. It was only a few months ago that Andron had arrived in town, seeking volunteers. He was one of the king's soldiers, and his goal was to train as many villagers as possible to fight and protect themselves. Gabrion was one of those volunteers, and he had shown great promise in a short amount of time. He was already strong from working his father's farm, but now he had developed basic skill and understanding. Andron had told him recently that he would be promoted and given a proper rank, so that if the need should arise, he could help lead the fight if war with Hathreneir actually did break out. The promotion would put him on the king's own payroll, and it was this that had prompted him to finally propose to Mira.

But he hadn't wanted to discuss this with Mira just yet. At least, not until they were settled among the flowers in the meadow.

He tossed some ideas around, wondering how best to avoid the subject until the right moment. "I think the king is doing his best, and it was a good idea to send soldiers to the towns to train us to defend ourselves. I'm sure if there was a greater danger, there would be actual troops here, not just little guys like us."

"Little guys?" she echoed with a slight laugh. "If you're little, I would hate to see the big guys."

He blushed congenially. "Still, there isn't anything to worry about, Mira. It's a beautiful day. We're together."

"Gabe—" she started but then stopped and sighed. "But what if something's out there and no one's really ready for it? What if—"

He stopped and turned her toward him. "I'm telling you it will be fine." He did his best to sound calm and confident and supportive. "Why is this on your mind today?"

"It's… on everyone's mind," she hedged. "Come on. Let's keep going."

Her behavior struck him as strange, but he drew in a deep breath and walked with her, wondering what was really bothering her. He debated pursuing the topic, to find out why it was troubling her so much on such a pretty day, but then she bent down to sniff some flowers, calling him to join her, and he was lost in the moment.

They continued along the path, and soon the meadow was in sight. Gabrion had grown silent with anticipation of his proposal. He reenacted the plan in his head again. He would pull out the sandwiches and open a small cask of wine. She would be surprised by the wine, but he would insist that it was a perfect day for wine in the meadow, and she would agree. Then he would tell her of his promotion, and they would discuss their future, after which he would set himself, in deference, on one knee, taking her hand and—

"Gabrion!" screamed a voice from far behind them. The sound rang out in terror, and he and Mira stopped cold. His name echoed down the path again and again.

Mira looked up at him, biting her lower lip, her eyes full of sudden tears.

He pulled her close and held her, but she just stood still, trembling. "It's nothing," he soothed, wishing with all his heart that he was right. "Be calm."

Footsteps pounded erratically in the dirt, and moments later a young teen came into view. He was badly out of breath and stained with something that Gabrion certainly did not want to see this day.

Blood.

He released Mira and turned to the youth. "Kaz, what is it?" he asked urgently.

The boy fell to his knees, dropping a sword to the ground. "This—" he gasped, shoving the sword forward. "We…we need you." He drew a deep breath of air to steady himself, then looked up into Gabrion's eyes. "The Hathrens. They're here. Killing. I barely got away to find you."

"No!" Mira gasped, eyes wide with stark terror. "Not like this."

But Gabrion could see that Kaz was telling the truth. He honed his ears and thought he could make out the sound of clashing steel in the distance. He knelt down and helped the boy to his feet. "Kaz, where are you hurt?"

"I'm not," he said, following Gabrion's gaze to the blood on his shirt. "No, that's old man Arinot's. He…was their first victim. He sent me to rally the others. I did.

Now I found you." He bent down and lifted the sword. "You left this at your place. I thought you'd need it."

Gabrion knew his duty. He needed to protect the town. Luckily, they were far enough away that Mira could find a place to hide until the trouble was taken care of. He turned to her now, a soldier—poorly trained but a soldier nonetheless. "Mira, I have to go. You have to hide."

Her eyes were fixed on the distant path, and she didn't seem to hear him. "I—I can't believe it's really happening." Her cheek twitched gently, almost looking like a bewildered smirk, as if she were thinking of something unrelated to the attack.

"Mira," he repeated, but she wouldn't acknowledge him. He figured she was seeing a vision of the town being torn apart. He didn't have time to shake her from her fear, so he did the only thing he could do. "Kaz, you have to get Mira to safety. Can you do that?"

The young teen nodded his head sharply and took Mira's hands, then bodily dragged her toward the meadow. Gabrion watched them for just a moment more, and as he turned, ready to sprint back to the village, he saw the picnic basket, set on the road, otherwise forgotten. He fished around inside it until he retrieved the engagement ring. He stuffed it deep into a pocket. "I'll take care of this mess, Mira," he said to himself softly, "and then we'll do this day again… properly."

With that, he ran back to the village to deal with the invaders in earnest, clutching his sword in his hand. His feet pounded along the path as he went, and he wondered how many warriors had come to ravage the town. The warriors he felt he could handle, even without years of experience behind him. Gabrion was more concerned about the other fighters, because his training hadn't yet prepared him for battling magic.

The sounds of yelling grew louder, and the path fell away behind him. He tightened his grip on his sword and braced himself for impact as he rushed headlong for his first quarry, a swordsman who looked barely old enough to cook for himself, let alone participate in a battle. The youth was intent on chasing the village baker across the road, and so Gabrion pushed hard and shouldered the attacker to the ground. It was a quick scrabble as the boy bounced back onto his feet, sword swinging wildly. He turned to Gabrion and slashed wickedly.

Gabrion parried the attack easily and thrust back offensively. The boy dodged to the side and spun, bringing the sword low, hoping to cut into Gabrion's legs, but he saw the move coming and hopped over the blade. Gabrion swung again, and sparks flew from the weapons as they collided. The boy cried out in frustration, but instead of continuing the move, which would have required Gabrion to pivot around, Gabrion abruptly punched out with his left arm, striking the boy across the chin and simply knocking him out cold.

"Take over!" he commanded the baker, who was still trembling but nodded. Gabrion sprinted off and found his next opponent.

As he approached, Gabrion assessed that the woman was some sort of thief or rogue, because she was very agile and fought with two daggers, a handful of pouches bouncing around her waist. She was scoring hits against Kaz's older brother, Bryn, who had volunteered with Gabrion for training. He was holding his own, but she was better.

Gabrion ran in to help his friend, but the rogue easily fended off both sets of attacks. Her daggers flashed in and out faster than Gabrion could follow, and she nicked him in several places within seconds. It was a tribute to his determination that he didn't drop his own sword from the shock of it. Instead, he firmed up his fighting stance and tried to communicate some sort of plan with Bryn, but he had no success.

The rogue didn't even seem winded as she pirouetted around, slashing both high and low, increasing her hit count. Each cut was superficial, but the combination was like hundreds of firegnats nipping and biting away, until each fighter was utterly distracted. Gabrion didn't know when she knocked him down, nor did he remember her stabbing him in the side, but when her eyes focused on him, he knew he was done for.

Bryn must have understood the predicament, because he wailed a fierce battle cry and bodily threw himself at the woman. And though he jolted her out of the way, one of the daggers struck him hard, and falling to the ground was his last great maneuver.

Bryn's sudden death didn't even register to Gabrion yet. He just knew there was danger and he needed to act. He threw a handful of dirt with one hand and followed it with his sword arm. She expected it and was ready, but Gabrion's strong foot swept out and crashed into her knee. She gasped and collapsed. As she fell, one arm lashed out, and Gabrion felt a searing heat graze past his shoulder as her remaining dagger whizzed by. He knew this fight couldn't end with simply knocking her out, and so he dashed at her with his sword and ended the struggle.

He had killed animals before. But this was different. It was a thinking person he had snuffed out. A lifetime of experience cast aside with a single thrust of his blade. Decades of future experiences that could never be had. A family, a set of friends and comrades who would never see her again. Before he knew it, he was on the ground, retching painfully, wondering why his world was crashing down so quickly.

"Gabrion," called a familiar voice. "Come now. Rise. This is a battle. You must rise."

He looked up into Andron's deep, dark eyes and saw the hardness in them. Soon, he would be the same, a trained killing machine. And though part of him protested this, he thought of Mira and knew he needed to protect her at all costs. If the village fell completely, then Mira too would be lost.

Andron helped him to his feet and understood the resolve that settled into Gabrion's gaze. "War is hard, son, but, yes, you must fight. Come. These piggons brought a mage with them, and we need to eliminate him before he burns everything down."

Gabrion tightened his grip on his sword, remembering the only advice Andron had ever given about dealing with mages: "Kill them first, unless a sword is aimed at your throat." He focused on his new goal and followed his mentor into the heart of the village.

The two of them ran full tilt, hacking and slashing as needed, plowing through in order to reach the mage. He was easy to find, for five warriors created a barrier before him, and he stood with arms raised over his head, waving them wildly, casting small fireballs left and right.

"We're in luck," Andron growled. "He's a neophyte. A stronger mage would have already incinerated this whole area."

"He's trying to burn the food!" Gabrion gasped. Without waiting for Andron, he sprinted ahead and barreled into the first of the five barrier guards. His sword slashed wildly, to little avail. These guards were better trained than even the rogue was, and each blow was easily parried. Worse, the nearest fighter openly mocked Gabrion's skill and managed to knock him down several times for sport.

His comrades were less fortunate, facing off against Andron, who was a seasoned soldier. He cut his way through three of the fighters with ease and grace, then turned to the fourth before getting hit full blast with a fire dart from the mage. It stung more than hurt, but it was followed by more blasts and an angry swordsman. Disoriented and coughing, Andron couldn't defend himself well, and he took more hits than he gave.

Meanwhile, Gabrion's attacker stopped toying with him as the guard's comrades fell, and he swished his sword forcefully at Gabrion. Scrambling madly, the inexperienced youth did all he could to keep out of the way until an opportunity arose. A few feet away, one presented itself in the form of a broken barrel. Gabrion grabbed at the various pieces of wood and hurled them at the fighter, causing him to slow his pursuit to bat away the debris. Gabrion righted himself and then charged, but he didn't charge with his sword arm. Instead, he jumped forward and dropped into a somersault, bowling the warrior over. He sprang up, twisted around, and kicked the sword from the man's hand, and then he dealt a deadly blow.

He didn't waste any time before pursuing the mage. The firecaster was still hurling fire darts at Andron, who was clearly struggling. Gabrion figured the mage would be easy to knock over and struck with confidence, but then his sword arm was suddenly useless. He looked at it quickly; it seemed the same, yet it was as heavy as an anvil. Its odd weight alone pinned him to the ground. He kicked with his foot, but when he touched the mage, his foot took on the same heaviness.

"Shield of Delminor," the mage said proudly. "My gift from the land of Hathreneir. And now you'll have to die." He raised his hands and bent his fingers into a strange pattern, preparing to cast some other woe upon Gabrion, but the spell didn't hit him. Andron jumped in the way, taking the full blast of a dagger-chain spell in the gut.

The spell binding Gabrion lifted immediately, and he sprang up to see that Andron had stabbed the mage, knocking him out but not killing him. Meanwhile, Andron was gravely wounded, as if he had been slashed with a hundred knives.

"Stupid... mages," Andron gasped.

A horn sounded, and there was a mad scramble as fighting stopped all around the village. Clearly, a retreat had been called. The villagers did not pursue them to finish off the rest. They had enough to tend to on their own. Gabrion was focused on Andron and the light that was now fading from his eyes.

"Hear me... Gabrion," the soldier said in a strained voice. "The king. He must... be told. The war..." He coughed blood and used his last ounce of strength to clasp Gabrion's hand and finish his decree. "It is... imperative the king learns of this. Do you... understand? Many others will share this... fate... otherwise. Do you understand?"

Gabrion hardened his jaw and nodded. "I do. If I must seek the king myself, I will. I promise. This can't happen again."

"Yes. You… must." With a gasp, Andron spoke no more.

Gabrion carefully pulled himself away from Andron's body and saw that the mage was still breathing. He debated what to do next, but he couldn't bring himself to kill the man in cold blood, despite the actions here today. He tore off part of the mage's robe and used the fabric to bind the man's hands and mouth tightly. He would have to figure it out later; there were other things to attend to first. He called over another villager to watch the mage, and then he stepped away to survey the damage.

He couldn't believe how much had been destroyed in so short a time. So many homes and lives were shattered now. He looked around and couldn't see how this place had ever been his home. It was so foreign without the cobbler's hut or the herbalist's storefront. Corpses littered the street, and he couldn't connect them with the people he knew. Not old Jeena, who told wild stories about flying horses and dancing flowers, nor young Tild and Howt, the only twins he had ever known. Pieces of his past were crumbling, and a new sense of purpose was coming over him. He would seek the king, and then he would seek revenge.

But just when he thought the pain was more than he could handle, one more wound was struck, deeply.

As he strolled aimlessly around, cataloging the carnage and helping a few of the villagers, Kaz came staggering in, covered in blood that was clearly his own this time. He sought out Gabrion, tears pouring from his eyes.

"Nothing," he wailed. "Nothing I could do, Gabrion!" He fell to his knees and bawled painfully.

Gabrion stared at Kaz as if he were a stranger, wondering if he had any sense in living anymore. Kaz was supposed to hide Mira. To keep her safe. But now…

Then one glimmer of hope cut through Gabrion's awareness.

Kaz looked up at the anguish in Gabrion's eyes, and he muttered, "I tried to stop them. But they took her, Gabe. I couldn't do anything. I—I'm sorry."

Gabrion's hand went instinctively to his pocket and pressed against the ring that waited there. A tear escaped from his eye, and he vowed to find Mira. To rescue her. To bring her home safely.

But he also knew that to do that, he would need help. A second tear followed the first, but he knew deep down that he needed to first seek out the king, to report this battle and gain aid, then find his beloved.

He wiped his cheek dry. It would be his last tear until he and Mira were united again.

CHAPTER 2

The Mage's Reprieve

DARIAK AWOKE SLOWLY to furious pain in his arms and back. He could hear voices nearby, and he could tell that he was tightly bound. It took a few moments of concentration to remember where he was.

His last recollection was of casting fire spells at a pathetic little village on the western border of Kallisor. Five guardsmen had protected him well enough, until the two maniacs had charged in. The brawnier one had intercepted a killing blow intended for the lesser warrior. And in the process, he had been struck with the fool's sword. His arm flashed in agony as if it agreed.

But Dariak felt he was fortunate because he was still alive. If his dagger-chain spell had killed the less competent warrior, he might be dead now. So, once again, the great forces of the world were with him.

He briefly tested his bindings and realized that he would really have to struggle to free himself. It was more important, he thought, to focus on the conversation taking place around him.

"—have much choice, Son. You have to go," a deep, resonating voice said.

"I know. But Mira…" There was a sadness there, Dariak noted. He might be able to use that.

"You said it yourself; you cannot find her on your own. You need help." There was a long pause and some movement. "There is still the issue of this one."

Dariak tried to control his breathing. He didn't want them to know he had awoken yet.

"I can't leave him here after he tried to kill everyone. He will have to come with me to the king and to the dungeons."

"But, Gabrion, we lost so many. We can't spare anyone to help you watch him and you're injured. If you take him, he may kill you."

"If I leave him here, he might escape and kill you and Mother and everyone who's left," Gabrion said quietly. "No, he has to come with me. If I have to hog-tie him to a tree every night with a knife at his neck, then I will."

There was a moment of silence before the father spoke again. "Son, I know what happened here was a tragedy. But don't lose yourself along the way. I hate hearing you speak like this."

"Until I get her back, I already am lost. Wake him. If I do it, I might wake him too hard." There was a flash of anger in the final words, and Dariak braced himself for a rough shake.

Surprisingly, Gabrion's father merely tapped his cheek until his eyes fluttered open. "Time for you to get up." Dariak noted that the kindness and concern were gone.

He moved slowly, partly for effect but also because he was truly hurt. He sat upright and looked around the dingy room. There wasn't much in the way of furniture, just a table and a few chairs, with a kitchen off to one end and a ladder leading up to a second floor, where he guessed the beds were. The man who woke him was strong and leathery skinned, and he'd clearly spent his entire life out in the sun. His sharp-jawed son, poised against a nearby wall, was a close replica of his father.

Gabrion was a tall young man, with short, messy blond hair and dark-brown eyes. He had small crevices around his eyes, as if he usually laughed all day long. He had to be only about eighteen years old, but his torso, which was uncovered except for a poultice on his left side and small cuts everywhere, was well muscled and rather intimidating to a mage who wasn't particularly athletic. If Dariak couldn't just summon the energy around him into a magic spell, he would have done anything he was told without question. He realized that with his hands and mouth bound, he actually couldn't cast a spell now, but that wasn't important.

It wasn't easy having a gag in his mouth either. It tasted dirty, and with his mouth open, he thought he must have been drooling like crazy. He found that it was annoying to swallow too, and he felt like choking. But he was in this predicament for a reason, and he needed to remain focused on his own goal. He reaffirmed with himself that he could have easily died in the battle, rather than get another chance to continue his mission.

Gabrion glared at him with pure venom in his eyes. The look didn't suit him at all. "You have a lot to answer for."

Dariak made a moaning sound around the gag and shrugged his shoulders a little. It was all he could do in response anyway. He felt a line of cold steel press against the side of his neck, and the gag was then untied, but he understood that the youth's father had a sword ready to cut him down if he tried anything.

"Why are you in this village today? Why attack us?" Gabrion demanded.

Dariak swallowed a few times and moved his tongue around. After clearing his throat, he gave his answer. "It was a job, and I needed the money and the experience." He watched Gabrion's muscles tighten as if he wanted to slap the mage. Dariak had the presence of mind to flinch timidly.

"That's no excuse. You invaded someone else's home and went wild, loosing magic all over the place." He shook his head. "It doesn't matter. We're off to the king. He will judge your crimes."

Dariak lowered his head and grinned inwardly. This novice warrior really did intend to bring him to the castle. That was fine with him; it was one of the places he needed to go anyway and part of the reason he had agreed to come into this kingdom in the first place.

"Father, are Andron's horse and saddle still intact?"

"Yes." The deep voice rumbled right by Dariak's ear.

"Good." Gabrion took the gag from his father and retied it around Dariak's mouth. "Let's go." He threw a tunic over his head and wrapped his scabbard around his waist, then guided the mage out with fingers pressed firmly into his shoulder. It wasn't a far walk to the village stable, but by the time they reached it, Dariak's shoulder was throbbing.

Three horses remained in the stable, but it looked to Dariak like there had been at least five others. Parts of the structure had fallen in, and some bore scorch marks from his own fire spells. He tried keeping his gaze downcast the entire time, but when he saw the saddle Gabrion grabbed from the wall, his eyes widened. The straps and buckles that kept the saddle astride the horse were not the only bindings.

After securing the saddle carefully upon a large, strong warhorse, Gabrion saw the dread in Dariak's eyes and nodded.

"Each of the king's soldiers rides a horse with a mage-saddle," he explained, reaching for Dariak and pulling him toward the horse. "They're rarely used. We usually just kill mages."

Dariak met his eyes for a moment and saw that this boy wanted him dead. He blinked a few times and thought of something dreadfully scary, hoping to make himself look at least a little afraid of the situation.

Gabrion held a dagger against Dariak as he removed two special gloves from the mage-saddle. Each was made mostly of leather, and bars of iron ran between each finger, keeping the mage from bending his hands to work a spell. Only a mild amount of flex was possible, which was necessary for staying upright on the horse. Usually, these gloves were strapped onto an unconscious mage, but Dariak cooperated when Gabrion slipped the gloves on his hands. He would have better opportunities to escape.

Once both gloves were in place, a leather cord was wrapped through and around the wrists, securing the gloves tightly. Gabrion was careful not to cut off the circulation, but Dariak could tell that it was a near thing. The leather cord was then laced through special hoops on the saddle. Gabrion hoisted the mage onto the horse, then pulled the cord tighter, dragging the mage's hands down, palms flat, to the saddle itself, right in front of his body. Gabrion was securing the prisoner's legs with two other straps when his father entered with saddlebags full of supplies.

"Be careful, Son," he said, handing over the provisions.

"Thank you, Father. I won't be long." Gabrion paused for a moment and then made his last request before leaving. "When Mira's folks return, please tell them—"

"I will, Son. They were lucky to be off on sojourn, but not so lucky in this. I will assure them that you will do everything you can to bring her back."

"No," he corrected. "I *will* bring her back." With that, he hopped onto the horse, behind Dariak, reaching for the reins and snapping them to start the horse on its way.

The stable was on the southern edge of town, near the bakery where Gabrion's first scuffle had taken place that morning. The horse sauntered under Gabrion's control, and the young man narrated for Dariak's sake and to resolve his own task.

"I managed to save the baker without killing the boy who attacked him. But if you look over there to that spot on the ground, that's where my friend Bryn was killed by one of your rogues. Then she—I had to…" He closed his lips for a moment, afraid he might get sick again, but remembered he needed to be strong. "Over there, that small shed with all the burns on it, that's old man Arinot's. Kaz said he was the first victim. Not bad enough he had to die, but then you went and burned his house. Down there"—he jerked his head toward the right—"three children were so terrified they went to hide, but then you all toppled that house next to it and crushed them. One of them won't ever walk again, but he was the lucky one; the other two didn't survive."

All through the village, Gabrion continued his narrative, and though Dariak tried not to listen, he couldn't help it with the deep, sad voice in his ear. He didn't quite feel pity for this village. He was a Hathren, and these were people who had warred against his homeland for countless years. He couldn't feel pity for them. Not until he completed his own quest; then he would pity anyone who crossed his path. He grinned at the thought.

"This spot," Gabrion interrupted the mage's musing, "was nearly your death. Instead, you killed the king's soldier, and the punishment for killing a member of the king's personal guard is severe. You should have died there." His voice was laden with guilt, for it was his own hand that allowed the mage to live.

"So all this blood and death, and you did it because 'it was a job'? For money? Experience? I can't imagine it was worth it."

He sort of had a point, Dariak thought, but it didn't matter much, because he had work to do and he was still alive to do it. He clung to his mission as Gabrion finally kicked the horse to speed. They darted from the village after Gabrion gave it a final wave farewell.

CHAPTER 3

Foray in the Forest

"WHAT'S OUR TAKE so far?" Kitalla asked as she rummaged through her pack. She skimmed over a handful of trinkets and objects the others didn't yet know about and pulled out a pair of matching crystal goblets. "I have these from last night."

"Oh, boyfriend went all out, did he?" Bostian joked, then quickly dodged away as she lunged for him. "Okay, okay, nicely done. I've got these." He brought forth a silver necklace and earrings.

"Well, at least you got them out of her ear this time, instead of taking half her head with you," Kitalla retorted.

"Yeah, that was a real mess!" Jafflin added. "Stupid things kept quivering a while."

"Knock it off, all of you," demanded Poltor. He was the shortest among the five, and he bore the most scars, many of them marring his face and arms. He reached around and claimed the treasures his rogues had collected, placing them into a satchel of his own. "This was a good grab, though," he said admiringly. "Well done."

"A compliment from the Mist," Jafflin said conspiratorially, looking around as if no one was supposed to have heard. He wasn't fast enough to move aside when Poltor smacked him on the head, but everyone else laughed. Jafflin was the only one who could tease Poltor at all, but then, they'd been working together since the beginning.

Kitalla sat back against a tree and looked up at the sky. "Smoke to the west."

"Been there all morning," Bostian agreed. "Something must have happened."

She rolled her eyes. "Obviously." She looked around at their band, which was missing only Heria, who was out scouting. She liked having Heria around more than Bostian. Not only was she another woman to talk to, her comments were less idiotic, though sometimes a little off in their own right.

Kitalla had been traveling with them for a few years now. It was a grander life than foraging in the woods or begging in the streets of a town. There was a fair share of danger, but she liked a good challenge, and thieving from the rich always made her feel a bit better. She pulled up a handful of grass and let the blades fall one by one, wishing she could rid the world of the rich and spread the wealth around evenly. Her mother had been a servant in one of the northern manors, serving the mayor of the area, but when she refused to perform certain tasks, she wasn't only dismissed from duty but sent to prison, and Kitalla was left to fend for herself for a time. Things grew worse after her mother was released, but Kitalla never dwelled on why. Hers certainly wasn't a glorious beginning, but at least her life had stabilized now. This was a well-trained group of fighters and thieves, and they never wanted for long, if ever.

"Out with it, Kit," Jafflin said, interrupting her thoughts. "You can't sit there smiling to yourself and not share. You got something cooking?" Jafflin was another one who could irritate her at times, though he was extremely useful in a fight.

For now, she ignored him and just kept grinning to herself.

Poltor intervened anyway. "Leave her be. She's earned a bit of quiet. She had the most lucrative catch last night."

Kitalla's grin widened, and she reached her hands behind her head, relaxing in victory. Earning the day's prize for best catch meant she would get first choice at dinner as well. It was a simple competition but effective. Poltor really knew how to manage this group of criminals. She once teased him that he shouldn't call himself the Mist, because he never "missed" anything, and she learned quickly that he wasn't one to be teased under any circumstances—except in small ways by Jafflin—even when laced with a compliment. She'd had bruises for days, but she'd also learned her lesson.

She turned her head to consider Bostian again. Though his inane comments could annoy her, he was a real powerhouse. Where Jafflin was quick, Bostian was strong. The bulky fighter preferred bludgeoning someone into submission rather than dealing with the situation tactfully. This didn't always suit their operations, but his talents were an important addition to the group. Kitalla had once been caught while on the job, fetching an expensive-looking golden bracelet, and the only thing that had kept the guards from killing her on the spot was a bull rush from Bostian. He had barreled through, hammer swinging crazily from left to right, with just enough control not to crash it into Kitalla's face. She would always be grateful to him for saving her life, and he'd done so several times.

She often wondered if she'd have survived those critical moments without Bostian. If she hadn't known he was near, would she have been a little more careful? Or would inspiration have struck and allowed her to craft a quick escape? Curious as she was, she didn't actually want the chance to find out.

As she cast her thoughts in another direction, Heria returned from scouting. Kitalla had always regarded her as a younger sister. She was only fifteen, but she had been hardened by a tragic childhood, and sometimes went into wild rampages. Poltor had tamed her somewhat, but a wild fire lit her eyes at times, and on those occasions, everyone in the group gave her a wide berth.

Today was not such a day, and she bounced back into camp as if coming to a joyous festival with the best of friends. "Travelers coming," she announced, long blond hair swinging behind her with each lively step. "On a king's war steed, no less. Not in too much of a hurry. Two aboard the mount. Should be here in about an hour."

"An hour?" Jafflin asked in awe. "How high up in the trees did you climb to see them that far off?"

Heria focused her eyes deep into his and grinned maliciously. He paled and scrambled to do something else for a while. She sighed and turned to Poltor. "The plan?"

While he considered for a moment, Bostian piped up, "Lost family in need of food?"

Heria frowned. "Boring. Beleaguered jesters traveling to the castle?"

Jafflin shook his head. "Nothing to juggle. How about the hag and the handmaiden?"

At this, Kitalla groaned. "Why don't we just tie you to a tree and have you call out for help when they pass?"

Poltor spoke at last. "No, it's been a while since we've done the hag and the handmaiden."

Kitalla pulled a face and shot Jafflin an angry look. Though the farce would work and always had, it meant she needed to rub ash into her rich brown hair and wrap it up in a bun, then powder her face with dirt and grime, because Heria matched the role of handmaiden much better than she did. She glanced over at Heria, hoping she would try to talk Poltor out of this scenario, but then she remembered that it was one of Heria's favorite acts, which was probably why Jafflin had suggested it.

She didn't even bother to argue. She had already earned first choice at dinner. Maybe this would give her a free pass for tomorrow's catch as well. An hour was much more time than they needed for preparations, but it didn't pay to risk missing the passersby. At once, the quintet went to work.

* * *

Leaving Savvron was harder on Gabrion than he thought it would be. He had been away from home before, sometimes with his family or friends and a few times on his own. This felt completely different. He wouldn't be returning to a safe haven anymore. His home felt tainted now that Hathren forces had ravaged it. He kept his anger in check, for the horse beneath him would just as likely start bucking with his frustration as bolt ahead on its own when he wasn't ready. He had ridden Tumbler before, and he had been thrown from the saddle the first few tries. Andron had at least taken care to train Gabrion in a hay-laden area, so the falls were less painful. It wasn't even that he was inexperienced on horses; he'd ridden them most of his life. But farm horses and warhorses were remarkably different, in size, power, handling, training, and temperament. This horse was so strong that the added weight of the mage didn't even seem to faze the beast.

Gabrion considered the mage for a moment. All he could see was the tangle of jet-black hair. Not once had the mage made any sudden movements to test his bindings. He didn't even try smashing his head back to break Gabrion's nose. It had happened once to Andron, so he'd already warned all his pupils to be alert for such a move.

Gabrion didn't like feeling suspicious all the time. He was much more of a jovial sort, but the recent events were too disheartening. He wondered at the mage's cooperation and whether he was missing key details that a more experienced warrior would see. Perhaps the mage was calm because he had been working his hands free, or maybe he had managed to work the gag out of his mouth, or both. It was an unsettling thought, so Gabrion decided to check. He called Tumbler to a halt and dismounted.

Gabrion decided that immediately checking the mage's bonds would show a lack of confidence in his ability, so he instead pulled a canteen and took a few drags of water. The mage must be terribly thirsty as well.

"Water?" he asked. The mage nodded eagerly. "Fine. I'll let you stretch your legs and such." He unbuckled the leg straps and then loosened the wrist bindings. He reached up and pulled the mage off the horse, but the man's hands were still linked to the saddle. He lowered the gag from the mage's mouth and gently poured in some water.

"Thank you," the mage croaked. After a few more sips, his throat felt much better. He wondered if it was worth trying a spell but decided that it wasn't the right time. He hadn't yet perfected the technique of casting without hand motions. "Any chance I could—you know—have some alone time in the woods?"

Gabrion had wondered about that complication. He didn't exactly need to watch someone else in that capacity, but he couldn't release his charge either. Pulling a rope from a saddlebag, he tied a line around the mage's neck, snug enough that it wouldn't fit over his head but not enough to choke him, and then he wrapped the other end around his own arm. "Sure, but I won't be far away." He realized belatedly that the mage would likely need his hands for the process. He unwrapped the bindings completely from the saddle, then asked, "Right hand or left?"

"Right, if you don't mind."

It could be either a ruse or an honest request. Either way, freeing a mage's hand was risky. He opted to remove the right glove and hoped he wasn't making a mistake. He had the mage bend his left hand behind his back, and he used the leather strap to secure it to his torso. Then they marched off the path slightly, until the mage had some privacy in the shrubbery, with Gabrion holding the rope a few yards away.

Though Dariak did indeed heed nature's call, he also made good use of his time. He hadn't swallowed since his last statement, and now he spat into the dirt, creating a tiny pool of mud. "*Jalicorith grienan*," he whispered quietly, curling his right hand like a corkscrew. Normally, this would produce a lubricating gel, but with the use of only one hand and being required to whisper, the mud barely congealed. He reached back and shoved as much of the mud up the left-hand glove as he could. He hoped it would stay moist a while longer. Since his hands were sweating inside the gloves anyway, it seemed a good prospect. The mud would help him pull his hands free if the moment arose. At least, he hoped it would.

The rope tugged on his neck, and he knew his time was up. He responded promptly and sauntered back to the horse. A few minutes later, he was fully bound again, and they were back on the road.

The journey was quiet, with only the chirping of birds and rustling of leaves competing for attention with the horse's hooves. Any other day and Gabrion would have lavished in the calmness of it all and the freshness of the afternoon air. And instead of an imprisoned mage, Mira would have been with him.

Although Gabrion was honestly troubled by the events in Savvron, maintaining an angry demeanor was exhausting.

He let his thoughts drift, relishing in the remembered scent of Mira's hair, the glow of her eyes, the grace in her step. She was everything he had ever wanted. The only thing he was grateful to the invaders for was that they had kidnapped her and not killed her. That was hardly a worthy concession, but it was the only glimmer of hope left to him.

Suddenly the mage wriggled back and forth to get Gabrion's attention. He looked over the mage's shoulder and saw an elderly woman huddled on the ground, with a gnarled branch beside her, and a weeping handmaiden trying to help the old woman rise.

"C'mon, m'ma, we gotta keep goin'," the girl said in exasperation. "'Tis only a bit farther."

The hunched woman rocked back and forth gently, nursing weary bones. "I cannae. Lemme rest a bit, lass."

Tears welled up in the girl's eyes. "Bu' nigh' will be 'ere soon. Then beasties. C'mon. Please!"

Gabrion slowed the horse down and noticed that the mage shook his head in warning. But he couldn't leave them there on their own. "Ho there, do you ladies need help?"

The young girl looked up with large eyes. "Oh, sir, please. It's me ma. He'p us!"

Gabrion hesitated for a moment and then made his decision. His father had cautioned him not to lose himself, and any other day he would have pitched in to assist them without delay. Hopping down from the horse, he walked over to them, seeing the mage shake his head again from the corner of his eye.

"What's wrong? What can I do?" Gabrion asked.

He didn't even see the girl draw her dagger, but there it was, pressed against his chest. "Your money, oaf."

Gabrion heard the mage heave an exasperated sigh through his gag.

"Your money," the girl yelled after his hesitation.

"Yes, now," added the hag, who didn't look so old now that he saw her up close.

Gabrion firmed his jaw and reached down for his money pouch, then rocked back on his feet and rolled over and away from the two women. He pounced and drew his sword swiftly, holding it before them. "I have no quarrel with you, ladies. Be off with you."

The girl, still brandishing the dagger, summoned more tears to her eyes, letting them drain sadly down her face. Gabrion felt completely awkward. It was hard to pull his gaze away from her eyes to focus on the dagger. Something compelled him to keep staring at those watery eyes.

He noticed movement in his periphery. The not-so-old hag was on her feet, moving in a strange cadence. It was a subtle type of dance, and he instinctively knew that although it wasn't true magic, it still had an effect on him. Something about the rhythmic movements was captivating in an odd way. He strained to fight against it, calling forth his need to save Mira to give him the strength of will he needed. At last, he broke free of the enchantment, and the woman muttered a curse.

His victory didn't last long, as suddenly they were joined by three men, each holding weapons of his own. The largest of them walked up to the mage, peering at him like he wasn't sure what it was.

"No, Bostian," warned Poltor. "That's no toy for you."

"Your lucky day," Bostian said to the mage before turning to Gabrion.

"But not yours," Poltor said to Gabrion. "Your belongings. Now. You don't stand a chance against us." He jerked his head toward the mage. "And it doesn't look like your 'companion' will be much help to you either."

"I'm on an important mission," Gabrion announced. "I'm taking this prisoner to the king. Don't interfere."

"We already have," Jafflin replied. He stepped up to Gabrion's sword and quickly snapped it out of his hand and examined it. "Cute blade. Not worth much though."

Shocked at the man's speed, Gabrion reached for the sword, but the man just laughed and backed away with it.

"See, now you're unarmed too," Poltor taunted. "It is time to end this."

"The odds are against you," the girl said.

"The odds have been against me all day," Gabrion said. His voice was calm, but even the rogues sensed a dark storm brewing within. "I'm not relying on odds anymore. Give me back my sword and go on your way."

"It's five to one," Bostian pointed out. "You can't really expect to beat us." For emphasis, he pounded his war hammer into his hand with a loud smack.

Gabrion brought his hand up to his face, as if to wipe his brow, but instead he stuck two fingers into his mouth and whistled sharply. Tumbler, the horse, knew what to do and reacted by biting the nearest person. Bostian screamed in agony, and the brawl was on.

Everyone was startled by the scream, and Gabrion was able to snatch his sword back and start attacking. He had no idea how he would defend against the rest of the bandits, but he didn't have much choice now. Jafflin's hands whirled around rapidly, and Gabrion had no hope of seeing where the man's weapon was. The apparent leader was suddenly nowhere to be seen, as if he had just vanished completely, but Gabrion knew he had to be around. The younger girl looked happier now that a fight was on in earnest, while the hag threw off her ragged shawl and picked up the gnarled branch at her feet.

There was only one option, really. Gabrion pounced for the horse, hoping to climb it and ride off before he was killed, but the horse was trampling about, trying to bite other foes. It knew the scents of Gabrion and the mage, so they were relatively safe from its attacks, but the thrashing beast was impossible to mount.

Dariak was jostled about fiercely as the horse rampaged, kicking its back legs out and then snapping its jaws forward. He immediately started tugging his left hand from the iron-and-leather glove, hoping the ensorcelled mud would give him enough leverage to be able to pull his hand out. He couldn't tell if the powerful thrusts of the horse under him were helpful or not, but his only goal now was to free himself.

Wild cackling filled the air as Heria went to work, leaping for Gabrion with her daggers. She jumped, dodged, spun, dipped, and leaped on her way to him, clearly intending to have as much sport as possible. Jafflin still had his arms in motion, but he knew not to interfere with the young girl when she was so excited.

Gabrion's arms whipped in all directions, blocking as many dagger thrusts as possible. Heria scored a few slashes against him, and he was reminded of battling the rogue that morning. He didn't want this to end the same way, but he didn't want to die either. He backed away and kicked at the dirt, trying to send something flying into the air but failing miserably. In a desperate effort, he turned and bolted toward a nearby tree, and his attacker roared in humor as she pelted after him.

Gabrion grabbed a small branch as he passed the tree and released it after pulling it back. The wood lashed out, and stray leaves scratched against the girl's face. Her hideous laughter turned into a groan of rage, and she dove through the air to impale him swiftly. But Gabrion had snagged a second branch, and he released it, smacking her in the midsection and knocking the air out of her.

He wasn't clear yet. Jafflin was on his way already, dodging left and right and keeping a wary eye for other branches the warrior might try to snap his way. Gabrion grabbed a fallen branch and wielded it in one hand and his sword in the other. He parried mostly with the branch, hoping some of its leaves would slow down the whirling blades of his foe. His eyes darted around for other assistance, but it looked like the rest of the fight would rely on his skill.

Back on the horse, the mage wrenched his hand and finally pulled it out of its harness. Bouncing painfully upon the horse, which had finished with the hammer-wielder and was now seeking another target, Dariak struggled to pull out of the leather straps holding his other hand in place. One kick of the horse's feet pushed the mage forward sharply, and the leather cord came free on its own. He quickly scrambled to release his legs, and then he launched himself from the raging horse to freedom.

But he wasn't free yet. The woman playing the old hag was upon him instantly. She knocked him around with her oversized branch, inflicting pain but not seriously damaging him yet. "Stop, stop, stop!" he called to her, burying his head under his arms and pulling off the second glove surreptitiously. "Listen to me!"

She pressed the end of her makeshift staff into his abdomen. "Why should I listen to you, mage?" she spat. "We may be thieves, but we're not scum like you."

"No?" he retorted. "What about your little dance moves? You think that's so different from magic, lady?"

Kitalla pressed the wood deeper into his stomach. "You tread a dangerous line, fool."

"Hear me quickly, then decide." It was hard to talk with the horse whinnying and thrashing around, but it also made good cover. His only hope was that he could appeal to her effectively and not be overheard by his amateur captor. "Follow us, and I promise you I can help you develop your skill into something more than just minor glamours."

"What? I have no intention of joining you. You try my patience," she added with an extra shove of her branch.

"Joining?" He pressed his hand to his chest in mock exasperation, secretly clutching for something sewn into his robe. "*Kathrahasslerad*," he muttered like a curse, shaking his head. "Don't be stupid. I said 'follow.' Trail behind us. This idiot thinks he is turning me in to the king. He doesn't know that he's taking me right where I need to go. Once I have what I seek, you'll see. I will be able to guide you to glory."

Her eyes narrowed sharply, but she didn't attack him further. "I can't possibly trust you."

He grinned. "True, but I can make *him* trust me with a little trickery. Help me up." He held out his hand. She hesitated for a moment, then took his hand.

Immediately, her arm pulled toward the ground. Dariak grabbed her other hand and then touched her feet as well.

"The Shield of Delminor works wonders, doesn't it?"

"You bastard!" she hissed.

The mage shook his head. "You'll see. I won't inflict much harm to your crew, but it will be enough to convince that fool to trust me. Then follow us to the castle. It will be worth it for you."

He dashed off, leaving her seething on the ground, unable to move. His arms whirled through the air, and arcane words tumbled from his lips, and suddenly each thrust of his hands released searing darts of fire. It was one of the only spells he could cast without spell components or deep preparation, and though it wasn't a strong spell, he knew it would be effective at any rate.

He followed the sounds of swords crashing together among the trees and found Gabrion in a poor position. If Dariak waited a little longer, his captor would be no more. But he needed the fool to get him through the castle gates and entering as a possible traveling companion was better than entering as a prisoner or a corpse.

He thrust out his hands and knocked Jafflin aside, allowing Gabrion to score a lucky hit on the man's thigh, which he followed up with a hearty kick. Jafflin crashed to the ground in agony. Gabrion wasted no time by trying to finish him off. He could tell that this crew outmatched him. He met the mage's eyes and nodded his thanks, then dashed back to the horse.

He whistled again, and the horse ceased its rampage and trotted over to him. Bostian had been destroyed by the horse's wild rampage, and Poltor had been toying with the beast to keep it busy while the rest of his crew dealt with the others. Gabrion shoved the mage belly first onto the saddle and then hopped up behind him. With a quick snap of the reins, they were off, putting as much distance between them and the rogues as the horse's stamina would allow.

After a time, the spell binding Kitalla faded away. She shrugged off an odd numbness that remained and then sought out the others to survey the damage. The carnage done to Bostian was horrible to behold. He looked nothing like the large fighter he had been. When Heria returned, she bent down and started examining the body's remains, but Kitalla turned away, unwilling to know what twisted ritual the girl was about to perform. She sought out Jafflin, who limped toward them, and helped him bandage his leg.

"I can't believe they got away," he complained. "Wasn't that mage a prisoner? Why help the guy out? People make no sense sometimes."

"I wonder," Kitalla muttered under her breath. Maybe the mage was telling the truth after all.

Poltor came over, also averting his gaze from Heria's bizarre behavior. "At least it wasn't a complete waste." He hoisted up the saddlebags. "Plenty of food in here. Once we deal with Bostian's remains, we'll feast tonight."

"You're so calm about his death," Kitalla said with heat.

"Death is part of our business, isn't it?" he answered coldly. "Haven't you killed your fair share?"

"He was our comrade," she persisted.

Poltor's eyes narrowed. "Leave it be, unless you wish to avenge his death. In that case, pursue that quest on your own."

They were few, but now Kitalla had options. She could continue on with the rogues and the comfort of the routine they had developed over the years. Or, under the guise of retribution, she could pursue the mage's offer and see how far it could take her. Avenging a companion's death was one of the few acceptable excuses to leave the group without Poltor's retaliation. However, it was risky. He might not ever take her back.

Twisted laughter came from Heria's direction. "So warm," she crooned. The others shivered, trying desperately not to imagine what the girl was doing.

Perhaps some time away from the group might not be a bad thing after all.

CHAPTER 4

The Sanctuary

TUMBLER RAN FROM the battle site at a solid pace for a while before slowing down. Gabrion held on to the mage's body with one hand and the reins with the other, clenching his thighs to remain seated on the horse. It was an awkward ride, but he needed them to be safely away before stopping to assess the damage that had been done. Once the horse reduced its pace, Gabrion decided it was time to stop. He tapped the reins, and the horse slowed to a canter then veered off the path into the cover of trees. They had cleared most of the forest in the mad scramble, but they still had a ways to go before reaching the castle.

Gabrion dismounted from the horse. It felt like he had landed on fiery spikes that lanced all the way up his body. He had been wounded several times during the day, from the dagger strike to his abdomen that morning to all the knife and sword cuts that had followed. He had lost a lot of blood, and his body started to rebel.

Moaning, the mage pushed himself from the horse's back, rubbing his belly tenderly and clutching his injured arm. "At least we got away," he said sourly. "But I don't think my stomach will ever work right again."

"We had to go," Gabrion said softly, closing his eyes and trying to calm the stabbing sensations coursing through him. "Thank you for your help back there. I was done for, otherwise."

The mage looked at the young warrior and shrugged. "How do you know I wasn't aiming for you?"

The question caught him off guard, and he laughed. "I guess I don't. But thank you anyway." He looked at the mage for a moment, then admitted, "You saved my life there, and I don't even know your name. I'm Gabrion."

The mage saw no benefit to lying. "Dariak." The mage eyed the numerous bloodstains on Gabrion's tunic and pants. "You're hurt rather badly."

"I don't suppose you know how to dress a wound?" Gabrion asked as he tethered the horse to one tree, then sank beside another. "I don't know if I'll be able to bandage myself. I may need a healer at any rate."

Dariak shook his head. "It's crazy that you're actually asking me for help. Aren't you still taking me to the king? 'To the dungeons'?" he repeated mockingly.

Gabrion pulled off his tunic to look at his more severe wounds. "I guess nothing's making sense right now." He tapped on his abdomen, where a thin trickle of blood was oozing. "Ouch. I can't exactly stop you from running away right now, can I? But could you at least grab me the medical supplies before you go?"

Shaking his head, Dariak went to the horse, then called out, "What supplies?"

Gabrion looked over and only then realized that the saddlebags had been stolen. "Damned bandits." A wave of frustration washed over him, and he growled in anger, clenching his fists around his tunic and pounding it into the ground. "What else could go wrong today?"

"Calm yourself before you rip any of your wounds wider," Dariak warned, eyeing Gabrion's torso. He considered his options. The warrior was definitely in no condition to stop him from doing whatever he wanted to do. It would be a simple thing to take the horse and finish the journey to the castle. But then what? He wouldn't be accepted into the king's residence without the warrior. Not in Kallisor, anyway. He knew he would most likely land in the stockade if he went into the heart of the kingdom unguarded. But was this young fool really the key to getting him in? It didn't matter much, because it was the only option currently open to him. Finding another fighter to bring him to the castle would probably end up with him dying first, and the band of thieves they had run into wouldn't likely assist his planned infiltration either. No, it was better to fix up this one who owed him a debt now and follow this through.

"Rest here a little bit," Dariak said after a few minutes of consideration. "I'll scour for some herbs and then help patch you up."

"I… don't really know what to say. Thanks." Gabrion started to feel hazy and only focused on the moments happening right then, not tying anything back to the morning, when this mage had been shooting fireballs at his hometown. Concentrating on the present was all he had. The haziness soon became dizziness, and his head started swimming around.

When Dariak returned from his search, he saw that Gabrion had passed out completely. He was slumped over in an awkward position, which wouldn't help any of his wounds heal properly. Part of him really couldn't believe he was about to patch this warrior up, but he reminded himself of his true mission, clutching his hand to the object sewn into a chest pouch of his robe. Dariak started by turning Gabrion's body and then laying him flat on the ground. He paused for a moment to admire the musculature of Gabrion's chest, then laughed at himself for getting distracted. This certainly wasn't the time for those thoughts.

He cleaned the wounds the best he could, using a few drops of water from a small canteen concealed beneath his robes. He scoffed again at his captor's lack of thoroughness. Didn't everyone know that mages kept all sorts of items within their robes? The warrior's ignorance had, of course, been helpful, yet he couldn't stop himself from complaining about the lack of standards anyway. He dabbed the more serious wounds with scraps from Gabrion's tunic and then applied various leaves of herbs before wrapping larger bandages around Gabrion's midsection and diagonally across his chest.

Dariak investigated further and found a gash on Gabrion's right calf, and so he dressed that wound as well. The warrior had been right; he would need an actual healer if he was going to survive all this. Or at least, someone a little more knowledgeable in the healing arts. All mages began their studies in herbology, especially since herbs were common spell components. Dariak had paid only the slightest attention in healing classes, focusing more on offensive spells and his one key defensive spell, but that one hadn't required much study, thanks to his father.

Gabrion moaned and roused himself as Dariak finished securing the other bandages and checking his own wounds. "You're pretty badly hurt," Dariak commented. "If you don't get treatment soon, you're not going to make it."

"Mira," Gabrion breathed. "No, I have to make it."

"Mira," Dariak mouthed sarcastically, rolling his eyes. "Listen, I know you're weak right now, but we've got to ride if you're going to get the healing you need. The horse seems all perked up again, now that it's eaten half the grass around here. So come on. Up, up." With that, he tugged Gabrion's arm, and the warrior acquiesced to the tugging.

It took time to mount the horse and get on their way. The sun was sinking low in the sky, but Dariak decided that they needed to make as much progress as possible each day if they were going to reach the healers in time to help Gabrion. The horse tracked the land much better than Dariak could, leaping over divots and branches and finding a quick path through the trees.

After another hour or so of hurried travel, Dariak guided the horse off the forest path once again and set up a makeshift camp. There was no threat of rain, thankfully, and the night was warm enough that they only needed enough fire to cook a meal. Despite his wounds, Gabrion managed to hunt down two rabbitats, which Dariak prepared and cooked.

They ate, slept, and woke early to continue the pace.

It wasn't an easy journey for either of them. Gabrion was mostly silent the whole way, which suited Dariak just fine. He didn't want to get too familiar with the fighter anyway, nor did he want to divulge any of his true plan accidentally. It was easy enough maintaining the ruse of being concerned, especially when Gabrion's face paled and he looked on the verge of simply expiring. But the warrior held to his own quest and found the will to keep going. Dariak found himself admiring the sheer bullheadedness of it.

It took four days of hard travel before the town loomed closer. The two men and the horse were thoroughly exhausted, but Dariak decided he wanted a decent meal before the night was done, and if they hurried, they could make it to the castle town before night fell in earnest. He nudged the horse sharply, and Tumbler bucked at first, but then opened to the wind and sprinted well.

Lights sparkled in the distance, and Dariak knew from the maps he had studied that they were well en route to Kaison, the town surrounding the castle of Kallisor. It was the second largest town in the kingdom, succeeded only by Pindington to the east, but that was only if the population of the castle itself was ignored. Within the palace lived a number of nobles and servants, plus the upper echelon of soldiers and healers, who each had their own barracks.

Dariak had also heard of the king's museum within the castle grounds, where relics of ages past were kept on arrogant display. He intended to pay the museum a visit upon his arrival, but doing so undetected would be the real challenge. He grinned to himself for his foresight in helping this warrior out of the forest. This plan could actually work.

As they neared the town gates, Gabrion slumped forward and pressed deeply against Dariak. The horse too grew weary, but the mage just straightened his back to keep from being crushed and tightened the reins, telling Tumbler that the run wasn't over yet. He knew a horse could keep up a fast pace for only so long, but reaching town was a greater priority to him than the health of a horse he wouldn't see much of soon.

The gates of Kaison were open, even in the dark of night. The guards at the post barely acknowledged their entrance, which made Dariak smile. Gabrion's initial goal had been to come here to warn everyone of the attack on Savvron and the possible start of yet another war between the nations, but without that warning, these guards were lax. That suited Dariak just fine, for if they had paid any attention at all, they would have noticed his mage robes, the wounds on the warrior, and that they rode one of the king's own warhorses. Grinning once again at the fact that the energies were with him, Dariak steered the horse inside and sought out the town sanctuary.

The best part of entering the town at night was that they didn't have to deal with throngs of villagers roaming aimlessly. The few passersby were able to guide them easily enough to the cathedral, and, when they arrived, Dariak handed the horse over to the stable hand and pulled a very groggy Gabrion from the saddle. He guided the warrior through the gates and looked around.

Like most churches of old, the cathedral was enormous for its purpose. The ceilings were extremely high and carved with intricate detail; they were a marvel to see. The countless hours of sculpting must have taken lifetimes by teams of artists. Those artists would probably be sad today, though, for the churches no longer served the same purpose they once did.

In the distant past, people the world over worshiped the gods, making offerings, praying devoutly, partaking in detailed rituals, and singing angelic hymns. Priests channeled the words of the gods and shared them with the populace. Clerics drew the energies from the patron gods of healing to cleanse and repair wounds, to eliminate diseases, and to produce some genuine miracles, according to all the legends. But the daily prayers of the people weren't ever truly fulfilled. Sure, the priests would claim that the great, almighty lords and ladies worked their miracles in their own ways, granting blessings that would give honest benefit to a soul rather than seeking to appease material desires, but after a time these words felt empty.

It had been about five centuries ago, Dariak recalled, when a massive famine spread throughout the entire continent, extending even beyond accursed Kallisor and beloved Hathreneir. People everywhere fell to their knees in supplication, begging for forgiveness from the gods who felt this need to punish them. The priests were hard-pressed to explain what the people needed to do to repent for their sins, for many didn't know themselves. When even the good souls were suffering, it was difficult to imagine they needed to do more than they were doing.

When prayers did little to alleviate the terrible circumstances, others rose up and fought back against the famine. They worked to till the soil, to find other means of growing food. And in becoming better farmers, they were able to push back and save the people from utter starvation. Some devout worshipers praised the gods for this lesson, saying that by giving the people a difficult challenge, the gods forced them to grow stronger, but those believers were few. Most people turned away from the gods entirely, trusting their own skills, and eventually the tenets of religion collapsed.

The greatest fear in that regard related to the clerics and their healing powers. What would become of their gifts if they turned from the gods? The clerics held on to the religious routines for a long time, continuing to channel the infinite power of the gods to bestow upon the people in need. However, skepticism abounded, for shunning the gods had not brought forth a dreadful wrath. Soon, the clerics ended their prayers but found that if they continued to reach for the energies and perform the rituals, they could still bring healing to the people.

As the years passed, others started to recognize the energy around them as well. Where once that energy was blindly associated with the will of the gods or god-granted talents, it soon became known as magic. Anyone who could feel the tug of the energy around them could manipulate it in some form or other. Those who did not feel the energy could often be trained through the old rites of the church, not in prayer but in the chanting and detailed movements. Eventually, magic became a common force in the land, but those who dabbled too strongly were alienated and often hunted down. Fear kept most people from exploring too deeply into the magical arts, and because of that, magical energy became somewhat diffuse in the land, and now it was extremely rare for anyone to gain too much power.

Hathreneir was unique in that it accepted magic users with welcome arms and even had a few magic schools scattered throughout its borders. Sure, there were restrictions for magic's use, but a mage could walk around much more freely than he or she could in other countries, Kallisor in particular. Yet as Dariak dragged Gabrion along the aisles, up to the altar where the healers awaited, he understood that even Kallisorians accepted magic when it suited them.

"The hour is late, brothers," said one of the healers. "I am Elgris. I bid you welcome."

"Greetings, Elgris. I am Dariak, and this is Gabrion. As you can see, he is in need of your services, and I am in need of rest."

The healer looked Gabrion over, and his brow creased in deep concern. "It seems you come none too soon, Brother Dariak." He waved his hand behind him, and two other healers approached and took Gabrion away. "You seem to need some attention as well. Please, do follow, and we will assess the damage, the repairs needed, and the cost for those repairs."

"Er, cost?" Dariak hesitated.

The healer frowned. "Do you think the work we do should go without compensation? Or that the material we use in our work is donated freely by merchants?"

"Of course," the mage acceded.

The healer guided Dariak through a doorway into a nearby room where the other two healers had set Gabrion upon an examination table and stripped off the majority of his clothes and bandages. Elgris quickly inspected Gabrion's wounds, then turned to Dariak.

"He will need quite a bit of attention, now that I look more closely." He gave Dariak a cursory scan as well. "It seems your wounds will hold well enough until morning. We shall focus on him first, then, if you do not mind." His tone made it clear to Dariak that his opinion didn't factor in. "Let me show you to sleeping quarters, and we will stabilize him for now while we determine what needs to be done."

Dariak grabbed the money pouch from Gabrion's things and then followed the healer down another corridor to a room lined with beds, some of which were occupied. After Elgris pointed out key exits, the location of the baths, and a small pantry with food, Dariak decided he was tired enough to fall asleep on the spot. He could tend to his other needs in the morning.

Chapter 5

Seeking Payment

Dariak awoke a few hours later, well rested but feeling sore. The sword wound he had received during the battle in Savvron throbbed terribly, and he hoped Elgris would find time to give his arm some attention. He also had numerous scrapes and bruises from the afternoon ambush with the bandits. No one had roused him, so he assumed Gabrion was well enough, and since there was no immediate pressure to get moving, he took his time about starting his day. Elgris had pointed out the baths, and so he ventured there first and soaked in luxury for nearly an hour before grabbing some food from the pantry.

At last, Dariak returned to the main foyer and sought out the chief healer on duty. "Good morrow," he said politely, remembering that a form of payment would be requested today.

"Greetings, Brother Dariak," said a vibrantly red-haired woman in a white robe. "You seem recovered from your late journey."

He pointedly turned his head to the bandage on his arm. "Mostly, yes, thank you." She simply smiled, then pointed to the door across the way. "Your friend is through there, if you wish to see him. Brother Elgris will attend to you both shortly."

Whether he wanted to see his "friend" or not, he understood her dismissal and went through the door. He walked to where Gabrion had been taken the night before, but Gabrion had been moved, so he poked his head into various doors until he found him.

Dariak had seen his share of magic rituals, but he wasn't ready for what he saw when he entered the room. Except for a small cloth about his waist, Gabrion lay naked on a sturdy bed that was waist-high off the floor. Fourteen chunks of rose quartz were placed on his body, accented with thin needles sticking out in numerous places, some of which pulsed with his heartbeat. Incense burned softly in the corners of the room and created a soft aroma that instantly made Dariak feel calmer. Sunlight came in through a window on the wall, was focused through a lens, then bounced around the room on mirrors, ending on a large, clear quartz poised over Gabrion's heart. The refracted light left rainbows all over Gabrion's torso. Four healers made continuous sweeping motions with their bodies, lunging forward on their legs and swooshing their arms ahead of them, all the while mumbling an incantation in perfect unison. They worked in a circle, sweeping energy down Gabrion's left side and up the right. Dariak could feel the pull and push of energy like a small tide on a beach.

He examined Gabrion's body more closely and saw that herbs lay over the deeper wounds and pockets of energy hovered over them, which suggested to Dariak that healers had earlier focused their attention on those locations, leaving behind residual forces that would help Gabrion's body to mend. A translucent jelly coated minor cuts and abrasions in order to prevent infection. The warrior's breathing was calm and very relaxed, and Dariak wondered if they had drugged him to keep him asleep so his body could focus on healing. Looking around, he saw many other implements in the room had been recently put to use, but he didn't have time to ponder them.

A hand grasped his shoulder, and he jumped, startled. "As you can see, your friend will be fine," Elgris said softly. "Come. Let us not disturb their work." He guided Dariak to another room, which looked more like an office than anything else. Bookcases lined the walls, lamps were aplenty, and a large, ornate desk spanned nearly the entire width of the room. Elgris took the chair behind the desk, motioning Dariak to sit across from him.

"You came to us late last night in rather a state," Elgris started. "You sought healing but had no thought to payment for that service. I don't know myself if healing is free in Hathreneir, but here you pay for services rendered."

Dariak struggled to keep his composure. Apparently, the healer wasn't as oblivious as the gate guards had been.

"You have had a good night's sleep, a bath, and food. Your travel companion is receiving the best care we can give. Yet we have neglected to tend to your own wounds, as I'm sure you have noticed."

The mage breathed deeply but didn't otherwise respond. Elgris had just referred to Gabrion as a "travel companion," not "friend." He wondered how much the healer suspected. Considering they had come in on a warhorse...

"These services are not free, Brother. They must be compensated for. And I am assuming that you do not have a store of funds with which to reimburse our efforts." He held Dariak's gaze for a moment. "The wound in your arm will indeed need serious attention; I can tell that much from what I have already seen and from the errant pulsing I feel from it even now. Your other hurts seem as if they will mend on their own. But though I wish I could do all this work out of the goodness of my soul, it cannot be."

Growing impatient, Dariak wished he would get on with it.

Elgris seemed to understand. "The fee to treat your wounds will need to be paid up front. I can tell you now that it will cost approximately seventy-five copper pieces." He smiled as he watched the shock appear on Dariak's face. "Your companion's wounds will be far greater, at no less than five hundred coppers."

It took a moment, but then Dariak laughed aloud and slammed his fist on the table. "It doesn't matter what his wounds will cost. I'll pay you to fix me. He can tend to his own bill."

It was the wrong thing to say. Anger lit the healer's cheeks a deep crimson, and his eyes hardened. "Perhaps you misunderstand, mage. Your presence here in Kallisor is barely tolerated. You are not simply free to go. Your ailments will not be mended until both sets of treatment are paid in full."

Dariak did not appreciate the threat in the words. He took Gabrion's money pouch and upended it on the desk, counting out the coins. "Sixty-three," he muttered. "Not even close. But you assumed that, and you have something else in mind."

Elgris sat back in his chair. "You're not a fool, at least. Yes, indeed, I have a means for you to compensate us." He opened a drawer nearby and pulled out a parchment. "We have need of supplies. Take back your coppers and procure as many of these materials as you can. We will buy them from you."

Dariak took the list and scanned it quickly. "These… These are some expensive things."

"It might take you several trips," Elgris agreed. "But I fear your options are limited."

"In other words, if I don't comply, you'll set the guards on me. How long do I have to complete this task?"

"Let us just say that the sooner you return with what we need, the less likely you are to die of infection from that wound. Since you are a mage, we expect that you will recognize quality materials, particularly among the spell components."

Elgris arranged his features into the most benign expression he could muster. "Have you any other questions, dear Brother?"

Dariak scooped the coins into the pouch. "Just one. Where do I get a map of the town?"

A short time later, the mage was wearing a spare healer's robe over his own. Elgris was right; he wouldn't survive long roaming around a town where mages were hated outright. He had chosen a set that was slightly longer than his own, which meant that it dragged in the dirt, but he didn't care. He didn't plan to run this ruse for long. As he meandered through the streets, seeking a local herbalist, he wondered if the healer's robe would allow him entry into the castle on his own. It was a long shot, but he decided he would at least give it a try at some point.

The pain in his arm was a good motivator, however. Part of him wanted to abandon all of his alternate plans and finish this shopping list so he could be properly healed. If only he had paid more attention to those first lessons, he might not be in this mess. But Dariak decided that the energies had been with him so far and this was just another aspect of the journey. He was so caught up in his musing he walked right past the herbalist and had to turn back to the quaint little shop.

A bell jingled over the door, and immediately he was blasted by too much incense. Sage, lavender, cinnamon, and apple did not work well together, and his nose kept wrinkling in disgust. He checked his list after wiping his eyes and sought out the wares he needed. He quickly found a potted aloe plant, but when he examined it, there were diseased spots all over the leaves. The others were no better. Scratching that, he turned to the other herbs, but everything in the store was of poor quality. It wasn't a wonder, then, that he was sent to find these items even though this shack was so close to the sanctuary. Ignoring the proprietor when she wafted in from the back room to greet him, Dariak turned and stormed out.

He had much better luck finding pottery a few stores down. He needed nine small pots with lids and four large bowls for washing. Unfortunately, it would require a sum of nearly two hundred copper pieces to claim all that at once. He tried reasoning with the potter, saying he could take the merchandise and return with the coppers, but the owner likened that to thievery with a promissory note. Dariak said it was worth a try, then spent a good part of the hour negotiating a solid price for the entire set. He took five of the small pots for his sixty-three coppers, assuring the owner that he would be back for the rest of it within a few hours' time.

Dariak returned to the sanctuary with the first purchase and was directed to a storeroom, where an acolyte tended the wares. Dariak received twenty pieces of copper per pot, giving him thirty-seven pieces in profit. He didn't say anything but cherished his luck and returned to the potter for the rest of the merchandise, crossing those items off his list.

Not every transaction was so smooth, and he discovered that the profit he had earned came mostly from his own bartering skills. Yet even when he couldn't negotiate a good deal, there were still a few extra coins in the payout from the sanctuary. On one of his trips back to the healers, Brenwel, in the storeroom, told him to skip ahead down the list to the bread and fruit, because they were running low and needed them for the morrow. Dariak bargained marvelously for peaches and cherries, but the bread was an altogether different issue.

Because it was late in the day, most of the bakeries in the area had run low on bread. He needed fifteen large loaves, and it wasn't looking good. With two bakeries left to try, he ended up at Stonewell's Dough-It-Yourself Bakery. He was skeptical about the name alone, but the throbbing in his arm propelled him to get this task done, and perhaps he could earn a little boon from Elgris for doing well this day.

"Greetings, friend," said a jolly, fat fellow at the far end of the main room. Dariak strolled right up to him and placed his order for fifteen loaves of bread, but the proprietor laughed.

"Look around, son. Do you see any loaves of bread?"

Dariak turned. He saw barrels of ingredients all over the place but no bread. "No," he said, crestfallen, turning for the door.

"No?" called the owner. "Well, I see lots of loaves! Why, in just one hour, you could have twenty loaves in hand, freshly baked and ready to eat!"

"Well, okay, then I need fifteen of them, please."

The owner, Stonewell, buried his face in his hands and shook with laughter. "Come hither, newcomer," he said, bringing Dariak by the arm to a barrel of flour near the front of the store. Beside the barrel, on a podium, was a thick cookbook. The man flipped it open to a basic bread recipe and pointed to it jovially. "Just follow the steps! Everything you need to make your bread is right here, including all the equipment. If you need fifteen loaves, just multiply the amount of ingredients by fifteen." His smile was infectious, but the prospect of suddenly having to do his own baking made Dariak uncertain.

"I think I should try Kettleburn's first. This seems a bit much for me."

Stonewell winked and patted Dariak on the shoulder. "I can save you time and tell you that you won't find fifteen loaves there if you go, unless you like them very well done—they don't call it Kettleburn's for nothing—but if you insist on checking, go right ahead. We'll still be open when you return. I'll fire up the oven right now, so it's super hot and waiting for you."

The man was correct on all counts, Dariak found. Kettleburn's seemed to be known for overcooking all their pastries. Everything had dark, crispy edges, and the loaves were very brittle to the touch. He could have gotten the required number of loaves, but he knew that they wouldn't fetch full price back at the sanctuary, if they were accepted at all.

When Dariak returned to Stonewell's, he saw another customer at the register with a bag of bread. Dariak couldn't help but notice that he was a good-looking young man, early twenties, with a commanding presence about him. Dariak's heartbeat picked up a little.

Stonewell was in the process of commending the young man. "You always do great work, Randler. I do love it when you're in town; this place always smells fantastic with your creations. Cranberries, raisins, and cinnamon today? You should give up singing and set up a shop, I tell you!"

"Stonewell, you old codger." Randler laughed. "You never do cease with the compliments."

Dariak practically melted with the quality of the man's voice. He took his time wandering up to the counter, enjoying simply watching Randler move as he fetched his money and paid for his goods. He turned, caught Dariak's eye, and smiled, glancing up and down appraisingly.

"New to town?" Randler asked.

"Just in last night," he said.

"Then you haven't seen my show!" Randler beamed. He reached into a pocket and pulled out a small parchment. "Four nights a week, including tonight. Don't miss it. Promise me?" He winked a cinnamon-colored eye that closely matched the hue of his neatly kempt shoulder-length hair.

Dariak took the small flyer with the details of the show and smiled back. "Sounds like a good time."

Randler stepped forward and whispered into his ear. "I can assure you a good time."

Feeling Randler's breath on his ear made Dariak shudder delightedly. "Wouldn't miss it."

The minstrel extended his hand and introduced himself properly, and Dariak responded in kind. He then watched Randler walk across the room and out the door, turning back to Dariak to wink one last time.

Stonewell was careful not to interrupt the moment for fear of losing this new customer. But once Randler was gone and a few quiet moments had passed, he came around the counter and followed Dariak's gaze. "Fine fellow, that one. Best singer I've ever heard. He seems to know the best ballads in the land, or maybe he just flashes them up with good words and music. Excellent baker to boot. Travels a lot; thought you should know." He then turned to face Dariak. "Now, about your bread. I've taken the liberty of figuring out the amounts of ingredients you'll need. Fifteen, right? I'll give you a hand; it's a lot of dough, but you're doing the bulk of the work."

Looking at the flyer one last time, Dariak suddenly felt that baking tons of bread seemed like it might be lots of fun.

CHAPTER 6

The Minstrel

THE LOAVES CAME out perfectly. Dariak wasn't too surprised, as following a cooking recipe was less demanding than most magic rituals, plus Stonewell had facilitated the process. Dariak gathered the bread while it was scorching hot and practically sprinted back to the sanctuary. He traded the bread with Brenwel for a lot more money than he expected—he must have really done a good job with it—and then he sought Elgris.

"Incredible that you've finished your entire task already!" Elgris mocked when he saw Dariak, knowing full well that he couldn't possibly have finished.

The mage showed him the list and drew the healer's attention to all the items that were already completed. "Of course not, but I've gone this far. And because I've done so much, I would like at least a poultice for my arm to slow down the infection. Surely that isn't too much of a request."

With a low hum of disapproval, Elgris considered the mage for a moment, then acquiesced. "Very well, but this should not deter you from completing this mission."

Dariak had committed himself to this task, and he saw no reason to waste time affirming as much. He just nodded and smiled expectantly, waiting for the promised poultice.

When Elgris saw the odd eagerness in Dariak's eyes, he altered his offer. "The poultice will cost you twenty-five coppers. Up front, of course."

Dariak kept himself from rolling his eyes or sighing, and he quietly dipped into the money pouch and procured the funds. Not long later, his wound was dressed with the poultice and he was rummaging through the supply cabinets for a cleaner healer's robe. He wasn't about to go off to see Randler in the same robe he had trekked about in the dirt all day. There wasn't time to wash his own cloak, but he donned it under the white robe again, after crushing some herbs and brushing them against the fabric to help deaden the scent. After transferring the bulk of his coins to a hidden pouch inside the mage robe, leaving only about fifteen pieces in the belt pouch, Dariak was off to the show. He needed a distraction from his injury, and with the shops closed, he couldn't continue bartering anyway.

He didn't want to get there too early, so all the preparation delays worked in his favor. He had already passed the tavern on his way back with the bread, so he knew precisely where to go. Dariak certainly had a lighter bounce in his step than he had felt for months. It was a good feeling.

Soon he arrived at the Rooster's Bane, chuckling at the sign of a rooster in full screech with a rising sun in the distance and bar patrons blissfully passed out from a night of frivolity. He pushed the doors open and saw that a few patrons had already arrived and were deep into their ales and food. The scent of a rich stew was quite exquisite, and he was eager to try some.

Looking around, he spotted the stage, so he worked his way closer to it, but not up to the front. He chose to sit a little closer than halfway and off toward the right side of the tavern. There weren't any chairs in his exact line of sight of the stage, and it was, happily, a shorter couple sitting in front of him anyway.

Within minutes, there were performers on the stage, tossing oversized rings back and forth, then scimitars, then flaming torches. Dariak paid them hardly any attention at all. His eyes were on the lookout for Randler and for a bar matron. The crowd thickened as he waited, and he made eye contact with one of the servers, who smiled politely and gestured that she would be over momentarily. Dariak settled deeply in his chair, happy to kick back for the first time in a while.

He was very surprised when the matron came to his table with food and drink. "Master Randler had this prepared for you," she said by way of greeting, and she placed before him a well-seared duck with potatoes and vegetables, a small bowl of dipping sauce, a plate of Randler's bread, and a tall glass of fine white wine. He wasn't much of a wine drinker, but one sip of the golden treasure made him want to gulp down the whole thing and ask for more.

While he ate the food, he grinned to himself. Randler had told them he would be coming and had a special meal ready for him. He'd even included some of the bread he'd made himself that day—and Stonewell was right; it was perfect.

They had barely even spoken, but here he was, like a little kid finding out the sweets store had free samples.

While he ate his delicious meal, his eyes darted around the room, wondering when his acquaintance would enter. Onstage, the jugglers had tidied their things and a comedian was rattling off a series of inane jokes, getting the crowd into a good humor.

"So the whole town came running out," the comedian called above the din. "Everyone was armed with something. Kids had their slings. Men had swords. Women had knives. My mother had her pot roast." He paused for laughter. "There they were, running right toward the ogre, charging on ahead like this beast had eaten their kids or something. Honestly, who'd eat something so dirty and wriggly?" Another pause. "Oh, that reminds me, don't order the sausage here." On cue, all the bar matrons turned and made a face at him. "So anyway, things got serious, and I could see they were going in for the kill. So it was time for me to step in at last. 'Hey, everyone,' I said, waving my hands like this. 'Don't you all know what time it is? Yeah, it's dawn.' So then I pointed at the ogre. 'That's not an ogre,' I told them. 'She just rolled out of bed; that's my wife!'"

Some of the patrons pounded their hands on the table, hysterically laughing, while others sighed and shook their heads. More than one wife glared angrily at an overzealous husband, and those looks made Dariak chuckle the most.

All of a sudden, the mage felt his heart start to race again. He looked around expectantly, and then from the wings came Randler, all decked out in proper minstrel garb, complete with a lute. His crisp brown hair spiraled down the left side of his head and swept just over his right shoulder. He was covered head to toe in a shimmery silk that reminded Dariak of a calm lake with just a few ripples disturbing the surface. His shoes were a vibrant purple, and upon his head was a poufy hat with wide green, violet, and azure stripes. If Dariak wasn't completely enamored with Randler's beautiful face, he probably would have laughed at the whole ensemble. Yet he understood that people expected a bard to wear something garish; plus, it probably helped a performer grab an audience's attention.

Unlike the other performances, the crowd fell almost completely silent with Randler's entrance. He hadn't even done anything, and yet they were completely his. Dariak was in awe. He wondered, if his pulse kept quickening, would he explode or just pass out? Bar matrons went around with orders, and a second glass of wine appeared at Dariak's table. He was slightly buzzed from the first one, so he took his time with the second. Cradling the glass in his hands, he wondered idly how its smoothness would compare to Randler's cheek.

A single note was released into the air. It held strong for a few seconds, then wavered and fell silent, followed promptly by a second note. This carried on a while, and Dariak wondered how a few simple notes could hold sway over the entire audience. But he didn't dwell on it for long, as the notes started coming faster, overlapping and creating pictures in his head of a wide, open field with a warm breeze blowing and flowers swaying gently. It was such a soothing melody that it could only belong to such a scene. And then something made it all the more beautiful. Randler began to sing:

> *Days long ago, when this tale unfolds, we see the pain of the lost.*
> *They were friends, companions to the end.*
> *Their destinies intertwined.*
> *Raising their hands to the woes of the world, they reached out to shine.*
>
> *Sword held high, it is where he showed his strength.*
> *Spells to bind, with her passion at her side.*
> *Joined in kind, the will to reach any length.*
> *Foes would die, for they simply could not hide.*
>
> *Victory was a futile goal to seek, for what's to do when war's done?*
> *These marvels took the world in hand.*
> *Each with a view of their own.*
> *She yearned for peace and a quiet home. Yet he prepared for more war.*
>
> *Sword held high, it is where he knew his heart.*
> *Spells to bind, with protection held in mind.*
> *Joined in kind, but drifting now apart.*
> *Foes would die, if there were any left to find.*

Years passed them by, as their dreams went away, lost upon destiny.
They lost their hearts in misery,
For they forgot why they'd fought:
To build a world where they could rejoice, to live out their lives with love.

Sword held high, it's the only skill he knew.
Spells to bind, fighting up against the tide.
Joined in kind, but the happy times were few.
Foes would die, even if they were inside.

They spent their lives living side by side, but not together at all.
King Kallisor always feared other wars,
While Lady Hathreneir seemed so meek.
Where once they were one and whole, now they were just incomplete.

Sword held high, where he lost himself in war.
Spells to bind, nourish all and one another.
Joined in kind, only up along their border.
Foes would die, even if it meant each other.

Now here we are, the children of these foes, who once were lovers of all.
Do we stay apart and hold to our own?
Or do we honor the love at the start?
Embrace the chance that we could be as they were once meant to be.

Sword held high, so let us put it away.
Spells to bind, just to heal us when we fall.
Joined in kind, let this be a special day.
Foes would die, but there are no more at all.

And by these words, let us not be the Forgotten Tribe any longer.

Dariak didn't consider himself an emotional sort, but something about this tale tugged at him. The nations of Kallisor and Hathreneir had been at war for ages, with the War of the Colossus twenty years ago marking a deep gash across their history. Dariak was only two years old when his father went off to fight at his king's side, never to return again from that one battle. He grew up hearing of the treachery of Kallisor during that fight and vowed to continue his father's work in his absence. But now, one mere song moved him to wonder about his motivation.

It took a few minutes for him to come back to the room from his thoughts. Randler was on to a new song, livelier this time, all about a child's toy that refracted light into different colors—"Crash, crash, crash, and the pieces fall away!"—but when the pieces were put back together, they became clear again—"Come together, and light another day!" It was whimsical and merry, and several patrons pounded their fists or tapped their feet with the tempo.

But voices carried over the din, and Dariak couldn't help focusing on them. "You're sure?" said one voice. "How do you know?"

"Definitely," replied a voice so gruff it was hard to understand. "Knew it afore, but now I'm certain. This thing's resonatin' somethin' fierce."

Dariak looked around for the sources of the voices, but quick glances made it difficult to spot exactly who was talking. No one near him seemed to be doing more than singing along with the tune.

"If it's him, then we hafta grab 'im afore he gets away, no?"

"Definitely," repeated the gruff voice. "And while he's unawares would be best too."

Dariak tensed, looking around desperately for attack. He knew he was a target in this town, being a mage. Plus, he had spent the entire day walking the streets in full view, albeit in disguise, not that merely wearing a healer's robe was much of a disguise if anyone somehow recognized his face. He nonchalantly lifted one side of his robe and withdrew the dagger fastened to his thigh. At least he would defend himself when the attack happened. He considered prepping a few spells, but the attack seemed imminent, and he wasn't particularly focused enough to control blasts of fire at the moment.

"So?" said the first voice a few moments later. "We have to get that back before it's missed, don't we?"

"Definitely," the other said. It seemed to be his favorite word. "Okay, brace yerself."

Dariak squinted and looked around for movement, but in a tavern full of people bopping to a peppy tune, movement was too easy to find. Several people were on their feet, serving drinks, heading to the middens, or adding dance moves to the song. He tried not to be overly suspicious in his search, because his attackers thought they had the element of surprise. When the attack happened, he realized that they actually did.

A group of four lithe men in leather jerkins popped suddenly into view, short swords and daggers poised for a quick and vicious assault. But they weren't headed for Dariak at all. The mage realized belatedly that Randler was the target. The minstrel didn't lose a beat in the song as the brigands darted toward the stage, but Dariak was relieved to notice that Randler had seen them coming.

The minstrel's stance changed dramatically as he swept his lute to the floor and lifted a mace that had been cleverly concealed inside the lute's case. He swung it around, alerting the attackers that he knew how to use it.

Most of the crowd screamed cheers at this turn of events, delighted they were now getting an impromptu performance on top of the other entertainment. Dariak used the cheer as a diversion and leaped from his seat toward the nearest swordsman, crashing him to the ground easily from behind. The move was met with raucous applause from the other patrons. He ignored them and scrambled to his feet to intercept another attacker, but he was less fortunate the second time.

Randler kept his mace in motion and parried the dagger thrusts of one rogue while another hopped onstage to approach from the side. Randler kicked his stool forcefully, and it flew into the man's face, knocking him to the ground. The bard seemed to be enjoying himself, though, and from the glimpses Dariak could see, it looked like Randler was trying to keep the beat going.

A short sword swung dangerously close to Dariak's face, but he pulled back in time to avoid the blow. Falling backward, he crashed a table to the ground, and the women sitting there yelled in protest. Dariak rolled to the side, bumping into a large man's legs and sending him to the floor. Soon, the patrons realized that this wasn't an act at all, and the screams of joy turned quickly to those of hysteria, followed by frantic shuffling and pushing toward the exit.

From the floor, Dariak hurled a tankard at the swordsman, shattering it against the man's skull and knocking him out cold. The first fighter he had felled was up again, his attention focused fully on Dariak now. The mage had to dodge three chairs and parts of a table before he could even get on his feet. As the fighter stalked closer, Dariak wished he had enacted his fire spell after all. Just then, the energies played with him, and a huge fireball lit the back end of the tavern.

Everyone turned to look.

Randler had a tankard of ale in one hand and a stage torch in the other. While Dariak looked, Randler took another sip of the alcohol and spewed it through the torch, turning it into a fiery blaze. The rogue he was fending off fell to the ground, thrashing in pain and trying to douse the many fires that lit his clothes.

Dariak used the distraction to his advantage, kicking his attacker forcefully in a rather sensitive area and following it up by bringing the hilt of his dagger down on the back of the man's head, rendering him senseless. With two men out cold and one writhing on the floor in fiery agony, the fourth fighter lost his nerve and bolted for help. Once he was outside the tavern, Dariak heard a sharp whistle cutting through the air in a staccato pattern. Help would be on the way.

Randler had the same conclusion. "Dariak!" he called out, rushing over to the mage and grabbing him in a strong embrace. "Not quite the entertainment I had intended," he added with a grin.

"Are you hurt?"

"No, I'm fine. Listen, there isn't time," the bard said, focusing his eyes on Dariak. "You need to get out of here before others arrive. You have to get to safety."

"What about you? I'll help."

"These guys have been after me for a while, Dariak. I know how to lose them, and it will be faster alone."

The mage pulled away sharply. "Go then."

Randler grabbed Dariak's shoulder. "No, listen first. I took something long ago, and they've been hunting me for it. I won't let them have it." He turned Dariak around to face him again. "You either."

"What?"

"I've been looking for companion pieces to the one I found, and I know you have one."

Dariak instinctively clutched the object sewn into the chest pocket of his mage robes, then cursed himself for reacting that way. "What do you know?"

"You felt it resonate, I'm sure. I knew you had it. They had one tonight, which was how they tracked me so quickly this time."

With his hand on his chest, Dariak could indeed feel the object pulsating. And all this time, he had thought his heart was only racing because of Randler. "I'm seeking them too," he admitted, not knowing what else to say.

Shouts echoed outside. They didn't have much time. "We came here for the same reason, didn't we? So stay, Dariak, and claim that piece."

"But—"

"There's no time. I'm heading north, once I lose their trail. Please," Randler asked, his eyes wide with sincerity, "take care of yourself and don't let them hurt you."

"Randler—!"

The tavern door crashed inward, and the minstrel grabbed Dariak and kissed him deeply before turning and darting up to the stage to grab his belongings, then bolting out the rear exit, leaving Dariak highly confused.

The guardsmen who came in only saw the last steps of the minstrel as he escaped through the back; thus they paid no heed to Dariak. He waited until the soldiers all left, and then he followed, barely peering his head out the door, wondering if Randler would be all right. The guards had already fled and turned down an alley and were lost to him. Utterly baffled, exhausted, and at a loss, Dariak made his way cautiously back to the sanctuary, where he sought a bed and stared at the ceiling all night long, wondering what was going on.

CHAPTER 7

Bartering

ANSWERS DIDN'T COME to him in the few hours of sleep he managed. Dariak awoke and rubbed his eyes, frustrated with the turn of events. He tried convincing himself that it was for the best, that Randler would have been a distraction from his quest, but then it seemed as if the minstrel knew of his mission, which wasn't possible. He hadn't told anyone what he was planning.

A patron of the sanctuary walked in and sat on another bed along the row and started sighing loudly, as if inviting Dariak to ask what was wrong. The mage took it as his cue to leave. He gathered his belongings and washed up quickly in the baths, then decided that he would finish off that list of errands so he could have his arm properly cured.

After his bath, he looked over the list, compared the destinations to the map, and counted the coins he had for all the shopping. Two things interested him. First, the healers were indeed paying him well, as he now had over three hundred copper pieces in his pouch from yesterday's errands alone. He hadn't expected to turn such a profit on this venture. Second, the rest of the items he needed would take him to shops near the castle gates. He wondered if he would be able to pass the guard station in the healer's robe. It would certainly reduce complications.

Dariak walked by Gabrion's room on the way out, noting that the warrior was still unconscious. The healers had to be keeping him sedated until Dariak's tasks were finished, because, on the whole, the wounds themselves hadn't been that severe, and the fighter had a strong will to keep going.

As he meandered through the streets to the candle maker, Dariak's mind wandered back to the events in the tavern. Randler seemed so calm about being hunted. Plus, he had known about Dariak's secret treasure and his mission to collect more of them. Dariak absently clutched the object at his chest and then scolded himself for doing so. He had learned something interesting, at least. It would resonate when close to others of its kind. That would be helpful, if he paid closer attention.

His thoughts then turned to Randler himself. Had Dariak really felt the fluttering of his heart when the bard was near, or was it just the resonance? But then he admonished himself. Randler was graceful, handsome, talented, apparently athletic, and—even more important than all that—an excellent kisser. Dariak's smile lasted all the way to the candle shop.

Because of all the funds he had accrued so far, Dariak was able to clear this order in one visit. The healers had requested a full crate of candles, though of various kinds, and once it was all put together, the shopkeeper tallied up a cost of four hundred and fifteen coppers. After some finagling, Dariak negotiated the price down by a hundred, plus the use of a trolley to get the crate back to the cathedral. Just a few more items remained.

After dropping the trolley off at the candle shop, Dariak made his way to the castle gate. He had to control himself as the gates loomed closer, for they were enormous. They opened like standard double doors but were made of wrought iron bars crisscrossing in an intricate pattern, not simply in chessboard style. They were easily the height of five men and had to weigh more than four horses fully decked out in battle armor, with riders to boot. Further examination revealed a chain-and-pulley system that clearly made opening and closing the gates possible. On either side of the entrance was a guard tower, carved of bright sandstone with the sheen of marble.

Dariak took a deep breath and decided to stroll right through, as the gates were currently open to the people. It was time to see if the healer's robe would be enough to get him inside.

Two steps away from the gate, a tall lance shot down and blocked his path. "Ho there. Where are you headed?"

He wasn't about to announce that he wanted to visit the museum to abscond with one of the artifacts, so instead he said, "The royal gardens call to me today, and I have need of nectar for the healers, which is available here."

"Oddly enough," the guard said, "I don't hear the gardens calling anybody. At least not without a proper admittance pass or invitation." He scrutinized Dariak for a moment. "Haven't seen you around before. New in town, son?"

"I have been working with the healers for some time," he lied. "My work has often kept me secluded."

"I see. So you should have known that you would need permission from the royal family in order to visit the gardens."

Dariak pulled a frustrated face. "But Master Elgris told me to come here for the nectar. What am I to do?"

Elgris was apparently a name the guard knew, for his stance shifted and he raised the lance. "I certainly have no reason to cross the will of the healer," said the guard, and Dariak struggled to keep the hope that this would work off his face. "So there is only one thing I can do."

"Thank you." Dariak bowed his head, taking a step forward.

The guard caught him with a powerful, gauntleted hand.

"The only thing I can do, son, is send you on your way."

"What? I don't understand. The nectar—"

Now the guard laughed. "You need a better ruse than that. Or at least, more current information. Master Elgris was already here this morning to visit His Majesty, and he made no comment of sending along an underling."

"But—"

"And Master Elgris had a perfectly clear writ of passage, so if he needed you to gather anything here, surely he would have seen to hand you one." A knock sounded on the guard tower door from the inside. "Oh, just a moment," he said to Dariak as he turned and took a sheet of parchment from someone inside. With a booming laugh, he turned the parchment around to show Dariak.

What Dariak saw was a very good likeness of himself, sketched out in coal.

"So here is what I suggest, friend," the guard said amiably. "Go run along and mind your own business, and never mind trying to sneak into the castle. If you do intend to sneak in, I would recommend you do so within the next two hours, because by then all the guards will have seen this portrait, and you can imagine that it'll be hard for you to pass through after that, eh?"

A bell rang over the tower, and the guard belted out another hearty laugh. "No, not two hours. Less now, I fear. That signal means someone tried to infiltrate the castle, so everyone will be on alert, and the captains will now head straight here to view this image of you."

Dariak shook his head in amazement at the efficiency of these tactics. They were simultaneously marvelous and infuriating. He let his face show his emotion this time but simply said, "All I wanted was to see the royal gardens before I died."

"Then you had better petition for entrance, which will take a few months. Or you could try hurrying it along right now and find the gardens quickly while the guard hunts you down. You'll die as soon as you're caught, of course, but you might catch that glimpse you're looking for." He was enjoying himself entirely too much. "Now if there's nothing else, move along."

So he did, carrying himself with an air of injustice about being treated so unfairly. Once he was away from the castle entrance, he dropped the farce and stormed his way to the town mystic, who sold all sorts of crystals and such. He sat outside for a few moments trying to calm himself before heading in, fearing he would lash out and ruin his chances at striking a good bargain.

Two other customers were inside, browsing aimlessly, talking about buying a piece of malachite so they could put it in their pockets and find money wherever they went. Dariak hated such stories, because they were far from the truth. He understood that crystals were suitable for channeling energy; he could feel that directly from his training. But people didn't realize that, in essence, they would need the ability to call for money on their own, and the malachite would just facilitate the process, like the healers needed rose quartz to help magnify their powers. The stones alone would do nothing more than amplify any excess healing energy nearby.

He did concede, though, that if the right person focused his or her thoughts on a gemstone, it was possible to re-create the semblance of an effect, but that was rare without real training. He thumbed through one of the books on crystals and, as expected, saw descriptions of the inherent healing powers but none of the warnings that they wouldn't work for most people. Still, it was a business, he guessed.

Shopping here was actually better than shopping in most places, because he could feel the flaws in the crystals and test how they would carry energy before he selected a piece. The proprietor offered several substandard chunks of mineral, and Dariak looked at her scornfully, shaking his head and pointing at other objects instead. She soon realized that he was a practitioner of sorts, and her demeanor changed completely. She became much more formal and less mystical, pulling out choice specimens for Dariak to examine. He checked his list and looked at her wares, nodding to himself. He could finish everything off here.

It took over two hours for him to select the gemstones and minerals the healers needed. He added to that the requested varieties of incense and a few dried herbs. Seeing the range of items he was selecting, the owner's demeanor changed again. She turned friendly, without being phony, and offered a bargain price at the start for the whole set, making negotiations all but unnecessary. Dariak didn't even argue the price, but he managed to get a polished cut of tiger's-eye thrown in for free. That one went into his pocket, for the colors reminded him of Randler.

With all of the items accounted for and exchanged with Brenwel in the storeroom, Dariak rubbed his arm in anticipation of meeting with Elgris for healing. He needed to wait a couple of hours before the healer was available, and Dariak used the time to gather his things and prepare to leave. After removing the healer's robe, he re-folded it as tightly as possible and stuffed it in the lining of his mage robe, thinking he might need it sometime. He grabbed a bite of food and, with an hour left before his meeting with Elgris, went for a long bath.

"Well, well, look at you," drawled a voice sometime later as Dariak soaked in the bath.

He looked around and saw a woman slinking out of the shadows with a very practiced and symmetrical motion. It was the rogue he had met in the forest ambush.

"I decided to follow you after all, and here you are, relaxing your life away."

Dariak started to speak but found that he couldn't. She was moving rhythmically, with subtle hand and arm gestures as she went.

"See, you recognized my talent, and I think that makes you too dangerous to live."

He was able to move, just not speak, so he gestured to his arm, then around him, finishing off with a shrug.

Kitalla dropped the dance with a sigh. "What? You look like a chicken flapping around in a trough."

Dariak cleared his throat. "We were injured, so we came here first. We weren't supposed to still be here."

"You had said you were looking for something? That with it you could help make me stronger?" She bent down and rested on her heels, crossing her arms over her knees and looking at him with a strange expression.

"Yes. It is in the castle. I need that oaf to get me in."

She shook with laughter, and it tinkled like glass. "Yes, your little attempt this morning was rather amusing. Trying to walk right into the most highly regarded castle in all the land? You're either brazen or a fool. Maybe both."

"You? Where were you?"

She laughed again. "It's my forte to be where I want to be without others knowing it unless I want them to. So, mage, what is it you're looking for?"

The time for his meeting with Elgris was approaching.

He ignored her presence for the moment and pulled himself out of the tub, which led to a raunchy whistle of approval by the rogue, who chuckled again as he rolled his eyes.

"I never thought you mage types would keep in shape, but I guess I've been wrong before."

"I'm no swordsman," he admitted. "But traveling around does force you to keep in some condition, don't you think?"

"Hmm," she debated. "Lots of merchants carry a belly about their waists, but then I guess they do often ride wagons from place to place." Her amused grin left her face, and she asked her question again: "Now, what are you looking for?"

Settling his robe in place and securing a rope around his midsection, Dariak decided to offer a hint. "I need something from the museum."

"Tell me what and I'll bring it to you," she said politely, with a hint of a smile.

It was Dariak's turn to laugh. "Sure, I'll tell you, you'll take it, then you'll keep it, thinking you can make use of it on your own."

Her smirk fell from her face; he had evidently guessed her intent. "You're going to need my help anyway, especially now that they know what you look like." She looked over her shoulder and groaned. "Someone's coming. I guess it's time for your little meeting. We'll continue this later." She strode off with an exaggerated swagger that blurred her appearance, making her difficult to follow. Dariak had to admit that she had an interesting grasp of the energies, and he was genuinely curious if he could help her channel offensive magic through her motions. Certainly, his father would have tried to investigate that further.

An acolyte fetched him for his meeting with Elgris, and off he went to finally have the gash in his arm cleaned of infection and sealed properly. They walked through a series of corridors and ended up in the office where Elgris had taken him before. The oversized table was littered with parchments and other paraphernalia that Dariak ignored.

Sitting with a cup of tea, Elgris listened to Brenwel report the status of the wares as Dariak took a seat.

"I see," Elgris said at the end of Brenwel's account. "Brother Dariak, it seems you have done rather well for us on your excursion."

"Thank you," he said, trying to remain patient even though he was feeling edgy after his encounter with Kitalla.

"So next would be the matter of your healing." Elgris grinned. "Once we have your payment, of course."

"My what?" Dariak shouted. "I did what you asked! I ran all of your little errands and brought back better quality things than you already have. I have given you your payment!" His face was flushed, and he shook with anger.

Elgris leaned back in his chair and touched his fingers together sagely. "I do recall discussing Brother Gabrion's treatment as requiring five hundred coppers and yours needing seventy-five, though I can already sense that you will need more than what I first estimated, so let us say an even hundred."

It took all of Dariak's composure not to start heaving spells at the healer. "What kind of place is this? You told me that if I completed your little shopping list that would cover the costs of the healing."

Elgris's voice raised considerably as he shouted back, "And I do believe you were given those funds for the completion of your tasks, so that you would earn the ability to pay for our services!"

"I—" he began, but then his arm shot him a stab of pain, as if reminding him of the real goal here. Defeated, Dariak pulled out the money pouch and spilled six hundred coppers across the table, keeping the rest for himself.

It took a few moments for the color of Elgris's face to return to normal. He looked over at the storeroom keeper. "Brother Brenwel, if you would." He then gestured aimlessly in front of him.

Dariak was seething, glaring at Elgris for this turn of events. He ignored Brenwel's approach, assuming he was going to take the money, but instead he threw a rope around Dariak and bound him tightly to the chair.

"Your wounds will be healed, mage," Elgris said, standing slowly. "We cannot send you to His Majesty oozing disease, now can we?"

"The— What? I don't understand."

"Your companion had much to say this afternoon about your attack on his village. To me, this is a warning sign of the next cycle of war. He will escort you to the king as he originally intended. And though our healing will therefore be in vain—as you will undoubtedly be executed—as I said, we cannot send you diseased and bleeding to His Majesty."

Brenwel had finished with the ropes around the chair and had started tying more effective knots around the mage's feet. He then forced Dariak's hands into fists and coiled rope around them.

"You swine," Dariak hissed. "Making me do all that work for you and now this?"

Elgris glowered at him in contempt. "I had suspected the order of events already. But then a messenger arrived from the castle gates, informing me of your attempted entrance under my name. Then speaking with Brother Gabrion set the other pieces into place. No, I feel we are fully justified in this course of action."

"Underhanded. Deceitful." Dariak growled. "Everything ever said in the stories is true about you Kallisorians."

"Be careful, mage," Elgris warned, his voice laden with venom. "Continue along these lines and your injuries just might overcome you before you can reach the king at all, if you get my meaning."

"More cunning and lies, killing me off because you're angry." Dariak spat on the ground, not aiming for either man, just needing to vent his disgust. "Very well, do what you will."

Brenwel shoved a gag in his mouth and placed a sack over his head. The chair tilted back, and he was dragged from the room, after which he felt the energies swirling around him as healers worked to fix his wounds. An herbal tea was shoved down his throat, and because it was laced with sleeping draft, it wasn't long before he was lost in darkness.

CHAPTER 8

Gabrion's Awakening

THE YOUNG WARRIOR faced himself in a mirror, boring into his own brown eyes, looking for answers. The day before, the master healer had awoken Gabrion, demanding to know of his injuries and the duo's arrival at the cathedral doors. He had recounted the mage's involvement in the attack on his village and then the mage's confusing cooperation on the journey through the forest, including the spells he had tossed at Gabrion's attacker to help him with his fight. And with Gabrion's wounds being so thorough, Dariak had ridden the horse hard to get them to Kaison and Gabrion to the healer.

"Then you trust your companion?" Elgris had asked at the end of Gabrion's story.

"I… don't really know. He confuses me."

Elgris had then informed Gabrion of Dariak's attempted entrance into the castle under false pretenses and his suspicions that the mage had an ulterior motive for being so helpful. The pieces had fallen into place, and Gabrion reclaimed his conviction to bring Dariak to justice before the king. His beloved Mira needed him, and he needed the king's help.

Fully healed and feeling strong, Gabrion turned away from the mirror and checked his belongings. His money pouch had been returned to him, with the same sixty-three copper pieces that had been there before, as well as a writ of passage into the castle sanctum written in Elgris's sharp penmanship.

The mage was awake, though mildly sedated. Elgris had assured Gabrion that the king would need to speak to the infiltrator, and keeping him knocked out would not support Gabrion's call to arms. The warrior spoke no words as he clutched Dariak's shoulder and dragged him from the cathedral, fully gagged and bound.

Two healers helped hoist the mage onto the warhorse, Tumbler, for it was important to return the beast to the king. Gabrion mounted up behind the mage to keep him from exciting the horse and making it bolt away. The two healers walked astride Tumbler, and off they went toward the castle.

It was a misty morning, the day after Dariak's wounds had been healed. Elgris had sent word ahead to the king of the arrival of these guests. As Gabrion rode through Kaison with the healers in tow, some of the villagers looked on at the procession in disgust. A few items were thrown at Dariak in anger, for someone bound in such a fashion, being paraded through the street, could only be the foulest of criminals. They reacted to a rage they did not understand, and soon the horse was followed by a small horde of travelers who now wanted to be part of the justice that would rid the world of one more thief, or murderer, or spy, or mage, whatever he was.

Gabrion was furious with the mage's ruse, and part of him wanted to be in the crowd, tossing things up anonymously. But he also owed his life to this man, both for the help against the forest rogues and the mad flight here. At the same time, he wouldn't have been in either predicament if not for the attack on his hometown in the first place. Yet now a crowd was angry with the mage for unknown reasons, and it felt unjust. Gabrion's tumbling emotions frustrated him greatly. He focused his thoughts on Mira, keeping Tumbler in line, and nothing else.

When they reached the castle gates, Gabrion showed the writ of passage and guided the horse through. The healers left them to their business, and one throaty voice laughed aloud and called out to the mage.

"Didn't take you long to find your way back here, did it?" It was the castle guard who had stopped Dariak yesterday. "Too bad you didn't try sneaking in; we would have enjoyed the chase!" His cackling laughter followed them in through the entryway.

Gabrion looked around at the massive walls in sheer awe. Though he had been away from home before, he had never set foot in Kaison, nor had he seen a place so grand. The walls of stone were enormously high, and he tried to look around without seeming like a lost child. Crenellations ran across each level of the castle, fully decorated with beautiful floral carvings. He could see a few shadows in those cutouts keeping watch on the courtyard below.

The yard itself was wide, with small structures scattered about. Some of these served as guard stations; others were gazebos for passersby. Gabrion could hear fountains on either side and thought it would be a beautiful place for a candlelit dinner with his love. Wondrously carved signposts were strategically placed so as not to distract from the visual balance or grandeur of the area.

Tumbler huffed a deep, rattling sigh, as if bored from it all. The horse also pulled to the right, toward the stable, and the motion distracted Gabrion from his thoughts, bringing him back to the moment. A stable boy jogged over and seized the reins from the warrior.

"Master Andron's horse," he said. "How fares the lord master?"

Gabrion wasn't sure how much to tell the lad, so he just frowned and shook his head sadly, lowering his eyes.

"That's a terrible shame, but I guess it explains why you're riding Tumbler. With a prisoner, no less. Come on, off now. You go in over there." He pointed needlessly to a grand door marking the entrance to the castle proper.

Gabrion dismounted, then pulled Dariak down. The mage's leg hit the saddle, and he fell in a heap on the ground instead of landing gracefully. Gabrion pulled him up and escorted him toward the opulent gold-and-crystal doors.

As they approached, the doors gracefully and silently swung open, held by two young pages in glimmering silk. They nodded their heads to the travelers while a guardsman walked up and took Dariak's arm to escort him gruffly behind Gabrion.

The young warrior stepped ahead through a line of marble pillars, trying not to fidget, and approached another set of doors. These were softly padded in red velvet, and he would gladly have pulled one door down to sleep on if someone challenged him; they looked so comfortable. These doors also opened automatically when he approached, and another set of pages nodded him through.

Apparently, the king had received Elgris's letter with serious concern. Twenty soldiers lined the walls of the throne room, four of whom wore special leather helmets and jerkins over their armor that looked to Gabrion as if they could repel any damage, including that from spells.

The king was covered in a vibrant bloodred cape that covered a shining plate of armor. The king's advisor stood nearby, as did several other court officials. It looked to Gabrion to be a massive trial, with a panel of witnesses who were in the king's employ. He approached the king and knelt down on one knee, bending his head in homage.

"Rise, champion of Kallisor," called the king in a somewhat high yet commanding voice. Gabrion did so and looked into a tired set of hazel eyes that scrutinized him deeply. The king's hair was a shiny, dark brown, and even though he was rather young, Gabrion could see threads of gray laced within.

He wondered idly if they were natural or for effect.

"Your Majesty, King Kallion," he replied.

"We received word from Master Elgris of the Kaison Sanctuary. What have you to say on matters?"

Gabrion recounted the events that led him there, cutting out superfluous details and sticking as close to the facts as possible.

"Indeed?" the king muttered when Gabrion was finished. "It is well that your first priority was to come inform us of these tidings. A lesser man would have pursued his lady, and not only would he and she be lost, but so would the great kingdom of Kallisor."

"Thank you, Your Majesty."

"Let us have a look at this foe of our land. And do allow him to speak."

The guard holding Dariak removed the gag but also unsheathed a dagger and pressed it into the mage's spine, clearly alerting him not to speak out of turn or act rashly in any way.

"I see. A mage from Hathreneir," the king said in disgust. "What have you to say of these crimes?"

Dariak's hands were bound tightly in fists, and he could feel his knuckles pulsing in agitation. "Sire, forgive me," he said. He lowered his head, knowing his only hope was to somehow appease the king. If only his hands had been released, he could have reached up to his chest in a feigned salute and summoned the Shield of Delminor. But realistically, it couldn't help him against so many foes. "I did knowingly enter this land to help a troop attack one of the border towns."

"Clearly," the king returned, a note of anger coming to his voice. "Perhaps I must ask questions of you more succinctly? What was the motivation behind your attack?"

"Sire, I merely needed money for food and experience to broaden my skills. I was hired by the group and joined them for that one foray so I could eat."

The king stood up. He cast an imposing figure as his cape swept outward and his armor gleamed in the sunlight beaming down from a cutout in the ceiling. "Tell me *why* this group infiltrated our lands. Was it a declaration of war?"

Dariak's answer had the benefit of absolute truth, and he didn't need to hide any words or dodge any meanings. "I don't know why the attack was ordered. But a hostage was taken from the village, so I would assume it had to be an act of war. Why else pillage the town? There was nothing impressive about it from what I saw."

Gabrion tensed at this assessment of his hometown but otherwise controlled himself. The guard pressed the dagger more deeply into Dariak's back, but he didn't cry out or flinch. He had actually expected more of a reaction.

The king paused his interrogation for a moment and started pacing. "How do we know for certain that this girl was taken as a hostage by the royal family of Hathreneir? How would we know that she wasn't simply abducted by one of the mercenaries to be—for lack of a better term—used?"

"No!" Gabrion gasped, horrified at the very thought.

"Silence!" the king demanded, and Gabrion struggled to calm himself. The king turned to the mage. "What are your thoughts on the matter?"

When Dariak hesitated, the dagger was pushed more tightly against his spine, and the pain made it hard to think clearly. It was bad enough he still had a mild sedative in him. He couldn't consider the pros and cons of honesty, nor could he fabricate any alternate story. The dagger dug deeper still, and he fell to his knees in agony, blurting out what he knew while straining to keep in his own quest.

"It was one of His Majesty's soldiers who brought the band together, and it was he who led the charge into your kingdom. I came to his call at the very last. I don't know his true intent, but I don't doubt he was of the royal guard."

The king stared at Dariak intensely for a few moments, then decided he believed the tale. "Curses," he spat, then nodded for the guard to bring the mage back to his feet. "You speak of the royal guard," the king started, and Dariak suspected what was to come. "You have slain one of my own, have you not?"

"I regret that I did," Dariak admitted. He truly did regret killing the soldier, because he was certain that it would now mean his own death, as if being Hathren and a mage weren't reasons enough for the grumpy king.

"That is a grievous crime against this kingdom, yet before I assign your punishment, I would hear again from the warrior who brought you here." He turned to Gabrion. "This mage infiltrated your village, slew your mentor and many people of your village, facilitated the loss of your lady, and attempted illegal entry into this castle. Yet you spared his life." The king's gaze turned cold. "How do I know you are not in league with him?"

Gabrion felt the floor drop away from him, and his mouth fell agape at the accusation. "Your Majesty!" he stammered.

"How do I *know*?" the king screamed, punctuating each word with anger. "You could easily both be spies from Hathreneir, sent to spark a revolt. Perhaps you are working together to incite this war for your own gains. Perhaps you wish to trick me into casting the first blow, marking us as the aggressors to your kingdom? I ask again, warrior, *how do I know*?"

Gabrion cast around for anything to stabilize himself before he spoke. No one was moving except for the king, whose chest heaved with his rage. The whole place seemed unreal to Gabrion. He lowered himself down to his knee again in homage to the king, not sure what he could say that would sway this irate master.

"Your silence says much."

"A—Andron, sire," Gabrion tossed out. "He said my training was going well. He said he was recommending my promotion, Your Majesty." He didn't know what else to say. "Wasn't I supposed to bring him here?"

The king remained quiet, waiting to hear more, but Gabrion, shaken by the king's attitude, couldn't find any more words. He looked up, agape, from the floor, completely lost. The king wasn't satisfied. He waved his hand out to the side, and one of the guards approached from the edge of the room. A blade was pressed into Gabrion's hand. The guard gave him a shove urging him to stand upright.

"This mage is clearly an enemy of our kingdom and must be dealt with as such. Show your loyalty to us and prove that you are not in league with him. Carry out his sentence now," decreed the king.

The guard holding Dariak turned him to face Gabrion while the warrior looked down at the jeweled dagger in his hand. It was such a pretty object; it was a cruel irony that it should be used for anything violent. It was obvious what he was meant to do. Trembling, he raised the knife until the sharp tip touched Dariak's heart. One thrust would show his liege that he was not in cahoots with the mage.

He looked into Dariak's deep-blue eyes and saw a firm resolve there. Even the mage knew what was coming, and he wasn't shying away from it. Gabrion swallowed hard and held the blade in place, but pushing it through didn't seem possible. The mage was responsible for so much, and Gabrion needed to continue on to pursue Mira, but killing the mage in cold blood didn't sit well with him. It wasn't why he was on this quest.

He lowered the blade. "I can't."

"Take them both away!" the king bellowed. "Order a public execution of these traitors. We will remind the citizens of their proper duty in the face of such as these!"

CHAPTER 9

Cold Stone

A GROUP OF soldiers roughly escorted Dariak and Gabrion from the throne room. Gabrion's sword was taken immediately from his side, but he was in such shock it wouldn't have mattered anyway. They were pushed and shoved down various corridors, up a flight of stairs, then down two others. They turned left, right, went down more stairs, and eventually Dariak was so lost he didn't think he would ever find a way out, even if he had a chance to look. He guessed it was more demoralizing to let the prisoners see they had no way out, rather than to blindfold them and escort them to the dungeon directly.

The final corridor was easily a couple of flights underground. The air was heavy and dank, and the stone walls were coarse and moldy. Crevasses lined the way with pools of oil, every other one lit with fire. The only other breaks in the walls were the cells themselves, plus an occasional guard station. Large iron bars ran floor to ceiling, only a handspan apart, with supportive crossbeams that prevented the bars from bending wider. Many of the cells held prisoners of various sorts, but only a few prisoners were alert enough to pay any heed to the newcomers. Most, in fact, pulled back from the passersby, as if afraid they were being summoned for execution. Only one older man thought it was highly amusing that more criminals were coming to a new home. His wheezing cackles echoed hauntingly through the dungeon.

The group pushed ahead to the end, where the hallway ballooned outward into sleeping quarters for the guards. Dariak's sedative had almost completely worn off, and he strained to focus on the room, in case there was anything of use there. He could see eight cots neatly arranged, each with a small footlocker. To the left was what he assumed were relief quarters, which probably included a bathtub of sorts. He could see three closet doors along the back wall, one of which was slightly ajar, revealing foodstuffs. It seemed that a number of the prison guards were forced to dwell here. He wondered if it was a punishment of its own for them. Off to the right was a heavily locked door, and Dariak assumed that it contained confiscated wares or weapons and armor for the guards.

Also in the room were four other guards, whose grim faces lit with the arrival of new prisoners. The burliest among them cast appraising looks over the two of them, and Dariak preferred not knowing what he was actually appraising. Two of the others pulled Dariak aside while the burly man and the fourth guard tended to Gabrion.

Having handed over the charges with instructions, the king's soldiers returned to the light of day.

One of the guards wrapped his strong hands around Dariak's throat, holding him steady while his partner disrobed the mage entirely, leaving only the ropes that kept his hands in fists. "Mages, mages, ever so clever," she snarled as she pulled the healer's robe from within the mage robe. "No spell components for you within your cell, I'm afraid. And no chances your friend has things you can use either," she added, nodding her head toward Gabrion, who was being similarly undressed.

The two were escorted back through the hallway past a few cells. Large keys jangled as one of the wardens opened a cell, where Gabrion crumpled in a defeated heap. Across from him and one cell down, a second door was opened, and Dariak was shoved inside, sprawling on the cold stone floor. As the bars clanked shut, he pushed himself up and eyed the jailer angrily.

She had seen that look before; she merely laughed, then pointed above the cell door. "See that there?" She drew a circle in the air to emphasize the large crystal dome that was set in the stone. "You may think it's there so you get some light in your cell, but these doors don't keep much out, you see. No, that there is a magic resonator. Try even the simplest spell, magey, and we'll know it. If that happens, we cut out your tongue and cut off your fingers, no questions asked. But do feel free to work yourself out of your hand bindings. You might need your hands for things in there." She chuckled, jerking her chin to the chamber pot in the back of the cell.

"It's cold in here," he complained. "What if I get sick, being all uncovered like this?"

"Aw," she said, affecting concern. "You needn't worry overmuch. It won't take but two or three days for your execution to be arranged and all that. It's not likely you'll die before then."

She turned to go, then stepped back for a moment. "Oh, and if you need anything, deary, just holler. We've all gotten good at ignoring the inmates."

As she passed by Gabrion's cage, she called out, "Hey, fighter friend, don't just lie there all curled over like that; your back will get a nasty crick in it. Healers don't come down here much, you know." Her piercing laughter echoed down the hall and started the old man laughing again, wheezing sharply.

Dariak gritted his teeth and started with the only task he could, freeing his hands. They had been bound this way for a day now, and his fingers needed release. He sat on the freezing cold floor, knees up so he could rest his hands against them, and began pulling and tugging and chewing with his teeth.

"You," said a solemn voice not too far away. "It's all your fault. Everything."

Dariak had expected to hear a little more rage, but the words were about right. "No, not everything is my fault."

"If you hadn't come to my village, none of this would be happening." Gabrion's voice was heavy and broken.

Dariak left his bindings alone for a moment and shook his head. "You're an idiot if you really think so. It isn't as if I was the only one in your village, or the one who orchestrated the attack. I just happened to be there with them."

That perked up the warrior. "Don't pretend you don't have a hand in this!" His voice rose.

Dariak sighed. "Sadly, my hands are a little busy right now." And he went back to biting at them.

"Stop with your silly quips, mage."

"Oh, 'mage' is it now? Are you upset with me, or are you more upset that you didn't kill me?"

Gabrion was silent for a few moments.

"The real problem is that this kingdom is full of crazies." Dariak snorted.

"Be silent!" the warrior yelled, earning a similar call from the guards.

"Fine, be angry, but you really ought to think about it." He tugged one rope free and stopped biting in order to rest his teeth. "I mean, you were being trained by one of the king's soldiers, right? And then your village was attacked and the soldier was killed. You go to the king to tell him about the attack, and he thinks you're working with me, of all things." He sighed dramatically, just for fun. "After all the years of deceit from this kingdom, even the king himself doesn't recognize truth anymore."

"Do *not* speak ill of His Majesty!" Gabrion responded automatically.

Dariak laughed. "I am sure he will be thrilled that you're defending him after he so casually tossed you in here with me." Dariak gasped expectantly. "Maybe he'll even pardon you!"

He could actually hear Gabrion seething from across the way. He wondered if it was worth truly enraging him to see if he could break himself out of the iron bars. Dariak snickered quietly, wondering if a rush of adrenaline would count as using magic. He looked up to the clear circle in the plinth. Could it indeed sense the use of magic? It could as easily be a lie, but he assumed others would have tested it, and if it wasn't a magic indicator, then they probably would have stripped his body of its fingers and tongue upon arrival, as the only real precaution that would guarantee safety. He shuddered at the thought.

Gabrion wasn't responsive to other taunts at the moment, so Dariak continued gnawing on his bindings. He gazed around the sparse room and understood that it was a well-crafted dungeon. He couldn't even detect a seam between the walls and the floor. It was as if the whole place had been poured into some magnificent mold. The iron bars had even been a planned part of the construction, based on how they were mounted. The poles went right up through the top and down through the bottom without so much as a crack in the stone. And though each iron bar was a separate piece, the crossbars holding them together were solidly welded in place.

It must have cost a fortune to create this dungeon.

A while later, footsteps echoed down the hallway. Dariak pressed his head against the bars, trying to see who was coming. A leather-helmeted guardsman strode purposefully by his cell and didn't pay him any heed. After a few moments with the wardens, the guard passed back and went to a cell a few doors down from Dariak. When the cell door opened, pitiful whining echoed into the hallway, accompanied by malicious laughter and the cracking of a whip. The prisoner was withdrawn from the cell, begging for mercy, wailing constantly in desperate fear as he was escorted from the dungeon. Once he was gone, only the old man's cackling remained.

"Oh, I do so wish I could see it," the old man lisped between spouts of laughter.

"See what?" Dariak asked.

"Punishment, of course." He wheezed again. "Sad, though. It wasn't even his time to go yet, but I think your arrival pushed up his execution. Too many prisoners in one place is never a good thing, is it? Ah, but what I wouldn't give to see a revolt."

"Didn't you just say you wanted to see the punishment?" Dariak was mildly amused by the old man he couldn't see down the hall.

"Punishment. Revolt. A little fluffy squirret. A sneaky lupino. There isn't much to see down here, sonny. I'll take any of it, sure I will." He slapped his knee and started his wheezing laughter again.

Dariak managed to eat through another rope and unwind part of it, which was a huge relief. He could already feel some circulation returning to his fingers. He appreciated the puzzle of trying to untie the ropes with the fewest cuts, for it appeared this would be his only real source of entertainment.

* * *

Hours drifted by. The new prisoners had missed the morning rations, which meant they would receive no food until the next day, according to one of the other inmates. Gabrion didn't say much but paced around his cell, trying desperately to keep warm.

He passed his time thinking of Mira. He could almost hear her giggling echo in his mind. He ran his fingers through his own hair, trying to pretend it was hers, but there was no comparison to the texture. She was like a goddess come down to the earth just for him. He pictured her flowing chestnut hair that took on crimson highlights if she stayed out in the sun too long, her deep pools of blue eyes that swam with joy when she smiled. She had a bountiful grace in her step, yet was completely clumsy when she tried to dance. But that made her all the more perfect to Gabrion's eyes, as if she were meant to fly on wings of gold. She liked to make her own fragrances with fruit and herbs, then try to have Gabrion guess the ingredients. And when he didn't get them right, she would blindfold him and slide samples of food between his lips. Sometimes it would take him several tries to guess the flavor, but he wasn't always trying his best. He chuckled softly with the memory.

"They say a man who laughs to himself has gone insane. It's a little early for that." Gabrion growled. "Leave me be, Dariak."

"Well, it's a little depressing down here. So if you find something funny, you could certainly share it and perk us all up."

"Hear, hear!" heckled a prisoner a few cells away.

"Thinking about Mira," Gabrion conceded. "I hope she's okay."

When Dariak's voice drifted to him from across the way, it was laced with compassion and wisdom. "I'm sure she's fine, Gabrion. If she was taken as a hostage, then she'll have to be treated well, or they won't be able to seek a reward or whatever they're after."

"You think so?"

"Definitely," Dariak agreed, then felt a shudder. Using that word reminded him suddenly of Randler and the fight in the tavern with the rogue who had kept repeating that affirmation. He fell silent, wondering now about Randler's safety.

Then he scoffed when he considered his own predicament.

"Now *you're* making weird noises," Gabrion commented.

"Just enjoying the atmosphere down here," he dodged.

Gabrion sighed and crouched down, unwilling to sit on the cold stone unless he had to. How had things turned out like this? Waiting to be executed for trying to alert the king about a real threat to the kingdom. And all because of Dariak. He ground his teeth, but then he wondered at the mage's earlier question. Was he madder at the mage or at himself? "I couldn't do it," he said aloud.

"Not following you there," Dariak said.

"I couldn't do it. I couldn't just kill you."

"Ah. Yes, well, I'm thankful for that." Then there was a pause. "Well, I'd be more thankful if it had landed us in a tavern or something less stony."

"I'm serious," Gabrion interjected. "I don't think I'm cut out for this warrior thing."

It was a few moments before Dariak responded, and once again his voice adopted a wiser, sager tone. "Let us first ignore the fact that we're about to die in front of a mob of peasants, and let's pretend we skip over that and go on with our lives outside of here. Being a warrior and being a murderer are two different things."

"Are they?"

"Nobility," the mage announced judiciously from his cell. "And, no, I don't mean the king or anything like that. At least, not the current king, but what nobles are supposed to be."

Gabrion grumbled. "What good is being noble when it gets you nowhere?"

"I wouldn't say nowhere. We did get to see the deep inner bowels of the castle, didn't we?"

Gabrion stood and scratched his head. "How is it you're not panicking down here? Lashing out with these things all the time? I don't understand how you're so cavalier."

Down the hall, one of the prisoners piped up, "I could use a cavalier down here; my cell is kind of dark."

Another prisoner moaned in annoyance. "You're thinking of a chandelier, idiot. Hush up, I'm trying to listen. It sounds like that guy's having a moment."

Dariak laughed, but Gabrion was frustrated. "Is it something with you criminals that makes you all like this? Laughing at your circumstances like you haven't a care in the world? Like nothing is more important than having a laugh at whatever's around you?"

Another cellmate, drawn into the conversation by the sheer passion in Gabrion's voice, jumped in. "Well, aside from the shape of my chamber pot, there isn't much here to laugh about otherwise."

The old man kicked up his wheezing laughter again, but it was enough for Gabrion. He shouted angrily and banged his fists on the wall. All the chatter among the inmates ceased but not because of him.

Footsteps echoed down the hall and paused in front of Gabrion's cell. The burly guard stared down at the warrior. "Problem, son?"

"I don't belong here!" Gabrion yelled. "I was only trying to deliver a message to the king. I am not supposed to be in here. I am supposed to be—" He stopped and composed himself as he looked at the uncaring eyes of the warden. "Is there any way I can petition the king?"

"Of course!" The warden beamed. "What, do you think there isn't a fair process in place here?"

Dariak snorted, but Gabrion's response covered the sound. "Then let me speak to His Majesty once again."

"Sure thing," the warden agreed. "You will have your chance the day after tomorrow."

"But isn't that—?"

"Yep. At your execution. You can petition all you want then."

Gabrion's hope was dashed as quickly as it had sprung up. He slumped down to the cell floor and buried his head in his arms.

"That's better," the warden said. "Nice and quiet. You're disturbing our game of dice with all your yelling. Keep it down now. You don't want me actually opening your cell and teaching you how to keep quiet, do you?" He waited until Gabrion shook his head before walking away.

As he sat there sulking, Gabrion could hear Dariak whispering to himself, "Deceit, deceit, and more deceit. Does this place ever stop with the lies and false hopes?"

Gabrion wondered.

CHAPTER 10

Day of Execution

DARIAK AWOKE SHIVERING, his body drawing in the coldness of the stone. He had freed his hands his first night in the cell, and even simply calling for the energies had indeed made the crystal over the door resonate. He was lucky the wardens had not seen it, though he had chosen a time when they were occupied by another inmate who had fallen ill.

The second day in the cell was odd. He had tried speaking with the warrior several times, but Gabrion was lost in his own thoughts. It was unsettling. Only occasional guard changes seemed to mark the time, but he suspected that, with all the other subterfuge in this kingdom, the guards changed at varying times rather than sticking to a set pattern that would allow the prisoners a sense of night and day. He also assumed that was the real reason for the living quarters at the end of the row, for the wardens never acted as if they were under any form of punishment of their own.

He had spent most of the second day examining the cell for defects, to no avail, and striking up conversations with the other inmates, but most either had lost their sense of self or were more interested in hearing about him, as a newcomer, and he wasn't in a mood to divulge much.

He thought his body was getting more used to the cold floor, but awakening this morning told him otherwise. His entire body was trembling uncontrollably; even his teeth were chattering. Food hadn't arrived yet, but his natural body cycle told him it was morning and time to rise. He wondered how long it would take him to lose that internal clock. How long, that is, if this wasn't the day of his execution.

Rousing himself, Dariak stood and jumped around, warming up and waking fully. He called out for Gabrion to do the same, and though the warrior didn't answer, Dariak heard motion in the cell diagonal from his. He did feel some pity for the poor boy. After all, he had learned that his monarch was as much a tyrant as all the stories of Hathreneir had said.

Footsteps focused his thoughts sharply as armored feet crashed down the hall. Dariak tensed, ready to be pulled from his cubicle to his doom, but determined to face it while also searching for an alternative. It sounded to him, though, as if Gabrion had resigned himself to his fate, for the young man had stopped moving around and was eerily silent.

Three guards in ceremonial armor, with gleaming chain mail over polished leather, paraded past their cells and sought out the wardens. Dariak strained to hear the exchange of orders, but they were carefully whispered. The anticipation was highly irritating. He turned around toward the chamber pot and looked at the shreds of rope that he had tucked around the base, wondering if he should claim them now, not that he could hide them. If he were stronger—and luckier, he frowned—he could probably use one of the lengths to strangle a guard. He could use another length as a component for a binding spell, but he would need a bit of dirt or mud to complete it. By the time he'd decided that it was worth the risk, one of the guards was at his door with the key to his cell, and he had no chance to claim the rope.

A catcall echoed as the guardswoman admired his physique. She pulled open his door slowly, tipping her leather-helmeted head to the side. "And here I thought you mage types were all about your books. It seems like I was a bit mistaken, eh?"

Dariak's eyebrows crouched together, for the comment sounded very familiar, especially after that whistle. It stood out particularly because he didn't think he was much more than skinny and so not much to look at in that respect. She stepped in and grabbed his arm, pulling him painfully from the cell and bringing him to the room at the end of the hall with Gabrion.

Most of their things were returned to them. "Can't have you beauties showing off to the people, can we?" one of the guards teased, waiting for the men to don their clothes. In the process of fastening his robe, Dariak could feel that most of his spell components had been removed, but some had escaped scrutiny, including the one sewn into the chest pouch. He couldn't help showing his relief, but the guards assumed it was because he wasn't to be executed completely naked after all.

Not long later, they were escorted out of the dungeon, both bound like mages with their hands immobilized and their mouths gagged. Dariak swore this would be the last time he would ever experience either form of binding.

The other inmates ignored the walking dead, each silently hoping his own day would never come. The old man wasn't even laughing.

Taking a less circuitous route out of the dungeon, it didn't take long before they were in the castle proper. A throng of people stood stone-faced along the pathway out of the castle to a more open location, where even more people could witness the event. Dariak was sad to see that it wasn't far from the Rooster's Bane, where he had shared his first kiss with Randler.

The guard ushering him to the raised platform, where the proceedings would take place, tripped unceremoniously and crashed into Dariak's back. The mage wondered at his luck, for suddenly the ropes binding his hands were free. He tumbled them around, grasping the rope, looking about to see if he could take advantage of this situation. The guard nudged him painfully in the back, pushing him upward onto the platform, where his death awaited.

He looked askance at Gabrion, wondering what was running through the warrior's mind. Gabrion lumbered up the three steps and simply waited to be directed by the guards, like a lost child. Dariak felt that wasn't too far from the truth; the poor boy did feel terribly lost.

The mage considered his options now that his hands were free. He looked around and opted for dramatics. With his last step up to the podium, he tripped himself and crashed face first to the ground, remembering to keep his hands locked behind his back but twisting carefully so they brushed the wood. The guardswoman picked him up by the scruff of his collar and set him on his feet, then led him to stand next to the dejected warrior.

Two nooses were lowered down, and the prisoners were secured in them, ready to be dropped through the platform at the king's declaration. It seemed obvious to Dariak that the king would first prattle on about duty to the kingdom, then spout about their crimes, and at last call for justice, at which point the floor would drop out and they would die. He didn't have much time to act, especially when trumpets sounded and the king came rounding the corner.

Dariak looked down and saw that the single plank of wood under his feet reached over to Gabrion's feet. So when one of them fell, both would fall. That was actually helpful. The rest of the platform was constructed similarly, with long planks extending from one end to the other. There were two posts on the edges of the plank behind him, and the beam across their tops carried the nooses.

He rolled his fingers together slowly, so as not to attract attention, feeling the bits of dirt he had scraped up during his staged fall. He rubbed it along the rope, recalling the words he needed for the spell. Timing would be critical, because he was still gagged and, therefore, could not utter the spell, but the burly warden had said they would have the opportunity to petition for release, so he held to the hope that his gag would be removed. Yes, everything would be in the timing.

As expected, the king rambled on for a while about threats to the kingdom and so forth. Dariak rolled his eyes through most of it, wondering how many times this monarch had uttered those very words in the name of justice. He knew no leader could be perfect, but the crimes of the Kallisorian nation were unacceptable. Not that he knew his own king's inner motivations, he admitted silently.

Gabrion's gag was removed at the king's request for confession and request of petition, but the warrior was so disheartened he said nothing but Mira's name. When Dariak's gag was released, a dagger was pressed against his throat by the guardswoman who had tripped into him. Quietly, so only he could hear, she repeated her earlier catcall. Dariak understood at once, and so he did not hesitate.

The mage threw his binding ropes at Gabrion and spouted the words of his spell, *"Darrethon nur pelliat kazs!"* In the same motion, he clutched his hand to his chest and added, *"Kathrahasslerad."* He grabbed the guardswoman and shoved her behind him as the king screamed, flailing his arms about, calling for the execution without delay. The soldier minding the lever panicked and pushed hard, releasing the floor under the prisoners.

As the plank under Dariak and Gabrion fell away, the guardswoman took a step forward, clutching the support post that held up the line of nooses. With the Shield of Delminor weighing her down, she wrenched the post from its board and the support beam for the nooses collapsed on Dariak's side. Simultaneously, the mage yanked on the ensorcelled rope to pull Gabrion toward him so the warrior's neck would not snap during the fall. Gabrion's noose slid along the now-slanted plinth and he crashed into Dariak with a hearty thud.

There wasn't time for anything but escape. Dariak took the dagger from the guard and slashed the nooses free. He then canceled the Shield of Delminor and dragged the guardswoman to her feet. She didn't need any further assistance, so the mage grabbed Gabrion's tunic and pulled him along tensely.

The trio ran under the platform and out the rear, crashing into the unarmed crowd and causing a mad panic. People shrieked as they toppled to the ground while the king's voice called out for order and demanded that his guards immediately capture the escapees.

They were only steps away from the immediate chaos when Dariak called out, "The castle museum. It's now, or it's never!"

The guardswoman laughed. "You're insane, but you're right. You're sure what you seek is there?"

"It has to be."

She led the way around a fountain, and they raced through the streets, Dariak still pulling on the dazed warrior's tunic.

"He's dead weight, mage. Let him go."

"I can't," he replied. "Come on, hurry!"

They raced quickly to the castle, which wasn't far away at all, and with the public execution, many of the regular guards were out protecting the king during his appearance among the people. They dashed past the guard towers, ignoring the cries of the soldiers still in place, and into the castle grounds they went. Having paid some attention earlier, despite his sedated condition, Dariak knew to head to the left, and so they did. They sprinted onward, barreling past people and knocking many of them to the ground in their haste, all the while avoiding arrows that had started to fall from the castle walls amid the ringing of the alarm bells. They dashed down a long corridor and turned at the end toward the entrance to the museum.

The doors were no obstacle as they crashed through, startling the few patrons who were too scholarly to care about public shows of force for political gain. Museum guards were present, and they acted quickly, but Dariak ignored them, releasing Gabrion at last and casting about for the object he sought. He remembered the night in the tavern and the information he had gained, so he pressed his hand against his chest and felt the resonance within his robe. While he concentrated, the guardswoman slapped Gabrion alert and pointed to the oncoming danger. Luckily, the warrior's training won over his despondency, and he crouched in a battle stance, ready to knock a foe down and claim his weapon so he could do real damage.

"Any time now," hissed the guardswoman, looking over a grid of knee-high rectangular bins, where various types of plants and grasses grew. Each was from a different region of the kingdom, with various scents and colors. The grid pattern would be easy to navigate, but it would also restrict their motions.

Dariak ignored her, turning slightly until he sensed a deeper vibration. "There!" He bolted off in that direction, seemingly oblivious to the threat around him.

The guardswoman grunted and turned to follow but noticed that Gabrion hadn't moved and a strange snarl had marred his face. "Damn," she muttered and spread her arms out wide, fingers extended far, and then with a forced calmness, she twisted slowly and drew in her hands, pumping her body to a slow rhythm she did not feel. Left foot, then right, right arm, then left. She moved with the grace of a cat and the care of the finest seamstress. She concentrated on the approaching guards, and they slowed down, confused, then started swinging about, attacking objects only they could see.

Gabrion rushed headlong into the nearest guard and toppled him to the ground. Claiming the sword, he went slightly wild, hacking and slashing to take out the rest. The guardswoman continued her controlled movements but did nothing else. Gabrion pounced from one place to another, parrying the errant attacks of the foes, then scoring his own dire hits. Once he was mobile, the guards didn't stand a chance. He took out eight of them with the help of the strange trance they were in, and the ninth fled to call an alarm.

Leather helm firmly in place, the guardswoman summoned Gabrion over, and she followed after Dariak. It wouldn't be much of a success if the mage earned his prize and left them behind to face the fury of the king. Through the room they went, racing to the back doorway as quickly as possible. The woman blasted through the entryway and saw Dariak at the rear wall of the next room, his arms moving oddly about him.

Jogging over, she asked, "Find it?"

The mage ignored her for only a moment as he finished his protection spell, then crashed his fists through the glass case. He scooped up a bluish crystal and shoved it deeply into one of his pockets. "Got it. Let's go."

"Got it?" Gabrion repeated. "What's this all about?"

"Later," the other two echoed, grabbing the warrior and turning him about.

Dariak summoned his fire-dart spell, since he was missing the components he needed for more powerful attacks, but he wasn't concerned. He led the way back toward the exit, shooting fire from his hands at the new guards who had entered the main room to stop them. Many of them dropped to the ground to avoid the flames, though the ones who received the full blasts didn't seem too fazed by them. Dariak knew it was more of a surprise tactic than an offensive skill, but when the guards-woman and Gabrion ran past him, weapons flailing, he kept calm, looking around to see if there were any materials he could put to use.

The room was full of flowers and herbs, which were great spell components in tandem with other objects. Scanning the room quickly, Dariak sought out one of the bins and combed his fingers through the soil, disturbing the contents as he searched with one hand and plucked leaves from a daisy with the other.

Gabrion barreled into one of the king's guards with his sword flailing about. He didn't think about his lack of skill compared to these fighters. He didn't consider his lack of armor and their abundance of it. He didn't ponder the ramifications of slaying his king's guards. The only thought he held on to in that moment was the temporary gift of life that had been given to him and the chance it offered him to get to Mira. The guards became obstacles, and he was determined to master them. He left open-ings for the guardswoman, who fought with him, but nothing else.

As the fight progressed, there came a sudden chanting from a few rows away. Some of the guards broke free from the group to interfere with the mage, but Gabrion released a feral cry and leaped over the nearest bin to stop them. He needn't have bothered, for Dariak shot his hands forward, casting his spell outward.

What Gabrion saw amazed him, for it started off as a foot-long earthworm, wrig-gling as it coasted through the air. The guard in front slashed it with his sword, cutting it in two. But both halves grew back to full size. One of them impacted another guard, and he thrashed about, trying to shove it to the ground, hacking it to pieces. Each of those pieces immediately puffed up and wriggled about, and soon the entire walkway was full of the writhing creatures.

Gabrion grabbed two of the giant worms and hurled them toward the guardswoman, who reacted by cutting them both in half and batting the remains at the soldiers facing off against her. Gabrion saw that nearly all the king's guards were occupied, so he bellowed, "Move out!" and bolted for the door.

Dariak knew the engorgement spell wouldn't last long, so he wasted no time hurrying out the door. The blinding sunlight required a moment of adjustment, and he could see his two companions several paces ahead of him. He pushed his body to run while his mind thought of the protection spell he had cast on himself before crashing into the glass case. It was still intact, except for his hands. He didn't have time to reset the spell, but knowing where the chinks were was enough.

Castle folk saw the mad dash from the museum and started screaming. The rain of arrows resumed as everyone ran for cover. The three escapees needed to get out through the main gate into the town of Kaison, then lose themselves in the crowds that were probably just disbanding from the aborted execution.

Gabrion's battle cry spurred Dariak onward faster, and he was lucky his protective shield was still intact, for three arrows struck his back, tinkling with the sound of broken glass, then falling to the ground and leaving the mage unscathed but less protected. He reached to his side and tried to feel around for another piece of shattered glass that he could use to erect another shield, but trying to accurately feel through various pockets while running for his life wasn't feasible.

The trio turned to the left as they fled the castle. Gabrion's face was red with strain, but he kept his sword arm swinging around, knocking down all the fighters he came across and clearing a path for the other two. Instinctively, he wasn't aiming to kill any of them, which was fortunate for them, because his blows certainly had the strength behind them. But his sword hit either flat or hilt first, and therefore most of his hits did not cut deeply. The concussion from each swing, however, was enough to knock the wind from anyone who crossed his path.

"This way!" the guardswoman called out, veering sharply left and then cutting between two of the permanent shops.

Dariak saw the mystic's shop out of the corner of his eye as he went, so at least he knew where he was if they became separated. His companions were still ahead of him, but when he passed into the narrow alley between the two shops, he stopped and let them get farther away. He quickly scrounged around and grabbed a spider that was scuttling up the wall. He wrapped the spider in one of the other leaves he had taken from the museum, and then he cast his spell, trying to ignore the twenty fighters who appeared in the distance, running hard for him.

"*Naarestigar engor shai.*" He spread his arms wide, making sure he touched the walls on either side of him. Feeling the energies take hold, he turned and jogged after his companions. Moments later, the other members of the king's guard crashed into a thin wall of webbing that bound them tightly and would hold them until the webs were cut away.

He knew it was only going to slow them down; there had to be other passages leading the same way. He lost sight of Gabrion's blond head and muttered under his breath, trying to run through the alleyway without stumbling. Breaking out through the other side, he saw the warrior a few buildings away, his feet pounding the ground earnestly. Huffing, Dariak followed. He sure hoped the woman knew where she was going.

Sounds of pursuit were not far behind. Dariak lowered his head and tried to let some of his body weight propel him forward. It nearly caused him to stumble, but it was all he had left. His lungs were burning, and he didn't think he was even taking in air anymore. He could barely feel his legs either, and he worried they might stop responding to his urgent demands to keep running. Turning down another alley and then pressing through to the other side, Dariak saw Gabrion run into a small hovel, so he went too.

"Come on, and quietly," the woman whispered as she led the two men to the kitchen, pushing aside the large oak table and lifting a trapdoor. "In."

They obeyed and clattered into a cellar while she followed them, pulling the trapdoor closed. She then reached for a rope and tugged on it hard, and because it was attached to the underside of a table leg, it pulled the table back in place, perfectly concealing them inside.

"We'll be safe here, for a little time anyway. So, catch your breath, boys." The guardswoman joined them at the bottom of the stairs and pulled off the concealing leather helmet.

Gabrion stared at her for a moment before recognition set in. "The old woman in the forest!" He stalked closer, his face curling in anger.

"Calm yourself, big boy," she replied. "Hey, mage, call off your dog."

"Gabrion, take it easy," Dariak intervened, gasping for breath. "She did just save us from a public execution."

Tensing his jaw while he considered this, Gabrion eventually relaxed and stepped away. "I keep ending up owing people who are trying kill me."

"Life is funny that way." She smirked, pulling off the chain mail she was wearing over her leather tunic. She was able to move in it, but she found it needlessly cumbersome and noisy. "I suppose introductions are in order? I'm Kitalla. You're Gabrion, and though we spoke in the forest, I don't know your name, mage."

"Dariak," he responded directly, rubbing his neck where the noose had pressed against his skin. "I'm glad you took me seriously and followed us."

Gabrion eyed the two of them suspiciously. "So then you do know each other?"

Kitalla laughed. "Hardly. But while you were fighting Jafflin, this one made a deal with me. It was interesting enough for me to explore, so here I am. Lucky for you."

"You had time for chitchat?" Gabrion was aghast.

"Recall, I was tied to the horse that started jumping around," Dariak noted. "When I freed myself, I fell, and there she was. It was bargain or die, really."

Kitalla didn't like the sound of that. "You do intend to hold to that bargain, don't you?"

The mage groaned. "Take the daggers out of your eyes, miss. I will. You have an interesting gift, and I'm curious about helping you advance it."

"Ah, the bargain that benefits us both." She nodded. "Shrewd."

Gabrion was annoyed, however. "I don't care much for what you two have worked out."

"You asked," Dariak reminded him.

Gabrion ignored him and changed the subject. "Kitalla, where are we? Is this truly safe?"

"It's Bostian's house, actually. Oh," she said to the blank faces that greeted her upon the use of her friend's name.

"Bostian was the big guy your horse mutilated."

"I—I'm sorry," Gabrion said with sadness in his voice.

She debated holding a grudge but decided that Bostian was dead and these two were with her at the moment. Suddenly Poltor's lack of emotion at Bostian's demise seemed like an act of prudence, not coldness. "We ambushed you. In the end, I suppose it was our fault he died. I must say, though, that was a well-trained horse."

"He belonged to my mentor," came Gabrion's haunted response.

Dariak made a face, knowing that the mentor's death was his responsibility. He looked at Gabrion wordlessly, wondering what the warrior was thinking.

Gabrion turned to look Dariak directly in the eye. They held their gazes for a while as the warrior debated his ghosts. He broke away and shook his head. "I can't figure any of this out," he admitted. "If I make a tally of all the times you've wronged me and compare it to the times you've helped me, the balance is somewhere in the middle."

"I beg to differ," the mage interjected. "You're alive, so I'm clearly on the upper hand."

Gabrion's jaw tensed, but then he forced himself to relax. "I still don't understand you. But, yes, I'm alive because of you. You could have left me back there." He stopped talking, but the others could tell he had more to say, so they waited for Gabrion to put the words together. The warrior looked from one to the other but spent most of his focus on the mage.

It felt like hours before Gabrion resolved his heart and his mind. He stepped in front of Kitalla and said, "You were fighting for your life, and you ambushed us so you could live. I don't agree with your method, but in the end, you came through for us both. Even if you're just following your own ambition, you fought hard to get us out of that mess and to bring us here to safety. You could have dropped to the ground and pretended we hit you. You have my thanks."

Kitalla didn't know what to say so she stared back at him.

Gabrion turned to Dariak with a much sterner expression. "You came to my village and ruined everything. Or at least, you were part of the problem. You did kill my mentor, though you were trying to kill me. If he hadn't jumped in the way, then his end would have been mine. But since then you've done several things to keep me alive. You certainly didn't need to risk yourself to drag me from the execution site, yet you did."

He stepped away and looked from one to the other. "My mission is to rescue Mira, who was kidnapped by the Hathrens. I know I can't do it alone, but if I must, then I will find a way. I don't know what your own missions truly are, but if they overlap and if your goals will take me closer to reaching mine, then I will work with you, if you will have me."

Dariak's eyebrows shot up. He was surprised by this declaration. He figured Gabrion would run off on his own. Kitalla was less surprised at the noble-hearted warrior who had tried to leave the forest ambush without a fight. She turned instead to Dariak and asked the question that affected matters the most: "So, then, mage, what exactly is your quest?"

CHAPTER 11

Dariak's Quest

THE ONE THING Dariak never wanted to share with anyone else was his quest. Staring at Kitalla and Gabrion in a dead man's basement, the mage started trembling, feeling he didn't have much choice. Part of him wanted the king's soldiers to burst in and take away this moment of confession. The rest of him wanted to keep silent and face the wrath of the two before him.

Kitalla saw the war going on inside the mage. She rolled her eyes and pouted impatiently. "Don't make me rethink my opinion of you. It's already obvious."

Gabrion didn't seem to think the mage's quest was so transparent, but then, he hadn't seen what Dariak took from the museum. As Dariak realized that she knew, he decided to explain. After all, Gabrion always seemed a little happier after letting his emotions loose. Why not himself? "I seek the Red Jade."

Kitalla didn't react, but Gabrion did. "What! That infernal magic device from the last great war? The one that summoned the colossus?"

"The very same." Dariak nodded.

"Ridiculous!" the warrior exclaimed. "Whatever would possess you?"

"Do you know the story?" Dariak returned.

"We all do," Kitalla moaned.

But Gabrion added more. "Yes, the war was in full effect, and one mage used the power of the Red Jade to summon a colossus to wipe out our forces. It was an obscene use of magic, twisting the powers of the world in a way they were never meant to be. The colossus decimated our troops but was slain in the end. The Red Jade exploded and killed our king. The pieces were scattered. How could you ever think to reclaim them?"

Dariak hesitated, yet now that he had started, the prospect of finally sharing his secret information felt invigorating. "No one ever knew anything about that mage, did they? All the stories say that your king thought a horde of mages summoned that colossus. But, no, it was just one man. One man who had poured his heart and soul into the magic forces. One man who had tried to support his own king with his talents in the only way he knew how. He wanted all the wars to end. He thought that if he created a means of bringing an invincible and powerful weapon into battle, he could stop all the wars, because enemies would realize that it was futile to fight against it. They would lay down their weapons and heed the will of our king. The fighting would stop, and peace would reign for the first time in countless years. The people would return to agriculture and to furthering their skills to improve life. There wouldn't need to be so much war."

He didn't know when his eyes had started leaking tears, but he ignored them. "Families would be able to raise their children, without fear of being invaded. Without fear that having a son would mean he would be sent to war to die so that the king could continue on. There would be no more pawns. Families wouldn't need to worry that if the capable men refused to fight, their wives would be taken as punishment. People who wanted to defend their nation would do so because they believed in it, not because they feared the consequences from their own leaders.

"So I seek the Red Jade, to reassemble it, to find that power again, so I can do what that mage could not do. So I can unite these two lands and smite those who would oppose peace. And if my path to get there isn't perfect, I don't much care. I know what I have to do. I know what lies at the end. And I know that I have the gift within me to achieve that goal."

Dariak reached into his pocket and withdrew the crystal shard he had obtained from the museum. "This here is a fragment of the whole. This is part of the Red Jade."

Kitalla and Gabrion had competing questions. Gabrion's focused on the object in Dariak's hand: "But it isn't red at all. If it's blue, then how is it part of the Red Jade?"

"Because the Red Jade was only red at its final moment, when the conjuration was complete, with all the spell components intact. It required all the forces of nature to work together before its power could be harnessed. This piece, I don't yet know what it does. The other one I carry"—he gestured to the concealed compartment on his chest—"is of the power of earth. And you've both experienced an aspect of its power; it can greatly increase the weight of what it touches."

"Your goal," Gabrion said slowly, "is to gain enough power to conquer both nations and unite them under your command?"

"Not really," Dariak admitted. "But I understand how you would see it that way. No, I want to stop war. Haven't we all lost enough because of war?"

"Fine sentiment," Kitalla interrupted. "Though I think you've missed something. If you have a big weapon, you'll just incite others to find bigger ones to take you down. It won't stop war at all. You'll make it worse."

"I know… The colossus wasn't supposed to be the end. It was meant to stop the fighting for the time. After that, other work remains to restore the balance of power throughout both lands. Only the united strength of the jades can accomplish that. The mage who summoned the colossus was not meant to die that day. He would have ushered in a new age where everyone would come to understand magic in a better light. If you Kallisorians didn't fear magic just because you were told to, then you would understand its uses and how best to counteract it."

Kitalla scoffed. "Sounds so simple."

"It isn't. I know that." Dariak held his impatience in check. "Hathreneir is turning into a wasteland in larger and larger areas. It's because the balance of magic is awry. With the jades, I can restore the land. We wouldn't need Kallisorian supplies. And for you, imagine how trade would increase overseas and in the south if your black-smiths could also imbue their armor with protection spells. Your own wealth would increase."

"No one here would go for that," Gabrion argued.

"Not at first. It would take time. That's also why I need the Red Jade: to give me the strength needed to endure. There's more to it all, but that's the premise." He paused. "And once it's all truly over, I could break the Red Jade again and give it to rulers who will maintain the peace."

"How will you figure out when it's all truly over?" Gabrion asked.

"I don't really know."

They were silent for a few moments before Kitalla wondered aloud, "Did I follow you for this reason? So you could bring the apocalypse? Did you intend to make me a queen? Was that how you were going to give me more power?"

The mage shook his head. "No, your skills draw the energies around you and cast them beyond your body. In some regards, you accomplish more with your dance skills than many mages can without tangible spell components and arcane words."

"Great. Thanks," she said, irritated. "This benefits me how?"

"In a few ways. First, I know offensive spells, and most of them require spell components. Yet if I can help you recognize the energies around you in more detail, perhaps you'll be able to channel them and use magic in your own way. You estab-lished a strong illusion in the museum. All the guards were baffled by things only they could see, and you had enough control to keep us from suffering under the same effect. That's an impressive skill. But I've seen you use those skills more than once now, and you're always defenseless while keeping the effect intact."

"Well, yes. It only lasts while I'm in the dance."

"Like a mage can only function if he is pulling the energy and translating it properly with words, motions, and using the components as catalysts," Dariak agreed. "What if you could augment your repertoire and add truly defensive spells to your arsenal, like a protective shield so you couldn't be harmed? Or what if you could launch fireballs as you move about?"

Kitalla scoffed. "I've seen your fire darts, mage, and they're not worth learning to cast, I can tell you."

"That's a minor spell, meant for lighting candles," he said. "I could incinerate a village block if I set my mind to it. You're missing the point though."

"I'm not. Your offer intrigued me before, and it intrigues me still. After all, I don't generally put my life at risk to break strangers out from under the king's nose."

Gabrion piped up at last. "There's still something that doesn't add up for me."

"What's that?" Dariak asked.

"My beloved was kidnapped from the village. I need to find her before she is hurt. I have to rescue her, or there is no point to me living."

He ignored the sarcastic faces the others pulled. "What about your quest?" he asked Kitalla. "What is it that makes it so important to you? You're clearly driven in a very determined way. What motivates you?"

Kitalla nodded. "Yes, that's a good one. My motivation is obvious. I want to be more powerful so I can stop playing the part of the hag and live a better life. What is yours?" she asked Dariak.

Dariak had known the question was coming. He wished it wasn't, because he felt stupid and weak for saying it, but there it was anyway. "No one knew the mage that left everything behind and went to war with the king to try to stop all the fighting with a grandiose display of power."

He paused for a moment, and his voice quieted. "Well, the mage's name was Delminor.

"He was my father."

CHAPTER 12

Preparation for Travel

GABRION AND KITALLA stared in silence at the mage's revelation, eyebrows raised. Most people had someone in their ancestry who had fought in at least one of the wars, but this was different. Dariak's father wasn't just some soldier or mage. He was the mage who had turned the tide of battle, the mage whose magic ultimately led to the demise of both warring kings. And now Dariak would follow in his old man's steps.

"That answers my question," Gabrion said, "but it brings up so many more."

"Yeah," Kitalla added, "because if he died in that war, then how do you even know what you're doing?"

Dariak grinned for a moment, then shook his head. "Instinct is a lot of it, but my father had a whole library of research, and he left many clues about what to do."

"But didn't he die in that battle?" Gabrion asked. "How could he clue you in on where to find what you're looking for?"

"You're not listening; I said a lot of it was instinct. One piece found its way back to me because a warrior brought it to me so I could remember my father. This second piece made sense. Don't all the stories say that the jade exploded and a chunk of it impaled your king? That he wanted all the pieces collected for the kingdom? If it wasn't destroyed outright, then the piece bearing the royal blood would be passed along to the new king, no? I'd heard in Hathreneir that a crystal was on display in the castle with other relics from previous wars, and I just knew what it had to be. Brazen king—wouldn't he put the object on display as if saying his people had survived even that?"

"Any clues of the others?" Kitalla asked.

Dariak pulled the tiger's-eye from the recesses of his robe, thinking of Randler and the brigands who were chasing him. "To the north."

"Mira is to the west," Gabrion interjected. "We have to save her."

Dariak looked at him and sighed. "We aren't strong enough yet. I need to tap into the power of this piece to find out what I can learn. I need time to work with Kitalla to strengthen her abilities. And you need to improve your fighting skills."

Gabrion wanted to argue, but the mage was right. "We can't do it here."

"We'll leave under cover of night," Kitalla announced. "Problem is, travel is dangerous the farther north we go."

"Why is that?" Dariak wondered.

"This far south and west have seen a lot of people over the years, so the creatures tend to stay away," Gabrion answered. "But the farther we get from the border of our two kingdoms, the more likely we're going to run into danger. Especially at night."

Dariak nodded slowly. "Ah, of course. I forgot you have them too. Sometimes I think the feral creatures are just Hathreneir's problem."

Kitalla shrugged. "Well, it looks like we need some materials then. Maybe some kind of armor for you?" she asked Gabrion. "Unless you want to try squeezing into that," she added jokingly, pointing to the chain mail she had gratefully shrugged off.

"I need materials too for my spells," Dariak agreed.

"Lucky I've got your money pouch then." Kitalla grinned, pulling Gabrion's pouch out of a pocket and tossing it to the warrior.

"That's great, but this won't get us far," said Gabrion.

"Why not?" Dariak asked. "There's over two hundred coppers left in there."

Gabrion shook his head, perplexed. "No, there's sixty-three in it. Same as when we got to Kaison. I checked it myself when Master Elgris gave it back to me." He verified that the pouch still contained that amount.

Dariak pounded his fist into his hand. "After all that bartering I did on his errands! And he went and stole the excess." He growled, then added, "I'm tired of this place. I can't wait to return to my homeland."

"No matter." Kitalla shrugged. "We'll just go and get what we need on our way out."

"I'm no thief," Gabrion objected.

"No, but I am. And if we're going to work together on this little mission, then you'd better get used to it." She stared at the warrior, waiting for him to challenge her. "We'll pay it all back later," she promised with an air of innocence, which Dariak ruined with a hearty laugh.

Gabrion heaved a sigh. "Fine. Whatever. But let's not kill people if we can avoid it."

Kitalla pouted in overdramatic fashion. "Then how am I supposed to have any fun? Really, warrior, I'm not an assassin. I kill if I have to, but only if. Are we resolved for now, then? Get some supplies, then head to the north?"

The next few hours passed quietly enough. Gabrion and Dariak first took a much-needed nap while Kitalla searched the cellar for food and supplies. Some of the things they needed were there, but not in the best condition. She tucked two knives into her boots and wrapped a length of rope about her waist. Because Bostian had been such a robust fighter, he didn't have many items of finesse in his secret room. Kitalla found a bottle of wine and sipped some while the two men slept, taking care not to imbibe too much and leave herself befuddled. All the while, she kept her ears trained for sounds through the ceiling, in case the king's guards found their trail.

But she had chosen their destination carefully. Bostian's house was maintained by an old acquaintance of the troupe for this very purpose. Kitalla didn't know the details of their relationship, but the older woman was more than happy to visit this place once or twice a week, light lanterns, and sweep the stoop to make it look occupied.

She also took care of paying the king's taxes from a coffer that Bostian replenished for the purpose.

Thinking of the coffer, Kitalla rummaged around the cellar, tapping walls and tugging on stones until one came loose. There was dirt and grime in there but also an iron box. Removing the strongbox, Kitalla opened the lid and was shocked to see so many pieces of gold surrounded by gems and jewelry. She intended to take funds for Gabrion, so he could put his conscience at ease, figuring a fellow of his nature would need time to adjust to a more free-flowing lifestyle. Keeping him calm and in line would make the upcoming task smoother, which would help. But then she saw that there was also a stack of parchments, neatly folded and bound with a thin cord. She untied the string and opened the first one.

Dearest Bos,
I hope this note finds you safe. I regret we must communicate in this manner, but you're right; I can't be caught up in your line of work anymore.
Sairre

Sairre, thanks. You'll always be my favorite. The rubies are for you, so enjoy them. Bos

Kitalla looked in the box and saw that there were no rubies. Sairre must have accepted them. She thumbed through a few of the other letters, and though they were personal, it didn't seem like a romantic relationship between the two. She thought of Bostian's death in the forest and decided she had to let Sairre know. She took a rod of coal and a spare piece of parchment and scraped out a message.

Sairre, I'm a friend of Bostian's. You should know there was an accident and he died. I'm terribly sorry. Thank you for keeping this safe house for him. But you should take what remains here and live your life free now. ~K

She folded the parchment and placed it on top of the contents of the box, then covered it and slid it back to its resting place, taking none of the funds from inside.

"Time yet?" Dariak asked over her shoulder, startling her. "It must be nighttime by now."

She appreciated that he hadn't asked what she was doing.

"Yes, let's move."

The three of them left the underground room, with Kitalla leading them stealthily. She peered out the front door of the house and noticed that torches lit various places along the street. "Not good," she murmured. "They have scouts in place watching for us."

"Not surprising," Gabrion said. "What's the plan?"

"Same. Just more careful."

"One moment," Dariak interrupted before they left. He fumbled through his pockets and pulled out three small, broken pieces of glass. He gave one piece to each of them. "Slice your finger just a little bit on the edge of it, and then hold it in your palm." He demonstrated what he meant, and then he placed his left hand over his right and chanted the words, "*Guaradair zuli haramanniav.*" A light glowed briefly from his hand, and when he opened his palm, the glass was gone.

Gabrion hesitated. "I don't know how I feel about this."

Kitalla took his piece of glass and scratched him with it. "You don't have a choice."

Dariak repeated the incantation before the warrior could protest, and then he set Kitalla's protective shield as well.

"Strange," Gabrion said moments later. "I almost feel like my whole body is wrapped in ice."

"You can feel that?" Dariak asked. "Good. When you're hit, those parts will go back to normal, so you'll know the shield's gone. Okay, now let's get moving."

"Handy," Kitalla said appraisingly, then poked her head out the door again. Glancing around, she could see that a few of the torches were moving. Apparently, some guards were in set locations, but others were patrolling. She didn't bother informing her companions, though. They all knew it wasn't going to be easy.

Waiting until it looked the clearest, Kitalla dashed across the cobblestones and into a dark alley across the way, keeping her body bent low. She paused only long enough for the others to reach her, then she continued. Their first stop was the mystic's store so Dariak could replenish some of his wares. Kitalla looked around, then pointed upward.

Gabrion looked and realized that she meant for them to cross on the roofs, which didn't seem like a good idea to him. His skepticism was clear, even in the darkness, but she urged him forward. He took two crates and stacked them, holding them steady so the others could climb up. Kitalla went first, springing from the second crate to the rooftop and pulling herself up easily. Dariak needed assistance from them both, and then Gabrion joined them. They crouched low as they scuttled across the roof beams, taking care not to step on any of the thatch, which would probably drop them painfully to the ground below.

The mystic's shop wasn't too far away, and when they reached it, Kitalla pulled up a few patches of roof and looked inside. It was a perfectly quiet store within. She turned around, bent low, and grabbed the beam before swinging her legs down and dropping safely to the floor. Dariak cringed at the motion but mimicked it relatively well, though he tumbled over upon landing. Gabrion remained on the roof as a lookout.

Having spent a few hours there before, Dariak knew where most of the merchandise was located. He pocketed some herb packs and gemstones first, then took a handful of incense sticks, which he wrapped in a sheet of parchment to lock in their scent. He poked and prodded through various other objects, taking only the best materials. He felt silly for doing so, but he fumbled through the books too and swiped a few of the smaller volumes that would fit in his larger pockets.

Kitalla wandered around, glancing out the storefront windows but also eyeing the merchandise. She found a number of interesting items and she secreted them away in her leathers where she could. Kitalla chose the items with care, ensuring she could barter easily with them in the future. On the far wall, tucked casually away from others of its kind, was a silver necklace, strewn with fragments of gemstones. There was nothing special or expensive about the style and it wouldn't fetch any reasonable price, yet she felt a compulsion to take it.

A sharp whistle sounded overhead, and Kitalla and Dariak dropped to the ground. A torch passed by the window moments later, and another went by soon after. They waited for a few moments, but it seemed like the guards had passed, until Gabrion came crashing through the ceiling.

"Archers!" he announced, pulling himself up from the ground and tugging on his sword. "One of them got me in the arm, but it glanced off because of that shield. But now they know we're in here."

"We're done anyway," Dariak decided, pulling out a dagger and preparing to defend himself.

"Got any spells rea—?" Kitalla started, but was interrupted as a soldier kicked in the front door. Gabrion charged forward and batted the man away, clearing a path for the other two. They sprinted out quickly and dashed across the street to dive into another alleyway. It didn't work as well as before, however, for shouts echoed down the street that the villains had been found. Gabrion scrambled to join the others. They made so much noise in their flight it was easy for the guards to follow them.

"Keep making noise!" Kitalla insisted, though Gabrion called ahead for them to be quiet. "Come on!" She grabbed a metal pole that was on the ground and banged it against a stone wall on her left. Not understanding why they would want more noise but willing to play along, Dariak grabbed a canister of debris and threw it high into the air and over Gabrion's head. It hit the ground with a resounding crash.

"Are you mad?" Gabrion hissed.

But Kitalla just smiled as she cupped her hands to her ear, signaling him to listen. Dogs were howling and barking at the ruckus they were making, alerting their owners, some of whom could be heard trying to quiet the dogs. Kitalla kicked a wooden box and shattered a piece of glass along her way, having a bit of fun with it. Gabrion and Dariak added to the cacophony, still somewhat doubtful about this plan.

Breaking through the alley, Kitalla cut a sharp turn to the left, smacking into a sentry. She recovered quickly and pounced on him, crashing him to the ground and banging his head on the stones to knock him unconscious before he could alert the others. Some of the frightened dogs started wailing like wolves, while others thrashed around their pens, desperate to get to the noises outside.

Jumping to her feet, Kitalla ran ahead, Dariak and Gabrion in tow. She broke into a house and ran right through it, out the back door and into the night, turning right and sprinting onward. If they didn't know any better, the others would have thought she was trying to lose them. They pounded their way through the living room, ignoring the cries of the children they had disturbed, and followed as closely as they could.

Kitalla's zigzagging didn't stop with the one house but continued across both sides of the street, until people and pets were yelling from all directions. Dariak admired the tactic as he went. If all the houses were calling for guards, those soldiers would find themselves rather busy.

At one turn, Kitalla dove inside a doorway but didn't run through at all. Instead, she pulled a full stop to catch her breath as Dariak and Gabrion joined her. "Quickly," she huffed, pointing around. It was one of the Kaison armor shops. They each scoured the dark room quickly, throwing on whatever would fit. Dariak hesitated before taking a leather jerkin; it would interfere with access to his robe, but he figured he could ditch the jerkin later if he couldn't make use of it. Gabrion grabbed an outfit of chain mail, minus the helm, and swiped the only buckler that wasn't locked to the wall with a chain. Kitalla added a set of leathers to the ones she was already wearing and then called the men to follow.

Out the front door they went, and three stores away, she dove inside the weaponsmith's shop. Dariak and Kitalla each pocketed a collection of daggers while Gabrion debated between a mace and a sword. Time was tight, though, so he kept to the weapon he knew best, taking a steel long sword with its companion scabbard. It was longer than the short swords he was used to, but it better suited his height. Kitalla stashed a whip on her belt rope, and they were off again.

This time they were spotted, and the alarm echoed through the ever-darkening night, punctuated by the occasional flight of arrows. Dariak had no idea how he was going to keep up with the stamina of these two, but he kept repeating to himself that if he stopped, he would die. It was enough to keep him moving for a while.

She didn't know how widespread the sentries were posted, but Kitalla assumed that the northeastern quadrant would have the largest concentration, since the three of them had run toward that area after the failed execution. Thus she veered through the streets, heading southwest as much as possible. Owl hoots sounded through the air, but all three knew it was the castle guard trying to send word out that the fugitives were on the run.

Kitalla charged headlong into a sentry who wasn't even looking in her direction. His torch fell to the ground, and she hefted it over her head. "Come on!" she urged the other two, running off. Holding the torch confused the other sentries as she reached them. They never would have figured the criminals would want to be seen. It was a crafty ruse, and it allowed Kitalla to best a few groups of sentries along the way. Gabrion kicked out at the guards, trying to keep them down so they couldn't follow, while Dariak focused his thoughts on just keeping his feet moving.

They made great progress through Kaison, with Kitalla at the head of the charge, torch blazing overhead, adding her own calls of alarm to the chaos. "Eastern quarter!" she bellowed to one group, who immediately headed off in that direction. Adding a panicked frenzy to one cry, she called, "To the king! They attack our king!" This led the sentries right into Gabrion's awaiting fists.

She ran ahead, prepared to barrel into the next group, but then something happened that she didn't expect. Her body crashed into an invisible wall of force, knocking the wind out of her. Dariak's eyes widened, and he dug within himself, for he needed to come through for them now.

They were outside the sanctuary, where the healers had gathered together, pooling their resources to face this trio of traitors. They had erected a wall of stillness by stopping the air from moving around and preventing movement through it. It was often used to keep a room quiet for recovery or to deaden the screams during particularly painful healings. Combined and overlapped in full force like this, it was a veritable wall.

But Dariak could take it down.

Skidding to his knees, he scooped up a fistful of dirt from between the cobbles and tossed it at the wall. The pieces struck as if against stone, but Dariak then grabbed the torch and swung it like a sword. *"Hazkhra bezhou!"* The speckles of dirt exploded in tiny bombs of force, powered by the torch, which instantly went out. The wall shattered against his shoulder, and he turned to face the healers, who were already swinging their arms around for another spell.

Gabrion couldn't help, for several soldiers had come around the bend. He pulled the long sword from its scabbard and swung it a few times through the air. It felt awkward, but he was ready. The buckler on his left arm was secure, and he crouched in a lunge, anticipating the first attack.

Dariak and the healers had their arms and legs flailing about, arcane words tumbling from their mouths. Most of Dariak's experience was with the power of the earth and some minor conjurations of fire. He repeatedly dug his fingers into the ground to pull forth the dirt as a component for his counterspells. The healers called to the humidity in the air, and a swirling cloud of mist rushed forth toward Dariak. He thought to dodge it at first, but he recognized part of their spell—*"casilar slumbreth nei"*—which intoned a call to sleep. He couldn't afford to be stunned during this battle, so he threw both hands out before him and scattered the dirt into the mist. Because the torch was gone, he couldn't explode the pieces to scatter the cloud, but he did something else instead.

"Jalicorith grienan!" he called, overlapping his wrists and curling his hands in the required directions. It was the same spell he had used back in the forest to turn the mud and water into a mild lubricant so he could free his hand from the mage glove. Then, the spell was weak, because he couldn't put force into his call and because one of his hands had been bound behind him. Now, the dirt clung to the mist and turned into a heavy sort of jelly, which promptly dropped from the sky and spattered to the ground. It was still potent and laced with the sleep spell, so he needed to keep his nose up and away from it until it dissipated.

Kitalla had recovered enough to enter a battle stance with Gabrion. The two of them faced off against three sentries, soon to be five, with the threat of more on the way. At least the arrows had stopped with the start of a melee bout; it wouldn't do for the archers to take down their own fighters accidentally. Kitalla dipped below one sword thrust and cut a dagger deep into the man's thigh. He toppled to the ground in agony. The next sentry sprang forward with an overhead hack, but she rolled out of the way in time, kicking up with her foot and sending him to the ground. Angrily, he rolled back up, his armor clanking, and he charged. Kitalla jumped high and pressed her hands on his shoulders as she sprang over him, then kicked her feet into his back to send him barreling forward into one of his comrades.

Gabrion swung his blade around and disarmed a younger soldier, who pulled back to let someone else step in. The warrior yelled aloud as he spun and slashed his sword, crashing it into one sentry's pauldron. It didn't stop the seasoned fighter at all, and Gabrion desperately raised his left arm to block with his buckler. He realized quickly that he needed a larger shield, for a second fighter came along and entered the fray. Gabrion swung his sword wildly, trying to parry two simultaneous sets of attacks. His mentor, Andron, had offered such training but not against foes of this caliber. He panicked and cried out again in defiance. He would not let them stop him from his quest.

Neither would Kitalla, apparently, for she threw a dagger with high precision. It struck one of the fighters in the neck, killing him instantly. She then glanced over her shoulder and assessed that Dariak was holding his own well enough for the moment. She pulled another dagger out and bounced and weaved as she pummeled into another sentry. From the looks of it, though, the alarm was directing the king's guard to their area, for more torches appeared in the distance and headed for them.

Gabrion saw this too, and he doubled his efforts, taking one of the short swords in his left hand and doing a wild pinwheel with both arms as he faced off against the next attacker. Seeing the imposing figure approach, the soldier lost his nerve and bolted away. Instead of following, Gabrion lashed his left arm out to another sentry and then followed it with a swing of his right arm. He then reversed these movements to take down a sentry who was intent on Kitalla.

With the sleep-mist spell ruined, some of the healers broke ranks and charged at Dariak with weapons. Staves, daggers, and a mace came lunging for him all at once. He rummaged quickly through his pockets for a root of blackwood, which he could use to cause blindness, but his hand struck something else, and a flurry of words burst forth from his lips: "*Sassrathallian vornier habberleese!*" It was an unexpected spell he had never heard of before, and in the time it took to cast, the healers had battered his protective shield into uselessness, then swung their weapons into him.

And through him, he noticed. His entire body reacted with the consistency of water. The mace pressed into his nose, then slowed down as it went through him, but it left him unscathed. He swung his arm out to block a dagger thrust, but he slid right through the attacker. The healers swung a few more times but started to panic, for they had never seen such a spell before. They weren't meant to be fighters anyway, and many of them fled.

Feeling a sense of success, Dariak grinned, realizing he had touched the new crystal he had confiscated from the museum. While his first crystal was of earth, this one apparently had powers of water. The water spell faded away, leaving behind an odd, deep exhaustion. He couldn't dwell on it for long, though, because a new, enraged foe appeared.

Master Elgris strode forth from the sanctuary, his eyes alight with anger. His arms swung up and around, and Dariak could feel the pull of the energies from the man. He struggled to pull them back, to somehow prevent the healer from casting whatever spell he was conjuring. But the healer pulled forcefully, and several balls of violet light glimmered within his fists. He spiraled them around in an intricate pattern that mesmerized some of the healers who were supposed to be fighting with him.

Dariak was too focused to be caught by a mere light show, however. He observed the pattern in a detached sort of way and then did his best to duplicate the motion. Mimicry was a vital skill for an ambitious mage, for if the magic user could not adopt specific body patterns quickly, then it wouldn't be feasible to learn more than a few minor spells. Fighting his exhaustion, Dariak bent his knees and swayed his body in time with the motions, then swept one hand down to his left pocket, pulling out a shard of glass. He wouldn't be able to create a protective shield with it, but it wouldn't help him anyway against the power being drawn now.

Gabrion and Kitalla bounded about as if they had fought together for years. She dove low as his sword swung high; then she sprang up as he spun about to kick out at another foe. Her daggers flashed like lightning, striking her opponents fiercely, while Gabrion's sword glided through the air like a gleaming moon, casting wider arcs of reflected torchlight that were just as deadly. Slowly, they took steps back toward the mage, where the sounds of chanting irked them both.

Elgris's muttering grew louder, but Dariak couldn't focus on the words the old man was using. He wouldn't be able to anticipate the intended effects of this spell, but he knew that Elgris thought Dariak was an instigator of war and deserved to die. Dariak continued to follow the motions of the master healer while also sputtering a few words of his own, and he clenched his fist on the glass shard and cut himself deeply, saying, "*Suocillipus mirollia petrica.*" The glass shimmered and vanished, but Dariak's left hand glowed dimly.

Roaring, Elgris shot his arms forward with a face creased in such fury he looked like a monster. Purple blasts of energy lashed out at Dariak with malevolent force. The mage held out his glowing hand while curling his whole self into a semicircle. The light struck his hand, and he felt the effects of the spell run through him. The energies called for the cessation of all of his life functions, the truest opposite to healing that there could ever be. He pulled the energies in thoroughly and allowed the shape of his body and the spell he had cast to act as they must. The power coursed through him, sickening everything and then racing back up and around to the glowing hand, where the violet light was reflected back out, seeking its originator.

Elgris didn't see it coming. He couldn't have fathomed that anyone could reflect such a spell back to its source. The light struck him with nearly the full blast he had released. The old man crumpled to the ground, instantly dead.

Dariak was badly weakened but very much alive, thanks to the reflective power of glass and the spell he had used to call to it. But he couldn't stand anymore.

Gabrion saw the mage fall to the ground. He slashed his sword behind him into one more foe, then turned to Dariak's aid. Kitalla sensed the shift in the warrior's focus, and she too altered her strategy. She slew the sentry before her and, seeing six more on the way, turned to help Gabrion. They hoisted the mage onto the warrior's back, and then she scrambled for a fallen torch.

Kitalla spun the fire around her body, kicking one leg into the air, then swinging her arm out to the side. She brought the torch down across her torso and then twisted so she could follow the flame with her empty hand. Around and about she shifted, pouring her concentration into every movement. She knew she was completely exposed now, with no hope of defending herself, but Gabrion and Dariak were both out of the battle now. If this didn't work, they would all die.

She leaped into the air and landed gently, bending her knees and folding over at her waist, dragging the torch in a graceful pattern with every maneuver. As the fighters approached, they were caught in her enchantment, and their eyes focused only on the fire as it moved about. But she couldn't stay there dancing forever. If others came too soon, their appearance would break this stage of the trance. Yet she also couldn't rush the effect, for that too would ruin it. Down and around the torch went, simulating the sun on its path through the sky, twisting and weaving as if affected by weather.

And then at the last, she threw the torch forward to startle them. What she didn't expect was the blazing fireball that erupted in their midst, severely wounding them.

Stunned, she turned around to see Dariak hanging desperately on Gabrion's shoulder, his hands outstretched in one last spell before he swooned.

Not waiting for any more of the king's reinforcements, they ran.

CHAPTER 13

Departure from Kaison

GABRION BOLTED FROM the battle site with Kitalla at his heels. They didn't have a plan of where to go, but they knew they needed to escape the town at all costs. Alarms flared all over, and though they had successfully dealt with a whole contingent of fighters, they knew they couldn't outlast them all. Kitalla didn't know of any other safe locations in town anyway, so if they remained, it would all be based on luck. Kitalla never chose to do much based solely on luck. The town wall was too high to scale under these circumstances, so dashing through the guard station was the best route.

Gabrion carried Dariak's limp body on his back, which greatly limited his mobility. His arms were under the mage's knees, and the mage's arms were hanging down Gabrion's chest. The warrior had to lean forward slightly to keep the mage from falling off. He pretended for a time that Mira was on his back and that he needed to get her to safety. He simultaneously thought of her waiting up the road and needing to reach her quickly. It helped him focus on anything but the pain he was feeling from the forced run, and it allowed his body to fall into the drill routines that Andron had put him through.

"Keep at it, son," Andron had said. "That wood has to get to town somehow."

"On my shoulder?" the young warrior had grunted in complaint. "At this pace?"

"Trees don't walk on their own, do they?" The soldier had laughed.

Gabrion grinned at the memory, for Andron had challenged him to cart back larger and larger branches across the field after a hard wind had torn some trees down. And Andron hadn't carried a single branch, making Gabrion and two others do all the hard work. They had all been sore for days, but now Gabrion realized that it was the hard training that had prepared him for moments like this.

His feet pounded along the ground as the guard station came into view. Gabrion had been practically unconscious when Dariak had driven them through on the warhorse days ago. He thought it ironic now that he was the warhorse and the mage was incoherent.

Kitalla wasn't thinking of anything at all except getting through the gate without losing a limb. As they approached, she could see that the guards had heard the alarms in town, and so their weapons were at the ready. But she also saw something that would make a stop here worthwhile: horses.

Having been to the town numerous times before, cataloging everything she saw each time, she had never seen more than six guards here. With a failed attempt at a public execution that morning, followed by an immediate break-in at the museum, she wasn't surprised to see that the complement of guards had doubled even that.

Gabrion was encumbered with the mage, so she knew the first attack would be hers. She pulled out half a dozen of her remaining knives and prepared them for assault. Sprinting ahead of Gabrion, she swung her arms in powerful arcs, releasing one dagger per foe with each pass. Only two of the daggers missed vital organs, but they still caused some damage. She reached for two other daggers and readied them for close combat.

Two of the uninjured guards spun around and faced the attackers. Kitalla drew their attention with a vicious cry and leaped toward them, daggers slashing wildly. She caught a lucky strike against one man, killing him instantly, but the other one stubbornly refused to give her an easy win. She faced off against him, bringing one arm up, then kicking out at his knee. He slapped her across her face with his free hand as he brought his mace around to finish her. Tucking low, Kitalla barely dodged the mace and followed up her move by slashing into his knee, taking him down. She tossed his mace to the side so he couldn't attack, but she didn't have time to finish him off.

Gabrion watched as Kitalla raced ahead and then took down half the guards with such fluid grace that it looked like a choreographed dance. He ran ahead, then grudgingly slid Dariak to the ground so he could help the thief in her struggle.

Having taken on the brunt of the assault, the other guards deemed her the greater adversary and focused mostly on her. The one guard who didn't met a quick end on Gabrion's sword. The warrior didn't hesitate to keep plunging ahead. He cut into the sword arm of one guard, then spun around and bashed the man's head with the buckler, knocking him to the ground. Kitalla was so exhausted she kept screaming as she lashed out with successive attacks. At moments like this, Bostian's wild charges had been most helpful.

Gabrion heard the sound of shattering glass in his head but ignored it as he turned to another attacker. The man was already wounded from Kitalla's first strike, but he was furious at these rebels, and his rage propelled him to a massive assault. Gabrion parried an attack that would have impaled Kitalla through the head; then he threw his body into the man to knock him away.

The guard recovered quickly, bringing his sword around and crashing it against Gabrion's shoulder. The warrior rolled aside and ignored the attack, focusing on ending this struggle quickly. He hacked wildly, and sparks flew as the two swords intercepted each other. The standoff was interrupted momentarily as one of the other guards tried to intervene, but Kitalla wouldn't allow it, tossing a dagger at the nape of the man's neck and bringing him down. She turned toward one of the wounded guards, but he held up his hands in supplication, desperately begging for mercy. He found it in the form of a dagger hilt crashing against his head, but it was better than the blade.

Gabrion's attacker saw that the guards had been decimated, but pride demanded he take down these rogues. He backed slightly away from Gabrion, keeping one hand actively poking and parrying with the sword, but his other hand reached in a pocket and retrieved a vial, which he crushed in his hand, and then he muttered some words. The man's sword took on a dim glow, and Gabrion noticed that the attack pattern changed. It was as if the guard had exchanged his weapon for one that was much lighter. He whipped it back and forth with increasing speed, and Gabrion was hard-pressed to keep from being hit.

Rather than demoralize the warrior, the illegal use of magic on the weapon infuriated Gabrion. He had never agreed with the tactics the old king had used in the War of the Colossus to secretly strengthen the arrows through magic. Now the act was being carried out against him. In the moment, it didn't occur to him that he too was protected by magic, for Dariak's spell was still intact.

Anger welled inside him, and his focus sharpened considerably. He heard the tinkling of shattering glass again and again, but it grew more faint, though he forced himself to concentrate on his foe. He eased his eyes slightly, trying to follow a pattern of movement from the faster weapon, and he delighted that he found one. He raised his sword and lanced it forward into an opening, causing the guard to jump back defensively. Gabrion dove to the ground and rolled forward, sweeping one foot out, but the guard was ready for the feint. The faster sword came around and down quickly, and it was all Gabrion could do to bat it aside. But the drive of the thrust sent the sword halfway into the ground, and there appeared Gabrion's advantage.

The warrior turned on his side and kicked one long leg up into the man's chest, detaching him from his sword. Gabrion then hopped onto his feet and took his foe's weapon in hand, noting, indeed, that it felt entirely too light for steel and seemed coated in a cushion of air. His assessment of the weapon cost him, though, for the guard threw a knife, and blocking it caused Gabrion to drop the sword. The guard rushed in, diving for the weapon, but Gabrion kicked it aside and then stamped his other foot down hard on the man's wrist. He followed the move with a boot to the man's head, ending the fight.

Gabrion turned around to help Kitalla with the rest, but there were no more. She had taken down the others or had accepted their surrenders, after which she quickly bound them. She had awoken Dariak and escorted him to the horses, telling him he needed to be strong enough to ride. To his credit, the mage did as he was told, though in a daze.

"I figured you could finish that one on your own," she said offhandedly to Gabrion, tossing him the reins to a sandy-brown steed. "Hope you don't mind." She then hopped onto a black horse and snapped the reins, Dariak close behind.

Gabrion looked around again at the carnage, shaking his head, realizing just how dangerous Kitalla could be. He shrugged off his small buckler and claimed a larger shield that hadn't served its owner at all, considering Kitalla's surprise attack. He mounted the nervous horse and left, following his companions.

The moon was high overhead, and Kitalla was both grateful and angry for it. While they would be able to find their way easily, they would also be easier to track. Still, they were in much better shape than they'd been without the horses. She stroked her mare strongly on the neck, trying to calm it down, for the horse was not pleased with its new rider. Glancing around, she saw that all three horses were fidgeting a bit, testing the mettle of the people on them, but only Dariak was in any real danger of falling off. She navigated her horse closer to his and reached out for his reins, hoping that keeping the horses closer together would make them feel more comfortable for this leg of the journey.

Gabrion rode well, especially after his time on Tumbler, and his mount realized quickly that the warrior was going to stay put. He guided the horse along with the others, but he kept peering over his shoulder for signs of pursuit. "We have to go faster than this," he said. "Dariak, can you manage?"

The mage's black hair bobbed up and down, but he didn't speak. Kitalla released the reins, and the three of them turned the horses north and snapped the reins for them all to run. Startled but compliant, the horses did as commanded, and the trio was on its way.

Gabrion wouldn't allow them to kill the horses by riding them too hard, so he periodically called for a halt or a trot, much to Kitalla's chagrin. She'd simply figured that when one horse died, they would either double up or grab a fresh one from the next settlement, but the stern light in Gabrion's eyes said she had figured wrong. Shrugging, she let the warrior decide their pace, allowing herself to relax in the saddle and sway with the motion. She eyed the mage during the night, noticing that he was gaining back tiny bits of strength. She knew that spells were draining for a mage, but she was the only one among them who hadn't taken a nap that afternoon.

The warrior guided them toward a small copse of trees, where they tethered the horses and settled down for a little rest. He seemed to be vibrantly awake, so he took first watch.

Neither Dariak nor Kitalla argued.

Gabrion knew he was pushing his endurance far, but he didn't have much choice. This wasn't like training, where it was possible to skip exercises if something was too difficult.

No, their lives were at stake, and so was Mira's.

He knew too that he needed to keep alert, so he started by assessing his wounds. He pulled off his chain mail and tunic and looked for gashes that would need tending, but he couldn't find any. It was then he recalled the sensation of shattering glass and the shield the mage had cast around him. It had deflected a good number of attacks, and the new armor had done the rest. He frowned then, for he had benefited from Dariak's magic and the stolen armor. There was little he could do about the use of the protective shield now, but he vowed he would pay back the armor someday.

Kitalla awoke an hour later and gave Gabrion time to rest. Her first act was to count her daggers, disappointed to find only eight remaining. She had reclaimed a number of them from the battle, but some had gone missing. Ideally, she kept at least a dozen scattered about her body, tucked into folds of the leathers she wore, lodged in boots, and hanging from her hips and anywhere else she could stash them.

She had always excelled in knife throwing, even as a child. Daggers were like extensions of her hands. During her time with her mother at the manor, Kitalla had been part of the entertainment by either juggling knives or tossing them into patterns on the wall.

She didn't want to think about her childhood right then, so she pushed the thoughts away and checked on the horses. They had calmed down greatly but were still skittish when she first approached. She laid a soothing hand on her mare and stroked the soft mane while crooning softly. It didn't take long, but the horse regarded her carefully, then neighed gently in response. The mare seemed like a leader, for the other two horses also stopped fidgeting once Kitalla's mare relaxed.

She didn't consider herself particularly good with horses, but she'd had experiences with them too, back at the manor. Usually, it was shoveling out the stalls and bringing feed, but once in a while she was allowed to ride one.

Kitalla stopped herself again and stepped away from the horses. She found herself fidgeting with the necklace she had claimed in Kaison, and she couldn't decide why she had taken it in the first place. Perhaps it was habit from working with Poltor, but it felt deeper than that, like a tucked away memory of a gift bestowed upon her by—

She knew how to stop the reminiscing, she decided. Kitalla looked out in the distance for signs of pursuit, grateful not to see any, and then stepped a little farther into the grove of trees, seeking some wildlife that could serve as food. Her hunt kept her occupied long enough to clear her mind fully. She didn't particularly like squirret meat, but it was a small copse, and they didn't have many options. She shook Dariak awake.

"Hey, mage, how about a little help with a fire here?" She nudged him toward a small pile of twigs she had already established.

He looked like he was in massive pain. His face was creased tightly, and his eyes were half-closed, and not solely from exhaustion. He murmured a few words and twisted his hands upward into the air, and a small flame flickered to life among the twigs. Kitalla had hoped for more, but she didn't say anything.

Gabrion awoke with the crackling of the fire. "Are you mad?"

"You like asking me that," she retorted, setting the skinned squirrets on the fire.

"They're going to see the fire and come right for us."

"True," she agreed. "But you must have noticed that the sky is lightening up, and they're going to find our trail easily enough anyway. Might as well have some food, right?"

"Hang on," Dariak interrupted, and Gabrion turned to the mage, glad that he was in agreement against this foolhardy plan. The mage reached into a pocket and handed some leaves to Kitalla. "Season them, please."

Kitalla chuckled at the look of betrayal on Gabrion's face, but then he caved in and helped with the food. It wasn't a great breakfast, but it satisfied their hunger. An hour later, they continued to the north, reaching the settlement of Warringer by nightfall.

CHAPTER 14

Respite in Warringer

THE VILLAGE OF Warringer came into view as a quaint town nestled among the hills. Torches lit up various homes and roads all along the way, and there was a welcoming tone to the entire entranceway into the town. Dariak and Gabrion were eager to find the inn and take a proper meal and rest, for three days on prison fare followed by a hard day's ride on horseback didn't do well for their strength. Kitalla had been to Warringer in the past, and so she guided them swiftly to the tavern, which was, thankfully, not far from the entrance. They tethered their horses alongside the inn and went inside.

Dariak looked around expectantly for Randler but then shook his head for the thought. It would be too much to hope for, finding the bard so readily. He walked over to the tavern master and ordered three plates of food and drinks, then requested lodging for the night.

The tavern itself was rather quiet. Only a few other patrons were there, and several were enjoying a hearty ale before heading home to their families. The mage earned a few scowls from the patrons as he joined his companions at the table they had selected away from everyone else, but he pretended he hadn't seen the angered looks.

Gabrion, however, had noticed. "That must be hard."

Dariak sat in the chair and agreed. "Yes, it could use a cushion."

The warrior gave him a look. "No, I mean everyone staring at you like you're some sort of criminal all the time."

"Aren't I?" Then he shrugged. "It goes with the territory. Literally. It isn't like this in Hathreneir. Well, some places, yes, but mostly we're as welcomed as anyone else."

Kitalla sighed wistfully. "I wonder if there's a kingdom for people like me, then. Where all the happy little thieves play all nicely with one another and don't worry about watching their backs all the time."

"I've... never really faced any kind of discrimination for just being who I am," Gabrion admitted. "Everyone in Savvron worked hard, and we all got along. But I see the way they look at you, Dariak, and I don't really know what to say."

The mage shrugged. "I guess I've always had to deal with odd looks from others, if not for being a mage, then for other things. It only bothers me when it gets me into trouble."

They paused as the barmaid came over with their food and drink. Each platter had a well-roasted breast of chicken, nicely seasoned with garlic, thyme, pepper, and salt; a mix of vegetables on the side, with sliced carrots and potatoes drizzled in a light gravy; and two slices of bread, one of which had been dipped into a lemony sauce to complement the chicken. The drinks were the standard tavern fare of house mead, but the beverage had a rich, frothy aftertaste that tempted them to just sip and pause so they could savor the sensation.

"You know, I never rightly thanked you back there," Kitalla said suddenly around a bite of chicken.

"Oh?" Dariak asked.

She had an odd tone in her voice, which Dariak couldn't place. "That fireball spell was perfectly timed. I was hoping to just make a run for it when I threw the torch, but I didn't need to. You turned my illusion into reality."

"About that," Gabrion jumped in. "When did you learn to do that spell?"

"The fireball spell? Years ago, why?" Dariak sipped his ale, confused by the question.

"You could have used it in Savvron and put an end to the fighting right away. Instead, you used that fire-dart spell and just scorched things."

"Ah." Dariak nodded.

Kitalla turned her gaze from one to the other and made a cooing sound. "Magey has a heart, does he?"

Gabrion scowled, but Dariak laughed. The sound drew the attention of a few patrons at a nearby table.

"What have you got to laugh about, mage?" one of the drunken men yelled.

Dariak ignored the comment, but Gabrion didn't. "Mind your own table, and we'll mind ours."

The man got up and staggered over, tankard in hand.

"Mages got no right to be happy."

Kitalla decided to intervene. "Hey, fellow," she said in a sultry tone, rising from the table. "I didn't see you over there, or I wouldn't have wasted my time on these two."

The man eyed her hungrily and licked his lips expectantly. "Well, er, hello."

Gabrion didn't know what to do, so he watched in awe as Kitalla poured on the charm. Her hand caressed the man's shoulder, pressing through his tunic. "Oh, strong fellow, are you?" She walked around him, dragging her hand across his back. "With the strength of a plow horse, I would say." She finished her circuit and pressed herself against him, gazing deeply into his unfocused eyes. "Where's your place, fellow? I could meet you there soon as I finish my meal."

The man stammered and snuffled deeply. "Over by the general store."

"Well then, hurry along, friend, and get the place ready for me. And hang your shirt on the front door so I know which one it is, okay?" She batted her eyelashes a few times promisingly.

He licked his lips again and eyed her body one last time before nodding and running out of the tavern to prepare for the tryst. Kitalla waited until he left before coughing deeply.

"Reeked of cow dung, that one."

Gabrion watched as she sat down. "You're not… really going to—"

She stamped on his foot and scowled, then tossed a pouch on the table. "You're an idiot. But at least he was nice enough to pay for dinner by way of apology."

Dariak choked on his mead as he started laughing. "You're something, Kitalla."

"Don't you forget it," she warned, rising again and swiping the pouch, this time to see if their rooms were ready.

Gabrion was still staring at the table where she had thrown the pouch. "I guess he deserved it after what he was winding up to do, but I don't know about all this stealing."

Dariak shrugged. "Then pay for your meal outright with your funds, if it makes you feel any better. As for me," he said, yawning, "I'm heading to bed." He turned around and saw Kitalla striding back with directions to their rooms.

They went upstairs, and Kitalla pointed to a room at the far end of the hallway, then turned into another room only halfway down. "Good night, boys." She went inside, and they heard a bolt snick shut.

The room at the end of the hallway had two cots inside, with musty pillows and blankets. Dariak didn't care. He locked the door and pulled off the leather jerkin he had claimed from the Kaison armor shop, and then he pulled off his robe, laying it open so it could air out somewhat. He watched Gabrion likewise undress in the moonlight, grinning at the show the warrior was inadvertently giving him.

Morning came too quickly. Groggy, the two men dressed and went down to break their fast with Kitalla. She was lively and appeared to have been waiting for them for hours. "You two do like a long sleep," she said by way of greeting, then added in a teasing tone, "or were you two busy all night long?"

Dariak blushed, but Gabrion didn't understand the reference. "Doing what?" he asked.

Kitalla shook her head. "You really didn't get around much growing up, did you? Never mind!" She put a hand up as Gabrion drew in a breath to rebuke the comment. "Food's coming anyway, and we have to figure out our next move."

An older woman came by with their meal. "Excuse me, miss," Dariak said in a warm voice.

"Miss?" She visibly melted. "Don't be silly, son. What can I get you?"

"This food smells as wonderful as last night's meal," he complimented her truthfully. "The only thing I wondered, though, was… Do you ever have any entertainment at mealtimes?" He ignored the piercing stare from Kitalla, who clearly wanted to know his reason for asking.

"Well, not often, I'm afraid," the matron apologized. "There was a minstrel here some time ago who drew in quite a bit of business, but then he left abruptly. And then he reappeared a few days ago, but just ate, slept, and was gone again without so much as playing a tune. He must be in some kind of trouble, I think, the way he keeps taking off like that."

"I see." He debated whether he should ask his next question and decided it couldn't hurt. "Did anyone come after him, do you know? Anyone asking about him after he passed through last time?"

She paused for a moment. "Not to my recall, but then I'm usually with the cherubs at nighttime." She turned her head over her shoulder and called across the room. "Barin, dear, has anyone been asking about that bard?"

"Just one," came a disembodied voice from the kitchen. "Paid extra for information, up front too. Told them he was headed east, toward Pindington." The thick-bellied tavern master came out to join them. "What have you to do with that bard?"

"He's a friend," Dariak said. "He told me he was heading north but not more than that."

"Some friend," Barin scoffed, then looked more carefully at Dariak, scrutinizing the mage robe that he was wearing over the leather jerkin. "So tell me, mage, if you will, when you saw your friend last, did you hear him sing?"

Dariak couldn't help smiling. "I did. He sang of the Forgotten Tribe."

"Aye." Barin nodded. "That's a good one, that. Mind, I think he knows more about the story than he lets on."

"Now, dear," interjected his wife, "are you going to keep chatting away over their meal, or are you going to tell them anything useful?"

"Bah!" He waved her away, then turned back to Dariak after eyeing the others. "He didn't say you'd be traveling with anyone."

Dariak tried to keep his heart in his chest. "Did he say which way he's going?"

"Didn't you hear? I said I told those others where he was heading."

"Pindington," Dariak repeated skeptically. "But that's not where he's going."

"No," Barin agreed. "You look a little like the one he described on his way through, but I need you to confirm it."

Kitalla reached for a dagger to speed things along, but Dariak intercepted her hand. "There isn't much I can say about him, really. We didn't have much time to talk. But he made the most delicious bread I've ever had, loaded with cinnamon, cranberries, and raisins." He didn't know why, but it felt like he had revealed a secret code to the tavern master.

"You're right about Pindington," Barin said. "It was to throw off those hoodlums who were after him. He went ahead farther north. You'll need to get near the Talonic River and then go west a little ways, find a rise, and then look for a cave in the hills."

"A cave?"

"If he isn't there, then he'll have moved on somewhere else. That's all I've got for you, I'm afraid." He tipped his head and left them to finish their food.

Once they were alone, Kitalla raised her brow. "Love interest?"

Dariak's cheeks reddened, and suddenly Kitalla's earlier comment made sense to Gabrion.

"He has a shard," the mage deflected.

The thief leaned back in her chair and put her arms behind her head. "I feel like we're doing a lot of hunting for your pieces of crystal there, but not much else."

"We will."

She threw her body forward and grabbed Dariak by the scruff of his robe. "I don't do things for promises. I'm not going any farther until I get a little something next."

"The more pieces I have, the easier it will be—"

"Likely story, mage," she spat, eyes darkening. They held their gazes in deep focus for a long time, while Gabrion stared at Dariak, digesting the new information about his interest in men. He'd never known anyone before who deviated from the norm in that regard. He wasn't sure how he felt about it.

With a heavy sigh, Dariak succumbed to Kitalla's will. "I will need to see you dance in force and follow the lines of energy you draw in. Then I'll be able to determine the best route to guide your training."

"In force?" she echoed. "So you need me not just to move, but to influence."

"Yes."

She banged her hand on the table. "I guess I could put the moves on this one"—she gestured to the warrior—"but he'll be harder to entrance now that he knows about it."

"Then what do you suggest?"

Kitalla looked around the tavern, and a grin crept upon her face. "Let's put on some entertainment here tonight." She looked at Gabrion. "How are you at standing still?"

CHAPTER 15

Kitalla the Great

THE TAVERN MASTER and his wife were so excited about the prospect of having entertainers that they offered free meals and boarding for each night they performed. Wisely, Kitalla said nothing about it being a solo performance. Barin ran to various spots around town to gather ingredients for food while his wife and children took Gabrion through Warringer, acting as criers. It suited Gabrion just as well, because Kitalla refused to tell him what he was going to have to do.

Dariak spent most of the day in the tavern, resting and preparing for the night. Though he wasn't going to be part of the performance, he would need to focus his concentration sharply to sense the energy flow around Kitalla as she worked in a room of rowdy patrons. In addition, he was still in pain from the vile spell that Elgris had used against him in Kaison. Sometimes parts of his body would tinge with agony for no apparent reason, yet when he read his own energy patterns, everything seemed fine. He also felt tired from the water jade's spell that had essentially transformed him into a liquid. His only hope was that these effects would wear off soon.

Kitalla seemed to be everywhere at once. The thief was full of enthusiasm for the upcoming performance. One moment she was in the tavern, checking viewing angles, the next she was out in search of a costume. Back to her room in the tavern to practice some moves, then off again to replenish her stock of daggers. All the while, her eyes and ears were wide open, and she absorbed information and sorted it as she went.

"You're wearing these." She handed a pair of trousers and a leather cap to Dariak on one of her flights through the tavern. "And we're going to smudge you up a little bit too, tie the hair up under the hat, stash the robe, a dagger or two on your hip, and… No, that should be enough," she decided with a tilt of her head. "Go on, now."

Even after such a short time together, Dariak knew such a demand wasn't to be denied. Up to his room he went, where he exchanged clothes, feeling very restricted wearing pants. They had pockets but nothing like the endless folds of fabric in his robe. It took him some time walking around the room before he felt at all comfortable. Kitalla did have a keen eye, though, for they were the perfect size, and he only tied the leather cord at the waist so it wouldn't dangle.

Once his disguise was set, he rummaged through his robe and pulled out the various spell components he would need for the night, and then he hit a snag. He had two pieces of the jade in his robe, and he didn't want to leave them unattended. He hadn't taken the earth jade from its sealed pouch since sewing it in at the start of his journey. He hated to take it out now, but he didn't have a choice.

Using one of his daggers, Dariak made a small slit at the chest pouch and pulled from within the slightly brown-hued jade he had been given as a token of remembrance. He absentmindedly brushed off some dirt that was on it, shaking his head as he did so, for more dirt immediately appeared in its place. It was an odd property of the crystal that constantly generated grime. Yet, though it was a constant supply, it wasn't endless. So if the dirt was left in place on the jade, none other would appear. It was one of the main reasons he had sewn it tightly into the robe in the first place. Without room to move about, it couldn't produce any more dirt. Loose in his pocket, it had kept regenerating the filth every time the cloth rubbed against it.

He actually needed some dirt, as per Kitalla's orders, and so he used it to smudge up and darken his face, neck, and arms, reaching down and covering his ankles in case his pants went up when he sat. Once he was satisfied, he shoved the brown jade into one of the tight pockets, pleased that he would be able to feel it at all times but also concerned that he could break it.

With one piece in place, he took up the other one. This newer addition had called to him in a moment of desperation and had given him the activating spell to give his body the consistency of water, thus he wasn't surprised to find it was perpetually damp. It had been soaking a small puddle into the robe pocket, but he hoped that when he placed it in the trousers, the confined space would keep it from regenerating water. He wrapped it in parchment first and then stuffed it into the pocket opposite the first piece. He layered the spell components in next and then set his daggers in place before heading downstairs for inspection.

Kitalla approved of the ensemble, merely tugging at the neck and wrists of the shirt to make the outfit look a little more worn in. "Will that suffice?" she asked, pointing to a small table off toward one corner of the stage.

Dariak paused for a moment, then did a double take.

"When did that stage get there?"

"You have your preparations, I have mine," she replied airily. "Will you be able to do your work from there?"

He walked over and sat in one of the chairs at his designated table. It did have a clear view of the stage, but he wanted a partial view of the crowd as well, so he pivoted it around until it suited him. "It's good, but some people might see my hands. Anyone paying any attention will know what I'm up to. I can't pass it off as trying to follow your rhythm."

She sighed lightly. "It isn't like anyone will be focusing on you, but that's a small detail anyway. We'll put a flower vase or a steaming tankard at your table to help block the view. Keep that chair there, and that covers the rest, I think."

"You're very good at all this," he commented.

She eyed him grimly. "Don't try to lead me to explain things. It won't work." Then she eased up her focus. "Besides, if this goes well, you'll have a chance to help me grow. Won't you?"

Those last two words carried a threat, and he knew it. Whether this event went well or not, he needed to find a means of increasing her powers through dance.

She didn't wait for an answer as she swept away across the room, turning some tables this way and others that. He couldn't imagine it would matter once people were filtering in; they'd easily bump tables aside, but he certainly wasn't going to point that out. She really didn't come across as a woman who needed any more power or ability than she already had. Yet on a similar note, neither did he, except for his own personal quest. He could take one of several jobs in one of the mage towers if the Council wouldn't take him back or perhaps seek the king's direct employ as mage chancellor, but his motivation was deep enough to cast aside those possibilities and take the larger risk. He just wasn't entirely sure what Kitalla's goal was.

He let his eyes wander around the room, and he was impressed by other subtle details she had surely demanded. Each table had a candle centerpiece, which served as good counterpoints to the few candles that Dariak had told her he needed for his spells. The fresh scent of lilacs was also present, which would help him hone in on the energies in the room by following their fragrance. The actual type of flower hadn't mattered, so long as it had a strong enough scent, so he wondered if there was a particular choice behind the lilac or if it had just been the easiest to find.

Gazing up, he saw that a few bedsheets had been repurposed to accent the ceiling, creating a tent effect over the impromptu stage. They were held in place by thin rope that wouldn't last the test of time but had a kind of elegance about it. Along the back edge of the stage was a row of square wood panels, but Dariak had no idea what those were for, except perhaps to give depth to the stage itself.

As he explored the alterations to the surroundings, Gabrion came in and was ushered upstairs quickly by Kitalla, who spoke fast but quietly in his ear. She came down a few minutes later, swung past the bar, and returned to Dariak's table with a full, frothy pitcher. "This one isn't for drinking. Just leave it here." She then placed a smaller mug on the table. "But this one you can have. It's the pungent kind, so at least swish some around and spit it, if you won't drink it. You need to smell like you belong here. Outside of that, you really shouldn't move from this spot." She took one last glance around the tavern, then went to her room to make her final preparations.

He took the hint, meaning he was locked at that seat from that moment forward, even though the performance was over an hour away. He sipped the ale and grimaced at its flavor, but it helped him set a gloomy expression on his face, and he felt that would help keep others from trying to join him at his table. Because it was evening already, some patrons were filing in for meals and libations, so Kitalla was right in that he couldn't move from his seat; he'd likely lose it to someone else.

As the crowd settled in, Dariak noticed that it represented perhaps every type of lifestyle in the town. He could see a group of three men, dark beards unshaven for days, hands kept on their weapons at all times. They looked like poor competition for Kitalla's thieving skills, even adding up all their best parts. A father and mother brought two of their children, who seemed so excited by the prospect of a show that their eyes might fall out at any moment. A pack of middle-aged women filtered in, chattering about their day and adding a pleasant, lilting laugh to the growing din. Couples of various ages entered, some with both members interested in the festivities, and others with one there to support the other who wanted to come, which was obvious based on the speed at which tankards were emptied. In one corner a strange blond man with a potbelly sat in green and purple silks, complete with a thimble-shaped hat that sported a gold tassel. Dariak was vaguely reminded of Randler, but it clearly wasn't him.

Then a group of young men entered, and Dariak felt truly stressed for the first time all day. They had sharp eyes that scanned the crowd, and they wore swords, shields, and armor, marking them as members of the king's guard. Their ever-moving glances told Dariak that their mission was to find the fugitives from Kaison, himself included.

The man in the out-of-place silks rose up when they entered. He spun once and approached them, bowing his head deeply and flourishing his hands as he brought them to a table in the center of the room. Two of them refused, opting to stand along the back wall, but the other three accepted the table. The overweight blond man bowed again and spun once more before returning to his place near the bar.

As Dariak followed the man's trail, he almost tipped over his table, for he suddenly recognized his traveling companion under all that silk. Gabrion was doing a fantastic job playing the jovial host as he shimmied this way and that, tending to the guards' needs and flirting with the barmaids who were already filling orders. Each time he swept past the guards, he would nod his head respectfully, which cleverly hid his face from full view. And each time, the guards would usher him away without a second thought.

It was a struggle stripping the smile from Dariak's face and maintaining a sullen expression, but he managed it with a few extra sips of the pungent ale. His own simple disguise had left him unremarkable. Though the guards looked all around the room at different intervals, not one stared in his direction for more than a moment. He blended right in, simply marveling at Kitalla's wit.

Thinking of her, he reminded himself that he had preparations to undertake. He leaned off to one side to pull a few herbs from one pocket, along with a handful of pebbles. He also poured a few drops of the ale on the table and pulled his table's candle closer after spilling out some of the wax. The growing chatter in the tavern covered his chanting as he ground the bits of herbs and placed them into the puddle, securing them in place with the stones. He made a decorative motif with the simple items, taking care to construct with perfect symmetry. Once the rest was in place, he glanced around the room before lifting the candle onto the stones, taking care not to drop any wax.

"Fathirassilur griena munillia forthren kye limonte kwerosh." He moved his hands and fingers with the rhythm of the words, bending one finger, then another, overlapping two others, and so on, in what appeared to be a random fidget but was just as carefully constructed as the motif. When he finished, he checked the room again, adjusted the large, foaming tankard that Kitalla had told him not to drink, then focused his gaze on the candlewick.

His spell was already working, for the lit wick pulled down into the candle, wax filling in atop it, but the flame did not extinguish. It traversed the height of the candle, which was about the length of his hand fully extended, and then the wick and flame poked out the bottom, hovering just over the ale, herbs, and stones. The fire spread out and licked toward the edges of the candle for a few moments, until it melted a domed cavern over itself, after which it remained contained.

The spell was a balance of essence, and he needed its power to help him analyze the energies that Kitalla would be pulling in around her. The ale and stones were the water and earth, while the hovering fire and air represented themselves. The herbs were a medium that would allow him to use his sense of smell in addition to his sight, and as he sent out a few other connection spells, soon he could feel the energies wafting around the lilacs and the other candles that were scattered around the tavern. It wouldn't help him determine anything until Kitalla pulled the energies into focus, and then he would sense the shifts.

Not long later, a few wolf whistles sounded through the tavern, and a veritable princess hovered into the room from the stairwell. Dariak's gaping jaw was mirrored throughout the tavern. Kitalla was ensconced from head to toe in such fine silk it was as if she were draped in a cloud. Her arms fluttered regally out to her sides, and her steps were small but precise. Dariak could already feel the pull of energies in the room, and he shifted his focus to study them carefully.

Kitalla took several measured steps toward the stage, then pirouetted three times, one arm bent tenderly overhead, then strode forth again. It took several repetitions for her to travel across the stage, then around its perimeter, finally coming to a rest at the very center. She bowed her head to the crowd, and they applauded her deeply. She had barely even done anything, and they already loved her.

The first thing Dariak noticed about the energies she used was that they were not flowing the same way that other energies flowed at all. While a mage drew power from the world around him and the spell components he used, Kitalla's forces were all supplied from within and spread outward. It was completely backward.

Gabrion wasn't idle either. He left his position at the bar and swept his way through the crowd, bending and twisting in comedic fashion, his fake belly bumping into the patrons and adding to the humor. He addled his way to the stage and took one of Kitalla's hands, holding it up high over her head. The thief—who looked absolutely nothing like a thief—spun on her heel, lifting one leg out to the side to help the dress flow wide. At the end of each spin, she bent her knee and did it again, slightly faster. Gabrion needed to quickly release and recapture her hand with each turn, and he did so perfectly, even as her dress billowed out and revealed an underlying flash of colors from the skirt. The crowd cheered.

Kitalla spent a while jumping and leaping around the stage while Gabrion assisted with lifts at times or by simply flourishing his arm toward her at others. They ended up at opposite corners of the stage, and she started spinning elegantly toward the center while Gabrion slid forward one step at a time, arms outreached as if intending to take her in his arms. Yet, when they met in the center, his hands snagged on her waistline, and as she spun away, a good portion of her dress came undone, leaving her in a much tighter outfit, still highlighted in silk but now of every color. Gabrion affected terror at the action, and comically looked from the garment in his hand to the woman, and then he ran screaming off the stage, which was followed by riotous laughter.

Dariak was really struggling to follow the energy patterns now, because part of him just wanted to watch the show. But he knew that if he didn't find some way of helping her to channel her abilities more offensively, then his quest couldn't continue. A surge of force called back his focus as Kitalla now strutted across the stage, sinuous and dangerous. Dariak's fingers bent and weaved, trying to match the new flow in the room so that he could remember the patterns later. It was a form of mage script, writing effects into his muscles and mind rather than on parchment.

The crowd quieted down as Kitalla sashayed her hips, pulling her arms sharply left, then right to counter each step. Her eyes smoldered, highlighted by careful makeup that covered her features with creative designs. She looked like a rainbow-colored bird of prey enticing its intended kill, catching it off guard and preparing to strike. She was drawing powerful energies with her movements, and the people were completely enthralled with whatever they were seeing. The moment ended when she stamped one foot forward and threw her arms out to her sides, elbows bent sharply to the floor, head snapped toward the stairs. She held the pose while the applause and whistles resounded.

Gabrion reappeared, clapping his hands, bowing awkwardly to her, and going around behind her until he reached the back of the stage where the wood panels were. He stumbled into one and kicked it over with a loud bang. When he tried to bend over to pick it up, he knocked down the next one, and because the others overlapped one another, they all fell down in a resounding crash.

Kitalla didn't budge, but the audience shouted in anger and dismay at this interruption. Gabrion waved his hands in the air apologetically, bending over and lifting one of the wood planks. Kitalla then clapped her hands, and Gabrion's back snapped up straight. She curled her arms into lurid waves, and with each undulation, Gabrion moved in response, walking to a specific location on the stage. She tapped her foot on the ground, and the silk-laden warrior bent over and placed the wood plank. A clap of the hands brought him back up, more arm movements guided him, and so forth until all the planks were arranged across the stage. The scene ended when she simultaneously clapped her hands and tapped her foot, which were competing signals, and he dropped to the floor with a thud and rolled off toward the stairs.

Dariak was grateful that the skit had not drawn energies to speak of, because he was hard-pressed to keep track of all her other moves. But he was indeed learning a lot from this exercise. He looked down at the candle and saw that the top of the wax was starting to pull inward. Once it reached the bottom, the flame would snuff and his connection to the energies would be over for the night. Yet, there was still some time.

With the wood planks set across the stage, Kitalla grinned and began her next number. She tapped her foot on the ground, which made a modest sound, and then she stepped back, kicking her other leg down to the same effect. But when her foot came down on the wood plank, the sound became a sharp whip crack with each kick of her foot. She built up a slow rhythm, tapping her feet carefully, and as she increased tempo, she pulled one length of silk from her outfit. Her arms moved in time with the beat she was establishing with her heels, and when she landed on both feet for a powerful crack, she launched the silk outward to the crowd. It had a small rock anchored at one end so it would sail easily, and as it fluttered over the audience, they oohed and aahed as if she were tossing out pieces of rainbow. Onward the staccato steps went, ever increasing in speed, with sashes sent flying at the end of each set, until all of them were gone and half the crowd was in tears with the beauty of all the flying light they could see passing overhead.

Dariak could tell that this was one of her strongest glamours, if not the strongest. The energy in the entire room pulsated with her steps, increasing more and more, and as he looked around, he could see that some people were breathing faster and faster, in time with the beat, while others' faces grew redder and redder as if from exertion, and he didn't doubt their hearts were racing. The silk sheaths became real rays of light to the observers, eye-catchingly beautiful and elegant, and something they could only experience in dreams. Dariak couldn't see the imagery itself, but the energies told him much. A hissing sound distracted him, and he looked down, surprised that the candle had already burned through. Apparently, the excessive energy she was drawing for this dance affected even the candles. He didn't have a way of signaling her that his spell was about to run out, but it didn't matter. He knew some things he could show her, and she would be pleased.

It took time for the crowd to recover and for the applause to begin. Kitalla was moving slightly back and forth, as if rocking impatiently, but Dariak could tell it was something else. The way the audience members were shifting, it seemed like they feared they were being ensorcelled, and even though the effects were astounding, they were rebelling against it. But Kitalla's little side sway drew them in and calmed those fears, and they focused on her, awaiting her next routine.

Gabrion was back, with a bit less bounce in his step. That morning, Kitalla had asked Gabrion how well he could stand still. It seemed time to find out. The warrior entered the stage and dramatically pulled up one of the wooden floor tiles, showing it to the audience as if to prove it couldn't possibly be anything else. He then took a place across the stage from Kitalla and held out the wood plank vertically at chest height. Kitalla, now wearing only leathers, withdrew a handful of daggers, showing them to the audience, who silenced quickly, realizing what was coming. Two daggers flew across the stage, hitting the wood plank near the center, and the audience cheered.

But she wasn't done. After removing the blades, Gabrion put the wood down and lifted a fresh plank. This time he held it in front of his head. Kitalla threw three daggers at the wood and then followed them up with five more, creating the semblance of eyes, a nose, and a smile. Gabrion lifted two panels side by side, and Kitalla threw daggers from her left hand at one panel and simultaneously threw daggers at the other panel with her right hand. The result was a perfect circle and a perfect square. She bowed and then stepped over in Dariak's direction.

She leaned over his table, whispering, "Be ready to run." Then she waved a blindfold in the air as if he had given it to her. She wrapped the cloth around her eyes, as Gabrion stood ready, rather nervously, across the stage. Kitalla took her time with the throws, but none of them missed the board, even though she could not see. And not only did they all hit the board, they were arranged in a cross pattern.

The astounded audience was on its feet, clapping, pounding, and begging for more. Kitalla reclaimed her weapons, tucking most of them away, except for two. She tossed the blindfold into the crowd and bowed several times until the audience members settled themselves, after which she pranced playfully around the stage, spinning here and there as she went. Gabrion was still on the far side of the stage, but he wasn't holding any more wood planks.

Kitalla's jaunty moves made the crowd laugh after all the dexterity she had shown, and she twirled once more and stood at the back of the stage at the center. Her hands flew up quickly, and her knives raced to the ceiling, slicing through one of the ropes holding the bedsheets in place. The fabric swooped downward gracefully, and the audience crooned. Before its flight ended, though, she tossed two more daggers in an overhead arc, cutting the other main guide rope and dropping the fabric completely. When it fell, it entangled the three seated members of the king's guard.

While the sheet was falling into place, Gabrion and Kitalla sprinted toward Dariak. Kitalla grabbed the bubbly tankard she had left on Dariak's table, and as she ran, she spilled it on the floor to her right side. Gabrion and Dariak followed on her heels, not touching the liquid, and shoved patrons aside as they made their way to the doorway. The crowd jumped to its feet with the theatrical finish, except for the guards who understood the moves were diversionary. The three under the bedsheets missed the trio's flight, but the two at the back wall acted at once and started navigating around the patrons to intercept them. Kitalla made sure she flung the tankard on the ground hard, so the pieces shattered, sending the rest of the liquid out in a wide pool. When the guards' feet touched the liquid, they slipped and fell hard to the tavern floor, for it was heavily laced with soap and lard.

The horses were not at the tavern's stable, for Kitalla had relocated them so the guards wouldn't recognize them. It hadn't taken her long to learn of their presence that morning, but she knew killing them would only make the hunt worse. Snubbing them by standing under their noses while blatantly out in the open was a much sweeter ploy anyway, in her opinion. She took her companions to the horses, where they mounted up and prepared to flee.

"My things!" Dariak protested.

Kitalla pointed at Gabrion, who tapped his excess belly with a grin. "Got it all, don't worry. Where to, then, that cave?"

The thought of going to the cave both thrilled and horrified the mage. Though he would love to reunite with Randler as soon as possible, the guards would be right behind them, and bringing them to Randler's secret lair was a betrayal he didn't want to commit. "No," he decided suddenly, remembering, "toward Pindington."

Not caring why, Kitalla kicked her mare off, laughing as the guards raced after them on foot. "Thanks for coming to my show, boys!" she called out to them. With that, she put the horse to speed, heading east, with Gabrion and Dariak close behind.

CHAPTER 16

Nighttime Menace

KITALLA RACED HER mare toward the far eastern town of Pindington, with Dariak and Gabrion urging their own horses to keep up. They each glanced over their shoulders for signs of pursuit, and it wasn't long before the guards followed on their own steeds. Pushing the horses hard, they moved away from Warringer into the dark night.

Deep howling echoed across the plain, quickly escorted by the sounds of massive paws beating into the dirt. The horses whinnied at the approaching beasts and struggled against their riders in terror. Kitalla's mare came to a full stop, rearing its legs into the air and nearly throwing the tired thief to the ground.

"Tether the horses together," Gabrion suggested.

"Great idea," Kitalla scoffed. "Then one bolts and they all do."

The howling echoed again, much closer than before, but it was hard to see in the darkness. "They're going to panic anyway," Gabrion insisted. "Better they stay together." He brought his horse toward Dariak's and reached for the reins, seeing that the mage had dismounted and was in the midst of a spell.

"*Carianna notiosa domenia klei!*" Dariak shouted after a few moments of wild gesturing. The ground underfoot started to glow ominously, illuminating the surrounding area so they could see the creatures stalking them.

"Fool," Kitalla hissed, dismounting from her horse and preparing to fight.

"Shadows may be fine for you," Dariak retorted, "but we need to see what we're doing."

Distant hooves approached from one side, as paws pounded from the other. The three companions brought their weapons about, linking the horses' reins gently so they would stay close, but if they ran, they wouldn't strangle one another either.

The illuminated ground gave Gabrion his first glimpse of a lupino. The beast was similar to a wolf in shape but had longer fangs and claws, wildly vibrant eyes, blue-tinted fur, and great agility. The massive paws looked powerful enough to swipe his head off in one shot. A long, barbed tail swished angrily back and forth as the glowing yellow eyes sized up the victims.

It wasn't alone. Lupinoes always traveled in packs, usually of at least five. Each pack had a leader, but it wasn't always the largest and strongest one. They had a strange sense of cunning, and the one with the greatest cunning was often respected the most. Though leadership was often determined through fighting and dominance, a well-placed bite and slash could immobilize a larger beast and end the struggle. Tails whipping expectantly, the pack drew close.

Dariak had already summoned the Shield of Delminor and his fire-dart spell as his instinctual defense. Kitalla scoured the six beasts, determined to pick out the leader and kill it first, hoping that would demoralize the others. The horses' eyes were wide with panic, and once the first lupino lunged in, they fled north.

Two lupinoes attacked each of the companions, roaring their war cries as they pounded in. Gabrion, amazed by their speed, barely escaped being eviscerated on the first swipe. He twisted his body sharply, bringing his shield about and completing the spin to crack the sword into one of the beasts' hides. The lupino howled in pain but didn't hesitate as it landed on the ground and jumped again for the warrior's throat. Its fellow lupino waited a moment and then lunged. Gabrion dodged the first creature and then threw himself on the ground as the second flew through the air. He tumbled desperately, righting himself at last and facing off against the monsters, better understanding their abilities.

Kitalla was exhausted from her performance, having drawn more energies about her in one session than she ever had before. Nonetheless, she was keen and sharp, and her daggers whipped around furiously at the attacking foes. One lupino jumped for her, and she ran toward it, rather than dodge aside, slashing upward and digging her blade into its forepaw and up into its underbelly. The monster screamed in agony and crashed in a heap, paws flailing to right itself and take revenge. Kitalla would have finished it off if not for the second lupino that charged her moments later. She tried to use the same tactic, but the agile creature had learned from its companion's mistake, and the large fangs snapped wildly as it approached, preventing Kitalla from repeating the attack.

The thief rolled to the side and kicked out at the lupino's rib, hoping emptily to knock the air out of it. She pushed herself up and threw one dagger sharply at the first target, catching it in the shoulder and causing another loud cry of agony to rend the night air. The distraction almost cost her, as the other beast pivoted sharply and nipped for her ankle. A fire dart struck the lupino in the face and saved her.

Dariak's arms were wildly swinging about. When his two lupinoes targeted him, he stood his ground, trusting the power of the Shield of Delminor. He weaved about to ensure he avoided the claws, but otherwise he let the beasts crash into him. They fell to the illuminated earth, unable to lift themselves off the ground. Their hind legs and tails were free, however—as were their jaws—and so Dariak moved away from them quickly. He shot a few darts to help Gabrion, then some for Kitalla.

"Halt, cretins, you cannot escape the king's wrath!" echoed an angry voice as the king's guards rode in. The speaker pulled the reins of his horse inside the illuminated circle, seeing at last the lupino threat. He called for his four companions to stop, debating whether they should let the beasts finish the work or intervene so they could take prisoners back to His Majesty.

The delay proved costly, and he realized his error too late. From the shadowy edge outside the ring of light, another lupino pounced and unhorsed him easily. He crashed to the ground, dead instantly. The fierce animal wasted no time and attacked the next rider, biting into the horse's neck and flipping its rider over to collapse head-first into the ground, snapping his neck. The youngest soldier among them was paralyzed in terror and survived only because his horse screamed and ran from the fray, taking the rider swiftly back to Warringer.

Two guards remained. They dropped to the ground for better dexterity, rather than wrestling with their frightened horses. Freed of control, the horses ran off, smelling the death of the gutted horse and not wishing to share its fate. A lupino bit one guard in the leg and took a sword thrust to its side. Wrenching hard, the man toppled, but the beast couldn't finish him off, as the other guard stepped in and dug his own blade into the creature's flank. Growling in pain, the lupino rolled on the ground, pulling the guard's leg over itself and raking his body with its powerful claws. The guard was finished, but the creature also met its end as the other guard punctured its exposed belly. The death throes of the beast sent its hind legs into the soldier, stunning him temporarily.

There wasn't much the mage could do other than distract the animals, for most of his spell components were in his robe, which was tucked inside Gabrion's tunic. He needed an exterior fire source in order to ignite a proper fireball, and so he was left with his darts. He could feel the Shield of Delminor starting to fade, and his two foes would soon be able to rise from their heavy state and destroy him. He tried getting in close enough to stick his dagger behind one creature's skull, but it was able to thrash around enough to make it impossible. On a second attempt, he learned the hard way that their spiked tails not only hurt, they were poisoned.

Very quickly, the feeling went out of his entire right arm, as if each beat of his heart thrust the poison through. He could no longer send out sparks with his right arm, so he backed off and focused all of his strength on launching stronger bolts from the left. Then a blood-curdling cry sounded from Gabrion, and he turned to see what had happened.

The warrior was on his back, covered in blood, screaming out fiercely. He clutched his shield in one hand and still maintained his grip on the sword in the other. He yelled again and rolled up to his feet, looking around for his next target. Apparently, it had been a call of triumph, for the two lupinoes he'd faced lay in heaps on the ground. Gabrion wasted no more time; he ran over to Dariak's side and hacked quickly at the two ensorcelled creatures, immediately ending their threat as well.

Kitalla needed help. She was using her dance moves to confuse the beasts, but they didn't work nearly as well as on humans. Still, they were enough of a distraction to allow her to escape the beasts' attacks, as the wounded lupino tromped slowly, while the other one skated in circles. When the motion fit the dance, she loosed daggers at the beasts, but they were often able to swat or bite them away. It was clear that she was running low on stamina.

Dariak fired off a few remaining fire darts and infuriated the two lupinoes, but it was Gabrion who charged forth and did the killing. He took out the wounded one first, rushing in with a loud yell and pouncing into the air, hacking at its head and thrusting his sword in through the creature's eye. The final lupino knew it couldn't win, but neither could it escape. Fire struck its paw, daggers hit its flank, and the warrior landed on its back, grabbing on to the dark-blue fur. The lupino thrashed wildly about, trying to unseat the man, but he squeezed his legs tight, slashing the sword backward and lopping off its tail, then turning the blade around to strike a killing blow. The beast denied its mortality for as long as it could, but then it crumpled to the ground, and Gabrion rolled away to safety.

They listened carefully and could hear another set of heavy paws hitting the dirt, but the steps were in retreat. Apparently, with the first line taken care of, the lupino leader decided this group was too fierce, taking the rest of its pack away.

Kitalla belted out her best summoning whistle, hoping her mare would hear it and return, preferably with the others in tow. She hadn't had much time to bond with or train the horse, but it was worth the attempt.

Dariak waved off help as he pointed over his shoulder, and Gabrion walked over to the last remaining member of the king's guard. Sword in hand, he waited as the man rolled over and stood up.

The guard dropped his weapon and placed his hands behind his head. "I cannot take you in, but please spare me. I have children."

"Kill him!" came a wild cry from Kitalla, and whether she was serious or calling out for effect, Gabrion didn't know.

"Please don't!" the man cried. "I am Hernior from Kaison, member of the king's royal guard. I admit we were to find and capture you, but we could not."

Kitalla hobbled over, having been cut and slashed in a few places. She held a dagger in her hand, eyeing it strangely in the pale light that was starting to fade. "Yes, yes, of course you couldn't. You didn't even recognize us when we were right in front of you. Maybe we shouldn't leave anything recognizable of you." She lunged forward, but Gabrion grabbed her shoulder.

"No," the warrior said calmly. Kitalla stiffened, but then the horses came trotting back, and she shrugged, going off to tend to them.

"What will you do with me?" the man asked.

Dariak wandered over, trying to massage feeling back into his arm. He examined the warrior and the odd expression on his face. "What is it?"

"I'm not going to live my life on the run," Gabrion said. "I went to Kaison to see the king in order to tell him that my town was attacked by Hathrens. He unjustly threw me in prison because I wouldn't kill you. And he ignored my call for help. Mira awaits, in enemy hands, and I can't go to her because we're pursued. This must end."

"Please, sir, I will testify to the king of your worth!" Hernior begged desperately. "I will do anything!"

"Just kill him already," Kitalla called, and this time Gabrion could hear a tone of humor in her voice. She knew he wouldn't do it.

Gabrion stared coldly at the man. "How much is your life worth?"

Wide-eyed, the guard looked up at the taller warrior. "Everything, good sir. Release me, and I will do whatever I can, the best that I can. I swear on my son, Erion, and daughter, Seliema."

"How old are they?" Gabrion asked.

"Erion is six. Seliema is four. Please, their mother died of fever three years ago. I cannot leave them alone!"

Kitalla walked over, lightly holding the reins of the horses. "Well, you left them long enough to go on a manhunt after a group of people who killed many of your brothers. You left for an indeterminate period of time and with no promise of return." She let her voice hang.

"The king ordered us to go!" he pleaded. "I would have chosen to remain at—"

"Enough," Gabrion cut in. "Listen carefully, Hernior." He added the name specifically to let the man know he had been paying attention to the details. "One of your group fled the battle. He will undoubtedly go for help, even if it means pleading with our merciless king. You must stop him. Convince him to leave this search undone. We were slaughtered by these creatures, and there was nothing left of us worth bringing back.

"And on the way, you will detour to Savvron. Speak to the oldest men and women you find. See the carnage that happened there and report it to the king as well. He might listen to one of his soldiers if not one of his peasants."

Kitalla groaned. "We don't know that he'll actually do it."

"I will! I promise!" the man groveled.

"Of course he will," Gabrion declared with certainty. "He has given us the names of his children. We know for whom he works. And he knows that we're able to escape notice if we so desire, even when one of us draws everyone's full attention, his included. He knows we're ruthless when we need to be. And we all know what he looks like. We'll find him if he doesn't do as required."

"I swear to you, on my wife's grave, that I will do as you ask. You all died in this tumult. I swear it!" His voice quivered, but his eyes were sincere.

"Go." Gabrion ushered him away to run in the darkness back toward Warringer.

"Well played," Kitalla commended, handing Gabrion's horse over to him. "We should get moving now, though. Those lupinoes might be regrouping." She turned to Dariak. "You all right to ride?"

"The feeling is coming back a little; I'll be fine." He struggled to climb upon the horse, but he managed.

Gabrion pulled the mage's robe from his tunic and handed it over, then mounted his horse. "Which way are you headed?"

"We're headed to Pindington, remember?" Dariak answered.

"No," Gabrion decided. "It's entirely the wrong direction. Mira is to the west."

The mage saw the determination setting into the man's eyes. "The group that was after the minstrel also has a shard, and they're heading east. If we intercept them—"

"Then we get closer to your absurd idea of peace!" Gabrion shouted. "Assembling the shards to earn great power to end wars? It won't work. No, we need to secure the border between our lands and stop brigands from crossing in both directions."

"Both directions?" Kitalla asked. "Don't you plan on crossing over that way first? For your lady?"

"That is different. She belongs in this land."

The thief sighed. "Everyone has their own reasons for all the things they do. They come here for one thing; you go there for another. How is your plan any better than his?"

Gabrion turned his horse around. "She needs me."

Dariak looked at the back of Gabrion's head. "We'll get her back. After this detour, all roads will go toward the west."

The warrior's head bent down. "But north too, then maybe into the mountains, and then perhaps waggling to the south. By the time we even get there, she'll be—" He stopped himself.

"Well, I'm not waiting around here anymore," Kitalla announced. "I'm bleeding, and I'm tired, and I want to reach Gerrish for a proper rest before making the extended journey to Pindington."

Gabrion said nothing, so Kitalla asked, "Are you sure? You're really planning to go it alone?"

"Yes." He looked back at the two of them. "You don't need me anyway."

"You're wrong," Dariak said honestly.

"Fine." Kitalla rolled her eyes, having reached her limit. "No long good-byes then."

Dariak couldn't believe the warrior was about to go. He had grown fond of the lug. He walked his horse over and grasped the warrior's hand, then cast a furious look at Kitalla to at least bid him a proper farewell.

Gabrion reached out for her hand. "Best of luck on your journey."

"You too," she said, reaching out with her right hand to clasp his. Then, before anyone could see, she swung her left arm out, dagger held backward in her hand, and clocked him in the side of the neck with the hilt, immediately knocking him out cold.

"What are you doing?" Dariak shouted.

"He's coming with us." She hopped from her saddle, unwound a rope from her waist and secured the warrior to his saddle, then remounted her horse, took the reins of both animals, and turned to the mage. "Do I have to knock you out too? Let's move it."

Stunned, it took a moment for Dariak to respond.

Apparently, the thief had also grown attached to the man. She could have easily let him go. Turning his horse and pressing his knees in hard, he raced after her.

"He'll kill you for that," Dariak called over to her.

"Let him try."

CHAPTER 17

The Warrior and the Thief

GABRION OPENED HIS eyes slowly, and the light striking them sent flashes of agony through his skull. He squinted for a while, then gradually let more light in until he could make sense of his surroundings.

He realized that he was lying down on a cot with a thin blanket pulled up to his chin. He felt weak and tired, but it seemed mostly from the pain in his neck and head. He pushed himself upright, and the blanket slipped down to reveal that he was no longer dressed as a silken jester. Several poultices were wrapped around various wounds, including a cold compress on his neck.

The room was tiny and made entirely of wood, from the walls and ceiling to the furnishings. The smell of pungent herbs wafted through the air, and light shone through a window cutout in the wall that had no covering and would allow rain to blow right in. His chain mail and tunic sat on a chair nearby, as did his sword and shield. He held his head for a while as he struggled to rise up and gather himself.

He remembered well enough what had happened. Kitalla had stunned him, and they had ridden through the night. He had only caught glimpses on the journey as he slowly recovered, but the pains had kept him well sedated. What he didn't know was where they were, but he suspected it wasn't Warringer.

Gabrion pulled on his pants and tunic, leaving the chain mail for later. What he needed most was food and something to alleviate the fierce pounding in his skull. Then he would deal with Kitalla and Dariak.

Stumbling through the doorway, he found himself in a larger house than he had expected, with at least eight rooms that he could see from his vantage point, including a seating area in the center, loaded with ferns and other green plants. He ignored as much of the throbbing as he could and approached a table off to the side, where an old woman sat with needle and thread.

"Ah, good, you've awoken," she greeted him. "You're a hardy one, my friend. My name's Pionalla. I'm the village healer. Your friends went out, but they'll be back shortly. You all looked worse for the wear when you crashed in last night. And your poor horses too. But everyone will be all right in the end, dear. You do look a bit peaked. Let me have a look at you." She didn't give him a chance to interrupt before pressing her hands against his temples, which hurt terribly. "Ah, you'll be fine, son.

Here, take a walk over there, and eat something. I'll get you an elixir for that head-ache."

Too achy to argue, Gabrion did as he was told. The fare wasn't bad, but he normally wouldn't have chosen to eat it.

The bread was at least a few days old, and the stew had also been around a while. It was grisly and had a strange tang to it. He tried to pretend it was loaded with healing herbs that would fix him up from the inside, but he doubted that was the case.

A large mug of warm tea was placed beside him, and the woman applied a cold towel to his neck on top of the poultice. "This one looks like it was for protection, if you ask me."

"I didn't," he grumbled.

She harrumphed and sat beside him. "I made them explain why you were tied to that horse and why everyone was wounded. Made a bit of sense, bringing you with them rather than letting you run off by yourself."

"It wasn't their decision!" he yelled, immediately regretting it as pain surged through his head. "I would have been fine… I will be fine." He crammed in a few more spoonfuls of stew.

"Yes, I don't doubt that," she agreed. "You're a strong one. Just don't be too rash. Think things through and do what your heart tells you. It's when you lose yourself that you're truly lost." Then she stood and walked away.

The words irritated him, for they reminded him of his father's warning. He didn't know what that meant anymore. At least he hadn't killed that last guard and had given him a chance to return to his family while hopefully convincing the king to call off the search. Yet he also wanted to abandon Dariak's quest and pursue Mira, to save her before it was too late. He had no idea how long the Hathrens would keep a hostage or why they had chosen her.

The tea soaked into the back of his throat and soothed on its way down. It calmed him, and that eased the throbbing in his skull. As he took the last few bites of stale bread, Dariak entered the main room, where Pionalla pointed in the warrior's direction.

The mage was wearing his robe again with a slight alteration, perhaps due to damage during the fight with the lupinoes. Instead of completely enshrouding him, the robe was left open and looked more like a cloak now, which gave Dariak more mobility while still allowing access to his spell components. It also appeared as if he had spent the morning stocking up on supplies, for the red cloth and underlying leathers were practically bulging all over the place. "Good, you're back with us."

"Not like I had a choice."

"She—"

"I don't want to hear it," Gabrion interrupted. "Not now. I need to rest." He pushed away his plate and bowl and then ignored the pleading look on Dariak's face before making his way back to his room. He shut the door and stretched out on the bed, tenderly rubbing his temples and waiting for the pain to subside.

Whether it was moments or hours later, he had no idea, but Kitalla was sitting on the chair, having moved his things to the floor. She sat with her legs crossed and her hands on her knee, as if he had summoned her to hear about his latest dream.

"Get out," he growled.

"Make me."

He sat up quickly, then regretted it as the pain swept back in full force for a moment, but when he was still, it was much better than earlier. "I don't want to talk to you."

"That suits me fine. I don't want you to talk. Just listen." She waited calmly until she read acquiescence in his expression. "You're very strong and very noble. That makes you uncommon and a bit stupid."

He opened his mouth to speak, but she waved him to silence.

"You're rash when it comes to some things, but you're consistent with other things. I knew you weren't going to kill that guard. We weren't in the middle of fighting him; you had no reason to. It's the same as when you tried to leave the forest without hurting us." To her credit, she held back a mocking laugh. "And you let that mage live even after he attacked your village. There aren't many men like you in the world." Her voice went oddly quiet, laced with emotion. "I couldn't let you run off to die."

"I wasn't going to go die."

She sighed. "Not in your head, no. But you forgot that Dariak stole something of value from the king's museum, didn't you? And I'm sure the guards were sent to retrieve it as well as us. Even if we had been killed, they would have taken that shard back."

Gabrion thought about it for a moment, then slowly shook his head. "Is no one honest in this world anymore?"

"I don't think the guard lied to you at all, Gabrion. I believe he will do what you asked, but when the king asks about the jade and there isn't one to return, the hunt will continue." She cleared her throat. "He probably knows that too."

"So the king will kill him."

She nodded. "Or give him the option of leading the next group since he knows well enough what we look like."

"How long do you think it will take?"

A proud smile crept over her face, and Gabrion wasn't sure at first how to read it. "You sent him off on foot, and then he has to talk down the other guard. Then you did the best thing you could have done. You sent him to your hometown. That in itself gives us a good deal of time, both for him to get there and then to return to the king. Because I do believe he swore honestly to you, and he will carry out his errand as you specified."

"And in the meantime, I'm just a dog following his masters."

"You were doing so well up to that point." She frowned. "Listen, will you? You weren't supposed to be talking anyway. I don't believe in promises. They're too easy to break. I've seen too many of them shattered for too many reasons." She cleared her throat. "I also know how men are, which was why it was so easy to disguise us all back at Warringer. One pretty dress, and I'm the focus. Unlikely outfits for the two of you, and we're all strangers, not a trio of brigands."

Gabrion was shaking his head. "Where is this going?"

"Shh." She rolled her eyes. "Some men are just stubborn too. Where was I? Ah, yes. I don't think the three of us have a realistic chance of entering Hathreneir and walking into the castle unscathed so you can collect Mira. But!" she exclaimed to cut off Gabrion's retort. "I do think that we have the potential to get there. Hear me out.

"Dariak needs the shards to gain more power. He spent some time this morning helping me to recognize the energy I draw in, which will give me the abilities I need to be stronger. Your skills improve greatly with every encounter, almost like you absorb the situation into yourself and then put it to use."

Gabrion blushed at this description of himself, as Kitalla knew he would.

"Given a little more time," she barreled on, "we will be strong enough to save her."

"Do you really believe that?"

She stared at him intensely for a while before she nodded. "Absolutely. Even without all the pieces of the Red Jade, we're all getting stronger. We've done so much so far. They won't be able to stop us. And," she said hesitantly, then stopped.

"And?"

Her eyes sank down, and she remained very still for a few moments before she spoke again, and when she did, it was as if she were letting out a part of her soul. "Your nobility is something I want to believe in. Something I lost a long time ago. But with every twist, you've always brought it forth. It's a real part of you. So I want to give it a try." His brows furrowed deeply.

She looked into his brown eyes, and he could see tears brimming there. "I promise you that I will help you get her back."

Gabrion's jaw firmed, and he gave a terse nod, which she returned. They each released a deep breath, and Kitalla stood up. "Good, that's done."

"Kitalla?"

"Hmm?"

"If you don't believe in promises, how can I count on you for this one?"

She smiled. "I guess you'll have to wait and see."

CHAPTER 18

Gabrion in Gerrish

THE HEALER OF Gerrish was skilled in her ways, but she had not the power of the clerics of Kaison. She couldn't pull the energies in and seal gashes or encourage the body to fix itself properly, thus the trio remained in the town for a few days.

Dariak and Kitalla spent hours together, discussing the differences between her arts and his magic. He worked with her on meditating and visualizing the energy flowing out of her, creating the scenes she was conjuring for her victims, but she hated sitting still for any length of time. She argued that she just thought of what she wanted people to see and her body did the rest, so challenging her to analyze it was like trying to feel how the mind tells the hand to bend into a fist.

When he wasn't coaching the thief, Dariak spent his time communing with the pieces of jade, trying to learn more about them, but his efforts with Kitalla were draining, so his progress was slow. He tried fitting the two pieces together, but none of the irregular faces seemed to match. The pieces resonated with perfect synchronicity, yet something was amiss.

With his companions busy, Gabrion walked around the village, learning where the shops were located and taking on tasks for the healer to help repay her kindness. Her practice depended solely on donations, and she never once asked them for a single copper coin, but Gabrion insisted on doing something productive for her.

The warrior was an experienced farmer, and so he put his skills to use tending the herb gardens that sprawled out the back of her establishment. She had rows of flowers and plants growing in wild patches, with weeds creeping in maliciously. A trowel, some shears, and the sun shining overhead were all the things Gabrion needed for a truly therapeutic recovery, both of his wounds and the garden.

Once he had tended to the soil and procured the supplies she needed from various vendors in town, Gabrion put his back into making repairs to some of the falling planks along the house. It was harsh work with his mending wounds, but he was careful enough not to reopen any of them. He couldn't convince the others to help, as they were focused on their own goals, but at least he knew he was doing what was right.

His father would be proud.

Gabrion's skills in the kitchen, however, were lacking. Chopping tomatoes usually resulted in a mess, and it became a bit of a sport for Kitalla to harass him during his attempts, after which she would apply her daggers in force and dice anything nearby with such precision Gabrion was always amazed. He was much better at larger, sweeping motions, but he needed to build finesse as well.

There was a training studio for wannabe warriors, and Gabrion attended a session one morning to try to learn some pointers. Warmaster Garroph refused to let the man participate against the younger lads, but he let the warrior watch from the sidelines. When Gabrion asked if he could spar against the warmaster himself, the man eyed the remaining poultices and shook his head, not willing to inflict any more damage until Gabrion was fully healed.

Among his rounds, Gabrion visited the village elder, but he was not permitted entrance until his fourth attempt. Something about routine and rituals not being followed, yet when he would ask around, no one would clarify for him. He tried bringing a gift of herbs on his third visit, but he was sent away, told the infirm needed them more.

Five days after arriving in town, Gabrion's wish to meet with the elder was granted. He was given a large smock to wear in homage to the town, and he walked barefoot into a wide room, where sand and stones etched a circuitous path toward the center of the room. Though it would have been much faster to take ten steps straight ahead to the old man kneeling at a table, he understood that he needed to traverse the longer path, and so he did.

At first, the steps were easy. The sand was perhaps an inch thick, and the river rocks along the side easily marked the path. He wound around to the left and followed the wall all the way toward the back, where the path turned around and led halfway down along the wall. As he went, the sand went deeper and deeper, until it was like walking along a beach, which Gabrion had done only once before, as a young child, when his family had ventured south to Benningor. He worked hard to maintain his balance in the sand, and when the path swirled around to the left and the right, the sand changed again.

Now shards of broken glass littered the sandy walkway, with scattered stones as well. The objects dug into his feet and set him off-balance. His arms floated out to his sides to keep himself from falling. The old man in the center of the room didn't acknowledge his struggle at all, and Gabrion didn't give him the satisfaction of hearing any complaints.

The path wriggled along the outer wall again and over to the right side of the room, where it swept around and back. As he went, the broken pieces of glass were fewer, and it was easier going. For a few steps, anyway. Then he placed one foot down and it sank. His foot touched a pool of water underneath the layer of sand. He noticed that he could stand for a moment before sinking in, so he took quick steps along the surface, practically jogging forward until the ground hardened again to a single layer of soft but firm sand. A few steps later, he dropped to his knees before the old man and waited.

They stared at each other for a few long minutes while Gabrion took in the shiny, bald pate, the gray eyes enfolded with countless wrinkles, and the fingers that kept tapping together as if expecting something.

At long last, the old man opened his mouth and asked, "Well, did you come all this way for some purpose, or did you just want to sit and stare at me for a while?"

Gabrion struggled not to laugh. "I only wanted to thank you for your hospitality in your village and to alert you to the prospect of war that is brewing to the west."

The old man drew in a deep breath and then poured out two cups of cold tea, passing one along to the warrior. "You notified my nephew of both things already. Yet you're here, interrupting my meditation anyway."

"I'm sorry. I just needed to tell you in person."

The old man scrutinized him carefully. "Yes, yes, I can see that." He sipped the tea, then reached over, plucked up a pinch of sand, and added it to his cup, swirling it and drinking again. "I don't generally see outsiders. They bring such trouble with them. And you're no different, mind. Tidings of war, indeed."

"But it's true," Gabrion said defensively. "They sacked my vill—"

"To the west," the elder interrupted, "is a town called Warringer, so named because it is the harbinger of war to us in the central expanses and to the east. When war erupts to the west, Warringer lets us know. What need have I of your news?"

Gabrion's eyes fell to the floor. "I wished to save your town from the same fate as mine, that's all." He stood up and turned to leave. "Forgive my intrusion."

"Now, now, don't get all uppity and go just yet." The elder waved for the warrior to sit and finish his tea. "I haven't known many visitors who wished to see me who didn't barge in or sneak in or bribe their way in. No, you just showed persistence, always respectful and optimistic that you would be allowed in to see me at some point.

"And then once you were in my door, you saw the path laid out before you, and instead of tromping your way directly to me, you took the winding path out of respect and approached me properly, all without a word of complaint." He tipped his cup in Gabrion's direction. "Too long has it been since someone showed such respect, and I thank you for it."

Gabrion sipped his tea and smiled, but before he could say anything, the old man spoke again. "Yes, you walked the paths of persistence, of patience, and of pain. It was well that you did so, for those are important roads to travel."

The old man moved the small table off to the side and lifted up a stick that was underneath. He drew a diagonal line in the sand between them. "The path of persistence is like the upward side of a triangle. It is supportive and strong and gives form and shape to the rest, yet on its own, it tumbles and falls. Rash action and blind rushing eventually fail in the end."

He drew a connecting diagonal line downward. "The path of pain is a part of life, whatever your vocation. A warrior takes injuries in battle. A child faces the eventual loss of his parents. A farmer sees the end of growth, where he must rip from the soil all of his hard work. Every birth requires tremendous pain to bring new life. And all of our choices have consequences of their own, to varying degrees."

He then drew a third line at the base. "The path of patience, upon which the other two rest. It is the foundation of rational thought and process, of finding a balance between when to rush ahead and when to face the agony. Without it, the other two slide and fall in time, collapsing in on themselves." He tapped the center of the triangle and looked deeply into Gabrion's face, studying him. "Your hand, in here."

Gabrion tentatively reached his hand into the triangle the man had drawn on the surface of the sand. He pushed his fingers inside, surprised to find a somewhat milky texture. Down his hand went until it stopped, brushing against a solid surface. Yet as he sat there, the sand around his wrist hardened, and he was trapped. "What?"

"Patience, remember." The old man poured himself another cup of tea and sipped it slowly, savoring the flavor. "What do you know of the Forgotten Tribe?"

"Not much," Gabrion admitted, sitting awkwardly with his hand stuck in the ground. "Dariak mentioned its name, nothing more."

"Have him tell you what he knows, then. But you should know this much: generations ago a man and a woman met and fell in love. They had grand wishes for the future to create a world together. But they fought, and they parted, and thus were born the kingdoms of Hathreneir and Kallisor. They never birthed the great nation they once desired, and therefore the people of that single nation never lived. It would have been a people in a land borne of love, not war. But instead, their love was forgotten, and so was its offspring. Hence, the Forgotten Tribe."

"So you're saying that the reason we're always at war with the Hathrens is because those two lost their way?" Gabrion asked.

"Indeed, and wasn't the War of the Colossus intended as a means of uniting the two kingdoms under one ruler?"

Gabrion flexed his back to reduce the knot that was forming from hunching over. "Then the Red Jade entered and ruined it for everyone again."

"Perhaps," the old man said cryptically. "Or perhaps its work was enacted at the wrong time or in the wrong way. Or the loathing of man was the greater force still. After all, it was our king's father who pressed his every advantage in that war." He paused for a moment. "Now, sit up."

Gabrion did so, pulling his hand from the triangle, clutching a glass-like object. He knew immediately what it was but didn't understand its appearance.

"Over these past days, young warrior, I have felt the vibrations of the jades in your party's possession, and I have wondered if I dared relinquish this one to your group or wait until you return for it later. It is likely, though, that your mage friend would have felt the resonances soon, so rather than turn it over to him, I hereby give this to you."

"I—" he started, swallowing hard. "But I don't want it. It's magic."

The old man smiled sagely. "Magic is a part of our world, Gabrion. To deny it is to deny your strength or the air we breathe. Embrace it, and you will achieve your desires."

"But, the king. He used magic illegally in the war. It cost us everything. We're all seen as deceitful, even among ourselves, I find."

"And the Hathrens? Do you not also feel they have acted wrongly in the past?"

"But that doesn't make it right for us to use this power either." He held the jade out toward the old man. "I don't know why you offer this to me."

The old man flexed his hands and, instead of reclaiming the jade, reached again for his tea. "I offer it because I can feel the flow of energy like any proper mage. Ah yes," he exclaimed at Gabrion's raised eyebrows. "I was a mage in our king's employ many years ago, when he outwardly upheld laws that denied my skills. Yet, secretly we worked to assist him, to give him an edge so that he could one day be victorious. I can no longer covet a secret power."

He glanced down at Gabrion's hand. "The jade calls to its brethren, seeking unification, and so I turn this over to you, rather than your friend, because I believe in your nature. I believe that you have the inner strength to reach the peace we have all sought for so long. Your own quest is based on that of love, on that one emotion that was meant to bind us all together. I feel that it is you who could help to restore the Forgotten Tribe and set us all upon the righteous path."

Gabrion's heart raced. "Me? But I'm just a novice at everything."

"Not of your heart, child. That, you know well." The old man leaned forward. "You may have been walking around town these past days, learning what you can, but as the elder here, I have those who report to me as well. And I know your plight, as well as the training your companions have undertaken in our midst. You would do well to set aside your reservations against magic and learn to work with it rather than deny it." He leaned back, seeing the conflict in Gabrion's expression. "Where the king of old failed and showed treachery was in hiding his magical strength and using it when unexpected. Show yours openly, if this troubles you, and your foes will have the opportunity to face you or not—by their choice."

The young warrior let out a deep sigh. "So you want the jade pieces to come together."

"I believe it is inevitable, and so I send this one with you to perhaps have an impact on where its energies will be directed, nothing more. Now, do you notice its color and its shape? Yes, feel that edge there. Is it sharp?"

Gabrion turned the jade over and saw that it was mostly white, with a hint of beige deep inside. He tested the edge, and it sliced his thumb easily. "Sharp indeed," he said, looking up, then sucked on his thumb to stop the bleeding.

"Yes, but notice now what just happened." The man gestured toward the jade.

When Gabrion looked, the blood on it was gone. "What?" He felt the crystal grow slightly warmer, as if trying to match the temperature of his hand. The outer edge took on a coarse, sandy texture, which he tried brushing off, but it reappeared.

"I don't understand."

"The jade has accepted your blood. Now it is attuned to you and always will be. This magic is old magic, and you will find a few oddities as you carry it with you, as I have done these past twenty years." He stared down at the jade, almost sadly, as if his only child were about to leave home forever. "That sandy exterior will always be so, no matter how much you wipe it clean. It will also grant you some power when you call to it, and perhaps your friend can assist you with that. And, this is a part that I entrust to you, which you should keep within unless you feel the need to share it: the blood rite is vital for its use. It is why many mages have failed to tap into the power of the crystal. But also, your children will be attuned to this shard, because it now carries your blood."

"Then that is why Dariak can access the other pieces so easily," Gabrion surmised. "I suppose I will have to at least tell him I have this."

"Well, yes, though if he is paying attention, the shards he carries will also tell him. He already has sensed that the jades in his possession are reacting oddly here, but I don't know that he has determined why."

"I see."

"Now, the hour grows late, Gabrion, so two more things before you run along. First, you will find that you cannot break that shard any smaller than it is. You see, these pieces are protected by the old magic, and no amount of force will crush them. And, though your shard lets off sand, its power is actually that of glass, which is a form of sand, if you think about it. Keep that in mind as you commune with it, and it will help you to determine its properties."

"Thank you, elder, for everything. You've given me much to consider."

"Don't forget the triangle either, young one. Perseverance will only get you so far, and every leap in that regard will have a balancing pain, but patience will hold you together."

"Time heals all?" Gabrion ventured.

"Of a sort," the old man agreed. "Now go on and join your companions. Oh, and don't bother with the long way. I've rather had enough time with you today." He smirked.

CHAPTER 19

Campsite

GABRION LEFT THE elder's house with the jade piece in his pocket, next to Mira's engagement ring. He felt it appropriate they should be together, as perhaps the jade would help him find her. He still wasn't certain he wanted to harness its power, but the way the elder had explained it to him, it sounded like if he was going to complete his mission, then he didn't have much choice.

"There you are! Finally," called Kitalla, fully suited up and jogging toward him. "Come on, we have to hurry. That group we were pursuing to Pindington has left and is on its way west. We have to intercept them before they go beyond our reach."

It really did appear that the jade shards were trying to reunite. Perhaps the elder had the proper handle on things after all. Gabrion followed Kitalla back to the healer's abode and claimed the rest of his belongings, putting on his chain mail for the first time since arriving. He fastened the scabbard around his waist and carried his shield on his arm until he could secure it to his horse's saddle.

Dariak knocked on his door. "We must hurry, Gabrion. Are you ready?"

"Let's go," he agreed, then ran off to thank the healer for all her help. He met the others outside and mounted his horse.

"Why are these things going berserk?" Dariak asked aloud, clutching two of his pockets, where his pieces of jade were calling out to the one in Gabrion's possession.

"Move out!" Kitalla called, snapping her reins, unwilling to wait any longer. Dariak groaned and hurried along after, followed closely by Gabrion.

"There's word they are heading west along the river up north," she called back to them, "so let's get there quickly." Her mare responded to her urgings by racing fast.

It took them over two hours to reach the riverbank, and along the way they avoided contact with a gaggle of gleese, large white birds with vicious tempers and a loud quack that could stun an enemy temporarily. They weren't nearly the same type of threat as the lupinoes, but even a large group of gleese could be overpowering.

The river came into view, and Kitalla swept to the right, heading east, hoping to intercept the fighters. Only Dariak had seen them in action back at the Rooster's Bane, but he didn't think they would pose much of a threat after the things his trio had already accomplished along its journey. Another hour of travel brought them into a deep-orange evening, with the sky changing so completely they wondered if the whole country was afire. Kitalla kept her eyes focused sharply, and she spotted smoke off to the southeast. It didn't take them long to get there.

The three of them rode in like kings, stopping before trampling the enemy's blankets and campfire. Dariak looked around eagerly and nodded. This was the band chasing after Randler. He recognized two of them easily enough, having fought them up close in the tavern. "Ho there!" he called out, alerting them needlessly. His group's approach hadn't been very quiet.

"What bother is this?" one of them asked, drawing his short sword and waving his hand for his friends to do the same. "Can't a bunch of campers be left to their own?"

"Not if they hunt a friend of mine," Dariak announced, jumping from his horse and enacting the Shield of Delminor. He wanted to also summon the watery shield, but there wasn't enough time to commune with the newer shard.

"Eh, it's you again?" The man spat at the ground as another sized up the mage.

"Him. Definitely." The rogue pounded his fists together, clearly angry about the missed capture in Kaison. "Ready, boys?"

"Not so fast," Kitalla interrupted. "You're way outmatched, so stand down." When they hesitated, she jumped off her horse and loosed two daggers as she landed, planting them at the feet of the two speakers. "Touch those and the next ones end up in your skulls," she promised with such aplomb they didn't doubt her.

"What business 'ave you with us?" asked the leader. "Somethin' important, definitely. I can see that."

"Two things," Dariak announced. "Hand over that crystal you have and stop your other pursuit."

This didn't have the desired effect, as they both started laughing. So far the other three hadn't budged from their places by the fire, but Gabrion kept an eye on them.

"On the first," the leader responded, "we don't have it now. It's back in Pindington, where we took it from. As for the other, we're not giving up a bounty of five hundred thousand."

"You might if you die," Dariak threatened.

Kitalla stepped forward, spinning one dagger around her finger as she went. "Pindington, you say. Whereabouts?"

"Won't help you none."

She launched the dagger, which grazed his temple and slashed off some of his grizzled hair. "I'll be the judge of that, thank you. Where?"

The man stepped back, fear lighting his eyes. "You'll never be able to get it," he warned.

Kitalla stalked closer, scowling, but Gabrion's voice called out, "To arms!"

Spinning around, Kitalla saw shapes closing in. Apparently, the monsters in the area had also sensed the campfire and were on their way for a meal. The three rogues at the campfire jumped to their feet, weapons in hand, turning toward the new threat and ignoring the three human intruders.

"Tigroars, reptigons, and eaglons?" one of the rogues called out. "Juuuust great."

Five large, catlike beasts stalked in, blue-and-green stripes mingling down yellow-brown fur. These tigroars had overextended jaws that could easily fit around a man's torso, as well as spikes along the outer facing of their limbs. They snarled with each step, and it was well known that the call of a tigroar could shake the ground and knock down an opponent. The secret was to be in the air just before the bellow.

That was where the eaglons came in, with giant metallic talons like miniature swords. Their wings were thick with feathers, and their bite could cause a stiff paralysis that rendered their victims' bodies useless for the time it took to disembowel them. It was worse than the numbing poison of the lupinoes' tails.

The added support of three reptigons made this a dirty fight. These lizard-like snakes had feet that carried them rapidly across the ground, and their wiry bodies, fringed with needles, could easily enwrap a foe, cutting deeply and causing severe bleeding. The serum in their fangs could put a grown man to sleep, but against a child, it was instant death.

Kitalla's dexterity and accuracy were unparalleled, and within the first few seconds of the attack, one eaglon died, a dagger through its heart. The others swooped more effectively, however, dodging her other projectiles.

Gabrion's sword led the charge against a tigroar, the sheer force of it frightening the creature and causing it to veer away and attack from a different angle. The warrior adjusted quickly and turned his body, bringing the sword around and nipping into one of its paws. Unfazed, the tigroar leaped for him again, jaws bared until they crashed into the upturned shield. Gabrion rolled backward, following the feline's descent and kicking up into its underbelly, winding it desperately. He pounced back onto his feet, pivoted, and drove his sword through its heart.

One of the rogues fended off a tigroar's initial attack, but he missed the reptigon's charge. It didn't take long for the two creatures to end his life.

Two other rogues worked in tandem, hacking and slashing with daggers and a sword. One of them cut into an eaglon's wing, causing it to spiral awkwardly to the ground, and the other followed up by cutting into its neck, killing it. They turned quickly toward a reptigon that was jumping toward them, batting it from the air and sending it in Kitalla's direction. She luckily saw it coming and met it with a dagger thrust, though its flying carcass managed to slash up her hands with its spikes.

The rogue leader and his second-in-command distracted a tigroar by throwing dust in its face, making it sneeze. The leader took a stick from the campfire and waved it into the monster's amber eyes, further blinding it, while his companion plowed into the monster's side, knocking it over. Not the wisest move, for the creature's paws furiously kicked in the air, scoring some hits, but the rogue leader jumped in and cut a deep gash along the creature's side, then struck again when he found that it wasn't deep enough.

The most difficult part of being a mage in a battle was the time it took to cast spells. Dariak pulled spell components from his pockets and put them to use, summoning a capture web similar to the one he had used in Kaison, though this one was generated from flour, which he moistened on his tongue. He had to spit it out at his target for it to work, but he was able to use it to take down an eaglon, after which his dagger did the rest. He then drew a rough rectangle in the dirt, bound it with magic to a grape, and waited for a tigroar to step within the border. It did, with a coordinated attempt from a reptigon. Dariak issued the final part of the spell and crushed the grape messily in his hand. The dirt within the rectangle became a swampy mire, dragging the two creatures in. They thrashed about and would have freed themselves if not for the help of Gabrion's sword, which slashed in from the side and vanished to attack another foe.

The warrior let his sword swing about from one creature to the next, knocking some of them down and slaying the rest. He yelled aloud at times, summoning an aggressive force from within that more than made up for his lack of experience. And with each swing, he learned a faster way to parry, a better way to twist, an easier way to dodge, and a keener way to stab. After a few quick kills, the creatures realized he was strong, and they went for the lesser foes.

The rogues fought hard, but once they saw the destructive power of the other three, they realized that the woman had been right; they were no match for them. They all worked in tandem to bring down the last of the creatures, ending the battle.

The leader grudgingly approached Kitalla after sheathing his sword. "Share our fire," he offered. "Anythin' you need, take it."

Kitalla paused long enough to catch her breath. "We intend to."

"You have a man down," Gabrion interceded. "And we have injuries to tend to first."

Kitalla considered pressing the matter, but the slashes she had taken did need attention. "Fine, but you'll talk once we're done."

"Definitely," the leader said, walking off with the other rogues to dig a grave for their fallen comrade.

Gabrion spent some time hauling the animal carcasses away from the campsite, once Dariak had claimed two to prepare as dinner. Kitalla helped the mage, keeping her eyes on the rogues.

Cleanup took about an hour, including patching their wounds, tethering the horses, and cooking the flanks of tigroar and eaglon, seasoned with some of Dariak's herbs. The seven of them ate silently, eyeing one another suspiciously as if waiting for the other group to attack. They also listened for additional wildlife on the prowl, but the scent of the dead kept most of it away, except a few scavengers. The feral creatures preferred live kills, not carcasses left out to fester. So though the decay that had set in quickly was irritating, it also served as a mild barrier against intrusion.

"So?" Kitalla asked, unable to wait any longer. "Where is it, if it isn't with you?"

The rogue leader frowned as if he regretted having to answer. Kitalla withdrew a dagger when he hesitated. "Okay, fine," he placated her at last. "I said before you won't get it. That's 'cause it's in the lair of Grenthar." He considered, then shook his head. "You'll never get it. We nabbed it once, but he knew it went missin' and upped all the security by the time we returned it. No, you'll never get it back."

"We could just send you back to fetch it."

"Ha!" the man scoffed. "We barely escaped as it is. Sorry, it isn' gonna happen. We 'ave better chances elsewhere."

"Not with the bard," Dariak interjected.

"Yes, mage." He didn't like the look Dariak made in response. "Maybe he's yer friend or something, but some things gotta be taken care of, like it or not."

"What is he to you?" Gabrion asked the rogue leader.

"He stole somethin' from our father." He signaled to his second-in-command. "Somethin' he was entrusted to keep, and when it went missin', our old man lost it. Ruined everything he'd built up for us all his life. It's revenge we seek."

"With a five hundred thousand copper bounty?" Dariak sneered.

"A rival of our father's boss offered it as an incentive for us to return it to her instead," said the leader's brother, after which he received a painful shot in the arm.

"Shut it!" the leader snapped. "It doesn't matter anyway. We're gettin' it no matter what. It's what we borrowed the other one for, to help us find him. Worked too, but if we didn't give it back, our lives wouldn't have mattered much at all."

"Grenthar must have owed you something big to let you even have it for that long and then to let you leave," Kitalla commented.

"You've heard of him?"

"All thieves have. Best there is. It makes sense he'd have a shard." She turned to her companions. "It won't be easy getting it."

"We'll manage," Gabrion inserted, to Dariak's surprise. He thought the warrior would declare the attempt fruitless.

"Fine then," Kitalla said casually. "I'm off to sleep. Dariak, Gabrion, do keep an eye on these idiots, won't you? Tie them up if you think you need to." She rose, stretched, and took off for the bedrolls, selecting the fluffiest one and falling into it quickly.

"Boys," the leader called to his men, "fall in, all of you. No sense in any of us losin' sleep tonight. These folk won' be killin' us in our sleep."

"Are you so sure?" Kitalla called out.

"Definitely. Because yer the one goin' to sleep," he explained, and then he and the others settled down, leaving Gabrion and Dariak alone by the fire.

They sat quietly for a while, listening to the others as their breathing calmed and they fell asleep. Dariak pulled the pieces of jade from his pockets and held them, his face a mask of confusion.

"What is it?" Gabrion asked.

"I think they're lying," he whispered, looking over to the five huddled bedrolls. "These are both vibrating more than before. They have to have a shard among them."

"When we left Gerrish, you said the same thing. Are they vibrating more than that?"

Dariak considered the question carefully, thinking it odd but also trying to remember. "No, it's the same as then."

Gabrion reached into his own pocket with one hand, pressing his finger to his lips with the other. He withdrew the shard the elder had given him and showed it to the wide-eyed mage.

"You! How?" Dariak struggled to keep his voice a whisper.

Gabrion explained briefly, letting Dariak hold it for a few moments before taking it back. "I'm holding on to this one for now." It wasn't a request, and Dariak was too stunned to argue anyway.

The mage looked at his shards and shook his head. "That explains that, then. But maybe they still have one?"

"They don't," hissed Kitalla's voice from behind them. "I checked. Come on, I would rather sleep with rats than these guys. Besides, you guys aren't keeping a very close watch tonight."

Gabrion breathed a laugh and followed her to the horses. Once again, they were off, pressing their way to Pindington in the east, with another shard to find.

CHAPTER 20

Pindington

THE JOURNEY TO Pindington was a busy one. The trio crossed paths with numerous groups of creatures. They took on several packs of gleese and reptigons, which were natural enemies but united in the face of new blood. A flock of eaglons was on the hunt for rodia, oversized, greenish mouse-like creatures that mostly fed on rocks and, therefore, had powerfully strong jaws and teeth. When the companions went near the feeding zone, the avian fiends turned to what they thought was easier prey, only to find they didn't have a chance. The only group of beasts that didn't require a battle was a small pack of lupinoes that focused its energy on herding their cubs away from the humans.

Kitalla commented that there was no way the rogue band had crossed so many attacks from the creatures, but Dariak believed it was partly a function of the three jade pieces they had in their possession. The resonances of the three pieces were strong in the beginning, as if they were excited to see one another, but he sensed the energy vibrations growing slightly less with each day they were together, like friends adjusting to day-to-day routines. Yet, still, the vibrations of the three together appeared to draw curious attention. They all wondered how frequent the encounters would become as they found other shards.

During the smaller confrontations, Kitalla tried making use of Dariak's training by pulling energies into her body before casting them outward during her dance moves. It wasn't easy for her to channel the energies properly, but she did start seeing some effects. Because Dariak had such skill with his fire-dart spell, it was the first one he shared with Kitalla. She drew the energies into herself and focused her thoughts sharply on releasing the flames with her movements. Though her first efforts were unsuccessful, she did begin producing sparks with her hands and feet. It was launching them that challenged her the most.

Gabrion worked hard during the battles, honing his fighting skills whenever possible. The warrior fared best when taking down larger beasts, such as a group of tigroars that attacked them one night. Swiping his long sword with all his strength worked well for clobbering massive bodies, but the smaller creatures could slip through more easily. He took advice from Kitalla, who offered suggestions for improvement. He even went as far as exchanging his shield for a dagger to work on his accuracy, but after numerous attempts, he found that he earned more damage than he gave.

When Dariak wasn't setting up protection spells for his companions, he worked to commune with the water jade to unlock the secrets within. He used techniques his father had recorded in journals and was able to unlock some new spells.

This was similar to his communion with the earth jade, which gave him access to his web-binding and dirt-binding spells, among others. While holding various spell components during his meditations, he could sense how some of their properties would react with the new energies around him. And so, when he was holding the water jade and a shard of glass, he found a protection spell similar to the one the earth jade had shown him, as well as a means of reducing the sharpness of an object.

Using jades was, of course, not the only means for mages to learn new spells. It merely facilitated the process by placing the activation words and motions directly into the mind. Dariak knew he still had a lot more to learn from both shards in his possession, but he hungered to know more about Gabrion's jade.

The warrior had not allowed him to hold it again but promised that he would in time. Gabrion did ask Dariak for advice in reaching out to the shard, and the mage assisted readily enough, hoping it would reduce the amount of time he would have to wait. When the two of them concentrated on their respective shards, Kitalla either practiced her moves or teasingly lamented that she wasn't allowed one of her own.

Their progress to Pindington took much longer than it should have because of the beastly interruptions and their own attempts to strengthen themselves along the way. Kitalla warned them that they would be facing large odds against the likes of Grenthar and that it wasn't likely they would all survive.

During the trek, Gabrion felt remorse that they were taking their time, leaving Mira in the hands of the enemy. But he trusted the words of the elder of Gerrish that the energies were coming together for a reason. He believed that Mira would be waiting for him.

Over a week passed during what should have been a three-day hard ride, but at last the skyline of Pindington appeared on the horizon. Even from a distance, they could see the town wall, with rooftops extending above it, as well as something that would have dwarfed even the castle of Kaison: the Prisoner's Tower. It was several stories tall, deep gray, with an oval base and a somewhat pyramidal structure that kept reaching up into the sky. Combined with the morning sun, the giant tower loomed over the town like an enormous sundial, its shadow extending beyond the town walls.

Pindington was one of the few towns or cities in Kallisor that Kitalla knew only by reputation. Even the experienced thief found herself on new territory as they guided their horses through the main gates, seeking lodging for their duration. Gabrion noticed that she squirmed a little more than usual, but whether it was the surroundings or the prospect of their task here, he didn't know. She had spoken words of caution when she talked of Grenthar, no wit or sass or frivolity.

The city had no less than six proper inns to choose from, with lower-class options available as well. Kitalla chose a place close to the center of town that could house their steeds and had an active tavern downstairs. The best way of staying hidden and informed, she explained, was to stay in larger groups.

As in Warringer, Dariak and Gabrion shared a room, while Kitalla took a separate space. She paid for their stay with money she had taken from the rogues who were hunting Randler. Once settled in, they each went their separate ways to explore the town, learn what they could, and obtain materials they would need for finding the jade.

Dariak spent the first part of his day replenishing his herb stores, as he had used numerous herbs on the journey from Gerrish for either spells or cooking. He located one of the mystic shops and exchanged a few pieces of rose quartz he had taken from Kaison for citrine and amethyst. From there he browsed for a new mage robe, but none fit him properly. He also searched for a leather carry case specifically designed for sorting spell components. He languished at the shop for a long time, for it felt a bit like being at home, having access to proper equipment. Kallisor, on the whole, may disapprove of magic, but shops like this could still have mild success. The proprietor offered him some good deals, and Dariak delighted in negotiating him down to even lower prices still.

Gabrion's day was spent quite differently. Because the healer in Gerrish had refused his coppers, accepting his labor as payment for services rendered, he still had his sixty-three copper pieces. He went to a jeweler and purchased a thick gold chain so he could wear Mira's engagement ring around his neck, keeping her close to his heart. It was important, because with each day that whiled away, he felt her chances of survival were slimmer. But if he kept that ring near his heart, she would benefit from it somehow, and so she would still be with him in the end.

He also visited the town sanctuary in order to receive treatment for a variety of wounds and bruises still left over from the incursions that had happened along the way. They were very official in their dealings with him, accepting a concise payment of thirty-four copper pieces for the injuries he had sustained. Three healers used magic to propagate the healing process of his lacerations while two others used pressure points to ease tension in his muscles, followed by a deep massage. He tried to pay attention to the healing used on him, and he surprised himself when he was able to sense the energies drawn from rose quartz, through the healers, and guided through his own body to match his circulation. Calm and relaxed, the young warrior returned to the tavern, unwilling to do more than enjoy the sensation.

Swendel's Lodge was a decent establishment, with mahogany accents along the bar, leather-topped stools, and cushioned seats for the patrons, as well as a variety of menu options throughout the day. It was uncommon to have such choices in a tavern, but Pindington was a large enough city, and with five other major inns to choose from, options were important.

"Swell to see you," greeted the proprietor. "Special today are the roast tigroar patties, seasoned with our own selection of spices and served with a rich red wine. What will it be?"

"The special sounds good, thanks," Gabrion said, walking over and selecting a table along the wall. A few other patrons were in the room, and he tried to eavesdrop without staring at anyone obviously.

"Then Battie won't give me the recipe, so Jalla's cake will be ruined!" said a woman at one table, her face flushed from rage.

"That's terrible, Marth!" commiserated her friend. "You know I can't cook for a rodia's tail, or I'd help you in a heartbeat. Oh, you poor thing!"

They continued nattering back and forth, and Gabrion aimed his focus elsewhere.

"—never seen the boss so miffed," commented a blond fellow around Gabrion's age, off to one side with two other young men.

"Yeah, tell me about it. Threw his dagger at me on my way out, he did," agreed the red-haired lad among them.

"Didn't even do nothing wrong."

"Didn't do 'anything' wrong, you idiot," corrected the third, dark-haired companion. "Seriously, I think he yells at you because you talk like an uneducated piece of street trash."

"Well, I *am* a piece of street trash, so whatever. Don't matter though. I won't be working for him much longer."

At this, the other two put down their drinks and stared in unison. "What do you mean?" asked the blond one.

"I'm getting out before there's trouble." He looked at his friends, aghast. "Didn't you see her?"

"It doesn't mean we have to hightail it out of here!" argued the dark-haired youth.

"No? Well, I doubt she's changed after all these years, but she was a menace back at—"

"Tigroar special?" asked a barmaid, dropping a plate down in front of Gabrion and interrupting his concentration.

"Do enjoy!" she said before whisking away.

Gabrion grabbed his utensils and tried to look like he was enjoying his meal, but the three young men had called the barmaid over to replenish their drinks, after which they changed subjects and talked about who had the best chance of taking her home.

The fare was better than he had had in a long while, especially considering he had eaten some tigroar on the road. The meat was juicy and perfectly cooked, and the red wine washed down the meal exquisitely. He wondered, if food this good was available in a tavern, what would a king's feast be like? He amused himself with the thought.

Some of the patrons shuffled around, either leaving when they finished or ordering a meal upon arrival. He expected Dariak and Kitalla to come through soon and wondered if he should check the rooms in case he had missed them. But then a quartet of singers shuffled toward one end of the room and sang of heroic deeds and distressed maidens, and Gabrion lost himself in their songs, feeling warmed with each victory told in the tales. Clearly, they had been paid to keep all the songs light and cheery for the patrons, as even in the most dire circumstances, the hero always prevailed. It seemed farfetched to the warrior, but it instilled him with hope. He got caught up in one of the refrains of a raunchy courting song and sang aloud with many of the patrons:

Shining bright in a dress of gold, all made of her hair.
The fairest maid that ever was made, gorgeous, standing there.
No garments ever touched her skin.
No tailor'd ever dare!
Oh, the copper I would have paid to see what's under there!

"I'm sure your ladylove would appreciate that," teased Kitalla as she pulled up a seat next to his, taking his fork and swiping a bite of food. "Still though, it is a catchy tune." She joined in the next repetition of the refrain.

The two were still singing when Dariak joined them, his stern face ruining the mood. "We have trouble."

Kitalla waved for him to sit down, out of the way of the performers, who had moved on to a light song about springtime. The one woman in the group accented the vocals with elegant flourishes that enticed everyone to bob their heads with her tune.

"I'm serious," Dariak interjected.

With a groan, Kitalla pulled her attention away and stared at the mage. "There are four detachments of guards working at all times in Grenthar's domain. He has installed new security measures, which means a series of deadly traps, and he intends to move the jade to some unknown location within the next few days. Yes, we have trouble."

Dariak frowned. "Well, you know that detachment the king sent to Warringer after us? Apparently, it wasn't the only patrol he sent out. They know about us here. Our faces are posted in the town square."

With a shrug, Kitalla replied, "Then eat up tonight and sleep deeply. We've a busy day tomorrow." She then smirked conspiratorially and jabbed Dariak in the arm. "Although, that fellow over there is rather dashing, don't you think?"

The mage glanced over at a redheaded young man sipping his mead casually. His face was well balanced between rugged strength and sensual charm. His large eyes drew Dariak's attention the most, for even across the way, they lit with humor when he grinned.

Kitalla yawned. "Sadly, he doesn't fancy my kind. Don't forget that we have pressing business tomorrow, but nothing says there's no time for a little fun too." With that, she stalked off toward her room, leaving her companions behind.

"I guess we should go too," Gabrion said hesitantly.

"You go. I need some food first." His eyes flitted back to the redhead. "And time to think."

The warrior went upstairs and sat on the bed, finding it full of duck feathers, which he had to pound into shape until it was more comfortable. The blankets were soft, but he wasn't ready to sleep yet. He'd had a relaxing day compared to the reconnaissance the others had done. He felt foolish for being so lax instead of gathering any useful information.

He was still staring out the window when Dariak came in over an hour later. "You okay?" the mage asked, bolting shut the door.

"I went to the healers today to clear up my wounds."

"That's good. You need to be at your best for tomorrow. Did you hear any good gossip?"

The warrior shook his head. "That's my point. You two were on point, but I went and tended to myself today."

Dariak waited in case there was something else, but the young man fell silent. "Well, Gabrion, we all did things for ourselves today. We just happened to pick up a few tidbits along the way."

"Kitalla picked up more than a few."

"Maybe you hadn't noticed, but she's a thief who specializes in being privy to what's going on. Besides, I think it bothers her that she's never been here before."

Gabrion turned around from the window finally. "I thought that too. It was weird though, these guys at the tavern earlier. I thought they were talking about her, but they didn't really say anything of importance. If it was about her, then they knew her when she was younger. They seemed frightened."

"It's a big city; they could have been talking about anyone. You probably thought it was about her because whatever you heard matched her in some way," Dariak concluded, lying down on his bed. "Or even if it was her, so what?"

Gabrion considered for a moment. "Well, if it was about her, then it seems like this task of ours is even more dangerous still. We don't even have a plan of action for it."

"Go in, take it, leave quickly."

Gabrion smirked at the retort. "Nice and easy, then."

Dariak noticed an uncertain look in the warrior's eyes. "Is there anything else bothering you, or is it time to go to sleep?"

Gabrion hesitated for a moment, but he couldn't find the right words. "Did you... go talk to that man?"

Dariak sat up and scratched his head. "Who? The redhead? No. Why?"

Gabrion shrugged, looking uncomfortable. "You seemed... interested in him."

"I like men. He was attractive, so I looked. What's wrong with that?"

"It's just creepy."

"No more creepy than you ogling that singer onstage. 'The fairest maid that ever was made,'" Dariak quoted, rising to his feet. "I saw you singing along like a big buffoon. It's really no different."

Gabrion stood up, glaring at the mage. "It's completely different. I wasn't ogling anyone. I was just singing a catchy tune! But you... you were staring at him!"

"Not exactly, but—" He stopped. "Oh," Dariak said as if enlightened. "You want me to stare at you?"

"No!" Gabrion grunted in frustration. "It just isn't right."

Dariak frowned. "And yet, back in Warringer, you were all upset that people judged me for being different."

"But this is—" Gabrion stopped himself.

Angry, Dariak sat on the bed, pulling the blanket around him. "I'm sorry for creeping you out."

"So, when did you decide this?" the warrior hedged.

"Which part?" Dariak huffed.

"Being into men."

"Ha!" Dariak said, struggling not to shout. "When did you choose to like Mira?"

Gabrion started an angry retort but then understood the intent of the question and paused to consider it. "I didn't. It just happened."

"Right," the mage agreed. "It just happened." Frustrated, he turned his head away and focused on the unadorned wall.

Silence hung in the air for a few long moments before Gabrion asked, "Do you ever look at me that way?"

The mage looked around and opted for honesty. "I'm attracted to men. You're a good-looking fellow and you're in great shape." He shrugged. "I'd be lying if I said I never did."

Gabrion's face curled into a scowl. "I think I like that even less."

"It isn't like I'd ever pin you down with the Shield of Delminor and have my way with you. At least, not without your permission."

Gabrion's jaw firmed for a moment before he shook his head. "Jokes like that don't help."

"Would you prefer a nice hug?" Dariak crafted his face into the purest farce of innocence he could muster amid his annoyance.

Gabrion groaned. "No, thanks." He regarded the mage for a moment. "I'm not used to it, that's all."

"Which part?"

"All of it," he admitted.

"You've gotten more used to magic," Dariak pointed out.

"I'll get used to this too," Gabrion promised. "You and other guys, that is."

"It isn't like I'm the only one, you know. There are at least… five others in the world."

Gabrion laughed at that. "Okay, I get it. Sorry for being an idiot about it."

Dariak shrugged. "You can really apologize by taking off those leggings." He wasn't quick enough to dodge the pillow.

"Idiot," Gabrion accused, rolling his eyes. "Go to sleep, mage. We have a busy day tomorrow."

"Okay, meat." Dariak laughed, throwing Gabrion's pillow back at him.

CHAPTER 21

Grenthar's Complex

A FEW HOURS before dawn, Gabrion awoke to Kitalla shaking him aggressively. "Let's go," she whispered.

Groggy, the warrior sat up and looked over at the door. "Wasn't that bolted shut?"

She pointed her thumb at her chest. "Thief, remember?" She then went and woke the mage. "Come on, you two, we have to get moving before they change guards again. Do hurry." There was an edge of concern in her voice as she drifted out of the room, heading downstairs into the tavern.

The mage and the warrior dressed quickly and followed her, shaking the drowsiness from their heads as much as they were able. "Heard something?" Dariak yawned.

"Guard changes at dawn, noon, dusk, and midnight. Those are our only chances to get in."

"You don't sleep much, do you?" Dariak muttered under his breath. "So what's the plan?"

She took out a small glass tumbler and handed it to Dariak. "Those glass shields would be nice." Nodding, the mage cracked the glass against the table, doling out the fragments for them to each bleed upon so he could bind the shields to their bodies. While he was at it, he added a second protection with the glass, thanks to the water jade, which would deaden the sharpness of weapons that made it through their outer defenses.

Gabrion noticed that his piece of jade trembled more intensely than before. "I feel all wet. But then I'll know when it's not working, right?"

Dariak nodded and turned to Kitalla. "What else?"

"Have some of your spells ready. There are several sets of guards who will try to stop us, and I'm sure there will be more than pressure plates on the floor that sound an alarm. Be alert, be quick, be wary." She drew in a quick breath. "Our goal is the piece of jade, correct? Good. Then it's important to reach it at all costs. If we fail, then we won't likely have another chance any time soon. Which means…" She let her voice drift off to silence.

Dariak frowned, and Gabrion looked between them. "Which means what? If one of us falls, the others just go on ahead?"

"Basically." Kitalla nodded. "And since we need the mage to unite the pieces when we have them all, I think that means we will have to cover him and clear a path."

Gabrion didn't like the sound of it. "This sounds like it's over our heads."

Kitalla shrugged. "If we can't do this, we'll never get past the king's guards in Hathreneir."

"She's right," Dariak added. "My king is also protected by mages, not just soldiers."

"Then let's get moving," Gabrion grumbled. "The longer we wait, the more anxious I feel."

The three companions strolled from the tavern as casually as possible, wending their way through the streets toward the western wall where the entrance to Grenthar's compound awaited. As the morning sun crept over the eastern wall, its light struck the Prisoner's Tower, which cast a black shadow on the ground. They kept within the shadow as it swept slowly toward the entrance to the lair.

From the outside, Grenthar's estate didn't look like much. It had a stone-and-wood facade, with torches on either side of the entryway. A guard stood underneath each torch at full alertness. The sidewall of the compound extended back, parallel with the barrier of the city itself. Looking quickly, it seemed as if the building just stopped and the outer wall continued back and around, but rather, the estate ran the entire length instead, painted and carved with masonry to make it seamlessly blend in.

The men weren't sure how the thief intended to breach the compound without notice, and they froze in place as two guards came from within while the other two walked off into town. Without a word, Kitalla crept along the edge of the shadow, signaling Gabrion to follow. The two new guards were bending and stretching gently, preparing themselves for a long stint outside the doors. Kitalla snuck right behind one and cracked him on the back of the head. She then leaped for the other guard, but she needed Gabrion to help keep him from shouting out an alarm.

Two thumps and the guards were silenced. The task wasn't done yet, though. Kitalla pulled out two lengths of rope, handing one to Gabrion and tossing the other over the torch bracket. She quickly tied knots around one guard and hoisted him up, securing him to the wall. After adding a gag to keep him quiet, she went and helped Gabrion with the knots. An additional length of rope went to tying their hands behind their backs, effectively immobilizing them until someone came along and freed them. At a quick glance, it seemed the guards were still on duty. Then, the trio went in through the main doors.

The interior of the compound was luxurious, even in the entryway. Gold-foil columns ran floor to ceiling at various locations around the room, creating a rectangular symmetry. With a door to the left, the right, and in front, they knew already that this was no straightforward task. Kitalla hadn't been in town long enough to learn more than the general location of the shard, and the path to get there was anyone's guess.

Kitalla stepped toward the door on the right, but Dariak stopped her. "Hold on." He clutched the jade in his pocket and slowly spun in a circle. He felt the strongest resonance when he faced the left door, and so they went for it. But two steps before reaching the threshold, Kitalla swung her hands out to stop her companions. She pointed to the floor, tracing in the air the outline of the floor tile, which was barely raised above the ones surrounding it and masked by a thin layer of dirt and sand. It was a pressure plate and would have been easily missed if she hadn't been watching for it. The trio stepped over the plate and pressed on into the next room.

Three torches lined the wall, but only one of them was lit. Kitalla kept low as she entered the room, noting a random assortment of weapons and armor along the walls and chests and crates along the floor. "Touch nothing," she whispered, inching her way ahead one step at a time. Gabrion and Dariak kept close behind her, wondering what had her so edgy in an obvious storeroom.

They worked their way carefully around a few obstacles on the ground, and Kitalla pointed out several pressure plates along the way. When they reached the center of the room, the middle torch burst to life, startling them. Dariak sidestepped, and his foot tripped a pressure sensor.

A whirring sound echoed in the walls, and small trapdoors opened at various heights, from which arrow shafts started to fly. The three of them ducked low under most of them, but they couldn't remain there for long. Overhead, an iron trellis loaded with spikes started its descent. There was nothing to do but run.

They leaped over boxes as they went, and Kitalla drew her knives, slashing them wildly in the hopes of fending off any close arrows. Gabrion's shield deflected a good number of the projectiles while Dariak followed behind, where the density of shots was the least. With each pressure plate they tripped along the way, the focus of the arrows shifted toward that portion of the room.

Kitalla sprang over the final pressure plate in the room and rolled into the next area, but Gabrion's foot struck the panel. An earsplitting crash sounded as a large portion of the floor fell away, sending Gabrion into a dark pit and out of sight. Dariak was close behind, and it took all of his reflexes to leap over the hole and land on the other side. He turned around and looked into the pit, but he could neither hear nor see anything within.

"No," he whispered.

Kitalla grabbed him by the arm. "Come on. Remember? We have to get to the jade."

It took time for the mage to compose himself, but there wasn't anything he could do without jumping into the pit himself and aborting the quest. No, he had to go on. He turned and followed Kitalla, wishing he could split himself in two and go both ways at once.

The new room brought with it a new challenge. A feral tigroar stalked along the back wall. That in itself didn't pose a problem, but the stone floor had several pools of liquid that smelled strongly of lantern oil, and along the stone walls were numerous candles on shallow perches. If they fell, the room would turn into a blazing inferno.

Seeing the humans enter the room, the tigroar snarled and entered a battle stance. Its front paws dug deeply into the rock, and its haunches tightened, ready to pounce. Kitalla stalked slowly into the room, as if the beast were a lost cat in need of rescue. Her eyes scanned around, wondering which candles were most likely to fall and which ones would miss the flammable pools. Dariak thought to cast a web spell to trap the creature in place, but as Kitalla walked closer, he understood the deeper threat.

Nervous at the unknown human's approach, the tigroar drew in a slow, rattling breath, ready to release an earthquaking roar, which would undoubtedly knock enough candles from the wall to light the whole place ablaze. Kitalla lashed out with her daggers, sending them flying at the creature's maw, but it turned its head to the side, and they only grazed its neck. Even more frightened now, the tigroar drew in another gust of air, readying its lungs for its attack.

Dariak could see that there wasn't enough time to slay the beast without the fire erupting everywhere. He bolted into the room, heading for Kitalla and tackling her to the ground. "*Sassrathallian vornier habberleese,*" he called as the tigroar released its bellow, shaking the ground and walls. One by one the candles fell to the ground, exploding upon contact with the oil. The unfortunate beast was caught in the aftermath of its own attack, and it spent the last breaths of its life thrashing about, roaring fruitlessly and filling the space with the horrid scent of burned fur and flesh.

The water jade responded to Dariak's desperate call as he repeated the spell several times while waiting for the flames to die. Until then, their bodies stayed the consistency of water, which allowed the heat and fire to pass right through them, but because the heat was so persistent, the spell did not last long. Kitalla remained as still as possible, allowing the mage to control this particular threat.

At last, the fire subsided, and they stood up, a little worse for wear but ready to continue. Averting their noses and eyes from the charred tigroar corpse, they worked their way toward the exit and the next challenge.

The first glance at the next area made Dariak wince. There was a large, empty pit spanning the length of the room, with no walkway across at all, not even along the walls. Instead, a series of ropes hung from the ceiling. He would need to channel his upper-body strength for this exercise, which meant he would rather face the tigroar again. He already felt the aftereffects of the water spell kicking in, and he realized his time was limited before he would pass out.

Kitalla didn't waste much time sizing up a path and taking flight. She ran and leaped for one rope, using its momentum to propel her forward, where she grabbed the next. Because the rope after that was far off, she veered to the left, swinging her legs wide to rock in that direction, and then she pounced, grabbing on.

Groaning, Dariak pushed himself to go. He ran and jumped, taking hold of a closer rope than the one Kitalla had started on. He swung back and forth and reached out for the next rope, grasping it first before transferring his weight and releasing the first rope. He certainly didn't travel with the same grace as the thief, but as long as he got there, he didn't care.

As they made their way across, they noticed an added complication. Some of the ropes were not properly secured to the ceiling, and because there was little light in the room, it was impossible to tell which ones were loose without tugging on them. Kitalla's speed saved her as she took a false rope in one hand, then lashed out with her other to grab the end of a nearby cord. She hung there for a few moments to catch her breath before climbing up and swinging onward to the next.

Dariak's progress was terribly slow, and his arms weakened quickly. He vowed to ask Gabrion to help him train his body physically once they were out of this mess. That was assuming, of course, that the warrior was still alive. He scolded himself for even thinking it, because, after all, without Gabrion, poor Mira would be left unsaved.

He allowed himself a slight chuckle before reaching out to the next rope. It was a false one, and he was able to let it fall without following it.

Kitalla struggled with a few more false ropes, but she was nearing the end of the harsh crossing. She swung her rope back and forth in wide arcs, building as much momentum as she could, and she launched herself forward, arms outstretched and ready to claim three ropes that were in front of her. Only one of them was false, and she released the cords to her right and swung on the left side. She brought her legs back and forth one more time and then propelled herself to the other side, where she rubbed her shoulders and looked back for the mage.

He wasn't even a third of the way across yet. Because he wasn't swinging and jumping, he was taking the longest route across, which meant a good deal of back-tracking and desperate clinging to the ropes. In the end, it wasn't a false rope that caused him to fall into the pit below but his exhausted arms.

With a cry of dismay, Dariak plummeted into darkness.

Kitalla rested for a moment, stretching to keep her muscles loose. Without the mage, it was somewhat useless to claim the jade, but she didn't think he was dead. Not just yet. Grenthar would have something in mind for his new toys, if everything she had heard was true. Though she had the option of going back now and finding a new path to glory, she was so close to this coveted prize, and losing her companions just to quit irked her. Besides, she had promised the warrior she would help him find his Mira. How silly she felt now for saying such a thing. With a grumbling sigh, Kitalla arched her back, stretched high, and then continued down a set of stairs to the next room.

The underground chamber was dank, and the oil sconces along the walls made the whole room feel even gloomier. She looked around, eyeing the surroundings and seeing immediately that there was an enormous pressure plate at the bottom of the stairs that she couldn't possibly avoid without being able to fly. Across the way, she saw three other large plates and an assortment of bricks, statues, and vases scattered about. Heading toward each plate was a narrow path, with pits of broken glass on either side to painfully catch an unbalanced walker. A nondescript stone door waited across the room, and she surmised the purpose of the plates easily enough. She needed to place objects on the plates in order to lift the door. Looking, she also saw small gaps in the right wall, and she wasn't surprised, after stepping on the bottom plate, that the holes launched more arrows.

Based on the regularity of the arrows, it seemed clear that some form of mechanism was launching them, rather than a skilled archer. That was a boon, because it wouldn't be able to target her properly. It also suggested there was a limited supply that would eventually run out, but she didn't count on that happening in the time she took down there.

Not only did stepping on the oversized plate start the arrows shooting across the room, it also caused the platforms with the objects to rotate and shift around. She had never seen such a mechanism before, and she had to admit that she was impressed by it. If only the moving walkway had been installed in the city instead of here.

She stepped off the pressure plate and onto the stone slab from which the other paths extended. She needed to grab objects from the left and right and bring them to each of the three pressure plates at the end, all while avoiding arrows and not falling into the glass pits. She grinned to herself, thinking that this was less dangerous than the lupino fight they had faced after Warringer.

Off she went, teetering along the leftmost walkway to claim a stone bust that vaguely resembled the king. It was heavy and cumbersome, but the sooner she lowered the three pressure plates, the sooner the door would lift, and the sooner she could continue on. Struggling, she dragged the stone with her along the pathways, flashing her dagger out with one hand to try to deflect the arrows she couldn't dodge by leaning or bending. It was rough going, but she managed to get the statue to the left platform and stand it on the pressure plate, which slightly sank down.

An ominous rumbling sound filled the room, and when she turned around, she could see that the walkways were now shaking back and forth slightly, adding to the challenge. A glance at the door told her that her task was far from over; it hadn't opened from the bottom, as she had expected, but slid a little downward from the ceiling.

Tiptoeing back to the central platform, ducking under arrows and balancing on the vibrating beam, Kitalla made her way toward another heavy object. This was a large ceramic urn with thick walls and hideous detailing all along the sides. It looked like it was meant to house a fountain for some garish garden, but it was so hard to look at that it was best suited to this dismal trap underground. She removed the lid from the urn and saw that the inside was empty. Smirking, she pulled the large urn over and flipped it upside down, climbing into it. Though it was heavier than the statue, and certainly more cumbersome, carrying it this way allowed her to focus on walking, because the ceramic urn protected her from all the arrows. With her chin tucked, she could just make out the flooring at her feet. Her breath made funny, echoing sounds inside as she wobbled on the right-side pathway and scuttled toward the pressure plate. It was hard work setting the urn down without shattering it, but she bent her legs until it touched the ground, then she bent forward, setting it as gently as she could before climbing out and righting the monstrosity.

Another deep rumble shook the room, and the door slid farther open. Then a trickling sound filled her ears, and she glanced upward and frowned. Upon the engagement of the pressure plate, a sluice had apparently been opened, releasing water into a series of channels in the ceiling. It didn't fall fast, but water dripped along every part of the shaking walkways, making them even more treacherous. Luckily, though, the density of arrows was decreasing, but she did still have to watch for them.

Next, Kitalla swiped an iron breastplate from the moving walkway at the edge of the room. She wrapped it around her torso and made her way to the central pressure plate, where she set it down, wondering what new threat would be unleashed into the room. Crunching sounds from below unnerved her as the glass-covered flooring started to rise. She looked quickly and realized that if the flooring came up all the way, it would be extremely difficult for her to fit down any pathway, but none of the other items would fit, and she would be effectively trapped. Time was running out.

Trusting her innate dexterity, Kitalla moved rapidly, dragging the next few items in place on the three different pressure plates. She realized at once that the more weight the plates bore, the more each plate's distraction increased. Adding a vase to the left plate caused the walkways to shake faster. Because of this, she decided to load up the rightmost plate first, until it stopped moving, figuring she could deal with the extra water. Soon she felt like she was in a severe rainstorm; the water was falling so fast.

The stone doorway could probably have fit her body if it were opening from the floor up, but there was no way she could pull herself up and wriggle through. And based on the amount it moved with each new weight, she still had at least three pieces to place before she could pass through.

The rising floor had caught up with the height of the shaking walkways, and the glass shards started spilling out, creating one more obstacle. She combated this by dragging her feet to kick as many shards out of the way as possible. This cost her some flexibility, and a few arrows came close to landing direct hits, but she managed to dodge them or deflect them before it was too late.

Because the rising floor was becoming a new obstacle in itself, she had to choose items that she could carry above the ground with some ease. She tried to take two body-length iron shields with her but she couldn't manage the weight of them both. Leaving one for her next trip, Kitalla fended off the dwindling arrows with the other as she made her way toward the left plate. She figured that with the floor rising up, the shaking platforms wouldn't pose as much of a threat, as she could use the walls for balance if she stumbled.

After placing both shields onto the left platform, the stone door opened enough for her to get through. But something irked her, so she took the time to add two more pieces to the left pressure plate and then brought forth three items to the plate in the center. She knew the plates could have held more than that, but the walkways were wobbling so strongly now she could barely move across them, especially with all the water that was still falling. Plus, the floors were rising so quickly that the passages would soon be highly restrictive.

She went to the stone door, which was now halfway down, and jumped up onto it and smiled at herself. The opening on the other side of the door was not as high as on this side, but she had added enough objects to clear the other overhang and allow herself into the other room. She had suspected as much, considering the difficulty of the room and the fact that someone could have managed to reach the doorway much earlier than she had. There had to be another obstacle. At least, if it were her trap, that was how she would have done it.

She rolled through the narrow gap and crashed in a heap on the floor of the next room. She pulled herself up and saw a pedestal in the center of the chamber with a silvery piece of jade sitting on a large satin pillow. But her heart sank when she looked around, for twenty men and women in full armor stood around the periphery of the room.

"Well done!" exclaimed an older man in a sonorous tone from a door across the way. "Passed every obstacle. Highly impressive."

Kitalla said nothing as she looked at Grenthar. His head was ringed with short white hair and long ears. His nose looked like it had been broken several times in his life, but though he was easily in his fifties, his body was highly toned and supple. His leather gear was tightly strapped on and looked more like a second skin than anything else. Kitalla could tell from the way he walked that every muscle was perfectly honed for his profession. No movement was without purpose.

"Nothing to say?" he asked, staying on his side of the pedestal. "But you didn't think you could actually get here and take my treasure, did you?"

Kitalla stood up slowly, keeping her hands away from her daggers. She didn't want him rashly executing her. Instead, she stalked forward, pouring her essence into her entrancing steps. Immediately, a strange, hazy feeling came over everyone in the room, and Kitalla continued her procession until she reached the piece of jade.

"No, no, no!" Grenthar screamed, jumping up and down and shaking off the peaceful illusions she had thrust upon him. Daggers flew from his hand.

Kitalla reflexively held out her arm to shield her face from the attack. The first dagger struck the glass shield and caused a soft shattering sound to echo in her mind. The next dagger thumped against her hand like a twig, but the third one slashed her deeply.

She couldn't maintain the trance while dodging the weapons, and the guards reacted quickly, rushing in to grab her. Kitalla pulled the jade inward with both hands and shoved it down her leather top. She didn't really think that would deter them from taking it back, but her mind was already on defense.

Daggers flew from her hands as she spun about, bending low and then jumping high, trying desperately to dodge the numerous attacks coming her way. But though she took down four of the guards, the others overwhelmed her. The glass shield shattered quickly, and her life was spared by the call of the master.

"Enough," Grenthar called, wiping his hand across his brow. "Detain her. Do not kill her." It took four guards to restrain her, one holding each limb. The old master walked over to her and thrust his hand awkwardly down her shirt, reclaiming the jade, scraping her skin deeply on the way up and drawing blood. "Nice attempt, young one. Very promising." He returned the shard to the pillow and waved his hand behind him. "Take her away."

She was dragged out through another door and down a long corridor, where eventually she was tossed through a hole in the floor into a blackened cell. They slid a stone slab over the hole, sealing her inside, alone and dejected.

CHAPTER 22

Into the Tower

GABRION FELL THROUGH the pit in the floor, frantically reaching up for the ledge, but he missed completely and plummeted down a dark shaft to a floor below. The room was pitch black, but he heard heavy footfalls striding forth, and then torchlight appeared in the distance. He knew he was about to be captured, so he rifled through his pocket and removed the piece of jade, stuffing it deep into his undergarments and hoping for the best. Moments later, a contingent of guards appeared, and there was nothing he could do to resist them.

"Rise up, scum," one of the guards spat, signaling to two of the others to claim the warrior's sword and shield. "Pretty times lie in wait for you, I think." He finished off with malevolent laughter.

Two spears poked Gabrion in the sides, and a third guard held a sword to his back. Four archers followed the group as the captain led the way forward through a narrow hallway. Several passages opened along the sides as they went, and Gabrion counted them as points of reference. They turned right at the seventh hall and walked for many yards before turning again. There was a slight bend to the paths, he noticed, so they weren't arranged as a simple grid. Keeping an eye out for markings on the wall, he tried to remember their path.

After covering quite a distance, they reached a large iron door. The captain pounded sharply on the metal in a rhythmic fashion, waiting for a detailed response, then pounded again. After that, locks clicked and slid and the door opened. Another pair of guards waited on the other side and became part of the escort leading up a set of clammy stairs. Gabrion debated stumbling purposely but realized it wouldn't get him far, especially with two of the archers purposefully hanging a few paces behind the rest.

The upper area was brighter than the dungeon area below, but it was still mostly enclosed in stone, with a few cutouts for sunlight to pass through. The torches were not lit in this hallway, as it was a bright day outside. Hesitating to step forward into the light earned Gabrion a jab in the back, which propelled him onward. Four more flights of stairs passed under them before they proceeded through another secured door that required a different series of knocks. He wondered idly if they were actually messages or just random banging meant to sound planned.

A holding room waited down the end of the hallway, where Gabrion was asked to register his name and hometown, after which his chain mail was removed and placed into storage with his sword and shield. They patted down the rest of him, but he didn't have any daggers concealed anyway, and they didn't find the jade, as if the shard had concealed itself from their prying hands. The guard did, however, tug on the necklace carrying his engagement ring for Mira, which caused Gabrion to beg for it.

"Wifey, eh?" the guard sneered.

"She's all I have left. Captured by the Hathrens," he added, hoping to be united at least in hatred of their common foe. "Please, it's all I have."

They took it anyway. "We'll make sure it's got no specialties to it, then we'll decide on giving it back to you. No chances, you know."

Defeated, Gabrion sank within himself and was led through another set of doors and down a range of hallways to another stone room. A door swung open, and he was shoved inside, where he curled into a ball and mourned the loss of the engagement ring. His quest seemed doomed.

The first thing Gabrion did once he composed himself was move the jade from its uncomfortable position back to his trouser pocket. He kept his tunic out loose so it would hide the bulge, but he couldn't have left the jade in his undergarments for much longer. He pushed himself upright and then stood, noticing that he wasn't alone. As if it were a signal that he had accepted his fate, one of the other prisoners approached.

"Greetings," the man said, "though there's not much happiness in it, I'm afraid. Cavall." He extended his hand.

"Gabrion," he said, acknowledging and returning the gesture.

"I know it's impolite to ask, but what are you in for? I'm here for taking too much of a liking to gambling. Well, I guess for not paying off my debts and then trying to fight my way out of it."

Gabrion wasn't sure what to say. "I guess for entering Grenthar's complex without an invitation."

Cavall backed away, clearly impressed. "And you're not dead! I won't ask more than that; that's enough for me." He lowered his voice conspiratorially. "Watch out for the scarred ones. If they hear you survived the labyrinth, they'll likely put you to their own test, if you get my meaning. They lost a few friends to that place."

"Thanks for the advice."

Cavall clapped Gabrion on the shoulder and brought him in among the others. The warrior saw that the outer wall was slightly curved and dotted with windows no larger than his head. The windows allowed a tease of fresh air and sunshine with the absolute knowledge that there was no escape through them. Patches of light beamed down upon a group of nearly twenty men, most just a couple of years older than Gabrion. Age wasn't the only thing they had in common; all of them were very strongly built. Cavall spent the next few minutes introducing him around. Most of them greeted Gabrion with a sympathetic expression. Only a group of three men in the corner offered no response. Horrid scars covered their faces and arms, and they waited until he turned away before continuing their hushed conversation.

"It's too bad you've come at this time of day," Cavall said companionably. "In an hour's time, we go to work, and they won't let you off because you're new."

"Work?"

"Yep. Lots of physical stuff, so if you have any limbering up to do, now'd be the time for it." He followed that by doing a handful of squats and side bends. Some of the others followed his lead, and soon a whole pack of them were running through a practiced warm-up routine.

The hour passed quickly, and Cavall's prediction was right; the guards put him to work with the rest of them. They were led out a long corridor, where rows of archers waited with arrows nocked and ready for any form of outburst from the prisoners. They were brought to a large yard, and Gabrion could see numerous floors above him that wrapped around the periphery and extended into the sky. This was the highest floor that had a central dais. And it was here they were set to work.

Because he was new, two guards escorted him around the yard and explained various facets of the work he was expected to do during his time there. All the while, he could practically feel the archers in the upper wings readying to take him down if he acted rashly. They weren't the only defensive structure, as the door through which they had come was now securely locked and barred from the other side, as were the other three exits from the area. Additionally, there were short cages along the perimeter that housed vicious dogs, some of whom pawed the ground when he passed, snapping teeth in anticipation of a kill.

One of the guards punched him in the shoulder, since he was too focused on the sights and not on their instructions. "Here is a bellows, as you can see. It keeps a healthy breeze to the lower quarters. It needs utilization throughout the day. Over here is the mill grind." The guard pointed to a cross-shaped wheel where four prisoners walked in a circle, turning the crank so an unseen mechanism could operate somewhere below. "On this side is the hydropump." It looked similar to the mill grind, but the men pushing it were straining even harder.

Around they went, visiting the various stations, including an area for chopping wood. It included two large axes that were well fastened with heavy chains so they could not be used against the guards, not that they would help with all the archers at hand. Cavall nodded at him from one of the stations.

"Over here, the boulders for the lift," the guard said next. There was a massive pulley over the ground, with an enormous chain running below. A thick stone basket on one end was up at the level of the floor, and peering into the other hole, Gabrion could see a similar basket on the other end of the line.

"Don't get any ideas of jumping down there," the guard said. "It's protected on both ends. When a call comes, you roll those into the basket. Simple," he finished, pointing to a nearby pile of boulders. "For now, go to the hydropump and apply yourself there." They gestured him back to the turnstile, where two others were pushing away, and he went, not knowing anything else he could do at the moment.

It was a long, grueling day at the turnstile. It was much harder to push than it looked, and keeping it going was truly taxing on his stamina, not to mention his equilibrium. The constant walking in circles made him rather dizzy. When a halt was called over an hour later, he fell to the ground until he recovered.

Stephen J. Wolf

There were three metal sluices that wrapped along the southern wall. They started from up at one of the guard stations and ended in baskets at the bottom. One sluice carried water, another bread, and the third a gritty sort of stew. Gabrion joined the line for the bowls and cups and took a share with the rest.

"Eat it all, trust me," Cavall warned him. "Ten minutes from now they flush them with water to keep the ramps from rotting with leftover food. So whatever you haven't eaten becomes pretty gruesome. But at least it leaves us with water for the day. They do, after all, need us."

A call went out to return to their stations. One of the hydropump workers asked to switch with Cavall, and he accepted, so he and Gabrion returned to the post and kept turning the wheel. During the whole process, Cavall didn't speak a word. He just leaned his body weight forward and kept pumping his legs in a rhythm. Gabrion followed suit.

The day was completely uneventful after the frantic morning. A new meal was sent down the sluices after a call was made to empty the baskets. They ate, famished, and put in another couple of hours of labor before being given a third meal and then sent back to their holding cell while a chilly night set in.

On the way back, Cavall commented, "Aw, no fireworks tonight." He turned to Gabrion, but the warrior wasn't listening.

Gabrion was so exhausted he passed right out. He was awakened late the next morning when it was time for the warm-up stretch, and then another day followed the first.

* * *

Dariak crashed to the ground in a terrible heap. His arms had completely given out; he couldn't even use them to brace his fall. He smacked to the ground, and lightning sizzled through his head, stabbing him with pain. He couldn't move; everything hurt so badly. Then, once he'd decided he was going to die there, the pain flashed up worse as his body was lifted into the air and carted away.

He had no idea how much time passed before the movement stopped. All he knew was that his robe was stripped off him and then he felt an odd, warm sensation that was somehow familiar. As the hours passed, he recognized that warmth as healing energy passing through him. He tried to pull himself together, but his arms and legs were strapped down to a wood table. Looking down, he saw needles sticking out of him, accompanied by a collection of crystals that facilitated the healing.

After another hour, one of the healers removed the needles and set aside the crystals, then bade him to stand up. He did so slowly and skeptically, keeping a close eye on the ten healers in the room and the eight guards. His robe was handed back to him, and he quickly covered himself up while trying to feel if anything had been taken. Strangely, it seemed like they hadn't touched a single pocket.

He was then guided down a series of corridors that wrapped in a counterclockwise arc. Nudged up a set of stairs, he entered a small laboratory of sorts, confused beyond words.

The room was made of glass on three sides. Two sides had views of what appeared to be observation rooms, where people could sit and watch him work. The third side opened to a wider room that had magic-dampening spells set on all the walls, the floor, and the ceiling. The laboratory itself had a desk and a bookshelf with a collection of books, as well as a bathing tub, bed, and chamber pot that emptied to an unknown place below. In one of the glass walls, he saw a collection of glass chutes with bowls at the end and smelled the faint scent of food.

"I don't understand," he said aloud to one of the guards.

"These are your new quarters, mage. Here you will work whatever spells you can. You may request any spell components you wish. But you are required to perform magic every day."

"What?"

"The amount and quality of food and water that you receive will be directly proportional to the amount and quality of the magic you produce. Want to eat? Start casting."

Dariak stared at the man in utter bewilderment. "You *want* me to use magic?"

"That, or die of starvation."

"But what if I use it to escape?"

The man laughed. "If you could, then you'd deserve it. But you won't be able to. Still, feel free to give it a try; if you do it magically, it counts toward your rations." He smiled widely and then stepped from the room with the rest of the guards. The iron door slid shut, and numerous bolts fell into place. Dariak then felt a horrible, wrenching sensation as an antimagic field spread across the doorway. No wonder they weren't worried.

Dariak's first reaction was to shake his head and lament, once again, the atrocities of this kingdom. They all refuted the magical energies of the land, touting the Hathrens as defilers of nature for their commonplace use of magic. And, once again, when the need suited them, the Kallisorians just tossed up a major spell to contain him. And, looking around again, he realized that the purpose of his prison was to give their mages a chance to learn more magic in the safest and most efficient way possible.

Dariak suspected that he would not be able to use the same spells over and over to earn his meals. They would likely demand greater and greater magic from him in order to best improve their own knowledge, but he would need to take care what spells he revealed to them over the next few days.

* * *

Kitalla struggled against Grenthar's personal form of punishment. Unlike the others, she was kept within his complex, for a time simply locked away in total darkness, except when food was dropped from above. Her only companion was a trickle of water that ran down one wall and into a drainage hole in the floor.

She didn't know what she was angriest about. It bothered her that she'd lost both of her companions on their way through the gauntlet. She was irritated that she hadn't anticipated a host of guards at the final destination. She was outraged that she was stuck in this small, dank cell. But most of all, she was infuriated that she had held the jade, only to have it reclaimed from her mere moments later.

Kitalla was kept in the cell for at least three days before time started blending together. She had no light at all, except for those brief moments at mealtimes, so she felt along the walls for any sense of deformation that she could try to exploit. But top to bottom, the circular walls were completely smooth, with a diameter wider than her body was long. There was no way she could even climb the fifteen-foot height to reach the upper hatch. She spent her time trying to keep limber and active, but it was hard with her only water supply a stale trickle down the wall that required her to press her tongue against the stone in order to capture any.

Perhaps a week after her imprisonment, a rope was lowered into the cell with a command for her to climb. It was smart of them not to use a ladder, for climbing a rope required her to use both hands, therefore preventing her from attacking when she reached the surface.

Sunlight cascaded into the room, and she squinted harshly against it. Two strong men grabbed her and dragged her forward along a corridor and into a room at the end of the hall. Her hands, feet, and neck were buckled into an oversized chair, allowing her to see and speak but not to move.

"Well, well," greeted a voice she hadn't wanted to hear again. Grenthar stepped into view and infuriated her by pacing back and forth, purposely walking beyond her field of vision with each passing. "I see you yet live, little pet."

"I'm no pet," she scowled.

"Temper, temper," he scolded lightly. "Like it or not, little pet, you've become one." He approached her and stroked her hair. She tried to bite him, but the restraining belts did their work well. "None of that, little pet, or I'll put you to other uses, and trust me, you would not like them." He made a suggestive expression, and Kitalla immediately calmed herself down.

"Better," he said. "If you could ask of me one question and any question at all, what would it be?"

"What do you want from me?" she hissed.

"Ah, now I expected a bigger heart from you! Not even asking about your friends. Tsk, tsk," he admonished petulantly. "Well, let me tell you anyway. You see, His Great Royal Majesty of Kallisor sent his elite force to our town to capture three fugitives."

He stepped outside her range of vision and brought back a parchment. "Look familiar?" he asked, holding out a wanted poster. "Well, you see, I handed over your friends to the guard for execution."

Kitalla's reaction betrayed her feelings. She writhed around in the seat, her chest heaving.

"Ah, so you *do* care for them. Pity." He shook his head. "If only I had known before, I would have secreted them away as well." He clapped his hands and sighed dramatically. "Well, nothing I can do now, I'm afraid. But this still leaves you, doesn't it? That was your question, after all?"

It took everything she had to calm down and tell herself that he was wrong about Gabrion and Dariak. "Yes," she said through gritted teeth. "What have you planned for me?"

"Ah, delightful!" he beamed, clapping his hands together again. "You are the only one ever to complete all parts of my little gauntlet and get your hands on my gem."

"The only?" she interrupted. "What of those rogues who had it before?"

Grenthar growled. "Those fools had the object on loan. Do not insult my traps with the likes of them. They would not have survived a single one of them." He paced back and forth a few times, trying to rid himself of the irksome memory. Kitalla wondered what the greater connection was between the two.

"Anyway," Grenthar grumbled at last, "because you made it through successfully, apparently my traps are not enough. So you will help me to devise better ones."

"Ha!" she barked. "I will not."

He ran up to her and shouted, "You will or you die!" He trembled in his anger.

"How?" she breathed.

It took a few moments for him to pull back. "You will run it again and again with the improvements that I make. And you will keep doing so until you die or until you claim that crystal."

She couldn't help herself; she had to ask: "What happens if I take the crystal?"

"Then you leave with it, of course."

She didn't believe him quite so readily. He was too shrewd to let a prize of that nature go. She assumed that if she claimed the shard either she would be detained and new traps would be created or she would have a second gauntlet to face on her way out. Perhaps both. She needed to be ready for the worst.

"I won't be able to help you in my present… living quarters," she ventured.

Grenthar laughed. "Smart, you are. It's no wonder you made it as far as you did. No, you will be relocated to a new cell. But don't doubt that you will have no chance of escape, except through that jade."

"What accoutrements will I have access to? If I'm going to really make your traps better, I need to be able to do as much damage as possible. No?"

The master thief smiled maliciously. "Oh yes, you will have a full complement of weapons and armor for the task. You see, no one will claim that prize after all I went through for it. And I know some of what you are capable of, and I will know if you are holding back in your attempts."

"No. I won't," she said confidently. "I will take that jade and escape with it. For Dariak and for Gabrion."

"Good then, my pet," Grenthar declared. "To your new quarters then, and your new profession, trap springer."

She was hoisted up by the guards after the bindings were removed, and then she was taken to a new holding cell that at least had some light. She was surrounded on three sides by stone and the fourth by a solid iron door, with barely a finger's breadth of space between the floor and the iron. And because Dariak had been working with her to sense the energies around her, she also knew that magical barriers had been put into place.

The only thing that gave her any hope at all was the scratch the jade had given her chest when she was captured. Though it had essentially healed by now, something about it remained with her, and she could feel it. The iron door itself seemed to have a pulse, and she instinctively knew it was because of the jade. Folding her arms and legs and opening her thoughts to her surroundings, Kitalla spent the next few hours in very deep meditation, reaching for and feeling the energies around her.

CHAPTER 23

Prisoners

DARIAK AWOKE ONE morning to a wild reptigon being brought into his glassy cell. He sprang from his bed and instructed the hunters to place it in a cage in the spell room. They left him then, glad to be rid of the beast, and locked the door, resetting the magic barrier that kept him detained within.

Part of him didn't really care. He gathered a few of his things and rifled through a set of notes he had made for himself, and then he glanced out the side wall to ensure that at least two mages were present for the viewing. Over the past weeks, he had learned that if his spells were not observed, he didn't receive his food and water. He had also discovered that if more than one mage was impressed by his work, then the food quality would improve. For one particularly crafty spell, in which he had used sawdust and his candle-flame spell to generate a sizzling firestorm, he had earned a small bottle of wine as a bonus. While the firestorm itself hadn't been utterly impressive, it was the creative combination of such a simple spell and component that had caught their attention.

Excited about the prospect of attempting a new spell, Dariak hurried his way into the other room, listening to the reptigon as it hissed angrily from its cage. He had spent a long time communing with his jades, which had purposely not been taken from him, and he knew that the structure of the serpentine's spine would suit a spell such as this. He looked over the cage toward the observers in the other room watching intently from beyond the thick, magic-proof glass. Today there were four watchers, which suited Dariak perfectly. As usual, they all had parchment and quill in front of them, and their bodies were covered from head to toe in thick cloaks that left even their heads in deep shadow. He understood that they wanted to remain anonymous in case he ever escaped, but still, it seemed overly dramatic at times.

He cleared his throat and his thoughts. He needed to remain focused here. Dangerously, he was combining the effects of three major spells, linking them with the components of lesser incantations. As always, he had already supplied a written description of the spell, required components, and the intended effects the day before. Glancing back at the viewers, he was admittedly surprised there weren't more of them.

Dariak placed his spell components out on a small table set there for that purpose. He opened a jar of spiders and took two of them, then mashed them together as he spouted his web-binding spell, casting it toward the reptigon. *"Naarestigar engor shai."* The slithering body was locked into place, its legs twitching to be free.

"Selucia froell nikrobar shath." This new spell was water based, and it coerced the creature's blood to flow in terse lines. This was why he needed the wriggling animal, because its spine would more readily adjust to the demands of the spell.

He took a short length of rope and knotted it numerous times along its length, making the rope as sturdy and immobile as possible. Because of the web-binding spell already in place, this spell added to the pinning effect, becoming a potent alternative to a true paralysis spell.

Dariak stepped forward quickly and opened the cage. If he cast the next spell with the reptigon locked inside, then the creature would be crushed to death.

"Sascrellia gorgola nuichi kasroth nyie," he spouted next, shoving pieces of flower buds into the creature's mouth. At once, the beast began to grow in size, keeping its form and intellect as it went. The forked tongue lashed out angrily, yet also with expectant hope, as its prey now seemed much smaller than before. Dariak's hands and arms whirled about, already into the next phase.

"Fabronie gravila martell breq kaie." It was the true vocal component of the Shield of Delminor, which he hadn't uttered aloud in a long time because he had been using the earth jade. But because he said it aloud and used a spot of mud to amplify the effect, he was able to send its energy outward and affect a desired target, rather than keeping it attuned to his body until he was struck. The projection component of the spell was relatively new to him, though, and something he had learned during his stay in the glass rooms.

The mud patch fluttered in the air as it drew toward its destination, the reptigon's fangs. Upon impact, the grossly oversized teeth became extremely heavy, dragging the reptigon's head to the floor with a loud thud.

Dariak pulled out a dagger and sliced his finger alongside the edge. This was an offensive spell he rarely used because it both cost him the dagger and hurt terribly within. He had only used it once in combat, during the siege on Savvron. *"Zharackatar impalliortus vreth coneai larrinkusa."* He threw the dagger outward, and it became a blur of smaller knives cutting and slashing at the reptigon, severing the teeth from its body, where they tumbled over. Searing pain laced through Dariak's body, but he wasn't done.

He took an empty glass bottle from the table and set it on the floor at his feet. Then he snapped open a container of thick molasses and covered his lips in it, making sure he left massive amounts in place. Gently placing his tongue against the paste, he stretched his hands outward and pulled in slowly, curling his hands as he fought against the pain of the dagger-chain spell. When the molasses broke and entered his mouth, he muttered the words while still drawing in his breath.

"Compallionus vacutious exthelia imprixicon ferinai." The fangs of the reptigon twitched and rotated around, and from deep within a thick, greenish ooze seeped out and arced across the room, landing into the glass bottle under the guidance of his fingers and hands.

Dariak quickly sealed it and set it aside before too much air could contaminate it. He then recast the web snare on the beast, as it was starting to move again, and drove his dagger deep into its neck to kill it. He could have used another spell, but he was deeply aching inside, and he also wanted to save longer spell chains for the days to come.

What he had now was a large container of reptigon serum that could be used as a spell component, a healing agent, or as a poison. Obtaining it normally was difficult, but this series of incantations had left him with a container similar to the extraction of nearly fifty beasts. Because he had used a vacuum-based spell to draw the serum, he had taken it all. Additionally, the water spell he'd used to pull it across the room kept it in its concentrated form, so when the engorgement spell wore off, its change in volume would vacuum seal the container without ruining its potency.

The excessive ritual earned him a rich meal, which was brought in by a team of guards, rather than cast down the food chutes. The carcass was also removed at his request, but he refused to allow the mages to have the serum. He claimed he would need it for better spells. The hunger in their eyes was unmistakable.

The vast drawings of energy, however, left him extremely weak, and he wasn't able to work magic again for a couple of days. Luckily his reward had included cheeses and breads, and he wisely stashed them away with a cask of water. Despite the success of his complicated spell, he would not receive more nourishment from the mages until he used more magic.

As he lay there three days later, noshing on a stale bit of bread, he wondered about his situation in more depth. Even in Hathreneir, he had never heard of a training ground such as this. Mages often used books and diagrams to learn spells, or they shared secrets with their friends or observed and absorbed spells from their foes. Nearly every mage kept notes, which became available to the populace after their deaths, unless they opened those pages to others during their lifetime. Yet a setup of this nature was unheard of. Practicing and creating great spells was left to theorists and wizened mages, not men like himself.

And though mages weren't precisely outlawed in Kallisor, he did feel restricted when it came to using his skills. Plus, the populace despised his kind. Just not in here. The blatant thievery of his spells irked him, but he also cherished the fact that he could push his skills to the limit. On a few occasions when his attempts had gone awry, healers had come in to seal his wounds and put him right again. He really had everything he could want here. Except for his freedom, of course.

He thought of his quest as he rummaged for a wedge of cheese. He wanted to follow in his father's footsteps and reunite the pieces of the jade figurine so that he could put an end to war. The enticements of the magic sessions, however, were diverting him well.

Curious, he rose and thumbed through his journal with all his notes. He wrote in it every day, keeping comments of the days passing as well as of all his spell ideas. He looked at the date and then had to look at it again. He had been there for almost six weeks already. Winter would be in full force, but he had no sense of it here in the tower. The realization of the spent time shocked him. He sat down but missed the chair and hit the floor. What kind of son was he to abandon his father's quest so easily for this freedom to use magic without prejudice or restraint?

He stood up, angry with himself, and started pacing furiously. The two observing mages lifted their hoods slightly, expecting him to start casting at any moment, but when he strutted from one end to the other without so much as a twitch of his mouth or hands, they eased back in their seats.

Two pieces of jade were in his possession. The earth and water forces could be channeled through them. He needed to use that to find a means of getting out of this place. But the walls were all fortified with strong antimagic wards that would prevent him from using spells on them properly.

Nonetheless, he needed a plan.

Walking back to his journal, he shook his head at the date and then flipped ahead to a random page, marking it with a single dot in the corner. By that day, he needed to make his escape.

The trickiest part, he knew, was beyond fathoming a way through the magic walls. No, the hardest part would be gathering what he needed without the rest of the mages knowing.

He continued pacing, pondering some options.

* * *

Kitalla crawled on the ground in the most unlikely of situations. Razor blades whirled overhead and along her sides, effectively boxing her in. She kept her head down and turned to the side so her cheek dragged along the coarse floor and slowly pulled her body up with the smallest form of crawling she could muster.

The task wasn't easy on the best of days, but today she was bleeding in numerous places and covered with deep welts everywhere else. She suspected one of her ribs was also broken from a recent fall, but none of it mattered. She simply had to succeed.

Ten. Nine. Eight more pulls. Seven. Six. Five. It was hard to count them but doing so helped her ignore the pain lacing through her body. She knew she had to hurry, though, for a fiery wall was catching up to her feet, not that she could see it in her position. Four. Three. Two.

With a final wrench, she pulled herself from the horrific gauntlet and sprawled on the ground. Ahead of her, she could see the pedestal with the jade upon it. She was so close now. Left arm out. Right knee up. Slide forward just a little. Right arm out. Left knee up.

Then something she didn't expect. From overhead, a heavy stone slab plummeted from the ceiling. She didn't have the strength to throw her body forward across the threshold, so she pulled back. But not quickly enough. Her right arm dragged back too slowly, and the stone crashed down upon it, flattening and shattering all the bones from her elbow to her fingertips.

She screamed. Her cry could have shattered the stone; it was so loud and heartrending. She couldn't breathe or see or feel anything else but a horrible agony that she would never forget. Her throat burned raw as she continued to wail and her eyes drained of tears. She couldn't move.

Only two things saved her at that moment. The slab was on a cable system that kept it just a few inches off the floor, so though it had broken all her bones, it did not do even worse damage. Also, Grenthar had an elite team of healers nearby for such an occasion, and they started first with sending the thief into a deep slumber. She grabbed for the unconsciousness desperately, but even when she was no longer alert, her body still cried out in agony.

It would take the healers a week to repair such major damage, if they could repair it at all. They had spent many days at the start of Kitalla's tenure analyzing and recording the aspects of her body, which had helped to facilitate the healing she'd needed as she tested each of Grenthar's horrific traps. They had also had much practice tending to the plethora of wounds she had already obtained on her passes through the dungeon, but whether they could ever properly restore her arm after this was a feat left unseen. If they didn't succeed, her usefulness to Grenthar would be at an end.

The wretched soul wished she could give up the fight and let her quest be over, yet the fighter in her would not allow it. Nothing else had ever defeated her—nothing that came to mind right then, anyway—and she was determined to succeed again. She had touched the jade once, and it had scored her chest, leaving her with an odd sensitivity to metal and an irrational desire to steal the jade away.

For Dariak, the weeks had blended together. Not so for Kitalla. She felt every terrifying moment of her new existence. Grenthar had started her small, testing single traps at a time, but he soon learned that she could conquer them rather easily, even when they were dangerous. He then added sets of traps to a room and pitted her against them. Even when facing off against two lupinoes in a maze-like labyrinth that had little room to maneuver, she'd still succeeded. Fire-tipped arrows in a chamber with a chasm and teetering poles as her only footsteps were also no match for her, even when she traversed them a second and third time with no more light than the arrows themselves.

Battering rams, fall-away floor tiles, whirling blades: she'd faced them all and lived. And so Grenthar added to the difficulty by stringing rooms of challenges together. Soon Kitalla struggled against two, then three, then four rooms of intensifying traps, all in the name of protecting his piece of jade.

But she knew she had to press onward, for if she truly failed a task, she would be slain. And as the challenges became more lethal, she knew Grenthar wouldn't even need to perform the execution, because the traps would do the work for him.

The master of the gauntlet kept the healers ready in order to cure her ailments quickly so he could send her out again and again, as if delaying at all would put his merchandise at risk. Kitalla had believed she was better than anything he could throw at her, but that stone wall after all the other obstacles had shown her otherwise.

As the extended healing period came to an end, Kitalla wondered if it was at all worth it. Her focus shifted from claiming the jade to wanting to send Grenthar through his own trials and see him fail within the first few seconds.

Revenge against him was no longer just in the form of taking his shard. She wanted also to repay him for her injuries.

Curled up in her cell with extra food to promote recovery, Kitalla rocked back and forth. Her arm was wrapped so snugly with bandages she couldn't really move it. Everything still stung inside, like dozens of fire ants crawling up and down, and she wondered idly if that sensation would ever go away. She looked around the cell, wishing she simply had someone to talk to, to lament with, to scream at. But she had nothing. Instead, she shifted her aching body over to the iron door and pressed her face against it. Since touching the jade, the iron had seemed somewhat alive, and though she didn't know if it was possible, she thought the door felt melancholy, standing there for all its life with people banging their fists against it in futility.

She knew pretty well how it felt.

CHAPTER 24

Escape from Prisoner's Tower

MIRA STOOD AT the end of the room with her rich brown hair billowing out behind her from a breeze that touched her delicately. She reached out her arm as her gown swirled gently around her, cascading in folds of opalescent white.

Gabrion stood at once and walked toward her, and she smiled, turning gracefully around and stepping away, almost hovering. He followed with a childlike smile lighting his face, but she was ever a hallway's length ahead of him, egging him on. Up and around she went, spiraling into the sky, with Gabrion keeping as close as he could, not letting her leave his sight.

At last, Mira stopped ascending through the air, and instead, her giggling laughter echoed toward him as she approached a watery wall. She stretched her arms wide, passing through the water and becoming a shimmering blur on the other side. Gabrion followed her, passing through the water without being drenched by it. Mira kept walking on, drifting into another chamber, where she stopped for a moment. While she stood there, Gabrion paused to admire her beauty.

Mira spun delicately, her dress flowing outward in cloudlike spirals, sparkling with each twirl. Then she stopped and laughed, and as Gabrion watched, her deep-blue eyes started to glow. They not only lit within her head, but they cast light outward, and as they did so, one beam of light remained blue while the other turned softly to brown. With a delicate leap, she bounded off again, Gabrion in tow.

Down she went now, spiraling again but floating closer and closer to places he knew. Around and down, with no barriers to impede her. At last she ran straight, and Gabrion doubled his efforts to reach her.

But Mira could not be caught. She entered a deep labyrinth with diamond and sapphire walls gleaming delightfully. She twirled as she went, turning down one passageway and then choosing another. Gabrion kept an easy pace with her now, for he knew this path. He had walked it before. Mira giggled again, her laugh tinkling against the diamonds.

She then spun once and ascended gracefully into the air again, and Gabrion scrambled to follow. The ground was suddenly slippery and hard to climb, but he needed to reach her. She was so close. Up he went, and off she drifted, bobbing and weaving through the room and settling into a doorway at the end. She reached into the room and withdrew a silver tiara, setting it atop her hair before pirouetting and tiptoeing over to another doorway.

Once inside, she lifted a glimmering gray shawl and wrapped it around her neck, and there the color drained down, turning her entire dress into silver white. As Gabrion approached, she smiled and fled toward his right, disappearing at last, and with the light from her eyes gone, the room went slowly dark.

He knew he couldn't follow her. He could only stare. But this time, something was different. Something happened that snapped him awake from his dream. He had been having it for many nights, and he had traced the same paths over and over until he could recall them during his waking hours. This time was different because as Mira drifted out that last door, she spoke.

"Now, Gabrion," her ethereal voice had whispered. "Now."

He sat up from his place in the cell, trembling. The room was dark, as dawn had not yet arrived. Clanging footsteps echoed from the entranceway, which signaled a change in the prisoners. The course of the past two months had been met with occasional changes, where either new prisoners were brought in or others were removed. Once, they had taken out a corpse, a man who had fallen victim to the scarred ones, who'd found something offensive in the man. Another time, a prisoner taken away ended up as one of the guards overlooking the work field, and then they realized that some of the prisoners weren't really under punishment. It was an effective and dangerous way of learning of escape plots, but Cavall had always taken it upon himself to quell any such talk.

He seemed to like his domain the way it was.

Each time the guards went by, Gabrion noticed that the one who had taken the ring intended for Mira always wore it around his neck, as if daring Gabrion to try to reclaim it.

"Now, Gabrion," Mira had said in his dream. "Now."

While the others slept, Gabrion stepped over to the doorway, standing to one side and tensing in anticipation. Slowly, the door swung open toward his face, and a new body was thrown inside. Gabrion grabbed the door and shoved it forward, knocking the guard to the ground. The new prisoner looked back, seeing the attack, and took full advantage of it. The red-haired youth stole the guard's sword and charged into the support team behind him, catching them all by surprise, so long had it been since a prisoner had revolted.

Gabrion kicked the fallen guard in the ribs and reclaimed Mira's ring and the chain from which it hung. He then took a sword from one of the guards the youth had taken down and followed, pummeling into anyone who got in his way.

The red-haired youth said nothing but fought with an unparalleled rage, taking up a second sword at one point and screaming as he continued lashing out at the other guards. He took some hits, but Gabrion couldn't get close enough to help; the blades were whipped around so frantically. One by one the guards fell until the youth sprinted off, leaving Gabrion behind as if he'd never existed. The warrior wanted to follow, to assist in his escape, but the lure of the dream compelled him to turn and go the other way.

Mira had spiraled up into the air, and he knew he needed to do the same. He found an alternate doorway, and it pressed open to his touch. He held his sword cautiously before him as he entered a quiet hall lined with various alcoves. He peered into them as he went. The ones on his left had windows facing away from the approaching dawn, and the right side held statuary. A doorway opened at the end of the hall, and footsteps rushed inside. An alarm must have sounded at the outbreak, and Gabrion jumped into an alcove on the right, pressing as far beside the statue as possible, hoping beyond reason that he wouldn't be seen.

The first few guards were running hard and stepped right past him, but then someone saw him and veered over for the kill. Gabrion leaped out to parry the attack while three others joined the fray. A war hammer swung low to knock Gabrion's feet from under him, but he jumped over the swing and kicked into the wielder's chest, sending him sprawling. As he landed, Gabrion ducked low to dodge a sword slash, after which he pivoted around to hack into one of the guardsmen's legs. It was a minor hit, but it offset the incoming ax. Gabrion rolled head over feet, causing one of the swordsmen to pounce aside, and then he sprang for the doorway at the end of the hall, figuring he might be able to use the threshold as a barrier to keep from being surrounded.

The ploy worked, and he fended off the four guards, until more footsteps thundered behind him as the alarm roused the entire tower. With two guards still fighting strong and at least five more on the way, Gabrion was effectively pinned. He decided it would be best to leap into the two guards and finish them; he could then pivot and use the doorway as a barrier again.

Then help came. Most of the prisoners from Gabrion's cell had gone down the main corridor, but the three scarred ones had seen the open doorway and turned to head off the other guards. The three of them worked like a symbiotic unit, bending and tumbling over one another as they kicked about and struck the two guards at Gabrion's front. The scarred ones eyed Gabrion appraisingly, then shoved him aside and raced headlong into the next pursuit of guards.

Shocked, Gabrion didn't react for a moment. He hadn't spent much time getting to know the three of them, and their help here was completely unexpected. But then he realized that they weren't helping him, per se. Whatever their goal was, they were seeking it for themselves; he was just a lucky beneficiary.

Gabrion claimed a second sword from one of the fallen guards, noting that the war hammer and ax were missing. The cries of outrage ahead easily told him where those weapons had ended up. He raced after the scarred ones to offer assistance as they tore through the hallway and fought their way up the stairs, weapons whirling with remarkable precision. They looked to Gabrion like a three-headed monster, devouring troops as they went. All he knew about them was what Cavall had told him that first day: they were skilled thieves who had lost some comrades during an attempted heist against Grenthar. Seeing them in action now, he couldn't imagine how they had been bested.

Along the way, Gabrion dealt with stragglers that had been knocked aside and left unattended. He mostly bashed them with a sword hilt and rendered them unconscious, but a few tried to rise against him, and those he ended up killing. He wanted to grab some of their unneeded armor, but time was precious, and his compulsion to follow Mira's dream flight propelled him onward.

The trio of thieves became a duo as one of them took an ax to the skull. Gabrion held back as the unholy cries of the other two shook the walls and they shredded the guard who had killed their companion. He met a horrible fate, as they practically turned him inside out in their rage, after which they continued their fast push through the halls until at last finding the place they were seeking.

Gabrion came upon them as one of the scarred ones battered down a door with his war hammer, splintering the wood and causing it to crash inward. The two of them took some form of personal revenge on the inhabitants inside and then sat on the floor, heaving deeply and clutching each other for support. Gabrion didn't dare disturb them. He wondered if the guards in that room had been responsible for the deaths of their other companions or perhaps had served to alert Grenthar about their infiltration into his compound, which had led to their capture. Whatever the case, it seemed obvious to Gabrion that they were out of the fight. The rest was his to do alone.

He needed to climb, if he was going to follow Mira's path from his dream, and so he rushed forward to the nearest stairwell and sprinted upward. As his foot touched the landing, he had to quickly drop aside to the floor, for a slew of arrows targeted him instantly. These were the same archers who perched daily around the periphery of the work field. There was a slight delay as the archers reloaded and fired again. Gabrion pressed himself against the wall and then dashed ahead, keeping low. He scooted under most of the arrows, but one caught him deeply in the left shoulder, and another grazed his cheek.

He wouldn't be stopped. Gabrion pushed ahead, throwing one archer aside into another one, then hacking the bow out of the hands of a third. He couldn't use his left arm, but he made up for it with brutal swipes of the sword in his right hand. It was the one bonus he'd gained working in the field all those weeks. The intensity had built up muscle tone and stamina, as well as a greater tolerance to pain.

The archers were highly skilled with their bows, but only a couple of them knew anything about melee combat. Those who relied solely on ranged attacks went quickly to the ground with each swing of the warrior's arm. The others deflected attacks with their bows, as they drew short swords or daggers to fend off the rest. But none of them could launch much of an offensive strike during the warrior's enraged assault. The archers struggled mostly just to survive with all their body parts intact.

Gabrion hurried from the room and propelled himself up the next flight of stairs. The corridor was lined with other prison cells, and here he found numerous women who had certainly had better days. He didn't think about his actions; he went over and lifted the bolts from the doors, warning them of the fighting and then hurrying on his way. Disbelief turned into excitement, and the women ran screaming and wailing from their cells, releasing other prisoners Gabrion had missed along the way.

The warrior jogged across to another doorway and up yet again. Traveling the distance in the dreamscape had been much more pleasant, but he kept focused and pushed onward. He knew he was nearing the pinnacle of the journey, but the appearance of more guards delayed him even further.

Gabrion didn't know why his dream always summoned him to the upper floors, but it did, so he made the same journey. Now, with the appearance of mages along with the fighters, he started to understand. Perhaps Dariak and Kitalla had been taken to the tower too. He had lost hope for them long ago, barely even holding onto his wishes to see Mira again until she had started appearing in his dreams. Though part of him honestly believed she was in his dreams because she was already dead, he didn't dwell on those thoughts when they surfaced. Nor could he dwell on them now.

Shards of ice cut across the room, streaking blue light along their paths. The radiance made him shy away, and the ice spears missed him, shattering on the back wall. When those missed, another set flew forth, this time backed by an additional blast of air power, which gave them better aim and more force. He zigzagged across the room as the fighters readied their weapons to protect the mages while he closed in on them. Another blast of wind lashed out, and this one struck him, making him gasp. It cut like a small knife, and he felt blood trickle down his cheek, matching his earlier wound. One of the mages pelted the ground with chunks of ice, purposely aiming for the floor to make a slick surface for the warrior, and though Gabrion struggled to remain on his feet, he managed it, while swinging his sword and trying to blast back some of the shards of ice.

Just a couple of yards away now, the fighters broke ranks and charged at Gabrion. He sidestepped and parried one sword thrust, turning and crashing his own sword on the man's back, sending him sprawling onto the icy floor, where he slid away, his armor scraping harshly on the surface. The next guard was not so easily cast aside and swung his flail viciously. Gabrion parried and grabbed the man's wrist, trying to twist it aside. The guard responded by kicking at the warrior, who fell back in pain. Gabrion hit the ground, then rolled backward onto his feet, bringing his sword around and banging it against the guard's helmet. With a roar, the guard flung his flail toward Gabrion, who batted it aside with his injured left arm and earned another wound in the process.

With a feral cry, Gabrion charged again but veered aside and lunged for one of the mages, who responded by unleashing another blast of ice darts into Gabrion's chest. He turned his left side into the attack, letting the bad arm absorb the damage and continuing the spin until he brought his sword deeply into the mage's chest, killing him instantly.

The other mage whirled his fingers around as the guard ran forward as well. The air around Gabrion's body condensed and caused him to slow down. It felt like a thick blanket being thrown over him, and all he wanted to do was cut through it, but his sword had no effect. The guard barreling in after Gabrion was caught in the spell, and his attacks struggled to find their mark.

Gabrion threw himself to the ground, finding that the air shield didn't reach to the floor. Out went his sword. The mage had to step aside, losing his concentration, and down went the spell. The guard reclaimed his normal speed, but he hadn't bent down with the warrior, and so his body flew forward and crashed into the mage with a yelp.

Scrambling to his feet, Gabrion readied his weapon, but the mage reacted quickly and flung his hands outward, sending fistfuls of sand and dirt at the warrior. As the particles flew through the air, they drew closer together, becoming a wall similar to the one of air cast moments ago. Gabrion could see that this wall wouldn't just slow him down. He surmised that the added sand and dirt would cause it to drag him down.

He felt a searing pain in his right pocket, where he kept the jade. It was vibrating so fiercely he dropped his sword and grabbed the jade, holding it aloft. He didn't know what compelled him, but he made a vertical slashing motion with the crystal. He felt a strange pull from within him, and as the sand particles reached him, they fell asunder, ruining the attempted spell.

He had to act quickly though, because the guard was up, flail swinging again. Gabrion dropped to his backside, kicking with one leg and transferring the jade into his left hand, all in one motion. He swiped his sword from the floor and brought it up into the guard's armor, impaling him in the belly and tossing him aside.

Tired, Gabrion launched his sword at the mage, cutting deeply into one of the man's hands, which made the mage cry out more in shock than in pain. A mage's hands were so important that he immediately fell to his knees and begged for mercy, splaying his arms out wide. Apparently, he would rather chance death than face further injury to his instruments of spellcasting. Having effectively bound Dariak a few times at the start of their journey, Gabrion made short work of securing the mage's hands and mouth before moving on.

The jade pulsated terribly, and Gabrion feared that it would shatter. His left hand was weak, but he kept the jade there, knowing he needed to keep his right arm ready for attack. Up ahead, a few doors lined the hall, and when he ran past one, the jade sent shocks into his fingers, so he turned back and went through the door.

The next challenge almost startled the determination out of him, for he saw a room of at least twenty mages, cloaked with thick robes and massive hoods. He dove into the room, hitting the ground in another roll to avoid any spells aimed for his heart. Yet as he spun around and came to his feet, he was stunned to see only two mages, who were summoning protection spells about themselves and not thinking offensively at all. A second glance around showed Gabrion that the seven other walls were all made of glass, casting reflections that made it seem like more mages were within, but he didn't have time to see more than that. The mages finished their initial spells and turned their attentions on the intruder.

"Hands down or you die," Gabrion warned. When they hesitated, he added, "I made it this far, didn't I?" The mages exchanged nervous glances, eyeing the blood pouring from his wounds that didn't seem to affect him at all. As one, they lowered their hands and put their arms out for him to bind them.

Throughout their journey together, Dariak had often commented about the lack of attention people paid to mages and their spell components. Thus Gabrion stripped the cloaks from the mages before tying their hands and mouths. He needed time to figure out the octagonal room, and because he wasn't running off right away, he had to take the extra measure. Once the mages were tied, he hit them each on the neck and knocked them both out, then slid their bodies in front of the only door.

Further inspecting the room, Gabrion saw that each transparent wall had another room on the other side, and except for a few notches in the glass, there was no passage between them. The jade in his hand was shaking so violently that it fell from his weakened grip and clattered to the stone floor. He set his sword aside and picked the jade up flat in his hand, as he had seen Dariak do before, and then he turned slowly around the room. But as he did so, he already knew which way to turn, because he remembered the image of Mira walking through a watery wall.

Not surprisingly, the jade practically bounced out of his hand when he oriented himself toward the northeastern panel of glass. He reached the jade outward and touched it to the smooth surface, but nothing happened. He wasn't aware of the antimagic field that covered the wall, but he wasn't going to let anything stop him anyway. He slid the jade into his pocket and took one of the wood chairs and whaled at the wall, cracking it slightly. But in the process, most of the chair itself shattered and fell to the floor in pieces.

He tried the sword next, but all he created were sparks on the glass, and he feared that he was deadening the blade. The jade still trembled, and he took it out again, focusing his thoughts upon it, wondering if even he could draw its energies out to work miracles.

But he didn't have time to commune with the jade. Running footsteps echoed outside the wooden doorway, and although they didn't yet know he was in that room, it wouldn't be long before they figured it out. He looked back at the ding that had been made in the glass, and he knew suddenly what he had to do. Gabrion wielded the jade shard like a chisel and cracked it into the glass with all of his strength. As he did so, he bade the wall to tumble like water, to shatter into pieces, so that he might continue onward to follow Mira's path.

Again he brought the jade down into the wall, and greater the damage grew. As he worked, the glass chimed with each hit, with each peal sounding less and less harmonious as his efforts ruined the flat surface. At last, with a cry of effort, Gabrion got the jade to break through; the glass turned instantly milky, then splattered to the ground like hailstones. Gabrion didn't hesitate. He transferred the jade to his pocket and retrieved his sword before crossing the barrier into the next room.

Before him, Dariak stood aghast. They hadn't seen each other for two months, and neither had truly known if the other was even alive. But everything the elder of Gerrish had told Gabrion was proving true. The jades were calling out to one another, hence the augmented vibrations of his shard. The jade could apparently feel its brethren at the top of the tower, and when the distance between them did not close, its radiant energies had started affecting the warrior's dreams. Because the jades could not be broken into smaller pieces and the crystal in Gabrion's possession had power over glass, he had been able to physically break the transparent surface, which interrupted the antimagic field in the room.

It took a moment for Dariak to register the warrior's appearance through his workroom wall, but then he was filled with such relief he ran over and gave the big man a welcome embrace. He pulled back, looked around, and realized that they needed to get moving immediately.

Dariak started by scrounging up various materials, but then he saw Gabrion's badly wounded shoulder and arm. "A moment!" he said proudly, reaching into his robe and pulling forth a sheaf of aloe. He placed pieces of it on the wounds and then wriggled his fingers quickly. *"Ferrathorian mentilion faloshir brea."* He inspected his work, and the lacerations had closed. "It'll have to do for now."

Gabrion flexed his arm. "Still hurts, but at least I have some mobility again. Thanks. Let's move out."

"What of Kitalla?" Dariak asked, taking his journal and struggling to fit it within the confines of his robe.

"I think she's next." Gabrion shrugged, feeling the strength of the door leading out of Dariak's sleeping quarters. "The jade is leading this charge." He pulled the crystal forth and felt its strongest vibrations when he touched it to the doorway. "But how to get through here?" he muttered.

Dariak closed his eyes and moved his arms in a circle, drawing them wide around and closer in toward his heart. "No good, this wall still has the magic nullifier in place."

But Gabrion's shard was again jumping around in his hand. "Watch for guards through there," he said, nodding his head toward the glass wall he had shattered. He then turned his attention to the shard. "Help me," he pleaded.

The vibrations of the jade ceased for a moment, and in that time, strange visions swept into Gabrion's head. He couldn't make any sense of them, but he described them aloud in a tongue he had never before used. The words felt awkward and powerful. "*Sharrasok kathzhak khalichoq,*" he murmured, feeling the jade tremble again, but now there was something new. His sword was also resonating with the jade. He lifted it, knowing suddenly what he had seen. He pocketed the jade and held the sword out firmly before him, and then he cut down swiftly into the iron door, severing a deep gash within the metal. His sword was now sharper than ever before, and with a few more strikes, he cut an opening from which they could flee.

Dariak was on his heels, not even asking about the sudden magic the warrior had used. He didn't need to, as he could feel the emanations from the sand jade. Gabrion raced down the stairs and plowed through one hallway after the next. Guards were scrambling along the lower levels of the tower, where most of the prisoners had escaped, and so their way was easy for a time. Each doorway they approached fell to the enhanced sword. Gabrion only feared when its power would run out.

Once they were two floors below the main dungeon where Gabrion had been kept, the guards became present. Gabrion's sword flew wide, cutting through armor like parchment, which demoralized the contingent of fighters. But they were well trained, and they avoided the dangerous weapon for as long as they could—at least, until Dariak arrived a few moments later and added his spells to the fray.

The mage's powers had, indeed, increased, and Gabrion recognized the effects of the Shield of Delminor as men and women fell to the ground under massive weight, though he had never seen the spell erupt from the mage's fingers before. To that, Dariak added other binding spells, locking as many guards in place as possible while Gabrion hacked away at those who refused to succumb. Though Dariak would have thoroughly enjoyed unleashing more powerful spells, the halls were too narrow and Gabrion would likely have been struck down in error.

Eventually they erupted into the labyrinthine tunnels where one path led back to Grenthar's complex. Dariak had been incapacitated then, but Gabrion had worked hard to memorize the way, which was fortified by the countless dreams of Mira floating about the crystalline hallways. He ran with purpose, slowing down only to give Dariak time to catch up. Left, then right, then left again, they hurried. There was little light by which to see, and most of it from other hallways boasting torches, but Gabrion ran on as if he had lived there for years. His sword wasn't vibrating as powerfully, but he needed its strength to cut through the final door into the compound.

He pushed himself harder, hearing Dariak falling behind but pressing himself to run faster anyway.

With a hearty crash, Gabrion's sword splintered the wood separating the tunnels from the master thief's domain. He could sense that the enchantment was fading away, returning the metal to a basic, nondescript soldier's blade once again. He focused on the jade while Dariak stumbled in and fought to catch his breath, but the jade would not cast the enchantment again, and he simply could not remember the arcane words he had spoken. It didn't matter. He still had a task to do.

He had fallen down a chute, so Gabrion felt around in the darkness until he found the base of it, and then he started to climb. Dariak followed and kept pace with the warrior. At the top, Gabrion pushed open a trapdoor that led into a large chamber with torches lining the walls.

After heaving himself into the room, he turned and pulled Dariak alongside, and then he refocused on the jade and turned toward his left, taking a step. But Dariak jumped and knocked him over.

They were in Grenthar's domain, and the traps were set. A large blade swept overhead, and once it hit the wall, it cut a rope that set off a series of three other blades across the room. Some of those oscillated back and forth, but one of them slashed another rope that started dropping sandbags from the ceiling, which broke floor tiles that fell to emptiness below. Gabrion eyed the contraptions quickly but realized that everything was happening too fast to ponder for long. He pounced over one set of fallen tiles and dodged under a swinging blade, and then inspiration struck as a sandbag plummeted onto a step in front of him. He slashed overhead to cut the bag, and then he thrust the jade into it, begging for it to freeze in the air.

The jade didn't respond, but Dariak seemed to understand the intent, or at least came to a similar conclusion. He threw a handful of webbing forward and cast his web-binding spell to keep the sand aloft, which prevented most of the blades from cutting any other guide ropes. It wasn't the best use of the spell, and he could feel the energies tearing quickly, so he nudged Gabrion in the back, and the two of them ran ahead into the next room.

But in Gabrion's dream, he hadn't gone through the whole gauntlet. He had detoured off to the side where Mira had claimed a piece of jewelry, a tiara in his last version of the dream. He looked around and saw a faint etching along one wall. He threw his body weight against it, crashing through a wood panel into a cold corridor beyond. Dariak was left in the trap room, where a flock of eaglons soared overhead and lava-like ooze poured in and bubbled up from the floor. He turned and jumped with all his might toward Gabrion, who reached out and clasped the mage's hands to pull him inside.

The corridor was littered with doors, so Gabrion again trusted the jade for guidance. Several rows down, on the left, the shard rattled outside an iron door. This time, they were on the proper side of it and the bolts were easy to slide. They pulled the door open and found a figure that was at the same time both familiar and hideously different.

Kitalla was covered in bandages, from around her head and arm, down across her chest, to along one of her legs. Where she wasn't bandaged, her clothing was badly ripped, revealing bloody welts and deep-purple-black bruises. Her eyes were closed and puffy, and her breathing was shallow and ragged. It was a marvel she was even alive.

Dariak used three healing spells on her in quick succession, just trying to get her conscious. He had practiced them during his imprisonment, but not deeply. Part of him hadn't really thought he would need them, but they were spells that had earned him food and water. Now, he plied his trade as powerfully as he could, drawing power from the earth and water jades to help seal wounds and improve blood flow. But there wasn't time to really fix her here.

Kitalla's eyes opened, and she reacted first by hissing angrily and trying to claw at Gabrion, but she wasn't strong enough to do any damage. He handed his sword to Dariak and then lifted Kitalla gently in his arms, knowing where to go next even without the jade. He continued down the hallway and burst into the chamber with the silver jade on the pillowed pedestal.

When she realized where she was, Kitalla awoke more fully, wriggling from Gabrion's arms until he had to bend and place her on the floor so he wouldn't drop her. She struggled to stand, grabbing the warrior blindly, her eyes focused solely on the jade. Staggering forward, Kitalla snarled at Gabrion when he tried to help. Instead, the warrior reclaimed his sword from the mage and looked around for the right-side exit that Mira had always used.

Turning to the door, Gabrion readied himself to run again, but he knew that Kitalla was in no condition to follow properly. Dariak was projecting other minor healing spells toward the thief, but they were barely effective at all.

Then, Kitalla's hand reached down and clasped the jade she had coveted for so long, recalling the pain and suffering she had endured to feel its embrace once more. She clutched it to her chest like a lost child, savoring its vibrations and wanting never to move again.

The door near Gabrion opened, and in rushed Grenthar with a contingent of fighters in his wake. The warrior swept his sword around, but Grenthar's agility was impressive, and the older man dodged easily out of the way, launching daggers from his hands in a fashion that reminded Gabrion vaguely of their flight from Kaison, when Kitalla had done the same thing. He brought his sword around to block the daggers, but he could not focus on the thief anymore, as the rest of the fighters stormed in, desperate to stop them.

Dariak turned to the side and aimed a fireball spell at the wall so that its blast radius wouldn't impact his companions. He roasted three of the fighters, one of whom took the blast in the face and was blinded. Five others turned toward the mage, swords and maces flailing about. He enacted the Shield of Delminor, as well as the pass-through shield spell of the water jade. He then used the natural dust and dirt in the room, summoning them to rush forth as unstoppable spears, which lanced through several of the oncoming foes.

His arms and hands gestured wildly as he drew back the used fragments of earth and sent them out again. It was difficult magic to reuse drained spell components in that fashion, but he had been practicing.

While the warrior and mage were busy, the thief faced off against her tormentor. Kitalla and Grenthar eyed each other viciously. "You'll never keep that," Grenthar taunted her.

"It's mine," she hissed, strengthened by both Dariak's continuing healing spells and this moment of achieving her goal. No stone doors would crush her this time. No well-thrown dart would stun her. No paralyzing mist in the air would stop her. She held the jade tightly in one hand and reached for a dagger with the other.

Grenthar sprang upon her fiercely, and she tumbled over, hitting the ground hard, still weak. Grenthar simply laughed and kicked her in the ribs, then made to bring his dagger down into her heart. But Gabrion broke away from his opponent and attacked the man, whose speed protected him more than his skill. He weaved and bobbed, and nothing Gabrion could do would allow him to strike the man down. Dariak ended his torrent of healing spells while maintaining the binding spells he had used on some of the fighters, and turned his attention to sending stronger versions of his fire darts toward the master thief. But Grenthar pounced and somersaulted and cartwheeled out of the way each and every time. He was too nimble to be hit.

During this, Kitalla pulled herself to her feet and withdrew her dagger again, then had to catch her breath as pain lanced through her. Grenthar had stepped in and slashed across her back to stop her. Gabrion blocked him from doing more damage and then turned to finish off one of the other fighters in the room, of which not many were mobile any longer.

The agile older man bounded from one place to another until Kitalla whispered, "Stop," and held her dagger out before her as if she were about to throw it. But instead of the dagger leaving her hand, the blade extended like a wild snake, growing and slithering through the air like molten metal. It lashed out and struck Grenthar down, killing him instantly. The dagger returned immediately to its original size and shape.

Dariak subdued the rest of the fighters with Gabrion's help, then pulled the last of his healing herbs from his robe and used them to aid Kitalla the best he could.

"No time," she rattled. "Must go."

Gabrion hoisted her over his shoulder with a look to Dariak, who understood that he was now taking point. They fled through Grenthar's door and raced through the safer areas of the complex. There weren't many fighters left in the compound, and the healers simply cowered in terror when they saw the fleeing trio. Dariak launched a few fireball spells on his way out, drawing energy from the torches and using them to hopefully raze the entire place to the ground. They approached the main foyer, and he remembered that two guards would likely be stationed outside the main entrance. He prepared his dagger-chain spell and launched it out to both sides as he flew out the doorway, striking both guards deeply and sending rending pains through his own body from the spell.

"She'll never make it at this pace," Gabrion assessed. "We have to hide."

Dariak agreed, and they sprinted through the streets of Pindington until Kitalla cried out in pain, begging them to stop. They didn't have many options, so they hurried to an inn and demanded a room. The innkeeper understood from Dariak's tone that it wasn't a request, and though he didn't want to comply, he valued his life too much to deny them.

Gabrion took the thief upstairs and set her to rest, still clutching the jade tightly in hand. He then returned to the main room and waited with Dariak, who was explaining to the innkeeper that no one was to know they were there, under any circumstance. The mage then wound up a spell, placing a vile curse upon the innkeeper that if they were discovered by any means, the innkeeper's heart would explode in his chest, and all other members of his bloodline would suffer a similar fate within days.

"I beg of you, no!" the man whined, crying desperately.

Gabrion tried to stop Dariak from such a horrid incantation, but Dariak finished it in quick form as the man cried pitiably, feeling his whole body throb under a painful and terrifying weight.

"I swear that I will do as you say. I beg of you, please release me."

Dariak eyed the man. "Food for us upstairs. And we will leave here as soon as we are able. Before I go, I will cast the countercurse that will ease up on your heart and return you to your health. Do not betray us, or the worst will befall you."

The man clutched his chest and nodded. He was already huffing from exertion. "I swear. You don't exist. Not here. Not ever. Go on, up to your rooms. Take whatever you like. Food, ale, yes, they will be there quickly. Thank you, master, but please, do rethink—"

Dariak cleared his throat threateningly, and the man shrieked and went to prepare their meals. Slowly, the mage walked away, ascending the stairs in dramatic fashion with a mortified Gabrion following behind. The warrior held in his rage until they reached the upper rooms.

"How dare you, you swine!" Gabrion hissed, grabbing Dariak's arm and shoving him.

The mage shook his head. "I see imprisonment hasn't changed you." He wrenched his arm away in annoyance.

"It doesn't give us the right to curse a whole family of decent people!" Gabrion struggled to keep his voice down.

Dariak couldn't take it any longer. He released a snorting chuckle, which enraged Gabrion even more. "Relax, will you? A little Shield of Delminor never killed anyone." He rolled his eyes. "A curse. Seriously. The things you Kallisorians believe…"

It took a moment for the truth of it to register with Gabrion, after which his face sank into his hands, shaking slowly. "You mages."

"Hey, Gabrion?"

"Yeah?"

"Thanks for breaking us out of there."

Gabrion released a deep sigh as they went into Kitalla's room. "None too soon, I'd say."

A pained expression fell over Dariak's face as he looked more carefully at Kitalla, still clutching the jade against her heart, even as she lay unconscious. "Maybe a little late too." He looked back at Gabrion. "We've a lot of work to do."

CHAPTER 25

Inn Wiego

THE FOLLOWING TWO-DAY respite at the inn was tense. Dariak spent most of his waking hours casting spells and sending Gabrion to obtain spell components. He was still in shock that he wasn't in his glass cage, but Kitalla was in such serious condition that he couldn't dwell on anything else.

Back in Kaison, when they had raided the mystic shop, Dariak had taken a handful of small booklets. He had intended to make Gabrion read them, to become more familiar with some of the aspects of magic so he would perhaps be a little more comfortable with its use. But the mad flight from Kaison, then Kitalla's grand performance in Warringer, and all the events after that had pushed the thought from his mind. Yet, while inventorying his supplies in the Prisoner's Tower, he'd rediscovered them, a bit mangled in places but still legible. He found one basic herbology booklet, *Wild Herbs and Their Mystique,* to be useful, reminding him of his early training in the healing arts. By requesting materials from the mage wardens, he had been able to build some fundamental skill. When the basic arts had no longer earned him food, he altered them, once using an anti-laceration spell to seal the binding of a book, which earned accolades again for the creative implementation.

Kitalla, however, would take much more work than he was prepared for, and it would take perhaps more time than he thought she had left in her. Each bandage covered major damage that had been partially healed by Grenthar's mages but needed much more work. He wondered if she had refused to work with the thief any longer, and so he had pulled back on the treatments, or, worse, if her damage was really just so bad that she couldn't be healed properly at all.

He refused to believe that he couldn't help her; he knew also that he wouldn't be able to do it hiding this way at an inn. Every couple of hours, he needed to reset the minor incantation on the innkeeper before it wore off and the man no longer felt compelled to hide them. This worked partly to Dariak's advantage, because the poor man would panic that the curse was getting worse and that he would soon be dead. This also led, unfortunately, to excessive pleading with the mage, thereby interrupting his work on Kitalla. But for now, it was all they could manage. Kitalla was barely ever conscious, and when she was, it took every effort to get food into her.

They clearly could not travel anywhere.

Gabrion came in with a new set of supplies for Dariak, as well as a tray of food. "Not many daggers left," he muttered. He had been using them to barter for supplies. "You look terrible, mage."

"She's still worse." Dariak shrugged. They'd had this exchange a few times already. They couldn't make use of the town healers because alarms had gone up through the whole city to be on alert for the prisoners who had escaped the tower. Apparently, the other hard laborers who had been trapped with Gabrion went on a rampage as they left the city, tearing down shops and breaking into homes, living up to their criminal pasts.

The innkeeper had shown Dariak and Gabrion a storage closet, which they had needed to use the previous morning when guards had stormed in looking for escapees. It was hard moving Kitalla, harder still keeping her from moaning in pain, but at least Dariak's ruse of the curse was working. For how much longer, he wasn't sure. Every patron at the inn set the two of them on edge, wondering if their time was up.

"Listen, Dariak." The warrior sighed. "I don't know if you'll be able to fix her like this."

"I'll figure it out." He tried to be flippant, but it fell flat.

"You've spent so many hours at this already. Take a break, Dariak. Go out; walk around. The innkeeper says there's entertainment at the Four Corners a few blocks over. Juggling and such. Refresh your mind."

Dariak eyed Gabrion suspiciously. "What is this about?"

Gabrion couldn't help himself; he started to grin. "That minstrel fellow you mentioned a while ago is in town."

It took a moment for Dariak to remember. He had put all thoughts of the bard out of his mind for so long. "Randler? He's here?"

"Four Corners," Gabrion repeated, picking up a pile of clothing he had brought in with the other supplies. "The innkeeper had these lying around. I say you disguise yourself as a normal person and go see your friend."

Dariak's cheeks lit red briefly. "I—I don't know what to say."

"Don't worry," Gabrion assured him, nodding toward Kitalla. "I've got her. She'll be safe."

Dariak clasped Gabrion's shoulder. "I don't doubt it." With a silly grin on his face he hadn't worn in a long time, the mage walked from the room to change out of his robe and into the common garb Gabrion had handed him. He hadn't thought to trim his hair at all, and he wasn't about to mess with that now, so he pulled it tightly against his skull and tied it at the nape of his neck, except for a tuft that he let hang over one eye. Though it was highly irritating, it kept his visage in shadow. He tucked his jade shards into a pouch he had obtained in Gerrish and slung the pouch around his neck, hidden under the loose tunic. After tucking a few daggers away, he scraped his fists along the wall, bloodying his knuckles, which he then partially healed with magic. He hoped it would look like he enjoyed a good bar fight. Lastly, he scraped a bit of clay and mud together with a few drops of water and painted himself a scar across his cheek, verifying with Gabrion that it looked passable before leaving.

Downstairs, he walked right past the innkeeper, who didn't make any note of recognition. Out the door and into the night air he went. He turned sharply upon leaving the inn, hoping no one would notice where he had come from. He wasn't sure exactly where he was going, only that it wasn't far. Patrols were out in force, tracing patterned routes but not entirely on alert. Some passersby were laughing, talking about going to see the performers, and Dariak nonchalantly veered his course to follow behind them.

The Four Corners was a large tavern that only served meads, ales, and wines, as well as some salty bread for noshing. A large, raised stage, complete with five steps leading up to it, stood proudly at the center of the room. Tables and chairs were scattered all around, and unlike other taverns he had seen, there was no main bar area on one side of the chamber. Instead, in each corner stood a smaller bar where barrels and tankards were piled high. Barmaids whisked quickly from the corner bars to the tables, with drinks on large serving trays. Numerous patrons had brought food in with them, and it seemed to be the norm. Dariak took a seat in the shadows near one of the corner bars so he could keep an eye on the majority of the audience. If guards were around, he wanted to be ready. He did remember, however, to keep his face looking a little vacant and sour.

Dariak anxiously awaited the arrival of the minstrel. All of his other woes were set aside for the time being. He just wanted to feel that special excitement again, though part of him was afraid things might be too different after all the time apart. He did muse, though, that it was uncommon for his heart to be so aflutter over such a brief encounter and one kiss, but he shrugged and tossed the thought away.

Flutes echoed through the air, playing a mournful tune. Dariak immediately focused his thoughts on the music, looking around for the source. The flute was accompanied by a soft drumbeat, a sad, lamenting horn, and a slowly plucked lute. From each sidewall, a musician stepped, with dramatic poise, toward the central stage. Patrons all settled down to listen to the moving sounds of the instruments, feeling pulls from deep within their hearts. For each person, the lament was different, yet it united the whole audience with only a few emotional bars of music.

Once the musicians reached the stage, their notes increased in octave with each step up toward the central platform, until the notes were so high some people started to wince in anticipation of higher notes. Then with elaborate flourishes, the music spiraled down to a jovial jaunt that replaced the sudden melancholy with a hearty thumping of feet. The four musicians stepped around one another onstage, kneeling, then rising and spinning again, performing a merry wedding dance while strumming and tooting away.

Dariak grinned up at the stage as Randler spun around and bowed to the flutist, who tipped her head and twisted back to the drummer, and so on. His heart raced with each graceful step the bard took, and he knew, without a doubt, that it had nothing to do with the resonating pieces of jade hanging around his neck. However, their rumblings informed him that Randler still had his shard. In the face of everything that had happened to him recently, though, that knowledge felt less important.

After the dance, the musicians settled onto stools, each facing one of the four corners. Regrettably, Randler's back was to Dariak, but the mage couldn't possibly shuffle around to the other side of the room without being noticed.

The instruments crafted another whimsical song, this time accompanied by the bard's soothing voice. Though he wanted to lose himself in the sheer quality of the man's tone, Dariak's training also pulled the words into memory, and he felt he learned more from the tale than those simply tapping along to the merry beat. With each repetition, one more musician sang along during the refrain, until all four were harmonizing the words and their instruments. By the time they reached the last refrain, the whole tavern knew it and sang along:

I sing to you a story of a little one named Roe.
She had a merry face, but her feet were just too slow.
She'd wave her arms about, and—alas!—there's falling snow.
But then she didn't seem to know which way to go!

And then you come up to a hill and then—whoop!—down.
You roll right in the mud, and that's where you are found.
You get up on your feet, and then you look around.
You never knew that this was the best way into town!

I tell you now a tale of a boy whose name was Kihel.
He stomped with his feet up a hill for quite a while.
He thought to overcome it, and then he could just smile.
But the pebbles underfoot just dropped him in a pile.

And then you come up to a hill and then—whoop!—down.
You roll right in the mud, and that's where you are found.
You get up on your feet, and then you look around.
You never knew that this was the best way into town!

Our two little tumblers were jumbled in a heap.
They really hadn't realized a hill could be so steep.
They laughed at each other, for the mud was really deep.
And then from that moment, a friendship, they would keep.

So then you come up to a hill and then—whoop!—down.
You roll right in the mud, and that's where you are found.
You get up on your feet, and then you look around.
You never knew that this was the best way into town!

A moment to reflect on them, their lives, they went ahead.
They each had their own dreams but went and shared instead:
To build up a world around, where everyone was fed.
And when they had their firstborn, this is what they said:

Oh! Then you come up to a hill and then—whoop!—down.
You roll right in the mud, and that's where you are found.
You get up on your feet, and then you look around.
You never knew that this was the best way into town!

The moral of this tale, in case you do not see,
Is not to be angry if you fall down to your knee.
Lift your head up high; it's an opportunity.
So don't forget your past; now, come and sing with me!

Oh! Then you come up to a hill and then—whoop!—down.
You roll right in the mud, and that's where you are found.
You get up on your feet, and then you look around.
You never knew that this was the best way into town!

The last refrain was sung three times, with the whole crowd joining in merrily, Dariak included. Whistles, shouts, stomps, and applause filled the tavern once it was all over. After several bows and promises to return after a break, the musicians left the stage to hearty pats on their backs while a set of dancers followed up the act with some spectacular stunts.

Dariak's gaze followed Randler on his way out of the tavern. He would have walked out too, but none of the other patrons seemed to be leaving. He ground his teeth and tried to look interested in the way three of the dancers climbed upon one another and then leaped off, spinning, into the arms of the others. He admitted it would have been impressive if he wasn't so distracted.

"You really shouldn't look so disappointed; they're really good," whispered a voice in Dariak's ear, causing him to melt instantly in his seat. Randler pulled over a stool and leaned on the table, feigning interest in the dance troupe. "Been a while, eh?"

Dariak sighed, keeping his gaze forward as long as he could, which really wasn't easy. "Too long."

Randler reached under the table and gently touched Dariak's knee for a moment. "I was afraid I wasn't going to see you again. But once I got to town, I saw you everywhere. Well," he admitted, "posters of you, anyway." He paused for a moment to applaud a thrilling aerial twist the dancers had completed. Randler leaned in and said softly, "You were supposed to rendezvous with me after Warringer."

Dariak looked at the bard's unreadable face for just a moment. "Complications," he said, turning back to the performance. "Guards were after us. I couldn't lead them to you."

"I'm grateful. But it would have been nice to see you sooner than this." His voice carried a smile. He waited for Dariak to say something, but the mage didn't know what to say. "How are your friends? The ones from the poster?"

"One's fine. One isn't." Dariak lowered his head, feeling a little guilty about wanting to abandon everything to cut loose and steal Randler away for the night.

"She'll be fine," Randler assured him. "But you need a better location."

Dariak turned a confused glance at the bard. "How did you know?"

"Who do you think told your friend to send you along tonight?" Randler winked, his brown eyes shining. "He wasn't too hard to follow either."

"Ah," Dariak said, then stiffened. "But then, you might not be the only one who followed him."

"True," the bard agreed. "I can take you all someplace no one will find you, if you'll let me."

After all the subterfuge and deceit and strangeness he had encountered along his travels in Kallisor, not even glorious Randler could win an immediate agreement. He stared at the minstrel for a few moments, biting his lip.

Randler patted Dariak on the back. "I know that look. I understand. So go back and speak with your comrades. I have another set to perform here. Once I can, I will head to your inn for a drink. I'll wait there for your answer. But if it's affirmative, then we'll leave quickly. Best not leave things to chance, right?" He rose, squeezing the mage's shoulder before drifting away from sight.

Dariak waited for a few moments before making his way out of the Four Corners. He meandered back toward the inn, checking over his surroundings in case he was being followed, but everything seemed fine. Even the guards patrolling the city were aloof to his presence.

When he entered the inn, he was greeted by an annoyed innkeeper, who pouted and stood with folded arms. Dariak rolled his eyes and walked over. "Hmm?"

The innkeeper kept his voice low so as not to disturb other customers in the tavern area. "Your 'curse' is gone. I want you out. I've already sent for the guards."

Dariak kept his composure. He had been gone longer than he'd thought if the spell had already worn off. "How would you know anything about when a curse runs out?"

For a moment, fear lit the man's eyes, but then he decided the mage was lying. "No, you're just a fugitive and a nasty sneak. And with you gone, the curse went away on its own. So get out now, and there won't be any trouble."

"We need time to gather our things," Dariak decided. "How long until the guards arrive?"

"I—uh, they—" he stammered.

Dariak laughed. "You didn't summon them in case you were wrong. No matter. We'll be out of here tonight." He then went upstairs to deliver the news to Gabrion, who was skeptical about the bard, but they really didn't have another option with Kitalla so broken. The next few hours were spent ensuring their things were ready to go. Dariak opted to change back into his mage robe, feeling that access to his spell components would be better than running through town incognito. Meanwhile, Gabrion spent time stretching and resting, knowing he would be carrying the thief to their new destination.

Periodically, Dariak checked downstairs for both guards and Randler. With each appearance, the innkeeper tensed and stared pointedly toward the door, but Dariak only nodded, scanned the room, and then returned upstairs. Eventually, he found Randler off in the corner, laughing with a small group of admirers. He approached cautiously, not wanting to interfere, but Randler waved him over.

"Don't worry, friend," he greeted Dariak amiably. "I don't bite. You're welcome to relish in my company now that my show is done. Join us for a drink!"

Two of the women giggled and raised their own glasses, sipping deeply. "Isn't he wonderful?" one of them asked Dariak.

"Oh, how I wish he could sing for me every day!" crooned another.

It was clear to the mage that Randler had the situation well in hand, but he didn't know how to convey his message with the groupies hanging around. Randler solved that riddle on his own. "So, newcomer," he started with a tilt of his head, "I assume you've heard my work, if you've come to pay your respects to me."

Dariak nodded, ignoring the women fawning all over him, crying out, "Oh, isn't his voice like a summer rain?"

Randler grinned and seemed to be partly enjoying Dariak's discomfort. "So who among you would want to join me on a wild adventure?" He nodded at the ladies, but his eyes bore sharply into Dariak's.

"Oh, Randler, you'd make any journey just lovely!" One woman clapped her hands.

Another added, "You'd even make monsters dance away so happily!"

The adulations made Dariak's face burn red from trying not to laugh. He decided then to join in the fun. "Ladies!" he interrupted them dramatically. "The very sun rises up and bears its light simply because he sings with such grace!" They all nodded with intense agreement. Dariak then looked at the bard. "And if your invitation was true, great minstrel, why, I would abandon everything and follow you this very night." He put such a lurid tone in his voice he earned sighs from the women. He had obviously impressed them with such a gushing show of appreciation.

Randler bowed his head. "Be careful, friend, because I could very well take you up on that."

Dariak understood that Randler was verifying the mage's acceptance of his help. "It wouldn't be a 'wild adventure' if I didn't just jump in, would it? Oh, if only you could let me live out the dreams of all of us at this table, my very soul would burst with joy!"

One woman looked at Randler with pleading eyes. "Oh, I do hope you take him with you! Not that I want you to leave, but think of all the new songs you would create with your adventures!"

Randler smiled, and he lifted each woman's hand and kissed it tenderly. "My angels, forgive me, for I would like to speak to my new companion here. But rest assured! I will sing of you all and how you marked the beginning of glorious days and wondrous tales ahead."

With a round of fluttering sighs, the women wished them luck, demanding that Dariak take proper care of the bard so he may return soon. He was gracious enough to promise them all deeply.

Once they were alone, Randler shook his head. "So your very soul would burst with joy, eh?"

Dariak smiled slightly, gazing into Randler's cinnamon-hued eyes. "If I didn't have a dying companion or the city guard waiting to kill me, then I would already have burst once I learned you were here."

"Then let's get you all to safety," Randler said, winking, "so I can see you live up to that."

The innkeeper wasn't sad to see them go within the hour. Gabrion left a few coppers and a dagger to help cover the costs of their stay, and that calmed the grumpy man enough that he opted not to call the guard when they left. Still, there were patrols in the city along every street. The guards walked in pairs, carrying torches and stopping everyone they passed.

Randler didn't seem at all fazed by the security. He walked with a light step, nonchalantly turning down alleyways or bending to fidget with his shoe. Dariak's eyes roamed around sharply, however, keeping spells in mind in case he needed them. He regretted that he couldn't send healing spells to Kitalla as she bounced around in Gabrion's arms, but he needed to remain focused on Randler.

The bard navigated the streets like a street urchin. He turned down corridors that didn't seem possible and wound his way through the roads and avoided every set of guards like a roaming shadow.

The thought of a shadow made Dariak take another glance around, and looking up, he saw the Prisoner's Tower looming with each street they passed. It was unnerving to be winding near the tower. He held his misgivings in check until their path continued to draw closer.

"Randler," he whispered as they paused in one dark walkway, waiting for Gabrion. "Where are we going?"

The bard pressed his fingers to his lips and shook his head. "You trust me, or you don't."

"I—I do, but it looks like we're headed there." He motioned to the tower with his chin.

"You'll see," was all the bard would say. He crouched low, waiting for a patrol to pass by, and then he stalked out and crossed the street, melting in the shadows beyond.

Dariak didn't like it. As he followed, he tugged a few spell components from his pockets, ready for a mad dash. His first act would have to be protecting Gabrion and Kitalla; then he would go on the offensive and fight off any oncoming guards. He wanted so much to trust the minstrel, but every step brought them back toward the tower. Gabrion also realized their path, but there was nothing he could do except abandon Dariak and take Kitalla elsewhere, and that wasn't much of an option.

The mage's worst fears were realized when they stepped from an overhang and Randler strode purposefully up to a thick stone wall. The Prisoner's Tower rose high into the sky, while the surrounding area was sparsely populated. They were out in the open; all it would take was a passerby seeing them and shouting for help. Not only that, but their goal was to flee the tower, not return to it. Dariak's heart fell, and he wanted to run away from this fiasco.

Randler pressed his hand against the wall and felt around for a few moments, then pushed and dragged his arms to the right. A dark crevice opened in the stone, and he waved the others to go inside.

Dariak froze on the spot. He wasn't going back into the tower. Not voluntarily. His head shook slowly at first, then angrily, his arms coming up to launch a spell. He didn't know what kind of spell it would be yet; he was so conflicted. Gabrion stepped forward and struggled not to yell in rage at the situation.

Randler sighed and spoke just above a whisper so they could hear him. "Either you trust me, or you don't." He gestured to the opening one more time, then looked around. "Either way, please hurry and decide."

The jade pieces were vibrating fiercely in Dariak's pockets. He knew Randler still had his piece. At the very least, by stepping forward, he could try to claim that shard. But at the worst, his pieces would be confiscated and his next sentence in the tower would likely end in death, after having escaped. He saw the sad expression on Randler's face as the minstrel's intentions were doubted so deeply.

Dariak had spent much of his quest mocking Gabrion's sense of justice and accusing his trust of others of being a real weakness. But when it mattered most, the warrior came through and had been responsible for freeing himself and Kitalla. Dariak wanted the world around him to be more trustworthy. He hated the deceit he found everywhere. He hated the warring everywhere he turned. And though his suspicions were running high, competing with his terror at reentering the Prisoner's Tower, he chose at that moment to put faith ahead of rationality.

He stepped forward and hurried through the opening, and Gabrion followed closely behind, grunting in annoyance but unwilling to lose Dariak. Randler stepped in last, pulling the portal closed and breathing a sigh of relief.

"Thank you, Dariak, for trusting me," he said, his voice heavy. "Come on, we still have a ways to go." A slight knocking sound filled the area, and sparks flew as Randler lit a torch. "This way, and stay close."

It was an exhausting hour of travel through stone passageways, up and down stairs, and into narrow doorways. By the time they reached their destination, Gabrion and Dariak were at the ends of their stamina, for they had both been busy during the day, trying to help Kitalla. Randler led them into a well-furnished room that had a large, comfortable bed on one wall and a small, makeshift pantry and kitchen opposite. Gabrion set Kitalla down gently, where she moaned and twisted about, then fell silently back to sleep.

Randler went to each of the three doorways leading out of the room, pulling heavy stone barriers into place and securing them with solid iron bars. He turned to the stooping mage and warrior. "We're here, and you're exhausted. No one will find us. Settle in and rest."

Gabrion eyed the bard for a moment and then dropped himself to the ground. "I swear to you, bard, if anything happens to me here, after all I did to get us out of this place, my ghost will hunt you down and make you wish you were never created."

Randler withheld laughter at the absurd comment. "Trust me. But if you don't, then bind me if you must, not that I'd prefer that."

"No," Dariak croaked. "We trust you." He stared at Gabrion until the warrior caved in. With a final shake of his head, Gabrion stretched out on the floor and soon fell asleep.

Randler stepped over to Dariak. "I guess I underestimated how much you've been through these past months. I'm sorry."

The mage stepped forward and leaned against Randler, reaching his arms around him for support. "I'm sorry it's not as magical as we both wanted."

Randler pulled back and traced his finger along Dariak's cheek. "Well, every spell needs practice, right? And the proper words and materials. We'll get there." He stroked Dariak's hair back and hugged him again. "Now, sleep."

Dariak breathed deeply and reached for Randler's hand. He pulled the bard to the ground and then stretched out, leaning against him, back-to-back. It didn't take long for either of them to fall asleep, warm and safe.

CHAPTER 26

Healing Kitalla

KITALLA'S CRIES WOKE them all. Her body was wracked with pain, and she writhed around on the bed, contorting into awkward positions, ever clutching her jade close. Gabrion responded by leaping to her side, wiping sweat from her brow with a rag, at a loss of what else to do for her. Dariak, meanwhile, fumbled through his pockets and pulled out various herbs and minerals, hoping he could manage to perform some miracle.

Randler stayed on the floor, turning to watch the three of them, as if he were recording this moment into memory while planning a song around it. He watched as Dariak set out a few small pieces of rose quartz, then slid an aloe leaf between her lips. His arms moved and swayed around in a rhythmic pattern, and all the while Dariak muttered quick healing spells.

After several minutes, Dariak's arms floated back down to rest. He walked away, sighing. "I'm not a strong enough healer."

"We have to help her," Gabrion said needlessly, looking back toward the thief.

"Magic," Randler said softly, "is based on certain principles, no? The cadence of the words, the motion of the arms and hands, the pulling of the energies from all around."

Dariak waited for more, but there wasn't any. "Yes," he answered. "That's common enough knowledge—even Gabrion knows it."

"But isn't it possible for mages to work in tandem, to pool their powers together and give greater effect to minor spells?"

Gabrion turned to the cinnamon-haired bard. "You're not a mage too, are you?"

Randler smiled and shook his head softly. "No, no. But as a minstrel, I am rather intuitive when it comes to resonance and dissonance. After all, when sounds don't work well together, they offend the listener. Well, doesn't magic contain a component of that? Wouldn't it be possible to increase the resonance of your spell by drawing from us?"

Dariak considered it for a few moments before shaking his head in denial. "You would need to be able to draw in the energies. Otherwise, all anyone would ever have to do is learn how to dance, in order to..." His voice drifted off as he looked back at Kitalla, who was able to do just that. "Well, it is true that non-mages can learn to harness the power, but..."

They waited in silence for a little while, listening to Kitalla whimpering in her sleep. Gabrion looked back at the bard and the mage and then decided. "I may not know how to summon any magic, but this piece of jade," he said, bringing out his beige-hued shard, "spoke to me when I needed it most and let me use its magic. Kitalla has a piece, and you have two, Dariak. Give one to him, and then we'll all have one. Maybe then, if we say what you do and move the way you do, the jades will help us along?"

Randler grinned. "That was along my thinking, friend." He then removed a dark crystal from his pocket. "Though I won't need a piece of yours, as I'm well attuned to this one." He held it out for them to inspect. It was unlike the other shards they had collected, in that the color of Randler's crystal was spread throughout most of the shard, rather than being faint and concentrated in the center. "The power of shadow," he declared. "It's what has kept me safe all this time."

Dariak immediately started pacing, hand rubbing his chin. "Earth, water, glass, shadow. And hers is obviously based in metal, if that attack with her dagger is any indication." He turned back to the bard. "You say you're attuned to it? How much control do you have over its abilities?"

"As I said, I am skilled in resonance and dissonance. With concentration, I can coax resonance with the jade and bring out its shadowy center, as I did when we ran here from the inn, lest we be seen. On the contrary, I can bring dissonance with the jade and dispel the darkness too. You might remember me lighting the torch when we entered here."

"That wasn't flint?" Gabrion asked.

"Well, it was." The bard bowed his head. "But I only made a few sparks. Mostly, I scraped the wall in order to hide the words I spoke to send back the shadow from the torch. It allowed the sparks to ignite the whole thing more easily. And this chamber here isn't properly lit by that one torch alone, is it? No, the jade is holding in its shadow so that we may see."

Dariak continued pacing during their exchange, hearing their words but also pulling his own thoughts together. "Gabrion, do you think you can reach into the jade again and pull help from within?"

He looked down at his shard, closing his eyes and breathing deeply. "No," he said at last. "It's stone-cold silent."

The mage had suspected as much. Gabrion had avoided magic all his life, and even though he had accepted some of its boons recently, they weren't enough to fully awaken his mind to the shard. The jade itself must have felt the need to loan Gabrion its magic when they were escaping the Prisoner's Tower, an act that had brought it within reach of four of its brethren, now that Randler's piece was among them. Still, though, he felt a sense of hope with the idea of trying to unite them to heal the thief.

"The body is mostly earth and water," Dariak said in scholarly fashion. "Our skin and bones, the earth. Our blood, the water. Through our noses we take in air. Our souls are empowered by fire, so some texts say. By linking these, healers pull the energies into the wounded, to remind the bodies of how they once were and encourage them to rebuild themselves. At times, a skilled healer can also seal wounds faster than they would heal on their own. Considering the extensive damage done to Kitalla, I fear we need to push for a rapid healing to at least give her a chance to succeed."

Gabrion shook his head. "Earth and water jades we have. Not the others."

Dariak managed a grin. "True, but magic doesn't only work one way. So your jade, which empowers sand and glass, can create a thin, transparent material, much like air itself. I will draw on it in such fashion, letting it represent air, if not being air. Randler, you will need to draw the shadow from within her, pulling out the pain and poisons that linger inside her. And if I can manage it, I will draw from her shard to strengthen her bones so they won't need splints. That's about all I can think of."

Gabrion handed his jade over to Dariak. "It sounds like you will need this."

The mage knew it was difficult for him to part with the jade after being hand selected by the elder of Gerrish to carry it. He assured the warrior he would soon have it back. Randler, however, did not likewise relinquish his shard, instead asking what else they needed to do. Dariak began by teaching them the words of incantation for the healing spells he would employ, as well as the hand and finger motions that went with them. Randler, a skilled wordsmith, absorbed the information quickly, but Gabrion took far longer. They stopped to eat when the warrior's frustration overpowered him and blocked his thoughts, but soon they arranged themselves and were ready.

They turned Kitalla's body so she was draped horizontally across the bed. This allowed Dariak to stand at her head and the others to stand at her feet. Because she kept the jade clutched to her chest in her right hand, Dariak had to fold her left hand similarly in order to maintain symmetry. He could have pulled the jade away and stretched her out, which would help circulation, but any tugging on the jade made her moan with a sense of loss, so he opted to work around it.

After propping Kitalla's head up on a pillow, Dariak set the glass jade on her chest to signify her breathing. The vibrations of the jade kept making it fall off, but eventually he was able to keep it in place. He set the water jade upon her belly, watching it rise and fall like a soft ocean tide. The earth jade he set on her brow, keeping it closest to himself, for he knew its powers more than the others. Kitalla's feet were separated slightly, and Randler kept his shard on the bed, midway between her ankles, keeping the line of jades running straight from head to toe. He seemed reluctant to set the jade down, but he needed his hands for the spell, and Gabrion was too focused on the incantations to even look ready to steal it.

Dariak accented the jades with other small crystals he had been gathering since reading about them in one of his handbooks. He set a small green kunzite on each of the three major wounds: one on her right arm, one on her chest, and one on her thigh. He set a dark-green tourmaline next to the jade she clutched to her heart, seeking emotional balance for her pain. From there he placed pink rose quartz among a number of lesser wounds. He then balanced the pink hues with light-purple amethyst and the green hues with yellow citrine along opposite sides of her body to complete the symmetry.

He could feel the pull of the energies already. They were mild in essence, but he felt the symmetry he had built was allowing them to work together. He looked at Randler as the bard smiled slightly, apparently sensing the resonances himself. Gabrion was glancing from one gem to the next, wondering if he was supposed to see something happen.

As practiced, Dariak raised his hands up in front of his chest and cast a sweeping motion down Kitalla's body. He then curled his fingers around and drew his hands toward his left side, following Kitalla's chest up to her left shoulder. Another sweep extended down to her left leg, where Gabrion was posted. Dariak then drew the energy up the leg and down the other, then back up to her right arm. He spiraled his arms around his own head, representing hers, and then pushed one final sweep from his right side and back down toward her heart.

In the process, he felt the energy follow his motions, but there were some flaws. He knew there would be, for she was covered in crushed veins, broken bones, sprains, and so forth. But more than that, he felt the external energy he was drawing in didn't have the right flow to it. So, he read the path again and adjusted several of the minerals he had set out around her before reading the energies again. It took a few tries to get a solid measure, especially when Kitalla's movements shifted some of the pieces, but eventually the mage was satisfied.

He stood again at her head and pulled his hands in close, palms together, signaling the other two that the process was about to begin. He had several spells he was weaving together now, and although he would be following the same basic path his hands had just traced, his fingers and hands would be bending and twisting in more complicated forms. While he made these motions, the others would mimic him, hoping to coax the energies into an impassioned form of healing.

"Hemoderishad farthinaritug klea noreth vatra-forfeth." The water jade responded by casting a pallid blue glow, facilitating the spell for improved circulation. Because the jade was at her navel, it acted as the central point of the spell. As Dariak worked the spell, the energies leaned in for support, anchoring the healing in a way he hadn't expected.

The next spell he spoke only upon exhalations, for it called upon the power of the sand shard to promote proper breathing. He hadn't spent much time with Gabrion's jade, but he could feel its power well enough to know it would hear him. *"Uliashios frethulie langshalas eriotho."* As he cast the enchantment, he kept his arms moving around her body in wide, healing sweeps, but now he bent and extended his knees in representation of breath.

Thankfully, Gabrion and Randler followed suit, and he trusted the warrior in particular to keep a constant pattern going, for his own thoughts were busy, and Randler would soon be tapping into his jade. With the two men at the other end of the bed slowly bobbing up and down, Dariak simply needed to match them and focus on the rest.

At this point, Kitalla started responding with painful moans. Dariak suspected that one of her lungs had been damaged, or at least the broken ribs were causing her pain, but he wasn't skilled enough to target a lung specifically. With her increased breathing, the pain in her chest amplified, and part of him wished he could cancel that part of the spell for her. However, there was worse to come. Dariak's only hope was that he wasn't going to injure her more.

Setting aside such thoughts, Dariak concentrated on the next spell. It was time to promote some actual healing, now that the energies, blood, and air were flowing. He glanced at the others, making sure they were continuing their bobbing stances and circling arm movements. Then he dove into the next portion of the spell.

"Sielios wai deownud carthra porthilos frajuliar mentiss." The jade poised on Kitalla's forehead cast an eerie brown glow that made her face seem more tan than usual. Under the slight illumination, Dariak could already see the beginnings of wrinkles at her eyes, signifying an increase in the aches.

He looked at the other two and nodded sharply. Now that the initial mending spell had been enacted, Randler and Gabrion needed to repeat it in unison with Dariak. Meanwhile, Dariak needed to sense other issues that required tending and then make adjustments along the way, matching up with the other two when he could, in order to keep the chant going. This would have been hard enough with three fully trained healers who could each pull in energies on their own, without having to rely on one single mage to perform the actual casting.

"Sielios wai deownud carthra porthilos frajuliar mentiss," they all said in unison, as Kitalla's moaning grew louder. She started twisting and writhing, but her body couldn't really move. The blood-flow spell was effectively keeping her still, because it was being powered by the energies surrounding her, spiraling around the center water jade. *"Sielios wai deownud carthra porthilos frajuliar mentiss."*

On his third pass around, Dariak felt a sharp, stabbing pain in his chest. He knew it was empathic because it shuddered and vanished, and when his sweeping arms reached that spot again, the pain started up once more. *"Fasethulineir habraniethan felniar."* At once, the pain lessened, and he knew one of her ribs had started to mend. Other sharp contrasts of pain arose, and he healed them the best he could.

They were all growing very tired, but there was much more to be done. He realized suddenly that they wouldn't be able to heal her in one such session. They would need to repeat this process numerous times to really bring her back to health. But he was determined to pour as much power into this session as he could, hoping his estimates were false and that she would recover soon.

A wound in her thigh drew Dariak's attention, and he realized that there was a form of infection brewing there. When his hands swept over the spot, he spoke the key word they had agreed upon beforehand, so Randler would know to draw the shadows from that location in particular. *"Drathnier,"* he whispered. The bard had already been pulling darkness from Kitalla's body, subduing some of her pain already, and so he was quickly able to shift toward the location and pull more forcefully. Kitalla's whole body lurched within its magical constraints, and she released an agonized wail that cut through their concentration and made it hard to keep going.

Dariak was ready for it, though, and it mostly mattered that he kept the energy flowing. So when Gabrion jerked upright and missed part of the incantation, the entire spell didn't collapse. It only took a moment for him to return to the cadence, keeping his hands swirling around and his knees bending and flexing.

Once several key injuries had called out for help, Dariak was able to sense other underlying problems. Kitalla's right arm was in shambles, from what he could tell. It was so wholly damaged that he believed the healers tending her had given up on it as a lost cause. He wanted beyond anything to prove them wrong, partly for her sake and partly for his. Mending the shattered remnants of bone would be, for him, like uniting the two kingdoms under a veil of peace—something that had never been done before but that he was just as determined to accomplish.

"Fortios mendiss jalledir brakent frearis." It was a call to the earth jade to bring the bone fragments together, rising up and mending back to their original form. And from the first moment that the spell took effect, a horrid cry erupted from the thief.

At once, the jade clutched to her chest started to glow. Dariak felt a strange heat building up from his side, and once it became unbearable, he had to reach his hand down and pull out a dagger from his hip. It was vibrating angrily, and he sensed that it wanted to strike at him, severing his spell and his life. He quickly tossed the weapon away, terrified at the rage he felt within it. He looked back at the silver jade, its light glowing brighter now, and then he understood. It was protecting her by trying to stop the one now causing her pain.

Dariak brought his arms up and around again, sinking back into the healing circle before its power was lost. As he approached her heart, he called to the metal jade, asking its forgiveness and inviting it to join to the energies surrounding Kitalla. It took numerous tries before the light diminished at all and the jade released a single wisp of energy to travel along with the rest, seeking the cause of Kitalla's pain. After a few circuits, the jade released more energy and focused it on Kitalla's right arm, fortifying the healing spell already in place. The two powers struggled at first to find harmony, but with a few passes through, Dariak was able to restore a sense of calm.

"Sielios wai deownud carthra porthilos frajuliar mentiss," Gabrion murmured, then coughed. His throat was terribly dry from the constant chanting, and his arms and legs were wearying from their continued motions. Likewise, Randler was sweating as he tried pulling more shadow from Kitalla's right arm, reducing the pain within. Looking around and assessing his own strength, Dariak knew they had to stop for now. He swept his hands around a couple more times and then brought them together before his own chest, stepping slightly backward and pulling himself out of the energy stream. The other two did the same. Dariak smiled to himself, because the swirling energies continued to spiral around, centered on the water jade and now supported by Kitalla's shard.

"Well done," he said softly, motioning them to step away. "That should continue on its own for a little while."

Gabrion hunched down with Randler off to the side of the room. "How much did we do?" the warrior asked.

"More than I could have hoped without your help," Dariak said proudly. "Still, though, she needs a lot of work."

Randler shook out his hands and rubbed his arms. "This place isn't known to many others. So stay as long as you need."

Gabrion looked at the bard questioningly. "It sounds like you're not staying."

"I'll return," he said. "But I have performances to run, and we will need supplies. And unlike you, I can walk around the city freely."

"Thank you for your help," the warrior said. "Though I wonder at your motivations for helping us."

Dariak frowned, but Randler laughed. "Of course you do. And that's all well and good. For now, just remember that you're in a safe place, away from the guards, and we've all worked together well to heal your friend. We all have our shadows," he said, holding up his jade, which he hadn't left on the bed with Kitalla. "But then we all have our light as well." He eyed the warrior carefully. "I see you're not convinced. Then let me tell you of this place, so at least one mystery is solved."

With that, Randler began to sing:

With deep regret, a man I met fell out of a tower.
He was a thief, and to my grief, he so needed a shower.
I turned my head, and then he said, "I've got for you a secret.
This prison here is rather queer, I think I'm gonna keep it."

Grendal, his name; stealing, his game; he said he was the best.
But spent his time for every crime inside a stony chest.
Was often caught, you would have thought that one day he would learn
To take a stash and not be rash, be happy with his earn.

Yet on the street, again we'd meet, so happy he would be,
Just walking on like he'd belonged, onstage up there with me.
He was a ghost, so said the most, a thief they could not keep.
So on his lap, he liked to clap, which added to the creep.

And then one day, he came to say, his time was running short.
I asked him why, he did deny but said he's off to port.
As he left, I felt bereft; he clapped me on the shoulder.
"Before I go, you ought to know, go press upon that boulder."

And so I did, and here I hid, one day when I was lost.
I walked about, and I came out, where prisoners are tossed.
This tower built, with hands so skilled, secret passageways unfound.
To hide from view, all you need to do is simply look around.

Randler finished, bowing his head and then chortling at the confused expressions on their faces. "Well, that's the lore of why it's the Prisoner's Tower, not the *Prisoners'* Tower," he said with a slight emphasis. "It was Grendal's tower, after all. He'd actually built a series of overlapping and crisscrossing paths that extended to various parts of the prison. So, when he would get captured with his loot, the guards would usually confiscate the goods and put them into a holding area while he was sent to a cell. He could slide the stones around and escape the cell, then steal back the merchandise from a similar hole in another room, and then wend his way out of the tower, safe and unharmed. Turned out he would hide here too under other circumstances."

"Remarkable," Gabrion muttered. "But wouldn't the guards notice he was missing?"

"Of course! He had to sneak back in at mealtimes." Randler chuckled. "He always seemed like the model prisoner, never making any noise. They would release him and then take bets on when he'd be back. One night, he got so drunk that he went in through his hiding place and curled up in his cell, forgetting that he wasn't under arrest at that time! That's actually what prompted his departure." He shook his head, amused. "If you do go exploring while I'm gone, let me give you some advice. Don't lean on anything unless you want it to open, in case you happen across a hidden doorway. And if you do pass through an opening, I suggest you put something in the way to keep it from closing. You won't likely find how to open it from the inside, and some of them can't be opened that way anyway."

Dariak took a deep breath. "Too bad we didn't know all this before."

Randler frowned. "Yes, I'm sorry."

Gabrion looked at the bard, his brows furrowed. "If you knew all that about this place, and you knew we were in here, why didn't you—"

"Bust you out?" Randler interjected. "Simple enough, and you can check if you'd like. The passages don't go up to where mages are kept. That way, if a mage blasts through something, it won't collapse the whole tower. I couldn't have gotten to Dariak. And forgive me, but I had never met you; would you have even accepted my help? Would I have even recognized you from a rough coal sketch posted in the city square?"

"There was nothing he could do, Gabrion," Dariak interposed.

With a grunt, Gabrion let it go.

"Very well then," Randler said. "I will return in a few hours with some supplies." He looked over at Kitalla. "Good luck with her."

He then walked over to the first entranceway and dramatically pulled aside a metal handle, lifting the iron cage before pushing the stone wall aside, showing them how to escape. He then bowed his head and backed out of the room, sliding the stone back in place.

CHAPTER 27

Randler's Tale

KITALLA SHOWED A large improvement after the first major healing session, but it wasn't nearly enough for the injuries she had sustained. Violent bruises splashed across her body in so many places that it was difficult to find an unmarked spot. Gabrion, Randler, and Dariak spent a good portion of each day recasting the healing regiment that Dariak had devised, propelling her body to faster healing. Randler left after each session to look in on his lodging and to keep up appearances at his nightly shows. He also occasionally didn't return for a day, claiming that he simply couldn't escape into the wall opening without being seen. Dariak accepted it well enough, but Gabrion had his reservations.

The warrior struggled with the new imprisonment. He wasn't able to directly affect Kitalla's healing, only perhaps amplify some of Dariak's work. He felt utterly useless, and so he took to investigating the secret passages.

The first thing Gabrion noticed was the passages were mostly very narrow, and he needed to traverse them sideways in many cases. It meant it would be impossible to carry Kitalla through them in the event of an emergency. But he kept his hopes high that he and Dariak would be able to fend off any danger. He also felt chill breezes seeping through the stony walls, his only reminder of the weather outside.

On one of his many excursions, Gabrion found a pathway that spiraled up and behind the archers' row that overlooked the prisoners' pit in the center of the tower, where he had spent a rough couple of months too recently to think about. He could easily see that a number of bulky men had been recaptured, but something else caught his attention. Cavall, who had shown Gabrion around when he was first tossed in, was now doing more than simply talking to the other inmates companionably. He had a whip of his own, and it looked like his duties had changed. From a few additional glances in, Gabrion decided that Cavall had not rebelled that day, clinging to his leadership position in the cell. And when the other prisoners had returned, the guards saw that Cavall wanted nothing more than to scold them for their desertion, and they rewarded him with the whip.

Gabrion tossed aside the thought that Cavall was a guard in disguise, because there was no real sense in him remaining there for so long. He wondered if one day Cavall would be offered such a position for his work keeping the others in line, but then he realized that Cavall would never accept such an offer. When left to his own devices, his life had fallen apart. At least here, he had a modicum of control and power while the temptations of the world around him were kept acutely away.

* * *

It took over two weeks of intense work for Kitalla to really come to her senses but another week before she had the strength to move on her own. She was surly all the time and distrustful of everything around her, her companions included.

"Back away, mage!" she hissed one day as Dariak offered her an herbal tea. "You're just as likely to poison me as kill me."

"Or heal you," he retorted, setting the mug aside for her to drink later.

"Likely, I'm sure!" she spat. "You've kept me in darkness long enough already. Who's to say you're not holding me for some other purpose? A victim for your experiments? To find out which of your concoctions can kill me without being detected? A fine ploy that would be. I'm trapped in here like any lost puppy. Can barely even move, and it's all because of you, I swear it!"

He knew based on her injuries that her fury was more directed at Grenthar, but her words stung anyway. It was all Dariak could do to clutch his hands into fists and keep his mouth closed.

But she wasn't finished. "Your quaint little ideals to save the world." She quivered for a moment, then pulled herself together. "You can't do it. You'll just get all that power and then turn on us and kill us all while we sleep or wake; it won't matter. You won't know what to do with that power when it comes to you. You'll annihilate us all! Damn you for keeping up this pretense of peace. Curse you for your stupid quest!"

The mage trembled, fighting to keep himself composed. At these times, Gabrion would sometimes step in and find a means of calming the enraged thief, but this time even his attempts were futile. When he approached her, she threw her mug at him, catching him painfully in the chest.

"And *you*," she shouted. "All to save your beloved Mira. You'd go to any lengths, wouldn't you? Even teaming up with a maniacal wizard seeking to destroy the world! You would use his power just to save your precious little cherub. And yet here you are, whiling away the hours in darkness, instead of being a real man and going off to fight for the woman you love. What kind of protector are you, sitting here and twiddling your thumbs? Admit it, you coward! You're too afraid to fight for her!"

"That's enough!" Gabrion bellowed, his face beet red and his veins pulsing noticeably. "You leave Mira out of this!" He couldn't take it anymore. He thundered across the floor and escaped into one of the passages.

"Ha, he runs again!" Kitalla shouted after him. She laughed and snarled, then whipped her gaze around at Dariak.

"As for *you*…"

He drew a deep breath and waited for the next portion of the tirade. It went on for some time while she belittled his sexual orientation and interest in Randler and then criticized his expertise as a mage, as well as doubted that his father had anything at all to do with the Red Jade they were seeking. He bore it all, trying not to internalize anything she screamed. Humming random tunes in his head sometimes helped, but she usually started throwing things when she didn't feel he was paying attention to her ranting.

Eventually, Kitalla grew weary, and her body collapsed in sleep. As always, Dariak took the first few minutes to calm himself, and then he turned his energies around to cast the next set of healing spells. It was harder this time because Randler was out and Gabrion had stormed off, but he still felt he was making progress. Though Kitalla was physically capable of walking on her own now, the process greatly weakened her, so she usually kept off her feet, venting her rage verbally until the rest of her body gave way. It would take a little longer for her to be strong enough to move for any length of time, but he knew he would have to fight against her tirades and heal her if she was ever going to get there.

Randler returned sometime in the midmorning and, sensing Dariak's mood, immediately started whistling a merry tune and acting goofy to break the tension. It took some time, but eventually the mage grinned and sighed, turning to Randler for a much-needed embrace.

Gabrion walked in while the two were locked together. He averted his eyes and set himself on the floor near his things. He fidgeted with Mira's ring, wondering if he would ever be able to bring it to her or if he would bury it in her grave, assuming he could find it. Time was ticking by, and with each passing day, he felt Mira was slipping from his grasp ever so slowly. When he was stuck in the Prisoner's Tower, he had given up hope that she would still be alive after all the time that had passed. Reclaiming her ring had instilled a new hope, but the shadow lingered within him, and returning to the tower only darkened his heart. Perhaps Kitalla was correct. Maybe he was a coward, too afraid to face reality. He would never win Mira back.

Dariak was crouching in front of him, and he hadn't even noticed. "Don't let her get to you. She's been through a lot, and she's taking it out on us because we're here."

Gabrion couldn't meet his gaze. "Easy for you to say."

"It isn't, Gabrion. Really." Dariak sat beside the warrior and looked over at Kitalla, who was sound asleep but clearly hurting. "We always knew she was astute. How else could she learn so much from a short tromp through town? But the things she says really cut to the heart. Maybe she senses our own doubts and throws them at us like daggers."

"At the same time," Gabrion said slowly, "she's right. I haven't pursued Mira directly. And saying I'm not strong enough is just a fancy way of not being brave. Look at the fights I've already gotten through, including breaking us both out of prison and her from her torture. So why am I still sitting here?"

"Because we're stronger together," Dariak said simply. "We just need to get her on her feet again."

Gabrion turned to look at Dariak closely. "You don't think Mira's still alive, do you?"

Dariak hesitated for too long.

"I see." The warrior's head hung low.

"No, Gabrion, she is still alive," the mage said in an attempt to comfort him. "I think you'd know otherwise."

Gabrion shook his head in denial. "Doesn't make any sense."

"Of course it does," Dariak insisted, grasping onto the chance for something positive after Kitalla's recent bashing. "We're all connected by the energies around us. We feel one another when we're close. We know inside what's going on with the people we care about the most. If it wasn't that way, magic couldn't work. We wouldn't be able to pull and push the energies to our will. If people didn't connect to them, magic wouldn't exist."

"You're reaching," Gabrion accused, stretching out onto his back and covering his face.

"I'm not," Dariak insisted. "Think of the jades themselves. They call out to one another, don't they? They resonate when they're near. They find ways of coming together when they're not; you said as much yourself with your jade in the tower. We're the same—people, that is. We resonate. We call out to one another. I think you call out to Mira because she calls out to you. It's as simple as that. So that means she has to still be alive, Gabrion. Or else you would know."

Gabrion was quiet for a time. "Like you and your minstrel, I guess."

Dariak blushed, turning to look across the large chamber at Randler, who was busying himself cooking a stew for them, nonchalantly unaware of their conversation. "I guess it is. So strange…" He sighed and let his voice drift oddly silent.

He struggled not to look at Gabrion.

It took a moment, but then Gabrion asked, "What's so strange?"

"It's strange that I'd find a bunch of Kallisorians that I can't imagine my life without."

It was a sweet sentiment that wasn't lost on the upset warrior. And Gabrion knew that Dariak meant it. He pulled himself together and reconsidered Dariak's words about Mira, wondering if the mage could be right after all. Perhaps he did call for her because she was still alive. He looked up at the mage, whose blue eyes had turned toward Kitalla in sadness.

"Well," Gabrion said, sitting up. "Don't think being all nice like that means I'm taking my pants off for you." He patted Dariak on the back and stood up to help Randler with the stew.

Dariak grinned. "Too bad. I'll have to try harder next time."

* * *

Being locked in a stone cell by choice didn't feel much different than being locked in by force. Still, Dariak and Gabrion made the best they could of the situation, comforting each other when Kitalla's rages were particularly vicious and combining their efforts to heal her. She was getting markedly better, they noticed, and soon she was on her feet regularly, walking around and stretching, wondering when they'd get out in the world and slaughter anyone who crossed their path. Her feisty moments often turned against them, but regardless, they ended with Kitalla crashing to the ground in a heap, too tired to move.

Along the way, Randler stayed true to the group, always bringing new supplies and stories of the events in the city. Pindington was the easternmost settlement of the kingdom, farthest from the king himself, and even though it was a trading port with other countries across the ocean, word from within the land itself sometimes took its time reaching Pindington. One afternoon, the bard came in with tidings he wished he didn't have to share.

"The king has called for war," he said sadly.

Gabrion's back straightened immediately. "What have you heard?"

"The attack on your village was verified by the king's soldiers, but he did nothing until other places were similarly attacked. When it was indisputable that the king of Hathreneir was on the offensive, at last our king decided to bulk up the defenses."

"We should wait it out," Kitalla offered. "Then go in for some easy looting." She was rocking back and forth anxiously, staring vacantly.

"War just leads to death," Dariak argued. "There has to be a way to compromise between the two. Stop all of this."

"That's a path that hasn't worked in centuries," Randler said mysteriously.

"Fine then, let's go out and kill them all," Kitalla said with an odd look in her eyes. She grinned, and then she groaned, shaking her head. "Ugh! Enough of this! I sound like Heria. I shouldn't listen to tidings of war."

"We can't stay here indefinitely," Gabrion chimed in. "I miss the sunlight, to be honest."

"Happy farmers!" Kitalla declared. "We'll all go be happy farmers!" She glanced at the strange reactions of the others and realized she was speaking nonsense again. It was a difficult transition for her, returning to life from the brink of darkness. Grenthar's punishments had pushed her beyond pain any mortal should ever have to endure, and just when she had thought she could take no more, she had been set upon his tortures again and worse. Sheer determination had driven her through the torments, shoving aside all rational thought of letting herself die and ending the misery.

Even the stone slab shattering her arm hadn't been the end of her trials. She had fought through numerous other horrors after that, and no one had come to save her, not even herself. Deep inside, something else resonated, some distant memory, but she refused to dwell on it.

After everything, when Gabrion had taken her from the cell and brought her from the pain, it didn't register as real. The healings she had received were nothing more than preparations for the next series of vicious traps she would have to face, and she had endured so much pain that seeing her companions made her feel more like she was imagining them than anything else, so lashing out was easier than accepting them.

Time had marched on, however, and the companions had remained, and the tortures had ended. She didn't fully trust it, but she was trying. Her nonsensical outbursts irritated her, but she had to admit that they were better than her impulses to hideously murder these people who had saved her.

"If any time called for the power of the jades," Dariak was saying, "it is now. We need to assemble the rest of the pieces and find a way of using them to stop the war."

Kitalla struggled to focus on the conversation, fighting off the lingering pain and memories. "Does anyone even know how many pieces of jade there are?"

"Very few made their way into Hathreneir," Dariak replied. "One went to me, two others to mage towers for study, and a fourth to the new king."

"So how many remained in Kallisor?" asked Gabrion.

Dariak hesitated for a moment, but then Randler answered, "Seven."

The mage looked up at the bard. "How could you possibly know that?"

Randler hedged but then shrugged. "It's my duty to know the lore of the land, as obscure as it can be sometimes. I hear things, I put them together, and I pull out the truth from the stories. Simple as that."

Gabrion wasn't satisfied. "Out with it."

Kitalla didn't do well with the angry tone in Gabrion's voice. She immediately twitched and reached for daggers that were no longer in her possession. Dariak had long since removed them after one of her tirades, during which she'd sent a few in his direction. Finding no weapons to pull forth, Kitalla growled and hopped onto her fists, as if ready to pounce on Randler.

He held up a placating hand and kept the fierce woman at bay. "Now, now," he crooned. "Settle down, and hear me out. It will all fall into place, all right?"

It took a few moments of hissing and seething before Kitalla calmed herself. They ignored her irrational outbursts, because they were becoming fewer and fewer with each round of healing, but they bothered her, and so she slid back from the rest, folding her arms onto her knees and pressing her head down to steady herself.

All eyes swept to the bard as he began his tale. "Long ago, my grandfather was part of the king's army. He served His Majesty as a general and trained the troops to fight alongside their liege under all conditions. He kept them well trained, even in the times when battles were few, because, as we all know, war is always imminent with loathsome Hathreneir."

Dariak cleared his throat at the description of his home, but Randler placated him with a knowing look. "I was very young when the last war took place, but I remember being fascinated by the stories my grandfather would tell."

His voice took on a grand, almost godly tone, as he continued. "And in walked the colossus of light, sweeping its massive arms and sending our troops into total despair. Simple as that, one brush of a hand, and men and women went sailing through the misty blue sky, never to be heard from again. The giant was unstoppable. Invincible to every attack, no matter how skilled the fighter."

The others nodded their heads, for their own knowledge of the war meshed. Randler continued. "He was a great storyteller, my grandfather, and it prompted me to take up this profession. We would talk for hours, and he would have me tell back the stories he'd told me, ensuring I could keep the details straight every time. Even though he was a soldier himself, he always felt that accurate storytelling was a better skill to have, for a good orator could uncloud the minds of the people. My mother didn't agree.

"No, Ma-ma wanted me to take up her mantle and secretly study the arcane and forbidden arts of sorcery." He looked to Dariak with a sad frown. "But I wanted nothing to do with magic, ever. She would insist on sitting me down with large tomes to study, and though I would repeat the words and flourishes, I never tried to pull the energies, despite what I told her."

"So then," Gabrion interrupted, "you *do* have some training as a mage, after all."

"Not much more than watching a fight would train me to be a brawler. I could mimic the moves, but that was all. At some point Ma-ma wanted nothing much to do with me, which freed me up to spend more time with my grandfather, telling stories. They never got along, those two, but he was my father's father anyway. He eventually took ill and died, but I owe my skills to him."

"What of the music?" Kitalla ventured softly from her perch, trying to focus on the conversation and keep calm.

Randler smiled. "My father was more the entertainer. He was part of a dance troupe, in which my sister also trained. I used to watch the performances and hum along with the music, and one birthday, my father put a lute in my hands to see what I could do. Pretty straightforward from there. After my grandfather and father died, I traveled with the dance troupe as one of the musicians and eventually ventured off on my own." Gabrion waited for more, but there was a long pause.

"That doesn't explain anything about the jade."

The bard looked like he wasn't going to divulge any more, but then he stretched and sighed and continued his tale. "Truth is, my mother never appreciated my father's line of work, which was why she delved into the arcane arts as a second means of income and security for herself. She knew it was dangerous, but she felt poverty was an even greater danger. My father died before the war, and she plied her craft to keep the family going. When my grandfather returned from the war, badly injured I might add, he brought with him a piece of the jade. He said he had intended it for me, but she felt its energies easily enough, and he handed it over, almost as payment for his residence with us."

"She sounds tough," Dariak commented.

The minstrel shrugged. "She was looking out for us all in her own way. In any event, she used the jade to increase her magic skills, which brought competition years later. There were secret showings of the practitioners' skills, and for some people, it resulted in their clandestine work for the current king, who benefits still from their knowledge."

Dariak grunted. "I just don't understand your kings, who all openly spurn magic but then have a storehouse of it hidden away."

"They come from a long line of soldiers," Randler answered readily, "but they know magic's value. Still, better to keep it controlled than to let it run rampant."

"Because Hathreneir is so wild," the mage murmured sarcastically, then waved his hand for the bard to move on.

"From the underground battles, Ma-ma became known as a strong force. And, as I said, she met competition. She had a few rivals, particularly when she turned down the king's offers. Apparently, she shared some of your ideology, Dariak, in that she didn't want to give magic knowledge to a king who shunned its use other than for his personal gain. It did lead to troubles for her, but she fended them off. I was off traveling around that time, so I only caught snippets of information when I would return home. I always offered a share of my earnings, but she only accepted funds if I earned them from performances—the troupe I was with didn't always receive their proper payments, so sometimes we went and, well, collected anyway."

"You stole it," Kitalla translated.

"Yes," he agreed reluctantly. "I don't like to admit that, but it did teach me additional skills, which later became far more important." He paused and gathered his thoughts. "One rival challenged my mother and nearly defeated her, which would have been a first. After all, she was using additional power and spells from the jade my grandfather had given her, so she only struggled against longtime practitioners. Not so when Halrone entered the scene. He was able to defeat nearly every one of her spells, and she was hard-pressed to keep him at bay. She was devastated by it, I could tell. So I decided to investigate."

"And you saw he had a piece of jade," Dariak concluded.

"Yes. And it took a few tries, applying all the thieving and cunning skills I had, but I eventually took it." He lifted his shadow jade. "Ma-ma was both furious and hungry. She wanted nothing to do with my 'foul and horrid deeds,' but at the same time, she wanted the extra power. I saw something break in her that day. She denied the jade I had stolen, but then she tried taking it from me through force. She was too conflicted between her set of morals and her desire for magic. We had a major scuffle over it, and before it could escalate to something unforgivable, I left with the shard."

"Wait a minute," Gabrion interrupted. "Those rogues who were after you…"

Randler nodded slowly. "Sons of my mother's rival. Hired by her to find this shard. With a huge bounty to ensure the task is completed. Clearly, my departure didn't settle well with her."

Silence fell as they all let the story fall into place. Then Kitalla stood up and paced around. "But you really didn't answer the question, did you? How do you know how many pieces of jade there are?"

He answered easily. "My grandfather knew of the soldiers and healers who took shards back with them. He told me."

"Easy and convenient," she said, her eyes narrowing into slits.

"Must all things be complicated?" he retorted.

"So you're collecting the jades too, then?" Gabrion cut in before Kitalla could start another tantrum.

"In a sense, yes," he said, hesitation creeping into his voice.

Kitalla raised an eyebrow. "What for, if you're not a mage and you're not planning on handing them over to your mother? Or are you?"

Randler glanced quickly at Dariak, then looked down at his hands. "No, I want to gather them and stash them away in a place where no mages will be able to use them ever again."

It struck like a knife deep into Dariak's heart. He stared at the bard like he was a complete stranger. His whole quest to unite the shards was in direct violation of Randler's own quest. And all along, he'd thought the minstrel was on his side.

"But you gave me advice to guide me to other shards," he stammered. "You're using me to collect them for you? So you can hide them away?"

"I'm sorry."

CHAPTER 28

Lightning Tower

THE NEXT FEW days were difficult for the group. Dariak refused to speak to Randler, who tried repeatedly to beg for forgiveness. The tension between them made Kitalla uneasy, which prompted spasms of pain as well as more lurid outbursts. Gabrion kept them all functioning.

Each chance he had, the warrior pulled Dariak aside to learn of any supplies he specifically needed, which Gabrion relayed to the minstrel. He then took the mage to Kitalla, and they summoned healing energies with as much passion as they could muster. Dariak was determined to repair Kitalla rapidly now and was grateful that the warrior at least helped maintain the energy flows.

All the while, Gabrion was torn between his ideals and his growing friendship with Dariak. A large part of him agreed with Randler's task and thought the jade shards should be secreted away and never found again. Yet he also felt that Dariak's intentions were true and that he would need the power of the Red Jade to bring peace to the land. While Gabrion doubted another colossus would help, the aftereffects that Dariak had mentioned about balancing resources and using the power to help both kingdoms thrive made some sense to him.

With the advent of war, many of the guards around the city made the pilgrimage to the western border to join the king's army. Not that Pindington was left unprotected, but the prisoners in the tower felt the change in their overseers.

Late one night, they started a revolt to rival Gabrion's own.

Loud, crashing noises awoke the trio. Bereft of Randler, who had a performance that night, they relied on Gabrion's scouting to determine the source of the noise. The warrior led them through a series of spiraling hallways until they could see the central dais where the turnstiles stood against the moonlight.

Gabrion scanned the area, and off across the yard he saw that the chain that operated the lift had broken. The pile of counterbalance boulders had been thrown against the support pulley, breaking it and dropping the mechanism to the pit below. Gabrion had worked the lift, and he knew that it was a decent drop from that height, but it wasn't impossible to survive unscathed. He glanced around again and saw, over by the axes, the corpse of Cavall. He'd met a bloody end, and his whip had then been coiled around his neck out of spite.

The fighting grew more intense, and even though they couldn't see any of it, it echoed through the secret passageways. Overhead, thunder boomed deeply, and Dariak gasped, understanding that the mages had joined the fray. He wondered if they were escaping prisoners or if, like himself originally, they were more annoyed that their studies had been interrupted. Either way, it wasn't good for the trio.

Gabrion led them through other hallways, until one wall crashed inward, nearly catching him in the face. He pulled back as two rogues bounded into the passage, weapons in hand. They didn't hesitate. Gabrion was an obstacle, and they lunged immediately upon him. The area was too constricted for them to do any real damage, but the warrior shouted in pain as one dagger slashed his thigh. He went down, and they clambered over him, kicking and jumping to escape. Dariak pressed himself against the wall to let them pass, but one rogue punched him in the face. They bounded over him and faced Kitalla.

The thief was already edgy from the noises reverberating all around them. This new threat, however, triggered a violent reaction. She fell back, kicking her foot up into the first rogue's weapon hand, knocking the dagger loose. Rolling onto her feet, she then leaped forward and plunged her hands into his neck and abdomen, not that she needed to do both to disable him. So strong was the force of her blow, however, that she crushed his windpipe, and he collapsed to the ground with only seconds left to live.

The next rogue shoved his comrade down and tried to continue fighting Kitalla over him. To stop him, she continued her forward momentum by bending down and flipping on her hands, bringing her legs up and grabbing the man by the neck with her feet. As he sailed one way and she the other, Kitalla twisted her body sharply, ending the bout with a loud crack to the man's neck. He clattered to the ground, and she turned her blind rage on Dariak, who did his best to look innocent and harmless. She pounced for him anyway, but Gabrion caught her, and though she clawed at his back and kneed him in the stomach, he withstood the attacks until she stopped.

The gaping hole in the wall was not going to go unnoticed for long. Their options were limited, and none of them wanted to actually head into the Prisoner's Tower. Gabrion took the lead again and brought them back to their main chamber, setting the locks, but with all the tumultuous magic being used, they all feared that these chambers wouldn't last long.

Randler ran headlong into the room as they caught their breath. "Hurry!" he shouted. "Grab your things; we must get out!"

"We'd figured as much," Kitalla commented, tossing blankets and pillows to the floor for the sheer desire to disturb something. She didn't have much in the way of possessions.

"What's happening?" Dariak asked, checking his pockets to ensure he had all the things he needed.

Randler scrambled to grab a few items left around the room. "A massive revolt within the tower, prompted by a mage at the top. Some spell of his went awry, and the inner wall started breaking and falling. They tried to subdue him, but the other prisoners took it as a sign, and they all rebelled. But the damage is massive up there, and the tower looks about to fall in on itself. We have to hurry."

Kitalla propped herself on the bed and eyed the bard sternly. "Weren't you at a performance?"

"It's rather late," he shot back, throwing a pack over his shoulder. "It ended hours ago."

"So you went into the tower to watch the mage's rampage?" she continued.

"Kitalla, this isn't the time for this. We have to move!" As if to accentuate the point, falling stone crashed outside the walls and shook the flooring. "Come on!"

She took her time getting up. "I just don't understand how, if this is all happening so fast, you were able to find out what transpired up there and then get down here to us."

Furious, Randler adopted an imposing stance and stared her down. "Blue-green lightning erupts from the tower, deep thunder echoes across the city, everyone wakes up and starts running around terrified. It's obvious where the source is. Pieces of stone falling everywhere, and prisoners screaming for their lives. What more do you want?"

"The truth," she demanded.

He rolled his eyes, exasperated. "Stay then, and ask the other corpses yourself. There is no other truth."

The ground shook violently; it was hard for them to even stand during the tremors. "Kitalla, let's go!" Dariak shouted. "There's definitely foul magic at work here. We'll sort it out later."

Gabrion suddenly leaped across the bed and threw Kitalla to the floor, which almost earned him a knife in the neck, until Kitalla saw the chunk of ceiling stone that had fallen to the bed. She stood up and dusted herself off, thanking Gabrion with a glance, and then stepped toward the exit at last. She pushed past the mage and the bard as echoes of her time in Grenthar's domain shook within her, just as the tremors shook the walls. She released a battle cry and charged through the dark corridor ahead. Debris was piling up, and other doorways in the passage had been blasted open, whether by spells, weapons, or crumbling walls, none of them could tell.

She leaped over the pieces she could, not allowing her body to claim weakness this time. She had bested Grenthar's every trap, or close enough anyway. One tumbling tower would not stop her. She pushed on through the darkness, turning left or right at Gabrion's calls from behind. They hurried past various openings, espying others running for their lives in other corridors.

Dariak hurried along, but something was amiss. He clutched the jade he had returned to his chest pocket and stopped. "Wait!" he called, closing his eyes and concentrating.

"This isn't the time," Randler argued, to which Gabrion agreed.

Dariak looked at them and then turned toward the nearest opening in the wall. "There's a piece of jade up there, and it's active. I have to go for it."

"This whole place is shuddering," Gabrion replied. "You'll never make it in time."

"Wait for the tower to fall," Randler pleaded. "We'll return and excavate the jade later."

But Dariak was determined now that he could feel his earth jade pounding so fiercely. "I have to go. You all go on ahead. I'll meet you later."

Gabrion saw the determination in Dariak's eyes. "Be careful, friend."

"You too." With that, the mage departed through the opening, dodging falling debris.

"Come on," Gabrion said, jogging to catch up with Kitalla, who hadn't slowed for them.

"I'm going with him, Gabrion," Randler said. "You two stay safe."

"Are you sure?"

"I have to." With that, Randler ducked through the hole and chased after Dariak.

The mage was surprised to see the bard, especially after their recent disagreement. He wasn't sure if he wanted to yell at Randler or hug him. Unable to decide, he merely asked, "You're coming?"

"One way or the other, I want you to be safe. So let's get the jade and go quickly."

It was good enough for Dariak. He nodded and turned toward a distant doorway. The halls were relatively dark, but lit wall sconces guided them along. Additionally, the open windows allowed flashes of light to cast eerie shadows down the path. Chunks of stone were falling everywhere, and the deeper they went toward the center of the tower, the more groaning sounds came from the walls and ceiling.

When they reached the center, a small group of guards greeted them, swords poised for battle. Dariak disabled them quickly with aspects of the Shield of Delminor, then ran on, turning toward a stairwell and taking flight upward. Along the way, some of the prisoners remained in their cells, pulling on bars and pounding on doors. Some of the growling and seething made them seem like fierce animals, but considering the plight of the tower, it wasn't surprising. "We have to release them," Dariak decided.

"There isn't any time!" Randler protested, but Dariak was on his way to the nearest cage, unwrapping a chain and pulling open a large gate. The men inside were filthy and bestial, and they rushed out with such force Dariak was splattered to the floor. It didn't matter to him, though. They might be criminals, but they didn't deserve to die because of the tower falling in around them.

After two other such stops in the area, Dariak felt a pulse from the jade, calling him to go onward. They found the nearest set of stairs and wound up them, stepping over the bodies of guards who hadn't survived an onrush of cellmates. Randler secured a quiver and bow for himself, and they continued upward. Most of the cells were empty, which suited the bard just fine. He didn't want to press their chances any more than necessary, but Dariak insisted on at least poking his head into a few cells along the way.

Three more flights up and the damage to the tower became more apparent. There were large punctures in the wall where blasts of energy had shot through, with more dead bodies strewn across the floor, including those of guard dogs and prisoners. The floors where the guardsmen slept were bare, for they either were off to the war or had struggled to reclaim peace within the prison tower. Dariak entered a storeroom long enough to abscond with a few extra daggers for himself, and then they continued the trek upward.

Once they passed the level upon which Gabrion had served, the going became much more difficult. The tower was supported now only along its outer oval, with nothing in the central column to keep it upright. Here, the spell damage wreaked havoc. Where walls had holes, now they dropped downward to the prison courtyard below, which slowly filled with more and more falling debris. At one such opening, Dariak peered outside and saw a spectacular series of flashing lightning streaking across the sky and exploding a gap in one of the inner walls, sending a shower of stones downward. The lightning continued whipping out in all directions, and he knew now just where he needed to go.

The problem was that many of the corridors were becoming impassable. A few stretches of ceiling had collapsed in completely, and the only way through was to take time to dig an opening. They veered around the obstacle, rushing through a mess hall where many tables still had food waiting to be eaten, and out another doorway. Around a bit farther, another stairway led up once more.

A deafening crash sounded, and the walls shook terribly. Screams echoed from afar, and the floor itself felt like it continued to move, even when the immediate tremors stopped. Dariak risked another glance and saw that the uppermost ring of the tower had burst apart and was collapsing in all directions. He could only see the portions falling inward into the central column, but he knew how large those chambers were up there, and he realized that portions of the wall would also be plummeting outside and into the city.

"Dariak, look!" Randler called, running over to a pile of fallen stone. At least three men were trapped underneath the rubble, their limbs flailing desperately to be free. The two of them immediately pulled chunks of rock from the pile, freeing the trapped guards, who each helped to free their fellows. Five men were rescued from the tumult, thanks to their iron-plated armor, but two others hadn't survived.

"Prisoners, flee this place," one of them demanded. "We have no time to deal with the likes of you. Go." He scrounged around for a sword and shield and then turned toward the doorway.

"We're heading up that way too," Dariak announced. "We'll help."

The guard looked back at them. "Then you're fools," he said. "Very well." Only one of the other guards was well enough to join them, and the rest made their way slowly down toward the exit.

With one guard ahead of them and one behind, Dariak felt like he was being escorted to another prison cell. If not for the explosions and vibrations around them, he would have avoided teaming up with these men. He knew it was more of a risk to tag along, but desperation was setting in among them all.

The guard captain raced ahead and took the stairs three at a time, disappearing until Dariak crested the stairwell. Some of the feral creatures were on this floor, roaring and screaming in terror. The cries of the three captive tigroars added to the rumbling walls, and the guardsmen split up to slay the beasts before their cries could make matters worse. Dariak wondered why they kept such a variety of creatures in the prison, but then he remembered requesting some of them for his own experiments during his imprisonment. He guessed that not all of these were for the sport of the mages above, and some were undoubtedly used as means of execution, but he didn't dwell on it for long, as a lightning blast shattered the right-side wall and the floor buckled underneath. The beasts were mostly still within their cages, but as the floor fell away, so too went the creatures, their terrified wails piercing the night air.

The four men pressed onward, climbing ever higher into the tower, which was teetering in the air with the endless assault from above. There weren't many more floors to go, but with each level they ascended, the crashes of lightning were more devastating, not only from the electric blasts but also from the reverberations of thunder.

The guard captain rounded a corner and opened a door, catching a searing blast full force and flying back, instantly dead. The guard at the rear bellowed in dismay and shoved Randler and Dariak aside with a war cry, charging ahead through the open door, ducking low and cutting down an adversary within. Dariak quickly summoned a few defensive spells for himself and the bard, and then they followed, the jade pulsing wildly against Dariak's chest.

Explosions erupted within the room as five mages stood around an altar, arms swinging frantically in unison. The central pedestal was aglow with greenish-blue light that flickered and then lashed out angrily in random directions. Most of the walls had already been decimated, and the next bolt flashed out near Dariak and rent a hole in the wall, opening the room further to the night air and the central column beyond, with a long, steep drop to the courtyard below.

Just in front of Randler, the guard lay dead on the floor, sword still clutched in his hand, its point stuck through the chest of a sixth mage. Dariak scanned around and saw several other mages and soldiers dead on the floor, one in particular whose body was so scorched and close to the altar that Dariak realized that he had been the one to activate the shard.

Blasts of lightning lashed outward, but the five mages around the room contained some of the power, channeling it away from them with their spells, sending it shooting out the walls. It didn't take long for Dariak to feel the flow of energy in the room and to understand that the mages were trying to contain the power emanating from the jade but failing miserably. At least they weren't the ones summoning its power. The next blast of lightning lunged right for him, shattering his glass shield instantly and leaving him with enough residual electric charge that his hair stood on end.

"What do we do?" Randler panicked, backing away from the horrible energy.

Dariak was already in motion. He first reset his protection spell, then enacted another just in case. Like most, he didn't know much about electric energy, but he quickly observed that it jumped toward the metallic objects in the room, including the guard's sword. He withdrew two daggers and tossed them toward the pedestal, watching as the lightning flashed out and struck them both in rapid succession. The mages eyed him suspiciously but didn't interrupt their own spells, for fear the lightning would incinerate them next. Too many other bodies on the floor had made that mistake.

The lightning blasted upward through a hole it had already made in the ceiling, bringing down more stone and wood and shaking the room with terrible peals of thunder. The mages caught another blast and contained it within the room, but it swept in a wide arc, building up more power before blazing through the inner wall and striking a portion of the tower across the way. A large expanse of wall fell inward, and the reverberations through the tower were frightening. Worse, the stability of the tower was weakening, and the swaying increased. With the supportive wall gone, the ceiling of the room across the way fell inward, as did the floor above it, and as Dariak watched from a distance, he had a sickening feeling that the tower had only minutes left. As each lower chamber fell inward upon itself, the ones above weakened, and soon the whole place would be tumbling down like a house of cards.

"Dariak!" Randler shouted, drawing the mage's attention as parts of their own ceiling fell in from a recent blast. "This is insane!"

"Can you douse some of the light?" Dariak asked quickly, reaching for earthen spells to strengthen parts of the walls and corner posts nearby. It wasn't much, but if he could at least stabilize the chamber long enough to subdue the errant jade, it would suffice.

The minstrel shakily withdrew his shard and focused on darkening the blasts of lightning, but with bolts of electricity erupting everywhere, it was too hard for him to concentrate. "I can't!" He jumped aside to avoid a falling chunk of stone.

The five mages kept their cadence going strong, but the never-ending lightning was the greater force. One blast overpowered their deflective measures and struck one of the mages in the chest, knocking him unconscious. The remaining four spell-casters increased their tempo and shuffled around the best they could to maintain a symmetrical placement encircling the jade, but it was obvious they didn't stand a chance against it.

Dariak tried encasing the lightning jade in a block of earth, but an inner explosion sent the tight shell ripping outward, shards of which cut into him painfully. He couldn't approach, for each time he did, lightning would leap out for him and break his outermost protection spell, forcing him to reenact it quickly. And he didn't have an unlimited supply of glass shards to keep resetting it.

Randler tried repeatedly to draw his jade's power and encase the lightning in shadow, but though he possessed some skill with it, he wasn't able to coerce it to his will under these circumstances. Meanwhile, more than half of the surrounding walls had been blasted away, and the ceiling overhead showed the floor upstairs rocking back and forth, ready to topple down and crush them. "Dariak!" he called out, rushing over and thrusting his own jade into the mage's hand. "Here!"

Dariak seized the jade and dropped himself immediately to the ground to commune with it quickly. He sought one power only, and so he was able to focus his thoughts into the energies of the jade and demand its response. His water and earth jades resonated fiercely, supporting his call, and soon the shadow jade answered.

Lightning impacted another mage, knocking him back through an opening in the wall to plummet down to the courtyard below. Only three of them remained now, and with the loss of each one, the defenses weakened greatly.

Dariak felt the deepening pressure, but mages were trained to handle such intensity as this. They needed to keep calm in the face of battles and dangerous incantations in order to successfully channel the energies and cast spells even when their lives were on the line. He called forth from the shadow jade and extended his arms toward the pedestal.

At first, a large, dark orb appeared around the altar. It was grand enough to fit Dariak if he stood upright. The deep purple color was highly transparent at first, but as he concentrated, he worked to condense the sphere to a smaller size. But the shadow jade was unfamiliar to him, so it didn't readily obey. He summoned bits of earth and water magic, drawing dust and moisture together to create a thin film around the shadow, and this he was able to press inward with better effect. The shadow pressed toward the glowing jade at the center, whose furious energy crashed against the darkness, trying to obliterate it.

Around him, the room was crumbling. Randler kept an eye on Dariak and twice reached over him to take the brunt of falling stone so the mage could maintain his concentration. The rumblings grew in intensity, and the floor above them, which had already suffered the collapse of the floor above it, started to buckle.

The three remaining mages took a moment to rest as Dariak contained the power of the lightning. But they didn't want to be caught unawares when its power burst through again, so they stretched quickly and then continued their chanting.

Sweat beaded on Dariak's brow as he climbed to his feet, arms swinging around, mouth sputtering quickly. He was maintaining three strong spells simultaneously, not even sure how he was managing it and unable to give it any thought anyway.

As the muddy shadow sphere grew smaller, the fury within intensified exponentially. He knew he wouldn't be able to collapse the power in on itself. But he didn't intend to stop the jade from functioning. Rather, he wanted to reach deep enough within that he could try to communicate with it and end its tirade.

His eyes pinned toward the center of the room, Randler scrambled about, pulling bodies and debris from Dariak's deliberate pace. He wished the other mages would abandon their posts and help, at least by coordinating with Dariak, but when he called out to them, they ignored his pleas.

A few streaks of lightning broke through the shadow barrier and, although dampened by the barrier, blazed with white-hot rage into the room. The three mages did their best to redirect the energy, sending it arcing from the room through the ceiling. It proved enough force to bring the upper level down at last.

As the walls and ceiling above crashed downward, creating a cascading collapse around the entire periphery of the tower, massive chunks of rock fell inward, and Randler couldn't possibly deflect them all. He was struck on the head and disoriented long enough to get trapped under another portion of the wall. While he struggled to free himself, Dariak was completely vulnerable, a fact that was compounded when two of the other mages were buried under debris.

The impact of the upper level falling through the gaps in the ceiling caused rents to form in the floor, pulling downward and breaking through to the lower level. All the while, other areas of the tower were still imploding, creating a constant rattling, which knocked Dariak to his knees. He pushed onward, trying desperately to reach the altar while maintaining the sheath he had created around the jade.

But then he felt the shield start to collapse and knew the massive energy within was going to escape. He knew it would be the end of them all, tower included. He needed to stop this force somehow. There wasn't much time, and he could barely concentrate with the rending tremors in the room. Randler had freed himself, so Dariak called out a quick order to him, hoping the bard would just obey.

Confused and terrified, Randler did as he was told. He snapped off a large section of the fallen guard's breastplate and gave it to Dariak, putting it in his left hand. The mage immediately curled his body, extending his backside away from the altar but leaning everything else inward. With a shout, he released the other protection spells, anticipating the incoming blast from the lightning shard.

He had already seen that the lightning most often struck objects that were metallic, large, and close by. With the breastplate in hand, he was the prime target of the enormous bolt that issued forth from the jade. He knew that the moment was practically instantaneous, but part of his mind tracked the bolt as it left the jade.

First, the bluish-white energy arced upward, then turned toward the shiny metal. It reached out with countless tendrils, seeking to shred its foe to endless pieces. The blast entered the breastplate and flowed right into Dariak's hand. A numbing force raced into his body, working its way furiously up his arm, ending all sensation as it went, which then turned into searing agony. The energy blazed through his shoulder, winding down and around his back and into his extended legs, then up again, circling around and seizing his heart. The electricity extended to his right arm and shot forth again, returning to its source with righteous passion. The shock stunned the jade, and immediately it started simmering and the light within began to fade.

But so too did Dariak. The light left his eyes as he realized that he had subdued the jade in its vicious anger. And because the energy had so thoroughly lanced through him, he felt the jade's own torment; the one who had enraged it had released its erratic power against its will, and now that Dariak had returned it, it was satisfied.

The reflective spell that had saved Dariak's life against Elgris's attack had now calmed the jade. But unlike the fight against Elgris, Dariak's body was not strong enough to withstand the amount of force it had taken in.

Randler watched helplessly as Dariak's body fell to the ground in a lifeless heap.

CHAPTER 29

Pindington's Woes

KITALLA AND GABRION raced through the outer chambers of the Prisoner's Tower, desperate to flee the falling structure. Exiting the hidden door to the town streets didn't offer them much safety, however. The tower itself was shedding massive hunks of stone, hurling them out in all directions. The ground around them was littered with broken debris and some of the citizens who had fallen victim to the projectiles.

The thief ran, jumped, and dodged automatically, using the reflexes she had honed so sharply in Grenthar's lair. But she acted without much rational thought, for those trials had always ended in horrific pain she didn't want to feel ever again. She ran on, Gabrion following the best he could, calling out to try to stop her. It was only when she crashed blindly into a fleeing family that she paused at all, trying to untangle herself from the others.

Gabrion caught up to them and assisted in righting the mess. The man, woman, and three children ran off screaming while Gabrion grabbed Kitalla and bore into her eyes, desperately trying to bring her back to him. "Stay here!" he yelled in her face. "I need you with me! Come on!"

The wild light in Kitalla's eyes subsided; she shook her head and apologized. "Why must I keep going berserk?" she asked.

"You'll get over it, but I need your help right now evacuating the people."

She stared at him incredulously. "You're mad!"

He actually laughed. "That's my line! But no, we can't let them suffer. Look!" He pointed up to the tower, where lightning blasted through the upper floors, sending more debris cascading to the ground below. From here they could see the upper tiers swaying back and forth in the tumult. "That's going to fall. We have to do something!"

"We could just save ourselves," she suggested, knowing what his answer would be. "All right, all right. But I officially object to this!"

"Duly noted." He grinned, then jumped aside as a bit of stone fell from above. They raced toward the nearest homes and screamed for the inhabitants to flee, only to find that these homes were unoccupied already. They took torches so others would see them more clearly as they ran through the streets nearest the tower, calling out an alarm for everyone to evacuate.

As they went, more blasts erupted outward from the upper floor of the tower at all angles. They had no idea how Dariak and Randler would even have a chance of surviving such a thing, but they couldn't do anything for their companions anyway. They rounded a corner and saw a few houses that had fallen from the impact and tremors. They raced inside the nearest one, finding some people trapped within.

Gabrion heaved wooden beams off one man while Kitalla strained to free a young boy from under a collapsed table. They had some injuries but were well enough to run off on their own, unlike the mother, who hadn't survived.

They found similar situations in other homes. One of them found a woman unwilling to leave because her daughter had taken a wooden slat through the chest. Nothing Gabrion could say would make the distraught mother move. She welcomed her fate at the loss of her child. When he tried forcibly to remove the woman, she entered a raging frenzy, kicking and screaming until he released her, after which she sank back down to lift her daughter's body to her breast, rocking back and forth solemnly.

Kitalla pulled Gabrion away, insisting there were others they could save. It wasn't easy, but he knew she was right. When they were a few steps away from the house, the topmost level of the tower erupted from repeated lightning blasts. The entire tier shot outward, raining death to the citizens below. More homes collapsed, and fires sprang up from overturned street torches. Soon, the citizens didn't need any rousing at all, but they needed direction.

Gabrion and Kitalla struggled to guide the people away from the tower. The people ran with such fear they paid no heed to which way they headed, so the two companions ushered small groups down a roughly clear road and shouted and screamed for the rest to follow.

Cries for help echoed through the night as the earth rumbled with the force of the tower's tremors. Gabrion and Kitalla assisted where they could, throwing burning wood aside or lifting stone chunks from fallen villagers. The number of dead piled up along the way, but Gabrion knew that many more would have amassed without their help.

They approached the damaged blacksmith's shop and ran inside, where the burly shopkeeper was hurriedly trying to shut down his forge. "Get out of here!" Gabrion called.

"The vent is ruined, and the pressure is building up inside," he argued. "If I can't get this fire doused, it will explode!"

Kitalla intervened. "It won't matter if everyone is away, so let's go."

The blacksmith gestured around his shop at all the weapons lining his walls. "And if this explodes, these all become projectiles too!" He tried again to wrench open the main door of the forge to release the pressure, but it was fused tight. Gabrion jumped in and took a sword from nearby, sticking its edge into the seam and pulling back, hoping the leverage would pry the door open, but the heat from inside the furnace had sealed it shut.

"It's no use!" the blacksmith shrieked as steam started squeezing through a small section of the furnace. "It's going to—"

And it did. The furnace erupted, sending superheated coals and sheets of metal flying through the air. From where they stood, Gabrion and the blacksmith took full panels in the chest, sending them flying backward and crashing to the ground. A host of smaller pieces broke through the ceiling and walls, sending weapons outward in all directions, including toward Kitalla.

It happened too fast for her to react. An ax and a fragment of the furnace shot right at her face. Her arms flew up defensively as she tried to fall backward out of the way, but she wasn't fast enough. The projectiles crashed into her hands with a dull, ringing thud, and as she hit the ground, she thought her arms must have shattered from the impact. But instead, her arms were only numb, and the metal had warped around her body like a soft bedsheet. She knew instinctively that the jade in her pocket had saved her.

Gabrion was badly bruised and singed from the impact, yet as he checked himself over, he noticed that the metal had shorn in half when it hit him. And though the momentum of the blast had knocked him over, the pieces themselves had fallen safely away. The shopkeeper was not as fortunate. Gabrion didn't know how he had managed to walk away from the explosion. The entire roof was gone from the shop, and nearly the whole stock of weapons had been cast through the air.

More blasts from the tower drew their attention, and when they looked into the sky, the white forks of light were simply terrifying to behold. Peals of thunder set them shivering from within, but they pulled themselves from the shop and continued trying to help with the evacuation.

There wasn't much else they could do, for Gabrion was struggling to breathe. The impact from the explosion had bruised some ribs, and he had twisted his ankle in the fall. He fought through the pain as much as he could, but at last he admitted they should try to find shelter for themselves.

They didn't have an opportunity to secure themselves away, however, before the real tragedy struck. Earsplitting blasts of breaking stone brought them to their knees, clutching their heads in agony. But they forced themselves to look toward the tower, which had reached its limits. The incredible structure teetered and folded in on itself, spraying the entire area with even more stone and mortar. It took forever for all the layers of stone to collapse, one upon the next, on the next, and when the stone couldn't implode any further, the rest of the structure wavered and then keeled over to the side, obliterating a good portion of the city in its wake. The cacophony was heard for miles and miles.

Gabrion's heart dropped from his chest, knowing Dariak and Randler were now gone. He fell to his knees, clutching his head in anguish. "I should have gone with them."

"To die alongside them?" Kitalla asked harshly. "It was a foolish act, jade or not."

He looked up at her, shaking his head. "Sometimes you're so cold."

Normally she would have shrugged off the comment, but instead she crouched down beside him, gazing off into the distance. "I've been through so much heartache and such ferocious pain. I have to be cold."

Gabrion stared at her for a while, watching as ghosts of memories flashed across her eyes. "You really have faced some incredible trials," he acquiesced. "But don't give up who you are. Not ever."

She covered her face and then released a rattling sigh. "Well, I'm not even sure which parts are the real me anyway." She stood abruptly and pointed toward the fallen tower. "Our companions may be lost to us, but I think there are enough people here who could use our help right now." She turned to Gabrion, who rose onto his feet. "Once we get things settled here, we'll mourn them properly."

He nodded sharply, firming his jaw for the tasks ahead. As he came to accept the pain, his senses widened, and he started taking in the sounds around them. Where people had been scared and running before, now there were violent shouts and terrified screams among them. Gabrion and Kitalla trotted along, making their way toward the tower itself, seeing a degrading sense of community with each step they took.

Rioting had broken out all over. Men and women were in the moonlit streets, fighting hard and looting the numerous shops scattered throughout the city. Members of the city guard struggled to subdue even the smallest incursions, so the warrior and the thief intervened and lent them a hand.

Gabrion rushed into a glassworks shop and interrupted the five men inside who were frantically grabbing merchandise from the shelves. They had clobbered the shopkeeper with his own wares, and he lay unconscious on the floor, his bald head bleeding from the impact. The warrior called for them to stop their antics, but instead of heeding his call, they turned on him.

The man nearest to him threw a glass vase at Gabrion, who batted it away with the sword he had taken from the blacksmith's shop. The glass shattered, raining down on him in a blinding fury. The other took the first man's lead and hurled other brittle pieces at the interloper. Swinging quickly, Gabrion was able to shatter each object before it struck him in force, but he wasn't able to make much progress at stopping them.

The shortest man among them grabbed a glass shard from the floor and charged ahead, trying to plunge it deep into Gabrion's side so they could continue raiding the shop, which had much less viable merchandise than moments before. The warrior jumped to the side but slipped on bits of glass on the ground, and he stumbled to catch himself. The short man shouted in rage and brought the glass knife down into the warrior's tunic-covered chest, expecting to plunge it deep within, but to his surprise, the glass disintegrated into sand.

Soon, all the glass sent in Gabrion's direction simply melted away to sparkling dust that hovered over the floor, creating a cloud that would likely shred their lungs if they breathed it in. Panicked at the mystic force the warrior was using, the five men abandoned their prizes and fled, covering their noses and disappearing into the night, demoralized.

Gabrion stepped calmly from the shop, purposely taking his time so he wouldn't draw in the glassy air, wondering how it had even happened. But even as he thought about it, the jade at his hip pulsed and reminded him of its presence. He pulled out the beige crystal, remembering its power over glass. Memories pulled his mind toward Dariak's own creative uses of the magic jades, when he'd tapped their underlying properties for otherwise unconnected spells. He remembered the metal furnace casing from the blacksmith's shop falling to pieces when it hit him. Considering the sharp edges of glass, Gabrion understood that the jade had enacted its power in order to protect the warrior, by making his body cut through the metal that would have otherwise killed him. And here again, the jade was working on its own to keep him safe.

While Gabrion was handling the glass shop, Kitalla had jumped into another fray with a young man and two women. Kitalla heard the pitiable cries of a middle-aged man as the three fighters hammered at him with random pieces of armor they had stolen from his shop. She offered them a chance to escape with their loot if they would just leave the shopkeeper alone, but then a guardsman charged ahead to take the fighters down and they turned their rage on him.

If they hadn't been beating the whimpering shopkeeper, Kitalla may have walked away. The guardsman, though well intentioned, was overmatched and would likely die at the hands of the three fighters. Kitalla decided quickly, keeping her daggers tucked safely away, and she bounded into one woman with her shoulder, knocking them both to the ground. Kitalla pounced back up and evaded a gauntlet thrown in her direction, then crouched down and swept a leg out from under the man. The guard rushed in as well, swinging his sword into the blocking shield of the second woman, who snarled and pushed back forcefully.

Kitalla realized quickly the three fighters were not mere peasants. They responded well to the blows they took, bending with the force of minor attacks and using the momentum to unleash their own. Their biggest handicap was that they hadn't anticipated a fight and so had no weapons other than the bits of stolen armor. The battle was much more of a brawl, and eventually the guardsman set aside his sword so he could grapple with the man.

The two women ganged up on Kitalla, furious that anyone other than a guard would intervene in their plunder. The shield bearer did well, blocking Kitalla's kicks and punches while also trying to pull the shield aside to land her own punches. The other woman, angry and sore from Kitalla's first attack, had picked up the gauntlet and slipped it onto her hand, adding weight to her punches. She had sharp-edged boots, which made her kicks potentially lethal against Kitalla's basic leather tunic.

But the thief treated this fight more like a warm-up exercise. She dodged and weaved, stretching her muscles and keeping as agile as possible. The two women couldn't land any solid blows, and the only reason Kitalla didn't either was because she wasn't really trying. She hopped over one low leg sweep and then swung her arm out to block the other's kick, after which she twisted around and landed a fist in the shield bearer's side.

She could have put more force behind it to knock the wind out of the woman, but deep inside, Kitalla knew a few things: First, under any other circumstances, she would have been among the thieves in the city, taking full advantage of the chaos of the tower's collapse, so how could she really fault these people for trying to enjoy their opportunity? Second, she was traveling with a noble warrior whose influence compelled her to protect the defenseless shopkeeper. But third—and most importantly to her—she was determined to conquer her recent bouts of uncontrolled rage, and by controlling her actions in this fight, she felt it would be a step toward reclaiming her self-discipline.

The three women danced around one another for a while as the two men battled full force. Eventually, the guard broke through the man's defense and was able to end their scuffle, cuffing the brigand's hands together with a cord. The guard then stepped in and brought the other fight to a close by grabbing the shield bearer around the waist and bodily throwing her to the ground. Kitalla took the cue that the battle was about to end and spun around delicately, avoiding a set of raking fingernails, and then clapped the woman's neck with her hand, knocking her out. While the guard took charge of the three looters, Gabrion rejoined Kitalla, and the two of them went off to continue their work.

Gabrion's grief welled up whenever they approached a family that had lost a loved one, and he veered off course each time to assist them in some way. Kitalla kept close by, sometimes making her own departures to help some group in need or to snatch up random pieces of forgotten merchandise from the road. Her instincts kept her claiming a few baubles along the way, for she knew her journey wasn't over and she would need items to barter with in the future. Part of her itched to run off full tilt for more impressive loot, but she wanted to keep close to Gabrion and that in itself tethered her temptation. She didn't know why his opinion and proximity were so important to her, but he had, after all, led the charge that had ultimately freed her from Grenthar's grasp.

The closer they came to the tower itself, the deeper the casualties became. Gabrion approached a crowd of people swaying and singing a mournful hymn beside a house that had been crushed by falling stone during the tower's descent. He learned that a family of six had met its end that night. Gabrion stood with the mourners and added his voice to their calls of woe, while Kitalla stood off to the side, watching silently.

Because the tower had toppled primarily toward the east, its entirety had fallen within the confines of the city. Had it gone the other way, the damage to the city proper would have been minimal, as it stood near the western wall. Instead, the fallen tower acted like a massive stone barrier, separating the northern and southern districts of the city. It was too immense to reasonably climb over. Many people had been instantly entombed with the tower's fall, leaving the citizens wholly shaken and full of unfathomable loss.

Numerous establishments had succumbed as well. One of the inns in which Randler had performed was so thoroughly buried under the tower no evidence of it remained. A mid-city animal farm was likewise eradicated, a fact that would horrify all the children who had visited it to pet the animals. The devastation to this part of the city was so complete Kitalla and Gabrion had a hard time even looking upon it.

Chants went up around town from angry citizens who had seen the lightning blasts before the tower's demise, and rage against the use of magic swelled strong. It was hard for Gabrion not to be caught in the flow of the words, for he had also grown up disliking mere hints of magical forces.

It pained him too, though, because Dariak had become a friend, and furious cries against magic felt like personal attacks on the mage himself. Yet, as Gabrion looked at the carnage caused by the tumbling of one single structure, he paled at the thought of the damage the mage could potentially do after collecting the jades and summoning the colossus.

He stopped himself before wondering if Dariak's death was for the best, but he scolded himself for even beginning the thought.

Eventually, Kitalla and Gabrion crested the top of the tower, where it flattened out lower than other sections because the upper floors had been projected farther. It was easy to see scorch marks where lightning had blasted viciously about. Debris was piled in random heaps all around, and dust still swirled in the air, clouding their vision of everything they looked at.

Cries echoed in the distance as other citizens tried to deal with the situation, but the area immediately around the tower seemed deadened by the dusty air. It was heavy and oppressive, with the still-settling rocks and dust looking like blood slowly leaking from the wounds of a dying stone giant.

Then Kitalla barked out a laugh, pointing ahead of her. It was a sound full of awe at the destruction before her and a bit of denial as she saw one section of the tower that had defiantly held itself together. "Look at that," she said in amazement.

Gabrion turned and saw immediately what she meant. With all the carnage around them, there stood a small cubical of stone, holding together against the odds, though lined with numerous cracks. They watched it for a while, and the cracks widened, at last giving way. The contradictory structure lost its form and tumbled down, adding to the debris all around. Gabrion and Kitalla both bent their heads in homage to the last vestige of the tower that had finally succumbed to its fate.

Voices continued to echo through the night air, but now something was different. Kitalla turned her head to the side and listened intently. Gabrion's expression confirmed her suspicions. Some of the voices, though very weak, were coming from the rubble, from the very spot that had just fallen apart.

They didn't hesitate. Scrambling over stone and rubble, Gabrion and Kitalla fought against the shifting debris, seeking purchases that were elusive and mobile. Several times, the stone gave way, and they slid back down, but the shallow calls for help propelled them onward. They slowly approached the chamber that had held together and peered timidly, expectantly, over the edge to the inside.

They saw numerous bodies strewn around within, most of them clearly dead. Two mages were still moving and waved their arms in greeting at the appearance of Gabrion and Kitalla. "You have to help us!" one of them called with a thick accent. "Please! These walls are collapsing! Hurry!"

Gabrion looked around and understood that either they would need to jump down and hoist up the mages, or they would have to lift them with ropes. "How many of you are there?"

"Five," the mage answered, waving his hand around vaguely. "Please hurry!"

Gabrion's eyes swept the chamber, and there among the fallen were the motionless bodies of Dariak and Randler.

Kitalla had already seen them and assessed what needed to be done. While Gabrion worked his way toward the lower lip of the chamber, Kitalla removed the rope she wore around her waist and secured it the best she could to the jutting stone fragments. She ordered Gabrion to remain aloft and act as a counterbalance for the rope, after which she swung her body down and slid into the chamber.

The two mages ran over to her immediately, carrying a third of their kind who was injured. The wounded mage took the rope in hand and, with the support of the others, made her way up into Gabrion's grasp. The two alert mages then turned to the thief. "Those two risked everything to save us. You must take them from this place." They went to Randler and dragged him toward the rope, looping it around his waist and tying it securely. The three of them then lifted the body as high as they could, after which Gabrion strained to lift the bard over the ledge. He tossed the rope down, and Dariak's body was sent up next, after which the mages and Kitalla followed.

The weight of seven bodies on the outer hull of the tower was too much, and the pieces started sliding and tumbling inward. Gabrion guided Dariak's body toward the ground while Kitalla focused on Randler's. The three mages kept close as a loud crash resounded with the collapse of the last chamber. They hit the ground and pulled the wounded from the area to safety.

Gabrion tried to examine Dariak's body, but the mages shoved him aside forcibly, with such determination in their eyes that the warrior was perplexed. He wanted to immediately retaliate and attack them, but their hands were already raised and moving, incantations spewing from their mouths in unison, and, after all the time spent working on Kitalla, he quickly recognized the cadence of healing spells. As he looked down at his companion, he saw that Dariak was already breathing shallowly, as was Randler.

"How is this even possible?" Gabrion stammered.

The mages finished a few rounds of spells, then lowered their hands. The man with the thick accent turned to the others. "Let us take them to a better location first, and then we will tell you, if that will suffice."

CHAPTER 30

The Determined Mage

FINDING VIABLE SHELTER so close to the crash site wasn't easy, but the group eventually came across a small house that had only minimal damage. The fireplace was still lit, though very weakly, and numerous personal items were scattered about, signifying a hasty departure. Gabrion carried Dariak's body to one bed while Kitalla and a mage brought Randler to another. The wounded mage hopped along painfully, supported by the third mage.

The heavily accented mage introduced himself as Quereth. "Frast, bind Lica's leg before she loses it." He turned to Kitalla and Gabrion. "Would you mind quickly putting on some tea? We've had a rather trying night."

"What happened to our friends?" Gabrion demanded. "Will they be all right?"

"I beg of you," Quereth responded. "Tea first. Food if there is any too."

Kitalla shrugged and went off to gather the provisions.

Once Lica's leg was bound and a few healing spells had been set in place and everyone was fed, Quereth called everyone together.

"Sit now," he suggested. "While we take a much-needed rest, let me relay what transpired in the tower."

Gabrion listened impatiently to the start of the tale, in which Quereth discussed how the jade itself had come into the possession of one of their brethren from an anonymous donor. They had experimented on it for a couple of weeks without success, until one remembered having seen one of their previous prisoners—who turned out to be Dariak, which had surprised them once they recognized his reappearance—communing with a shard. The lead mage had pulled the energies from within, and the shard's power escaped violently, and then the rest of them circled around the room to subdue the unleashed power. But of the twelve mages who had begun the process, only the three of them in the room were left.

"Along the way," Quereth continued, "your companion arrived, but we could not help him, since we needed to redirect the lightning blasts. He tried several variations of spells to quell the magic from the jade, but nothing worked. My compatriots were falling, as was the tower. It was our hope to stop the jade from destroying the city, but we realized we were doomed. Your fellow then made one last effort and drew the energy through himself, and the shock struck the jade, effectively neutralizing it, but then your friend collapsed to the ground. Dead."

211

Gabrion and Kitalla both leaned forward. "But he was breathing just now," Gabrion argued.

Quereth nodded slowly. "Remarkable. I never would have imagined. As frantic as the rest of the night was up to that point, it was at this moment that the real miracles happened." He paused to drink his tea and ask his companions how they were faring.

Gabrion grunted in annoyance. "You do intend to reveal the nature of these 'miracles'?"

The older man smiled slowly. "Patience now. As I said, it was a trying night. A moment to compose my thoughts, if you will."

It was only minutes, but to Gabrion it felt like hours before the man continued his tale...

* * *

Randler watched in horror as Dariak's body drew in the lightning blast, then collapsed in a heap on the ground. The entire tower was shaking terribly, and the one remaining mage was unable to offer any assistance.

"Dariak, no!" the bard screamed. Scrambling desperately, Randler made his way over to Dariak's body, feeling around for a pulse that was no longer there. The mage's deep-blue eyes were unfocused and unblinking, his chest unmoving and without breath.

Devastated and angry, Randler pulled Dariak into an embrace, then set his lifeless body down gently before turning to the altar and the lightning jade that sat upon it. He grabbed the jade, his whole essence focused sharply, and he turned back to Dariak with it, pressing it against him. Quereth, across the room, saw the bard trying to summon the power of the jade and stepped forward to stop him, fearing he would release the lightning storm yet again.

Randler ignored the approaching mage, whose progress was hindered by the walls that shook and trembled erratically. He knew it was pointless to try to help Dariak, but he preferred they die together, and not because of the jade itself. The bard picked up the shadow, water, and lightning jades and pressed them all against the earth jade that was inside Dariak's tunic, so close to his heart. Randler could feel the resonances of the jades as they welcomed one another, but he sent his thoughts deeply into the shadow jade, pleading with it to pull the darkness away from Dariak.

The jades pulsed around more deliberately with Randler's request. He wondered if the shards could truly communicate his will between them or if they just responded to his own energies. He closed his eyes and begged for the return of Dariak's life, knowing it was an impossible appeal but seeking it anyway. A bright light bore through his eyelids, and he opened them to peer at the jades in his hands.

The lightning jade glowed vibrantly, with sparks leaping across its surface. Randler's fingers went numb from the bursts of electricity, but he tightened his grip so he wouldn't drop the shards. The light intensified with each pulse of the jades, until it was so blinding that Randler had to look away.

Quereth realized he couldn't intervene in time, so he started casting his protection spell again, waiting for the lightning to blaze out of control.

Once the light reached a crescendo, a bolt of electricity shot forth into Dariak's chest. The mage's whole body lurched with the impact. The light built up again, and a second bolt blasted into Dariak's heart. After the fourth shock, Randler heard a sound he'd feared he would never hear again: Dariak breathed deeply. After the mage was resuscitated, the lightning jade dimmed and pulsed softly in time with his heartbeat. It took a few more moments for Dariak to open his eyes.

Randler pulled him close and hugged him, then looked around at the shaking walls that dropped more and more rocks as the moments ticked by. "At least we can be together for this," he said apologetically.

Dariak was disoriented and weak, but he pulled himself upright as the tremors increased. A major crash sounded as other portions of the tower imploded across the way. A quick glance showed him that large sections of the tower had collapsed completely, pulling on the surrounding walls and slowly toppling them. The chamber they were in rocked precariously and shuddered dangerously.

There wasn't much he could do, but Dariak was determined to try. He clutched for the earth jade and begged for its help. They were surrounded on all sides by stone, which was within the jade's providence. He had already fortified a few sections of the chamber to keep it intact. Now he extended the call for even greater power. The earth jade hummed within his pocket, and he felt the energies reaching out, but alone, they weren't enough.

Dariak saw the awed look on the other mage's face, and he called out for help. "Together, now, or we don't stand a chance!" With that, Randler helped him to stand, and Dariak and Quereth faced off, the older mage mimicking the younger. Dariak's hands and feet swept about as he shouted the words of his spell over the clamor that echoed around them.

"*Forticulus combrinor cagarion. Hossrathen derrethock saei.*"

The room itself teetered sharply toward the inner column of the tower, and at last its inertia was too great to recover. The whole structure fell over like an enormous tree, crushing all the rest of the floors in its wake and splattering itself across the city.

Dariak's spell, however, called to the stone immediately around them, and with the aid of the other mage, they were able to pull fragments of wall together into a stony cage that kept the rest of the tower from crushing them. They were tossed around inside, however, and Dariak and Randler were knocked unconscious in the tumult.

Once the major rumblings stopped, Quereth sent a few exploratory spells into the mage and bard, assessing internal damage, then followed the cursory glances with some healing that would allow them to recover over time. He turned to the other mages in the chamber, finding only two other survivors. Together, they worked to open the wall to the air before they all suffocated or the fortification spell faltered and the walls fell in.

* * *

"And that's where you came in," Quereth finished. "Without these two, we all would have perished. I care little for their own intentions with the jade, but your friend, as you called him, seems to have an innate knowledge, and there must be some reason for it."

"He does," Gabrion acknowledged, but didn't elaborate. "How badly hurt are they?"

"Not badly at all, considering the circumstances. The three of us will tend to their wounds after a brief respite. You'll all be ready for travel soon."

Quereth's estimate was accurate. The three mages spent the majority of the early morning hours casting a wide variety of healing spells, curing all the major wounds the team had sustained. Dariak received the most attention for his ailments, until he banished them from his side, eager to gather his thoughts and accept that he was truly still alive, despite it all.

Gabrion used most of the following day to help the citizens and Pindington guards while his companions took care of their various needs. The entire city pulled together to help those families who had lost loved ones in the tower's collapse, though all the while, complaints against magic echoed everywhere. The guards recognized Gabrion as one of the prisoners from the tower, but they made no effort to detain him, especially when they chanced upon him digging away large braces of stone and rescuing people still trapped within the debris.

"Surprised to see you still hanging around," one of them commented.

The warrior finished moving a large stone and dusted himself off before examining the speaker, but he couldn't place exactly where he knew the guard from or if they had ever actually met at all. Perhaps the man had only seen the wanted posters and thought it surprising any criminal would tarry. "These people need help," he responded simply.

"Indeed, but it isn't every man who would risk his freedom for such a task."

Gabrion shrugged his massive shoulders and gestured to the rocks behind him. "You're welcome to try taking me in, but I'd prefer we work together on this instead. What say you?"

The man grunted and clapped his hands together. "I say we get digging." He introduced himself as Ordren, one of the captains of Pindington's defense patrols. The two of them spent a good portion of the day at hard labor, and other guards who witnessed their cooperation realized that Gabrion was no longer to be treated as a felon.

Randler spent his afternoon in a very different state of mind. So many lives were shattered in Pindington that mourning would carry on for long periods of time. He went through town, plucking his lute and crooning softly to the needy souls, stopping in open streets as crowds gathered for a distraction from their personal woes. He sang of spiritual journeys of the dearly departed, of glorious afterlives that promised peace and warmth for all eternity. Upon request, he increased the tempo and brought cheer and laughter to some who needed a dose of levity. Yet everywhere he went, he touched the hearts of the men, women, and children he passed, easing their pain if only for a few minutes at a time.

Kitalla's day focused on the morrow. She returned to the decimated blacksmith's shop, absconding with various weaponry that lay strewn about the ground. She bartered with the armorer and flirted with a tavern master for travel packs of durable food. As she went, she listened to the tidings of war to the west, knowing they would soon be heading in that general direction. The people were worried that the war might extend as far as Pindington, adding to the horror they had just experienced, but many argued that if the fighting ever came their way, not only would it be a long time off but they could always take to the ships and leave.

What troubled Kitalla the most were the groups of distraught citizens talking about the mages in the tower and their role in the destruction of the city. More and more people turned their grief into anger, and a rising sense of unrest emanated everywhere. The desperate men and women yearned to find those responsible for the devastation, and accusations rose all around. Some took shreds of posters from around the city and turned the blame toward the featured criminals. Disguised, Kitalla slipped into numerous conversations and realized that they needed to all get out of the city as swiftly as possible.

Dariak, on the other hand, remained with the other mages, resting and keeping out of sight. He described the pain he had felt when the lightning crashed into him and killed him, then the added pain he'd felt when the same power returned his life to him. He never wanted to experience such a thing again. The four of them spoke of their spells, and Lica, Frast, and Quereth all admitted to witnessing some of Dariak's abilities during his imprisonment within the tower, as well as their wholehearted disappointment when he had first escaped.

"We were learning so much from you," Lica said, stroking her hand through her graying hair.

"If we only had a means of practicing without having to go to such lengths," Frast added. "We've all taken turns playing the part of prisoner just so we could have the chance to cast at will."

Dariak's brows scrunched together. "You couldn't practice?"

"Not like that," Quereth acknowledged. "We could keep our skills refined in case of emergency, but we were not to free cast like the prisoners."

"No," Frast agreed. "My brother let the powers get to him, and after watching many other mages go wild within the prison, he started experimenting. The other guards reported him, and he was slain in his sleep. So we must always keep secret and adhere to the confines of the job."

"Then why let prisoners do what they will?" Dariak asked.

"In the event they find a way of turning the tides," Lica answered. "Our king would not deny a true opportunity, but I think that successful mage would find himself at the front line to do his work, dying rather quickly once it was over."

Dariak shrugged. "I've said it countless times since journeying here: I don't understand your king. Listen, trouble is brewing out there and there isn't much time to prepare, so could I ask a boon of you, to show me some of your healing spells? Mine are rather feeble."

For the rest of the day, Dariak paired off with the mages, rotating partners throughout the day and soaking in whatever spells he could in the short time. Meanwhile, the mages prepared a hearty meal for the four travelers. They brought in a large table from another house and cooked a wide range of delectable foods, from fruit spreads to lemon-dipped chicken with sides of wild vegetables seared to perfection. Wine flowed readily, complementing the worldly flavors that each mage concocted for Dariak and his companions.

"A toast," Quereth announced halfway into the feast that night. "To a wondrous mage with insight beyond that of the greatest sages. Without your bravery, we three would have perished. Without your gifts, we all would have joined the tower in its final throes. Without your wit, the lightning jade would likely still rampage upon this city."

Dariak let his cheeks burn red, raising his glass and sipping deeply. "I regret I could not help more of your brethren."

"Yet if I read the energies correctly, brother, you will," Quereth returned, receiving curious looks from the others.

He nodded sagaciously and raised his glass briefly toward Dariak. "The jades resonate with you. There is a distinct connection. A mage of your potential has the means of breaking our chains here in Kallisor and opening the land wide for our magic to reach from shore to mountain to distant valley."

Kitalla breathed a heavy sigh. "No, I'm not so sure that's right. Not after the disaster here. Do you really think people will want magic blossoming left and right after a crazy lightning storm killed easily over a thousand people when it knocked down the tower? They're already rallying together to find those responsible."

Randler yearned to voice his agreement with her assessment, but Dariak was finally speaking to him again, so he remained silent. Instead, Gabrion filled the awkward silence that followed. "Dariak saved you three—well, five, really with himself and Randler—but Kitalla's right. The rest of the people see this as magic going awry and bringing the end of their livelihoods. And they're right. It was indeed magic that brought this all about. It has to stop."

Quereth shook his head. "If we were allowed to practice our craft, we would have had a means in place to prevent this tragedy. The people will come to understand."

"You're right," Dariak muttered softly, staring at his wine. He realized from the confused expressions that they didn't know with whom he sided. "Kitalla and Gabrion have the right of it. I've seen too much of this wretched country to think anything else. If I could have kept the tower from falling, then maybe. But no. No, even with the power of the jades, I wasn't able to save these people. I couldn't do more than rescue a handful of us, no more. This won't further our cause, brother. We can already hear them rising up in anger. I am sorry."

"But we'll make them understand!"

Dariak simply shook his head. "Coercion won't help either."

"That isn't what I—" Quereth stopped himself, then sighed. "Then what do you suggest?"

There was silence for a time as everyone looked around, seeking inspiration. Dariak's eyes settled on Randler. "You want the jades hidden away, untouched ever again by mages. But how will that help us?"

The other mages erupted at this announcement. The jades were physical manifestations of their innate abilities; to cast them away was unthinkable. Besides, Dariak had used their powers to save their lives. Such a gift could not be squandered.

The bard tolerated the noisy barrage for some time before the anger ran its course. He simply endured it, accepting the hurled insults and awaiting his chance to answer. When he spoke, his tone was as calm as Dariak's had been, as if they were discussing the best types of flowers to accent a front yard. "Our nations have seen torment since the beginning of magic, once our forefathers left the gods behind. We abandoned them, and they left us to fend for ourselves. Our ancestors found the paths to magic, and our land has ever been divided."

Dariak interrupted him. "Your tale about King Kallisor and Lady Hathreneir."

Randler smiled, pleased that Dariak had listened so well to that tale. "Yes, indeed. The great lady was a mage and had vast magical power, but the king was a warrior, and they could not coexist."

"That does not mean we must ever be persecuted," Quereth interjected angrily.

"I can't convince you," Randler started, "because I don't even know if it's the answer either. But if magic dissipated, we might be able to resolve our problems without fear of mystical forces."

"Psh!" Lica sputtered. "Nonsense! Our problems would resolve if people realized that magic isn't as bad as they think it is. If they knew more, they would understand that the worst among us is no more fearsome than the worst among the tyrants. A charismatic leader is a much bigger threat than a mage who can summon a giant."

"Besides," Kitalla threw in, "no one has any trouble turning to the healers." This led to quite a bit of agreement from the mages.

Gabrion couldn't take the arguing anymore. "This isn't getting us anywhere. Whether we assemble the jades for their power or bring them together so we can lock them away, we're still gathering the jades to keep them from others who could abuse them. I can't say anything about what the best option is, as much as I distrust magic. But yes, it's been useful too. Then we have our king, who threw even me into prison without a spell at hand, completely irrationally, while he employs others who train in magic for his use in other regards." He paused for a moment, realizing he was going in wide circles. "No, I think we all have a single goal here but different ways of getting there."

"Oh?" Quereth asked skeptically.

"Yes. Don't we all want the wars to end? Hasn't there been enough fighting? Haven't enough people been lost?" Gabrion choked on the last word. "I can't say what the best solution is, but I think that these jades are coming together anyway. So let's bring them together, and if the circumstances change, then we will alter our course."

"Who determines that?" Randler wondered. "Whose call is it whether to use the jades or not?"

"Let Gabrion decide," Kitalla suggested, laughing. "After all, his quest is for Mira. As for the jades, he isn't firmly set in either direction. He's a neutral party; who better to decide?"

It wasn't a popular notion, and the room erupted in angry shouts. In the end, only Dariak was able to restore order. He stood up and removed the jades from his pockets, placing them on the table before him. He set the earth, water, and lightning shards out in the open, turning to his companions expectantly. Kitalla added her metal jade, Gabrion set his glass jade, and Randler placed his shadow jade. The pieces were already resonating from their proximity, but freely set upon the table, they shook and twisted about, aligning together determinedly.

"They point to the west!" Gabrion announced in shock.

"Not to Mira." Dariak hated breaking it to him. "Though they do point in her general direction, they actually point to their nearest brother."

Randler released a deep sigh. "My mother," he said. "She has a shard."

Gabrion made a face. "Will Mira ever be our destination?"

"Yes," Dariak answered. "We will head west now. This next shard is just a detour. We are gaining our strength and we will reach her."

Kitalla tipped her head toward Gabrion and responded to the mage. "We'd better or this guy is going to leave us in the dust and save her himself. And after I promised to help him too."

"We can't delay much more," Gabrion added. "There's no telling what condition she's in."

Dariak looked at the group and nodded. "Okay. As for the jades, keep your piece, Randler. And you, Kitalla and Gabrion, keep your shards. Even if we travel together, they aren't quite united. You saw that yourself in the tower, Randler. I needed possession of your jade to truly activate it, and you can't argue that I wouldn't have used its power if I could have."

"No, not under those circumstances," the minstrel admitted grudgingly. "Then we'll follow the warrior's advice. Take the rest and see what happens." His voice was sad and resigned.

"So you intend to collect the shards?" Quereth ventured after glancing around at the companions.

"Yes," Dariak answered coldly. "Even Randler knows that with the three pieces I have, I could locate all the others and use their powers to eventually claim the rest. Even if they all want to argue, they can't."

Gabrion grimaced deeply at this declaration and stared at the mage, fighting an innate anger. Yet as he watched, he saw that Dariak was turning his gaze determinedly around the room, but there was a deep sadness in his eyes. Gabrion realized that the mage was simply bringing an end to the debate, allowing no one to argue the point any further, which would only serve to create even deeper rifts within the group. Gabrion wondered if he would have the same inner strength under the circumstances. Kitalla realized this too and sank back in her chair.

Quereth ignored the nonbelievers and focused on Dariak. "We are in your service, Master Dariak. We will go forth and assemble the underground mages, and we will join your fight."

"You will join in my victory," Dariak responded officiously, accepting the offer. "Once we've claimed the next shard, we will head west to break into the land of Hathreneir in order to assemble the other jades. We could use your assistance in that endeavor."

"You will have it," Quereth agreed. "And when, once again, you've assembled the shards into the whole, we will be at your side then too."

With the agreements made, the companions sought a deep and silent respite, but the city's echoes of grief and anger weighed upon them. The night passed fitfully and the morning was met with further unrest.

Mobs had formed in the streets and the hunt began to find those responsible for bringing down the tower. The disheveled citizens roared with outrage and crashed into one home, then the next, seeking the mages who had brought doom upon them.

The companions gathered themselves as the rioting drew near. The door crashed open, enraged faces filling the entrance.

"That's them!" one man cried. "They're on the posters!"

Another shouted, "Look! More mages in there!"

"Die, heathens!" the mob screamed, pushing into the small house.

Quereth, Lica, and Frast reacted quickly, casting out webs of paralysis and turning to the others. "Flee this place before your quests end here."

"What about—" Dariak started.

"We'll be fine. We can hold off this lot. Flee, Master Dariak!"

Kitalla grabbed Dariak's shoulder. "Get me out of here before I murder them all, mage." Her eyes raced wildly left and right and Dariak knew she was struggling to control herself.

"This way," Randler called from the rear exit.

"You're coming?" Gabrion asked as he hurried past.

The bard nodded. "It isn't safe for me here anymore either."

Dariak hesitated a moment longer until Frast turned his head and assured him they could handle these people. Clutching the jades in his pouch, Dariak followed his companions into the troubled streets of Pindington and the next leg of his journey in Kallisor.

The Saga Adjourned

MERIAD CLOSED THE large tome and pushed it aside. Her grandson sat anxiously in his bed, clutching the blankets firmly.

"Are you all right?" She chuckled softly.

"I can't believe he died… *and* came back!" the boy gasped.

"Indeed. He wields some great power, don't you think?"

"It's amazing he didn't end up taking over the whole world!" His eyes were wide with awe.

Meriad chortled. "Perhaps he did and you don't know it."

He paused to think about it for a moment. "Did he?"

Now she laughed openly. "We will see, as the tale unfolds, what happens to Dariak and his friends."

"I'm wide-awake, Gran-mama. Tell me more. Please!" His pleading eyes tugged at her heart, but there was no more to be said for now.

"You understand that reading this tale takes a lot out of me. It is time for me to return home to tend to some things there, but you know I will be back to continue."

"Yeah, I know," he said in his sulkiest tone. "But Gran-mama, what happens to Pindington now? It's all destroyed and lots of people died, didn't they?"

"Indeed," she answered gravely. "Unfortunately, with all of Dariak's skill, even he couldn't bring the dead back to life."

"But he came back to life!" he protested.

"That was very different and under specific circumstances, mind you. We have all lost people in our lives, love, but we must remember to keep them alive in our hearts."

His head sank low, and he nodded solemnly. "I know."

"So what do you think of their decision to find the other jades?" she asked.

He perked up as he thought about it. "I think it's a great idea. Then Dariak can do all sorts of things."

"You're a fan of Dariak, I see."

"I—well, he's from Hathreneir, like me."

Meriad cleared her throat in an annoyed fashion. "Haven't I told you countless times that we must not discriminate against people just because they were born else-where?"

"I know."

"That's your phrase of the evening, I see."

"I suppose," he said with a grin.

"Some people would say your ideas are a little funny."

"Why?" he asked indignantly.

"Well, some people would discriminate more against Dariak because he likes other men. And they would applaud Gabrion for pouring his life and heart into the love of a woman. That doesn't bother you?"

"Sh—should it?"

Meriad smiled warmly. "No, dear, it certainly shouldn't. There is nothing wrong with Dariak's interest in Randler, but also there is nothing wrong with those born in Kallisor. I need you to remember to judge people on their actions, not 'what' they are."

"I'll try."

Meriad bit her lip. She believed he would really try, but it would be so much easier if she could take him with her and show him another lifestyle, where the character of men and women meant so much more than their birthplace. Still, she did her best the only way she could.

"Gran-mama?"

"Yes, dear?"

"Would it be weird… if I wanted to be more like Kitalla?"

Meriad laughed. "Tell me which attributes you would emulate first, and then I'll decide."

His face scrunched in confusion. "Which attri—? Emul—? Huh?"

"What part of her do you like?" Meriad explained tenderly.

"Oh! Well, she's so fast. And determined. She really just does whatever she has to do to survive. Every time you tell me what's happening to her, I think I could never survive it myself. But then she survives it. I want to be like that."

Meriad reached out and hugged him. "That's inner strength and believing in yourself. And that's totally within your grasp."

All of a sudden, the young boy yawned, and his eyes dripped tears in the process. "Gran-mama?"

"Yes, dear?"

"I can't wait to find out what happens next. Please come back safely."

With a soothing hum, she leaned close and kissed his forehead. "I will, dear. Now sleep, and I will see you in a few weeks."

The Shattered Shards

Recalling the Start

MERIAD SAT ON a soft, cushioned chair in her grandson's bedroom. The young boy was sitting excitedly at the head of the bed, while Meriad was on the side, close to the foot. In front of her, Meriad had propped up a large, dusty-looking book. It seemed too large for someone of her age to carry, but she hefted it without any complaint.

Beside her was a tray of food, still steaming and ready for her to eat. She had only just arrived for her visit with the boy and he had, as usual, whisked her away to his room, keeping her all to himself. It didn't matter, for she wasn't there to visit with anyone else and her presence was merely tolerated because she was family and she had been given a task to do. As usual, guards awaited outside the room, listening to her words, ensuring she did not stray from her task, though her grandson was unaware of their presence.

"You remember the War of the Colossus?" she asked, reaching for a small loaf of bread.

"Yes. It's the war when the Kallisorians almost took over Hathreneir."

She sighed. "You still say that with disdain. Do I have to remind you every time I see you that the Kallisorians are not our enemies?"

He protested. "They did bad things to us."

"Yes," she agreed. "But we also did bad things to them. That sort of makes us even. Now, tell me what else you remember."

He pushed himself more firmly into the pillows to get comfortable. He knew this tale well; it was one of his favorites. "Well, there was a lot of war between our two kingdoms and then the kings decided to put an end to the fighting once and for all. They chose to battle to the death and whoever won would take control over both kingdoms. The Kallisorians tried to win by poisoning the Hathr—"

Meriad cleared her throat, obviously disappointed.

"Without the king's permission," he edited, "some of the Kallisorians acted on their own and poisoned the Hathren troops."

"That's better," Meriad accepted, selecting among a collection of finger sandwiches. "Go on."

"Well, it's called the War of the Colossus because a mage named Delminor used this piece of magic called the Red Jade to summon a huge monster, which killed a lot of people. He was defeated and the Red Jade broke into a bunch of pieces and then people from both sides took the shards."

Meriad nodded. "That much of the story you've known for a while. What happened after that?"

He bit his lip, then dove in. "Well, twenty years later, there's Gabrion, a warrior from the Kallisor town called Savvron. His girlfriend, Mira, was kidnapped during a raid on his village, and he wants to try to save her, but he doesn't think he's strong enough yet. Dariak's the son of Delminor and a Hathren mage who's trying to collect the jades, and he and Gabrion teamed up eventually, even though they started off as enemies. Then there's Kitalla, who is a thief with a special dance skill. She can do a form of magic that no one else can do. She wants Dariak to help her become stronger. They all traveled together and made their way to Pindington far to the east of Kallisor. A whole lot of stuff happened there and they got separated for a few months. After that, they joined with Randler, a bard, and then… then the big tower in Pindington fell."

"Because?"

The boy wrung his hands together. "Because magic went bad and it broke the tower and the tower crushed and killed a lot of people."

"So magic is evil then?"

"Well, no," the boy argued, "not really. I guess it depends on how people use it, but the thing that happened in the Prisoner's Tower was really an accident, wasn't it?"

"In some ways, yes," Meriad acceded. "Now, you mention that Dariak is questing for the jades. Do you remember which ones he has already?"

The eleven-year-old paused for a moment before answering. "Well, Gabrion has the glass jade. Kitalla has the metal jade. Randler's got the shadow jade. And I think Dariak has the earth and water jades."

"Don't forget the lightning jade," Meriad added.

"Right, and they have five more to find. But, Gran-mama… Doesn't Randler want to get rid of all the jades and magic?"

"It does seem to be his goal."

"Then how can he and Dariak love each other?"

Meriad smiled, a haunted look in her eyes. "Love can be a funny thing."

They sat quietly for a moment, then Meriad set aside the last few bites of her meal. "Very well," she commented. "I think that brings us to where we were before. Shall we continue?"

The boy beamed and nodded his head vigorously, a big smile lighting his face.

CHAPTER 1

The Four Companions

PINDINGTON LAY IN ruins. The easternmost city of Kallisor was the center of trade with countries across the great ocean, but now it was in shambles. The unnaturally tall Prisoner's Tower had succumbed to a vast explosion of magical forces and the stone structure decimated an entire section of the city. A dusty pall still floated in the air two days after the tower's collapse, a sad reminder of the many citizens who had perished.

Magic was barely tolerated in Kallisor, and mostly only in healing sanctuaries. The eruption of magical energies and the subsequent fall of the tower led many people to riot in the streets, angrily seeking those responsible. Those who were not lost in mourning gathered together to seek their own form of justice.

The angry citizens crashed from one home to the next, seeking any evidence of magecraft and, upon finding any, destroying it. The few people in mage robes shed them swiftly and sought refuge wherever they could.

Many prisoners had also escaped during the catastrophe and every chalk or coal drawing posted among the guard stations and notice boards was taken by the gangs. All unsavory people would be victim of this cleansing.

The mobs swept through the city, often dragging the official guard force with them for support. They rushed toward the collapsed tower and followed its corpse as it led to the northern district. House upon house was violated by their rage, but they would not stop until the city—their home—had been cleansed and purged.

A pack of hunters approached a small wooden house not far from the uppermost level of the fallen tower. Their shouts echoed wildly as they forced open the doorway. Peering inside, they recognized Kitalla, Dariak, and Gabrion from their wanted posters and the mob's excitement escalated. A bard and three other mages accompanied them, and the city's defenders pressed inside.

The mages acted quickly, paralyzing the mob, after which they called to their companions and compelled them to flee. Four travelers burst out the back door and sprinted away.

Nineteen-year-old Gabrion, blond farmer turned warrior, pushed ahead of the others and cleared a path through the growing throng of people. He kept his weapons away, simply using his powerful hands to get through.

Kitalla followed on his heels, keeping her hands off her daggers so she wouldn't feel compelled to launch them. The brunette thief had been through too many trials in her twenty-six years, and her most recent experiences in Grenthar's lair had left her dealing with random outbursts. She kept her eyes trained on Gabrion as she ran.

The bard, Randler, came next, also with his weapons away and his shoulder-length brown hair flying side to side with each step. Twenty-four years of experience had shown him enough angry mobs and he knew their best chance to escape safely was to stick together and not stop running.

Lastly, Hathren mage Dariak trailed the group, eyes focused on the warrior as he led them away from the wooden house. Dariak's mind reeled with the recent explosion of magic in the Prisoner's Tower and he knew the people of the city had suffered enough. He had to escape with his companions without causing any more harm. Like his father, the twenty-two-year-old's goal was that of peace, though his methods to reach it weren't always peaceful.

There was little time to think with the angry mob chasing them and hollering for reinforcements. The companions refused to attack and cause further damage. Instead, Dariak fumbled through his pockets, reaching for the water jade. He touched its permanently wet surface with one hand and twisted his fingers with the other. "*Shassalorian fretha kaie!*" he called. The cobblestones behind him cooled until the humidity of the air turned to a fine sheet of ice. The chasing mob slipped and was deterred.

It didn't give them much time, but every bit helped. Gabrion led them toward a guard station. Kitalla protested, but the young warrior insisted. He had spent the previous day helping the people to recover some of their losses and he hoped his efforts would pay off for them now.

The city guard was overwhelmed and the station was barely manned. Gabrion put his hands aside his mouth and shouted, "Ordren!"

A younger soldier peered around a doorway. "Can I help you?"

"Is Ordren here? I need a favor."

The dark-haired teen shook his head. "The captain is out, I'm afraid. Is there something I can help you with?"

Gabrion requested a loan of horses. Kitalla chimed in, adding that their goal was to assist the people in the southern district of the city, and that mounts would make their trek through the streets faster, particularly because of the rioting. The soldier wavered, but he had seen Gabrion and Ordren working together briefly and he acquiesced.

Gabrion claimed a dark chestnut steed for himself, while his companions chose their own mounts. Kitalla gravitated toward a black mare, against which her leathers blended perfectly. A palomino chose Dariak—who was eying a different horse altogether—by strutting over and resting its nose on the mage's head, claiming him so thoroughly the other horses all stepped away. Randler strutted toward a steed that was stark white and mounted it easily, patting its neck affectionately.

The team pressed their horses swiftly through the city, avoiding the throngs of angry people whose shouts permeated the air. A few chased after them, accusing them of treachery, but the horses outpaced them well and facilitated their escape. At last, the troubled walls of Pindington were left behind and the team pushed onward into the wild.

Randler took the lead, guiding them toward his hometown where his mother held a shard of the Red Jade and wouldn't likely surrender it without a confrontation. He veered toward the river, angling along its bank and crossing over at a narrow ford. The bright sunshine helped keep the feral creatures at bay, but Randler also used the power of the shadow jade to obscure their passing. They could almost feel hungry eyes scanning for them, eager to take down the intruders, but the attacks did not come.

The group made camp alongside the river at the edge of a row of trees. They could have either entered the wooded area or remained out on the plain, but Dariak opted for the border of the two. He spent the good part of an hour setting up protective enchantments while the others prepared the campsite itself.

There wasn't much game in the woods and Kitalla and Gabrion returned empty-handed from their hunt, but the thief pulled some wrapped tigroar steaks from her travel pack and handed them over for Randler to cook. Of the four, he had the best talents when it came to food, gained from all the places he had visited and the different varieties he had experienced. Gabrion cleared the dishes away, washing them in the river before packing them again.

"Let's go, mage," Kitalla said some time after dinner, grabbing Dariak by the arm. She led him from the campsite, into the woods and toward a clearing she had found earlier.

So much had happened to them, Dariak had forgotten his promise to teach her how to draw the magical energies through herself. They started by reviewing the steps she already knew, and soon her hands and feet were lit with fireballs that glowed with every dip and turn she took, warding off oncoming attacks. But she wasn't satisfied. She wanted to be much stronger.

"Do you feel the energy?" Dariak asked, and when she nodded he continued. "Good. Now, what you need to do is pull in the direction of those energies, draw them through you, and repeat. Mages use spell components and words to help us channel the energies, but you have to draw them differently. The more complicated and powerful the spell, the more the energies must overlap and work cohesively."

She reenacted her dance, straining to do as directed, but it was difficult for her. She hadn't grown up thinking she would use magic of any form, and her dance skill had manifested itself accidentally, though she had learned to develop it over the recent years. Every attempt to pull the fire around her failed, and only her hands and feet took light.

She dropped to the ground and pounded the dirt. "I don't know if I can do this," she muttered. "I feel everything pulling together, but it isn't doing what I need it to do."

Dariak paced back and forth, thinking hard. Fire spells were basic manifestations of energy and were among the easiest to summon. There was no substance to move with a fire spell, only energy. That she could create the fists of fire at all was amazing, but he knew she had other talents within her. The woman's swinging hips and arms had done everything from confuse fighters, obscure her from view, and implant vivid images into the minds of others. Yet protecting herself was not a skill among them.

The only other energy she had drawn was in Grenthar's domain when she had claimed the metal jade and its power lent itself to her so that she could project the dagger's edge outward, seeking its kill.

Dariak smacked his forehead loudly, drawing Kitalla's attention. "Take out the jade," he said, "and a dagger. Now close your eyes and feel that shard in your hand. Sense its energies as it runs back and forth across its surface."

"I feel it," she said. "But I have for a while and it doesn't come to my call unless my life is in grave danger." She recalled the exploding blacksmith shop in Pindington and the metallic projectiles that had essentially turned molten when they struck her and left her unscathed.

"Yes, but now feel the energies of the dagger blade."

She looked at him oddly, for there were no energies from the dagger. He waited until she gave it her full attention, but no matter how hard she concentrated, she couldn't feel them.

"Next, trace the jade's energy over the dagger," he instructed, undaunted that she couldn't sense the dagger. "Imagine that the other energies are there and following along. Go on."

She did so. She let her mind swipe back and forth across the top of the jade and also across the dagger. Nothing happened, but the process required vast repetition. She stood there for a long time, focusing her mind on both the shard and the blade, pulling back and forth, back and forth.

At last, something inside the jade resonated with the energies and the dagger responded. Its blade elongated slightly with a deep internal vibration that shook Kitalla's arm. It broke her concentration, but the dagger had changed subtly. She could see that it was visibly longer yet just as sharp. She smiled up at the mage. "That's great, but—"

"Shh," he interrupted her. "It's only the first step. You've channeled the jade through you and into the dagger. Yours is the jade of metal, so it affects the metal. You were able to create a gentle resonance with your mind. Now, do it again with your body. Find that same cadence with your steps. Move yourself in time with that process and do it all over again."

While Dariak and Kitalla continued their work, Randler and Gabrion settled themselves back at the camp, watering the horses and stashing their belongings. The young warrior examined the bard carefully. They had been companions for a short time and the minstrel had been useful to the group, especially in terms of helping to heal Kitalla, but Gabrion felt he knew little of the man.

"Randler," he said slowly. "Do you really think hiding the jades away will work?"

The bard considered for a moment, then shrugged. "I don't know, but most towns seem to get along fine with proper governance and no mystical forces. And if you take that tower into consideration, it's pretty easy to see that magic is just too erratic and destructive."

After a pause, Gabrion said, "I'm sorry."

It was an odd reaction and Randler screwed up his face in confusion.

"You and Dariak," Gabrion explained. "You seemed so happy at first, but now there's this rift between you."

"Ah, yes. I guess we don't see eye to eye on this."

"Do you think it's more than your relationship can handle?"

"I—I don't know," Randler answered. "I hope not, but it's difficult. I have seen how bad magic can be. Haven't we all? And though I want to believe that he is different, once someone has power, you never know. I don't want him to be tempted by it and then lose himself in it. I wish he could find another way to achieve his goal."

"Hmm," Gabrion hummed. "The people love you. Everyone seems to know of you all over. You did great work in Pindington with your songs, easing their pain."

"Yes?" the bard said hesitantly, confused again.

"I know I'm not making much sense. My thoughts are all scattered, so bear with me." He bit his lip. "Dariak told me about that song you sang right after you two met. About the Forgotten Tribe."

"Ah yes, a good tale I've told in many ways over the years."

"You're not the only one to mention it. The elder of Gerrish said something of it to me, too. What's happening now feels like the things that happened then. You had Lady Hathreneir who was a mage and King Kallisor who was a warrior. They loved each other, but they let their differences interfere with their relationship and it tore them apart. That rift started the wars we still have today."

Randler nodded slowly. "Dariak told you well. Yes, that was basically what happened."

"So here we are again," Gabrion continued. "Dariak is the mage who wants to use magic to unite the people, but you want the world to be without it. You two clearly have a deeper connection, though you really haven't had much time to explore it."

"That's true," the minstrel said, interrupting Gabrion. "I recognized him as a jade bearer because mine was pulsating, but I didn't realize that when we first met in the bakery. He just caught me, I guess. I wanted to push everything aside and get to know him."

Gabrion nodded. "He and I weren't friends when you two met. I was still bound to turn him in to the king for attacking my village. But when I think back, he definitely had a bit more bounce in his step after meeting you. You two have this special something. So how can it all be happening again? How can the debate of magic or no magic be at the center where it could tear you both apart?"

The bard blinked several times. "I hadn't looked at it that way."

"More than that, though," Gabrion plowed on, "these jade pieces are coming together on their own. I believe that now, especially with how you and Dariak went in to the tower and he claimed the lightning jade, literally dying in order to take it, and then it brought him back. We're working together right now and the jades have been protecting us all along, like guardians. My jade hid itself from the guards and then helped me to break out of prison with Dariak in tow, and then it saved me again when that furnace exploded. Kitalla has had similar protection, as have you. I can't deny that they're helping us as much as we're helping them."

The minstrel released a deep sigh. "Then you've decided that you're siding with Dariak in assembling the jades so he can wipe out the armies and 'bring peace.'"

"I think the jades have to come together anyway. We might as well have a hand in how they are used. It isn't as if you don't make use of the shadow jade, right?"

The bard pursed his lips. "True."

"But, Randler, those mages in Pindington were also right about something else. A good speaker can affect people more than brief shows of power, no matter how strong. They can influence the heart and mind and bring people to do things they might not have done before, and not because they're afraid of retaliation, but because they believe. Even just walking through in Pindington with your lute, you helped many people in ways sheer force could not."

Randler waited while Gabrion searched for his next words.

"So you see? What if Dariak gains the ability to summon the colossus, but he doesn't actually use it? What if, then, *you* step in and reach the people the way you were born to do, and help them realize that all this warring is for nothing? It's just killing us all off, keeping our lives a constant mess."

"Save the world with a song?" Randler scoffed, but though he tried, he couldn't discard the thought.

"The connection you and Dariak share is new to me."

"What of Mira?"

He squirmed awkwardly. "Between two men, that is. But I see how you two are with each other and I see that it's real. Neither one of you can let this disagreement come between you. Not for yourselves and not if we're going to put an end to the fighting."

"Funny thing for a warrior to say."

"I know," he admitted. "I've always been better lifting things than anything else and I would have been a farmer like my father if it hadn't been for the skirmish years ago."

Randler raised a brow. "What happened?"

"A few of the older boys in the village, Mira's brother included, went off to explore parts of Hathreneir. They crossed the border illegally and went into the desert, just looking, really, but hoping to find some kind of treasure to take back as a memento. They were seen by local guards." Gabrion's voice turned solemn. "The fight didn't last long, and only one of the boys was left alive, so he might return to the village to warn the rest not to invade their lands again."

"Mira's brother?" Randler ventured.

"No, Kyrell didn't return. Most of the villagers were horrified, both that the boys had gone and more so that they had all been killed, save one messenger. Hosreth couldn't accept his fate, that he was allowed to live while the others died, so he… rectified that shortly after returning to Savvron."

"I'm sorry."

Gabrion cleared his throat and pushed onward. "For the most part, everyone accepted the warning and from then on we were all bound to keep far from the border. Except for Mira's parents. They went and petitioned the Hathren king to take back the bodies of the slain so they could be put to rest with their families. He wouldn't allow it, but he instead gave them a writ of passage that permitted them to visit their son's grave once a season. Mira stayed with us at first; she and I were already very close, even then. Then she started traveling with them sometimes to see her brother's grave. It's been, I guess, about seven or eight years now.

"That's where Mira's folks were when the Hathrens attacked that day," he said quietly. "Mira had chosen to remain behind and she would have been alone in her house if we hadn't been on our way to the meadow. She was taken away that morning, but I wonder if she would have been safer if I hadn't pulled her from her home. Or maybe she would have died instead."

"You can't wonder such things."

"I know." He shrugged. "It's been so long since then, Randler. She's a village peasant. Her family isn't renowned for anything. There is no reason to ransom her off. I can't imagine she still really lives after all this time."

Dariak stepped in from the forest, Kitalla close behind. "You can't give up hope, Gabrion."

The warrior jumped. "How long have you been listening?"

"I heard most of it," he said, with a glance toward Randler. "But really, you need to keep your hope alive."

Kitalla smacked her hands together. "Yep, I promised I'd help you save her, didn't I? I can't do that if you give up on her."

Gabrion dropped his head into his hands. "It's hard to be hopeful. My brain says one thing, but my heart can't imagine spending the rest of my life without her. I know you mock me for saying things like that, but it's true."

Dariak glanced again at the bard and clapped Gabrion on the shoulder, "No, I think part of me understands what you're saying."

Randler looked up at the mage and smiled softly.

Kitalla rolled her eyes. "Well, I'm going to go vomit off in the woods while you all get mushy."

"Don't you go anywhere, Kitalla," Dariak chuckled. "You're part of this love-fest too."

"Not happening!" she said, raising her fists.

Gabrion couldn't help but laugh. He stood up and looked at his companions. "Strange how things can change so quickly sometimes. If Kyrell and the others hadn't gone off and died, our village wouldn't have felt as deep a need for protection from the Hathrens. We already had some men who were trained to protect us, and a few of the older children who followed their fathers. But that tragedy prompted the king to eventually send soldiers to organize the fighters in the towns and after a while they started seeking volunteers among the rest of us to train as warriors. At least, that was how Andron said it went.

"So I wonder sometimes: If Mira's brother hadn't died, would I even be here on this quest? Would I have trained to fight at all? If not, would I have been among the casualties when Savvron was attacked?" He shuddered. "I know it doesn't help to wonder such things, but sometimes I have to. Am I just a victim of circumstance or do I have a choice in my destiny?"

"Gabrion—" Dariak started, but the warrior cut him off.

"No, I'm not really asking. I have to remember why I'm here. I could have died so many times along the way, but I didn't. I fight for Mira. Her safety is my goal and, you're right, I have to keep her alive in my heart until I learn otherwise. I have to be strong and push ahead to the next step along the way. If I stop now, I'll never know if I could have saved her. I would regret it forever. I won't be another Hosreth, ending things because I cannot face them. Because I regret what I did, or didn't do."

He coughed and then breathed deeply. "Sorry. After everything we went through in Pindington, I'm tired, so if you don't mind, I'm going to get some sleep. We have a big day ahead of us tomorrow, don't we?"

Randler nodded. "A hard ride tomorrow will bring us within reach of Vestular by nightfall." Without another word, Gabrion turned toward the woods, settling himself down out of earshot. He lay on the ground with his back to a tree, gazing out across the river until he fell asleep.

Once Kitalla realized she wasn't going be the victim of any random hugging, she tossed back her hair and stretched. "You two go chat a bit. I'll take the next watch when you're done. Just promise you'll keep an eye out once in a while for monsters."

"Other than you?" Dariak teased.

She responded by spinning and bringing her arms up her body slowly, fountaining them out over her head and sliding them down low again. Caught off guard, Dariak and Randler both succumbed to a chilling sensation that ran down their spines, like being tossed into a cold waterfall. Kitalla then stalked off, laughing, on her way to grab some sleep.

Left alone by the fire, Randler and Dariak stared at each other for a long time. Neither one wanted to break the silence that was both comfortable and awkward all at once.

At last, Dariak had to ask, "Do you think we stand a chance, Randler?"

He knew the mage wasn't referring to the upcoming battle against the bard's mother, or the larger goal of ending the war. "I think your warrior friend is right. We have to find a way to work through this."

Dariak lowered his eyes for a moment. "I would like to."

They reached out and linked hands for a time, watching each other in the waning firelight. "Back in the tower, Dariak, I was tested like never before. We weren't going to make it. I was purely terrified, but you held it together. It was remarkable."

"I couldn't let you die up there."

"Nor I, you. Truly, I've wanted to gather the jades so I could hide them away and stop other mages from unlocking any of their secrets. Yet when the test came, I thrust the shadow jade into your hand because you were stronger than I was. I couldn't do it. All I wanted was to scream and to die with you, together, because I didn't see a way out. Then that lightning struck you and you fell…" His voice choked.

"I wasn't sure what I was doing," Dariak said.

"You knew enough to trick the lightning to come right to you, keeping the rest of us safe. After you fell, I didn't know what to do or how to react. I thought the lightning jade owed you. It had to bring you back. That's the only reason I brought it over to you."

He smiled. "It was lucky you did."

Randler squeezed Dariak's hand. "The warrior's right, I think. We need to find a way to be together and not let our differences interfere."

"That's easy," Dariak said. "Just agree with me about everything."

It took Randler a moment to realize the mage was joking. "I would like for us to be able to give this a real try."

"So would I."

There were a few moments of silence while the two gazed at each other. When it seemed like neither was going to move again, Kitalla called to them from the trees, "Kiss him already, you idiot!"

"I wonder which of us she's talking to," Dariak said, grinning ear to ear.

"Let's not find out," Randler whispered, leaning in and kissing him deeply.

CHAPTER 2

Vestular

TRAVEL WAS DIFFICULT the following day, as rain clouds rolled in and turned the landscape into a muddy field. The horses trudged along the best they could, but the team made slower progress than they would have liked. Because of the darker sky and the wet weather, creatures behaved differently than normal. Where some nestled in their dry lairs, others went on the prowl.

Not long after their departure, a vicious pack of lupinoes charged at the group from the cover of trees. Dariak drew upon the water jade and pulled on the rain, creating a protective curtain around the group, which effectively blocked the assault. Because the rain continued, he was able to constantly refresh the water shield until the beasts turned away.

However, the same tactic did not work against the massive ursalor that pounded from its cave and raced across the muddy landscape toward them. The bearlike monster was too strong for the water shield and its huge claws raked right through and scored a gash in Dariak's horse. The terrified equine threw the mage to the ground and ran off. Dariak wasted no time in casting his next spell. He pulled the rain toward the ursalor into chunks of ice, cutting into its thick hide, but the spell only enraged the beast.

Randler rode his horse off a ways and turned about, pulling out his bow and lobbing arrows through the air, careful not to hit his companions. He compensated well for the rain and a few of his arrows struck home, but still the ursalor did not seem affected.

Kitalla sprinted off after Dariak's horse as Gabrion turned and drew his sword. He raced beyond the creature and struck its spine with a mighty thrust. The ursalor roared angrily and swiped out at Gabrion's horse, finding it gone before it could land a hit. Dariak weighed down the beast with the Shield of Delminor but was surprised when it had little effect. He wondered if it was a complication of the rain, but then the ursalor stood upright on its hind legs, reaching a towering fifteen feet into the air, and he realized that the added mass from the spell simply hadn't mattered.

Gabrion couldn't fight well enough from horseback, so he jumped off and ran toward the bowed legs, slashing at them powerfully, hoping the ursalor would fall over. His sword bit deeply, but the beast merely swatted at him like a gnat and roared again into the sky, then turned back to the mage.

Dariak was sore from his fall and the mud made him sluggish, but he kept his hands and arms swirling about, first adding personal protection spells in case the ursalor came too close. He then drew the rainwater together into pools around the monster and urged them to freeze, creating treacherous patches of ice upon which the creature slipped and crashed to the ground. Gabrion pounced immediately, driving his sword into the creature's side, loosing a gush of blood that splattered him with its warmth. Unfortunately, the attack now marked him as the more dangerous target, and the ursalor turned its huge body over, swinging all four of its powerful claws and spraying mud everywhere. Gabrion jumped away, brandishing his sword and trying to damage the meaty paws that could cleanly sever his head if they connected.

Kitalla had returned and she handed off the horses to Randler, whose arrows were essentially ineffective anyway. She hit the ground, striking a powerful stance, and began a new routine. She stepped forward once, then back, after which she switched legs for another step forward and back. Her arms reached in directions opposite to her feet, and all the while she kept her head and torso perfectly erect. It was difficult doing the steps with the mud clutching at her boots and interfering with her rhythm. Dariak pulled the water away from the area, drying the land temporarily until the rain soaked it again. Still, it allowed Kitalla to complete her preparations and draw the energies about her.

Gabrion wasn't sure what she and Dariak were doing, but he knew that his sword wouldn't be enough to subdue this monster. He hoped his companions had a plan, so he parried attacks and nipped at the creature's legs when he could, keeping its focus on him at all times. Then all at once, Kitalla screamed and raced across the distance separating them, yelling for Gabrion to flee. He did so, turning only when he heard the ursalor shriek in pain.

Kitalla was covered head to toe in metallic spikes, not unlike an angry porcupus. She had charged and leaped into the air, throwing her whole body into the beast's backside, effectively stabbing it hundreds of times simultaneously. While single wounds barely affected the beast, the large-scale assault hurt it badly. Gabrion returned to the ursalor, realizing suddenly that even though it couldn't reach its paws around to swat at her, if the creature toppled onto its back, Kitalla would be crushed and it didn't look like she was having any luck dislodging herself.

The warrior yelled aloud as he ran in, waving his sword in challenge and cutting into the ursalor's belly. He hacked again and again, bending out of harm's way as the front paws swung for him. He could hear Kitalla straining to free herself, as Dariak chanted spells of his own from a few paces away. In the end, Randler saved Kitalla. The horses had mostly settled and the bard rushed in, grabbing carefully around Kitalla's outer spikes, and pulled her free. She hit the ground with a thud and the two of them sprinted off to catch their breaths. Gabrion, meanwhile kept batting at the bear, preventing it from running after them.

"Ferrizonniar hydallicos binndicus!" Dariak screamed, sweeping his arms in wide arcs before his body. He repeated the incantation three more times, stepping closer to the ursalor with each repetition. The creature's actions grew slower and slower as Dariak worked to freeze the creature's wet fur, trapping it in an icy prison all its own. The difficulty lay in the immense size of the monster and its powerful muscles that kept breaking through the ice itself.

Even slowing it down was helpful to Gabrion, however, and as the ursalor struggled against the freezing menace, it toppled over again, shaking the ground, but making itself more vulnerable. Gabrion dashed around the flailing limbs and sought the massive skull. It was larger than the fully unhinged jaw of a tigroar and he didn't want to think about how much of his body could have fit inside at once. The head tossed around in frustration as Dariak also froze the mud underneath the creature, adding to its slow confinement. The ripping fur echoed as the ursalor tried righting itself, but the pain alone kept it grounded. Gabrion at last reached its skull and he called to the jade within his pocket, declaring his need of a sharp impact at this moment. He didn't know if the jade responded, but he plunged the sword into the creature's head, just below the base of the skull and deep into its brain. With a final spine-chilling wail, the ursalor fell still.

Without waiting, Dariak ran to his horse and threw healing spells in its direction, mending the gashes it had received. Sensing its new master close by, the palomino stood as still as its wounds would allow. They luckily weren't particularly deep and a few repetitions were all Dariak needed to ensure the steed's safety.

Kitalla was particularly exhausted from her dagger-spike routine and quietly mounted her horse, clutching the reins and waiting to be off again. Not long later, the rest of the team joined her, and Randler took the lead toward Vestular.

The best part about their battle with the ursalor was the blood smattered all over Gabrion's clothes. When other creatures ventured nearby and whiffed the scent, they turned and fled. Apparently, if he had survived an ursalor attack, then they were no match for his prowess. Several groups of beasts charged the group, only to scurry in fear once the wind carried the stench to them. Dariak made a mental note, thinking ursalor blood would probably make a powerful spell component, not that he was about to head back toward the monster's corpse and try to claim some.

They pushed the horses hard throughout the wet day and reached Vestular in the middle of the night. The town was dark with the exception of a few street torches, but Randler knew the way to the All Tumble Inn. He let Gabrion enter to negotiate rooms, as he needed to remain incognito. Though there were no other guests at the inn, the keeper only offered one room for lodging and access to the stable for the horses. Kitalla was still weary and didn't even try picking the lock of another room so she could have her own private quarters. The four of them stripped off their wet belongings and wrapped themselves into blankets before settling down for the rest of the night.

Gabrion awoke first the next day and he went to the innkeeper, requesting four meals, which he then brought up to the room. The innkeeper was unhelpful, providing the food and drink but making Gabrion take three trips to carry it all upstairs himself.

The companions ate solemnly, feeling much better now that they were dry and rested, yet knowing a difficult day lay ahead. "We can't tarry here for long," Randler reminded them. "People will be inquisitive and we won't escape notice. If we're going to make a play for the jade, it has to be soon. She must be caught by surprise or all is lost."

Gabrion shook his head sadly. "To think you speak of your own mother with such loathing." He looked at Randler who was about to argue back. Then he remembered Randler telling them about the mercenaries his mother had hired to hunt the bard down. "Sorry, just thinking out loud. You've already explained."

Within the hour, the four had filtered from the inn, one at a time, meeting at a discreet location of Randler's choosing. Once they were there, he pointed out the path that led to his old home, where his mother would be tending to her garden or hiding in the basement with her spells. The only thing they couldn't agree upon was who would go first. Gabrion argued that it should be himself, that he could be a lost traveler in search of aid. Kitalla reminded them that her greatest skill was that of stealth and so she would be the best to lead the march, even though she was still weak and aching from the spike dance. Yet Dariak overruled them, claiming that only he could truly assess the protective wards she would surely have in place. There wasn't much they could argue to that, and so Dariak went ahead with the others not too far behind.

From the outside, Randler's home was disheveled and small. It seemed as if there was only one main room, perhaps a sleeping quarter and a kitchen area, but nothing else. It wasn't tall enough for a second floor and Dariak thought back to Randler's tale of his father being a performer, suddenly realizing that the man had been raised in total squalor. Patches were missing from the roof and the door didn't fit its hinges properly. In some regards, it appeared deserted, but the energies surrounding it said otherwise.

Dariak stretched his hands out wide, sealing his eyes shut to feel the energy patterns. There was an intricate quilt of protection woven through and around the structure, something that must have taken years to properly establish. He wondered how much of it was perpetual and how many aspects of it needed periodic resetting. Yet he couldn't dwell on it for long, for as Randler stepped forward, a particular section of the shields trembled in reaction.

"Stay!" Dariak hissed, trying to wave Randler back. The violet light weaving through the house reminded Dariak vividly of the death spell that Elgris had tried using against him. To think a trap of such magnitude surrounded the house, targeted specifically for Randler! "If you walk through that door, you die," he said over his shoulder. "But how?"

As he pondered a counterspell, the need for one evaporated. Randler's mother opened the front door and crossed her arms in front of her, leaning against the doorjamb, taunting them. "Well, well, well, my little boy returns."

Dariak felt immense power emanating from her. She wasn't a tall woman and her brown hair was a dusty mockery of Randler's. She carried a bit of girth about her waist and her back was somewhat hunched over, as if she had spent too many years poring through spell books. Her clothes were plain, but Dariak couldn't help but wonder if it wasn't intentional. There was too much strength exuding from her for her to be weak and poor.

Randler stepped forward. "Greetings, mother. I hear you've been looking for me."

She cackled with a haughty laugh. "Oh, how droll." She swept her hand across the threshold, inviting them inside. Dariak could sense that the protective spells in the doorway were disrupted now that the portal was opened, but they weren't dispelled. Once that door closed, he knew the death spell and all the others would be back in place.

"This isn't safe," Randler muttered to Dariak.

"It's either walk away or go inside. We can't exactly start attacking, can we?"

"Well?" she demanded, stepping back and holding the door open.

Rolling her eyes, Kitalla pushed past Dariak and Randler and strode inside. The others followed close on her heels. When the door closed, Dariak felt the weave press shut, sealing them inside completely. He wondered how long it would take for him to dispel enough of the enchantments so they could even escape.

"Welcome, friends of Randler, I am Sharice. I would offer you a drink, but no doubt my son will have warned you of poison or another such form of nonsense." She stalked across the room with purpose, heading toward a dividing wall in the center of the floor plan and leaning against it.

"We have come for the shard," Dariak declared, deciding to end the charades.

Sharice cackled wildly. "Have you now? You're powerful enough. Challenge me for it." Her toothy grin was unnerving.

"It's a trap," Randler warned.

"Trap indeed," she nodded. "But then you don't have a choice, really." She turned to Dariak for confirmation. "You already know how well this place is secured."

"It's true. What, then, are the terms of your challenge?"

"My jade for all of yours," she grinned. "Oh yes, I could feel them all quite well when you entered last night. Who was it, do you think, that taught Randler how to find the rest?"

"You lie!" the bard yelled defensively.

"Do I? Well, it isn't like you ever needed my help claiming the shards anyway."

"What do you mean?" Kitalla asked, focusing on the woman's use of the plural.

Sharice clutched her hand to her heart. "He didn't tell you of his great plunder of Halrone's lair?"

"We know of it," Dariak said.

"Mother," Randler interrupted. "Hand over your piece before you're hurt. You have no need of it any longer."

But she wasn't fooled. "How much did he tell you of his heist? Not all of it, I presume?"

Randler stepped forward, face burning red and fists clenched. "I told them what I took and how you tried claiming that treasure from me. I couldn't let you have it."

"'That treasure'? Son, you do craft your words well. I see now that you told them only a part of the whole, isn't that so? Shouldn't you entrust your truth to your companions?" She twisted her fingers and threw a silencing shroud over Randler. Dariak noticed she hadn't spoken any words aloud, a sign of a truly gifted mage.

Sharice shook her head and sighed. "My dear son took not one shard from Halrone, but three. He has one with him, I sense." She then looked at Dariak. "Oh, and he gave you one too."

Randler averted his gaze from Dariak, still unable to speak. The mage looked from son to mother. "What do you mean?"

"That one with the sparks. Yes, he took that from Halrone. You didn't know?" She delighted in the colors of Randler's face as the information struck home.

Dariak kept himself composed but Gabrion spoke at last. "Wait! Quereth said they obtained that piece from an anonymous donor." Sharice lifted her spell, wondering how her son would react to the tension suddenly filling the room.

"Yes," Randler warbled. "I had the lightning shard and I turned it over to one of the mages when I reached Pindington. It wasn't supposed to end up in the tower until later, but the mage was apparently too eager to examine it." He faced Dariak, awaiting the brunt of his betrayal.

The mage drew in a steadying breath and released it slowly. Instead of addressing Randler, however, he turned to the bard's mother. "It is in my possession now. Give me your shard and I will let you live."

Sharice laughed and clapped her hands together. "How wonderful! Yes, yes, come along!" She walked around the wall, heading toward a set of stairs that led down.

"Dariak—" Randler started.

"No. You were set on separating the jades and keeping me from uniting them. That was before we even reunited in Pindington." He stepped toward the kitchen and the door into the basement, but then he looked over his shoulder. "But if you do have another one stashed away somewhere, I hope you will lead me to it next." Without waiting for a response, he followed Sharice into the darkness below.

Dariak kept his senses alert and discovered strong magical energies emanating from the walls. He didn't detect any malice in the spells, and he reasoned that they were in place to support the upper and lower structures. His guess wasn't far from the truth, and he realized how close he was when he stepped into Sharice's work room.

The underground chamber was vast. It spanned many yards across in both directions with a high ceiling that held up the house and her land. Worktables and benches lined the walls with blue-lit torches hovering eerily overhead. They cast a strange pallor to the room, making everything seem coated in mist. The tables themselves were covered with numerous spell components and a wide range of exotic plants, complete with massive, thorny vines hanging about.

The woman strode across the floor toward a staff that leaned against the wall. It was a well-whittled staff from a much larger branch, fortified with streamers of wrapped steel and topped with a glowing crystalline crown. Even from where he stood, Dariak could feel the power of the jade within the staff. She had done well to unlock its secrets and, from its pulsing light, it was eager to lash out.

Before the others could join them, Sharice lifted her arms and the stairwell behind Dariak closed shut with an impenetrable wall. It sounded like sliding stone but the odd material was translucent and cold to the touch, not quite glass but something he hadn't ever felt before.

"Once I have your jades," Sharice said by way of greeting, "I will hunt down the rest, starting with the three your friends have with them."

"You know much. You would make a better ally than a foe."

"Only a fool who is about to die says such things," she taunted. "I will have the jades and none will stand in my way." She turned the staff in her hand, creating a large circle of light in front of her. A fog appeared and she was blurred from view.

Dariak pulled his energies tightly around himself and set up some protective spells, not yet understanding what form of attack she would unleash. "I would rid this land of its ban on magic, Sharice. Then you and I could work our skills to their best advantage."

She barked a laugh. "And what makes you think I don't do so already?" She tilted her staff forward and a streak of light shot across the room, piercing through Dariak's outer enchantment. He heard the glasslike sound shattering in his head as part of his protective spell was defeated, but he focused more on how the shield felt as it collapsed, sensing the power that touched it so he could plan a better defense. He then immediately reset the spell in preparation of the next volley, which came soon after.

"You waste your talents here in the underground," Dariak said, trying to keep her using small spells until he learned enough about her magic. "You belong in the world above."

"I don't disagree with you there," she said, lashing out with three spikes this time. Though her spells weren't powerful, she was baiting him into a false sense of confidence, holding back her other skills until the battle erupted completely.

Yet, Dariak wasn't fooled. "You should join us."

Her laughter echoed menacingly in the large room. It hit the walls and bounded back, growing louder and louder, until Dariak was distracted enough that her next spell caught him unawares. The full force of the spell shattered his enchantments, cutting through all but the Shield of Delminor and knocking him down. He knew their conversation was over and he reset the protection spells one last time, knowing that once they were up he needed to attack properly.

Sharice swept her staff around, sending blades of force streaking through the air. Dariak pulled his hands up sharply, magically lifting stones from the ground to block the attack, after which he punched forward, sending the bits of stone at his attacker. Sharice easily dodged the assault, but Dariak launched ice spikes and caught her off guard.

The woman threw herself to the ground, bringing her staff over her body, further obscuring her from view. To Dariak, she was merely a glowing blur across the way and he knew that if she set down her staff he might not be able to see her at all.

He called to the moisture in the air, drawing strength from the water jade. The humidity deepened until a slow rain fell inside the chamber. A fierce wind retaliated and blew the rain into his face, blinding him. However, he had expected it, having sensed the power of air behind the initial attacks. Dariak drew the water from his eyes and spun it down his body, linking it to the protective wards already in place.

Sharice was on her feet again, tightening the air into sharp darts that she sent through the room, chipping into Dariak's shields. She summoned with such fury that Dariak was hard-pressed to deflect them all. A few slipped through the wards, breaking a chink in the Shield of Delminor and scoring a hit on his arm. It was minor, but if she could cut through him with simple air darts, her stronger spells would be fearsome indeed.

Once the rain spell ran its course, Dariak pulled the energies toward him, cooling the wet floor until an icy coating was left behind. Sharice cursed as she lost her footing, but she recovered quickly enough by blasting into the layer of ice with more air darts, breaking the surface into a slushy mess. Swinging her arms around her body, she summoned a tornado, which carried the slush toward Dariak, pelting him and knocking him down.

"Is that all you have, little mage?" she yelled. "I haven't even begun yet!"

Dariak stood up, thoroughly soaked. Sharice set her staff on the ground and raised her hands, chanting aloud for the first time. Her fingers curled angrily and lashed out at Dariak, sending searing bolts of lightning across the room. She cackled madly during the blinding flash, walking forward as her eyes readjusted to the light, ready to step up to her fallen foe.

But Dariak was uninjured. The lightning jade drew in the energy and hummed deeply within Dariak's pocket. "I see you spent some time with the jade before you lost it to Halrone," he commented.

She snarled. "Lost it? Fool, I loaned it to him. How else could I become stronger unless I had others who could challenge me? You don't become powerful by squashing ants." She eyed him dangerously, then growled again. "I see it takes a liking to you, protecting you. No matter."

While she spoke, Dariak readied his next spell. He reached out for the blue flames along the wall and pulled their energies forward into a blazing azure inferno. Sharice caught the brunt of the blast and toppled over. Angrily, she brought her hands up, redirecting the air in the room to send the flames toward Dariak, who then pushed his hands away and returned the flames to their source.

Sharice reclaimed her staff and drew an intricate symbol in the air with its crowning light. At once, the air thinned and she all but vanished from sight completely. Dariak prepared his fire dart spell and sent out cursory shots, trying to locate her. She laughed mockingly from behind him, but when he turned and fired, no one was there. Her laughter sounded randomly throughout the room, as if she were in all places at once. He remembered the way her laughter had echoed from the walls at the start of the battle. With the added control of air in the room, he realized she could manipulate her sounds.

Dariak pulled another fiery blast from the blue flames and lit a blazing fireball toward one end of the chamber, hoping he could at least sequester her into a smaller zone. Wind blew in and scattered the flames, but he tried again anyway. With each successive fireball, he noticed the direction of the wind and he used it to locate his target. The floor was still wet and, waiting until each fiery blast distracted her, he turned specific patches to ice again.

Yet the wind wasn't erratic or purely defensive. Sharice was slowly creating a large whirlwind through the room and Dariak didn't notice until too late. The wind whipped at him, snagging his robe and heaving him up into the air. He hovered toward the ceiling and then plummeted harshly to the ground. Before he could recover, the process repeated itself, leaving him bruised and gasping.

Cackling echoed around the room and Dariak reached for more spell components from his pockets, but his supplies for protection spells were running low. He withdrew a knob of blackroot and cast it outward, seeking to blind her from where he thought she stood. He felt the spell take hold, glad at least that he had correctly ascertained her position.

"Fool," she accused again. "Shadow magic? Don't you think I had access to that jade as well? Here, let me show you shadow magic!"

The room filled with the ominous sounds of malevolent chanting. Dariak slapped his hands onto the ground and stood up, drawing the stony floor with him. He didn't send it outward this time, but spun in a deep circle, continuously pulling the stone closer and closer until it covered him from head toe, essentially turning him into a rock golem.

Sharice was caught in the throes of her spell and unleashed a bolt of darkness that drew all the light from the room, seeking Dariak next in order to draw the light from within him as well. His stony coating deflected the spell, but she had anticipated some form of defense and was already casting the spell again. Dariak didn't have time to reset the stone shield before the next death bolt flashed forward.

Dariak withdrew the lightning jade, fanning the outer sparks with his hand and pleading for help. The electricity shot up and around him, binding him in a glowing cage that numbed him when he touched it. The shadow struck the light and a violent boom shook the walls.

Sharice screamed in fury, racing toward him, staff in hand and no longer obscured by darkness. She moved impossibly fast, propelled by the wind she summoned, making her body light and fluid. The staff crashed into Dariak, ringing his head with a deep thud. He kicked out, but she was already gone, circling around and batting at him again. He raised his arm, calling the earth for protection. His arm solidified and when the staff struck it cracked loudly as if hitting stone. Sharice pulled back and swept again, moving too quickly for Dariak to stop her.

Pulling energy from the water and earth, Dariak created a thick muddy paste and tossed it up and around him, hoping at least to slow her down. Two slices through with her staff, however, and the mess was gone. He tried turning the mud into a sticky sludge, but her speed overpowered it and it didn't slow her down at all.

With each swing of the staff, she added another spell. Air darts pelted him from above, after which thorns appeared, shooting out from vines that were hanging on the wall. Dariak deflected the attacks the best he could, but the onslaught was so fast he wasn't sure he could fend them all off.

The staff struck his arm painfully, disrupting a shielding spell he was summoning. He had survived the crumbling Prisoner's Tower; how could this one woman be beating him into submission? Furious with himself, Dariak reached deep within, touching each jade in turn and asking for help. He lingered with the lightning jade, whose power was still new to him. He pulled it forth and beckoned to the flickering light.

Sharice balked at the feeble sparks leaking from the jade, then doubled her efforts by encasing Dariak in a dark, blinding sphere and continuing to float around rapidly, striking him hard. She reached across the room with her powers and drew on the plant life that waited so tamely on her workbenches. The vines were already spewing their thorns, but now she called for the flowers to release their toxins. She channeled the disruptive fragrances with sharp jabs of air, bringing the poisonous fumes directly within Dariak's darkened globe.

He could smell the poisons before they fully came within his area, thus he drew as deep a breath as he could manage, then held it as he focused the rest of his thoughts into the lightning jade. He knew he needed something explosively powerful in order to defeat Sharice, and the earth and water were more defensive than offensive. Calling to the torches had proven fruitless, and though she had used an electric blast of her own, Dariak doubted she had ever seen the jade unleash the level of fury he had witnessed at the top of the Prisoner's Tower.

As the poisonous fumes surrounded him, making his eyes water terribly, Dariak concentrated to block out all other sensations. In a detached manner, he understood that while he remained within the shadow orb, he was exposed to noxious fumes that would give him only moments to live. He also realized that Sharice was compressing the air around him, making him feel heavy and sluggish. Plus, she had her flailing staff in hand, its glowing head cutting through the darkness occasionally and cracking against him.

None of it mattered. Without the strength of the lightning jade, he would run out of stamina soon anyway, even if he escaped the darkened sphere and found clean air. Channeling his mind into the sparking crystal, Dariak recalled the searing pain that had lanced through him at the tower, and not just the initial moments of numbness followed by scorching pain; he remembered the pain he felt of dying. He called to the lightning to give him the strength he needed to overcome this foe and to live. He knew it was risky, for the lightning jade had taken his life once. That time it had restored him, but there was no guarantee it could revive him a second time. He would have to entrust the quest for the jades to his companions, hoping they would fulfill his destiny if he could not.

The jade sparked with blinding fury, and with a deafening crack, the air within the shadow globe vanished into a vacuum. Dariak felt his insides pulled apart from the force and rather than fight it, he accepted the call of the electricity, which erupted from the jade and ran through his body. He felt the power tingle from head to toe, erasing all his physical memories of how things felt and worked. He no longer had legs or arms. There was no sense of sight or sound.

He became a throbbing ball of energy.

All Dariak could do was will himself in various directions, but he couldn't see where he was going, only sense disturbances of power. Surrounding him was a spherical field that hindered him, so he willed it asunder and so it went, obliterated by the light he had become. The torches called to him from the sides of the room. He leaned toward one and his body streaked across the chamber to the blue flame, trailing deep thunder. Nothing happened when he struck the fire, however, so he hesitated, building up his strength and sensing another disturbance nearby.

The vines and flowers continued to release their thorns and toxins, and Dariak flashed over to them, burning them instantly to ash. He couldn't control himself more than that. One tilt and he blasted across the room, eager to bring destruction to the next flux of energy. He could only sense a narrow pathway in front of him, however, so he couldn't tell quite where in the room the other jade was located. He knew nothing of Sharice, but felt energies being pulled from one end of the room toward the other. Eagerly, he followed them.

With a blinding streak, Dariak's electrified body shot across the vast room, chasing after a flurry of energy that whirled in a tight cyclone, but it wasn't a true source of power, he realized after reaching it. It was a spell meant to contain him. But he was pure energy now. He couldn't be contained. He tilted back and blazed across the room, his powerful thunder shaking the walls and threatening to bring them down.

Each passing across the room weakened him. He knew that much but not much else. More power existed in the chamber and he pushed ahead, crashing into the barrier Sharice had erected at the stairwell and exploding it into pieces. He was vaguely aware that it was a supremely dense wall of air held together by her will alone, but he couldn't appreciate the craft of it, for a sheath of darkness fell over him.

The barely human aspect left of him told Dariak that the dark magic should have killed him. It was full of malice and the intent to paralyze his life functions, making them all forget their individual jobs and leaving him a lifeless mass on the floor. The rest of Dariak, however, saw the attack as a violation of its own invigorating strength. The lightning traced the spell back to its source and Dariak hungrily leaped across the room, searing a violent path of his own.

As he reached the great source of the power, however, something distracted him. It was relatively small, but it drew him so forcefully he couldn't stop himself. He crashed against a thin filament and wound upward in a tight, deep spiral, cresting at the top and exploding outward. He heard a terrified scream and it took him a moment to realize it wasn't his own and that there was someone else in the room with him. He understood slowly that as the lightning faded away, his own senses started to return.

Fear welled inside of him, for he knew that with all the force rushing through his body, he was due for a terrible amount of pain once he could feel again. He didn't want it to happen. He focused his thoughts on the other energy sources in the room, finding one very close by and flashing himself toward it, seeking to add its power to his own, thereby prolonging the spell. But he didn't have the strength to pull the power from its source, perhaps because it was Sharice, tightly curled in a ball on the floor, badly burned and using every protective spell in her arsenal to keep herself alive.

Without an ample power supply, the lightning faded and Dariak crashed in a heap, his body blissfully numb for the moment. He glanced around the oversized chamber, seeing burn marks streaked all across the floor and ceiling in numerous directions. The distance he had covered! Beside him, near Sharice's huddled form, was her staff with the winding metal bands that had drawn him in and forced him to spiral up its length until he erupted out the top of the staff. Though the upper portion of the staff was blown apart, the jade itself lingered, pulsating wildly with Dariak so close by. He reached out and claimed the clear jade, feeling an odd breeze exuding from its surface. Without a word, he pocketed it, turning at last to Sharice.

The woman was covered in massive burns from head to toe and energies swirled around her body, so tightly woven to protect herself, she probably didn't even realize that the fight was over. Dariak reached out to touch her tentatively, but a shadowy outer covering prevented him from making contact. There was nothing he could do for her; he couldn't even stand on his own.

But at least he had claimed her jade.

CHAPTER 3

Dinner with Mother

THE WARDS ENCASING the house were still intact and because Sharice hadn't willed them to leave, the travelers were trapped unless Dariak could find a way to undo them. The mage was exhausted, however, and his body wasn't responding well to his demands. Gabrion had to practically shout in his ear to be heard, but Dariak had no suggestions yet for what he needed. Gabrion propped him up on an armchair, making sure he was secure before helping the others with Sharice.

The woman's body was hard to look at, she was so burned. Layers of flesh rolled back, some of it fused with patches of cloth. Ash and steam rose from her frizzled hair and her head lolled limply as they moved her. If she wasn't still breathing, they would have assumed the worst.

Randler was at a loss. His mother had rejected him, sending bounty hunters after him to claim his pieces of jade even if it meant killing him. Yet seeing her in this condition broke his heart all over again. He wanted to help her somehow, so he tried drawing her pain away with the shadow jade as Kitalla gently tapped her face to awaken her. It took a while, but her eyes opened, then widened fearfully once she realized she was bound. Moments later, pain followed the fear, as tears streamed from her eyes. Randler couldn't bear it, so he pulled the gag from her mouth, asking what he could do to help.

"Where is he?" she hissed.

"What? Dariak? Over there."

"Alive?"

"Yes."

She growled, muttering under her breath. "Release me so I may heal myself." When he hesitated, she snarled, "Now!"

Kitalla had daggers ready as Randler untied the ropes. Sharice immediately cast a few spells to numb her agony, then set about promoting healing within her. As she felt the extent of the damage, she grumbled again, knowing she would need more help than her ability alone could handle.

"Is there another mage among you? No, what am I saying," she answered herself. "Yet you each carry a shard. Very interesting." She sniffed at Kitalla. "Haven't met yours yet. Mind handing it over and letting me look at it?"

"Sure," Kitalla replied sardonically, "but it won't help your quivering corpse much." She emphasized her threat by whirling her daggers around her fingers.

Sharice grinned. "Well then, maybe some other time. So where is he?" It was a needless question as he was across the room in a chair, straining to bring the energies about himself, especially now that she was on her feet again.

Dariak clenched his fists and sought the power of the earth jade, pulling dust toward him in the only form of protective shield he could muster. He eyed the charred woman ferociously, hoping at least to portray a sense of strength, even if he didn't feel it.

"Peace, mage," she said, coming closer. "You defeated me fairly. Killing you now would prevent me from learning more from you. You do recall my comment about squashing ants, don't you?" She stared at him carefully. "You'd be better off putting your skills toward healing than defense. I'll help." And she did, bringing her hands about and sending healing energies into him.

The two were greatly weakened from their bout, but as they sent healing back and forth, they regained enough of their strength to move about freely, though Dariak still struggled to hear anything. The burns on Sharice's skin looked horrible, but magic stopped them from becoming infected and from hurting. Hardly any of the plants in the basement had survived Dariak's lightning blitz around the room, and so Randler, no longer needing to keep his identity hidden, went to secure some herbs from town, knowing he could do so the quickest.

The next few hours were tense as Gabrion and Kitalla kept a constant vigil on Sharice, ensuring she didn't act in any untoward manner, though they understood that their knowledge of spells was so limited they wouldn't know a harmful spell until too late. Still, keeping weapons trained on her made them feel safer, and Dariak seemed content with the situation. When Randler returned with all the supplies they required, the team worked at creating salves to mend Sharice's burns and to tend to puncture wounds Dariak had suffered from the air darts and thorns, as well as his scrapes from being tossed by the powerful winds. With all the major work out of the way, Randler made a quick meal, needing to eat but anxious for them to be on their way again.

"So, what happens now?" Sharice ventured once the food was gone.

"We continue our mission," Dariak said.

"Collecting the other shards, no doubt?" she surmised. "Randler, dear, where did you put that other one?"

The bard shook his head. "I'll tell them once we're off, mother."

"Oh, don't want my pets finding it first?"

Kitalla snorted. "Those rogues you sent? Don't make me laugh. Even if they did get to it first, they wouldn't manage to keep it for long."

"Well, I can see that's true, especially with him around," Sharice commented, looking pointedly at Dariak. "Very powerful, indeed, young mage. You're almost like a conduit for the jades. A very rare skill, I must say."

"Mother," Randler said with a warning note in his voice.

"I'm just paying the man a compliment. Mind yourself, child," she scolded. "Yes, my husband's father told great, wild tales about such things. Perhaps Randler has shared some with you on the journey?"

It felt like an ominous opening to a new branch of conversation and no one really wanted to engage with the woman, but sitting in awkward silence was worse. "Of course, Sharice," Dariak said, feeling he should keep the focus on himself. "We've heard quite a few good tales."

She cleared her throat and set down her glass, then she spoke in verse, unable to sing well:

With bloody blade, the thirsty king did slay a host of men.
He cut them down, then faced the next, and did it all again.
He razed the towns, instilling fear, no end was there in sight
until a single lady friend happened upon him there one night.

Friends they were when they were young, meeting in a glade.
Parted then for years to come, while he fine-tuned his blade.
She begged of him to change his way and seek a greater peace
ensuring him a better way for him to find release.

The two were wed among their dreams of starting a new land
in which the populace would come to think was rather grand.
But how they sought that foolish wish could not have been more wrong,
for in the end the two of them simply could not get along.

The children born within those years were scattered now between them,
with an angry borderline that tore apart their kingdom.
The girl went with her saddened mother to hone her magic gift
and so a war was rashly fought to ensure their family's rift.

The boy, left with his father, rode at his father's side
so he was there that very day, the day his sister died.
A mage, she was, thus casting spells gave her a greater strength
and so the nasty king did tear her down at any length.

Horrified at watching his poor father's butchery,
The little boy left him then, seeking sanctuary.
He hid for years, grew to a man, gave birth to many sons.
Most of those did die in wars, except the peaceful ones.

They carried on their lineage from times so long ago,
where their blood did soak the lands, with nowhere else to go.
So who among those children lived to carry on and strive?
Perhaps that is the answer to the Long-Forgotten Tribe.

"So you're saying," Gabrion spoke at the end, "that a descendent of Kallisor and Hathreneir is still among us today?"

"Oh yes," Sharice agreed. "But good luck figuring that one out. It does trace back quite a few years."

"You're not suggesting that Dariak is descended of the line?" Gabrion asked. "You said he was a conduit for the jades and all."

Sharice laughed. "Dear me, no. Were you not listening? The line of the Forgotten Tribe is loaded with cowards! Dariak is no timid child. Well, it's all fantasy anyway, passed down through the years with no way of finding out how much might ever be true."

"Yet you bothered to learn it," Randler commented.

His mother chortled. "With all the times your grandfather sputtered such nonsense, how could I not?" Randler's seething seemed to delight her. "Now, there was a point to telling you that in any event. Bloodlines matter. If you, young mage, have a link to the jades, then you must be connected to their past."

Dariak withheld the information that his father was the mage who had summoned the colossus in the last Great War, though part of him wondered if she suspected it anyway. "Perhaps that could give me an edge," he said instead.

"Certainly so," she said, disappointed with his vague response. "With your gifts, you would do well in the Underground."

Dariak nodded and rose to his feet. "That may be, but as I said earlier, I would rather not have to. In any case, we need to be moving on."

Sharice pouted. "Come in, swipe my jade, and run off without so much as a thank you. Such poor manners."

"Because attacking my friend was mannerly!" Randler shouted. His rush of anger caught the room off-guard, but Sharice laughed at the outburst. "Come on," he said to the others, heading for the door.

With a shrug, Sharice lowered the defensive wards, which allowed them to depart unhindered. "Good luck, little boy," she called out to Randler. "Once your task is done, do bring ma-ma the jades, won't you, dear?"

It was an awkward departure and Randler stalked off angrily, chased by Dariak, whose body ached thoroughly despite all the healing. "Where to now?"

"Ha!" the bard barked. "Got one shard, off to the next!" He shook his head. "Is it a hunger for you mages or what?"

Dariak's tone was cold and his eyes unflinching. "I was rather thinking of a place to spend the night, but if you'd prefer heading right off, I can manage."

Randler turned to look at Dariak. "It's—I… I'm sorry."

Kitalla stepped in and shoved the two of them apart. "Enough of this nonsense, you two. Get me to a place with some ale." She winked back at Gabrion. "Do you feel up to putting on a show tonight?"

The warrior thought back to his role as jester in Warringer and he chuckled. "I think I'll pass. It's not like you've been practicing your throwing lately."

"True, true," she said, grabbing Randler's arm and dragging him from the spot. "So, maybe you could help me with some new music. The ones I play in my head need more tempo. I was thinking something along the lines of this…" She made fast clucking sounds as they stepped away.

Gabrion patted Dariak on the shoulder. "He's upset. He'll be fine."

The mage sighed. "I suppose. When you see how the power turned her into something wild and hungry, it's not hard to imagine why he's worried. You should have felt the amount of energy wrapped around her house and how she pulled force from all directions during our battle. I couldn't beat her without the jades. I needed all three of mine to keep up with her, and she was barely using hers."

"She's had more practice."

"Yes, but what will become of me once I've had that practice? Would I let a foe walk away so he can become stronger, in the hopes of facing off against him someday and defeating him? Will I become someone just living to become more powerful?"

Gabrion stopped and turned Dariak to face him. "You might. If you were alone. But you aren't. We're with you, Dariak, and we'll keep you in check."

"But how can you be so sure?"

"You're conflicted about it, so you have a conscience. I'll keep reminding you of that." He nodded toward Randler up ahead. "Besides, I think his opinion matters enough to you that you'll be more careful than his mother."

Dariak took a deep breath. "Thanks, Gabrion." He eyed the warrior warmly. "You know, Mira's a lucky girl."

CHAPTER 4

En Route to Randler's Hideout

THE BATTLE AGAINST Sharice left Dariak feeling terribly weak. They remained in Vestular only for a few days, avoiding further contact with Randler's mother, then heading off again for the next piece of jade. Randler promised Dariak to lead him to the other shard he had claimed, which was resting in his hiding place to the southwest, where the innkeeper in Warringer had tried directing Dariak long ago.

"It will only take us a few days to reach it," the bard promised.

Dariak nodded, holding firmly to the words. He needed Randler to be on his side now more than ever before. His whole body was disobeying him and he wondered if he hadn't permanently harmed himself in his battle with Sharice. "We'll get there," he said simply.

Kitalla was also fighting against her pains. Though she had received an unprecedented amount of healing in Pindington, her body still raged against Grenthar's tortures and her efforts against the ursalor. It irritated her endlessly, and seeing Dariak in a similar state both angered her and gave her solace. Her impatience with herself occasionally manifested itself in outrages against Dariak's whimpers. Yet other times, she was the most nurturing of the group.

Gabrion, meanwhile, pushed ever onward with a vacant look in his eyes. "Mira is gone from me now," he had confided in Randler one day, "but I would seek her anyway, to know for certain where her end came." Beyond that, the warrior said little.

Rain had come and gone, tamping the dirt down firmly and giving the horses a solid ground to tread. The foursome made respectable progress toward Randler's hideout, until Gabrion called an alarm. "Reptigons approaching."

"And more," Kitalla added with a nod toward the west, where a pack of firegnats swarmed in. The tiny fliers were practically impossible to stun or avoid and their bites were laced with a mild venom that wasn't overtly poisonous, but caused the sensation of severe pain in the area of attack. They were more of a distraction than a threat, but with the fierce lizards nearby, they were a distraction that couldn't be afforded.

Dariak, twitching and cursing himself for it, swept his arms about, calling forth to the earth jade in his chest pocket. He drew the spell around himself and then projected similar blocking shields around his companions. Though he didn't feel much up to the reptigon attack, at least the Shield of Delminor would protect them from the firegnats.

Randler's bow sang with arrow flight. Deadly projectiles soared through the air, reducing the imposing threat before any melee could even begin. His prowess with a bow was impressive indeed, and he attributed it to the strength of his fingers from years of strumming his lute. A constant rain of arrows fell from the sky, as Kitalla and Gabrion dismounted and readied their weapons.

Kitalla's recent success with her dance patterns filled her with a longing to use the power again. Yet the attack against the ursalor had left her whole body aching with tiny pinpricks. She wasn't ready to try such an attack again, and reptigons weren't known for their intellect, so she figured her other moves would be useless against them. Daggers in hand, she crouched low as the reptigons hurried closer on their speedy legs and prepared to pounce.

Gabrion slashed out with his long sword, beheading two of the slithering beasts with one attack. The wiry bodies kept wriggling forward as if denying the death that awaited them. Dariak called out and warned him not to touch the ichor that oozed from the wounds, for it was highly acidic. The mage still had the super-condensed venom in his robes from his experiments in the Prisoner's Tower. He hadn't yet decided upon a use for the serum, but he knew well that the blood of the reptigon was not to be carelessly tampered with.

The horses were becoming more accustomed to battle, but Dariak took the reins of the others to ensure they didn't bolt. Gabrion's horse, however, seemed to feel that its master was more important and it stalked away to remain near the warrior, which unfortunately put it in line with the incoming firegnats. Seeing the plight, Dariak cast another Shield of Delminor around the horse so the insects wouldn't bite it and cause it to start thrashing violently. Much to Dariak's surprise, however, the firegnats were easily able to breach the protective spell and the bites sent furious pain into the equine friend.

The horse's cry of terror rent the air and created panic among the others. It was all Dariak could do to keep his horse calm and not lose the reins of the other two beasts of burden. He tried weighing the horses down with the earth jade, but he was simply too weak to pull the energies forth properly. He cast his thoughts to the other jades, wondering if water would soothe the bites of the firegnats. With a sweep of his hands, he called to the humidity in the air to condense around the afflicted horse, and to his surprise, the horse was doused with water. He didn't have time to contemplate the effect, for the other horses were pulling away. Randler intervened, running over and grabbing his mare and soothing her, then taking the reins of Kitalla's mount. With deft hand strokes, the bard was able to calm them almost immediately.

Kitalla, heeding Dariak's earlier warning, dipped low under a leaping reptigon and batted it toward Gabrion with the flat edges of her daggers. The warrior side-stepped and swung his arms down, knocking the creatures away from the group. Only a few remained, and it wasn't much later that the team was able to regroup and continue on their way.

The firegnats followed them relentlessly for the next few hours, nipping forcefully at the horses and the humans. Dariak's protection spells were all but useless against them, and as the failures piled up on his conscience, he sank into a sullen mood that he could not shake. Of all the spells to fail him, his father's own shield spell was the most painful to endure. His randomly twitching muscles didn't help matters, and he feared he would have to return to Sharice to seek treatment from their battle. He figured she was the most experienced mage in all of Kallisor and so she might have some sort of answer, though he would probably have to battle her for it.

But it wasn't an option at the moment. The team progressed to the southwest and, though the firegnats were constant companions, they weren't taking any detours unless absolutely necessary. It helped that Dariak knew the lore of the firegnats and that their stings were only temporary and brief. Of course, that didn't stop the cries of pain when the little creatures hit their marks.

Thinking of Sharice, Dariak turned his mind toward the wind shard he had claimed from her. He called to it and twisted his fingers into the air to create a small whirlwind that would distract the bugs, but he hadn't spent any time communing with the jade, and the need wasn't so pressing that it would offer its strength to him on its own. The amateur puffs of wind were no more than useless zephyrs, and Dariak wondered if the firegnats merely laughed at his attempts.

As the day wore on, even the firegnats grew bored, or at least enough of them had eaten from the team's flesh that the swarm moved on at last. The four of them rode on a little longer to ensure they were clear, and then they set up a much-needed camp. It had been an annoying ride all afternoon and the chance to relax was a welcome one.

Gabrion and Randler went off for food while Kitalla and Dariak arranged wood for a fire and prepared the cooking utensils. "What are you doing?" Kitalla asked.

Shrugging, Dariak kept striking flint to stone. "Starting a fire."

"Yeah," she said slowly. "But you can do that by twiddling your thumbs, can't you?"

"It's more of a flourish of the fingers," he corrected solemnly, "but I don't know that I can do it today."

"You live and breathe that fire dart spell. Why stop now?"

He lowered his head but didn't answer.

She saw his distress and she lowered her voice to ask, "Something wrong with your magic?"

He nodded imperceptibly. "The magic I have the most experience with and knowledge of, and I couldn't do anything with it all day." He looked at her confused expression. "Those firegnats should have bounced right off of us."

"I figured that's what you meant," she frowned. "I wonder why."

"That... fight. Against Randler's mother. Something happened to me there. I became this wild ball of energy. It's put my whole self off. I keep twitching and feeling numb at odd times, in random places. Like, this spot right here is suddenly numb," he said, pointing to the center of his forearm. "I think I overdid it back there. I mean, what if I don't recover?"

Kitalla growled and shoved him hard. "Shut up! You're an idiot if you think you're done for. And if you are, then roll over and die right now! I have no use for you, pathetic scrap." She paused, realized what she was saying, and grabbed her head uttering a deep groan. "No, no. Not what I wanted to say."

"True enough, nonetheless," he admitted. "Enough self-pity for me. I have a job to do anyway, don't I?"

She eyed him for a moment and then nodded. "Assemble the jades? Save the world?"

"That's the one."

She smacked him again. "Ha!" she barked. "You're only alive because you have more to teach me. Quit now and I'll kill you myself."

He bore into her eyes and realized that though she was teasing him, part of her was serious. "So what's your deal anyway? Why the lust for power?"

Kitalla's answer was to hit him a third time and stalk off, leaving the mage to his own thoughts. He poked at the timid fire, feeling its energy pulsing within the sticks and twigs. His disappointment from the day kept him from considering the jades at the moment. He wanted control over his twitching, numbing body, pulling himself together to keep from falling apart. He had been questing for so many months now that he wasn't entirely sure he knew what he wanted anymore. The sovereigns ruled their lands in ways they saw fit. Did it really matter if magic was never freely used in Kallisor? Wasn't Hathreneir a good enough place for mages? Weren't there plenty of opportunities for mages to wield their craft in his homeland?

It was the endless warring that was the problem, he reminded himself. Though the people of the land had apparently spawned from the ideals of two royals centuries ago, if Randler's tales were true, they couldn't abide each other's company. He needed to finish his father's work, to assemble the jades, and to remove the need for war.

Yet Randler's arguments were right, as well. Force wasn't going to fix things. Summoning the colossus wouldn't be the end of the matter. He needed a means of making the two kingdoms respect each other. Months ago, he would have scoffed at the idea, feeling that Kallisorians were all worthless and needed to succumb to great Hathreneir. Yet working with Gabrion, Kitalla, and now Randler, he saw merit in their ways and he understood they were people, not any different from those in his own land.

He thought then of the team's dynamic. Where he bolstered the team's offense and defense—when his magic didn't fail, that is—Gabrion went in with a pure heart and sheer force. Kitalla's cunning and agility, plus her mystical dance skill, gave them all an edge he couldn't match on his own. He knew full well that her actions had protected and saved them all during various battles. Then there was Randler, adding his knowledge of lore to the group and proposing alternate ideals to his own. His skills as an archer and an entertainer helped keep them in high spirits, for not only did they sing and clap at camp, but just as with the reptigons that day, the bard managed to weaken the enemy forces before they needed to engage them at all. Not to mention, he smiled to himself, the man was extremely alluring.

They were a team because they each contributed their strengths to the whole unit. It was like the jades themselves, each with their own abilities that would come together to create the colossus. So, too, must the people of the land find ways of working together across the borders. They needed to find and share their strengths for the greater good, to share resources, to end the wars, and to start out on a new path.

Dariak was so caught up in his epiphany, he didn't realize he had been swinging his hands, inadvertently augmenting the fire in front of him. Now, it rose to a blazing, spiraling column, swirling in the air and alerting all the land to their presence.

"Put it out, you moron!" Kitalla shouted at him. "You *want* all the patrols to come take us in? Not sure if I can break you out of the royal dungeons again! *Turn it off!*"

Embarrassed, Dariak reversed his hand motions in order to quell the pulsing energies. To that end, he tapped the water jade with his mind, seeking its help, and soon the campfire returned to its complacent glow. Gabrion and Randler sprinted back moments later.

"What was that?" Gabrion gasped. "Are you sure you're fine?"

The mage nodded, abashed. "I was lost in thought. Sorry."

"Not to worry," Randler chimed in, "we were heading back anyway. You just got us here a little sooner." He cast warning glances at Kitalla and Gabrion, who shook their heads and dismissed the issue.

At once, the team set about preparing dinner and laying out the next course of action. They still needed to reach Randler's cave and retrieve the last of the jades he had claimed. After establishing the order of the watch for the night, the team settled into their routines, hoping to pass the night peacefully.

But Dariak's inadvertent signal had indeed alerted the nearby patrols. Magic use was essentially forbidden in Kallisor and no other explanation would hold for a display of that magnitude. Randler had taken first watch as usual, pulling out his lute and strumming a warm lullaby. He continued the tune for a while, pausing only to stoke the fire and take some water. But soon the night air filled with the sounds of horses and clanking armor.

Alert for such an attack, Kitalla was already on her feet when Randler sounded the alarm. It took seconds for them to ready their weapons and to arrange themselves into a fighting stance, keeping the horses behind them and out of harm's way. The patrol was coming from the southeast, but they suspected it wouldn't be the only one that would arrive.

"Halt, fiends!" the guard captain sneered upon arrival. "I place you under arrest for the use of magical energies. Lay down your weapons and come peaceably or meet your doom."

Gabrion whispered back to Dariak, "They're well protected against you."

"Silence!" the man demanded.

Kitalla released a loud sigh. "There are only nine of you. You don't stand a chance against us. Go home and have your wives bake you some bread. Better that than dying here."

"Impudence!" he barked, but he didn't issue the order to attack. "Whatever your skills, you will succumb to the law of our lord king. Now stay your weapons!"

Kitalla turned to Gabrion. "I don't think he understands. Can I kill one of them to make my point?"

It took all of the warrior's concentration not to laugh at her flippant retort. "If they raise a sword against any of us, you can kill the usual four."

The thief grinned and added a malicious cackle for effect. "Raise your sword, armored one. Go on, I dare you! Please!"

The sheer audacity of it broke the man's resolve. His horse sensed his hesitation and stepped back a pace as he glanced at his troop, wondering if the companions were all bluff. He was a seasoned soldier and he could sense the deep camaraderie between them. He wavered only for a moment more before raising his sword and calling for the attack.

True to her word, Kitalla's hands flicked forward and daggers sailed through the air, killing two soldiers instantly and unseating two others. Randler had a mace at the ready, for arrows wouldn't be much use at the moment. Gabrion's sword flashed and dispatched two more fighters from their mounts. The captain, bewildered by the instant turn of events, snapped his reins and ignored Kitalla and Gabrion, racing directly for the mage among them.

Dariak had been pulling on the energies through the entire verbal exchange, even knowing that his spells had been failing or going haywire all day. The Shield of Delminor was ineffective, but because he had witnessed it earlier, he looked for the fault in the energy weave and sensed immediately that it wouldn't do more than protect him from a scraped knee, if even that. Thinking quickly, he brought his arms up and wide, mimicking the swell of a tide, and then spun full circle, reaching out for the oncoming soldier. A gush of water issued forth, spraying horse and rider, but they weren't deterred at all. The man and horse were covered in special magic-resistant armor, not unlike the protective wards in the Prisoner's Tower that had kept him trapped within. The spell struck and fell, dampening the land, but not hindering the attacker at all. Randler tried to intervene, but Dariak insisted otherwise, sending him to join the rest of the fray.

Dariak didn't want to do it, but the horseback rider was coming closer so fast, he didn't have time to think of other consequences. His twitching and numb-patched body understood the need, and so it cooperated with him as he tapped into the lightning jade. The erratic energy of the jade raced instantly through his body, but he had no intention of turning back into a ball of chain lightning. Instead, he sent the energy burst forth out of his body and into the air between himself and the rider. A blinding sphere of light blazed to life and terrified the man's horse, causing it to buck and veer away. The spell didn't last for long, but at least it had saved the mage. Unfortunately, its light acted as a second beacon, and another nearby patrol rode in minutes later to investigate.

Gabrion and Kitalla, meanwhile, were dipping in and around the remaining guards. It was a tougher fight than others they had experienced against the king's soldiers. As he slashed and ducked, then spun about, Gabrion wondered about it, knowing he ought to be focused instead on the battle but unable to stop himself. It seemed to him that the king was not sending the best fighters off to the war, but rather the lesser ones. The more-seasoned of the troops were instead kept near the king's capitol city in order to protect himself. At least, so it seemed as he took a few hits and doled out several of his own.

Kitalla had come to the same conclusion but was less surprised by it. Instead, she focused on lunging and stretching as much as possible, keeping herself limber and ready for more. She understood that Dariak's second blast of unnatural light would ensure they had a busy time of it tonight.

"Incoming!" Randler hollered moments later. He faced off against one of the wounded soldiers from Kitalla's first attack, but his sensitive ears heard the hooves from the north. He smashed his mace against the man's helmet and pulled back, turning to help Dariak who was struggling against the guard captain.

The man had fallen from his frightened horse and he moved a little sluggishly through his pain, but he had an angry glimmer in his eye that alerted Dariak to the man's determination. This battle was going to end in death—either his or the soldier's. The mage summoned his fire darts, casting them outward to distract his foe, but the guard had clearly been trained for such things, and he trusted deeply in the protection his armor gave him. His only reaction to the fire darts was to squint against the light.

Dariak backed away, fumbling in his pocket for a dagger. He wasn't ready for this. He relied on his magic. There wasn't much he could do here. A quick glance showed him that the others were busy, especially as the northern patrol rode in and joined the fray. Even Randler was splattered with blood from his bouts. No one could help him now.

The soldier sensed it too and he gave a toothy grin. "Time's up, mage." He took a teasing jump forward, causing Dariak to stumble in his haste to step back. He had his dagger at the ready, but he knew already it was no match. With a yell, the broad fighter rushed forward and brought his sword around, a crazy light flaring in his eyes. Dariak stepped further away, then remembered something Gabrion had done back in Savvron. As the fighter ran toward him, Dariak daringly lurched forward into a roll and snuck under the man's attack. He brought his dagger up into the man's belly, scoring a wound but not a fatal one. In fact, the move only enraged the man further.

The mage kicked with his feet, trying to knock the sword from his opponent's hand, to no avail. The soldier grabbed one of Dariak's ankles and stamped his foot down into the mage's crotch, sending waves of searing agony through him. As he recoiled, the soldier laughed lining up his sword and preparing for the final blow.

Dariak looked once more for help, but his friends were hard-pressed. He had little option left. He cried out to the jades among him, begging for their help in this battle. He felt the sizzling response from the lightning and though he feared the repercussions, he accepted its hunger. The electricity seared through him and tugged at his essence, desiring to change him again into the ball of energy.

But the other jades refused. Dariak could sense their interference all at once. The earth and water jades raced through him and held his body together in material form, thwarting the efforts of the lightning jade. Even the air jade whipped around and battered against the sparks. Three against one, the lightning lost and was quelled once again.

This didn't help Dariak against the sword seeking its way into his flesh. A biting, searing pain cut into his chest as the tip of the sword pierced through his tunic and punctured his skin. With the mage essentially immobilized, the soldier was delighting in making this thrust as painful as possible, and though he could have killed the mage quickly, he enjoyed the horrific screams now filling the night air.

His torment of the mage led to his own undoing, however, for Dariak had another ally he hadn't counted on. Sensing its master's pain, Dariak's horse tore free of its post and rammed the soldier to the ground, nickering angrily and biting with terrible force. Taken unawares, the soldier went down, where his arm landed under a stomping hoof and was badly broken.

Dariak couldn't move for all the agony he was feeling, but he coerced his thoughts to pull on healing energies. He swept them through his chest and the jades helped by augmenting the spell. It was only enough to seal the wound from inside out; the pain lasted far after. Dariak rolled onto his side, clutching his dagger and eying the captain, who was again on his feet and slashing wildly at the horse. He couldn't let his protector be harmed, and so Dariak sent sparks toward the soldier, drawing his attention back once again. But one glance told the man that the horse was the greater threat, so he thrust and stabbed again, scoring some hits on the larger beast, but not striking anything vital.

Dariak pulled himself onto his knees and then found his feet. Whatever hurt he felt was irrelevant if the man scored a kill against the horse. Not thinking about what he was doing, Dariak leaned forward and let his body weight pull him forward, arm outstretched. With a thud, his dagger penetrated the captain's armor from the back, and with a startled cry, he fell dead.

With the threat gone, the horse immediately calmed down and nuzzled against the mage, whose body gave way and dropped to the dirt. The injured horse stood guard over the unconscious Dariak, keeping him out of harm's way.

By this time, the others had drawn closer together to better protect themselves. Gabrion's sword swept wide and his shield blocked many incoming blows. Randler defended more than he attacked, but he kept his fair share of attackers busy, wounding many of them along the way. Kitalla was the major killing force among them. While Gabrion and Randler drew and deflected attacks, Kitalla leaped forth with deadly strikes, bringing down their foes quickly.

A third patrol had joined the fight, but with the piling bodies around the field, they were reticent to get too involved. Two of them were archers and they launched a few volleys into the trio, scoring hits on Randler and Gabrion, until Kitalla unleashed her daggers and snapped their bowstrings with careful tosses. It wasn't until a fourth battalion entered the area that the team grew truly concerned.

Heartened by additional support, the third group of fighters became enthusiastic in their efforts, sweeping aside other fighters and trying to get close enough to score hits against the fearsome threesome. Kitalla called forth to her jade, which increased the accuracy of her metal blades. Similarly, Gabrion sharpened his own sword with his shard's help and Randler obscured the enemy's sightlines with a bit of darkening magic. They couldn't control the powers well, especially within the heat of battle, but the jades themselves were somewhat willing to assist and so they did.

The fourth set of soldiers was fresh and the team was weakening. Dismounting and readying their weapons, the soldiers waded through the other fighters, giving them well-earned respites, seeking the rogues in the center. They too had seen the mage-fires in the sky and if they weren't mages themselves, it was clear they were in league with one.

Desperation set in and Kitalla started screaming with each major thrust of her daggers. Her supply was running low, too. Another fifteen fighters remained to take them down now that the fourth troop had arrived. She believed in herself and the others, but she sure wished a large fireball would appear all of a sudden and level the field. Thinking of the mage, she glanced around but saw no sign of him.

Gabrion received some nasty wounds from his attackers, who saw him as the biggest threat with his wide sweeping arcs. Doubling up against him, they were able to keep the nimble warrior constantly moving, and he was starting to tire. Gashes appeared on his legs and arms, with a slice scored on his right cheek adding a sharp sting as sweat dripped within. He refused to admit defeat and kept pushing onward, taking down another soldier and then another.

And then another sound filled the air that took the hope from him. More horses were nearby, rushing to enter the battle. He raised a ferocious cry and spun in a wide, dizzying circle, felling all the soldiers within range with his crazy, blind attack. He needed erratic action now in order to combat the endless parade of foes. He thought too of Dariak and the spells that could save them now.

As the fifth group of fighters approached, the rest of the king's men redoubled their efforts. Randler took a sword hilt to the head, collapsing in a heap. Gabrion's retaliatory strike kept the attacker from killing the bard, but the move cost Gabrion some of his defensive posture. Kitalla more than compensated for it with a hasty dagger throw, after which she turned to finish her newest opponent.

The soldiers on the outskirts trying to get inside to kill the rogues were furious when a horn sounded, calling for a halt. They shouted back at the newest commander, insisting that a mage was present and needed to be taken in at once, but the horn blast repeated in reply. It took time to disentangle the fighting, but Kitalla and Gabrion held their own and pulled Randler between them once they had the chance. Dariak was too far away to likewise protect, but they could see the mage's horse standing over him.

"Stand down!" ordered the newly arrived officer. "This is my jurisdiction. Defy me and face the consequences."

Kitalla sneered but refused to lower her weapons. To her shock, all of the other fighters set aside their weapons and stepped away. They created a wide, safe berth, though she could have breached it easily with a good toss. However, it wouldn't benefit her in any way with all the fresh fighters in the area.

"Signs of magic were seen in this vicinity. I shall meet with the perpetrators now," he commanded. Gabrion eyed the man oddly, tilting his head and squinting. The soldier dismounted and handed his sword to one of his men before approaching Gabrion and Kitalla unarmed.

He came very close to them and looked briefly at the carnage they had created. The duo was panting heavily, still ready for attack even with everyone else backing away.

"Greetings to you," he said somewhat congenially from behind his helmet. "I understand that magic was used in his area and justice must be served."

"You won't take us with you," Kitalla assured him coldly.

"I will. And you haven't any choice." He shrugged. "That or death, in any regard. But fear not, for you will not be harmed within my troop. I assure you." He then lowered his voice so only they could hear. "I beg of you to comply."

"We surrender," Gabrion said after a moment. He looked sorrowfully at Kitalla. "We really don't have a choice."

She didn't like it. But there wasn't anything else they could do. If they struck the man down, they would certainly die when the others retaliated. If they resisted him at all, he would have no choice but to coerce them or kill them. Going peacefully might give them a chance.

The soldier waved a hand to his men, who rushed over and claimed the prisoners, steering them away from the other fighters who had lost comrades to these two. Randler and Dariak were also recovered, as were their horses and belongings. The compliance of all the other guards left Gabrion and Kitalla with no doubt that this soldier was indeed at the head of jurisdiction in this area. They departed the scene moments later, leaving the rest to tend to the wounded and dead.

It was a quiet and formal march away from the battle for the next hour. The dark night overhead added a solemnity to the procession and as the minutes ticked away, both Gabrion and Kitalla doubted the situation more and more. At last the leader called a halt and the rest of the men set up camp for the remainder of the night.

The prisoners were pulled from their perches and set together on the ground, after which their binds were cut. Kitalla rubbed her wrists as she looked up suspiciously into the leader's helmeted eyes. "What's this about? Now that we're away from the rest, will you kill us? Why release our hands?"

At last the man pulled the helmet from his head, which prompted a sharp gasp from Gabrion. "No," the soldier responded to Kitalla, "I won't kill you. Not after you spared my life," he added, looking at Gabrion.

The warrior smiled despite the hectic night. He remembered the man whose life he had spared after their mad flight from Warringer where they had then battled the lupinoes. "Hernior?"

"The one and same," he nodded. "You've been missing for quite some time, but I've kept an eye out for you, friend. I did as you bade me and delivered your messages. I fear that it prompted the onset of war in earnest. After that happened, I requested a transfer to Warringer proper to maintain order in light of 'hard times.' The king accepted and I have been scouring this land since then."

"To what end?" asked Gabrion.

"As I said, looking for you. I intended to shelter you from other patrols that are still hunting you. It may be half a year later, but the king has not forgotten your transgression."

Kitalla laughed mockingly. "He has a whole war to oversee but he's still petty enough to want to kill us personally?"

"Basically." He looked down at Randler and Dariak. "Will they be all right?"

The thief nodded. "They're both breathing. Just tired and in pain. But what happens to us now?"

"Put your faith in me tonight and sleep deeply and eat well. We are already prepping a stew. Tomorrow," he added with a grin, "you will unfortunately escape and go on your way."

"I'm not sure I can trust you," she replied.

"I can," Gabrion refuted. "Thank you, friend. Upon your visit to Savvron, did you speak with the elders there? Did you relay all that I asked you to?"

"Yes, and your father and mother are proud of you."

Gabrion breathed a sigh of relief. It was months-old news, but it was the only word at all he'd had of his home. "Any word from them?"

"All they had said was that Mira's folks had not returned from sojourn but that a messenger had brought them a letter saying they were well." Hernior shrugged. "Your father said he didn't know more than that, but the handwriting was legitimate, so he felt they were safe."

This confused the warrior. "But Mira had been captured."

Hernior nodded, "Your father said he wrote back to them, but hadn't heard a response yet. He didn't feel you should worry, not that he thought I would see you again anyway."

"What does that mean?" Kitalla asked.

Gabrion shook his head. "I have no idea."

A member of Hernior's troop stepped up cautiously, so as not to upset the warrior and thief. "The sup is ready, Commander."

"Thank you, Jeron." He turned back to the other two. "Wake your friends and eat, then sleep. We can discuss this more in the early morning. If you'll pardon me, I have to send off a team to obscure our trail from the other patrols." With that he left.

CHAPTER 5

The Cave

THE TEAM WAS roused in the early morning by Jeron, Hernior's second-in-command. "Get up, quickly now. Time to move. Another patrol is closing in and we need to be gone before they arrive." Apparently, hiding their tracks hadn't worked.

The mad scramble went smoothly, despite the injuries Dariak and Randler had sustained in the battle the night before. They groaned through their pains and pushed ahead to the waiting horses, which had already been saddled and stocked with supplies by Hernior's men. Gabrion kept ahead of his wounded comrades while Kitalla stayed at the rear in case the other patrol slipped through Hernior's forces. Yet the four of them understood they couldn't remain with the guards for long. It would ruin the soldiers' reputations and make their journey tedious.

Recognizing the need to break apart, Gabrion rushed ahead to consult with Hernior. He wondered if it would be better for the troop to simply lose the team or if they should stage a battle and escape from it.

"A great man, you are," Hernior commended, "looking out for our well-being in the king's eyes, though you've no more stake in what happens with us." He considered for a moment, keeping his horse running onward as he deliberated with himself. "I fear you will be pursued in either regard."

Gabrion nodded. "Then we slipped out in the middle of the night. Better you have to fake one reprimand for a poor watchman instead of losing face for falling in a battle against us. Besides, we would rather not harm any of you, even superficially."

"Nor have we the time," the soldier agreed. "Very well, friend. Take your comrades onward and I will have my men raise a ruckus at your escape. Be speedy, for we will not be able to hold back our brethren for long."

"Understood." The warrior tugged his reins and the horse slowed instantly. He rejoined the others and passed his message among them. "We ride, quickly now. Away!"

As the four of them broke away from the host of soldiers, Hernior called out an alarm and guided his troop slightly toward the east. The twenty men fanned out, partly to cover the others' westerly escape, but also to suggest some confusion as to where to go. They slowed down and spun about, turning instantly into a hunting party that was purposely going in the wrong direction. And when the nearby patrol caught them, Hernior spurred them onward to join their search in vain.

They had barely enough time and trees to escape notice. Randler's head pounded fiercely as his horse thundered beneath him, but he took the lead, guiding them toward his secret abode and the jade awaiting them there. At least they had made some progress southward, but now it was a quick sprint to the west.

They passed a few clusters of creatures along the way, waking a family of gleese from a morning snooze, but they blazed past all the foes and hurried on. Though the speedier lupinoes kept up at first, they lost interest once they realized the pack leaders had stayed put. It took about two more hours at a hurried pace before the river came into view and, shortly after, Randler dismounted his horse and stalked carefully onward.

Despite knowing what they were looking for, it was difficult for them to see the cave, even for Kitalla who had a few stashes of her own. Randler knew its location well and he walked with purpose toward a slight hill, nestled within a row of trees and marked by a large boulder. He stepped closer and nudged the enormous rock aside, revealing that it was mostly hollow.

Kitalla laughed and shook her head. "Such a juvenile disguise, but perfect, being so."

"Uh, thanks?" Randler grinned. "The horses won't fit, but everyone in."

Gabrion tethered the horses to a tree and followed the rest of the group inside. He was stunned to see that there was light within the underground space. As he looked around, he saw crafty holes in the ceiling that would probably look like nothing more than divots in the land above, but from here they were reinforced with iron shafts to prevent them from filling in. Though it seemed relatively dark after being out in the sunlight, once his eyes adjusted, he could see well enough.

"It's all rock, the walls," Randler was explaining. "Tollimar, from one of the troupes I traveled with, found this place as a child. We spent a while here together, long ago when we were on the run." He subtly turned away from Dariak as he gestured to the ceiling. "He said this was all open to the sky when he literally fell into it one day. He and some friends made a roof overhead and used it as a hideout for themselves. Storms and time covered over the roof and sealed it in pretty well."

Kitalla interrupted him. "I'm surprised you're not singing all this. Sounds right out of an old fable or something." She adopted a mock bard's tone and added, "O darkened place of ill repute, I find you sitting here all mute. I cover you upon your head, so I can then hide here instead."

Randler chortled. "Indeed! Tollimar had quite the set of verses for this place. I figured you had enough of my singing for the moment, but if you'd rather..."

Kitalla waved her arm for him to continue his tale.

"Well, Tollimar and his friends were a bit of the rough-and-tumble type, and they landed in some trouble. Tollimar's friends were killed in a scuffle and he managed to run away, hiding here for a few months until he felt safe. No one found him, but he knew he couldn't realistically hide here forever. He played a good beat and sang decently, so he traveled and joined different performance troupes. He broke away a few times over the years; he was a bit hard to get along with, and he wasn't particularly... accepted... by everyone," he added with a roll of his eyes and a slight gesture toward himself and Dariak. "But eventually he met up with a group that welcomed him, and then me, and because we were alike in some ways, we got along fine."

"More than fine, it sounds like," Kitalla added with a wink, knowing the comment would irritate Dariak but saying it anyway.

The bard hedged, but nodded. "Yes. In any event, after learning of this place, and venturing from it a while later, Tollimar lost himself in a tavern one night. Drank until he had no idea what he was doing, and eventually angered the patrons so much they called the town guard. He was carted off and eventually died in the dungeons."

Dariak looked at his companion, feeling the sorrow that issued from the man's lips. He stepped closer and wrapped his arms around Randler, comforting him.

"So no one else knows of this place?" Gabrion asked a few moments later.

"No," Randler answered, greatly relieved at Dariak's support and keeping his arm around the mage.

"I don't agree," Kitalla commented. "This place looks… disturbed."

Randler frowned and Dariak closed his eyes. "The jades aren't resonating with anything new here," the mage said. "You're sure the jade is here?"

The minstrel realized that Kitalla was right. "No…" he breathed. He pulled away from Dariak and touched random places around the cavern, lifting a small urn in one corner, opening a box in another. He later slid aside a stone panel that blended well with the wall, and after that he sank to the ground and buried his head in his hands.

"What is it?" Gabrion asked, knowing the answer but asking anyway.

"It's gone. All of it. My songbooks. My extra lute. My money. And the jade." He looked up at Dariak, whose jaw tensed with the announcement. "I swear to you, it was here. I promised you I would bring you to it. It was here. But I can't prove it," he realized suddenly, his voice growing faint.

Kitalla continued her own investigation. "He's telling the truth," she commented, much to Randler's surprise.

"How could you even know?" he asked, incredulous.

"I recognize some stuff," she said vaguely. "Besides, it's been months since you've been here; anything could have happened in that amount of time. Not so hard to imagine someone else stumbled in and took your things."

"Especially if the tavern master in Warringer knew of this place," Gabrion added. "Kitalla, what else do you see here?"

"Evidence that a friend of mine paid a visit, actually, if I'm not mistaken." She said it with such confidence, there was no room for her to be mistaken. "See these patches of darkness on the floor in that strange pattern? Definitely her work."

Randler followed her gaze. "True, I don't recognize that."

Dariak stared at the odd patterning. "It looks like an energy conduit, as if someone was trying to channel magic in here."

Kitalla nodded knowingly, but Gabrion asked, "What's it drawn with?"

"Blood," the mage answered, crouching nearby and examining it more closely. "Not particularly long ago either."

"That's a good thing, anyway," Kitalla stated. "At least it means we have a chance of finding her. Of course, I doubt even she would have gone far from her usual places."

"Who?" Gabrion asked.

With a snort, Kitalla replied, "The handmaiden." Gabrion's eyes opened wide with the recollection of his first meeting with Kitalla in the woods when Dariak was still his prisoner. "Yep," the thief acknowledged. "Heria was here, doing some sick and twisted ritual like always."

"But *blood* magic?" Dariak hissed. "That's so erratic and doesn't work nearly half the time! What's the point of it?"

Gabrion wondered, "Haven't you cut us a dozen times on shards of glass so you can set up protection spells?"

"That's different." Dariak shook his head. "That ties the spell to you. It's a connective force at that point, not a power supply for the spell."

"Blood is powerful," Randler suggested. "It's why kings and queens have heirs. Their blood means more than others'. Besides, without it, we don't live very long, do we? So many wars are fought over rights of blood."

"Yes." Dariak dismissed the history lesson. "But blood isn't a proper conduit for magic in and of itself. Recognizing the energies and working with them... that's the way to go about it. Why would she seek power through such a method?"

Kitalla shrugged and answered with a cool nonchalance that irked the others. "She was a young child when she murdered her father, albeit accidentally, then watched as her mother suicided. She has some sick fascination with blood. She's deadly in her way, but it's after the killing that she creeps people out." She held up her hands before anyone could speak. "Don't even ask for details."

"Wasn't going to." Randler frowned.

"You're sure it's her, not some other fanatic?" Dariak asked.

Kitalla pointed to the design. "Absolutely. See how there are four flourishes going upward in one direction, then two pooling out to the sides, and a final one aiming downward? She drew that all the time. The downward one represents herself and the two out to the side are her parents."

"Ah," said Randler, "then the other four are siblings?"

The thief tilted her head back and forth from side to side, maintaining a slight detached manner while talking about her previous traveling companion. "Two of them were: older brothers. But those four in particular were the first four men she killed out of revenge for... violating her during her youth. I think one was a lord and the other a servant or an uncle, but I forget."

Gabrion was horrified. "Outrageous!"

Kitalla barely registered a nod. "Her father would have been among those others if he hadn't earned his own special place as her first kill. She used to say she was the family pet. Anyway, Poltor was the only man ever to earn her true respect, not that I have any idea or interest how. She tolerated the others we worked with out of respect for Poltor, but she would have killed them in an instant if he hadn't expressly told her not to." She clapped her hands suddenly, making the others jolt upright. "In any event, we know who has that jade now, so I have to go find her to get it back."

"You?" Gabrion echoed, shaking himself alert. "We're a team, Kitalla."

Maintaining her flippant attitude, she gestured to Dariak and Randler. "These two boys are hurting and need time to recover. If she sees you, she'll try to kill you. I have to go it alone."

But the warrior was determined. "I won't let you face this alone."

She raised an eyebrow. "Don't trust me?"

Gabrion's reaction surprised her. He started yelling, his face burning a deep crimson as his rant escalated. "Trust you! Who was it who infiltrated our king's personal dungeon, impersonated a guard, and freed us from capture? Who used her skills in the museum to thwart the guards and keep them at bay so we could fend them off? Who scored us a set of new equipment in Kaison as we ran for our lives? Who protected us by felling a half-dozen guards as we flew from the city? Who has kept us alive at every single turn along this journey? Who got us out of Warringer under the guards' noses? Who defeated countless horrific traps set up by a maniac? Who took down the ursalor to keep us all alive? Who fought at my back every step of the way, protecting us all when our own battles kept us detained? Trust you? Are you kidding me? My life would have ended long ago without you, you idiot! Trust you?" He fumed and huffed but he stopped yelling at last.

Something about his response shook her. The phony mask she had adopted to talk about Heria suddenly crumbled and she looked almost stricken with the warrior's outpouring of raw emotion. Tears leaped into her eyes and it was everything she could do not to cry with his overwhelming support of her. She had felt respected, but hadn't expected this.

Dariak saw her inner armor break away at that moment as she digested the words. It was a subtle change, but it was almost tangible. She looked back at Gabrion with such an odd expression, it was as if some definite truth had just been shattered within her and replaced by something better. Though he had raged in disbelief, Gabrion had said the exact thing she needed, without anyone even knowing she had needed it.

The room was silent for a while as Kitalla stared at Gabrion and everyone stared at Kitalla. At last, Dariak felt that something needed to be said before the silence grew painful or awkward. "She's right, Gabrion. We're too injured to rush off at the moment. You two should go."

Kitalla didn't even argue. "We could leave at dawn. One more day won't change the trail much. Heria has a few haunts she likes best."

Gabrion took a deep breath. "I guess that settles it, then. We leave in the morning."

CHAPTER 6

Hunting Heria

IT WASN'T, PERHAPS, the ideal situation, but Kitalla knew that finding Heria would be easier with a smaller group and waiting for the bard and mage to heal from their injuries would only make it harder to find her one-time companion. They left while Randler and Dariak slept deeply. After all their injuries, any sleep they received was necessary and it wasn't worth disturbing them anyway.

Silently, she rode her horse to the south, with Gabrion dutifully in tow. She was grateful he hadn't asked any questions, despite being on the road for a few hours already. Although she might have picked up some information in Warringer, Kitalla opted to skirt around it, so as not to alert the local patrols. Their presence in the area was already known, and though she trusted their ability to escape unharmed, there wasn't any sense in risking it.

She knew that Heria had five particular hiding places that had personal interest, and so she guided the warrior to the closest one, hoping beyond all that their journey would end after a single attempt. The metal jade in her pocket rode silently alongside her. After all the time spent with Dariak talking about resonances, she knew its silence was a bad sign. Perhaps she should have had Dariak point them in the right direction before they had left.

Kitalla wasn't accustomed to relying on others for any long-term purpose, but riding along on Dariak's quest had made her journey a bit easier, perhaps too easy. She was protecting herself in battle. But she was ultimately just a follower now. Even trusting the jade to guide her felt like a betrayal to her own instincts, and it was part of what kept her quiet along the way. She couldn't confide in Gabrion that she wasn't certain with this first destination. Still though, he never complained. She looked over her shoulder and watched his blond hair bouncing with every one of his horse's steps, but his face was set in stone, and it didn't fit him.

She thought of Gabrion's naïveté when she'd first met him back in the forest. He had blindly trusted her guild's ruse and fell into the ambush, accompanied by a mage who was no ally of his at the time. Every odd was stacked against him, yet he persevered through it all. And here they were riding off together on their side quest, and she fully trusted him to protect her at all costs.

The thought sent chills down her spine, but warmed her, too. She hated relying on him even in a fight. And though she had intended to take this task alone, his determination to accompany her made her feel accepted in a way she had never been before.

Except that once, something inside whispered, but she rejected it.

With an accidental tug of her horse's reins, Kitalla groaned with the tumbling thread of her thoughts and nearly unseated herself. The horse whinnied and stamped its feet, wondering what had upset its rider so. But the thief shook her head, snapped the reins, and they continued onward. In the few seconds of hesitation, Gabrion rode ahead, and Kitalla watched him, unable to look away.

The warrior's quest for Mira was fodder for children's tales, as far as she was concerned, yet he clung to his ideals at every turn. She hadn't met anyone quite like him before. Sure, men had gotten into brawls over women, but she hadn't realistically heard of anyone traveling the world over trying to find the strength he needed so he could infiltrate enemy lands and recover his lost love. It had been over half a year since they had met, and in that time, he had never wavered from his ultimate quest.

She thought about her own motivations and instantly tried to dismiss them. She knew she couldn't change the past. She wasn't trying to save anyone anymore. She wanted so much to undo the hurt of her childhood, but before she dwelled on it for too long, she shoved her thoughts away, focusing instead on Heria, the insane child who had found a home with a group of thieves.

"Over there." Kitalla pointed to the distance with relief. "That cave over there is one of her places."

The warrior silently nudged his horse in the appropriate direction, saying nothing. Kitalla wondered about his silence. It felt very unnatural to her. Perhaps he was intent on finishing this hunt quickly, or perhaps he regretted his outburst in Randler's hideout.

She pushed ahead of him and guided them toward the cave. The journey took another couple of hours, but it was otherwise an easy trek. They focused on the destination, while Kitalla also batted away her racing thoughts.

It had been a long time since meeting up with Heria. She had phenomenal eyesight and instincts, and so Kitalla suspected they would not be able to sneak up on the teenage girl, whatever they did. Kitalla thought of all she knew of the deranged waif, wondering what kind of greeting she would receive, assuming, of course, that Heria was even at this location.

The cave loomed closer and Kitalla slowed her horse to a trot, watching the area for signs of the girl. She didn't really expect to find any, but then Gabrion called out, "Look there!" He was pointing at the stone surrounding the entrance where dark stains marred the surface.

Kitalla drew close and nodded. "Blood again."

"It doesn't look very new."

"I agree. I think it's a warning not to enter. But," she said as she hopped off her horse, "that's what we came here for, so let's go in." They tethered the horses and Kitalla lit a torch that was near the entrance before guiding the warrior inside.

The cavern was small, but it was clear that Heria made use of it with some regularity. A ratty-looking potted plant rested against one wall, its soil dry. Crumbs of food littered other areas, giving off a foul scent of decay to the chamber. A wood plank, presumably serving as a table, lay flat on the ground. The surface was covered with countless knife cuts and was stained with blood. An altar of sorts stood nearby in front of a torch brace. The upper portion of the altar was carved in the same pattern they had seen on the floor at Randler's cave, and it seemed obvious to Kitalla that if a torch was lit behind it, the shadows of that design would dance across the floor.

They spent some time scrounging around the meager furnishings, but they found nothing at all, except for one pouch of shiny stones. Gabrion brought the pouch to Kitalla for inspection.

"These look like they're from the Talonic River," she said, turning them in her hand, noting gold flecks that sparkled with her torch. "She was born near there, and seems to be drawn to the area at times."

"Should we have gone there first instead?" he asked.

"It's the wrong season for it." She shook her head. "Winter, maybe, but not now."

"Winter," he echoed. "So odd that we missed it completely."

Kitalla didn't want to think back to the reason why, for she was undergoing Grenthar's tortures. But Gabrion had an odd look on his face and she couldn't deny his concentration. "What's wrong?"

"The winter didn't seem to hit us in Pindington. It was cold some days, but our group was working so hard every day, we didn't even feel it. If it snowed at all, it never fell in through the tower." He lowered his gaze. "Mira was a winter child. She loved the snow. We never got much, but when it hit, she was the first one out in it."

Kitalla eyed him carefully. "You're talking about her in the past tense. You haven't given up on her, have you?"

"Of course not," he replied automatically, but there was no feeling in his words.

"That's good to know, because if you are giving up, we'll drop you off at home and go on without you." She said the words with a sharp bite to them, hoping to shake him into a response.

But his tone was unchanged, "I can't return home until I find her."

"Well, then let's continue on our way. There isn't anything worthwhile here. And though these stones suggest she went north, I think it's more likely a ruse, if she even planted them at all. Come on, let's be away from this foul place."

"Yes, let's. The stench of death here is irking me."

Over the next several days, Kitalla rode them further west, seeking another of Heria's locales, but it was hard staying focused on the journey. Gabrion spent his time in one of three ways. He was sometimes resolutely silent and would only answer with hand gestures or nods. Other times, he was monotonous and emotionless when he spoke. And most irritating of all was when he tried getting her to talk about herself, so he could escape whatever was troubling him.

She could practically feel his pain in the way he went about the days and she wasn't entirely sure how to react to it. In some sense, she felt that Mira was a driving force for him on his quest, but as she saw sorrow drowning him, she also wondered if he would be better without Mira as a goal. Though he probably wouldn't have a reason to journey with them then, he was certainly a capable warrior and didn't need someone else as a reason to be successful. He was talented in his own right and should accept as much.

On the other hand, when he did talk proudly of Mira, his whole demeanor brightened and invigorated him. He was much happier when he spoke of times they had shared together. For some reason unknown to her, sometimes those looks of joy made her skin crawl. Dwelling on the reason why meant tapping into her own thoughts, and she wasn't ready for that.

They were nearing the location anyway. The edge of the forest was to the south of their long-ago fight against the lupinoes, but further west than the castle town of Kaison. The area was loaded with a massive network of trees that reached high into the sky, intertwining so deeply, it was practically impossible to know which branch belonged to which trunk. This was one of Heria's favorite places because her agility allowed her to scale the trees easily and hide within the canopy above.

Kitalla called her horse to a halt and Gabrion trotted up behind her, still silent. The thief dismounted and scoured the area, checking the ground for signs of recent activity. She was surprised to find footprints in the dirt, an indication that a traveler had recently come through.

She should have suspected it. More so, she should have reacted to it. But she didn't. A snap sounded nearby and a huge net fell from above, having launched itself outward from a larger tree. The thick rope smashed her to the ground, trapping her effectively. She managed to flip over and start pulling the net aside, muttering under her breath at her carelessness, but Heria warned her to stop.

"It will kill you if you keep doing that, you know," said a playful voice. "Laced with toxins, that rope. The more you move it, the more you touch and breathe. Soon, there will be nothing left of you." She paused. "Mmm, on second thought, keep writhing so I can see if it's strong enough."

Kitalla immediately stopped moving, but looked for Gabrion, noting that he too had fallen prey to the trap. She couldn't see clearly, but she realized that a dart was also sticking out of his neck and he was pressed tightly against his horse.

How could she have let her own musing interfere so thoroughly with her search for Heria and the jade? Kitalla banged her fist into the ground, and with it, she smelled a pungent whiff of the poisoned rope. There wasn't much she could do at the moment, especially as her hands started itching from contact with the irritant.

"Better," Heria said. "Now, what is it you're looking for?"

"Don't recognize me, Heria? I was looking for you." Kitalla didn't even hear the girl approach, not that she expected to. They had both trained under Poltor in the art of stealth and he had insisted they learn to move in total silence.

Heria's response was to utter an odd, twittering laugh. "The hag? Delightful! I didn't think to see you again."

"We've much to discuss, Heria. Let me up, will you?"

It took a few moments of inner debate before Heria decided. "No. I think it's safer this way. And more fun, of course."

"Of course," Kitalla laughed, adding a false sense of amusement to the sound. It was never good to be at Heria's mercy, and something seemed even odder about the girl than usual. Kitalla listened intently to her instincts after having ignored them moments before, and so she made no attempt to loosen a dagger to cut the net apart. Heria would expect as much and would likely retaliate. "How is the rest of the gang?" she asked instead.

"Oh," Heria said with a strangely distant air, "haven't seen them in a while. After you left, Poltor went about looking for others, but it never worked out." She clapped her hands suddenly and chuckled. "Then again, I think it was more my fault than anything. No one liked hearing how Masher was mashed to a pulp and how some parts were more mashed than others." She giggled sickly. "Eventually, he dismissed me."

"Oh, I'm sorry." She truly was. Poltor was the only person she'd ever known who could keep Heria remotely sane.

"No, I've been happier now," she answered cheerfully. "At least, none of my findings end up in his pocket. Not that he appreciated all of them. You know, you *do* look rather uncomfortable under there."

It felt like bait, so she dodged it. "I'm fine," she replied, keeping her tone light and friendly. The conversation wasn't progressing well, and she knew it needed to move along in order for her to be freed from the trap. She peered over toward Gabrion, regretting again that she had let them both fall victim. "It's an interesting poison you've applied to the rope."

Heria lit up. "Isn't it? It took me a while to find the right combination. Sometimes people died from it, but not when I wanted them to. So I had to add other things to make it take longer to kill someone. At least, so I could do what I needed to first, anyway."

"Oh? Does this mean you're planning to add me to your list of experiments?" She said it to be funny, but the look on Heria's face said that the girl was actually planning on it.

Heria smiled. "Of course! You've got that very interesting skill, don't you? I always wanted to know more about it. But you, you'd never tell me."

Her heart sank. "I don't really know much about it or a way to describe how I do it."

"No matter," Heria dismissed. "I've got my own methods."

"I see. What about him?"

The girl rubbed her hands together. "He's rather cute. I think I can find uses for him. But enough of this. We need to get out of here. This air feels orange."

"Orange?" she asked, unable to stop herself.

"Don't you ever smell something and it reminds you of something else? This reminds me of orange. Not too fresh. Not too musty. A little pungent."

"That could be the rope," Kitalla offered.

"True!" Heria laughed, stepping closer, pulling a thin tube from her belt. "But that's enough for now. 'Night." She blew the dart and it took only moments for Kitalla to pass out completely.

CHAPTER 7

Dariak and Randler

DARIAK WAS GENUINELY sad to see that Kitalla and Gabrion had left that morning without waking them, but he knew he had no strength in him to join them. He hoped they would find the jade without too much trouble, then return as he and Randler recovered completely.

He looked over at Randler, who was cleaning up from breakfast. The bard was trying hard to keep positive, even though his private hiding place had been desecrated. He occasionally whistled whimsical tunes, but they didn't last for long. It was clear that Randler felt violated.

Dariak wandered over to the bloodstain Heria had drawn and traced it with his hands several times, letting his fingers splay out in a matching shape. It didn't feel right at all. He couldn't sense any benefit to the pattern in terms of drawing energy, which implied to him that if she was indeed performing blood rituals with this pattern, then they weren't very successful. She was likely doing them for a sense of inner enjoyment. He shuddered.

Randler joined him, wrapping his arm around him, looking sadly at the stained floor. "I used to sit there a lot and dream up new tunes. Not any more, I can tell you that."

"We'll clean it up," Dariak assured him. "Not that it would erase the memory of it, but at least the reminder will be gone."

It was a good challenge. The blood had soaked in thoroughly, so Dariak and Randler set about mixing different concoctions, trying to make a cleaning agent that would work. The mage applied his vast knowledge of herbs and used a few spells, but the stain was resolute.

As he fumbled through his pockets, he came across the vial of reptigon serum and chuckled to himself. "I was a prisoner when I extracted this," he explained to Randler's confused expression. "I used quite a series of spells to engorge the reptigon and then to extract its venom, while then drawing it into the vial and sealing it before the engorgement spell ended. Such a process, it was."

"What does it do?"

"This? Many things, depending on how it's used. I think a few drops will help us here, though."

The bard looked at him intensely. "Dariak, don't waste it on something like this."

"Waste?" he smiled. "This is your place and it deserves to be cleansed. I wouldn't call that a waste." Without waiting for Randler's response, he popped the vial open and a caustic whiff of venom filled the area. Dariak poured a few drops onto a leaf and then rolled the liquid around until the leaf was coated fully. He stoppered the vial, intoned a spell, and waited as the activated venom released a puff of smoke, sapping the leaf of its hydration. As it did so, Dariak flipped the leaf over and started scraping it against the stone.

A thick, acrid purple mist rose as the venom touched the dried blood. Holding his breath, Dariak applied as much force as he could without ripping the leaf. Over the patterns he went, tucking his head into his robe to draw in more air when needed. Randler had backed away coughing and with his eyes streaming from the smell.

It took time, but in the end, the stain was gone. Dariak withdrew the recently acquired air jade and called forth a breeze to clear out the cavern, but the fickle jade barely responded to his call. He felt frustrated that one spell would work and then another would not.

"Maybe I am broken after all," he muttered later that day. "These spells are randomly working and failing. That battle against your mother, and then those soldiers. I don't know. Maybe I'm not whole anymore."

"Dariak…"

"No, really, there's something very wrong." He looked at Randler woefully. "I might not be able to call upon the jades effectively at this point. My quest might be over."

"I don't know what to say, Dariak." Which was completely true, as he wanted Dariak to fulfill his dream but also wanted the jades left unused. "All I know is that you used some spells well enough."

"Some," he echoed. "That's my point. Not all. Even the Shield of Delminor failed me. But then I summoned up all that water against the soldier, which was pointless because of his armor. But the spell itself worked otherwise."

"Same thing against those firegnats," Randler recalled. "You know, why not try a water spell right now?"

"What? How's that—?"

"Do it," Randler interrupted him. "I have a feeling it will work fine."

With a sigh, Dariak complied. He curled his hands toward a nearby pail and spouted the words, *"Kathra hydallos spirrilious."* As directed, the water rose in an ascending spiral, then splattered back down when he dropped his hands. Bolstered by the success, he focused on the power of earth, *"Temmular rothribak fau shei."* But the pail did not tip over at his command, though it did shudder for a moment. He groaned in annoyance.

"Resonance and dissonance," Randler said with a smile lighting his voice.

"I don't see how this failure makes you so happy," the mage grumbled.

"You *don't* see it, that's why." He beamed. "But you're looking at it from a standpoint of power and ability. Not from the overlap or lack of overlap, for that matter. It's like when a lute and a drum play together, one can overpower the other at times, but finding a balance so they work in harmony makes for better music."

Dariak stared at the bard, not knowing what to say, but amused nonetheless by Randler's sudden excitement. "Put it in mage terms, if you can."

Randler laughed. "The jade you took from ma-ma is that of air, yes? And you have the jade of earth with you. Aren't they opposing forces? Wouldn't they cancel each other out in some way?"

The truth of it struck him and relief washed over him all at once. "Yes! Yes, that would fit! Just like in the tower when the lightning jade was going berserk and I tried containing it with the power of shadow. I thought it was because I was unfamiliar with your jade. But no, that makes sense. They couldn't contain each other completely, and since I had less experience with the shadow, I was even less effective on my own. Yet when I added the power of water and earth, I was able to enclose the lightning for a time. Yes. Randler, yes!"

The bard delighted in the sudden illumination in Dariak's eyes and then he was puzzled as the mage thrust the air jade into his hands.

"Hold that for a moment." He then stepped away and summoned the Shield of Delminor, sensing it for weakness and now finding none. "Yes!" he laughed. "Oh, it isn't me after all!" His relief was palpable.

He spent the next few minutes summoning minor spells, ensuring he was in full control, but Randler's mind was on to something else and he hesitated to bring it up. "Dariak…" He decided to remain true to the mage and so he pushed the words out instead of letting them fade away. "Dariak, if the jades can interfere with each other and cancel each other out, then how can you possibly bring them all together and unite them? Won't they just prevent each other from functioning?"

Dariak's mood crashed with the question. The light went from his face and he dropped himself to the ground heavily. "I have no idea how they can be united. Do I wear them all around me or do I have to fuse them magically together? And how are they to be arranged? Is there a way they are supposed to line up? I don't have any information about that."

"They must, somehow, right? Line up, that is."

Dariak looked at the bard and shrugged. "Yes, they must. Of course they must, because it was done before."

"Yes, the mage who summoned the colossus," Randler said solemnly. "I wonder if he left any records of his work."

Dariak realized at that moment that Randler didn't know the connection between himself and that fateful mage. He rarely spoke of it himself, preferring to keep his father's work tucked safely away, but apparently his companions hadn't brought Randler up to speed either. He wondered why. "What do you know of that mage?" he decided to ask.

The bard tapped his lip and considered the question for a moment. "The stories all speak of a cold, heartless mage, gathering the energies of the land in a desperate rush to slay our king. Even stories I've heard from Hathrens hold him in a similar light, that it would take a mage of great power and arrogance to call that much power forth. But…" and his voice drifted off to silence.

"But what?" Dariak prompted.

"Well, I haven't thought much of it since then, really, but when my grandfather returned from the battle he spoke of the mage with a sort of reverence and respect. I always thought back then it was because of the massive power he had held. But listening to my memories now, it sounds different."

"In what way?"

"That moment wasn't the only time my grandfather had met that mage on the battlefield. The war had raged on for some time and there were other skirmishes before the colossus came about. My grandfather always commented about the use of mages on the other side of the line, and the lack of offensive mages on our side. Sure, we employed many healers, but the outright firecasters and such were abominations of the enemy. Yet he noticed on the field that the other mages rallied behind one in particular and seemed to take his lead in some areas. Admittedly, war is chaos and following simple plans isn't likely to happen, but my grandfather saw that when the magic became dangerous and erratic, the mage would calm the others."

"The same mage?" Dariak asked.

"I think that was what my grandfather was hinting at, now that I'm dwelling on it. He used to say that the enemy in front of us isn't always there by choice. Duty drives people to do what they must, not what they desire. Maybe he understood something about the mage that others didn't."

"Maybe," Dariak supplied, "he wasn't intending to wreak havoc on the land; maybe he wanted to just stop the fighting?"

Randler's voice escaped in the whisper, "Maybe." He stared at Dariak for a while in silence, wondering at all the horrible tales of that mage and then thinking of them again. He knew his words were powerful at times and could sway emotions one way or another, but perhaps the mage behind the colossus had another story.

Dariak let the silence sit for a moment before posing, "Perhaps the mage summoned the colossus because Kallisor troops infiltrated Hathren camps and poisoned the people within? Maybe the fighting was about to become truly vicious and horrific and so he brought out the jades and tapped into them, hoping to scare the enemy away, rather than decimate them."

"I'll admit, I've never allowed myself to consider that as an option. He was just a violator of natural law and good riddance at his death."

Dariak drew in a breath of air and released it slowly, trying not to let the declaration upset him. "The mage's name was Delminor. He worked personally for the king and most of the mages in Hathreneir looked up to him for his work. He was a cautious mage, but also curious. Sure, he experimented with numerous magical methods, but he always did so with as many safety precautions as possible. Sometimes he would bring in teams of mages to not only watch his progress, but also to help with the protections in case things went awry. And things did often go awry."

"Delminor," Randler echoed. "That's the name of the shield you summon."

"Yes. He was among the first mages to do so with the power of earth. Sure, others would cast walls of force by bending air or calling rock over in front of them, or by reflecting the damage back. But Delminor broke through the basic uses of magic and applied them in unique ways. The Shield of Delminor not only blocks projectiles from getting through, it magnifies their weight, thus grounding them and trapping them. He discovered it by communing with the earth jade, among others, and watching its effects on the objects around him. He saw patterns where other mages didn't and then he was able to manipulate the world in a very different way."

"Randler nodded his head slowly. "He sounds creative and talented when you tell it this way. You must have looked up to him, too."

"At heart, he was a very kind man. Deeply loving and protective of the people around him. He didn't necessarily develop the Shield of Delminor as a means of protecting soldiers in war. In fact, he was working with the castle engineers to develop a better lift system. The Shield would augment the weight of a passenger or stone and, depending on that weight, the lift would respond. No need for muscled slaves hoisting rocks, like Gabrion was forced to do in his imprisonment.

"But as you've noted before," Dariak continued on, "our nations have always been at war, and so every practical application was also bent toward battle, and Delminor did his work well. He created his spells and then worked with the soldiers to adapt them for use in a fight. He wasn't able to create for the sake of creation. If he had been, who knows where we would be today?"

"I wonder if my grandfather saw a bit of that in him, too, even from afar."

"He had the jades for years before anyone ever knew about them. Not all of them at first, but he had a good team of treasure hunters who would seek them out. They also employed the talents of bards for help in locating and deciphering obscure hints and locations." He tipped his head in respect toward Randler. "Though some mages wanted to use the jades for themselves, they couldn't harness the power within, and Delminor's team managed to claim them all in the end, sometimes by force."

"You know much. Are these tales taught in Hathreneir?"

"They are," Dariak acknowledged, "but that isn't how I know them. I knew Delminor personally. He showed me his work when I was just a tiny child and I was awed even without knowing what he was doing." He grew quiet for a moment. "But my best memories of him were when he would come to me at night and tuck me in. Then he would make all the candles glow different colors and swirl until I fell asleep."

Randler gasped with realization. "He was your father!"

"Yes." He then let silence hang in the air until Randler processed the information.

"And you're looking to continue his work," the bard said some time later. "You want to stop the warring so you can go back to seeking spells in their own right. That's why you thrived in the Prisoner's Tower and didn't try to escape. You were finally in a workspace where you could step closer to your true purpose."

"Now you have it," he agreed. "War or not, I need the jades to continue my father's ingenuity. But I would rather fulfill his life's goal, which was to show the world they could get along without fighting. If we could power lifts with magic, we wouldn't need slaves. People could work where they wanted to and not have to subjugate others. I want the same thing. He never wanted to bring those jades together in that colossus, but in the face of all else, he had little choice."

"You must have been too young to know any of this when he died."

"Of course, but he kept detailed journals, and mother would sit and read them to me, so I could have father's words with me growing up, even if he himself was gone. When I came of age, she gave me the earth jade, which had been returned to us from the war. So, I followed his path and worked with his apprentices to learn what they knew of his spells, until I was able to understand the texts myself. Then I spent some years working his magic until I was ready to venture off on my own. But now that we're gathering all of these jades, I'm at a loss of what to do with them."

Randler looked down at the air jade Dariak had handed him earlier. "Your father's notes didn't say?"

The mage shrugged. "I knew the jades I needed to look for, but not specifically where. I know the mage towers in Hathreneir have two, and they will bequeath them to me when I arrive there and prove myself worthy of them. It is my right as Delminor's son and as a member of the Mage Council. But at the start of my quest, I knew so little aside from the words. And I planned to bring the jades together in my father's laboratory anyway, so I could consult his texts with the jades in hand. So, I don't know if he actually wrote down how to bring them all together or not. However, if he could unravel the mystery himself, I'm sure I can find a way, too."

They sat quietly for a while and the sun tracked its way through the sky. "That's a lot of information, Dariak. I will need to process it into a ballad so I can remember it all clearly. Would you mind if we stop for now and eat something? Then, after, perhaps we'll spend some time with our lore and see what we can do to get the earth and the air to cooperate with each other. I feel it must link in with dissonance, but it would take time to find out."

Dariak's eyes opened wide. "You would help me unlock their powers further?"

The bard smiled hesitantly. "I'm still worried you might try to destroy the world or something, but if you do and I helped along the way, maybe even I'll be immortalized in a song." He winked.

Dariak shook his head. "I think you're more likely to be the voice of reason, when it comes down to it. But yes, enough of this for now. I'm famished, too."

CHAPTER 8

Heria's Mercy

KITALLA AWOKE, BADLY sore and bruised. Above her was a dank, musty ceiling and it smelled as if sewage ran through the room. She could barely turn her head, for a leather strap pinned her skull to a large wooden board that was slightly angled upward from the floor. Her legs and arms were stretched outward and bound with numerous bands, preventing all hope of escape. Large straps were secured about her torso, so tightly it was hard to breathe.

The angle at which she was raised allowed her to see Gabrion across the way, bound in similar fashion. He seemed to be asleep, for his chest rose and fell in a very slow rhythm. Kitalla didn't recognize the place from the view she had, but her biggest concern was trying to get free.

She tugged, twisted, and pulled from every direction, but nothing gave way. Heria had apparently wrapped each strap around her before securing it, thus there was no leeway when she tried to move. The thief was completely at the maniac's mercy.

Kitalla listened intently to the chamber and heard a trickle off to one end, no doubt the source of the odor that made her want to gag. Nothing else gave her any indication of her whereabouts or any means of escape. As she lay there, she could sense that Heria hadn't taken the time to disarm her. Perhaps she hadn't trusted the sleeping potion to keep Kitalla asleep for long enough, but when she tried her bindings again, it wouldn't have even mattered if she were a mage, she was so tightly secured. Or maybe, the thought skittered through her mind, the metal jade had effectively hidden itself and her iron daggers from prying eyes and hands. It was a fleeting thought but she couldn't dwell on it anyway.

Despite the restraints pinning her down, she refused to give up. Her trials against Grenthar had prepared her for such as this. No mere teenager would defeat her, even when it looked so grim. Kitalla tensed and loosened her body from head to toe, progressing from one muscle group to the next. The bindings were indeed tight and restricted her, but leather was leather. It had a breaking point. If she could find one weaker segment, her way to freedom would be at hand.

As she wriggled about, Gabrion awoke and tested his own prison. Unlike Kitalla, he pulled frantically and groaned in frustration until the thief whispered to him. "Keep quiet or she will hear you." He fell silent at once.

Kitalla, meanwhile, continued trying to stretch and release, hoping to build up some sweat that might soak into the straps and perhaps let her break through them. What she didn't know was that Heria had laced the leather with a mild sedative and the more she perspired, the easier it was for the poison to seep into her skin. Soon, the thief was disoriented and she ground her teeth against passing out again.

Footsteps echoed from afar and Kitalla focused on them carefully. She needed to be alert now more than ever. She stopped trying to wriggle about and forced herself to lie still, waiting for her captor to join her.

Heria bounced into the room from the side near the trickling sound. Skipping and whistling a children's song, she went to Gabrion's holding platform and then she whirled around Kitalla's, laughing when she saw evidence of Kitalla's struggle.

"That isn't going to work!" she sang merrily. "You should have figured from the ropes earlier that I would poison those too. Be still, hag. Be still, this won't take long. But you need to be awake for it, so relax. Just relax."

"What do you want from us?" Kitalla breathed.

Heria responded petulantly, "I already told you! Why is it, when you dance, you make things happen to people? I want to do that, too, so I'm going to find out how you do it, so then I can learn. See?"

"You don't need him. Let him go."

Heria laughed and pounced across the room to Gabrion's plank. She pulled off a leather strap from his midsection and then rubbed his belly. "But he feels so nice and solid. Even here in the meal bucket. No, I want to find out more about him." She touched her lips to his navel and laughed. "He even tastes different. Oh, look at him wiggle!" She cackled as Gabrion tried to writhe away from her touch, but of course he couldn't go anywhere.

"How did you get us here?" Kitalla asked, trying to distract Heria.

"Not easy! Not easy!" the girl cooed. "I had to use the vines. Yes, they don't much like me, but when I threaten to kill them, they do what I say in the end. It all evens out."

"Vines?"

Heria clapped her hands. "Well yes, they listen to me sometimes. But like I said, not always. That's why I didn't tie you up with them. No, I had to use the straps. My poor friend, Zerra. But it did give me lots of meat to eat."

"Zerra?" The name was completely unfamiliar to her.

"Yes, yes, like a sister of mine, but a boy, so more like a brother, really," she corrected herself. "Big fellow in every way. His parts were more jiggly than Masher's. But he's more useful this way, holding you down."

The realization—and horror—set in slowly. "These straps aren't leather?" she had to ask.

Heria only laughed in reply. "But I thought you wanted to know about how you got here? Though, I could certainly tell you which parts are which if you'd prefer. Why, sometimes I like to try to reassemble—"

"No!" Kitalla cut in, trying not to vomit at the thought of it all. "So the vines," she coughed, "they helped?"

"Well, some," Heria admitted, enjoying her story. "I had to prod them almost every step of the way, but they know I'm stronger and faster than they are. So they do listen in the end. Oh, I've said that already. No matter, it's all important. You see, the horse was terrified of the vines. Kept squealing, it did. Like a piggon. Ever hear it? Funny, because even quiet, timid, tiny rabbitats make the same sound when they're scared out of their minds." She followed this with some high-pitched squealing sounds, before clapping her hands and laughing again.

Kitalla concentrated very hard on straining and loosening her left leg. If the straps, whatever they were made of, were covered in poison, then they wouldn't penetrate her leggings as easily. And if she could loosen one foot, she might have hope for getting something else loose. She tried to keep Heria talking as she worked. "Yes, that reminds me of gleese too."

Heria barked a laugh. "Ha! Only when they're yelling at each other, not when they're scared. No, a gleese is more like a low honk. But what were we talking about?"

"How you got us here."

"Right!" She snapped her fingers. "The horse carried him most of the way until it nipped at the vines and they struck back. I couldn't exactly stop them. It was really amusing, when you think of it. Vines and horses fighting. The world is strange sometimes."

Kitalla did everything she could not to agree out loud. She let her thoughts wander to her foot, but she couldn't sense any progress.

"Well, it was a matter of getting you both here in spurts. Took a while. And a fair bit of draft. If you've a headache, it's because you've had at least half a dozen doses of the stuff. But you're alive, so at least you're not allergic to it. Well, the vines won't come in here, no matter what I threaten them with, so that's another reason Zerra was needed."

Kitalla did not want to be reminded. "You've gained a tremendous amount of skill already, Heria. I'm very impressed."

The girl started giggling, which turned into loud maniacal laughter. It took a few moments for her to calm herself down and wipe her tears away before she could reasonably speak again. "You don't really think flattery is going to help, hag?"

"No," she lied. "Just stating the obvious."

"Hmm. Well, I don't know. How are you feeling, by the way? Nice and awake?"

"Yes, of course," she replied, then remembered what Heria had said before about needing her to be awake. "But that poison is something powerful."

Heria mewled for a moment and then decided. "No, I think you're nice and awake. Yes, very nice. Very awake. You'll be able to tell me lots of things now." She stepped away and then came back. "Hold still and don't go anywhere." She laughed, then left the chamber.

"Gabrion," Kitalla whispered. "Are you hurt?"

"No," he growled. "But I can't move."

"She's probably going to focus on me first, so keep trying when she isn't looking. Feet first, I think."

"I've been trying. But she really knows what she's doing."

"Unfortunately for us, I'm afraid," Kitalla said. "Gabrion, listen, just do what you can to get out of here. Never mind me, when it comes to it."

"We're both done for here, Kitalla."

"Don't say that!" she hissed. "Stop giving up on your quest, warrior! Mira needs you more than ever. Find her within you and find a way out of this. Then rescue her. She waits for you."

His response was silence, but she felt it was more of a concentrated silence than one of hopelessness. She continued shaking her leg, feeling the dagger still tucked into her boot. She wondered if somehow she could manage to shake it enough for it to cut through the boot, then the strap itself. She also wondered, mocking herself, if Heria wouldn't just get bored and let them go. It was hopeless, but it was all she had, so she kept working her leg up and down fractionally.

A strange baying entered the cavern, followed by footsteps. The baying ended in a shriek as Heria tossed the animal into Kitalla's view. "Hard to find, those. Only feral ones nearby, but one sheep should do the trick."

Kitalla thought of the feral version of the sheep, the sheeliope, whose wooly body was so sticky, it was almost impossible to detach from it. They were nasty biters too, and once a victim was stuck to one's body, others in the flock would come over for a feast. In contrast, the sheep here was docile and unaware of its surroundings, trembling in fear for the rough handling it was receiving from the girl.

Thinking of all the other evidence of blood rites Heria had left behind, Kitalla had no doubt about the reason for the sheep. Its blood would help the girl channel whatever energy she could into the next ritual that would somehow allow her to get a sense of Kitalla's unique dance skill.

Heria spouted a few strange words that sounded nothing like magic, but nor did it sound like any spoken language in the land. Her teeth clicked a few times and she grabbed the sheep by the scruff of the neck, then slashed its throat, catching its life-blood in her hands. She continued to murmur strange phrases as she drew her symbol on the floor, right in front of Kitalla. The poor sheep thrashed in its final moments and all Heria did was chuckle under her breath when it stopped.

The girl stood upright in the center of her drawing, the four upper prongs aimed directly toward Kitalla. She then clasped her dagger, point up, in between the palms of her hands that looked otherwise poised for prayer. She hummed a few more odd phrases and then stepped toward her old companion.

It was all about to happen, Kitalla realized. As Heria drew closer with the knife, panic welled within her, true and strong, in a way she hadn't felt in many years. The trials at Grenthar's were less fearsome than this, for at least then she had the ability to defend herself and use her skills to escape. But now, she was trapped, pinned, immobilized. She violently tugged her leg forward, hoping to burst through somehow, but nothing happened.

Heria saw the motion and laughed again, touching the side of her own face in mirth, smearing the sheep's blood all over it and not caring. "Oh my," Heria taunted, her voice light and flowery. "You didn't really think you'd get out like that, did you? No, no. Soon, your worries will all be over, hag. Don't worry. The poison on this blade will sting, yes, and it will kill you, yes. But then it's over."

"You can't!" Kitalla protested. "What if you're wrong? What if I die and you don't learn anything? I'm the only one who has this ability. Kill me and it's lost forever!"

Heria whistled a jaunty tune. "Sorry, dear, I don't respond well to begging. You know that." She took another slow step forward and flipped the dagger over in her hand. "All I need are a few layers of your skin so I can see where things are happening." Then her tone filled with malice. "And then I'll really know where to dig."

Unable to control her fear, Kitalla clenched her jaw and her breathing intensified. She knew she could close her eyes against the oncoming foe, but the thought of not knowing when the girl would strike was worse than seeing it coming. She was utterly helpless as Heria leaned over her, sniffing various parts of her body before finding one she liked and bringing down the knife.

The dagger was held horizontally over Kitalla's left forearm and Heria swiped it back and forth sharply in the air, clearly marking out the path of her first incision. She lowered the knife more and more. It was like a bladed pendulum, dropping inevitably lower with each swing until, at last, the blade struck against her skin.

Kitalla clenched her whole body against the onrush of pain, blocking out all sense of it when it happened. She felt the pressure of the blade and the beginning sparks from the acidic coating Heria had applied to the edge, but then that was it. Her body must have shut down like all those times after Grenthar's trials, she guessed. But when she looked up, Heria had the most curious expression on her face.

It was a mix of anger, amusement, and utter bewilderment. She swept the dagger again over Kitalla's arm, but the blade did not bite into her skin. It warped and glanced off it instead. She tried it a few more times to be sure. "What is this?" she wondered aloud. Then anger sank in, for this was interrupting her ritual. "You *will* be cut!" she demanded, thrusting the knife deep into Kitalla's chest.

But as the blade passed through the binding straps and Kitalla's tunic, it changed. The metal warped and became liquefied, dribbling away from the hilt and rolling off her body and eventually to the floor, where it hardened again in a nondescript puddle.

With a feral scream, Heria brought the hilt of the dagger down onto Kitalla's face, breaking her nose. She screamed again and bashed again, and there was nothing the thief could do to stop her. When at last her rage played out, she turned to the metal stain on the floor and tried to pry it up with her fingers.

"I should have known you were cursed," she said absently. "Such a strange one to begin with." She tugged harder and managed to free the metallic disk. "Whatever caused this to happen, I wonder?" Ignoring Kitalla's moans of pain, she turned to Gabrion. "What of you? You're not cursed too? No, you smell too innocent to be cursed." She stalked closer and Gabrion, who had been trying to free himself, watched with the same inability to move.

Heria stepped up to him and sniffed him as she had done to Kitalla. "Yes, you smell so different. No curses there. You'll bleed, won't you? You'll give me what I need, won't you?"

Kitalla forced herself to speak. "He doesn't have the gift you're looking for."

Heria screamed and reacted by bringing the metal disk down onto Gabrion's belly, with the sharpest edge in the lead. Yet when the disk touched his skin, it broke like glass and clattered to the floor. But that wasn't all. The glass jade in Gabrion's pocket had sharpened him with the threat on his life, and like the blacksmith's forge that had exploded against him in Pindington, so too did the metal and all of his bindings fall away from his body.

"No!" Heria gasped, backing away.

Gabrion pushed himself upright, sore and stiff, but ignoring it. He had no weapons, save one. He withdrew the jade from his pocket, remembering the words of the elder of Gerrish that nothing was sharper than that jade. He brandished it like a knife and lashed out at the girl, who bounded away, slow only because of her shock.

Gabrion chased her away a few steps before turning and slashing away Kitalla's bindings. The thief rolled painfully to the floor, clutching her nose and trying to quell the bleeding. Gabrion turned and saw that Heria was armed with new daggers.

"You already know those won't help you," he warned. "Stop now and we'll spare you."

Heria cackled and rolled forward, swinging her arms out, trying to strike him. He parried and blocked her attacks, not entirely sure if the jade's protection was still intact and taking no chances. Weakened from all the poison, it was all Gabrion could do to keep up with the nimble girl, but he kicked and twisted about, making sure she didn't have a chance to get to Kitalla, her real target.

This was Heria's hideout, though, and she was ready with more than just daggers. She rolled off to one side, feinting easily, and when Gabrion moved, she dove the other way, seeking a tile on the floor. She smashed her dagger onto the tile, breaking it, which opened a series of trap doors in the floor, one of which opened right under Kitalla. The thief reacted instantly and rolled on her side onto a solid part of the floor, where she curled up for a few moments more until the blood stopped gushing from her nose.

Gabrion leaped over the holes in the floor and sought the mad girl with vigor. The more he moved, the more his body wanted to move, warming up to the exercise, eager for more. He tried watching for more trap releases the girl might press, but he didn't really know what to look for, so he focused instead on bringing her down. Heria made a good show of fighting him in earnest, but she was only pretending. She already believed he couldn't be harmed by her daggers, so she needed to do something else.

With a few fancy leaps and spins, Heria made her way across the room, Gabrion following close, his jade clutched tightly in hand. She cracked another floor tile and he heard a loud groaning sound overhead. Gabrion looked up reflexively as the girl rolled low and under the plank that had trapped Kitalla. All the warrior could see was darkness ahead, but then a hot sticky sludge splattered through the room. It burned him on contact, but worse than that, the tar stuck to the floor and made it extremely difficult to move.

Heria cackled wildly. "I may have needed a sheep earlier, but that doesn't mean sheeliopes don't have their uses too! Good luck moving in that."

"No problem," Kitalla whispered in her ear, grabbing her tightly and pressing a dagger against her throat. Kitalla had tracked her movement and dove under the plank behind her as the tar fell from the ceiling. "It's about time to end the fun, little girl."

Immediately, Heria started to cry. "All I wanted was to learn how to protect myself." She sobbed weakly. "I know I didn't always go about it right, but that's all. That's all I wanted. So I wouldn't be hurt anymore." She wailed pitifully, but Kitalla wasn't fooled.

"That's enough out of you, murderer," she said coldly. "After all you've done, you don't deserve any pity."

Heria cried louder. "So that's it, it ends like this? Huddled like an animal in a cage? You'll cut my throat out and that is all?" Kitalla could feel the girl's tears dripping onto her forearm.

"Like the sheep," Kitalla agreed, tightening her grip.

"No, please!" she begged desperately, and the sound tugged on Gabrion's heart. "Kitalla…"

"It's a ruse, Gabrion," Kitalla responded. "Help me with her. She isn't done yet. These tears are fake."

"How *could* you?" Heria sobbed. "Everyone turns against me. No one ever trusts me. No one ever wanted to understand me. Why?"

Gabrion worked his way over, his boots making loud sucking sounds with each step as he pulled up from the tar. He was careful in his steps so as to avoid all the pitfalls the girl had opened. He saw the ultimate sorrow on Heria's face, and the stream of constant tears falling down her dirty cheeks, cutting lines through the sheep's blood on one side. She looked a mess.

He couldn't help himself. He reached in to pull her out from under the plank, as Kitalla knew he would. She was ready for it, and when warrior took the girl in his arms, Kitalla came quickly to his aid.

It was in a flash that Heria jabbed her dagger into Gabrion's side. Once her arm was free, she acted without hesitation and even Kitalla's anticipation of the move wasn't enough. The warrior fell over into the pitch, clutching his side as Heria laughed and pulled away easily. Her shoes were laced with talc that resisted the pull of the tar and she was able to easily bounce away to another floor tile. As Kitalla bent down to examine Gabrion's wound, Heria's cackle echoed once more, cracking the floor tile and opening another set of trap doors in the ceiling. Instead of releasing tar, these dropped numerous flasks of liquid, and when they crashed upon the stony floor, noxious vapors filled the chamber.

"Not much time left now!" Heria sang. "Fresh air is what you'll need! That toxin is stronger than the rest. Pity that I won't be able to learn your dance steps, but my life matters more." She twirled and leaped toward the exit, oblivious to the two daggers Kitalla had sent through the air. They struck the girl in the back, bringing her crashing down.

"No pain, Gabrion," Kitalla said, trying to ignore her own. "Try not to breathe either. Come on, let's go."

It was a challenge pulling him up from the floor. The wound in his side would need serious attention and soon, but with the horrid vapors filling the area, they needed to get out first anyway. Kitalla could hardly see through her squinted eyes, but she did her best to find patches of floor that had less tar than others. Gabrion drew breaths through his hand and tried to hold them for as long as he could, but each step forward tugged on his side and made him gasp. Soon the two of them were coughing and retching, pushing harder to reach the exit.

As they went, Heria also struggled to rise. The daggers had struck full force, but hadn't hit any vital organs. She hated herself for not expecting the attack, even more that the foolish hag had been the one responsible. She didn't have an antidote to the poison on her. The vines had seen to that on the journey there. But if she could get out, there was still a chance she could survive. She got to her hands and knees and slogged forward the best she could.

It became clear to her that Kitalla and the warrior would reach the exit first, so Heria reached into her tunic and removed the last of her daggers, trying to take them down in one last attempt. Kitalla was ready this time and she shoved Gabrion ahead a step, then dodged aside as the dagger hit the wall.

"No!" Heria screamed. "No!" She pulled forward, but started gagging as the toxic air swelled around her.

"We've got to do something," Gabrion gasped.

Kitalla knew it was coming. "Keep going, I'll get her," she snarled. She shoved the warrior one last time and he took the hint to keep moving onward. She then turned toward the teen, who didn't understand what was happening and started thrashing about in defiance. "Settle down, little fool," Kitalla said, reaching to pull her up.

But Heria wouldn't have it. She kicked out at Kitalla's leg and swung one arm upward with all the strength she had, which wasn't much after the dagger strikes to her back. The pain clouded her eyes and Kitalla knew that between the wounds and the poison, this girl didn't have much longer to live. Still, Gabrion would never forgive her if she didn't try. Kitalla reached down again and yanked the girl to her feet. She then shoved her harshly forward, closer to the exit. Heria flopped down onto the tar in a heap, coughing and sputtering and crying in earnest now.

Kitalla went to her again, taking breaths through the sleeve of her tunic, hoping it might block some of the poison. Heria responded like an old doll, limp and with no more fight left in her. Kitalla hoisted her up and carried her the rest of the way, where Gabrion grabbed hold and dragged as well. Soon, the three of them were free of the underground cavern.

Fresh air met their noses eagerly and their lungs drew it in with raging hunger, making them cough deeply until the fumes were cleared out. They felt nauseated and wanted nothing more than to pass out from their trials, but there was more to do.

Heria lay in a heap on the ground, barely breathing at all, as Kitalla wrapped Gabrion's midsection with his tunic to help slow the bleeding. They would need to do more but it would suffice for now. There wasn't much to do for Kitalla's nose, but at least it had stopped bleeding on its own.

"No," Heria whimpered. "Not like this." She coughed and spat blood, then looked up at the others. "You were all supposed to die at my hand. No one left alive. All gone. I would have done it too. I would have won."

Kitalla bent down and gazed sadly upon the writhing girl. "It's over now, Heria."

Gabrion joined her. "Come on, we'll help you fix your wounds. Get you to a healer."

But Heria was somewhere else. As she stared at Kitalla and Gabrion, her eyes welled up in sorrow. "Papa, you mustn't hurt Mama any more. I didn't mean to kill you. I just want you to stop hitting her. Please, Papa," she cried.

Gabrion could see that her eyes were glazed over and that her end was near. He leaned closer and took the girl's hand. "I promise, dear heart. I will stop now. You have saved me. And I thank you."

Heria then faced Kitalla. "Mama, I don't know why you don't love me. Why you took yourself from me when I needed you. Why you left me. All I wanted was for you to be safe. Why did you go?"

Kitalla trembled and took Heria's other hand. "Child, I was wrong to leave you. But we will be together soon, the way we were all meant to be. Go in peace."

A small part of the girl's pain healed with those words and she closed her eyes for the last time.

Gabrion and Kitalla sat there a while longer as the last breath left Heria's body and the lifeblood stop seeping from her wounds. Kitalla tried to convince herself that her tears were from the pain of her broken nose, but she knew even Gabrion wouldn't believe her.

"At least," he said, frog-throated, "she received some mercy at the very end."

Kitalla nodded.

CHAPTER 9

Early Homecoming

GABRION AND KITALLA were too damaged to give Heria a proper burial. They first searched her things for the nature jade, but they already knew from the lack of resonance of their own jades that it wasn't there. They dragged branches and rocks atop her body, wishing in some way they could do more for her, but their own need was pressing.

The dagger wound to Gabrion's side was deep, and even with a tight wrapping, it still leaked blood. Kitalla's nose was a fiery mess from Heria's bashing, and as she started to bruise, the pain grew worse and her eyesight diminished. She wasn't certain of their location, for it was a hideout Heria had never shared with her during their earlier travels, but as they looked around, Gabrion gave a start.

"I know where we are!" he gasped, clutching his side. "We go southwest from here."

It was good enough for the thief. They had no supplies to take with them and so she wrapped her arm around him to steady him and they walked slowly away from the torture chamber, Gabrion trying desperately to keep alert and focused. Their lungs ached from breathing the poison and their bodies rebelled against the journey, but their determination won out and they stumbled along for a good hour before Gabrion pointed ahead.

"There." He could barely speak. Kitalla turned her head to gaze out from her lesser-puffed eye and saw a hint of silhouette along the horizon. She nodded so Gabrion would know she understood and then she helped drag him toward the destination.

"Halt, travelers!" called a young man as they approached a few hours later. "What business have you here?"

"Desperate need of healing, friend," Kitalla returned as amiably as possible, but the young man seemed skeptical.

"You do look worse for wear, both of…" His voice drifted off as he looked them over again. "Gabrion!"

Kitalla could barely recall the next few hours as they were ushered in to Savvron, Gabrion's hometown. Their wounds were dressed and tended. They were fed and bathed and laid down to rest. She knew there were no magic healers in the town, based on the quality of the ministrations, but she didn't care. She turned herself over to whatever hands were nearby that poked, prodded, and then massaged her ailments away. It was morning when she came to again, alert enough to question her surroundings and to take an actual interest in this destination.

She sat up on a firm bed, inches off the floor and covered with a thick blanket that did little to cushion her from the straw underneath. Her body ached from head to toe, particularly the nose that had been so badly beaten. She tentatively touched it and felt that a poultice had been applied to it to help facilitate healing.

The room was bare of furnishings, with only a chair in the corner and a table off to the side. The door was open and allowed a view of a larger space beyond, but it, too, seemed barren. She didn't really expect to see much, having previously spent a number of days trying to ambush travelers in the area, Gabrion included, but as she looked around, she was appalled at the sheer lack of anything valuable.

With a gentle push, she rose to her feet and paced the room, feeling terribly dizzy and pained from her injuries. After a few minutes of walking, she ventured from the chamber and saw an older woman sewing together scraps of leather into a tunic. The woman was focused on her work and didn't acknowledge Kitalla until she reached her workspace and sat down.

"Feeling any better, dear?" she asked in a grandmotherly voice. It made Kitalla cringe.

"I've been worse. I've been better. May I ask where I am?"

The woman smiled. "You've entered Savvron, sadly in a time of war. Skirmishes break out all the time, now, and I do hope you are able to flee to safety before the next one starts."

"What of you?" she couldn't help but ask.

The woman gestured to a pile of clothes behind her that Kitalla hadn't noticed. "I have work that needs doing here. And if the Hathrens see fit to slay me for it, then my time will have come anyway. If not them, then a falling beam or a wayward cart. But until then, best do what I can." She made a few tight stitches and Kitalla was impressed with the quality of the work. The woman looked up, "And what of you, dear?"

She wasn't sure what to say exactly, so she ventured the truth. "My friend and I were injured and needed healing. He's from here. Gabrion. Perhaps you know him?"

She chuckled warmly. "Of course, dear. The boy grew up right outside my window. Gentle soul." Then her voice grew heavy as she added, "But so, war changes even one so light."

"He was badly hurt. Do you know how he is?"

"Oh yes, dear. He will be fine." She then leaned forward conspiratorially. "Though I admit that he would be better off with a magic healer instead. Too bad about that, really."

"Too bad?" she asked.

"Well yes." At last she set down her work and stared into Kitalla's eyes. "The only magic healers nearby at all are in Kaison, near the king. But—oh, I do not think it really my place to say so, but if you know Gabrion then you already know his heart and won't think ill of him regardless. You see, he is a wanted fugitive of the king. Quite the scandal, really. He broke out of the dungeons and freed all the prisoners then spat in the king's face on his way out!"

Kitalla's eyes lit with amusement, recalling that the events had been rather different. "You don't say! I always knew he had great courage, but to think! Did he really?"

The older woman devoured Kitalla's interest. "So they all say. Why, a soldier visited here some time after, seeking his parents to say they'd met on their journey and that he was off fighting lupinoes, of all things. I knew the boy was special, but taking on a horde of lupinoes, saving that soldier's life in the process! What a marvel. But," and her voice grew sad again, "since he left, the king has sent others trying to locate poor Gabrion to escort him back to the dungeons. To finish him off for good. You would think that with a war going on, he'd let a silly incident like that go for now. After all, it was, what, eight months ago? Really."

Kitalla nodded, agreeing full-heartedly. She also wondered at the exaggeration of Gabrion's prowess. Had the guardsman not mentioned the others on purpose, or was this doddering woman just focused on the one soul she knew personally? She hoped it was the former, for that would better protect herself and Dariak. "Do you know where Gabrion is right now? I would like to see him if I could."

"Why, dear, he would be next door, of course. You certainly should go and see him for yourself. But do return after. It has been a delight to talk with you."

Kitalla bid farewell and walked into the blinding morning sun. She could hear the sounds of the small village coming awake and though she knew they were near the frontlines of war, she felt more calm than she had in some time. To the west, the sky was faded with smoke from campfires in the distance. Whether from Kallisorian troops or Hathren, she couldn't possibly know. There was a calm solemnity to the villagers as they went from place to place. They weren't frightened or fearful, exactly, just wary. Several of them eyed her suspiciously, wondering if she was a spy for the Hathren forces. More than one changed directions upon seeing her. It suited her just fine.

She walked over to Gabrion's house and rapped on the door. A well-muscled man opened the panel and invited her inside. Kitalla inspected him carefully. He had the same chiseled features of his son, though his skin was a bit darker and more leathery from the extended years outdoors. Age suited him well and he carried himself with unabashed pride and confidence. He had no secrets about him. There was no darkness in his essence in any way, and Kitalla envied him for it.

"Kitalla, I presume. He's asked about you a few times," he said with a deep, resonating voice. Gabrion had inherited that, too. "We assured him you would be here when you were able."

"Thank you. May I see him...?" She let her voice hang expectantly, waiting for him to introduce himself.

He obliged. "Terrsian. My wife, Galdina, is out gathering supplies, but you will meet her soon, I am sure. Come, this way."

Like the old woman's house, this place was sparsely furnished and everything in it was well-used. The house itself was in better repair, no doubt because of Terrsian himself. The ground floor was a little larger and had three rooms extending off the main area. He led her inside to Gabrion's temporary room, as he was unable to ascend the ladder to his usual space. He then backed out and left them alone.

Kitalla eyed the warrior from head to toe, tracing the lines of his arms and torso, watching the gentle rise and fall of his chest. It filled her with such peace to simply know he was there, alive and recovering. His determined spirit was not gone from the world. His quest had not yet ended. She reached out and placed her hand on his chest so she could feel his heart beating strongly. She listened to her own heart as his beat beneath her hand, and she tried to calm her breathing so that they also matched. His skin was warm and soft, and as she stood there over him, she realized suddenly that she had fallen for him.

With a start she stood up and covered her face in her hands, turning away. It was ludicrous. He was only a boy, really, and his heart was devoted to another. Besides, her heart was dead and cold inside her chest. She couldn't care about anyone. Not again. Not ever again.

"Kitalla?" he whispered, clearly in pain. "You're here."

She couldn't look at him. "We made it, it seems," she said, her voice also very quiet. "Nice place."

"It's home," he replied. "Help me up, will you?"

"You should stay down," she decided, still facing away.

He strained to push himself up, but he was too weak. "Kitalla, please. Help me."

Grinding her teeth, she turned and did so. She pretended he was some feeble old man with gross sores and moles all over his body, but touching him felt like magic. His skin was silky, stretched over firm, solid muscles. She had to consciously stop herself from pressing her lips to his shoulder. Once he was upright, she stepped away, leaning in the doorway, looking anywhere but at him.

"You look a mess," he said, trying to make her smile, but she didn't. "You're hurt pretty badly, are you?"

"No healers here," she returned flippantly. "Got to make do, I guess."

"We're a small village. We never really had use for healers before. Not that we usually rely on magic of any kind here."

She nodded. "But embarrassing and sad that your village is in the line of fire and the king doesn't see fit to send even one here as a backup."

Gabrion grunted. "Now you're channeling Dariak. How do you think they're doing?"

She tried to be funny. "They've probably figured out by now that they can't make babies and have gone off to find a home instead. I wonder who will do most of the cooking?"

"Randler," Gabrion decided. "But as usual, Dariak will offer up some extra herbs to season it with."

"That's true. That's true."

"Kitalla, what's wrong?"

She knew the question would arise at some point; she just wished it was later. "I guess I'm tired and hurting, Gabrion."

"It's more than that. What happened?"

She looked at him and smiled weakly. "I'm fine," she lied. "But what about you? How long until you're ready to continue on?"

He considered for a moment, gently touching his hand to the wound at his side. "I don't really know. I certainly can't use a sword for some time, not without healing anyway." He watched her fidget in the doorway for a few minutes, wondering what was troubling her so. He hoped she would tell him so he could help, but there was no point trying to force it out of her. He'd come to understand how fruitless those attempts could be.

"Gabrion, Kitalla, would you like some food?" Terrsian called from the kitchen area.

With relief, Kitalla readily agreed, as did Gabrion. He couldn't stand on his own, however, so Kitalla walked over and reached her arms under his as if she were going to give him a great hug, then she pulled up and back, while he pushed with his legs. Together, they got him upright, though unsteady, and it a took a few moments with her holding onto him before he felt secure enough on his own.

He thought he saw her blush as she turned away, but he figured it was from the strain of helping him up. He couldn't dwell on it, anyway, for taking steps forward tugged on his wound and sent sparks of pain shooting up his side and he insisted on eating at the table. He worked his way into the other room and struggled into a chair, after which he needed a few minutes before he could focus on the food in front of him.

Terrsian didn't seem particularly interested in Kitalla or any of their adventures, instead catching Gabrion up on town gossip, which thoroughly bored Kitalla. She never minded catching up on news, but for a town imperiled with frequent skirmishes, Terrsian had very little to say about even that.

"Old Gavinod gave the bakery over to his son soon after you left, saying that he couldn't pretend things hadn't changed. I don't think he's stepped inside the place since. He's been helping with the wounded, mostly. I guess he feels it's his penance for failing that day."

"He can't blame himself," Gabrion chimed in, remembering that first actual battle. "Besides, he did step up in the end and guard the boy."

"Not really. Not in his eyes," Terrsian clarified. "But anyway, Frenith has done a good job with the bakery ever since. Has a real knack for it, I think." From there, he talked about the smiths and the other farmers. They discussed the year's crop of his own farm and how different it was harvesting it alone again, with Gabrion gone. "Not that I'm complaining. It was good for me," he boasted, flexing his arms. "Though… your mother missed you."

"I wish I had returned under better circumstances."

Terrsian nodded. "Bleeding profusely at our doorstep was not quite the welcome we had planned for you." After what seemed like all day, he then shifted his attention directly to Kitalla to address her. "And I wholly thank you for protecting him on his return journey."

She tilted her head in acknowledgement, then slid Gabrion a glance. "We've done a fair share of protecting each other along the way. He's quite the capable warrior. Though I regret that your lives were turned upside down with the fighting, I think it would have been a shame if he had never really experienced some actual battles. He's very talented."

Terrsian harrumphed. "We could have done without the fighting, but I'm glad he has proven himself in your eyes."

Something about the way he said it irked her. She couldn't tell if he suspected a deeper connection between them or perhaps he knew of her life as a brigand in the area. Whatever it was, it made her uncomfortable.

As did Gabrion when he shifted the conversation. "Father, has there been any word at all? Of Mira? Her parents? Anything?"

Terrsian shook his head. "Not much."

"But Hernior told me you had received word from them."

"Ah, the soldier. So you met up with him again?" He grinned, despite himself. "He seemed intent upon fulfilling your wishes. He said you had specifically challenged him to speak to all the older villagers and tell them of your travels."

"I didn't want to single you and mother out, just in case. But I figured at the least, even if he told old Klerra, word would reach you."

A full smile lit Terrsian's face and Kitalla saw that it had some of the same innocence that Gabrion kept with him, too. How alike they were! "Yes," Terrsian responded. "But we all came together at his arrival and we introduced ourselves to him directly."

When he didn't continue, Gabrion prompted for more.

"Very well," Terrsian grumbled. "Mira's parents went to Hathreneir to petition for Mira's release. However, something went wrong and, from what I could tell, they became prisoners themselves. Their letters were genuine enough. I recognize the writing. And there wasn't strain to the wording or the penmanship, so they were writing on their own. But I've had only two letters from them. One was to say that they and Mira were safe. The other was to demand I stop trying to reach them."

Gabrion was aghast. "Demand?"

"Yes." Terrsian shrugged. "I can only imagine it was for my own good, so that the Hathrens wouldn't come hunting me down to stop me from asking too many questions."

"Do you know where they are?"

Terrsian squinted. "You may have ventured out across the land, son, but seeking your way through enemy territory is a completely different matter. I advise against it."

"Father…"

There was hesitation as Terrsian regarded his son. Kitalla looked between the two, glad of the distraction, for the mention of Mira had made her stomach flip over. After all, she had promised Gabrion she would help him rescue her. And then what, lose him to her?

Shaking his head, Terrsian acquiesced. "The messages came from the Hathren court. I believe they are in the castle itself."

Kitalla couldn't help herself. "For a ramshackle little town, you sure seem to know a bit about royal processes."

Terrsian was not offended. "Ramshackle little town, perhaps. But we're close to the border so we receive some messengers through here en route to either king. It helps to know the real messengers from the scouts and spies."

"Then what news of the war can you impart to us?" she asked. "You've said so little in that regard."

He stared at her for a moment before answering. "I have little interest in the actual war, just how it directly impacts us. And it isn't as if the messengers clear the details with us before traveling on. There isn't much I can tell you."

"But you're under siege," she insisted. "Or at least, you've been hit a few times."

"Father, is this true?" Gabrion gasped.

Reluctantly, Terrsian nodded. "The Hathrens have attacked numerous times since your departure. Roughly twice a month, but we've held them off each time and haven't had… many casualties. It feels as if they're just making a show of the attacks."

"Not many casualties," Gabrion echoed. "But some. Who?"

"Son, don't trouble yourself with this now. You have more important things to worry about, such as recovering. No, I won't speak further on the matter." He stood abruptly and then turned a sharp eye at Kitalla. "Escort him back to his room and then assist me with cleaning this up."

Kitalla wasn't used to such directives and she wanted to rebel against the command, but she was still healing, herself, and she didn't have the fight in her. She pulled Gabrion's dejected form from his seat and guided him back to bed, where he laid himself down and fell promptly asleep.

It took some time for Terrsian to speak to Kitalla after she joined him in the kitchen area with the leftover dishes from breakfast. He did stare, though, which she found unnerving, but she knew several times when Gabrion had struggled to find the words he wanted to say, and so she scraped the food away, then placed them in the basin until Terrsian figured out what he was trying to say to her.

She wasn't disappointed. "What are your intentions, Kitalla?"

"Just scrubbing these clean," she said offhandedly.

Terrsian's voice tightened as he continued. "With my son. Will you lead him to Hathreneir? Will you bring him to his doom?"

She turned and bore deeply into the man's brown eyes. "You underestimate him if you think such a journey would bring about his doom. He's grown much since this adventure started. Believe in him, and you'll see he has greater potential than you could imagine."

Terrsian regarded these words carefully before speaking again. "You should know that his heart is set on another."

"Mira." She nodded, turning back to wash the cutlery.

"I fear he will be devastated if he meets up with her again." Kitalla listened intently to the man's voice, and realized that it pained him to admit this to her. "He always idolized her, but we always thought he would outgrow it. Yet, still he quests for her after all this time."

"It has kept him strong, believing in her," Kitalla said.

"If she is within the king's company in Hathreneir, then I don't see how their union can ever be met with joy. Some letters came," he confessed, "but…"

"What are you saying?"

Terrsian shook his head. "No parent wants to see their child hurt. He has clearly been through much already. I couldn't bear it if his heart shatters over a woman. Especially one who never confessed herself to him, as far as I knew."

Kitalla almost dropped the fork she was scrubbing absently. "You mean to tell me that she didn't share his sentiment?"

"They were great friends. Always were. Maybe she did. But I don't think they had the same connection my wife and I had."

"'Had,'" Kitalla echoed. "She is one of the casualties you mentioned earlier."

Terrsian's silence was all the affirmation she needed.

"I won't tell him. It's your place to do so when you feel the time is right. But won't he notice her absence?"

"Not if he continues to sleep like this, no. But once he is able, I must ask you to escort him from here. Take him to safety, I beg of you. Do not bring him into harm's way by guiding him across the border." Here, he grabbed her shoulders and spun her around, then locked her in place so he could drill his gaze into her. "You may be a very skilled thief, but don't steal my son from me. He is all the family I have left."

She staggered for a moment, her jaw opening and closing at random. "How—?"

"I may only be a farmer to you, but I keep my eyes and ears open. Your antics have affected others of this village, not just my son." He wouldn't release her, not yet. "But he has clearly found something in you to trust. And I trust my son. I will not turn you in or seek retribution from you. I only ask that if there is any morality left in you, you will use it to keep him safe."

Kitalla looked away from the piercing eyes and thought about her revelation that very morning. Gabrion meant more to her than she cared to admit. She pulled herself out of Terrsian's grip so she could stand on her own before she answered. "Morality or not, I will protect him."

Terrsian closed his eyes and nodded in relief. He then awkwardly patted her shoulder and strode from the room, heading toward Gabrion's chamber to change the dressing on his wound.

C H A P T E R 10

Savvron

TWO DAYS WENT by quickly for Kitalla and Gabrion. She spent as much time as possible avoiding the warrior, hoping some distance would help her restore her personal sense of composure. This prompted her to walk about town and familiarize herself with its layout, which felt much more like reconnaissance than hiding, anyway. She spoke with the villagers who would open up to her and she focused the conversations on the previous skirmishes they had defended against, hoping in turn to provide them with some insight to further their efforts.

Gabrion, meanwhile, spent a majority of the time eating and sleeping. His body had shut itself down in order to recuperate from his recent trials. Terrsian withheld the loss of Gabrion's mother from him, regretting he would someday soon have to break his silence.

Kitalla stayed with the old woman, Klerra, sometimes helping her with her sewing. The thief was impressed to learn that Klerra also knew a fair bit of healing skills and had been the one to stitch up the wound in Gabrion's side after their arrival. "The least I could do," she had said after telling Kitalla about it, "was to try to keep him from scarring too much."

Gesturing to the fine needlework she was exacting on the clothes, Kitalla had replied, "No one will ever know he was hurt, you're that good."

She had to admit that the old woman was growing on her, even in such a short amount of time. Klerra had no love for the king, especially after accusing Gabrion of treachery and leaving their town without royal soldiers to aid in their defense against Hathren attacks. But her loathing extended back to her childhood and the previous king, who had later died in the War of the Colossus. The great and powerful leader of their kingdom had come to their village, stolen a handful of maidens, and all but one had been lost forever.

"And when Merla returned, she was just broken, she was," Klerra recalled. "Nothing sensible came out of her again." She leaned in toward Kitalla, as she seemed to enjoy doing, as if the thief was a close daughter of her own or some wild conspirator. "She had a bit about her of being bewitched, I say. Beating and physical terrors don't put a ghost in the eyes quite like the one she had. Poor thing."

"That's why this village despises magic, then?"

"It's a fair reason, indeed. Not the only, of course. It is, for all intents and purposes, forbidden, you know. The king may claim mages are free to roam about and do minor incantations, but—woe!—if a mage is seen in his craft! Never heard of one to survive being discovered, I can tell you."

Kitalla had, of course, heard of such a mage. These past couple of days, she had all but pushed Dariak and Randler out of her thoughts, knowing she couldn't do anything about them until Gabrion was feeling stronger. If the town was away from the battling, then maybe... But here they were and the villagers were growing tense, as if a fight was scheduled to occur any day.

As she finished her evening stroll through the village, Kitalla stopped by Gabrion's house to spend a little time with him. Terrsian welcomed her with a plate of food seasoned with his own herbs and vegetables. "It's a wonder Gabrion isn't better at cooking," she teased.

Terrsian smiled sadly. "He was better keeping the field in line. Galdina challenged me to learn early on, insisting she wouldn't marry a man who couldn't surprise her with a delicious meal." He abruptly cleared his throat and took Kitalla's empty plate to the kitchen, clearly finished with her for the time being.

Kitalla went in to Gabrion's room and he was sleeping once again. The flickering candlelight danced over his body and made her feel as if she were watching his dreams. If so, he was running wild and free in a desert sun, laughing merrily and enjoying every moment of it.

The dream ended abruptly with a loud crash outside. Kitalla turned and was nearly bowled over by Terrsian as he raced for the door. Shouts echoed in the early night air, and it was easy to see that torches were guiding a Hathren troop in to town.

She shoved past Terrsian and bolted through the streets, raising an alarm of her own. The few villagers who had taken her seriously during her stay grabbed their weapons and makeshift armor, then followed in her wake as she gauged the arrival of the invaders. The herbalist's hut was the easiest for her to scale, after which she leaped over to the tanner's store and then crouched down low to assess the situation better. As she did so, her escort gathered below in the defensive formation she had described, awaiting her orders.

"Six archers, and I wouldn't put it past them to send lit arrows on a night like this." She continued counting and calling out the tally. "Eighteen fighters, swords mostly, but a couple of lances, too. I don't see any mages with this set, but they could be waiting until we're fully engaged with the others. Rogues, also. Four of them. Those four will be the best trained in taking down a foe, so be wary and leave them to me."

Her nose and face felt no pain as she prepared herself for the battle. She ignored the demands of the village's fighters and issued orders of her own. "You will obey me or you will die," she warned them. The light of experience in her eyes was compelling and most fell in with her strategy right away. The rest needed some mild convincing, but once she laid the groundwork, they could tell she knew what she was doing.

They hadn't had time or real inclinations to build any elaborate traps, but the villagers already had a few lined up. Covered pits and projectiles swinging from trees were about the extent of them, but in the darkening sky, they could still prove effective.

Kitalla guided her forces to key areas, sending three off to rouse the rest of the town and to prepare barrels of water for dousing fires. It was the one precaution that saved the village from total destruction, for no sooner had the archers come into range than their fiery arrows rained from the sky.

Cries went up from the townspeople, but Kitalla sharply reminded her fighters to stay in line. "If they ignored the warnings, let the fire teach them to listen better next time. I assure you, if we do not put an end to this here and now, these attacks will continue. Let's free this place from tyranny!"

The echoing cheers gave the opponents pause, for they were unaccustomed to such a unified front from these people. Indeed, the soldiers sent to attack the town were of lower caliber than Kitalla had originally expected; not that they weren't skilled, but they were no elite force.

As the arrows dwindled, the fighters and rogues ran into Savvron, weapons drawn and fury in their eyes. Kitalla's daggers were ready, and with a quick toss, the first two casualties were scored. Enraged, the next in line turned right for her, but she welcomed them eagerly. She had felt too helpless for far too long, from being injured in Pindington, finding herself useless against Randler's mother, nearly dying at Heria's hand, and spending the past days here in reclusive recovery. With each flash of memory, her actions sharpened and she became a veritable death-wielding blur.

She didn't realize it, but she was channeling energy through her body and her dance skills kicked into gear as she raced into the fray. Her arms swept from side to side as her legs propelled her forward. She dipped below sword thrusts and kicked out at sweeping legs. The energy whisked about her as she went, obscuring her from view, and turning her almost to shadow.

Four, five, six bodies fell at her feet and she kept rushing onward, reveling in the beauty of each dodge, parry, and strike. Every movement connected to the next, not like a brawl at all, but a carefully scripted ballet. Seven, eight went down. Nine turned to run, but she didn't let him get away. Ten tripped on his own foot and impaled himself on his sword.

Then the foes scattered and the weaving shadow lost its way. Kitalla slowed down to find the next target, seeing now that she was alone with her carnage. The sounds of fighting echoed and she turned to notice that she had sprinted away from the town in her bloodlust, leaving it in the hands of its own defenders. She raced back to help them.

The fighters of Savvron held true to the tactics Kitalla had imparted to them. They remained close together, refusing to be separated, and moving as a group toward their foes. They worked in solid sets of two and three, pressing their advantage against the invaders and driving them off. Soon, the troops became demoralized and the remaining six Hathrens called a retreat and vanished into the night. Kitalla debated going after them, to complete this task, but with the sudden thrill gone, her body reminded her that she wasn't at her optimal strength. She needed to rest.

The villagers thanked her for her efforts and took care of their wounded. No one had died on their side. It was the first time no one had felt death's bite in these skirmishes. Kitalla made her way back to Klerra's, hoping to clean up and then find a way to sleep, for she knew that the next day would be a busy one. Not only would they need to bolster their defenses against the next attack, which would undoubtedly include a stronger force, but they would turn to her for help.

With a single fight, she had proven her worth to them and had ensured they all survived. She thought back to Gabrion's words at Randler's cave when he was shouting at her, telling her how important she was to them all. Yet, she didn't want to be important. She didn't want anyone to rely on her. She was meant to be free.

She approached Klerra's home, but then veered and went to Gabrion. The tumult outside didn't seem to have fazed him. Standing beside his bed, she struggled to keep in her tears.

"I can't do the part of the hero. That's your role in this. I'm no hero. You wouldn't be hurt if I were. No, Gabrion, this isn't a life I can lead here. I can't stay." She crouched down to the floor, her back pressed against the wall. "But how can I leave you here? I can't let you abandon your quest. I can't leave you here unprotected.

"I joined the mage's little quest to gain power. I never expected to be changed by someone else, least of all a naïve villager, trying to protect his home. But I don't want to change. I can't go back to being the protector. It wasn't ever what I was meant to be." Her face sank into her hands and she cursed herself for feeling so confused.

But Gabrion wasn't asleep. "You don't want to be the protector, but you won't leave me unprotected? That doesn't make much sense."

"I—" She drew in a deep breath and tried to steady herself. It had been too long since she had allowed herself to dwell on her feelings. She didn't like it.

"Kitalla, you've been the protector all along on this journey."

"No," she breathed. "The protector was always you. I'm just a tool. A means to an end. A way through the fight so we can get to the next fight. So I can learn offensive skills. So I can—" She stopped herself.

"Go on."

"No," she whispered. "I won't do this." She cleared her throat and battled against her emotions. "We each have our roles to fulfill. You're the protector," she repeated. "I am not capable of such a thing."

He turned his head so he could try to look at her, but she was covered in shadow. "We have different ideas of what it means to be a protector."

Her voice took an icy edge. "Enough. I won't have it. Your town needs to finds its own protector. It won't be me." She pushed herself up.

"Don't leave, Kitalla."

"What would you have me do instead?" she asked with a flash of her old self. "Tell you a bedtime story? Something about bunnies drinking tea?"

"You could. But I'd be fine if you just sat nearby for a while."

"Protecting you?" she asked petulantly.

"Mira's gone. Dariak and Randler are gone. Don't you go, too."

"You're being childish, Gabrion. Grow up." She took a step toward the door.

"Please, Kitalla. Don't go."

She breathed it quietly, but he heard her anyway. "I have to."

CHAPTER 11

Champion of Savvron

GABRION KNEW SOMETHING was terribly wrong when Kitalla disappeared for the next few days. She didn't visit him anymore, but he knew from the resonance of his jade that she hadn't gone far. Perhaps he had said something offensive, or maybe she was striving to teach the villagers proper defense. Either way, she was gone and he missed her company.

What he received instead was attention from the town's healers, including his father and old Klerra. Everyone asked him endless questions about his injuries and they poked and prodded when he least expected it. When he shooed them away, he struggled to calm his thoughts and drift off to sleep. It was difficult because it wasn't only Kitalla's absence that was on his mind. He still hadn't seen his mother. Terrsian avoided the subject at all costs, deflecting Gabrion's questions either by offering a meal or saying she was off somewhere.

"Father, level with me," he finally demanded.

The tall, solid man crumbled like a heap of clothing. He sank down on the edge of Gabrion's bed and buried his face in his hands. "There isn't much to say. She's gone, son. I couldn't save her."

"What happened?" he asked.

"It was maybe two months ago. The Hathrens came to town with a pair of mages. They played with us, mostly, shooting spells at the children to make them run. The soldiers kept the adults from coming to their aid. But your mother wouldn't have it. She ran out there, kitchen knife in hand, and she ordered them to stop. She accused them of becoming heathens, no longer Hathrens. They didn't appreciate the word-play. They told her off, but she refused to back down until the children were safe. I tried pulling her back but she wrenched herself away from me. Before I could inter-vene, they…" his voice drifted off and he shook his head. "I was too slow, when it comes down to it. I should have gotten her out of harm's way. She didn't need to die that day."

"If not her, it would have been you. Or both of you," Gabrion said.

"Better me than her," Terrsian retorted. "The troop left after her death. It's been like that ever since that first attack. They come, kill someone, then leave. Only your friend was able to break that chain."

"We'll end it for good," Gabrion declared, his voice sounding haunted. "You'll see. Savvron will be safe."

Terrsian was silent for a time. He reached out and placed his hand on Gabrion's knee. "Son, you're no longer a farm hand, are you? You've gone across this land and you've developed fighting skills, but you've also grown. Your heart is stronger. Your determination is more focused. Seeing you hurt like this was hard for me. I feared I would lose you, too. Yet, already, you're coming back to yourself and regaining strength. Son, I believe in you and your quest, whatever it may be. If you set your mind to it, I know you will succeed."

Gabrion's eyes shimmered but tears did not fall. He grasped his father's hand and held on to him tightly for what felt like the last time. He knew his childhood was gone from him then. His father had granted him ascension into manhood. When their hands released, they were no longer father and child. They were men, respectful of each other, and honor-bound to protect those around them.

Some time later, Terrsian crafted a midday meal as Gabrion stretched and walked through the house, fondly remembering his mother's presence with every step. He was gaining mobility again and it felt good being able to rise and sit on his own, without the excruciating pain he had arrived with. The wound itself was healing nicely, though it was taking its time; he would still need a while before he could brandish a sword in any meaningful way. He didn't venture outside yet, though, fearing the waves of weariness that still overtook him randomly.

As evening approached, the main door crashed open at Kitalla's touch. Gabrion opened his mouth to greet her, but she interrupted him, her eyes lit anxiously.

"You have to get out of here," she commanded with a slight note of panic in her voice. "This very moment, well or not. Terrsian, grab some essentials and take him from here. Head south or east, but stay away from the north."

"What is it?" Gabrion asked.

"Danger," she said simply. "Don't argue with me. Just go. Keep yourself safe."

"What of you?" he pursued.

"I have work to do here." With that, she turned and stormed out, pulling the door behind her so Gabrion couldn't call after her.

Terrsian looked at his son, wondering if he should heed the woman's warning. "Your thoughts?"

"I think she means it," he answered. "It must be bad."

"Anything we can do to help?"

Gabrion drew in a deep breath and immediately felt searing pain lancing through him. "Nothing *I* can do, in any event. Slow walking, sure. Very helpful."

Terrsian sprang into action, grabbing a satchel and loading it with food and waterskins. He grabbed a sword for his waist and a walking stick for Gabrion, though the young man protested it at first. They pushed their way to the door and stepped outside in the dwindling daylight. Gabrion looked northwest and saw a strange series of blue-white streaks blasting across the sky, battling with the sunset itself. Thunder echoed deeply, but he had enough experience to know that the sound wasn't the result of lightning, but of booted feet walking in unison. It seemed that Kitalla's recent victory against the Hathrens had spurred a full-force retaliation.

Kitalla was darting about when she saw Gabrion emerge from the house, leaning on the walking stick. She ran over to him and grabbed his shoulder. "You stay alive, and so will I. We have a promise to keep, remember?"

"To save Mira," he replied.

"To save Mira." She slapped his cheek and winked at him, then ran off, trusting him to take cover.

"Son?"

He stared after her for a moment before turning back. "She's right. I'm not ready for this. But I will say, it would have been a glorious fight." They strode off, after calling to the nearby elders to join them. As a pack of slow-moving villagers, they ventured toward the forest for cover.

Meanwhile, Kitalla had taken over the town's defenses completely. No one stood against her after the past few days of setting traps and training the men to fight. She had left Gabrion's side after the last skirmish, deciding she would keep his home safe since he presently wasn't able to. After that, she knew she would have to move on, whether he was ready or not. But for now, she had a goal in mind. It was a challenge, a trial, nothing more. Grenthar himself could have set it and it wouldn't matter. She was ready.

Fire-laced arrows were the first line of attack once again, but the villagers were ready for them. Every home was stocked with barrels or pails of water with one non-fighter dedicated to the purpose. The projectiles themselves were still dangerous, but old Klerra had been working on tarps that spanned the roofs across the houses in order to catch the brunt of them. The northern quadrant of the village looked like an oversized tent.

Their first volley thwarted, the Hathrens moved in closer. Packs of swordsmen flooded the streets and the fighting began in earnest. Kitalla was not among the first wave of defenders, as she was making other preparations, but she had trained the young men hard and they had been eager and capable learners.

Swords and shields crashed one into another, raising a cacophony that broke the spirits of some of the villagers, who then bolted and ran for the forest. However, the majority of the townspeople banded together and held the line tight, striking back to save their homeland and to keep these invaders from harming any more of their own.

Lancers raced into the forefront next, but Kitalla was ready for them. Their longer weapons would be a greater threat, for they could puncture the defenders from safer distances. With an owl cry, Kitalla alerted the brave boys and girls who were in the northern trees. They were perched on high, watching the archers and the swordsmen pass below them, knowing their homes were in jeopardy, but holding true to their orders. With the owl cry, they knew it was time for their part. The children cut or untied key ropes within the canopy of trees, releasing branches from their tethers and sending them crashing into the forces below. Many of the warriors who passed by were caught unawares, for the children released the traps from the furthest distances first. The fighters in front had no idea of the peril approaching systematically from behind.

The specialist archers, who had little to do until the villagers burst through the front lines, turned their attention to the children in the trees. Taking aim, they sought to bring down the scoundrels and prevent them from taking any further action. Some were successful in their endeavors, but most of the children had released their trappings and immediately fled.

Kitalla was perched atop a taller house so she could view the battlefield. She called out various animal cries, informing the villagers to tighten their defenses to the west, or to refocus their efforts in the north. Yet as she watched, she could see that even with all her preparations, they would be overwhelmed when it came down to it. The leader of the Hathren army was taking no chances with this foray and had sent his best fighters in to take down the village.

She wouldn't let them.

With a battle cry, Kitalla vaulted off the roof and landed on the ground in a careful roll, pulling out two daggers as she rose onto her feet. Charging forth, she burst through the western defenders and evened the odds by felling two Hathrens with quick jabs to their throats. She leaped over a sword thrust and pivoted around, driving one dagger into the man's chest, while bringing her other arm up to deflect another sword. Bending low, she tripped another swordsman and let a villager finish him off. She pounced back up and smashed the hilts of her daggers together into the temples of an archer who had taken up a comrade's sword, and brought him promptly to the ground unconscious.

"Finish them," she called out, leaving the villagers to continue the fight. She sprinted off toward the eastern sector, where a set of three youths was standing back to back, swinging their swords wildly, trying to fend off their attackers. Kitalla let a dagger fly across the field, catching one man in the back and bringing him down. She then lashed out at two others, before a horn sounded in the distance and drew her attention.

It wasn't the sound of retreat, she knew. She didn't expect this group to pull back, and certainly not so soon. It was a call for reinforcements. Help would be on the way. She glanced around assessing the damages already scored. The Savvrons were holding their own, but they weren't trained for this. A few days of sparring wasn't enough to build proper stamina for a continuous flood of troops.

She left the younger defenders on their own as she raced ahead to the northernmost houses. She rapped on the door in a specific rhythm and the portal opened to admit her. "Gavinod, it's your hour of redemption," she said to the one-time baker. He looked at her with grim determination and nodded sharply. "Await the signal, but it won't be long now." After giving similar warnings to two other houses, Kitalla darted to the center of town and whistled loudly.

As best they could under the circumstances, the defenders drew nearer to Kitalla's location after her call. They continued battling their foes, drawing them closer to the center of town, but working to dispatch them, too. Casualties mounted on both sides, but that was an unfortunate law of war. A law Kitalla was determined now to overwhelm in their favor.

The footfalls of reinforcements grew closer and the fighting intensified in anticipation. Kitalla helped slay the Hathrens and soon few were left in the immediate vicinity, giving some of them a chance to catch their breaths. But Kitalla did not rest. She kept a wary eye up north, awaiting the next wave of invaders, hoping they weren't mages.

Luck was on her side, for a battalion of foot soldiers came marching forward, their swords gleaming in the fading sunset. She drew her hands beside her mouth and called aloud in her best imitation of an angry eaglon. With a loud crash, the back walls of the three northern houses fell toward the oncoming troops. Large barrels rolled down the makeshift ramps and plummeted into the midst of the foot soldiers. They looked at the obstacles in wary confusion, but when nothing happened, they ignored them and moved them aside or circumvented them, assuming the barrels had just been meant to knock them down.

What they didn't know was the contents within each barrel, and with the fighting on in full, there wasn't time to investigate anyway. Kitalla had designed them herself, inspired by some of Grenthar's more devious traps. Each barrel contained several small oilskins, each full of lantern oil and a fuse. Also inside were parchment-wrapped packets of flour, which Kitalla had included upon the baker's insistence, as well as a decent number of knives and other sharp projectiles. Right after knocking down the outer walls of the houses, a small torch was tossed within the barrel, and then the cover was hastily banged into place and the barrel was sent rolling down the wall-ramp. As it sat there on the field, being passed by the soldiers, each barrel burned from within until the lantern oil caught fire and dramatically increased the barrels' internal temperatures.

Then all at once, the barrels exploded, amplified by the flour dust, instantly slaying dozens of Hathren soldiers. It was a demoralizing bloodbath that gave the enemy pause. As they struggled to recover, additional sets of barrels were loaded and set into the fray. Wiser with the second batch, the remaining fighters took cover, but it wasn't quite safe for all of them. The barrel-rollers waited until the troops started moving again, but they didn't anticipate the forces splitting in two, trying to skirt around their houses and enter the village from a different angle.

Kitalla had expected it, though, and the first unfortunate fighters fell headlong into deep pits, lined with brambles and broken pieces of wood. It wasn't enough to stop them all, but their comrades certainly took better care entering behind them.

The Savvron defenders were doing well, but their losses were piling up, too. Kitalla realized that they could withstand another wave decently, maybe two, or until the Hathrens brought in their mages, after which there would be little hope.

She rallied her forces and reminded them of their victories this day. She cheered them all as heroes, challenging them to reach deeply within themselves and pull forth the powers of their ancestors to save their village once and for all. Cries echoed in the night air even as the next round of swordsmen rushed in.

Kitalla helped fight them off, but then her heart lurched when the blue-white bolts of lightning that had filled the sky earlier rose up again, not far away. Now that the villagers were tiring, the mages were coming. Kitalla pulled back, knowing only she had any hope of fending off the magic-users. The villagers of Savvron, having shunned magic so strongly, knew little about how to battle against it. Even Kitalla was uncertain in the thick of it, but she knew she had to do something. Without her, all would be lost.

She refused to let Gabrion's home die.

She gave orders for the defenders to pull the fighters toward the east and west, clearing a safer path to the north for the mages to enter. They would need a line of sight to cast their spells in any case, but she wanted them to focus on her specifically. Kitalla prepared herself by taking two fresh daggers in hand and stomping her feet. Left foot. Right foot. Up went her left hand, then right hand. She spun, bringing both arms down, lunging to the dirt. Around she went a second time, then she spiraled her daggers about her body, pulling the energy around her like a blanket.

The mages came into view, hands sparking with energy. They saw her and called out to each other to attack, seeing her movements as a bigger threat to their powers. They couldn't know of her dance skills, but she was clearly drawing energies and so she looked as much like a mage as they did. Fireballs and ice darts leaped across the way, arcing through the air, all seeking Kitalla.

The dancer focused sharply on her movements. She felt the offensive energies filing in from the distance, and she drew them toward her, still spinning herself around, pulling, ever pulling. The fire and ice shot toward her, then were caught in the streams of power she swept about herself, deflecting out and down into the dirt, impotent.

Enraged, the mages called for more powerful spells, staggering them so as to maintain a more steady flow of magic. Kitalla kept time in her head, spinning carefully about, trying to ignore the growing dizziness from all the turning. She managed to cast aside summoned rocks and binding spells alike. It wasn't particularly clear to her how she was doing it, but she held on to Dariak's words of so long ago. He had told her after observing her in Warringer—where she had dressed Gabrion up as a jester of sorts—that she dealt with energies in a way that opposed magic. Where mages manifested their spells from the outer world, in terms of their incantations and spell components, Kitalla's power was generated from within. Both were empowered by the caster's will, but the mages required more powerful components for more powerful spells. Kitalla, however, had the strength of will to defeat them all, so she told herself.

She could feel the spells aimed her way growing in intensity and she knew she wouldn't be able to deflect them much longer. She hadn't seen the lightning spells yet, but that was just as well after the story Dariak had told of lightning being drawn so easily toward metal. It was why she clutched her daggers during her dance, for she intended them to disrupt the lightning by casting them outward when the energy blasts were unleashed. Of course, that would only help with one or two such blasts. In theory.

Kitalla was concentrating fiercely and did not see the baker, Gavinod, leave his barrel post to strike down the mages directly. He lunged at them with a short sword, killing two who were in the throes of chanting, and wounding another who was rummaging for spell components. A fireball aimed at his chest ended his heroic charge, however, and he fell with a peaceful grin, feeling he had at last done his part to protect his homeland.

The dizziness grew overpowering and Kitalla had to stop spinning about. Releasing a cry to alert the other defenders not to look, she let the energies dissipate, but only for a moment. She immediately summoned them again as she sashayed her hips from side to side, controlling her arms in a fluid gesture. The effect was instantaneous and the mages were confused. Spellfire lashed out in wild directions as they attacked foes that suddenly sprang up before them. She was tired, but Kitalla focused and kept the moves going, picturing herself multiplying on the battlefield so the mages would pursue one of her summoned doppelgangers and not the villagers.

The illusion couldn't last for long against mages, who were much more accustomed to mystical forces than fighters or commoners. But the ruse helped lessen their numbers as some defenders broke through, following Gavinod's lead to strike the mages down. Yet, the mages weren't entirely alone either. More soldiers were entering the fray all the time, trying to protect the mages and take down the defenders.

The Savvron resources were dwindling, Kitalla realized. The mages were also chanting in unison, which boded ill. If they channeled their strength into a combined spell, she wouldn't be able to defend against it. At least, not more than once, she decided grimly. She clapped her hands and raised a hooting call above the din of battle. The children who had cut the tree traps raced back into action from their hiding places. Each carried a metallic sheet of some kind, whether once a shield or part of a breastplate or some other object. The blacksmith had been working endlessly to produce weapons, armor, and to fulfill Kitalla's odd request of metal sheets. Only her adamancy convinced the smith to fashion them.

The children, essentially unprotected behind the flimsy sheets, all gathered around Kitalla, sitting close together so their panels overlapped just barely. They hunkered low, but kept their sheets up high. Kitalla, now surrounded in somewhat of a metal ring that reached up to her belly in height, dug into her pocket and withdrew her jade at last.

Having considered all the times the jade had acted in her favor, Kitalla knew how to call for its power in a moment like this. It wasn't far-fetched for her to believe her life was in danger, so she looked at the carnage in the village and she allowed herself to feel a sense of panic. She then turned her gaze toward the mages, whose swirling arms and frantic chanting was indeed frightening.

She felt the jade react to her call and she welcomed its instinctual advice. Still dizzy, she started to spin again, letting the jade reach out to the metal sheets surrounding her. She could feel them resonating with the jade, with her. The metal sheets linked together where they overlapped, while the energies dashed across their surfaces and united them into one massive shining circlet. Kitalla stopped spinning abruptly, but her part was done anyway. The metal ring hovered and started spinning, following the energy maelstrom she had created. She held still, her arms outstretched to her sides, her body facing the mages whose spells would seek her death. Unbidden, the children, now unprotected, scattered for the deepest recesses of the village, away from the fighting at last.

A vicious tempest erupted from the mages. Wind, sand, dirt, rain, and lightning all swept forth with devastating and unruly force. The unified spell was set outward to do its work, no longer under the mages' control. Exhausted from the effort, they fell to their knees to catch their breaths and to regard their work.

As it struck, the tempest eradicated everything in its path. The northern houses were flattened, debris sent flying everywhere, killing attackers and defenders alike. A deep rent was scored in the earth as it traveled, and every scrap that was lifted by the storm became another weapon at its disposal. Bits of wood pelted off into the distance; rain splattered the houses and distant trees. Unchecked, it would have leveled the entire village, leaving behind a scarred memory.

But Kitalla's spinning metal ring drew the lightning like a clarion call. The storm wavered but sought out her location, obliterating everything in its wake. The metal shield whirled around her and though she could still see over the ring, just barely now that it was hovering in the air, she didn't let herself get distracted by the oncoming terror. The metal spun like a wild, oversized metal belt. When the edges of the tempest struck, the sound it produced was deafening.

The metal jade warmed in Kitalla's hand almost beyond bearing. She held it tightly, though, knowing instinctively that to release it would be to end its effect. The metal banged hard against the stormy winds and particles and then Kitalla felt a strange flash of inspiration. Polished metal was highly reflective, so she wondered if the metal couldn't just reflect back the magical energies it was taking in. Heightened by the idea, the jade shook more forcefully and Kitalla had to bring her arms together to clutch it in both hands to hold it.

The banging against the metal intensified and then the storm was redirected along its original path. The metal ring spun for a short while longer, but then the threat on her life was gone and so the jade calmed and the protective spell ended. With a crash, the metal sheets detached and splattered to the ground, and so too did Kitalla, whose body had sustained the effect with her own inner strength.

The mages flew from their posts and only a few of them fell victim to their own spell, but the swordsmen and archers were not as fortunate. Sadly, a number of Savvron defenders fell during the tempest as well. There was little else anyone could do now.

A villager followed the destructive path of the tornado and saw the fleeing mages, but then he spotted something else that terrified him. He ran back to Kitalla, shaking her to rise. "You must get up! He returns to finish us off! You must stand up to him!"

Eyes blurry, Kitalla pushed herself up to her knees, wondering how she was supposed to find the strength to fend off the new threat. She could see blasts of blue-white lightning and orange-red flame flashing not far away. She knew what needed to be done. As when she had battled against the ursalor, she needed to pull the metal jade's energy through herself and let it pull all the metal in her body to use by extending it out in sharp spikes. It was exhausting and painful, but with it, she could run blindly into the new foe and hopefully complete the turn of the tide and give Savvron its victory.

Climbing to her feet, she held the jade tightly and focused on the steps she needed to channel the energy once again. It was a very deliberate pace she needed to maintain, and it left her entirely unprotected. She hoped the villagers would rally around her and keep her safe, but she didn't have the strength to call them to her aid. As she stepped, stepped, moved, and posed, she could hear the increasing number of death throes. Villagers were dying. She wasn't going to be able to complete her final rush without it being a suicide attack. No one would be left to defend her.

As she realized the futility of it, her step faltered and the jade went silent. She tried to call to it again, but it denied her. Looking at the encroaching mages, she begged for help, for some kind of defense, but still the jade did not react. She glanced at the field but even the failing defenses weren't enough to spur the jade into action. Or perhaps its recent action with the metal ring had exhausted its own supply of energy. Kitalla guessed that must be so, and thus she reached again for her daggers and took a moment to compose herself before the new threat was fully upon her.

"You're not alone, Kitalla," said a voice very close by. She looked, shocked to see that Gabrion was with her. He was covered in blood, some of it his own. The dagger wound in his side had reopened and he was bleeding painfully from it, if the expression on his face was any indication.

"Why are you here?" she gasped.

"It's my home," he said.

"You're an idiot."

He just laughed.

She drew in a few extra breaths of air, letting his mere presence fill her with a sense of protection. "It isn't over yet, you know."

He nodded. "We can do this, Kitalla. Come on, let's get you up." But he needed as much help as she did.

They rose up and supported each other, readying their weapons and preparing for their final battle. The villagers were overwhelmed and were retreating now, leaving the remaining attackers for Kitalla and Gabrion to fend off alone. With the pressure on, the jades responded. Kitalla's daggers flew with greater accuracy and Gabrion's sword cut with the ease of a hot knife through soup. Anyone who came within reach died quickly and soon the Hathrens backed away from the duo, waiting until their strange prowess showed signs of weakening.

Then the new set of mages came for a final round. Spells flashed about and Kitalla and Gabrion both swept their weapons through the air, hoping somehow to cut through the energy forces and survive. Gabrion grew silent during the assault; his pain was so great he took gasping breaths and held them, fighting not to pass out. Kitalla, on the other hand, battled her exhaustion by adding her voice to each swing and stab.

The mages were clearly perplexed by their antics, for some of the spells took down their own fighters. The Hathrens were crumbling and soon they all fled the scene. Kitalla and Gabrion turned to the leading mage, whose glowing hands alerted them to their impending doom. Kitalla's daggers flew, but it was a useless attempt. The mage simply swatted them away in midair.

Gabrion couldn't lift his sword, he was so tired and in such agony. Instead, he pulled Kitalla close against him and they turned to face the glowing mage. The warrior drew one breath to announce his challenge, "We've slain the vast majority of your forces, villain. Flee now or we will kill you, too."

The remark was met with laughter. But it wasn't a malicious laughter. It was oddly familiar. The glowing hands dimmed and the mage stepped closer, black hair shaking in dismay. "Can't leave you two alone for a minute," he scolded. "What a mess you are!"

CHAPTER 12

Reconnection

THE SURVIVORS OF Savvron didn't know what to make of Dariak's entrance. Some remembered him as the mage who torched their town all those months ago. Others were grateful for his assistance wiping out their enemies. Whichever view they held, everyone was bewildered by the veritable army he brought with him.

Randler turned on the charm as soon as he appeared, introducing himself lavishly and asking where he could be of the most assistance, while also finding resting places for the fighters and mages accompanying them. He managed to find sleeping quarters for everyone before lighting up the dark night with a bonfire in the center of the village, paying homage to the fallen with a deep, melodic dirge.

Dariak, however, escorted Gabrion and Kitalla away from the scene as quickly as he could, after which he tapped into his reserves and spread healing waves about them. Dariak already knew where Gabrion's home was located from his one-time imprisonment, and found it hadn't changed by much in the interim, except the added damage.

"How are you here?" Gabrion asked once the majority of the pain subsided with the mage's spells.

"And what's with the army?" Kitalla added.

"When you see them, you will recognize most of them, actually," Dariak commented. "The mages from Pindington. You remember Quereth and the others? Also, Gabrion, that guard captain you worked with after the tower's fall… Well, when the mages moved out to meet up with us, he took a pack of volunteers and joined them."

"Ordren," Gabrion remembered. "He wondered why I didn't flee the city once the Prisoner's Tower had emptied, then his soldier gave us horses when we left."

Dariak nodded. "It seems he wasn't satisfied with his lot in life. The mages had promised to help us cross the border into Hathreneir once we had claimed the jade from Randler's mother. We hadn't decided any official means of communication, but they estimated the travel time well and journeyed west. Randler and I had a bit of a tussle with some thieves on the road, and when I used a few spells, Quereth turned and found us not long after. True to their word, they've joined our cause."

"A tussle with some thieves?" Kitalla asked. "Sounds interesting."

Dariak grinned and, having rested for a few minutes, summoned up the energies to set another round of healing through the pair of them before he answered her. "It wasn't the same without you two there. Randler is good in a fight, but nothing compared to your skills, either one of you. We were trying to lay low on the way, but it was magic or die at that point. A little lightning blast and they ran off."

"You're controlling the lightning now?" Gabrion asked. "I thought you would avoid it after Sharice."

"I intended never to use it unless I was desperate, but Randler reminded me that my goal is to unify them all, so I need to be more familiar with them. Right after you two left, we worked to untap some of the powers in the jades we had with us. He certainly has a gift for seeing things differently than I do. He compares magic to music all the time, and I'm starting to wonder if there isn't a greater connection between them after all," he added with a smile.

Randler found them then, walking in and sitting with Dariak and embracing him warmly. "You two look better now than earlier. I'm glad."

"A pleasure to see you again, Randler," Gabrion replied.

"You're just in time," Dariak cheered. "I was about to tell them of our journey."

The bard laughed. "It isn't much of a tale unless you count the times we were ambushed, by friend or foe. Sometimes I thought the shadow jade was playing pranks on us to see how we would react."

"Who else ambushed you?" Kitalla wondered, amused at the look on his face, and feeling so much better now that her wounds were being properly healed. As Randler spoke, Dariak focused more energy into his spells, easing all the flashes of pain she was feeling from the battle.

"A caravan of merchants heading to Pindington—at least that was uneventful. A pack of thieves who wanted all our gold—we gave them steel instead," he chuckled, "and Dariak followed that with some magic, which prompted the mages to find us. Another set of bandits appeared at one point, but Dariak talked his way out of dueling with them." He turned to the mage, "You never did tell me how, you know."

Dariak lowered his hands and shook his head, looking at Kitalla. "They were part of your old cohort. We recognized each other and the leader said he wouldn't mind catching up with you again at some point to see how you're faring. Apparently, he suspected you ran off to follow me."

"Poltor was always a few steps ahead of anyone else," she said. "Did he give any indication where they were headed?"

"Ask him later," Randler inserted. "He followed us, though at first he did so secretly until it was driving us mad wondering if they were planning to attack or not. I was able to convince them to join the festivities. Ah yes, so the mages arrived and behind them were soldiers of Pindington. But they came in two waves. The second wave split off, looking for others to aid us, and they found Hernior and his band, who then brought another couple sets of defectors. Little by little, the forces grew into this little army we have now."

"We missed all of that while we pursued Heria?" Gabrion said in awe.

"Timing is everything, I suppose." Randler shrugged. "We hadn't intended to leave the cave until your return, but we were invaded."

"Our first ambush was by reptigons," Dariak explained. "They would have killed us in our sleep if Randler didn't have bell-traps set up in his lair."

"Lair," Randler echoed with a laugh. "But yes, they prompted our departure, and so did the jades."

Dariak withdrew a new jade, one with a hint of green glowing within the center and giving off a mild, fragrant scent. "It sensed its brethren, I supposed, and they responded in kind. This is the nature jade you sought, so we already know you weren't able to reclaim it. It was further north from Randler's cave and well-protected by a number of devious traps."

Kitalla's head bobbed slowly and she turned to Gabrion. "I was wrong, then. Those stones we saw in that first cavern really were from the Talonic River."

"There was no way to be sure," he dismissed. "Besides, tracking her down kept her from seeking us, right?"

"There's that," she said.

"But if she didn't have the jade with her," Gabrion started, "how did she manage to control the vines the way she said she did?"

Kitalla shrugged. "She did say she didn't have good control over them and that they fought back."

"Interesting," Dariak said. "Perhaps some of her bloodletting rituals allowed her brief glimpses into magic after all."

"Or she was hallucinating," Kitalla considered. "I could definitely see her walking the horse into a tree and then thinking the tree itself was striking back. Besides, if she had any real connection to the nature jade, would she have ever put it down? I doubt it."

"We'll never really know," Gabrion said softly.

After a moment of silence, Kitalla shook her head and looked at the mage and the bard. "So you left the cave to pursue the jade, and then?"

"It was en route to the jade that the mages found us," Randler continued. "Once we had it, we changed course to try to find you."

"Then the jades started going berserk," Dariak put in. "It felt like something was terribly wrong, so we doubled our efforts to find you, letting the jades guide us on the way. They led us here, obviously, but because we were a bit further north when we approached, we stumbled across some of the Hathren troops. I regret taking down my own people, but we weren't given a choice."

"It's true," Randler chimed in. "They were attacking anyone they didn't person-ally know. Once Dariak and the mages used their spells, they were confused by it, but then assumed it was a ruse by our king, and they fought back all the harder."

Dariak continued, "Ordren, Hernior, and the others protected us while we held their mages at bay. We probably could have taken over their outpost completely, but it didn't make sense to remain there, especially with the jades pounding as they were."

Randler pulled out the air and shadow jades. "They were starting to sound like a mix of drums and wind chimes, they were vibrating so much. Even I could tell some-thing was awry."

"We traveled along the border, blazing new trails and taking rests as briefly as possible while maintaining our stamina. Then today we came to one outpost that was already empty except for a token guard and the captain himself. We interrogated him, but didn't learn much more than that he had sent everyone here to slay you all."

"He almost did," Kitalla offered. "If you hadn't arrived, I don't know that we could have finished the rest of them."

"The jades propelled us," Dariak said. "I used the earth jade in the negative, reducing my weight instead of increasing it, and that allowed me to join Randler in a hearty sprint, as he was empowered by the air jade. The other mages used what spells they had to stay with us, and the fighters all ran with utmost speed. You must have already taken care of the first wave and the Hathren mages because they were starting to retreat when we arrived. We joined in to help you and I could tell everyone was confused. The rest of our fighters arrived a little after that. I wish we could have gotten here sooner."

"We are certainly grateful you got here at all," Gabrion commented. "And the healing you've been doing. That's helping so much already."

"The nature jade is assisting me right now, which is why I've been able to do so much during this little reunion. But tomorrow, the other mages will finish the job and get you both ready for the march into Hathreneir."

The prospect of leaving Savvron so soon tore at Gabrion's conscience. He had just returned home, deeply wounded with battles on the horizon. Plus, there was the news of his mother's death, and leaving his father's side didn't seem like the right thing to do so suddenly. He didn't say any of it aloud, but the others seemed to understand.

"If you've cleared out a number of troops along the border," Kitalla was saying, "then now really is a perfect time to infiltrate your homeland, Dariak."

"It's funny when you say it that way, but yes. We need to pass through and then seek out the castle and the mage towers. The remaining jades are there and we must claim them so I can find a way to assemble them into one."

Randler spoke up again. "There is also your father's laboratory to explore. He may have some clue as to unifying the pieces."

"Mira," Gabrion whispered, then raised his voice so the others could hear him properly. "My father believes she is held captive at the castle. If the captain who led your original attack here, Dariak, was of your king's guard then it does make sense she might be there. She—she could still be there, waiting."

Kitalla looked pained, but she agreed with him. "She will be waiting. And you will free her from her bonds." She then turned to Randler and Dariak. "I can't speak for anyone else, but this evening was thoroughly exhausting for me. Might one of you help me to sleep, either with a lullaby or a sleeping draft?"

Randler took the challenge and escorted Kitalla to Klerra's house next door. She didn't explain why they went there instead of remaining at Gabrion's home and he didn't ask as he settled nearby and sang of flowing green fields on a sweet spring day.

Dariak and Gabrion were also tired, but they remained awake a little while longer, until Terrsian returned at last from the forest. He greeted his son with a deep embrace, after which he fixed his gaze on Dariak.

"It wasn't so long ago that you were at our mercy," Terrsian stated. "I am grateful that Gabrion listened to his heart and did what he believed in."

"As am I," the mage couldn't help but reply.

"And here you return, not to burn our village to the ground, but to support us in our time of need. You've healed my son, who should have died tonight considering his injuries and the fervor with which he left my side to defend our town. Mage, I thank you. Dariak, you have a home here, if ever you need it." And as he had done to Gabrion moments ago, Terrsian grabbed Dariak in gratitude.

Flustered, Dariak said nothing, but turned a bright shade of red.

Terrsian laughed then and clapped Dariak's shoulder with a mighty hand. Within seconds, the mirth left his face and he sobered completely. "What are your plans for departure?"

"We aren't welcome to stay?" Dariak hedged.

"I just offered you a place in my home," Terrsian rebutted. "But it's clear you do not intend to remain here. Not with the forces at your disposal and this quest you two are on."

"The four of us," Dariak corrected, "but yes. The longer we remain, the more likely the borders will close completely and make crossing into Hathreneir practically impossible. Right now, there are gaps through which we can penetrate."

"Then sleep tonight. Make your preparations. Venture out when you must."

"Father…" Gabrion started.

"I trust you, my son. Your success is in your hands and I believe your hands are truly capable ones, especially with the friends you have at your side." He stared deeply into Gabrion's eyes as if trying to confirm his thoughts, then he nodded. "I will say this again, so that you do not ever forget. Along your journey, son, never forget who you are."

CHAPTER 13

Into Hathreneir

A DAY OF recuperation and strategizing didn't feel like enough, but if the group didn't hurry, the Hathrens could fortify the border and their opportunity for a quick entrance into the neighboring kingdom would be lost. Quereth, Lica, and Frast, along with the other mages they had brought with them, completely healed the wounds Kitalla and Gabrion had sustained. They also offered their services to the badly wounded villagers, though there wasn't enough time to heal all their injuries.

The king's soldiers who had joined the fight worked with the citizens to lay the dead to rest. It was a way of paying homage to their own comrades who were fighting on the frontlines further north, but it also brought the community together as a unit.

"I will remain here," Hernior decided that day, sharing the news late into the evening meeting with Dariak and the others. "A handful of my men will ensure that this town is secure from retaliation."

Gabrion gaped. "I don't know what to say. Thank you."

"We will miss your support," Dariak confessed, "but at least we won't have to worry about this place when we go."

"It was my hope to ease that worry," he said. "But also, I need a place to be now. I cannot spend the rest of my days scouring the countryside. I may send for my children to join me."

Terrsian clapped him on the shoulder. "Your family is welcome here."

"Along those lines," Ordren cut in, "we may need to send a group to keep the northern outpost out of enemy hands. If we can establish a firm hold, the Hathrens will no longer be a threat in the vicinity."

Kitalla shook her head. "We can't disband and thin ourselves out at this point. We have more to do first."

"She has a point," added Poltor, her one-time mentor. They had spent a portion of their day catching up on their time apart, and the lure of new adventures in Hathreneir enticed the master thief.

"We are over a hundred strong," Ordren argued. "Sending even ten wouldn't weaken us. Besides, won't you need a way back in to Kallisor?"

"Not if Dariak is successful, no," Kitalla retorted.

Randler released a troubled sigh. "What if there are complications and we do need to still come back? I think it wise to err on the side of forethought and preparedness."

Quereth grunted. "We will spare two mages to join the fighters securing the line. That should give the Hathrens pause if they attempt to reclaim the outpost."

"Quereth, you're not leaving, too?" Dariak asked, his eyes widening.

The older man laughed. "And miss a visit to the famed mage towers of Hathreneir? I would not miss such an opportunity. But there are some among us who are reluctant to leave Kallisor and they would be perfect candidates for the post."

When Ordren's gaze flickered away from the group, Dariak realized the impetus for the man's suggestion. "Very well," the mage surrendered. "It would be good to keep the door open, so to speak. I will leave you to the details, then."

The group slept fitfully that night, but they were on the move soon after dawn. The townspeople themselves had awoken early and prepared a veritable farewell feast, after which the village of Savvron returned to quieter times.

The start of the journey began solemnly and with purpose. They had decided to head north toward the outpost in order to fully secure it before the western journey into the opening desert of Hathreneir, for if the Hathrens had received support from another outpost further along, then a small band might not have been able to claim it. When they approached, however, they found it abandoned completely. They made a cursory search of the area to ensure that traps hadn't been set and left, but the place was ready for the reserve troop to take up residence and fortify the area. The remaining eighty or so fighters, mages, and rogues took to the road and stormed off.

Randler noted the grim, uncertain glances from some of them and decided it was best to unite everyone and to give them a bit of hope. He didn't have a lute with him, so he settled for tapping on his waterskin, and soon the men and women mimicked the beat.

No one knows the future of the place we mean to go.
And thus we travel onward, so carefully and slow.
No warriors will stop us. No mages have their spells.
No creatures there can harm us, wherever they may dwell.

And so we travel onward, through the night and day.
Nothing there can interfere as we head on our way.

Our swords are ready, sharp and strong, to decimate our foe.
They simply cannot stop us once we've chosen where to go.
The power in our hearts is a beacon through the night.
For we will find the strength to succeed in every fight.

And so we travel onward, through the night and day.
Nothing there can interfere as we head on our way.

Light the fires, send the word, that we are coming through.
I swear you cannot stop us; there is nothing you can do.
United, we are strong with a purpose grand of mind.
A stronger mesh of army you will never ever find.

And so we travel onward, through the night and day.
Nothing there can interfere as we head on our way.

The song caught on and others in the troop created their own verses and sang them loud and strong as they pushed their way across the plain and approached the beige horizon that shimmered to the west. Dariak couldn't help grinning and stepping to the beat of the song, but as he did so he kept his wary eyes open for the border guardians, whose whereabouts were elusive.

Because the mages in Hathreneir were encouraged to practice their craft, they were able to make use of a wide variety of spells. It was a lure for an aspiring mage to enter the land and seek out a mentor willing to offer training. The unworthy, however, could be overpowered by the magic they tried so eagerly to control. A broken mage had a strange connection to the energies and could rarely control them again, thus they could never truly venture into Kallisor without being hunted by mage-haters. Yet they were also shunned by the Hathrens for being too eager, arrogant, and weak. Their means of survival were limited. They could scrounge for scraps around the lands, hoping for sympathy; they could surrender their bodies to study within the mage towers; but the majority opted—or were coerced—to join the order of border guardians.

The guardians themselves were often solitary, and how they reacted to visitors was individual. Some welcomed passersby, eager for bits of news and gossip. Others fought off anyone who looked ready to approach. Others still encouraged people to pass across the border, only to then give chase and kill them when they weren't expecting it. Their duty, however, was the same; keep people from passing. There were exceptions, of course, for Hathrens were generally allowed to freely cross their border in either direction, and those with proper writs usually made it through unscathed. A very few were able to sneak across undetected, but those were rare.

As the group approached the sandy border, a hobbled old man crawled into view. One of the swordsmen pointed and laughed, but Dariak called an immediate halt. It was too late, though, for the man heard the laughter.

Trembling, the old man rose up on his spindly legs and fire swirled around his belly. The guardian stamped his feet and the ground nearby rumbled ominously, threatening them as they faced his wrath. "You laugh? You laugh? You laugh at poor Arricon?" crooned the old man, the fire growing brighter and spreading to cover him completely.

"We mean no harm," Dariak called out regally. "I am Dariak, son of Delminor, and I seek to reenter my homeland."

"Not alone! Not alone! You are not, not, not alone!" The guardian bounced up and the fire blasted outward in all directions. The entire troop ducked low to avoid the ring of flames, except for Dariak who allowed them to crash into him. "Oh!" said the old man.

"Please, allow us entry. We mean no harm to this land, good guardian."

The old man crouched back down to hands and knees and rocked from side to side. "Oh, what to do, what to do, I wonder?" he mumbled. "Surely I cannot let them all go."

Poltor stepped over and whispered in Dariak's ear, "What's the delay? Dispatch him and move along."

"Dispatch! Dispatch!" the old man cried. From his position it seemed impossible for him to have heard, but his expression grew from wary to angry. He rose up again on his feet and brought his feeble arms out to the sides, lifting sand from the ground as he did so.

Dariak frowned. He had hoped to avoid an actual confrontation, but the man was incensed and the energies whipped frantically, filling the air with a strange tingling sensation.

"What is this?" Kitalla asked.

"Wild magic," Dariak answered. The sand hovering in the air between the man's arms and the ground suddenly changed. Some particles turned to fire, while others splattered as sludge. The fiery pieces flew out at random and more sand was brought up from below and likewise altered before being cast about. Dariak waited patiently, sensing that this was only for show, despite the sting of the fire.

"Dispatch!" the old man cried, swinging his arms and pushing them forward. The majority of the troop dodged down again to avoid the next wave of attack, but the ice darts that left the guardian flew backwards instead, impacting the sand safely the other way.

"Look out!" Dariak called, pointing to the ice darts. Where they struck the sand, odd creatures rose up and stalked forward. They looked like giant scorpions, complete with claws and tails; however, Arricon's magic gave these sandorpions the ability to leap powerfully through the air, and the poor beasts didn't seem to have any control over it. Two of them pounced overhead, but Dariak had to let the fighters tend to them, as the guardian was moving oddly again.

The old man had knelt down, his knees and hands sunk into the sand, his eyes wide and unfocused, and his mouth hanging agape. Swinging side to side again, fire swirled up and spun in a growing whirlwind, bolstered by more sand. It wasn't a particularly large firestorm, but Dariak could sense that it was powerful.

The mage stepped forward as a few more of the ensorcelled sandorpions leaped about. He knelt beside the guardian and mimicked the man's posture, pressing his hands into the soil on the Kallisorian side. "Border guardian of Hathreneir, I beg your forgiveness and seek entrance into the great and noble land. I bow to your graciousness and your power. Admit us through, for only you can see us safely to the other side."

The fiery whirlwind sputtered and vanished. "Well, that is true," the old man cackled. "Why, without me, you couldn't possibly go through, could you? Could you?"

"We could not. Of course we could not. So I pray you let us pass."

The old man pulled his hands from the ground and stood up, gesturing for Dariak to do the same. They stared at each other for a few long moments, while the sounds of fighting continued behind the mage. Apparently the sandorpions were giving them a hard time, but he knew that if he turned to assist them, then they wouldn't be able to pass this way. Not after failing the guardian's initial challenge, anyway, if it could be called that.

Then at last the old man started laughing. The sound echoed strangely in the air. The sun overhead darkened into a bloody crimson color, casting a strange ubiquitous glow. As he continued his laughing, the old man's jaw widened and then he fell again to his hands and knees. Laughing. Ever laughing. The sound soon became irritating and louder, until everyone covered their ears with their hands. The guardian's mouth opened wider and wider, and as it did, so too did the cackling increase, until the air shook as if it was full of thunder.

Dariak stood as firmly as possible under the circumstances, but the ground shook and shifted underfoot. Gusts of air kicked up as well and Dariak realized that the border guardian was now permitting their entry. Staying focused on the guardian despite the peril to his comrades must have pleased the wild mage after all.

"Hurry!" He stepped forward along the sliding sand with the wind propelling him from behind.

"This is crazy!" someone shouted.

"Then stay behind," Kitalla hissed, finding her footing on the shifting sand and following Dariak. One by one, the others followed and Arricon kept the magic flowing until the last fighter was within the Hathren border. The old man cackled once more and increased the flow of magic, pushing the small army further into the sandy desert.

Sometime later, they were dropped to the sand in a heap. Dariak stood and turned, trying to ensure that the guardian was going to depart peaceably after having delivered its cargo. The fighters and mages dusted themselves off and pulled away from the location, getting a head start until Dariak was satisfied with their safety, after which he trotted to the front.

"That was disconcerting," Kitalla said when he approached.

"It was only a passage," he said offhandedly. "And lucky we had it, too. There were more creatures in that part of the sand than those sandorpions. He propelled us through them."

"How could you tell?" Gabrion wondered.

He shrugged. "I live here."

"I don't understand it," the warrior commented. "How could we ever invade your land with defenses like that?"

Dariak chuckled and shook his head. "They aren't always there, for one thing. They steer clear of our own outposts, and most attacking armies would seek out those places to conquer for shelter. The guardians can also be overpowered. If we had a full-sized army, the guardians would probably cower and hide; they're not likely to work together. Also, we were seeking polite entry, which made him more curious in a way, wary in another. He was willing to test us though we are a united force, but we passed his test and he kept us from harm overall. As I said, there are other dangers along the borderland. But when it comes down to it, the guardians are completely irrational beings. The mages in the towers try to contain them and keep them focused from afar, but it isn't easy. They are a means of defense, just not wholly reliable."

"He reminded me in some way of Heria," Kitalla murmured. "Completely crazy, but he knew what he was doing."

Gabrion rubbed his face, complaining, "I'm not sure I'm going to fit in here with magic like that around."

Dariak laughed and clapped him on the shoulder. "Not to worry. Most of the time, the magic is used by people who know how to wield it more effectively."

He looked back incredulously. "That's supposed to make me feel better?"

CHAPTER 14

Traveling Through Hathreneir

OVER THE NEXT several days, Dariak guided the troops toward the southern town of Marritosh. The desert heat was tempered by the faded winter, and it helped that Dariak and the other mages were able to draw moisture from the air, keeping everyone properly hydrated along the way.

"So desolate," Poltor complained in the late evening. "Not a scrap of life anywhere. What do you hunt? How do you survive? Where do you gather riches?"

"You look under the surface," Dariak replied casually. "There are hovels and springs where you least expect them. But the whole country isn't desert like this. Just the eastern edge and parts of the south."

"Ah, the great droughts of ages past," Randler nodded. "Their mark is still felt on the land, I see."

With a solemn nod, Dariak gestured toward the distance. "Yes, and it has been spreading. It's an unnatural desert, though, so it is also cooler than it ought to be. Soon we will approach an oasis where people have found the means to survive. It is a place I used to enjoy visiting as a child because it was different than my home. Fewer mages and more warriors. Many of the king's guard come from there after training in their childhoods to be strong. I never understood why they would work so hard to learn how to swing a sword." He laughed. "I thought back then that magic could do anything."

"But everything has limits," Kitalla said unexpectedly, looking down at her clenched fists.

They set up camp that night. Dariak enlisted a team of fighters to dig a two-foot-wide trench surrounding the army, after which he and the mages solidified the channel and then filled it with water from the air. "This will help keep out the sandroaches," Dariak said. "They hate water."

"Sandroaches?" Gabrion said.

"Remember those sandorpions this morning? Imagine them a bit smaller, unable to jump—which was Arricon's fault anyway—but with an appetite for nibbling on humans. We're easy targets asleep and you would barely see them in the sand itself."

The warrior shook his head. "Give me a reptigon any day."

"We have those, too; don't worry." He grinned, turning to start a fire in the center of the campground. "Keep this lit throughout the night," he alerted Ervinor, a strong young man of twenty-two who had been under Ordren's command until the parting at the outpost. "It will keep out the nightflies," he added, feeling that empty orders were less likely to be followed than those with reasons. The fighter saluted and set about arranging the order of the watch, adding his own instructions about the fire.

As the camp settled down, Gabrion sought out Kitalla. She was seated within the watery border, tossing pebbles across the surface and watching them roll in the sand on the other side. She started when he sat down beside her.

"What's wrong, Kitalla?" he asked softly so as not to wake anyone else.

"Nothing, I was concentrating on my throws." She emphasized by sending another stone across the way. "What about you? We're getting closer to your destination."

His face contorted with her evasion but he answered her anyway. "It is hard to believe that within a week we could find Mira and take her home."

"What if—" but then she coughed and stopped herself.

"If what?"

She shook her head and remained silent.

"I don't understand what is going on with you lately. You talk even less than before."

She shrugged. "I keep wondering when Dariak will keep training me to channel the energy. It looks like his own journey is nearing its end. He may not feel the need to assist me any longer."

Gabrion looked at her hard. "Maybe you don't understand friendship, Kitalla, but lying to me about what's going on isn't the way to go about it." He stood up and stormed off, not waiting for a response.

The thief's head sank low and she breathed the night air deeply, trying to remain calm. She wanted to prepare Gabrion for the worst—Mira might not want to return home—but didn't want to hurt him if she was wrong. Then she considered what she had told him about Dariak and her training, wondering what had interrupted her own plans and when she had stopped caring as much about growing her dance skills.

Annoyed at herself, she rose up and sought out Dariak, but he was already asleep, with Randler sitting nearby humming softly. The bard saw Kitalla and followed her as she walked silently away.

"Restless?" he called to her.

"I didn't realize he was asleep," she said, turning away.

He followed her back to the watery border. "I have spent the majority of my life seeking remnants of the stories of the Forgotten Tribe. Something about them always resonated with me."

She groaned. "Please don't break into song right now. I don't need a lullaby."

"It wouldn't be a lullaby anyway. The story of the Forgotten Tribe is one filled with great pain and loss, with very little hope for the future in the end."

"That doesn't seem to fit with the way you have been singing it all along."

"I spin it into something that suits me better," he said. "What fun is it to think that the founders of our nations were bitter rivals who sought each other's destruction with no hope of redemption?"

She tilted her head to the side to consider. "That would certainly bring fewer people back to the show." She then turned to look at the bard in full, admiring how he could look so kempt even after the day's sandy travel. "So then, in your heart, what's your take on the story?"

He smiled seductively. "If I tell you that, will you share what's aching *your* heart?"

She stiffened and scowled. "Always, everyone trying to dig things out of me. Leave me alone."

He grabbed her shoulder and it told him much that she didn't pull away. "My mother never put much store in my feelings. She never cared about what I wanted. So I try to honor others around me. I'm sorry. I won't ask again. Please, sit with me a moment."

She sighed dramatically and then threw herself to the ground, bringing up her knees and wrapping her arms around them, then settling her chin upon her forearm. "Go on, Randler. Fascinate me."

He sat down with her and gazed out in the distance. "The gist of it is this: Lady Hathreneir and King Kallisor fell in love but they couldn't agree on how to get through their differences. He loved to fight. She didn't. He was brawn. She was heart, but she also had a brain. She didn't need massive armies to protect herself because her magic was enough."

"I've heard this part before," she moaned.

"Perhaps," he shrugged. "But King Kallisor did feel threatened by her power. So he sought to build an army. But an arrogant man would also want his lineage to continue."

"Not just arrogant men," she said with a hollow tone. "Good men do, too."

"Of course," he acceded. "But a good man doesn't go about impregnating dozens of women. He finds one he loves and he raises a family with her."

"Well," she breathed, "he tries to."

He wanted to ask about her responses, but she seemed particularly edgy tonight, so he bit his tongue and nodded. "Yes. Well, King Kallisor had many heirs but only two with Lady Hathreneir."

She focused on the story. "Your mother told us of them. The boy and the girl. The boy stayed with the father and then accompanied him as they went and killed the girl. Then the boy and his offspring went into hiding for generations."

"You listened well," he commended. "I always wanted to be the heir of the Forgotten Tribe. I wanted to have something special within me that marked me as different. I wanted to be able to stand out from the rest and not be mocked or shunned for being who I am."

"Bards are well-renowned through both lands," she said. "You have nothing to worry about there."

He smiled. "Thank you. But that didn't help much while I was growing up. No, instead, I thought I would find this inner *something* and make my way with it. In a sense, I wanted to have a bit of magic in me, but different from what my mother wielded. It's partly why I have trouble with Dariak's vocation. In some way, he's just another manifestation of that power I never wanted."

Kitalla laughed emptily. "Don't they always say we end up falling in love with our fathers and mothers? I guess it holds true even in a case like yours."

"Perhaps," he shrugged. "But that's an awkward thought, dating my mother. I won't thank you for connecting that image into my mind."

This time her chuckle was genuine. "No, I wouldn't think so." They fell quiet for a few moments, looking out to the dark horizon. "Randler? I know your mother said Dariak couldn't be the heir of Kallisor and Hathreneir, but what do you think?"

"I have tracked the genealogies as far back as the lore permits. There are certain strong family lines that end abruptly and others that continue down to this day. The problem is the accuracy of those records. They are rarely written down anywhere."

She shook her head, boggled. "I don't see how you could ever know you're following the correct bloodline, with all the people in the world, not even just the ones here. Do you follow the ones who travel across the eastern sea? Or those who venture to the far south?"

"It has been daunting, yes. But as I said, I've become a bit of an expert on the Forgotten Tribe. Their lines are marked in unique ways throughout the generations. So as long as the lore is true, then it can be followed to some degree." He stretched and rubbed his temples. "What I think is that an heir will be pivotal when the time comes to unite the two kingdoms. I'm not sure what the role will be, but I can't shake that feeling."

She looked deeply at him. "And you wanted it to be you," she echoed. "But you know it's not you."

He tried to keep the disappointment from his voice, but it was a lifelong hurt. "I'm just meant to gather the information and share it with those who will hear, apparently. And whether the unification occurs in my lifetime or not, it's my duty to keep learning what I can and then disseminate it."

She thought back to all the songs she could remember him singing. "Every song has been related to the Forgotten Tribe, even that war song yesterday."

"Except rare occasions, yes. You were unconscious when I sang of Grendal and the Prisoner's Tower."

The name sent shivers down her spine. "Grendal?"

"Yes," he answered. "Father of Grenthar, I'm afraid. He taught his son all he knew in the art of secret passages, traps, and thievery. Grenthar excelled, of course, and delighted in taking things to an even further extreme."

"I'll say," she muttered, absently rubbing the arm that had been shattered by the falling doorway in Grenthar's domain. "You really do catch all the details of things, don't you?"

"I wouldn't be a good bard if I didn't," he said proudly.

She clapped him on the back. "You're an excellent bard, Randler. You even brought me out of my slump this evening. Thank you."

He winked back at her. "See? I don't always have to sing the words for them to work."

* * *

The troop watch was diligent through the night, heeding all of Dariak's warnings about the creatures that would be in the area, and so they did not raise any false alarms, even when a pack of shadowcrows floated overhead cawing in the darkness. Shadowcrows only ate during the daytime, Dariak had insisted, and when they attacked, they would only attack small creatures, not people. Nonetheless, the dawn was a welcome sight, though it meant a hot day ahead.

The biggest concern of Gabrion's was walking into Marritosh with a full contingent of fighters and mages, but Dariak assured him that it wouldn't be a problem at all, though he didn't explain why. The warrior remained close to the mage's side during the morning march and avoided Kitalla when she approached to greet them. Randler whistled a merry tune, which Dariak interpreted as a signal not to ask any questions, so he kept quiet.

It was another two and a half days before the town came into discernible view. There was a low outer wall that served to keep feral creatures out, but was easily scalable otherwise. Dariak reminisced the days when he couldn't see over the top ledge, he was so small. Now he could pounce over it without much effort.

Beyond the wall were the sandstone huts of the village. The roofs were made of tarp or treated wood that wouldn't burn easily. Everything was well fastened to combat the strong winds that would pass through during the winters, and as they approached they could see that some places were in need of repair from some recent storm.

Dariak greeted the entry guards with a Hathren salute, which included a flourish of the hand, a glowing fireball in his palm, and a low sweeping bow that exposed his neck to attack. The guard acknowledged him with a nod and asked him his business.

"We are traveling through, but need a moment's rest within. We mean no ill will."

The guard looked over Dariak's shoulder, eying the line of soldiers behind him skeptically. "From where do you hail?"

"I am Dariak, son of Delminor. These companions are visitors from Kallisor, under my guidance and protection." He spoke with deep authority and purpose. Gabrion kept extremely still, doubting this plan. He had wanted to send only a small group into the town to gather the supplies they would need for travel westward to the mage tower.

"That's a large number of visitors you bring, Master Dariak," the guard commented heavily. "But you are within your right to do so, by order of the Mage Council. I trust your destination lies there?"

"It does indeed, good sir," Dariak nodded. "It is why we have come here first, for supplies."

The man paused for a moment, scratching his chin, and then nodded. "You would do well to steer clear of Vesille's Inn at this time. Otherwise, abide the laws and be on your way through."

Gabrion was dumbstruck as the guards stepped aside and admitted them freely and without escort. They hadn't even questioned the others of their purpose or names. He felt it was rather foolish, but it also challenged him to look at Dariak anew. While traveling through Kallisor, the mage had been bound several times, treated as a prisoner, sentenced for execution, and chased across the land as a traitor. Here, he was so highly respected he could bring a contingent of enemy forces right into a Hathren town.

His musings blinded him to the surrounding area and so he missed the destitute rise and fall of homes along the way. The required repairs they had seen from afar were nothing compared to what really needed doing in the town. As the vicinity worked its way through his awe, he realized suddenly why such a group would be welcomed after all; they would bring much-needed revenue to the town.

For three coppers apiece, every man and woman was secured with a place to eat and sleep, and many did so in resident houses, paying the owners directly for their hospitality. Dariak's fee was waived, as he was a citizen of Hathreneir, but he donated the funds anyway, knowing they needed it more. Only Poltor and his band were reluctant to part with any coin; they only acquiesced to the demand when Dariak intervened and told them clearly that they didn't have a choice in the matter.

"There isn't any loot here worth the price," the master thief growled in response.

Dariak shushed him. "You'll have other opportunities. Don't make a battleground here for any reason. They may look decrepit, but they know how to come together in the thick of it. We would not be wise to disrupt their ways. That said, we should find some ways to assist them for a while if we can."

"I won't," the man stated.

"If you keep your hands clean while we're here, and that includes your followers, then that will suffice for me." Grudgingly, the thief agreed. He took his band to a tavern and they remained there for nearly the rest of their stay.

Dariak took his three companions to seek one of the four town elders. The old woman was wrapped in a thin silk shawl from head to toe. It tugged against her hips and left little to the imagination, much to their chagrin. "Greetings, Imerelda."

"Dariak, my boy, you return at long last!" she said with a gap-toothed smile. "We always knew your return would come, but we never knew when."

"It is always a pleasure to be here," he replied with such feeling. "We were wondering, while we're here, if there is anything we can do to help? We have a fair number of able hands at the moment, if you need us."

The woman's whole face lit with enthusiasm. "What a delight! Indeed, we could! This winter was a massacre with all the winds. Surely you felt their raging energies?"

"I was away," he answered regretfully, thinking back to his incarceration within the Prisoner's Tower. "What could we do?"

"Simple. We have been rebuilding many homes already but more work needs doing. The king has taken a fair share of the strong ones for the battles against Kallisor. A shame they would start rebelling when our need is so great."

Gabrion drew a breath to contradict her, but Kitalla jabbed him in the side for silence.

"We would be delighted to help," Dariak said.

It was difficult convincing the Kallisorians to work toward rebuilding the village, but the four companions managed to convince a good number of them to do so anyway. Their arguments were valid; after all, their land was being attacked by soldiers who were grown and trained from this very town. Building it up seemed like a direct violation against their own country, but Dariak demanded it and they were serving him.

Once they began, the mages had the most fun of all of them. Not only were their spells allowed, they were encouraged, something they had rarely experienced in their lifetimes. White-haired Quereth swept his arms about, tightening the bonds between roof and wall, while Frast and middle-aged Lica drew added support from the earthen floor to secure those walls in place. The other mages also worked in tandem, some with the soldiers, to fortify the various homes. Most of them started with the huts in which they were staying, but eventually they fanned out around the town and did what they could for the better part of the day.

Dariak didn't begrudge the thieves their abstinence from the construction work, knowing he would have other things to lay on their shoulders in the future. He didn't think they would as easily gain access to the castle once they reached that far, but the thieves would provide at least a distraction, if not the key to breaking through the king's defenses.

He didn't like that line of thinking, but he expected there would be resistance when they approached the castle. However, their next goal was Magehaven, where the Council was housed, and he expected a warm enough welcome there when they arrived. His only hope was to recover their jades without much incident.

The day ended and the villagers showed their appreciation by preparing various meals for their visitors. The whole town felt united and the precarious division between Hathrens and Kallisorians was blissfully set aside for the night.

The next morning, they stocked up on supplies, further contributing to the town's finances, and then by noon they were off again to the west, with Randler crafting some tunes on a lute he had purchased. He also procured a new mace that had a diamond-shaped head and fit his hands better. The troop left reenergized, in high spirits, and feeling good about having assisted the people.

In truth, it went better than Dariak had ever hoped it would. He wanted everyone to see that they were all just people with different needs but that they could work together. Randler saw it, and eventually so did many of the others. It gave them something to think about as they braved the hot day and the feral creatures that came out to greet them.

Indeed, the creatures seemed determined to make the journey to Magehaven as difficult as possible. Luckily, the troop was able to fend off the attacks easily, but there were many of them. Eaglons and reptigons appeared with the sandorpions and shadowcrows. The mages were hesitant at first, but Dariak led the way, spraying the air with fireballs and ice darts, windstorms and rock bullets. He encouraged everyone to use all their skills to the fullest, and so they did. Some of the warriors opted to practice their archery or lancing skills. A few put their swords away in favor of daggers, working with the thieves to hone their close melee battle tactics, though they often ended up wounded and bleeding. However, the mages tended to their needs promptly, keeping everyone strong and ready for the next barrage.

It felt as if the country of Hathreneir had no shortage of creatures. They fought for hours, with only brief rests between each foray. The fighters didn't mind as much, but soon the mages grew weary. They weren't accustomed to utilizing their spells with such rapidity. Yet everyone encouraged them to push through their weariness and keep the magic going.

Kitalla also practiced her dance moves, understanding that they would be less effective against the beasts than they would against the army itself. Still, she drew the forces around her like a cushion, envisioning the effect she wished to convey to her targets, and then casting the energies outward from herself to ensnare her victims. The eaglons seemed the most affected by her attempts and she was able to confuse a good number of them throughout the day. At one point, she convinced a pair of them to chase after each other, much to the amusement of the fighters below who laughed as the large birds flew in figure eights trying to catch each other.

Gabrion warmed up well to the fighting. He was grateful his injuries had been so fully healed back in Savvron after the mages had arrived. The pain was gone completely now; only the fear of it remained, and he was determined to banish that before he was engaged in a real battle. He kept twitching when he would turn to the side, fearful of reopening the side wound Heria had scored, but it was gone and healed and there was no wound to open. Still, the intensity of the pain stuck in his memory, so he kept repeating the maneuvers until he relaxed at last.

Through most of the fighting, Randler played his lute, rattling off numerous variations of battle songs, keeping the troops well motivated even when they started to tire. Each time a wave of weariness swept over them, Randler increased the tempo and inspired greater action from them all. He also took turns setting the lute down and launching some arrows or swinging his mace to keep his skills sharpened, but when his music was gone for a while, the fighters called to him for more. In a way, he inspired them more than did the need for survival.

Many of the creatures were salvaged for food, which they needed in addition to the dry rations they had obtained in Marritosh. Though they weren't mages, Poltor and his gang focused on the recovery of the reptigons so they could claim the poisonous drops of serum before it decayed too greatly. They knew its value to the right mages, and they hoarded the rewards as they went, finally feeling like this journey might prove worthwhile after all.

It took a few days for them to reach Magehaven. The nights were much easier than the days. They set up the necessary protections at dusk and fended off the occasional intruders, while the days were fraught with continuous fighting. The battalion adjusted its strategy on the second day, where only a third of them fought at any given time, unless the odds were overwhelming. This allowed them to remain as fresh as possible while also protecting the group as a whole. It was an effective strategy and the troops credited Ervinor and Gabrion with its derivation. Soon, they were seen by most as the mutual leaders of the army, though the two of them in fact responded mostly to Dariak's cues.

It was evening as they gathered at the base of Magehaven, which rose over ten floors high with a wide wall of force that kept them out. The wall had also obscured the tower from sight until they were nearly upon it. Dariak gathered his companions. "The four of us will need to enter together. I have the right to be here as both a citizen of Hathreneir and a mage. You three will join me as bearers of the jades. We will be admitted if we go together."

Ervinor saluted proudly, "We will await your return, Master Dariak." The young fighter escorted the four to the barrier wall and watched as they clasped hands. As one, they stepped forward and passed through the invisible wall, where they vanished from sight completely.

CHAPTER 15

The Thief Unmasked

KITALLA LOOKED AROUND the oaken room, staring in awe at the high ceiling overhead and the luxurious tapestries that lined the walls. Sheer fabrics decorated the windows, teasing the room with multicolored light as the sun shone through. High shelves wrapped the perimeter, adorned with statues and figurines of all shapes and kinds. She tried to turn toward them, but someone tugged on her arm, so she looked back and upward into admonishing eyes.

"Be still, child," the woman said tersely. "You'll have a chance to look later."

"Yes, mama," she replied, remembering why they had come in the first place. They had left their hometown in the north and ventured to a local city where the mayor was seeking a wide array of workers, from cleaning servants to engineers. The prospects were exciting, even to the six-year-old, whose life had already been a struggle. She had no recollection of her father, but when her mother was able to sneak herself some wine and she loosened her tight grip on her emotions, she always spoke well of the man. Kitalla wondered when he would return from the war and when he would lift her in his arms and spin her around like she saw other fathers do.

A tug refocused her and it was months later. Her mother was enwrapped with aprons and rags, scrubbing a mess on the floor. "Such a careless thing to do!" she scolded.

"I only wanted to see, but he wouldn't let me."

The woman growled in annoyance. "It isn't your place to have your way. It is your lot to obey the will of the masters. I won't have any more of this nonsense."

"But mama, they were saying things about you."

The woman reached up and slapped the girl across the cheek. "Their words mean nothing at all, foolish child. Keep your tantrums in check or I promise you, I will send you off on your own." She then forcibly calmed herself and pulled young Kitalla close. "Please, dearest. We need to make this work."

"Yes, mama," she said, and not for the last time.

The years drifted by and Kitalla's mother was put to more and more grueling tasks, from scouring the chamber pots to cleaning out the animal stalls. She never knew that Kitalla spied on her when she could, listening to what was happening and absorbing all the information. One cool autumn evening, the servant was crying to a sympathizer over a bottle of mead they had taken from the kitchens.

"You know I can't leave," Kitalla's mother wailed.

"You're better than this. Neither you nor the girl needs this kind of turmoil in your life! Pack your things and go!"

But she was resolute. "I only had to clean up after him. I can clean. I can do that for us."

The other woman hissed. "He murdered the boy, tore him to pieces, and *you* had to go in and make it all disappear. This is outrageous. If he wasn't the mayor, I swear!"

"Keep your anger down!" Kitalla's mother insisted. "It was—it was an accident."

"So the story will go, but you saw it happen! What kind of life is this for your daughter?"

The response was miserable, "The only one I can afford for her. No, I can survive this." She wiped her tears away and straightened her back. "She has to grow up strong. She must. I can't live on the street and still raise her to be strong."

"Bah!" the woman protested. "You'd be better off elsewhere. Take her juggling act on the road. Join a troupe. Earn money that way and get help raising her in the process, I say."

Horror filled the woman's eyes. "You would send me off to wander the land in a circus? Oh, I pray you're only too far into the mead to be speaking clearly."

"Clearer than you, at any rate," the woman scoffed, after which they dissolved into meaningless banter.

The terrible secrets continued and the burden placed on Kitalla's mother grew more dangerous, but she didn't know what to do other than follow through with orders. Meanwhile, Kitalla's knife-throwing talents were discovered and the mayor periodically brought her in for performances before large audiences. She once dared to refuse and received such a violent beating she didn't think her skin would ever return to its usual color. She submitted to the commanded performances, unable to do anything as a child. What she did notice, though, was that as her throwing skills brought money in to the mayor's hands, her mother's trials seemed to lessen.

As Kitalla grew older, she paid less and less attention to her mother's troubles. They had accepted their lot and the periodic fiascos that arose as a result. The mayor's temper led to a number of random deaths through the years, and more than once the town guard sought Kitalla's mother as a suspect. The men handled her roughly, but would end by leaving her sprawled on the floor, which was an improvement over escorting her to the dungeon.

Time flashed forward again.

"You're… really talented," said a kind young squire one day. Kitalla was sixteen and he wasn't much older himself. His cheeks were red with embarrassment and though she didn't have time for him, she couldn't help but feel intrigued.

"Am I?" she grinned, tucking her daggers back into their hiding places. She had just finished a wild performance, tossing her knives and cutting fruits into evenly sized chunks. Partway through, the mayor had risen up, apparently bored, and strode from the room, after which the other nobles had followed, all save this one boy.

"You really are," he affirmed, then he held out his hand in greeting, which clearly wasn't the proper way to greet a girl. "I'm Joral."

"Kitalla," she replied, looking over his shoulder at the empty room. "Sir, shouldn't you be off with the others?"

"Perhaps, but meeting you was more important," he said, his cheeks flaring red again. "And… It's Joral."

"You've taken too much wine," she accused.

"Not a drop," he swore.

She noted his hazel eyes and the funny curl of his reddish-brown hair. "I'm just a knife thrower, Joral. Bastard daughter of a serving girl, really," she explained, determined to cast aside his interest.

"I don't very much care where you come from or who your family is, Kitalla. It's you I want to know better."

She didn't know how to respond, his sincerity was so blatant. "I—" She cleared her throat. "Look, I have to go before I'm punished for being late."

"Then go," he said kindly, "but I'll find you again and we'll talk then. I won't forget you. Don't forget me, either. Promise?"

Kitalla laughed. "Very well, Joral, if you insist."

True to his word, he scoured the town until he found her the very next day. She was off buying food for the servants and he approached her timidly from the side. They made a day of it, bartering with the merchants, and arguing over the best ways of making salads or debating the finer points of daily life in the city.

They became close very quickly after that and were together at all times. They had some passionate disagreements, but they always worked through them in the end.

"Kitalla?" he said one afternoon, nearly a year later.

"Yes, Joral?" she replied dreamily, lying beside him on the hill outside the city, watching the clouds float effortlessly by.

"Kitalla, I love you."

She laughed and sat up so she could see him properly. "That isn't news, Joral. I love you, too."

"I would give this world to you if I could."

"Hitting the wine again?" She winked.

He turned to her and took her hand in his. "I want you in my life forever, Kitalla. Let me love you. Let me protect you. Let me honor you, for all time."

"J—Joral?"

He kissed her hand and offered her a traditional engagement bracelet that only nobles exchanged. It was simple in detail, but its intent was clear. "Will you let me, Kitalla?"

Her astonishment turned to joy and she threw her arms around him and kissed him deeply. "As if you ever needed to ask! Yes! Yes!"

They were too young to wed and their respective parents didn't take particularly well to the news. Joral's parents demanded he cancel the engagement with the lowly peasant, stating he deserved better than such filth, but he swore that she was more than just a peasant at heart. Introducing them actually worked to his advantage, for they could see that she was at least pretty, and she did seem intelligent. Still, it took time.

Kitalla's mother, on the other hand, took it as a personal affront. "You're trying to desert me after all I've given up for you!" she bellowed one night. "What I've endured for you! And you would run off with some infant out of spite!"

"It isn't spite, mama!" Kitalla screamed. "I love Joral. He means everything to me that father meant to you!"

She received a slap for the comparison. "How *dare* you imply that you know *anything* about your father, you demon child."

"Mother, why won't you listen to me?" she cried.

"It is for me to protect you, daughter. You will sever this tie at once! Had I known it was more than a mere dalliance, I would have put a stop to it months ago."

"Mother, I—I can't." With that, Kitalla started trembling and the reaction caught the woman off guard.

"What is it?" she asked hesitantly.

"I'm with child," Kitalla whispered.

* * *

"No more," Kitalla moaned.

"Yes. You must heal these wounds," an ethereal voice echoed.

"I won't. Don't make me."

"You don't have a choice."

* * *

"Mother, what is it?" Kitalla asked, her hands pressed to her noticeably expanded belly. "You're an absolute wreck."

Distraught, the woman grabbed her hair, tugging wildly. "We will have to get you out of here, that's all. Yes, that has to be it. There isn't time, Kitalla. Go, go!"

"Mother, will you please explain? Why are you in such a panic?"

"The mayor," the woman gasped. "He is out of his mind, Kitalla. I have held him off for as long as I can but time is running out." She moved away from her daughter and started rummaging through their belongings, completely unfocused in her search.

Kitalla stepped forward and grabbed her mother, turning her around. "Please stop, you're making me nervous. What is it?"

Tears streamed from the woman's eyes. "The mayor. He has… wanted you for some time now. I've distracted him for as long as I can—"

Realization set in. "Wait, mother! You haven't—"

The pain was obvious. "I wouldn't let him touch you, Kitalla. It didn't matter if he used me, not if it kept you safe."

"Mother!"

"But now, now he's decided to take you anyway. He is perverse. He has a greater interest in a woman with child. You must go, Kitalla. You must."

Kitalla steadied herself, finding an inner strength she didn't know she had. "Mother, let's both go. We'll be free of this terrible place. We'll go. Come on."

"I don't know that I can."

In the end, they did, with Joral, who first tried to talk them out of fleeing, but then refused to let them go alone. They escaped during the night and sought refuge in the nearby forest. None of them had ever been pursued before, and so they were unprepared for what awaited them. Guards rushed into the forest, waking them in a panic and spurring them to run. Joral propelled Kitalla onward faster, but Kitalla's mother didn't have the strength. She fell and was promptly killed. Kitalla screamed but Joral pushed her forward. She wrenched herself out of his grip and spun around, a fire raging in her eyes. Daggers flew from her hands, taking down the unsuspecting guards in seconds.

"What have you done?" Joral gasped.

"Mother!" Kitalla cried, running over to her mother's body. It was too late. The light had already left her eyes and all ties to Kitalla's family were gone.

"K—Kitalla, please. W—We can't stay here." Joral nervously retrieved her daggers and dragged her from the scene.

* * *

"Stop," she begged weakly. "No more, please. Please."

But the voices were resolute. "You're nearly there."

"I can't."

"You will."

"No…" she whimpered.

* * *

Kitalla and Joral were pursued relentlessly. The mayor was enraged not only over the loss of his servant and his intended plaything, but also at the insult he received at the loss of his guards. The longer the hunt continued, the heavier Kitalla became with her child, and soon the mayor decided to join the pursuit himself, racing forth on the fastest horse he could procure from his citizens.

With only weeks before the child's birth, they were finally overtaken. Kitalla was vomiting in the woods and they didn't hear the approaching men. Soon they were surrounded and there was nothing they could do as they were each pressed against a tree. Even Kitalla's daggers were useless as the guards bore large shields and thick leather armor, not that she was particularly focused.

The mayor rode in, cackling wildly. He was a short, overweight man with frayed white hair on the sides of his head. He slipped off his horse and strode forward, ready for his conquest. He made lewd gestures toward Kitalla, who was now tied to her tree, standing over her lost breakfast. Stalking forward, he pulled one of her own daggers from her pocket and he used it to cut through her clothing.

"Leave her alone!" Joral shouted, but the mayor only laughed.

"Be sure he can see this."

Joral thrashed about and tried to pull himself free. Kitalla screamed but there was nothing she could do. With a violent rage, Joral wrenched one hand free and used it to knock out the guard watching him. He freed his other hand and staggered forth with the binding around his feet. The other guards laughed at his struggle. The mayor finished his deed and turned, knocking Joral to the dirt and pressing his foot against the young man's face.

He thrashed around and freed himself, but the mayor scooted out of his reach. Joral immediately went to Kitalla's side, trying to pull her torn clothing over her body. "I'm so sorry," he wept.

"We'll… get through this," she breathed.

He drew strength from her, secretly taking one of her daggers and folding it into his palm. He nodded his head and turned, eying the mayor with malice. "You had your fun. Leave us."

The mayor laughed raucously. "After that look of horror on your face? I may take you both back just to repeat the whole experience!"

"Y—you wouldn't," Joral said.

"Guards!" the mayor replied, raising his hand haphazardly into the air.

Joral panicked, throwing his hand out and sending the dagger through the air. The sharp blade sliced the mayor's cheek, enraging him at the audacity.

"No!" Kitalla cried, watching from her imprisonment as the mayor unleashed a hideous roar and raced toward Joral, fists flying. The young man fell, clutching his face. But the mayor didn't bother to finish him off. One of the guards came in and restrained Joral as the mayor strode back to Kitalla.

"Such impudence, denying me. Thinking you can better me. You are pathetic and worthless."

"No, I beg you," Kitalla pleaded. "Let us go. We will flee. You'll never hear from us again."

The mayor hesitated, seeming to consider.

But at the same time, Joral brought his hands back sharply into his guard's belly, stunning him. "Kitalla!" he said, coming forward. "I promised I would protect you."

Kitalla's sudden scream was ear-piercing. Joral raced forward as quickly as his tied feet would let him, but the mayor stepped aside, laughing wildly. "Too late!" he crooned in a sing-song voice, moving away so the young man could see the results.

It took a moment for Joral's eyes to focus. All he saw was blood pouring from Kitalla's belly. Her binds were cut and she collapsed, clutching her stomach desperately, but knowing it was fruitless. "The baby," she wept. "The baby."

"N—no!" Joral called out, reaching for her.

"And to think," the mayor chortled. "I was about to give you your freedom until you wrenched yourself free there. Tsk. Tsk."

Kitalla looked at Joral with fading eyes. "You failed me," she murmured, clutching her stomach.

"K—Kita—" he started, but never finished, for the mayor brought a sword down and slew him.

She watched as the light left his eyes and all her hopes for the future died.

Slowly, she focused in on the mayor, who was talking to his guards. "Patch her up and leave her there. Let her carry that corpse to term and remember that I am the power here."

She felt hands pulling her belly together and wrapping poultices around her. She let them, but only because she didn't know how to do so herself. Yet once they were done, her hands flashed out and three guards splattered to the ground. Moments later, even the mayor lay dead.

She couldn't look at Joral's body. He had failed her. Worse than that, she had failed not only him and her mother but also their baby. She knew it was dead inside of her. Every dream she had ever had faded away, horribly and terribly lost forever.

CHAPTER 16

Crystal Chamber

RANDLER'S TRIAL WAS nothing like Kitalla's. He didn't relive any old memories or experience any emotional torment. Instead, he was trapped in a crystalline room, hexagonal in shape with pointed apex and floor, and with no memory of who he was. His feet slipped down the smooth surface and rested painfully within the sharp point, and so he pushed himself upward and tightened his legs to remain aloft. It was uncomfortable.

As he moved, though, each contact with a panel of wall generated a distinct note. There were eighteen variations among the walls. He also found that touching a vertex resulted in a harmonious combination of the neighboring sounds. What else he needed to do, he had no idea. Tapping produced rhythmic cadences that echoed all around him, but no portals opened to him.

Securing his feet along the sloping floor, he reached out his hands and struck the side walls, learning their specific notes and then pressing them again to create a song. The notes sang, bouncing off the inner walls and growing in volume as the sounds interfered with each other. He stopped when the noise became uncomfortable and it took a while for the chamber to return to silence.

He hummed a few stray notes, hearing their sounds echo back to him clearly. Turning created a bit of musical noise but he was trying to get a better bearing on his surroundings. He could see the panes of the crystal, but only a dark void existed beyond the walls. It didn't make any sense.

Crouching down, Randler sank into the base of the oversized crystal and tried to remember from where he had come. Vague images wafted through his mind. A glimmering wall of light he could only see as he passed through it. Someone clutching his left hand, but then letting go. His body flying upward into cold night air, spinning wildly until the crystal gathered one pane at a time, enclosing him within. That was all. Nothing else existed.

He held on to the thought of a "before" and decided that there must be something outside the crystal that he just couldn't see. He reasoned that it must be important, or why else separate him and lock him away from it? Yet no matter how hard he tried, he wasn't able to remember.

Resting his head back sent a deep reverberation through the chamber. It warbled in a strange sort of spiral, first climbing to the apex and then winding its way back

337

down. Curious, he bopped his head against the crystal again, trying to follow the sound as it traveled. The note was merely reflecting off each panel until it ran out of energy, but then he could almost feel it as it went.

He turned and rapped his fist purposely on the wall, sensing the path of the sound once more. It was no different, except in its initial volume. A gentle tap also produced the spiraling effect, but he could barely hear it, as its amplitude was so low.

Alternating fists, he pounded on the wall, hearing the tones chase each other up and around. Then he shifted his focus, pounding on two neighboring walls and listening for a difference. The two tones harmonized, just as when he had pressed on the crease between them, but now the sound propagated through the chamber.

It was an elaborate musical device, he mused, strumming the different panels and letting the reverberations echo wildly. Then his foot slipped from under him and he crashed downward, shaking the whole structure vibrantly. The rattling irritated him and he covered his ears until the noise settled down.

Though unable to remember who he was, he decided he must be linked to the music in some special way. How else could he follow it so well as it went up and down? Why else would it both please and trouble him so? He connected the two ideas in his mind; that he was a musician and he had something waiting for him outside this cell.

Standing, he could easily reach the upper panes that stretched to the apex. The design of the chamber allowed him to touch any part of the panel to produce its sound, so he didn't need to strike the exact center, for instance. This gave him some freedom; his motions wouldn't have to be precise.

He thought of the songs swimming around in his head, trying to make some meaning of them, but the answers were too elusive. So instead he reattempted his first venture of producing a song within the crystal. After testing the panels he would need for the proper notes, he secured himself against ones that would remain silent. Then he tapped with finger, hand, toe, or shoulder, as required, calling up a jovial song about a boy and a girl meeting after sliding down a hillside and then becoming fast friends. The crystal seemed to learn the song and after he finished the main verse, the walls kept singing the tune for a long while.

But nothing else happened.

Ransacking his brain, he dug for another one, hoping that some song that was tucked away would somehow serve as a key for his escape. He vaguely recalled the tale of King Kallisor and Lady Hathreneir, with swords held high and spells to bind. He searched for the notes he needed and then banged them out in order. Once again, the panes reverberated for a long time, singing the tune back to him with unnatural vigor.

Song after song issued forth, from children's fancies to tales of eccentric thieves. Each one was accepted by the chamber and returned in force, but still nothing else transpired.

He wasn't sure if he could physically do it, but he tried playing two different songs simultaneously anyway. To his surprise, some part of his brain was able to control his body with two completely different tasks. The result was an odd conglomeration of notes that either amplified or diminished as they overlapped.

Something about the additive and subtractive qualities of the sounds was meaningful to him, so he sank back down to think about it for a while. He couldn't come up with anything concrete, however, so he returned to mixing up parts of various songs, amused when the crystal would accept the offering and then return it, louder and clearer, moments later.

Perhaps his lot was in fact just to create and play various melodies for the enjoyment of those listening on the other side of the crystal. But if there was another side, then he knew he belonged there instead, remembering again that he had been holding on to someone before.

Then randomly he leaped upward as high as he could, crashing his arms into the apex and sending a strange mix of sounds cascading through the crystal. He didn't really think he would break through, but he would have felt terribly foolish if he hadn't at least tried. The action may not have released him, but it did change the orientation of the crystal.

He leaped again and the crystal pivoted some more; now the flat walls were all lying horizontally and there was a pointy apex on either side of him. It was more comfortable having a flat surface underneath, but he couldn't fit standing up. He compromised by sitting down and crossing his legs, stretching to ensure he could strike every panel if he needed to.

The cell was clearly designed for him, for all eighteen facets could be touched without much effort, now that he was centered along the side wall, which had become the floor. He played a few tunes to test the musicality of the chamber, and it hadn't changed at all. He was both grateful and disappointed. If the sound quality had been altered, then maybe his goal was to rotate the crystal until it opened or cracked. But since it sounded the same, he surmised that it remained unchanged.

There needed to be more than tapping and sounds. He had a purpose, if he could only remember it. He slammed his hands down, generating loud sounds that bounced forcefully off the walls. Then he banged again and again, adding to the noise as frustration set in. He didn't like the sound, so he calmed himself and waited for silence to return once more.

He thought again of the songs playing in his head and how the crystal echoed them back to him clearly. Perhaps the key was in a song after all. He tested the eighteen panels one more time, setting their positions into his mind so he could strike them in the correct order. And once he was ready, he launched himself into it, singing as he did so.

The ages are past. The hours are gone. The terror fades away.
Our power can last. We must be strong. We linger every day.
For we are braver than our foes and we will always win.
We can do what none of them knows and so, let it begin.

A magic within. Hidden quite deep. We'll bring it forth one day.
And then we begin. Awaken from sleep. Ushering in a new way.
For we are wiser than we show, and we will find the path.
It will lead us as we grow, and cleanse us like a bath.

Stephen J. Wolf

The swords will rise. The blood will flow. The warring, it will last.
The men will all die. The women will weep. The stones will have been cast.
For brutal strength is not enough, it cannot solve our woes.
The meekest peasant has proven tough, and that's where the courage shows.

As he continued to sing, the crystal echoed the melody in perfect harmony. It reflected off the walls and amplified as the sound waves overlapped. Each verse he added grew louder and louder until his ears pounded against the volume. He wanted to stop and cover his ears, but the song kept singing in his head and so he plodded onward, keeping the melody flowing.

A sliver of truth. A glimmer of hope. Perhaps we can find a way.
We listen to youth. We yearn to cope. Let peace come in to stay.
For holding on just to the past, we're trapped in darkened pain.
We need to find an answer fast, so that we may survive again.

Louder the crystal echoed, making it hard for him to concentrate on the words he was spewing forth. He focused himself, keeping his limbs tapping the notes out in harmony as he pushed onward.

An answer is here. A voice shall call. A sacrifice will be made.
Don't shed a tear. For the good of all. We seek the shards of jade.
For with the power deep inside, united they can find
a means to make the bitterness hide, a gesture made in kind.

To give up your heart, you must first release. You must survive your pain.
The healing must start. A blind treatise. Scrub out a stubborn stain.
For only then can you be free, to look at the world anew.
With gentleness that you can see, while knowing what to do.

He heard a shift in the timbre of the song. The crystal changed slightly. A bit of dust fluttered down and then more. The augmented tune rattled terribly among the glassy surfaces, pounding against him, but he persisted in his effort. And as he strummed the notes again, the energy was too great for the crystal to contain. With a great discordant cacophony, the crystal shattered, raining down in millions of pieces. The tiny bits each carried a scattered note and, like a musical rainfall, they showered him in song.

Eagerly, he looked around, but with the crystal gone, he saw only darkness. His body hovered in the emptiness, unable to go anywhere. Sadness immediately overwhelmed him, for his one companion, that wonderful crystal, was now gone. Here he would spend the rest of his life in solitude.

But what of that someone holding his hand before? He struggled to reclaim his memories, fighting against the loneliness that was swallowing him. He reached within himself and recalled the tune that shattered the crystal, bringing its notes to mind and pointedly adding another verse.

I still have my heart. And I will be strong. I know I will find my way.
I have played my part. It will not be long. I will find the light of day.
For I am a man who loves another. I will not take a gibe.
As we have come to respect each other, we reveal the Forgotten Tribe.

He held on to the words, not quite knowing if they were true, but admiring them all the same. They instilled him with a pure hope and they resonated with his heart in a way he hadn't thought possible. He breathed deeply, bringing the feeling through his mind, and as he exhaled, the darkness before him parted.

At first, the room was a blob of odd colors, but soon they resolved into known shapes. His memories also flooded back, as did the words of his impromptu song, and he smiled to himself, remembering Dariak and cherishing him in his heart. As two men, their relationship was frowned upon by some others. As citizens of opposing countries, they would further be shunned. Yet, he knew that they were a good and solid fit, a strong union of two different worlds. Indeed, they represented the message he had been hunting all his life. In their own way, they were the Forgotten Tribe, the union of Hathreneir and Kallisor, unbound by land, united by love.

The truth of it filled him with such joy, he laughed aloud, unable to contain himself. He sat up and swung his feet to the ground, not recognizing the chamber, but not caring either. He could practically feel Dariak's presence nearby, a hall or two away. Rising up, he stepped lightly toward the door, throwing it open, and seeking out the mage not far beyond.

Finding Dariak, he threw himself against the man, burying his head into the man's shoulder as he squeezed him tightly, after which he kissed him with such passion, Dariak was lost for words. They held each other a while, enjoying each other's presence, delighted that, for once, everything could feel so perfectly right.

CHAPTER 17

Dariak in Magehaven

AS THE COMPANIONS stepped through the invisible wall surrounding Magehaven, Dariak felt a searing heat from his hands, after which a brilliant light flashed and he found himself alone. When he turned around, the small army was still beyond the wall of force, setting up defenses against feral creatures, but his companions were gone. He smashed his fist into his hand in annoyance.

"Trials," he hissed. "I should have known." He wasted no time running toward the entrance of the tower and throwing open its massive doors. "Stop!" he called aloud. "They are with me!"

Three acolytes were in the foyer and they stared at Dariak, aghast at his arrogance. Two of them stalked forward, hands swinging upward to summon defensive energies, but Dariak ignored the magic, shoving them physically aside and stamping his feet as he approached other mages beyond them.

"To whom must I speak?" Dariak shouted over the din within the room.

Practice spells fizzled and fell away as the casters were distracted by the authoritative call. Two older mages stepped forward slowly, their bodies shimmering with all the protective magics that enwrapped them. They were necessary precautions in a practice room, but their presence irritated Dariak all the more.

"Who so addresses this chamber with anger?" called one of the men.

"It is Dariak, son of Delminor. I have returned at last. Yet my companions were taken from me and I would have them released before they are bound to the Trials."

The two mages looked at each other with concern, and then ushered him to follow. "There is little time, then," one muttered.

They hurried up a flight of stairs and the older of the two mages waved his hand before a wall panel, which then melted away, revealing a hallway behind it. He stepped through without hesitation and Dariak followed as the other mage took up the rear. The walls were carved of wood and though there were no light sources, the air itself glowed with a faint glimmer that made it easy to see. Dariak's nose wrinkled in annoyance and he realized they must have been using the glow sacs of lightflies for the luminance.

The corridor ran the length of the oversized chamber that was on the other side of the wall, then the hallway started to branch off in various directions, including down and up. The leading mage turned sharply right and ascended six stairs, then stopped to wait.

Dariak stood beside him, with the other mage close behind. As one, they turned and stepped forward, but rather than traverse the steps back downward, their feet landed on an invisible set of air steps that guided them upward to another landing. It was a secret passage that would make their ascent much quicker than going the normal route. Dariak was glad he was with these masters who could access the secrets, for he knew his own spells would not work any longer. To avoid unwanted infiltration, these quick-routes were bound to passwords and spells that were changed by the Mage Council periodically. Only those within the upper echelon were permitted to even learn them.

Though it didn't take long to wind up eight flights of the tower, Dariak couldn't help feeling that they weren't moving fast enough. Still, they had accepted his claim without hesitation, as was his right, and his demands were being promptly met. There was little he could actually complain about.

Once they reached the upper quadrant of the tower, the mages introduced their guest to an elder in the room, after which they left Dariak and returned to the practice chamber below where their talents were needed for training.

Dariak turned his gaze around the room, noting that a number of the elite mages had changed since his time there. They kept to tradition, wearing long flowing robes of various colors, each one signifying the mage's preferred element. In his time here previously, Dariak wore a deep brown robe lined with crimson florets that decorated the sleeves and hem. Many mages debated the wisdom of wearing their colors so openly, for it would alert others to their strengths and suggest their weaknesses, but proponents insisted that if they had earned the right to wear them at all, then anyone would be hard-pressed to take them down, even with that information. It was a difficult argument to win without admitting a personal weakness among one's own defenses.

The eldest of the group was also an earth mage, with water droplets sewn along the robe in a gentle swirling pattern. He stepped forward and clasped Dariak's hand warmly. "It is good you return, young Dariak."

"Thank you, Pyron. It feels as if it has been ages." He lowered his gaze in homage. "Before we reconnect, however, I must ask a boon. My three companions were taken by the barrier. I assume the Trials are in effect? I would have them protected from such a thing. They are here with my support and guidance."

The wrinkled face turned downward. "I am sorry, friend. They were unrecognized by the perimeter and set within the Trials with utmost haste."

"No one spoke to them first?" Dariak asked in shock. "They were just inserted immediately?"

"The Council has seen fit to make some alterations to deny those who would unwittingly intrude upon our grounds," he explained, then leaned in so that only Dariak could hear. "Once you left, Farrenok joined the Council." It was explanation enough for Dariak, remembering the spritely youth whose paranoia woke him at all hours, spewing spells at random. He had learned to control the errant energies, but the fear had never left.

"Can't we interrupt their Trials early?" he asked, already knowing the answer.

Sad gray eyes confirmed Dariak's intuition even before he spoke, "No, Dariak, I am afraid not. They must endure the tasks set upon them. But take heart, for other changes have also come about in your absence." He turned away and motioned for Dariak to follow.

The other mages waved greetings to him or eyed him cautiously, in the event he turn out to be some sort of imposter. None were permitted to speak yet, though, as Pyron had not welcomed their attention to the visitor. It was an old custom that had occasionally brought them trouble, but as the leader of the Mage Council, the old man had the right to speak first and uninterrupted. There were, of course, ways for the other mages to indicate interest in the conversation, but it was still the elder's decision to permit their words or not. As of now, no one had anything pressing to add.

Dariak took an empty seat at the table where some of the others were gathered. They continued their muted conversations, albeit half-heartedly in the presence of Dariak. "You say there are other changes?"

"Yes, indeed. You know already that the Trials are initiated by a single element, be it fire or water, or some such. However, we have been making use of a different element altogether. It is one we had not thought of using for such a purpose, but in many ways it has proven to be more effective than others." He was delighting in the revelation he was about to unleash upon Dariak, and he built up suspense by waiting.

There was nothing Dariak could yet do for his friends if they were being subjected to the Trials. They would each have to endure them in their own right and succeed. But the joy in Pyron's eyes awakened Dariak's curiosity. He considered for a moment and then realization struck. "You tapped into the healing shard!"

"Indeed!" the old man clapped his hands. "I knew you would understand. Always astute, like your father. Yes, we managed to unlock many of the secrets of the healing magic and then Olissa beseeched the Council to link its power to the Trials. It was a curious enough thought that we voted and agreed."

"Though you say it has been effective?"

"Delightfully so. A number of ill-minded travelers have attempted to breach our walls, but once they have been cleansed of their pains and ailments, their goals shift, sometimes slightly, other times drastically. Regardless, each one has understood that taking our power is both impossible and foolish. Several have remained on to study our ways, while others have gone abroad to teach the populace of what good we can bring to them."

Dariak didn't know whether to laugh at the description or be concerned. "Are you altering their minds?"

"No, no, fixing their wounds," Pyron assured him. "But it is a healing of the inner hurts that they face within the Trials. It is not the mending of cuts or breaks they face, but the broken parts of their souls. After all, what is a thief other than a man damaged by circumstance seeking to better himself by taking from others? Show him the error of his way and he no longer seeks the same target. He finds he can rebuild himself and live anew."

Dariak let the words sink in, wondering what ailments the healing Trial would find within him. He had hurt others along the way, and not just the men and women he had killed in Kallisor along the journey. There were childhood hurts and pains. "But don't we grow into who we are by how we deal with the things that go awry?"

Pyron's brow furrowed. "I did not expect you to question this method, Dariak. These people do not lose themselves. Rather, they find themselves as they truly are meant to be. They find a means of repairing the hurts that give them a false focus. They are then free to live as better people."

He shook his head. "Something about it doesn't seem quite right."

Pyron shrugged and his tone grew slightly terse. "Considering that the previous Trials pitted unsuspecting visitors against any number of horrors that, in many cases, led to their deaths or hysteria, I think we've moved to a better system. Come and see." Without waiting, he guided Dariak from the room.

They walked in silence, spiraling up another three floors before coming to the Chambers of Trials. Rarely were more than a handful of chambers ever in use and, at present, only Dariak's companions were undergoing the Trials.

He had been here before. Admittance to Magehaven was often challenged, and even in Dariak's case, he had submitted to testing by the resident mages. He knew that a few floors higher up there was a group of mages whose sole purpose was to provide the energies for the Trials. When their protections were not needed from intruders, the Chambers were attended by willing members among the mages who wished to prove their worth in order to seek advancement. Completing a successive series of Trials was a requirement for a mage wishing to join the Mage Council.

Dariak's admittance had been contested because he only engaged in two Trials; one upon entrance and one to earn a place among the Council members. But his bloodline was thick with the work of his father, whose experimentations had greatly furthered the mages' goals and so Dariak's place was all but secured. Though he hadn't needed to submit to either Trial, he offered to do so in order to prove himself to others. He was among the youngest members of the Council then at the age of nineteen, but it wasn't uncommon for a few members to be young.

The Trials themselves were arranged to push a person beyond their usual limits, not necessarily to annihilate them. Those with weaker abilities were challenged against somewhat lesser tasks, but Dariak wasn't certain what that would mean for his friends, for each of them carried at least one shard of the Red Jade. He didn't know if the jade's power would amplify the Trial's difficulty or if his friends would even be able to channel the jade's energies at all.

His own Trials had been harrowing in their own way, but he never regretted attempting them. Instead, he rose to the challenge of battling against numerous elements at once, summoning paralysis spells against fire arrows and binding spells against creatures. He had exhausted his spell supply during his tasks, but they had also helped him to prepare for greater challenges ahead.

Two years after his admission to the Council, he had participated in the empowerment of the Trials. Linking with a handful of other mages to draw energy through a large diamond seemed silly to him at the time, but once the energies swirled around and they pulled through the mineral, he could sense the countless array of abilities that were available out in the world.

Pyron's voice cut through Dariak's reminiscences as he led the mage to a central platform that housed a crystal column extending upward through the ceiling. The floor was a murky white, like frozen milk, and it reached around in a wide circle, with Chambers extending off at set intervals. The walls of each Chamber were transparent from the central area, and Dariak could easily see his friends within their own cells, separately engaged in their own Trials.

The companions' rooms filled with blurred visions from their thoughts, projected haphazardly upon the walls. Each was a manifestation of the energies coursing through them, which the walls drew in and mimicked temporarily. He could see a reflective bluish glow in Randler's chamber, whereas Kitalla was surrounded by a wildly changing set of scenery. Gabrion's quarters reminded Dariak mostly of Savvron, with the occasional appearance of blurred people, including himself, that he'd met along the way.

"I don't recall this," he said.

"As I said, changes have come," Pyron gleamed. "We no longer need to send specific spells down into each location, for the energies themselves interact with the participants and create a world completely contained within their minds. The walls are enchanted with the power of fire to draw the energies into patterns of light that we can see. It allows us to have a sense of what transpires with them."

"I don't understand," he muttered. "Where are the spell chambers? Where are the battling mages? Where are the beasts or traps?"

"Be calm, Brother Dariak." Pyron clapped him on the shoulder. "Those rooms do exist for the men and women who prefer such challenges, but for the errant trespasser, these Chambers suffice."

"What control do you have over what happens to them?" he asked, suspecting the answer.

Pyron hesitated. "Little, I'll grant you. But no one has succumbed to death or despair since we have begun with this work. We owe it to the healing jade. The magic we have derived from it has allowed us this progress. Oh, it is progress, don't deny that," he said, seeing the refutation building in Dariak's face. "We may be able to control the feral creatures within our walls, but it is a cumbersome trade to begin with, and now we lose fewer specimens than ever before."

"Perhaps I have been away from my kind for too long," he murmured. "This seems so foreign to me, otherworldly." He pointed to the flashing images on the wall. "And that seems like an invasion of their private inner-most thoughts."

As he watched, his companions were writhing about, fighting off their own internal demons. He noted that Gabrion was often pressed down to one knee or that he moved with a solemn grace. Kitalla, on the other hand, fared the worst of them all, if her pained expressions were any indication. He wanted nothing more than to break the connections and release them, but he knew he couldn't. Even without the advanced magic they were using, disrupting the energies during a Trial could be disastrous for the participant and the empowerers above. Now with the energies twisting so intimately with each person's experiences, he feared the repercussions of even speaking too loudly.

Pyron guided him from the room a short time later. "I know why you have come, Brother."

"I must take the jades," he replied.

"Yes. They are yours, by right," the old man affirmed.

"I hear hesitation in your voice."

"Some of the Council members have been reluctant to adhere to some of the old laws, including those of your return and what it would forebode."

Dariak stopped mid-step. "Forebode? They think I would take the power unto myself in order to, what, bring them down instead? Aren't all mages joined in our goal of unifying these two nations?"

Pyron shook his head. "No. That was your specific emphasis of the goal. The Mage Council would prefer that magic be freely used—with governing exceptions against wild magic and cruelty—in both nations."

"That's essentially the same thing."

"It isn't and you know it."

Dariak scowled. His biggest dream was to end the wars by unifying the nations, which demanded acceptance of mages across the lands. He wanted them to be free to see the port of Pindington to the east, though the lure of the impressive Prisoner's Tower was now lost, and to visit the imperial museum within Kallisor Castle proper. "Are you saying that the Council won't let me have the shards?"

"Some… may wish to challenge your worthiness," he said.

"Let them," Dariak answered with seething anger. The jades were all his by right, having been assembled, tested, and utilized by his father. The mages had access to them on loan, to further magical education. They were never meant to be hoarded away and kept from his hands.

Footsteps echoed down the hallway and Dariak turned to a vividly passionate Randler, who enwrapped him so tightly he struggled to breathe, and then was further besieged with a deep series of kisses. The bard didn't even seem to realize the old man was standing beside them.

Pyron cleared his throat and waited for them to disentangle. "I see you have overcome your Trial." He gave a pointed glance to Dariak for doubting the new variation on the method. "You will no doubt need sustenance and rest."

"Wait," Randler gasped. "Dariak, it's us. You and me. We're the ones! I figured it out. We're the heirs of the Forgotten Tribe. It's up to us to do this after all!" He beamed with joy and it was all Dariak could do not to join in.

"The Forgotten Tribe?" Pyron's eyes narrowed. "That is a false tale. There are no more bloodlines extending from the originators."

But the bard would not be covered in shadow. "Each group has its own history," he dismissed respectfully. "You would have different aspects to consider if you were tracing the lines yourself. I've spent my life gathering information on my own."

"You are welcome to consult our libraries, but you will find disappointment, I'm afraid."

"Say what you will, sir, but it was the answer to my imprisonment. It's what freed me from that crystal prison. I say then that it is true." He took Dariak's hand. "It means we will succeed, Dariak. You understand that?"

The mage smiled. "It sounds wonderful. Once we have the rest of our friends and the shards, we will be close to our goal."

Randler scanned the area. "Gabrion and Kitalla? Where are they?"

"Facing their own Trials," Pyron offered. "Perhaps they will be as fortunate as you to find a quick freedom."

However, they were not as fortunate. Kitalla's Trial was wrought with such pain and disappointment that her passage through the Trial kept her detained for the better part of a week. Merely reliving her past had not been enough to permit her release and she struggled with whatever answer the magic was seeking from her, not that she understood that aspect of her imprisonment.

Considering what he knew of the current Trials, Dariak had somewhat expected Kitalla's struggles, but Gabrion's were a complete surprise. The warrior was locked away with no sign of emergence. He would undergo fits of furious fighting against unseen beasts, and then hunker away to silence, barely breathing. When he spoke, it was unintelligible, making sense only within his inner reality.

Kitalla awoke first and slid from the Chamber silently, seeking solitude where she could find darkness and silence for a time. Dariak found her easily within the tower and he brought her food and drink, offering his support and friendship for when she needed it. She nodded, accepted the nourishment, and then tucked into the food without word. The pattern continued for a couple of days.

While they waited for the companions to recover, Randler and Dariak talked of plans for the future, of what it would mean to unite the two kingdoms properly. They were fanciful dreams and though some of the mages delighted in the discussion, many steered clearly away.

The unexpected delay made the waiting army nervous outside. Early on, Dariak convinced Pyron to at least allow the two dozen mages to enter, though each needed to submit to a Trial, and most did so eagerly. Then Dariak himself ventured out to speak with Ervinor. "I have no idea how much longer we will be detained here, I'm afraid. I cannot gain admittance for the rest of the forces here, either."

"I understand. We will need to relocate. If you deem it wise, we would return to Marritosh and seek refuge there until your return."

"It would be the most prudent course," Dariak agreed. "Keep the men in line and the townspeople happy and you should be welcomed."

Poltor was affronted by the suggestion. "Neither your tower nor that town suits us," he decided. "For now, mage, we part ways. Not as enemies, don't worry. Rather, we will venture toward the castle and scour the area so that you may return at ease."

He didn't like the idea of sending thieves into the heart of the castle but he didn't have much choice. "Fare thee well, friend. I would rather ask you to keep your hands clean in my hometown, but instead I'll ask you not to harm the people."

Poltor raised an eyebrow. "We will defend ourselves as needed, but we will also feed our nature. Until next we meet." He gave a sweeping bow, completely unbefitting him, and then turned to disappear in the crowd of fighters.

Ervinor bit his lip. "I would have preferred keeping an eye on him, but the truth is, he has been tainting some of the men."

Dariak wasn't surprised. "He joined us for adventure, not sentry work. I will have to hope he remembers that he has no rights here at present and so won't be reckless."

"We are all a bit timid in this foreign land, Dariak, but we all trust you for our various reasons. For one, I believe that Gabrion's heart is true and he is dedicated to you, and so I'm yours. The others follow one of you or the other. We will remind ourselves of your valor when we recommence in Marritosh, and when you return, we will be ready for whatever task awaits."

"Thank you, Ervinor. I pray we won't need force in the end, but we may need to defend ourselves long enough to survive so that we can be heard. It's why we need you. This isn't my battle alone. It's one we all fight so we can earn true peace between our kingdoms and stop living in needless fear."

Ervinor saluted proudly. "I see you and Gabrion share a common heart. Be well, Dariak."

"And you, Ervinor."

He hated the call that Ervinor made to summon the troops together and the following sounds of packing up the tents and supplies so they could hike again through the desert and reach Marritosh. Before he returned to Magehaven, Dariak took out the vial of reptigon serum from his pocket. He had been saving it, without knowing why. And though he may need its strength at some other time, he opted to use it now.

He didn't have the air jade with him, but he knew enough of the jade's power to call to the wind directly. He summoned a small cyclone to stand before him, which pelted him with bits of sand, but he ignored the discomfort. With a dagger, he cracked the vial, letting the serum escape into the swirling wind. "*Fathrinor surruscavitar farthrin kaie garrinnoth.*" The reptigon serum vaporized and was swept up completely by the cyclone, which then raced outward and traveled with the small army, surrounding the whole battalion and keeping the feral creatures at bay. It gave them a safe journey back to Marritosh without a single skirmish to fight along the way.

He had been casting many spells lately from energy alone, supported by the jades in his possession. Tapping into a spell component reminded him in a way that he was just a man playing with powers that were greater than he was. It was an important distinction for him. Returning to Hathreneir was far from humbling, he was so well-known. He needed such reminders to keep his dreams in check so that he could find a realistic means of making them come true.

He turned around and faced the tower, seeing a few stray faces in the upper windows gazing out at him. Or perhaps they were watching the army disappear into the distance, he didn't know. But they would have sensed the magic he had cast, and whether they approved of his actions or not, he didn't care. His mission was greater than the petty wishes of a few close-minded mages. For those who supported him, all the better.

His next mission, though, was to help Kitalla break her silence and to assist Gabrion with his Trial in some way. After those tasks were complete, he would officially request possession of the jades. Two of them were stored here, he knew, partly from history and partly from the resonance of his own shards. From Pyron's comments, he expected some sort of difficulty, but he would have to deal with it at its own time.

For now, his friends needed him.

CHAPTER 18

Trials Continued

LIVING IN MAGEHAVEN for even a few days was difficult for non-mages. Wherever they turned, objects would erupt into flame or float through the air without notice. Randler was more accustomed to it, having Sharice as his mother, but he had left that part of his daily life behind long ago. Watching it happen all again in such a commonplace manner irked him. Taking Pyron's advice, he thus ventured into the mages' library.

The library was broken into two sections within the tower, with the more advanced subject matter closer to the tower's apex. The lower floor was only about three sets of stairs up from the base of the tower, and it held the larger works of historical documents the mages had recorded throughout the years. He decided to peruse them first before venturing up to the eleventh floor where the more advanced works lay.

The layout of the library was deceiving. The stairs brought him to a landing that opened into a large rectangular room. There he could see tables and glowing lanterns scattered about and a few mages absorbed in study. The back walls of the room were brightly painted and punctured with numerous archways. As he stood there at the stairwell, some mages walked down from the upper floors and nudged their way past him, looking over at him with a bit of a sneer. Apparently, not everyone felt that the library should be open to all visitors.

He turned about and saw that the arches extended in every which way and none was marked with any form of explanation, at least that he could see. His search would take him forever without any guidance. Turning toward a nearby mage at one of the tables, Randler stepped forward and introduced himself.

"Good day, fine sir," the bard said with casual grace. "I am a bit lost here, and I was wondering if you could perhaps lend me a hand?"

The mage didn't acknowledge his presence, but kept reading through his text and making notes in a personal log. Randler tried again, but it was useless. When he ventured toward a few others, he found similar reactions. It felt to him as if they were driven by a mad hunger and would brook no interruption. The thought made him wince.

He couldn't just quit, he decided. He would go blindly into the stacks and see what he could find. There wasn't anything else he could do right then, anyway. Kitalla was still keeping to herself and Dariak was trying to speak with the other mages about intervening with Gabrion's ongoing Trial. No one knew what was taking the warrior so long, but the mages were adamant there was nothing to do but wait.

Plunging forth, Randler stepped purposefully toward the nearest archway and his jaw dropped out from under him. Away from the central room, he could see the vast rows of shelves housing innumerable books and sheaths and scrolls, extending much further back than he would have guessed. In fact, the entire outer perimeter of Magehaven was loaded with volumes, extending all the way around the massive structure. He had initially thought the main room was the larger part of the whole, but he was sorely mistaken. Easily a hundred mages could wander inside the library and never once bump into each other, it was so expansive.

The task before him felt overwhelming, even more than moments ago. But he reckoned there must be a system for the mages to follow. It couldn't all be haphazardly scattered around the place. Approaching some of the mages left Randler feeling unwelcome, from the anger in their responses to the continued moments of being ignored. They seemed an altogether unfriendly lot.

Stretching his hands and stepping forward, he walked toward one of the bookshelves and touched the leather binding with his finger, turning his head to the side to read the title. *Mystical Myths of Magical Mayhem*. Beside it, *Mysticare's Most Magnificent Marvels*. He glanced at a few other titles and was overwhelmed by the rampant alliterations. The words all started blending together, but he had the feeling that he wasn't necessarily in the historical section of the library.

He randomly pulled a book from the shelf, *Simple Spell Songs Sung Softly*, and flipped open the cover. The writing inside was a deep and carefully drawn script. He had feared that the written language of the mages might differ from the one he knew, but he was pleasantly surprised that it wasn't the case, at least for this piece. The songs in the book reminded him of the odd cadences his mother had him practice as a child. He thumbed through, wondering if any of them would actually be the same as the ones she had taught him, but he knew it wasn't likely. These seemed to be lullabies for little children to ease them from pain and to send them to sleep. Whether they were actual magic, he doubted it even mattered.

Randler investigated, glancing at titles occasionally, slowly coming to understand part of the organization of the library. It housed everything from nursery rhymes and songs, to simple and complicated spells, mages of great import, geographical variations in the land, and so on. Not everything was arranged alphabetically, but it was all together by topic. As he perused further, he also noticed that older works were located higher up on the shelves than the younger ones, offering a sort of chronology to the displays.

At last he came to the founding stories he was looking for. He started with a tome at eye level that touted itself vaguely as *All You Need To Know*. A quick inspection revealed that it was part of a series that the authors had crafted, perhaps for use in lessons with children. The writing itself was simpler and often included diagrams of the events. He flipped through a few pages and smirked at the recollections within.

One page in particular caught his attention, as it was a rendition of the War of the Colossus. There, the great magical giant towered over the land, glowing with a radiant orange hue. Its arms were upraised in supplication, but the army drawn in at its feet was merciless. They were painted in shadow, with vaguely sculpted angry faces. The rendition clearly showed that the opposing forces were evil and raving mad, whereas the wide-eyed giant was trying to be some arbiter of peace. He read the caption under the drawing:

And so the mighty Colossus stepped in to protect Our King, but alas the enemy's Treachery was vast. With empowered arrows, they pierced the bodies of Our King, bringing his imminent Doom. Turning then upon the Colossus, the Army of Kallisor used its own hidden Mage Forces and eventually brought the great Colossus to its knees, never to be seen again.

It was an uncomfortable interpretation of the events. True, his king's forces had infiltrated the Hathren troops, but most of them had acted of their own accord in order to bring an end to the fighting. And though the Kallisorian king had always shunned magic, he secretly employed it to his advantage. It would always be a point of contention between the realms, for at least the Hathrens had always acknowledged their magic powers. Growing up, however, the alleged treachery of his king was seen as necessary force against a greater, invading foe. After all, who would want their land ravaged by a colossal giant of light and energy? It was a terrifying tale told to children to keep them in line, lest the colossus come for them.

But to see this caption written with the colossus being a savior, taken down by evil forces, made Randler shudder. He knew there would be other sides to the story; of course there were. Seeing it in print, in a tell-all text, made it feel more real than he expected it to be.

Despite his discomfort, he flipped to the next page, which depicted the eruption of the Red Jade, scattering pieces in all directions. Men and women were lying dead on a battlefield, yet the scene centered on two figures. The first was his king, dying from the impact of the jade as it exploded. The other was the mage who had summoned the colossus—Dariak's father.

Before he could look at the caption, he pressed his face closer to the drawing, hoping to see some defining characteristic in the depiction of the man who had fathered Dariak. Of course, it was impossible to see any real detail in the size of the drawing, but he tried anyway. Perhaps there was a text here about the man himself with a better rendition. Considering the work Delminor had done for the mages, he assumed there would be volumes. He first scanned the caption below the picture.

The evil king slew the great Mage Delminor in the midst of his spell, thereby casting Energies out wild and killing many who need not have died. Then, stealing the Mage's Spell Components, the king ordered his men back to Kallisor so he could be buried with his kin. Delminor died that Fateful Day, leaving his young family behind to fend for themselves.

Curiously, the book didn't specifically mention the jades. He flipped through the rest of the volume, but they were never named. They were only referred to as spell components. Whether this was to preserve the safety of the jades or to augment Delminor's perceived abilities, Randler could only guess. Yet part of what he wanted to learn more about was the jades themselves. So though this text was illuminating in its own way, he shelved it and searched for one that was more detailed.

* * *

Kitalla meandered through the upper floors of the tower, seeking places to hide away from others. She spoke as little as possible to anyone who crossed her path. Her hands slowly rubbed her belly all the time, wondering at the life that was lost to her so long ago. She had heard of warriors who had lost their limbs in battle, but still felt tingles from where those limbs once were. She had felt the same, and she had worked tirelessly to block the sense of loss. Yet now it was all back with her. The pain. The sorrow. The unfathomable loss.

Her footsteps carried her, while her mind swam sadly back and forth. Much of her understood the situation better now, but there was no going back to fix it. There was no way to repair the damage that had been done. This was a pain she would have to endure.

The room before her was much brighter than the ones she kept hiding in. She had visited this place a number of times, seeking a reason for her recent flood of unwanted memories. The chamber was brightly lit and enwrapped on all sides with chambers that faced the central column. She knew she had awoken in one of these rooms several days ago and she understood that the resurrection of her pain had begun here, too. Yet as she entered the area, as always, her thoughts turned away from her own turmoil. It was one of the reasons she kept returning.

The chamber itself was loaded with healing energies. Walking in to it was uplifting in its way, but she was starting to feel an emptiness with the slight euphoria, for it never lasted once she walked away. No, her reality came back to her outside these walls. But still she was lured within.

Over the past few days, there were numerous people engaged in their own Trials. She recognized them as mages from their own small army, but she kept her head down and never spoke to them if they emerged in her presence. Most of them would spend hours or days thrashing about in whatever was presented to them, but all of them eventually left.

Save one.

It wasn't a mage she visited. It was Gabrion. The protector. The one she had come to rely on without realizing it. He was a stronger version of her Joral. In many ways, he was what she envisioned Joral could have been as a man, or, rather, what she lamented he should have been. Nothing deterred the warrior from his quest. Not for long, anyway. When his hope for Mira waned, he still pushed onward, determined to find her, living or not. He would not rest until she was with him again.

She ached with the thought, for she wanted such a man for herself. In her teenage frivolity, Joral was that man to her, though they were both too young to know they had much more growing up to do. But all of her childhood fantasies of a husband had been of someone as strong as this. Someone who fought for what he believed in, without fail.

"So why are you still trapped in there?" she whispered, touching her hand to the thick glass that kept him enclosed. His body was at rest now, which was a welcome relief. She had seen him several times while he was in some sort of battle, jumping and twisting about. It was too much commotion for her right now. She needed peace and tranquility until she could find her center once again.

She didn't know how long she stood there before he moved. Slowly, he flipped over onto his back. His days of thrashing about with his shield and sword had torn his clothing in many places, but any wounds on his body had been healed by the energies in the room. She caught herself trying to catch random glimpses of skin as he turned about, wondering how it would feel if she could touch him. She tried casting the thoughts away, but they were persistent.

Nor could she turn away as he launched into another aspect of his Trial. Rolling up onto his knee, Gabrion bent his head low in homage to an unseen power. She wondered who it was, but the glimpses that appeared on the walls offered no suggestion. The room was filled with snippets of Gabrion's recollections, and she always felt a wave of warmth when her own visage floated by.

Two other women in particular appeared throughout her visits to see him. One, she assumed, was Gabrion's mother. She had a strength to her, as well, and though she wasn't classically beautiful, her inner power radiated like sunshine. Kitalla regretted that such a woman was gone from the world. Like so many others.

The other woman who appeared in the images had to be Mira. The girl was pretty, Kitalla had to admit, and it made it harder for her to witness the moments that flashed by. There was usually laughter on the girl's face with such innocence it made Kitalla's heart ache. Yet there were also moments where the girl was curled in terror, with tears pouring from squinted eyes. Always at those times, Gabrion would pull her close and comfort her.

Watching these scenes unfold again filled Kitalla with conflict. She wanted to take Mira's place and be coddled by the warm farm boy. Yet at the same time, she despised the girl for taking all of Gabrion's focus for herself. The tenderness in his projected memories were always of Mira. Kitalla and Gabrion had shared some tender times, too, but they were never represented in what she saw.

"Your quest really is just for her, isn't it?" she asked under her breath. Something within her tensed with pain and she grabbed her chest in response. "With all we've been through, I'm not there with you, am I?"

Footsteps scraped up behind her, intentionally loud. "Kitalla, you're here," Dariak said softly.

She shook her head. "I was leaving."

"We have to try to help him, Kitalla. He has been in there for too long."

She turned her head slightly so her words were aimed at Dariak, but she refused to turn and look at him. "I'm not his protector."

Dariak frowned at the remark. "Kitalla, I could use your help with this. Please, let's do this together."

Her hair swished gently from side to side as she shook her head again. "I told you, I was leaving."

The way she said it irked him. The words cut through him in a way he couldn't explain. "Kitalla…"

Her chin sank until it rested on her chest and then she turned away, walking slowly toward the exit without meeting Dariak's gaze. "If you fix him, tell him I wish him well."

"You'll tell him yourself," Dariak retorted. When she didn't respond, he stepped forward and grabbed her. "You're not leaving!"

At last she met his eyes and he could see the anguish overwhelming her. Then she drew in a deep breath of air and a hollow mask fell upon her. She lashed out with her fist, knocking the wind out of the mage, crumpling him to the floor.

"Stop me," she challenged sarcastically, dropping a leather-wrapped object in front of him. It was her shard of jade. Without a backward glance, she stalked from the room, winding her way through and out of Magehaven.

CHAPTER 19

The Mage Council

THERE WAS NOTHING Dariak could do to stop Kitalla from leaving. Even as the healing energies swirled around him, he felt that she needed to go. Keeping her would only make her resent them all and she would truly be lost forever. Perhaps she only needed some time apart.

He wished he knew the contents of her Trial, but with the internal method the mages were using, there was no telling, only speculation from the projected images. Even the mages powering the Trials had no knowledge of the actual inner workings that took place. It never used to be that way. Previously, the Trials were well-controlled by the mages, who took active part in administering them. The mages who supplied their strength through the pinnacle diamond once had some influence. But no longer.

Dariak stood before the rest of the Council, feeling more like a visitor than a past member. His own mage robes were tattered in places and ripped along the seams, acting more like a pocket-filled cape, the deep crimson color of the fabric a misleading indicator of his strongest element. He wished he could have procured a brown robe for this occasion, but in the end, he didn't think it would make the argument any easier.

"Ladies and gentlemen of the Council," he called once his presence was officially announced. "I come today to discuss with you the procedure in use among the Trials."

"What have you to say, Master Dariak?" asked a bored-sounding, older member named Kerrish. "Surely you understand that in your absence, you abdicated your voice with the Council in such matters."

Dariak kept his poise. "I did not realize that pursuing my father's legacy would render me silent among my colleagues here." The comment had its desired effect; a number of the older mages fidgeted in their seats.

"Go on, then," Kerrish prompted. "Better we get through this."

Pyron had warned Dariak of resistance, but he hadn't even begun and they were challenging him. "Days long ago, this tower was far grander than any other in any land. From here we could oversee the affairs of the nearby king and attend to the defense of this kingdom through the powers we extend to the border. We have secured the southern lands from intrusion as well, and no forces ever attempt to breach our walls. Within our own home, we have precautions in place to protect ourselves from harm. But I wonder at the new procedures.

"Upon our arrival, my friends were taken from me and cast instantly into the Trials without so much as a request for their names. Since when have we cast aside humanity to treat every visitor like vermin?"

Farrenok leaned forward in his seat, his eyes darting from side to side. He was younger than Dariak and his lack of worldly experience made him a curious choice for the Council, but he had apparently proven himself through the gauntlet of Trials in order to earn his seat. "Things are different, Master Dariak." He stammered slightly. "Even when you left you knew there was a change in the air."

"It was why I left," Dariak agreed. "We all sensed a shift in the energies. It was our time to act. To strike out and gather the shards of jade so that we could reunite them and find peace for our realm."

"Our lands are cursed," sputtered an old mage, Lorresh. "There will never be peace here. Better we turn our energies toward what we can." Some of the others rapped their hands on the table in agreement.

"With attitudes like that," Dariak reprimanded, "you'll only prove it to be correct. But I have another belief."

Kerrish yawned loudly. "We've heard your diatribes all before, young master. Find the jades, bring about a semblance of peace, and somehow convince the Kallisorian fools that we can all work together if they'd only let mages into their midst. And we've choked over the arguments that have followed, that if we *did* put mages into their midst, then they will assume they are spies and they will rebel. It is an endless cycle and we are done entertaining the idea."

Dariak's jaw set. "You're right about one thing, anyway. It's an endless cycle the way it is now."

Farrenok saw an opportunity. "And we daresay that the feeble-minded mages of Kallisor really made certain that the citizens of Pindington will yearn for mages among them."

"I beg your pardon!" Quereth shouted from the audience area. A silencing spell was immediately placed over him to prevent any other outbursts and he sank back to his seat in utter outrage.

Dariak had warned the mages not to speak under any circumstances. "I apologize for my friend's outburst, dear Council members. Were it not for the work of Quereth and the other mages with us, all of Pindington would have been lost to the unleashed power of the lightning jade."

"Ha!" Farrenok barked. "And who was it that released that energy in the first place? Answer me that, mage," he called to Quereth whose silence shroud was lifted.

"It was our brethren, I regret to say," the old mage answered honestly. "Yet it was not his intent to bring down the tower or to free the wild energies into the air."

"Intent or not, his actions were of severe consequence," Farrenok said. "In your land, magic is basically outlawed, isn't it? Yet it was magic that brought the tower down and killed a large percent of the populace."

"It is an error we can fix," Quereth assured. "Until that moment, we were working well with the people."

"A lovely sentiment," Farrenok scoffed. "But people cannot unsee something like the fall of that tower. Wild magic like that leaves a lasting impression."

Dariak was trying to maintain his composure, but the arrogance was getting to him. "I recall a time, Master Farrenok, when wild magic was a common problem of a certain mage. Yet he overcame it and now sits upon the Council itself."

Rage flushed the young mage's face and his twitching worsened. "You dare!"

"Gentlemen!" Pyron intervened at last. His voice boomed over the muttering din, magically amplified.

Dariak spoke into the brief pause that followed, cutting Farrenok off before he could speak. "I only raise the point to remind us that we can overcome all adversities when we set our minds to it."

Kerrish saw that Farrenok was fuming and so he responded. "Very well, Master Dariak. Let us say that the irreparable damage in Pindington can be overcome." His tone clearly questioned the possibility. "It is only one step upon the mountain. How do you plan on convincing the king himself, who persecutes our kind in his land?"

Dariak knew a question like it would arise at some point. It was one he had been thinking about through all of his journey in Kallisor. "I admit that it will not be easy. But the kings of Kallisor have always vested time into the research of magical powers. They have underground societies from which they pull experienced mages into their fold. They established the mage compartments in the Prisoner's Tower so they could learn from other mages. The people know that the ban against magic is a farce, when it comes down to it. They adhere to the principles because their king says it is so.

"But there are many who explore the magic anyway, and they will be the voices within the land that will support our call. I have met many of them along the way, and I have seen that they are respected by their fellows. When they join the ranks of the people around the nation, the king will see that it is pointless to deny his people."

Kerrish offered a slow, deep, mocking clap. "Beautiful sentiment, Master Dariak. If only the pride of man could be so easily swayed. His pride runs generations deep and you will see that you will fail, just li—" He stopped himself with a cough.

It took a moment for the unspoken phrase to echo in Dariak's mind. He looked around and a number of the other mages averted their gazes when he peered at them. Then it all fell into place. "You think I will fail… like my father failed, you were going to say."

With a sneer, Kerrish realized he had erred. "He did fail, did he not?"

A dead silence fell over the room. Dariak struggled to hold his emotions in check. He had never heard a Hathren mage speak ill of his father. Now he was surrounded by several who thrived off what they had learned from Delminor's research, yet still they were tagging him as a failure. He couldn't believe what he was hearing.

When he composed himself enough, he spoke clearly and succinctly. "Since my return, all I have heard is how things have changed in the past year. I see that procedures are not the only changes." He shook his head in disbelief. "Very well then. I will make two requests of the Mage Council and then I will be on my way."

"The Council will hear your requests," Pyron said in his most official tone.

"First, I would ask that my companion, Gabrion, be released from his Trial."

"That cannot be done," Pyron denied. "The risks are too great."

But Dariak would not be swayed. "Then I will assist in his removal so that my failure will also be at my cost."

"It can't be done," Farrenok sputtered. "You will destroy the empowerers and your companion all in one."

Dariak bore into the youth's eyes and quelled any further reactions, but he spoke aloud for the rest of the gathering. "The empowerers can leave their posts. I will replace them. From there I will do what is necessary to free my friend."

"It is suicidal," Kerrish argued.

Dariak turned a cold gaze on him. "Only if I fail." He waited for Kerrish to challenge him again, but the determination in his eyes balked the older man. Dariak turned back to Pyron. "Once we are ready to leave, I will require the remaining pieces of jade for my quest."

"They are not yours to take," said another mage among the Council.

"They are mine by right," Dariak said. "You base all your work on my father's legacy. I will have those shards for my own work. As I learn more, I will bring my knowledge back to the Council for your use, as was always the intention in the past."

"Bold words," Farrenok murmured. "And no way to prove their worth."

"It is true that things have changed here, but until my departure, I was a well-standing member of the Council. It is with that word that I make this vow. I pray that trust has not left us among our own kind." Having said his piece, he clasped his hands behind him and waited for the Council to deliberate.

Pyron swept his hands about, tossing a bit of dust into the air. The tiny particles flashed in numerous colors and swirled around the Council table as the mages discussed their thoughts behind the silencing force field. No one on the other side of the table could hear, but they could still see the silhouettes of the mages raising arms and apparently shouting at one another.

Dariak held his place and did not flinch or look at the assembly behind him. The mages who had joined him from Kallisor sat transfixed at the wild display of magic, but they realized that it wasn't actually wild at all. Each fleck of glowing dust represented opinions and thoughts of the mages arguing behind the screen. The colors swayed from one hue to another as the tide tipped in favor of Dariak's demands, and against them. After a while, the dust fluttered to the floor. The decision was made.

Pyron stood up with the proclamation. "Master Dariak, the Council has decided upon your requests. In the case of your companion within the Trial, the Council feels that it would be prudent to discover whether a participant can indeed be removed safely from the challenge. However, we feel that you will not be able to accomplish this task on your own. We will ask for volunteers to empower the session."

Quereth immediately stood up from his place in the audience. He remained quiet even though the silencing shroud had been removed, but his intent was clear. Lica and Frast joined him, as did two other mages with them.

But Dariak knew they wouldn't be allowed to help, for they had no training as an empowerer. He looked around, wondering if any of the resident mages would stand to support him. The wait was unbearable, but he didn't care if none stood up. He would do it alone if he needed to. Pyron scanned the crowd, seeing only Dariak's traveling companions rising in support.

"No one, then?" Pyron asked.

At last, one mage stood up, and it was one that Dariak did not expect. Kerrish rose from his perch and glared at Dariak. "I will empower this attempt, lest you die."

Dariak didn't understand the motivation and wondered if the mage would try to interfere with the process. More likely, he was curious enough about whether Gabrion could safely be removed from the Trial and his curiosity won out. Kerrish had his own ghosts to deal with. Unfortunately, some of those ghosts despised Dariak directly.

Pyron waited a moment longer but no other mages offered to assist. He faced Dariak again with the next announcement. "As for your second request, the Council has decided that you must prove your worth in order to receive the jades."

Enraged, Dariak couldn't stop himself. "This is preposterous! Very well, then. First I will release my friend from his Trial and you will see that I succeed. Then I will personally engage in a mage-battle with any member of the Council who has denied my request for the jades."

This challenge incensed the Council. Dariak's supporters hated the injustice of it, whereas the mages who denied him were insulted by his words. Pyron rose up and called for silence in the chamber.

"Your challenge is unacceptable," Pyron declared.

"So is your denial of my rights," Dariak said. "Let them face me themselves if they think I am unworthy of possessing the jades. Let them see my inner strength as I seek to fulfill my father's life goal. Let them see my determination as I prove my worth. There is no other way to convince those who doubt me. Pit me against them and I will show them."

Pyron looked around at the Council to mixed reactions. The men and women who had denied him were either afraid of such a challenge or eagerly looking to squash this upstart mage. Pyron wondered what course of action would be best for his tower. He saw the inner fire in Dariak's eyes and he decided. "You make a convincing argument. The Council will deliberate. I will offer two choices to the Council now. First, we will vote again on allowing you the jades as requested. Failing that, those who oppose you will stand against you in battle."

The Council was furious with this turn of events, but the fiery deliberation wall was set up again. Dariak appreciated this measure, for the weaker mages on the Council would likely change their votes in his favor, and it might be enough to grant him the jades without the fight.

The discussion went on for some time. Dariak waited as patiently as he could, but it was irritating. He wanted to leave this fiasco and start making plans for helping Gabrion. He had no idea how he would go about it, but he knew he would find a way to succeed. The trick would be to disconnect the energies from Gabrion's mind. Somehow. It wasn't much different than the problem facing the errant mages who lost their way and became border guardians.

At long last the glowing wall dissipated and Dariak waited for the final decision. Pyron rose up again and announced, "Upon completion of your first task with the Trial, you will then face the five mages who have decided against you." He gestured to the Council and the five mages stood up, including Farrenok and Kerrish.

The decision made Dariak even more suspicious. If Kerrish was deciding against him, he wondered once again if the mage wouldn't try to impede his success with freeing Gabrion. He would have to keep himself on alert.

The Council was dismissed and Dariak turned to explain the situation to Quereth and the others. "Your support means much, friends, but we can't insert you among the empowerer station without training, and we simply don't have time for it."

"I understand." Quereth looked sadly at the room as it emptied of its participants. "I always yearned to be part of the mage circles here in Hathreneir. I always wanted to learn from them and then bring my new knowledge back to our people. Yet now that I have seen some of these inner workings, I realize that men and women here are not so different from those at home. I regret that these people cannot see your noble heart."

"Thank you, friend." Dariak smiled. "It is not everyone, though, as you well understand. For some, it is a fear that the jades will be gone from them forever. Or worse, that there really is no hope for peace. Whatever they say, we all want true peace, not just freedom for mages."

Quereth nodded. "But you also forget that some are jealous of you. Be wary of them, Dariak. They will hurt you if you aren't careful."

"It's a good point. An unfortunate one, but good nonetheless."

CHAPTER 20

Healing Gabrion

DARIAK AND RANDLER spent the next few days with some of the acolytes in the library, searching for information regarding the Trials. Though Dariak knew much already, he feared that his planned intrusion into Gabrion's mind would render them both senseless. The research was disheartening, for all anecdotes relating to breaking into a Trial led to the loss of mental faculties. No one had ever accomplished it, but he knew he would have to find a way.

It didn't help matters that Kerrish would be the backup support. The old mage had always quarreled with Dariak in the past, and his arguments during the meeting with the Mage Council made him a poor choice in Dariak's eyes. However, he also knew that Kerrish had lost two sons, a daughter, and a handful of trainees, either to the Trials themselves or to their own failings. Some of them had died; the others became border guardians, not that they would recognize Kerrish any longer. Some mages secretly felt that Kerrish's teachings must be flawed, but his own magic was ever flawless. If Dariak could succeed in this attempt, it might give the mages a means of preventing further damage from the overuse of spells, or perhaps to find a way of healing those whose minds had broken.

Dariak assured Randler that Kerrish's selfish goal would keep him level-headed during the intended healing. He didn't expect Kerrish to turn and sabotage the proceedings. At least, he convinced Randler as much, though in truth he wasn't actually so certain. He didn't tell Randler that Kerrish objected to Dariak's sexual orientation; it would only make the bard worry.

Quereth and the others offered as much support as they could muster, both in researching the library when Dariak's eyes grew weary, or by sparring with him in preparation for the battle that would occur after his success with Gabrion. Lica orchestrated those, mostly, focusing Dariak's thoughts on success and the aftermath. It was a brilliant scheme that kept Dariak sharp and feeling as if he could indeed safely free his friend from the Trial.

When the time came, Pyron called for a halt of all magic within the tower. He assured everyone that it would be a temporary respite, and he urged them all to fill their bellies and take their rests, so as not to disturb the energies that would soon be engaged.

"Ready, little mage?" Kerrish sneered as they gathered together in the chambers of the Mage Council.

"Of course," he replied confidently. "Aren't you? You seem a little shaken. Not nervous, are you?"

The old man scowled and strode off toward the rear door, which led to a set of stairs that wound up toward the crystal chamber near the top of the tower. Dariak followed solemnly, touching his pockets and feeling all the items he had with him. Mostly, they were for defensive spells to help keep him grounded here as his mind ventured forth, but he also had some offensive magic planned just in case Kerrish tried taking over.

Dariak had asked for several concessions leading up to this moment, but only one was granted to him. He only hoped it would be enough. Randler went to the chamber where Gabrion was essentially entombed and set himself on a chair with his lute, some food, and water. There, he would try to maintain a sense of calm while Dariak was working his magic unseen from above.

Kerrish and Dariak spiraled up the stone steps and reached a level flooring that was wide open to the nighttime sky. A soft breeze swept through the room and Dariak breathed in deeply, cherishing its scent. Kerrish turned to him and then sighed with exasperation, but Dariak would not be rushed.

Once he felt sated, Dariak strode toward the center of the room, where an enormous diamond rested on a crystal altar, reaching halfway up to the ceiling. Winding around the altar were several chairs, benches, or beds, and upon them were four mages who were busy empowering the tower's defenses, including the Trials. Kerrish was not one to lie down as he worked and so he took an empty chair and propped himself in it officially. He glanced back at Dariak and prompted him to take a seat and to begin the process before the night wore too thin.

But this was Dariak's task. He had chosen nighttime for the darkened sky so that the light would not fluctuate during the process. No clouds passing over the sun or even the motion of the sun itself would interfere. He had been in the chamber when the sun's rays had struck one facet of the diamond and reflected the light painfully into his eyes. But once tied into the diamond, it wasn't easy to let go, so the shock hadn't pulled him from the empowerment. It was a safeguard of the system, for if the mages could be so easily disrupted in their work, the defenses would falter. Still, he didn't want to risk even that much of a distraction.

Dariak also chose a chair for today, though he usually opted for a bench so he could shift and stretch out if needed. He closed his eyes and drew the air in more deeply, while he heard Kerrish murmuring the chant that would grant himself access to the diamond. A dim blue glow shone a few paces away and Dariak knew that Kerrish had connected. It was up to the old man to send the four empowers back into themselves and to await further command. He did so with such efficiency, Dariak was admittedly impressed. Within a few minutes, only Kerrish himself was connected to the diamond. Now it was Dariak's turn.

He pulled three items from his pocket; a small piece of diamond that had come from the larger gem itself, a flask of water, and a miniature lute that Randler had given to him as a memento. The bard had been carving it at night while Dariak meditated, and he hoped it would help them to maintain a semblance of a connection during this task.

Dariak sipped from the water and held the diamond shard in his left palm. *"Correnectus rizhulier harrethorian factentius enshirthen orrulus fathrinhorius shashtennei."* The diamond shard glowed and he reached it forth until it touched the larger mineral. The facet of the diamond took on a deep blue hue and Dariak felt himself pulled within.

The sensation was as jarring as he remembered. His mind leaped from his body, almost like waking slowly from a dream and finding the will to pull himself back into slumber. It was an odd disconnection from reality, where the only emotion he felt at first was sheer panic that he would never be whole with his body again. Soon, logic reminded him that he had done this before and he was only channeling his thoughts.

Kerrish appeared soon after, taking the form of a swirling black and red cloud. Though he spoke in the language of mages, it sounded perfectly intelligible to Dariak. "Begin now your ceremony. Dally not longer than you must." A red bolt shot forth and the energizing blast filled Dariak with strength. Kerrish clearly wanted this task over with promptly and was going to ensure that Dariak's strength would not wane. With a nebulous nod of his own, Dariak focused his thoughts and let himself spiral downward into the floors below.

He had traveled this way when empowering the Trials, but he knew the pathways had changed with the new regime. His mind tugged toward the left but those were no longer the Trial rooms being used, so he sharpened his thoughts and bent them to the right, where his mind slipped through a narrow opening and plummeted into the next few floors below. A vast white expanse opened before him and he felt a strange, yet familiar, warmth nearby.

As he contemplated the warmth, he could sense a pleasant melody wafting through him. He knew instinctively that it was Randler, offering his support the only way he could. He wanted to listen to it, but there wasn't time. Kerrish reminded him of the urgency with a few quick jabs of energy.

Dariak scoured around and followed another source of warmth nearby, knowing it would have to be Gabrion. He twisted himself around and floated forward, following the sensation until he entered the warrior's prison. But though Dariak had prepared himself for many possibilities, the one that occurred had not been one of them.

Once Dariak was fully inside Gabrion's chamber, he was immediately whisked within the warrior's thoughts, and his own self diminished so greatly that he barely remembered why he was there or that this was, in a sense, unreal. Thus when Dariak's magical self was dropped into a gray-brown town, he knew vaguely that it was Savvron, but he knew little else.

His essence reshaped into a body as he examined the surroundings. The buildings were ramshackle huts, but they were well-used, not untended. He couldn't see more than a few yards away, and he kept rubbing his eyes unsuccessfully for clarity. It was as if a thick fog lay beyond, obscuring the information he needed most.

A warbled scream echoed and Dariak turned sharply toward its source. A young woman was running in terror, and she wasn't alone. Several other villagers ran with her, one of them knocking her down in the process and continuing on. Dariak ran over and hefted her back onto her feet, then he looked to see what chased them, but whatever it was existed beyond his range of vision. He took a few steps forward, but someone grabbed his shoulder and turned him around.

"No, you mustn't," cried out a middle-aged man. Dariak wondered if he knew him at all, but he couldn't place the frightened visage. "Flee while you can!" As if Dariak couldn't understand, the man tugged on him once more in demonstration.

With all the terrified screaming, fear soon gripped him. There was mass panic everywhere and the emotions swept him along. It didn't help that he could barely see and had no real idea where he was or why everyone was so scared. He turned and ran with the villagers, surprised to see that the fog stayed with him. As he ran forward, the misty ring remained equidistant from him. He wouldn't be able to see anything unless he was physically close to it, he realized. That meant, of course, that he wouldn't be able to see the oncoming terror until it was completely upon him, and then it would be too late.

To make matters worse, some of the running villagers who were coming toward him fell and were swallowed up by the fog, as if the monster on the other side was reaching out and grabbing them, drawing their careless forms into its maw and devouring them. Dariak screamed and bolted, crashing into a woman and knocking her senseless. He didn't dare help her up, but continued sprinting for his life.

He kept running and, moments later, he saw a young man approach another fallen woman, helping her to her feet, then ushering her onward. Dariak gaped at the young man as he stood there at the edge of the fog and awaited his doom. He looked like he was about to head out into disaster, so Dariak did the only thing he could do. He ran over and grabbed the man's shoulder, spinning him around, and urging him to flee. But the young man wouldn't listen. He stood there resolute, almost bewildered, so Dariak tugged on him again as the cries of terror echoed through the village, then he ran off by himself, unable to help the poor fool.

The mage sprinted onward in a blind panic. Tears streamed from his eyes, clouding his already foggy vision. All he knew was that people were fleeing, but no longer aimlessly. No, now they were running from him. He must have terrified them with his own fear, but he called out to them and told them to calm down and that he meant them no harm. He was just a visitor and he had no idea what was happening.

At the edge of his foggy vision, he saw a girl fall and he wanted to reach out to help her, but another youth stepped in and righted her, sending her on her way. Dariak yearned to approach the boy, the one brave soul among all of them, himself included. He wanted to know why the boy was so strong, so sure of himself. Then a taller man approached the boy and tried unsuccessfully to pull him away. Dariak was grateful, for he wanted to meet the boy and ask him… Ask him what, he didn't know. But as he drew closer, the boy also lost his nerve and ran.

With a roar, Dariak followed, his feet thundering against the ground, his heart racing, and his mind reeling. None of this made any sense. He told himself he should stop, but the panic was too great. He ran onward, reaching out to the villagers for help, but he succeeded only in trampling them, after which they disappeared. He ran and ran, and at last when his lungs gave way, he collapsed in a heap. It took time to catch his breath, as people ran past him, arms flailing, mouths opened wide with their shrill cries.

But he was helpless on the ground now and whatever was chasing them would now be upon him. He tried scrambling to his feet, but his exhausted body would not listen. He turned over and watched a woman fall down not too far from him, and as a young man bent down to help her up, Dariak called out for assistance. The terror was coming and he didn't want to be swallowed in it. But when he thought the young man would hear him, someone else approached the savior and yanked him away, or tried to at least. Then moments later, the young man saw his doom and bolted off, leaving Dariak yards away in a heap on the ground. He turned over, unable to rise, and knew that soon he would die.

The foggy edge of his vision wavered as a giant stumbled carelessly in, stomping about aimlessly. Dariak looked up and realized that it was some sort of overgrown ogre from the south. Ogres were vicious fighters and purely heartless, when it came down it. They were known for eating their prey alive, delighting in the horrific screams. Well, Dariak conceded, there were certainly enough cries here to sate the beast. Its massive feet pounded into the ground, and the vibrations made some of the fleeing villagers tumble to the dirt. Huge hands lurched around, trying to catch the fallen victims, Dariak included.

Though he was essentially mindless with panic, Dariak did note that the ogre seemed to be completely blind. It kept reaching up and wiping its eyes, then leaping out toward the loudest villagers. It made Dariak want to curl into a ball and stop shrieking, but he was too scared to not cry out loud. He forced his eyes open as he drew in another breath and he saw, to his dismay, a massive foot plummeting down on his face and snuffing him out.

But the weight of the foot did not kill him. Instead, it pushed him through the ground where he popped into another setting altogether. No longer was the ramshackle town surrounding him. No longer did the cries of fear pierce the air. Instead, he was curled on the ground in a forest clearing, with a tall ring of trees blotting out the surroundings, rather than the obscuring fog.

In the center of the ring, he could see a blazing campfire, sparkling myriad colors and casting strange shadows on the ground and surrounding trees. A few people were also there with him.

Dariak pushed himself upright and surveyed the solemn group. His eyes were immediately drawn to the oversized ogre sitting hunched over in front of the flames. Its eyes were milky white with giant tears streaming forth and rolling down its mottled chin. Dariak filled with such remorse at the beast's pain that he immediately walked over to console the poor thing.

But as Dariak approached, the sounds of conversation came into being. Or perhaps he was now close enough to hear them; he wasn't sure. Everyone was talking at once to the ogre; it was an unintelligible cacophony. The ogre rocked back and forth, clutching itself into a tighter ball on the ground, as if the motion would protect it from the onslaught.

Stepping closer to the beast, Dariak noticed a shift in the conversation. Some of the people were yelling, others were consoling, and others still were seeking help. As the moments passed, though, their mouths released more than words. Light and mist flowed from within, showering the forest area with an ominously dense feeling with shifting light that was more impressive than that given off by the firelight.

The ogre growled low, trying to decipher it all, but Dariak could see it was terribly weakened. There were no obvious wounds, but by the way it rocked itself on the ground, Dariak assumed that the pain was internal, and most likely mental.

There weren't any magical spells that worked on the minds of sentient beings, because the mind itself would deny the effects. It was a primary reason that Kitalla's dance skill was so interesting. Dariak frowned as memories of his own started coming back to him and he remembered that not only had he stopped trying to understand Kitalla's dance skill, but she had left the group entirely and he would no longer be able to learn from her.

With a forceful shrug, Dariak wrenched his thoughts back to the ogre. He wasn't here to dwell on Kitalla, but the oddness of her skill lured him to consider it further. He wondered when it had first developed within her and when she had truly come to master its effects. He remembered the spell he had conjured in Warringer during her exhibition so that he could trace the way she drew in the energies. Perhaps if he tried replicating the process—

Dariak stopped himself again and focused his thoughts on the whimpering ogre and the growing noise of the other campers. Still, though, Kitalla's face wafted into view unbidden, tinged with a faint crimson glow, and then it was that Dariak understood. Kerrish, empowering the spell now, had overheard the shadow of Dariak's thoughts and was trying to learn about the dance skill for his own purposes.

With a nod to himself, Dariak sent a thought back to his body, where he reached into a pocket and withdrew a small twig. He snapped it between his fingers, and released an odd fragrance in the diamond room. Briefly intoning an incantation, he cast the scent toward Kerrish's body to confuse him. Not expecting it, the elder mage was indeed distracted and Dariak was able to continue his search.

The interruption was a beneficial one, though, for he had forgotten his purpose for being there, and the reminder that this was not his own Trial helped him refocus himself properly on the surroundings.

His eyes went back to the sad ogre, who sat there under the barrage of words that visibly floated through the air toward it. Because the giant was the focus of the attacks, Dariak realized that the ogre was an inner manifestation of Gabrion himself. But why had his inner psyche turned him into a misshapen, ugly beast?

The mage joined the ogre, encircling the creature's shoulder with his arm, or as much as he was able to reach, at any rate. At once, the contact brought them together in a strange way and Dariak was drawn into the ogre's experience directly.

Sitting there in a huddled heap, the ogre's misty eyes wavered as it looked toward the firelight. It could hear distinct voices calling to it from across the way, each one a memory or a construct that may not have specifically happened, but the same essence was there.

On the left was Mira. Dariak could only see a mental image of the woman, as the ogre's eyes could not see and he was linked to the ogre now. Mira laughed and her voice tinkled with delight at jokes and stories she heard from Gabrion's past. Dariak sensed she was pretty with a sweet, gently flowing voice that carried the words softly to the ogre's ears.

"Oh, Gabe, you're such a riot sometimes. I don't know what I'll do without you." She laughed.

"You'll never need to know," the ogre replied. "I'll always be with you, Mira."

"Always so sweet, ever the gentleman. But, Gabe, you never know where life will take us. If the Hathrens come—"

"Mira, that's why I joined up. It's why I'm training to fight. I'll protect you. I'll protect the village. The Hathrens won't lay a finger on you. Don't you ever worry."

She giggled. "You always sound so noble when you talk like that. But the... dreams, Gabe. They warn me—"

"They're only dreams, Mira," the ogre comforted. "Everything will be fine."

"Maybe you're right," she said, but to Dariak, she didn't sound very convincing. He wondered about the comment of her dreams. Perhaps she knew more than she had let on, or perhaps Gabrion had simply refused to listen. He also wondered if Mira had had any such dreams at all, or if Gabrion had constructed the idea of dreams to give credence to something he didn't understand.

The conversation changed to menial aspects of the day and the ogre stopped focusing in on it altogether, shifting over and participating in another chat. Dariak noticed that once the focus was off Mira, he could no longer picture her through the ogre's inner eye. And also, he heard Mira's voice echoing softly in the background, starting that fragment of conversation all over again, endlessly repeating itself.

"Yes, your majesty," rumbled the ogre. Dariak brought his focus back to the beast and listened intently, sensing an odd familiarity. The ogre viewed itself as in a pose of fealty, on bended knee, offering up its service and life to the defense of the kingdom, but the king himself was doubtful of the ogre's intent.

"Ogres do not protect this land," scowled the king. "How can I possibly trust what you say?" The domineering king leered over the ogre, and then his face lit up. "Ah! A test!" One regal hand gestured to a slave that had been brought in with the ogre. "Use your might to squash the life from this insignificant insect and show me that you will obey my every command!"

The ogre turned its milky gaze and sensed the scrawny form held out for it to kill. Dariak couldn't see the slave clearly and didn't know if it was a man or a woman, adult or child. It was gaunt and wrapped in a thick cloth that offered it no real protection from harm. Something about the slave irked Dariak as he witnessed the muddled event in the ogre's mind. Something about it was entirely too familiar.

The ogre flexed its massive hands and then turned to face the slave, but the creature stood stoically, ready for its execution. It wasn't defeat as much as a challenge of its own. The slave knew the ogre would have to obey or face dire consequences. But all the ogre sensed was a pathetic, harmless creature, standing there, ready to be killed by the will of a tyrant.

Dariak could feel some of the emotions wafting through the ogre at that moment. The king was the upholder of peace in their land. He saw to the safety of the villages and towns. He sent soldiers to ward off Hathren attacks. But this was complete injustice. Killing an innocent person just for the ogre to prove its loyalty? No, the ogre couldn't do it.

The giant lowered its hands. "Ask anything else, but not a mindless murder."

With rage, the king shrieked, "Traitor! Guards! Kill him now!"

A strong, searing pain pierced Dariak's neck and chest, but when he looked down, there were no actual wounds. They were snapped back to the campfire and the cacophonous voices around them.

The change was so quick and sudden, the mage was disoriented for a time, but the ogre had been enduring this nightmare for long enough, and it just turned its attention to another voice calling out to it. Dariak tried to breathe and process the events he was witnessing, but the next moment dragged him speedily away.

In it, the voices were unfamiliar. They were all terrible cries of death and despair. Dariak still could not see clearly through the ogre's eyes, but he had the sense of running, weapons in hand, his arms swinging wildly and killing everything in his path. It was different than the first vision of being in Savvron. This was a more advanced town with cobblestone streets and well-trained fighters coming to the town's defense against the terrible ogre that was rampaging through.

The recesses of the ogre's mind echoed the words, "Ask anything else, but not a mindless murder." It was followed with a scream that was cut short as the ogre's mace crushed the fighter. The words echoed again, and slowly the tone shifted to that of the king's, and rather than a plea, it was loaded with mockery. "Mindless murder. Mindless murder." Each swing of the ogre's weapon; each life erased from the world. "Mindless murder." The king's voice raised in pitch and it echoed horribly like a shrieking eaglon. Dariak cringed under the sound and willed the ogre to focus on something else.

The killing continued unabated for some time before the ogre pulled itself back to the campfire and turned its focus elsewhere. Dariak recognized Kitalla right away but he struggled to place when the memory occurred. They were talking, in a forest, not unlike where the ogre was currently seated. Randler's name was whispered, so Dariak determined that it was some time after the fall of the Prisoner's Tower, for that was when the bard had joined their party.

As Dariak listened, he found that the words themselves were unintelligible. He wondered if they were speaking a different language for some reason or if the ogre's hearing was now malfunctioning. Yet the tone of the words came through, and he sensed a stern tenderness in them. They were consoling each other somehow, but without being too emotional. Each was being strong for the other and a strange sense of warmth came from the exchange.

Then Dariak realized why he couldn't understand the words; they were irrelevant. It was the way in which they spoke to each other that mattered. He then remembered when the group had reached Randler's hideout and Kitalla opted to venture off on her own to find Heria and the shard she had stolen, but Gabrion had erupted with an angry passion, demanding that Kitalla was part of their group. Now it struck Dariak differently. As he thought about it, the scene replayed itself in the ogre's mind, and though the words alone were mumbled gibberish, Dariak could feel a strange heat burning through his veins.

He felt the ogre moan and bury the imagery, summoning Mira back to the fore-front. "Oh, Gabe, you're such a riot sometimes…" she repeated, and Dariak tuned her out, focusing instead on the ogre.

As the memory replayed itself, Dariak could feel an intensity in the ogre's reactions to Mira, but it was an altogether different kind than the one that emerged with

Kitalla. They were both passionate in their own right, but the essence within them was different. Mira flowed with loving energy of the world and people around her, and the ogre basked in its desire to be included in that. Yet it also cherished the seriousness that was Kitalla, whose focus was always in the moment, sharp and ready. Where Mira could be swept away by the sheer beauty of a rainbow, Kitalla was an arrow, ever on target.

The scene switched again, and Dariak went along for the ride, curious what would be next. It was Kitalla's turn, and apparently she and Gabrion had spoken during their quest for Heria. Then Mira surfaced again, a semblance of her beauty washing over Dariak and making him smile for the sheer grace of it. They were having a picnic, he surmised, and the ogre was calm and happy.

Dariak expected Kitalla to be the next focus, but she wasn't. Instead, it was a black-haired man with vibrantly beautiful blue eyes. Dariak could sense a strange annoyance from the ogre, but the mage was delighted in the visage that was conjured up before them, and then he laughed once he realized that it was himself.

The ogre seemed affronted at this intrusion, as the memory of Dariak ogled him from across the room. "Stop watching me," the ogre groaned.

"But you're fun to watch. I can't help myself. It's like putting gold in front of a thief and asking him not to take it." His grin widened. "Keep going, just a few more layers."

Listening, Dariak chuckled. Their conversation hadn't quite played out that way back in Warringer, but Gabrion's skewed recollection wasn't far from the mark. Yet at the same time, he wondered why it was surfacing now during the duel between Mira and Kitalla. He didn't need to wait long to learn why.

"Is that the only reason you let me travel with you, mage? Because you like the way I look and move? It's disgusting."

Both Dariaks frowned at the remark. "Not at all, you idiot," said the memory, hurt and sad. That Dariak turned away, burying his head and sulking. The real Dariak, however, sensed that the scene would soon end, as it had in Warringer. And though it would be a calm ending with a resolution to the dilemma, Dariak decided that something was here that needed to be addressed.

He wasn't entirely sure how he did it, but he focused his thoughts on his blurred image within the ogre's mind and he strained to become that memory. An odd icy coldness shook him, but he took that as success. Before the moment passed, he spoke to the ogre sitting on the tavern bed. "I travel with you for a great many reasons, Gabrion."

"Gabrion?" the ogre wondered.

Dariak ignored it. "You're a strong and powerful fighter, and you've saved my life many times." As he said it, he remembered the recent recollection of the ogre and the slave and he realized that Gabrion had been reliving their audience with the King of Kallisor. "You saved my life at the very beginning, before we really knew each other."

"So if I stop saving your life, you'll stop staring at me?"

"I'd be dead, so I suppose I would," he retorted. "But that's beside the point. You're extremely gifted and you grow with such astounding skill, I'd wager you will become the greatest warrior in the land, second to none."

The ogre grunted and pounded its fists. "Now you're making fun of me."

"You know me well enough at this point. You know if I'm poking fun or if I'm serious."

The ogre considered for a moment and realized the truth of it. Rather than feeling bolstered by the compliment, the ogre's back hunched over further. "So I'm a great killing machine. Wonderful."

Dariak mentally slapped his forehead. This was harder than he thought it would be. He wasn't speaking directly to Gabrion but to this manifestation of the warrior that wanted to hold a grudge and to be miserable. He needed somehow to reflect back Gabrion's true self and dispel this hideous mask the warrior was wearing.

"You've killed," Dariak admitted. "Not always by your choice. You were never one to just walk into a place and start hacking off heads. No, always it was in defense of others, including us, your friends."

The ogre shouted in response, "That gives me no more right to slaying another man than if I was in a blind rampage!"

"I don't agree. You are fighting to protect the things that matter to you, and that does make them important. We all try to protect what matters, but sometimes that means we have to fight for it. And when others don't see to reason, it might mean our weapons come to hand and they are defeated."

The ogre's back hunched lower still. "Who am I to judge what's right?"

"You aren't," Dariak decided, remembering something Gabrion had said to him after the struggle against Sharice. "That's why I'm here. That's why you aren't alone. We all agree in what we believe in and we agree that you are right in your actions."

A fleeting image of Mira flashed, followed by one of Kitalla. The ogre shook its head and grumbled low. "We're no different than the people who set our countries at war."

"We *are* different. We seek to unify the land by showing the people how we can all come together in harmony. Our respective kings hoard their lands and refuse to open their doors. We seek a wider, more peaceful world."

"Peaceful," the ogre scoffed. "But all this killing." In the background an echoing chant of "mindless murder!" started up.

Dariak struggled to remain within his ghost and he knew this conversation wasn't going where he had intended it to go, but either way, time was running out. "Gabrion, listen. You are a kind and noble man. Yes, you have killed, but that's the world in which we live and there is no escaping it. No, listen!" he interrupted as the ogre opened its mouth. "At every turn in our journey, you have shown your true character at all the right times. Think of that battle against the lupinoes after Warringer, when you spared Hernior's life. Think of all the work you did restoring the healer's abode in Gerrish. What of the people in Pindington? You risked your own freedom and faced the threat of further imprisonment to help bail out the stricken citizens. They were people you didn't even know, but you helped them because they needed helping. You're a strong and noble man, Gabrion. It's those parts of you that I've come to love." He blurted out the words, not expecting to say them, but as he did, he understood why this memory had appeared when it did.

The ogre did not take kindly to the declaration. It stood up high and pounded the walls, screaming in rage. "Love? You disgusting filth! Men were not designed to love other men. They were not created to ogle the bodies of other men. Your wandering eyes should be removed at once!" The ogre snarled and stepped toward Dariak.

The mage had no idea what to do. He couldn't abandon his ghostly self and leave it to the ogre's rage. Even if it was only a memory, he worried that if the ogre damaged it, it might fray his friendship with the warrior. The young man's history might be rewritten in this mystical prison. He didn't know the scope of the Trial's influence but he was wise enough to be cautious. He cast his thoughts about, but he couldn't move.

The ogre stamped closer and Dariak only had words at his disposal. "You claim that a man loving another man is disgusting, but you're wrong. Think of brothers. Of fathers and sons. Think of your love for your liege—before you met him, at any rate. You had a blind devotion to the king, but he ignored that and he broke you. He shattered your image of him and he left you wounded."

The ogre hesitated and looked as if it was about to submit to the logic. But a strange reddish glow swirled in its eyes and the fire burned anew. "The love between brothers is not the love you feel for me, you letch. Don't mince the truth to suit your purposes. Your interest is foul and unnatural."

"Foul and unnatural?" Dariak yelled back. "To care for you because you have integrity and a passionate heart? I don't see your logic, ogre. There is nothing wrong with my feelings, toward you or any other."

The crimson light in the ogre's eyes intensified and it looked as if the creature was about to enter a berserker rage. Dariak tensed unsuccessfully, then grasped for more words, but it was the ogre who spoke next. "You cage your lust in a claim of cherishing a noble spirit, but your lust is a travesty of the land. If men were intended to love other men as you do, your bodies would be able to grow children and keep the population moving forward. No, nature is against you. And you will be ended."

In all of his years of hearing angry taunts against his orientation, this one argument had crossed his ears only once before. He was a young teenager and already knew that his romantic interests were different than those of other mages. He had become close with one boy in particular. They had experimented in some forms of cuddling and were discovered by an irate mage who happened upon them. The fury with which the man berated them sent Dariak's friend from his life forever; he never knew what became of him. But Dariak was the son of Delminor, who had perished protecting their land, who had given so much of his knowledge freely to the mages; because of his strong history, Dariak did not cower under the man's tirade.

As he recalled this, the scene within the ogre's mind was temporarily suspended. He didn't know how, but it didn't matter. He had always thought Gabrion had come to terms with Dariak's interest in men, and the ogre's insistent denials seemed out of place. The reddish eyes and Dariak's own memory connected the two.

"Kerrish, that's enough!" Dariak shouted out. "You may be empowering this process but it does not give you the right to intervene like this. Keep your personal opinions to yourself."

The ogre's voice changed momentarily as Kerrish asserted himself more directly. "Your foul antics of ages past cause conflict even now. You've confused this poor farm boy with your affection. You sense it, don't you? It's one of the main issues keeping him here trapped in the Trial. If it weren't for you, Dariak, your friend would have been fine long ago."

He wondered, but not for long. "Gabrion does have qualities I admire and would cherish in a beloved. But his heart is elsewhere and it's there he is conflicted. Leave us to this and you will see."

Kerrish chuckled through the ogre's oversized lips. "You don't hear him like I can right now."

"Then release him and let him speak."

But the older mage seemed bent on ruining this moment. He continued to probe the ogre's mind and lash out at Dariak with choice thoughts that stung the mage. Yet Dariak knew the true source and he knew he needed to act. He kept one mental hand grasped firmly within his ghostly self and then he reached his other hand back toward his body. It was like trying to watch a completely different scene with each eye and making sense of both. Into his pocket he reached, where he withdrew a vial of spiders' eggs. At least, that's what he thought he was grabbing. Uttering the activation words, he urged his body to lob the vial across toward Kerrish's body, hoping to bind the man tightly and force his thoughts back to the real world.

The spiders' eggs, however, were in a different pocket and Dariak in fact withdrew a container of dead firegnats. The activation spell that was meant to break the spiders' eggs and release a thick web-like goo instead inverted the firegnats and released their inner venom sacs, which erupted into a blazing inferno, aimed toward Kerrish's prone body.

Dariak couldn't receive any actual information from his senses, for the ogre lunged forward angrily after Dariak's last response. His ghostly self was wrangling with the beast, trying to keep the flailing arms away, but of course the mage's physique was no match for the power of the giant. The hits rained down and though he was within a shadow of the ogre's memory, the pain seemed very real, though not long lasting. A sliver of thought attributed that aspect to the healing energies supporting this Trial, though they were unable to prevent the pain outright.

Then, all at once, the pummeling stopped and the crimson light faded out of the ogre's eyes. It pulled back, then touched its hands one after the other, wondering what it had done. Anguish erupted on the creature's misshapen face, for once again it had succumbed to the senseless beating of another man.

Dariak saw the despair building and so he called out, "Gabrion, I'm fine, really. You didn't do me any harm. I'm fine."

The ogre looked toward the voice, its eyes again a pale milky white. "I never did understand your proclivities and part of me was uncomfortable with the way you would devour me with your eyes. But I never meant to hurt you."

"I know, Gabrion. You're much more a protector than anything else."

The description summoned a vibrant image of Kitalla, which the ogre brushed away. "No, I'm not done with you yet. Tell me, Dariak. What is your will with me? I need to know."

"I—" He hadn't really considered having to define it before. "I would be honored to be your friend, now and forevermore."

The ogre needed more. "Just friend? What of your other desires? Wouldn't you be interested in pursuing those with me?"

Dariak blushed. "Delighted," he drawled humorously, but then he pulled himself together. "Listen, Gabrion, it's true that I've come to love you, I won't deny that. And I'll admit that I find you attractive, too, and not just physically. But you're not interested in me in that way and so I would never pursue you in that regard." He thought also of his love for Randler, of how he wouldn't want to hurt the bard, but he didn't think the ogre could understand that at the moment.

The ogre stared down at him and though Dariak knew the beast couldn't actually see him, he kept himself resolute and firm anyway. "Then what if I was curious about your way of things? What if I wanted you to teach me?"

It was a question Dariak never could have expected. "I— I—" he stammered. He knew the correct answer to say, but he also knew the answer that was in his heart. He found he couldn't hide the truth, though he struggled to do so for fear of the ogre's reaction and of hurting Randler. It seemed the healing energies insisted he speak honestly here. "Well, I would want to show you. But really, Gabrion, if it came down to it, your friendship means so much more to me than one dalliance with you." He shook his head. "No, I wouldn't risk our friendship over such a thing." He paused and then added, "But I know you, Gabrion. There isn't a single part of you that would seek such knowledge anyway."

The ogre actually smirked. "I know. I just wanted to know how you would react."

It was the first thing the ogre had said that sounded at all like Gabrion himself. Dariak smiled and found that he was ejected from his ghostly host. The scene dissolved and Dariak saw that they were back at the camp. The ogre was still seated by the fire, staring blankly toward the flames. Its head turned from left to right as it debated the series of conversations that were happening all around it.

Dariak stepped forward and sat beside the ogre. He felt like he had repaired a rift in his friendship with Gabrion that he hadn't known existed. He felt lighter, having confessed himself, and then he chuckled to himself for all the times Gabrion had done the same thing during their travels. He turned toward the large ogre and shook his head, wondering how such an innocent thing could be so mired in self-doubt.

"Gabrion?"

The ogre ignored him.

"Gabrion?" he said louder, and the ogre pulled its attention away from its distractions. "Gabrion, listen. You still need some help in there. I can help you if you will let me." The beast grunted in response and Dariak realized that since he was no longer within its thoughts, it was treating him like a stranger again. "You have things to deal with and I may be able to help if you let me." The ogre didn't seem to respond, so Dariak pressed further. "You need to come to terms with the fighting. And you need to resolve your feelings for Mira and Kitalla."

At this the ogre screamed and scuttled away from Dariak as if he was afire. But the mage followed calmly, repeating his offer for help every step of the way. Several minutes later, the ogre crashed into one of the trees that locked them into this area and it cowered there as the mage stepped closer.

"Take my hand and we will do this together." Dariak reached out, knowing he could not force his help upon the lost soul. Doing so might free Gabrion of his current Trial, but it wouldn't fix the underlying issues that were at odds with each other. They had come to some kind of understanding and Dariak was banking on that. The ogre would recognize him and would accept the help, even from a deviant such as himself. He didn't know how he would be able to repair the warrior's pain, but he knew that if he kept trying then something was bound to work. Besides, in some way, it felt good that he was actively reaching out to try to save Gabrion's life.

But the ogre was blind and he could not see Dariak's offered hand. The massive body sat for a long time, unmoving. Dariak remained there, waiting.

* * *

"Come, young bard, you need a rest."

Randler's fingers were numb from strumming the lute for so many hours. He had emptied his jug of water but he kept playing the lute, knowing that Dariak needed his support as he tried to free Gabrion from his Trial. Frast's intrusion snapped the bard awake from a mild trance, but he shook his head in denial.

"They need me."

Frast approached the bard and rested warm hands on his shoulders. "You're extremely tense, exhausted, and you need food. You're no good to them in this condition. Come away now and rest, then you can return."

Randler looked up, confused. "You make it sound like they aren't coming out any time soon."

Frast only shrugged. "We have a meal ready for you, Randler. Come on, now."

"A moment," he agreed. Frast walked away as the bard stood up and stretched, then walked toward the sealed doorway into Gabrion's chamber. He felt a heavy sorrow within himself as he looked upon the warrior's writhing body.

"So you've claimed Dariak's love, have you?" He swallowed hard, frowning. "And nary a thought of me." The resonance of his music with Dariak's energy, amplified perhaps by their respective jades, had allowed him glimpses into what the mage was seeing and hearing. He had heard the passion with which Dariak declared himself to Gabrion, and he knew enough about the Trial that it was based all in truth. Lies would not have held together.

He didn't know what to make of it or if Dariak's claim that a fraternal love was all it was. Still, he found it unsettling. He wanted to pull Dariak from the Trial so he could ask about it. He didn't want this feeling to linger on even a moment more.

But Frast was right; he was too tired to help right now or to make any sense of his own thoughts and feelings. He considered Dariak's words one last time before turning away.

With a deep, pain-ridden sigh, he walked away, "Well… I suppose it would make a fine, heart-wrenching ballad, in the end."

CHAPTER 21

After the Trial

DARIAK KNEW HE had been working for far too long. He was exhausted and for some reason felt utterly alone. Yet there he was with the ogre at the camp with the visions of others by the bonfire. The ogre had changed greatly, though, and it mostly resembled Gabrion's true self now, save for a few misshapen oddities. There were still some hurts that needed mending, but he felt that the warrior would be able to tend to them on his own now.

He approached the man and placed his hand on a shoulder. "Gabrion, it's time for me to go. The rest is up to you."

The young man nodded and looked up into Dariak's concerned eyes. "You've done much for me, Dariak. I thank you. Until we meet again on the other side."

"Until then." Dariak smiled. He closed his eyes and allowed his thoughts to drift apart. Swiftly, the tendrils of his mind floated back to his body, where they yearned to rejoin. It felt like usual, as if he had jumped off a cliff and was about to crash far below. His mind raced rapidly back to his body, increasing in speed until that moment of impact where his body jolted in anticipation, though not actual pain.

He was terribly stiff and his eyes wouldn't immediately open, though he saw a dim reddish glow that told him he had worked through the night and it was dawn. The acrid scent in the air, however, was unexpected. Rubbing his eyes, Dariak breathed deeply and gagged. He looked around and was horrified by what he saw.

The benches, beds, and chairs that usually encircled the diamond all lay in dusty piles, including the one upon which he sat, which left him awkwardly dropped on the floor. Dariak rose up cautiously, his legs shaky, and he looked over toward Kerrish, but he wasn't prepared for what he saw.

The mage's body was curled on the ground in a charred heap. The skin was blackened and the robes were all but burned away. He checked himself but he was untouched by whatever fire had erupted in the room. He knew it was pointless before walking over, but he checked anyway for signs of life from the older mage. Stepping around the chamber, all the wood in the room was burned or badly scorched and much of it had been devoured by fire. The diamond itself was unharmed and so was he, which puzzled him more. He frowned as he realized he had dropped the carved lute Randler had given him. It was burned badly and barely recognizable.

He walked over to the stairs and the open windows but there were no signs of trouble elsewhere. Baffled, he sat down and tried to remember what had taken place. His thoughts had been within Gabrion's Trial, but his body should have also been alert to some of what was going on in the chamber. All he could remember was trying to block Kerrish's intrusions twice.

He reached into his pockets to check the spell components and when he found the spiders' eggs, a chill raced down his spine. Searching, he noted that the firegnats were gone and then he knew what had happened, or at least in part. Erupting the firegnats would not have created such a disaster. In the end, he decided that either someone had been present and added to the spell, or Kerrish had pulled himself from the empowerment and tried to counteract the explosion.

As he thought about it, he decided it was Kerrish who had augmented the spell. Firegnat venom needed to be quelled and drained of its power, not snuffed out like a regular blaze. Containment allowed the venom to concentrate itself before erupting outward again.

It also made sense, then, that he was unscathed but Kerrish had succumbed. The Trials were powered by the healing jade at present, and because Dariak was connected through the diamond, the jade would have continuously healed him as he burned. Kerrish, on the other hand, had to have disconnected himself, since he had been slain.

He felt little remorse over Kerrish's death and felt calm though some part of him believed he should be distraught. He wasn't sure why he felt so detached from what he was seeing. Yet he couldn't feel sad or angry or anything at all. It was just something that had occurred. He wondered idly if the healing jade was keeping his emotions in check, especially after spending hours trying to do the same for Gabrion. Regardless, though, he soon realized that there was a bigger problem anyway. How would he explain all of this to the Mage Council?

Dariak paced the room briefly but nothing came to him. He had to leave this area and seek a location without the calming influence of the jade. But before he did, he checked to see if the jade was physically here. He didn't expect to find it, yet searching didn't take long anyway. Empty-handed, he headed for the stairs and descended them.

As he left the upper chamber, everything started wafting back into him. He recalled all the angst and torment from within Gabrion's Trial; the intrusions Kerrish had made during his empowerment, trying to learn some of Dariak's secrets; the use of spells to quell Kerrish's intrusion; and taking the wrong ingredient from his pocket and unleashing the accidental fire spell. Remorse swelled over him and he wanted nothing more than to run back up to the diamond chamber and feel the calming effects that were there.

Shaking his head, Dariak pushed himself on. Down the stairs he wound, seeking the new Trial chambers, hoping Gabrion had arisen from his imprisonment at last. He approached the area and was sad to see Randler's empty chair. He had hoped for some support from the bard, but he couldn't blame him for not being there; the process had taken all night, after all.

Gabrion lay in his chamber, breathing slowly and at ease. The crystalline barrier leading to his chamber had fallen and so Dariak was able to walk right in and crouch beside his friend. He took Gabrion's hand and whispered his name to awaken him.

The warrior hadn't spoken aloud in some time so he sputtered at first, but then he looked at the mage and smiled. "Thank you, Dariak."

"We need to find Randler, and we have to be ready for a fight," Dariak warned.

"What happened?"

Dariak briefly explained. "And once the others hear of Kerrish, they will deny me the right to take the jades."

"But it was an accident."

Dariak nodded. "More than that, my father already knew the dangers of firegnat serum and the mages here are trained to deal with it. Kerrish should have known to respond differently. He was a true master in his craft. Unless…" A look of dread appeared on Dariak's face.

"Unless what?" Gabrion asked when the mage fell silent.

"Unless he did it on purpose, in order to prevent me from obtaining the shards. Unless he was seeking to end our journey here and now. I was scheduled to face him in battle after freeing you, but he wouldn't have won. Maybe this was his way of defeating me." As he said the words, they felt true. "That must be the case," he decided. "Gabrion, are you strong enough? Can you stand? This won't be easy."

He did so, responding to the tone in Dariak's voice. "What next, then? We have to alert our friends, don't we?"

"Yes. I must also abscond with the jades that are here. We won't be able to get them any other way."

"Can't you petition with the leaders or something?"

Logically, he knew he should try, but he also knew that with numerous members of the Council already against him, the sudden death of Kerrish would only incite them further. "My father's legacy has lost favor among the mages. I don't know why. I don't have the respect here that I once had. My initial petitions were refused. Conditions will only be worse after this. I—" But he stopped, shaking his head.

Gabrion stared at him for a long moment. "Your goal is to unite the kingdoms, Dariak. Don't you think that warring within your own country and among your own kind is the wrong way to go about this? There has to be another way."

"True," he conceded, falling silent for a time. "Very well, I will seek out Pyron. Go find Randler and alert Quereth and the others that they should prepare for a sudden and immediate departure."

Gabrion's brow came together, noting one particular name missing from the list. "What of Kitalla?"

Dariak reached into a pocket and withdrew the metal jade that Kitalla had obtained back in Grenthar's domain. "She left us, Gabrion. I do not know if it's forever or just for a time, but leaving me with this says much."

The warrior winced. His Trial had made him face his growing feelings for the thief, and though he hadn't yet resolved them against his love for Mira, this loss was a painful blow. "Where did she go?"

Dariak shook his head. "I was on the floor when she stormed out. Her comrades headed toward the castle, so maybe she went to find them. Otherwise, perhaps she ventured back to Marritosh with the army."

Gabrion considered for a moment. "If she needed to get away from us, she wouldn't have gone to the army," he decided.

"Marritosh is a bit closer, so she may have gone if she felt she needed supplies." Dariak frowned, his whole self feeling heavier than usual. "Gabrion, go, alert the others. I must speak with Pyron." He gave some basic directions and then strode off toward the adept's chambers.

Some of the mages were surprised to see Dariak walking about and though they asked him of his success, he ignored them all. Back straight, eyes focused, he strode forth like he was the leader of the Mage Council and their words were intrusions to his business. The others were confused by his haughtiness, but they mostly accepted it, deciding they would hear about it soon enough anyway.

As he went, he debated the wisdom of seeking the mage first. There was no guarantee that Pyron would really listen to his tale or that he would be believed by anyone who mattered. Facing Pyron was risky and it might lose him the opportunity to freely obtain the jade shards that were here.

However, if he sought out and claimed the jades now, he would ruin his reputation with the mages entirely. Kerrish's death would be viewed as intentional if he went off to steal the jades. Neither option suited him, but at least speaking with Pyron offered a chance for success and reconciliation.

Not long later, Dariak knocked on the door to Pyron's chamber. "A moment," grumbled the old man from beyond. Dariak could hear the shuffling of a chair and, moments later, the portal opened.

Pyron stared down at Dariak and raised an eyebrow. "You return, Brother Dariak. I assume this means you were successful? Surely you aren't here already to call for the first of your mage battles?"

"Master Pyron, we must talk."

"Come in then. We were having breakfast, if you'd like some."

Dariak hesitated on the use of the plural. He looked over the old mage's shoulder and he saw several Council members munching away on bread and jam, sipping juice, and telling stories about spells they claimed to have invented. "Master, I would prefer to speak with you alone."

Farrenok was among those assembled, and he saw Dariak trying to cower in the doorway. "What's this, Pyron? Has our little visitor given up trying to rescue his friend?"

Old Lorresh slammed a mug on the table, "Well, mage? What is the outcome, then? And why isn't Kerrish with you?" The wrinkled face scrunched in suspicion.

There was no way to avoid the inevitable without rousing more distrust, and so Dariak explained. "I was able to help my friend, but there were complications."

Utensils and cups scattered to the table. "What happened, Dariak?" Pyron demanded, his voice sated with anger.

He opted for the truth. "While I was working, Kerrish kept insinuating himself into the energies and distracting me from my mission. His goal seemed more to learn what I knew than to help empower the process so that I could save Gabrion."

"Slander!" Farrenok accused.

"It isn't," Dariak insisted. "He kept pushing my thoughts in other directions, which would have been disastrous to all three of us in there."

"So you say!" Lorresh shouted. "No one has attempted such an undertaking before. How were you to know what the danger was?"

"Silence!" Pyron snarled. "Dariak, go on."

"I used a spell to temporarily distract him, which allowed me to continue my work."

"That's impossible!" Shelloni sputtered. She was one of the mages on Dariak's side, but this sounded preposterous to her. "Once your mind is locked with the diamond, you cannot cast spells."

Dariak shrugged. "It was a lot like being in the midst of a battle but thinking about cooking a meal at home. I sent some thoughts back to my body to cast the spell, and it did. Meanwhile, I kept making progress with Gabrion." The explanation was simplistic but clear enough for the time. "Later, though, Kerrish took direct control of my friend and tried beating me within Gabrion's mind. I then sent another spell to—"

"Master Pyron! Master Pyron!" an adept called, running toward the assembly. Usually, the elder would not have tolerated such an intrusion, but the girl's urgency was palpable. "It's terrible! Master Pyron!"

"What is it, Gianne?" he asked in a soothing voice, meant to calm her hysteria.

"The empowerment chamber! It's all ash and cinders! And… and… Master Kerrish. He's a charred hulk. Dead."

The gathered mages shrieked in horror, turning to Dariak, "What did you do?"

Dariak stayed strong and he looked Pyron in the eye as he answered. "I must not have concentrated well enough when I tried to stop Kerrish's second intrusion, but I pulled firegnat serum out instead of the spiders' eggs I was seeking."

"You killed Kerrish? With a fire storm?" Farrenok asked. He didn't let Dariak answer before shouting out, "Murderer!" The other mages erupted into babbling.

"It was an accident," Dariak insisted. "He must have used the wrong counterspell against it—"

But it was no use. The other mages were in an uproar, and those who had sided with him stared in horror at this realization. Farrenok and Lorresh wasted no time spinning the tale to make the act seem intentional; that Dariak wanted to slay Kerrish when he was defenseless.

"It's one less foe he would face now that he succeeded with the Trial," Lorresh raged.

"Leave it to the wanderer to kill a man while he is entranced!" called another.

"Any number of you could have been there to support and protect him, but you were all cowards," Dariak retorted.

"He—he threatened my life if I offered to help with the empowerment," one mage invented, pointing at Dariak.

"Me too!" someone seconded.

"He would have killed all of us if we had been there!"

"Yes, he wanted us there! Easy kills!"

"Poor Kerrish!"

Pyron was unable to restore order with words alone. He summoned the energies and dropped a veil of silence over the gathering, which outraged them more. His arms swung wildly and he fused their feet to the floor to keep them from storming him or Dariak. "Silence and be still," he commanded. He turned to Dariak. "This is a serious crime against us, Dariak."

"It was not my fault, entirely," the mage defended. "All mages here know the signs of a firegnat spell, thanks to *my father*," he added for spite. "Kerrish augmented the spell on purpose."

The accusation angered even Pyron and it pushed him over the edge. "How dare you, Dariak! I tutored you as a fledging mage and have championed you since your arrival, but I will not tolerate such a claim. May your poor mother never learn of this, for her sake." He refused to listen to any of Dariak's words, deciding that the young mage was twisting the truth now. He drew his silencing spell over Dariak before he could have a chance to deflect it or defend himself further. "You will pay for your crime, mage. You will answer for the murder of Council member Kerrish."

Dariak had known his confession would not be received well, but if he could have spoken to Pyron alone, he might have been able to explain properly. Words would have sufficed. He hadn't set up any protections against spells, partly because he was exhausted, but also because Pyron would have at least listened before bringing the situation to the Council. Now, with the eager eyes of nine other mages, Pyron could not just hear the tale. The master mage whipped his arms around, pulling spell components from his pockets with such dexterity, only a practiced mage would have noticed. And with a jolt, Dariak collapsed, his body enwrapped in thick, magic-resistant chains.

"Your friends will share your fate, Dariak," Pyron declared, "for it seems now that your intent was all along to infiltrate this place, to insinuate your crew among us, and to eliminate your former adversaries among the Council. From striking out against Master Farrenok at the Council meeting to this heinous murder of Master Kerrish, your actions have shown you to be a rogue among mages. Your comrade could not survive his healing Trial without your assistance, and even the lowest of thieves have come through them in the past. It shows us the caliber of your character more than you know."

Farrenok snarled, speaking up now that Pyron had removed the silence shroud from them. "To the border guardians, I say."

"No," Lorresh argued. "Quite the opposite! Do not let him feel magic's warmth any longer. Seal his powers."

Shelloni had tears in her eyes, but her jaw was firm. "I once admired you and your father, Dariak. But these atrocities must be repaid." She turned to the others. "You cannot seal his powers, for we have seen others break through the seal, and this one is wise and resilient enough to find a way. No, I say he should feel the bite of a sword through his heart."

The other mages called out other tortures and torments to use against this traitor. Pyron let them carry on, eying Dariak as he lay on the ground, but unable to read the man's eyes. At last, the elder had heard enough. "The final punishment will be decided in Council. Dariak will be an example to other mages not to reach above their stations and not to seek retaliation within our ranks. The rights and privileges afforded to Delminor's kin will be hereby revoked." The others agreed. "Gianne," he said next, "send word. Capture and bind his companions. All of them. Then alert the king for a guard escort."

"It will be done," she said, bowing her head and running off.

On the ground, Dariak lay in a tightly bound heap, tears streaming from his eyes.

CHAPTER 22

Within Magehaven

GABRION LEFT DARIAK to go find Randler. Luckily, the mage had given clear directions, and it wasn't long before he located the bard's room. Knocking on the door, Gabrion walked in, a little surprised to see that Randler wasn't alone. Frast was there too and they were talking over the remains of a pastry they had shared.

"Gabrion!" the bard exclaimed. "Then Dariak was successful!"

"Yes, but there's trouble." He explained the situation briefly, immediately dampening the relief in the room. "There isn't much time, from what Dariak said. We have to hurry."

Frast stood up abruptly. "I'll alert the mages. You two should go support Dariak. It sounds like he'll need it."

"He was adamant that everyone is ready to leave right away," Gabrion said, shaking Frast's hand in gratitude. "Be safe."

"You too," the mage said, running off.

Randler was already on his feet, rummaging through the room and gathering his things. "There shouldn't be anything for you to get together, Gabrion. I believe all of your belongings are still with you?"

The warrior checked his equipment, noting a strange tone in the bard's voice. "Yes, I have everything."

"Good. That will save time." He wrapped his lute in a velvet cloth before storing it in its case.

"Need any help?"

"No, you've done enough," Randler said. Then he shook his head before Gabrion could respond. "Sorry, I need a little time to sort this out. My thoughts, that is. But that will have to wait."

"I don't follow."

The bard stood up and shrugged. "Let's say that I heard some of what Dariak said to you in your Trial and I didn't care to hear it, or what it meant."

Gabrion's brows furrowed for a moment, then he understood. "Randler, it's—"

"No, Gabrion," Randler cut across. "Not now. And it's Dariak I need to speak to about it, in any event." He hefted his pack onto his back and stepped forward. "For now, let's go to his aid."

There wasn't time to argue. With a stern nod, Gabrion turned and followed Randler as he hurried across the room and out the door. They didn't go very far before a strange occurrence stopped them.

"Randler! You're glowing."

The bard turned and gasped. "You are too." They looked at each other and their skin had faded to a greenish hue that started to shimmer. "It's showing through our clothing too," he noted with a frown. "This can't be good."

As they looked around, Quereth ran up to them, his skin also bearing a verdant glow. "Good, you're still here. Frast is alerting the others, but we don't have a moment to lose."

"What is this?" Gabrion asked, lifting his hand.

"Some kind of light marker they're using to identify those who don't belong here. I don't know how, but they have managed to illuminate the life force within us." Quereth stepped forward and adopted his most ominous presence. "This means we will not be able to hide here. They will know exactly where we are and they will find us."

"It doesn't matter," Gabrion dismissed. "Dariak needs us and we're going to get him."

Footsteps echoed not far away and three acolytes sprinted into the room. "There they are!" Arcane words sputtered from their mouths and a variety of spells flew across the floor toward them. Gabrion sidestepped a web-like projectile and Randler dropped to the floor to avoid a thick black ooze, but neither was ready for the spark ball that exploded over their heads and rained down on them. The glittering sparks bit and stung violently and made it hard for them to get their bearings. Quereth, on the other hand, had protections in place and he was already casting various counterspells.

After setting spell shields for Gabrion and Randler, the older mage focused his attention on the acolytes. They shouted their spells to add power to them, which signaled to Quereth that they weren't particularly experienced, which was helpful. He pulled a parchment-wrapped package from his pocket and hastily opened it as he sputtered the words, *Fethrinus incarsatier magilliar ruptus.* With that, he threw one of the dried frog tongues from the pack and as it drifted through the air, it expanded and erupted into a veritable swarm of flies. The acolytes had never seen the spell before and they were immediately distracted and unable to retaliate.

Quereth turned to his companions. "I know your intentions are to save Dariak, but there is nothing you can do for him now." He interrupted Gabrion as he tried to object. "This tower is filled with hundreds of mages who have practiced magic for years and are much more experienced than this lot. I cannot fight them all myself, and without powers, you two will soon perish."

"We can't abandon Dariak," Randler said.

"You won't be able to hide with this magical green light," Quereth said, fumbling in his pocket for more spell components. The acolytes were succumbing to the swarm, but he knew they were just as likely to break free of it.

"My jade," Randler said, pulling the shadow jade from his pouch and calling for its darkening strength. He set a thick globe around himself so he could be completely obscured from view. "There."

"No good," Gabrion groaned. "That green light is dimmer but still shining through. I can still see you." He waited as Quereth sent another spell toward the acolytes, then asked. "What do we do?"

"Do as Dariak bid," Quereth hissed. "Flee. It is our only hope for survival."

One of the acolytes escaped the swarm and ran forward, arms pinwheeling as he launched a series of fire darts. Unlike Dariak's usual fire dart spell, these were loaded with small cutting knives. Gabrion ran forward, determined to end the mage's charge, but though he managed to avoid the brunt of the spell, a number of the blades still cut him. Moments later, he was disoriented, too. Apparently, the blades were also poisoned.

Randler sent an arrow back in response and would have killed the acolyte if he didn't have a protective shield around himself. His comrades freed themselves from the swarm and as a team they bore down on the intruders. Quereth coated the floor with grease, which made the unsuspecting acolytes slide in a tangled heap. Randler grabbed a torch from the wall and threw it toward the grease pile once Gabrion was away.

The acolytes screamed in pain and the others turned to flee. The mages weren't badly hurt, just stunned. Their protection spells were strong indeed, and one of them was already upright and countering the flames with a water spell that quenched the heat.

Quereth grunted angrily and tossed another frog tongue into the fray, but this time he laced it with a bit of acid so that when the swarm hit, their bites would be stronger. He grabbed Randler and Gabrion and pulled on them to run. "These are only acolytes! What chance is there against others? We do not have a choice. We must go!"

"But Dariak," Gabrion complained.

Quereth's thick voice was panicked. "I know your strength and your bravery, Gabrion, but I am telling you that we are not capable of surviving this place. If you think the energy unleashed in the Prisoner's Tower was great, then you have no idea what these mages will be capable of. Let us flee, lest we die."

"Down!" Randler shouted as a series of ropes flew overhead. They hit the wall and stuck there, instead of falling to the ground. Clearly, if they had been struck by them, the ropes would have bound them solid. "Gabrion, this is madness."

"I do not wish to leave Master Dariak behind," Quereth assured. "But I am no match for such a horde as this. Please see to reason."

One of the acolytes broke ranks and charged the team. Gabrion raced to meet him, reaching out his mighty fist to knock the wind from him, but instead it felt like he had punched a castle wall. The mage merely laughed and started chanting. Randler shoved the mage aside, just barely, and pulled on Gabrion's collar to hurry him along.

"Gabrion, Quereth is right. Let's move!"

"After what he just went through to save me, I—" the warrior started, then he grabbed for Randler and yanked him out of the path of a lightning bolt. But his hand was in terrible pain after striking the mage's protective shield, and the searing agony told him that he really was no match for this fight. "If only Kitalla—" he started, then he rolled aside and avoided a glowing ax that whirled through the air toward him.

Quereth was already tiring and Gabrion realized that the mage didn't have an endless supply of spell components in his robe. He couldn't pull the spell energy from a jade like Dariak had been doing for a while now, and there certainly wasn't time to try. Thinking of the jade gave him an idea though, so he dragged Randler over to Quereth and screamed for help from his jade. The only effect he knew he could summon was that of sharpening, and so the three of them became a rending force that was able to cut through some of the spells coming their way. The warrior knew he couldn't sustain it for long, so he tugged on the others and ran.

"No, this way," Quereth guided, tugging toward the right. Gabrion let him lead, keeping his mind focused on the jade as much as possible. Angry, the acolytes followed, casting their energies toward them repeatedly.

They reached a stairwell and Quereth stumbled as he tried to descend. He fell from Gabrion's grasp and rolled down the stairs, ending in a glowing, green heap at the bottom. Randler disengaged from Gabrion and went to the mage's aid, glancing about and seeing chaos everywhere.

Mages were battling fiercely from every direction. In most cases, it was five or six mages to one glowing intruder. The odds were clearly insurmountable, and seeing the green light from every one of their army's forces made Randler realize that they had absolutely no chance of rescuing Dariak. They might not escape with their lives.

Gabrion came to the same conclusion as he pulled out his sword and shield, then refocused the jade's energies on them. He ran toward the nearest group of mages and felled two of them who were too focused on their own foes to turn and protect themselves.

Others did not fall so easily. The room was a frenzy of magical energy and even when spells were not specifically targeting him, it was nearly impossible not to sustain damage. Gabrion blocked whatever spells he could, trying to take down some of the mages when opportunities arose. Most were protected front and back, though, so his efforts were often in vain. An ice dart seared his arm, but he channeled his thoughts away from the pain and turned them toward survival.

He broke up a couple of groups and the glowing mages he had saved were grateful, turning their healing spells on him or their offensive spells against the enemy. Quereth received enough healing to rise up and support the flanks. And just when they thought they had a chance to turn the tide, reinforcements came.

Fifty war hounds pounded into the room, howling like tigroars and stomping like giants. Three mages controlled them from the entryways, that much Gabrion could see, but they also had a flank of other mages protecting them. The war hounds raced into the room, growling and biting angrily. Despite their demoralizing appearance, Gabrion was grateful for their arrival, for they were not magical beasts and his sword would be effective against them. He needed the rush of success to bolster him, so he swept the legs out from under one mage but then abandoned the magic-users altogether to take down the other creatures.

Randler's mind took a similar path and he turned his attention to the war hounds as well. They were large dogs and would be at least as tall as he was if they stood on their hind paws. They were powerfully strong and fast. Randler recalled a song with a rapid tempo and used it to keep himself focused on a dance of dodge, parry, and strike. Whenever possible, he blinded them with the shadow jade, but he found that the magical green light emanating from his skin seemed to pass through even that. Soon, he stopped spending effort on the jade.

Quereth ran off to a corner to catch his breath, but there was no hiding place for them. Their glowing skin was a truly effective beacon and no amount of coverage blocked them from view. Quereth noted, in fact, that as he looked up and down, he could see nearly two dozen other green masses on different floors. It was terribly unsettling, especially as he watched one verdant light wink out.

Gabrion and Randler took down nearly all of the war hounds and were ready to turn their attentions toward the mages again, but the beastmasters summoned more monsters into the fray. Reptigons joined the war hounds, as did some sandorpions. No, this was an endless army, and they had to flee. Gabrion raised his voice as loudly as possible, "Kallisorians, retreat!"

It was as if the glass jade allowed his voice to cut through the entire tower. All the green blobs of light seemed to take notice and they stopped trying to fight back. Each looked for the nearest exit and ran. Gabrion made sure that Randler, Quereth, and the other mages they had traveled with were at the exit before he dove down the stairs. The mages gave chase, ushering all the forces to the lower floors.

Green comrades raced along and Gabrion called out to them, urging them to escape. His sword and shield deflected whatever spells they could, but the warrior couldn't fight back against such a wave of magical energies. Even as his companion mages came together, they were no match for the extraordinary forces within the tower. Floor by floor they raced, losing some of their friends along the way, but pressing ever onward, desperate just to live.

The lower floors of the tower had more novice mages than the upper floors. This allowed more of the fleeing forces to survive as they neared the exit. The verdant group banded together on its way out the main gate and into the night air. Quereth called a halt before they reached the giant mage barrier that surrounded the tower. Considering the barrier had claimed them on their way in, he assumed the mages would use its energies to entrap them once again. He had no way of knowing that the mages empowering the barrier were focused on maintaining the life force illumination spell, and so there was no danger of being whisked away, but he found Frast and Lica, both of whom were badly injured, and enlisted their help.

The three Pindington mages combined their efforts and erected a force tunnel that bore through the mage barrier, after which the survivors funneled through to relative safety on the other side. Once they passed the barrier, the odd green glow faded. The mages turned and added their support to Quereth's spell, widening the path and allowing everyone to get through before the mages in the tower pursued them. They needn't have hurried, for none of the mages actually left the tower, as if doing so would weaken them and render them vulnerable to attack.

Once they were on the other side, the mages collectively combined their healing powers and bolstered the group as much as they were able. They were down to less than twenty of them, plus Gabrion and Randler, but at least they had survived. Dariak was lost to them, but the warrior and the bard knew there was no way to have rescued him. The only recourse left to the group was to rejoin their fellows back at Marritosh.

CHAPTER 23

Randler's Advice

SUNLIGHT SEEPED IN through the window, waking Gabrion reluctantly. His body ached with the hurried flight from Magehaven, not to mention the countless wounds he had taken in the battle leading to their escape. Quereth and Lica were nearby, clearly exhausted after the frantic journey and hurried healing they had administered with the help of others. They had been pushing themselves hard and weren't accustomed to so much activity at once.

As quietly as possible, Gabrion tiptoed from the room, following the scent of food wafting through the air. The next-door bakery was already cranking out pastries for its morning patrons, and the warrior couldn't resist the allure. He shielded his eyes from the sunlight at first and then made his way over the dirt path and into the small hut across the way.

"Good dawn," greeted the matron of the place. Her hair was tied up in a funny bun above her head, keeping it clear of the food but looking more like a misshapen beehive than anything else. Gabrion made his way to the counter and peered around for a selection of wares. The woman smiled warmly. "Only breakfast rolls with jelly this time of day. Would you like one? We also have some apple-berry tea to go with it."

With a nod, Gabrion passed over some coins and stalked to a seat, where he tried to clear the grogginess from his head. He wasn't accustomed to being so tired, but as he reflected on it, he knew that he had been in worse shape along the journey. His adventure had truly taken some unexpected turns, and now he was missing the two companions who had been with him since the beginning. The more he thought about it, the more he felt as if his life was doomed to loss in every regard.

"Such a sad pout," admonished a welcome voice. Gabrion looked up to see Randler striding in to sit with him. "We've been in better predicaments than this, but with that scent in the air, how can you possibly be so gloomy?"

"What do you have to be happy about today?" the warrior grumbled. "Everything is lost."

Randler reached across the table and clapped Gabrion's shoulder. "All is not lost, Gabrion. We aren't finished yet."

The matron brought a pair of pastries and tea for them, hovering politely until Randler paid for his. Gabrion took a quick swallow of the sweet tea, choking as it was scalding hot.

"Careful now," Randler warned needlessly. "If you're too rash, you'll hurt yourself."

"You're rather cheerful this morning, considering we left Dariak back at the tower to die."

The bard's grin faltered for a moment, but he pasted it back on promptly. "He will be fine. They need his knowledge before they kill him, don't they? They may have turned against him and his father, but they still know the value his knowledge brings. No, I think Dariak has some time before they turn him into one of the border guardians."

Gabrion scrutinized the man for a moment. "You almost believe it, don't you?"

Randler sighed. "Almost," he admitted. "So that's me. What's wrong with you?" He lifted his pastry and bit into it heartily. It wasn't the most delicious thing he had ever tasted, but it was pleasant in its own right. The tea was much better by comparison.

The warrior lowered his gaze for a moment, but the bard wouldn't let him remain silent. After some prodding, Gabrion finally relented. "Everything has been slipping from my grasp. It started with friends I knew dying in Savvron the day Dariak swooped in. My mentor, Andron, died saving my life. Mira was taken. Later, Savvron was sacked and my mother was lost. All those people in Pindington when the Prisoner's Tower fell. Crazy Heria. Then Kitalla ran off. Now Dariak is lost to us. And you're mad at him, on top of it, because of me. I feel... cursed."

"I—" Randler started, then shook his head. "Well if you're going to put it that way, sure, sulk."

Gabrion looked up at him, brows furrowed. "That's helpful."

"No, no, don't let me bother your darkened thoughts. Keep at it and maybe you'll make it rain, or perhaps you'll find an answer when you stop beating your head against the wall."

"It's too early in the morning for this, Randler."

"Gabrion, you have an army here at your disposal. Your beloved Mira is thought to be at the palace. Go and get her. It seems simple to me," he said, popping the last bite of pastry into his mouth.

A glimmer of hope flickered into the warrior's eye before clouds whisked it away. "They follow Dariak and his mad quest for the jades."

"Ah, you're wrong there. Most of the fighters here follow you or Ervinor, truth be told. And if the young man is right, the troops are most eager to be off doing something. They might as well seek out your princess."

"Princess?" Gabrion echoed with a laugh. He then stared intently at the bard for a moment. "Ah, Randler, you always manage to break through our armor and earn a chuckle."

"We are all on this journey for different reasons. For some of us, our reasons have changed along the way. Take me, for instance. I wanted at first to find the jades and secret them away. I haven't always gone about it the right way, like when I gave the lightning jade over to the mages in Pindington." He shook his head. "At the time, it seemed like the best way to keep them busy while I looked for the other jade in the city. Then I ran into you, and you reunited me with Dariak. Now I'm trying to help him fulfill his dream of uniting the lands with the jades."

"Even though you're mad at him?"

Randler frowned and fidgeted with his tea mug. "I was hurt initially that he threw himself at you, so to speak."

"That's hardly what happened," Gabrion scoffed.

"Well, he declared that he loves you and would enjoy your physical company if given the chance. Besides, it wasn't like he said anything about me then. That doesn't exactly do much for my self-esteem."

"As if you need to worry, Randler." Gabrion now reached across and grabbed the bard's shoulder. "I assure you that his love for you and his feelings for me are two totally different things. Randler, he was inside my head, surrounded by all my own thoughts and emotions. I sensed him as much as he sensed me. He might like who I am and what I look like, but you make his heart skip a beat."

Randler couldn't help but smile. "Skipping a beat isn't usually good in my profession." Yet as the words sank in, he found his grin remained.

"Randler?" Gabrion stared hard at the man and tried to choose his words carefully. "I think you're right: I need to go after Mira. My quest has gone on for so long. I need to see it through so I can start living properly, whatever that is. If I find Mira, we can start a life together. If I find she's gone—"

"Don't say that, Gabrion. Keep hope."

"I am hopeful, but it's something I have to be prepared for, Randler. If… if I can only see her, alive and well. Then I'll know everything is going to be fine. Then I'll know that all these trials were worth it in the end." His eyes lost focus as he pictured her glowing face. "To have her nearby again. To hear her laugh and sing. It's that hope of having her with me again that keeps me going on. It's that part of me realizes that it's been about a year now since she was captured and there is a good chance I won't ever see her again."

Randler stayed quiet for a moment, eying the warrior as he spoke. "I think that's it, then, Gabrion. Just now, as you spoke of seeing her, you were alive and vibrant. The thought of being without her, and you fall into shadow again. So, I urge you: go. Rally the men and go to the castle. Find her if you can. It's clear that you need to."

As he thought about it, a sense of calm washed over the tormented warrior. "It seems a crazy thing to bring an army to the king's doorstep."

"Perhaps. But you aren't likely to secure an audience or to make your request unless you have strength to support you. Besides, I doubt they are enough to seriously pose a threat upon the king's own forces, so it isn't like you're announcing war or trying to bring down his castle. You're simply there with support, showing your strength so that he will take you seriously."

Gabrion nodded. "It does make a bit of sense."

Randler tapped his finger on the table, biting his lip gently. "I regret to mention it, but would our king have imprisoned you and Dariak if one of you had forces waiting outside the castle gates? I would wager that he would have bargained on better faith than he did if he felt any sort of threat of retaliation from your supporters outside the walls."

"It's true that I was just a body to be kicked around." He clapped the bard's shoulder again. "Thank you, Randler. You've given me a new focus. I truly needed it."

"I'm happy to oblige." He smiled, tipping his mug in homage.

"Now," Gabrion said, sobering quickly. "You've given me this task to carry out and all the while, you said that I would be going, not we. What are your plans?"

Randler's face flushed, caught off guard. "Very astute, Gabrion. You've really grown on this journey." He cleared his throat and answered, "I intend to go after Dariak."

"I'm not surprised, but how? Those mages will destroy you if you go back there."

"It's a risk, I know," he admitted. "Yet, Frast and I have a plan in mind that may work. We know the mages have been irrational in some of their dealings. However, when faced with new knowledge, they stop, learn what they can, and then discard what they no longer need. I spent a good bit of time in the library there and the history that precedes them echoes these practices."

Gabrion considered for a moment, then gasped. "You're going to offer Frast as a hostage, exchanging his knowledge of spells with Dariak's life!"

"Not quite, though we did think of that," he teased. "But Gabrion, you need to put us out of your mind right now. You have to focus on Mira and you have to find her. Until then, you won't be able to reconcile a new tomorrow. You will always be stuck in yesterday. Now is your chance to find her. Don't make her wait any longer."

The warrior stood up without a word, and Randler was momentarily perplexed, thinking Gabrion would run off at once. Instead, he walked over to Randler and hoisted him up onto his feet before wrapping his massive arms around the bard. "Thank you, Randler. I know you're worried about your own plan, having avoided telling me about it. Just promise me that you'll be safe."

Randler returned the embrace and nodded. "You too, Gabrion. You too."

* * *

Gabrion walked around Marritosh, feeling resolute with his new direction. The sun shone brightly overhead and his mind was clear once again. He was no longer the moping, lost warrior with no purpose. He hadn't realized how draining his time in Magehaven had been until this moment of clarity, with his goal lay bare at his feet.

Many of the warriors that had come with him from Kallisor were already awake, stretching or sparring quietly so as not to disturb the rest of the people. Gabrion was amazed by how well his fighters were accepted into this place. However, it was a warrior's town and the children were all raised to be as strong as possible so they could one day become members of the king's guard. The people understood fighting, and having so many able-bodied battlers among them must have felt like a giant homecoming of their kin.

Indeed, Gabrion was slapped on the back so many times he grew numb to the sting. The residents themselves welcomed him with smiles and friendly nods, seeing that he and his crew were not a threat, but merely warriors needing a respite. It was the only place other than Savvron that felt even remotely like home.

After wending his way through the streets, Gabrion sought out Ervinor, who had taken up residence at the home of one of the town's elders. Gabrion knocked on the wooden door and was admitted by an older woman, whose apron depicted a sword cutting a prize choice of meat.

"A good morning, deary. Yes, we were waiting for you. Your friend is out in the back, if you'll go on through there." She pointed the way across a lavishly decorated main room, which housed all sorts of trinkets the elder had collected during her husband's tenure with the king's guard. Gabrion couldn't help but stop to admire the collections of goblets on one wall, arranged by size rather than by the importance of the deed for which he had obtained it. A collection of bronze coins had been crafted in the man's honor and were housed in a glass-covered case to keep them from dust, and to reduce the desire to spend them. Of course they weren't proper currency, but in a quick transaction a careless merchant might accept them.

The far wall, which led toward the rear yard, was an oddly undulating surface of shiny metal slats. As he walked closer to it, the sunlight beamed through an upper window and reflected off the wall, casting myriad rainbow shapes on the floor. It was as dazzling as it was beautiful. As he stepped closer to the shifting wall, he realized that they were, in fact, weapons. Each long sword and spear was highly polished and they were hanging from the ceiling close together. To keep them from clanging into each other, they were spaced into four receding rows, but he could only see that from up close. Also, the bottommost blade along each strand was secured to the floor with a slightly loose rope that would allow only a little movement; just enough to give the shimmering effect from across the way.

"Each one," the elder's wife narrated at Gabrion's prolonged pause, "was given to Herchig at the end of a successful battle. Not all of them have shed blood, but each represents a time when he would have died without it. Come now, son, you may look at this later."

He allowed himself to be ushered from the room and into the backyard, which was one of the few in town that was enclosed with a fence. Gabrion had never seen a wood fence this tall surrounding a house such as this. His ogling eyes were noticed.

"Built it myself, I did," said a gruff old man, who sat in a rocking chair on a wooden deck. A small table rested by his hand with the remnants of his morning meal. Beside him sat Ervinor, a welcome smile on his face.

"Greetings, Gabrion," the young commander said, rising to greet his companion. "It has been too many days, indeed."

"I agree. It has been some while. How do you fare?"

Old Herchig slammed his tankard on the table. "Close your mouths and sit a spell. There's time later for you two to yammer on about the time you've had apart. It's only been a week or two anyway. Not like it's years or as if you'd never reconnect. No, not like the time I was off to the battle at Sarrithon, leaving poor Nesseria here with the little ones. Frian was almost old enough to go off for advanced training and, after the mishap with Sheina before him, I knew she wouldn't want to deal with it on her own. And it didn't help that the sandorpions were going wild because a mage had lost his wits and was sending them every which way. Blasted thing nearly took off my hand. Lucky it only got half a finger instead. Why if I hadn't been missing my Nesseria so much then, I might not have charged that mage to kill him. I might not have been wounded that day; I might have all my digits, but then again, the fight might have gone another way entirely. But as I was saying, no sir, you weren't facing things like that when you two parted, from all I've heard, so sit a minute and stop your blabbering."

It took everything Gabrion had not to start laughing at the windy tale and he could see that Ervinor was having the same kind of struggle, though he'd clearly had more practice. The warrior took the offered seat and readied himself for a long morning.

"Now your friend here," Herchig started right away, jerking his thumb toward Ervinor, "said you've brought this army here for a couple of reasons, but I have to tell you that you've got to focus on just one goal or else you'll be wandering all over the place. See, it happened once to General Therrius back when I was a trainee. He wanted to squash an uprising at the border, but he also wanted to plunder one of the northern caves. He didn't have a true goal in mind, so while he was planning to tackle one task he was dividing himself without knowing it and trying to plan the other excursion. No, if you're off to fight, you can't think about the loot. And if you're off to loot, you're just a damned fool anyway, but if that's what you're into you have to go for it and not stop to defend the kingdom on the way. It's the same here with you."

Gabrion nodded. "It's true that we have been focused on too many things at once. It's—"

"That's a good lad, fessing up to your elders and admitting your mistakes. But I have to warn you," Herchig said, aiming a gnarled finger at Gabrion's eye, "that you have to keep yourself in check with how much you admit you're wrong. Why if you don't, you'll end up like jolly Jonifer. He was promoted before his time and he made sure everyone knew he wasn't ready for the task, so he kept apologizing for things left and right, blaming his ignorance or what have you. Thing is, when you're in a fight and you need a leader, you can't have your leader send you off and say they're sorry if they're doing wrong by sending you that way, but hopefully it all works out right for you. No sir, you can't be all apologetic all the time. Sometimes you have to decide and let your errors be things only you know."

Ervinor couldn't resist. "Whatever happened to Jonifer?"

"Oh he took quite a beating from his fellows and their families, he did. They dressed him up in lurid clothes, apologizing all the while for not being able to find him something more suitable. Then they tied to him to a pole 'accidentally.' And kept throwing sticks, punches, and stones over his head, but they kept missing at missing him. Oh they rightly pummeled the poor thing, and every time they made contact they said they were sorry for actually hitting him. They stopped before they outright killed him and he lost himself that day. Never picked up another weapon again, I heard. Had to find himself a woman who was willing to cut his meat for him; he wouldn't even pick up a knife. On the up side, his indecision led him into entertainment and he became a bit of a slapstick performer for a while. True, some days people would throw things at him for his show, but at least he wasn't tied up anymore. Quick runner, if I recall."

Gabrion's mind was already reeling. He had already forgotten why he had come.

Herchig didn't seem to need the warrior's input anyway. "So you've got yourself an army here, and I've seen them in training and they're a far better set of fighters than the ones I first traveled with. No, we were more likely to spear ourselves in the back with a missed thrust than by the enemy. But yours is a good, coordinated team, and Ervinor here has done a great job of setting up responsibilities among them. Sure, a man follows orders for a time, but when he's working toward something, then he really gets the job done. It's why my father freed his father's slaves when I was a boy and grandpaps died. He offered them all a piece of the land they had worked on all their lives, offering them to live there if they kicked back some of what they produced. All but one of them stayed on to live in freedom because it was something of their own to work for."

"And the one that didn't stay?" Ervinor prompted, sliding a humorous glance at Gabrion who was starting to squirm with all the long-winded responses.

"Fool couldn't recognize a good opportunity. Found himself another farm to work at and was enslaved without knowing it. Yep, he went in, offered to do some work for some food. That's all a slave really does anyway, right? But when he got tired of it, which wasn't long, out came the whips and then the chains. He didn't live much longer after that. He'd dug himself a grave and pulled the dirt in on his own head. They only found him because his chains went into the ground. At first they thought he had just run off, but he didn't turn up anywhere nearby, so they finally did some digging and were horrified by what they found."

Gabrion slammed his eyes shut at the thought and wondered how he could focus this conversation a bit more.

But he had paused for too long. "Right, so this lad here," he reached out toward Ervinor again, "did a right smart thing and made captains and such among the men. Why, in fact, he did such a wonderful job of it, most of the folks here decided he was a better commander than the king's commander, and that's not a light thing to say. Why back in the day, the king's commander was a position to be feared above all else, and if you spoke ill of it, you were drawn and quartered. Ever see a man drawn and quartered? No? You're lucky. It's not an image you ever forget." He paused briefly to shudder. "Today's commander, though, has been focusing on hunting errands for the past few years now and the cohesion of the king's guard has crumbled. Why, if Ervinor here took over the king's guard, he'd fix it right up, I'd say."

"Hunting errands?" Gabrion interjected. "Don't you mean invasions into Kallisor?"

Herchig shrugged and sipped his drink again. "Call it what you will, but one man's plunder is another man's hunt is another man's duly assigned task. The king has been sending his guard out across the land in search of a precious treasure, more precious than any other treasure, so it's said. Sure at first it was just something for them to do to keep limber but then it didn't stop until a year ago. Since then we've been sending fighters to the border to keep the Kallisorians on their side. Now that gets rather boring after a while and a man needs variety in his life." He looked over his shoulder and smiled, "Except in a woman like Nesseria. No, that's not something you mess with, I'll say. Why, I remember the time I was late for meeting her and not only did I hear about it, so did the whole western quadrant! Passing through there every day, all I heard were jeers and cheers, urging me to be on time and not to keep the lady waiting!" He laughed to himself for a moment.

Gabrion grumbled. "They wouldn't need to be guarding the border if they hadn't invaded my town in the first place and kicked up this war."

"Bah, both sides start the wars each time. It's never one over the other, not really. Why it's like a game of cards. There's a deck just sitting there and one guy picks it up and shuffles it, but whatever he does with the cards doesn't mean anything until the next guy sits down and joins in. They wager, they gamble, they win or lose and in the end someone goes home unhappy with his night. Sometimes he turns around and knifes the guy who was at the other side of the table." He lifted his tunic, exposing a deep scar over a wrinkled belly. "Lucky I had some good reflexes, even when I was drunk, or I wouldn't be here today, I'd wager. But our kingdoms go to war if someone sneezes too loudly."

"Well, it has to stop," Gabrion said.

"Right, right, of course it does. Then you have to wonder what all the fighters will do once there's no more fighting to keep them in shape. Maybe they could start up games of skill and such and just compete that way. Hmm, now there's an idea…" He paused for a moment, but then prattled on. "Your friend here told me of your rescue mission, though, and I think it's noble of you to want to ride in and save her if she's still there, but it's just another big sneeze, if you ask me. It's only going to lead to more trouble for the Kallisorians at the border already fighting. And more trouble for them means more trouble for us and that means more of our children are dying."

"That's why I need to confront the king, so he can try to right the wrong peacefully and without creating more war. Then he can go back to hunting for his treasure and leave my homeland in peace." Gabrion looked at Ervinor, who nodded his head in support.

"You're a noble lad there, son, and you remind me of young Gethric. He had great lofty ideas in his heart and he would go around to all the houses trying to collect supplies to help the people in need. He would have been great if not for the thief, Kelsh, who merely grabbed him and slit his throat for all the things he had gathered. I always wondered what the world would have been like if Kelsh hadn't made that strike. Would this world be more wholesome or would another Kelsh have risen and done the deed anyway? Or would Gethric have been overwhelmed by the poverty in this world and succumbed to it? Or maybe, maybe, what if he had succeeded in getting his message across? Where would he be today?"

"Hopefully, he would have succeeded the king," Gabrion offered. "A peaceful regent with an eye toward altruism would be the best way of turning our countries away from war."

"Indeed, that is quite the fantasy you have there in your head. Not as wild as the ones my little Leeda once fancied, but that's a tale for another day. Yet let us say that a kindly king sat upon the throne, what then of the neighboring tyrant? He would crush us surely as glass and there would be blood. Endless blood."

"There already is endless blood. And if this Gethric could have overcome the odds within the land, then why not within other lands as well?"

"Well…" And for the first time, Herchig fell completely silent without a story to tie in.

Gabrion took the opportunity. "Ervinor, I intend for us to visit the castle, as a united force. There, I will ask for Mira's return and the king will have to listen to us. He will have to surrender her."

"The men will be excited with the prospect of moving on. They will have to be ready for resistance, though. The king may not quite welcome us with open arms."

Herchig laughed at that. "No, he certainly will not, especially when he sees that the rest of Marritosh is on your side! It has been a long time now that someone has spoken of peace. Of change. It's many years since I ever believed in the chance to make a difference. I grew up here in Marritosh and raised like any good crop, like all the other children born or sent here. Here we break many of our family ties and reconnect them to the king and the kingdom itself. For a long time, we have been the well from which the king has drawn the water drops that are his troops. Upon hearing you now and your hope for a different tomorrow, I feel you're just like that one man so long ago whose vision changed this land forever."

Gabrion bit his lip. "One man with a vision of peace…"

"You'll know all about him, of course. And you'll know about him because his work ended in the most paradoxical way. He was the man who summoned the colossus at the last major war."

"Delminor!" Gabrion gasped, then realized he should have known.

"You know his name! I am most impressed. Yes, that man opened many eyes wide, but greed can often be more powerful still. And though I hope you can do right in your quest, I fear it too that you may fall to greed. If you reach your peaceful agreement with his majesty, will you then seek to cast him out and replace him, or would you walk away? In the moment you may not react the way you expect. Circumstances may forbid you from doing what you think right now you'd do. I know not how your books unfold the story of the war, but I was one who knew Delminor in his prime. His heart was pure and true and strong, and he was powerful indeed, but like Gethric, the deeds of others defeated him in the end. You may be striking out on this quest, young warrior, but be wary that your odds of success are minimal, and your odds of survival are infinitesimal."

Gabrion nodded sternly. "And yet, I have to try."

Herchig bore into Gabrion's eyes with his own, as if trying to read the warrior's soul. Gabrion did not flinch away, knowing this was some challenge of his inner resolve. He knew he could do this now. He wasn't traveling alone; an army would march with him. And it was an army that had been augmented in his absence.

Ervinor sat as still as stone, not wanting to intrude upon the contest of wills he was witnessing. It wasn't as tense as he imagined it could have been, but he knew a pivotal decision was in the works here, though he couldn't know what it would be. Perhaps Herchig would know of other troops to summon on their behalf, or perhaps he knew some leaks in the king's defenses.

At last, the old man sat back in his chair, releasing Gabrion's will. "Your heart is strong, young warrior. I will call upon my brethren to aid you. Give us until tomorrow or so before you plan to depart, for it will take until then to fit your army properly."

"Fit us?"

"Kallisor lives without the blatant use of magic, but here in Hathreneir, the king is well-guarded, and you will need defenses against the king's mages. We will give to you what armor we have and it will aid you against their spells. If you succeed in your discourse against the king, you may keep the armor for yourselves. If you fail, you will die and the armor will find its way back to us in the end."

"We will not fail," Gabrion assured him. "I will not fail."

"If I thought you would, then I would not be offering you this boon. For, if you die, then all this armor will once again be stained with blood, and like the time in my thirties when we…"

As he rambled on now, Gabrion didn't mind. He listened instead, trying to pull the underlying wisdom from beneath the story layered on top. He grew to understand why Ervinor seemed so amused by the old man, for Herchig had seen so many hopefuls rise up and be squashed, and yet the old heart still had hope as its guide.

The antimagic armor would help him in his quest for Mira, and once he had her by his side, he would swiftly race to the mages' tower and rescue Dariak—and Randler and Frast if their plan backfired. He could not seek them out first, for Herchig's offer of the armor demanded he first meet with the king, something the old man reaffirmed in one of his tales later that day.

Yet Gabrion wasn't worried. Hope swelled within him again.

CHAPTER 24

Subterfuge

RANDLER AND FRAST left Marritosh a few hours after the bard gave his advice to Gabrion. It wasn't easy escaping the town without notice; everyone was on alert for one reason or another. The mages were wary of retaliation from Magehaven and they spent much time together, trying to share spells and build a stronger set of defenses. The army was anxious to be off doing something productive, as were the natives of Marritosh who had fallen in with the visitors from Kallisor.

Dodging Lica and Quereth proved the most difficult. They had been working closely with Frast for years and they sensed something was amiss. But Frast was determined to make this work, for Randler's sake, and he evaded his colleagues the best he could, deigning to meet with them in the evening to lay it all out for them in detail. They accepted his delay, not realizing that he would be gone before then.

Packs on their shoulders, weapons close to hand, the minstrel and the mage trekked off to the west. The sun was blinding on the hot sand and made travel difficult, but they pressed onward, discussing their plans quietly as they went.

It wasn't long before the creatures in the area noticed them. Randler alternated between his bow and his mace, depending on where the enemies were. Frast was of average skill with a short sword, which he used mostly in order to preserve his strength for the spells he would soon need when they reached the tower. The reptigons and sandorpions fell to their attacks, but then an eerie silence surrounded them and Randler's skin tingled nervously. Sandorpions and reptigons, they expected; a young pack of lupinoes, they did not.

The clever cubs gathered around the duo, tracking them slowly, gauging their steps. They tromped along with the sun at their backs so the two men would hardly be able to see them. Wisps of sand swept up and concealed them further, and Randler wondered if the lupinoes themselves were kicking up the sand intentionally. The cry of an eaglon overhead disrupted the mounting tension and one of the lupinoes gave away its position by growling in response. Randler let loose with an arrow and took the cub down with a shot to its paw. It howled in agony as it huddled in on itself and tried to pull the arrow out.

The others, however, did not wait. As a unit, the remaining lupinoes charged inward. Randler let three more arrows fly randomly, hoping for a lucky kill before he had to switch weapons. One muffled cry seemed to indicate a victorious hit, but that was all. Slinging the bow over his back, the bard withdrew his mace and slashed it through the air to remind his arms of the balance they would need for this dance.

And a dance it was. He had spent a lot of time with Kitalla, trying to devise new songs for her that would focus her own skills, and Randler had watched her movements in awe. He called to the music now, feeling the frantic beat swelling inside him, and then he let his body follow the rhythm. As a bard and performer, he was already a decent dancer onstage. Now the dance would save his life. Down, up, spin around. Swipe, thrust, duck, bend. Leap, twirl, smash, dive. He was barely aware of what damage he was causing, but he knew he was striking his foes.

Frast was having a harder time. He saw Randler swing into a semi-trance and he stepped a few paces away to give him room. The mage brought his sword up with two hands and brought it down in a wide, sweeping arc. He batted away two lupinoes with the move, but rather than disabling them, he angered them. The cubs rushed in again, growling and spitting as they did so, and Frast almost fell for it. Something in his mind reached out to him and he turned sideways and saw another lupino sneaking up on him while the other two held his attention. It was a lucky move, for he was able to dispatch the one sneak, and then defend against the others.

Randler felled three pups and the eaglon before his first focused attack wore off. He glanced over to Frast, seeing his plight, but he couldn't help as a pack of sand rodia scrambled into the brawl. He turned away from Frast and focused on the new menace. Unlike the green-skinned rodia in Kallisor, these blended well with the sandy ground and were hard to see, save their dark eyes that never blinked. Randler gauged the enemy. The lupinoes were confused by the appearance of the rodia, but they quickly regrouped to fight in earnest.

The bard hummed aloud as he dove into a new song. Frast picked up its tempo and the two of them came together as a unit and battled back against the creatures. Some of the rodia slipped through the defensive maneuvers, seeking to chomp the victims with their powerful jaws, but Randler's mace proved faster. It helped that, as more creatures fell, their will to fight lessened. One of the lupino cubs howled a retreat and the rest of its kin bolted away. The rodia did not follow suit and instead remained, hoping to claim a victory, but only meeting their doom instead.

Huffing, Frast sank to the ground. "I knew we'd have to defend ourselves, but that was a bit much."

Randler joined him, flipping open a waterskin and sharing it. "Indeed, but it shows we have the skills we need to get through this task. Are you injured at all?"

Frast checked himself. "No. Just scrapes and bruises. Nothing major. You?"

"No, I'm okay." He sighed with relief. "I don't know what we would have done if I hadn't spent all that time with the others, Kitalla especially for this case. I felt like I was channeling them during that battle."

Frast smiled and placed a hand on Randler's shoulder. "They are your closest and dearest friends. I'm sure they were with you."

"Thanks," the bard smiled. "I also know that I could not have survived this without you. I'm glad you're with me on this trip."

Frast blushed and then cleared his throat. "Onward then?"

The journey to the west was difficult for the two of them. Fending off small packs of beasts was manageable, but it seemed to be an endless parade with little time for rest in between. Part of their plan called for them to circumvent the tower and approach it from the northwest, but after a solid day of continuous fighting, Randler decided against it.

"It won't much matter if we're successful getting around the tower," he said to Frast, as much as convince himself as the mage. "They will recognize me anyway. It won't matter the angle at which we attack."

"I still say a disguise is worthwhile."

Randler shook his head. "I need to be fully free to move about. And in this heat, anything I apply to my skin to alter its appearance will just melt off or drain with sweat." For emphasis, he wiped his brow. "No, there's nothing we can do in that regard." He looked up at the horizon. "Oh, but that, we *can* do something about. You ready?" He pulled out his bow and nocked an arrow.

Frast moaned. "Eaglons and… are those swallomers?" The deep, curved wings of the swallomers made them more suited to flitting between trees than bearing the heat of the desert. Like their docile kin, the swallow, the swallomers were vividly colored, which added to the strangeness of their appearance here. "What are they doing in the desert?"

"Dying, by the look of it," he responded, letting an arrow fly, but slaying an eaglon instead. It seemed the two avian groups were battling each other. "Swallomers may bite and draw blood, but I'd prefer to face them than those eaglons." He let another arrow loose, striking a larger bird and felling it.

Once the third arrow sailed through the air, the birds turned toward their new adversaries. The eaglons shrieked and some broke away from the swallomers to dive at the humans, metallic talons clawing for them angrily. Frast was ready and though the eaglon twisted deviously as it approached him, he adjusted and cut into the bird's chest, killing it instantly and splattering the mage with blood. Luckily, it was the eaglon's salivary glands that carried the paralyzing venom and not the blood. He didn't hesitate for long as three eaglons went into a spiraling dive, forming a sort of braid. Randler shot one down, but missed the other two. Frast cut forward and threw himself on the ground to avoid being struck.

They focused on the eaglons and ignored the swallomers. Indeed, when a couple of the smaller birds flew by the bard, he hesitated with his bow, aiming for the larger and scarier threat. The swallomers misinterpreted this, but their confusion worked toward the humans' advantage.

One swallomer tweeted a merry tune and the others left their own clawing brawls to rally together. Randler watched in fascination; he had never seen them act that way in Kallisor. He wondered if it was a learned skill here in the brutal desert or if he had simply missed such a concerted effort. The lead swallomer tweeted again and more birds joined behind it. Frast looked up nervously, wondering if the avian pests were gearing up to take them down, but the eaglons recaptured his attention.

Randler avoided switching to his mace at all costs. The eaglon talons were too sharp to chance getting so close to strike. The nature of the feathery attacks, though, forced the birds to swoop down and away each time and melee moments were brief anyway. Randler dodged nimbly and kept grabbing for more arrows.

At last, the swallomer swarm was ready. All fifty-something birds screeched and dove forward, cutting through the air like a scythe. The eaglons in their path were stunned by the loud cry and then destroyed by the countless beak and claw strikes of the smaller foes. Randler couldn't help but chuckle about composing a song touting a heavy rain of eaglons. Once the large birds were defeated, Randler replicated the bird call and the swallomers turned to him, circling overhead. He called up his thanks and whistled delicately in what he thought would be gratitude. The birds dove lower, flying rapidly around Frast and Randler; then, after a few moments, they darted off toward the horizon to continue whatever quest they had already been on before the eaglon strike. The bard and the mage followed suit.

Evening approached and the sun dipped behind the horizon. The duo opted to set up a small camp, taking advice from the citizens of Marritosh who lived in this brutal region. Because they were a group of two instead of a host of a hundred fighters, survival tactics were a bit different. They dug a trench deep enough so they could lay within it and not breach the surface of the sand. Once the pit was ready they shared a quiet meal of bread and cheese, then they arranged some defenses, mostly made of brittle twigs they had brought with them arranged in a perimeter around their campsite, about which they set a few spare daggers and broken shards of pottery. With any luck, nighttime invaders would step upon the sharp objects and howl, and if that didn't awaken the two of them, the snapping twigs would help.

This, of course, did not protect them from avian attackers, but the Marritosh soldiers had also explained that the birds would not typically swoop down at level ground, hence the trench and a sand-colored tarp Randler had procured in town. Frast lay inside the trench first, clearly nervous about this refuge, while Randler secured the tarp into the sand before crawling in next to the mage and rolling the tarp over them. He could feel Frast trembling in the darkness.

"Relax, it will be fine."

"I don't feel protected here at all," he returned.

Randler agreed, but he couldn't let it show. "Close your eyes and relax."

"I'm sorry." He shook, trying to breathe deeply and to settle his nerves.

There wasn't really any room to move around, for they hadn't dug a particularly large trench. Randler shifted and turned toward Frast, where he placed a calming hand over the mage's heart. He then sang a gentle lullaby.

Close your eyes.
Find your dreams.
The darkness is just a veil.
The sun will rise.
And you will be
Rested and calm and safe.

I am here.
You have no fear.
I shall watch over you.
You will see;
Count one, two, three.
Warm and secure and safe.

The path ahead
Is in your mind
You can take it if you choose.
Dancing trees
Swaying flowers
Happy and sound and safe.

He felt Frast's pulse calming as he sang the song, but then a noise outside alerted them both. Randler halted his song, tilting his head to listen to the approaching foes. He was baffled at first, for it sounded like high-pitched lilting music and then it dawned on him that it matched the song he was singing. He hummed along and reached up to peer through the tarp, despite Frast's silent protest. Randler freed his hand and then rolled the tarp back, still humming the sweet melody.

Their small campsite was lit well enough by moonlight for Randler to see the swarm of swallomers, perched all around, just inside the ring of twigs. Some of the smaller birds had their heads tucked into their wings, clearly catching some much-needed sleep. The larger swallomers looked at Randler, not entirely sure what kind of creature would be humming from beneath the ground, but then recognition set in among them both. The birds continued whistling the melody as Randler smiled and sank back below the surface.

He quelled Frast's question by answering in verse, keeping the melody flowing strongly, yet with a tender softness underneath:

The birds,
They've come.
They are guarding our camp.
Fall to sleep
Fade into night
Tomorrow we both shall rise.

The mage shook his head in disbelief, but the confidence of Randler's words and tone comforted him anyway. He turned on his side, curling slightly, believing in the minstrel and hoping beyond all that they would survive the night. Randler buried his own doubts as he turned the other way, resting one hand on a dagger, just in case.

The night passed quietly, save one moment where the swallomers fended off a swarm of firegnats. Cawing and howling awoke Randler, but he couldn't move at first. Groggily, he felt himself held down by a tender embrace, arms trapping him, a warm body pressed lovingly up behind him.

The screeching of the swallomers awoke him further and he pulled himself up to peer cautiously through the tarp, but retreated once he saw the flurry of feathers swatting away the tiny mites. He certainly didn't want to attract any of the venomous fliers into the trench. He lowered himself down, still with a pair of arms clutching him longingly.

"Dar—" he started, but caught himself, remembering that it was Frast, not Dariak, trapped with him. The mage was still sound asleep, clearly exhausted from their day. As Randler settled back down, Frast clutched him more tightly, and he curled himself against the bard as if he would never let go. He remembered how nervous the mage had been settling down and so he closed his eyes, letting the arms remain where they were, holding him tightly.

In the morning, Frast awoke, finding himself deeply entwined with Randler's body. He enjoyed the warmth and the security he felt, the slow rise and fall of the bard's chest under his hands. He nuzzled his cheek against Randler's neck, holding on to the moment for as long as he could. A gentle cooing sounded outside as some of the swallomers also awoke for the day, and Frast mentally wished them to be silent, so as not to awaken the bard. He thought he could feel Randler's life force racing through his body and the sensation filled him with a great hope for the day.

Randler was awake, however, and he wasn't sure how to disentangle himself from Frast's advances without hurting the mage's feelings. He liked Frast, but his heart belonged to Dariak. Opting for a deep yawn and a slow stretch, Randler gently pulled himself apart from the mage.

"Good morning," he said quietly, turning to face Frast. "Sleep well?"

"I—um, yes, thanks. You?"

"Not bad. It was helpful having the swallomers out there," Randler acknowledged.

"I suppose so, though I felt better that you were here." He tried not to blush, but his cheeks gave his feelings away anyway.

Randler smiled softly. "Clearly, you were rather comfortable. You slept soundly."

Frast's face burned a deeper crimson yet. "I—I'm sorry for grabbing you so tightly."

He wasn't sure why he felt the need to do it—maybe it was because he had needed support once too—but Randler pulled Frast's hand into his own and held it tightly. He leaned in and gently kissed the mage's cheek, telling him without words that there was nothing wrong with mage's feelings but that they were not reciprocated. At first, Frast didn't understand. He tried to pursue Randler's lips but the minstrel smiled and teased him instead. "Now, now, we have a journey ahead of us today."

Randler didn't think Frast's face could burn any redder, but he was wrong. "We could… start off a little… later, if you want." Frast tightened his grip of Randler's hand, sliding his thumb gently back and forth.

"Frast, I'm sorry," Randler shook his head slowly. "If circumstances were a little different, then maybe. But my heart is elsewhere. I can't do this. It wouldn't be right."

To his credit, Frast took it well. "I know, Randler. I know. I just… I've never met anyone like you. I—" He paused to gather his thoughts, then he sighed. "I know I shouldn't finish that thought."

"Which thought?" he asked.

Frast chuckled once, then smiled oddly. "The one where I list all the things I like about you." He stared into Randler's cinnamon eyes and then he looked away. "You even charmed the birds into keeping us safe. Any idea how we should thank them?"

Randler accepted the diversionary question and hummed in thought. "I guess we'll have to protect them, too. Come on, let's get started." He sat up and pushed aside the tarp, which startled a few of their avian friends, but they settled quickly.

Randler stood up and stretched into the morning sun. "We can eat as we go," he decided.

"Sure," Frast agreed, trying not to think about the way Randler moved as he stretched.

The day started off well and few beasts approached them at all, which was a welcome relief. Randler wondered idly if it was the complement of swallomers that kept the enemies at bay or perhaps the defeated lupino clan had spread the word that these two men were not to be trifled with.

They had enough food for five days' worth of travel, but they realized after the second day that it wouldn't be enough to get them to the tower and back. Because it was only the two of them, and neither was a stout warrior with endless stamina, they couldn't make the journey in the same amount of time as before. All told, four days passed them by before they approached their destination.

Though Magehaven was tall, its security field kept it obscured from view. With the recent attack on the tower, defenses were heightened and Randler already knew that they would have a hard time discerning its exact location until they were very near. His eye for detail scoured the lay of the land and he judged that they had a few hours more before they would be near enough to the tower to start enacting their plan. He thought of the swallomer swarm and grinned. It felt to him like luck would be on his side for this journey. The birds had periodically flown off, presumably to hunt, but they always returned to the bard, particularly when he would sing.

As the afternoon waned on the fourth day, they paused briefly to eat and then continued onward until at last they were close enough to the tower. Frast opened his pack and pulled forth the beige tarp. He made sure he gripped it tightly for its color matched the sand so closely he would lose it if he let go. Randler unpacked his lute, a flute, and a small drum. Then he helped to enwrap Frast in the sand-colored cloth until he was neatly obscured from view.

"I hope they don't use that life force spell again," Frast muttered. "It would ruin this whole endeavor."

"They won't. Or if they do, it won't matter. Remember? It stopped working once we were beyond the defensive border. It won't reach us." Randler eyed Frast sharply and then poked and prodded him until the shadowy folds of cloth were smoothed out. It required much fondling for the cloth to sit properly and Frast stood there, his face burning brighter and brighter with each pull and tuck of the cloth. Randler noted the mage's reaction and he sighed in mock exasperation. "Now, now, don't you look adorable, dressed as a lump of sand."

"I—" He stopped himself, realizing that he was blushing. "Okay, okay, I'm ready. Forgive me for getting caught up in the moment. It's been keeping me from being nervous. Okay? But I'm ready for this. The plan is still set. We've got this."

"Do you have all your spell components ready?" Randler smiled, hoping Frast truly was prepared. There wouldn't be a second chance and if the mages discovered the ruse before he managed to get in to the tower, then Dariak would be lost to him. Thinking about it, he wondered what kept himself so calm, considering what lay ahead. He turned away from Frast, as if searching for the answer.

"It's all ready," Frast assured him. "Are we waiting for nightfall or is dusk close enough?"

When Randler turned back, his face was grave. "It's now, actually. Look over there." He pointed off in the distance toward the northeast.

They were far enough away not to be a hindrance yet, but clearly a contingent of soldiers was approaching. Their heads were beyond some of the dunes and they seemed to be marching with purpose, though they weren't racing ahead. Randler wondered if it was a security patrol or if the mages in the tower had summoned support from the king after the recent events. Luckily, he and Frast were to the west of the troop and so they were lost in the sunlight and went unseen by the approaching forces. Additionally, late afternoon was a good feeding time for the swallomers and they were away, unseen.

"No time to waste, Frast. Let's get to it. Once I'm inside, I beg of you to run for safety. Don't let them see you." He grabbed the mage's shoulders firmly as if doing so would keep him safe when he would need it most.

Frast controlled the urge to grab Randler into an embrace, fearing he would try to sneak a kiss if he did so. Instead he sharply nodded his head and dove into the necessary spellcasting. He started by squashing a dead spider between his thumb and forefinger and tracing a pattern in the air, "*Sesspinnar trallin uluf callinor.*" He traced the spider's remains around his own lips, shrugging off the discomfort. After that, he established a protective ward with a shard of glass, like Dariak had done countless times. Randler withdrew a hollow ball from his pocket, which had already been severed into two even halves. He held them aloft while Frast enchanted them.

"*Echkinar repeallio modicallium fasthris binniar.*" He then took one of the halves and pocketed it, handing the other half to Randler. Frast enacted a few more spells, trying to ignore the approaching army and the upcoming task. Remaining focused, they completed their preparations and then glanced once toward the northeast, ensuring they still had time before the soldiers arrived. It would be close.

The air shimmered slightly to the west and Frast could feel the pull of the barrier that surrounded Magehaven. He approached as closely as he dared and then signaled for Randler to stand there. He stepped behind the bard, slightly off to one side, and dropped low. The sandy tarp tucked all around his body blended perfectly with the sand and Randler made only a few last adjustments to keep the man hidden. He then lifted his lute and strummed a few piercing notes.

"Behold, mages of the tower. I come with knowledge that you seek!" Randler bellowed aloud. He strummed a few more notes. "Admit me peacefully, and I will share with you my knowledge."

It didn't take long to receive an answer. "There is no knowledge in your head that will improve upon the stores of information in our vast library! Be gone from here before we share some of that knowledge with you. I assure you, it will hurt."

Randler was undaunted. He strummed his lute and sang briefly.

The fires of the sun, upon the earth they turn.
See them twisting, writhing there, suddenly they burn.

On command, a swirling column of flame erupted from the ground, and as Randler strummed lower notes, the fire tilted to the left. When he twanged on the upper register, the flames danced to the right. He then played a looping pattern and the flames moved and spiraled around him. He released the lute strings and as the music fell silent, so too did the flames die away.

"What trickery is this?" cried the tower mage.

"No trickery, I assure you. I have studied the patterns of energy and of sound and I have found a unique connection that no other has ever exploited." He wasn't even lying by much. His Trial in the tower had shown him a connection, but also his time with Kitalla had shown him another. It was her dance skills and their ability to pull energy into a form of magic that had inspired this ruse. Of course, his music held no actual power over the energies. Instead, the music was Frast's cue for which spells to utilize and how to manipulate them. The spider remnants on Frast's lips trapped the sounds within his mouth, keeping him essentially silent.

When the tower mage stood transfixed and doubting, Randler lifted the drum and rapped a staccato beat.

Barrier of magic, strong and tall
blocks your foes, one and all.
With these notes, I do command:
now before you, here I stand.

With that, Randler stepped toward the protective barrier, hoping the mages had not altered its magic. Upon his first passing through the barrier, his body had been ripped away from Dariak and the others and they had been subjected to individual Trials. Randler surmised that he wouldn't be carted off to an additional Trial because he had already completed one. It was the same reasoning why Dariak hadn't undergone another Trial. The tower mage didn't recognize Randler from his previous visit, and so he wouldn't realize that the bard would not be tested. So Randler hoped.

He kept his doubt from his face and posture as he took those steps forward, but no invisible force whisked him away, and the mage at the door stood agape that this bard could so easily pass their defenses. He called over his shoulder for help from within. Randler waited patiently until the help arrived. There was no need to rush things now, even with soldiers approaching the tower.

Randler kept himself composed even as the help arrived in the form of Master Pyron. The old mage snarled when he saw the bard. "It is foolish of you to return here."

Only years of training kept Randler's voice strong. "I came seeking an exchange."

The mage brimmed with hatred and disgust. Randler didn't know of the death of Kerrish or how that had imperiled Dariak, but he sensed a great danger here. Still, he couldn't leave without trying and if the mage killed Randler as well as Dariak, at least they would be together in the afterlife, if one existed.

Pyron glared viciously. "You have nothing with which to barter."

Randler had hoped to be admitted inside after duping a lesser mage. He didn't think the musical ruse would work against a master, but he had to try it anyway. "Watch, then." As he lifted his lute, Pyron instinctively raised some additional defenses around himself. Randler strummed a set of notes and then sang aloud.

Even when the ground is dry, there's moisture in the air.
Pull it, drag it, summon it, and it appears right there.

A few paces in front of Randler a small puddle of water appeared. As with the fire column moments before, when he played different notes on the lute, the water moved in unison, this time jumping upward in the desired direction and splattering back to the puddle.

The expression on Pyron's face belied his curiosity. "A trick," he decided, just like the tower mage, who was still watching the show. "I felt the energies enacted, yes. But something is amiss here."

Randler was ready with his response. "It seems amiss because you have not seen it before. You feel the energies because they come from me." This, too, was almost true. Frast was casting his spells into the half sphere he had enchanted, and the other half in Randler's possession projected the energies back out, while the spider spell kept Frast's voice hidden.

Pyron was clearly intrigued by the concept but he wasn't convinced. "Let us pretend for a moment that this 'skill' of yours is real. Is this what you propose to exchange?"

"It is," he agreed, surprised at being asked this so soon.

"And for what do you bargain?"

"Dariak's freedom," he answered firmly.

Pyron didn't respond immediately. "What good is your knowledge to me? We have the ability to cast spells without the need of silly instruments." To demonstrate he gestured with his hands and launched a set of ice darts in Randler's direction.

Trusting entirely to Frast's defensive spells, Randler only grabbed his drum and beat a tense pattern upon its surface. The ice darts struck the air in front of the bard and shattered, leaving Randler unscathed.

The minstrel commented flippantly, "Did I mention that I do not need the words and that I was merely singing them so you would know what to expect? Shall I demonstrate another?" Pyron immediate swept his arms up into what Randler recognized as another defensive spell. "You need not fear me harming you, Master Pyron. After all, if I injured you, who would honor my plea?"

"Who indeed?" the old mage growled.

Randler and Frast had worked on nearly two dozen different spells to enact during this exchange, but when Randler lifted his flute and played a jaunty tune, he did not expect the results. Instead of a harmless dancing ball of light, a flock of twittering birds appeared. The music had apparently carried itself to the swallomer flock and they fled their resting place and came to Randler's side. He kept himself in check as they arrived, pretending he had summoned them directly.

"Foolishness," Pyron harrumphed. He lifted his hands, calling upon the beast jade that rested within the tower and he threw the energies over the swallomers to bid them to fly away. However, their connection to Randler and his music was stronger and the master mage was unable to deflect the birds as they flew toward him. "What is this?" Pyron gasped, trying to control the flock to make the birds deviate from their flight path, but despite his experience with the beast jade, he could not affect the flock.

Randler whistled into the flute, hoping the swallomers would turn aside and not attack the mage, for that would be disastrous to his plot. The birds heard the change in the tempo and they stopped, trying to discern its meaning. From the positions of Randler and the mages, it seemed as if the bard was under attack, and they wanted to protect him. They chirped in confusion and flew back to Randler, hovering over his head in great circles. He hummed the lullaby he had sung to Frast a few days earlier and the birds picked up the tune and sang along.

"Perhaps we should speak after all," Pyron said hesitantly.

Before he agreed, Randler made one demand. "Show me that Dariak is well and then I will share my knowledge with you."

Pyron laughed aloud. "Perhaps we'll just surround you once you are inside and torture you until you reveal your knowledge."

Randler shook his head in disappointment. "Very well then, I will depart and spread word of my findings to all the populace of the land. I will teach all people to draw upon the energies through the use of music and when I return, I will collapse this tower, and all the mages across the land will be obsolete."

The threat struck Pyron deeply. "You wouldn't!"

"Nor would you disgrace the mages in your care by treating me with anything other than courtesy. Not that it would matter, with what I know."

Conflict warred across the mage's face. Though he still had doubts of Randler's apparent skill, if it was real he couldn't chance its knowledge reaching the masses. The sheer aplomb of the bard was unnerving. Clearly, the minstrel had learned much on his last visit to the tower.

They stared intently at each other for several minutes while the mage decided. The swallomers grew bored and found perches along the crevices of Magehaven. It was an unintended act that pushed Pyron's decision in Randler's favor, for if the birds felt so comfortable resting on the walls, then Randler's skill might be more powerful than he had let on. The thirst for this unbidden knowledge won out. The old mage muttered instructions to the other mages who had gathered at the doors by then.

"Very well, bard. You will enter under my protection. Yet your actions will be scrutinized upon entry."

"Indeed," Randler said easily. "I will cause no harm to your fellows nor steal any of your treasures or secrets. I am not here for them. I am here for Dariak and you will give him to me of your own accord. My knowledge for his freedom."

Pyron hesitated, for he had no intention of releasing the murderer, but he yearned to know of this link between the music and the energies. "I have agreed only to show him to you unharmed. The rest... we will see."

"Fair enough," Randler shrugged carelessly. He hadn't expected even this much cooperation up front and it was only when Pyron cast a few odd glances to the swallomers that the bard realized that they were the impetus for this exchange. "Thank you friends," he muttered softly.

As he passed by old Pyron, he heard one of the other mages whispering to her elder, "Master Pyron, the king's guard approaches."

"My eyes function, Nera," he said sourly, not taking his eyes off of Randler. "We shall deal with our visitor with haste so that we may accommodate the guard."

"But Master—"

"Tend to your duties, Nera. We have a couple of hours before they arrive." He then walked inside the tower, leaving Nera to gather herself. The Master waved his hands side to side, signaling various mages within. Some merely bowed their heads, though others ran off to assigned posts.

Randler was recognized by several of the mages and it was a testament to Master Pyron's power that they held themselves in check, for clearly they wanted to lash out and strike him down. For Pyron's sake, Randler loudly hummed a melody, which he hoped the mage would take as a warning. The anxious crowd didn't understand this procession as Randler was guided, unbound, to a meeting chamber on the third floor.

The room was coated in well-polished brown stone. The striations in the stone made it look more like petrified wood, but wooden structures were dangerous in a tower where fire could literally flare from the fingers of its inhabitants. This at least gave the semblance of being an oaken study with a grand table for greeting important guests.

"It will not be long before Dariak arrives." Pyron offered a glass of red wine, which the bard refused, then he sat across from Randler and shook his head. "It is remarkable if you think you will be able to take Dariak alive from this place, after what he has done."

"And what, indeed, has he done?"

"He accomplished what he set out to do," Pyron explained, his voice growing cold and menacing. "He murdered Kerrish. One opponent down with no hope of defense or protection. He will be escorted to the king for execution."

"I see." Randler remained calm. "That would explain why you have summoned the guard then. I had thought it was merely a result of your defensive routines."

"Well, it is a—" Pyron stopped and narrowed his eyes. "How would you know of our defensive procedures?"

"I am a bard. I soak in information and turn it to use as needed."

"A walking library, then?" the mage scoffed. "You think of yourself too highly."

Randler knew he needed to keep the conversation going and that he had to avoid speaking of his apparent abilities at all costs, for Frast was still outside and would be unable to provide the spells now that Randler was out of range. "I only know that I was welcomed to this magnificent tower and given free rein to walk around, to explore the library, and to speak with its denizens. You have factions here that are straining against each other, even on your own Council. There are those who would experiment with wilder magic, and those who would quell the very thought. The part that confuses me the most is why Delminor's work has been cast aside and is so horribly disdained."

Pyron's lip twitched, for the minstrel was too astute. "There is no cause for me to discuss these issues with the likes of you."

"Of course not; however, it does seem as if you mages have been locked in this tower for far too long, if you have forgotten your roots. People disagree all the time, but that's a natural course of humanity. That is how we grow, by having conflicting theories and exploring them. But can you truly tell me that Delminor's work is at the heart of evil? That his son is seeking some vicious revenge?"

"Dariak arrived and demanded the jades, but his request was thwarted. A key member of the opposition was then alone with Dariak and with that opportunity, Dariak murdered him."

Randler shook his head. "It sounds too convenient. Dariak was trying to free Gabrion from the Trial, if I recall. Kerrish was needed for that process to happen, and volunteered himself to the task."

Pyron rose to his feet, his face flushed. He slammed his hands on the table as he shouted, "And once the task was complete, Dariak summoned a powerful firestorm that eradicated his enemy!"

"That isn't the Dariak I know," Randler said. "Though I would have assumed that an accomplished mage who serves on the Council would be able to counter such a spell, and being the elder of the two, probably had a deeper understanding of the spell itself."

"Enough! You will not spin this tale on its head, young bard."

The reaction told Randler much. Pyron was holding on to one version of the story for some specific reason and wasn't willing to consider any other options. He wondered if it had to do with alliances within the Council or perhaps there was some other complication with Kerrish's death that only this mage knew. His vehement reply also suggested that Pyron had considered the alternative and was actively denying it. Randler wondered how strong the mage's conviction was to hold on to that tale.

"I did not mean to anger you, Master Pyron," the minstrel apologized graciously. "I was merely making conversation until my friend arrives."

"Bah! Conversation indeed. If you wish to speak to me of important matters, then discuss your powers with me. How are you channeling magic through music?"

"As I told you already, I will share that knowledge once I see that Dariak is well and not before then. But I will tell you that it was Dariak's own insight during our journey together that led me to this discovery. You would be a fool to kill him and lose all the advances he could bring to the mages."

Enraged, Pyron lost his temper and before he realized what he was doing, he lashed out at Randler with a set of lightning flares. He'd only had a few seconds' notice when the mage's finger sparked, but Randler reacted before the bolts were released. He withdrew two daggers and jabbed them into the armrests of his chair. He then grabbed his drum and strummed a fast, erratic rhythm upon its surface. By then, the mage had drawn enough power and unleashed his blast. As he had hoped, after watching Dariak deflect the lightning bolts back at the Prisoner's Tower, the lightning veered toward the daggers. What he didn't know was that Frast had set up a reflective shield around him, which took the lightning and turned it back toward its caster.

Pyron accepted the blast and fell. The mages along the walls who had remained silent and out of sight rushed in to their master; all save one, who rushed forward and firmly grabbed Randler's shoulder. The bard slightly turned his head to speak with his captor. "I merely defended myself. I spoke only words, yet he attacked me. Remember this moment for it will surely portend much."

The hand clutching his shoulder gripped more firmly, causing him to wince. "Shh."

Randler half expected Pyron to rise up, make some wild accusation, and then send him for execution along with Dariak. What he did not expect was Pyron to hoist himself up, dust off his robes, and laugh.

"Crafty, bard. Crafty. I will give you that much." He rubbed his arm to combat a twinge from the shock and then he sat down. "I did not expect your form of magic to work so speedily, but you did well."

"That was a test?" Randler asked skeptically.

Caught, Pyron frowned. "Of sorts," he evaded. "But your skills do seem to extend well. Reflecting magic is usually difficult to do and requires mimicking the movements of the caster, yet you merely tapped a pattern on your drum."

"Ah, well, it was the tempo of the pattern that turned the spell back toward you. Here, I will play it for you again," which he did.

Pyron listened intently and his brows furrowed. "It certainly cannot be as easy as that. What was the purpose of those daggers?"

Randler grinned. "You call me crafty, yet here you are trying to get me to divulge my secrets without honoring your part of the bargain."

"If there were a society of bards, such as we have a Council of Mages here, I would name you among the most prominent members. You are no mere warbler of tales. You have true insight and a definite gift." Randler tipped his head at the compliment as Pyron continued, "And I see now that I will not succeed without showing you what you wish to see. But I must alert you; Dariak is a dangerous mage and he is bound so that he cannot utilize his powers. You will see him alive, but he will not be able to interact with you. We cannot release him."

Randler was affronted. "You can't simply bring fifty mages together with spells at the ready and allow him to speak? That is absurd."

"He would kill us all as likely as not and there may not be enough time to react if he did. Enough of this, though. Come." He paced across the room without looking back. Randler followed, noting that the mage who had been grabbing his shoulder stayed close by, cowl pulled low, only grunting at the bard and shoving him when he hesitated.

Randler wasn't happy ascending another two flights of stairs, for it meant the exit was that much further away. Each delay also gave the king's guard more time to approach, and that was an added complication he hadn't anticipated. He hoped Frast was safely out of sight as the night deepened.

The cold iron door swung open and admitted them to a holding room. There were bars lining the walls, but they were only decorative, from what Randler could see. This wasn't a cell, just fashioned to look like one from the inside. There were no scuff marks anywhere from prisoners trying to escape or spells being cast. It was simply a cold, dank sort of room.

In the center was an odd sight. Randler's eyes focused on the warbled mass that rested on the floor. A strange cloth-like coating enwrapped the outer husk like a large cocoon. Silver bindings wound through the hull, creating a pattern that repeated itself all along the shell. He approached and felt a warm emanation from it, then he hesitated for a moment. It was a blessing that he could sense it, for if he had walked right into the energy, his claim of channeling magic through music would have lost its merit, for it would have alerted Pyron that he had no connection to the energies after all.

Stepping cautiously, Randler moved around the mass and nearly crumbled when he saw two puffy blue eyes peering up at him. Dariak was so tightly entombed, only the bridge of his nose up to his forehead could be seen. His mouth was covered and he clearly had no hope of speaking, much less of casting a spell.

"This is outrageous!" Randler gasped. "How does he eat or drink?"

"He doesn't," Pyron said coldly. "What need does he have for such things when he is to be slain anyway?"

Randler was stunned. "But it's been a week since you captured him. He has had no food or drink in all that time?"

Pyron's voice was emotionless. "It has taken longer for the king's guard to arrive than usual."

"Release him, so I may hear his voice!"

"You do not make demands here, bard."

The door opened and several other mages entered. Pyron acknowledged them with a nod, but some were angry. "What is the meaning of this, Pyron? You would give the friend of this murderer visiting rights?"

Pyron answered, "Easy, Farrenok, this situation is under control."

"Indeed!" the petulant mage responded. "*His* control! Dariak's death has already been delayed for long enough. Now he gets to play with his friends? You're not fit to lead us any longer."

"Here! Here!" cackled old Lorresh. "Let's put an end to this now."

"Calm down. There is no harm being done here!" Pyron shouted over the muttering that started. "This bard has a knowledge of a skill that he will trade merely for seeing Dariak alive."

"You skew our agreement, mage," Randler warned. "I was to take Dariak."

Now Pyron roared. "And I did not commit to that!"

"What skill?" asked Shelloni, who had been one of Dariak's supporters before the news of Kerrish's murder.

Pyron calmed enough to explain. "He is able to cast spells without the use of spell components or the old language."

"Impossible!" cried Farrenok.

"Preposterous," echoed Lorresh.

"Show them," Pyron challenged, turning to Randler.

The bard frowned. Now he was stuck. "What good will that do? Will your thirst for knowledge stave off your hunger for blind revenge? Will either Dariak or I walk free from this place? Safe from you, who all have bloodlust in your eyes?"

The mage who had gripped Randler's shoulder in the other chamber stepped forward and repeated the gesture harshly. Something then poked Randler in the back, and the bard assumed it was a dagger.

He had no choice. He chose the flute, for if this would be his last song, he wanted it to come from his last breath of air. "My greatest lament is that we could not solve this any other way." He breathed deeply and blew across the mouthpiece, crafting a slow, melancholy tone that tugged at everyone who heard it. What surprised him, though, was the unbidden coldness that fell from the ceiling of the room. The mages collectively gasped as snow fluttered down, created solely from the wailing notes on the flute.

"I—I don't believe it!" Farrenok fell to his knees.

"How are you doing that?" Shelloni demanded. "I feel the energies coming from you, but you uttered not a single word."

Randler needed a moment to think of a response anyway, for he was as surprised as they. It was a moment, however, he did not receive, for in the huddled mass in the center of the floor, Dariak suddenly moaned, drawing everyone's attention. Randler tried to step forward, but his shadow grabbed him and yanked him to the floor, smothering him. Seconds later, all Randler could hear were gasps from the other mages and shouts and cries to bolt the door. Then spellfire flew across the room and mages screamed in agony.

Yet Randler could not see them, pinned as he was. He struggled to rise up, but his captor wrestled him well and kept him down.

"Kill him! Kill him!" Farrenok panicked, but then fell to the floor with a hard crash. Lorresh fell soon after.

All Randler could feel was the mage lying on top of him casting incessantly, though he uttered not a sound. Soon the chaos ended and the mage pulled himself slowly away, then withdrew his hood.

"Frast!" Randler gasped. "I don't understand."

"There's no time. We have to move. Now!" He grabbed Randler's arm and dragged him toward the door.

"But Dariak!"

"There's nothing you can do for him right now. We *have to* move! Go!"

CHAPTER 25

The Castle Town of Hathreneir

TRAVELING TO THE castle took a few days but it was a relatively easy journey for a group of skilled fighters and mages. Creature attacks were fended off without casualties, just minor injuries in some cases. Gabrion rode astride a horse, bedecked in the antimagic armor he had received from Herchig. Nearly one hundred of the fighters in the group had been fitted for the special attire, meaning that over two-thirds of the sword-bearing army were ready for battle. Beyond that, the thirty or so mages wore their own vestments so they could reach their spell components more easily.

Gabrion still marveled that any of the citizens of Marritosh would join his cause, but in talking with the defectors, he came to understand why. The king of Hathreneir was a strict ruler and, like Gabrion's own king, caught up in his own affairs. Whenever the kingdom required soldiers, for instance, they were taken from the surrounding populace, and because Marritosh was the closest settlement to the castle, they were the first victims. Many stepped up nobly and served with honor and for a touch of glory, but the stores of men in such esteem had long ago joined the king; for several years now, the volunteers were anything but voluntary.

Taxes were also higher these days, especially after the recent insurgence of fighting with Kallisor. At last, the people had grown tired of the pillaging of their town by their own monarch and it was those rebels who joined Ervinor's side while they had waited for Gabrion's return.

Upon arriving, Gabrion looked at the castle and wondered at its construction. He only had Kaison to reference in terms of strategic defense, where his king's ancestors had enwrapped the castle with a vast city that would be trampled by invading forces long before anyone would reach the castle gate. Here, the situation was different.

The castle itself was designed more for military defense than architectural beauty. Battlements lined the walls like teeth, but not in the decorative manner he had seen in Kallisor. These looked menacing, like a giant maw ready to devour invaders. He withheld a shiver at the thought, scanning for any signs of movement, though they were still some distance away.

There was a defensive wall, too, surrounding the castle, but it was low enough to seem barely useful. He wondered if there was a deep moat surrounding the wall that he couldn't see, or if the kings of Hathreneir were arrogant enough to leave such a low barrier. Had he consulted the mages about it, they would have told him that other defenses hovered about the stone, though they would be unlikely to identify them without being much closer.

In front of the wall was a marketplace. It wasn't a bazaar with tents and lean-tos, but the stalls were set firmly in the ground and made of stone. There was little organization to the layout of the shops themselves, which made bargain-hunting a bit of a chore, but was probably arranged purposely by the merchants themselves for that very reason. Between the rows of shops on either side was a cobbled square and it was here the army stepped with poise.

Gabrion and Ervinor dismounted and approached the nearest guard. The young man was suited in the finest emerald satin and though he held himself with purpose and strength, he looked as if he had never done more in his life than stand still and await orders. He saluted the newcomers with precision and asked them their business.

"Greetings, friend. I am Gabrion from Kallisor and I come to entreat with your king."

The young soldier appraised Gabrion's attire, then looked over the warrior's shoulder at the armed forced waiting behind him. A deep frown flickered on the young man's face before he cleared his throat and spoke clearly, "I am Azosh, page to the king of Hathreneir. Do you come with peaceful intent or otherwise?"

Ervinor laughed despite himself. "If we came meaning harm, would we announce it?"

Gabrion nudged him to silence. "There is no need for us to fight. I have two requests for his majesty and then we will depart. I bring my supporters only to give weight to my requests."

Azosh focused on Gabrion. "And if the king refuses these requests? What guarantee can I have that your forces here will not retaliate?"

"You have only my word." Gabrion held the man's stare and it was here that he understood why this unimposing youth was at the gate's entrance. Like his contest with Herchig, he felt his soul being scoured during the silent exchange.

At last the man nodded. "Very well. Then your safety within the walls will be assured for the duration of your stay, so long as you remain to your intent and raise no trouble within. You will be allowed to enter, but your presence and intent must first be announced to his majesty. Settle your troops out here and I will fetch you when the time is nigh."

He couldn't ask for more than that. He agreed and the man whisked away down a flagstone path and toward the castle, where he disappeared.

"That went well." Ervinor snorted. "At least we weren't banished immediately, right?"

"I wonder if I will actually meet with the king or speak with a chancellor or something," Gabrion agreed. "Keep your eyes open for additional guards entering the marketplace. They might be delaying us so they can prepare an ambush."

"It would seem the best course of action on their part. That and he took notice of our armor, so they must be extra suspicious of your purpose." Ervinor then turned and barked out a few orders to his lieutenants, who in turn set the troops at relative ease. They were to mingle casually among the market, but remain alert for the order to reassemble. In groups of four and five, the army dispersed, though a number of them remained in the central square.

Gabrion admired Ervinor's command of the army. Sure, he had spent time getting to know them, too, but Ervinor held their utmost respect. He still believed they were more Ervinor's troops than his own. After all, what had he actually done to bring them together anyway?

Much of Gabrion's quest had involved waiting and this request for an audience with the king was no exception. He adopted a stoic pose and focused his energies on his purpose for coming. He would request Mira's release and he would ask about the piece of jade remaining here. Dariak might currently be stuck in Magehaven, but he trusted Randler and Frast to find a way to free him. They would still need the jades if their hopes to bring peace would come to fruition.

"Deep in thought," mocked a voice Gabrion had not heard in some time. He started at the sound of it, and turned to look at the thief who had snuck up behind him so successfully.

"It's been a while, Poltor. I'm glad you're well. Have you seen—?"

"Shh," the man interrupted, keeping his voice low and menacing. "Ask not of people I may or may not know. I will not tell you anything in either regard, but I'd rather not be connected to anyone else in any form. However, you're someone I respect in some way and so I will enlighten you about some recent events since my time here."

"Any light—"

"Shh," Poltor hissed again. "I'm not telling you anything that's newsworthy if you're in the know. And if you're seeking to speak with the king, then you ought to be in the know."

"I've only just arrived."

Poltor jabbed him in the ribs before Gabrion even registered any movement. Apparently, The Mist still had all of his skills in check. "There was some sort of attack on Magehaven not long ago. The foolish mages sent for help. I guess their skills were not strong enough."

"Sent for help?" Gabrion asked, already knowing about the altercation, having played a major part in it. It was unnerving to think of troops approaching Magehaven while Randler and Frast attempted to rescue Dariak.

"Indeed. Defensive measures here require the king to dispatch a troop of soldiers to their defense. They've already left and should be reaching the tower by now if they haven't already." The thief pressed Gabrion's shoulder as a warning not to move. He then stepped off and disappeared in the shadows.

Moments later, the verdantly clad page appeared and saluted to Gabrion. "His royal majesty of Hathreneir will hear your request. He has accepted my council and you are to be admitted alone."

"Alone?" he balked, remembering the last time he had entered a castle without help, over a year ago. "Surely I am permitted a handful of my men as a show of good faith."

The man frowned. "Very well. You may bring two others. I will collect you an hour hence." Azosh clicked his heels and stormed off, annoyed that Gabrion hadn't accepted entering alone, though clearly he hadn't been expected to.

Before the warrior could think about whom to bring with him, Poltor was back, standing behind him and whispering in his ear. "Leave your commander here. He will need to maintain order in your absence. Take another soldier and one of your mage friends, so they can watch for subversion while you are inside."

"How about you?" Gabrion breathed. "You'd be a better bodyguard than anyone."

Poltor scoffed at the notion. "I do not show my face without good reason. Besides, I have other work to attend to. Go and choose wisely, but ask your mates if they've heard news. I must be off." And with that, the thief was gone.

Gabrion cleared his head and sought out Ervinor to update him on the situation. He agreed with Poltor's advice and suggested that Gabrion take Quereth with him and Morrish, an orphan of Kallisor who felt tremendous pride for his homeland, despite the harshness his life had shown him.

"But before you go, the others have heard some interesting things, Gabrion," Ervinor noted. "A faction was sent off to support the mages. Also, some major scuffle happened within the castle recently, but no one knows what it was about or what happened. Defenses have been ramped up because of these things. Apparently, sending troops off to Magehaven didn't sit well with some people in light of other events. Everyone is on edge."

"That probably explains why they tried to get me to go in alone."

"I'm sure it does," Ervinor agreed. "But there's more. The biggest news, Gabrion, is that the fighting apparently hasn't been going well at the border, so though they're on alert here, many fighters have been dispatched to the east."

"That's either good or bad for our visit."

"Yes. So be careful, Gabrion. If we have no word from you by nightfall…"

Gabrion clapped Ervinor's shoulder. "Be at ease, friend. If I am well and night approaches, I will send word to you so you'll know." They established a set of secret messages and if none of them was included in the missive, then Ervinor would know that Gabrion's safety had been jeopardized.

Azosh approached Gabrion at the end of the hour. "Are you ready, my lord? These are the two who will accompany you?"

"Yes. Quereth and Morrish," he said by way of introduction.

"Very well," he responded with a hint of impatience. He then strode purposely forward while Gabrion and the others followed closely behind.

The inner sanctum of the castle was as cold and hard as the external walls. Gabrion wondered how anyone actually chose to live with such stark features and jutting lines everywhere. There was a militaristic elegance to it, but he would have preferred a little more softness here and there. He wondered idly if the king sat upon a rock-hewn throne or if at least the throne room would have better furnishings.

Of course, the castle was designed as such to keep visitors on edge. Most of the castle grounds were loaded with lush tapestries and rich gardens, but this direct passageway toward the audience chamber and its anteroom were kept bare of any welcoming elements.

They hadn't had much time to strategize, but Quereth gently touched Gabrion's left shoulder blade, an indication that magical wards were protecting this room, but that there was no immediate danger. Had the hand touched Gabrion's shoulder, then the warrior would have gone on deeper alert. Morrish spotted no hidden guards and so kept his hands to his side and his eyes wide.

After a short delay, the three were brought to King Prethos' chamber. They walked in respectfully, with heads slightly bowed and backs held straight. Gabrion noted a richer atmosphere in this room, but it was still mostly barren and uninviting.

Two elegantly carved wooden thrones awaited at the end of a slate walkway that was highlighted with cobblestones on either side. It looked more like a town road than the welcome carpet to the king; nonetheless, he walked with pride and knelt briefly in respect.

"Rise, citizen of Kallisor. My page tells me you have requests?"

The king's voice cut like steel and held more power than arrogance. He truly sounded the part of a man whose word was rarely questioned, if ever, and whose decisions were enacted without hesitation, yet with respect. His own king had sounded abrasive and bullying, compared to the rich tenor in this man's voice.

"Greetings, your majesty. Indeed, I do have some requests."

"By what intent do you enter my court to make these requests? Come you here by the will of your king? Does that explain the presence of your troops at my gate?" He never raised his voice, but Gabrion could feel the anger anyway.

"No, sire. In the end, I seek a means of ending all the warring."

Before he could continue, the king laughed mirthlessly. "Unless you possess the authority of your king to subjugate your country to mine, then that is unlikely to transpire."

"I do not come at the behest of my king," Gabrion returned sharply. "His will isn't one of compromise, and I'm hoping that your mind is more open to a peaceable resolution to this ongoing threat to our lands. We endlessly lose resources, both in the lands that are trampled and the people whose lives are lost. There must be a way of ending this conflict."

The king tilted his head ever so slightly. "You do not speak like a conqueror. Come then, ask me of your requests."

"I have two, your majesty. In the first, over a year ago, your forces invaded my homeland of Savvron and you took a close friend of mine as prisoner. I would have her returned to me unharmed."

The king's brows furrowed. "We have no prisoners here, young warrior. Certainly not from some unnamed village in Kallisor."

Emotions swirled up within Gabrion. His pride took a hit for the comment about his town being unnamed, despite having just offered its name, yet that blow was the least of what he felt. His heart felt like he had been stabbed, for if there were no prisoners, then surely Mira— He pushed the thought away, but it persisted. Mira's face swirled into his thoughts but he already knew—of course he knew—that she was gone. Keeping a maiden from a random village prisoner for a year? Thinking about it now, it made no logical sense to him. Part of his conscience mocked him, while another piece crumbled miserably. A searing pain burned in his heart and all he wanted to do was fall to the ground and cry out in agony. All his questing, all his tribulations, and here at the end, there was no Mira waiting for him. Gabrion felt suddenly empty and he didn't know what to do or why he was there.

"Your other request?" the king prompted.

There was something else he was supposed to ask for. Something important. Something that mattered. But all he wanted to do was raise his sword and cut down this man whose forces had attacked his village and taken his one true love away from him. And all this time later, the name of his village was insignificant to the man. It didn't register to him. It mattered nothing. He wanted to skip the second half of his request and call out for Ervinor to set the army on the castle; to take down the fighters who were here and to simply destroy them all.

He wanted to leave them as empty as he felt now.

A hand clutched Gabrion's shoulder tightly and brought him back to the moment. Morrish was shaking him, trying to bring his focus to the king. Glancing around, Gabrion could see that a few of the king's guards had stepped forward with the warrior's reaction to the news. His silence was clearly disturbing, but so was his hand, which was clutching his sword hilt so tightly his knuckles were white.

It took tremendous strength of will for Gabrion not to lose himself in the loss of Mira. Suspecting it and hearing about it were very different things. Now it was a reality and his world had changed. But, he reminded himself, his whole purpose in coming here was to help the world to change. He needed to continue Dariak's quest and from there forge a new land.

He composed himself and cleared his throat. "I am sorry. She was a dear friend and—" He stopped himself and breathed deeply. "Since the one request is denied me, perhaps you will see fit to make retribution by honoring my second request."

The king sat back in his throne, but he was clearly tensed and ready to move, in case the emotions warring on Gabrion's face erupted physically. "Go on, though I make no promises."

"At the end of the War of the Colossus, the mage Delminor summoned a giant from the power he claimed from the pieces of jade. Those pieces were scattered across our kingdoms. One such shard lies here in your possession. I ask for that piece of jade."

The king stared at him intently and then laughed wildly. Already wounded by the first bit of news, Gabrion tensed into a fighting stance, though luckily he neglected to pull his blade. Quereth and Morrish both grabbed him to restrain him just in case. "Oh, young warrior," the king said with an amused smirk. "Even if I could give you that jade, I would not lightly hand it over to one such as you. As it happens, it is no longer in my possession."

Gabrion scanned the man's face and realized that he spoke truly. "It is vital that I find it."

"You're no mage who can wield its power. Or is your friend here the one who would do so?" He looked over at Quereth.

"No, my lord." The old mage bowed his head. "But his quest is true nonetheless."

"I see." The king narrowed his eyes and considered Gabrion thoughtfully. "I will tell you this much, young warrior, in the hopes that you will recognize truth when you hear it and thus leave this place afterward. The jade was stolen several days ago and I do not think it likely you will find it anywhere within my castle or its immediate surround—"

A guardsman entered from the western door and strode purposely toward the king, ignoring the visitors. He leaned into his monarch's ear, whispered something, then fled as quickly as he had come. The king's face turned to stone and he lost his path of thought as he looked at Gabrion and the others. Then he blinked several times and waved a hand in the air. The Kallisorians pushed themselves to alertness, wondering what was coming next.

"Forgive me this intrusion," the king said with a dramatically formal tone. "An urgent matter has come to my attention and I must interrupt our audience momentarily. If you will follow my page here, I will reconvene with you shortly." He then spoke to the page who appeared at his side, "Berral, take our visitors to the gardens."

Gabrion didn't care. All he knew was that he would be able to have a moment to digest his conversation with the king and take a few moments to grieve before planning anew. He needed the hiatus, so he didn't argue at all. He nodded to the king and silently followed the page out the eastern door, trying to hold himself together.

CHAPTER 26

The Imprisoned Mage

DARIAK LAY ON the cold stone floor, cursing his luck. He thought he could talk to Pyron, but with the other masters in the room, he didn't have a real chance. He wished now he had just gone for the jades.

As the magical bindings were set around him, he had crashed to the ground and anguished tears fell from his eyes. He had sworn never to be incarcerated again, and yet he was helpless at a time when he needed to be strong. The bindings trapped him like giant vines and he could feel the antimagic spells contained within them. They were designed to absorb magical energy and to cast it outward, inert. The energy came off in the form of heat and the more magic he tried to use, the hotter his cell became.

Also covered was his mouth, thereby limiting a majority of his power. No hands to form and shape the energies. No words to empower them. He was at a severe loss. He had a few spells he could call that would respond to his thoughts alone, but, like most nonverbal spells, they were not enough to effect an escape.

For the first couple hours of his newfound imprisonment, Dariak tried the few spells he could, hoping to work his way out from the spell-trappings. Yet neither fire nor water were helpful forces. The ribbons would not burn, and even wet, he was not slippery enough to wriggle out of them. Of course, he understood well enough that the bindings themselves were likely bound to him as if they were more alive than simple rope. It would be a complex spell, but he was in Magehaven. There would be no reason for them not to use their strongest abilities to ensnare him.

What he didn't understand at first was why they didn't just kill him for his alleged transgression. If he had truly murdered Kerrish, then why let Dariak breathe for even a moment more? Surely some of the others immediately petitioned for Dariak's execution. And perhaps, he considered, his death would be made into a show against all who would thwart the Council. Considering some of its members, Dariak conceded that it must be the case.

It took time for him to calm himself enough to rationalize. There wasn't time to postulate who would want him alive and who would seek his imminent death. He couldn't waste effort on weak spells that were doomed to fail against his bonds. Yet the stress of helping Gabrion escape his Trial, the realization of Kerrish's martyred suicide, and sudden imprisonment all took their toll on him.

Perhaps it was a day later—or maybe hours, he had no idea—when he could think calmly again. No one had come to his cell and it confirmed his suspicions of a public execution. He had no idea of the assault on the tower that Gabrion, Randler, and the others had led while trying to flee. He was unaware of all the other mages who had died during that escape. All he hoped was that his friends were gone from the tower and off somewhere safe.

Part of him didn't want to acknowledge it, but he wasn't entirely sure that their group could have escaped unscathed, not with the hundreds of mages who lived within the tower who could rise up and protect against those intruders. And though he didn't want to consider that Gabrion and Randler had fallen, he had to admit that it could have happened. If he didn't accept it as a possibility now, then it would swell up against him when he least expected it and, considering his predicament, he needed to be sharp and ready.

Hunger pains set in, though the bonds pressing against him helped alleviate some of the discomfort. There was no water to be had, so he worked to pull moisture from the air. Every enactment of magic caused the coils to heat up, but he didn't care. He needed the water. Because his mouth was sealed, he had the added complication of condensing the liquid inside his nose and then trying to guide it magically in toward his mouth without choking on the drops. It was painstaking, but it kept him busy.

Because of the nature of the bonds, he could not establish a set of spells that would continue to hydrate him in that fashion. The magical threads drew the magic away and each casting was like trying to climb a mountain during an avalanche. Yet he stayed firm and pulled the moisture when he needed it most. As time went on, though, the need grew stronger and stronger.

Eventually, Dariak's survival instincts inspired him. Hadn't he been traveling with the jades all this time? Couldn't their powers overcome even this binding? He felt foolish when the thought crossed his mind, for he hadn't considered seeking the jades' help. Sharice would scold him, he admonished himself, and then he smiled at the thought of her. She was ruthless, difficult, and unbending. Yet when Dariak had proven to be stronger, she folded. But, he reminded himself, it was the jades that had given him their power. He hadn't done anything more than allow himself to be an open conduit for the lightning jade. The experience had shaken him and he only recently had stopped having random tremors from the residual energy.

Yet times were desperate again. He needed to turn into a bolt of electricity right now and blaze his way out of the bonds. He needed that energy to escape. Without it, he was lost. Dariak closed his eyes and communed with the jade that was still in his pocket. It resonated with his thoughts and he smiled. Pyron had to have known that Dariak possessed the jades, yet they were bound with him and not removed. He wondered if it was fear. They would have needed to undo his restraints in order to fish around for the jades and perhaps in that time, Dariak could find a way to escape. He wondered, and not for the first time, if the jades themselves had protections that kept others from seeking them on his person. Or perhaps, more simply, their attention was elsewhere. Indeed, several mages had needed healing or burying after the escape of Dariak's companions, not that he knew that.

Dariak breathed deeply through his nose to steady his thoughts. He called to the lightning jade and shared with it his desperation. He could feel the anger within the crystal thrashing about, seeking release. The mage opened his mind wider to allow the lightning to possess him, though he also had to focus his thoughts so as not to allow other ideas to intrude. It was one of the earliest mage-oriented lessons his father had taught him, through his mother who read Delminor's memoirs to their son. Opening the mind to the energies allowed them to fill him, but it would also let them run rampant if he didn't control them. He thought of it like an inverted funnel, where on one end there was a vast open expanse, ready and waiting, but to get there required passing a narrower channel.

The lightning sparked through his body. He could feel it running down one leg and up the other, leaving a trail of sharp numbness behind. It was like a fine knife cutting into his skin, followed immediately by a healing spell that nullified the pain, followed moments later by that unshakable feeling like when he would sit with his legs crossed for too long. He ignored all the discomfort that came to him, and begged for the jade to continue to strengthen him.

Drawing the electricity through him brought the strange numbness to all of his limbs and then to his chest and his face. He could feel the energy starting to flow through him. It was an agonizingly slow process, considering that in his fight against Sharice, the change had been so sudden. He strained to pull the energies upward, through, and around, egging them on to flow frantically on their own. All he felt for his troubles was his body temperature increase from the effort. Soon he was sweating, and with his dehydration, he knew it was dangerous. But without the lightning, he had no idea how he would escape.

In the end, he couldn't maintain the electric flow. His body did not turn into lightning. He did not escape his bonds. Dejected, he grunted in annoyance, unable to think clearly at first. However, once his anguish subsided, he realized that the magical coils had been absorbing the energy from the lightning jade, and that's why his body had become so hot. He was essentially cooking himself.

But now... now what? The mages had included elemental counterspells in the restraints. He understood now that there was no way he could use the lightning, earth, or water jades. Hopelessness began to well within him. His father's name was being destroyed by these mages whose very spells were those invented by Delminor. And here he was, trapped by a set of those same spells. This, then, would be where he died.

He hated to wallow. It infuriated him, but he couldn't deny his disappointment. His body grew weaker as time went on. Soon it took tremendous effort to pull any moisture from the air and he wondered what was worse; dying of dehydration or dying alone. Perhaps pitying himself was the worst feeling of all. It made his heart and will feel weak.

He was stronger than that, he told himself. Hadn't he done the unthinkable, by entering Gabrion's mind through his Trial and helping him to free himself from his own inner prison? Hadn't he made the most of his time in the Prisoner's Tower by crafting a wide array of complex spells, such as the one he used to extract the rare reptigon serum? Wasn't he the son of Delminor, who had unlocked the secrets of the jades and summoned the colossus in an attempt to end the wars?

Dariak's resolve strengthened. He compared it to one of Gabrion's swords, resting at first as a lump of molten iron, then poured into a mold, and later hammered into shape and sharpened to perfection. He was the same. He was once just a boy who loved his father. Now he was the one chance left in the world of restoring Delminor's name by completing his work the way it was meant to be. But to do so, he needed to be strong now. He needed to be sharp so that he could break through these bindings.

Gabrion had the glass jade. The mages might not have a counterspell set up against that, but it wouldn't help him now. He didn't have the strength to try to use that jade's magic on his own. Besides, for a working like that without the jade, he would need spell components to unlock the energies, as well as his fingers and voice. No, he needed something else that was obscure. He needed help from a source that the mages would not have anticipated in their haste.

Dariak's blood tingled. He thought at first that it was the lightning jade rising up to his call, but this was different. It was inside of him. And yet it wasn't. He closed his eyes, half delirious at this point, and allowed his mind to flow along with his bloodstream. Through his head, then down to his heart, he plodded along. Then down the left side and again up toward the right. It reminded him of the energy flow that he had established to heal Kitalla all those months ago. The energies followed his blood's circulation, but nothing else was happening.

He knew what the problem was. He wasn't listening. He was just along for the ride. He was letting other thoughts get in the way and carry him. Mind wide, but focused, Dariak reminded himself. The journey started again and as he went, he felt tiny glimmers all along the way, like a multitude of stars shining inside his body. It didn't make any sense; there wasn't any untapped power within him. Randler was so focused on the Forgotten Tribe and the lost generational line, that Dariak suddenly wondered if maybe… maybe…

But Sharice had been adamant. Dariak was too strong-willed to be a descendant of the Forgotten Tribe and those cowardly sons who had fled the warring to save themselves. Could those stories even be true? It wouldn't matter anyway, for if they were, Dariak was not descended of them. His lineage traced back to other lines, he was certain. No, it wasn't him. He didn't have some dormant power within him that was trying to call to him now.

He groaned. His thoughts were rambling and because of that, he was losing his control. He could still feel the pinpricks within his blood, but he couldn't make sense of them, especially if his mind was wandering. He bit on his lip gently to try to help himself concentrate. He had seen Gabrion do that when he was deep in thought and it make him chuckle for a moment, the big tough warrior, lost in thought. Not that Gabrion wasn't smart, but sometimes he looked the part of a bungling oaf, naïve and trusting his surroundings. He even saw it in himself, considering his appearance within the Trial as a blind ogre. He—

Dariak grunted again. Hunger and thirst were making this so difficult. Logically, he knew a number of days had passed by. He had fallen asleep several times without realizing it, and the thoughts continued when he awoke. No one had come to check on him, and unless his estimate of the time was grossly wrong, then it meant that something else had happened. Yet the more time he wasted here in thought, the more likely he would never escape.

After many attempts, Dariak's desperation empowered him to follow the stabbing pains within his bloodstream. He knew they weren't because of malnutrition or dehydration. There was a distinct difference between them and the other ways his body ached. The pinpricks were becoming more persistent and harder to ignore. Perhaps it was a signal that he was dying and that the blood was poisoned, but he didn't dwell on it. Instead, he pushed his mind into his blood once more.

Down, around, up. Down, around, up. Down, around—wait!

He felt an extra pulse in his hip. No, not *in* his hip, against his hip. He hovered there for a moment and felt a pulsing energy that flashed with his heartbeat. He tried to remember what was there. Only a few minor spell components and the jades were with him. The jades were useless, though. The magical restraints were deflecting all their energies away.

The pulsing continued, so Dariak opened his mind wider and he reached out toward the source. An odd sensation overtook him, and he had felt it before. He was indeed contacting a jade, but it was one he had only recently claimed. It was a jade that had been near him, but he hadn't spent much time with at all, for Kitalla had kept it close to her heart ever since she had claimed it from Grenthar's dungeon.

Dariak let the metal jade pull him inside. It communicated to him in a strange manner. All he sensed was a rigid lattice with tiny gnats fluttering so rapidly he couldn't follow them. And as he looked, the lattice was able to weave and bend and reshape itself. It reminded him of that odd thought that had occurred to him days earlier about one of Gabrion's swords. He wondered now if the jade had planted the thought, trying to encourage him.

A sword was solid and rigid. It was powerful and could slice through anything, but a sword needed room to swing so it could build enough momentum to strike. Dariak was tightly enwrapped and had no room to swing. He didn't let hope fade away. He focused on the idea of a sword. If struck too hard, it could shatter. The pieces could be reassembled and mended. Yet to do so, they needed to be melted down a bit, or perhaps completely, in some cases. Iron, unlike wood, could withstand great heat and instead of burning, it would start to melt. It would draw in the heat and it would liquefy.

A bright light pierced Dariak's eyes, and he groaned against it. He thought he heard voices, but he was so focused on the metal jade that he barely paid them any heed. An image of Randler flashed before him and he was too disoriented to wonder if the bard was in his thoughts or if he was actually nearby.

It didn't matter anymore. The answer came to him. The pinpricks in his bloodstream called out to him, and he realized that there must somehow be metal inside his body, for why else would any part of his inner self resonate with the jade? He had had cuts before and sucked on the wound; hadn't the blood possessed an oddly metallic taste? He reached his mind into the jade and gave himself over to its power.

Yet nothing happened.

Scrabbling, Dariak reconsidered the sword and iron image. To fix the sword, it needed—

Dariak held on to the metal jade and kept his thoughts centered there, but he released a part of his mind to the lightning jade again. It was difficult being in two places at once, but he had partially succeeded doing so during Gabrion's Trial. He would be completely successful this time. He called to the lightning jade, demanding its energy to strengthen him.

The odd numbness started again, punctuated by the sharp spikes in his blood. None of it mattered, so long as the process worked. Then Dariak remembered that electricity was drawn toward metal, and part of him smiled. He channeled his thoughts differently, now, letting his consciousness spread fully through his own body. As he went, he triggered various metal buoys for the lightning to follow. The electricity chased eagerly, but the magical restraints did their work and drew strength from the lightning, which Dariak counted on. The bonds surrounding him heated up greatly and his body gained in temperature.

When he thought he would pass out from all the effort, Dariak reached into the metal jade, begging for his body to lose its form, and the metal jade drew on all the heat within him and obliged.

Dariak's thoughts whisked back to his head in time to see the world through his hazy eyes. It was a quick glimpse of mages surrounding him with two standing very close by. He felt a strange kinship to those two, but he couldn't recognize who they were at the moment. Suddenly, all the pain within him was gone. But so was the sensation of even having a body.

When the lightning jade had subjugated Dariak in the fight against Sharice, all he felt was energy. His physical senses ceased to function and he was drawn to places of energy and toward various metals. This experience was different in some ways, for he felt incredibly heavy, yet able to move. Like a rolling sludge, Dariak willed himself away from his restraints, and suddenly he had the sensation of tumbling wildly, like he was trapped in a lopsided barrel speeding down a steep hill. He couldn't control where he was going, but as long as it was away from the bindings, he was grateful.

The journey stopped all of a sudden, and so he tilted himself in another direction, and the rolling sensation turned into rapid somersaults. As he went, he felt energy strike against him, but rather than stop him, he gained momentum from the blasts. His rolling increased with each attack, but he had no sense of where anyone or anything was located. His only thoughts were of getting away from the restraints and escaping the room.

Despite the ceaseless spinning, he slowly gained a sense of other lifeforms in the area. He didn't know how he could be tumbling so much yet still have any inkling of life around him, but a snippet of thought wondered if it was the same metal in other people that he was sensing. As he rolled himself along toward one such lifeform, he felt searing heat strike against him. This angered him, but, as before, it also made him roll faster. He crashed into the mage and toppled him. He couldn't be sure of what was really happening, but he felt as if he was a rolling sludge of molten metal and that the mage died when he plowed into the man. At least, the sensation of life certainly ended after the contact.

Dariak felt the other lifeforms retreat away, or perhaps he was shrinking to an impossibly small size, he didn't know. Whatever the case, he knew only that he needed to escape. If they were fleeing, he needed to follow. It was hard to control his exact direction, but he kept tilting his thoughts toward those distant pinpricks of life energy and, with some effort, he made his way after them. He felt encouraged as he drew nearer, for it meant that he wasn't actually shrinking.

His awareness of the surroundings was better as a metallic blob than it had been as a bolt of lightning. Perhaps his density slowed him down enough that he could sense a little bit, but he soon realized that he was under attack. He had no way to counter the spells that were hurled toward him, so he leaned toward the sources until the spellcasting stopped. He was led through Magehaven and he had the sense that he was brought up several flights of stairs. They were difficult to traverse, but the added blasts of energy kept him going.

Part of him was amused that the mages kept throwing spells his way, not realizing that they were giving him what he needed to continue. But eventually, the run would end. All things did.

The life sparks started to dwindle after a while. His new form became very sluggish. He pushed hard to reach the next source of energy so that he could continue his rampage, and he was aware enough to understand that he was indeed rampaging. He couldn't stop yet or he would be completely unprotected. He had no idea what the aftereffects of this transformation would be, but he had to wait as long as possible before finding out.

One being was ahead of him and no others were nearby. This one person wasn't launching spells his way, so he guessed the mage figured out the secret. Without spells shooting at him, his tirade would end. He reached for that spark of life, but it was ever out of reach. Rolling forward, then sideways, then diagonally led all to the same unsatisfying result. Then he realized what must have happened. The person must have climbed up onto something, so Dariak tried to follow, but his heavy metallic self was unable to follow.

The one bit of food was all he could sense anywhere nearby, but it was beyond him. He could feel the effects of the jade starting to wear away. He tried to maintain this form, but he didn't have the strength to do so. He couldn't figure out anywhere to run to, for he was unable to sense walls and doors. Several attempts to roll away splattered him unsuccessfully against an obstacle, and he was too disoriented from the hunt to try to retrace any part of his path. He was also too tired and frantic to think of something methodical, like rolling along the walls until he passed through a doorway.

No, the jade's power was fading and when it was gone, Dariak lay defenseless in a heap on the floor, unable to move, and at the mercy of the other person in the room. His last thought before passing out completely was that even though he was about to die, at least he had escaped the restraints.

CHAPTER 27

Reminiscence

THE WARM SAND spread out in all directions and even under the nighttime sky, it held some of the warmth it had gained from the day. There was little commotion, as the men and women were asleep, save the few who remained on watch. The creatures of the desert were also still, avoiding the host of warriors, for they were a well-trained group that sprang to immediate action, even though they were not the king's elite forces. Feral monsters or not, they sensed the power here.

Yet though the host was calm, they were on a mission from the king and they pursued it with pride. It didn't matter that they expected to arrive uselessly beyond the time they were needed; their king required them and so they went. Perhaps their skills would be necessary anyway. While they slept, they dreamed of winning the king's favor, which could only improve their lower standings and thus conditions for their families who relied on their tenure of service to the crown.

Only one among them had thoughts wandering off in a different direction, and because she had to remain still while on watch, she could do nothing to distract herself from her reminiscence. Indeed, she had tried doing minor exercises to remain limber and to keep her mind quiet, but the captain had scolded her for the commotion. Rather, she was forced to battle within herself.

Leaving Magehaven and the life she had come to know was hard for Kitalla. Traveling with her companions had instilled her with a hope she hadn't expected to feel, and she had built a camaraderie that rivaled her thieving days with Poltor. Worse than that, though, were the growing emotions for Gabrion, whose noble spirit drew her despite all she knew about herself. No, she had made the right decision after her Trial in Magehaven. She couldn't afford to let her heart sway her so powerfully any longer. Besides, Gabrion wasn't even available to her anyway. He yearned too strongly for a ghost.

Kitalla punched the sand, then glanced around to ensure she hadn't disturbed anyone. She could leave this troop as soon as she wanted, but it was more convenient to travel with them for her current mission. She still couldn't believe she was doing it. Hadn't she just said to herself that she couldn't afford to let her emotions control her actions? She scoffed, shaking her head.

Her departure from Magehaven had been a rash decision, but with all the emotions she had been forced to relive in the Trial, she didn't have much choice. She had left the metal jade with Dariak and she missed its company. Something about the cold shard resonated with her, and she wasn't sure if it was its uniqueness, its loneliness, its power, or just her own need to feel close to something. Kitalla gritted her teeth with the last thought.

She had stormed from the tower and made directly for the castle. Though she was aware Poltor and the others had gone to Marritosh, she knew her old master well enough that he wouldn't remain in a small village for long, not when a ripe castle town wasn't far away. She had jogged toward the palace to reach it swiftly, ever ready to pull out her weapons to slay the desert creatures on her journey. But now that she was thinking about that trip, she barely remembered the fights at all. She had fended off reptigons and sandroaches without hesitation. Partly, she was grateful, because it echoed the ruthlessness of her thieving days. Yet it also meant there was no point to it, either.

The thief grabbed a fistful of sand and let it drift slowly between her fingers like an hourglass. It reminded her of how even Poltor had slipped away from her upon her arrival at the castle. It frustrated her deeply. Sure, she knew him well enough to locate him in the castle grounds, even dressed as a filthy manure merchant. However, he had treated her like a stranger in the daylight, using a broken dialect he had picked up in the dingier parts of Marritosh. So she had pursued him at night after doing some reconnaissance of her own.

The master thief hadn't received her well. Poltor expected her arrival, having denied her attention that day. Kitalla fell prey to the traps purposely so she could talk to him. He was all she had left in this world.

"If you continue to follow me, I will have you slain," Poltor had said by way of greeting.

"I wish to resume our old practices," she had responded.

"It's impossible. You've become too well-known in our kingdom and even here. You won't be able to escape into the shadows as in the old days. No, I won't have it, I'm afraid. It's a shame, though, for you were always talented."

"I'll prove to you I can—"

"No, Kitalla," he had said harshly. "You made your choices a year ago when you assisted that mage and left us all. Your ambitions are greater than the petty thieving we do, and you know it."

Her eyes had fallen low as the truth of it hit hard. "And you only followed us here so you could reach this place and start anew."

"It was an opportunity I could not deny." There was a long silence. "Out of respect for you, you may sleep in the loft here tonight, but then you and I are no longer acquainted."

She hadn't taken him up on it. It took everything she had, as she sat there on watch on the sand dune, not to grumble with aggravation and loss. Instead, she grabbed more sand and watched it rain down endlessly from her aching fists. Everything was rushing out of control.

She spent a few days in the castle town and within the palace itself. Unlike the alarmed gates in Kallisor, most citizens were allowed easy access to the castle grounds. It took wearing a crest in some prominent location to be allowed entry. It was something only the people of the area knew, but Kitalla could easily dig up information.

Obtaining the crest itself had taken a little effort, but sneaking into a hawker's hut and swiping a bandana took relatively no time at all.

She wore the bandana as a bracelet on her upper left arm, just below her shoulder. The image of an open, judging eye was surrounded by rays of a fiery sunlight, with birds wafting all around. She figured the eye represented the king, the sunlight signified the magical prowess of this country, and the fluttering birds were the citizens who would scatter under the king's wrath if they disobeyed. She didn't know if her assessment was at all accurate, but it amused her, nonetheless.

With the armband in place, she walked straight through the gates and into the castle itself. She spent a couple of days perusing the halls and getting a feel for the layout, while also surveying the castle's defenses. She hadn't decided what her goal was, but the information would be useful to her some day in some way, she just knew it.

Kitalla visited the well-kept library on two occasions. The first was an accidental turn down one corridor as she was attempting to trace an escape route from the kitchens, but because others were in the area, she didn't feel she could turn and go another direction without arousing suspicion. Her second trip was more purposeful.

Though the thief was distracted by her immediate quest of learning her surroundings, the past year kept swaying her thoughts. When she thought she had put enough distance between herself and her companions, some comment from a passerby or some basic magic spell sputtered from an acolyte always reminded her of Dariak and the others. She felt almost haunted by them.

The library beckoned to her after her first visit, for Randler's stories and songs swirled in her mind when things were otherwise quiet. He had spent so much of his life learning about the Forgotten Tribe that even Kitalla's curiosity had been piqued. She wondered if the library here would have a better record of the original king and queen's lineage than the library at Magehaven. She didn't really expect to find it, but the descendants of the king would probably want a historical record kept close to the castle.

Though she needed to maintain an authority about her while walking through the castle, it was perfectly acceptable to be lost within the library itself. There were a few scholars roaming around who were more than glad to help the less-educated find the tomes they sought. Kitalla didn't ask directly for a copy of the lineage, but instead sought guidance for the historical texts.

Mearan, the lanky scholar who helped her, was overjoyed to show her the section she was seeking. He practically floated through the library in dark black robes that were slightly too long, even for his tall frame. They were belted tightly around a narrow waist and Kitalla couldn't help but wonder if he would vanish if he turned sideways, he was so thin.

Once they were in the section, Kitalla practically ignored the scholar and let her eyes dart about, hoping to avoid wasting days in her search.

"For what period are you searching particularly?" Mearan asked.

She tried hard to keep a straight face when he spoke, for he pronounced things differently than most, and clearly it was a ruse to make people think he was more erudite than he was. For instance, he set heavy emphasis on the wrong vowels in most of the words, like the 'i' in 'period' and the 'u' in 'particularly.'

She composed herself quickly, "Well, I'm not entirely sure, now that I think of it. There was some incident my grandfather once spoke about that his grandfather had told him, from his own childhood."

"Do you have any recollection"—he started, pronouncing each letter individually, which forced Kitalla to bite her lip—"as to the nomenclature of the presiding liege at the time of interest?"

"The king… er, I don't, actually," she frowned.

"Hmm," Mearan had pondered for a moment. "It may have been Hallibar or Demollia, or perhaps Forithius, depending upon the longevity of your own family line." He then turned and pulled a book from a shelf and handed it to her. "Unless you have more specific details as to the time period in which you seek, then perhaps it would be best for you to peruse this volume and narrow down your search. Would you like my assistance or should I leave you this for the moment?"

Kitalla glanced down at the book and nearly dropped it in shock. He had handed her a copy of the royal family tree. She flipped open a few pages and saw an intricate number of lines and notes, such as "lineage continues on sheet 48" and "from hence the line has ended." It was exactly what she was looking for, but she wasn't entirely sure it would make sense.

"I think I will spend some time with this first and when I need you, I'll come for you." She touched his arm softly and winked enticingly, which made the scholar flush a deep red and scurry off to another section of the library, though she knew he would remain somewhat visible so she wouldn't have to look hard to find him. It was her way of ensuring he didn't sneak up on her.

Thinking about the scholar's reaction made Kitalla snort aloud, which in turn alerted one of the sleeping warriors, who turned over and looked at her. She shrugged apologetically and waved him back to sleep, then grabbed more sand as she considered what she had learned from the lineage.

Which was to say, she hadn't learned much from it. Randler's mother, Sharice, had claimed that no one would be able to trace the lines of Hathreneir and Kallisor down through the ages accurately, but this one immense book did a fine job of it overall, though the constant flipping of pages to the next generations made it somewhat tricky to follow. Whoever crafted the tome did an excellent job of marking years in an effective way, so that it was relatively easy to see who was alive at the same time, though it did sometimes require flipping ahead or backward three to fifteen sheets to see the connecting pages. Surely the genealogist trained apprentices solely in the keeping of this work, for its organization was very precise.

In the lineage, she looked for the people she knew, which wasn't an uncommon thing for visitors to do. Yet none of Dariak's, Gabrion's, or Randler's family were even remotely connected to royalty except through service, which of course did not appear in this book. She did lose herself at times with names that seemed familiar to her from her childhood, including the dread mayor who had murdered her unborn child and her beloved Joral. As those memories had started filling her again, she closed the book and replaced it on the shelf, unable to continue.

Upon the sand dune, Kitalla grunted quietly. Now she wished she had looked further. She knew Joral had been the son of nobles. She wondered now if perhaps his family would have been in that book. If so, then her unborn child's name would also have been written there on the pages someday.

It was a painful thought and she struggled to push it away. The Trial in Magehaven had ripped her protections away, leaving her raw and hurting from all the old woes. She wondered, and not for the first time, how she had ever moved on from that tragedy, and more so, how she had allowed herself to become close to Gabrion, even a little.

She looked up at the night sky and breathed deeply. As she exhaled, she cast her sorrow from her and pushed it away. It didn't do her any good to dwell on it. She certainly couldn't talk about any of it with any of the people near her. It would have required admitting she was from Kallisor, for one.

That made her grin.

After a couple of days roaming the castle under the subtle eye of the guard, who never interfered with her wanderings or the wanderings of others, Kitalla had bumped into an opportunity. She overheard an angry conversation between two members of the guard that was taking place in one of the vacant hallways; that is, vacant except for Kitalla.

One of the guards was furious with the captain for refusing to allow her time away from her post to visit with her family. The other guard was a friend who was commiserating by yelling with just as much outrage.

"It's like they don't even *have* families!" the friend had raged. "They protect the kingdom, sure, but aren't we doing this for the people we love?"

"Exactly!" hissed the scorned guardswoman. "And I asked only for a few days! Enough time to head for Geraul, spend a day with my man, and then return. I wasn't asking for a month off!"

"Inhuman! I just don't understand why not."

"'We gotta protect the king,' was all he said. 'Trouble's coming from the east. No one can take a leave now.' I can't *stand* it!"

"I know!" agreed the friend. "It isn't like this is a new threat, by any stretch of the mind. And one guard won't change the outcome of a major battle, not really." Then she added quickly, "I'm not saying that you're not an amazing fighter; I'm just saying—"

But her friend growled and cut her off. "Never mind. If I didn't need this employ, I would go anyway."

"There's got to be something…"

"I told you; if I leave, I'm a traitor. Not only am I out of a job, but they'll come and kill us all." She shouted in anger again. "I haven't been there in months and Keel's last letter begged me to come home."

"What if you were sick, Jareesa?"

With a sigh, "No, it would be too obvious now, wouldn't it? Dammit, what am I to do?"

Kitalla had chosen that moment to intervene. "A moment, ladies, if I may?"

It had taken a bit of convincing, but Jareesa's need and anger were great enough that she conceded to Kitalla's plan. Her friend, Haasa, loved Jareesa so much that even she agreed to the ruse. And so, after two hours of preparatory work, Kitalla was suited up in Jareesa's guard outfit, given an outline of her duties, key passwords she may need in the event of an emergency, and with a two-week plan in mind, Kitalla became Jareesa.

Kitalla still hadn't any plans for herself at the time, but she felt it wouldn't hurt to know the inner workings of the castle. Jareesa's role was more of a common guard, and with her willingness to depart her post for a tromp with her lover, Kitalla wasn't surprised she hadn't gone up the ranks. Part of Jareesa's personality was sharp, so there were times Kitalla could say what was on her mind without having to play very nice, and her portrayal of Jareesa was close enough to fool most of the people around her who didn't care much for her anyway.

After only two days in the position, Haasa and Jareesa were reassigned to another part of the castle, which suited the situation better, because they both needed to learn new routines under a different captain. Now it would matter even less if Kitalla slipped. Everything was working well. The only thing missing for Kitalla was a purpose.

She had infiltrated the castle in Kallisor by clobbering a guard and stealing the uniform she had worn, and it was all to free the wild mage who had promised to show her a way to tap into her innate skills. Everything had been done as a means to an end. Now there wasn't such a focus and it left her feeling empty. She wondered if she could take a role like this and not need a bigger purpose for fulfillment. But she was too antsy to think she would last long at all, and part of her wondered if she would get through this stint until the real Jareesa returned.

Her new patrols hadn't taken her too far into the castle, but from her ever-alert eyes, she was able to estimate the locations of key rooms within the castle proper. She also happened on Poltor one afternoon as he was scouring a hallway that was not open to the public. She carried herself with such authority that he responded with the bewildered tone of a wimpy child until he realized who she was. He had admitted that he was surprised at her new line of work, but she only winked at him before giving him time to flee ahead of the next patrol.

Kitalla chuckled to herself as she remembered the expression on Poltor's face. He had trained her himself to assume others' roles and it was a deep compliment to her skill that she had fooled even him. Once recognition had set in and she sent him on, he had whispered something in her ear that she hadn't expected, and it had given her a goal for her temporary new position. Though, it also meant that she would be reconnecting with her recent past.

Kitalla's new uniform didn't have many pockets or much room for growth. She couldn't conceal the number of daggers she liked to have on her person, so her next goal would be a bit trickier if things went awry. She couldn't ask for help from anyone. Clearly, Poltor's tip was the only assistance she would receive from him. Haasa was devoted to the guards, despite helping to conceal Jareesa's sojourn; Kitalla couldn't ask her to violate any other rules of the crown, but her support for Jareesa would provide a perfect alibi. And once the real Jareesa returned, no amount of questioning would reveal what had happened, except possibly her own departure from the castle.

It took a little time for Kitalla to make the preparations. The hardest part was finding the right color rope that she could conceal along the seams of her uniform without it appearing obvious on quick inspection. She ended up having to dye the rope to match the leather jerkin of the guard, after which she stitched it loosely along the seams of the tunic. She ran the rope up one arm and down her side, around her waist, and then up the other side and down her other arm. The symmetry of it helped make it less conspicuous and, if she kept her hands at her sides, which was mostly required in the job, then no one would see it at all.

Haasa and Jareesa had the midnight shift. The moon was low and hidden by thick clouds in the distance. The entire castle was tense with word of forces breaking through the border defenses. Some scoffed at the mages for their lack of protective ability, despite their use of the border guardians, but others were edgy for fear their land would soon be invaded in earnest. Haasa grew nervous like all the others and Kitalla played along and added to some of the disquiet. Haasa was so upset at times that she seemed to forget that Kitalla wasn't actually Jareesa, which Kitalla used to her advantage.

"What if some crazy person gets in and tries to kill people?" Haasa asked that night, while they paced the wall.

"I know," Kitalla said with a tremor. "It's a scary thought, really, especially with some the guards off celebrating. But it's a good thing we're up here to make sure it doesn't happen."

"I'm glad you're here, Jareesa. I couldn't have imagined if we had been separated." Then she remembered. "Oh, well, you know what I mean, *Jareesa.*"

"Of course I know," Kitalla snapped in Jareesa form, "we've been friends for so long."

"You're right." Haasa nodded, stopped, then laughed to herself.

Before Haasa could admit she was growing to like the new Jareesa, Kitalla pointed out in the distance. "Do you see something out there, Haasa?"

Panicked, the woman looked, squinting hard and trying to find the disturbance. There was some darkness fluttering around out there, but whether it was invaders, shadows, or feral creatures, she couldn't tell. "I—I don't know."

"Do you think I should report it? 'Anything suspicious' right? Or do you want to do it?"

Haasa was a bit afraid of their captain, despite her willingness to cover for Jareesa, and she didn't want to face a reprimand if raising an alert led to wasted time. "Um, why don't you go?"

Kitalla hesitated as if she didn't want to go. "What if I'm wrong? Worse yet," she added with a whisper, "what if she recognizes that I'm not Jareesa?"

Haasa's face went white, and Kitalla could see it clearly even in the darkness. "I—" but she didn't say more than that.

"Oh never mind, I'll just go do it," she snapped slightly. "You wait here and keep a lookout just in case."

"A—Are you sure?"

"Yeah. She probably wouldn't know me from a bucket anyway." That made Haasa chuckle and relax, after which Kitalla stalked off with no intention of actually alerting anyone of anything, especially not wind in the distance blowing over the sand.

Three doors, two hallways, and a set of stairs flew under her feet as she went. Eventually she came across another sentry who asked her business being there. "Nature calls," she answered him, pointing off toward the middens. He shrugged and continued gazing out at the stars.

Once she turned the corner, Kitalla vanished into the shadows. She slid behind tapestries when she had to or ducked into archways, mimicking statues or suits of armor. She eluded several other guards, some of whom were roaming sentries and others who were posted outside specific doorways. Kitalla checked her mental map of the castle grounds and decided it was time to head down one floor. But she knew there wasn't a floor beneath her, which was why she needed that concealed rope.

With a few tugs, the loose threading gave way and released the rope from her tunic. She secured it along a shadowy parapet and then slid down the side of the castle onto the rooftop below. It wasn't easy hiding from some of the guards, but she had chosen tonight for this adventure because of a recent wine shipment that had come in. Everyone had talked about its upcoming arrival and the revelry that always ensued on the night of opening the crates, and she wasn't disappointed. Some of the crates were scattered even here and she found refuge behind them as needed. But also, it was the upper echelon of the guard that was invited to partake of the goods, and though a number of those more elite guards were still on duty, several had earned the right to join the festivities.

Kitalla worked her way through the secondary kitchen and into the rooms beyond. There weren't many more places left to go before reaching her destination. This area was established for the king's private quarters. The small kitchen was set up for personal snacks among the king's family and closest advisors. Soon, she would be near the king's chambers and her goal.

Kitalla kept alert for hidden guards or traps. There had to be some protections in place and they had been scarce so far. She worried that she was going to miss something, so she focused her eyes more sharply and she drew a steadying breath, reaching for the metal jade and its support, forgetting for a moment that it was no longer with her. She had hoped it would help her sense anything amiss, but she was truly on her own now. It didn't matter, she reminded herself; she had survived worse.

Creeping forward, she heard a soothing voice not too far away. It was a woman singing softly in the night. The melody was pleasant and sounded oddly familiar to her, though she couldn't place it at the moment and didn't want to, either; not until she was safely away. As she crept past the room, the words and melody permeated through her and burned themselves into her ears.

Rest now my child.
You will be strong.
Rest now my child.
You will one day be grand.

It was beautifully sung and held such deep love. She could remember someone humming it, but right now she couldn't recall *who* had hummed it, just that it wasn't Randler. Kitalla shook her head; if she didn't remain focused right now, she would be caught and killed for treason. There wasn't much more distance to cover.

She kept low as she passed the singer's door so as not to be seen. As she went she could hear the soft crooning of a happy baby in the room, and Kitalla realized suddenly that it must be the queen and her child in there. She stood up on the other side of the door and peered in, but all she could see was a woman leaning over a crib and a strong man standing with her, his hand on her back. Apparently, the king was there as well. Other movement within the chamber alerted her to guards who were with them.

The thief kicked into action. She made her way down the hall and burst into a room near the end of the hallway that had a crest carved on the doorway. The room was not empty. Four guards staggered for a moment at the intrusion but quickly realized what was happening and attacked.

Kitalla dodged a spear that lunged for her as she rolled aside and crashed purposely into another guard while also shoving the door closed. She grabbed the sword that fell from the man's hand and threw it across the way toward another guard, who interrupted his charge and batted it aside. The fourth guard drew a breath to sound the alarm but Kitalla pulled off her bowl-like helmet and threw it at him like a disc, cracking his jaw. She then pulled a dagger that was wound in her hair under the helmet and drew another from her boot before rolling forward and defeating the spear-wielding guard.

As his body crashed with an echoing thud, Kitalla realized that the sound would alert any other nearby guards even without a call to arms. She couldn't penetrate the iron armor of these soldiers, but her daggers worked well enough against their faces. Two of them rushed her, hoping to grab her, but she crouched down low and then pounced up as they drew near, making it impossible for them to nab her. She thrust one dagger upward into the back of one man's neck, killing him instantly, but she couldn't do the same for the next guard because a small fireball lashed out at her and knocked her over.

So, one of them was a mage, she thought to herself. It didn't change much of her strategy, though. She realized that the man who had received a beating from her helmet was launching another spell, so she pounced at him and tackled him, bringing up her knee sharply between his legs and disabling him for a moment. The other guard had recovered and ran toward Kitalla with a battle cry, bringing his sword down onto Kitalla's back, but she rolled aside at the last moment and the guard pierced his sword through the mage's armor, killing him. Kitalla pulled off the swordsman's helmet and cracked his temple with the hilt of a dagger, knocking him unconscious.

She didn't have much time, but she didn't need it either. The chamber was beautifully furnished, and though there could be many hiding places, only one made sense to her. She jumped onto the king's bed and rifled through the drawers of one side table, finding only lavish bits of jewelry and an ornate comb. She rolled over to the other side of the bed and ransacked the drawers, finding the object she was looking for and taking it.

Noises filled the hallway and she knew others were coming. There were no windows in this room, presumably to keep the king safe, but there had to be an escape passage. No king would allow himself to be trapped in a dead-end room all night. Kitalla pictured the layout of the castle in her mind, which wasn't easy to do with the impending doom, and decided that the passage had to be on the side wall that was nearest the king's side of the bed.

She ripped down the tapestry and tapped on the stone frantically, hoping a loose brick would move or something, then she shoved aside the low reading table that was there and saw one part of the wall that was slightly different from the rest. She dropped down and pushed the brick inward. It slid back but that didn't open the doorway. She didn't care; Grenthar hadn't always made his escapes easy either. She felt inside the hole and found the catch, popping it and feeling something smash onto her finger. She recoiled for a moment but ignored the sensation, seeing that the seam in the wall was more pronounced. With a heavy shove, the door opened, but so did the door from the hallway. Guards poured into the room as she made her escape.

There wasn't a long hallway to follow, only a doorway that was as thick as the castle wall itself. Kitalla went through, and then pushed the door back into place until it snapped shut, which would force the guards to unlock it on their end. She looked around, pleased with herself, for she had correctly identified the escape route. Over toward her right side, hidden in shadows, was the rope she had used to climb down the wall. Sprinting to it, Kitalla leaped and ascended the rope as nimbly as she could. She crested the wall, pulling the cord up and tossing it aside. With a light jog, she hurried back through the corridors and found the castle on alert.

She made her way to Haasa, who was pacing feverishly. "Jareesa!" she cried out in relief. "Hurry up!"

"Where are we going?" Kitalla asked. "And where is the captain? I couldn't find her anywhere!"

"It seems you were right! There *was* something out there and it snuck into the castle. We have to help." She ran and Kitalla followed, still massaging her finger. She looked down and saw a small cut. Something had fallen on it when she had released the catch. Hoping the mechanism had only broken and wasn't poisoned, she continued on.

"Halt!" cried out a sharp, steel voice. It was the captain.

Haasa whimpered and stopped running.

"Where do you think you're running off to?"

"To help!" Haasa replied sheepishly. "We're answering the call to arms!"

The captain's eyes narrowed but then softened. "Back to your posts, you fools."

Kitalla decided to play Jareesa's part in force. "But there is a call to arms. Aren't we charged with defending our king? What good are we pissing on the walls?"

"You will follow orders. Return to your posts."

Kitalla made as if to protest, but Haasa grabbed her, "Jareesa, no! Let's go."

They made their way back to the wall and once they were there Kitalla decided to complain. "She thinks we're not good enough to protect the king?"

"I don't… think so. No, it's—" she stopped and then realization came over her. "No, I remember now. Don't you, Jareesa? If we were on our old post then we would have gone in, too, but this new post means we have to stay on the wall. I forgot all about that."

Of course Kitalla had remembered that. It was one of the delightful things that had changed when they were given this new position. Rather, one of the demotions. It had also allowed Kitalla the opportunity to carry out her little scheme because she was supposed to remain at the wall, watching for intruders, not rushing in to the castle for any reason. Luckily, Haasa wasn't particularly bright and never questioned Kitalla's absence amidst all the confusion.

Things hadn't gotten easier after that day. There was some disturbance at Magehaven and they had requested assistance from the king. Grudgingly, he sent a battalion to the tower, but like the king of Kallisor, he only commissioned his lower guards to leave the castle, keeping the stronger forces at home. Thus, Kitalla, Haasa, and a number of others were currently en route to offer support to the mages.

Kitalla's watch was almost up. She shook her head at the turn of events and then looked over the group of men and women she was traveling with. The sleepers were still dreaming, but soon it would be her turn for a break. She woke Haasa up to take over the watch. Dutifully, Jareesa's friend agreed, and Kitalla pulled out her blanket and rolled up in it.

As she did so, she tucked her head under the cover and pulled something from her pocket, partly to ensure it was still there, but also to look at it in amazement. In just a few days she had turned her back on her friends, abandoning the quest for the jades, and now she had infiltrated the king's own bedchamber and stolen the one jade he had in his possession, the jade of fire. And with this journey back to the tower, soon they would all be reunited.

Trying carefully not to snicker, Kitalla placed the fire jade back into its pocket and then went to sleep. The tower was only a day or so away.

Chapter 28

Ervinor of the Kallisorian Army

The castle town of Hathreneir faced a darkened day. The sun beaming down from above did not illuminate the land as it should, for tensions were high and the people looked around nervously for shadows that might jump at them.

The war had already been raging for some months and the citizens felt the drain on their resources. Merchant caravans arrived with fewer wares for the populace, as most of the quality goods were brought directly to the king. Guard patrols were staggered through the town on a purposely erratic schedule, so that thieves could not track the guards' paths and undermine their attempts at maintaining order. Food supplies were rationed out, though a surplus still allowed people to purchase in excess of their individual needs, but products with longer shelf lives were sold in limited quantities. The older citizens read the signs that the king expected a siege sometime soon.

As the months carried on, new recruits from neighboring towns had been ushered into the castle proper for military training. Many of these younger men and women made up the town patrols and wall guards, and their lack of true experience did little to calm the populace. Though it wouldn't be hard for anyone to see Kallisorian forces marching across the land, it would take a more practiced eye to spot a scouting party, and such knowledge could be the deciding factor in a battle.

Additionally, recent events at Magehaven had demanded a host of guardsmen to vacate the castle and offer assistance with some unknown trouble. It wasn't unheard of for the mages to request the help of the king's forces, but with all the other cards in play, losing any fighters for any reason made people even more uncomfortable.

And then there was the arrival of the small Kallisorian army.

The force was comprised of roughly a hundred men and women, but the people saw that villagers of Marritosh had joined their ranks and the fighters were equipped with magic-shielding armor. Clearly, something terrible was on the horizon and the people were afraid.

Ervinor watched as Gabrion entered the castle with Quereth, Morrish, and the king's page, and he worried that he would never see Gabrion again. It was irrational, he knew, but he worried all the same.

Fretting wouldn't help them to be ready for an attack, however. So, Ervinor set himself in motion. The army had dispersed among the nearby vendors in small packs so they wouldn't look so imposing to the people. After all, if they had a chance to deal peacefully, all the better.

He noticed that the Kallisorians kept an eye toward him, waiting for any signal from him. It was almost amusing that he would be at the head of the army, second only to the companions of the jades themselves. He was only twenty-two, average looking, and with a standard childhood. He didn't think he was particularly special or that he should command such respect from these people. But the more he thought about it, the more it made some sense to him.

Ervinor had grown up in Beltriss, which was to the southeast of Kallisor castle. His parents had taught him well from all the old stories that had been passed down through the generations, and his dislike for the Hathrens was the same as all the villagers he grew up with. The folks ensured that he was well-versed in lore and they trained him to fight so he could always defend himself. Yet his childhood was not filled only with war and anger. There were many times his family and friends were together laughing wildly at some jester or at the town play or during an afternoon picnic. His life was richer than most, and not because of money.

It was that way of life that brought him here. He cherished every aspect of his life in a town that saw no actual fighting in his time there. He wanted the war to end so all children could grow up as he had. Too many of the men and women he met had lost relatives to the fighting. Gabrion's own mother was dead from a skirmish in Savvron. Dariak's father had died over twenty years beforehand in the War of the Colossus. Randler's father had also fallen in that war. He didn't know of Kitalla's parents, for she never mentioned them, but he assumed they too were gone. Ervinor felt unique in that his entire family was still alive. His sister had married some local tailor and they had three children. His brothers were still schooling themselves on the world and would come of age soon enough if the war allowed it.

Indeed, he hadn't really dealt with much loss, but some part of him took that as a means of preserving the life around him. He was confident that he could protect people and it was his confidence that made him such a leader among the rest. They recognized his heart and his dream, and though the army was following Gabrion's fantasy of ending the war, they resonated well with Ervinor, who instructed them in the ways of teamwork and cooperation when Gabrion and the rest were away.

As he thought of these things, Ervinor meandered through the castle town and tapped various colleagues on their shoulders, asking about the selections at different booths. The merchants eyed them all suspiciously but barely bothered to interact with the Kallisorians. Some thought they could turn a profit from the newcomers, but most realized that the men and women were there for another reason. A cloth merchant nodded at Ervinor abruptly, signaling that he had no intention of selling to a Kallisorian even if he had money.

Ervinor didn't care. His goal was to keep his army calm and dispersed. Assembling them in the courtyard would be seen as a threat, but letting the men and women wander for too long without word wasn't safe either. He didn't know why he understood this, but he did. Perhaps it mimicked the way his parents had kept him and his siblings in line. So as he waited for Gabrion's return, Ervinor made a few circuits of the promenade.

Time passed slowly for the troop and Ervinor worried that Gabrion and the others had been taken prisoner. He perked up his ears, trying to listen for any unrest within the castle itself, but he knew that was a fruitless venture. The king knew full well of the forces stationed here and he wouldn't risk the security of the castle by alerting the army to danger.

Though Ervinor stayed on alert, he worried that he had missed some sign. He started pacing and had to consciously control himself to stop. Pacing would only make his soldiers restless. He needed to wear a face of aplomb. He could practically hear Herchig prattling on about some errant general who had paced himself off a cliff in his worry.

Ervinor chuckled to himself, but he couldn't shake the feeling that something was terribly wrong. He wandered to a signpost and leaned against it, keeping a wary eye on the castle gates.

CHAPTER 29

The Metal Jade

THE NOONTIME AIR was tense for a reason Kitalla could not explain. Though she was imitating another woman, her own skills were still finely tuned and she realized that something was about to happen. Ignoring the chain of command, she shouted for the troop to hurry on their way. "To the tower!" she cried. "Waste no time! We must hurry!"

Panic spread and the captain ran over to Kitalla and demanded an explanation.

"There's no time!" She tried to turn away but the captain caught her arm. The thief squared off sternly and insisted, "If I'm wrong then reprimand me after it's over, but I assure you that we have to go now."

The unease had already prompted too much action from the resting army for the captain to call them to stop. Besides, it would be better to complete this errand quickly and return to the castle. Grudgingly, she growled and focused the men and women as they prepared for fast travel.

Kitalla couldn't shake the feeling. Something within her was trembling and she couldn't understand it. She wasn't as prone to nerves as others and simply being close to the tower would not have agitated her so. No, there had to be something more to it, but there wasn't time to ponder. She grabbed her haversack and rushed ahead, pushing past others who were still preparing to leave, carving a trail for the rest to follow.

Jogging through sand wasn't particularly easy, but they were determined and trained well enough to endure the strain. They only paused briefly when they needed to, and not as a unit. Kitalla's drive compelled the rest to press on. She wondered if they all thought she sensed some calamity against their country and that they would all be heroes for overcoming it. It didn't much matter, especially as she had no idea what drew her either.

As evening set in, the army crested the last dune and they could hear commotion from behind the mages' protective barrier. It was enough to propel them onward in a mad sprint to the main gates, Kitalla still at the lead. She wondered idly if any members of the army would be taken up into Trials or if, perhaps, they had all been cleared of such an ordeal. Spellfire flew from a window high overhead, and Kitalla reassessed the situation; the mages were simply too busy to call the Trials into effect.

The first floor of Magehaven was sparsely populated. Only a few specialists remained, ready to blockade the stairways and other passages. The army was greeted with welcome relief.

"Hurry! There are intruders upstairs and no mage has been able to contain them. We need your help! Go!"

Kitalla ignored the captain's orders when she split the forces to various points of entry, for the thief had her own destination in mind. The captain didn't much care, for Kitalla had chosen the stairway that seemed closest to whatever danger lie ahead, and if she died in the process, it was one less thing for the captain to deal with later.

Up the stairs Kitalla leaped, taking them three at a time with ease, even after the hurried journey here. Her pulse was rushing faster and faster, and the driving force compelled her more strongly now. She couldn't understand the urgency of the innate call, but she accepted it and flew through the tower.

Lightning bolts crested the air near her as she hit the fourth floor. Glancing quickly, she could see two mages aiming for her, but relaxing once they noted her armor. "Over this way!" they directed. "Please hurry! We're taking casualties!"

Sounds of battle were closer and closer as she approached the next floor, but she felt that she wasn't near her goal yet. Lupinoes and mages were running wildly, and she couldn't tell if they were working together or if they were themselves engaged in a fight. Fire erupted in front of her and she leaped into the air and rolled to safety a few feet away. Another blast of fire followed and she realized that she was under direct attack now. She looked and saw two older mages stalking closer to her, alternating their spells to keep up a more regular fighting pattern. She guessed that these mages had seen her with Dariak previously.

One mage altered his attack frequency by unleashing staccato blasts, similar to Dariak's old fire dart spell but with much greater intensity and accuracy. The other mage spread her arms wide and obscured the fire darts with larger orbs that crackled and sparked as they approached Kitalla.

Avoiding the attacks was simple for the experienced thief. She rolled to one side and pounced over three darts, then landed with a twisting motion to avoid a larger orb. With each step she took, she drew closer to the mages, challenging them to try harder. Daggers launched from her hands and caught the man in the chest. The woman beside him screamed and released a massive burst of flame.

Kitalla couldn't avoid it, so she stamped her feet on the ground and extended her hands before her. Thinking quickly, she recalled one of the songs Randler had taught her and she applied the beat to her steps, pulling with her hands, spinning in a twirl, and then thrusting her hands forward again. She repeated the process once before the fireball struck her and smashed her to the floor. She winced in pain but it didn't linger. She pushed herself up and looked toward the mage, who also lay in a heap on the floor. It had been a quick pulling of the energies, but her innate dance skills had helped her reflect some of the power. Wasting no time, she struck the other mage to disable her and then continued up to the sixth floor.

She didn't quite understand what she saw when she approached the landing. Numerous bodies were sprawled on the ground in awkward positions. Some looked as if they had been struck by errant spells, while others appeared to have been smothered to death. There was a clear path through the destruction which led upward, so she followed, stepping cautiously over human and creature corpses alike.

She could hear fighting somewhere nearby, but she was listening to her instincts, so she ignored the other noises and followed the path of bodies that led higher up into the tower. She risked a glance behind her, wondering where the rest of the army was at present, and whether any of the survivors on this floor would rise against her. She didn't have time to subdue any of the writhing bodies; not if she was going to complete her mission.

Mission? She shrugged the idea off, wondering if it was a remnant of her recent stint in the Hathren guard or something else entirely. Even if she had wanted to consider it further, the moaning ahead of her drew her focus. She crouched low, trying to remain unseen as she made her way up yet another flight of stairs.

Mages were sprawled all over the floor, some in worse shape than those she had seen already. A quick assessment, however, showed her that fewer mages had tried confronting the mysterious enemy on this floor, perhaps because there were less of them in the area, or more likely because they had fled in the face of a foe they could not defeat. For all their grasp of the energies, Kitalla often felt that mages were cowards at heart, fighting from afar and rarely ever engaging in true battle. It was the proximity to another life that gave a fight true meaning, of trying to anticipate and overcome reactions within a moment's passing, without distance offering any time for contemplating a defense.

This wasn't the time for such thoughts, she reminded herself, as an ice dart crashed against a wall. She looked around and saw a young mage on the floor, badly hurt and dying, but still trying to defend his home. He summoned whatever spells he could, but Kitalla could already see the light fading from his eyes. He was reacting instinctually now. She flipped him over so his magical flailing wouldn't inadvertently strike her down.

Only a few of the bodies remaining here were alive, but those that were seemed to be heavily seared from spell blasts of every variety. It looked to her as if the mages had turned against each other, fighting to the death, however unlikely it seemed. She hurried on.

Another flight up revealed a similar setting with fewer bodies to avoid. Kitalla heard screaming and she hid against a wall as a young mage ran away from some unknown enemy ahead. The mage was in a terrible panic, looking over her shoulder and casting spells when she could, but the mage she battled was quick and returned her volleys of energy with utmost speed, knocking her down. Kitalla hesitated for only a moment before running ahead and looking at the foe who had taken her down. She wasn't ready for what she saw.

Five mages had surrounded a writhing metallic blob. They launched spells toward it and some were reflected off its outer surface while others were absorbed. Kitalla wondered if there was some pattern to it, but there clearly wasn't time to determine one. There were no sounds of struggle behind her so she felt temporarily safe from being flanked. Instead, she focused on the anomaly before her.

The silver sludge splattered forward and struck one of the mages. The woman had no defense against the attack and she crumbled in a heap, apparently dead. The other mages panicked and started backing off. Kitalla sprinted ahead calling for a ceasefire, only to receive a few spells aimed in her direction. A lightning blast struck her left shoulder and bit painfully, but she focused her strength on avoiding the rest of the barrage of attacks.

Turning away from the metallic ooze led to the detriment of two of the other mages, who succumbed to the being's wrath and died at its touch. Kitalla noticed that it lurched ahead with each victory as if it had been boosted momentarily by the kill. Something about it was eerily familiar to her; she followed but remained cautious.

The other mages had given up trying to stop either Kitalla or the silver liquid. They bolted away, shoving against each other in their haste to escape. Moments later, Kitalla was the only person close by. The metal blob responded by turning its attention toward her. She nimbly leaped away, wondering at its ability, while mindfully seeking an exit for herself. The ooze pursued her almost instinctually and with a sense of desperation. She could use that to her advantage as long as she was careful.

She debated trying one of her dance skills against the sludge, but she remembered that the other mages' spells had either been absorbed or reflected and the creature had only been bolstered by them. She made her way to the nearest stairwell and the ooze followed her, becoming more and more sluggish with each rolling step. Curiously, Kitalla grabbed a candlestick nearby and lobbed it at the goo, but nothing happened. The blob kept heading for her and the candlestick remained behind after passing through the silvery mess without any hint of effect.

Kitalla stepped carefully up the stairs and reached a storage chamber. There were several exits in the room, but she didn't open them. Instead, she watched intently as the metal made its way toward her, struggling up the stairs. By the time it reached the top, it moved languidly. Kitalla decided that it was feeding off the energy blasts and the lives of its victims, so all she needed to do was stay out of its reach until it had exhausted its resources. She scrambled up a number of crates and kept a close eye on the silvery blob that could not follow. Though it had been able to ascend the stairs, the crates were too tall for it to climb. It tried several times to reach her, each attempt more feeble than the last, until finally the puddle settled on the floor and started to change.

The silvery luster faded first and Kitalla tensed in anticipation, but she started to suspect what was happening. As the metal hues were lost, the ooze coalesced into a more human shape. Before long, Dariak lay coiled on the floor, barely conscious. Suddenly, the urge to reach her goal subsided, and she thought she knew why. The metal jade had been active and after all the time she had spent with it, she had felt a resonance with it, even from outside the tower.

She approached Dariak cautiously, in case there were some residual energies cascading around him, but she need not have worried. The metal jade drew her attention and gave her a sense of safety and completion. She withdrew it from Dariak's possession and held it tightly, despite its increased temperature at the moment. After placing it into her own pocket, she rolled Dariak over and tried to awaken him.

He looked terribly weak and undernourished. The jade at her hip was pulsing and she could feel it trying to help despite its own exhaustion, though she wasn't entirely sure how she understood its intent. She fumbled through Dariak's belt and retrieved the other jades, placing them at key locations on his body, as guided by her metal jade. She let her hands hover over the mage's body until her jade pulsed, and then she set the gem down. The earth jade was set at Dariak's belly and the water jade on his heart, with the nature jade over his forehead. She held the metal jade aloft over his body and she could feel a series of pulsations emanating from it, reaching down and interacting with the other crystals.

Free from the restraints, the jades were able to draw energy from the air and their innate abilities strengthened the life force within Dariak. Moments later, his eyes opened and he breathed deeply.

"What?" he said dryly. "Kitalla?"

"Rest for a moment. You look like you need a break after your ordeal."

"What… happened?"

She looked over her shoulder and listened for signs of pursuit, but there were none, though the tower itself was far from quiet. "I'll venture a guess," she said a moment later. "Remember when you turned into that electrical pulse when you battled Sharice? I think you underwent a similar change with the metal jade."

"I—" he started. "Yes, that… makes sense. Where… are we… now?"

"Temporarily safe. The jades are trying to heal you."

"Randler. I saw Randler. Is he with you?"

Kitalla shook her head. "I was essentially summoned here by the metal jade. This one was guiding me." She withdrew the fire jade and flashed it before Dariak's eyes.

His jaw fell open. "How?"

"I'll fill you in later when there's time. It led me straight to you. How are you feeling?"

He tried to sit up but could not. "Heavy. Very heavy. I don't think I can stand." He breathed deeply for a few minutes but he still couldn't move. "How did you come to be here?"

She laughed. "It's a long story. I'm more concerned about getting you out of here, and if Randler is here, then we have to find him as well. I just hope he wasn't—" she stopped.

"Wasn't what?"

The thief cleared her throat. "There were a lot of casualties on my way up here. And there were sounds of fighting elsewhere, which still seems to be going on." She looked at him intently. "I should go and see if Randler is there. But I can't take you with me if I do."

"I'll be fine," he said, trying to sound confident but failing miserably. "Just tuck me out of the way."

"I've retaken the metal jade for now, in case you start missing it." She said it sharply, almost challenging him to resist.

But he didn't. "Take it. It'll let me find you when this is over."

She smiled despite herself, then set about sliding some crates in front of Dariak and disguising them to look untouched. On her way out, Dariak could hear her moving the other bodies away from this room, covering the traces that would lead others here. Before she left, she called to him, "Rest up as much as you can, mage. There's no telling what's coming next."

"Kitalla," he replied. "Be careful."

With that, she left.

C HAPTER 30

The Beasts Within

"I DON'T UNDERSTAND," Randler hissed. "Dariak went *that* way," he pointed.

"And there's nothing we can do for him right now. But I suspect he will be fine," Frast said.

"You suspect? That isn't good enough."

Frast grabbed Randler's shoulder. "Dariak is a mass of pure energy right now, which in itself doesn't make sense. You couldn't see what was happening in there. He was absorbing energy from every direction and it was empowering him. No one will be able to stop him, Randler. And while they're busy, we have something else we must do. Come on."

Frast crouched low and ran across the landing, keeping out of sight. Randler groaned but followed, after casting one last look toward Dariak's escape path. He didn't agree with this, but Frast had risked his life to keep Randler safe by knocking out the acolyte Nera outside the tower and donning her cloak before following the bard and Master Pyron inside. He had then remained at Randler's shoulder, pretending to scold him and keeping him in control. Because of the enchanted eggshell, only Randler was able to hear Frast anyway at the time, but Randler hadn't noticed the exact source of the voice under the circumstances. It had allowed Frast to enact other magical defenses and demonstrations when Randler would otherwise have been defenseless and cast aside as easy prey by the mages.

The thoughts flashed in his mind as he skirted across the room. He tucked himself behind the mage and waited for the next opening. The two dashed across the way and flew up a nearby set of stairs.

Mages were running in panic and spellfire was erupting around the area. Some of them were in control of minor beasts, who were trying to help quell their terrified comrades, but no one was listening to reason. A few mages had seen Dariak's transformation and were lucky enough to flee, but they erected force fields and defensive spells that erratically harmed their nearby colleagues.

Frast and Randler tried to make use of the chaos by sprinting in a similarly crazed run toward another hallway, but errant spells crashed into them and knocked them down. Frast hit the ground hard and rolled aside. Randler fared better and was on his feet quickly as a war hound raced toward him, snarling in anger. The bard was immediately recognized as a traitor.

No subterfuge would help him now. Randler grabbed his mace and crouched low as the hound charged. The beast leaped for him, jaws snapping wildly, and Randler stepped one foot forward while dropping his back to the ground. This allowed Randler to get under the beast where he jabbed upward with the mace and used the dog's momentum to push it further along. A howling screech echoed through the chamber and alerted some of the terrified mages to a greater threat.

Frast was on his feet again, arms and legs working to channel the energies into offensive spells. He ripped a wooden shelf from the wall and flung it like a disc toward a trio of encroaching mages. *"Extenninar staructis fibricular spanse."* The wood stretched oddly as it flew and dismantled itself into thousands of sand-like particles. He followed the spell with a small burst of fire and a conflagration erupted in the chamber.

"Hurry!" he called to Randler, who complied immediately, pulling himself away from the war hound as it tried to continue its attacks, despite its wounds. The bard and the mage bounded up the stairs, leaving the mages below to tend to the fire damage.

They were followed by a few brave souls who recognized the need to stop these intruders from reaching the jades upstairs. Randler had his bow ready by the time he reached the top of the stairs and, with a few careful shots, he disabled the pursuers without killing them. He trusted they would not be able to heal themselves quickly enough to trouble them any time soon.

Meanwhile, Frast was tossing ice and fire at the mages he faced on the new level. Randler turned his bow around and launched a few volleys at the mages. One of them seemed to be a master of the wind and he was able to divert the projectiles with great ease. Frast altered his tactics immediately and enflamed the arrows and guided them toward the less-skilled mages. Robes caught aflame and distracted the acolytes long enough for Frast and Randler to focus on the master.

The mage was well-protected against all of Frast's spells. He wielded air like an iron curtain and cast the energies aside as they approached. Randler rushed forward, drawing his daggers, but a gust of wind buffeted him like a club and knocked him to the floor. Frast bombarded the man with more magic and Randler tried to launch a dagger while the master was distracted with his counterspells, but he was too skilled. Randler turned to the acolytes, who had overcome their fiery robes, and leaped at them, bringing them both down in a heap. He grabbed one's head and banged it on the floor, knocking him out cold. The other mage grabbed Randler and tried to disable him the same way, but the bard was too nimble. His powerful fingers clenched the mage's wrists and twisted until the younger man cried out in pain. Randler frowned apologetically and then loosened one hand and used it to crack a blow against the mage's neck, rendering him senseless as well.

Frast stepped slowly toward the air mage as he kept sweeping his arms around and sending more and more magic forward. Each step was harder than the last, for the mage's shield pushed back with powerful gusts, even as it shoved the magical energies aside. Frast was tiring, but he needed to get past this man. He lowered one hand to a pocket to withdraw a necessary spell component, keeping his other hand in motion to maintain his barrage. Randler glanced over and thought he recognized the stone Frast had pulled out. He knew what was coming, so he readied his mace and a dagger, tensing in preparation.

Muttering, Frast pulled his hands down, which ended his attack on the mage and allowed the gale forces to crash into him. He stood as firmly as he could against the wind, forcing the words from his lips and coercing his body to obey. *"Lutrimos embelliosh catramorillous!"* He then threw the stone downward and a blinding flash of light erupted in the room. It was energy the wind shield could not penetrate, and though it caused no direct harm, it blinded the air master for a moment. Randler capitalized on the chance by lobbing a dagger through the air with one hand and sprinting forward with a battle cry, mace at the ready. The air mage directed his defenses toward the sound of Randler's voice, but the flying dagger was not stopped. It pierced into the mage's shoulder and he screamed in agony.

Once they knocked the mage unconscious, they continued their frenzied ascent. Frast seemed to know exactly where he was leading them, so Randler gave way and took the rear. The mages in this part of the tower had no idea of the commotion Dariak had caused but they were responding to the noises on the floors below and to the intrusion that was Frast and Randler.

The mage and the bard had surprise on their side as they turned corners and blasted spells or arrows at unsuspecting mages. They were trying not to kill any of them, but the mages retaliated with all their skill. Ice, fire, and lightning all erupted around them and it took finely honed reflexes and defensive spells to keep on the move. Only a few of the mages were trained in physical combat and when they appeared, Randler's mace was put to the test.

One mage in particular was an expert staff fighter. She struck out with one end of the staff, whipped it around her body, and used the momentum to crack Randler's side with the other end. Each tip of the staff was wrapped in steel and the carved head was shaped like a falcon, with a biting beak that lived up to its likeness. Randler kept on the move and was hard-pressed to score any hits against the longer-ranged weapon.

Frast was busy with his own adversaries. The excessive spellcasting was wearing on him, but he couldn't let his guard down. Fire bolts impacted him and he drew energy from the heat and wove it into a stronger defense against future attacks. It was a complex twisting of energy and it prevented him from attacking directly, but it allowed him to absorb some of the spell damage for a time. Once the energy built up to a level he couldn't control, he funneled it away from himself, unleashing it back to his attackers and overwhelming them. The drain was too great and he collapsed to catch his breath.

Randler ducked underneath the staff, then leaped into the air to avoid the next sweep. He swung his mace at the woman but her wildly twirling weapon deflected it easily. Randler took a step back and tried to feign a lunge, but she anticipated it and rapped him on the thigh instead. He threw himself to the ground in the direction of the attack to try to reduce the damage, after which he bounded back up, scanning the area for anything he could use for defense. Unfortunately, they were in an open hallway that was sparsely decorated. The one wall tapestry was too far away and he doubted he would have enough time to even rip it down, never mind reorient it and smother the woman with it.

The whirling staff drew closer and Randler breathed deeply and charged. He took several running steps before pouncing into the air, but the mage cracked him on the side of the head and brought him down. He dropped his mace so he could brace his fall. With a hearty crash, he hit the floor and slid to the wall, in too much pain to move. His vision blurred as the mage stepped closer, laughing as she did so. "Invade *us*, will you?" she taunted, bringing the staff overhead to deliver a fatal blow. Randler tensed, knowing he had no defense against this attack. It was over.

The woman screamed one last time and then the staff fell, but not into Randler. The woman crumpled, dead, with a dagger protruding from the back of her neck. Randler couldn't understand it, and he clutched his head as his vision slowly returned amidst a throbbing skull.

"Can you stand?"

He knew that voice! "Kitalla!"

"You took a pretty bad hit. Can you stand?" she repeated. She held out her hand to help him up. It wasn't easy, and he struggled, but he eventually regained his feet. Frast was also up and he approached the bard, offering some minor healing spells so they could press onward.

"How are you here?"

"Long story," she smirked. "Dariak's back to normal, sort of. He's hiding." She turned to Frast. "How much further away is it?"

The mage stammered. "You… know where we're going?"

"For the jades," she answered impatiently. "How much further?"

"Stop them!" voices called from the distance. "Release the hounds!"

Kitalla cracked her knuckles and laughed. "Time for some exercise. You two get moving; I'll hold them off."

"But—" Randler started.

"Go!" she insisted, pulling her daggers out. "I'll be right behind you."

As Randler and Frast went on ahead, several mages approached from the lower levels. Kitalla noted a difference in the tactics of these mages; they did not rush the floor and unleash a torrent of spells. She assumed they were well protected and that her daggers would do them little harm at the moment, but she wondered why they were waiting.

The massive clamoring of footsteps echoed moments later and soon a swarm of creatures flooded the area. She spotted young lupinoes, war hounds, and sandorpions. The beasts ignored the mages and sought Kitalla instead. She grinned; this would be a good challenge, one that even Grenthar would envy. Before the battle began, she watched the beast army approach her as if in a parade procession with each flank shown for greatest effect. It reminded her of a tale Randler had sung one night: the Battle at Rigweld. An ominous force of enemies had encroached upon the fortress, slowly, stealthily, demoralizing the people within. Then they halted for a brief moment before launching into a wild attack. It was a massacre. Rigweld lost many of its inhabitants, but not all. Not all.

The fierce battle music pounded into Kitalla's mind and raced through her body. The rhythm became her soul. Every step was another beat of Randler's drum. Each slash was a frantic, yet controlled, note on his lute. Kitalla became a killing machine.

The creatures seemed to have expected the single woman to cower in fear, but her change in stance and the fire in her eyes told them otherwise. The animals broke rank and charged. The war hounds were the fastest and the heaviest, but they did not pose the greatest threat. Kitalla ran toward the nearest pair and twisted her body to pass between them. The confused beasts snapped at her as she drew close and they managed to lock their jaws together from the effort. Kitalla brought her daggers down simultaneously into their spines, causing them to thrash about in agony. She withdrew her daggers and scooted away before she was crushed between them.

The lupinoes held back for the moment, obviously calculating a better time to join the fray. Kitalla admired their inherent cleverness, but it wouldn't help them today. However, her first target was the sandorpion, writhing its way toward her, oversized tail held over its head, ready to strike. She couldn't afford to take a hit from the paralyzing poison in the tail, so she dodged left, then right. She dove toward the ground, right into the sandorpion's face, where she grabbed its cranial shell and twisted with all her body weight. A hideous crack sounded as the neck broke and the tail immediately went limp and fell away.

Two lupinoes charged in, thinking Kitalla was trapped under the carcass, but she kicked one lupino in the face with a foot and knocked it into its companion. She then righted herself and let the beat of the music in her head guide her. She lashed out with her left hand, twirled, jumped, then bent low with her right hand. Leaping aside, stabbing again, spinning a second time, and kicking out forcefully, she took out two lupinoes and another war hound.

She maintained the dance maneuvers as she pirouetted around a sandorpion and evaded its pincers and tail, then she stopped abruptly and killed it from behind. She didn't stop for long, though; three steps later she took down a small lupino, which she then lifted into the air and heaved through a doorway. The mage on the other side of the entryway staggered and tried to get out of the way, but the unexpected move caught him successfully and he fell. Several of the animals hesitated, momentarily bewildered as they tried to seek their target.

The freed lupinoes immediately realized that Kitalla was too big of a threat and they started a retreat, but the fallen mage reclaimed his footing and brought the energies about him again, regaining control over the creatures and impelling them to continue the fight. Kitalla was not discouraged. The key would be to disable the mages and then destroy the beasts that did not flee.

Kitalla's body wove through the room like mist, felling creatures each time she turned. She earned a few scratches and scrapes, perhaps a bruise or two, but these animals were unable to fight at their best while they were being manipulated by the mages. Part of Kitalla hated killing these beasts, for they may not have crossed paths if not for the mages. She wasn't in the habit of killing slaves, after all, but her survival required her to continue until she found a way to take the mages down.

A lupino leaped for her and she grabbed its chest and turned it aside, bringing it down with a thud. The beast whimpered but its snapping jaws told her that it wasn't finished yet. Kitalla swung the creature around and lifted it by its ribcage, after which she hurled it through another doorway, knocking another mage aside. She wasted no time; while the mage was on the ground, she pounced through the doorway, clearing his defenses, and she punched him in the face, knocking him out cold.

One by one, Kitalla took down the mages until the lupinoes themselves rebelled against their masters. The gray wolfish creatures strained against the controlling magic but their own survival instincts were strong. The remaining mages recognized their loss of control and bolted away, the lupinoes chasing after them.

It had lasted for quite some time and now that it was done, the battle music faded to silence. Kitalla considered the vast carnage surrounding her and wondered how she could possibly have had the stamina for all that fighting, especially after the mad dash to reach the tower, the frantic ascent as she chased Dariak's damage path, and then the pursuit of Randler and Frast. And though she was winded, she still felt strength coursing through her.

She turned to follow Frast and Randler when it dawned on her. The fire jade was pulsing strongly.

Eagerly.

CHAPTER 31

Gabrion's Audience with the Hathren King

THE CASTLE WALLS were a soft gray stone and they enwrapped the royal garden with a delicate embrace. The stones caught glimpses of the sunlight and sparkled gently from a crystal dust that had been scored into the stone itself. The effect was dazzling as it cast rainbows all throughout the floral yard. A soft breeze whisked through and illuminated the air with the vibrancy of life itself.

Yet amidst the flourishing energy, Gabrion was a miserable wretch, curled in upon himself, trying to erase the thoughts passing through his mind.

Quereth and Morrish eyed the warrior cautiously, not sure what to do. The young man looked clearly broken by the news from the king, but neither seemed to quite understand why the pain was so intense for him.

He couldn't possibly explain it to them. No one would truly empathize. Perhaps Dariak might, he considered, since the mage had occupied his thoughts during his Trial at Magehaven. Or maybe Randler, who sang of deep romances and sweeping heroic sagas. Even Kitalla would acknowledge his loss, for she had risen up to protect his homeland from invasion before their journey into Hathreneir.

But overall, Quereth was just a grumpy, jaded mage. And Morrish knew even less. They couldn't comfort him. He was utterly and completely alone as the truth burned through his heart. The king hadn't taken any prisoners from Savvron. Mira was lost to him. His whole entire quest was for naught.

Why fight to protect the world if Mira could never be a part of it?

Why endanger himself to protect a memory that was now forever lost?

Why even inhale another breath when his whole purpose for living was eternally gone?

He had no answers. The beating of his heart felt like a hammer crushing his chest to dust. Yet also, he felt utterly empty, as if the banging would ring across an open valley for miles. But if so, then that banging should reach Mira's soul and she would appear from whatever Otherworld she was in and she would find him, as he knew he would eventually find her.

She had come to him in his dreams during his incarceration in the Prisoner's Tower. She had guided him on a path of escape through the tower, saving Dariak along the way.

But it wasn't Mira, he finally admitted to himself in earnest. It had been the glass jade that guided him to Dariak. It had tapped into his mind and he only thought he saw his dearest love leading him safely through. No, it hadn't been Mira at all.

Yet he had convinced himself that some part of her was still with him. Still guiding him. Still loving him with the same careless freedom his heart shared with her. It made more sense that her soul was part of him. They had grown up together. They had spent so much time together. They were so rarely ever apart.

But now he felt torn asunder. Mira was truly gone.

Quereth and Morrish walked through the garden and only glanced occasionally in Gabrion's direction. They didn't try speaking to him as he rocked back and forth, trying to make sense of his loss. Though Gabrion didn't know it, Quereth understood his pain keenly. And he knew the young man would need some time.

Time, they received. It took over two hours before any word returned to them from King Prethos. The page, Berral, finally joined them in the garden and called to the three visitors to rejoin his majesty in the throne room. Pale and empty, Gabrion needed Quereth's gentle guidance to comply.

The page led them back to the throne and there the king sat upright. It was as if he had been lashed during his absence and now it hurt too much to rest back on his opulent chair. Yet also, a searing anger burned in his eyes.

"Visitors from Kallisor," he spat. "Have you the courtesy to cease your lies at present? Will you now speak with clarity and avoid misconstruing your intent here?"

Gabrion furrowed his brows and responded half-heartedly, "What are you talking about?"

The king's voice lowered and it was hard for the three of them to hear him. "You say you came not to engage in war, but to seek other knowledge. Knowledge of an unknown prisoner and the piece of jade that was already lost to me. Knowledge only."

"It is as we said," Gabrion acknowledged, tensing with the increased suspicion creeping into the king's voice.

"And you proclaim your peaceful intent, though you arrive with a small army of your own, garbed in magically protected armor, which you clearly pillaged from one of my own settlements."

Gabrion's face twitched in annoyance. "We did not pillage any of your towns. These garments were given freely by the people who believed in us and our quest."

"And what, may I ask, is your quest?" the king sneered.

Gabrion stepped forward clenched his hands into fists. "I came here to reclaim my beloved. I came also to find a way to end the warring between our countries. Securing your piece of jade is the means to that end. I did not come here to start a battle with you. My forces outside are merely to lend credence to my claim. I have already explained all of this."

The king barked a laugh. "And you claim not to be here under the command of your king. That this quest is your own."

"It is so."

The king laughed again. "The evidence is to the contrary. As your army awaits in my courtyard, you have reinforcements arriving from the east. Clearly you are a diversion here, set to disable us until support arrives."

"Reinforcements?" Gabrion looked confused.

The king's eyes squinted in anger. "Take your subterfuge elsewhere, warrior child. There was no logic to your claim but scouts have shown us your true purpose here. You will leave my courtyard immediately or else my archers will shoot down your forces where they stand."

"You're mad! If you did so, you would slay your own merchants and citizens in the process."

"It is worthwhile if it prevents you from scoring an early assault. No, young fool, you will all leave these grounds at haste and you will—"

A clattering sound echoed from the western wall of the room. "I demand you let me through!" shrieked an exasperated woman.

"But! You can't!"

"Nonsense!" The woman stormed across the floor toward the throne. She ignored the three visitors tending the king and spoke to her husband, whose face flushed in a mix of anger and bewilderment. "Is this true?" she demanded.

The king composed himself and addressed his queen with utmost patience, though not even he knew where he found it. "My lady, clearly you can see that this is not the time for an interruption. I am nearly finished here. Wait outside a moment longer."

"I will not be blindly escorted to some hidden location for fear of attack. I will remain where I can best assist!"

"Let me finish with my guests," the king insisted. He gestured to Gabrion and stopped when he saw a bizarre look scrawled on the young man's face.

For Gabrion, it was as if he had fallen asleep and entered a dream. No, a strange nightmare. He watched the woman stare down the king, her hair enwrapped with a misty white veil. He couldn't breathe as he registered her face. Her delicate cheeks. Her soft brown hair. He hadn't recognized her voice for she had never spoken in such tones around him. But he knew her. And he knew he wasn't awake any more, or perhaps he had died without knowing it at all.

It took all his strength to pull in the air he needed to utter a single word. "Mira?"

But it couldn't be. It was impossible. The king himself had said there were no prisoners from Savvron here. This woman was merely close in resemblance to his beloved Mira. And she was foremost on his thoughts, so of course he mangled her features in his mind so that this woman resembled Mira. That made more sense to him than the momentary thought that she was standing mere yards away from him.

The woman turned to him and her brows furrowed. "Do I—?" Then she gasped. "Gabrion?" She hesitated for only a moment before she floated those few steps that separated her from the warrior, after which she threw her arms around him and laughed merrily. "Gabe! It *is* you!"

He didn't know what to do. Who else would know his name? It had to be her, not some charlatan that only looked like her. As she laughed, the sound echoed through him and reminded him of his childhood and all their joyous times together. But he was dreaming. This wasn't real. It was some form of mage trickery or some foul magic that had never existed before. He then glanced around to see if maybe Kitalla was nearby causing strange illusions just to play with him.

Mira disengaged and she looked at him, gazing deep into his eyes. "You've—you've really grown a lot, haven't you?" she asked. "Oh, Gabe, I can't believe this! How are you here? What brings you here?"

While he tried to find even a single word, the king asked, "My lady, you know this miscreant?"

"Miscreant?" she retorted with a laugh. "Hardly! Gabrion is harmless, my lord. We grew up together, he and I."

The king connected the pieces easily. He turned to Gabrion with a questioning gaze. "This is the prisoner of whom you spoke?"

"Prisoner?" Mira asked.

Gabrion could only nod.

Mira laughed. "I'm no prisoner, Gabe."

"She is my queen."

Chills raced up and down Gabrion's body. He shook with a cold fright. He couldn't explain it. Something was terribly wrong here. "But you… You were kidnapped. From Savvron."

"No, Gabe, you don't understand." Mira chuckled. "I met Prethos," she said, gesturing toward the king, "on one of the sojourns I took with my parents. We've known each other for some time now. The attack on Savvron was…" She paused, trying to find the best way to explain it, but she wasn't sure.

The king finished for her. "I had told her that I wanted her as my queen and that I love her deeply. She knew it would entail relocating here. Thus I sent for her."

"Oh, it was quite a rush, Gabe!" she said. "His scouts rode in to the forest in Savvron and found me and we rode off that very moment! It was beautiful. I knew he would be waiting for me here."

"You… you what?" Gabrion asked, perplexed. "Don't you remember all the fighting?"

"It was all staged," she dismissed. "They were all trained to make it look like a skirmish. That's all, to make it more exciting. You ran off in a panic but you saw, didn't you?"

"No," he said in disbelief. "It was no false battle, Mira. Don't you know how many people died that day?"

Her expression flickered for a moment. "What?" she asked, pausing in her glee for the first time.

"I barely survived, myself," he said, exasperated. "All this time, you really thought it was a fake battle? Mira?"

The king looked at his queen and shook his head. "Kallisorian nonsense," he pronounced. "My fighters were well trained and would not have harmed a single man, woman, or child in a defenseless town like that. He is lying."

Mira looked torn. "Gabe isn't known for lying." She turned to her lifelong friend, as if reevaluating him suddenly.

"I have quested since that day to find you and to bring you home," Gabrion stammered. "You've been here all this time?"

"Yes, Gabe. Of course. My parents are here as well."

The warrior paused for a moment, recalling what he had learned from his father. Mira's parents had been on sojourn when the attack occurred and they hadn't returned. Only letters had come back to Savvron, and only briefly until they had stopped altogether.

"Your parents knew."

"Of course they did," she smiled. "They accepted the king's proposal for marriage before he came for me. He wouldn't have sent for me otherwise."

"But you were kidnapped," Gabrion muttered. This made less sense to him than her being dead. He needed it to make sense somehow. "You were stolen away. I had to find you."

"Gabe, that's very sweet, but I wasn't kidnapped. Not really." She turned and smiled at her husband. "He simply had me brought here to my new home. With him."

Fire welled inside of Gabrion and as he swallowed, he felt as if knives cut through him as well. He had yearned for her so lovingly and for so long, yet her heart had not been his. She hadn't yearned for him. She hadn't expected him to find her and rescue her. She had barely given him any thought, it seemed, for she hadn't even written to him over the past year.

She seemed oblivious to Gabrion's plight. Instead, she clapped her hands and laughed. "It's so good of you to come. We should celebrate our reunion."

Gabrion was dumbstruck. Clearly, Mira had been brainwashed by this tyrant king. But as he looked at the two of them, he realized that he was an utter fool.

That very day she was taken, Mira had kept asking Gabrion whether he thought the armies would come. She had kept looking around as if she expected them to arrive at any moment. Perhaps she had an inkling that her king would come for her while her parents were away. Perhaps she had agreed to go but wasn't certain of when her escort would appear. The more he thought of it, the more he remembered her pensive moments, her odd sighs that hadn't made any sense back then. She clearly had struggled to tell him about her love interest, for she had not once hinted about him. She had avoided Gabrion's own advances, but he thought she was merely being shy or playful.

It started making sense now. All along this journey, his companions had teased him time and again about chasing a ghost. Though when they saw the comments hurt him, they had withdrawn. But here he realized that he had indeed been chasing a ghost all along. The Mira in his mind hadn't been real after all.

"Gabe, what is it?" Mira asked, fear making her voice quaver.

He reached deep into his pocket and withdrew the one object he had carried with him all this time. He kept it clenched tightly in his hand as his eyes darted back and forth from the king to the queen. "I die this day," he declared.

"Gabrion?"

"The world around me is a false one. Your troops invaded Savvron and slew many of our people, just so you could steal away the one person I truly loved with all my heart."

"Gab—"

"I die this day, now that I see that you are blind, Mira. That you could believe in any way that an assault on our hometown would bring no casualties. That young Kaz found us on our way to our picnic covered in blood, and you would dismiss it. You are blind that the king sent Andron to train us to defend ourselves, so that when the Hathrens attacked, we did rise up to defend ourselves. And many of us died that day."

"Gabe, stop!" Mira demanded, clutching her head with her free hand and turning away.

"Our homes burned and that one skirmish led to the increased fighting of today. It also brought me out of Savvron to travel the world, in search of enough strength that I could come to rescue you. You, who cared nothing for me."

"That isn't true, Gabe!" she cried. "You were my closest friend!"

"So close, you could never tell me of this man? So close you never wrote to me once over the past year to tell me what was happening or that you were all right?"

"I—I did!" she retorted. "And you did not return my letters. I told you of Prethos and our wedding and that I became queen—"

"Nothing ever came to Savvron!" Gabrion interrupted. His gaze slid to the king. "How is it that none of these supposed letters reached Savvron?"

The king merely shrugged. "Messages between our kingdoms do not pass easily, especially if you incited your king against us. But I assure you, I left no orders to interrupt any letters my beloved Mira would send."

Gabrion shook with the man's use of 'beloved Mira.' His soul trembled as he looked at them, calm and in disbelief, doubting his own story. The distrust in her eyes made her seem unnatural to him. There was something wrong and he couldn't discern its source. He glanced again to see if there were signs of mages casting charms over her, remembering fleetingly that such magic did not exist among the mages anyway.

"My lady," the king said. "This friend of yours seems utterly confused. He is a lovesick child who went on some mad quest to pursue you."

"I don't know what to believe," she said. "But I don't know why Gabe would lie."

"I wouldn't," the warrior said. "Visit Savvron and see the destruction for yourself."

"There's no way of proving when any such destruction occurred," the king dismissed. "It could have been from a recent battle or a bad storm."

"The people will tell her," Gabrion insisted through gritted teeth.

"My lady," the king sighed. "You came running in here because of the dreadful news that has befallen us, did you not?"

Mira shook herself alert for a moment. "Yes, the Kallisorians broke through the eastern defenses and march upon the castle."

"Indeed, and this young 'friend' of yours also brought a small army of his own."

Mira turned her wide eyes on Gabrion. "Is that true?"

"Yes, but—"

"And he came demanding the fire jade from my possession, on top of that."

"Gabe?"

"I did, Mira, but—"

"Isn't it clear," the king said in a loud tone, "that this boy has used your presence here to seek audience with me so that his forces can weaken us before the main army arrives? He seeks to destroy us, Mira."

"No!" Mira gasped with tears in her eyes.

"No," Gabrion echoed. But he could see that she believed her husband's version of the events. The burning within him faded to an icy coldness and he felt a sensation he had never truly experienced before. Loathing.

Mira backed away as the look in Gabrion's eyes changed to a feral sort of rage. He lost all sense of humanity as he stood there fully accepting that his whole quest had been based on a lie and, worse than that, that Mira's new life was also based on a series of lies that she clearly chose to believe without trying to listen to him at all.

"Mira, come home with me," he said in a strange voice that wasn't his at all. He sounded as if he had risen from death and his throat was barely working.

She stepped further away. "No. You monster. Leave this place!" Distraught, Mira spun on her heels and bolted from the room, tears streaming from her eyes.

The king rose to his feet and four guards approached from the wings. "Your stay has ended," he declared. "I should slay you outright for the pain you have inflicted upon my queen. Take your forces from these walls and pray I do not order the guards to eradicate you once you are in the desert."

"What have you done to her?" Gabrion snarled. "How can she have forgotten the battle in Savvron?"

"Her Highness is of no concern to you, commoner. Be gone from this place before I slay you here and now." In response, the guards drew closer still, swords at the ready.

"This isn't over."

"Oh, yes," the king returned sternly. "It is certainly and undeniably over." With that, the guards rushed Gabrion, Quereth, and Morrish out of the throne room, where heavy doors slammed decisively shut.

CHAPTER 32

Deeper into Magehaven

THEIR BODIES WERE riddled with minor injuries, but Randler and Frast sprinted away and raced toward their goal. Randler hated leaving Kitalla behind to fend off the beasts and mages by herself, but he also knew that she would be up to the challenge. He was elated that she had suddenly shown up and he understood full well that she wouldn't do so just to die now.

Randler hadn't known Kitalla until after her torture in Grenthar's domain, but his bardic talents had kept him informed even then. Rumors had swept through Pindington of the happenings in the thief's lair and after he came to know her, Randler easily connected the tales. Seeing her in combat, he had also determined that the whispered stories hadn't quite lived up what she must have really endured.

Frast tugged Randler's shoulder. "Hurry!" He was fiercely directed in this sprint, which seemed a bit unlike the mage to Randler. Still, he had served as a great protection within the tower. He could not have entered to rescue Dariak without his help or without the risk to their lives.

Magehaven was coming alive with more sounds of alarm. Additional defenses were triggered, but there were no portcullises that fell to pin intruders, no trapdoors or secret arrow holes from which they were attacked. The defenses were all based in magic and now that the warnings had spread, the defenses came on in earnest.

"Follow my steps precisely!" Frast yelled suddenly. He hopped toward the right and then jumped forward and to the left. He sprang wide across and almost lost his balance, then he turned and leaped again. Randler did not ask; he simply followed, pouncing in the same intricate pattern.

After dozens of erratic leaps through the room, Frast teetered after a landing and he went down on his knee. Fire erupted floor to ceiling where his leg touched the stone floor and he screamed in pain, jumping back, ready to land on yet another square outside the invisible safety zone. Randler saw the plight and pounced ahead, grabbing Frast and holding him tightly to keep him from falling. The mage pressed healing magic toward his knee hoping to quell the agony, but the fiery column had some form of disruptive spell that made healing difficult. Frast couldn't pull the energies properly and the pain grew worse.

"Tell me where to go," Randler said in Frast's ear. "I cannot see the runes like you can."

"A moment." Tears streamed from the mage's eyes and the throbbing grew worse. "No. Leave me, Randler. I'm no good to you. Make a run for it and don't stop. It's the only way." He gasped in agony as the pain extended to his calf and thigh. "It's getting worse. Go! You have to. I'll follow once the pain subsides."

Randler didn't entertain the idea at all. He looked around and saw the door. It was too many paces away to walk to and he doubted he could carry the mage while making a run for it. "Frast, I'm not leaving you here, but we can't stay. I don't care how badly it hurts; you have to run with me."

"No, I—"

"No choice, mage," Randler cut in sternly. "If you collapse here, we both die. I'm not leaving you. Let's move."

Frast tried to put weight on his injured leg and screamed. Randler shook him and insisted that he had no choice. But Frast wouldn't make a move. He looked like he would fall over at any moment, giving up because of the pain.

Randler wouldn't have it. He didn't care about the repercussions. They had to go. He gauged the door, braced himself, and then shoved Frast ahead with all his might. As the mage stumbled pitifully, the room erupted in a torrent of magic. Randler bolted across the room, grabbing Frast as he went and dragging him, using the mage's momentum to get them both to the door.

Blasts of electricity and fire erupted all around the room as they made their escape and the bolts did their damage. Both the bard and the mage were badly seared by the energy and the pain receptors in their bodies flared as they collapsed on the other side of the doorway. They were completely immobilized by the magical forces. The agony grew in intensity and spread throughout their limbs, threatening to overtake them completely.

"Not like this," Randler hissed. He could barely see through his tears but he did his best to ignore it. He summoned up the tales of Kitalla's suffering in Pindington and tried to convince himself that he could survive this as she had overcome that. He thought of the battle dances he had shared with her and channeled his thoughts on the heavy beats of the drums. Focusing his thoughts helped him to set the pain aside, at least until he moved and everything flared up again.

"Come on, Frast," he gasped pitifully. "Come on." He coughed as a spasm of fire erupted within him. "Counter this magic. Somehow. Some way."

But the mage was lost in his suffering. He curled in on himself and wept sadly, unable to fight the waves of agony.

Randler felt bereft. He had only minor skill with magic, and mostly just theoretical knowledge. He couldn't fight a spell like this. He reached for his shadow jade, yearning to withdraw the pain, but he couldn't focus on it strongly enough to have an effect. Randler thought of his friends and remembered that each of them had faced horrible challenges and yet pressed onward. Dariak was off somewhere in the tower fighting to survive, though the snippets Frast had given him about Dariak's metallic condition were disheartening. But he had pressed on through the lightning battle against Sharice and he had proven victorious then, and Randler knew his mother's skills were terribly strong. Dariak had survived.

All along on the quest, Gabrion had pursued his missing lady and, despite all the odds, Randler believed the warrior would find her. Nothing deterred the young man's quest nor broke his spirit. He had faced harsh doubts but still he strove.

And there was Kitalla, who had seen the worst of it all, ever fighting alone in the world, and often proving herself as the greatest defender amidst their group. Even at their best when all four of them were in their stride, Kitalla outshone them all with her agility and cunning. She never surrendered to her surroundings; she took control and dominated them.

Randler was determined to do the same, even as his mind argued against him. The pain kept increasing though he was nowhere near the initial runes. Magic skill or not, the bard would beat this.

The minstrel clutched on to any rational and irrational thoughts that might grant him survival. He realized partly that there had to be a counterspell to this effect, for if any acolyte or master inadvertently triggered the defensive spells, they would have to be cured. Thus, there was an answer somewhere. He rocked back and forth, considering battles he'd seen, stories he'd heard, toys he had played with as a child; none of it helpful.

Only one fleeting thought held anything substantial for him. From his own Trial upon entering the tower his first time, Randler had experienced the resonance and dissonance effect of sound. In some way, perhaps he could apply that to this spell. The only sound Randler had was his voice, and though it would be laden with intense pain, he pressed words to his lips and he chanted.

I'll never let the pain succeed.
I'll never let it win.
Just release the agony.
It will not start again.

I'll never let it win.
I will use my inner strength.
It will not start again.
I will go to any length.

I will use my inner strength
To release the agony.
I will go to any length
To never let the pain succeed.

The challenge of crafting the oddly repetitive pantoum focused his mind deeply on the structure of the lines. He felt the echoing lines resonate within him as he chanted them again, twisting some minor variations here and there. As he chanted repeatedly, he heard Frast moaning in the background, but it wasn't the random moaning of a man suffering. He was matching the tune that Randler was murmuring and Randler focused his energy on the words again. He uttered them over and over, building a resistance to his own pain by giving strength to the pantoum. As he did, Frast pulled healing energies and wove them into the melody, letting the repetition stack the spell into a stronger incantation.

It took time but the pain started to subside. The two of them focused their efforts and soon they were free of the torture. Frast decoded that the pain spells had been fortified with firegnat serum, hence the long-lasting effects. He would have to try to remember that as he considered a better counterspell. They hesitated for a few minutes to let their bodies readjust and then they had to press onward. Randler looked over his shoulder, but Kitalla had not joined them yet. He feared the other defenses may have harmed her, but then he dismissed it. No, she would only be delayed, not stopped. He knew.

"Let's go," the bard decided and Frast nodded, greatly relieved to be able to move and think clearly again. The two men dashed down a rounded corridor, while Frast kept his senses alert for more magical traps.

They approached a room in which three mages were tensed and ready for intruders, though they were perched back-to-back so they could face all of the doorways at once. When the duo entered, the mages pivoted around and fired off their first round of spells.

Randler jumped to the left and entered a roll, pouncing back onto his feet and pulling out his mace. He had to split the mages' attention so Frast could better neutralize them. He feinted to the left and then charged forward, as the apprentice brought his hands around and issued forth a binding web. Randler dodged it easily with another roll, but it landed him in dark sludge a second mage had set on the stone. The viscous liquid clung to Randler's clothing and weighed him down. It reminded the bard of the Shield of Delminor that weighed down its victim, thereby immobilizing him. He tried to brush the ooze off himself, but succeeded only in spreading it.

Frast, meanwhile, was channeling energy like a master with many more years of experience than he had. Desperation pushed him to spells he didn't know he could cast. When he had entered the room, two of the mages launched their defensive spells in his direction. Fire and ice darted toward him. He considered deflecting them, but he wasn't sure which way Randler was headed at the time. Instead, he sputtered a quick incantation and breathed deeply as he clapped his hands. The effect brought a quick tug of air together, forcing the fire and ice to collapse and dispel each other in a sizzling mist.

The mages growled and thrust their hands into their next volley, taking care not to fall prey to the same tactic. But Frast was slowly moving closer, subtly approaching them as they focused their spells. He hoped they might misjudge the distance and that it would give him an advantage. He listened intently for the key spell words, hoping to discern their attack before it was on in earnest. He hadn't heard '*contronor*' or '*relliashinos*' before but the rest of the keywords clued him in to a sort of binding spell.

Frast dipped into his cloak and popped the cork from a small vial of thick oil. He smothered the liquid on his finger and called to the substance in the ancient tongue. "*Encirrisiculous brevitishe forthranetricant shallious.*" It was an inspired enchantment that he hadn't ever attempted before. He didn't know if his inspiration came from his earlier studies or from being exposed to the abundant energies in the tower itself. He released the last thread of the incantation and while the spell hesitated a few seconds before commencing, he set his mind to an offensive strike.

Randler continued to dodge the increasing fury of the mage he faced, barely able to consider an alternate strategy to defend himself. He considered tossing his mace at a second mage, but he doubted he could fend off the two of them with his agility alone, and he wasn't fully recovered from his burns. Instead, he settled for duping the mage into a false security; he only hoped he wouldn't distract Frast in the process.

When Randler's attacker sent a volley of thorns flying forth, the bard collapsed, moaning in pain. He heard the brief snicker of the mage, who immediately set upon augmenting the venom within the thorns to further paralyze and contain his victim. Randler recognized a few of the intoned syllables and he reacted accordingly, though not a single thorn had actually touched him. He curled within himself, groaning madly and hoping that Frast would remember his recent cries of actual pain and understand his ruse.

Frast, however, was too engaged in his own spell-casting to pay much heed to Randler's plight at the moment. While the bard tried keeping one mage detained, Frast was working to take down the other two and if Randler fell in the process, then he would have to find a way to help him later. For now, the mages' paralyzing spell fell flat as it impacted Frast's delayed lubrication shield. The mages had counted on the paralysis, for they had paused in their casting to gather themselves for the next volley.

But the inspired delay Frast had placed upon his defensive spell gave him the time he needed to pull the energies around himself and cast them toward his attackers. He drew upon the powers of wind and negated heat to chill the air and to create a freezing snowstorm. A flurry of snow blinded the other three mages and Frast ran forward in an attempt to overwhelm them.

Randler took the opportunity to drop his ruse and to spring to his feet, mace first, smashing his attacker and then turning to tackle the others. He struck hard but not fatally. The mages could heal themselves, but by the time they had healed enough to pursue them, it would be for naught. Moments later, Randler and Frast were on their way.

Exhaustion was taking its toll on the two of them as they made their way up a flight of stairs. Frast kept offensive spells at the ready so he could instantly strike any others they approached. Likewise, Randler nocked an arrow and drew his bowstring, hoping his aim would be true enough as he darted upward.

Frast called a halt as they crested the landing. He sent a wave of ice to his left, focusing more on the floor than any living target in the room. Randler peered over the mage's shoulder and saw a slightly opened doorway from which the growling of beasts could be heard. The ice would cause the poor creatures to stumble as they entered, giving Frast and Randler a chance to subdue them. The ploy worked, though two lupinoes leaped over the icy flooring and stalked Randler angrily.

The bard fired off his arrows at the other beasts first, letting the lupinoes scope out his skills. He had time before the wolf-like creatures would attack. By then, he hoped to have the rest of the horde eliminated. Frast added more ice to keep the creatures stumbling as they tried to stand, but he, too, was wary of the lupinoes.

A cry echoed from behind Randler and he turned reflexively toward the sound. The lupinoes reacted instantly, racing for the bard to slay him in his moment of distraction. However, Kitalla veritably flew up the stairs and intercepted them easily. She had a slightly wild look in her eyes and the lupinoes halted in her presence and then cowered like timid puppies, after which they turned and fled.

"Didn't think you'd have all the fun yourselves, did you?" she said by way of greeting.

"Kitalla!" Randler gasped with obvious relief. "How we've missed you!"

"Never could do anything without me." She looked at the pile of slain beasts and nodded. "I stand corrected. You have done well, you two. But let's get to those jades and get lost before the magic here overpowers us."

Frast nodded and led them toward one of the doorways. He sensed an electrical surge from the entryway and he disarmed it with a defensive shield he summoned up from a fragment of bark. He marveled at the spells he was calling, but only for brief moments, because the next challenge was never far behind.

Kitalla dashed past him and sprinted down the corridor, setting off all manner of rune traps. Light blazed in the room and Frast shielded his eyes until the brilliance dimmed enough to see by. The magical energies had been expelled and Kitalla leaned against the far wall, inspecting her fingernails as if she had been there all evening. Randler chortled as he and Frast jogged to catch up with her.

"We're almost there," Frast said needlessly. Both Kitalla and Randler possessed jades that pulsed with the proximity of another shard. Also, though, the next set of mages was ruthless in its defensive strike. Some of these were masters of the arcane arts and they thrived on tugging the energies in unique ways to disable their foes. Kitalla dispatched one of them quickly anyway. The other six ignored the death of their comrade and kept chanting.

Frast detected a protective field in front of the others; a ward they had erected moments too late to save their fellow. Physical attacks weren't likely to get through the wall and Frast was uncertain how to proceed. He traced the energies swiftly, seeking a hole in the balance, but finding none.

Yet as Frast investigated their defenses, the mages were working insidiously to trace Frast's own energy patterns. One of the masters was able to follow a keen line and tug on it sharply, which sent Frast tumbling to the ground with a stabbing pain in his side. It was very like the chamber that had harmed him earlier. He was determined to stand against this torment better than before.

Without delay, Frast withdrew the vial from his pocket that held a vitreous oil and he smashed it to pieces on the floor. He grabbed a shard of glass and sliced his hand with it, tying himself to the piece. The spell he cast was not entirely a defensive spell, but it was similar in some way to the reflective spell Dariak had cast long ago against the healer Elgris back in Kaison. Where Dariak had drawn the energies through himself and cast them back to his attacker, now Frast was using the reflective property of glass to mimic a similar effect. Doing so, he was able to counter the intrusive twinges that hurt so much.

Randler and Kitalla were hardly idle during all this. The thief and bard, their cooperative skills honed after countless battles together, entered a dueling trance that would have impressed the mages if they hadn't viewed these two as intruders. Kitalla and Randler drew upon the same battle dance and the bard emphasized the beat by striking his mace or boot on the floor when the timing permitted.

The mages themselves were seeking the weaknesses of their enemies and they were calling the energies forth into a concentrated spell that would obliterate the three foes while keeping themselves unscathed. It seemed in some ways that they were chanting to maintain a wall of force, but even Kitalla and Randler could feel the other energies at work. It wasn't often that mages combined their energies to enact a major incantation such as this, but it wasn't unheard of either. Indeed, the mages of the Kallisorian army during the War of the Colossus had done the same.

Kitalla realized that she couldn't directly penetrate the barrier. She also noted that Frast would have a hard time taking down six masters collectively standing against them. But Kitalla knew something that the gathered mages did not know. She possessed a unique skill that no mage had yet been able to produce through any magical means. And so, with Randler's lead, she danced.

The fire and metal jades called to Kitalla so she pulled them into her hands, where they flared with inner light. Her hands and arms swept sensuously around in the air and her hips cleverly dodged in other directions. She stepped lightly, spinning when the music hit particularly high notes, bending when the tempo slowed. It was a song Randler had sung some nights, and though he only hummed the notes and beat his mace on the stone to keep the rhythm, Kitalla had all the cues she needed.

In her mind, she pictured a vast, open landscape. The trees swayed serenely in the breeze and bent low when the wind gusted. Flowers followed the dance of the trees yet when the wind kicked up high the petals released from their birthing homes and floated into the air, carried delicately by the wind. Crimson, gold, white, and lavender all fluttered around one another wildly. The colors blended into a fleeting rainbow that was gone all too soon. A deep longing followed their sudden flight away and a misty rain fell from the heavens, like tears of sorrow for the loss.

Kitalla's body and mind worked in unison to maintain the imagery as she moved about, now otherwise defenseless. She had full faith in her companions to protect her, but there was little need. The master mages were enthralled and Frast was able to break through their defensive barrier without much effort. It was as if the weaving itself had unraveled and invited him within. He and Randler wasted no time knocking the mages to the ground, stunning them to unconsciousness.

A great sense of warmth ran through Kitalla. It was a sensation she had felt before, though it had never been this pronounced. Her belly twittered and she touched it gently, protectively. The sensation suddenly irked her and reminded her of the horrors she had been forced to relive as part of her Trial here. The pain of loss would always be with her, but using her skills now suddenly felt so right. So completing. Not even the memory of the death of her unborn child could ruin this sense of contentment. Some part of her had felt it before, but it had always been blocked beneath the memories she had fought to deny.

She knew there wasn't time to dwell on it. Carefully, she set the thoughts aside, not intending to bury them this time; just to keep them waiting until she could explore them.

Randler was looking at her oddly, wondering at her hesitation, but she smiled drolly and shrugged before running off ahead.

They had reached the inner sanctum, finally, where the jades were stored. Frast was already puzzling over the defensive wards that protected the jade, but Kitalla gently nudged him aside. She still held the fire and metal jades in her hands, and now she reached them before her, pointing them toward their missing comrade on its pedestal in the center of the room. She felt the energy coursing through her and pulling her closer to the middle. Frast intervened, and rightly so. Even two more steps and an explosive fireball would have engulfed them all.

Randler felt a similar pull from the shadow and air jades. He pulled them from his pocket and held them aloft as Kitalla did. Their four jades emanated powerfully and the pulsations coursed through his whole body. He subconsciously started tapping his foot to the rhythm.

The lonely jade in the center of the room called to its brethren, longing to be reunited with them. Its power radiated sharply from its perch, almost crying out to be rescued. Kitalla couldn't bear it any more. She stepped forward, escaping Frast's attempted block. It didn't matter. The metal jade drew the harmful energies away, and those that could not be drained were burned by the fire jade.

Frast stepped back in awe. "If you could only see the energies," he murmured to Randler. "It is almost as if she is a conduit for the energies in this room. They cannot touch her, not harmfully anyway. It's… uncanny."

The bard nodded. "The jades call for each other. They protect their masters, too. Whether it's because she has two jades or some other reason, they are working in unison to reunite. Frast, don't get too distracted. We aren't likely to be alone here for long."

"Indeed," he nodded. "And once the mages who have been calling on this jade for support can no longer do so, this place is going to become even more dangerous."

Despite Randler's warning, the two of them couldn't tear their eyes from Kitalla's deliberate advance toward the central pedestal. Frast watched as the threads of energy in the room alternately dissipated or absorbed themselves into Kitalla with each step. As he observed more closely, he reaffirmed that the energies were not going into Kitalla exactly, but the metal jade was channeling the energy and it was then coursing through her body safely.

Her hand touched the jade on the pedestal. The beast jade. She could hear a slight growling from within it as she held it, or perhaps just a low vibration; she didn't know. The glossy surface felt like several textures all at once; feather, fur, leather, skin, claw. It was all there. This jade would give dominion over the feral creatures. It was different than Dariak's nature jade, which connected its energies to inanimate life. Yet she knew instinctively as she held the new jade that it would have no power over people.

No power over minds. It meant that her dance skill would still be unique. Somehow that seemed important to her, but she also knew that now was not the time to dwell upon it. She set the thoughts aside as the defenses in the room collapsed.

She blinked at Randler and Frast as if waking from a slight trance, then took a deep breath and released it, but it was Frast who spoke, a slightly dour expression on his face. "I was hoping both jades would still be here."

Kitalla nodded slowly. "That means trouble for Dariak. Let's get going."

CHAPTER 33

Rush of Honor

THE FEELINGS BURNED within Gabrion as he and the others were led through the hallway and toward the castle's exit. Part of him felt completely dead inside, but not all of him. He knew deep within himself that Mira's memory had somehow been altered. He didn't know how it was possible, but it had to be so. There were no rumors of such magic, yet it was all that made any sense to him. Besides, hadn't he seen strange things happen with magic? Hadn't Kitalla's dance skills influenced his own mind?

Perhaps he could reach Mira's true memory if he just talked to her, but the king's tone was definite. He wouldn't get another chance to see her. There was no time to act but this very moment.

Four guards ushered them forward and although everyone was silent, Gabrion decided that he had come too far to quit now. He had to know for certain. He needed to try.

"Quereth, Morrish," he said lowly and calmly, "tell Ervinor to prepare for attack."

"What?" Quereth gasped.

Gabrion didn't hesitate. He stumbled awkwardly and crashed to the floor in a heap. Two guards pushed Quereth and Morrish ahead while the other two berated the young warrior's clumsiness and knelt over to hoist him onto his feet. They barely drew close before Gabrion lunged back up and tackled them both fully, clobbering them with outstretched arms and swallowing them with his assault.

The other two guards reacted promptly, shoving their captives off-balance and then turning to defend against the warrior. Morrish recovered and turned to fight, but Quereth denied him the chance. "No! We mustn't! Morrish, we must get out of here!"

"But—"

Gabrion grabbed a guard's arm and heaved the man around behind himself and then turned to reach for the next one. He eyed his hesitant comrades and called out. "Get out of here! Alert Ervinor! Immediately!" He ducked a sword swipe and leaned forward to punch the assailant in the stomach. "Now!"

Quereth shoved Morrish ahead of him as the guards called out an alarm. The soldier bolted onward at last, lowering his head and barreling his way toward the door

469

in the distance. He didn't turn to ensure that Quereth was with him, for Gabrion had commanded them both to flee and he knew the old man would be right behind him.

But he was wrong. Quereth rooted himself where he stood once he saw that Morrish was on his way. He then fumbled through his robes and withdrew whatever spell components came to his fingers and from those he crafted a number of spells.

Gabrion was both angry and relieved. This was supposed to his fight. His rebellion against the injustice. His rescue of his beloved Mira. Quereth had no right to interfere, not even to make his mission a success. Yet at the same time, Gabrion knew he would be overwhelmed without help.

Ice darts flashed through the air and lanced into a guardsman that was charging for Gabrion. The warrior had already started a defensive attack but he shifted his weight and brought his sword toward the next target. The guard was caught unawares and took a slice to the cheek, which enraged him. He shouted ferociously and tightened his grip on his sword, charging Gabrion with all his strength. It was a foolish move, and one that Andron had trained Gabrion to defend back in Savvron. Battles were better fought with a clear head, not anger. Gabrion parried the strike and kicked his foot out, tripping the emotional guard and casting him to the floor. What Gabrion didn't anticipate was the counterstrike from the falling guardsman, but the warrior pounced over the attack and was left unscathed.

Quereth's casting continued as Gabrion dodged about. Finding three spiders, the mage used aged sap from a tree with a complex incantation and as he stretched the doughy sap, the spiders grew in size, their pincers clicking in anticipation. Quereth set them on the guards that were starting to arrive then turned his mind toward the next spell.

Gabrion pulled himself away from the growing pile of bodies that were falling around him. The narrow hallway kept the guards from completely surrounding him, but it made escape nearly impossible. Still, he did his best to incapacitate the defenders without killing them. They may have aligned themselves with this king, but perhaps if they had a choice they may turn their services elsewhere, as had the citizens of Marritosh.

"Whatever you're planning to do," Quereth gasped between spells, "you'd best get on with it. This place isn't defensible for long and more guards are on their way." He shot a fire dart down the hallway to intercept an archer. "And they're not just swordsmen any more. Gabrion, it won't be long before the mages arrive. You must move!"

He debated quickly. Whether he left now or saw this through to the end, the king would retaliate by firing on Gabrion's army outside. He had to finish it. "Quereth, go! You're needed out there with the rest."

"You're a fool if you think I'm leaving you to deal with this on your own." He moved his arms in a wide circle and Gabrion thought he actually recognized some of the words the old man uttered. Indeed, it was a protection spell very similar to the ones Dariak had used on him. "Stand there any longer and I may kick you myself to get you to move!"

Gabrion nodded, then tightened his grip on his sword. He drew a deep breath and then ran back toward the throne room, his legs pumping powerfully and carrying him more swiftly than Quereth could follow. The mage gave chase, hoping to offer continued support, but he had his own troubles soon enough. Reinforcements arrived from side halls and Quereth was hard-pressed to stop them.

The mage drew an empty vial from his pocket and cast a spell, then smashed the glass to the floor. As it shattered, the bits of glass spread out finely and created a powdery coating on the ground. Quereth then added an icy layer atop the fragments and the floor became slick. The rushing guards pounded inward and lost their footing on the slippery surface, tumbling half a dozen of them in a heap. The mage did not wait for them to recover. He ran after Gabrion.

The warrior, however, was beyond the mage's reach. He had already crested the archway into the throne room, much to the dismay of those inside. Twenty guardsmen and four mages erupted from their posts to protect the king, who had been pacing the room as he sorted out the recent events. Gabrion swept his sword side to side and sought a clear passage across the chamber. Five guards surrounded the king defensively, but Gabrion wasn't heading for them. Instead, he sought the rear left exit and the door that would lead to Mira.

Adrenaline rushed through him as he bolted across the chamber. Six guards intercepted him, but he barreled through, ignoring the cuts and scrapes he earned from them. His sword lashed out and crashed into them, bruising and stunning, but not killing them. He didn't even think about it. He knew why.

The glass jade in his pocket was beating fiercely with each pulse of his heart. He knew it was going to protect him, as it had at every turn on his journey since the elder of Gerrish had given it to him. Its power wasn't unlimited, thus after the jade had freed him from Heria's bindings, she had been able to strike him. He knew for now that sword thrusts from the guards would be turned aside because he would simply cut through them, and because he did not want to harm any of them in the process, the jade blunted his blade so that his attacks would not be fatal.

Ice darts, fire bolts, ensnaring webs all flew at Gabrion from the mages, but he had survived the fighting within Magehaven where the spellfire was much more concentrated. These attempts would not stop him. He would find Mira. He would find her and he would help her to understand. He pressed onward.

As Gabrion approached the door, he heard two simultaneous shouts, but he couldn't focus on either one. His objective was clear. He dug his heels in and eluded two more guards on his way to the door.

"He isn't alone!" echoed one of the guardsmen by the main entrance to the throne.

"He is after the queen!" shouted the king. "Stop him! Kill him!"

The spells launched in his direction increased in intensity, but his magic armor defeated the potency of the spells. His skin tingled with numbness from the electric blasts, and he felt the heat from an exploding fireball, but it was more like he was reliving a tale told by a great bard, rather than feeling any of it himself. It was a curious sensation, but the door was approaching and he needed to invade it deftly.

He punched a guard in the face and ducked under another's sword, while still making his way forward. A guard from the rear of the room cut his poleax through the air and it connected solidly with Gabrion's chest. The strike should have killed him.

But the glass jade did its job perfectly. As the large weapon touched Gabrion, the warrior's body sharpened immensely. He was knocked back a few steps from the impact, but the weapon itself shattered into limitless pieces and the astounded guard just looked at the remnants in utter bewilderment. Three other attacks met Gabrion with the same reaction and the king cried out in horror.

"What foul magic is this? What are you, demon?" He waved a hand outward and three more men charged Gabrion with all their might, but each attack fell impotently away and the warrior was essentially untouched. "There isn't protective armor that strong!" the king raged. "Who are you?"

The attacks on Gabrion ceased as the guards and mages realized that he could not be harmed. They encircled him with their weapons ready, as if some sign would tell them if he became vulnerable, but it was fruitless. The king, too, realized this.

"Stop," he called out to his guards. "Lay down your weapons." He stepped toward Gabrion. "I do not understand your defenses, young warrior. But I do see now that we are helpless before you. State your demands that I may entreat with you and have you gone from this place."

Gabrion eyed the king menacingly. "You have showered me with lies and accusations. Why would I believe you now?"

The king narrowed his eyes and focused intently upon Gabrion. "Clearly, yours is a skill unknown to my castle. You have cut through every defense you've encountered thus far. I obviously have no way of stopping you. Yet, even on this rampage of yours, you haven't killed a single one of my men." He struggled with his next words, as if they were hard to say. "I would rather deal with you rationally before you turn your power into a killing force and eradicate my defenses."

"My intent here was never to kill anyone or to start a war," Gabrion said, lowering his sword but keeping it in hand. "I told you earlier that my intent was to find a means of ending the wars between our kingdoms."

"Barging back in here in a berserker rage is hardly a proper way to communicate your intent," the king growled.

"Mira," Gabrion said. "What have you done to her? How have you bemused her? I must speak with her."

The king's jaw set firmly. "I don't know that I can deny your request, given your defenses. What would you speak to her about?"

Gabrion knew the king was stalling, but he didn't care. Nothing was going to stop him from his goal. "She must know the truth of what happened to our hometown. She must understand that this"—and he gestured around, unable to find the words—"is all a farce."

"Hardly," the king muttered. "You claim she is bemused, but perhaps you're a fool. Perhaps you're mistaken. Speaking to her will offer you no solace."

Gabrion straightened his back ever so slightly. The king recoiled in honest fear, unsure if the young man would attack. "Lead me to her or don't. Either way, I *will* speak to her."

They stared at each other intently and at last the king conceded. "Very well, young one. I will bring you to her, but prepare yourself. You may not hear what you are hoping to hear." The king ignored the protests of the guards and he strode to the door, opening it and stepping through with Gabrion close behind.

They walked through a series of passages, greeted by confused soldiers along the way. They eyed Gabrion suspiciously, but the king demanded compliance. The corridors were all fortified with stone but most were decorated with lavish wooden struts and beams that were purely aesthetic. Flowers lined various alcoves, bringing a soft fragrance into the castle, while scented oils burned softly, adding their perfume as well as light to the path. Gabrion, however, saw only the path ahead.

As they reached the end of the journey, Gabrion heard singing. It was slightly muffled, for it emanated through a door, but it was clearly a song he had heard before. The voice wavered as if it was upset, but he recognized it as Mira's.

Sleep my beloved for night has come to us.
Close your dear eyes and turn your thoughts inside.
Dream now, for there you will see the light and the hopes of your tender heart.
You will be at peace as you drift through clouds of wonder and harmony.

Rest now, my child.
You will be strong.
Rest now, my child.
One day you will shine.

No one can harm you while I am here by your side.
No shadows can fall here for I am your light.
Your dreams will guide you to your morrow and you will be safe with each step you take.
You will achieve all that you wish and all of your desires will be filled.

Gabrion froze in place as the song echoed in his ears. The king merely stared at him, wondering what the man's reaction meant. Memories swirled in Gabrion's mind but they were muddled by everything he was feeling at the moment. He wanted to hold on to the innocence of the song, of the times she would sing it to him when he was sick, of the times he would hum it softly because it reminded him of her, of the times she sang it as they walked through Savvron. He knew he had hummed that song a thousand times over the past year; surely his companions had overheard him often.

But now the song was painful. He couldn't shake the sudden feeling that he did not want to pass through the door. He didn't want to confront the truth. Though he needed to see her and to speak with her, he was terrified that the king was right. But he couldn't be.

Gabrion pressed his hand to the door and it opened silently. A waft of air swept through the room and alerted Mira to the presence of visitors. She straightened and turned around and when she saw Gabrion, she set her jaw.

"What is it?" she asked. Her voice was cold, having shed all the warmth it held as she had sung.

Gabrion stepped inside while the king waited in the hallway. "Mira, please. Listen to me."

She shook her head. "You want me to believe in the horrors you were telling me of before. Why would you want to hurt me, Gabe?"

"I don't," he pleaded. "But you can't live in a lie, Mira. This isn't where you belong."

Mira rolled her eyes. "What lie, Gabrion? This is my home. Don't you see? This *is* where I belong."

"At what cost?" he asked, his heart aching.

"Gabrion, we—" she stopped and tried to find the words.

He reached into his pocket as he had done earlier and he withdrew the object he had kept with him all along. "That day, Mira, I was going to offer this to you." He reached his hand out but he couldn't step toward her. She was half a room away from him, but for all it felt like, she was in another kingdom entirely.

Tears welled in her eyes when she realized that he held an engagement ring. "Gabe." But she did not step toward him. "I'm sorry, Gabrion. I never… I didn't…"

He didn't need her to finish the sentences that were catching in her throat. "I see." He lowered his hand and choked on a knot of his own. "But Mira, even still. This isn't right."

"Gabrion, stop!" she cried. "This is my place. These are my people. This is my home."

"But how can you say that after all we had? After Savvron?"

The answer came, but not from Mira or Gabrion or the king, and Gabrion instantly knew why he had felt trepidation before entering this room. He knew why Mira so willingly believed the altered version of events concerning the battle in Savvron the day she was abducted—rescued—it didn't matter.

The answer was in the room with them, behind Mira, fussing now that she was crying and no longer singing her lullaby.

It was Mira's child.

She saw Gabrion's eyes turn toward the crib behind her and motherly love pulled her around where she reached in and lifted the infant into her arms, cooing and humming to settle him. She faced Gabrion again and introduced him.

"Our son," she smiled proudly. "Perrios."

Gabrion could see the tiny face enwrapped in its silk blanket and he estimated the child to be two or three months old. He couldn't offer congratulations to her. He knew he was supposed to. It was only polite. But she was denying all the pain to the people in Savvron, and himself, for the sake of this little child. She was ignoring the suffering from that day one year ago when she was taken from the village. One year ago. One year ago.

He couldn't offer his congratulations. Instead he warbled in a strange tone, "You didn't wait very long to produce an heir for your king, did you?"

"Gabrion!" she gasped, horrified. "How dare you!"

He couldn't stop himself. "Was it the very night you were brought here? Did you even wait until you were his queen?" He knew he was asking hurtful questions, but his heart was crushed and each beat hurt more than the last. He wanted her to hurt; to understand the pain she was causing him. "Do you have a second one already brewing within you?"

Tears rolled unchecked down her face. "Gabrion, stop. Please, I beg you." Her voice teetered between sadness and rage.

"Do you think begging and pleading kept the people of Savvron out of harm's way when your lover's army attacked?" His voice was cold and sharp. His pain was almost palpable.

"No more."

"Do you think ignoring the truth will make everything all right? That your… *spawn* will have an honest life because you've lied about how you became its mother?"

Mira strode forward, deeply hurt, and slapped Gabrion across the cheek with all her might. But where her hand should have struck his skin, instead it shattered. Blood sprayed everywhere and she screamed in agony, nearly dropping her baby in the process. The king rushed in, sweeping the child from her hands while trying to catch her as she fell.

Gabrion looked aghast at Mira's hand. Or rather, at the stump that ended at her wrist. The glass jade was channeling his anger and hurt, and it had lashed out at her in force. He knelt beside her, horrified by the injury, but the jade still pulsed strongly. When he reached out for her, his fingers sliced unhindered into her shoulder and side. He retracted his hands fearfully, blood splashing everywhere. Mira howled in agony and the baby echoed her cries.

"No!" Gabrion trembled, watching the gaping wounds pour blood all over the stone floor. The king was hollering for help from the mages, but Gabrion heaved and tried to breathe against what he was seeing. His beloved Mira, bleeding out, and it was his fault.

The mages came in and dove into a furious set of healing spells, while others wrapped the wounds to quell the flow of blood. Mira's cries grew quieter and quieter, but Gabrion realized that it wasn't because of the healing.

It was because she was dying.

Soon the room was full of the sounds of chanting and the wailing infant. The king tried to calm the child, to no avail. It seemed to know definitively what was happening. Gabrion stared in shock, unable to fathom what he had done.

Mira's blood soaked the floor, looking like a deep, thick wine that could not be contained. She fell silent and her body stopped thrashing. She shuddered one last time and then it was over.

She was dead.

CHAPTER 34

Dariak in Hiding

DARIAK FELT TERRIBLY weak. He was curled up in a heap behind a pile of crates, barely able to move after his stint as a metallic blob. All around him the sounds of fighting echoed, but he was powerless to do anything except wait.

Kitalla had left him some time ago after moving a few of the wood boxes to block his view of the stairwell. True, it also prevented others from spotting him, but he was essentially blind and the way the battle sounds echoed off the walls, he wondered if he would be discovered at any moment.

No, he had to remain positive and strong here. It wasn't the time to give up or to be pathetic. Indeed, someone may come into the room, perhaps also to hide, and he had to be ready to defend himself.

He started by putting his effort into regaining control over his limbs. He tried lifting his hand up, to no avail, and then settled for flexing his fingers. He still felt weighted down by the metal, but he reminded himself that the effect was over and now his body was back to normal. There was no reason he couldn't be up on his feet.

He smirked at the thought, remembering how long it had taken for him to recover from his transformation into electrical energy in his battle against Sharice. Even weeks after, he felt numbing shocks of pain that coursed through him. He hadn't felt them recently, but he wondered if that was because he had healed or just that he wasn't noticing the surges any more. Probably the latter. To distract himself, he turned his thoughts elsewhere while he continued to flex his extremities.

Kitalla had come back to them. He wondered what had happened. Her Trial in the tower had obviously affected her deeply, but he had no idea of the depth of her pain, nor the circumstance. It wasn't something she had shared with him before she had knocked him down and stormed off.

Perhaps she had only come for the metal jade. She had battled great peril to claim it; maybe she felt she could not live without it. It was sort of like his earth jade, the first one he had ever possessed. He had a deep connection with it, though he hadn't drawn much power from it recently. It was like a safety net that he could fall back to when he really needed help. He didn't need its constant support; its presence was enough.

He thought of Kitalla returning just for the jade, but he dismissed the notion. Her demeanor may be aloof to her emotions, but the smolder in her eyes was evidence enough that she cared for her companions. He had no idea in which direction she had run off after leaving him, but he knew in his heart that it hadn't been toward the exit of the tower. She had gone further in to... to...

He wasn't sure exactly. His thoughts were still leaden, but he had remembered Randler nearby for a fleeting moment. He wondered if Kitalla knew that Randler was here and she went after him. At the very least, she knew of the other two jades and she would seek them out.

The other two jades. The last two. The beast jade and the healing jade. Then collectively they would have all eleven of the shattered shards. They were so close to their goal.

He knew their next course of action would be to seek out his father's laboratory and find the hidden references to the assembly of the jades. He knew the texts were there, but he hadn't consulted them in detail before. He knew only the number of jades and their basic powers. Finding the means of combining them would be the next challenge.

He wondered what it would bring to the land. His father's summoning of the giant colossus had brought decimation to the warring armies, and a temporary end to the fighting, yet it was almost as if years' worth of suffering had been condensed into one moment and all lives that would have been lost over that period of time were instead lost all at once.

It was a strange thought. There was no such way of altering time or life forces like that. But it helped him to rationalize the unintended effects of his father's last great use of magic. So many had died. But what would have been the cost had the war continued unabated? Surely, as terrible a cost as it was, his father had saved them from a truly endless war.

But what would happen when it was Dariak's turn? Would he also become a giant? Would his summoning also bring chaos to the land? Would hundreds or thousands die because of him? Would any of his good deeds also be cast into shadow because of the fateful colossus? Or would he morph into some other being entirely? He had no idea.

The fighting outside the storeroom waxed and waned and waxed again. It seemed as if the conflict was changing tides rapidly. Swords clanged together and spells exploded violently. He wondered exactly who was fighting here and who was winning.

And as soon as he had the thought, he wished he could take it away, for someone entered the room, huffing heavily as if he had been running for some time. There was a slight wheeze to the man's voice, and Dariak estimated that he must be an older mage. None of the warriors with their flailing swords would sound like that, he was certain.

Dariak tested his limbs, but he was still very weak. He had regained minor mobility, though not enough to truly defend himself. He reached his thoughts into and through his body, seeking help from his inner spirit, and also from the jades in his possession. When Pyron had imprisoned him, he hadn't taken the jades away. Instead they had all been wrapped tightly together, and it hadn't mattered anyway for the shielding had kept him secure for all those days.

Now, however, he was free of the magical bindings and he could call upon the jades at will. Unfortunately, he wasn't sure they would respond, considering what the metal jade had done to him. He had noticed such fickleness before from the jades. It was as if they had wills of their own.

The gasping man had calmed himself and settled on the ground near the doorway so he could spy on the exit. Dariak didn't care, as long as he didn't take to exploring here. A few moments later, Dariak heard some minor incantations being cast, complete with flourishes of robes and snapping or breaking of spell components. The mage had apparently caught his breath and was preparing to run off again into the fray, whether to fight or flee, Dariak couldn't tell.

A few minutes more and he would be safe again, left alone in hiding. Just a few—

But then Dariak's leg had a spasm and he kicked out uncontrollably into one of the crates. The older mage snapped to attention. "Who's there?" he demanded.

The blood drained from Dariak's face. It wasn't just some older mage. It was Pyron himself! Dariak knew he was doomed. His thoughts raced frantically for a potential means of escape but there was nothing he could do.

"Who is it?" Pyron asked again, fumbling through pockets for offensive supplies. He stepped closer to the crate pile where Dariak cowered and he gasped when he saw the young mage curled on the floor. "You!" His eyes lit with rage.

"Pyron," Dariak returned with a determined stare, knowing he must look ridiculous in his position. "It is good you survived. But leave me."

Pyron cracked a laugh. "Leave you? After you destroyed half the Mage Council with your antics? You're as daft as your father."

Dariak cringed at the slight against Delminor, but he held his retort in check. "Who's to say I'm not ready for more antics if you don't get out of here?"

Pyron backed up a step in fear, but he reassessed Dariak and decided the man was bluffing. "You're in no condition to do anything, fool. I don't know how you accomplished what you did, but know this, Dariak, you die here. Now."

"I'll just draw your spells into me and send them right back at you, Pyron. Don't be stupid. You can't defeat me here today. Be gone." He said it with enough conviction that the master mage took another fearful step back and looked away as if to examine an escape path.

But Dariak had done too much harm to Magehaven. The demise of Kerrish was only the beginning. He had defiled the Trials by entering into them. He had started massive fighting within the tower itself. His presence had drawn up terrible unrest within the Council. His arrogant claim for the jades had merely provoked Pyron's own rivals to rise against his wisdom, weakening his posture as Council Leader. Then the infiltration by Dariak's companions, and Dariak's own escape from his magical bindings and his eruption into the metallic ooze that devoured the people around him; no, Pyron was certain that Dariak's end was to come now. He didn't respond in conversational tongue, but sputtered the incantation for a spell instead.

Dariak tensed as he heard the key words that called for intense flames. Fitting, he thought to himself, that Pyron would try to burn him as Kerrish had burned. The fleeting thought was followed instantly with thoughts of defense. When the inferno erupted from Pyron's hands in swirling waves, the flames reached for Dariak but were sharply doused by the water jade.

Pyron roared as the flames fizzled. Lightning crackled from his fingertips next, but the earth jade drew the room's dust quickly around Dariak to shield him. Pyron screamed again as he launched a volley of poison darts from his fingertips. Here, the nature jade nullified the poison, though it could not stop the spikes from cutting Dariak.

Mad with rage, Pyron stamped his feet and ran toward Dariak, determined to kick the mage's brain in if he had to, but the Shield of Delminor stunted the attack and augmented Pyron's body weight, dragging him down.

Dariak wanted this stalemate to end. He wanted Pyron to flee and he needed to rest. The jades were drawing some of his energy for their defenses; he hadn't ever noticed it before, but then he hadn't relied on their powers so desperately when he had already been drained by one. Perhaps they always drew on his life force when they acted. He would have to explore that notion later.

Pyron readied another assault. Dariak could tell that it was going to be a combination of effects and he wondered if the jades would be able to work in tandem to repel the attack. But in his heart, he felt that if Pyron completed his incantation, then there would be no defense against it in his condition. He begged the jades for help, knowing now that they too were feeling his exhaustion. His only hope was that Pyron would be satisfied with his victory and that he wouldn't bother to search Dariak's body. His friends could then reclaim the jades more easily, but whether they would know what to do with them, he had no idea.

Futility overwhelmed him. His body wasn't responding to his wishes and he couldn't even roll over or lift his head from the floor. He was going to die here in mere moments, once Pyron finished. It was like watching the mage in slow motion. He heard each carefully pronounced syllable. He saw each flourish of hands, arms, and feet. He watched as numerous spell components appeared from pockets and then were consumed one way or another. Doom approached. And the last thing Dariak saw before Pyron completed his spell was a flash of light.

Pyron collapsed against the wall, the smell of charred flesh rising from a badly wounded body. A massive burn mark marred the mage's chest and he lay, apparently dead.

Dariak knew the source of that light. He felt it draw on his life force to unleash its power. The lightning jade had risen up once more to defend its master, but at the cost of Dariak's remaining strength. He held on to consciousness as long as possible, trying to determine if Pyron was alive or dead. He didn't seem to be moving, but it was hard to tell as his vision started to fade.

Soon, everything was black and Dariak knew nothing more.

CHAPTER 35

Gabrion's New Quest

MIRA'S BODY LAY motionless on the floor as all watched the last moments of her life drift away. The king, holding his only son, knelt slowly down to his queen's side, tears streaming in hopeless agony. He touched her cheek gently, caressing her one last time before her carcass would be carted away. Everyone stood so silently, only their breathing could be heard. Time seemed still, threatening never to resume.

The mages had finished their attempts to save her life, but they stepped back to give the king a wide berth. No one dared offer to hold the child, for the king clutched the boy to his chest in a locked embrace they feared they could not break. He would not release the infant and it would have been worthless to try.

Gabrion's eyes echoed his own immense pain. He barely knew who he was at that moment. He was no great warrior, no hero swooping in from the sagas to save his beloved. He was merely a killer. A useless murderer whose single-minded quest destroyed the one thing that, to him, had been worth living for. Yet there she lay, cold on the stone floor, gone. Irrevocably gone.

He had felt such anger at her betrayal. Such rage that she would turn her back on their past life together. It made no sense to him that she could deny the attack on Savvron to Gabrion's face, as if she truly believed that the fight had been staged.

Perhaps it was, he considered for a moment. Perhaps it was all a falsehood. The people who had died that day hadn't truly been killed, but maybe drugged and then escorted away. And perhaps Dariak, the one mage who had remained, son of the one man who had brought the last major incursion to its bitter end, had been planted. The entire quest could have been a farce to distract Gabrion from Mira so he would forget her and so she could accept her new life wholeheartedly with no thoughts of ages past.

It was absurd, he knew, but how he wanted to believe that this too was a ruse. For, if all the killing in Savvron had not been real, then perhaps this moment was also false. Her shattered arm, her emptied corpse, her lifeless eyes; they were all part of an elaborate scheme to release Gabrion's obligations, so that he would be free to live life on his own without some errand leading him on.

His body shook in revulsion. How could he try to rationalize this moment? How could he even attempt in any way to ease his own suffering after killing her?

And he knew he had indeed killed her. It hadn't been her fault for striking him. He couldn't even blame the jade. His anguish caused this destruction. At first he knew of only one recourse. He was clearly unsuited to this existence. His quest would have to end now, this very instant. Her death should have meaning in that the monster in his own heart would also be slain. He would free the land of his own evils, the kind that had decimated countless men and women in battle, the kind that ended the lives of free-roaming creatures in both Kallisor and Hathreneir, the kind that rose up in fury and channeled the jade's power into such a terrible force that Mira's mere touch destroyed her.

He turned his gaze to the king, unaware of how long the monarch had been staring at him. Gabrion opened his mouth to speak but he couldn't find any words. The king merely held his gaze and waited. The guards and mages tensed in anticipation of what would come after this grievous act, but those who had witnessed Gabrion's invulnerability kept back in fear of what else this strange warrior would conjure about himself.

He knew what he had to do. Gabrion reached into his pocket and everyone tensed with the motion. He withdrew the shard of jade and held it in his hand, staring at its striations for a time, turning it over and trying to remember anything about himself that wasn't connected to death. He thought of the elder of Gerrish who had tried to guide him by offering a philosophy he could follow if he so chose. The three paths: Perseverance, Patience, and Pain. None could exist for long without the other two, the elder had said. Gabrion had been vastly patient, hoping and dreaming of Mira. He had been incessantly perseverant, meeting every trial head on with the will to survive so that he could save Mira. He had never expected that it would end with such pain.

He held the shard out to the king. "Take it," he croaked.

The king already knew what the object was based on how it had protected the young man. He had no need to break his gaze. He held Gabrion's eyes in thrall and hissed, "Why?"

"Take it. I am not worthy of it. Take it and slay me. You won't be able to do more than scratch me if you don't take it."

The king's eyes narrowed. "What would be the point of killing you now?"

Gabrion glanced down at Mira's body. "I deserve no less for what I have done."

"You certainly do not deserve an easy release from your pain either." The king's lip curled into a snarl. "You have come into my home and you have slain my wife and destroyed any hope our son had of a full and happy childhood. He will forever wonder about his mother and how she died. And I will have to either confess to him that I was weak and could not defend her, or I will have to lie to him and craft some wild tale. Either way, he will feel that I am not competent, for he will seek to challenge my power or he will discover my deceit and lose trust in me forever."

The king paused for only a moment to let the words burn into Gabrion. "No, you have not just killed this dear woman. You have ruined her son as well. He may rise up one day against the Kallisorian who infiltrated the castle and slew his mother. He may well become a tyrant like your own king and neglect reason and honor."

"Honor?" Gabrion croaked. "Where was your honor telling me you knew nothing of Mira when I arrived? When I asked about the prisoner from Savvron?"

"Mira's past had little relevance here and the name of your hometown was meaningless to me. Also, you asked for a prisoner, and as you may realize by now, she was no prisoner here." His tone was biting but he did not raise his voice as he spoke.

"It's all too convenient," Gabrion muttered. "No word from her. Her belief that the fight was staged. But none of it matters now."

"People choose to believe what suits them best," the king pronounced sagaciously. "She could not bear to think of pain in her past, and why should I encourage her to? As for her letters, I already informed you that there was no preclusion on her sending them. I know not why you failed to receive anything she sent."

Gabrion stared at the king angrily. "You imply she never sent any."

"I imply no such thing," the king returned.

"You altered her somehow. Changed how she thought."

The king's eyes narrowed. "Is that why you killed her?"

A surge of emotion overwhelmed Gabrion and all the pain fought its way to his face again. He wanted to end this moment and have no more moments afterward.

"Ah," the king said. "There it is again, young warrior. Your agony. Your furious, burning pain. That utter loathing of what you did. Yes, *that* is why I will not kill you. Doing so would be a petty revenge for me and my son and our land. But that self-detestation you feel—that is a more fitting punishment."

Gabrion shook his head, unable to think. He set the jade down on the ground and backed away from it. "No. I deserve death."

The king, still clutching his child, leaned forward and lifted the jade from the floor. He then stepped over and slapped Gabrion hard across the cheek, completing the strike Mira had intended to give. He then shoved the jade into one of Gabrion's pockets. "Take that sting from Mira. Leave Hathreneir and never return. You have harmed us enough."

The king then addressed the rest of the people in attendance. "This warrior and those with him are to be escorted from the lands unharmed. If he provokes a fight, you are to flee, not engage him. Make no attempt to kill him. Let misery be his quest now."

He turned back to Gabrion, whose face was creased in utter dismay. "Leave this place, murderer. You have caused enough harm to my family. Begone."

Gabrion stood up slowly and wavered. "What's to stop me from finishing what I started by killing you as well?"

The king met him eye to eye and challenged him. "Go right ahead."

But the king knew Gabrion's anguish well enough. He had dealt with enough men in death and war to know the haunted look in Gabrion's eyes. He would likely never kill again, even in self-defense. No, the king sensed a noble heart beneath the horror of what took place that day, and he knew that Gabrion would now suffer terrible inner tribulations that would keep him docile, unable to stand and strike down the men around him. In essence, by releasing him now, he was sending a strange sort of ally back into the world. Or, at least, someone who would harbor no more hostilities to his people.

Gabrion's shoulders sank with the weight of it all. He saw no escape other than the one made for him by the guards. He looked at the king one last time and focused his gaze for a fleeting moment on the infant in the king's hands. The child had wailed so shrilly at first, but the strength in his father's grip had calmed him, though the baby fussed as if it knew something was still amiss.

Then Gabrion stared down at Mira's mangled body and he traced the lines of her corpse, closing his eyes and burning the image into his mind so he would never forget. All his questing had done was shred apart anything that had mattered to him, and damn this king for forcing him to live and suffer the pain.

But the king was right. He deserved to suffer. Death was too easy and Mira, befuddled though she must have been, deserved more.

Gabrion turned at last to start to trek away from this place. The baby moved and let out a gurgling cry. It was just a normal baby sound. It meant nothing.

But it haunted Gabrion.

CHAPTER 36

Ervinor's Sacrifice

THE HOURS PASSED slowly as Ervinor waited for Gabrion to return. A messenger had come to inform him that there had been an interruption in the audience, and he bore one of the agreed-upon missives that meant Gabrion was safe. Ervinor's edginess did not subside, however, and he bided his time checking on the others and returning to his signpost to watch the entrance.

Then Morrish came running from the castle and chaos ensued.

The rogue shouted at the top of his lungs, calling his comrades to arms. Ervinor rushed over to him for an explanation, looking over the man's shoulder for Gabrion and Quereth; or worse, for the king's soldiers.

Morrish panted frantically. "Gabrion! He went back in! Guards and mages! We have to help him!"

"Calm down and speak clearly," Ervinor demanded in a voice that summoned years of experience that he didn't possess.

Morrish's panicked eyes flickered for a moment and then he pulled himself together. "The king met with us, then he took other news while we waited. Then Gabrion… he went sort of mad. The girl he has been looking for. She's here! She's the *queen*! She wouldn't listen to reason and we were going to leave, but then Gabrion decided to go back and talk to her. Fighting broke out everywhere. Quereth and I were running to escape but the mage turned back. I had to get here to warn you. Rally the forces! Gabrion needs us! Hurry!"

Ervinor closed his eyes for a moment and strained his ears, hoping to hear anything in the distance that would validate Morrish's story. There was nothing. He didn't doubt Morrish, but if Gabrion had since quelled the fighting inside, then arriving with armed troops would not bode well.

"Come on!" Morrish implored. He then turned and shouted to the courtyard. "Kallisor, march!"

"Hold!" Ervinor interceded, angry now. "We can't infiltrate the castle. We'll be slaughtered."

"There's no *time*!" Morrish then called to the rest. "Who's with me? Charge!" And he drew his sword and ran back toward the castle.

The men and woman looked at Ervinor and then at Morrish. The young leader shook his head, but some of the feistier Kallisorians took Morrish's lead and charged inside. There was little Ervinor could do to stop them. He feared that this would be the end of their chance for a peaceful visitation. With a heavy heart, he lifted his sword over his head and then pointed it toward the castle.

With a rushing cry, the hundred men and woman left their positions and made a mad dash forward. Ervinor ran as fast as he could, trying to catch Morrish and the few who had gone with him. They broke through the main gates without any resistance, for Morrish had taken care of the door guards upon his exit, and then they entered the main entryway.

Several bodies already lay on the floor, including some oversized spider carcasses. The ceiling was dripping from some magical defenses that had been expelled. Ervinor directed the forces to split up along the smaller corridors to fight off additional guards, while the rest of them made their way forward into the throne room.

The throne room, however, was loaded with warriors and mages alike. The entrance of the Kallisorian forces distracted them from whatever held their attention and they went into a battle stance at once. Mages threw protection spells around themselves and the warriors, and then they shifted into the rhythm of casting offensive spells. The oversized throne room played host to over twenty fighters from each side.

Ervinor kept his sword moving at all times. He cut high toward one guardsman and then ducked low with a short spin to avoid another's attack. He did his best to disable one guard while making his way toward the half dozen mages at the back of the room. If they could interrupt the mages, the rest of the fighting would be easier. It was the first battle tactic anyone ever learned.

The ground in front of Ervinor grew sharp spikes and he sprang to the left to avoid them, crashing into a guard who was righting himself. Ervinor turned swiftly and cracked the man on the side of the head with his hilt, then pivoted, pressing onward. A quick glance showed him that most of his army members were also trying to reach the mages, though a few engaged the warriors out of necessity. It was good they had practiced these tactics.

Soon the room was filled with various spell effects, including a freezing rain that stung the skin on contact. Ervinor didn't care; he pushed onward, trying to get past the defenders so he could take down the spellcasters.

A dagger cut into his arm and he spun around to deal with the assailant. She parried his attack and kicked at his kneecap, but he pounced back and avoided it. He brought his sword down into her shoulder but her armor deflected the blow, though it set her off balance. Ervinor then spun clockwise and crashed his sword into her midsection, cutting deeply and felling her instantly. He continued his spin until he faced the back of the room and lowered his head as he charged forward.

Fire blasted at him from the side but the special armor reduced the impact so that it was only irritating. However, the mage seemed to know that his armor was shielded against magic, for the fire dart was followed by several more, each targeting the same location on the armor. Enough hits would surely break through the anti-magic enchantment and then the fire would cause its intended damage. To protect himself, Ervinor had to turn his body as he ran so the darts would impact him in different locations, but it greatly reduced the effectiveness of his charge.

Two guards intercepted him and he enacted a trick he learned from Kitalla, dropping down and cracking the fighters on their thighs, then leaping up and bashing them in their faces. Stunned, the fighters fell backward and Ervinor pressed onward, reaching one mage and throwing him down, where his head cracked on the marble floor and knocked him out.

Ervinor disentangled himself quickly, rolling to the side to avoid an overhead sword strike. He kicked up a foot and connected with the attacker's wrist, but it wasn't strong enough to loosen the blade. Ervinor then pounced onto his feet and sprinted toward the next mage, jumping over a water trap and catching the mage by her shoulders. He punched her in the face until she stopped fighting back.

He was weary but he kept pushing onward. His troops fought bravely but he could already see some casualties. Three other Hathren mages had been taken down, and the last mage responded by trying to summon a firestorm. Ervinor couldn't reach the mage so he threw his sword with all his might. The blade cut into the mage's protective barrier and interrupted the casting long enough for another warrior to get to the spellcaster.

Weaponless, Ervinor had no way to defend himself from the fighter who leaped upon him, dagger swinging wildly. Ervinor grabbed the man's arm, trying to deflect the blade, but he was outmatched. They wrestled, with Ervinor trying to push off the ground with one leg to roll over and disengage himself, while also keeping a firm grip on the ever-encroaching dagger arm. The blade came terrifyingly close to his jugular and he tried to wriggle aside from under the massive guard, but he couldn't get away. The dagger came down, cutting into the side of Ervinor's neck and erupting a fiery blast of pain and a thick wash of blood.

Help came too late as the guard was attacked and pushed off of Ervinor. The young warrior heard a bandage hurriedly ripped and he felt it pressed against his neck, which only added to his agony. He then heard incoherent babbling, after which a strange warmth permeated his body. Moments later, the pain reduced and he was able to focus his eyes on old Quereth, who chanted frantically to quell the bleeding.

The fighting was still going on and they were not safe. Ervinor saw a dark shadow approach from behind the mage and the shine of an ax flashed in the air before it came crashing down. Ervinor grabbed Quereth and shoved him aside, saving the mage's life, but taking the attack himself instead. The blade struck deeply into his right shoulder, cutting through bone and sinew.

Time slowed for Ervinor as he took a detached look at the result of the attack. His eyes turned toward an object on the floor beside him. He saw part of his own tunic and armor. It was roughly cut off and it— He looked again. Yes, it was covering something. Something that was twitching. And as he continued to look at it, he slowly came to realize that it was his arm. He didn't understand—his arm shouldn't be lying on the floor. He was vaguely aware of Quereth's panic and increased summoning of the magical energies. But still, there on the floor was unmistakably his own arm, completely severed from his body.

As he looked around in his time-skewed vision, he thought he saw Gabrion stride in from the rear door. There was something oddly different about him. Gabrion ignored all the fighting and didn't once try to help any of the Kallisorian forces. Ervinor tried to call out but his throat injury prevented him from it. The warrior paced the room and headed for the exit, completely unscathed by any of the weapons flying around.

He didn't know what was more strange: Gabrion's detached, plodding stroll or his own arm lying on the floor, disconnected from him. He looked up and saw the tension on Quereth's face as spittle flew from rapidly chanting lips. It was almost funny. A little bit of magical rain falling down as strange sensations swept through Ervinor's body. His vision grew hazy and Quereth's face tightened further.

Ervinor tried to tell the mage how funny he looked. Or that he should go find out what was wrong with Gabrion. Or that it was weird that his arm looked like it had fallen off somehow. He wondered idly if he would be able to keep the arm and maybe reattach it with a rope. It would be a great gag in a tavern. Perhaps a little gruesome, but not something just anyone could do.

He opened his mouth to tell Quereth to relax, but the haziness took over him more and more. Soon, he couldn't remember what he had wanted to say, or even where he was.

No, the darkness was inviting. He should go to it and find refuge there. No one would find him in the darkness. He would be safe there.

Ervinor closed his eyes.

CHAPTER 37

Leaving Magehaven

KITALLA, FRAST, AND Randler left the jade chamber at a sprint, guided by Frast's references to magical traps. He had witnessed the miracle, in his eyes, of Kitalla drawing the energies in through the metal jade and safely dispelling the defenses set to keep the beast jade safe. However, now that the jade had been reunited with some of its kin, the desperation within the jades instantly faded. It was as if they started communing with each other and would no longer support the humans who carried them.

Randler remembered something similar happening before to Dariak. Even more so, the beast jade and the metal jade seemed to be opposing forces, meaning their skills would interfere with each other until a symbiosis was established. After explaining this to Kitalla, she handed the beast jade to Frast.

With the beasts no longer under the mages' control, sounds of battle erupted throughout the tower and it seemed the very foundation might crack under the tumult. Randler nervously recalled the Prisoner's Tower and its collapse, but Dariak was not here to protect them in case the same fate befell this place.

"Where is Dariak?" he asked as they sprinted toward a stairwell, leaping across the room like gazellions as Frast avoided more rune traps. "We have to get out of here."

"What of the other jade?" Kitalla asked, keeping her eyes alert in all directions in case mages appeared.

"It should have been up there," Frast answered. "It's where they store them. Something must have happened."

"Let's get to Dariak," Kitalla said.

One flight down they met resistance. The floor was coated with a murky sludge that slowed their movements, similar to the trap Heria had used from sheeliope fur. Kitalla walked on tiptoes the best she could, but still she was terribly sluggish. Across the way, the mages who had set the ooze swept into motion with their spells.

Only their feet were detained, so Kitalla was able to bend and sway around the magical blasts that shot at her. She pulled daggers from her tunic and launched them at the mages, but because the mages were unhindered by the sludge, she missed completely.

However, Frast made use of those fallen daggers. He channeled the energies and summoned a blast of lightning to skitter across the room. The energy was drawn toward one dagger, then the other, and Frast added more strength to the incantation and soon the lightning whirled into a möbius chain behind their foes. The charges whipped through the air behind them and Kitalla grinned at the panic of the mages. She tossed a third dagger into the ground in front of the spellcasters and the lightning obliged by reaching for it. Screaming, the mages collapsed, pulling healing energies about them. Meanwhile, Kitalla pressed forward with Randler and they clobbered the mages unconscious. The sludge did not dissipate, so the trio struggled through the room and beyond until their shoes were free of the binding substance.

The next chamber had three possible exits. Frast had toured the tower well during their first visit, therefore he led them onward, pausing only as they reached new chambers to assess the dangers within. The further they traveled, the more dangerous it became.

Kitalla had arrived at the tower with a small host of soldiers from the king's army. She had sprinted ahead of them while the captain sought counsel on what help was needed. It had taken time for them to organize and then to dispatch themselves to various layers within the tower. Kitalla's own mad flight up toward the jade chamber called more troops in her direction than other locations, but Frast was leading them down through another path anyway. Still, soon they faced soldiers as well as mages.

Kitalla was still wearing the uniform of the Hathren soldiers and she tried using it to her advantage. "Hold!" she called as she entered a room. "I must see the captain! There is trouble up above!"

One of the soldiers ran up the stairs behind Kitalla to investigate while the others remained, eying her skeptically. "Who are these two?" another guard asked.

"Mages from the tower," she snapped. "Look, if you don't believe me, go check for yourself. But we're here to get reinforcements."

"Ollino, go down and summon the captain," one man said to the youngest member of the troop. He turned back to Kitalla. "Lead the way; we're right behind you."

"Finally!" Kitalla said with exasperation, turning back the way she had come. Randler and Frast hesitated only for a moment before following her lead. They approached the stairs, knowing that the first scout would see the downed mages above and would return swiftly. Kitalla tripped on her way up the stairs and Frast used the distraction to blast a fireball behind himself, felling the soldiers.

"Let's keep going," Randler said needlessly as they turned back and continued down on their original path. Frast tried not to look at the roasted guardsmen he had so casually blasted. They hadn't even had a chance to defend themselves, nor had they attacked. But there wasn't time to mourn now.

A ferocious growl sounded from the chamber below. Frast looked around their room and shook his head; there wasn't another helpful exit so they had to go forward. One growl was then echoed by several more and the trio knew that the next fight was going to be a rough one. Even Kitalla was showing signs of fatigue now that the fire jade had calmed down. There was no point in delaying. They pushed ahead, defenses at the ready, eyes alert. They were startled by what they saw.

Instead of a pack of wizards with their controlled beasts, they saw a pile of dead bodies with the creatures fighting amongst themselves. The lupinoes were circling around the outside while sandorpions shot poisonous darts across the room, their tails whipping frantically. There was even a baby ursalor in the middle of the room, too bewildered to do much more than yell in consternation. It took a number of blows from the sandorpions and the two diving eaglons, but it didn't fight back much. Its massive paws pounded through the air, trying to knock down the avian foes and to bat away the sandorpions, but it missed most of the time.

The lupinoes saw the newcomers first and the growls erupted anew, which added to the fierce tension in the room. The wolf-like beasts turned and stalked the human prey, sensing it as easier fodder than the other beasts, who were preoccupied anyway.

Kitalla was already on the move. If she could disable one lupino, the others may turn their attentions away. She raced ahead, leaping over sandorpion tails and claws. Within seconds she reached her target and she crouched down so it would snap its jaw low, then pounced over its head, laying her hands on its neck as she cartwheeled through the air and cracked a landing on its spine. Her hands held the thick neck firmly, telling the poor creature it didn't stand a chance.

Its only defense would have been to flip onto its back, but the lupino knew that she might kill it before it finished the move. Plus, if it flipped over, it would be defenseless until it could right itself again. Thus, after a brief consideration, the lupino lowered itself to the floor in submission. The other lupinoes acknowledged the act and turned their attention back toward the sandorpions.

Kitalla could have made her way across the fray and down the stairs, and Randler might have also been able to get through, but Frast was another matter.

He wasn't used to all this fast-paced hustling and he was wearing out. He pushed himself to follow along the room's perimeter, calling up defensive shields to protect himself from the sandorpion venom and to dissuade the eaglons from approaching him. Without launching a massive attack, he wasn't sure how he would get through.

But as he went, he slowly realized that the creatures weren't pursuing him at all. Some of their attacks flew his way erroneously, but the creatures went out of their way not to crash into him. He hadn't had personal experience with a jade before, but Randler understood what was happening. The beast jade was shielding its current owner from harm, so Randler grabbed Frast's hand and pulled him toward the exit.

The closer they came to Dariak's hiding place, the more chaotic the tower was becoming. The mages no longer controlled the beasts, except those few who had a natural proclivity toward that form of magic. Mage and soldier alike were engaged in a wild torrent of battling the beasts that had, until now, helped keep the tower safe against intruders. Some of the chaos allowed the trio to slither from one location to the next. Other times they were forced to interject their talents in order to get through the beasts, while trying to avoid the soldiers and mages where possible.

Eventually they made it to the storage room where Kitalla had left Dariak. He had passed out, but he was definitely alive. The air had a strange scent in it, like after a massive thunderstorm. The air itself felt charged, but there was nothing else of note. Frast sent some healing spells through Dariak, hoping to awaken him, but his exhaustion was too complete.

Their only other option was to carry him. "Too bad Gabrion isn't here," Kitalla lamented. "But, it's a good thing Dariak is trim." She lifted up the mage's shoulders and recoiled uncertainly. "He's... he's really heavy!" she said, confused.

Frast and Randler tried to help lift Dariak up, but his body was still affected by the hyperdensity of the metal, as if all the energy he had absorbed during his flight to this room was now turning into mass.

"What do we do now?" Frast asked. "We can't stay here and we can't move him."

"We're not leaving him," Randler declared, not that the others would suggest it.

"Well, Frast," Kitalla said, shrugging, "we need a pack mule. You've got the beast jade. Surely you can figure something out."

Randler protested. "He doesn't know how to call on its abilities. There has to be another way."

Frast pulled the jade from his pocket and looked at it. "It seems wrong to enslave the beasts here to satisfy our own need. I don't know if I can do this."

It took effort for Kitalla to keep herself from rolling her eyes. "We're open to other ideas, but time is limited. Look over there." She pointed out the doorway where spellfire, streaked across the room and was met with angry snarls and shrieks. Swords and spears also clattered as they fought against the feral foes. There wasn't going to be much time before they were discovered.

Frast bit his lip. "What do I do? How do I call to the jade for help?"

Randler saw the warring emotions in Frast's eyes and he hated having to push him in this direction, but their lives depended on an escape right now. He placed a comforting hand on the mage's shoulder. "You have to find a balance with the jade and then you have to sort of let it into you, if that makes any sense."

As a mage, Frast was more accustomed with the idea than Randler expected. "What then?"

"Communicate your intention to it, your need. Show it what you need done and if it can, it should comply."

Frast nodded and closed his eyes. It wasn't entirely different than focusing the effects of a magic spell. It was important to visualize the outcome of a spell, else its effects could erupt carelessly in ways that were unintended. Generally, a spell would not hurt its caster because the natural survival instinct already placed that into an incantation. But whether a fire spell was launched in darts, erupted in a cone of blaze, or exploded in a wide area fireball depended on the wish and skill of the mage. Yes, Frast could commune with the jade and he knew it would listen to his plea.

At first the jade seemed distracted by its reunion with its brethren, but Frast was persistent, pleading for help. The shard turned away from its musings and reached a tendril of its power into Frast's mind. The mage grabbed that glimmer of strength and wrapped himself in it. It was a wild experience, for he sensed all of the hundreds of beasts within the tower all at once. Their emotions were erratic and purely primal. Some were seeking refuge in darkened corners, bewildered by their sudden freedom from control. Others raged angrily against their captors, while others still turned against the beasts around them, for they were natural enemies. The flood of emotions was overwhelming and Frast cried out in shock.

Kitalla and Randler couldn't console the mage, for his cry alerted the nearby foes. A call of "Who goes there?" turned into a blast of electrical energy and the fight was on.

"Who do you want: mages, beasts, or soldiers?" Kitalla asked Randler as they drew their weapons.

The bard smiled grimly. "I was going to let you handle them all yourself." He then fired off an arrow toward a guardsman.

"Mages it is, then," Kitalla murmured, sprinting down the few steps from the storeroom and across the floor. Four reptigons skittered in her direction, but she did not pause to intercept them. With a groan, she leaped over the critters and ran pell-mell toward a pair of mages on her right side. One mage had erected a wall of fire as protection, so Kitalla first took out the other mage, who was slower in defending himself.

Randler's bow sang with several more arrow shots, but time was running out. The guards were fighting off the beasts that were attacking, but three guards slipped away and pursued the bard. Randler threw down his bow and drew his mace while calling up a frantic battle song. He then bent his head down and charged.

The guards were not expecting the man to be as agile as he was. Randler bashed one guard's arm and jammed another in the shoulder, then he dropped and spun about, sweeping the legs out from under one of them. As the guard fell, Randler rolled aside and hopped back onto his feet. He dodged a swinging sword and had to pull back as an eaglon swooped in to kill him. The guards took advantage of Randler's back step and lunged forward. One kept his flail low to prevent the bard from getting past.

Kitalla saw his plight from across the room but she was too far away, even for a well-placed dagger throw. Instead, she whistled powerfully and distracted the guards, for it was the same call the captain used to get their attention. It was only a split second of interruption from their assault, but Randler capitalized on it by rolling aside and grabbing onto a reptigon. The beast immediately thrashed about, trying to free itself from Randler's grip, but the bard held on tightly and then swung the creature around and released it into the guards' path. They veered away from the angry reptile and Randler was back on his feet, sprinting over toward Kitalla's side of the room.

Hardly idle herself, Kitalla was struggling with the fire-encased mage, for his shield also had a physical barrier that kept her from launching her daggers through. It was a powerful set of defensive spells keeping the mage protected while allowing him to send offensive bursts outward. The fire flared up and shot darts at Kitalla and the beasts, which were attacking the other mages. Kitalla realized that she would not be able to penetrate the barrier without magic of her own, but now wasn't the time to engage in a dance. The numerous beasts and spell blasts erupting around the room would undoubtedly strike her if she tried.

Instead, Kitalla wove her way through the beasts, trying to let them see that she meant them no harm. Unfortunately, there were no lupinoes here that would actually notice the maneuvers. These critters fought on instinct and every living thing that wasn't like itself was seen as a threat. Thus three eaglons dove in, screeching madly, talons reaching out to slash at Kitalla and the other creatures around her. Likewise, the reptigons were biting and scrambling about the room. Three mages lay dead from the feral assault already, and four others were defending themselves.

The companions didn't know whom to attack first. Each of the warring factions had a right to be there. The mages lived in the tower. The animals were prisoners here, seeking escape. And the guards had been summoned for protection. But all in all, Kitalla decided that the mages would have to be disabled first, for they had imprisoned Dariak and the beasts and they had called for the reinforcements from the king. Take out the mages, and perhaps the rest could be abated.

Randler was almost at her side, his mace battling the rampant beast attacks. Kitalla, meanwhile, felled a mage by cracking his neck with a fist, after which she dodged the reptigons that swarmed over to ravage the fallen body. The fire-shielded mage realized that the beasts were not the major threat now and turned his attacks toward Randler and Kitalla. Blasts of molten metal struck the floor, making it difficult to walk upon, and then he sent bolts of lightning cascading toward them. The blasts hurt terribly, but they couldn't escape the attack.

Kitalla yelled and charged forward. She had had enough. The protected mage would fall. She avoided the molten patches on the floor, which slowed her rush, but she needed to take him down. Seeing his situation, the mage drew fire from the shield and launched it toward Kitalla, but it did not stop her. She pushed harder and rushed into the flames, tackling the mage's barrier, and knocking the man over entirely. The fire-shield enwrapped Kitalla with blistering energy, but she did not care. This mage needed to stop so she drew out her dagger to break through the defensive barrier even as the fire burned her with its searing heat. The mage panicked and whimpered pitifully as he tried to set up other defenses in the few seconds he had before she broke through. He hadn't seen anyone with the mad look that Kitalla now had in her eyes. He knew deep down that she would kill him.

At last, Kitalla broke through the protective barriers, though the fire shield still scorched her, and her dagger slipped through the air. But she did not bring the knife point into the mage's eye as it looked like she would. Instead she swept her hand downward to keep from killing him and then she brought the hilt backward, cracking into his skull and knocking him out. At last, the fire shield dissipated.

Her body ached deeply from the heat but as she looked, there was no charred flesh. The fire jade had kept her whole, though it had not protected her from the pain of the fire. Perhaps it was exhausted from propelling her into the tower as they sought its companion on the upper floors. It didn't matter. She had overcome pain before and this would be nothing new.

The fighting in the room continued and she could see Randler struggling between the feral and human opponents. She was disoriented from the agony for a moment and could not assist him, but the bard had learned well from her over the course of their adventure. He used one guard's momentum to flip the man overhead into the sandorpions on the other side. Randler then turned and ducked the next attack, while dodging another eaglon strike. The large bird took the brunt of the sword thrust that Randler avoided and it crashed to the ground, wailing miserably.

Two more mages fell to the onslaught and, with only one remaining, soon the rest of the fighting would turn into a brawl with the random bursts of energy erupting around the room. Randler dipped under a sandorpion tail and rolled over to safety on the other side, but an eaglon caught him and bit his shoulder deeply. Screaming in pain, the bard grabbed the oversized bird and pulled, hoping that the eaglon's claws had not pierced his skin. The bird's grip on his shoulder was strong, and wrenching the beast off created terrible damage to his shoulder. He blacked out from the pain and collapsed.

Kitalla was already by his side as he hit the ground and the eaglon was dispatched. Desperation set in, but the jades seemed unresponsive to their plight. Claws and swords all reached for the thief, and she fended them off as best she could, but she was getting weary.

Then, all at once, the beasts stopped, as if someone had turned them off. Momentum carried them forward to crash into walls and each other, but otherwise the room fell oddly quiet. The four remaining guards stumbled over the beasts and Kitalla called aloud for them to stop fighting. They knew her only from their journey to this tower and realized that she had infiltrated their troop, but they were exhausted and lowered their weapons.

Kitalla first shook Randler awake and assessed his shoulder wound. It was a deep gash that would take more healing than she could do on her own. He was bleeding badly, but she didn't have anything with her that would help. "Frast!" she called, then turned to ensure the guards had not resumed their attack.

The mage was smiling at his success over channeling the power of the beast jade, and impressed with the absolute obedience the beasts were showing him in the room. His joy was short-lived as he saw Randler and he sprinted over and enwrapped the bard with healing energies. Kitalla turned and approached the guards.

"We're leaving this tower and you're not stopping us," she stated.

One of the guards shook his head. "You'll never get out alive. We won't let you, nor will the mages."

Kitalla looked at the horde of beasts that were standing still, eying the surroundings but otherwise completely enthralled. "I think we have a chance. Care to test your theory?" She grinned evilly and twirled a dagger in her hand deftly.

"We cannot let you go."

"I would rather not kill you," Kitalla frowned. "But I will if you leave me no choice."

"Fesh, come on," piped up another guard. "We don't stand a chance against them."

"Our fealty requires us—"

Kitalla had enough. She pounced forward and punched Fesh hard, dropping him to the ground. "Anyone else suffering from duty?" For emphasis, she pounded her hand into her fist.

"We—we are honor-bound to stop you," said another guard.

Kitalla growled. "So only one of you has any sense. Fine. Come at me. I will try not to kill you."

"Not me," said the other guard. He looked at the other two. "I'm all for defending the kingdom, but I'm not going to die here needlessly." He looked back at Kitalla and then threw down his sword. "I don't care if it makes me look like a coward. I'm not fighting you. But I can't just walk out of here either."

Kitalla understood his underlying plea and she stepped forward and knocked him out. "Next?" She eyed the other two who felt completely overmatched by her. They swallowed hard, debated silently, then they too dropped their weapons and waited for Kitalla to clobber them.

"He's going to need more healing than that, but it's all I can do right now," Frast said as Kitalla approached.

"If he's going to live for now and you don't think he'll lose his arm, then let's get moving."

Randler was barely coherent, but he was able to walk and follow. Frast communed with the beast jade again and now he called for a different kind of action. With Kitalla's help, a set of reptigons dragged Dariak's magically heavy body from its hiding place. Four eaglons gripped Dariak's torn robes and helped to ease his weight by lifting him upward, though they were not strong enough to actually carry him. Frast guided the beasts to work in unison to carry the sleeping mage from the room. It was, perhaps, the oddest litter any of them had ever seen.

Randler and Frast were both distracted, one by pain and the other with keeping the beasts in line. Kitalla was hurting but focused. She led the group onward, down through the rest of the tower. The fighting on the lower levels had quelled, for Frast's interaction with the jade had stopped all the creatures in the tower from attacking. The mages and guards were now tending to their wounded, rising up only as Kitalla and the others approached.

On the fourth floor, Kitalla intercepted the attacks that came from a mage but the fight did not last long. The mage could see that he had little chance of stopping them, so he turned and fled. Kitalla hoped he wasn't going to call reinforcements, but she didn't have the inclination to pursue him to make certain. Instead, they continued toward the next floor.

"Jareesa!" called a familiar voice as they crested the landing.

Kitalla couldn't believe it and nearly forgot her role. "Haasa! Thank goodness you're safe!"

The guardswoman looked over Kitalla's shoulder at the progression that was following her. Her eyes went wide. "What—what's all this?"

Kitalla looked back at Randler and Frast who were staggering along behind the beasts that were struggling to carry Dariak. "It's what the king sent us here for," Kitalla replied easily. "Those two mages in the back are controlling the creatures."

"I—I see," Haasa said in a strange tone. "What of him?"

Kitalla shook her head after glancing back at Dariak. "One of the mages on the Council. Badly wounded and barely alive. We must take him to the king."

"But—"

"Haasa, there's no time!" she interrupted with intentional impatience. "If he dies before he gets his message to the king then the war with Kallisor will be lost. He has vital information that no other mage has and it's imperative that we get him safely away from here!"

"But the other mages. Surely they can heal him first?"

"No time, no time, no time!" Kitalla raged in her best Jareesa tone. "I wouldn't want to be responsible for his death!"

Haasa always responded to such off-hand threats. She paled at the thought of angering the king directly. "Well I— Oh, Jareesa, what should I do?"

Kitalla loved this woman for her lack of intelligence. In the heat of the moment, she seemed to have forgotten entirely that Kitalla was not Jareesa at all and that she really owed her no allegiance. "Go ahead of us with the guards and secure a path out of here. No more fighting is needed. We have to get to the king posthaste! The other mages can start looking for wounded in the tower and healing them."

"All right," Haasa agreed, then turned to share this information with the other guards nearby. They looked at Kitalla, recognized her, and nodded, running off to carry out the orders.

Amazed at their luck, the group moved onward and downward until they were in the main foyer of Magehaven.

"Halt!"

Kitalla knew that voice. It was the captain's. There was no chance of duping her like she had Haasa. "Captain!" she replied, snapping to attention. "Urgent message for the king from this mage here," she said, gesturing to Dariak. "We must hurry onward to the castle."

"You don't give the orders here," the captain sneered. She looked over her shoulder and called out to someone in the shadows. "Is this claim true?"

Kitalla's heart sank as Master Pyron strode over, his robes charred and gaping. Kitalla thought back to the storeroom and the odd electrical after-smell that had been there. Perhaps Dariak had not been entirely idle in that room, which would explain his added convalescence.

As the older mage approached, his eyes widened and he drew breath to start casting spells. Kitalla leaped forward and stabbed him with her dagger, breaking through a defensive shield. She struck again rapidly, shattering a second, then a third, layer. At last, her dagger bit into his flesh and though he cried out in pain and staggered back, he did not fall.

Outraged, the captain drew her sword and pursued Kitalla. The thief knew the captain was an accomplished fighter, but she was in no way the best fighter in the king's service. Her sword swipes were wide, though powerful, and she had an undisciplined sense about them. Gabrion easily fought better than she did and would bring her down with little effort at all. Not that he was here.

Instead, Kitalla grabbed Pyron and spun him around even as he summoned a freezing snowstorm into the room. The captain's frantic charge could not be stopped and her sword thrust its way through Pyron's belly, almost impaling Kitalla on the other side. The old mage screamed and coughed up blood.

Panicked, the captain withdrew her blade, worsening the wound. She then threw it aside and grabbed for the mage. Meanwhile, the screams alerted the rest of the people in the area that the trouble wasn't over yet. Mages and guards readied for battle and approached.

They were going to be overwhelmed shortly. With Pyron's death, there would be no escape, though it was technically the captain who slew him. Kitalla glanced around for inspiration and then she stopped suddenly, agape.

Pyron was already back on his feet, his face contorted in anger and pain, but he was very much alive. His hands gestured wildly and the snowstorm he had summoned grew more intense. A bitter wind cut through the room and the falling snowflakes were denser, splattering icy patches of water everywhere.

The captain recoiled from the mage, horrified and partly relieved that he was alive. But she didn't understand how it was possible. It was so far beyond her comprehension that the fight went out of her and she backed away until she hit a wall, still stepping backwards in order to keep away.

It was obvious to Kitalla what had happened. Pyron had the healing jade with him, which was why it wasn't on its perch on the upper floor. However, she had no idea how it would be possible to stop him, especially if he could overcome such a wound as the one he had just received. Kitalla could hack away at him over and over and the jade would keep him alive and healthy. No, she wouldn't be able to defeat him now. They had to escape, recoup their resources, and try again some other time.

There was nothing else to do. Pyron was already casting another spell, but she didn't want to see its effect. She called back to her companions, "Frast! The beasts! Attack! Attack!"

The mage was caught up trying to support Randler and Dariak while maintaining the calm of all the feral creatures. He wasn't focused on tactics, but he heard Kitalla's plea and he snapped himself to alertness and then complied. He pulled on the energies of the beast jade and he bade the creatures to flock to this room and take down the mages within. Straining against a budding headache, he maintained a separate set of commands for those beasts that were transporting Dariak.

Kitalla was lost in the flood of creatures that poured into the chamber from side rooms, upper floors, and from outside the tower itself. The reach of the beast jade seemed immensely powerful, but it was something to be explored later on. She couldn't get back to the others, but she didn't need to. Frast was already having the beasts open the way toward the exit while still overwhelming the mages in the room.

Pyron saw what was happening and he understood the cause. Infuriated, he manipulated his snowstorm spell and soon each bit of snow that hit the ground exploded, spraying venom everywhere. Man and beast were soon covered in agonizing poison, but Frast remained focused despite it and he commanded the beasts to take Pyron down. Reluctant lupinoes sprinted toward the elder mage and slashed and bit into the man's skin. The healing jade kept him from suffering any damage from those wounds, though he still felt the pain of each nip and cut.

Frast was tiring from all the concentration, but they were getting closer to the door and their freedom. He tugged on Randler's sleeve and the beastly entourage led them and Dariak's unconscious body from the tower. Kitalla was already outside taking care of a couple guards posted by the door. The way was clear. Frast kept the animals within the tower active so the mages would be unable to pursue them. Kitalla decided instantly that they should return to Marritosh rather than the castle. They would have less chance to rest and heal at the castle, especially with the increased security that would undoubtedly be in place after her bit of thievery there.

Once they were outside the invisible boundary of Magehaven, the strength of the beast jade waned significantly. Frast could no longer maintain a hold over the creatures within the tower and it was difficult to control the eight beasts that were carrying Dariak. If he didn't prioritize things, he would lose them all, so he released the beasts within the tower and encouraged the group with him to move all the faster. It was hard for Randler to keep up, but Kitalla dragged him along while keeping a lookout for attack. Luckily, the beast jade's power was active and the desert's feral creatures let them pass without incident.

It took nearly two days for them to actually reach the town, and they had barely slept along the way. The beast jade kept Frast's wishes active even in sleep, which was a welcome relief. But once they reached Marritosh, Frast at last released the beasts from their duty. They almost immediately turned back to attack him, so he summoned the jade's power for one more command. They were to flee the area and go into the wild. Only then did the companions have a chance to catch their breath.

CHAPTER 38

Recovery

THE TOWN OF Marritosh buzzed with excitement. The arrival of the Frast, Kitalla, Dariak, and Randler gave the people a new sense of hope that they hadn't realized they were missing, and they greeted the four travelers with a cheering bellow. With Gabrion, Ervinor, and the Kallisorian forces off to the castle, not much had happened.

Dariak's body was less heavy after the two-day journey and the villagers swarmed in to carry him. They reached the healers' hut and the visitors were set inside on cots. Dariak's overly heavy body crushed his bed instantly, so they tucked a pillow under his head and tossed a blanket over him. Three mages swooped around Randler and immediately started tending to his deep shoulder wound. Kitalla glanced over and frowned, worried that he might never be able to play the lute again; Frast was no real healer and they hadn't had time to stop and tend to him properly.

Frast only requested a blanket and some water, but he was asleep before the cup was even brought to him. That left Kitalla with nothing much to do.

"Rest, my lady," said one of the healers. "Your journey must have been harrowing and we will tend to your needs while you are here." He noticed the burns on Kitalla's tunic and asked about damage to her skin.

But the fire jade had protected the thief from burns. Kitalla shook her head. "What I need is information, healer. I don't need your services otherwise."

"Then what information do you require?"

"Tell me everything that's happened since I was last here."

It took some time for Kitalla to refresh the man's memory and it was necessary to bring in a few others who could update her on the recent events, but she pulled the pieces of information together the best she could.

"I see," Kitalla said after a lengthy recitation. "So all it took was Gabrion to pull you together before he went to see your king? Have you all truly thrown your lot in with Kallisor?"

"Not exactly," said one of the healers. "We have sided with your Gabrion and his beliefs that the war must end. We understand that it means we must support the Kallisorians in order to reach that end. Or, at least, your comrades."

"We're all tired of the wars," chimed in another mage. "This is no way to live our lives."

Kitalla looked around at the six men and women who had gathered to update her. "What do you expect us to be able to do? We're only a handful of people. How are we going to change everything that has been in effect for centuries?"

One woman walked up to Kitalla and took the thief's hands in her own. "We believe in your spirit. It is what you seek to do that awoke us all from our stupor. We know that you have it in you to succeed despite all else."

"It's going to take more than belief," Kitalla explained. "We're all going to risk dying if it comes to a conflict. Are you ready to die for this cause? Can each of you really say your life is a worthy cost for success?"

They were quiet for a time but then the youngest among them, Ylior, nodded. "I could not fight, in the eyes of the king." He lifted his robe and showed Kitalla a withered leg that he had been born with and that magic had not been able to repair. "I would have been slain if not for the chance to join the healers, dismissed by my own 'protector' because I was deformed as an infant. I would like the chance to prove that his arrogance was wrong. I would like the chance to fight in my own way. And if I must die in the process of defending what's right, and it somehow helps us reach a victory, then yes, my life would be an acceptable cost."

Kitalla kept her voice level. "And what if we can't achieve that victory?"

"Don't you believe we have a chance?"

She shook her head. "It isn't that. For me... I don't know. There is much I can do, but I also know that there will come a time when I won't succeed. There will come a time that I fail. Completely. And I will die." And she added in a whisper just for herself, touching her belly, "As I have died before."

She cleared her throat. "I'm not here to end any war. I'm here to fight. To grow stronger. I know that I may not win. But I fight anyway. I know I may meet an opponent who is faster than me, or that my luck or skill won't be enough. But I fight anyway. It's a reality of what I face each time I battle. You have to accept that you might die a senseless death. You have to understand that you might not survive. And you have to admit to yourself that it might all be for naught."

They stared at her in silence, their eyes wide and uncertain.

"Randler is better at this sort of thing, but try to understand me," she implored, unsure why she was even talking. "Each day we live, we have sunlight and we have nighttime. You cannot deny the darkness of night and still call each day a day. You have to know it's there. You have to accept that it's coming sometime in the future. It isn't that you only focus on the darkness. But you don't deny it, either. Yet if you come to understand it and keep both halves together, you have a better chance of living in the daylight. If you ignore the night, then it sneaks up on you and you're lost in shadow when you need to be ready.

"So ask yourself again: If you die in this fight and we are not victorious, is your death worth it?"

There was silence for a while and Kitalla didn't even realize that everyone in the healers' hut was listening intently to her words, including her comrades who were nearby. She felt embarrassed but didn't let it show.

Then the deformed healer spoke again. "My death would still be worth it," Ylior decided. "Because I'll be standing up for a safer future. If we fail, others won't. Maybe it won't be for another decade or century, but if no one ever rises up, there is no hope for success. So I will fight. I will rise up and I'll do what I can to help those around me who need me. If that means I heal Hathrens and Kallisorians, mages and warriors, men and children, then that's what I will do. For me, I fight; not to win, but to bring us all closer together."

"Aye!" echoed someone else. "That's a goal even I could get behind. A lot less fighting and a lot more of us getting along."

"Hear! Hear!"

Kitalla listened, amazed that she could incite such passion in them. She hoped she wasn't instilling them with false beliefs, but then she remembered that she didn't live her life on hope, belief, or speculation. She dealt with facts and cunning and preparation. Almost single-handedly, she had arranged for the defenses in Savvron before they had entered Hathreneir, and it was because of those defenses that Randler and Dariak's small army was able to gather safely in the first place. She could do the same here. She could help them to prepare for the road ahead, though they weren't the young, fit warriors the kings would send into battle.

Kitalla could level the field. She knew it.

CHAPTER 39

Healing Forces

MORNING DAWNED IN Marritosh and Dariak was uncertain of the day. He felt as if he had been incapacitated for at least a month. He reached his arms outward and rubbed them gently, still feeling an oddly heavy sensation in his skin. He knew people had died when he had slathered over them in his metal form and he wished he had been able to prevent those deaths, but there was nothing he could do about it now.

He remembered nothing of the others bringing him to Marritosh. Randler had filled him in on the whole frantic journey, complete with Frast's control over the beast jade so the creatures would carry the mage safely. It seemed absurd, like something out of one of Randler's own ballads, but in his heart he knew the truth of it.

He hadn't really been there for a month yet. It only felt that way. Everything seemed strangely slow to him, even when people were talking to him. He remembered the amount of time he had needed after his recovery from a similar transformation through the lightning jade, so he understood full well that he had to wait it out.

This morning, though, he felt better mobility. All the mages in the town were working hard to restore the companions to their full health. They had succeeded in repairing Randler's shoulder wound. He sported a garish scar now, but he hadn't lost any of his finesse, thanks to the concerted efforts to heal him.

Kitalla seemed her usual self to Dariak, and in some way that felt odd. She had run off in such a state, leaving the metal jade behind, only to swoop in and reclaim the jade, all the while saving them in the process. Her battle skills were legendary, but she wasn't exactly known for altruism. However, they had become a tight-knit family.

The only part he didn't understand was Gabrion's delay. The elders of Marritosh had visited with Dariak and informed him of Gabrion's departure to the castle a week earlier, taking several of the villagers with him. They were concerned he hadn't returned yet.

Not much took place that day as the companions all took turns helping Dariak to his feet and reminding his body how to walk. Randler spent a good portion of the time testing out various instruments and making sure his shoulder worked properly. He was often stiff and sluggish, but it was nothing that time and a good deal of stretching wouldn't fix. Frast held back a little, especially if Randler was visiting with

Dariak. His own feelings for the brown-haired bard had grown on their mission to save Dariak, and he feared they would swell out of control and at the wrong time.

In the predawn hours the next day, the calm healing period ended. The army returned from the castle, haggard, worn out, and depleted of nearly two dozen fighters. Most of the mages were carried on stretchers, though not because of injury. They had spent the entire return trip pressing their energies to the limit trying to heal any of the injured they were able to reclaim from the castle.

Kitalla's eyes scoured the group as it entered the town, but there was no sign of Gabrion. Her gaze was drawn aside by one particular stretcher, around which five mages were poised, arms weaving in unison. She examined the enwrapped figure under their care and was both relieved and saddened that it wasn't Gabrion. But she soon realized it was Ervinor and something was terribly wrong.

The men carrying the mages and Ervinor hurried to the healers' den where the injured man could be tended by a more skilled set of practitioners. The stretcher was brought inside and set near Dariak, who gasped when he saw Ervinor's fate.

The healers went immediately to work, supported by Lica and a few other mages from Kallisor. They tore off Ervinor's tunic and cringed at the sight of the damage. The shoulder simply ended in a ragged gash. The mages had done well to preserve him, but they hadn't been able to repair any actual damage and the little healing his own body had done was nothing compared to what remained.

Though the healers were mostly mages themselves, they employed a wide array of techniques, especially in a case like this. They started by cleansing the wound with several buckets of clean water, while one mage worked steadily to help regulate Ervinor's blood flow and to keep it from gushing out of the shoulder. There was a constant trickle, but it was slight and actually necessary, for his lifeblood was needed for the healing process.

Needles were prepped, as were several cloth towels, a packet of herbs, and a host of gems and minerals. Another healer concocted a strong sleeping draft, the scent of which made Dariak woozy from across the room. He tried following the action, listening intently to whispered instructions from the main healer. It looked to Dariak like a hopeless cause, but the healer wasn't going to give up just yet.

The sleeping tonic was administered to Ervinor slowly. He was unconscious already but the work they were about to do would otherwise awaken him. Even with the draft, there was little chance of him remaining still. They took a few precautions and secured Ervinor's body to the table with leather straps, but because of the locations in which they needed to work, they knew the bindings wouldn't have much effect.

Two mages stood opposite the main healer and directed their energies toward Ervinor's belly, which Dariak thought was odd considering the location of the wound. Then another healer came in and started cutting a large round layer of skin off Ervinor's stomach. It was gruesome to watch, but the layer was needed to help seal off the shoulder wound. Already, Ervinor started trembling in his sleep.

Dariak could feel the healing energies amplifying in the room. The magic tugged at his senses and he yearned to be a part of it, but he knew it wasn't a good idea after his recent ordeal. He continued to watch, amazed at the efficiency with which they tackled the injury. He understood basic medicine and healing but the level of skill in this room impressed him. At least a dozen men and women were tending to Ervinor's needs. The room was in constant motion.

But as the healing became more invasive, Ervinor started to rouse from his stupor. They tried adding more sleeping draft and tightening his restraints, but the pain was too great and soon the young man was howling in agony, his body writhing and thrashing on the table, knocking over pieces of rose quartz in the process.

Ready for this, a few nearby villagers ran in to help subdue the thrashing, but the exuberant youth was too strong for them. The mages who were using their healing powers couldn't turn their energies toward keeping him sedated, else the healing forces would falter and they would lose him entirely. Saving Ervinor would apparently take more people than they had available.

Dariak knew what he had to do and he didn't care much about the consequences. "Help me up," he called out to one of the villagers, persisting until the man came over. Dariak made his way over to Ervinor, then he sent his helper off to gather a few items he needed. The other healers didn't protest Dariak's appearance at the table. Poor Ervinor thrashed about so rashly, the healers could barely do anything at the moment but hold him. Three of the bindings had already snapped and those that remained were barely fulfilling their purpose.

Soon the supplies Dariak needed were in his hands. He cast an incantation over a thick twig, *"Connioshtose joierinus umblasser, porial."* He proceeded to coat the twig with a greasy syrup, taking care to press the viscous liquid into the nooks. *"Proteis, rathrafar helliosh nai."* He grabbed a pinch of talc next and coated the sticky twig until it was smooth and soft to the touch.

He then bent the twig in two and moved on to his next spell. *"Bendinariosh fruthic kai morrish santhrineir."* One of the twigs grew warm and slightly malleable. He turned his attention to the other half. *"Absorifice rectiss menarr farrithoni lea shhar."*

The main healer looked up from his work. "What do you think you're doing? Stop this instant!"

"His need is greater than mine. I will be all right."

"But you—"

Ervinor screamed and thrashed on the table, and the healers surrounding him were unable to do anything to subdue him. If he continued, all their efforts would be in vain and he would likely die of massive infection or loss of blood. They maintained their healing spells in the hopes of aligning with the young man's own natural healing powers and finding a means of repairing him.

The main healer acceded. "I cannot argue with you, as his need is indeed great. But I recognize parts of your spell and it worries me. Take great care, Dariak, if you intend to succeed."

"I do. And I will." He nodded his head sharply and then brought one half of the twig to Ervinor's jaw, setting it between his teeth. To some, it looked like a precaution to keep him from breaking his jaw, but Dariak's ensorcelled stick held a strong spell set, similar in some way to the one Frast had used to help Randler's ruse at Magehaven. Dariak made his way back to his bed and then set the other half of twig into his own mouth. *"Commellious."*

Instantly, the pain in Ervinor's body was absorbed into the wooden stick and transmitted to Dariak, sending the violent spasms of pain into the mage. He immediately began screaming and thrashing about. It startled the other healers in the room, but the main healer drew their attention back to their current patient and demanded they ignore the new sounds of agony.

Dariak no longer knew anything except for his intolerable pain. He felt a searing emptiness on his right side, and he knew his arm was gone. He couldn't see with his own eyes, for they were tearing endlessly, blinding him. He felt the ax cutting downward, scraping metal against bone, severing the bond of life that was never meant to be cut. It was a wound like no other.

Then other pains were alive everywhere. The cutting of his belly, pinpricks at his slashed shoulder, welts all along his body, a deep laceration in his throat. Everything was a war field and he had no defenses against any of it.

But that wasn't true, he tried to remind himself. He had chosen to accept this pain, for it wasn't real, at least not for him. He was only connecting the pain to his own self so he could calm the fighter enough to allow the healers to do their work. He could also send information back along the connection. He only had to remember... remember...

Something jabbed into his shoulder and he vaguely heard voices calling out in dismay. He had no idea what was going on, but he could sense a great distress. He tried to open his eyes, but he was still unable to make sense of anything. Spellcasting filled the room in tense panic.

It was that sound that helped Dariak to remember. He was a mage and though he was not proficient at it, he could be a healer too. It was a matter of drawing the balancing forces in the world and pulling them through himself, guiding the energy through the conduit clenched between his teeth and then releasing it into Ervinor where it was most needed. The syrup and talc coating he had given the stick before breaking it in two would prevent the energies from extending outward errantly. He clung to this image and strained beneath the torrents of agony to seek the knowledge buried within his own mind.

Dariak started with a basic healing spell. It was only good for reducing the pain of a sting, like after slapping a table with an open palm. It was a tiny wisp of power, but it was enough to remind him of who he was. He called again and reached more deeply within himself, seeking the old spells that he hadn't spent much time studying after the rudimentary skills.

He found a spell for sealing a slight laceration. It wouldn't do much for the great damage to his—to Ervinor's—shoulder. But every bit would help. He knew it had to help. Gently flowing power enveloped his mind and he let mental hands mold it into a brighter light. He cast it forward, into and through the twig, where it leaped over to Ervinor and swam around his body, leaving traces of healing at random points.

Dariak felt a bit of success, for some of the pain within him began to lessen. He opted to continue his efforts, drawing power from some unknown source and casting it outward, wrapping Ervinor in its light and healing him, ever so slightly. Wave after wave, Dariak pulled and released, keeping his thoughts as calm as possible all the while.

The pain within him grew weaker and weaker. He was glad, but it worried him, too, for he wasn't entirely certain that it was a good sign. Sure, it could mean that the wounds were closing, but it could also suggest that Ervinor was dying and that the weakness was a form of his body shutting down. He tried to listen for the others in the room, but the blood was rushing through him, fighting off the pain he still felt. He could only continue his work and hope somehow that he was helping.

Dariak had no concept of time, and not just because of the aftereffects of his transformation with the metal jade. The spell linking him to Ervinor pulled the young man's haziness into himself as well and, in essence, Dariak realized that he was also feeling drugged by the sleeping draft. Maybe that was why the voices had started shouting moments ago. He wasn't sure. He couldn't hear them anymore. There was no reason to stop, so he pulled and drew the energies around himself, then he cast them off to Ervinor.

At some point he wondered how he was able to use so much magic at once. He hadn't used any spell components. The few things he had taken from the villager were part of the binding itself. He wasn't entirely sure what it meant, but he vaguely told himself that he must be using the jades somehow. They must have sensed his distress and sought to help him, like all those times before.

The thought comforted him and he relaxed his concerns, pulling in more energy and sweeping it all through the room to bolster the efforts of the other healers while also sending a few tendrils specifically toward Ervinor. The pain was still decreasing and he knew he wouldn't need to work at this for much longer.

Then, all at once, he felt a searing pain rip through his whole body. It was unlike any of the other pains that had buffeted him so far. This one originated at his jaw and bolted like an angry snake through every part of him. He screamed aloud, now feeling his own pain, which was completely different than Ervinor's. He tossed his head around, reaching for his jaw, trying desperately to reduce some of the hurt. There was a figure nearby and he strained to focus on it. Something pounded against his ears, and as he struggled to tune into it, he realized that it was only sound. A voice. It was speaking to him. It was strong and soothing all at once, with a frantic urgency hiding underneath the words.

"Dariak, let go. Stop your spells, now, Dariak. You have to let it go."

He knew the voice. He knew it well, and it still warmed him and comforted him like nothing ever had in his life.

"Dariak, release your magic, now. Let it go. Stop your spell. Dariak, listen."

His response was warbled. "Randler, I—"

"Dariak, do you hear me? You have to stop. End your casting. Stop using magic, right now. Please, Dariak. Please stop."

"But Ervinor—" he pushed through his aching jaw.

"Shhh. Just listen to me, Dariak. Obey me, please. Stop your spell. Release the magic."

It was all Randler seemed to care about, and Dariak couldn't understand why. Didn't everyone want to help Ervinor? Wasn't that worth his own sacrifice? But Randler was insistent. He held tightly to Dariak and he repeated his plea over and over. At last, Dariak obliged. He closed his eyes and he pulled mental hands aside, disrupting the swirling energies within himself. He felt the powers stagnate and start to fade away.

"Good, Dariak," Randler consoled. "Wait here. I will return."

Dariak's gaze followed the shadowy figure as he stepped away. He wasn't content just letting Randler go, however, so he pushed himself upright a little, propping up his head and trying to focus across the room.

It took a while for his eyes to adjust, but there was far less commotion here now. The healers had stepped away from Ervinor's body and were seated on the floor, it seemed, resting after their hard work. Randler was checking on them before returning to Dariak.

"Did it work?" the mage asked.

"Ervinor should live," Randler said with a strange grimness in his voice.

"What is it?" he asked uneasily.

Randler bit his lip and looked over his shoulder before answering. "I think everyone is going to be fine, Dariak. Just know that."

"What? What is it? What happened?"

Randler reached out and took Dariak's hand. "Your spell. Somehow it affected all the others who were using magic on Ervinor. From what I understand, there was a terrible backlash among the mages. They all seemed to feel what was happening to Ervinor and their healing spells were pulled from them. The non-mages had to take over entirely but we couldn't free the other mages from their spells."

Dariak's eyes went wide. "I—I thought I was drawing power from the jades."

"I think you were, which is why the magic overflowed into them all. They're coming around. It's going to be all right."

"I—I had no idea."

"I know. I think they know, too. They all seemed to be feeling everything you were feeling and I don't think any of them will blame you. But, Dariak," Randler's eyes turned into warm pools of deep concern, "you really ought to get some rest now."

"I didn't mean to hurt them," he said absently. The idea of rest washed over him and his body responded hungrily. His feet and hands tingled in anticipation of a deep, restful sleep. "Randler, tell them, I— I—"

"I will, Dariak. Now rest."

CHAPTER 40

Wounded Struggles

A LITTLE OVER two weeks passed after Dariak's efforts to heal Ervinor. The young warrior was much stronger physically, but adjusting to the loss of his arm was proving difficult. He spent most of his time locked away in one of the villager's homes near the healers' workstation so they could tend to him often, and they did, especially deformed Ylios. Food was also provided to him, and his friends stopped by frequently. Each tried in his or her own way to comfort the damaged warrior, but they all understood that his healing journey would be a long road.

"I can't carry a sword like this or use one in battle at all," he lamented one afternoon to Frast, who had come to visit with him. As usual, the windows were covered, blocking out the warm, beautiful sunlight. "I'm useless now. I'm not going to be any good in the coming fight once Dariak claims the remaining jades, either."

These complaints were not new, and it took all Frast's patience to remain calm and play his role carefully. "Nonsense, Ervinor. You are resourceful and a smart young man. You will find a way through this."

"How can I swing a sword like this?" he gestured toward his severed right shoulder. "One swipe and I go off-balance. I'll spin like a top and my enemies won't fall, except in laughter."

"I don't believe that."

Ervinor raged, "I can barely walk on my own feet, mage! I should—I should just go home."

"I don't think that's where your heart is, Ervinor. You know that."

"My heart," he echoed. "I've lost it, Frast. There isn't anything I can do now."

A dagger flew into the room and struck the right side armrest of Ervinor's chair. "I disagree," Kitalla argued from the doorway. "You certainly dodged that knife well."

Ervinor scowled. "Not today, Kitalla. Not today."

She turned to the mage. "Frast, you've been summoned. Dariak and Quereth need your help over in the tavern."

The mage scrunched his brows. "In the tavern?"

"Maybe it was the middens or the weapon smith, I don't care; get out," she added, lifting a sack from the floor. Frast responded quickly.

"Kitalla, not today," Ervinor implored.

"So dark in here," she commented absently, striding over to the window and tossing the curtain aside. A blast of sunlight flooded the room, causing the young warrior to wince. "Much better."

"Please—"

Kitalla ignored him and dropped her sack on the floor. "The healers all say you've had more healing pumped through your body than this entire town has seen this past year. They also assured me that you may be in some pain but that you're quite capable of getting on with things. So, I'm here to make that happen."

Ervinor grabbed the dagger that was lodged in the armrest and he threw it with his left hand toward the thief. The throw was badly aimed and fell wide of its mark. "I'm finished, Kitalla. It's time we all accepted that."

"I agree."

He hadn't expected that response. "Y—You do?"

"Yes. You are finished with all this wallowing and self-pity. It is time you get on your feet and start training. We need you, Ervinor. Every single one of us."

His confused expression turned to one of annoyance as Kitalla ignored his resulting pleas and started rifling through the sack she had brought with her. "What do I need to do to make you leave?" he yelled.

"Only indulge me for an hour. That's all I ask."

He squinted suspiciously. "One hour?"

"Yes, though the time does not start until I'm suited up, so you'd best give me a hand over here."

He didn't know if she had chosen those words on purpose. "I can only give you one hand, remember?" he noted sourly.

By now, Kitalla had inverted the sack and pulled out a strange tunic. It was stiffly made of a thick leather and one sleeve was noticeably longer than the other. She drew the tunic over her head and pulled it tight against her torso so that the longer sleeve enwrapped her right arm. There was a metal clip along the waistline and she used her left hand to slip the excess portion of the sleeve through the loop. She then fumbled when it came to securing the loose end.

"Your assistance, please," she called over her shoulder.

Ervinor could already see what she was planning to do and he didn't like it. "Don't mock me, Kitalla," he grumbled. She responded with an impatient look and waited until he hobbled over and helped her to tie off the excess fabric, which effectively pinned her right arm against her body, rendering it useless.

"This certainly isn't the same thing, I realize," she stated, "but I'm not about to cut off my own arm for you at a time like this."

"Very funny," he said in a tone that was far from humorous.

"I had this tunic specially made for us. It was ready a few minutes ago and I haven't had any time to practice in it yet, so let's get to it."

"Practice what?" he asked, though he knew the answer.

"Fighting, of course. Now, you prefer a sword, yes?"

"Kitalla, this isn't going to work."

"Not with that attitude, no. But you promised me an hour, warrior, and I expect you to do your best."

"If I refuse?"

"I'll make it two hours. No more talking. Get your sword."

She bent over awkwardly and reached for a sword that she had brought with her. She tipped over too far, however, and crashed to the ground.

"You did that on purpose," Ervinor accused. "It isn't going to win you any victories with me."

"So chivalrous to help a fallen lady," she murmured as she brought her legs under her and pushed herself upward. She tried to reach out with both arms to stabilize herself, but her right arm was firmly secured against her side. She staggered again, but managed to keep from toppling over. "Interesting."

Ervinor shook his head, not believing any of it. He made his way across the room and found a sword to use for himself. He held it at his side and used it as a cane as he stepped back toward Kitalla.

"Not your common use for a sword, but effective, nonetheless." She ignored the angered look on his face, bringing her blade up and casting a few swings in the air. "Now you."

Rolling his eyes, Ervinor spun his sword around. His whole body went off balance and he crashed into the nearby chair, almost splattering himself to the floor. "This is pointless!" he growled.

"Swords always have a point, actually," she taunted. "Now again, but this time, set your feet a little farther apart." She demonstrated what she meant and he mimicked her movements, finding himself a little more stable, but only just so.

"Wonderful," he said sardonically. "So I haven't fallen flat on my face."

"Oh," she said, sounding perplexed. "I thought you had; I did always think your nose was a little flat."

"You're not funny!" he snarled.

"I'm not trying to be," she said. "Now parry." She swept her sword forward and Ervinor made a jerky movement to intercept her attack. He missed, but so did she. Her whole body lurched forward and she stumbled.

Ervinor laughed at her faulty step. "Not as easy as it looks, is it?"

"As if you could do better," she sneered. "Never mind, I'll get it. Parry again!"

She swung her sword and this time the blades connected. She stepped forward to press in, but Ervinor anticipated it and he stepped backward, allowing her imbalance to overtake her again. As she staggered past him, he slashed his sword across her backside and knocked her flat.

"Well, if that's how you're going to play, then let's stop fooling around," she challenged. After reclaiming her footing, Kitalla charged toward him suddenly, surprising him. Ervinor took a step back to dodge the thrust and he made a jerky motion to intercept her. Kitalla recognized the move; he had instinctively tried to use his missing right arm. The instant frustration on his face was even more evidence, but she didn't let him dwell on it. She spun and brought her sword in front of him again. He twitched but he didn't raise his arm until a few seconds too late.

She didn't let him stop to think. Kitalla kept her feet wide and pressed another attack. He had to concentrate to stop her, but he managed it. She let him taste the one victory but only for a moment. She spun and brought her sword about, but her body went off-center and she turned too far, missing her target completely. Ervinor saw the opening and he stepped forward clumsily to smack her with the flat of his blade. Kitalla recovered by spinning further and coming around to defend the attack. Ervinor wasn't ready for it and he toppled over, crashing down on top of Kitalla and bringing them both to the ground.

"It's no use, Kitalla," he breathed into her face.

"It's no use, Ervinor."

"I know."

"You're much too young for me," Kitalla continued. "Throwing yourself at me like this won't get you anywhere."

"Throw—Kitalla!" he gasped, his emotions somewhere between bewilderment and rage. He struggled to disentangle himself from her and then he rose up to his feet and walked over to his chair, where he dropped himself heavily down. "The hour is up," he declared.

"Hardly," she barked a laugh.

He pounded his left fist on the armrest. "When are you going to listen to me? It's over. I'm finished. I cannot fight anymore, Kitalla. You can show up here with any crazy contraptions you want, but it won't change the fact that I lost my arm. It is gone and I can't get another one. Don't you see? I'm useless now. I can't guide this army onward any longer. I can't help you all in your quest. It's just plain over."

She paused as she stared at him. Defeated, she reached over and untied her special tunic, casting it lifelessly to the floor. "I see your point."

"Do you really?" he questioned skeptically.

"Yes, I do. You don't even want to try. You've given up. And it has nothing to do with your missing arm. No, Ervinor, you're just a coward."

"I'm what?" he shouted. "How dare you!" His face curled into an unpleasant mask of rage. Such anger truly did not suit him. "After all the things I've done, how dare you!"

"All meaningless!" she badgered back at him, her words biting and sharp. "Nobody cares about what you did 'yesterday,' you fool."

"Of course they do! If it wasn't for me, there wouldn't have been an army for Gabrion to bring over to the castle in the first place. Who remained here with them keeping up morale and organizing training sessions while you were all tromping off in Magehaven?

"And what about everything after that?" he fumed, rising to his feet. "When Dariak was captured and you ran off to who knew where? You abandoned everyone and do you even know how crushed Gabrion was that you were gone? How upset we all were?

"But no, we all pressed on. Randler and Frast went to rescue Dariak. Quereth, Gabrion, and I went to the castle and we brought the army with us. And who was it who kept the troops in line as we waited all those hours for Gabrion's return, sitting right there in the midst of the enemy forces?

"You call me a coward, Kitalla? I raced in to the castle to find Gabrion and I knew there was little hope for escape. We were surrounded on all sides and inside the castle there could have been any sort of defensive structure to stop us.

"But I went in," he seethed, pacing as he spoke.

"The fighting was still going on," he continued, heated in his tirade. "Everything was in chaos and Gabrion was nowhere in sight. Did I turn around and leave to go home? No! I stood my ground and I fought. And Quereth... Poor Quereth. He was clearly exhausted. He tried to help me, but that soldier, he was coming in too fast. There was nothing else I could do. I pushed Quereth out of the way and I paid for it with my arm!"

He knelt low and pressed his face into Kitalla's. "Does that sound like the act of a coward to you?"

His breath was hot against her face and his chest heaved with exertion. He glared at her viciously for a few moments before rising up and turning away.

Kitalla crooned a hideously mocking laugh.

Ervinor snapped. He spun around, hefted his sword from the ground, and attacked her with all his might. His swordplay was erratic as he fought with his untrained and weaker left arm. But he did his best to adjust as Kitalla sprang to her feet to defend herself, still laughing in that demeaning, careless tone.

Ervinor dipped low and struck hard, missing his target. Kitalla was no longer bound to the restrictive tunic, and so she took advantage of Ervinor's misstep. She crouched low and then swept her sword upward, almost knocking his weapon out of his hand. He grunted and brought the sword back sharply and Kitalla had to flatten herself to avoid it. She rolled to her feet and backed away momentarily before adjusting her grip and lunging ahead.

Ervinor pivoted to the side and her attack missed. He then kicked out his foot, catching her thigh and knocking her down. But Kitalla was unhindered now. She hit the ground with her hands first and allowed her momentum to carry herself into a roll. She pounced back to her feet and turned to dodge Ervinor's next attack. He was unsteady and he wavered, but his anger kept him from noticing.

Kitalla grinned inwardly as he approached. She twisted in a motion similar to his recent move, and then she brought her fist into his chest, causing him to drop his sword.

Ervinor's rage still burned brightly and he brought up his knee into Kitalla's stomach. She doubled over and grabbed him around the waist, pushing him off-balance. He staggered back and fell to his backside. Now Kitalla was upon him and he swung his left arm at her head, but she managed to stop the attack. He then brought his right knee up and she rolled off him then pounced away.

Ervinor needed more time than that to right himself, but not by much. He looked for his sword but it was out of reach. He glanced back at Kitalla, but she wasn't in a battle stance. Instead, she was leaning against the wall as if she had been waiting there for a long time.

"I'm not finished with you!" he roared.

Kitalla inspected her fingernails intently. "I'm glad to hear it. You may be a little hotheaded right now, but you're fighting excellently, if you pause to think about it."

He took two steps forward and then stopped. He looked around the room at the lump of tunic on the floor, the two clattered swords, and the furniture that had fallen over at some point. He hadn't even noticed it.

He turned back to Kitalla but she was gone.

CHAPTER 41

A Plan Develops

TIME PASSED SLOWLY for the group as they mended their wounds in Marritosh. Ervinor was less depressed over the loss of his arm, though he was far from accepting it. He moped at times, but made himself useful as well. The elders of the town found excuses to call on him for aid and he obliged most of the time.

Dariak was also feeling much better. His efforts to assist Ervinor's healing process had drained him more emotionally than anything, for he hadn't intended to cause suffering to the village healers. He had approached them all to explain, but each one had felt his intentions during the spell, and no one blamed him directly, though some now eyed him cautiously, if not a little fearfully. His power was certainly strong, and he knew he needed to be more mindful of his actions.

Randler spent time in the town, boosting morale in his own way. From sweeping tunes on his lute to deep, heartfelt ballads, he brought the people in touch with themselves and, in doing so, he was able to help them face their ailments. Even Ervinor had propped himself up in the corner of the tavern to listen to Randler's music and words.

The injured members of the army were also recovering well. Their wounds were staunched and their spirits were lightened. Yet everyone worried about the next move. There were too many unanswered challenges to face and, when they allowed themselves to admit it, they were a tiny force, all told.

"Time is going to slip away unless we start doing something," Kitalla cautioned one evening. The thief had spent many hours keeping her skills intact by sparring with the warriors in the village. "We can't remain here much longer waiting."

Dariak nodded and whispered, "I know." He breathed a heavy sigh and looked at the council table. The major players of his forces sat with him, as did the elders of Marritosh. They knew that if the army fled, then the king's forces would swoop down and reclaim the town.

Old man Herchig slammed his tankard on the table. "Why, this reminds me of the time I was captain of a small force myself. We were lying in wait to ambush a group of brigands. We were hunkered down for what seemed like weeks and then we grew restless. Sure, we had to maintain the ambush or we would lose the thieves. But in truth, we were getting so anxious to be on with it that we started getting sloppy. Blasted brigands turned the ambush around on us and gave us a good teaching, I'll tell you. Now sure, we're all hunkered down here licking our wounds and gathering our plans, but the more we sit tight the more likely we'll get complacent and just lose ourselves too.

"Now, I know you young people are all worried about the king taking away the rest of our freedom, and he may do just that. But you have other things you need to do in the meantime if you're going to put an end to this for good. Why, that blasted group of thieves was led by a vicious scoundrel and it was the general of the army who realized we couldn't stop the caravan attacks by trapping a few measly sellswords. No, he let the defenses slide where he had to so he could mount a larger assault and take down that bloody scavenger. Sure, it nearly cost me an eye; why this one day—"

"Herchig!" one of the other elders cut in. "We'll be here all night if you're going to recount your life history. Make your point."

"He has, Imerelda," Ervinor muttered softly, his eyes focused on Herchig. Ervinor then turned his gaze to his companions. "He's right. The king may come, but you have other things to do."

"Ervinor..." Dariak started.

"No, it's fine," he retorted. "I won't be of any use to you right now; not until I regain some of my skill. And confidence," he admitted openly. "I will remain here and help to protect these gracious people."

Herchig smiled. "Now that's a lad and a fine man, too. Yes, sometimes it's not the battles we seek, but the battles we know to avoid, that measure us. When I was but eleven years old—"

Imerelda slammed her fist on the table, "Herchig!"

The old man sputtered for a moment and then he released a deep sigh and sank back in his seat, clearly dejected.

"Dariak?" Kitalla prompted.

"The real question is figuring out what the priority is. We then need to tackle it efficiently."

Randler decided to enumerate the options so there were no misunderstandings. "We have Gabrion to find, naturally. We have been without our friend for far too long and I'm worried. There is also the healing jade to obtain from Pyron, though based on our last attack on Magehaven, it won't be easy. We have to fortify our defenses here in case the king sends forces to quell the rebellion before troops from Kallisor hit the castle proper. We also need to bolster our forces, and the best way to do so will be to turn the Kallisorian troops to our cause."

Quereth snorted a laugh. "Sorry, all. Just hearing all that, I have no clue about where to even start. Perhaps my recent ordeal has taken the fight out of me, but we're only a handful of people here."

The statement cast a sudden pallor on them all, for it was the one thought each had buried within but none wanted to face.

Dariak broke the silence. "I have to go after Pyron before he develops any more skill with the healing jade."

"I'll be by your side," Randler immediately agreed.

"Good." Dariak smiled. "I'll need your help with the resonance and dissonance theories, as well as your company. Frast? Would you join us?"

The young mage snapped to attention in his seat and he bit his lip as he looked from Randler to Dariak. "I— No, I'm best suited to work here. I'm in need of a respite from the excitement." He cast another furtive glance toward Randler before lowering his eyes and shaking his head. "I'm sorry."

Another silence filled the room before Dariak turned to his earliest conspirator on this quest. "Kitalla?"

"You already know," she said. "Yours is a magical fight and though I may score a lucky hit with my daggers, Pyron needs to be taken down by magical forces."

"You're remaining here, too?" Frast looked up, confused.

"No, mage," she said softly.

Randler nodded to himself. "Perhaps on your way you can try to persuade the troops to join us? If anyone can, it's you."

"Actually," she added, still noting that Frast hadn't figured it out yet; his cheeks were still flushed from his glance toward Randler. "I'll let Gabrion do the talking. He may be a simple village boy, but he knows the locals better than I do." Her lilting tone was amusing only to those who knew her best.

Ervinor opened his mouth in protest but Dariak laughed. "You sell yourself short, hag. You know the locals quite well enough."

She winked in reply and then turned to Ervinor. "When I return with Gabrion, I expect you to be ready."

"Ready?"

"You're in charge of things here." Her tone went from light moments ago to sharp and domineering. "There's no point in changing the chain of command. The army needs someone they know they can trust, and if we're all heading out, then that leaves you. So I expect you to be ready."

"Kitalla, I need more time," he argued.

"You don't have it," she replied.

"We'll help," Frast said. "Won't we, Quereth?"

The older mage hedged. "I will do what I can, but as I said earlier, I'm losing my will to fight."

"Defense," Randler offered. "Just work with the rest of the mages and help them sharpen their skills for defense. You don't need to do more than that."

"Until Ervinor needs more," Kitalla said with a grin. She then returned the incredulous looks she was receiving. "What? I expect to come back here to our forces holding strong. I don't intend to come back having to fight my way in. No, I will return and you will have a nice cold tankard of ale waiting for me, and perhaps a few of Herchig's mint rolls. Yes, that will do nicely."

Herchig released a sudden belly laugh that caught the assembly off guard. "Why, lass, if you only knew how I even came upon that recipe!"

Before he could dive into the tale, Imerelda intervened, "Then it seems like we're set. Are there any other issues we need to address this eve?"

Everyone chuckled, including Herchig. "Very well," he conceded. "I'll tell you that one when you're back with our friend Gabrion."

"It's a deal," she agreed. "But I fully expect to depart tomorrow with a pack of those rolls for my journey."

Herchig rose to his feet swiftly, despite his age. "Nesseria's going to make me sleep out on the cobblestones tonight. Fire up the oven, Ness! We've got rolls to make!"

* * *

It wasn't easy for the team to split up again so soon. They gathered together a couple of days after the meeting, having assembled their supplies and preparing to set off once more.

"You keep practicing," Kitalla said to Ervinor. "The fight is in you and you'll be back up to speed in no time."

"So oddly serious." He grinned. "I have a lot to do here and I'm glad for it, really. It should distract me enough so I don't focus so much on missing an arm. Before you know it, I should be able to ride horses backwards and then fly through the clouds on the back of an eaglon."

"Blindfolded," Kitalla added with a wink.

"Is there any lingering pain?" Dariak wondered. "If you need, I could—"

"No, Dariak, I'll be fine," the young man answered. "There are plenty of healers here who can help. I get the sense that I will always feel like the arm is there. I keep trying to reach out for things with it or try to scratch it because it itches. But I don't think even your magic can fix that."

"Perhaps the healing jade will."

"I won't count on it. I can't. I have to focus on what's to come."

Dariak accepted that and nodded. "Frast, you're sure you want to stay here? We could use your help against Pyron."

He tried his best not to glance at Randler and mostly succeeded. "My place is here now. Quereth isn't up to rebuilding the army and Lica's been focused on healing. We need a mage in charge of the other mages. I think I qualify."

"More than enough," Randler said, clasping Frast's shoulder in earnest. The mage flushed gently.

"Well, I guess it's about time." Kitalla sighed. She reached into a concealed pocket and withdrew one of the two jades she had in her possession. "We hadn't discussed this, but I think this shard would be more useful to you, Dariak." She reached out and handed him the fire jade.

But the mage refused. "I can't take it right now. The dissonance would prevent me from using the jades I am already familiar with, and I don't have time to commune with it."

"Besides," Randler added, "you can use it as a beacon for us when your task is complete. Light up the sky and we will see it. I'm sure of it."

She tucked the shard back into her pocket. "I hope you don't expect me to offer the metal jade next, because I have no intention of parting with it now."

"Resonance," Randler smiled. "The two of you work too well in harmony after all you've been through. You support each other, and Dariak and I know that."

The mage nodded. "Yes, and after my stint as a coagulated lump of iron, I think I'm fine with you holding on to it for a while."

Kitalla smiled and tipped her head toward him. "You never have explained how you have managed to 'become' these jades."

The mage shuddered. "It isn't exactly something I either control or enjoy. In that moment of sheer desperation, it senses my need and takes over my body. First in the battle against Sharice when I became a roving lightning storm, I lost all sense of myself. And when I was bound in the magical shroud by the mages, I was being starved and my body wouldn't hold up much longer, then the metal jade took over. Instead, it sensed that I would die and it did what was necessary to protect me. It's a horrible experience, really. I don't recommend it."

Randler added, "That's going to be our challenge against Pyron."

Frast drew a sharp breath. "If he channels the healing jade like that…"

Dariak nodded. "Yes. It won't be easy to stop him."

Kitalla frowned. "Perhaps, then, it would be necessary to give you all the jades. My two and the beast jade."

Frast instinctively clutched the jade in his pocket. "If it would help."

"As I said," Dariak argued, "I don't know those jades well and they would hinder me. Randler and I have some ideas, anyway."

"Aside from that," Ervinor chimed in, "you all need those jades for another reason: To be able to find each other again."

"That's the truth of it," Frast acknowledged. "We may not be able to stay here in Marritosh for much longer. And not just because I grow weary of this desert heat."

Dariak grinned. "Don't worry. Our next base of operations will be on a glacier."

The others laughed. It was forced and uneasy, but it was a necessary show of mirth.

"You remember how to focus them?" Dariak asked Kitalla.

She rolled her eyes and pouted like a petulant teenager, but she deigned to answer. "Yes, of course. And it will help that I have these two, as it will help me to triangulate Gabrion's position. I just hope he still has the glass jade."

"Whatever happened to him and wherever he went, he wouldn't lose it," Dariak decided. "Even in the Prisoner's Tower, he hid it and I doubt that the shard would let him leave it behind." He reached down and touched the earth jade, nestled along his hip in the special belt Randler had made for him. "Somehow, I think they want us guiding them together."

"You… speak of them almost as if they're alive," Ervinor ventured.

"I can't explain why," the mage said, "but I think in some strange way, they are."

"It would explain a lot," Randler agreed. "But I don't know of any tales about that."

"Well, bring your lute, then." Kitalla winked. "Someone needs to write the first one." She glanced up and gauged the sun. "If Herchig is right, then this is the best time for me to head off. The sandorpions should be in a glorious daze, basking in the late morning sun."

"Not looking to fight them?" Ervinor teased.

"Not needlessly. After all, if I destroy them, won't the border guardians or the eaglons or the reptigons become too numerous or something? Food chain and all."

They all clasped hands one last time and then the three factions went their separate ways. Kitalla would seek Gabrion and try to bring reinforcements from the east. Frast and Ervinor would strengthen the army in the south. And Dariak and Randler would venture to the west to seek out Pyron and claim the last of the pieces of the infamous Red Jade.

A Boy Reflects

"Dear, are you all right?" Meriad looked in concern at the boy. His face was drowned in tears and a stricken pain. She set aside the book and reached for his chin. "We shouldn't continue."

In denial, he shook his head. "No Gran-mama, I'm fine. It's just a lot. Too much happening. Too much feels too real."

"I see. Perhaps it is best that we stop here then."

"I just don't understand it," he wailed suddenly. "Gabrion. Protector. Hero. One of the good guys. *He killed her!*"

"Yes, dear, he did," she said with a deep solemnity. "But I don't think he meant to."

He punched his pillow. "You always try to tell me that the Kallisorians aren't evil, but *he killed her!*"

"Listen, child, and listen well, for this is very important. Not everything happens the way we expect it to. But in many ways, things happen for the best of reasons—"

"They what?" he interjected, tears streaming anew.

Meriad's voice hardened. "Now, you will not speak to me in such tones. I will not return to complete this tale if you speak down to me."

It took a few moments for the boy to collect himself, but he did so at last. "I— I'm sorry. I just don't understand how you could say something so… horrible."

The old woman drew a deep sigh. "Me either, if you must know. But if we move past the one moment and look at the rest, then you will see that there is more at stake than her life."

He clutched his jaw and then shuddered. "I don't know how. How am I supposed to not hate him for what he did?"

"Well, just keep a few things in mind, perhaps. What Dariak said about the jades was true; they sensed his need and acted accordingly. Think now about the pain Gabrion felt at that moment. He did not intend her any harm."

He made a low rumbling noise in the back of his throat. "You're saying he— that the jade did it? You're saying that the jades are evil?"

She patted his shoulder affectionately. "I am not quite saying that, but there is something mystical about them. None of them knew what."

"We don't even know now, Gran-mama. You even said yourself that no one really knows about the jades. They've all been forgotten."

She grinned. "Perhaps, young one. But perhaps a select few people know quite well."

The boy's eyes opened wide and he asked in wonder, "Are you one of them?"

She reached out and placed her hand on the large tome. "You might say that I have learned. And it is a lesson I intend for you to learn as well."

He sat upright and poised himself strongly. "I am ready, Gran-mama."

"Oh! Are you, really?" she asked, bemused. "Well, I would agree, else I would not have ever started this tale with you. But my visit here has come to a close."

He moaned. "I know."

"But worry not, for I will return in a month's time and we will continue the journey together. Try to keep an open mind about poor Gabrion, despite the terrible crime he committed."

"I—" he started, then slammed his jaw shut. If he argued too much, she might not finish the tale with him. "All right, Gran-mama. I will see you soon."

"Good night, love," she whispered as she kissed him gently on the cheek and rose to her feet. She took the tome in her hands and made her way to the door, turning to watch him as she did every night of her visits. He was pensive this time, and she hoped that he was taking her advice. She knew he needed to keep an open mind and heart. If he shut down too early in the face of pain, then he would be no different than any of the heartless kings who had ruled the lands of Hathreneir and Kallisor.

"No," she muttered to herself. "He will understand one day. He must."

The Assembly

A Year Recalled

TWO LONG MONTHS had passed and the winter was blowing harshly outside. Old Meriad hated the bitter chill and her soaked riding cloak clung to her fragile frame. She always traveled with a supply caravan when it was transporting thick blankets, for she could curl up in the cloths and keep herself as warm as possible without a fire. She never worried about the feral creatures in the land, for the caravans she chose always traveled with a contingent of well-trained guards.

Her grandson welcomed her with a running embrace, knowing she could no longer hoist him into the air. He remembered to ask all the pleasantries before gently tugging her arm toward his room, where she would continue the tale of the Red Jade.

She allowed herself to be escorted by the child, knowing full well that he would have food waiting there for her. His actions were presumptuous for a little boy, but she had honestly arrived only for him. She had no other purpose to visit this place and they both understood it.

Seating herself and enjoying a few sips of warm soup, she asked him about his studies, his health, his exercise regimen, and the other things she felt required to investigate before turning to the purpose of her extended visit. He obliged her questions with as much patience as an excited boy could muster.

Then came the question he both loved and detested. "Remind me what has happened so far."

"Years ago, there was the War of the Colossus. The Kallisorians, who hate magic, used some anyway to defeat the Hathren king. Hathren mage, Delminor, assembled and used the power of the Red Jade to summon a giant colossus that put an end to the fighting. Both kings and Delminor died that day and the Red Jade split back into eleven pieces that were scattered.

"Delminor's son, Dariak, went on a quest to find the shards of the Red Jade so he could use the power to restore the balance of magic in the land and bring peace between the nations. He didn't really start off the right way, but he ended up meeting Gabrion and Kitalla in the beginning. Gabrion was a warrior from a small town and he went on a quest to—"

Meriad lifted her eyes from her meal, wondering why he had stopped speaking. The boy's face was contorted in a mask of pain as he recalled other parts of Gabrion's journey. "Keep going," she said.

With a nod, he did, though he changed his focus. "Kitalla was a thief who wanted to get stronger so she would never be hurt again. Terrible things happened to her when she was a teenager and she lost everything she had." He paused again.

"Is something wrong, dear?"

The concern in her voice frightened him, only because he wanted to hear the rest of the tale and if she felt he wasn't ready to handle it all, she might not continue reading to him. He swallowed hard and pressed on. "They met Randler, a bard, and the four of them traveled through Kallisor and into Hathreneir to collect the jades. They were joined by a small army and they made camp in Marritosh. Ervinor sort of took over the army so Dariak could to go Magehaven and Gabrion could to go Hathreneir Castle."

The boy steadied himself with a rattling breath. "So much happened in both places. But in the end, Dariak managed to get all the jades except for the healing jade. The master of the tower, Pyron, escaped with it. As for Gabrion, well… he found Mira. And he…" The boy cleared his throat and added, "He ran off and no one knows where he went."

Meriad smiled at the boy. "Succinct and well-remembered," she commended. "However…"

"Uh oh," he moaned.

"You tell me."

But he didn't want to so he shook his head.

"When I left here two months ago, I challenged you to think about Gabrion's motives along his journey and the ultimate fate that befell him. And your hesitation leads me to believe that you haven't come around to understanding what truly happened."

He tried hard not to yell in frustration. "But he *killed* her, Gran-mama. Even if the jade was really just using his anger to hurt her, he was still that angry."

"Not angry so much as hurt. But you raise an interesting point."

"I—I do?"

She grinned warmly and twisted in her chair so she could lift the heavy tome from the floor. She set it on the edge of his bed as always, then gently flipped through the volume until she reached the place where she had left off. "Yes, you do. However, I still challenge you to release your own feelings on the matter and try to see the rest as well. It is an important skill you must learn."

He sighed and then nodded his head. "I'll try, Gran-mama. But it isn't easy."

"No," she agreed. "It never is."

CHAPTER 1

A Troubled Friend

A COOL ZEPHYR swept through Jortun, bringing with it the promise of a snowy winter. The air was bitterly crisp and heralded the onset of the deepest cold. Felluria pulled her shawl around her aged bones, muttering in the breeze. She truly hated the winter and spent a good amount of her wealth just to keep her home warm on the coldest of nights. She didn't care how many trees were killed for one season's worth of heat; she could pay for it and so she would have it.

Despite the drain on the town's resources and her sometimes severe attitude to the villagers, Felluria was well-respected as a leader. She accepted the title Matron from those below her, deciding long ago that she knew what was best for them and that they needed her guidance. Adopting a motherly role, she had nursed a dying village back to health, sometimes with difficult decisions that were met with dissent. But, as with a misbehaved child, she punished those who thwarted her, then offered forgiveness and a chance for redemption.

The town was nestled near the base of the northern mountains, far from the warring to the south, and the fierce winds brought every whipping storm imaginable. Sand and rain were not a problem. The one thing she could never change, however, was the blasted winters.

Felluria's father had been an able carpenter and bricklayer. She had apprenticed under him and learned his skill well, bringing that knowledge to a people that lived in feeble huts of straw and poorly-secured slats of tender wood. Now the homes were built to withstand the force of the storms.

To an outsider, the village itself looked strange. Many of the houses were misshapen and twisted. The roads were rarely in perfect rows. Channels ran along the front of each house, weaving back and forth as they traced through the town and led to a deep reservoir not too far away. When the sand and wind whipped through the village, it was guided along the odd pathways, branching randomly and therefore weakening until each gust of wind was mightily tamed and set softly aside. If sand built up, it would eventually run off as if in an hourglass. During the spring and autumn rains, the channels carved into the roads brought the water to the reservoir, which serviced the town's needs for long periods.

But snow just fell. It clung to the buildings and the ground. It clogged the channels and needed to be constantly cleaned out by the villagers, who knew it was best to stay inside when the winds were strong, or risk being swept along with them. No, the snow fell hard in wintertime and it blocked the roads and trapped the people in their homes until the worst of the storms died down.

Felluria shuddered and readjusted her shawl, as if it could warm her thoughts and keep the snow from ever coming. It was the only thing that made her feel mortal. "More wood!" she called out to a young man lingering nearby. Silently, the muscled youth went off to do her bidding.

She breathed the crisp air again, trying to separate its beauty from its warning. It was a scent most people would crave, inhaling to savor the perfect clarity. Indeed, she had done the same when she had first arrived decades ago. Until the snow. The accursed snow.

Felluria moved away from the front porch of her house and walked the few yards to the woodshed. The structure was the size of a normal villager's house; in fact, it had been someone's home several years before, but it was handed over to the Matron so she could combat her bane. The old woman pulled the front door open and stepped inside, eying the rooms full of chopped wood as she walked from the front of the house to the back. The breeze did not touch her here, for the walls were strongly fortified by stone and oak. The entire place was filled with the scent of wood and she breathed it in as if it would prolong her successful, contented life.

She made note of a few places where the piles could be higher or stacked more neatly to accommodate more wood. Those corrections would have to be addressed soon, for the winter could sometimes surprise them with an early visit, and she refused to be caught unawares.

Felluria left the wood house and returned to her massive abode, which was over twice the size. She didn't have servants, per se, but several villagers regularly helped her with menial tasks and preparing her meals. She was perfectly capable of doing these things herself, even at her age, but she didn't argue with the assistance. It was fitting the people paid homage to her, as well as taxes.

Afternoon tea was set out for her with a handful of cakes that she loved. They were buttery in flavor and very soft, which was important, for some of her teeth had gone missing over the years. Upon each cake was a sugary icing and slices of fresh fruit, today cut into stars. She admired the creative flourishes of the young baker and encouraged her to practice her craft so she could find true success at her natural vocation. Bakers wouldn't ever earn more than her accumulated wealth, but people needed to eat and so a baker's livelihood was secure.

Eventually, the woodcutter returned with some well-chopped logs. Felluria made her way to the door to observe as he dragged the wood to the small side house and disappeared within to stack it. The blond-haired youth made a few trips to bring all the wood from his chopping area, and he worked silently, without a smile or grimace with any step.

Behind her, Felluria could hear her helpers chattering away and though it irritated her, they spoke what everyone was thinking. Perhaps that was what irritated her the most. This strong young man was a mystery even she couldn't solve.

"—Nobody knows, Aissla, you know that," one voice whispered.

"I know, but *somebody* has to know *something*," Aissla insisted.

"Nope. He just showed up one day and started working."

"I don't trust him, Veldi."

"Well, Matron seems to accept him, so should we all."

Listening intently from the doorway, Felluria smiled, imagining that the two teens were a little more than enamored with the young man's looks and physique and were more frustrated that their attempts to get to know him had utterly failed.

"Accept him? But he won't even tell us his name. How can we trust someone who won't speak?"

"Maybe he can't, Aissla." Then Veldi's voice went even quieter, making it hard for Felluria to overhear. "Maybe they cut out his tongue."

Aissla gasped in shock. "No. He wouldn't have let them."

"He couldn't help it," Veldi decided, enjoying her friend's reaction. "They grabbed him, pinned him down, and did the deed. Chop! Like cutting a carrot. And poof, no more talking."

"You're toying with me. Look at him. He's way too strong to fall for that. And the way he hacks away at the wood. Have you ever watched him?"

Veldi nodded. "Who hasn't?" she drawled.

The girls twittered with laughter. "But he looks like he really knows what he's doing with an ax. You know? The grace in the way he moves. The power in his arms."

"You're drooling, dear," Felluria interrupted caustically. She stepped inside and closed the door. "The young man's presence here is a mystery. There is a pain in his eyes that runs deep, and I think that's why he doesn't speak."

"Can we really trust him, Matron?" Aissla chanced, earning a motherly eyebrow from Felluria.

"Indeed, we should keep an eye on him," the old woman said, then amended. "That is, perhaps the men should keep an eye on him to ensure he doesn't harm anyone."

The ladies giggled. "He doesn't seem the sort, Matron, does he?" Veldi commented, looking at him through a window as he continued bringing wood into the oversized shed.

"No, and that's what puzzles me. Where does his pain come from?"

All three turned and stared at the young man walking solemnly into and out of the storage house, his arms and chest bulging with strength and purpose, but his face lacking any emotion at all.

"I have to know!" Aissla decided suddenly. She separated herself from the other two and she strode out the door and stalked across the way to where the man was lifting another bundle of wood. "Excuse me!" she called, determined to succeed today despite failing previously.

The man paused and looked at her, his body straining as he held the logs aloft.

"I—ahem, my name is Aissla. W—Who are you?"

The man blinked at her but he said nothing. After a few seconds, he turned and walked toward the shed. Not to be cast aside so readily, the girl stamped after him.

"That's rather rude, you know? We've put up with you here for weeks now. We've given you shelter and food, and you haven't told us your name. Is that so much to ask?" She stood with her hands on her hips, watching as he silently stacked the wood. He deliberately adjusted the cut logs so they would fit more neatly. Then he turned to get more.

"Are you dumb?" she asked. "Or is Veldi really right? Did they cut out your tongue?" But as she asked the question, she knew the answer, for she had already spent a number of meals watching him eat in silence when he thought he was alone, and he certainly had a tongue.

She waited inside the shed for him to walk out, gather a few more logs, and then return. Aissla reached out to touch his shoulder, but he suddenly jerked away before she could make contact. He staggered and dropped the load of logs, then lost his balance completely, crashing against another stack of wood and knocking it utterly to the floor.

Aissla rushed to his aid, but the young man scrambled away before she could reach him. "I won't hurt you!" she called to him. "Stop a moment. You're bleeding. I can help you."

But the young man kept moving away from her, despite her persistence. They crossed the floor of the house and the woodsman realized she wasn't going to stop. He made his way toward the back door and slipped out, slamming the door behind him and keeping her inside.

"All right, fine, don't tell me your name, but at least let me try to patch up your wounds." Her voice was muffled through the door, but she was certain he could understand her.

The door remained shut fast.

She sighed with exasperation. "I'm only trying to help." At last, though, she surrendered. For now. The young man waited as Aissla walked through the house, crossed over the pile of logs, and then vacated.

He opened the door and entered, turning to lock it shut behind him in case she opted to sneak in the back. He then closed the front door, locking himself inside. The piles of disturbed wood lay scattered on the floor. Without even a groan of annoyance, he bent to his task of resetting the stacks, one finely cut log after another.

It took him the rest of the afternoon to restore order to the chaos, and when he was satisfied with his work, he opened the front door and made his way to the Matron's house.

Felluria greeted him with a nod as she had come to do as a sign of respect for his own silence. She eyed him carefully, trying to scrutinize him for some sign of his intentions here. But none of her previous inspections had revealed anything to her either.

"Food and bandages await in your quarters," she said. "Aissla won't trouble you again. Mind, she was only trying to be friendly. You shouldn't count that against her."

The young man turned and met her gaze for a moment, but he gave no indication of what he was thinking. A moment later he retired to his room, where he slowly ate the meal and then dressed his wounds. Had Aissla been spying on him then, she would have admitted that he seemed experienced at treating his cuts, as if he had done so before.

Light still filtered into the room, but it had been a busy day and he was exhausted. He decided to let his weariness guide him and so he began his routine. Though the Matron's house was kept immaculately clean, his room had a pile of sand in the corner. He had placed it there his first night, and he replaced it each night since until Felluria realized that he was bringing the sand in himself, and she told her helpers to leave the pile untouched.

He cupped the particles in his strong hands and spread them across the floor. Into the sand, he drew a large triangle, with the base facing him and the apex pointing away. Over and over again, he traced the shape with his hands, as if doing so would help him to make sense of it. For all its simplicity, the design confused him terribly. He ached when his hands moved over it sometimes. And other times he felt soothed by it. But every night now, he followed this routine until his eyes blurred from exhaustion and his body begged for him to sleep.

The triangle made no sense to him. But he knew it had meaning. Just, it had failed him. Now it was only a drawing, a pattern. He felt the grit of the sand beneath his fingers, waiting for that moment as his body grew more and more tired. That moment was fast approaching.

He made a dozen more passes over the sand, tracing the triangle religiously, his eyes heavy-lidded and his breathing becoming labored. His back ached, for he had been sitting this way for hours now. Then it happened, like it had happened every night since... then.

The sand firmed into bits of broken glass. His hands traveled through the shattered pieces, but instead of being cut by them, the glass bits popped and cracked and crashed into tiny pieces again, as if his fingers were mashing a vase to a fine powder. He passed his hands along the path again until the tinkling of broken glass filled his ears and then eventually faded away to silence.

And as the silence sated him, his body lost its battle against the weariness and he slumped upon the sand, drifting to sleep at last, lost in darkness.

Chapter 2

The Bard's Prediction

RANDLER AND DARIAK left their friends behind in Marritosh, heading to the western edge of Hathreneir in search of Pyron, who had claimed the healing jade. They had traveled for a few days through the treacherous desert, battling all manner of creature on the way. Dariak made use of his spells, while Randler focused more on his bow. Having two ranged fighters in a team made some fights harder than others, but when the need arose, Randler pulled out his mace or some daggers while Dariak defended him magically.

"It wasn't this bad before," twenty-two-year-old Dariak commented one afternoon.

"What wasn't?" asked the bard.

"The monsters. The mages in the towers kept the beasts at bay so we would only need minor protection. I wonder what happened over the past year for things to have degraded so drastically."

Just two years older than the mage, Randler looked at the concern on Dariak's face and it pained him. "I wish I knew, but I can only guess at it."

"Take out your lute and let's hear it, then."

The cinnamon-haired bard chuckled and shook his head. "We've been attacked almost hourly every day so far, and you want me to stop and sing? Well, if you insist." He reached back and withdrew his lute, tuning it with nimble fingers while Dariak set a few defensive spells around them in case they were attacked.

Days long ago, when this tale unfolds, we hear the fear of the weak.
They once were strong and their reach was long,
but now they flash in a streak.
Fear guides them now like ne'er before, and soon they will all lose heart.

Once they were strong. Now they all just fall away.
Their leader has passed. So they do not have a guide.
Each one is lost. And so they try to hide.
They don't belong. Now there's panic every day.

Mages united under Delminor, a man whom many esteemed.
He was wise and brave and kind
but some just saw him as meek.
Obeying his king, he worked for war, though the mage only sought peace.

Once they were strong. But they pushed the mage away.
Their leader has passed. Because they pushed him aside.
Each one is lost. They were swept up by the tide.
They don't belong. For they fear pain every day.

Delminor's heir ventured from the land, seeking his father's path.
He gathered jades and he hoped one day
to unite them to end the war.
Yet when he left, so did the path, and the other mages fell astride.

Once they were strong. But they now worked all alone.
Their leader has passed. For they do not accept his claim.
Each one is lost. And so their fates will be the same.
They don't belong. With only magic skills to hone.

With their pride so turned inside, they no longer save the land.
Now they pursue their own desires
which weakens them all the more.
Without a leader to guide them forth, soon they will all be gone.

Once they were strong. Now the beasts take o'er the land.
Their leader has passed. And they wish none at their side.
Each one is lost. Until each one of them has died.
They don't belong. For no one now guides their hand.

These are the trials that exist to us, as we seek to end all war.
How do we lead the rest of those
who would rather decay and fall?
Our journey must complete with success, so you can gain your honor.

Once they were strong. And they soon will be again.
Their leader has passed. You will rise up in his place.
Each one is lost. To be found soon by your grace.
They don't belong. You'll give purpose to these men.

And in the end, they will come together, bound as one, ending war.

Randler played a few final notes and then set his lute aside, looking at Dariak for his reaction. He was making a few assumptions in his tale, like the mages turning away from unity and therefore allowing the beasts to overtake the land, but it seemed reasonable to him.

Dariak seemed to agree. He pulled Randler into a strong embrace and kissed him. "You give me hope," he said. "Hope that I really can focus the mages toward other endeavors, so we can end the fighting once and for all."

Randler stared into Dariak's azure eyes. "I believe in you, my love. Once you have reunited the jades, you will find the way to utilize the power to bring everyone together. It was a chance lost to your father because his duty was to his king. I believe if he had been able to explore the jades properly and not use them in the War of the Colossus, then things would be very different today."

Dariak just smiled, not knowing what to say.

Randler grinned at the look on the mage's face. "The only regret I would have if Delminor had succeeded, is that I wouldn't have met you."

"Nonsense," Dariak said, running a hand through his jet-black hair. "We would have won over the kingdom and you would have come to craft a tale of our accomplishments. And like that time in the bakery where I met you, I would have been yours immediately."

Randler blushed and kissed him. "I sang that melody to you before."

Dariak remembered. "Yes. At the Rooster's Bane in Kaison. You sang of the Forgotten Tribe instead though. But I did remember the tune."

"This story isn't so different, actually. That's why I chose that music."

Dariak considered as they continued walking westward. "In the Forgotten Tribe, you tell of King Kallisor and Lady Hathreneir who fell in love, had dreams of building a new land together, and then tore each other apart because of their differences."

"Indeed."

"And when the king and queen were no longer united, their two nations turned against each other in war. Fight after fight, for all the years since."

Randler nodded and let Dariak continue.

"My father was a prominent mage and researcher for Hathreneir. Many spells came from his own crafting, and he inspired others to do the same. But his work ended in failure. He couldn't defend the king and he lost the jades in the process. He was lost to the mages and they started following their own ways."

"That's what I think has been happening, Dariak," Randler agreed.

"But the mages I knew growing up were kind to me. I was even admitted to the Mage Council when I was nineteen. It was a good couple of years. How did it all go awry in the one year I spent in Kallisor?"

"I think the seeds of decay were already there. You had adversaries, didn't you?" the bard asked. "But people kept their agendas hidden from you, perhaps in case you were as powerful as your father, or worse, more powerful. They feared you, I think. But once you were gone, they no longer needed to put on airs. Things can change rapidly when people are motivated to change them."

Dariak grunted. "I never should have left Hathreneir."

Randler placed his arm around the mage's shoulders. "I think that only would have delayed the process, and then it would have hurt you more when it did happen. Dariak, I heard a lot of things in Magehaven. These beliefs weren't new to most of them. They were just unspoken."

"Even Pyron, who had been a mentor of mine, now has turned against me. You must be right, Randler. Though, it'd be easier if it was some sort of spell gone awry: I'd find the counterspell and fix everyone."

Randler chuckled. "I thought there was no magic to alter a person's mind?"

"True. There isn't." Then he hesitated and made a concession. "Except for that skill of Kitalla's. She can influence people with the energies she draws upon in her dances. I wonder why?"

"You'd never heard of that before?"

"No. Have you?"

The bard thought for a time as they walked, but then he shrugged. "There are tales of people who charm others to do their bidding, but it's usually some type of charisma, respect, or fear that changes the followers. Who knows if there is real magic behind it, but I think you mages would have heard stronger whispers about it if it were true. Certainly my mother would have mentioned something," he added wryly.

"Ah, Sharice," Dariak bobbed his head slowly, remembering the vicious battle he'd had against her in Randler's basement. It was there he had fully channeled the lightning jade and turned into a bolt of energy, which itself nearly killed him. "I wonder if she will come around some day."

"To your line of thinking?" Randler asked. "She may. That is, if you're able to out-battle her in the future, too."

"Relieving the restrictions on mages in Kallisor would help as well, I'd wager."

"Yes, I think so. Though, she does enjoy her time in the Underground. It makes her feel part of something special. Still, though, freedom for your kind should be allowed."

"Thanks," Dariak smiled, placing another kiss on Randler's cheek.

Randler grabbed Dariak and stared into his eyes. "Dariak, you know I really mean that, don't you? I don't say it lightly."

The mage nodded gently. "I remember. Your original quest was to gather the jades and bury them away somewhere so no one could ever find them or use them."

The bard nodded. "At first, you convinced me that it was folly because others would eventually find them and I was just putting off something inevitable. But I came to realize who you are and what you stand for, Dariak. It's what I fell in love with. It's why I'm here now."

"Randler—"

"But I'm still worried at times," the bard cut in. "Like in that battle against my mother, and again in Magehaven. Those times where you 'are' the jade and become a manifestation of its energy."

"I've recovered each time."

"Yes, but I don't want that to become part of who you are. I want you to remain Dariak, not some tool of the jades, carrying out their whims."

"It isn't like that, Randler. The jades are protecting me at those times."

The bard shook his head. "It goes too far when you lose yourself, though. I want you to remember to be here. Not to give yourself over like that. I don't want to lose you."

"You won't," the mage promised.

"But those two times, I almost did lose you."

"There… was a third," Dariak confessed hesitantly. He hadn't told Randler about it because it had happened before the bard had joined them in Pindington. "I was escaping Kaison with Kitalla and Gabrion. The healers were gathered together, launching spells at me and attacking with maces. I had no defenses, but the water jade called out to me. I had just claimed it from the museum, so I didn't know much of its power. But I became a sort of manifestation of water, and the maces passed right through me.

"I never really thought about that spell much and it never occurred to me again after that. But like the lightning and metal jades, I can't summon that power on my own. It activates when my life is in dire need. And once the healers were finished attacking, I was so exhausted I collapsed. It didn't take as much time to recover from that experience as the others, but I didn't turn into a complete ball of water; I became the consistency of one."

Randler listened carefully and gently bit his lip when Dariak was finished. "We've known all along that the jades resonate with you, but for whatever reason they are able to affect your body completely. Dariak, I beg of you to be careful."

"I know. And I try. Believe me, those stints as lightning and metal were not fun once it was over. And during the process, sure I felt great surges of power, but I had such little control that I wouldn't want to do those things on purpose."

"That's mostly what I wanted to hear. I'm just worried; that's all."

"I know. And now that we're talking about it, there is something else that worries me."

Randler raised his brow. "Oh?"

"Pyron. What if the healing jade reacts to him as the other jades have reacted to me? What if he *becomes* healing energy? I have no idea how to stop him if he can heal any wound instantly. How can we defeat him if he *is* healing?"

"I have no idea, but we don't really understand how far along his resonance is with the jade, do we? Dariak, you were oblivious when we pulled you from the tower. You might be able to see something we couldn't. You'll find a way through, I'm sure of it."

Dariak allowed himself to chuckle, though his fears weighed on him and he didn't actually feel like laughing. "Well, you did predict that I would be leading the mages one day."

"That I did, Dariak. That I did."

CHAPTER 3

In Pursuit

KITALLA COMBED HER fingers through her long, dark hair wondering vaguely if the sun overhead would add highlights or leave her untouched. She pulled the long strands together and examined them, but they were as dark as always. She shrugged, not particularly caring about it. It just meant that some day when her hair showed signs of gray, she wouldn't be able to blame it on the sun.

She looked back over her shoulder toward Marritosh, though she had been traveling a while already and the town was gone from sight. Part of her wanted to remain there and work with the fighters, training and honing their skills. The endless parade of willing combatants was exciting, and knowing they wouldn't purposely kill her helped make it a little more of a challenge, for she had to restrain herself. She also reveled in her own stamina and the fact that she could better half a dozen young men before needing to rest herself.

Thoughts of pride in herself always tore her in two and she tried not to dwell on it for long. As a teen, she had failed to protect her family, but ten years later as a woman, she survived countless torments. She allowed her mind to focus on her horrific time in Grenthar's domain, where the psychotic rogue set up numerous traps and then released her to defeat them. Spikes, flames, and barbs of poison were but a few of the tortures she had avoided. And after each run, a team of healers worked to restore her strength so she could be put to trial again. She wondered where her bullheaded perseverance had come from.

It was penance, she realized suddenly. It hadn't made sense to her before where she found the strength and courage to push through the tortures time and again. She hadn't understood what inner motivation had nudged her to live despite the desire for it all to be over. The endless cuts and bruises, even the time her arm was shattered by a falling stone slab; Grenthar had put her through such a gauntlet that it would always be a part of her.

After recovering from those trials, she had thought that Grenthar had brought out her inner strength. But then she and her friends were trapped in the magical Trials at Magehaven, and the power of the healing jade had caused her to face her true pain, and though she didn't want to dwell on the horrific losses of her mother, lover, and unborn child, she knew that her failure to protect them gave her strength now. Now, she had the power to overcome all tribulations.

It was a blessing and curse, though, she mused as she looked across the sand and saw movement among the shimmer visions in the distance—apparently the creatures were awakening from their noontime slumber. Kitalla was blessed because her agility and stamina were incredible compared to most people around her. But she was cursed because she couldn't remain idle for long without a burning need to battle something.

Turning her attention back to the distant movement, Kitalla pitched forward slightly and entered a solid jog, determined to work out some of her energy on a good scuffle, whether the beasts wanted it or not.

The sand shifted before her, revealing several sandorpions. The large, scorpion-like creatures sensed her approach and turned to meet her, poisonous tails raised overhead in the hopes of a quick strike.

They didn't know Kitalla.

The one-time thief leaped into the air and came down in a roll, dodging three lancing tails and bowling into a fourth sandorpion, knocking it onto its side. The large beast squealed and its limbs flailed about as it tried to right itself. The five other sandorpions responded angrily, as pincers started clicking together in anticipation. Kitalla was already on her feet again, daggers in hand, pouncing onto the hard shell of one of the creatures. Another sandorpion struck at her, but Kitalla pounced into the air and let the tail strike into her ride's spine. A second keening wail filled the air.

Kitalla didn't remain idle, especially as other sandorpions in the vicinity heard the pained cries of their brethren and turned to join the fray. The rogue didn't care. She dove low under a sweeping tail and rolled to the side to avoid another's set of pincers. She brought her dagger up into one beast's jaw and cracked a fang to pieces. The bones fell and Kitalla avoided touching the blood, for some sandorpions carried a blood poison that was fatal to humans.

The wounded sandorpion thrashed around and Kitalla grinned when she saw the beast inadvertently topple two of the others. She didn't hesitate, though, leaping forward and bringing a dagger down between the monster's eyes, killing it instantly. Its body collapsed heavily to the sand.

Two of the other sandorpions hissed in rage, tapping their lower feet in warning. Kitalla sized them up and determined that these two were some sort of leaders of the rest. The other sandorpions responded to the tapping sound by mimicking it and swaying side to side. With ten more of the creatures nearby, now swaying in synchronization with each other, Kitalla felt unnerved.

Her answer was not to leap and attack but instead to join their dance. She reached out her hands and pulled them close, trying to feel a sense of calm that belied her predicament. The sandorpions moved faster and faster, and Kitalla knew instinctively that in a few moments, they would pounce all at once and she wouldn't likely escape.

So instead, she dropped to the sand and reached her arms out in front of her, snapping her fingers in the same fashion the creatures were clacking their pincers. She raised her left leg up, supported by her right leg, and bent the knee, then tried to sway it left and right in a slight arc, mimicking the sandorpions' tails. She used her breath to try to keep her thoughts calm and to reach for the energies in the air around her. Kitalla was no mage, but her unique dance skill called to the energies as if she were. She pulled them into focus, keeping the rhythm going and trying to forget that most creatures did not fall prey to her illusions.

She targeted one of the two leaders and ignored the minions. Outward she sent her thoughts, creating an image of herself off to the side, while mentally concealing herself under the likeness of a small sandorpion. She had only moments to hold the image before the beating feet double-stomped the sand and the rush took place.

Kitalla had to hold the image and the motions carefully, for once she released them, so went the energies she channeled. It was the greatest weakness of her skill because she was completely vulnerable while maintaining any sort of dance posture. She had joined Dariak's quest over a year before, hoping he could train her to extend her abilities and to give herself offensive power with the dances. She had only succeeded in briefly spewing small bits of fire and once turning herself into the semblance of a metallic porcupus, but then they hadn't had much time to explore her unusual gifts on the journey.

With a thunderous reverberation, the sandorpions sprinted ahead and Kitalla heard a crash, reminiscent of stone grinding against stone. She rolled to the side to escape a sandorpion whose body had been upended by its fellows. Apparently, she had chosen her target well and the leader had more intellect than the minions, for it was duped into attacking its own mate.

Daggers flew from her hands, striking two sandorpions in the eyes, and as she pulled more knives from her boots, she rolled and then pounced onto the leader itself. The other sandorpions turned and slashed at them both and the leader screamed, trying to regain control of the other creatures. However, the minions had followed its command to attack and kill the first leader and now a sort of mutiny arose. Kitalla felt the sandorpion trembling in fear beneath her and she realized it was time to flee.

She waited for the first creature to strike, then she leaped backwards off the sandorpion and sprinted away, breathing heavily. She risked a glance over her shoulder and saw the smaller creatures ganging up on the larger one, tearing it viciously apart. There was no telling what the rest of the creatures would do once they had finished their task, and Kitalla decided that she didn't need to kill all of them right then. It was good, perhaps, that the lesser sandorpions were rather stupid, else they might have saved their revenge for after taking care of the human.

When she was a safe distance away, Kitalla crouched and dug a shallow hole, after which she crawled in and covered herself, keeping a scrap of cloth over her head so she would have some air. The people of Marritosh had dealt with the sand creatures before and they had instructed the visiting Kallisorians how to disguise themselves from the predators temporarily. Her scent could still give her away but being under the ground would keep them from seeing her, and many of the sun-dwelling creatures relied on keen sight for verification.

She rested for nearly an hour before deciding it was time to continue onward. Sitting up, Kitalla looked around for signs of movement, but saw none, save the natural shimmer visions of the hot afternoon. As trained, she watched those visions carefully to ensure they wavered symmetrically without breaking. A disrupted pattern would indicate more beasts.

Kitalla reached into her pockets and withdrew the fire and metal jades. She set them on the sand in front of her and gently placed one hand on each. She couldn't feel much vibration from them, so she pivoted around slowly until the metal jade shook with a minor tremor. She turned a little more until the fire jade also twitched, ever so slightly. She pushed the jades gently into the sand and then released them, after which she reached her hands forward and carved two lines forward in the sand. After reclaiming the jades, she closed her eyes and held them out before her, letting the energies course through her the best she could. Pivoting slowly once more, she confirmed the first set of readings to ensure they weren't aberrant. Because the tremors aligned with the first set of marks she had made in the sand, she knew the right way to go. After a few sips on her waterskin, she was off to continue her search.

It was a lonely journey, and she did her best to keep her thoughts focused on her goal. She needed to find Gabrion and learn what had transpired with the warrior to make him run off from the others. Kitalla wondered if he had learned of Mira's whereabouts and went off in a mad rage to find her. She chuckled at the thought of him running rampant, arms flailing over his head, calling out Mira's name.

But then she stopped chuckling, for she felt a pang in her chest. It wasn't a physical pain, but she checked herself anyway for a wound. No, it was a pain inside of her; an emotion she thought she had banished from her soul ages ago. She cursed the healing jade and the mages of the tower who had used its power to draw out her innermost memories.

Yet those weren't the aches she felt now, she realized. It wasn't the past plaguing her, but the present. It was Gabrion. No, not specifically him, she amended. His quest for Mira. The pain lanced through her again and she nodded. She hated to admit it to herself, but she was jealous.

During their time together, Kitalla had pandered Gabrion every time he spoke of his love for Mira. She scoffed at him, saying it was absurd to cling to the girl so fiercely. He needed to sharpen his skills, not pine after some childhood sweetheart. And as they had quested together, Gabrion's nobility was always present. He fought when his life was in danger but he did not kill needlessly. He strove to always find his beloved and to save her, regardless of the personal cost.

Kitalla hated Mira for it. Not because the girl had been captured or that she needed to be saved. Not because she and Gabrion had grown up together. Not even because Mira had Gabrion's heart.

Kitalla hated her because no one had ever given everything for her. Sure Joral had risked his future as a nobleman by running off with her when they were so young. But he hadn't been able to protect her the way Gabrion sought to rescue Mira. Joral had run away with her, but he had died, unable to defend her or her mother. Gabrion hadn't died. No, after all this time his quest still went on strong.

No one had seen Gabrion since he had run into Castle Hathreneir, but Kitalla knew he was alive because a spirit as pure as his would never die until his quest was over. And the jades guided her toward the north, toward him, the protector.

Kitalla screamed suddenly and dropped. She felt broken and unable to control her thoughts. She was supposed to be the most disciplined among the group, not prone to these emotional pains. It frustrated her greatly to not only feel jealously of Mira, but to be contemplating its source. She was never one to dwell on such things, and she wasn't happy to do so now. Pounding her hands into the sand did nothing to sate her angst, so she stood back up and ran.

Her body ached with the effort after a time, but she pushed herself harder and harder, pumping her arms to keep in counter-balance with her feet. She welcomed the fiery pain running up her legs and back and used it to push herself onward even further. She was stronger than the silly emotions that were coursing through her. No one would see her weakened from mere thoughts.

It didn't matter that no one was nearby. It was pride kicking in again, and she reached for it, remembering Grenthar's domain and claiming the metal jade at long last, using its power instinctively to slay her captor. Her dagger had grown and lashed out like a whip, cutting down her terrible foe and freeing her at last from her torment.

Yes, freedom. She felt it now. Around her, the world seemed suddenly open and vast. The desert spread out before her and begged her to travel its surface. The sun was falling from the sky and night would be upon her soon. She pushed harder, ignoring the growing agony in her body. Somewhere in her mind she knew she needed to stop running and build herself a quick shelter before she was too exhausted to protect herself. But her body had never failed her when she needed it. She would run to the end of the kingdom if she had to, but her thoughts would plague her no longer.

But run as she might, she could not escape them. Jealousy burned in her breast, mocking her. She didn't know how to turn it into a power for her own use. It bore her down, weakening her and bringing back that empty ache of loneliness. Her throat clenched from the tension. Running was of no use anymore and her legs gave way, dropping her harshly to the sand.

Kitalla smacked down and crumpled in a heap and—though she fought against it as much as she could—she wept deeply, her body wracked with pain and not from her fall. Her sobs echoed solemnly as the sun dipped out of the sky, deserting her like everyone she had ever loved.

CHAPTER 4

Ervinor's Army

"COME ON, NOW. Time to wake up, Ervie," said Lica, a middle-aged woman from Kallisor, whose magic skills had tagged her an outsider as a child. She had joined the Mage Underground at the age of fifteen, where she teamed up with Quereth and later Frast, and she had been working with them ever since. "It's already midday and the troops need their general."

"Don't call me that," Ervinor complained.

"As long as you make me play the role of mother, then I'll call you whatever pet names I want." She pulled open the curtain to let the sunlight in and hovered by the door to ensure he was getting up.

"Thanks, ma!" he called out playfully as she closed the door behind her.

It was never easy for Ervinor to rise out of bed. His body was so different since he had lost his right arm when he had pushed Quereth out of the way of a falling ax in Castle Hathreneir. Everything was harder to do, and it still felt as if the arm was there, ready to help him move the sheet aside and allow him to push himself up. But no, it was gone, and every time he awoke he had to remind himself that this was his new norm.

He sat up and turned his body, setting his feet on the floor, after which he spent some time stretching and getting ready for the day. Lica had teased him, both with a nickname and a title. There were about a hundred men and women who were unofficially under his command, gathered together for the united goals of Dariak, Randler, Gabrion, and Kitalla. During his time in Marritosh with the warriors and mages, Ervinor's own passionate leadership had drawn the eyes of the people in the town. Though it was a Hathren town, the people banded together with the Kallisorians, with the hope of bringing about an end to the constant war.

In a sense, he was indeed their general, even though, at twenty-three, he was young for the job and didn't exactly look the part, especially now that he was missing an arm. One of the town elders had told him that he possessed an old soul and a wise spirit and that's why he was born to lead these others, especially while the companions were away. Ervinor didn't see it as a burden, just something that needed to be done. He had served for a couple of years under Ordren in Pindington, so he had a sense of how to lead them. Although he sometimes thought his experiences with his siblings had been better preparation.

He reached over to scratch his right arm, then realized belatedly that he didn't have an arm there anymore. The healers had stopped the major pains, but they had only prescribed time to heal the itching sensations. Already a month had passed. He wished they had been able to give him another arm instead of empty promises.

He grunted at himself for his thoughts. Kitalla would draw her daggers and battle him right then and there at the start of a good wallowing. That is, if she were around. But no, his friends were off on their own quests, each for good reason, but he was stuck here instead because of his missing arm.

As he considered it, though, he wondered what he would have done if he hadn't been injured. He could have either gone off with Kitalla to find Gabrion or with Dariak and Randler to seek the healing jade. But that would have left the army without a leader, unless they divided it into two, or—

He stopped himself, knowing it was pointless to debate it. Most likely, he admitted, he would still be here in Marritosh, fortifying the town's defenses, training the army, and ensuring that when the others returned, they would be ready to march to their true goal.

With that, he stood up at last, teetering a little to the side with his new center of gravity. It would take some getting used to, he reminded himself. He knew he had dallied long enough; if he didn't dress and fetch food soon, Lica would come back and really let him have it.

Marritosh was unique from other places he had been to because it had four elders who oversaw the events in the area, instead of only one. They worked together in a close-knit team and rarely disagreed when it came to major decisions. Ervinor had grown closest to Herchig, an eccentric old warrior who belabored everyone with long-winded tales, whose meanings always related but were sometimes hard to find. The respect between them was mutual and after Ervinor's dread injury, the old man and his wife, Nessaria, had taken it upon themselves to craft something special for the young soldier. They had waited until the day after the companions' departures to present it to him.

Ervinor went to the special armor now. It was a set of leather leggings and tunic, hand-crafted for his unique situation. He started by pulling on the leggings and tugging a special drawstring with his arm and looping it through a ring until they were snugly secured. He didn't have to fumble with tying the drawstring or buckling the belt, for the simple mechanism worked perfectly.

The tunic was more complex in design but easy enough to put on. He pulled the darkened leather over his head and slipped his arm through the elbow-length sleeve. But there was a lot more to the design than having one sleeve removed and closed off. Wound around the leather was a greenish corded strap that served several purposes. Along the right side, the straps linked through small ringlets, each of which could carry a dagger. The handles would face forward, which would have been a terrible hindrance for his right arm.

The straps continued onto the back and wound upward diagonally from his right hip to his left shoulder. Inside the straps, Herchig had fastened in a scabbard, which would allow Ervinor to draw his sword over his shoulder for a quick strike.

He still struggled with sheathing the blade safely, but Herchig had assured him he would figure it out soon enough.

The emerald-hued strap continued downward across his chest, meeting again in the metal loop at his right hip. The chest strap was flatter than the rest, and had small holes cut inside, where Ervinor could store poison-tipped blowdarts. Each dart slipped in at a downward angle, the tip hidden inside a folded layer of the strap. Herchig had ensured him that he wouldn't accidentally stab himself with the darts, for the leather was secured against punctures.

The green strap then made one last weave across his belly to a metal loop on his left hip, where he could tie in the leggings if he needed to wade in water or some such thing. But the tunic had one more function that Herchig and Nessaria had included just for him.

"Now that there is a unique piece of armor," Herchig had announced proudly. "Shielded against magic, and all these places for weapons, which you can easily get to with your left hand. Took a bit of forethought to get it all worked out, but when there's an important thing that needs doing, you buckle on down and figure it out. Why, when Nessaria and I got married, you should have seen her! The detail gone into setting up her hair; even the wind knew not to blow it out of whack. And all the work that went in to putting that wedding dress together. An army's worth of work. Sewn by her own hands, no less. Family tradition, she said, and not that it was a tradition in her family for the bride to make her own dress, but that she was starting one.

"But that there tunic will keep you well protected, I'll tell you. Daggers, swords, poison darts, and that's not all. Now I know you're not one for the darts, but you've got to be able to defend yourself, and that's just what Nessaria and I were trying to do. Now maybe some poor fool will come at you, thinking you're some disfigured beggar, but not so in my armor. No way. See, even if you lose your sword and your daggers are stolen and you run out of darts, there's one more trick to that tunic. That green cord there, wrapped all around yourself. Well, if you're in a real bind, it's detachable and you can use it as a rope or a whip if you need it. But I daresay don't be trying it unless you're desperate because it'll be a trick to get it back in place.

"Got to give Nessaria credit for that little addition, I have to admit. It was an idea she had when she was just a lass, really. That wedding dress I was telling you about? Well, she worked in a strap like that one there and—well, I'm not very well going to tell you how we made use of it." He had ended with a wink.

Once Ervinor was fully suited up, loaded with weapons, he strode out into the fresh noontime air. Walking through town brought mixed emotions. Most of the faces were those of fighters he had traveled with since he had left Pindington with Ordren's group. Some, though, wore pitied frowns meant to express their sorrow for the loss of his arm. As if he needed constant reminders.

He made his way through the streets toward the edge of town where scents from the best bakery around called to him. As he approached, he noticed that it was a popular spot today and there was quite a crowd milling about, enjoying various breads and cakes. He was glad for the crowd because it meant Dellina, the baker's daughter, would be too busy to spend much time with him. She had doted on him during his first visit to town, but after his injury, her attentions had turned more toward smothering.

"Ervinor!" her voice called above the din of customers. "Come sit!" she offered, turning to a soldier and abruptly asking him to move. "We've got a great selection of sweet rolls and jelly cakes today. There are some coming out of the oven in a moment; we've been so busy today! I'll bring you one; do you want juice with it or water?"

"Thanks, Dellina," he said, not even hearing her question. Before he sat down, he stepped over to the soldier who had been ousted from his seat. "Carrus, you don't need to get up for me. Sit back down."

The soldier was a decent-looking fellow, about twelve years older than Ervinor. He saluted with a callused hand and replied, "Thank you, sir, but I'm finished; the seat is yours."

"You're sure? I can certainly wait."

"Yes, sir, I'm sure." He waited until Ervinor took the seat. "Sir, may I say something?"

"Of course."

"Sir, I served under King Kallisor for over half my life. I spent a number of years in the stables. I trained and worked to earn a place in the king's army. I spent about two years in his personal guard before asking for reassignment to a patrol group. In all that time, sir, he never once addressed me by name as if I was a real person."

"Of course you're a person!" Ervinor sputtered in disbelief.

"Yes, sir. Thank you. There were many reasons I left my home to join this venture and several reasons I've stayed despite the odds. You've gotten to know us all. We're men and women to you, not mere pieces to be moved around. I hate to be one of the gawkers, sir, because I know you've suffered a great loss in your arm. But that act alone shows me and all of us that you're the man we're here to follow."

Ervinor didn't know what to say. He eyed the man suspiciously for a moment and then asked, "Did Herchig put you up to this?"

"I'm sorry?"

Ervinor realized his mistake. "No, Carrus, I'm sorry. Thank you for your kindness. It means a lot to me. How is Jarrul—"

"Here you are," Dellina swept in with a tray for Ervinor. She gave an impatient look at Carrus as she set it down and then hovered.

"He is fine, sir. If you'll excuse me." And with that, Carrus left.

"He didn't give you a hard time about the seat, did he? After all, you're like their leader, aren't you? I shouldn't even have to ask anyone to get up so you can get some food, now should I?"

"It wasn't—"

"Well it better not be or else I'll start charging him double if he wants to sit while he eats. Here, eat up, you haven't even tried anything yet."

Ervinor found her incessant rambling to be highly irritating. She was only sixteen and hadn't yet figured out when to keep her mouth shut, but when he took a bite of the first pastry, he remembered well why he put up with her at all. The raspberry tart was warm and buttery and made of the freshest fruit he had ever tasted.

There was a light cinnamon flavor wrapped into the pastry that made it impossible to put down for even a moment.

Meanwhile, Dellina was prattling on. "Today's the last day for the raspberries, I'd wager, with everyone coming in for them. We always have to grow them out of season because it's so hot all the time so winter's the best time to grow them here, but the rest of the time we import—"

It happened all so fast, Ervinor didn't register it at first. A loud crash sounded and an enormous fireball exploded not far away, scattering debris everywhere. Part of a wooden crate flew through the air and impaled Dellina, catching her through the back, and putting an end to her babbling forever. Blood drizzled from her mouth as her body collapsed.

After a moment, Ervinor shouted, "To arms!" He jumped up from his seat and ran toward the impact site of the fireball. Looking overhead, he could see more spells on the way. "Take cover! Quickly!" he yelled, diving toward the nearest house and crouching in the doorway.

Four concussive blasts shook the ground and debris rained through the streets. Ervinor ran and surveyed the damage. Two homes had been crushed under the spell-fire, but he couldn't tell if there were any other casualties. Lightning flared against the blue sky and confirmed that they were under attack.

Soldiers gathered around him, awaiting orders. "Assemble teams Sparrow, Eagle, and Raven," he called. "We're going to need the mages today. Hurry!"

Ervinor ran ahead to find the source of the offensive magic. The initial explosion could have been an errant mage's spell gone awry, but the ensuing blasts signaled much more. He struggled to maintain his balance as he ran, often crashing into unsuspecting villagers who were fleeing in the opposite direction.

"What do you see ahead?" he tried asking, but no one wanted to pause for questions.

He wasn't alone on his run. Carrus and a few other soldiers joined him on his mad dash to the trouble. "Sir, let me take point," the warrior offered, keeping his sword sheathed until they were closer to the mages. Without waiting for a reply, he jogged ahead and cleared a path through the townspeople.

It wasn't long before they reached the source of the trouble, for the bakery itself was close to the western edge of Marritosh. There, about fifty mages stormed in, arms swinging wildly with angry fire in their eyes.

"Spare no one!" cried one of the central mages. In teams of five, the mages gathered closer together. Three of those groups worked in tandem to create a magical barrier for defense, while the other groups channeled their strengths into destructive spells. Only one group remained inert, and Ervinor assumed they were healers, ready to tend to any wounded.

"Carrus, hold!" Ervinor shouted, and the warrior stopped suddenly, having drawn his sword, ready to charge in.

"Orders, sir?"

"There is little we can do, just the few of us. The mages will focus their attacks and obliterate us. Get the rest of the villagers out of here until reinforcements arrive."

There weren't many people left in the area, but a few of them either tried to protect their homes or cowered within them, terrified by the invasion. Three houses were demolished by the fireballs and it was only a matter of time before others followed suit. Eying the mages in the center of the invading force, Ervinor saw that some were directing their blasts blindly upward, not caring where the spells struck within the town. Angered, Ervinor pulled a dagger from his right side and launched it into the foes.

As expected, the mage barrier deflected the simple attack and the mages turned to focus on him as a new target. He had no real defenses against the mages, but if he could keep them from wildly launching spells at the innocent villagers, then it would be worth his efforts.

A bolt of searing blue lightning lashed out in his direction, barely missing him as he threw himself toward the ground. He rolled a few times and sprang to his feet, tumbling slightly to the side as he tried to right himself. He grabbed another dagger and held it at the ready, while trying to focus on one of the nearby mages who might send a spell at him next. He thought perhaps the defensive shield would drop briefly to allow their spells through. He did his best to time a shot with an angry younger mage whose dark eyes focused intently upon him. Ervinor had seen the mages in his own army cast fire spells enough times to know the motion that would release the blast. He waited for the hands to recoil to the mage's chest before lashing outward at the intended target. Ervinor wound up and released his dagger.

His timing was accurate and the dagger crossed paths with the magical barrier, but his hopes were dashed, for only the energy-powered spell made it through, while his dagger hit the invisible wall and fell. He didn't wait for too long before launching himself sideways to avoid the flames. Luckily, it was a fire dart spell and did not explode when it impacted the ground.

Two more homes were destroyed, one of them by a mage who channeled the power of the earth and caused its support beams to crack and tumble. The other was battered with strong blasts of air until the walls were so weakened that the structure collapsed. Ervinor off-handedly remembered the damage that had been done to Marritosh by sandstorms, which his troops had spent some time trying to repair over the past two months. It seemed that after this ordeal, they would be put to the repair task again.

Ervinor brought his thoughts back to the fight, wondering how he would be able to break through a defensive shield that was powered by fifteen mages working in unison. It was a tall order for a fighter, and he feared the answer.

"Sir, everyone's away," Carrus called out, approaching swiftly. "Reinforcements are coming. We need to—"

Ervinor pounced and tackled the man, barely saving him from a spray of thorns released by two of the mages. Carrus reacted quickly and caught Ervinor, rolling him around so he would be able to stand up easily.

"There is nothing we can do without our mages," Ervinor decided. "But we won't die here. Keep alert!"

"Sir!" the soldier acknowledged.

Ervinor looked around for anything that would help, but only bits of stone and wood remained after the mages' spells flared up. "Grab that debris and hurl it back at them!"

Ervinor, Carrus, and the other soldiers who had followed him there went swiftly to work. They grabbed anything that was manageable and heaved it toward the mages, hitting the barrier, but causing no harm. "Keep at it. We need them distracted."

The tactic was working, for the defensive mages went into a deeper chant, their words echoing more loudly as they fought against the thrown materials. Four mages from the center stopped lobbing spells into the town and ran to the front line, adding their voices and steps to the defensive cadence.

Fire and lightning were the primary attacks, but a few mages threw in water spells as well, dousing the ground and zapping the puddles with electric shocks. Two defenders were caught in one such attack and collapsed. Soon, though, reinforcements arrived.

Lica and Frast each raced in with a contingent of at least twenty men and women, some of them mages. Immediately, the magic-users set up their own defenses and hurled spells back at the invading forces.

The team of mages had infiltrated into the town and were making steady, but slow, progress as Ervinor and the soldiers threw debris at them. Now, with the support of his own mages, Ervinor was determined to end this battle swiftly.

"Eagle squad, east side. Sparrows, south. Ravens, with me!" Lica split off to the right, while Frast's Sparrows dug in where they stood and entered a battle stance. The Raven squad hurried after Ervinor and threw protection spells around him, augmenting the defenses of his own armor.

"We need to break that shield," he said to one of the mages among the Ravens. "What's the best way to go about it?"

Gresh assessed the situation. "It won't be easy with that many mages, sir. That team there is working in unison. But the more we hit that barrier, the harder they have to work to maintain it."

Ervinor nodded; he was on the right track with the debris. He ordered the soldiers to continue lobbing everything they could find at the invisible wall. "Carrus! I'm leaving you in charge here. Keep up the assault and if the barrier breaks, only then should the fighters charge in."

"Yes, sir!"

Ervinor sprinted off to Frast's group. The mage was deep into a water spell, drawing vapor from the air and dropping it at the base of the magic shield. He looked up once he could. "We have to disrupt them," he heaved, then he called over his shoulder to the other mages in Sparrow. "Ice spells, now!"

Six sets of ice darts flew overhead and pelted the wet surface, freezing it solid. The mages behind the barrier paid it little heed as they continued their methodical progress. They were moving so slowly and uniformly that it was unlikely that any of them would slip on the icy patch, but that wasn't Frast's intention.

"Earth, now!" He brought his own hands up and around, sweeping out to the sides, making fists, and then drawing his hands upward in front of his chest, almost like grabbing a massive tablecloth to wipe his chin. Ervinor glanced around; four other mages in the group were doing the same thing. *"Ferishonok crallikos, norresh shai fathrinos, nok!"*

Ervinor turned to watch the result, as the frozen earth erupted into millions of pieces, creating a shaky surface. The defensive mages lost their balance and, for a moment, the shield fell.

"Quickly!" Frast called.

"Charge!" Ervinor shouted, drawing his sword at last, running pell-mell toward the stumbling mages. Ten soldiers sprinted with him, as the Sparrow mages immediately began casting offensive spells.

The warriors broke through the defensive line, even as the mages swept their arms around to reinstate the field. Ervinor's sword crashed haphazardly into one mage, and he used the momentum from the strike to pivot around and take down another. At close quarters, the mages were less confident, but some of them cared less about their comrades and simply launched their spells at the attackers, even if it hit their own allies.

Ervinor could see that members of all three groups had penetrated the barrier before it was restored. "Focus on the outer rim first," he commanded, for taking down the wall permanently would allow the rest of the Marritosh defenders to assist.

Lica and Frast remained on the outside of the barrier but Carrus was inside, long sword swinging powerfully and with control. He had clearly earned his right to serve on the king's personal guard, and Ervinor was grateful to have him along now.

The chaos around him was difficult for Ervinor, for his mind was still straining to keep him balanced as he lurched from one attack to the next. He turned one too many times, however, and his equilibrium left him as he collapsed, severely dizzy. It took a moment for him to regain himself, but in that time, two mages targeted him.

Carrus saw his plight and screamed a battle cry as he raced over to take one mage down, the fire spell shooting wide. Ervinor struggled to get out of the way of the second spell, and he knew he wouldn't have time. He grabbed at his chest and flicked his arm out toward the mage, sending a poison dart flying through the air. It didn't catch any vital organs, but the sting distracted the mage enough to disrupt the spell. Ervinor pushed himself to his feet, reclaimed his sword, and then turned to face the next foe.

The mages started to panic. Spells flared randomly and once the protective barrier fell a second time, they abandoned it altogether. The rest of the Marritosh fighters stormed in and the invaders were quelled soon after.

Ervinor was terribly weary from the battle. He was young and resilient but his body needed more time to recover before engaging in such scuffles. Still, he pushed himself to remain alert, making note of the wounded and checking that the prisoners were properly secured.

Lica and Frast double-checked the mage binds, ensuring the invaders wouldn't be able to use any spells in the meantime. Then they reported to Ervinor.

"Not the attack we were expecting," Lica said dourly. "But it looks like I woke you up in time."

"Good thing, I guess. This isn't a detachment from the king then?"

"No," Frast answered. "That mage there," he said, gesturing to a seething wizard with wild eyes, "is Farrenok, who openly opposed Dariak's claim for the jades over at Magehaven."

Lica chimed in, "We think they came here hoping to eradicate us for the damage we've done to their facility."

Frast nodded. "It would make sense. We stole their beast jade, killed a number of their friends, and broke Dariak out of his imprisonment. It would have been easy for them to know where we were camping out; we never did try to hide it."

Ervinor hadn't been allowed into Magehaven, but he was aware of the events. "It's a shame they would open up and try to decimate this place because of us."

Lica sighed. "Indeed. It seems that little upstart was the instigator though." She motioned back to Farrenok. "They were deferring to his leadership during the fight."

"Then he's the one we need to talk to," Ervinor decided. "Send word to Herchig; I'd like him to suggest a place to hold this Farrenok. As for the others, corral them in one of these fallen houses. The villagers won't like it, but these mages should have to see their destruction for a while. Have Eagle team stay with them."

"Got it," Lica acknowledged and moved off to follow the orders.

"Frast, you're in charge of Farrenok." He was going to say more but a wave of nausea swept over him and he grabbed Frast's shoulder for support.

The mage responded with a quick healing spell. "Ervinor, you've got a few wounds, but it's your other injury draining you right now. We'll manage here; you go get yourself ready for Farrenok."

"Some general I am."

Frast shook his head. "You got us all here in short order and you hit upon the best strategy to subdue them. No more arguing; get moving."

Carrus saw Frast's signal and he jogged over to take Ervinor away. "We did it, sir," the soldier said proudly. "Hardly any casualties on our side, mostly a few people stunned or scraped."

Ervinor groaned. "Not many, but some. And the villagers here were hit badly too."

They made their way through the streets, passing several damaged sites. Each time, Ervinor and Carrus stopped to examine the situation, offering some help where they could, but it was Carrus' goal to get Ervinor back home.

"There is little we can do now, sir."

Ervinor didn't care. These people needed help and he was just weary. He could push a little more. The villagers banded together and pulled debris away, freeing some people who were trapped, and others who had died. They passed the bakery where Dellina had been among the first victims of the attack.

The baker sat hunched in a chair, his establishment otherwise empty. Sobs wracked his body and Ervinor walked over to him and sat with the man.

"I told her," Yerra cried, "that life as a baker was safe. That the worst she would ever face was a hot tray or an angry patron." He blew his nose into a cloth and continued. "Never did I expect such a terrible thing. How could this have happened? Will it happen again? She was our oldest daughter. Our little princess. Oh, Dellina…"

There was nothing Ervinor could say but he remained there with Carrus a while until the baker asked them to go. They meandered through the streets, heading slowly back to Ervinor's house. He was determined to assess the damage before returning, but his body had a different idea. After several massive dizzy spells, he eventually swooned. Carrus gently hoisted him in his arms and brought him home to rest.

CHAPTER 5

The Silent Woodsman

DURING HIS FIRST couple of weeks, the task of felling trees, chopping wood, and stacking the logs in the woodshed had kept the woodsman physically busy and tired. He never spoke and the continued silence unnerved the villagers, not that he seemed to notice.

But the shed was now full and there was little to keep him occupied. He spent a good portion of the day trying to make minor repairs around the village when the people allowed him near their homes, but at the end of the day, he wasn't tired at all.

Each night before bed he drew his triangle in his pile of sand, trying to understand where he had gone wrong. But his body yearned to be active, to wear itself out so he could sleep. Once it was clear that there were no more major tasks for him to do, his body started acting on its own.

Late each night he staggered out of the house in a dreamy daze. A few villagers who saw him didn't notice a difference at first, for he never acknowledged their calls to him anyway. But he walked behind the Matron's house and into the forest, then a short distance north to where the base of the mountain began.

All that the town heard at first were wild cries of massive pain. People awoke and looked out their windows for the source, fearing that the fighting had gotten so bad that the war had crept to this haven for the first time in a century. The cries echoed again and again, and those who listened beyond the screams heard a strange cracking noise.

Night after night this continued, and a few of the braver townspeople followed the silent woodsman to his place of torment, where they saw something horrifying. The young man pounded his fists into the side of the mountain, crying out someone's name in a deep moaning keen. With each punch into the rock face, pieces broke away.

A crowd gathered outside the Matron's house one morning when the woodsman's bizarre actions continued unabated. "We must do something!" said a young mother. "My child is terrified!"

Felluria scoffed. "Your babe could use some toughening up, I say. No, I won't have it. He hasn't hurt anyone. He stays for now. Be off with you."

"Matron!"

Rage flared in her eyes and her wrinkled mouth curled into a furious sneer. She stamped her foot on the ground and spat each word of her reply, emphasizing each syllable angrily. "I will *not* be questioned."

The townspeople withered under her furious glare, fearing retribution if they lingered at her door any longer. She grabbed a nearby cane and cracked it against her house until the walking stick shattered as she worked out her rage. She then threw the pieces at the retreating crowd and clenched her fists tightly.

"Breathe, Felluria," she sneered. "They're only children, after all."

She waited on her stoop for nearly a half hour until she stopped seething at the disrespect she felt she had received. The villagers kept out of her line of sight, which was challenging for those who lived closest to her. Seeing them scamper away helped improve her mood, though, and at last she turned to her house and went inside.

She was grateful no one was tending her at the moment, for she needed to be left alone a while, not unlike their silent visitor. He was in his room, determinedly drawing a triangle in the pile of sand he had brought with him. Sure, she was curious about this young man, but she wasn't about to tell him to vacate because he was sleepwalking, even if he was somehow strong enough to chip away at a rock wall barehanded.

Besides, he had taken care of her wood problem in no time at all and without a single hint of complaint. She certainly wasn't about to cast him away. As long as he didn't hurt any of her children.

Some time later Aissla and Veldi arrived to cook for them. The two girls were solemn after the earlier events and they practically tiptoed around the house getting things ready. Felluria sat in a chair, eying them hawkishly for anything to berate them over. Despite their flighty affectations, they were attentive and they prepared a simple steak dinner, diced into small cubes, with a hearty chopped salad for accompaniment. A deep red wine was also served and once the girls plated the food, they left.

Felluria preferred it that way when she was in a snit. It gave her the option of eating right away or waiting, but tonight she had something else in mind. She brought the plates down to the woodsman's room and she sat behind him on his bed after handing his plate to him.

"Not sure what's going on in that blond head of yours, but some of it's starting to leak out," she said sourly, stabbing a steak cube with her fork and nudging it between her remaining teeth. "I know you're not going to tell me anything but you've got no right not to listen to me. Understood?"

He lowered his head and took a deep breath, then he tucked into his food.

"Good," she murmured after choking on a piece of lettuce and scowling at the rest of the salad. "I've been around a long time. You might have guessed." Her tone was informational, not emotional in any way. "I look out for these people here. They're my children. Well, good as, anyway." She paused to wrestle around another piece of steak.

"You've frightened them," she said. "And it leaves me with a decision to make on their behalf. I don't like it any more than you, but you're a real mystery here and you've amused me. But now I wonder what's wrong with you."

He looked up from his plate and turned his head to look at her, then he continued eating.

"Mm," she grumbled. "I don't think you're dumb or anything, mind you. I can see the pain in your eyes. And now that you're not chopping wood for me, you're acting out, did you know that?"

He set his fork down and tilted his head. After a moment, he gently shook it side to side.

Felluria almost dropped her plate, for it was the most direct answer he had ever given her in six weeks. "Well, you're dreaming something awful and, like a little kid, you're dreamwalking out into the night. Right through the forest to the mountain, same place each time. And you're pounding on the stone like an animal. None of this sounds familiar?"

He shook his head again, just barely.

"Figures," she huffed. "You think I'm making it up, don't you?"

He didn't respond and she took that as affirmation.

"Well while you're doing it, you're wailing like some sick ursalor." She chewed another piece of steak, making loud squelching sounds on purpose, her eyes focused on the back of his head. "You keep calling out a name, over and over, with each hit to the mountain. 'Mira!' 'Mira!'"

The young man jumped to his feet and he backed away from her, bumping into the wall, his eyes flicking about wildly. His breathing came in heavy gasps and sweat beaded on his brow.

"Eh, you see? I'm not making it up, am I?" she said, pleased with herself. She stabbed into a piece of steak and then flung it at him. He didn't even twitch as it smacked against his face. "See, there you go, being all daft again. Sit. Eat."

She stared at him with her most petulant gaze until he acquiesced and finished his meal. When he was done, she merely took his plate and left him there with his sandy triangle.

"Well, that was productive," she muttered to her herself as she slammed the dishes into the wash basin. Felluria went to the window and looked at the setting sun. She usually liked to have some tea around this time, but not tonight. The old woman walked by the woodsman's room and refused to look in at him, merely passing by to reach her own quarters. There, she closed the door and set herself down for an early sleep.

A few hours later, she heard the echoing cry in the night and Felluria woke herself up, slapping her cheek until she was alert. She hadn't been awake this late in years. The night was chilly, and with a mild curse under her breath, she gathered a thick shawl about her shoulders. Choosing a cane to accompany her, she carried herself out of the house to finally see what the young man was up to each night.

Some villagers were awake, too, despite the late hour, but no one dared ask the Matron her mission, nor did they offer to guide her to the wounded man. Guidance was unnecessary anyway, for his cries clearly drew her toward his location. A few people tiptoed safely behind her, keeping quite a distance, wondering what would happen.

Felluria hadn't expected to be unnerved by what she saw, but the villagers hadn't been exaggerating. The blond man stood there next to the wall. He cried out, "Mira!"

with tremendous pain, then lunged toward the rock face and plunged his hands into the stone, breaking off numerous bits of debris. He pounded again and again, tirelessly, his throat growing more raw with each cry.

For all her inner coldness and bullheadedness, Felluria felt his anguish. He crushed the wall to snuff out some insidious pain that crept through him. And for all his silence, the only word he uttered was laden with such heart-wrenching sorrow, she thought the mountain itself would start to weep.

She stepped over to him as he pounded against the stone, and she could see that he wasn't quite himself. Perhaps he truly was asleep and unaware of his actions. It was all fine and good having him dig a new cave with his bare hands, but if he ever turned that mystical strength on her children, she would never forgive herself for having let him stay.

Punch.

"Mira!"

Punch.

"Mira!"

Punch.

"Mira!"

She watched him hammer away like some odd automaton, endlessly pounding, like a watermill ceaselessly grinding wheat. But it had to stop, she knew. At first, his silence had been enough, but now it wasn't. Soon, even this release may not suffice for him. She looked around and carefully bent over to heft a stone the size of her fist. Her walking cane supported her as she pulled herself up roughly. She then stepped as close as she dared and then heaved with all her might, aiming for his head.

Whatever strength protected his hands as he struck the wall did not also protect his head. He collapsed with a thud and rolled around, moaning. Felluria wandered over and jabbed him with the butt of her walking stick. "Wake up, you hear me? Look at where you are and what you're doing." Her voice cut through him like a whip. "On your feet, woodsman, and look at this." She gestured to the mountain wall, dimly lit by the moon.

Grudgingly, he rose to his feet and let his gaze examine the wall.

"See there? That's your pain right there, little one. If you want to beat the stuffing out of that mountain, then go right ahead, but from now on you've got to do so when you're wide awake."

He stood transfixed on the rock.

Felluria wouldn't take silence from him now. Her voice screamed with rage. "Do you hear me, boy? You *will* answer me."

But he still made no acknowledgement.

Not to be disrespected twice in one day, Felluria stalked up to him. "I'll teach you!" she scowled, reaching out a gnarled hand to slap him.

He saw the motion from the corner of his eye and he leaped away in panic, clutching against the mountain, shaking his head in dismay.

Felluria looked at him oddly, then she glanced at her hand. "Ah, I see. I know your pain, then. You beat your lady something senseless, didn't you? Nice fellow like you. Lost your cool, let your fists fly a few times."

She seemed to enjoy the way he cringed with her accusation. "Did you beat her if your food wasn't warm?" she hissed acidly. "Or if it was too hot? Did she never wash your clothes the way you wanted? Folded them wrong? Did you smack her if she looked at another man? Even if he was only a merchant? Is that what your fists have done?"

He continued to slide slowly away from her, pain and fear outlining his face even in the darkness.

Felluria's rage swelled the more he stepped away from her, and she pressed onward, keeping the distance between them from increasing. "Did she deny you when you were in the mood? And then did you beat her down until she was hurting and weak, unable to stop you? And then did you violate her? Take from her that precious part of her soul that no one has a right to take without consent? Is *that* why you try to break your fists on this rock? To erase the times you defiled her?"

Tears slid down his cheeks, but he kept backing away.

"You vicious monster!" she spat. "You heathen. You dare defile someone so pure, so young? Someone who adored you and wanted to be your partner? But you denied her, didn't you?"

Her voice echoed ominously in the night. "You wanted to control her, to dominate her. And when you couldn't have your way, you beat her into submission." Her voice turned menacing. "You crushed the bones in her body and you left her to die."

Fire burned in her eyes as she stalked closer, her voice grinding viciously, "And then—you *bastard*—you walked away."

He had stopped moving, except for the wracking sobs that shook him miserably.

Felluria was lost in her rage and she stamped up to him, brandishing her cane over her head and she swung.

"But she didn't die, you fool!" she screamed.

Smack.

"She fought back!"

Smack.

"She lived!"

Smack.

"Despite everything you did to destroy her!"

Smack.

"She lived!" she echoed. "She lived!"

Smack.

Smack.

Smack.

Smack.

And when the cane shattered to pieces and the woodsman lay bleeding on the ground from various head and chest wounds, Felluria dropped to her knees and pounded on his skull with her hands until all her fury had played out on this unsuspecting victim and her vengeance was sated.

And with nothing left to hold onto in this life, she passed on to the next.

CHAPTER 6

Forest Folk

"RANDLER, NOW!" DARIAK shouted, curling his fingers and lashing his hands outward. Streaks of fire blazed forth, reaching the five arrows leaving Randler's bow and lighting them. The projectiles crashed into piles of dried leaves, igniting them easily.

From across the way, a foreign voice called out, "Nossa, douse that fire. Poech, you're with me. Charge!"

This was the fifth set of forest sentries the mage and bard had come across. Each trio was stationed at various waypoints along the edge of the desert, leading to lush forests beyond. The trick, however, was getting past them before the beasts came.

The previous battles hadn't gone well and, each time, Randler and Dariak had needed to flee. The defenders didn't pursue them beyond a certain range, as these people were highly territorial.

Dariak swept his arms wide over his head in a great pinwheel, lunging to his right side, and bringing his hands low and across to the left while dragging his heel through the dirt. "*Bastronoss gorifich eperatus!*" he intoned and a trench cracked into the earth in front of him.

Randler kept his arrows flying, trying to knock the burning leaves away from the woman who was trying to put them out. The giant squirrets in the forest hated the smoke and it was the easiest way to keep them from joining the fray.

The two men charging at them saw the hole Dariak had created and pounced over it, but the mage was ready for them. He was already sweeping his hands into a spiraling pattern, calling upon the power of the air to buffet against the leaping men and knock them backwards. They tumbled in a heap and moaned.

Nossa had doused two of the fires and only one remained. Dariak responded by activating his fire dart spell, blasting her with low-power bursts while trying to reignite the other piles. "No!" she hissed, dropping and rolling purposely in the dirt to snuff the flames.

"Poech, get off me and draw your sword!"

"Right, Datch." The oafish warrior disentangled from his leader and drew his weapon. Dariak splattered him with a large ball of mud by fusing together the powers of earth, water, and air. Poech staggered back and collapsed again onto Datch.

Randler was nearly out of arrows, and because so many of them had burned, he wouldn't be able to reclaim them. Success here was more important than the hours it would take to whittle new ones, so he loaded his bow, took aim, and fired. His target this time was a meaty vine hanging from one of the trees behind the defenders. His shot was true, but the vine was too thick to fall with the one shot, so he fired again.

Dariak, meanwhile, called the three spells he needed to reenact the mud ball, which he launched into the trench, trying to secure the men inside. He followed it with a blast of ice and another layer of mud.

Randler had the vine down now. Nossa rose up and dusted herself off, the flames doused. She saw that the attackers had lit the other piles of leaves again and so she bodily threw herself onto one pile to smother the flames. She rolled to put out a second pile, but when she went for the third, she found she could not move.

With the vine lying on the ground, Dariak called to it to enwrap the woman's feet. Like a snake, the vine slithered toward her, binding her ankles, and then worked its way up to trap the rest of her. Randler had chosen well, for the vine was thick and long enough to cover the majority of her body.

But Nossa wasn't ready to quit. Without access to her arms or legs, she wriggled on the ground like an inchworm, striving to snuff out the last bit of flames. Closer and closer she went, so Dariak projected the Shield of Delminor across the expanse, effectively pinning her at last.

The bard and the mage waited tensely, eying both prisons to see if any of the trio would escape. After a few minutes, a solitary set of applause sounded in the distance. Randler and Dariak relaxed.

"Well now, you've got my attention, guests. You may enter." A set of shrubs melted down into a bridge, welcoming them to cross.

They scrambled over the land bridge, its only purpose to guide them toward the heart of the forest, for the landscape itself was easily traversable. The sand disappeared as trees swept by them and the desert heat was whisked away to a light, welcome breeze.

It had taken them over a week to cross the desert of Hathreneir, especially with having to skirt to the north to avoid Magehaven. The beast battles had been a constant challenge, even sometimes into the night, which was unexpected. Typically, they should have been able to hide below the surface without being noticed.

"The jades," Randler had said two days earlier. "Just like after Pindington when the beasts came out of hiding and tried to take us down, the ursalor included. They're drawn to them, I suppose."

They had tried Randler's trick of hiding themselves with the shadow jade, but it hadn't been enough. Dariak used a complex series of spells to create a concentric set of shields around them, but the effort needed to maintain it prevented them from making much progress anyway. No, they simply had to deal with each threat and push onward.

Crossing into the forest, however, had become almost as difficult as dealing with certain border guardians. Dariak was frustrated and irritable over the increased difficulties they had to face as they journeyed through his homeland. A scouting party en route to the king had informed them of the new defenses of the forest and the challenge set forth by the forest master to win entrance. The trouble was, without prior knowledge about the rules of the challenge, it was almost impossible to win, hence their first couple of failed attempts.

Dariak shook his head as he watched the trees pass by on their way to the center of the forest, remembering the conditions for winning. They had needed to defeat three fighters and prevent beasts from joining the fray, and do it without hurting anyone, which included knocking them unconscious. It hadn't been easy.

"Do you think anyone figures out how to get in?" Randler asked, sensing Dariak's train of thoughts, which wasn't a hard stretch after their ordeal.

"If they're determined. Maybe most are turned away. Or killed off. Or worse yet, maybe they're enslaved to be involved in the next skirmish. I could see that. They replenish their forces by making a prison sentence out of it. Win fifteen battles and you go free."

Randler laughed. "It could also explain that rule about not harming anyone."

"But why not specify the rules?" Dariak wondered. "It was a rough enough task already. Why make it harder?"

"I don't know. Maybe to keep out the army from Kallisor."

It was Dariak's turn to laugh. "I think an invading army would be able to muscle through."

Randler winked. "Not against those squirrets."

"True. I never did like them. Some kids have stuffed toys made to resemble them. But shooting rocks from their tails like that? I always wondered what the rocks themselves were made from, and if you think about where the tail is connected to their bodies…" He shivered. "My mother wouldn't confirm my guess that the rocks were anything but stone."

The heart of the forest wasn't much further along. It wasn't at the center of the wood, rather a place near enough to the desert border where a group of people had created a home for themselves. The rest of the forest was completely wild and difficult to navigate without using the numerous paths and markers carved in stone. The village came into view and Randler whistled low in wonder.

The people here had truly adopted the forest as their home. Huts were made of leaves and twigs, supported between pairs or triplets of trees, overgrown with a thick mossy coating. Many huts spiraled up into the trees where branches allowed for them. Passageways between the huts were all natural, often part of the branches themselves that made natural ladders. Even from his vantage point, Randler could tell that the trees had been carefully cultivated over the years so additional supports would grow in the directions they were most needed.

Thousands of vines were interwoven overhead, creating a massive green sky that wriggled in the breeze, easily simulating thick, billowy clouds. Light flickered in from gaps in the vines, and under each such opening was a giant funnel made of woven twigs and leaves, its purpose clearly to catch rainwater. As he considered that this was a poor source of hydration for an entire village, he could hear a running stream not far off.

He wondered idly how long they would need to remain here. For the past many days they had been surrounded by the golden sand and azure sky. Here, he was inundated with green and brown. The difference was stunning.

"Welcome, guests," greeted a forest girl of about eighteen, her hair threaded with numerous flowers, her skin a rich russet. She almost looked like a walking bouquet.

"Thank you, I am Dariak, and this is Randler. We humbly accept your welcome and will honor this forest as our own."

She tipped her head. "We thank you. Our forest is sacred to us and any who would harm the wood shall face our fury." She said it politely, but it was a definite warning. "Come. You must bathe."

"Bathe?" Randler sputtered.

The girl tinkled with laughter. "You smell of the desert and of death. This way." She guided them to the running stream that wound behind the village.

About a half mile away, the stream emptied into a pond, which then continued flowing into a narrower stream at the other end. The water was clear and babbled incessantly from some unseen source. The air here was mildly humid, but it was fresh and slightly fragrant with a host of wildflowers. What surprised the bard, though, were the twenty or so villagers—men, women, and children—all bare to the skin and soaking in the water. Their guide stripped off her own outfit and strode casually to the pond and dove in.

"Dariak?"

"We go in." The mage nodded, opening his robe and stripping down.

"The jades?" Randler whispered, unfastening his tunic and pulling it over his head.

"They should be fine," Dariak replied, slightly hesitant. "But we promised to honor the forest, and this cleansing is a part of their custom."

Randler eyed the host of people bathing in the water. "Clearly."

"You seem nervous."

"Well, I've never quite bared it all for such a large audience."

Dariak nudged him. "The more you think about it, the worse it will be. Personally, I just hope the water isn't cold." With that, he pulled off his shoes and walked toward the water, jumping in to get it over with.

Randler sighed and followed. After he was in the water, he scrubbed himself down and watched the others, seeing them simply bob up and down in the water's flow, not a care in the world. They looked so calm, so refreshed, and he wondered if things would ever quiet down enough that he could feel the same.

After some time, their guide swam over. "You no longer smell of death or sand. You may follow me now." She climbed out of the pond on the side opposite to where they had entered.

"I need to get something first," Dariak called out to her.

"No," she said softly. "You will come this way."

"But—" Randler started.

"This way," she interjected, her voice sharpening ever so slightly.

They were tired and they knew they had to follow her, though it meant leaving their supplies, and the jades, unattended. Dariak feared if they turned to claim their things, the whole village might run them out.

The two men pulled themselves from the pond and traced the path of their guide. She brought them to a small hut, where numerous cloth drapes were hanging.

"Visitors are often uncomfortable here, and so you may don one of these for your stay."

"My robe?" Dariak asked.

"It will be returned to you shortly, with all of your belongings intact. It is not our intent to rob those who enter here. Come. You will eat and you will rest. Later you will meet with Astrith. It is why you are here."

"We were hoping to pass through," Randler said, finding a cloth long enough to cover himself, and slipping it over his head.

"Only Astrith can grant such passage."

Dariak's brows furrowed. "We could just follow the paths, couldn't we?"

"Astrith will guide you. But for now, come eat and sleep."

They felt like prisoners of a sort, but they needed both nourishment and rest, especially after the six harrowing attempts to pass the absurd challenge that had admitted them in the first place. They worried most about the jades, but, as promised, everything was returned to them after some much-needed cleansing.

All that remained was for them to wait to meet Astrith.

CHAPTER 7

Kitalla's Journey

KITALLA LOOKED UP at the sky, deciding it was past the middle of the day. She turned her eye downward and scanned the horizon. Shimmer visions shook the air, but there was also other movement beyond, and it was neither friendly nor beastly. Just over the next rise, she could see a large regiment of Hathren troops.

She knew that the closer she came to the border, the more likely she would run into the armies engaged in battle. She had avoided a few sets of sentries and two skirmishes between the Hathrens and Kallisorians, who had slipped across the border hoping for an easy win.

Her mission was for Gabrion. She couldn't engage in any battles that would tip the balance of power right now. Besides, she needed Hathreneir to keep its eye focused on this eastern edge of its land, and for Kallisor not to be defeated.

She judged each battalion to host around fifty fighters on each side, with the Hathrens utilizing mages. In some way, it meant the Kallisor forces were stronger, for they held their own without the added effects of powerful spells. Yet she also knew that the king of Kallisor had outfitted his troops with magic-resistant armor and at least two healers to give each troop a chance to withstand the magic.

Part of her yearned to joined the fighting, and she laughed to herself when she realized that she didn't care which side she was on. She just wanted a good scuffle, not keeping herself hidden like she was doing now.

In the desert, there were no boulders or trees behind which she could hide. No shadows to disguise her steps or allow her to blend into the surroundings as she went. No buildings gave her any shelter at all.

Instead, she had buried herself in the sand, up to her neck with a beige kerchief veiling her dark brown hair. She could turn her head, but that was about all. Her hiding strategy had kept her safe for days, though once in a while a sentry passed closely. Today she knew she would be safe, for the fighting was engaged to the south and to the north and both skirmishes would keep the fighters busy.

She needed to wait a little while longer, for once the sun moved a little further, the sand creatures would awaken from their noontime respite and they would be the distraction she needed to head further east.

The fire and metal jades guided her faithfully. She needed to head further north as well, but she couldn't do so until she crossed into Kallisor. It meant Gabrion had crossed into their homeland, but she didn't know if he had done so on his own or as a prisoner. Actually, she couldn't tell any more than the basic location of his glass jade, but that was another matter.

Clicking and scraping sounded not far off and she grinned, for the sandorpions were awakening. They were most hungry after their slumber, and she intended to use that to her advantage. She turned her head around to see how many were nearby; only three were close enough for her purpose. The creature to the west was coming right for her, drawn by the scent of her sweaty bandana, as was her plan. The other two wandered more aimlessly, and she hoped they would remain aloof.

In the distance she could hear a horn blow, signaling a break in the fighting between men while they dealt with the beasts. This was her chance. Kitalla kicked her knees and arms, and sand flew off her body. She rolled out of hiding and kept low, so as to appear from far off as just another critter. She scurried toward the nearest sandorpion, carrying her trap in her hands.

When she reached the clacking claws of her foe, she smirked, for the beast was less interested in Kitalla personally and more so in the bleeding shadowcrows she had caught earlier that morning. They were hanging from the end of a fallen sword she had claimed after a skirmish she had passed along the way. The scorpion-like creature was so distracted by the easy meal that it didn't address Kitalla, even as she leaped onto the beast's back, hunkered down, and held the sword out over its head.

Sandorpions weren't known for their intellect, and she had doubted this would work, but it was the best plan available to her. The stupid creature kept walking forward, trying to grab the ever-elusive shadowcrow carcasses hanging two feet out of reach. It was hard for her not to laugh.

As the creature rolled across the surface of the sand, another caught the smell and made its way closer. The sandorpion's first instinct was to run faster, but the hunter kept pace well enough. Kitalla could feel the writhing body underneath her tensing in anticipation, the tail wagging back and forth to propel it, or perhaps it was readying its venom to fight off the attacker.

Her mount was too slow to escape the other sandorpion, but Kitalla didn't think it would be wise to let them fight, or to try to switch beasts. The other one could have been smarter and not fall for the tethered meal. She reached one hand for a dagger, while keeping the sword in place with her other hand, and she lashed out, catching the invader in the eye. The beast screamed in pain and thrashed about, but its pursuit ended. Kitalla shook the sword with the shadowcrows playfully, making sure her new friend would remember its hunger and keep moving.

After nearly two hours, the sandorpion seemed weary and less interested in the almost-meal. Kitalla looked over her shoulder and judged that she was far enough along anyway. She pulled the sword in slightly, letting the beast get its much-awaited snack, then pounced off its back, jogging off to let it eat. She felt it was only fair not to kill it, for it had provided her escape. "Just don't come after me for making you work for that lunch, you hear?"

Her journey through the desert hadn't been easy, and it had certainly taken her longer to reach this point than it had taken the army to pass the other way and reach

Marritosh. Then again, the host of men and women had been able to simply march across the sand and fight off any threat without losing much time, plus the border guardian that had transported them into Hathreneir had shaved off a portion of their journey with its rushing wind and sand.

No matter, she decided, for the horizon was flecked with green. Kallisor was only perhaps an hour away with a light jog.

She half-expected a border guardian to appear and challenge her passage into Kallisor, but then she remembered that the warped beings mostly protected against entry into the kingdom, as they worked for Hathreneir. She trotted along to the edge of the desert and reached lusher ground without incident.

Once she had put the desert behind her, she sought out a tree, simply to sit under its shade for a time and rest. She hadn't seen a tree since entering Hathreneir, and she marveled at how much she had missed it. Not far from the tree was a small pond, though as she drew closer to it, she realized it was leftover rainwater from a recent storm. It was a little muddy, but she ran her hands through it anyway and splashed it on her face to cool down after her day.

Night was coming and she was hungry and tired. In about two hours, she could reach the outpost where they had parted ways with Ordren and other members of their forces that hadn't wanted to leave Kallisor. Or she could head south in about as much time and find herself in Savvron.

She fantasized about Savvron as she splashed more muddy water onto her skin. She had pulled the villagers together to defend their home against the Hathrens, trying to protect Gabrion's hometown while he was out of commission after their experience with her old colleague, Heria. They would welcome her back as a hero. Old Klerra would knit her a scarf and then outfit her a new set of leathers, just because. The baker would lavish her with a feast and the blacksmith would hand over two dozen newly crafted daggers. Terrsian, Gabrion's father, would greet her with open arms, after which he would prepare several days' worth of supplies for her journey. Hernior, who had defected from the king's guard to remain in Savvron, would ride with her and clear the roads of Hathrens so she could simply fly to Gabrion and convince him to forget his quest for Mira. Kitalla should be his quest now. She had earned it. She had earned him. She wanted—

Kitalla shook herself awake. She hadn't meant to doze off, certainly not in the middle of a clearing, half-laying in a muddy puddle. Perturbed at her carelessness, she grunted and woke herself fully by stretching, doing some squats, and then entering a light jog.

She watched the sky as she went, judging it to be after midnight, based on the moon. Night creatures were on the prowl, but there were fewer of them in this area than in the Hathren desert. She only hoped there were no lupinoes this far west, for they could give her some trouble in her current state. Hopefully she would reach the outpost bef—

Searing pain lanced through her side and she collapsed in agony. She felt as if she had been stabbed with a heated sword, the pain was so great. She clawed at her hip urgently, struggling with the strap on her pocket. It was hard not to cry out in pain, despite her tolerance to it. After fumbling frantically for a few moments, she ripped open her hip pocket and pulled out the two jades, throwing them on the ground.

The fire and metal jades vibrated angrily, each glowing more than usual. She couldn't touch them, for the fire jade was exceptionally hot and the metal jade shook so violently, it was impossible to hold.

She looked around, trying to find something to wrap them in so she could continue onward, but there were only some random leaves nearby and they burned instantly when they touched the fire jade. She had to wait it out and that took a couple of hours.

The same thing happened each night over the course of the next several days. She didn't know what it portended, but it frightened her and she hastened her steps to find Gabrion.

CHAPTER 8

Taming the Mages

ERVINOR ONLY SLEPT for a couple hours before he was strong enough for his next task as general of the army. Carrus had delivered him home as ordered, removing the tunic for fear Ervinor would roll over and stab himself with any of the remaining weapons. But Ervinor was going to face Farrenok now, and he needed to stand strong. He donned the tunic again and equipped enough weapons so that there were no empty straps left.

He wondered what he would do, but it would partly depend on Farrenok's responses. The mage had infiltrated the town and their forces had slain innocent people. But, in all fairness, so had Dariak and his companions invaded Magehaven, creating their own list of casualties. There was a difference, but Ervinor had to consider both sides.

Making his way through town was difficult, for remnants of the attack were everywhere. The western edge had seen the most damage, but that one cluster of mages had lobbed countless spells into the town, not seeking any particular target. Here and there, homes or shops had fallen, sometimes harming the inhabitants within. Not many had died in the assault, but Ervinor hated that anyone had been slain. The attack was needless.

Winding his way toward Herchig's home, Ervinor understood that he needed to be strong and face this situation. Dariak would have tended to the matter himself if he wasn't off questing after the last piece of jade. He wondered what Kitalla or Randler would do under the circumstances, but he believed they would have deferred to Dariak. Gabrion, though, would have found a way to work through to a truce. But Gabrion had run off, leaving Ervinor and the others to battle on their own in Castle Hathreneir.

He knew something must have happened to make Gabrion flee. Something major.

But as he approached Herchig's house, he had to thrust the errant thoughts aside. He called for a mask of aplomb, so he could deal with the invader carefully. Frast, Lica, Quereth, and a few others were already waiting for his arrival.

Frast greeted him first. "Are you ready, Ervinor? This won't be easy."

"I'll do this with one arm tied behind my back," he retorted, trying to channel Kitalla's sarcasm. The others didn't know how to respond. "Yes, I'm ready."

Ervinor had requested that Herchig find a suitable place to hold the rogue mage, and the old man had opted to keep him in his own home, surrounded by a handful of Marritosh citizens. Each kept a wary eye on the aggressive man, anxious for a chance to strike him. His hands and mouth were tightly bound, but even if they weren't, he wouldn't likely have attempted anything with the guards hovering over him. Four of the captured mages were also in attendance, each bound and guarded.

"He has been cooperative," Herchig announced, gesturing toward Farrenok. "Which is to say, he ate, drank, and filled a chamber pot."

Ervinor waited for a spinning side-tale, but there wasn't one. It boded ill for the situation. He had never known the old man to withhold recollecting some memory in response to any predicament. Instead, sad eyes waited for whatever the outcome would be.

Ervinor turned to his mages, all of whom had fled Pindington with him. "Lica, Frast, cast protection spells. Quereth, mind the energies to ensure he doesn't conjure anything silently." After that, he turned to one of the soldiers in the room. "Pull off his gag."

Farrenok eyed Ervinor with such malice that the young warrior doubted he would make any progress at all. "Scum," the mage hissed.

"I'll have you gagged again if you prefer," Ervinor said. "I would rather, however, that you have the chance to verify the events I will summarize for you. Let me know if I should preach to you or talk with you."

Farrenok snarled but then he angled his head for Ervinor to continue.

"Dariak is the son of Delminor, the mage who summoned the colossus in the last great war. Delminor was a prominent mage who sought peace with his research of magic."

"Peace?" Farrenok interrupted. "His spells were always turned to war."

"Turned, yes," Ervinor commented before the others spoke up. "But his own goal was not of war. I see you disagree, but let us move on. Delminor's work with the jades unlocked a hoard of magic spells that mages have successfully employed for decades now."

"It wasn't only *his* work that led to the advancement of magic."

"Hmm," Ervinor hummed, reaching back and keeping Lica in place. "Do you deny Delminor's contributions?"

Farrenok eyed the man viciously, but acquiesced. "No."

"Without Delminor's work, mages would not have the skills they have today. Is that correct?" He waited for affirmation before continuing. "Unfortunately, the mage was lost in the great war and he could no longer further your cause. However, he left behind his progeny."

With this, Farrenok released a guttural tone and Quereth took a step forward to ensure he wasn't casting a spell. "His progeny," Farrenok sneered, prompting Ervinor to continue.

"Dariak was raised to use magic and he became deft at the trade, joining the Mage Council when he was nineteen."

Farrenok cut in. "*I* was admitted to the Council at eighteen. *His* entrance was a farce, promised to him by old sentimental mages who pitied Delminor's kin."

Frast couldn't hold back. "Perhaps you were pitied, too."

Ervinor gritted his teeth. He needed the mages there to witness this, but he didn't want them to skew the events. He looked at the other four prisoners, hoping they were paying close attention to their leader. "Delminor was the only man in recorded history to assemble all eleven pieces of jade."

"Yes, so?" Farrenok acknowledged.

"He consumed many resources to gather those jades and spent countless hours learning their secrets and disseminating the information to the rest of the mages."

Farrenok squirmed in his seat but he did not interrupt.

"Before he mastered them all, he was called to war, where he did the unthinkable; he brought the jades together and became a massive giant, capable of defeating any spell or attack, then he used his will to defeat his enemies."

"Accurate," Farrenok conceded.

"And then those shards were lost. But because they once belonged to Delminor, it was decided by the mages of the time to bequeath them to Dariak, though not all of them were in their possession. You can't deny that fact, can you?"

It almost visibly hurt the mage to say, "No."

"So Dariak was in his right to seek those jades, wasn't he?"

There was a moment of delay. "In a sense."

Ervinor laughed coldly. "In a sense, you say? No, I think he had every right, and damn all of you who turned against him. Does any one of you even understand the purpose of his quest?" He eyed Farrenok and the other four mages, two of whom avoided his gaze. "Let me spell it out for you then. He seeks to gather the jades, to unite them, and to use their power to end the war."

"Nonsense!" Farrenok raged. "Look at every action he has taken! He stormed into the tower and demanded that the time-honored Trials be canceled for his friends. No one entering the tower has been exempt from them. No one! Then he demanded the jades themselves, callous and uncaring that we need them for our defenses. It's with the jades that we defend ourselves from intruders, be they creatures or thieves. No, he would rob us blind and leave us with nothing."

"Nothing?" Quereth scoffed. "Haven't you got a host of spells at the tips of your tongues? Can't you band together to defend yourselves? You rely on a piece of ancient magic to keep you safe, not your own skill? What has happened to the mages of Hathreneir?"

Farrenok seethed with anger. "You have no idea how we are tested by the creatures of this land. The ogres to the south, the border guardians, the rogues out for treasure, the king himself seeking to bolster his own defenses. No, we need those jades."

"The border guardians?" Frast barked. "Aren't they errant mages who have lost control of the power?"

Farrenok hedged. "Well, once they are broken, they must be controlled."

"Ervinor, I'm sorry," Quereth qualified, then turned to Farrenok, "but didn't Dariak say something about you losing yourself to wild magic?"

Anger lit in the mage's eyes and he scowled. "You speak of things you do not know, old man," he hissed.

"Enough," Ervinor intervened. "This deviates from our purpose here. Let me tell you this, mage. I care nothing for your personal struggles. I couldn't scrape together an ounce of care for your ambition, either. What I want is for people across our lands to grow up in peace and happiness, troubled only in their daily woes, not looking over their shoulders constantly for calls to war. Hasn't there been enough war? Haven't enough people died over nothing? Haven't our two kings bled our kingdoms enough over the centuries?"

Farrenok interrupted him with mocking laughter. "You speak like a child, begging mommy and daddy to send away the evil monsters under your bed. Look around you, fool! We have real monsters in our land. Vicious creatures tearing apart anyone who ventures away from any town. We have brethren who fight their way into our homes and kill our colleagues to claim some artifact to use for their own gain. Haven't enough people died over nothing? You're insane. You don't even see the truth all around you."

"I see this," Ervinor said calmly, cutting off the responses of his comrades. "I see you there, with a small mind, inciting a group of malcontents to do your bidding. I see you dragging them out to take down a man you hated as a child because you envied his fame. I see a man duping his colleagues into decimating a town full of innocent people because your own ambitions got in the way. And I see you here, barking back at me like an angry dog, unwilling to hear anything I have to say."

"Shut your mouth, you armless freak!" the mage screamed. "You'll never take us down! The mages of Hathreneir will kill you where you stand. The jades will be ours and your pathetic Kallisor will fall to our power. The people who died here died because they sided with you and your disgusting view of the world. Peace? What good is peace? Nothing comes of it. It's war where we prosper! It's when there's a stronger enemy to defeat that we rise up and challenge our ways. It's there that magic becomes stronger, not in peace. You're fooling yourself if you believe that peace will bring anything other than famine and misery. We will stagnate and never grow beyond who we are. Hear me! Hear me!"

Ervinor turned his gaze to the other four prisoners in the room. "He led you here. Do you also feel as he does?" Four sets of eyes turned away.

Farrenok laughed wildly. "They're only afraid because you have them bound. Release them! I dare you! Release me! I will show you the truth."

Ervinor nodded his head and the ropes binding the four prisoners were cut, much to the dismay of Ervinor's colleagues. The four mages stood and rubbed their wrists, shaking their heads.

"So many have died," one of them said, her voice pained. "For nonsense like this. For absurd claims. How did I ever follow a madman such as you?"

"Madman?" Farrenok challenged. "Why, you were perfectly willing to follow me once I visited your bed. You got your wish, sweetie, didn't you? All you need to do is support me."

She turned her face away, abashed.

Ervinor ignored the exchange and focused on Farrenok once again. "You have a chance to atone for your crimes. I can release you and you can work to rebuild this town. Or you can return to the tower and teach your brethren a new way, one without your ambition. You can seek a new peace."

Farrenok burst into laughter again. "I guess when they cut off your arm, they took part of your brain as well. You're a fool. You'll never unite our kingdoms. Everyone sees things as I do. Each of us is here for our own self. Our own well-being. Our own families. We grow children to take over for us. We seek power to maintain our ideals. No, your kingdom will fall to ours and you will become the slaves to the mages. It's what your king fears the most, don't you know? That the magic-users will be so strong, his little swordsmen won't be able to stop them. Doesn't he work in secret with a host of mages so he can keep us in our places? That's the irony, isn't it? He despises us but he relies on us also.

"No, you simple-minded, armless freak. There will never be peace between our kingdoms. You will die at our hands, just as the people of this village fell today. You will never rise up against us. You are too weak to do what must be done, be we are not! We will succeed where you—"

At that moment, Ervinor truly accepted his role as general. He understood that the fighting needed to end, even if it meant that some people had to die along the way. He knew the madness spouted by the mage was not uncommon, but was the same poison that permeated the land and maintained the hatred between the two peoples. It had to end.

Perhaps it was more symbolic to him than anything, but Ervinor pulled out one of his daggers and thrust it into Farrenok's heart, quelling his incessant badgering. He half-expected the other four prisoners to react immediately, but their silence said much to the young soldier. They, too, wanted peace, and the crazy ramblings simply had to stop.

He had never killed in cold blood before, but Ervinor knew in his heart that he had helped Dariak's cause. He only hoped he would never have to kill a defenseless man again.

                            CHAPTER 9

Turmoil

THE WOODSMAN AWOKE several days later and his face was a mask of pain. Every
part of his body ached and he knew he shouldn't even be alive. He both thanked
and cursed the glass jade for protecting him. Throbbing coursed through him, reminding him of every pain he had ever suffered.

He remembered the old woman reaching out to strike him, but he couldn't let
her do it. It would kill her, as it had ki—

Then she had berated him, accusing him of things he had and hadn't done. He
realized she had lost herself in her own suffering, but too much of it had been his as
well. After all, hadn't he lashed out and grievously hurt—

Then the cane swept in, clobbering him mindlessly. Beating and beating him to
a bloody pulp. He deserved nothing less after the devastation he had caused when
he had kil—

And then she died, her aged body collapsing on top of him, finally releasing the
rage she had gripped all her life. It had motivated her and kept her functioning. Her
personal agony was clearly a deep secret she had never shared before. It was a fury
that had given her a unique strength to overcome any odds that stood against her.
Yet once the rage was gone, there was nothing left to keep her pressing forward.

He faced that now. His quest was over. He had ventured out to gain greater
strength so he could rescue… her. But a year had passed and she was only a mere
peasant. Who would have kept a peasant alive for so long? It hadn't made sense and
he had come to terms with it along the way. She wouldn't be waiting for him, but he
quested anyway just to learn what her ultimate demise had been.

Instead, he had found her, alive and well. Happy, even, despite her first entrance
back into his life where she was raging at the king—her husband—for trying to
secret her away to some safe haven, far from the fighting.

Hadn't he wanted to do the same for her? To protect her?

But then she ran off, refusing to believe the truth of the attack on Savvron, their
hometown. He couldn't fathom how she had blocked it from her memory, the
blood, the dying.

But she hadn't seen any of it. Not really. Kaz had been covered in blood, but it
wasn't his own. He had said as much. To… her… it *could* have been staged. And

though Kaz was later injured, that could have been after her abduction—or rescue. She really may never have seen, may never have known...

But he had to make her see. She had to know. Hathren troops had killed many people they both knew and loved. She needed to understand that her... husband... was a tyrant, as bad as their own king. He needed to be defeated.

She needed to return to his side and be with him, like he had planned. Like they were destined.

So he sought her out, despite being turned away by the Hathren king. He burst in, found her, and she denied him. She denied his truth. She denied his love.

She crushed him.

Devastated him.

In that moment, he had died, though his body continued to draw breath.

He couldn't explain it, until he saw... *it*... the child... her child... with *him*. *His* child.

The pain welled up and echoed through his new injuries. He wanted to cry out, to change the past, but he knew he couldn't. He had to admit it to himself. He had to. He couldn't escape the truth any longer.

He ki—

He—

He hadn't wanted to, but he had wounded her so badly. Betrayal: hers, his. He didn't know what was worse.

He was nasty to her, belittled her, destroyed her...

She slapped him, but the glass jade channeled his pain and...

He kil—

He—

No.

He wasn't ready.

He couldn't say it. Not even in his own mind.

No.

Not yet.

Maybe not ever.

In his memory, a baby gurgled softly.

CHAPTER 10

Astrith

DARIAK AND RANDLER were awoken after a long nap and guided to meet the leader of the forest people. In homage to the people around them, the mage and bard wore simple cloth drapes that were so thin they left little to the imagination. They supplemented the outfits only with their jades. Randler wore his shadow jade on a cord about his neck. He handed the air jade over to Dariak, who put it with the others in a special belt Randler had made for the purpose.

The meeting place was in the center of the forest village, where they had arrived that afternoon. In the dark of night, the place looked eerie and uncertain. Firegnats had been harvested for their stinging venom, which glowed for many hours if it was preserved correctly. Hundreds of such firegnat lamps were strewn about the area, highlighting each hut, each major walkway, and little else. In the center of the clearing, however, was a well-controlled bonfire, tended by six forest folk to both maintain its strength and keep it from growing too strong.

Astrith sat nearby on a simple bench carved from a log. He was an older man, with jet-black hair that matched Dariak's, save numerous vibrant gray streaks. "Welcome, guests," he said. His voice was scratchy like bark and his skin was as dark as the ground in which his feet rested. "I am grateful for your presence here in our wood."

"And a warm welcome to you, as well. I am Dariak and this is Randler. We are—"

"Sit, eat," Astrith interrupted, "while I look upon you. And, I daresay, do not refuse this offering, for other provisions will not be available to you until morning."

He watched them for a long time and Randler couldn't help but wonder what he was looking for. It seemed as if the forest leader was making mental notes of how they looked—of his own bark-hued eyes and hair, of Dariak's black hair and azure eyes. Perhaps he was more interested in how they moved, or the manners with which they ate. Maybe the man sensed the deeper connection between them, that they were more than just travel companions or friends.

"You fought well today," Astrith commented after they had finished their meal. "In tandem, you relied on each other's strengths to achieve your goal. It was a worthy contest and I was glad to have witnessed it."

"You were watching?" Dariak asked, unsurprised, but needing to say something after being ignored during the meal.

Astrith nodded deliberately. "I am known here as the one who sees. Patience must be yours, though I sense your task is rushed."

"Indeed," Randler said. "We had not expected to be detained at all before passing to the western lands."

"Detained," Astrith echoed with a smile. It wasn't a sinister grin, but it irked the two of them nonetheless.

Randler bowed his head and wondered what was wrong with himself. Usually, he could navigate the nobles better than this, but he felt irritated and edgy. "I apologize if I choose my words poorly."

"You do well to seek a more patient stance, young one. For the forest is as old as time and these trees have stood for centuries. To rush our meeting would be to deny the very forest and life around us." He raised his wrinkled hands in homage to the trees around him. "We are a vast community here and we work together to maintain a steady calmness."

"Your ways are legend," Dariak said. "I've only heard stories of your people and haven't visited you until now. My goals were different when I was younger, but this always seemed a place I would want to visit."

"Legend," Astrith repeated, his lips curling into another smile, but he said nothing else.

"Yes," Dariak added, confused, but pressing on. "Your people have been here for a long time. Some stories say decades; others, centuries. You live with the land, not off it. You have a symbiosis with nature and a gentle peace."

"Indeed, your legends speak well of us," Astrith said. "Though your understanding of our ways is limited from such tales. It makes little difference, however, for we will ever be here, growing with the land and connecting to this world in ways that even you mages cannot do."

Randler furrowed his brow. "The famine of ages past, which destroyed the land east of here, turning it to desert… You don't fear something ever happening to you and your people?"

"No, for nature will not turn on us so long as we live with her. As she protected us in the past, so will she protect us in the future, despite the encroaching desert."

Dariak shook his head. "I don't understand it."

"Stay with us, child, and you will come to better learn our ways."

"No, that isn't what I mean. You're here, in the center of Hathreneir. You have the ability to challenge passersby with your own guardians and thus keep them from your land. But when I was growing up, people came through here all the time. There were no restrictions."

"There were restrictions," Astrith assured him. "However, times have called for us to be more cautious."

"But you are not cautious enough, perhaps," Dariak pushed. "You allowed a dangerous man to pass through these paths and you did not stop him."

Astrith squinted in confusion. "I know not of whom you speak."

"Pyron," the mage answered softly. "He is a mage of the southeast tower. He carries with him a power that makes him impervious to damage. He came this way, passed through your land, and awaits somewhere beyond, growing stronger with each day."

Astrith's calm demeanor slipped. "You cannot claim to know who has come through our land, not today or before. Other paths exist."

"Pyron would not have gone north to traverse the mountains," Dariak said. "Nor would he have gone south to cross by water. You may not have dominion over the entire central expanse, but your land is the easiest path. And I know he is to the west."

"And by what means do you have these assurances?"

Dariak assumed they already knew about the jades, since the forest folk had cleansed their belongings, so he did not hesitate. Yet when Randler and Dariak withdrew the shards, Astrith's reaction said otherwise.

"What is this!" the older man exclaimed. "How is it you come to possess these relics?"

"Relics?" Randler asked. "They have been out across the land for many years. They were assembled roughly twenty years ago. Knowledge of them isn't entirely uncommon."

"Those were supposed to have faded from the world by now," the man said sadly. "We were meant to move on from our ties to the past, to seek our own fortunes as a people that had learned from history and did not need to repeat its mistakes. I should have known better."

"I don't follow," Dariak said.

Astrith waved his hand in the air and an attendant brought over some herbal tea for them, the flavor of which was somewhat lost in the rough wooden tankards in which they were served. He sipped heartily from his mug until he needed a second serving.

Randler spoke, not believing the unspoken words, "Are you suggesting that the jades were meant to be hidden away?"

"Yes."

The bard didn't know how to react, for secreting the jades away had been his original purpose. Sure, he had gone about collecting them first, but his goal was then to find ways of removing them from the world, even if it meant taking a ship out of Pindington and dropping them into the vast ocean. He had been forced to barter the lightning jade there to keep the mages and thieves off his back, but at least he knew where it would be until he could reclaim it. His quest hadn't procured enough of the jades on his own, but Dariak's journey had corrected that. Though, by then, his goal had changed, to allow Dariak to possess the jades so he could bring an end to the war.

Yet Astrith intimated that the jades were meant to be lost, and it shook Randler's soul.

"You can't be serious," Dariak scoffed. "The jades came together two decades ago. That alone says you don't know what you're talking about. If they were going to be hidden away, then clearly those events erased that possibility."

But Astrith shook his head. "The Red Jade erupted and its parts were lost. Of course they were not lost to memory, and some mages would seek their powers. But little would come from possessing any one jade, and each would be a simple keepsake until their powers were forgotten."

Dariak considered for a moment. The water jade had been kept in a display case in Kallisor's castle museum. Likewise, the Hathren king had kept the fire jade as a bedside keepsake, and the elder of Gerrish had hoarded the glass jade. Randler's shadow jade and Dariak's earth jade were mostly mementos to them; Randler because pulling on the darkness hadn't often been helpful while fighting in a team, and Dariak because he knew the earth spells without having to rely much on the jade. Randler had hidden the nature and lightning jades away, unused at all. The thief, Grenthar, once owned the metal jade, apparently knowing its worth, based on the expenses he had spent on devising traps to protect it, to Kitalla's misfortune, but he hadn't used its actual power at all. Only the mages in the tower had tapped into the healing and beast jades, but then it was the mages themselves who empowered the tower's defenses. The jades had only guided them.

"Only Sharice," Dariak decided, recalling his battle for the air jade. "Only she had been trying to use the jades to any real extent."

"So though they flared into our minds recently," Astrith concluded, "knowledge of their powers was ready to fade away." He then eyed Dariak's jades as they lay on the dirt in front of him. "Now, though, I see I was mistaken."

Dariak struggled under the disapproving tone. "Ignoring the jades would not end the war. It would still be mage versus warrior. Hathreneir versus Kallisor. Eventually, some mage would wonder about the jades, seeking to turn the tide, and the hunt for them would begin anew." Then his voice grew quiet. "Like it had for my father."

Astrith's eyes lit up. "Your father?"

He usually withheld the information, but he felt shaken. "Delminor. The one who assembled the jades in the great war."

The older man stood up, arms curling threateningly, hidden muscles bulging forth. "It was he who wrested our jades from us. He who sent the warriors and mages in to burn this wood, to find the jades at all cost."

"W—what?"

"You have no idea how many lives were lost, man and swallomer alike. Trees that stood for thousands of years, torched and burned to cinder. Men and women who died at the hands of metal swords and vicious spells, my wife and daughter included. You cannot know the pain of this forest, the agony we felt that day, as poison ran through our veins, cursing us to defeat."

"But you thrive here now," Randler inserted, seeing the pain in Dariak's eyes.

"We thrive because we know these woods. And though we can guide some things with our hands, we cannot commune the way we could. No, the nature jade in your hands, was once ours. As was a jade that allowed us dominion over the beasts so we could keep them at bay. In the years since, we have had to kill some of our neighbors, because the creatures did not understand our wish to live together."

Astrith paced back and forth. "It is not our way to leave this forest to pursue our foes. We live here and we focus our energies here. Thus, when the jades were taken we could not follow. And though you show me this jade this evening, I feel no right to reclaim it, for it has been lost to us for some three or four decades.

"Yet here you are, son of the man who came and killed us. Son of the man who tore these forgotten pieces from our protection. Son of the man who doomed this world to despair by bringing these dread pieces together with their brethren, wreaking havoc upon the land. You are here, son of Delminor. His price is now yours to pay."

"No..."

Dariak looked physically wounded and Randler didn't know what to do. The claims could be true. Kallisorians told stories of Delminor being a slayer of men, hoisting magic upon the people and eradicating them. But Delminor was Dariak's father, and since Randler had gotten to know the mage, he felt that Delminor was a completely different person than the tales had claimed. Even his grandfather had seemingly respected the great mage after several encounters on the battlefield.

Yet when it came down to it, Astrith's story made sense. Delminor had to have gotten the jades from their resting places, and if those jades had been here, then surely they had been taken. When Randler looked around, seeing the huts with the interlocking branches that offered both support and a means for scaling the trees safely, and the protective canopy of vines overhead, along with the lack of violent feral creatures in the area, he had to admit that the nature and beast jades had probably been here for a long time before Delminor had claimed them.

Dariak seemed to come to the same conclusion. "I don't understand. Father, he... yes, he sent for the jades, but... he..."

Astrith analyzed the pain in the mage's eyes, wondering at its truth. He gestured to the forest people nearby and, moments later, Randler and Dariak were escorted back to their chamber, but now they were under guard.

Dariak was too stunned to do anything and Randler's worry for his friend superseded anything else. It wasn't until later they realized that Astrith had kept the jades.

CHAPTER 11

Disturbance

KITALLA SHUDDERED IN the chilly air, but she needed to press onward. The fire and metal jades no longer burned fiercely at night, but they maintained deep vibrations at all times. At least she was able to handle them in this state, unlike those uncontrollable outbursts in the dark of night.

She had ventured north from the murky puddle and pressed hard to reach her destination, avoiding contact with the outpost, which she felt would only delay her. Something compelled her, much like after she had claimed the fire jade and it urged her to reunite with the metal shard. She hoped it was just the jades trying to reconvene and not that something tragic had happened to Gabrion.

But she would find out soon, she realized, for as the mountains loomed closer, so too did she espy signs of a village. Plumes of smoke rose in the air from numerous sources, and though they could have been from a battalion, soon huts also came into view.

"Ho there, visitor," called a middle-aged man as she approached. "Be warned; this place isn't safe now. You should turn back."

Kitalla looked around. "Few havens are safe these days, friend. What's your trouble?"

He looked immediately disturbed, as if he had expected her to turn away with his warning. "Uh, nothing the likes of you can thwart, if you'll pardon my say so."

"I don't pardon you. And you couldn't detain me if you wanted to, so you might as well welcome me in and be done with it."

The man stammered and stepped back a pace. "We can't abide another crazy visitor. Please go."

Kitalla's eyes lit up. "Another visitor, you say? Introduce me."

She didn't want to use violence against a clearly peaceful town, so when the man refuted her still, Kitalla took one step forward, another step to the side, and swept her hands deliberately around. Her eyes pierced the man's and after a few moments, his panic faded and he shook his head.

"You poor thing, you must be hungry. Come inside. My name is Nathe and you'll be safe with me for a time." He gestured her to enter the town and then guided her to his home. If he wasn't right about her rumbling belly, she would have moved on immediately at the behest of the jades.

"Very well," she said, joining him for a plate of old stew and a tankard of rather tasteless cider.

"You look so familiar, dear," he said halfway through the meal.

She had imprinted him with the suggestion that she was his late grandmother, and the image had held in some way after she released her dance steps. Kitalla wondered what it meant. Perhaps her skills were growing. Maybe he was daft. Or, she decided once she looked around his meager home, he was very lonely. "I am a friend, Nathe, and you have no need to fear me. This stew is excellent," she lied. "However did you make it?"

Pleased by the compliment, Nathe talked about hunting for the rabbitats and squirrets he needed, then how he bartered half of his catch for the vegetables. Collecting the water and filtering it through a sheet of cloth had provided the basic stock. His tale was utterly boring to her, but she needed to finish getting the food down and give her stomach a chance to settle after the terrible meal. He must have made the dish days earlier, based on the way her stomach wanted to reject it.

A scream echoed outside, followed by much commotion. Kitalla reacted instantly, leaping from her seat and striding from the room, Nathe too flustered to watch her go. He simply put his head down and muttered, "Not again."

Two dozen villagers jogged through the darkening streets, seeking the source of the cries. A young woman's voice cut through the evening air; Kitalla followed it easily. She stepped awkwardly in one of the odd grooves running through the road, twisting her ankle in the process. She muttered under her breath and ignored the pain.

In the center of a road on the far eastern edge of the small town, a girl was collapsed on the ground, wailing hopelessly as blood poured from a severely wounded hand. Kitalla pressed through the crowd and saw that no one was trying to help her.

"Bandages!" she called, and when no one responded, she grabbed the nearest man and ripped off a piece of his tunic.

"It won't help none," the man murmured, not even resisting.

Kitalla knelt and she could see that the girl wasn't just bleeding, but several fingers were missing. She wrapped the wound with the bandage, but the bleeding continued. She applied pressure to specific places on the girl's wrist, hand, and arm, but nothing she did could stop the flow of blood. "What is this?" she asked, bewildered, raising the girl's arm up high over her head. "Why won't she stop bleeding?"

The villagers only backed away and then lowered their heads minutes later when the girl died. An older woman approached Kitalla and placed her hand on the rogue's shoulder. "Easy, child. There was nothing you could do to help her."

Kitalla pressed the girl's eyes closed before rising to her feet. "What's going on here?"

The old woman's voice was heavy. "Poor Aissla was attending the woodsman tonight. He must have awoken while she was dressing his wounds. A shame. She only wanted to help the poor fool."

"Woodsman?"

"Yes, yes," the woman answered as two men removed Aissla's body and brought her into the woods to prepare a burial site. "He came here some time ago—"

"I need to see him," she cut in.

The woman eyed her shrewdly. "I don't like your tone."

"I'm sorry. But it's important."

The woman's face curled unhappily. "More important than the sudden death of a caretaker? Very well, impatient one. This way."

The old woman led her to a nearby house, which was the largest one Kitalla had seen in the village. They went inside, the woman nattering the whole way. "First Felluria died, but I think her heart just gave out, the poor soul. Then he was moved back to her house and his wounds were dressed the best we could. Presh, our best healer, was the first one to die while tending the woodsman's wounds. He was changing the bandages, cleansing the wounds with water and herbs, then setting new dressings in place. But the woodsman's eyes fluttered open and then something happened to Presh's hands. The man hadn't moved, yet Presh's fingers were gone and he was bleeding out surely as Aissla died tonight."

They were inside the house and four men stopped them from walking down the narrow hallway to the woodsman's room. "He is awake. Now is not the time. Turn back."

"No," Kitalla said, and the fire in her eyes dared them to challenge her.

"We wish no others to die tonight because of this intruder."

"Boys," the old woman crooned from behind Kitalla. "There is no way you can actually stop her, you realize. Better she face him and find her fate like Felluria, Presh, Jerrisha, Veldi, Morv, and now Aissla."

Kitalla hesitated for a moment. "You've lost that many to him, yet he lives? Why try to heal him? Why haven't you killed him instead?"

"We can't," one of the men answered. "Nor can we move him from here."

"Show me."

They stepped aside and allowed Kitalla to pass, after which they pulled away from the woodsman's door, in fear of what would happen next. Lost limbs and broken weapons might be the least of their worries, especially after what he had done to the mountainside.

Kitalla stepped forward cautiously, fighting a rising fear within her. The jades in her pocket throbbed maniacally and she knew already who the woodsman was. Still, as she crossed the threshold and saw him lying there, she gasped.

"Gabrion!"

His face and torso were badly bruised, with numerous bandages scattered around the room, some of them actually on his wounds. Pools of blood dripped off his hip and leaked onto the floor. Kitalla could see the trail of blood that had followed Aissla as she fled the room after being cut by this man. But she didn't see any weapons nearby at all, just debris.

"Gabrion," she repeated, stepping closer.

"Go away," he breathed, his voice ragged and heavy with pain.

"Gabrion, it's me. It's Kitalla."

He closed his eyes and breathed again, "Go away."

Kitalla stepped forward slowly, reaching her hand out to him. "Gabrion."

"If you touch me," he warned, "you will die. Like all the rest."

She pulled back and looked around again. She could see dried patches of blood around the room, as well as broken swords and staffs. Some of the bedding was charred as if they had tried to light him on fire and hadn't succeeded. His exposed wounds were a couple days old, but they didn't seem infected, from what she could tell. "What happened to you?"

"Go away."

She stared at him for a few minutes, trying to digest it all. He was clearly wounded, but not just physically. Something had indeed tormented him and she guessed at its source. "Did you find her, Gabrion? Did you find Mira?"

The name summoned a terrible reaction. He howled in pain and thrashed about on the bed, his hand swiping through the air and catching the wall, tearing a gaping hole in it. His body trembled and thrashed for a time, until he eventually calmed himself, turning on his side and curling his knees up to his chest. All the while, tears streamed from his eyes.

Kitalla had never seen him cry. They had talked about it one evening, that when Mira had been captured, he swore he would never shed another tear until he found her. Now they poured from his eyes like the blood had drained from Aissla's body outside. She crouched down and lowered her head, feeling his anguish as it resonated with her own. He hadn't said it in words, but she understood that Mira was dead. Like her unborn child was dead. She didn't fight the tears this time. She let them fall and coat her hands, like she hadn't done since that time all those years ago.

One of the men in the antechamber stepped up to the doorway, fearing the worst. "Are you… all right?"

Kitalla turned her anguished face. "You may go," she whispered. "I will tend to him."

"But—"

"He is a friend," she explained. "I will tend to him."

Grudgingly, he turned around and Kitalla waited until the five sets of footfalls stepped outside the house. She breathed deeply and looked upon Gabrion, the protector.

"What happened, Gabrion? Talk to me."

He didn't respond, so she stood up and stepped closer, trying not to walk in the blood on the floor from the others who had died tending to him. "Go away," he murmured.

"After everything I went through to find you, that's not happening." Taking the last step away from his bed, she started to sit down.

Gabrion jumped away from her. "No! Don't touch me! You'll die like all the others."

She didn't know what to say. "I saw Aissla out there. Gabrion, how—? No, I know how. But why, Gabrion?"

He shook his head slightly. "Go away."

"I won't!" she yelled indignantly. "You're part of the team, Gabrion, and you will snap out of this and talk to me!"

She waited, but he didn't respond at all. "If you won't talk to me, then I'll make you talk."

"You can't do anything to me," he said, almost sadly. "So many have died because of me. You can't hurt me. But I can hurt you. Go away."

His body was tense, so she sat very still for a few moments, waiting for some of the tension to fade. With a deep, distracting sigh, she slid her hand over and placed it on his knee.

"No!" he screamed, pulling his leg away from her.

"Yes!" she insisted, moving closer to him. "You're being an idiot. Stop moving."

"You can't. Kitalla, no!"

She paused for a moment. "So you *do* know who I am then. Good. Then you'll also know that I'm going to win this one."

He shook his head. "…You'll die."

"After everything Grenthar put me through, *you're* certainly not going to be the one to kill me."

The words pierced through him and he wailed in agony. "No, don't."

Kitalla thought for a moment, then put it together. "I see, Gabrion. Then this punishment makes sense to you, doesn't it? You've gone from protector to someone who kills those trying to protect you. That's some penance you've thrust upon yourself. But don't you think it's a bit misguided? A bit foolish? There's a bigger task at hand here, you know. You can't be hiding here in denial, tormenting these pathetic villagers every night. It's not who you are."

"Kitalla, go… away."

"Make me!" she challenged. "Go ahead and try lopping off parts of me, like you've been doing to these people."

"I—I don't… mean to."

"Well you're obviously raw from some major hurt, and I'm here to wake you up. It can't be as bad as you think it is."

"I…" But he couldn't say the other two words to finish the sentence.

Her tone was sharp and prodding. "You what? Go on, Gabrion. Say it. What did you do?"

"I—no."

"Knock this off, silly farm boy," she sneered. "You think you've had it rough, do you? You think you've had pain? You don't have a clue. Stop cowering there like a witless waif. Get on your feet and let's continue our quest."

"Kitalla…"

"Gabrion," she replied sarcastically. "Fess up, boy."

"I can't."

"If you won't tell me, then I'll wrestle it out of you."

"No, you can't. If you touch me—"

"Ha!" Then, fully fearing that he was right but also believing in her past experiences, she grabbed his arms and tossed him to the floor.

Gabrion sprawled in a heap, sobbing. "Kitalla, no! Don't die!"

She looked at herself, but her hands were fine. No cuts. All ten fingers. Smug, she hopped onto the floor and jabbed her foot into his side. "Get up, idiot."

"Kitalla, you have to stop, before I—"

"Stop hedging," she demanded. "Say it!" For emphasis, she grabbed his torso and flipped him over.

He pounced to his feet. "Stop, before I kill you!" he shouted, after which he collapsed again.

"There, that wasn't so hard," she scoffed. "Now tell me what's really bothering you."

When he refused to answer, she dove at him again. This time he rolled away from her, desperate to avoid contact. She persisted, though, matching his feint and grabbing his wrists. He kicked a leg out toward her belly, but she avoided it, then she dipped low and flipped him over her shoulder, dropping him on his back with a thud. She didn't stop there. Twisting around, she grabbed his left arm and pulled it over his head, pinning it with her foot. He tried to roll away, but she grabbed his leg as it swept over and she yanked it upward and over his head, flipping him onto his stomach, trusting to his own skills to angle his neck to keep it from snapping.

"How?" Gabrion gasped. "How are you touching me without dying? How?"

Kitalla refused to answer his question. "Who else died, Gabrion? Who? Tell me."

"No, I can't."

"All right then." She geared up, taking a deep breath, and Gabrion knew her attacks were going to get worse.

But he didn't want to hurt her. He couldn't let her continue this battle. He didn't know why she hadn't been cut like the others, but it could happen at any moment. After all, hadn't the villagers been able to tend to some of his wounds, but not others? It had seemed so random, so out of his control.

Kitalla pounced for him, but he was ready. He sprang to his feet, entering a battle stance, eying the dagger Kitalla had at the ready. "That won't help you," he cautioned.

"I'll be the judge," she taunted, then jabbed at him. The blade cut through the air and Gabrion jumped backwards to avoid it, but Kitalla stepped in again. The room was small and there wasn't far for him to go before he hit the wall and she struck him.

Her dagger blade couldn't penetrate his skin; however, she had suspected as much. She could feel the dagger trembling, as if it wanted to shatter, but she knew that wouldn't happen either. Instead, the sharp blade banged against his skin and fell to the side like a wooden spoon. She tossed it when she recognized the bewilderment on his face, and she closed the distance between them, grabbing his shoulders and shaking him.

"Tell me!" she spat.

Everyone who had tried touching him had died... since that moment. Every weapon had shattered on impact with his body. Even the healers who were seeking to cure him felt the fury of his touch if he was awake. But he was awake now and Kitalla was shaking him to awaken him further. No one had been able to touch him. No one. Not since.... since...

"I... killed Mira." The words tumbled out of him and crashed upon their ears. His body trembled and shook, and he doubled over and started retching violently, spilling food to the floor. His keening wail pierced through the town, not unlike the cries he had unleashed as he had pounded against the mountain.

Kitalla crouched down and tucked his head into her lap. She stroked his hair tenderly, letting him unleash his pain into the air. All the while, tears streamed unchecked from her own eyes.

CHAPTER 12

The Siege at Marritosh

SEVERAL DAYS HAD passed since the mages had infiltrated Marritosh, wreaking havoc among the villagers. Ervinor was greatly weakened by the fighting, for even with the help of the healers, his body was still adjusting to its loss. He paced around his room, massaging his right shoulder. He thought he could almost feel the arm still there sometimes, and he knew he had to stop looking for it.

He didn't know if his agitation today was due to the people around him or his actions after the battle. He had murdered Farrenok to quell his words. But had he turned the mage into a martyr for others to rise behind? His closest advisors didn't think so. They had witnessed the interview and they agreed with the action he had taken.

Even Herchig had clapped Ervinor on the shoulder on his way out. "The enemy cut off your arm and you pressed harder to fight back. Now you have cut off a limb of this insurgence, but they may fall instead of rise. What you did may or may not have been right. But it was necessary for the goals of peace. In war, some sacrifices are needed. He was one who could not open his eyes to the ways of peace."

It irked Ervinor when Herchig didn't drown him in rambling, yet related, tales. "How does my action make me any better than the kings, Herchig?"

The old man grinned solemnly. "Indeed, how? It may not. But know this, young general: Someone needed to silence him, and it would not have been Dariak or the others, save maybe Kitalla. In this moment, where the battles increase across the land, where the jades are nearly assembled, decisive action is needed. Don't let it weigh on you, but also don't lose your humanity."

Ervinor had sighed then, and he sighed now. Most of the mages who had accompanied Farrenok had heard the details from their colleagues who had been in attendance, and they agreed that Farrenok had taken the wrong path to make himself heard. Only a few held true to Farrenok's vision.

"You'll kill us next, here where we stand," one of them had claimed.

"No, for I hope that you will see reason," Ervinor said. "Your friends have opened their eyes and it is my hope that you will too."

"In the end you'll kill us all. You'll wipe us out because we don't agree!"

"I'm no tyrant," the general had said. "You have your lives. What you do with them is yours. But ask yourselves: Does killing the people in this town fulfill you? If it's battle you want, take it to the front lines. Don't be underhanded by doing it here."

"What of your murder of Farrenok?" another had challenged.

"He committed a crime against your crown and he paid the penalty."

"What of your own crimes against our king?"

Ervinor had nodded his head slowly. "Indeed, we will be judged in our time too. For now, however, meditate on this: What is your goal for the world? What would you change in our lands if you could? How can you accomplish that in the best way? What defines your best way? Killing helpless civilians? Exerting your magical forces over those who cannot defend themselves? Or negotiating peacefully with your neighbor, even if he is your enemy? How would you achieve your goal?

"It is that which you must decide, each of you, for yourself. Then find those who are like-minded and band together with them. That's what brought me here. I seek a world where our two nations can stop the fighting and find a balance. If it means I must defend myself, then so be it. Yes, we marched upon the castle, but it was not our intention to fight. Our friend was attacked and we went in to assist him. Then we retreated here to lick our wounds." He gestured toward his missing arm.

"But now," he had continued. "Rest for a few days, then go back to your tower and consider my words, your actions, and what you see here. Decide your future and your fate."

However, two days after speaking to them, forces had arrived from the castle, and none of them had left yet.

A knock on the door interrupted his musing. "Come," he said officially.

The door opened and Frast entered. "Ervinor, it's time. And you're not dressed. Here, let me help." The mage persisted as he grabbed Ervinor's tunic and held it aloft for him. He then enwrapped the treated leather around the slim torso and fastened it tightly. He claimed various weapons and helped stash them in the numerous slots upon the tunic.

"What's the situation?" Ervinor asked as they made their way to Herchig's house.

"Grim," Frast said. "Farrenok's men aborted to the other side, as we thought they might, but they were assumed to be spies and were slaughtered outright."

"Fools," he muttered, and he didn't know if he meant the mages or the king's soldiers. "How are our defenses?"

"The northern walls are still holding, but only because of the mages who turned to your golden tongue. They have allied well with us and are keeping the archers from piercing through."

"Have any mages appeared yet? I expected them long before now."

"Only a few," Frast reported. "Strange that the king would send a hundred men to take this village, but not send the forces necessary to win."

Ervinor shook his head. "No, his army is spread too thin. Even with five thousand men, they are scattered along the border, they are protecting the castle, and they are patrolling the kingdom. He wouldn't have many to send here, mages least of all if he wishes to win the war."

"You sound like we're in a bad way."

"We are." They reached Herchig's house and entered. "Frast, relieve Quereth's team, if you will?"

"Yes, sir," he said, already planning to do just that.

Herchig and Nessaria welcomed him with a plate of food. "Keep up your strength, young master. Times are tight."

"Indeed." Ervinor nodded. "Herchig, have you any other advice for me?"

"I've told you before, lad, that now it's up to the young folk to fight. You've taken all the precautions you can with the town, and you managed to enlist the aid of some of the invading mages. I think, whatever happens, you've done well for us all."

"I feel like I'm trying to stop an hourglass. It's been, what, three days now? We've lost two dozen fighters already. They trickle in new reinforcements, but we have no allies to call in ourselves. The men are tired and soon it will all collapse."

Herchig tried to smile. "Well. There is only one thing to do when an hourglass runs out."

Ervinor nodded and rose to his feet. "Turn it over, start anew." He paused and then turned toward the door. "Thanks, Herchig."

"Ervinor!" the old man called out before the general stepped away. "When I was but a lad myself, my mama took us down to the sandy beach, far southwest of Magehaven. We played there for hours in the sun and burned our skin to a crisp. We scooped water out of the ocean and plied it to the sand, molding it and shaping it into castles and beasts, something quite fantastic. Ah, it was the most wonderful thing we ever could have done, even if it was more fantastic in our minds than in reality. It didn't matter. We worked on it as a team and we loved it. And then there was a disturbance in the ocean and the water washed up higher than before and it verily ate our castle away. Tore it right down in seconds. We were devastated by it, let me tell you. But though the water withdrew some of the sand, pulling it into the ocean, most of the sand was left behind. And you know full well what we did then. We pulled that sand together and built another castle, but with a nice trench for a moat!"

Herchig then met Ervinor's gaze and held it firmly. "You've come to know me well these months, Ervinor. You know what I'm telling you."

Ervinor set his jaw and closed his eyes for a moment, then he nodded sharply and stepped outside.

As he made his way toward the northern part of town, he passed various soldiers and issued new orders. They were perplexed with the change of assignment, but they acknowledged their general and heeded him well, passing the word along. He tried not to look at the townspeople that remained as he made his way to his army.

Frast and Lica waved their arms in unison with a dozen others, building a steady defensive barrier above the meager stone wall that was only waist high to keep out the sand creatures. The town was never meant to withstand a siege. As Ervinor looked through the shield, he could see the king's forces readying themselves for a unified strike. Archers were ever on alert, for if the magic barrier went down, they could reduce the numbers without much effort, but the longer the wall was up, the more exhausted the mages became.

"Frast!" Ervinor called out, and when the casting permitted it, the mage turned his role over to another.

"Yes?"

"That beast jade in your pocket. Have you had any luck with it?"

The mage shook his head. "Barely at all and I can't figure it out. I had great control over it in Magehaven, but after we reached here, my skill with it essentially vanished."

"I think Lica's theory may be accurate."

Frast nodded. "The energies in the tower itself let me tap into the jade, but also all the other spells I was using, and I agree that Dariak's jades probably kept this one active when we were bringing him back here."

"But if you've had no other success with it, then we can't count on it, can we?"

"I'm sorry."

"Be ready for new orders, Frast. Get Sparrow squad ready to move."

"Sir?"

"Just be ready." Ervinor then went off to Lica and gave the same warning. "Lica, be ready to let the Eagles fly."

"I don't like that look in your eye, but will do!"

He sent similar word to Nightingale and Wren, then he called the Ravens to meet with him. They gathered around closely, Carrus hinging on every word. "Ravens, we have a difficult task ahead and I need your commitment now or not at all."

After a brief explanation, Ervinor and his group moved into position. He then pulled his short sword from the scabbard on his back and he waited for a moment, peering again at the king's forces on the other side of the magical wall. They were still gathering together, but they weren't yet unified.

It had to be now.

He slashed his sword down through the air and four of his fastest runners sprinted to the leaders of the other four groups, delivering their new instructions; meanwhile, the other fifteen men and women gathered themselves into a battle stance, with the three mages in the back pulling spell components to hand.

Lica hurried over to Ervinor. "Are you mad?"

"Go! That's an order." He could see the denial in her eyes. "Do this, Lica. I need to know I can trust you to follow the instructions."

She growled at him. "Fine, but you owe me an ale and I intend to collect! Eagles, fall back!" She glared at Ervinor one last time and jogged off to the south, her troop falling in behind.

Sparrow, Nightingale, and Wren all left the front line and the defensive barrier collapsed with a pop. The king's army was startled, but they responded quickly. Arrows launched through the air, but so did responding fireballs and ice darts. Ervinor and his battalion raced forward, every weapon flailing with each fighter up against five or six others. He didn't care about the odds. This wasn't meant to be a victorious battle.

Screams filled the air as swords collided and sparks flew. Ervinor dove forcefully, keeping as much focus on himself as he could, for he only had one fight left in him right now. This fight. This one way to turn the tide back in their favor.

He felled three fighters, taking only minor damage himself. His sword swept in a frantic pace, and he glanced around, seeing his troops fighting with as much passion. Carrus's face was blood red from the exertion, his body pumping hard with each swing of his long sword and parry with his shield. He clobbered foe after foe, like in the battle against the mages. The arrows raining from the sky targeted him and he took two of them in his left shoulder. He paused only to yank the projectiles out, then continued his fight as a nearby mage swept her hands around and sent healing toward him.

The surprise attack only gave them a short bonus, and soon the king's army came together as a stronger force, ready to subdue these traitors and insurgents. The casualties mounted and when Ervinor looked around, nearly half of his team had already been defeated.

"Fall back!" he called out, bringing his fighters together inside the boundary of the village. The king's guard had already succumbed to the defensive traps in the town on their first foray three days earlier. Most of the traps had not been reset and, even if they had, Ervinor knew they wouldn't be of much use now. As his battalion clustered closer together, the arrows fell more heavily upon them. Some of his fighters had shields and they came together, hoisting them overhead and blocking the deadly rain.

There wasn't much time left for them, but they needed to keep the king's men distracted a little while longer. The plan would fail if they fell now. He looked left and right and whistled. His team broke into two halves and they sprinted a few lanes into the town and then scattered and hid behind the nearest houses, taking a quick respite from the battle.

Laughter echoed in the air, and Ervinor hated it. The king's commander mocked them for cowering. Their hiding place wasn't even well concealed. A fireball flew into view and Ervinor's team dropped down to avoid the brunt of the explosion. More laughter followed. At last, the commander grew tired of waiting, and he rushed his forces in to kill the rest of the Marritosh defenders.

Ervinor grabbed a tripwire and pulled it sharply. The poisoned wire cut into the legs of three warriors, knocking them down while the poison worked to stun them. The mages launched their own projectiles, as fighters drew bows and let poison-tipped arrows fly. It reminded Ervinor of the War of the Colossus. But he hadn't broken any codes of war using poisoned arrows. The Hathrens would simply brand him as an evil general. Yet once he was dead, he wouldn't much care about his title.

Eighty fighters broke into view and Ervinor launched several daggers and poison darts before returning to his sword. Already, his body protested the excitement. He hated feeling so weak all the time. He had to really concentrate, to focus his thoughts on parrying the attacks that were coming toward him, and dodging others nearby.

Carrus went down, Ervinor noted, though he couldn't tell how bad the damage was. There were only six others fighting with him now. It was coming to an end soon. He was determined to be the last one to fall, so he pushed onward, growling in rage and screaming when an ax sliced into his side. It wasn't deep and he rushed on, thrusting his sword into the wielder's face. Another sword swept in, and he dodged to the side, losing his balance. The weapon would have cut his right arm, so he was spared another wound, and as he toppled over from the move, he gashed the man's leg.

"Get up!" he yelled at himself, as his equilibrium opted to play tricks on him. His vision swam dizzily, like landing in the ocean and not knowing where to find the surface. His legs knew the ground, so he trusted them and pushed upward, bringing his sword around.

A hand reached out and grabbed him, dragging him back down. "Ervinor, look out," Carrus moaned, making one last move before pain overwhelmed him.

The general couldn't see what Carrus was talking about, but he heard the enemy commander yell in panic. The air filled with a terrible crackling noise and Ervinor rubbed his eyes, trying to see. Light blinded him but he also felt a swelling heat. Stabbing the earth with his sword, Ervinor pushed himself onto his feet, then prepared to run to the nearest enemy and slay him.

But there was no need. Before him, the town was ablaze and the king's forces were trapped in the center of it. The northern-most houses had been lit first and then the flanking homes and now these. Horrific screams cried out as men and women were overpowered by the conflagration, their bodies consumed by the flames.

A few escaped the fire and Ervinor and his fighters cut them down. "Ravens, rally!" Ervinor gasped. "Check... survivors."

His one remaining mage ran over and loaded him with whatever healing spells she could, then she tended to Carrus and two others who were hurt but still alive. They worked swiftly, for the neighboring buildings were catching the blaze and adding more and more power to the heat. The eight remaining members of the Ravens dragged themselves from Marritosh, heading solemnly to the west to rejoin the other four battalions who had been ordered away.

Just beyond the border of dying Marritosh, Ervinor paused and faced the inferno. "Bless you, Herchig. This sandcastle may have fallen, but I will secure you another. I'll reset the hourglass. Somehow. Farewell, dear friend."

CHAPTER 13

Solitude

GABRION AWOKE AND gazed around his room. It felt different and some part of him wasn't sure why. Then he remembered; Kitalla had been there and she had touched him.

Despite himself, Gabrion cracked a slight smile, but then banished it from his lips. He had no cause for celebration. Sure, he was relieved to see Kitalla, but he had caused so much harm for the village and the people around him that he doubted he would ever have the right to smile again.

His emotions wavered but he decided to get up and try to do something to help the people he had harmed. He made his way out of Felluria's house, keeping his mind focused on his goal. Kitalla was in another room, and he realized that if he sought her out, he might not do anything else. Slipping from the house, Gabrion ventured into the town.

He knew he wasn't welcome here and the people shied away from him in fear that he would come closer. It didn't matter; they needed help and he was capable of giving it. He hoped.

"Does anyone need wood?" he called out. "Does anything need to be dismantled? Broken down? Does something need to be moved? Please, anyone, let me help."

"You could help by getting yourself out of this place!" shouted one irate villager. It wasn't an unexpected taunt.

He heard the sound of chopping in the distance and so he made his way toward the noise. A young man held an ax in his hand and he hacked away at a set of logs, breaking them into usable pieces.

"I could assist you," Gabrion offered.

The youth jumped nearly out of his skin in fear when he saw the warrior. "I— I'm fine."

"Really, with the two of us working together, we could get this job done in no time at all." He stepped forward, not wanting to take no for an answer.

The villager pounced aside so as not to come too close to Gabrion, and he glanced nervously over his shoulder, checking for some form of escape from this situation. "I think I hear my sister calling me."

"Come, let's tackle this together first." He stepped forward and measured an approximate foot of length on the larger log. "Is this a good length?"

"Uh… s—sure."

"Good. You work on that one and I'll handle this," he said in the most helpful tone he could muster. Then, with a chop from the side of his hand, he sliced into the wood. No ax was needed for the jade-empowered warrior. He repeatedly brought his hand down like a hatchet, making the dent grow larger and larger in the process. Two dozen strokes later and the log was separated.

He turned around to see if the young man approved, only to find that he was alone and the ax lay abandoned on the ground. Gabrion closed his eyes, putting himself in the villager's shoes, and he admitted that he probably would have run, too.

So many people had tried to help him and they had perished because of the magical cuts he made. He deserved the isolation from them all. Perhaps it was a mistake Kitalla had found him.

He had interrupted the youth's chores and sent him skittering away in terror. Maybe he was watching from a window or cowering under a bed. It didn't much matter. Gabrion decided to finish the original task and he reduced the tree trunk down to the same size the villager had already been making before his intrusion. It took a fraction of the time with much less exertion than whiling away with the ax.

Gabrion sat and pounded his fist into the soil. He didn't know what to do with himself. He hated feeling such sorrow. He didn't know how to be a positive force anymore.

Growing up in Savvron had been so easy compared to life now. His father had pushed him hard to labor well, building strong muscle tone even as a young lad. Terrsian had been raised as a farmer, passing his skills to his son, and Gabrion had excelled. He had a natural gift with the soil, almost as if he sensed when its nutrients needed time to rest, or which berries would take seed based on the amount of rain he sensed in the air.

Tilling the land had been hard work, loosening the soil and turning it over, ensuring he had dug deep enough until the dirt was damp. They had done well with the food they produced and were well-respected among the villagers, but they never would have amassed much wealth.

Gabrion remembered lamenting one summer that other farms had better plows and beasts to pull them, yet they were doing the work by hand. His father had claimed that the better goods were managed by a man's sweat and tears and he had simply refused to improve their equipment.

At first, Gabrion hated Terrsian for his obstinacy and he had stormed off, wanting to run away to some better place. Yet as he lay in bed that night, he heard his father talking to his mother, his voice heavy with sorrow that they simply couldn't afford the things Gabrion wanted. She had tried to console him, offering to speak to their son about the situation, but in the end there was no need, for Gabrion now understood the truth.

He had pushed himself after that, striving to make his father proud, trying to help them earn enough profit to make their lives easier. It was grueling, but Gabrion bent himself to the task.

He had also always wondered why he was an only child when most farmers bore a host of helpers for their fields. This, too, he overhead one night when his mother was upset that she was unable to supply Terrsian with any other children.

No, Gabrion was meant to work alone.

He lifted his gaze from his reverie as he examined the logs he had cut with his bare hands. It felt so empty now. He barely exerted himself as he cut the pieces apart and wasn't even honing his muscles in the process. He never strained himself or struggled for breath. The jade took all of that away.

Just as it had helped him to take Mira away.

The truth was all around him; he truly was meant to work alone. Now, he only needed to convince Kitalla of that and then send her on her way. Feeling defeated, Gabrion stepped away from the chopped wood and he wandered aimlessly along the outskirts of town until eventually he found his way back to Felluria's, where he sank down in his room and let the sorrow overwhelm him.

CHAPTER 14

Astrith's Decree

RANDLER AND DARIAK were detained in the forest for a couple of days while the elder decided their fate. He had seemed willing to talk to them, then release them on their way, but once he discovered Dariak's lineage, things had changed for the worse.

Dariak was distraught at the stories of his father's conquest of the forest people and of the theft of their jades in the process. Whether he had come himself or sent minions to do the work, it didn't much matter to the mage. It was hard for him to accept a tarnished view of his beloved father, the one man who had truly and unconditionally loved him.

Randler tried soothing Dariak's woes with stories and songs, but he also learned that sometimes it was best to leave the mage alone with his thoughts. Not everyone needed a tune to get through their pains.

They had some freedom to walk around the village, but they were always accompanied by three men each, some of whom they had battled during their attempts to enter the forest. This gave the guards an advantage, for they had seen the two prisoners act as a team and had witnessed some of the variety of their skills. Even if Dariak was in his right mind at the moment, they would have a difficult time of escaping.

But their first priority would be to reclaim the jades. They had laid them out in the open for Astrith to see. It was something Dariak had insisted upon before their meeting. Any secrets they kept would mark them as enemies of these people, whereas forthrightness might get them through unscathed.

Each morning, they were escorted to the bath, where they were expected to cleanse themselves of the previous day. Dariak complied, for resistance would only make things worse, not that he could imagine how. His father... his father.

In the midafternoon of their fourth day, the mage and the bard were summoned before the forest leader. Astrith sat on his log, clothed only in vines that wrapped around him, concealing little. Two women were similarly dressed, flanking him.

"I have considered your quest and I am undecided," he announced. "You claim a man has passed through this realm and that his actions are housed in danger. It is true that a man of power did pass this way some time ago, but his energy was that of healing."

"Pyron has the healing jade," Dariak said. "But his intentions—"

"I have not invited you to speak," Astrith interrupted. "You are impulsive and you do not honor the forest with your ways. You are the son of the man who disrupted our way of life, and though we have come to build our own rapport with the forest, it was a difficult process. Some creatures of the wood were weakened and perished forever, whereas others grew stronger and overtook parts of the woodlands. Whether it was all the will of the forest remains to be seen."

He waited as the two attending ladies lowered the trays in their hands. "These are your pieces of jade, as you can see. I have communed with them the best I can, and I see that they resonate with you to some degree. This, however, does not alone give credence to your claim."

Dariak tried not to frown, but he failed.

"No, the energies within could resonate with you for many reasons. They could sense power in you and wish to channel it to their purpose. We cannot know their reasoning."

"You speak as if they are alive," Randler couldn't help saying.

"Indeed, for in some way they are and they are not. There is a tale in this land that connects these jades. It is one you have heard, I can tell, for your words have echoed through the trees. Your tale of the Forgotten Tribe is that story."

The bard's eyes shot up. "But it's only a legend. A fable, meant to give us hope in some power yet to be known."

"Almost," Astrith agreed. "You have sung with emotion when your lips share this song. The errant love between King Kallisor and Lady Hathreneir. Their children: one dead, the other who ran away. Yet you say little of the rest of Kallisor's descendants. You focus only on the one. And that one is the ancestor of your Forgotten Tribe."

"It is true, the king had numerous descendants," Randler commented. He had said as much to Kitalla one night along their journey. "But their tales are not told."

"Indeed, for their lines have all ended. But not the one line. It has still continued, despite all."

Dariak joined in, "Have you any idea who is a member of that line?"

"Not precisely, no. But there are many lines that branch off, and it is possible that more than one descendent remains now." He eyed the both of them critically. "I see hope in your eyes, but it is unlikely to be either of you, for the originator was the king of Kallisor himself, and even if his child ran from him, the nobility would be in his line. I believe neither of you has any noble blood."

Dariak's father had been a prominent mage and worked closely with the king of Hathreneir, but he hadn't been a nobleman. "We are not."

"No," Astrith echoed. "What you seek is that descendant now."

Dariak was growing impatient. "We seek to assemble the jades, to bring their power together and to stop the war."

"Ah, but the forest has told me, as the one who sees, that your task cannot be completed without the heir to the Forgotten Tribe."

Randler, who knew the lore the best, was crestfallen. "But how can we even find him?"

"True, you may not be able to seek the person out directly, but I feel you will be brought together in the end."

"Like the jades," Dariak muttered. "They too are drawing together, despite our actions."

Astrith's face went grim. "Indeed. You have done well to claim this set of shards, but more remains ahead of you."

"Will you return the jades to us so we may continue our journey?"

"Not yet, but nor can you remain here." Astrith eyed them both cautiously. "Since your arrival, the forest creatures have gone on the offensive. We have been put to task to fend against them. We will do so as needed, but I regret the loss of the beasts."

"They are drawn to the jades," Dariak explained. "Return them to us and we will depart your wood immediately. Things will return to normal for you."

"Will they?" the older man wondered. "A fanciful suggestion, but I am still not ready to relinquish them to you. No, your father did a greatly evil deed to our land and so I must challenge your resolve to set things right."

"There isn't time," the mage said.

"Impatience will be your undoing."

"What is this challenge?" Randler asked, determined to keep things civilized.

"Your goal is to leave the forest and seek this mage, and so you shall. I will permit you to depart."

"What's the catch?" Dariak asked.

"You will go without any objects and you must make your way by communing with the forest and utilizing it without harming it. If you so reach the western edge of the wood, my followers will return your belongings, including these," he added, motioning to the jades.

"Without any objects?" Randler asked. "No weapons to defend ourselves?"

"No weapons, no clothing, no food. You will walk into the woods as a babe. Whether you emerge as men, only your actions will tell. You may leave at any time within the next three days, for if you wait any longer, I fear we will not be able to hold off the creatures."

"Why bother with this, then?" Dariak asked, frustrated. "Trust the jades and—"

Astrith rose to his feet. "I have decreed, and you will obey. I suggest you rest well tonight and feast as fully as possible before you leave. You will be protected within the confines of this place, but when you are ready to embark upon this quest, you must shed all material belongings and venture forth."

Astrith didn't wait for a response. He walked away, leaving them to consider their options, which weren't many. If they did not accept his challenge, then they would need to locate the jades and steal them back, but finding them would be difficult without the resonance of a shard to guide them. They could head back to Marritosh for Frast's jade, but because it was the beast jade, they worried that Astrith would claim it for his clan.

In the end, they knew their target lay to the west, and they needed to meet the elder's task head on, while respecting the forest along the way. They resigned to leave early the next day, right after the morning meal. It would mean they wouldn't have to hunt until later in the day, and if the forest held fruit and proper herbs, then that would be even better. They returned to their hut and curled up in each other's arms, needing the extra support before the next part of their journey.

CHAPTER 15

The Anguish of Life

KITALLA REMAINED WITH Gabrion in Jortun, trying to convince him to continue his journey. Their reunion had been painful, and they spoke little in the days that followed. Kitalla remained able to touch the warrior, but no other villagers dared to try. She tended his wounds and ensured he ate properly, hoping she would succeed soon.

"You must be terribly bored," she said one afternoon. "The people won't talk to you, and you don't do much but meditate in your room."

"If you're restless, then return to the others."

"You're not getting rid of me that easily, Gabrion. Come on, we made a break-through. But you haven't told me any more than that. How long will it take until you to break your silence?" She teasingly poked him in the ribs.

"I can't rejoin the quest. All I do is cause pain." His head drooped low and Kitalla responded by rolling her eyes.

"Wallow, wallow, wallow." She shoved him hard and he nearly fell off his chair. "I know I can't reason with you about this. But whatever it takes to convince you to move, I will do it."

He turned to face her. "Like what, dance and make me see ponies galloping in a meadow?"

Her face lit with excitement. "Yes! That's perfect! And we'll have a picnic, and the bunnies will sing songs while the squirrets play a game of catch."

Gabrion shook his head. "Crazy."

"You started it. But it's what we're reduced to while we sit here staring at each other."

"Then go do something."

"I can't," she said. "Gabrion, you picked the most remote, boring town in all the world. After I spoke to two people, I knew everything this town knows. They have no reports on the war. No philosophy about which side should win, which is insane because we're in Kallisor. They don't even have good recipes for honey buns."

Gabrion snorted a laugh. "You're ridiculous."

"Well, you were apparently having fisticuffs with a mountain, so you'd be the authority on ridiculous."

His smile diminished. "Every time you make me laugh, you go back to that."

"Until you come back with me, you're right. I am going to keep asking about your pain."

He slammed his fists on the table. "What of you? What about the times you've been quiet and aloof? What of your pain? What is it you're hiding, Kitalla?"

Her face went stone cold. "I may be mysterious with you at times, but it's what got me to where I am today. What am I hiding? I won't tell you. Not like this. Not now."

"Then why should I tell you anything either?" he growled.

"Because you always talked about your feelings. And bottling them up now is making your jade lash out at the people around you."

He blinked. "Everyone but you."

She sighed. "Gabrion, it's no mystery. The metal jade is keeping me whole when you would otherwise destroy me. I thought you would have figured that out by now."

He hadn't. He was so consumed in his own hurt, he hadn't even tried to understand. "That—I see. How did you know it would work?"

She shrugged carelessly. "I didn't."

He smirked, despite himself. "But you risked yourself anyway."

"Yes, Gabrion. Because—" She stopped herself and tried to find the right words. "Because you're dear to me. I have come to rely on you in ways I shouldn't. And it isn't just me; it's Dariak, Randler, even Ervinor and Frast. We've all rallied behind you, but you don't even realize it."

He scoffed. "You rally behind Dariak and his quest for the jades."

"No," she said softly. "You know full well that we each joined this mission for our own purposes. Dariak wanted to unite the jades. Randler wanted to bury them. Ervinor, Ordren, Lica, Frast, and Quereth all wanted a new way of being. I wanted to gain more power so no one could challenge me again. And you, Gabrion, your own quest was for Mira." She ended there purposely and watched him sink into his chair.

"Then my quest is done. She is… gone."

Kitalla touched his shoulder tentatively. "I don't agree. You sought her out of love and devotion, but all the while, you strove to end the needless fighting that had taken her from you in the first place. And you never lost yourself along the way."

"Just the once, Kitalla. But it was enough. I am no longer… me."

She waited, hoping he would continue but he fell silent again. "Tell me," she prompted in a whisper.

"I can't."

Kitalla rose out of her chair and she stood close to him, not sure what to do. She needed him to be strong for her. She had come to rely on his prowess and his focus. Seeing him this way was painful. Yet there was something else even more painful deep in her heart.

She had come to know him as the protector and during their stay in Savvron she realized she had fallen in love with him. His bullheaded quest may have been cause for ridicule from her, but his devotion had touched her soul. He pursued Mira relentlessly, despite the odds against finding her. And apparently he had reached her at last. He admitted to having killed her, and his reaction had been so violent she didn't doubt its truth.

What shook her deep down now was, how could she still love him for his devotion to complete his task of rescuing Mira when he himself had ended the journey by killing her? How could he still hold her heart captive if he couldn't be trusted to protect it? What if he turned on her next? What if this was something that was twisted inside of him, maybe some side-effect of dealing with Heria, or being ripped from his stable life to join the adventure? What if he was shattered inside and she would find herself his next unwitting victim, like these helpless villagers who had only tried to mend him?

It was why she needed to know what happened. She had to understand what could have caused him to betray Mira so completely. It had to make sense. It couldn't just be some glitch inside of him. She needed to know, at any cost.

Her decision made, Kitalla took one of Gabrion's hands in her own and she placed it upon her belly. At first he twitched to pull away, but she persisted and he succumbed.

"When I was about sixteen, I fell in love," she whispered. Her whole being shook, barely believing she was going to say this out loud. It took more courage for her to continue than it had facing any of Grenthar's tortures. "He was a nobleman, Joral, maybe a year older than I was. My mother was against it. She served the mayor of Wroque. He was a vile little man, but she needed the job... for me."

She cleared her throat and continued, in the same voiceless breath. "Joral and I were a perfect match. We both knew we were right all the time and we both loved trying to convince each other of that fact. Every fight ended passionately. Then one day he proposed.

"My mother was against it," she repeated. "She would have killed him, if she could. But I hadn't told her about the engagement right off. Not until..." She tightened her grip of Gabrion's hand as it pressed against her belly.

"The months passed and my pregnancy started to show. The mayor wanted me, to..." But she didn't say it aloud. "My mother wouldn't have it, and we decided to run off. Joral came too. Mother fell shortly after we left. I defended us. I killed the guardsmen who slew my mother. My first kill."

She shuddered as the memories swirled in her mind, so recently stirred by her Trial in Magehaven over two months ago; memories she had suppressed for nearly ten years. "Joral and I, we ran. We eluded the mayor's guards for months. Then I was too burdened down by our child and we were caught."

Her grip tightened further but Gabrion made no motion to pull away. "The mayor was there. We were pinned against the trees. He... had his way with me, with my child floating around inside of me. Joral was forced to watch. He tried... he tried to save me. But he wasn't strong enough. The mayor retaliated.

"There was nothing I could do to defend myself. There was nothing Joral could do either. The mayor took one of my own daggers and then stabbed me here." She squeezed his hand tighter. "He killed my baby. Then Joral. He had his guards bandage me up, to make sure I carried my dead son to term."

She took a deep breath. "I don't know where I channeled the strength, for I was so terribly weak. But I killed them all right there. I threw my daggers. I stabbed the ones I only knocked down. And I drove a dagger into each of the mayor's eyes."

There was a pause. "I should have gone insane that day. Maybe I did. I don't really know. But I swore I would never be defenseless again. I would find ways to protect myself from harm. Soon after my son was buried, I started training. And during that time, I discovered my dance skill. I blocked the pain of my past deep within myself. I used it to power everything I've done since then.

"Only recently was I forced to go through all of this again. Those Trials. I hurt all over again every day. It's like those first days... after. The wounds are raw and they threaten to tear me apart."

She swallowed. "But then I see you, Gabrion. I see the way you stand tall. The light in your eye. I always knew you were on a mission of love for someone else, that it could never be me, but I fell in love with you anyway.

"I promised to help you find her," she remembered. "Back in Gerrish. I wasn't able to be there with you when you met. Had I been there, it would have been different."

Gabrion's voice cracked. "No. It would have been the same." He hesitated, but continued. "She had secretly been trysting with the king of Hathreneir while she and her family were on sojourn to visit her brother's grave. I never had a clue. That day in Savvron, she was whisked away by her knight. Well, by a servant of her knight. They were reunited permanently; they wed. She was happy, Kitalla. So very happy with her life. Everything about her radiated joy."

He pulled his hand from her grasp so he could rub his face tersely. "She had to understand that it was all based on a lie. I had to make her see that I was there for her, to save her. She had to know that the battle in Savvron was no farce, that people died. But she didn't want to see it. She blotted it out of her mind like it never happened."

He rubbed his hands on the table, clutching into the wood. "Then... I went back in to make her see reason, to understand. The jade made me impervious to the king's guard. I simply went through the throne room and showed the king he couldn't stop me. He brought me to her, so I could see her once again. Mira. But she was distraught when she saw me. She was supposed to be overjoyed, not impatient. And then I knew why.

"Behind her, there was a baby boy. He was hers and the king's. And I was so hurt. Devastated. Crushed. I lashed out at her—not with a sword. I insulted her. I said such horrible, terrible things. And then she came over to strike me. That was when it happened."

His head sank down. "As her hand struck my face, it shattered. Her hand was just gone. She fell, bleeding. The wounds were so sharply cut by the glass jade that even the mages could not heal her. I tried to lift her up, but I cut her again and made her end come even faster."

He turned his face up to Kitalla's and he realized that she felt as exposed as he did. "She was my reason for this quest. She was everything I strove for, and I killed her. I killed her because she did not love me back."

Kitalla dragged him out of his chair and wrapped herself around him. He responded in kind. "We're not meant for happiness, maybe," she said. "But I'm tired of hurting, Gabrion."

He held her tightly for a while, then pulled away and looked into her eyes. "I can't love you."

"I know," she breathed.

"I can't protect you."

"I know." Before he could speak again, she pressed her lips to his, fully expecting him to push her away. Yet he pursued her. He tightened his grip and his lips crashed passionately against hers.

Their souls were already bared. It wasn't long before their bodies were, too.

CHAPTER 16

Magehaven Revisited

WITH MARRITOSH REDUCED to cinders and no allies left in Hathreneir, Ervinor made the only decision he could. They had to return to Magehaven and somehow seek asylum.

The journey to the tower was difficult for the troop, for they had lost many friends in the town, and they were escorting hundreds of unhappy villagers. Ervinor kept two of his five battalions on alert at all times, and they dealt with the beast attacks when they occurred. Luckily, there were few actual incidents with the creatures of Hathreneir. The villagers, however, were another matter.

Most of the townspeople of Marritosh had thrown their lot in with Ervinor's forces, but not all. Numerous families had held their devotion to the king, praying for his victory against the Kallisorian forces and finding peace through domination. Those villagers were angry with the destruction of their home, feeling the troops should have surrendered themselves and left the village quietly.

Brawls broke out randomly as the competing factions came into contact with each other, and Ervinor was forced to assign a third battalion to quell the disquiet. There, he cycled through the five groups to maintain alertness on the trek to the southwest.

It took nearly five days for the enlarged group to make the journey, mostly because the complacent villagers refused to push through the trek. This too led to many arguments among the people, but Ervinor always intervened and ensured the villagers that everyone would reach the tower safely if only they would stop the infighting.

"We're here," Frast said at last, and Ervinor couldn't help sighing aloud. "How will we do this?"

The invisible barrier surrounded the tower and Ervinor stood inches away from it, wondering about the consequences if they all passed through. He knew about the Trials from his companions, but if three hundred people crossed the border, would the mages be able to endure the flood?

He was grateful for the interruption to his musing. An acolyte appeared at the entrance to the tower. "What is the meaning of this invasion?"

Ervinor bowed low and spoke clearly. "Forgive us, great mage, but we are in need of shelter."

The woman eyed the large group and she had no idea how to react. "You can't storm in here and take us over, even if there are mages among you. We are strong enough to defeat you, should you try."

She was clearly worried and bluffing, Ervinor assessed. "We intend no harm. Only shelter."

"I can't grant you that!"

"Is there someone within who can?"

She bit her lip and tugged at her reddish hair. "Wait there, and I mean that!" Then she disappeared inside the tower.

Lica approached Ervinor. "I don't think we're going to be allowed in."

"It doesn't matter if she is afraid. Someone will see that even they can't turn us away."

Lica shrugged. "Sometimes you sound like Gabrion. But times like this, you sound like Dariak."

"What does that mean?"

She grinned. "It means I can take a bath tonight."

Moments later, one of the Council members emerged from the tower, his body covered in so many protective enchantments, even Ervinor could sense them. He was an older man with an unkempt mess atop his head and hanging from his chin. His robes were a mustard yellow, signifying his dominance with the electrical magic drawn from the similarly colored lightning jade. Unlike other masters, he bore no secondary colors or imagery, suggesting he dabbled only in the one school of magic.

"Greetings, friend," Ervinor bowed again.

The old man eyed the general suspiciously. "I am Vinnek and this is not the first time you stand at our door."

It was true, for Ervinor had accompanied Dariak and the others on their first visit. "Yes," he answered, "though I have not entered your halls myself."

"And why would you attempt entry now? Surely you understand that your comrades wreaked havoc here."

Ervinor knelt. "I ask not for myself, good sir, but for your own people. With us"—he signaled over his shoulder—"are the survivors from Marritosh. Surely you saw the blaze in the nighttime sky; it burned for two days without rest. These villagers were cast from their homes and require a place to stay, temporarily, so they can gather themselves and then venture out to start anew."

A skeptical eyebrow raised. "I believe all of Hathreneir saw the destruction of the village, for it was a grievous loss to our liege. How are we to know that you didn't set the blaze yourselves and that you don't intend to do the same here?"

He had anticipated a rejection and was ready with a response. "There are some of us from Kallisor here and we are allied to the ones who visited you recently. If we're unwelcome, then we'll camp in the sand. However, there are two hundred men, women, and children whose only crime was living in Marritosh while we were there. Give them shelter and compassion, for their homes were destroyed and they had no say in these events."

"Compelling," the old man said. "I have little authority here, but that barely matters today, for our greatest members have disbanded." He paused.

Ervinor waited for a time and then realized that he was supposed to explain something. "Farrenok and his companions came to Marritosh to tear it down. We held them off. Farrenok is dead, by my hand. His closest followers died at the hands of the king's men. The rest have joined me, at least for this journey back to their home. I will not speak for their commitment beyond this excursion, but you may question them."

The old man's nose twitched. "Farrenok was a close-minded fool, immature and motivated by personal growth. His death means little to me personally, but I would speak with the others." He deliberated for a moment. "Very well. We will allow entrance to Hathrens only, but they will be confined to the first level. Anyone who ventures to any other area will be decreed an enemy and will be killed on the spot. We will need some time to make arrangements. The rest of you will remain out here until we can better determine your purpose."

"Fair enough." Ervinor bowed his head, disappointed not to gain full access from the start. The old man staggered back inside, after which five mages emerged to keep an eye on the people.

Lica frowned. "I was wrong. No bath for me tonight. I thought for sure we would be able to enter."

He smiled. "Then I channeled Gabrion today, you're saying? I can't blame them for being cautious but at least they are compassionate enough to accommodate their countrymen." He then set his commanders to the task of sorting the families from the rest so their entrance into the tower would be as smooth as possible.

It took three hours for the mages to make preparations to admit the citizens, but eventually they all went in. Each person passed one of a dozen mages who cast some sort of spell, which they claimed would signal out anyone from Kallisor.

"Nonsense," Quereth grumbled later that evening. "There is no such spell to find a person's origin."

Ervinor was gathered around a small fire with Lica, Frast, and the old mage. "Perhaps they've discovered some special magic here, like that life force spell you encountered before."

"No," Quereth persisted. "That spell was a combination of healing and lightning magic, if you break it down. The healing magic tapped into the bloodstream and the lightning magic caused the light."

"Okay, I'll bite." Frast grinned. "How did they separate us from the mages who lived there?"

Lica shrugged. "Basic protection spell, taught to the mages who reside there for that purpose. It is a well-guarded secret and delivered to the others only by the Mage Council."

"How do you know that?" Frast wondered, impressed.

She smiled toothily. "While you were fawning over Randler, I was getting to know the mages inside. I may be a little older and weightier around the edges, but I still have my charms."

Frast's cheeks burned red; he didn't think anyone would have noticed his infatuation with the bard. He turned to Quereth. "You don't think they can tell a Kallisorian from a Hathren?"

The older mage sighed. "It would be impossible, really, even if they had a keen ear and listened for accents. No, I think they're enchanting them with some sort of barrier that will allow them to be found by that life force spell."

Ervinor shrugged. "I don't know why they would need it, if the mages are already protected against the spell."

"They could be setting it up with a different color to differentiate them from us," Lica ventured. "Or it could have nothing at all to do with the life force spell. To be honest, I couldn't really care. I did really want a bath tonight."

The others laughed and a warrior ran over to them, pausing until Ervinor acknowledged her. "Sir, Verna has asked for you."

"Is there trouble?"

"She said it was urgent." She waited until the general agreed, then returned to her post.

"What could it be?" Lica asked.

"It's too early for the Wrens to come off watch," Ervinor said, "so it's either fighting or something with the mages." He rose up and left the campfire.

Lica turned to the other two. "You know, I never thought to ask him why he gave us those names; Wren, Nightingale, Eagle, Raven, and Sparrow. Did any of you know he was a birdwatcher?"

Quereth chortled. "Hardly. He was just a grunt back in Pindington, but he was always a wise lad. I had a few run-ins with him there, but luckily nothing ever serious. He was certainly no birdwatcher, though. No, there is another reason for the names."

Frast tuned in intently. "Go on."

"Well, it's difficult for a general to know where all his men are at any given time, so why not name them so you can find them easily?" He gestured to Lica. "Don't your Eagles get assigned to the east?" He turned to Frast. "And your Sparrows go south. He knows where he assigned you because the names are based on compass points."

"And Raven," Frast guessed, "almost sounds like a spin on his own name."

Lica clapped her hands together. "I may have to start calling him 'Eravenor' to see if he responds."

Frast laughed. "I bet the Wrens are happier with that name than Warblers or Woodpeckers or something."

Lica agreed. "And yours could have been team Swallow."

"Yes, well, before we get lost in all the bird names we can think of," Quereth interjected, "perhaps we should help set up some enchantments for tonight?"

"Of course." Frast beamed, shifting his gaze to Lica, "we wouldn't want to have any Egrets."

"I'm too old for this," Quereth grumbled.

"Yeah, I thought you were going to retire from this fighting business?" Lica asked.

He nodded slowly. "It is true. I know I promised Dariak I would follow him, but we've been so long without him that I wonder what work I'm really doing right now. And with everything we've seen here, all the fighting and the mad dashes we've had, I think I've gone past a point where I can really be helpful on the front line."

Quereth paused, staring off to where Ervinor had walked away. "But my life was about to end in that castle. That boy saved me, and it cost him his arm. So, I'm holding on for as long I can, at least until I can repay him. If that means leading one of his battalions, then so be it. My brain still works and so do my spells. However, once things quiet down…" He sighed wistfully.

"You saved his life, too," Lica offered. "He needed to push you out of the way because you had dropped all your offenses to heal him in that fight. I don't think he'll hold you to this task if you want to step down."

"He said the same to me, Lica. The difference is, he still paid a price." Quereth stretched and stood up. "Let's get those enchantments in place."

* * *

Ervinor made his way to the western edge of camp, where Verna waited for him. Most of the army was settled down for rest or sleep, but the members of Wren were stationed around them, keeping an eye out for beasts or invaders.

Verna was standing tall, her red hair fluttering in the evening breeze. It was mostly a tangled mess upon her head, and she often laughed that no matter how much she brushed it, it simply had a life of its own.

Born in Marritosh, Verna was raised as a warrior by her father, Vathros, who served in the king's army along the eastern border. He went to war because he had no choice, for if he had remained in the village, then the king would have demanded that Verna report in his stead. Most families didn't have that option, but Vathros had served Hathreneir well even during the War of the Colossus twenty-one years before.

In some ways, Verna was irrational. She would laugh one moment, but snap the next, yet Ervinor had come to know her during his time in Marritosh, and her outbursts were often justified. Perhaps she would benefit from more tact, but she was a smart fighter, strong and well-trained. Many of the villagers who had joined up in Marritosh needed the familiarity of someone like Verna, and of the fighters he had worked with during training, Ervinor felt she was the best choice to lead one of his battalions. Promoting her also gave her a sense of purpose again, for her mother had died years earlier, her siblings had either left or died, and guarding the town hadn't been particularly fulfilling.

He approached her slowly, trying to gauge her mood. "Verna," he said by way of greeting.

Her back was already ramrod straight, yet he swore she somehow straightened up more at his arrival. "Sir, the mages." She pointed needlessly ahead of her.

Ervinor watched as a team of nearly twenty mages swept and moved in practiced rhythms on their side of the mage barrier. He could hear muttered chanting in the air, but only another mage would have any chance of deciphering any of it.

Verna anticipated his request. "I had Nurial and Osso try to puzzle out what they're doing, but they had no idea." Then, just as quickly, her tone changed to the biting sting of a whip. "Leave it to mages to keep secrets."

"Surely you don't suggest that Osso and Nurial withheld information?" He knew she hadn't but he needed to be certain.

"No, sir," she said without malice, then her tone flipped again. "Just look at them, waving about like that. They could be doing anything over there and we're just watching." She realized what she said and her voice switched back. "Sir, I don't suggest we invade or attack. I am merely saying that they're acting against us without provocation."

"I understand. And I understand their actions as well. We're an army. Some of us have been inside that tower before and things went badly. Many of their kind died because of the mages among us who entered that place. Their presence here does not surprise me. Rather, I would be more concerned if they weren't there."

"Sir?"

"It would suggest they were plotting something much more devious against us. For, if they trusted us, they would have invited us inside. To keep us out here, they need a show of force against us to keep us in check. I would rather watch them dance for hours over there than worry that they're scheming inside."

Hazel eyes turned to him. "But we don't know that this isn't some kind of ruse too. They could just as well be planning something inside."

Ervinor smiled and clapped his hand on her shoulder. "That's why you're in charge of Wren squad. You have a keen mind and an alert eye."

Verna didn't wilt with flattery but drew strength from it instead. Ervinor had recognized early on that she needed occasional compliments to battle some emotional scars from her childhood.

"Thank you, sir."

"Keep an eye on them and send word if their pattern changes much. I have a feeling they're maintaining a barrier against entry. If I'm wrong, their postures will change and then the spells will fly. Keep Osso and Nurial nearby and alert."

"Understood." She stepped away from Ervinor to scold one of her fighters who had opted to lie in the sand to stretch out a few kinks in his neck, then she was back at her post after sending the man to fetch her mages.

He stepped away from her, looking over his shoulder one last time as the wind swept her hair around. She was a pretty woman, he admitted, and that alone helped keep some of the men in line, but it was her attention to detail and her standards that truly rallied them. He had chosen well, giving her command of the Wrens.

As he returned to his Ravens for some sleep, he grinned. Somehow, his own attributes had outshone the fighters around him, and he became the de facto general of this army. He wondered if, one day, Verna would succeed him.

However, he reminded himself, if things went correctly and Dariak assembled the jades, then there would be no need for an army and Verna would have to find something else to do. He set himself down to sleep, trying to picture her as a seamstress, a candlemaker, a potter, a gardener, a singer... And though putting her into these roles seemed absurd considering her personality, it distracted him from the day so he could drift off.

CHAPTER 17

Guilt

HE WAS NOT supposed to feel happiness after everything he had been responsible for. Leaving Savvron had opened the way for his mother to be killed in a raid. In part, his presence in Pindington had contributed to bringing down the Prisoner's Tower, for if he hadn't freed Dariak from his spell chamber, perhaps the lightning jade never would have gone haywire. If he had handled events differently, Kitalla's old crony, Heria, may have been tamed instead of slain.

No, he was not supposed to feel happiness or joy, and yet he had spent the entire night in Kitalla's embrace, shedding his pain while allowing her to release hers as well.

Countless soldiers had perished at his hand. Guards who had trained for years with a sword had died because his cuts were faster and more precise. He had the drive to take the life away from others and to end all the possibilities those people would have brought to the world.

Who was he to end people's lives?

And the villagers in Jortun still saw that food was left at his door though half a dozen of them had been vanquished while trying to help him. He assumed they fed him to keep him from rampaging through the town, but it meant they sacrificed their needed water to support him, the village murderer. And how had he expressed his remorse at their losses? Bedding Kitalla.

It was wrong and he didn't deserve it.

His attempts to help around the town were unwelcome. Everyone turned and ran away and he didn't know how to overcome their fear while holding on to the one thing that he felt he needed to maintain: his pain.

Perhaps he should leave the town after all, but not the way Kitalla intended. If she had her way, he would flee to Dariak's side and tag along with the mage's quest to the very end, but he knew he was better suited to scampering off to the top of the mountains where he wouldn't be able to harm anyone at all.

He turned his eyes toward the glass jade in his hand. He opened his palm and turned it upside down, but the shard did not fall. Shaking his hand and trying to fling it away did nothing either. He could shift it around his body but it wouldn't come loose from his skin. He didn't understand why the jade couldn't be removed, but it

609

had done the same to him before when he had been imprisoned both in Pindington and by Heria. At times, he couldn't see it as it revealed its inherent transparency.

Gabrion slid out of bed, leaving Kitalla behind. He dressed himself, wondering idly why the glass jade allowed him to touch his clothes but not the townspeople. Why could he protect his modesty but not the people trying to care for him?

He staggered out into the morning and he called aloud for the villagers to awaken. His voice shook with emotion and he wailed as loud as he could, rousing them all without fail. Some peered from their windows, as others braved the road he traveled on while still maintaining a safe distance. He raised his voice and called out the names that mattered most to them.

"Felluria!" he shouted. "She was your Matron, who grew this town from a tiny hovel. She was a fiery spirit and she was a dangerous foe. You couldn't cross her without suffering at her hand, and yet she loved you all, each and every one. You obeyed her because you knew her feelings for you. You knew her struggles and you knew that she would keep this place together for an eternity." He could see they were listening, mixed expressions on their faces. Then Gabrion slammed the final point home. "She died because of me."

He paused for a moment, ensuring he had their attention. "There was Presh, one of your most accomplished healers. He tended my wounds despite the fear I bring to you all. He saw the damage and, as a true healer, he did what he could to bandage me and to cure me. And for his efforts, his body was slashed open whenever he touched my skin and then his blood washed over the floor and he couldn't heal anyone any longer." Murmuring echoed in the street.

"Jerrisha," he said next, seeing each visage turn more and more enraged. "Kind and warm, barely old enough that no one still called her a child. A fruit-bringer, she tried to make sure I had everything I needed to survive in that house. She sacrificed her family's wares to feed a stranger who had murdered your kin, and for her kindness to me, when she touched my hand to see if I was awake, she was cut so deeply she could not heal and there she also perished, her whole life stolen from her.

"Veldi—"

"Shut up!" someone yelled. "You defame their memory by speaking of them! Get out of our village!"

"Veldi," Gabrion persisted. "Curious about my past, she watched me as I chopped wood for Felluria. Her terrible fate was sealed when she cooked a meal for me and stumbled when she delivered it to my room. She tripped and her cheek brushed against my leg as I sat on the floor, and it sheered the flesh right off. Her death was painful and it took time for her to die."

"What do you hope to accomplish with his morbid summary?" an old woman hissed.

"Morv," he said next. "He tried to talk to me and wanted me to answer, but I wasn't able to speak. It's only now that I can get the words out. He sat on the floor and drew images in the sand, pointing and trying so hard to communicate with me, to find out if I was some cursed fool or if I truly meant to harm any of you on purpose. His mistake? When I responded to one of his drawings by pointing at a landmark I recognized, and he slapped my knee in delight. His drawings were drowned in blood as he died."

Gabrion watched as the fury rose among the villagers, but he wasn't finished. "Then Aissla, dear friend of deceased Veldi. Aissla tried the hardest to get to know me. She followed me around, watching every move I made, trying to assess what I was. Perhaps she was also a foolish girl with a crush, unable to reason through her actions. Why else would she have reached out to me like she did? And for being a warm-hearted girl, her reward was her blood spilling all over the cobblestones, screaming in horror that her life was coming to a screeching end."

"You monster!" a child shouted. "She was my sister!"

"You can't get rid of me because you're afraid I'm here to take you down one at a time. Maybe you're right. Maybe I can't be moved. Maybe I've got your whole village set up in my head so I can continue ending your pitiful lives one at a time, keeping you ever wondering who will be next. Will it be you?" He pointed at one random person, causing her to jump. "Or you?"

"Stop trying to terrorize us!"

"Trying?" he echoed. "Haven't I succeeded? I was cutting holes in the mountain with my *bare hands*. Who among you didn't have nightmares about that? Anyone? I thought so. So why don't you do something about it?"

"Like what? You said yourself we can't touch you without dying ourselves."

"Come at me. Get whatever you can carry that you don't need. Show me what you feel after all the killings I've done so far."

"You'll kill us like the rest!"

"Don't let me touch you but do your best to take me down. You know Felluria would order you to do it if she were still here, don't you think? Or would she tell you to lie down and die? I don't believe so." He added an edge to his voice as he called, "Come at me!"

A stone flew and smashed against Gabrion's face, breaking apart and clattering to the road as pebbles. It was one object that started an avalanche of rage among the people. Some made quick trips into their homes grabbing for things that were broken and beyond repair and then they returned to Gabrion and did their best to tear him down.

Buckets and brooms smacked against him, breaking in the process. Horseshoes clanged loudly and fell, warped, to the cobbles. Rope, tankards, planks of wood. Each object was hurled with such anger and dismay, and as they struck the enchanted warrior, the villagers felt a small sense of release, though they could see their efforts had no direct effect on hurting Gabrion. Yet there was a freedom in their actions, for they could strike and strike again and take out their aggressions on him without the guilt that would come if he were normal.

Some villagers lined up repeatedly, scrounging for anything they could find that would fly through the air and strike him. A few focused on metallic objects, for they made a ringing sound when they hit. And Gabrion stood there, chanting out the names of the fallen, egging them on to continue the onslaught.

Some part of him wanted them to succeed at harming him. His life couldn't return any of those who had died due to his actions, but if he perished, then his heart would no longer be so conflicted and pained.

"For Jortun!" he called aloud, raising his arms upward as object after object crashed against him, then fell away, leaving him unscathed.

It was cathartic for the townspeople and at last Gabrion felt he had done at least one thing to help.

CHAPTER 18

Into the Woods

DARIAK AND RANDLER awoke early, ready to begin Astrith's challenge. Their guide, Yehyona, met them without a stitch of clothing on. Her rich russet skin glistened in the sunlight that flitted through the overhead vines and slinked across her delicate curves. Her voluptuous figure was blocked only by a tray of food she brought to the visitors, but only long enough for her to veritably float into their hut and then bend to her knees to place the tray on a low table. Most men would have wilted at her grace and beauty, but to Dariak and Randler, her nakedness was only a reminder that they also needed to meet the day without adornments.

Astrith had apparently sent word to all his villagers to abide the trappings of nature, for as they left their hut, the mage and the bard noticed that not a single person was clothed in any way. They tried their best to keep their gazes firmly upward, feeling severely out of place in the lacy cloth they still wore. With a sigh, they surrendered to the requirement of the elder and stripped down as Yehyona glided in front of them, bringing them to the start of their path.

"Beyond these walls, you venture forth into our domain," Astrith began with a booming voice that rattled the air. "You enter there as you entered life, helpless but for your ability to grow. You have no parents to guide you here. Therefore, you must use your wits, skills, and experiences to get through. Though you may not bring any belongings with you, you may gather things as you go. Yet, you must not harm the forest."

"If we're attacked, may we defend ourselves?" Dariak asked.

"Of course, but do not kill needlessly, for it would upset the balance in the woods. You will also need sustenance, so, unless your herb-lore is strong, you will need to hunt." Astrith clapped his hands. "Yehyona, if you would send them on their way?"

She stood before them and nodded her head to each, then broke into a powerful dance. She tapped her feet left and right, bending low, clapping her hands, reaching up to the sky, and spinning around. She drew her hands sensuously down her body, her face lighting in ecstasy as she moved. Her luxurious black hair cascaded around her as she dipped at the waist and swept to the side. She danced around the two adventurers, clapping her hands again to a staccato rhythm, her feet tapping in time.

She twirled and stopped before Randler, then she stepped forward, pressing herself fully against him and kissing his cheek, after which she did the same to Dariak. Stepping away from the blushing men, she crouched and touched her forehead to the dirt, where she swept her hands out wide and back, encasing herself in a circle drawn in the dirt.

The other villagers were gathered around and they knelt to the earth, then bowed until their heads struck the ground. They, too, swept their hands around in a giant circle, even Astrith. Dariak understood rituals well as a mage and he immediately followed suit, Randler only moments behind. They dipped low and swept their arms around, waiting there until Yehyona rose up and placed a gentle hand on each of their heads. "Be safe on your journey," she blessed them. "The forest provides for you. The forest protects you. But if you do not respect her, then the forest will lose you. Go now."

Without word, Dariak and Randler stood and followed her gesture toward a path that led from the village. They took one last glance over their shoulders. All the village was still pressed to the ground, save Yehyona, who had taken a half step forward into a lunge, then reached her hands crookedly over her head, fingers flourished outward. In her own way, she looked very much like a tree; supple, strong, everlasting, and just a little wild.

They walked the path silently until the village was gone. Their first order of business was to cover their bodies. Randler eagerly hunted for fallen leaves while Dariak meditated for the spells he would need to pull them together.

"I can't figure out the best way to ensure they fit well," the mage said, "so lie down." Randler did as he was told, while Dariak set leaves across Randler's chest and waist. He then took two leaves in his hand, after which he spit on one and started casting. *"Fabrithius oskallor benirrilo nosh karrai."* Bringing the leaves together, he touched their edges and allowed the spittle to roll between them, creating a seal. As he did so, the leaves on Randler's body fused together.

Looking at the creation, Dariak realized he needed to make some adjustments, and create the tunic first, for the top and bottom halves had joined and wouldn't be very comfortable. He also had to use more leaves, for when they linked together, they covered less area. Trying again, he crafted fronts and backs for each of them, which he then linked together with more leaves. By the time he molded shoes from the foliage, he moved much more rapidly.

The leaf-clothes were itchy for a while, but they both felt more protected by them. "Perhaps we should just go naked," Dariak suggested after an hour of scratching.

"If I knew it would only be the two of us, then maybe," Randler muttered. "But who knows who else we'll run into here and I'm not really up for the public shows."

Dariak made an admonishing ticking sound. "I have no idea why you're so shy; you certainly have no reason to be."

Randler hedged. "I guess I don't want you distracted."

"You would have to pluck the eyes from your head, the grace from your step, the voice from your throat, the mind from your skull, and—well, I'll stop there."

Randler shook his head. "You're hopeless."

"Hopelessly in love, you mean." Dariak moved closer to kiss the bard, their leafy clothes crinkling in annoyance.

"What of Gabrion?" Randler asked suddenly, pulling away from Dariak's advance. "What about the things you said when he was in his Trial at Magehaven? You're attracted to him, aren't you?"

Dariak grabbed Randler's arm and stopped him from stepping away. "Are you serious?"

"Well, you said that you hungered for his body and that you loved him as a person. Didn't you admit you would 'be' with him if you could? If he had any interest?"

"Randler," Dariak gasped. "It's not—"

"Never mind. It's stupid. Let's go on."

"No way. Not like that!" But the bard pulled away, agitated. Dariak raised his voice, "Randler, this is absurd!"

He shook his head. "You were in that Trial but I could hear some things. The music resonated with the energy in that room. I could feel you. I could hear you. I knew things you were saying. I knew what you were feeling. I know how tempted you were when he asked if you wanted him."

"Then you also know I would never act on it," Dariak insisted. "You would have felt that too."

Randler nodded softly. "But not because of me, Dariak. You wouldn't act on it because of him, because it would ruin your friendship with him, because he isn't into men. I wasn't even in your thoughts then."

"I—I can't believe this," Dariak stammered. "Why haven't you said anything about this until now?"

"There's been a lot happening. And talking with Astrith has given me a lot to think about. This has been on my mind but it isn't something easy for me to talk about."

"It's also wrong, Randler. Stop walking away!" Dariak jogged forward and grabbed the bard. "Would you listen to me? Or do you want to hurt?"

"You can't change those feelings, Dariak. I felt them through you. I hated it. Another twisted piece of magic."

Dariak clutched Randler tighter, preventing him from pulling away. "I will explain this once and you can do with it whatever you want. I was there inside Gabrion's mind, completely swallowed up in his memories. Every part of my being was trapped in there with the things that were tormenting him, which included me gazing at him, yes. When he started confronting me about it there, Kerrish intervened and made Gabrion lash out to attack me, and though I was caught in the energies within Gabrion, I had to also reach back and fight off Kerrish. I could not have done that without your support. I had the lute figurine you carved for me in hand. It gave me the strength I needed to get through that task. Maybe I didn't interrupt my tenuous chat with Gabrion to tell you how much I adore you, but Randler, you're crazy if you think I'm interested in him. You're the one I want to be with, don't you know that?"

Randler wrenched himself away. "I... need some time. I don't know. Something about being exposed back there... I don't know. I don't know."

Dariak watched him walk off, crestfallen. He had no idea how to convince him aside from tackling him and demonstrating his feelings, but he sensed that wouldn't help right now. Perhaps there was something else troubling the bard, but until he opened up, there was nothing Dariak could do.

With a heavy sigh, he took a few steps to follow, then realized that they would need weapons, so he set himself to looking for fallen branches. It wasn't long until he spotted some that could be of use. He grabbed them and stripped off the smaller twigs by hand. It wasn't easy to do while walking, but he needed to try to keep pace with Randler. Dariak only stopped to rub dirt along the branches so he could cast a spell to fortify their strength.

It felt good to draw upon the power of the earth, for it was the first element he had learned as a child, thanks to the earth jade. He touched his chest, where the jade had spent a good portion of his journey. Now he felt naked without it, and he wondered if, perhaps, that was Astrith's lesson for him. He had become so reliant on the jades over the past year that he had lost part of himself, part of his creativity. Now, would he lose Randler, too? He frowned.

Dariak looked around for some rocks and magically attached them to the ends of his makeshift staffs, giving them added strength, after which he jogged up to Randler. "Here," he said simply, thrusting one of the enchanted branches into the bard's hand. He wanted to say more, but the pained look on Randler's face kept him quiet. They walked silently for hours.

Eventually, hunger set in. Randler still had not spoken, but Dariak could hear the bard's belly rumbling. He moved off from the path and sought various herbs and mushrooms, many of which were good spell components, too. Years of training allowed him to navigate away from the poisonous plants and seek nourishment among the rest.

They didn't have any water to wash them down with, but he found a few places where rainwater had collected on large leaves. It was enough to allow them to keep traveling onward, though he hoped they would happen across a stream sometime soon. Sips of liquid here and there wouldn't get them through the whole forest.

Movement in the wood made them stop and look for beasts. Dariak noted that there were deer skittishly fleeing. Some rabbits and squirrels also hopped about and he couldn't help but smile. They had been inundated with feral creatures on their journey, attacked at every turn. To see their docile kin eased his heart.

It had an effect on Randler too. "They look so peaceful," he whispered.

"I agree. Maybe this would be a good place to camp for the night. The sun is starting to sink low."

The bard nodded.

"If you can gather some more leaves and branches, I'll do what I can to make a tent."

Randler moaned. "More magic. But we have little choice. I will return."

Dariak felt a pang in his chest as Randler turned from him and stepped away, staff in hand. He wondered if the bard would insist on having two tents or if he would simply opt to stay awake while Dariak slept. He needed to do something to bridge this sudden rift. He sat on the ground and folded his legs in, resting his hands upon his knees and entering a meditative trance.

"Dariak!" Randler shouted some time later. He sounded panicked.

The mage roused himself and grabbed his staff, listening for Randler's call, but he didn't shout a second time. Calming himself, Dariak focused on the sounds of the forest, trying to distinguish some disturbance that would lead him to Randler. But there was nothing. He knew the basic direction the bard had taken and nothing more.

He needed to act, but if he went off in the wrong direction and Randler was in trouble, he would arrive too late, so he bent down and grabbed a handful of dirt where Randler had stood, which he then placed in his mouth. It was difficult not to gag on the flavor and harder not to reflexively swallow. He called the words to mind and then blew the dirt into the air, chanting aloud. *"Whirricant kai brethros forrilus, nortch corrus, benn'ai."* He coughed and spat the rest of the dirt from his mouth, dragging his tongue on his arm to help remove it.

The dirt wafted into the air and swirled around momentarily. He curled his fingers and swept his hands about as if he were shooing away flies. A summoned breeze tickled Dariak's skin and as it tossed the floating dirt ahead, he followed. It was a tenuous spell, for he was linking earth and air magic together, but Randler had helped him better understand the aspect of dissonance, using music so he could hear how disparate sounds could actually complement each other. Now, he needed these elements to work concordantly to guide him.

Randler had stood still on that one patch of dirt, and Dariak's hope was that some sweat had leaked through the makeshift shoes, which would temporarily allow Dariak to link the earth to the bard. The gentle wind allowed the dirt to reach for Randler, as long as Dariak was careful not to disturb the breeze with his own motions.

It took some time, complete with crunching through underbrush and ducking under branches, but at last Dariak found him. Randler lay in a heap, eight dead squirrets nearby and numerous pelt marks on his skin. He had apparently stumbled upon their nest and they defended themselves admirably.

Dariak set his staff aside and knelt beside Randler, gently shaking him until his eyes creaked open. "Hold still," the mage murmured. He rummaged for some leaves in the area, which he set over Randler's deeper wounds. He called upon his meager healing skills and drew the energies through Randler's body, trying to restore his strength.

"I feel so stupid," the bard said.

"Never mind that; you're okay. That's all that matters."

Randler spouted a quick verse.

Squirrets of the north,
Pellets in their tail,
Shooting ever forth,
Like ever-falling hail.

"I swear they blasted me fifty times for each one of my swings back. They flat-out overwhelmed me. It never should have happened."

"You've been upset all day," Dariak said. "I wish I could help you understa—"

"Don't," Randler cut in, looking away.

Exasperated, Dariak stood up. "Fine, then. Give up this quest and go home. I don't need you getting in the way." He stormed off, leaving Randler behind.

He was exhausted and wanted a full meal and some sleep. But he couldn't stop. He was angry, hurt, and utterly confused. Didn't everyone have errant thoughts? Didn't people filter them out and not share them with the world? Was he really to be shunned because he thought Gabrion was attractive and a worthy friend? Because he had entertained the idea of being intimate with the warrior? Should Randler be allowed to hold such a grudge for thoughts Dariak would never act on? He didn't care right now. He crashed his staff into the earth and dragged himself onward, barely aware which way he was headed since he was no longer on the path.

Soon a new sound filled his ears and he was grateful for it. It was the endless babbling of a stream. He hastened his steps and threw himself at the water's surface, drinking his fill until he gasped for breath. Sated, he curled up beside the river and set a protection spell, using a dried leaf as the main component, so that an intruder would make a loud rustling noise that would awaken him.

He wondered idly if Randler really would turn around and go home. It seemed so petty. It didn't make any sense. He tossed and turned through the night, the crinkling of his leafy tunic spooking him repeatedly.

CHAPTER 19

The Outpost

SHE KNEW IT was a bittersweet victory, but Kitalla lavished in Gabrion's attentions. For days, they indulged themselves in each other, always with Gabrion apologizing to her for not loving her. Part of her didn't care. She had had a fair share of partners over the years, all for sport, save her first, Joral. Gabrion had never been with a woman. He hadn't ever touched a girl passionately, despite all his yearning for Mira. He had been the utmost perfect gentleman with her, but Kitalla enjoyed her time educating him. She teased him that his prowess would far exceed his battle skill any time now.

They needed to move on from Jortun, though. Kitalla tried to reason with him, but he wouldn't listen. He gazed at her hungrily and with a few crafty touches, she melted in his arms. But she decided at last that their quest had to continue. She didn't discuss it with him. She simply announced that the next time she woke up, she was leaving and he had better follow her.

Midafternoon, Kitalla rose from bed, dressed, and ventured out into the town. The villagers hated seeing her, because she was a friend of the murderer who had slain their friends and family. They bartered with her for supplies, then she paid a messenger to run to Felluria's house to tell Gabrion that she was leaving. She knew if she tried to tell him herself, she might not go anywhere.

Jogging softly in the cool autumn air, Kitalla made her way toward the south. Trees were scattered here and there, birds chirping at her intrusion. She laughed, feeling lighter than air.

It wasn't long before Gabrion joined her. "Come back, Kitalla. Where are you going?"

She eluded his grasp. "I told you! We have to return to Dariak."

Gabrion's face collapsed. "I can't do that. You know I can't. I can't fight anymore. Not after what I've done."

"Nonsense," she scoffed. "You can fight if you have to. You have more to protect in this world. We all need you, Gabrion."

He shook his head. "I—I can't."

"Well, I'm going on," she said. "I expect you to come with me. It's as simple as that."

"Kitalla…"

She winked sensuously and then turned around, swinging her hips wildly side to side. Gabrion was wholly entranced, and she wasn't using her dance skill to enthrall him. He hesitated, eying her hungrily, then surrendered and followed.

They didn't talk along the way, nor did they make any contact. It was an unspoken agreement between them for the time being. All the while, Gabrion looked over his shoulder as his recent sanctuary faded away into memory.

"Eaglons!" Kitalla announced, pointing at several floating forms in the sky ahead of them. "You didn't even bring a sword."

"I can't fight. I told you that."

She wished she hadn't bartered away the sword she had used to wrangle the sandorpion. She only had her daggers and Gabrion refused to fight at all. Perhaps when the battle was on, he would forget his vow and join the fray. The beasts flew closer and attacked.

There were eleven of the feathery creatures hovering around and they worked as a concerted team to assault them. Gabrion ducked and weaved about, avoiding each one, but Kitalla had her daggers in hand, trying to cut the oversized birds without being cut in return. The poisonous claws would do serious damage, especially without a healer nearby to cure the poison.

Two birds were taken down and a third veered away before she could kill it. Gabrion continued to feint left and right, which broke Kitalla's flow. She was used to having his help in a fight, and his useless thrashing about was irritating. She tossed two daggers into the sky and pulled two more from her pockets. The eaglons avoided her blades, but as they veered, she leaped into the air and slashed at one creature, while kicking her foot toward another. The eaglons swept in and one crashed into her belly, knocking her down. She grabbed the bird and cracked its neck, then checked herself for wounds. Finding none, she rose up, coughed painfully, then assessed the next attack.

Five eaglons flew in formation and charged for her, while the rest sought Gabrion. She considered trying to bewitch them with her dance skill, but the birds were diving in fast. She tossed a dagger into their midst, knowing it would only cause them to swerve out of its way, but she was counting on it. The leading eaglon twisted to the side, slightly breaking formation, which allowed Kitalla to turn sideways and slip between two of them, bringing her hands up and knocking them out of the sky.

The other three creatures in the formation screeched and swept around to strike again, but Kitalla had collapsed.

She knew it was a risky move, but her leap between the eaglons hadn't gone as well as she had hoped. Her left hand caught on the talons of her victim and ripped jagged cuts through her skin, leaking poison into the veins. The blistering pain was instant and it raged up through her arm and toward her heart. Few would survive a gash like that, for she had been sliced with several talons and had taken in a large amount of poison.

She wondered idly why the metal jade hadn't saved her, but even as the idea occurred to her, she could feel it pulsing at her hip. It reacted somehow with her bloodstream, trying to fight off the poison. But the metal had no providence over poison, she thought to herself. It couldn't heal her.

"Gabrion," she gasped.

He raced over, ignoring the rest of the eaglons as they circled overhead, ready to strike again. He saw the gashes on her arm. "No!"

"The outpost, Gabrion. Healers." She felt the metal jade pulse more wildly and a wracking pain shook her as the shard took control of the metal in her body and drew her into a deep stasis. The fire jade assisted, drawing the heat from her skin, slowing her down. Her breathing stopped, as did her blood flow.

"Kitalla!"

The eaglons sensed his helplessness and they dove down, determined to end him, too. Squawking viciously as they dove, the eaglons aimed for Gabrion's heart. One after another they pelted him, and subsequently shattered like glass. Each creature erupted into bits, like the unfortunate villagers of Jortun. Like Mira.

His jade hummed powerfully in a suddenly different rhythm. He examined Kitalla's lifeless body and felt the frantic pulsing of her metal jade. Instinctively, he knew she wasn't dead, but he didn't question how. He scooped her up in his arms, trusting her fire and metal jades to protect her from his touch.

He didn't want to go to the outpost. It would bring him closer to the war. To the fighting. And the killing. The endless killing. He didn't want to be the warrior any longer.

But Kitalla needed him. She would die without help and she had called for the outpost. Indeed, it would be the only place nearby with any healers who might be willing to help them. He had to save her. He had failed Mira, but he would not fail Kitalla.

He ran and ran, his glass jade empowering him with its energy. He pressed onward with barely any food or water for nearly two full days. Beasts in the area drew close to him, but they sensed an unnatural threat and they fled before engaging him at all. Kitalla never stirred along the way, her body held in stasis.

As he approached the outpost, he his body slowed down. Perhaps the jade was out of energy, or maybe his frantic run was coming to an end. The ground was littered with the remnants of armed forces that had been camped there not long ago. The troops had since entered Hathreneir to take the fighting across the border, leaving the grass here trampled, beaten, and littered with debris.

The outpost was in sight and he struggled to keep his feet moving. He had to reach it. The white stone glinted in the fading sunlight and he pushed on further, carrying Kitalla, her body eerily cold against his skin.

A scout called out to him. "Halt! Identify yourself!"

He stopped running because his body refused to continue. Collapsing to his knees, he replied with heaving gasps. "Gabrion of Savvron. Friend of Ordren. Help us. Healers. Help."

He wanted to pass out, but the jade wouldn't let him, for Kitalla wasn't yet safe. The scout eyed him and considered Gabrion's words. "Come."

Pushing himself up felt like trying to lift the stones of the outpost all at once. He managed it through sheer strength of will, bringing Kitalla's body to the three-story barrack and seeking an audience with the soldier from Pindington.

"Gabrion!" greeted a familiar voice.

"Don't touch me, friend," Gabrion called out, seeing the man approach to clutch his shoulder. "No one must lay a finger on me. I'll explain later, but for now, you must call your healers." He set Kitalla's body on the stone floor. "Eaglon poison."

Ordren eyed the young man oddly, but he drew his attention toward Kitalla's wounds and hissed through his teeth. "Gabrion…"

"Healers," the warrior insisted. "They will be successful, but you must hurry."

The soldier whistled over his shoulder for help. "What of you, Gabrion?"

"I am uninjured, but I need a place to rest. And some food." He watched as a team of men carried Kitalla away to the healing room. "But I insist, Ordren, that no one must touch me. It will only cause them great and irreparable harm."

"Yet not her?" he asked, gesturing needlessly toward Kitalla.

"She is… protected against my curse."

"You're sure she can be healed?"

"You know of the jades, don't you, Ordren? They are protecting her, and the healers would do well to abide any advice they feel from them. The jades will know how to help her." Gabrion looked over Ordren's shoulder. "Promise me you will heal her."

"We'll do what we can," he answered skeptically. "But you have to realize, no one really survives eaglon poison."

"Forget that and heal her." His voice was edgy and forceful and Ordren took an involuntary step back. "Sorry… Food. Bed. Please."

Arrangements were made and Gabrion alerted everyone he saw not to touch him for any reason. They eyed him fearfully, but they obliged.

The only room that was open at the time was a cell in the dungeon. He accepted it, not much caring where he had a chance to crash. Bread, stew, and water were brought in and he devoured them like they were roasted chicken and herbs fit for a king. Every part of his body tingled with the anticipation of a deep sleep, but it didn't come.

Hours drifted away and he was able to see the moon through a small cutout in the cell. His thoughts tossed about, but he was so overtired he couldn't pin down the threads of what he was trying to think about. He had mental glimpses of his home, of Mira, the jades, Dariak, a tiny infant, Randler, and Kitalla. They flashed so quickly, they reminded him of the overlapping conversations that had plagued him during his Trial.

He had failed Mira because his anguish had channeled the jade's power and caused his body to be so sharp, her arm had essentially exploded when she had tried to strike him. She died because the wounds were so perfectly and magically severed, the mages couldn't overcome them. Now Kitalla was poisoned and dying, locked in some freakish stasis because he had decided he could never fight again.

Was he doomed to destroy all the people around him?

That one thought kept returning to him, and he hated it. It was worse than one of Randler's songs being so lodged in his head that he kept singing it relentlessly. He was tired of guilt and pain. He wanted to shut it all away and just…

But he didn't know what. He doubted he would be able to tend a farm any longer. His life had taken such a violent turn, he suspected he would never have the patience needed to till the land or tend the crops. He didn't want to fight because he had killed so many things already, many of them people. The killing must stop, even though he excelled at it.

Pacing around the cell didn't help, nor did lying down. He kept trembling, wondering if Kitalla would survive the night, while simultaneously knowing she would have to because of the jades. Even his jade had kept him safe. Or had it?

Perhaps the jade was to blame for the way things were. Without the shards, the team would have died long ago, whether in a fight against beasts, or after the crash of the Prisoner's Tower in Pindington when the blacksmith's furnace had exploded. If he had died, he wouldn't have had to feel all this raging pain that tore at his soul. His quest for Mira would have ended unfinished, rather than ending murderously.

Absentmindedly, he caught himself drawing a large triangle on the stone floor, his finger cutting into the surface, each side with its representation: Patience, Pain, Perseverance. He carelessly dug deepest into the edge representing Pain until his knuckle sank into the stone and he realized what he was doing. The triad still didn't make sense to him. The more he hurt the people around him, the more he had to be patient? The harder he had to persevere?

Dawn crept through the window and distracted him, thankfully. He stood up, his eyes bloodshot, and he left the cell to check on Kitalla. One of Ordren's soldiers pointed him in the right direction. Gabrion pushed the door open and he saw her lying on a table, a white sheet covering her up to her chin. He watched carefully and saw the slow rise and fall of her chest, and a deep relief washed over him. The healers had succeeded.

Finding a chair and settling down, he watched her, his mind suddenly and blissfully blank.

      CHAPTER 20

Verna's Mistake

SEVERAL DAYS PASSED awkwardly outside Magehaven. Ervinor and his team remained on alert against the mages who refused to allow them to enter. The young general wasn't entirely sure what to do; he needed to keep the army intact for Dariak's return, but he had no idea how to do so while camping out in the sand when a shelter stood literally yards away. He considered leaving this area, but he had no clue where to go. The only other places known to him in Hathreneir were the castle and Marritosh; his last foray to the castle had cost his arm, and Marritosh lay in ruins.

He watched the dance of six Hathren mages this morning as they maintained whatever spells they thought were necessary for their protection. He had not seen any of the Council members since their arrival, but he had expected some form of parlay by now. His troops were antsy and eager to be anywhere other than lying in wait.

He scanned his remaining forces, proud how they were faring despite the circumstances. Lica's Eagle group was on patrol of the area, watching for desert creatures. Quereth's Nightingales were posted closest to the magical barrier that surrounded the tower, keeping an eye on the mages on the other side. Ervinor's Ravens and Frast's Sparrows were on rest, many of the men and women taking the opportunity to eat or sleep. Verna's Wrens were also assigned a break, but she had decided to keep her team limber by engaging them in some sparring.

The sounds of clanking swords echoed, as did the banter of their commander. Amused, Ervinor decided to inspect the training session, so he stepped away from his perch and approached them.

Most of Verna's group was composed of Hathren fighters, with only a couple of mages. The fighters were mostly swordsmen, for it was the most common weapon forged in Marritosh and easier to train with than spears or axes. Daggers were less useful in a large-scale battle, and then only if things were bad and close melee was required. As Ervinor walked up to them, he could see teams of two or three in close-knit sparring, making use of a wide range of battle tactics. Some were more aggressive with thrusts and stabs, whereas others blocked well enough to keep the blades away. Now and then, they swapped roles, and Ervinor could see the differences in skill levels between them.

The mages among them kept their spells in check outside the tower, at Ervinor's request. Defensive spells were allowed, but shows of force were discouraged at the moment. He didn't want to risk an incident with any errant spells that might cross through the barrier. Instead they wielded staffs and swung them sluggishly to defend themselves. The maneuvers would only be useful against tired fighters, but perhaps if the mages managed to slow the swordsmen down first, then even these defenses would suffice.

Verna screamed at one of the younger fighters in her group. "Sword higher! If you parry like that, you will die." She lunged in with a vicious blow and the poor teenager panicked and threw himself down to avoid the strike. "No! No! No!" she wailed, chasing him with her sword as he frantically rolled away. The blond youth glanced up as she roared and thundered after him, stabbing her sword into the ground every few paces. He didn't have a chance to get to his feet during her pursuit.

"Ho there," Ervinor interrupted before she could connect.

"What?" she shrieked angrily, turning to face him, her crimson hair swinging out carelessly. She eyed Ervinor and lowered her gaze. "Sorry, sir. Just training."

He watched the young soldier rise to his feet and skitter away, gasping in panic. "I see. Keeping your men on their toes is wise, though some may need more basic training first."

"You question my technique?" she raged. "As general, I would think you would want these fighters at their best for our purpose."

"Watch your tone, commander. I do admire your skills, but I am still in charge here."

It took a moment for her to calm herself before she apologized and nodded her head. "What would you suggest, sir?"

"Don't train him by fear, Verna. That's all."

Her voice raised despite her efforts to control it. "But when we join the fighting, we will all be empowered by fear if we become its master."

Ervinor considered for a moment and nodded. "Yes, but it shouldn't be you he fears."

Her lip twitched and her voice grew husky. "So he should wait until he is in the midst of a battle before he ever truly has to defend himself?" Her voice escalated. "He should die then because we're too afraid now to teach him what it means to be truly and ruthlessly attacked? He will die without being prepared! Is that how I should train these men?" She started screaming now, her voice echoing in the morning air. The members of her battalion stood tall and turned to face her, weapons still in hand. "Every single one of them will die! Not a one of them will live to see another day!"

Ervinor squared his jaw and set his gaze angrily upon her. Her words were uncalled for and when she paused to look at his face, she knew she had crossed the line. However, it was how she felt. The fighters needed to be prepared for the worst.

Unfortunately, she had summoned the worst with her shouting.

Perhaps the mages had only heard the last part of her impassioned speech, but those words, coupled with the fighters around her armed and ready for battle, prompted the six mages beyond the barrier to cease their repetitive casting. Breaking formation, they scattered and each pulled the energies about them for offensive spells. One mage began by launching fire darts toward Verna's group, while the other five spread their attacks around toward the rest of Ervinor's army.

"Halt! Halt!" Ervinor called, trying to keep his troops in line. However, within moments, spells erupted everywhere and mages poured out from the tower itself to join the fray. Apparently, the disruption of the unified spell was signal enough to the mages within.

Sandorpions were summoned with desert rodia and a pack of eaglons, controlled by a team of mages who targeted Verna's group. Ice rained down from above onto Lica's forces, while Quereth's team took the brunt of the electrical charges. The rest of Ervinor's army came abruptly alert and took up their weapons to defend themselves.

Ervinor tried to restore order, but the chaos erupted too quickly. He pulled his sword from the sheath on his back and used it to bat away a swooping eaglon. Verna's team pressed themselves into the sand and assaulted the rest of the creatures with relative ease. The rodia were dispatched and only one fighter took damage from a sandorpion. Even the eaglons were no match for them.

As they fought, Ervinor tried to reach Frast so he could use his magic to call a ceasefire. Three lupinoes raced from the tower and headed right for him, clearly sent out to take him down. He swept his sword toward one and rolled away from the other two. They circled around him, snarling, their silver-blue fur glistening in the sunlight. The smallest of the three charged in, head low and ready to bowl the man over. Ervinor was not duped by the attack, however, for the other two lupinoes separated and stalked toward him, and if he focused all his attention on the small beast, then one of the other two would ambush him.

He ran forward and leaped into the air, inadvertently catching his foot in the lupino's eye. It offset his leap and he tumbled, tucking in to roll. The injured creature howled and spun about as its companions did the same. Ervinor thrust his sword into the ground at his feet and reached for two poison darts that were secured along his chest. There wasn't time to pull out the blowtube, for the trio raced toward him again. They kept their heads high this time, preventing another leap.

When they reached him, Ervinor fell backward and hooked his feet under the front legs of the center beast. Rolling frantically, he flipped the creature overhead, sending it through the air, where it landed awkwardly in the sand, its neck snapping. Also as he rolled, he lashed his arm out and threw the two darts, which struck one of the flanking lupinoes. Winded and dizzy, he righted himself and reclaimed his sword to finish off the last lupino as it charged him with snapping jaws. Perhaps if the beast wasn't being controlled by the mages, its raw power and instincts would have allowed it to fight more strategically, but as it was, Ervinor was able to meet the charge with a deep sword thrust through the lupino's brain.

There was no time to catch his breath. This battle had to be stopped. He pushed himself up and scanned around for his commanders, but each was out of sight amidst all the commotion. The mages used their skills well, sweeping the sand into the air and creating a blinding sandstorm off to the south; a wild set of vines smacked repeatedly at three fighters who hacked away at the husks to keep from being entangled; fire, ice, and lightning erupted everywhere, sometimes combining into powerful attacks. The field was complete chaos, worse than the mage attack on Marritosh.

He had no idea how to stop it except to find one of the mages and try to be heard. He sheathed his sword and made his way toward the tower, keeping his hand over his head in a nonthreatening manner. His Ravens gathered around him and he explained his purpose. Three stayed with him, but the rest disbanded to deliver word to the others. Ervinor pushed onward, seeking a team of mages ahead of him who were crouched low and offering healing to fallen comrades.

Crossing the mage barrier offered no ill effects, save a strange popping sound in his ears. He realized absently that they could have entered the tower at any time instead of languishing in the desert. Shrugging away the thought, he made his way forward with his small entourage, all with weapons sheathed. "Hear me, mages!"

One of the mages looked up and panicked at his approach. She immediately jolted him with a blast of air, which was followed by a bolt of lightning from one of her fellow healers. He endured the pain, determined to show that he meant them no harm, but they were caught up in the moment and their attacks continued. Ervinor and his Ravens fell to their knees in pain, lucky that the offensive spells were not terribly powerful and that their antimagic armor worked. As another barrage erupted from the healers, help swooped in.

Verna's team had dispatched the summoned beasts and the mages who had called them. Now she guided her team toward Ervinor as he approached the healers. She misunderstood his intent, only seeing him fall to his knees from their spells. She rushed in, sword flailing, and moments later all three healers were dead. She didn't spare Ervinor much attention, turning instead to other foes nearby who were on the offensive.

Ervinor tried to call out to her, but he was too weak. His Ravens hadn't gotten the message to her, but he could tell that the rest of his forces had obeyed. The sounds of fighting behind him grew weaker, but Verna pressed on. She made her way toward the tower entrance, her Wrens in tow, and they entered the structure and disappeared.

Healing energy swept around him and Frast helped him to his feet. "This is bad," the mage said needlessly.

"I must go in," Ervinor decided. "I have to stop her."

"I'm coming with you. And don't you dare protest. You need me." For emphasis, Frast cast another healing spell and Ervinor admittedly felt bolstered by it.

After sending the rest of his Ravens to reaffirm the ceasefire, Ervinor and Frast jogged to the main door of the tower. They passed several dead mages, fighters, and creatures along the way; their deaths all for naught. The massive doors stood silently open, and when Ervinor stepped inside, he wished he could go back to the first light of morning and change the horrible fate that had befallen the place.

When they had arrived at the tower days ago, the mages had allowed the Marritosh refugees inside, sequestered to the main floor. As he entered the main chamber, he looked around at a mass of fallen bodies. The townspeople who had lost their homes lay in lifeless piles on the floor. He didn't know how Verna could have butchered them all so swiftly, or why she would have done so. Clearly, madness had claimed her.

"Even the children," Frast whispered in a hollow tone. Neither man could bring himself to walk further into the room.

Ervinor fell to his knees, horrified by the butchery. Verna was a bit wild, but he had never suspected that she could be capable of such blind rage. He had no idea how he could compensate for this tragedy to the people of Hathreneir or to the mages. He knew it would have to start with finding Verna and bringing an end to her insanity.

"Let's go," he said, pushing himself up and crossing the main chamber.

"Wait!" Frast interrupted, his face scrunched in confusion and his eyes darting wildly about. "Ervinor, there's something strange here."

They walked farther into the room, drawing closer to the fallen bodies. Ervinor inspected one man whose limbs were tangled. "No blood."

"How—?"

"Stop!" shouted a voice across the way. "Lower your weapons, Kallisorian scum."

Ervinor recognized old Vinnek, whom he had not seen since their first meeting days ago. Numerous mages crowded behind him. "Our weapons are away, friend."

"Friend?" the mage scoffed. "What friend attacks another? Have you no sense of honor? No amount of patience to wait until we had deliberated?" He seethed with anger and sparks flickered along his fingertips. "This outrage demonstrates once more the treachery of Kallisor. Perhaps Farrenok and the others were right to eradicate you all."

"No, please hear me," Ervinor bowed low. "This whole battle was a misunderstanding."

"We heard your threat!" the old man barked. "We defended our home. You will all perish for your actions."

"So that's it?" Frast shouted. "You won't even listen?"

Vinnek shot bolts of lightning across the room, missing them intentionally. "Why should I listen to barbarians?"

"Because if we don't speak, there will be more useless killing," Ervinor said. "Hear me first. Strike me down later."

"We already dealt with the scouts you sent in ahead of you," Vinnek informed him. "Your demise will soon follow."

"You overheard part of a conversation and you acted on it. Verna was not threatening the mages here. We were discussing training tactics, albeit vehemently. Your mages broke formation and launched the first assault. I never ordered the strike and I immediately tried to quell it once it broke out." He looked around at the bodies littering the floor. "I can't believe it came to this. How could she have killed these innocent people? She grew up with many of them."

Vinnek looked perplexed as Ervinor gazed around the room. Then he laughed. "These people are not dead, you fool."

A glimmer of hope flickered in the general's eyes. "Then what?"

Frast snapped his fingers in understanding, which caused Vinnek to flick another lightning bolt toward him in warning. "I get it now. When you brought them in, you ensorcelled them so that if we attacked, you could put them to sleep and they wouldn't be able to join the fighting. And the mages outside," he surmised, "were keeping the sleep spell from activating. When they broke formation, these people fell and you determined that the fight was on."

"Astute," Vinnek said. "And since you don't have access to these reinforcements, you should understand full well that you can't withstand us at all. We will finish what was started here and your army will be terminated."

"You're not listening," Ervinor said. "We never intended for this fight. These people here are refugees only, not fighters. Not one of them is under my command."

"Then what of the party that erupted through our doors?"

"They acted on their own, without my orders, I assure you."

The mage snorted. "Convenient."

"I want peace, Vinnek. Not this fighting. It's the fighting we're trying to stop. It's why we're gathered in Hathreneir in the first place. It's what Dariak's quest is all about. We're to be his support and defense while he needs us. We were never meant to battle you, not here or anywhere. I urge you to hear me."

The anger in the old man's eyes flickered. "Send your mage back out to the rest of your followers. Take these mages with you," he said, signaling behind him. "They will bind the hands of your allies and they will be brought inside where we can better watch them."

Ervinor agreed. "If you can, cast the same sleep spell over them as you did these people. Then you can shut us down just as surely."

"Very well." Vinnek withdrew a rope from his robe and he used it to tie Ervinor's arm behind his back, anchoring it about his waist. "For now, you come with me."

CHAPTER 21

Nightmares of the Warrior

As Gabrion sat in the healing chamber, with Kitalla breathing normally nearby, his body fell into a deep and immovable sleep. He felt himself swimming around in his mind, trying to escape the utter darkness of his thoughts. He reached out with mental arms, trying to sway from one side to another, seeking a light that would free him of the stifling emptiness of his mind. Yet, wherever he thought he turned, the same blankness met his inner vision.

He floated there for a time, trying to understand why he was drifting in the first place. He vaguely recalled a harrowed journey and multiple days with jade-empowered stamina that prevented him from sleeping. And here his body was plunged in darkness to recover a semblance of his usual cycles.

An image of Kitalla flickered into view and Gabrion seized upon it, looking at the exhaustion on her face. She was much younger and seemed immature compared to the woman he knew. She didn't quite have the same determination in her eyes, and he wondered if he was viewing her past somehow.

The young thief ran in the black emptiness and she kept glancing over her shoulder in panic. Her clothes were a shifting mix of styles, from elegant princess to struggling peasant. Each moment, some facet of her appearance changed and the more Gabrion strained to watch, the faster everything transformed.

Kitalla kept running and shifting appearance until her belly widened and extended forth, echoing the child she once had carried. Gabrion had never known much of her past, for she had kept it guarded well against her companions, but now he knew of the darkness in her memories and, as he considered it, he realized that he was trying to make sense of the information.

In slow motion, Kitalla continued to run, her body weighed down by her unborn child. He saw a blur beside her, as if someone was running with her. She hadn't been alone when she was fleeing her pursuers, he recalled. The mist of color resolved itself into a young lover, though as he stared, it was his face upon the body instead.

From the blankness arrived an attacker and as Gabrion observed the scene, he saw that he was also the villain, chasing the young couple, his face a mask of rage. He opened his mouth and tried to call out to warn them, but pregnant Kitalla spun around, her arms becoming massive swords and she slashed into the pursuing Gabrion, tearing him to infinitesimal pieces.

Shuddering, Gabrion pulled away and the image changed, though some part of him wished it wouldn't. The buildings of Savvron rose up from the ground, growing out of the soil like flowers. Each structure waved lazily back and forth. He floated overhead, watching as a version of himself scampered around the village, batting at enemies with a blunt knife that was no longer than his thumb. His replica jabbed as hard as he could; the enemies laughed and pushed him away, and each time they did his body shrank in size. When he was no larger than an apple, a Hathren general stomped over, chortling, and squashed him.

As Gabrion hovered, he saw Mira pass his flattened corpse, skipping and frolicking merrily, a yellow ribbon in her hair. Young and free, Gabrion's beloved twirled with such overwhelming glee that, for a moment, he knew he loved her still. Then she laughed and the tenor of her voice was malicious and scheming. Gabrion's parents hurried over to her, bringing gifts of flowers and fruits, and Mira took the overflowing baskets from their hands, after which she pinched their faces and collapsed their heads until they were as small as Gabrion. Then with a kick, she punted Gabrion's mother into the air, where she exploded like glass.

Gabrion's mind cried out in horror, for he understood why he envisioned such a death, having shattered Mira's body. He reached out but he had no hands, no voice, no way of stopping the visions from coming.

Mira spun and spun, laughing as she went until Gabrion looked again and realized that she was now Kitalla. His mental body descended and the two of them stood in Jortun, Kitalla's body marred with countless wounds.

He tried to ask her what had happened, but she shook her finger as if to ward off his question. Then, beckoning him to follow, she guided him to a dark, dank cave in the mountain. Traversing into the stone, Gabrion realized that it was the same place he had been hacking away at outside the town, though the gap was certainly much larger than he could possibly have carved on his own.

Just under a league later, Kitalla stopped and she stood before him, suddenly naked. With her arms and legs outstretched, her body rose up into the air, light emanating from her fingers, hair, and toes. Then her body rotated as if she were cartwheeling, centered on her navel, faster and faster until she was a veritable disc of light. Her belly exploded outward and absorbed the illumination from the cavern, leaving only a tiny flickering spark in the center of the room. Gabrion struggled to see in the twinkling flame, but all he realized was that suddenly, Kitalla was gone.

He didn't know what it meant. His mental form slowly drifted into the rocky ground. He reached up, trying to remain in this place where Kitalla's last glimmer of life had burst apart, but he still had no limbs and he could not resist the pull.

Like a man falling into an ocean with a large rock tied to his foot, Gabrion panicked, thrashing around to put an end to the horrid visions. He felt the pressure of the stone swallow him ever so slowly, crushing against his legs, his stomach, his chest.

But he had the glass jade, he recalled, so he shouted for it, begging for help. It could easily cut through this stone and release him from the impending doom. He tried and tried again, but his mental body had no voice. The glass jade refused to hear him and he had no means of escape.

He slid further and further down, no longer able to feel the parts of his body that were below the surface. The rock touched his chin, yet he sank further still. Then his mouth was covered. As the stone approached his nose, he drew in as much air as he could, wondering how he could possibly survive the crushing prison.

Then his nose was below the surface and he realized suddenly that he didn't feel anything from his cheeks downward. His body was perhaps being devoured by a pack of tigroars, though he couldn't hear their screams from below.

Up and up the stone went, reaching his eyes. He slammed them shut, fearing the sensation of rock scraping against an eyeball. And as his eyes went down, he lost them and didn't know what they felt.

He tried to move, tried to free himself. Soon his whole head would be gone and he would be lost to oblivion.

He felt a soundwave shake against his head, but he couldn't decipher it without his ears. Yet his mental self told him what that sound was and he tried not to hear it inside his mind. He wanted to push it away and never hear it again.

But as the rock dragged him down and his essence was erased from existence, he heard Kitalla's voice repeatedly condemning him. "You failed me. You failed me."

CHAPTER 22

Caravan in the Forest

A FEW DAYS passed after Dariak separated from Randler in the forest. The mage was hurt and upset, but he couldn't face the bard, and he did his best not to wonder too much about him. He kept his thoughts on the path ahead, while also seeking shelter and sustenance when the needs arose.

He knew Randler was on his trail, but keeping his distance. They did not have their jades to find each other, but Dariak could hear him just out of sight, hunting and following.

The forest was mostly peaceful as Dariak wound his way along the path. Forest creatures were rare, which was fine, except when he was hungry. Eating herbs throughout the day was not particularly fulfilling.

As he went, Dariak spent time communing with nature. He sat down often to listen to the forest, the wind sweeping the leaves gently overhead, the animals chittering in their holes, the insects buzzing softly. He never quite felt alone.

Growing up, Dariak had spent most of his time in towns or the castle proper. His mother kept close tabs on him as she oversaw his magical training. The earth jade was bequeathed unto him in his teens, once his mother felt he needed to begin his training in earnest. Since then, the earth itself was much like a companion that responded to his needs.

He missed the jade now, for it had been a friend to him at times when he was otherwise alone. He had other boys and girls to play with, but some had stayed aloof because of his father. Perhaps their parents feared that Dariak's life would be as doomed as Delminor's. No one wanted ties with that.

Memories swirled in his mind of his childhood and the time he spent with the earth jade. Without anyone ever telling him to do so, he kept it hidden from others. It was a gift from his father and part of a legacy that Dariak wished to restore. Delminor's work gave the mages of Hathreneir deep skill sets, allowing most mages to dabble in multiple elements, rather than having to specialize in a single one. The flexibility opened new possibilities with magic, allowing even healers to better practice their craft, for they could tap into the earth powers to mend bones while healing energy reduced the pain.

Dariak frowned, irked how the mages had turned from his father for having lost the jades in the great war. Perhaps that was what had bothered the mages the most; Delminor had lost most of the jades to Kallisor, whose forces were stronger at the time the colossus was defeated. The mages wouldn't be able to focus their work as intently into the lost elements.

Few, however, understood the blood connection of the jades, that the artifacts needed to absorb part of the mage's life force to fully protect the bearer. The bond alone had allowed Dariak easy access to the powers of each jade he contacted, and not because he had blooded himself on them, but because he was connected to them through his father. It was uncommon knowledge that Dariak had never heard spoken by others. He doubted more than a handful of mages had discovered it.

Dariak thought of his motivations for his quest. He wanted to restore his father's good name, now that he understood how the mages of Hathreneir had turned away from Delminor. He wanted mages to be accepted wherever they went, regardless of what king sat upon a throne. He wanted the fighting to stop, so the lands could grow and the people could thrive. He wanted magic to be balanced across the kingdoms so Hathreneir would stop turning into a wasteland.

He regretted that his actions had partly spurred the current insurgence. He had joined the patrol that went to Savvron, and it was that battle that became the impetus for Kallisor's retaliation. Now people were dying and he was too far from the front lines to effect any change. He needed to leave the forest, seek Pyron, and claim the final missing jade before reassembling with his comrades.

Sounds echoed around him and Dariak pulled himself from his reverie to examine the area. It was more noise than Randler would make and different than a feral stampede. He grabbed two fistfuls of dirt, calling defensive spells to mind in case he needed them. He also clutched his staff, spilling some of the dirt in the process.

The sounds grew louder and he spotted a covered wagon and a ragtag team of adventurers slogging along one of the nearby paths. Dariak estimated they would meet up a little further ahead.

"Greetings, travelers," he called when the paths drew closer. "How goes your journey?"

"Well, friend, for our profits have never soared so high," returned a jolly woman a few years older than Dariak. "These woods are ripe with supplies."

"Is that so? In what materials do you trade?"

"Have you any coins?" one of the others asked.

"None on me," he confessed, "though my curiosity is sharp nonetheless."

The man grunted and turned away while the cheerful woman shrugged and responded. "Never mind Gaff; he's never happy. Give him a diamond the size of his fist and he will look for one that covers his arm. I am Lurina."

"I am Dariak. Pleased to meet you and your crew."

Lurina introduced the others. "Gaff and his brother Garr are our fighters." The two men were in their thirties and sported scars along their arms and faces. Dariak wondered idly if the scars were the result of countless battles or amateur fighting skill. "Old Tassa there is our weaver. Give her a handful of sturdy twigs and she will twist and bend them and craft anything you can think of. Her mate, Hetch, is a mute, so don't be bothered if he doesn't answer your questions." She pointed to the couple and Dariak noted there must be over twenty years between them. "My daughter, Ellie, is asleep in the back with my son, Frew. And lastly, this is Buckles," she finished, with a kind pat of the horse's neck. It was a mottled steed, and it looked beleaguered, as if it had been pulling the wagon for decades without rest.

The mage smiled warmly. "I've spent too much time in tense situations and haven't received such a warm greeting in a very long time." It was all too true, and as he looked at the group, he felt no threat from them at all.

"And you? You travel alone?" Lurina asked. "Large wood for wandering."

"I'm separated from my companions at the moment, though one is nearby." He absently looked over his shoulder, wondering if Randler was indeed close.

"You're welcome to walk along with us for as long as your path heads in the same direction, though first we would ask to meet your friend."

Dariak nodded slowly. "We had a disagreement the other day, so I don't know if he'll join us readily, but I can try."

"Please do, for having another mage among us would be welcome."

Dariak raised his eyebrow but he did not respond. He had already sensed energies among this group, and he assumed Lurina and the weaver were both practitioners. It was comforting and notable that she had sensed his own skills; she was no mere novice.

As they exchanged a few more pleasantries, Gaff ran off the path into the woods, his feet thumping heavily in the dirt. Dariak didn't know if the man was just clumsy or if he was purposely signaling his presence to any creatures or people in the area. He was gone for the better part of an hour, meeting up with them again later, his arms loaded with twigs, which he set in the back of the wagon.

Dariak had bargained for time to speak with Randler. He did so by delivering news of the war and a light overview of his own quest, which whittled down to his need to find a friend to the west. They traveled for a few more hours until the sky above the trees darkened enough to signal the onset of evening.

"Garr will have rustled up some food, if you'd like to gather your friend now," Lurina offered with the implied proviso.

He couldn't delay any longer, so Dariak retraced his steps, keeping his senses sharpened as he sought Randler.

The search did not take long, for the bard was busy rummaging in the wood for food of his own. He had chased a pair of squirrets toward their nest and his arms were swinging his staff around to crush their skulls.

"Randler."

The bard straightened sharply and the squirrets scampered away without meeting their doom. "I'm not ready to talk to you."

The mage kept his annoyance in check. "I don't care. Come, I made some friends and we're about to make camp."

"I don't know if I'm ready to rejoin you."

"You're only sharing a campsite. You can talk to them all you want; it doesn't mean you need to speak with me." Randler hadn't turned around to look at him yet. "Whatever's bothering you can wait for one night."

The only response he received at first was the bard hunching over, defeated. He nodded slowly and then followed Dariak silently back to the wagon.

Once introductions were made, Lurina ensured them they would be safe for the night so long as they kept their business to themselves and they made no attempts to touch their wares. Leery, Randler remained awake for half the night, after which he shook Dariak alert for a second watch. Dariak said nothing, but he complied with the bard's unspoken request.

The group traveled together for the next few days and as they went, Randler added some songs to the journey. They were deeper ballads, wrought with emotion, and it clued Dariak in to some of the bard's thoughts. Still, though, the two barely spoke.

The caravan itself had come up from the south and was winding its way through the wood for supplies, after which it was heading north to ply its trade. They made all sorts of wood products, from furniture and weapons to armor and utensils. Old Tassa was a strong earth mage, and she wove the twigs together with a practiced skill that Dariak envied. He spent some time with her, discussing the earthy magic, and she indulged his questions for a time before she began seeking her own form of payment. And because Dariak had no interest in her advances, their conversations all but stopped.

Randler found it amusing when Tassa tried to seduce the mage. Her gnarled hands tugged at her wrinkled face, as if she could flatten the skin to make herself glamorous and enticing. She didn't even seem to care when Dariak admitted his interest in men. She assured him that she was good with her hands, despite their appearance.

Lurina's children thought Randler was fascinating. They adored his velvety voice and they asked him to sing and sing for hours, not caring about the content at all. Only they were truly able to break through his sullen mood and make him laugh, which warmed Dariak's heart.

Roughly a week passed by as they wound through the woods before Randler's silence toward Dariak broke. The mage sat cross-legged by the campfire, his hands entrenched in the dirt. Deep breaths lifted Dariak's torso high and he folded in on himself as he exhaled. It looked as if the earth was trying to devour the mage and he was only mildly trying to escape its grasp.

Randler sat down beside Dariak, staring off down the path. He folded his hands around his knees and considered his words carefully. Dariak didn't dare interrupt him.

"I'm sorry for the way I've behaved," Randler started.

"You don't need—"

"Shh," he said softly. "You've always looked out for me and I pulled away from you. It hurt you, but it hurt me, too. It's all rather foolish."

Dariak looked at him in the dim firelight and kept silent.

"There was… a man in Vestular when I was growing up who was sick and twisted. He… did things… to boys and girls, things that never left visible scars, but hurt them anyway. He… gave them experiences they weren't ready for."

Dariak's jaw sank open but he could see pain on Randler's face and he wanted to offer support but it seemed as if Randler needed silence for now.

"I knew a few of the victims. They talked about what he did to them, touching them in adult ways." He hesitated. "Some of them spoke openly, but most were terrified. It was secret from the grownups and I never knew why they entrusted me with it because I wasn't one of them. I was only their friend."

Randler grabbed a handful of dirt and let it sift through his fingers. "We sort of knew it was wrong for an adult to do those things to them, but we were young and too scared. I couldn't tell my mother, as you can imagine. First, she might not even listen. But worse, she might have gone after him and killed him."

He paused for a time and Dariak waited patiently. "I didn't know what was worse. I was... jealous in some ways, that they were getting that attention from him. But I could see that they were changing. Our games weren't as fun anymore, and they seemed preoccupied with how people looked at them, as if others would glance at them and suddenly know what was going on. We all felt out of place for one reason or another.

"This one day, my friend Creus came to my house and he tried... showing me some of the things he was... learning. I freaked out. I knew it was wrong and I wanted no part of their little... cult. But I did, too. I didn't want to be the only kid in town who wasn't 'in the know.' It was a strange war in my head and I ended up lashing out and punching Creus. We beat each other up fairly well and when my mother found us, she was livid. I lied to her. I told her Creus tried to steal something from me. I guess maybe it was true in a way."

"What happened?"

"My mother went crazy and stormed right over to Creus' house and raged at his parents. He ran off and hid, and I went to my room and cried for hours. They eventually found him and asked about what he was trying to steal.

"Well, no," he amended. "They found him. But they couldn't ask him anything because he had killed himself out of shame. And in the dirt he wrote: I'll never tell."

Randler rubbed his face roughly. "I thought he deserved it for what he tried to do with me. But I also felt responsible and I didn't know what to do. Eventually I told his parents what was going on, at least in part, and I told them that other kids were in the same trouble."

"That must have been hard to do."

"It was terrible. I was... eight? It was bad enough that all those kids were being molested. After word got out, some of the parents beat their children for hiding it from them. Not all, just two or three. Some were horrified by it and swept their children to other towns. But my mother... First she beat me for keeping the secret, even though it hadn't been happening to me. Then she healed my wounds, after which she beat me again for lying to her about Creus. Then she blamed me for Creus' death, more so than his own parents did. I took a few good hits for that, and for waiting to confess. It was... unbearable at times."

He breathed deeply. "What made it worse was the agony in her eyes. I could see she was rattled by the events. She was hurting that I hadn't been protected from such a sick thing, but she didn't know how to handle it aside from taking it out on me."

He looked at Dariak. "That was really when I came to despise her magic, because for every wound she caused, she sealed it up and made it go away. And though she got rid of all the pain too, I still felt every bit of it first. I know, in her own way, she was trying to teach me a lesson, to never hide such a tragedy again. And knowing that she was really looking out for me… I don't know how to explain it. It pulled me close to her and pushed me away all at the same time.

"She never struck me, aside from that one set. Never before and never after. I know people whose parents beat them and they became broken. I don't feel broken because of her actions against me. But I do feel worse pain because of what happened to the others. Because I could have intervened long before the damage really affected them, long before Creus ever died."

"It wasn't your fault, Randler."

"I know that logically. But deep inside, I knew what was happening was wrong, and I did nothing to stop it. I've run into a number of those kids as adults. Some seemed fine, but others were mired in their baggage. Some removed themselves from others, becoming hermitic. Others became obsessed in the same behaviors that had been thrust upon them. A few adjusted decently, though they admitted they had these deeper urges they struggled to control. One of them even tried to seduce me, just for the sake of touching someone. None of them ever should have had to endure any of that. No one should ever have to."

Dariak opened his mouth to speak but Randler shook his head to silence him. "I've been irrational with you because of your infatuation with Gabrion—even if it isn't as strong as I was making it out to be; or even if it is. It isn't the same thing at all, I know, but how could that sick bastard shower his 'affections' on those children? Not just one child, but over a dozen. The multiplicity of it is the connection to Gabrion; however shallow that may seem, that's how it hit me.

"But what brought this on now was our time in the forest village, with all the people freely bathing in the nude, regardless of age, and our departure from there. Children and adults so casually undressed, together… it reminded me of things I pictured happening with my childhood friends. All so open, so… blatant. All by the decision of one man, Astrith.

"And I realize that most people have few qualms about their nakedness. But after all that happened—and I wasn't even part of the actual… events—I just… it just… I can't imagine what the inner turmoil must be for those whose bodies were violated. And he… ran off, free from judgment. I—I should have… done something. I— I—" His words failed him and he shook his head, sinking to silence, tears carving lines down his face, scarring him in the flickering firelight.

CHAPTER 23

Kitalla's Wounds

KITALLA LAY STILL on the bed, her body feeling strange and her thoughts in turmoil. She didn't want to talk to anyone and so she feigned sleep when others were nearby. A few times, she cracked her eyes open to see if she was alone. Well, more alone than usual, she corrected. For, even with people around her, she felt disconnected and solitary.

She had thought, foolishly, that her loneliness had come to an end. Her connection to the companions had shown her she could rely on others again, at least for travel and adventure. Recently meeting up with Gabrion had suggested a new path of light, one she never thought she would experience again. Their days together felt wonderful and exciting, until that fight with the eaglons, where the warrior simply refused to battle and she was poisoned.

Someone stirred in the room, and she understood that it was Gabrion himself, keeping vigil until she recovered. She had called him a protector. It was sweet, but she had had enough with the emptiness of his actions. To stand there doing nothing while the eaglons attacked? It said more to her than anything else.

It was hard not to cry as she relived the pain in her heart. She wasn't meant for happiness, she supposed. Why else would everything in her life be so stacked against her? Her absent father. Her servile childhood. Her stolen betrothal. Her murdered baby. Her trials with Grenthar. Now, too, her aching heart.

Kitalla had spent years on the road, struggling to survive, learning to engage in petty thievery. She had stumbled upon a caravan once, pillaging some food, only to be caught in the act. But instead of taking vengeance on her actions, the caravan had taken her in and trained her with better fighting and thieving skills. Soon after, she ventured off on her own until she came across Poltor and his band of misfits. Despite appearances, they were all highly skilled thieves, who simply chose not to engage in higher crime. They could have managed it, though, but it wasn't their goal.

Poltor had explained it best. "What's the point of stealing the king's treasure? We'll be hunted for it by other thieves. We'll end up spending it on defenses, and so it defeats itself. Besides, then what do we do with our days? Knit? No, I prefer it this way. Take when we need. We're better off not reaching too high. If we're caught, we're dead. No, as long as you're with me, you will keep your goals in check."

And he had never been caught, she knew. His philosophy worked well, for they had good times together. But her own travels had made her a target in her own right, and her recent attempt to rejoin his team was met with rejection. He couldn't risk his own safety by associating with her again.

Kitalla groaned. She had also lost her mentor. It was unbearable and something had to give. She peered through half-opened lids to check the room. No one was there, save Gabrion, who was fast asleep.

It was time. She got up from the bed and looked at the young warrior, so peaceful as he slept, even curled awkwardly on a bench. She wanted so much to curl up with him, caressing his skin and indulging her desires.

But indulgence had only brought her pain, she reminded herself. If Gabrion would not play the role she needed him to play, then she would leave him behind to sort out whatever was left for him to sort.

Two major tasks remained, however, so she stretched her fingers and examined Gabrion again, this time seeing him as a target for her skills. She looked more closely, seeking out the location of the one precious thing he kept with him. Her fingers reached out and probed gently, careful not to wake the warrior, and then she found it. Removing the glass jade from his pocket was not easy. At first the shard was elusive, as if it didn't want to be taken, but she persisted, her two jades empowering her. Gabrion shifted around as she fumbled with the shard, but he did not awaken. Moments later, the jade was in her own pocket and she made her way to the door.

She looked at him one last time before she left. He looked so innocent again, despite everything he had been through the past year.

She couldn't spare any more time for him if she was going to make her escape. She stepped through and closed the door, but before she walked away, she broke off the door handle and fidgeted with the mechanism, effectively locking Gabrion inside.

It didn't take long for her to find Ordren. He was dining with his soldiers, discussing plans for continued defense of the outpost.

"Kitalla, you're awake!"

"Yes, and thank you for your help. I could not have recovered without it."

"I think your jades had more to do with it than anything," he confessed. "My healers were baffled by their magic."

She couldn't dally so she changed the subject. "What's the state of things here?" As he responded, she took a seat and gathered herself some food from the serving plates around her. It was nothing fancy, but it would sustain her.

"The king has left me in charge here," Ordren said. "At first, there was some chaos, for we were not recognized by the king's troops when they first arrived. We convinced them of our duty to Kallisor and, after some time, I was entrusted with the defenses. Mostly, a contingent of fighters arrives once a week, camps for a day or two, and then ventures elsewhere, sometimes into Hathreneir."

"Then this place is secure for now," Kitalla said. "But the time for action is coming."

The commander's face curled into a scowl. "Dariak's foolish quest is still underway then?"

She looked at him incredulously. "Why else would we have come here? It's time to gather the rest of our supporters. The jades are nearly united and Dariak will need to show his strength to the kings."

Ordren shook his head. "I don't know that I can resume that old quest."

"You abandoned the king when you left Pindington and joined us in the first place. This is no time to change your mind."

The older man was clearly angered but he kept his voice under control. "I am the first line of defense for our kingdom now, Kitalla. I am not some security guard in a quiet port town, breaking up bar fights. No, here I have a purpose. I've taken over well here and have earned the king's own praise."

"Such that it is."

He glared at her for a time. "Not all of us are free to wander the land."

She shrugged. "Perhaps. But the healers you have here, the mages. Were they also approved by the king?"

Ordren paled. "That isn't the point."

"It's exactly the point that Dariak was always trying to make. And it shows me that you've not only thrown your lot in with the king, you're acting like him, too. Secreting away the mages at your side, using them when it suits you, but otherwise pretending they don't exist. It's shameful."

"It's not the same." But for the life of him, he couldn't explain how.

Kitalla waited but he said nothing else. She sighed deeply. "Fine. Don't aid us directly, but at least fulfill part of your oath to Dariak. Send word that we're assembling in Marritosh over in southern Hathreneir. Anyone who would join our cause should come together, breaking allegiance to both kings and seeking a new way."

"That is a hard word to get out without being marked a traitor."

"Surely some of the men under your command were with us in the battle at Savvron and will be able to comply. It's the least you can do, Ordren." She looked around at the other soldiers in the room, most of whom were engaged in their own conversations.

He frowned, then banged his fist on the table. "Very well."

"Try to get a mage to venture out, too," she suggested. "There is a whole underground of magic users here and they may be willing to lend a hand."

"It sounds as if you and Gabrion are heading on your way again so soon. Don't you need more time to recover?"

Kitalla's voice went hollow. "Gabrion should be escorted to his father in Savvron. I have his jade and I will deliver it to Dariak."

"Escorted?"

"Yes. I will gather a few things and then I'm off. He's asleep and will not be accompanying me. Tell him..." She hesitated. "Tell him to take care of himself."

"He doesn't know you're leaving..."

"Nor will you tell him until I'm long gone."

CHAPTER 24

Ervinor's Plea

A FEW DAYS had passed since Ervinor was brought within Magehaven as a prisoner. He was fed and allowed to wash, but that was all. He had no contact with anyone of importance, and all his attempts to speak with the guards resulted in a stern silence.

At last, Vinnek agreed to meet with him, and Ervinor was taken from his room and brought to an official-looking chamber within the tower. The chairs were plush and ornate. The walls were carved of wood, and, based on things the others had said, wood anywhere within the tower was rare. Most of the walls were made of stone, clearly fortified with magical spells; such a tall structure would have otherwise buckled underneath the weight of it all.

While Ervinor waited for Vinnek to arrive, he studied the intricate details in the wood. One panel was full of etched leaves, each its own size and shape, angled in its own direction, like a random pile composed from the leaves of dozens of trees. It reminded him of his little army. Each fighter with his or her own background and goals, coming together for training and battles, but remaining individual otherwise.

Another carving was of mountains overlaying each other endlessly into the distance, but when he tilted his head, he thought the crests and troughs looked like the silhouettes of men and women. Whether he was projecting his own imagery into the carving or if it was the intent of the artist, he had no idea. It evoked a sense of the years of work and effort that was needed to build a kingdom, or even this tower. Countless nameless faces stacked one atop another.

The thoughts irked him so he stepped away from the walls and set himself into one of the plush chairs. It was undeniably comfortable and he wondered if most of the tower was furnished with them. It was unlikely, he knew, but when it came to mages, nothing was certain.

He remembered his first encounter with magic. Two mages were in a tavern in Pindington and had a disagreement over the best components for an engorgement spell. At first their dispute was kept in hushed tones, for magic was never openly encouraged in Kallisor. But the ale had been flowing and it wasn't long before their words erupted into action.

Ervinor was a simple guard back then and he wasn't even on duty at the time. He'd had a few drinks of his own, but he saw the growing agitation at the mages' table. They pulled out strange objects and though he knew he couldn't properly identify them, he tried anyway. They looked like peas, dried worms, various leaves, a marble, pieces of bark, and so on. One mage would push three components forward and claim their importance, then the other would shove them aside and signal to four others. In their stupor, they forgot their place and the mages started chanting while crushing various components and drawing the energies from them. A roach running across the floor was the first critter to be enlarged by their spells. Initially, Ervinor thought he was too far into his ale, but then the second mage enlarged a spider too much and the creature splattered all over the corner of the bar, dripping sticky webbing everywhere with the spider's engorged guts.

The tavern patrons were furious and they pulverized the mages while Ervinor stepped in to try to stop an all-out brawl. He took a chair to the back of the head and collapsed, waking later to find the fight was over and the mages had been taken into custody. He remembered being a little frightened that a few crazy words and items could allow them to do something like make a creature larger, but he also thought it was interesting.

Since then, he had sought out a few other mage-related incidents to try to learn more about magic without seeming too interested. He pursued knowledge, but carefully. Even though he didn't have the aptitude, he didn't want rumors floating around that he was a mage sympathizer. It would have ruined his career.

As the next two years rolled by, he saw the levels of injustice enacted upon the wizards. The spells in the Prisoner's Tower alone showed that there was some tolerance to magic, but on the streets it was all but forbidden. The dichotomy upset him. As long as the mages weren't hurting anyone, why should they be cowed? When a group of suspected mages was hunted down by a band of rogues and the rest of the guard helped only by cheering on the thieves, Ervinor knew his time with the troop was going to end soon. He started sneaking in to mage dwellings to learn more about magic, and once word reached him about Dariak's quest, he joined eagerly, hoping one day to help build more equality among the people.

He found it ironic that he was now sitting in a Hathren mage tower, at the mercy of mages who thought he had commanded his own army to attack them. Nothing could have been further from his intent.

Vinnek's strategy seemed to be to keep people stewing, for he did not show up for another hour or so. Ervinor did his best to keep the agitation from his voice when the old mage entered.

"Greetings, Vinnek."

"I realize that the time has come for us to discuss matters," the old man said. He still wore his mustard colored robe, but he was fidgeting with his hands and that made Ervinor nervous.

"I hope to clear up the unfortunate incident," Ervinor started.

"No need. No need."

"But you think we set out to ambush you and we did not. We seek only sanctuary here for a time."

"Yes, yes, so you've said before." The mage made his way toward a chair and dropped heavily into it. "The truth is, young Ervinor, that I don't much care right now."

"I don't understand."

"The Council. It... it is in a weary state. So many of our members are gone or dead. The few of us left have little conviction to do more than to close our doors to the world until we recover our strength. I'm inclined to follow suit at this point."

"But the world needs you," Ervinor said. "The mages of Hathreneir can't simply turn and hide away. What about the things Dariak is trying to accomplish? How can he help achieve peace in Kallisor without all of you in the mix?"

Vinnek raised an eyebrow. "Did you think we were going to rally behind Dariak and support his quest?"

"I—" He stopped and pursed his lips. "I guess I secretly hoped so. He's going to need more than the fighters I have with me if he's going to be able to infiltrate the war and bring an end to the fighting."

"You are... young," Vinnek said. "You dream of a fantasy world where mages live freely and peacefully amongst the commoners."

"Well, yes. Aren't mages welcomed in Hathreneir? Can't you walk around without fear of being attacked because of your skills?"

"Foolish boy. Yes, we are welcome, but only in small numbers at any given time. Exceptions are made, of course, but the things we can do strike fear in the hearts of men. It is why we have our towers here in Hathreneir. They are the safest places for mages to be, even now."

Ervinor considered for a moment. "I didn't think you all faced persecution here as well."

"It isn't as if we're escorted to the king's dungeon with any spell we cast, but if a mage shows he is losing control or being too ambitious, then yes. He is subdued."

"But that sounds reasonable. Don't we do the same for warriors or thieves? If the fighter brawls with the weak, he's taken away. If the rogue steals a great enough treasure, a true hunt begins to find and stop him. So why not also stop a mage who's on the verge of becoming dangerous?"

Vinnek looked at the young general. "Point taken." He then leaned forward. "You have an interesting wisdom about you. It is... refreshing."

"Then tell me what's wrong here."

"Very well. There is no point in refusing, for word is spreading quickly anyway. We have lost access to all the jades now. Because of it, our powers here are weakening."

"Really?"

Vinnek shifted in his seat. "Yes. We kept at least one jade in the large room upstairs to empower the barrier and the Trials that visitors must endure. All, that is, except your group. Yes, in all the years since the Trials were instated, yours is the only group of people to escape their tests. That alone has made the mages here nervous, for we have no assessment of your strengths or intents."

Ervinor kept his cool. "I have tried to explain our intent."

Vinnek waved him off. "Yes, yes. But at least one jade was always here. Now that every shard is gone, the power is waning and the spells we have been practicing are weaker and they sometimes fail completely."

Ervinor remembered Frast talking about his last excursion to the tower, where he had ultimately claimed the beast jade. Along the way, he had spouted out a wild variety of spells with much more ease than he was used to. And after leaving the barrier, those spells returned to their regular strength. He had spoken of it in conjecture only, but now Ervinor received confirmation. The energies within the tower had made him stronger.

"There is panic mounting," Vinnek said. "Some fear the day our powers will die completely. I don't think that's likely, for mages have lived away from the towers for years and still command their magic."

"Towers," Ervinor echoed, emphasizing the plural. "I have only seen this tower."

Vinnek accepted the tangent. "That's not entirely true, for Kallisor also housed a mage tower, though its use was altered long ago."

Ervinor's eyes widened with realization. "The Prisoner's Tower in Pindington."

"Indeed. Only magic could have allowed such a structure to remain aloft for so long. And only powerful magic would have brought it crashing down."

"The lightning jade," Ervinor recalled, shuddering. The decimation of the city had prompted him to follow Ordren in support of Dariak's quest.

"And there is another tower in the northwest," Vinnek finished. "It's out of the way, however, and fewer mages train there. It's almost as if it has been bleeding for years, slowly dying a silent death. Nowadays, the oldest of our kind go there when they wish to work with new spells. It's safer to be away from others if and when an aged mind forgets key parts of an incantation. Some also go to practice our craft without the augmentations that have been here."

"I see."

"I fear some of our current residents would escort a few Council members there come morning, if they could. Me among them."

"Why you?"

Vinnek snorted. "My ideas are mildly popular here, but I'm not. No, I've come to taking my time about things, as you have no doubt witnessed yourself, and though I own up to that, some see me as weakening."

Ervinor shook his head. "It hardly makes sense to me to send mages away from here when you're already having a hard time. Wouldn't it make matters worse?"

"You're an interesting young man, Ervinor. Not many people without magic are as supportive as you."

"I want to help, if I can. But I know that Dariak will also need your help when he returns."

Vinnek buried his face in his hands. "Harping on Dariak's quest will only lose you favor among others here. The mages have turned from Delminor for losing the jades. Some are angry that he died and could no longer supply them with easy routes to magic. And because the anger has been so strong among some, those who support Delminor are all but silenced. You will have difficulty in your quest, I fear."

But Ervinor wouldn't accept it. "That's nonsense. Even if they can't realize their folly in turning away from Dariak's father, they need to see reason about this current task. They need to understand that we have to unite our lands in peace. We all need each other."

"Indeed, young one, though I'm surprised you understand the depths of it."

"I grew up with everything I ever needed, but I didn't grow up blind. I listened. I watched. I saw that other kids in town didn't have the life I had. And I knew others had it better. Kallisor thrives because the land is fertile essentially everywhere. We can grow any kind of food you can imagine. We have roaming herds to supply our meat, too. Water is plentiful enough."

Vinnek added, "Whereas here, we need mages in every town to help ensure the crops will hold, that water is purified, and that the beasts are kept out of our towns."

"I knew things were difficult, but things sound much worse here than I thought." Ervinor's brows furrowed. "It makes me wonder why my king would want to own this land at all."

Vinnek chuckled warmly. "Perhaps you have never wondered where glass trinkets come from or large slabs of immense marble, like the ones that exist in your king's castle. Many of those resources are from here originally, and many cannot be obtained realistically without the help of mages. This is obviously an overly simplistic view on our two benefits, but it is at the heart of the conflict."

Ervinor scratched his head. "Then why ban mages? You would think the king would make use of them to harvest the land."

"Unless those mages were once responsible for turning parts of this land into desolate waste, untillable, infertile, useless. Those same mages might kill the lushness of Kallisor, no?"

"But—"

"No, Ervinor. No more of this topic. It irritates me."

He choked down his words and turned toward something else before Vinnek decided to end the interview altogether. "You say the mages here are panicking. What can be done to help them?"

Vinnek wrung his hands together. "There is very little that can be done, I must say. Without any jades to power the barrier and enhance the energies within, our powers will wane."

"But not completely."

"No, no. But as I said before, everyone would feel disastrously weakened after all the time they've spent here relying on those augmented energies." He sighed. "It would make more sense if you were a mage."

Ervinor stood and squared himself with Vinnek. "I don't think so, Vinnek. You see, all my life, I counted on having two arms. Eating, playing, and running all depended on two arms. I'm weakened now that one's gone, but I haven't given up. And it's silly to hear that you mages with your ability to pull energy and make things happen with your minds… and you're giving up because the work is a little harder. I don't accept it."

Old Vinnek made a face like a child being admonished for swiping extra dessert. "I… don't know what to tell you."

"Cooperation, Vinnek. That's what's needed. By everyone. We need to work with you. You need to work with us. And the factions of mages here with different views need to work together, too. Let's come together as one unit and build this place back up. Let's rebuild the confidence of the mages here. And once they see they can succeed and that cooperation is the key, then they will follow Dariak when the time comes. Because in the end, that's what we're seeking: cooperation of all the people in these lands."

The mage stood up and met Ervinor's gaze. "I don't understand how a one-armed upstart like you can light a fire in an old man like me. Very well, Ervinor. Let's go speak with the Council. Let them hear what you have to say. Though, don't expect much."

Ervinor nodded. "I expect to be heard. And that should be enough for the doubters."

"Perhaps, my feisty friend. Perhaps."

CHAPTER 25

Gabrion's Awakening

WHEN GABRION OPENED his eyes, he felt different. The world seemed heavy and painful. Something drastic had changed, but he didn't know what. Rising from the bench, he stretched his back to work out the kinks, breathing deeply to clear the sleep from his lungs. His dreams had felt empty and aimless, but he didn't dwell on them.

The room was brightly lit and the air wafting through was magically purified by the healers residing at the outpost. None of them was in the room, but they periodically swept in and called the air to swish about, bringing healing energies to every corner. After months of doing so, the room itself almost seemed to breathe with life.

Once he fully wakened, Gabrion noticed that he was truly alone. The treatment bed was empty and that meant that Kitalla had awoken at last. He discarded the thought that she might have been moved instead, believing he would have heard the commotion of taking her out.

A smile crossed his face as he stood up. Kitalla was all right. They would be able to share some time together again. She had opened his body to a world of new experiences and it seemed as if she had much more to teach him. And he was eager to learn.

He didn't let thoughts of Mira cut into his musing. He remained focused on Kitalla only, letting lust consume him, for it helped to reduce his pain. He wondered idly if she felt the same, but once the thought popped into his mind, he shoved it aside, not wishing to dwell on it. Why not just have some fun?

Gabrion made his way toward the door and tugged on the handle. The iron bar did not turn like it was supposed to. Pressing on it again, Gabrion tensed. Something was wrong.

With two hands, the warrior yanked on the handle again, but nothing happened. He strained and tugged on the bar, but it didn't budge at all. Annoyed fists pounded on the heavy metal door but there was no effect. Something was really wrong.

Surely his fists crashing into the door should have caused enough damage so he could push it away. His hands had cut into a mountainside! This door was softer than that rock and he should be able to make his way through without a problem.

Yet, bang and bang as he might, the door didn't even dent. Frustration overwhelmed him as he threw his shoulder against the obstacle, again and again.

Gabrion moved aside and banged his hands against the wall, expecting the stone to chip away. But still, nothing happened except for the growing pain in his hands. He hadn't felt such pain in a while. Not since the incident with Mira.

Chills ran down Gabrion's spine as the realization slowly sank in. He knew it would be fruitless to try, but he searched himself anyway.

Kitalla had taken his jade.

Emotions fountained within him and he had no idea which ones to address first. Outrage flared the strongest and he pounded his fists against the wall. How could she have stolen the jade from him? He hadn't been able to set it down; the jade hadn't permitted it. It had behaved like a tacky glue that shifted around his skin, unable to come off. Yet it had gone with Kitalla.

He felt betrayed. The shard was the only thing keeping him alive. And people away. No, she couldn't have taken it from him—it couldn't have chosen to go with her—not when he still needed it to keep his distance from others.

Fear crept in next, for it reminded him that he would now be vulnerable to attack and to others. People would be able to hunt him down and exact their revenge on his actions. They deserved their chance, he felt, but he feared it, too. He didn't want to die. But he deserved it after all he had done.

He had failed his quest in the worst possible way, and his one means of dealing with his self-loathing was taken from him. He didn't know if he wanted to scream at Kitalla or to crumble and fade away.

The warrior stepped back from the door, no longer wanting to leave this sanctuary. It was his last haven. Outside these four walls, nothing would protect him. He needed to stay here, whatever the cost.

But then he thought of the pleasure he had experienced with Kitalla, and he suddenly hated himself for it. It was wrong to indulge himself with her. What did he deserve of happiness in any form? Even using those moments as an escape should not be allowed. He hadn't earned safety, happiness, or pleasure.

And during those times, Kitalla had seemed so joyous, so playful. Did she suspect there was more to his motives than just escaping his pain? Had she suddenly realized his game? Was that why she had run off?

Shame weighed down on him and Gabrion bent to his knees. Nothing made sense right now and he was tired of it. He had wallowed for so long and it had gotten him nowhere. Instead, he only hurt more people, from the poor villagers in Jortun to Kitalla herself.

And in the end, hadn't he been punishing himself too? Yes, but he had earned that much. Not the rest, though. The other people should not have felt any aspect of his pain. They did not need to carry his burden in any form, whether by dying as Mira had died or by helping him to hide.

When he left his home to embark upon this journey, his father had told him not to lose himself. It had sounded like silly advice, even when it was repeated on his later visit to Savvron. But now it made more sense. He was lost and confused and he didn't know what to do.

Gabrion sat fully on the ground, folding his legs and resting his hands in his lap. Then he asked himself a question he had never asked before. It was one that would help him, he knew. It wouldn't be a distraction like the three-sided diagram the elder of Gerrish had shown him. It wouldn't be a mindless activity meant to wear himself out. It also wouldn't be errant slaying of the people around him who were just trying to help.

It was a simple question with a complex answer. And as he pondered it, he thought back to his childhood. He thought of his friends growing up. He considered how he had developed along the journey with Dariak. All the triumphs and failures washed over and through him and instead of drowning in them, he examined them.

Whenever his mind went silent, he asked the question again and he challenged himself to respond in some form or other. He would not let the question go unanswered any longer. Not until the pieces fell into place. Not until he had discovered some form of truth.

The question echoed within him for hours.

"Who am I?"

C HAPTER 26

Trouble With Triggans

D ARIAK AND R ANDLER continued traveling with Lurina and her caravan for several days, winding their way through the dense forest, taking a serpentine path that seemed to carry them forever through the wood.

"How much further?" Dariak asked.

"Two, three days," Lurina shrugged, unperturbed by the duration of their journey.

"It's taking too long. We need to be elsewhere by now."

The middle-aged woman eyed him critically. "To find your 'friend?'"

Dariak noted the emphasis on the last word; she knew his goal was not necessarily a peaceful one. "I must find him, and soon."

"Will you kill him for what you seek? Torture, maybe? Perhaps threaten him with a few spells?"

"It isn't like that."

Lurina was silent for a moment. "I could be wrong. It might be five or six more days. Some trees have fallen up ahead."

Dariak frowned, for they had been met with numerous delays already. Some of the pathways were improperly marked, leading them in wide circles that weren't obvious at first. Rain had fallen and slowed the wagon to a grinding halt, its wheels mired in mud. Now trees blocked the way, probably from the same storm. It was frustrating.

"Your quest is clearly important," she mused. "Surely it's worth the effort to keep going."

"At least this can be handled more easily than the mud." Dariak hopped down from the wagon and jogged to the fallen trees. The trunks were tall and they blocked the path well. The horse and wagon had no chance of getting over the debris, and with the shrubs off the path to either side, there was no way of them getting around. The hearty trunks had fallen atop each other and were nearly as tall as Dariak as they lay in a heap.

Kneeling, Dariak dipped his fingers into the soil, reaching his mind within to feel the natural energies. After some contemplation, he felt the telltale tingling in his fingers that signaled the powers within the soil itself. He hummed a low note and let his mind wander, trying to determine the best course of action for removing the trees. He then snapped off a small twig and laid it in front of him.

"Depfrithorious kreenahn ruhl, rostobar kethric korrios tanz. Frustigar allevios pynator karrathos rostrall." As he spoke, he dug his left hand into the dirt under the left side of the twig and scooped it into a pile on the right side of the twig, repeating the motion until he had dug a ditch and erected a mound. The power coursed through him and he felt the energies of the earth respond in kind. Massive creaking echoed in his ears, but he could not look yet. He needed to keep digging, to keep piling, to keep reaching into the energies and bending them to his will.

A scream echoed off in the distance. "Look out!" The next thing Dariak knew, Randler tackled him and desperately tried to scramble out of the way. The effort was followed by a terrible cry of pain.

Dariak shook himself alert and disentangled himself from Randler. The bard was screaming, tears racing down his chin. It took a few moments for the mage to make sense of what had happened.

His spell was tied to the earth before him and as he dug his hand into the soil, so too did a large mass of earth move from under the trees in front of him. Little by little, the giant trunk tilted upward from the spell, but apparently the ever-increasing mound was unstable and the trunk rolled forward. Randler shoved Dariak out of the way, but the bard's legs were crushed under the falling tree.

"Randler!" Dariak gasped, immediately drawing healing energies into the bard. He sensed great damage in the legs. He couldn't focus on that yet, though. He needed to get Randler out from under the tree. He recast the digging spell and created a small indentation under Randler, after which he pulled the bard away.

Randler was incoherent with pain, his legs badly mangled, and his arms flailing about, as if he were trying to flee the agony, his cries piercing through the air.

Dariak threw some dirt onto the bard's legs and he immediately began chanting. *"Mentithoss kaie patrithos mellurian bindicus forthri notra-pollus."* The dirt around Randler's legs hardened. "Forgive me," Dariak whispered, reaching for Randler's legs and tugging them into a more proper position. He strained to ignore Randler's thrashing and screaming, calling to the energies again and fortifying the dirt by drawing in some sticks from the very tree that had crushed the man's legs. He magically fashioned two splints, then he set his focus to easing Randler's pain.

He didn't have any supplies and despite the times he had tried to train with the other mages along his journey, his healing skills were still relatively weak. It didn't stop him from trying. Scrambling for herbs nearby, he grasped them and used their inherent strengths to draw healing into Randler, but mostly to set him to sleep. It was all he would be able to do.

Eventually, Randler fell into a fitful slumber, his body twitching and igniting pain each time. It was only then that Dariak remembered they weren't alone. The rest of the caravan was paces away. Why hadn't they come to help? Why was he facing this trial alone?

He rose up and scanned the area. The wagon was stopped and no one seemed to be onboard. Closing his eyes, Dariak focused on the sounds of the forest, hoping to determine what was amiss. Voices echoed off in the distance, followed by the sounds of a scuffle.

Dariak was torn. He looked back at Randler and knelt beside him. "I need their help. I can't heal you without them. I—I have to leave you here. But I'll be right back. Please, Randler. I love you. Be strong."

He wrenched himself away from the fallen bard and ran toward the sounds of fighting, swinging by the wagon long enough to grab his staff. The team was far off the path and he could hear shouts and grunts as the battle went on. Dariak raced through, keeping his head low to avoid the branches.

"Garr, go left!" Lurina's voice called out. "Tassa, hurry!" She then dissolved into hurried casting.

Dariak arrived to see one of Lurina's children unconscious on the ground and the other hovering over him protectively, her face and arms badly scratched. Gaff was sprawled on the ground, blood seeping from a bad wound. Old Tessa was also injured, and she was only upright because silent Hetch made it possible. He held her up with one strong arm, being sure to allow her arms freedom of movement for spells, while his other arm held a buckler, which he used to fend off attack.

Dariak then noted their foes. It was a ragtag mix of forest creatures, from squirrets to eaglons, though only a couple of each. The true foe was one Dariak hadn't seen before, and had only heard tales of as a child: Triggans.

Triggans were natives of this forest, protecting its borders from centuries of conflict and life all around. They were rarely seen by humans and many regarded them as a myth. But as Dariak looked upon them, he knew he should have paid more credence to the tales. Each triggan looked like a miniature walking tree, with four arms apiece and a wild mangy head of unruly leafy hair. Overlong legs carried them swiftly when they needed to, but the appendages served other purposes as well.

Two squirrets launched rocks at Dariak and broke his reverie. He rolled and charged at the little creatures, cracking one in the skull and stunning it. The other critter scampered away to its last remaining companion, where they teamed up against Garr, who was also fighting off an eaglon.

Another eaglon swooped toward Lurina, and Dariak could see that she was deep into casting a spell and could not defend herself. He leaped in the way and swung his staff at the unsuspecting foe, causing it to swerve aside and miss its mark. With a screech, the eaglon pivoted in the air and dove for the new threat. Dariak kept calm and focused his thoughts on striking the bird. He didn't want to use any magic, in case he inadvertently interfered with Lurina's spell. The bird swooped in and Dariak swung, but missed. He spun and brought the staff up again as he did so, clipping the eaglon's tail. The bird shrieked and landed on a triggan briefly to gather itself for another attack.

The triggan didn't seem to notice its visitor. The tree-creature was barely taller than Dariak and stalking toward him, no obvious weapon in hand, aside from the sharp-looking branches extruding from its torso. Three other triggans stalked closer, branches waving threateningly, but they weren't exactly charging. As Dariak realized this, the eaglon left its perch and dove for him. Like before, he swung with a sidestep and brought his staff around to attack the eaglon from behind. This time he connected with the creature's torso, striking it from the sky and taking it out of the fight.

Garr struggled against his adversaries. He was highly distracted by the eaglon circling over his head, and he kept swiping at it with his sword. Frontal attacks were rarely useful, Dariak had come to understand, for the avian creatures were agile and maneuverable. As the bungling warrior focused on the attacker above him, the squirrets pelted him with rocks, gaining an advantage as they started to overwhelm him.

Dariak sprinted over to help, but he never made it. Lurina and Tessa finished their joint spell and the ground shook, knocking everyone to their knees. A rift opened in the ground, creating a deep trench that separated them from the oncoming triggans. Unaffected by the earthquake, the eaglon swooped in and Garr was finished.

"It didn't work!" Lurina cried out. "They still come!"

Dariak's gaze swept around and he agreed that the rift in the earth was not going to deter the approaching triggans. Their long legs would allow them to simply hop over the trench as if it wasn't even there. Dariak struggled to his feet and ran to Garr's body, crashing his staff into the eaglon as it continued to rip into the man's flesh. Dariak then claimed the sword and scared off the disoriented squirrets before rushing back to Lurina, who was still on her knees.

"What do we do now?" he asked.

"I—I don't know," she stammered. "Must be… something." She reached for rocks and twigs, but she made no indication to Dariak what she planned to do with them. Tassa and Hetch had collapsed and made no effort to rise up again.

"This doesn't end here," Dariak decided. He swept the sword through the air to get a feel for it, then told the others to get back. He brushed some dirt on his hands and erected a minor protective shield around himself. It wouldn't be nearly as effective as ones empowered with a shard of glass, but it was all he had.

The first triggan reached the chasm and, as Dariak expected, easily leaped over it and continued on. Its face was made of cracked bark and it looked angry. All four arms waved through the air menacingly as it stalked forward. Dariak wondered why it didn't run ahead and end him, now that the other creatures were subdued. Perhaps the tree-like creature was afraid of his sword.

Charging, Dariak shouted a battle cry and chopped his sword through the air, cutting off one of the triggan's arms. He turned aside and sprinted out of the way before the being could strike back. He had rarely used a sword before and attacking with it now was foreign. He knew he had to strike quickly and get away, then reassess. As he looked, he smiled at his successful cut, but the joy didn't last for long.

The fallen branch hit the ground and lay there for only a few moments before it too rose up. Broken bits of wood reached outward, becoming feet, while its own small branches became writhing arms. He hadn't hurt the triggan at all; he had spawned a new one.

He couldn't let it dissuade him. Perhaps cutting off the head would be more effective. His protection spell was still intact, so he charged in, cutting horizontally into the skinny trunk. The injured triggan's head simply fell off. It felt more like cutting a flower's stem than a walking log. It didn't take long for Dariak to see that the attack did not have the desired effect. Indeed, the triggan head pushed itself on its side and used its branches as legs and arms. Meanwhile, the rest of the trunk continued to lumber onward.

Dariak sensed that these creatures could run if they needed to, but that was it. They didn't need to. The rift in the ground was meaningless to them, for they clambered over it, as the other triggans were now doing. Chopping them down only created more of them. It reminded him of earthworms and their ability to regenerate. No, the triggans didn't need to run right now; they could meander forward until their quarry was captured or destroyed.

He backed away slowly, trying to think of another plan of attack. Lurina at last unleashed her next spell, launching a flurry of rocks and twigs as if she herself were a squirret. The projectiles impaled a few of the triggans, but did not stop them. One branch was dislodged; it hit the ground, then rose up to join the encroaching foes.

Desperation took over and Dariak called to one more spell that was sure to work. Sweeping his hands around, drawing the energies from the air, he summoned his fire dart spell. Though it wasn't strong, the blasts of fire struck the triggans and they burned like kindling. Dart after dart flew from his fingertips, draining his own strength as he launched them. Each triggan looked like a torch, hobbling along in pain.

Then they started to run. Fiery man-like trees rushed toward Dariak, burned leaves and branches falling away and striking up smaller fires among the woodland debris. Dariak readied his sword and swept it left and right as the triggans approached. He knew it would cause them to multiply, but they would be smaller and hopefully easier to subdue. Lurina hurried over to Tassa and Hetch and helped to pull them back toward the wagon.

Dariak spun wildly around, hacking and slashing the burning triggans, bringing their bodies to the ground. They pushed onward, however, and he grew weary. But the fires were magical in nature and they did not diminish easily while kindling was available. As the triggans were cut down and their pressing forces lessened, the fires consumed them more quickly. Dariak kept his sword swinging as much as possible, stopping only to douse himself of flames when one of the triggans came too close. Then at last the fire overwhelmed the creatures and they were slain.

Unfortunately, though, the trouble wasn't over yet, for the errant fires splattered everywhere and the dry leaves and sticks in the area caught the fire hungrily. Soon the whole area was ablaze and Dariak knew in his heart that the whole forest would be in jeopardy of burning down.

And it would be his fault.

"Lurina!" he called, but when he looked around, she was gone. Every second he waited, the fires spread more violently. Fully grown trees took the flames and acrid smoke started to build up.

Earth was his strongest element, but he didn't know how it would help him now. He couldn't smother the flames with enough dirt, nor cause enough trees to fall to break the fire chain. He knew he needed water, but he wasn't sure he could manage it without the jade.

Fire burned all around him and he wanted to run off and avoid the danger here. But he needed to right this wrong. He hadn't meant to destroy the forest, just stop the triggans. Perhaps, he wondered, the forest itself was all one big triggan living here countless centuries ago, its branches and leaves falling and sprouting up as the other trees, which in turn made others. Now they were all sharing the same fate.

Dariak pulled frantically on the energies, reaching with all his might. He had expended a lot of effort trying to clear the trees from the road, then trying to offer some relief to Randler, and now this fight. He didn't know if he could do this.

The water jade had been the second piece he had ever owned, taken with Kitalla's and Gabrion's help back at the Kallisor museum. He had communed with it and had become a watery sort of substance during a fight soon after claiming it. However, he hadn't ever really devoted a lot of time to its properties, and though they worked well with the earth, it was like trying to recall a story from when he was a little child. Parts of it he could sense, but the rest was out of his reach.

The fire crackled and hissed all around him and he shouted any spells that came to mind, but he had no way of making it rain, or drawing from some unseen stream to quell the flames. Instead, he needed to do something more drastic.

"Randler, forgive me," he muttered. "I hope someone else can tend to you. But... I have no choice."

Dariak reached his hands out wide and he closed his eyes. Ever so slowly, he turned in circles as he chanted over and over, *"Drathinius marrusth ettrinox endinnior kaie. Drathinius marrusth ettrinox endinnior kaie."*

Crackling fire echoed louder, but he kept his eyes tightly closed as he continued turning slowly around, arms outstretched. Heat welled up around him as the forest burned and he responded only by chanting the spell louder and louder, fighting against the pain that reached for him.

Within moments, his hands ached and burned as if he had fallen into a campfire. The heat and pain reached up his arms, spiraling in toward his heart. He chanted and he turned, keeping his arms out to his side, despite his desire to drop and roll in the dirt to douse the flames.

The fire licked at his makeshift clothing and he felt the leaves burn away. His legs also drew the heat from the forest as he turned about. The feeling left his fingertips first and he knew it was because he didn't have fingers anymore. The fire had consumed them. But he did not shout in pain, for he deserved this torment. His fire darts had started the blaze. Now he drew the flames back within himself, but he pulled all the new fires too. The energy raged throughout his body, but as long as he achieved his goal, he didn't care.

He repeated the chant again, *"Drathinius marrusth ettrinox endinnior kaie."*

It would be for others to unite the kingdoms now. His destiny was here, to rescue this forest from his folly. It wasn't what he had set out to do, but if he couldn't save a single forest, what chance would he have had at uniting two warring kingdoms? No, this was fine, he decided. He had made his share of mistakes and had caused others plenty of needless pain. This was his due.

All he could feel now was the world spinning around and his body in raging agony. There was nothing else to hold on to. He couldn't feel any more energies in the area and so he cracked open his eyes. The forest around him was scorched and hurting, but it was no longer ablaze. His own body, however, was surrounded by fire.

It was time.

Dariak's slow spinning had two purposes. One was to allow him to draw in all the flames from the area, but the other was to cut a ridge into the soft earth. As the fire overwhelmed him, he allowed himself to drop within that circle like a pile of useless ash.

And there the fire was extinguished.

CHAPTER 27

Kitalla's Detour

LEAVING GABRION BEHIND was a difficult decision, but she had no choice. The jades needed to reach Dariak soon and the warrior had become a liability. She was angry and hurt by his actions, standing there as she faced the eaglons, even when she took a hit. She knew his pain was deep, but so was hers, yet she pressed onward. It may have been difficult, but she knew it was right.

It didn't take long for her to cross the border into Hathreneir. She specifically chose to follow in the Kallisorian army's footsteps, for Dariak had told them long ago that the magical border guardians generally hated large groups, so she felt it was more likely that this location wouldn't be watched.

There weren't any extra horses at the outpost, so she was on foot again. Without help, it meant another week of travel before reaching Marritosh. She tried not to think about it, but pushed on instead. Something would inspire her and allow her some means of reaching her destination faster.

In her pocket, she felt for the jades. She now had the metal, fire, and glass shards, but she barely knew how to activate them on her own. The metal jade resonated the most with her and she felt she could trust it for protection, but what she really needed was for the jade to magically become some sort of metal horse and carry her across the desert. She laughed at herself for the thought.

The sand was well-trampled by the set of fighters who had crossed this region of the desert into Hathreneir. She felt as if the fighting drew closer to the castle, but it was hard to tell for certain. Encampments could be seen off in the horizon and she needed to steer clear of them if she was going to make it to the others.

Kitalla was about to veer toward the south to avoid being spotted by distant scouts, but then she reconsidered. "No," she said aloud, grinning. Setting her sights on the nearest tent, she dipped her head low and entered a jog.

Some time later she was met by three guards in full royal armor. "Stop, trespasser, or die."

"I'd like to see you try," she challenged. "Besides, I'm not here for trouble."

"Your presence is not known to us. You must speak with the captain."

Kitalla shrugged, rolling her eyes carelessly, but taking a survey as she did so. Her ears picked up sounds of discontent, though she wasn't sure of its source. She could linger a while and discover if the troops were sour about the leadership or the state of the war itself, but she didn't plan to stay for long.

"Captain, a visitor."

Kitalla was shown into a large tent and a burly man sat by a table with a noticeably barren map laid out before him. Several daggers were jabbed into the parchment to mark the locations of troops: green handles for Kallisor, black for Hathreneir.

The captain responded to the intrusion by throwing a blanket over the table. "What is the meaning of this?"

"You're the captain?" Kitalla asked in mock politeness. "I was told I needed to speak with you, though I was only passing through."

The heavyset man stood and tugged on his mustache. "We're at war, little lass. No one is 'passing through' right now. Except maybe traitors."

She sighed, bored. "Whatever. Neither side is going to win this war anyway."

"What!" the man raged. "Traitorous scum."

Kitalla dismissed his anger with a wave of her hand. "You warmongers never understand. All you do is set up battles, fight, let people die, and then go home calling it a victory."

"Who are you?"

Kitalla stepped toward the table and flung back the blanket from the map. The captain eyed her cautiously but did not stop her as she studied the layout. "This is all wrong," she said. "This battalion will be dead by morning and this one will fall soon after."

The man's face lit red. "How dare you. You will die for your insolence."

"See, now you're being pigheaded by not even asking me why."

She could see the warring expressions on his face. He wanted to strike her down where she stood, but he also wondered if she was right. "Fine… Why?"

"These troops are facing the west and the sandorpions will surprise them from the east. While they're busy fighting them off, these Hathren troops will overtake them. As for this group, they're set closer to the castle so the Hathrens have more forces there to send in. Pretty simple, really."

The man scanned the map and looked up at Kitalla. "How do I know you're not some Hathren spy sneaking in here to give me bad advice to set up an ambush?"

Kitalla shrugged. "You don't. It doesn't matter though. Fight all you want; neither side can win like this."

The captain's voice lowered to a growl. "What do you suggest as an alternative, surrender?"

Kitalla laughed melodically. "You really don't have any forethought, do you? How did you even make captain?" She raised her hands in supplication and waited for him to calm down. "I will give you two options. First, call for a meeting among the commanders and negotiate peace, refuting the kings."

"Preposterous! What you suggest is more traitorous nonsense and you will die where you stand."

"Option two," she continued, undaunted, "is to send your battalion to this location and capture the commander within, holding him for ransom, giving you time to pause the fighting long enough for reinforcements to arrive from Kallisor."

"That's… absurd," he said, but the expression on his face said otherwise. Kitalla waited as he worked it out. "This could easily be a trap for us."

"No matter. I'll go in alone and bring the commander back. All I ask is that you don't interfere and when I'm done, you give me a horse."

"Now it really does sound like a trap. How are you supposed to infiltrate their ranks alone?"

"I got in here, didn't I?" Then before he knew what was happening, Kitalla leaped over the table and tackled him, covering his mouth so he wouldn't scream. She pinned one hand behind his back and breathed hotly in his ear. "You're all fools, don't you know that? Letting me in here like this, so easily. Look at your guards over there. They don't know if they should charge and take me down or watch to see what happens. This is why you will never win."

She then shoved him away and straightened her tunic. "Easy, boys, I've made my point." She then turned to the captain, who lay on the ground rubbing his wrists. "Option one or option two. And don't dare ask for option three; you won't like that one at all."

He saw the crazed look in her eye and decided that option three wouldn't bode well for him. Whether she was a Hathren spy setting a trap or a Kallisorian sympathizer trying to help, he knew she had the ability to kill him if she desired. "Take a horse and get out of here. I don't want any trouble from you."

She looked disappointed. "You don't want me to go kidnap a Hathren commander for you?"

He shook his head. "It won't end well. Just go. Leave here and if you enter this camp again, we won't hesitate to kill you."

"You can try. Pity, though. I was in the mood for a fight today." She stepped toward the exit and grabbed one of the guards by the top of his chest plate. "Get me a nice horsie, okay?" She then shoved him outside the tent and then looked back at the other guard. "It's your job to make sure I leave here safely, understood?"

The young man glanced at his captain, after which he nodded feverishly, his eyes wide.

"Good," she smiled, turning back to the captain. "So you know, I'm no Hathren spy. But I've come to realize that this war business is just a way for us to kill each other by the hundreds. I intend to help stop the fighting on both sides. How many soldiers have you already lost? How many more do you project losing? Think about it and come up with new tactics. Otherwise, we're doomed to fight this war for all eternity."

A horse nickered outside and she swept out of the tent and pounced upon the offered ride. Without hesitating, she snapped the reins and bolted away from the camp.

She wasn't sure which way to go at first. Partly, she wanted to enact her plan of capturing the enemy commander, but she also realized that it wouldn't necessarily work out in her favor. She trusted the jades would protect her as much as they could, but she had no idea when their abilities would give out. Her own skills she understood better, and in many ways she relished the challenge of the attack.

Deep down, however, she knew she couldn't afford to be rash without proper backup. She needed her companions for a task of that nature and so she turned the horse southwest and entered a hearty gallop. Better to be away from the camps than to chance getting involved after all.

The Kallisorian horse wasn't well trained for the sand and it struggled to find its footing for a while. The beast pushed hard at her command and eventually it found its way. Encroaching sand rodia were ignored as the horse pummeled past them. She urged the horse onward as hard as she dared, stopping when necessary to give the creature some water from her own canteen.

Camping at night was a challenge, for she had no way of securing the horse from running away. Plus, she had no defenses against any nighttime attackers. Instead, she coaxed the horse to sleep and then lay a few yards off, buried in the sand. When creatures whisked by, they mostly ignored the horse, and those that didn't were scared away when Kitalla screeched wildly and jumped up from her hiding place.

With her mare, Kitalla reached Marritosh in two days, arriving at its border in the evening. The majority of the town lay in ruins. The scent of death lingered about the place and she took some time to investigate the charred husk of the town after tying the horse to a post to keep it still.

First she noticed evidence of random fires, all striking the western faces of the buildings, suggesting a magical attack rather than a natural blaze. She wondered if the king had sent troops to circle around the village first or if the mages at the tower had simply lost their minds and unleashed their fury upon the people. Houses were smashed and ruined at random; she couldn't imagine the king would sanction such destruction, even with Kallisor reinforcements camping here. Plus, they more likely would have attacked from the north.

Testing her hunch, Kitalla wound through the village toward the northern end, keeping her senses honed for movement. As she reached the central part of town, the damage grew far worse. Blood stains marked the paths and the stones. Homes were razed by vicious fire. And there, between a row of disintegrated houses, she saw a pile of bodies, charred husks picked by carrion birds and noshed upon by sand rodia and sandorpions alike.

The remnants of armor and cloth upon the scavenged bodies signaled the Hathren king's forces, and from the pile of carnage, she realized that the town had been purposely torched to subdue them. There were no sounds of life nearby. Once the corpses had been cleaned, even the scavengers had moved on.

Kitalla checked a few places throughout the village for survivors, but there were none to be found. She located the bodies of several older villagers, including all four elders and their closest companions. They had banded together at the end, bringing the calamitous fires upon their home to end the fighting and, she surmised, to give Ervinor and the others a chance to escape.

Night fell upon her while she looked for survivors, so she found a house that was in reasonable condition and there she set herself to sleep. In the morning, she would gather whatever supplies she could find and head out in search of the army. Where they would have ventured, she could only guess. North to the castle seemed unlikely, but so too did west to Magehaven, especially if the mages had come and unleashed a barrage of their own fire upon the town. Kitalla was exhausted and she put the matter aside, as she had learned to do many years ago. It was a time for sleep, and though she had left the horse at the eastern edge of town, she did not return for it until morning. She didn't like the thought of walking through the dead town in the middle of the night.

This once, she allowed herself to feel scared and alone, so she curled into a ball on a broken bed, breathing deeply until her heart rate calmed and she was able to clear her mind of worry. Each breath was tainted and cloying. The night was perfectly silent and utterly dark.

CHAPTER 28

A General Idea

THE MAGE COUNCIL was reluctant to meet with Ervinor, but Vinnek convinced them to at least listen for a time. The fighter was brought to the meeting chamber alone, with no support from his army, who waited in captivity in the lower levels. Ervinor didn't mind. If it gave the mages comfort, then so be it. He wasn't trying to hurt anyone and when it came down to it, he was at their mercy regardless.

For nearly an hour, he stood in the center of the chamber, awaiting the arrival of the Council members. Like Vinnek, they seemed determined to keep their guests waiting. He shifted from one foot to another, but refused to otherwise show his impatience. Three mages guarded him, but he made no effort to speak with them. They hadn't said a word on their ascent to the room, except to tell him to keep moving.

Ervinor hoped to break through the distrust and hatred among them. He needed the leaders to hear him out and understand why working together was so important to them all. It seemed silly that he would have to spell it out, but many people in the world were close-minded and focused only on their own small purviews. Even the kings.

At last, the rear door to the chamber opened and eight mages filed inside, Vinnek among them. Each wore colored robes, hoods drawn over their heads, obscuring them from view. He didn't understand why they needed to hide from him, but he withheld comment, wondering how he would reach them. Vinnek had hinted that it wouldn't be easy to make them understand. Seeing them now, covered head to toe with their faces in shadow, Ervinor realized he had underestimated their resistance.

Vinnek stood after the other mages had settled into their chairs. His cowl also masked his face. "The Council recognizes the arrival of Ervinor, general of the army from Kallisor. State your business."

"My lords and ladies of the prestigious Mage Council, I thank you for your time here tonight—"

"Shut it," croaked one of the mages. "If you're going to butter us up all day then get out of here and go back home to your lousy king. What is your business here?"

Ervinor straightened his spine at the remark. "I am not here at the behest of my king and I have little love for his involvement in this war."

Another mage piped up. "Yet you come here with an army that you intend to use in the war, do you not?"

"My intent is to help stop the war, and that is why I need your help."

A third mage groaned. "This fool reeks of Dariak. Send him out."

"Give me a chance," Ervinor implored. "Allow me at least that much."

"To what end? You'll just try to kill us when it comes down to it."

"That's what you think? That I came here to betray you?"

"Isn't that what Kallisorians do to Hathrens and mages?"

Ervinor looked around at the ten of them. "So that's five of you who are unwilling to listen to what I have to say. What of the rest of you? Are you all as petulant and dumb?"

"Now see here!" one of the mages cried out, rising to her feet. "You beseech our help, do you not? What right have you to speak as such?"

Ervinor waited while a few of the mages chimed in and then bickered about the wisdom of even meeting with him. At last they settled down and Ervinor couldn't help feeling annoyed that Vinnek hadn't spoken at all in his defense. Clearly, the old man was afraid of his peers.

Another mage rose to her feet. "Friends, let us put our bitterness aside long enough to at least hear him out." Grudgingly, the others agreed. "I am Shelloni," she said to Ervinor. "I once supported Dariak, but his recent murder of another master has caused me to reconsider his motivations. You are not likely to sway me. Yet I agreed to hear you. So speak, but be efficient in your words, fighter."

Ervinor nodded his thanks and then carved the most important information from his mind to present to this temperamental Council. It wasn't how he had wanted to talk to them, but they left him little choice. "The warriors of Kallisor are numerous and strong. They will overwhelm your forces without mage support. You mages here are weakened by the loss of the jades. Countless men and women will die in the fighting, you among them."

"Preposterous!"

"Outrageous!"

"Vinnek, you will suffer for the outrage of bringing this man before us."

"Foul treachery! Threatening us in our own tower."

Ervinor held his hand up in supplication, waiting until the mages calmed themselves to listen further. Now, though, he felt some were merely biding their time until they could strike him down with some spell or other. He didn't let it bother him. "At least now I have your attention. I have no intention of killing or assisting in the killing of any of you. My alternative is to find a way for us to all come together, put an end to the fighting once and for all, then go on to start a family of my own in a world where my children won't have to be trained for war."

"You seek the impossible," Shelloni accused. "It can never happen."

"You're wrong and I have seen it." The mages all turned to face him now, curious despite themselves. "A mage from your own breast came to Kallisor seeking a goal that only he knew in his heart. He traveled the land, gathering jades, hoping to reunite them into one so that the people could also band together as one."

"More Dariak nonsense," one mage grumbled, but no one joined in this time.

Ervinor continued. "Along his way, he made some mistakes, but he always held true to his goal. He made friends as he went; friends with the sworn enemy. And those friends came to accept his ideals, despite his ties to Hathreneir, and despite being a mage. He first united a small band of travelers, then gained the respect of many others. We came together to defend a helpless village from a needless attack, then we ventured here to your land.

"The people of Marritosh first welcomed us for the bartering we brought, but they came to understand Dariak's desire. They stood with us in many ways, despite other trials we faced here on your soil." At this, he pointedly looked at his severed shoulder. "There were casualties on both sides, and in many cases it was because no one would listen.

"Dariak had a claim to the jades, but you refused his request. It led to an accident where one of your kind died, but instead of investigating the incident properly, you bound Dariak and refused to let him speak. It led to more misunderstandings and more needless deaths.

"Around that time, I was at the castle, and because of more confusion, people died and I lost my arm. It was the people of Marritosh who truly put me back together. They not only mended my body and kept me alive, but they mended my heart and reminded me why I am on this journey.

"Then, mages left here and attacked that village, killing your own citizens who could barely defend themselves against you. My troops held them back and, yes, I served as executioner of Farrenok for his deeds. Perhaps I had no right to do so, but his siege wasn't unlike a grown man striking and slaying his young child out of frustration. He had no right to attack those people.

"We then were beset by the king's forces, who came down from the castle to put an end to our uprising. But it was a token force and they refused to speak with us before they attacked. We defended ourselves, but it brought on the self-sacrifice of the remaining people of Marritosh, who gave their lives so that we might complete our quest. I would have died that day to defend these people, gladly, but Herchig and the others saw fit to keep me whole.

"We came here, seeking your help. Who else in the land but a mage can see beyond the petty squabbles that keep the kings at war? But I was wrong. You mages are a sorry lot. It took a misunderstanding to gain my people access to your gate. A misunderstanding that led to the death of one of my commanders and those who followed her in here. Again, it was a lack of communication that led to those losses. I had no intention of attacking you. Your mages outside overheard part of a heated conversation and they acted on it in error.

"Yet at the same time, it's my fault, too. Verna was not well-trained yet, not for my army at least. She didn't know when to hold back and when to strike. I regret her actions as if they were my own; I should have been able to prevent what happened.

"But in some way, I'm grateful for her rashness, for now I stand before you. I'm not some Kallisorian general, seeking to usurp your power and put an end to your freedoms. No. I am a man who believes in an ideal that we can find a common ground, if only we put aside our differences and learn to speak with one another.

Learn to listen. Learn to hope. Learn to look past what makes us unique long enough to find a way to cherish those unique qualities.

"I didn't grow up around mages. I was told to fear them and to scorn them. But it was a mage who truly opened my eyes to a better world, to a bigger and brighter hope. And I didn't doubt what was right because he was a mage or a Hathren. No, I put aside my petty prejudices and I followed my heart to seek this ideal future that we have all earned. I have traveled with mages for a long time now, and I am a greater man for it. The irony of it is that *they* follow *me*.

"I know the reason why. They believe in the future, too. It's why I'm standing here. It's why I'm alive at all. The people came together and protected me and healed me in my times of need. And I did my best to protect them in return. Now I ask of you to join us. I ask you to look within your hearts to figure out what kind of a world you want to live in. If that world is like the one we already have, then great. Stay here and have your way.

"But if the lot of you want something better, something real, something safe, then consider the future I describe. Put aside your prejudice and find a way to band together with me. With Dariak. So that way, when he returns with the jades, we can stop the war and the world can be one that we all create together, without all the bloodshed and all the death and deceit and despair.

"I ask you to stand with me."

CHAPTER 29

Ordren's Maneuver

WITH KITALLA GONE, Gabrion remained at the outpost, anguished and alone. He avoided the other fighters as much as possible, surfacing only to eat when mealtimes came. Most of the time, he languished in the darkness of the cell in the basement, where no one disturbed his musings.

At last, however, Ordren went down to see the ailing young man. He stomped his booted feet on the steps, alerting Gabrion to his presence long before he was in the room. "The darkness does not suit you, friend."

"Leave me," Gabrion muttered.

"I *have* left you here and you have done nothing but mope. I'll have it no longer. You are a drain on resources and morale. It's time for you to earn your keep." When Gabrion didn't move, Ordren swept in and grabbed him by the arm and hoisted him to his feet. "You will *rise* when spoken to by a superior officer."

"Ordren…"

"Sir!" Ordren corrected him. "I am a commander of the Kallisorian army, and you will respond to me with proper respect. You will address me as 'sir' when you speak, is that clear?"

"This is ridicul—"

Ordren punched him in the gut, knocking the wind out of him. "You will not question me again, soldier. Now, on your feet!"

Gabrion eyed him oddly but he pushed himself upright and waited. Strange voices echoed in his memories. He had relied on them at one time but now they were nondescript.

"Soldier, stand at attention!"

He knew what Ordren meant, but he didn't know why he was being ordered. The commander raised an eyebrow with Gabrion's hesitation, so the warrior responded by straightening his back, squaring his shoulders, and snapping his heels together. "Yes, sir."

"A troop is heading in from Kallisor castle in the morning. They are a fresh lot of fighters with little training, so I'm told. I need my men here to show them the proper meaning of discipline. Is that clear?"

"Ordren, I—" he started, but then found himself on the floor again, doubled over in pain.

"I asked you, soldier, is that clear?"

Gabrion coughed. "Sir. Yes, sir."

"I expect you to be upstairs within the hour for training. Gather your wits and come above." Without waiting for a response, Ordren spun on his heel and ascended the stairs.

Gabrion had no idea why Ordren was suddenly acting this way, but he didn't dwell on it for long, for as he sat there, the indiscriminate voices in the back of his mind surfaced again. He focused on them and reached for them. They reminded him of home.

Get on your feet, and try again. Don't lower your guard. Keep an active stance. You may all be farmers and tinkerers, but you can learn the basics like anyone else. I won't hear you complain about the work; you volunteered for this assignment. Get up, get up, get up. Arm yourselves. The enemy won't wait while you roll in the mud. Get up!

The memories swept over him and Gabrion pulled himself to his feet. Andron had come to his hometown from the king's guard to train the people of Savvron to fight and defend themselves from attack. Because they were further south, they were not a direct line of invasion, but their village was relatively close to the border and that put them at risk. Andron had ridden in on a large warhorse, speaking of valor and triumph against their foes, and Gabrion had immediately become enthralled.

Rise up, youth of Savvron. Take arms. Defend your homes and your families. The king has little to spare in terms of troops for your aid. I am here as that aid. I will train you, those who are willing. I'll make you strong.

Gabrion was among the first men to enlist in the training sessions. His mother hadn't wanted him to do it, but he intended to keep them safe and the promise of riches, or at least payment from the king, was enough incentive beyond keeping them protected. He would use that money to start his life with Mira, as her husband.

Find that something to fight for that only you have within you. Find a reason to push through to be stronger than you ever thought possible. You will ache. You will hurt, but when it comes to a fight, if you train well, then you will live. Hear me and learn from me. I will guide you and train you.

Training had been rigorous and sometimes dangerous, but Gabrion had learned that he had a natural proclivity for fighting, even early on. Andron often sparred with him personally, then had him train some of the others. He wasn't necessarily the best of the group, but he was young and energetic and that bolstered his inherent talent.

I am not your friend, but I am here to bring out the greatest warrior in you that I can. I will hurt you along the way. Your challenge is to not let me. If you see me attack, get out of the way. If you cannot dodge, then parry. When you have an opening, strike. If there is no opening, create one.

Gabrion stretched himself in the dungeon, thinking back to those simpler days when the war was only a threat. Those days, when his biggest worries were about training sessions and maintaining the farm with his parents. Those days, with Mira.

War is ugly and there will be death. Some of you will die and there will be no glory for you then. Glory does not follow the dead. Once you die, you are gone. Only the living matter, so you must fight and struggle and live. That is what I am here to teach you.

Mira was gone. His mother was gone. It was possible that his father had died by now, if the fighting kept migrating south to Savvron. He had lost so much in the name of war. He knew the fighting needed to end and he had hoped that running from the battles would bring him peace. But it hadn't. It had only drawn Kitalla to him and then his inaction drove her away.

The war will never end. This is something you must know. If you think you can face one battle and then sleep happily, you're a fool. Our land is a breeding ground for war. Even in our times of peace we fight with each other; over land, over prices, over lovers. War is in us and it will ever be. You can either be on the losing side or the winning side. Pick up your weapon if you wish to live. Otherwise, go run home, where you will die, defenseless.

Andron's voice kept echoing in his mind, repeating the various speeches he had given during the training sessions and at town events or in the tavern. The hardened soldier had never wavered from trying to recruit new fighters, though it meant more work for him to train them. He reveled in the work, Gabrion realized. He needed it. It gave him purpose.

Gabrion had sulked for long enough. Walking up the steps, he pulled himself from the dungeon and sought out the war room, where Ordren would command his fighters. Gabrion was no real soldier of the army, but he would at least do this, in honor of Andron, who gave his life to save Savvron.

Ordren stood at one end of the room while nearly thirty fighters gathered in groups in front of him. They stood tall and strong, ready to support each other through whatever their commander required. Gabrion could feel the camaraderie among them but he was entirely left out. He didn't know how to ingratiate himself into the groups, to be counted among their number. So he stood there, slightly off on his own, watching, listening.

Ordren looked at the gathering. "Fighters of Kallisor, tomorrow another host arrives from the east. I have word from the king that these are younger than the last crew. They will need some fine-tuning in the art of war. Most haven't seen battle and will likely panic at their first scuffle. It's imperative their fear doesn't occur against the Hathrens."

Gabrion listened to the plan that followed and though he had some reservations about it, he understood the need. When the meeting adjourned, he waited as the fighters left, Ordren included, then decided he didn't want to be alone. He wanted a new purpose. He decided he would be a part of the plan.

Striding from the room, Gabrion walked the stone hallway to the armory. It wasn't loaded with a wide array of weapons and armor, but it didn't matter. He was still cloaked in the magic vestments Herchig had given him in Marritosh. All he needed was a sword.

The weapons themselves were in some disrepair, but a notched sword would do the job until it cracked, and the weaponsmith assured Gabrion that these weapons had been tested for durability and would last at least a few more battles before they needed to be melted down and recast.

Gabrion made his way to the training pitch and limbered up with a few sword strikes against a wooden practice dummy. He hated to admit it to himself, but it felt good to hold a sword again. Even without the protection of the glass jade, he knew he was skilled enough to keep himself safe. Strike, strike, parry, bend, roll, strike. He went through a series of motions, dodging and weaving around the dummy as if it pursued him.

"Gabrion, is it?" asked a young fighter named Urrith. "Want a real sparring partner?"

Urrith was a wiry lad, barely seventeen, but his skill suggested he had been fighting since he was born. With a wild crop of black-brown hair masking his face, Gabrion wondered how the young man saw anything at all. Urrith favored a short sword, which gave Gabrion an advantage with his long sword, but Urrith's agility more than made up the difference.

Swords clanged as the two men sparred, dodging and weaving and keeping out of each other's reach. Some of the other fighters stopped their own matches just to watch these two in their bout.

Gabrion brought his sword across low and Urrith leaped over it, following with a strike of his own. Gabrion dodged to the side with an upward kick that struck Urrith's forearm, but he didn't lose his weapon. Urrith responded with a flip in the air, landing with the sword in his left hand, cutting wildly out to the side. Gabrion barely dodged the blow, not expecting the change of hands. He deliberately fell backward and rolled up onto his feet, bringing his sword to bear.

Urrith grinned as he turned, keeping the blade in his left hand and inching toward Gabrion. The crowd cheered them on, alternating between the two fighters in support. Urrith jabbed ahead, then spun, sweeping the blade around. Gabrion backstepped out of the way then dropped his sword. The crowd gasped, seeing that it was over.

But when Urrith laughed and leaned in for the final strike, Gabrion pounced forward, sliding around the blade and grabbing Urrith's arm. The warrior brought the youth's arm up and then down sharply, dislodging the short sword, and pinned the arm behind him. Gabrion reached his left hand around and grabbed Urrith's throat, after which Urrith yielded.

They disengaged and Urrith turned to Gabrion. "You're really something in a fight. I thought I had you when you lost your weapon."

"I didn't 'lose' it. I threw it down," Gabrion said. "Gave you a sense of confidence, didn't it? It also gave me the advantage."

The young man laughed. "I have to spar with you again, and soon. Maybe after tomorrow's welcoming ceremony."

Gabrion thought about it for a moment and he was surprised at how happy it made him feel. "Yes, that would be good." Urrith saluted him and he and the crowd scattered off to other tasks. Some of them returned to sparring, trying to incorporate some of the techniques they had just seen. It made Gabrion smile.

You have to train against fighters better than you, Gabrion, if you want to grow as a warrior. Yet I do not begrudge my time here with you rookies, for I pass along my knowledge, in the hopes that you will each become my better and then you will come back and train me to be stronger too. Only in working this way can we all grow.

"It didn't make much sense to me then, Andron," Gabrion muttered under his breath. "But I think I understand now."

Evening came and went, with the usual army rations for dinner. The men engaged in some leisure activities, like playing dice, but Gabrion didn't join them. He went up to the wall to sit with the night watch, knowing he had work to do in the morning with the rest of the fighters. The night air was crisp and vibrant, and he felt the cold winter winds coming in from afar. It wouldn't be long before the season changed completely and though he knew there wouldn't likely be snow here so close to the desert border, he wondered what this place would look like blanketed in white.

Morning came swiftly and one of the night guards shook Gabrion awake where he had fallen asleep against the battlements. Off in the distance he could see movement, which signaled the incoming troops. He went downstairs, grabbed a quick bite to eat, then met up with the rest of the men to engage in their assigned duty. Ordren alone strode from the outpost to greet the newcomers.

There were fifty or so fighters among them, guided by one of the king's messengers, not a knight. Clearly, even the king didn't have high hopes for this group. Sending them to battle was almost like an execution of these poor souls, and the few Hathrens who would be defeated in the process would hardly be worth the loss.

Gabrion cleared his thoughts. He needed to be focused here. Keeping his eyes on Ordren, he stayed silent and sharp. Soon they would greet the new forces. It would be any moment now.

There! Ordren raised his hand in greeting and then slashed it down. Gabrion and the others threw open the doors and gave their most frightening battle cries and flashed their weapons brazenly, diving into the impromptu fray. Most of the new fighters met the challenge; only a handful panicked and bolted away. Swords and daggers clashed in the morning air, ringing in a vibrant staccato to awaken them fully. Gabrion took on three fighters, using their momentum against them, batting them with the flat side of his blade rather than striking outright. The others, however, fought fiercely and it took all Gabrion's skill not to take or deliver any damage.

Urrith had learned a lot from Gabrion's maneuvers the night before, and he used this time to practice the skill as much as he could. He parried and dodged, but then he swept in alongside the fighter's defenses and disarmed him, one after another. The goal was to pin each new fighter and not to seriously harm any of them. The added challenge was good for the more seasoned fighters, for it honed their control.

After some time, Ordren blew a deep horn and called a halt to the battle. He then properly welcomed the new recruits into the outpost to clean up and to feast. They were bewildered with the reception, but eventually they settled in. Ordren gave them time to eat, then he set Gabrion with his next set of instructions.

Once the afternoon hit full force, Gabrion approached the new recruits and took them to the training ground, where he channeled Andron's lessons and set about training the young men and women who had been drafted into the king's service. Like his own mentor, he asked them each their background and why they had enlisted, but then he told them to put their pasts aside, as Andron had said to the trainees of Savvron.

"We go to war," Gabrion said. "We fight for our futures. It doesn't matter what brought us here today. It only matters what we do from this point forward. In your hearts, hold on to what drives you. In your minds, hold on to your training. In your bodies, hold on to your skills. We will pave a new path to freedom with our victories. We won't all survive, but each of us has a role to play. The better we play that role, the more of us there will be who see tomorrow. Be strong and we will survive. We all have something within us to live for. So let us train hard and be ready to face what lies before us. Together, we'll create a future we can all be proud of."

The new recruits raised their arms in cheer and Gabrion stood there, ready to begin their training now that he had instilled them with hope. He almost believed his own words.

Almost.

CHAPTER 30

Wood and Stone

PINPRICKS OF PAIN skittered up and down his body, reminding him of every torment he had felt in his life. Scrapes as a child. Cuts as a man. And now a truly powerful flood of raging inner fury. He was barely aware of his surroundings, but felt
some glimpses of sunlight searing him. It seemed like sunlight, anyway. It could be
the light from a close torch or a fiery poker from a wild blacksmith. The light flickered sporadically, teasing him, tormenting him, trying to make him wince and shy
away.

He also felt a touch of wind against his aching body. Its presence reminded him
that he wasn't entirely alone. Some other force was nearby in the world. It also told
him he was still alive, not walking through the stony corridor of death toward a
nondescript glimmer in the distance. The zephyr was fleeting but enough to distract
him from the rest.

Cracking his eyes open proved challenging, as did moving his limbs. He knew
he could feel them, but that was part of the problem, for nothing felt right or whole.
He lay there, struggling to piece together what had happened.

Pressure shook against his ears and his brain told him he should understand
what it meant. He didn't want to know. Not yet. He wanted to hold on to this co-
cooned state for a while, for he feared what would await him if he awoke fully. But
the pressure was insistent. Demanding. Deeper, it tried to penetrate into his skull
and he moaned against its assault.

"Are you whole?" he heard, piecing the vibrations together.

He didn't know how to respond because he didn't know the answer.

"Can you stand?"

Standing seemed impossible. Not after what he had just been through. No
power in the land could grant him the ability to rise up on his own feet, not now.

"Here, let me help."

Before he could push words of denial from his mouth, he felt something crash
against him, rousing his body from its huddled state and wrenching him apart. He
didn't want to let go. He didn't want this voice to pull him from the ground. He
wanted to lie there a while longer.

"Come on. You can do this."

The world spun as he was dragged upward. Teetering wildly, he wondered if this new sensation would always be a part of him now. He didn't like it at all.

"Up!" the voice insisted. "Yes, come on."

The ground beneath him escaped his grasp. That one surface had kept him steady and safe, and it was being dragged away from him by the relentless tugging of the voice. He reached his hands out to hold himself down, but the soil slipped through his fingers and he found no purchase. He couldn't see well as the dirt fled away and he ascended upwards, upwards, away from this haven.

"There you go."

He wavered, feeling something against him, supporting him. He wasn't drifting endlessly up to the heavens after all. He felt strange and weak and his body rebelled against this new position. Yet something about it felt better than where he was moments before. This was more right, in a way. The way it was supposed to be.

Light seeped into his cracked eyelids and slowly the blobs of color amassed into shapes. The breeze still struck his skin and found its way into his nostrils, reaching deep within his aching lungs and seeking to cleanse them.

"Yes, breathe."

Around him, there was a mix of browns and greens. He sensed the trees and the dirt but he couldn't yet make them out with his eyes. He tried to blink but his eyes were swollen as if he had been crying for a long time.

The air wafted in, bringing a distinct scent. It was both clean and unclean. There was something wrong with the air itself, as if it didn't know what it wanted to be. Ignoring the voice whispering to him, he focused on the breeze entering and leaving him. There was life in it. And death. Hope. And despair. Joy. And fear.

"Open your eyes."

He tried, not just because he was told to. He wanted to see his surroundings. He wanted to understand the dichotomy of the air. It needed to make sense somewhere. Somehow. Concentrating was difficult, but he focused his efforts into widening his gaze, drawing in the light and reassembling it into shapes that made sense. The light cut like daggers, but he persisted.

Trees. Shrubs. Dirt. Leaves. He pieced it together slowly, remembering he was in a forest. A place of foliage and creatures. A place of life.

Then he saw the scorch marks marring the area. Dark blotches upon the verdant landscape. Branches that should have boasted wild-growing leaves now lay in crackled husks on the ground. A place of death.

Little by little the area resolved itself to him. He stood in the middle of the forest where a battle had taken place, where someone—he—had fended off attackers with fire. Fire that reached out and burned the defenseless trees. And then he had drawn that fire into himself, taking the pain away from the woods and sparing it. And he had crumpled, consumed by the flames.

"You're looking better," the voice said. "Can you stand on your own yet? Here, take your staff."

A shaft of wood was placed into his hand. It felt oddly familiar and safe. He shifted his weight to lean against it as the voice then pulled away, releasing him from its hold.

"I almost lost you," the voice explained. "It was all I could do to keep the fires from destroying you."

He coughed. "Wh—" he sputtered.

"Easy. You'll need some water. Can you see me? Do you remember me?"

He turned toward the voice and he was surprised at first, but his mind was clearing from the fog and he realized he shouldn't be so startled. "Lurina."

"Yes."

"I thought you… went off."

"I came back once Tassa and Hetch were away with my children. You were standing there, pulling these flames in toward you. I could tell what you were doing and that it would kill you. So I heaved some stones your way and wove a protection spell around you. The fire was great, however. The pebbles melted together, basically, and they coated you in a rocky skin. The fire ate through it in some places, but mostly the stone absorbed the heat and then the fire was gone. You collapsed and I've been trying to revive you for some time now. Dariak, are you whole now?"

The mage's body felt stiff and was still tingling, but the pain was less. "I believe so." He touched his hand to his forearm but it was strange, as if he was touching her instead. And at the same time, it was as if she was touching him. "Odd."

"It should wear off once the spell is completely gone," she shrugged. "A difficult spell to pull off, but the need was great and the earth magic responded to you as if it wanted to keep you safe."

"The woods. They didn't burn?"

She smiled and looked rather matronly doing so. "No, Dariak. You fought off the triggans and then you saved the forest from the fires. I know you didn't mean to set the blaze, but you were willing to sacrifice yourself to save this place."

"I—I couldn't let it burn. I had to protect it."

"It is good you did, for this place is very old. It has seen generations of travelers and residents alike. And it should be here for generations to come."

"I don't want to kill things," he said suddenly. "I've had to, to get this far. But I don't pursue it. I don't want to destroy the things around me. The people. The creatures. Homes. Dreams."

"It showed in how you responded here."

"But the triggans. I just swept in and destroyed them."

Lurina tossed her head to the side. "Maybe a few, but like the times we cut down a tree for firewood, we find other trees to grow in their place. A sapling here and there, and a bit of tending and protecting, nurturing through time, and then we have more trees and an ever-living forest. Triggans are very much the same—these were, at any rate. They keep mostly to themselves, but when we stumble upon them they will defend their homes. It was unfortunate, but without your actions, we would have been overrun and then what? Most of the triggans you defeated are gone, but their ashes may ignite new offspring."

"You're in a consoling mood today."

"Yes."

He remembered the events of the fight in the forest. "The others?" Then he gasped. "Randler?"

Lurina's face fell. "My son was defeated, as was Garr. The others are hurt and are resting."

Dariak waited but the woman didn't elaborate on her own. "What of Randler?"

"Badly hurt, Dariak."

The bulk of a tree trunk had crushed the bard's legs. Dariak didn't deceive himself; he knew the damage would be severe. "Is he dying?"

"I don't know."

It wasn't the answer he wanted. "I need to see him."

"Maybe." She saw the ire rise in him, but she placed a placating hand on his shoulder. "There is little you can do for him right now."

"Where is he?" he insisted.

"Sit down," she offered, pointing to a log nearby. He realized his body was exhausted and drained. He needed to sit, like it or not, so he allowed her to escort him over. "Dariak, why are you here?"

"What do you mean?"

"Here, in this forest, traveling with us?"

"We were on our way to meet up with Pyron."

"Why?" she pressed.

He hadn't revealed the true nature of his quest to her before now, but he was too weak to hold back. "He has the last piece of jade and I need it to complete my quest. I must find him."

"He is not in the forest."

Dariak wrinkled his brow. "Yes, that's why we were traveling through the forest, to reach him."

Lurina shook her head slowly. "We have not been going through the forest, Dariak. We have been navigating within it circuitously."

He looked betrayed, but he wasn't entirely surprised by the admission either. "Astrith's challenge," he realized. "He said he would be watching."

"Not him specifically, but yes."

"And the jades. You have them. In the wagon, I wager? That's why we were never allowed to look inside?"

Lurina frowned. "They were. But no."

"Level with me, here. Randler could be dying, Lurina. Where is he? Where are the jades? What's the point of all of this?"

"You needed to prove your worth in this forest. You needed to prove your willingness to protect this place. But after all the time on the road, you were only muddling through, getting by. The jades were brought back to Astrith days ago. It was felt that their closeness was holding you back."

Dariak's eyes narrowed.

Lurina continued without prompting. "Tassa and I have been creating the roadblocks that have kept us spiraling through the wood. Gaff and Garr have been the messengers, sending word through a network in the trees. But we needed to make sure you didn't sense the jades were here, and that was Hetch's role. He is a Silencer, though I doubt there is another person like him in all the world. He has a unique tie to magic and he can shield the energies from others. He has used that skill to block the jades from you."

"The children?"

"Really mine, though now…" She withheld her tears, as if this conversation with Dariak were more important somehow.

"I'm sorry."

Lurina cleared her throat. "Hetch is with Randler now, using his masking skills to try to shield Randler from the pain. It isn't the same as healing or anything of the sort, but he can sometimes draw the energies away from things. They are not here, though. They are already en route to Astrith and whatever healing he can provide for your friend."

"I have to help. Which way do I go?"

Lurina placed her hand on Dariak's knee and a deep pain echoed in her eyes. "What can you possibly do for him? Didn't you already try to heal him? What skill do you have against the damage that was done?"

Dariak closed his eyes and pictured Randler, lying there in pain after pushing Dariak to safety. He had indeed pulled his skills together to try to heal the bard, but he knew he wasn't capable of the work that needed to be done, if even Randler's legs could be mended. His only hope was that Kitalla had suffered a similar type of injury after one of Grenthar's trials and a team of skilled mages had been able to fix her. Perhaps…

"I don't have the ability, even with the jades." He looked at the agonized expression on Lurina's face and he knew she understood what he was going to say next. It pained him to acknowledge it, but he knew he had little choice. "I have to go after Pyron. The healing jade is the only chance I have."

"It means abandoning Randler," she said. "If you choose to seek the jade, you can't afford to waste any more time. Randler may not survive that long as it is."

Dariak stared at her intently and he tried to reconcile his decision, but he was distracted by the anguish he saw within her. "What is it?"

"We set the roadblocks," she whispered. "But we didn't mean for him to be hurt. He wasn't meant to be harmed." Her eyes shimmered with tears that she willed not to fall. "Nature is a place of balance."

His lip curled in bewilderment, but then he understood. "Your son was the price."

Her head sank low in affirmation.

"That isn't right. What happened to Randler was an accident. Your son… No, that's… no."

"He will return to nature and be born again from her womb, though it may not be my womb."

"But Randler didn't die. Why should your son's life be the balance?"

She lifted her head and trained her eyes on his. "Thank you for your compassion, but outrage is unnecessary. It was the will of the forest to bring my son into the soil. I cannot say I know why. I cannot change his fate. Whether it was a direct counterbalance to my error, I can only guess. It may be something else unrelated to me at all. I can only come to accept it, as all of us in the forest must do."

"It's unfair. I don't understand."

"You are not of this wood," she said as if that was explanation enough.

"Let me at least help you to bury him."

"It has already been done."

Dariak felt empty and confused. A boy's life traded for Randler's injuries? It made no sense to him, but Lurina seemed to believe it. He couldn't argue; it wouldn't do any good anyway. But he had to pull his thoughts away. He had to commit himself whether he would seek the final jade on his own, abandoning Randler to Astrith's care, or go to the bard's side and do what he could to help with the healing process and to ease the pain. Surely, he could find a means of gathering assistance from Magehaven so Randler would survive, limbs intact. It might be a struggle, but Randler was worth that.

It just wasn't a guarantee. The mages may not cooperate, and if they did, they may not have the skill to repair the damage.

His brain told him to seek the jade, for its power would repair Randler's legs, if any power could. His heart told him to be by Randler's side, regardless of what else he would be able to do.

"I will take you directly there," Lurina said solemnly, watching the war on the mage's face. "Just tell me: west or east."

CHAPTER 31

A Mage's Regret

KITALLA AWOKE THE next morning, stretching into the dawn and breathing in the odd scent in the air. It was a mix of freshness and decay, intermingling into a sense of something familiar. She knew where she was and that she was alone, but memories of her childhood swept through her thoughts.

She didn't think of her early days often, for they were empty and foreign to her. Her father was a misty shadow in her mind, and she assumed she only imagined his appearance from things she had overhead, making up the rest. Yet something about this scent in the air reminded her of him. She couldn't place it, so she shook off the feeling and stretched until she was wide awake.

Marritosh was dead. She had given it a cursory search upon her arrival and knew it was pointless to look for survivors. Still, the cloying, yet fresh, scent propelled her to dig around more before leaving the desolate place.

She started by heading toward Herchig's home, for he had been their greatest ally in Hathreneir. His abode wasn't far from her location and she reached it within minutes. She knew what she would find, but she hoped beyond all that she would have a chance to do something miraculous; something as wonderful as what she assessed had happened here.

Because Herchig's fenced-off home was near the center of the mass carnage, it was utterly destroyed. The fence itself was burned and blasted apart. The house had collapsed in on itself, and when she dug through the debris, she thought she could tell where the old man and his wife had stood when they had lit the powderkegs that exploded in this area. The walls were cracked and destroyed and only her memories made anything recognizable. Broken bits of bone and cloth were littered around her and she knew her suspicions were right. The villagers who had remained here had given their lives to end whatever threat had come.

She stopped by a few other locales, but the story was the same. Bits of wood and stone lay scattered everywhere with the remains of the people who had buried themselves with the town that had been their home for so long. She wondered idly if she would ever feel so strongly about any one place. Or person. So far, she had yet to truly experience it.

After a while, she gave up her search and returned to the eastern edge of town where the horse waited for her. The poor beast had apparently suffered some minor attacks during the night. It seemed relieved when she walked up to untie it and lead it away.

Kitalla realized that the others had to have headed toward Magehaven after the decimation that took place here. Northward would have brought them to the castle and the evidence of battle in the northern edge of town suggested to her that they would have avoided that direction. And though they could have gone east or south, those options seemed unlikely, for the south was loaded with larger beasts that would have been hard to defeat, and the east was too close to the Kallisorian border and would probably draw them into the fighting. Aside from all that, the jades pulsed toward the west, though their signal was mixed as to whether she should head more north or south.

She mounted the mare and trotted around Marritosh rather than travel through it, mostly out of respect for those who had fallen defending their homes. She then snapped the reins and hurried to the west.

On horseback, she was able to make the journey before the day was out. She expected trouble when she arrived at the tower, for her previous visits had brought much unrest. Yet there were no obvious defenses set up as her horse cantered closer. She even crossed the barrier with only a mild sensation that there was a barrier of any kind. She was grateful not to be whisked off to some other Trial. She didn't think she had it in her right then to delve into her psyche again.

Kitalla dismounted the horse as she approached the gate and two mages came outside to greet her. They seemed to recognize her, and she assumed that had to be bad, considering her last visits here. However, they took her horse to a small inner stable and then brought her deep within the tower without any threat to her wellbeing.

"Just stay here. He'll be with you shortly," one of the mages on her way out.

"'He' who?" Kitalla asked, but she did not receive an answer. Instead she walked around the stony chamber, finding crevices here and there, perhaps from fighting or spells gone awry. The table and chairs were utterly ordinary and she had no desire to sit in them, preferring to stand and be at the ready in case something went amiss. Perhaps the calm with which they greeted her was good, for it meant no ill will. But it also could be a ruse to put her off guard.

It wasn't long before the door opened and an older mage stepped inside. "You must be the thief, Kitalla."

Her eyes narrowed at the greeting, her eyes tracing the lines of his mustard-colored robe. He held no obvious weapons, but mages didn't need them. She wondered what protective spells he had about himself and whether she could break through them and take him hostage long enough to effect her escape.

"Peace, peace," he said holding his hands openly in the air. "I am Vinnek of the Mage Council and you are here as a friend."

"A friend you address as thief? A friend you sequester in a locked room? I don't buy it."

He smiled sadly. "Easy now. We could just as easily have turned you away or made your entry difficult. But before I release you to the rest of this tower, I must know your purpose here. There are no more jades within."

She knew he was lying, for her jades were pulsing more strongly now inside the tower. Yet he didn't seem particularly deceitful. "Where is everyone?"

"All around, I assure you," he answered carelessly. "Come now. Your purpose?"

"To seek my friends. The ones I was to rendezvous with in Marritosh. Perhaps you know that the town was destroyed. I would guess my friends came here."

His eyebrows furrowed. Kitalla didn't like it. "I saw you here before, young lady. Weapons flashing around like a wild assassin, and you took with you our colleague Dariak—"

"Whom you imprisoned," she cut in.

"Ah, indeed. But you killed a fair number of our mages on your way. How am I to know if your intentions here now are as innocent as you say? And why should I risk our safety?"

Kitalla straightened her back. "You said I was here as a friend and would be released. Was that a lie?"

"Do not banter with me, child," Vinnek said. "Many of my friends are dead at your hand. What's to stop me from adding your life to the death toll?"

Kitalla barked a laugh. "Go right ahead, you old fool. I never had a gripe with you mages. Not as a group anyway. But you hurt my friend and for that you were hurt in return."

"Petty foolishness."

"And what of this? You'll strike me down because I hurt mages here before? Is that not also petty?"

Sparks flared at Vinnek's fingertips. "We incarcerated one of our own for a murder he committed in our tower. You trespassed here and slew our defenders! There is a world of difference."

Kitalla made a horse-like sound and turned away. "Do what you will, but stop hesitating about it. If you're planning on punishing me, get it over with."

"So flippant."

"Shouldn't I be? You welcome me here all calmly under a false sense of security so you can execute me here in this room? I'm only looking to reunite with my friends. Point me in the right direction and I'm out of here."

"My wife and son were among the losses," he growled. "In what way should I let you be free?"

"Do it!" she screamed at him. "If you're going to kill me, then go right ahead, you old goat. No more of your useless prattling about loss. Do it!"

His hands twitched and his fingers curled. She could tell he truly wanted to hurt her, so she urged him on even more.

"That's right, Vinnek, go ahead and splatter me with your spells. You couldn't defend this place on your own, so you might as well go on and take me down now, one on one. I'm not even armed, you weak oaf. Do it already. It's your hesitation that's your biggest enemy. Not me. Because you held back, your wife is dead. Your son is dead. But blame me for it. That's right. Go on! Do it! Kill me!"

The rage boiled in him and he struck his hands out toward her, his face twisted in fury. The glimmering sparks of lightning at his fingertips banded together in a raging torment that fluttered swiftly across the room, aiming for Kitalla's heart. She made no attempt to get out of the way, instead standing firm, her eyes locked with his.

The air shook with a loud thunderclap which made Vinnek wince and when he looked again, Kitalla stood there, glaring at him, shaking her head slowly. She was unscathed.

"How?"

"You're an idiot," she said. "Now where are my friends?"

"How can you stand there unhurt? How is this possible?" He trembled now, slowly dropping to his knees. "What are you, thief? You come, you steal, you kill. But you will not fall. What are you?"

"I will fall," she said. "One day. But not at the hands of a weakling like you. Where are my friends?"

Vinnek scrambled for answers, but was too upset to think clearly. He looked at Kitalla as some freakish being able to absorb his magic and render him impotent. Like all those times when intruders were in the tower and he was too slow to join the fray. He always arrived moments too late to be of help, seeing only the heads of the fleeing enemy and the bodies of the fallen. He had no courage of his own, no will to do more than get through his day without any more bloodshed. But this one should have died for all the pain she had wrought. It wouldn't restore the rest, but it would give him some peace to see her die.

"Where are they?" Kitalla repeated as he crumpled on the ground, sobbing.

A flash of clarity pierced through him and then he understood. He gasped, trying to push himself up. "I see. You have the jades. They have shielded you."

"Obviously. Why else would I wander in here all 'hey guys, what's up?' As I said, you're a fool. Show me to my friends. I know they're here." When he hesitated, she added, "Don't make me get... persuasive."

"Yes, your friends are here."

"Thank you. Now tell me which way."

He stood up and held her gaze. "I meant here now, in this room, and I am not among them."

Kitalla looked around but saw only the table and chairs. "Stop messing around."

"A woman like you has no friends," he said coldly. "You take when you want something. You strike when you don't get your way. You ally yourself with those who bring you power. You don't connect with people. You have no friends. You don't even know what friends are."

"Shut it."

"You're an empty shell, aren't you, thief? You've killed enough men in your life to populate a town, haven't you? You've stolen enough treasure to rival a king's hoard. Even now, I hold you from what you want and all you want to do is tear me down."

"I said, enough."

But Vinnek did not relent. "There is little left you can take from me anymore. I have no possessions. I can't even have my vengeance against you. You already took that away. Had I a dagger, I bet I couldn't even penetrate your heart. If there is one within you."

Kitalla stood rooted to the spot, unsure why she couldn't move. "Where are my friends?"

"There's that word again," he dug. "You came here alone. No support. No friends. You're all alone in this, Kitalla, aren't you? Standing here, facing me without a single ally. Well, except a piece of magic in your pocket. Does it love you? Do you love it?"

"You're on dangerous ground, old man."

He kept talking, kept poking at her and making her want to bleed. "Where is everyone, child? Why have they all abandoned you? Isn't it because you're not worth their time? Not worth the effort? Aren't you really just trying to find a place to be, a place to be accepted? Because you're not wanted anywhere."

"You're wrong," she denied, trying not to think of Gabrion.

"They why stand there and listen? Because you know I'm right. You're broken. You're unloved. Alone."

"And so are you."

"Thanks to you," he said. "You killed them. Your hands. Ripped the souls right out of their bodies. They were only defending their home and you just pressed your knives in and cut their lives out like they were pits. No regard for life. Because you have nothing to live for."

"Everything I've ever had to live for was cut from me."

"So this is retribution?"

Her cheek twitched as tears filled her eyes. "What do you want?"

"I want you to feel my pain. I want you to lie down and die at my hands. I want my wife and son back. I want an end to the uselessness of this life. I want a purpose again." His eyes tore through her. "What is your purpose, Kitalla?"

"To end it."

"To end what?"

"To end the pain."

"That only happens when you die."

She clenched her fists and closed her eyes. It seemed so simple. If she died, there really wouldn't be any more pain. No more suffering. No more losses because of her. Her heart couldn't be cut open by Gabrion or the others anymore. She would be at peace.

She touched her hand to the pocket with the jades. All she needed to do was remove them and lay them on the floor and they would no longer protect her. Then Vinnek could deliver peace to her at last. Kitalla opened her eyes and saw the hungry look on the old man's eyes as she pulled open the pocket flap. It was a mad look. Dangerous.

"No," she whispered.

Vinnek raced toward her and shoved her arm aside, reaching for the pocket to take the jades himself. He was no match for her speed and strength and she eluded him easily, after which she pushed him down to the floor.

"Good try, mage, but I do have something to live for: life itself." She debated kicking him in the ribs to make him suffer for his insolence, but she changed her mind. "If you won't tell me where my friends are, then I will find them myself."

Old Vinnek laughed in a deep guttural tone. "There is no need."

"This again?"

"No," he said, pushing himself up slowly. "Ervinor said you would come."

"So where is he?"

"I wanted you to die. Even as we try to make changes here, I wanted you to pay. I am such a fool."

"That's the smartest thing you've said so far. Now… where is Ervinor?"

"*Fathrimiac bartilius crathentar!*" Vinnek's body lit with a burst of lightning. He blasted it into the floor underneath him. The stone cracked and splintered and at last it fell away, taking him with it.

Kitalla leaped in and grabbed him. She snagged his yellow robe, but he simply raised his arms over his head as the ground fell away underneath him. He crashed lifelessly to the floor below.

CHAPTER 32

Unexpected Reunion

THE DYNAMICS WITHIN Magehaven had more structure than Ervinor had realized before now. The mages within found representation among the Mage Council through its members. Mostly, fire mages banded together under Rothra's leadership, the earth mages supported Shelloni, and so on. Some mages did cross disciplines, for it wasn't a stern rule to be within a particular faction. For instance, Vinnek led the lightning mages but many older mages also turned to him as their leader, regardless of their affinities.

In most matters governing the tower, the Council members decided and the mages within their factions abided the rules as decreed. Years before, there was an influx of fire mages and the training rooms were being overrun by them, which made water mage training difficult, among other things. The Council set a fire mage training schedule to parcel out the sessions in the rooms and because Rothra had agreed to the calendar, the fire mages obeyed their restricted times, but the other mages also had to clear the room during fire sessions. Not everyone was happy with the result, but it did offer a better balance within the tower and the people eventually saw the greater wisdom in the decision.

Today was a harder day, however. Ervinor had won a majority vote with his impassioned speech to the Council, but it hadn't been unanimous. Zelldin, who had assumed a role on the Council after Farrenok's sentence had been carried out in Marritosh, had decided to keep to his predecessor's inclination to thwart any plans aligning with Dariak. Likewise, Shelloni, who once openly supported Dariak, stood her ground after Dariak had killed Kerrish and she refused to join the fight. The other Council members agreed to work with Ervinor.

Then the question came up about the mages under Shelloni's and Zelldin's jurisdiction. What if they wanted to volunteer and join Ervinor? The Council agreed to allow them to join the struggle, but they did not consider the reverse. What if Rothra's mages didn't want to fight? Would they be allowed to remain behind?

At first the answer was a flat-out no. Because their Council member had offered support, the mages were committed, but there were some fire mages who wanted nothing to do with any of this, preferring to stay behind at the tower and practice their magic. Ervinor gathered each faction together with its leader and explained why he needed them all. Many were swayed by his passion, but not everyone.

Since then, he had been working with the Council members to separate the mages into well-balanced groups, so that healers were present in every pack of fighters, and so on. As evening fell, his head pounded from all the personality conflicts on every side. Sometimes it made no sense, for the mages would agree that the destiny of their lands was to be united, but they wanted no part in making it happen.

"And what if you're thirsty?" Ervinor had asked, frustrated. "Do you just wish for it really hard or do you walk over and pour yourself something? This is more important than a simple glass of water, obviously, but it's the same principle. If you want things to change, you have to help make it happen."

He grew tired of trying to convince people to do the right thing. He had to remind himself that the majority of the mages were content with helping; it was a noisy few who made things so difficult. It would be so much easier to ignore the naysayers and send them off somewhere.

In front of him sat four healers who already had concerns about being out in the field, stating their skills weren't honed enough yet, and they needed more training. He let them blather on about how inadequate they were, but they were not novices. They simply didn't want to be in danger, though they wanted to be ready to help the wounded. He let them talk longer than he should have, but he was weary of the spiraling conversations.

Then the discussion came to an abrupt end. The door crashed open and a mage rushed in, panicked, "It's Vinnek! Come quickly!" Ervinor hopped out of his seat and followed her closely as she raced toward the scene.

There, in a heap, lay old Vinnek, stripped of his robe, his body broken from the fall and battered by debris from the ceiling. Ervinor looked up and saw the hole that peered into the empty room above.

"How did this happen?" he asked.

"We have the culprit!"

"Murderer!"

"She's done this to us before!"

"She'll pay for his death!"

"No one's safe here anymore!"

"Stop!" Ervinor called out. "Who is responsible for this? Show me."

Shelloni arrived then and walked up to Ervinor. "She has already been brought to the dungeon."

"That was expedient," he said sourly.

"Wouldn't you have done the same? Besides, she was being carted away as a message was sent to you, so it isn't as if much time has passed."

"Take me there, Shelloni."

She shook her head. "This is our matter, Ervinor. We will deal with it."

"Not this time," he argued. "The Mage Council agreed to grant me access to the happenings in this tower, and so I will oversee this as well."

"Well, *I* did not agree to give you such power. But very well. I'm curious to know what you'll do with this situation."

He didn't like her tone. "What do you know?"

She only smiled and turned away. Ervinor shook his head and followed her to the dungeons. Because she was on the Council, she knew the privileged enchantments that opened secret passageways, which allowed them to reach the dungeon in less time than it had taken Ervinor to reach Vinnek from the meeting room.

The mage dungeons looked much like other cells he had seen. They were made of stone with heavy bars locking the prisoners within. The main exception here was that there were no doors in most of these cells. Shelloni saw the curious look on Ervinor's face and opted to explain. "Most mages have spells that will allow them to move the bars somehow. Fire mages can melt them and then reform them. Earth mages can warp them or raise them. We have other cells elsewhere in case we're overrun with healers who can't manipulate the bars and need conventional locks and keys."

Ervinor squinted. "So if I were imprisoned here by a fire mage and then for some reason he left and only healers were here, I couldn't get out?"

She grinned. "Basically. Just a little further." She gestured down the corridor.

They reached the cell and Ervinor's eyes lit up excitedly. "Kitalla!"

"Oh, so you really are here," she answered dourly. "Good. Now get me out."

"Not so fast," Shelloni said. "As far as we know, you killed Vinnek."

"I did no such thing." She then explained how Vinnek had met with her in the room and then later blasted himself through the floor with a lightning burst.

"Convenient," Shelloni sneered.

"That doesn't mean it isn't true," Ervinor said.

"Perhaps."

Ervinor turned and stared the mage sternly in the eye. "Are you trying to change what's happening here? Are you looking to set Kitalla up as a scapegoat so you can sway the rest of the Council?"

"How *dare* you!"

"I can see it now," Ervinor pressed. "Vinnek's gone, so you get Wylan to step up for the lightning mages. He has no interest in the quest, so you garner more support in favor of keeping the mages at home. Then you pin the blame on Kitalla for Vinnek's death. That's a double benefit, because she supports Dariak and she 'killed' Vinnek, so clearly Dariak's cause is a fraud. And when I try to step in to defend her, I'm also seen as a traitor to the mages. The Council loses confidence and a new vote keeps the mages home. Crafty, Shelloni."

The mage's face was lit with rage. "You insolent swine!"

They glared at each other for a time and Kitalla watched the two of them, curious about the outcome.

At last Shelloni broke. "Do you know what I hate most?"

Ervinor shook his head. "No, what?"

"Your little plan would have worked and turned everything my way, but it didn't even occur to me." She struggled with her next words and Ervinor saw her lips tremble as she tried to form them, so he waited. "Fine, Ervinor. I don't even know how you know about Wylan's views or any of the other effects you mentioned. I can't outwit you, not in this. There's no point in denying it. The evidence points to the accuracy of her story, anyway. Vinnek's been a strange old man lately. He very may well have killed himself trying to hurt her."

"He did try," Kitalla spoke up at last. "He said I killed his wife and son when I was here to rescue Dariak. Maybe I did; I don't know. But he got lost in despair and there you have it."

Shelloni's brows furrowed. "His wife and son died years ago during a raid. I guess it wasn't unlike what happened here. He must have confused the two, the doddering fool. Still though… What's to keep me from holding you in there for the lives you did take when you were here?"

"Shelloni," Ervinor warned.

"Just wondering is all." She then raised her hands and intoned, *"Rizzithur nock-trus."* As she lifted her fingers, the bars rose up, allowing Kitalla to leave the cell.

"Much better," the thief said, stretching. "Thanks."

The mage rolled her eyes and they turned to leave when another voice echoed down the hallway. "Ervinor? Is that you?"

The general's eyes widened and he turned around. Shelloni tried to stop him but then submitted to following him, Kitalla in tow. Many yards down the hallway Ervinor stopped and gasped, "Verna? They said you were dead!"

At this, Shelloni laughed. "I believe Vinnek told you she had been taken care of. Not dead. Dealt with."

And it wasn't just Verna; it was her whole squad. "I can't believe this! You've been down here this whole time? Vinnek never said anything about it."

"Looks like you showed the mages what for," Verna sneered, sliding a glance to Shelloni.

"Nonsense." He eyed her darkly. "There was no call for you to enter the tower at all. You reacted poorly to the events outside and people died because of it."

"But the mages attacked," she retaliated. "We had to defend ourselves!"

"It was a misunderstanding. Regardless, you had no authority to cross the barrier, yet you went in. And not only inside the barrier, but you led your team into the tower itself. You acted on your own, without my command."

Her back straightened. "So it would have been better for us to die, then? Is that it?"

Ervinor shook his head. "Once we called a ceasefire, the fighting stopped. It would have stopped sooner if not for your charge into the tower."

"But I thought—" She stopped herself, seeing the anger on Ervinor's face.

Shelloni turned to Ervinor. "I suppose you want me to release them too?"

"No," the general said. "Clearly, she needs more time to mull things over."

Verna's jaw dropped and she stared in disbelief at Ervinor.

"You know you were wrong. You know you broke orders."

Her voice was tight. "I wanted to check on the people of Marritosh but they wouldn't listen to reason, *sir*. They left us rotting outside for days, *sir*. No word, *sir*. What was I supposed to do? I had to defend them, *sir*!"

Kitalla stepped up to the bars and looked at the wild eyes. "You know, Ervinor, she really doesn't listen well, does she?"

"How dare you!"

"Enough! Enough!" Ervinor barked. "I can't take any more of this today, any of you. I've hit my limit." He turned to Shelloni. "Verna and her group will be released, but I will let you decide if it's now or later."

Without hesitation, Shelloni cast the spell to open the bars, then she chortled. "Seeing the chaos this Verna person brings, I can't wait to let her go. You're free, honey. Go on now, and make sure you thank me by taking up your problems with Ervinor at every convenience."

Shelloni then stepped to the other cells and released the others. Unlike Verna, they accepted Ervinor's judgment that they had acted in error and they waited for his command. Verna, however, stepped up to her general and glared.

Kitalla could see how exhausted the young man was, so she opted to end this feud. "Verna, you're with me."

"You can't give me orders."

Kitalla grinned. "Nope, but I can surely give you a beating. Now move!" She shoved Verna aside to show her strength and then led the woman from the dungeon.

"I can't wait to see how this develops," Shelloni gloated.

"Just tell me where these fighters should go." He gestured to the rest of Verna's Wrens.

"Come on, all of you," the mage said, then she led them from the dungeon with an extra little bounce in her step.

CHAPTER 33

The Course

GABRION ACCEPTED HIS current role as trainer at the outpost. He used his own experience and Andron's old lessons to teach the newest recruits how to battle safely. Gabrion set them to menial tasks at times to help them to build focus, thus they rebuilt an old wall with small roughly-hewn bricks and homemade mortar. They groaned against the labor, but the soreness of their muscles the next day taught them they needed to build more strength and endurance.

Veterans who remained at the outpost to keep the place functioning joined Gabrion's training sessions, rebuilding their fighting edge in the process. For a long while, they only had each other for sparring, so having new responses to test their mettle was refreshing. Also, though, Gabrion rallied the men and women by setting random teams each day and pitting them against each other in miniature tournaments.

Along the way, he also instilled in them the need to obey orders. It wasn't easy to train a ragtag team of fighters to heed a single man's voice, especially when chaos erupted all around, but Gabrion did his best to demonstrate why it was so vital.

"Today, half of you will be blindfolded," he called to the morning gathering. "The rest of you will have your ears padded. Urrith and I have designed an obstacle course and the deaf will lead the blind through the course. If you are among the blindfolded, then you must heed the instructions of your guides. If you are among the deaf, your duty is to guide your partner through the obstacles safely. There is real danger in there and if you fail each other, there will be pain. Now, pair up and meet me inside at the northern exit."

Urrith was already there with the equipment they needed for the day. He grinned widely when Gabrion arrived. "You ready for some fun?"

"Dangerous fun, but this will be interesting."

"We made it through," Urrith said playfully, slapping Gabrion's shoulder.

"Sure, but not without some scrapes and digs, and we were the ones who built it."

The trainees approached them and Gabrion noted once again that a handful of veterans were in the mix. It seemed odd to have them there, but he didn't mind their presence. Guard duty was dreadfully boring and surely these men needed some form of entertainment.

"Blind, to my left. Deaf, to my right," Gabrion called. "Stand against the wall, facing your partner. When we're in place outside, you'll begin when I swing the flag. You may not remove your gear until everyone is through and we give you the signal to do so. Now, while we bring you the accoutrements for today, place your hand on the fighter beside you so that we can lead you out to the course. Don't mix up the order or you will lose your partner before we even begin." The blind side set their right hands on the shoulder of the person to their right, while the deaf team did the same with their left.

Urrith bounded down the right side of the aisle, plunking a padded helmet atop each fighter's head. The padding inside was thick at the ears, which made the helmets hard to get on, but he wriggled them into place, trying not to hurt anyone in the process. Meanwhile, Gabrion went down his line and blindfolded each participant. Sixteen pairs faced this challenge. It was hard not to smirk at the odds of anyone making it through unscathed.

The trainers walked to the head of the line. Urrith called out, "Deaf marchers, step forward and follow me."

Nothing happened. The blindfolded soldiers murmured, "They really can't hear anything."

Urrith then stepped in front of the leader of his row and tapped her to follow. The rest of them followed suit, keeping their hands firmly planted on the shoulder of the fighter in front. Gabrion waited for a few minutes to ensure the deaf group was gone and set into place. "The others will have figured this out by now, but you won't have a clue, so I will tell you: You and your partner will not be traversing the course together. Instead, your partner will be walking along the sidelines calling out instructions. They will not be able to help you."

A few of them gasped in shock and annoyance, but they quickly quieted down. Gabrion led them outside. He took the hand of the first man in the line and tugged for him to follow. "Don't lose your grip on this part of the journey," he reminded them. "Move out."

He took them outside to the field, and then turned sharply right to have them line up with their backs against the outer wall. He then spent the next few minutes spreading them out, removing their one last grip of help as they were forced to disengage from each other. Urrith had divided the first group in half, setting them at the sides of the course. They planned it so the partners would be as close to each other as possible at the start.

Gabrion gave one look out over the field and grinned to himself. The obstacle course itself wasn't difficult for any one of them if they were fully able to use their senses. Scattered around the course, there were three walls to climb over, each of varying heights, but one was angled backward. The walls had knotted ropes hung over them to assist the ascent and descent. Two sets of wide-plank balance beams sloped upward and downward a few times. A suspended plank crossed over a mud pit, which the course-goers would either have to climb over or under to pass. At the halfway point there was a rope net hung horizontally high enough off the ground so that if anyone's legs fell through, they wouldn't reach the ground. The last obstacle was a trench filled with jagged rocks, but zigzagging pathways of slate would allow safe passage if navigated correctly.

"Runners, are you ready?" Gabrion called out. Each of the sixteen blindfolded fighters raised a hand in acknowledgement. The warrior then fetched a nearby pennant flag and held it aloft, ready to swing it down to open this first full run of the course. "Ready in three… two… one… go!" And he swept the flag down.

Excited by the idea of the race, several of the blindfolded runners immediately bolted from their position at the wall and tried to rush into the course without awaiting instructions. One of them ran smack into the first wall and staggered back with a bloody nose, but he did not quit.

At the same time, though, the guides began calling out orders and it was such a cacophony that no one could understand a single thing.

"Jarraf! Jarraf, go forward ten paces! Jarraf, no! Ten!"

"Shena, there's a wall a few steps ahead of you. Shena, are you listening?"

"Paasa, grab that rope right there. Come on, it's *right* in front of you!"

"Jog a few steps! Listen up, come on, jog! Go go go! Would you listen to me? *Jog!*"

Urrith had joined Gabrion in the center of the field to help him keep an eye on things. "This isn't going well, Gabrion."

But the warrior looked at the craziness and frustration and he just smiled. "No. It's perfect."

Some of the runners gave up on their guides and tried to navigate the course without them. One man, Helris, made it past three obstacles before he veered off course and smacked into the boundary fence that separated the course from the runway the guides were using. His partner eventually caught up to him, furious that he was ignoring her, and after ranting for a few minutes they shrugged it off and continued onward.

Soon the guides used fewer words. They called sharp, succinct commands with the name and the direction. Or the name and an action to take. They learned that long strings of complaints only confused the runners and they had no chance of following any instructions.

The runners themselves had a terrible time trying to decipher the noise. They could hear the shouts of their partners, but also everyone else's partner. Additionally, the runners kept calling back for clarification of what to do, forgetting that their guides had been made deaf. Cutting through the noise to hear a single voice was terribly frustrating, just as the guides were agitated that their charges struggled to obey.

They pushed on, however, and Urrith also started to smile. No one had given up yet. There were some injuries, including what looked like a sprained ankle on someone trying to leap off the sloped climbing wall. His partner was generous in asking if he was all right to go on. They agreed to pause for a few minutes to let some of the others go on ahead so the injured runner could focus more easily on his guide's voice. He was able to catch up with the rest of the pack soon after. He pushed through and was one of the first six to reach the end.

The cargo net in the center of the course was, perhaps, the most difficult obstacle on the course. The net itself was a challenge because of the flexible rope, but once a second, third, or fourth person was also climbing across, their movements made the whole thing unstable. Several people were hung up in the rope and, more than once, Gabrion and Urrith had to intervene to untangle a few.

As each pair reached the end, they were allowed to sit and relax, but not remove their gear. The teams who finished first paired up so the guide could narrate the events to the runner. Having been through the course with the noise, the runners communicated to their guides to keep the narration quiet so as not to disrupt the others still in the race.

The course took a grueling two and a half hours for all the groups to get through with their enforced disabilities. The fastest groups finished an hour ahead of the last pair.

Gabrion stepped into the finish zone and waved his arms about to get the guides' attention. He then mimed lifting a helmet off his head. "You may now remove your gear, but please hold onto it. We're going to rest here for a couple of minutes before we head back inside."

"Some of us have already been waiting a while. Why do we have to sit here longer?"

"I didn't open the floor for questions, soldier." The man opened his mouth to complain but his partner shushed him.

After a few minutes, Gabrion asked the contingent to stand up. He ran them through a series of minor exercises and stretches. "Now, we're ready to head back."

As one, the group sighed in relief and immediately started to break formation. "Hold!" Urrith shouted above the mumbled voices. The fighters stopped in their tracks. "Not like that, soldiers."

"No," Gabrion echoed. "You were blind and deaf on your way out here. You will be deaf and blind on your way back. You're going back in through the course, in reverse roles. Switch gear with your partner and suit up."

They were too stunned to argue. Helmets were plunked onto the original runners' heads, and they then took their cloths and blindfolded their original guides. Urrith and Gabrion ensured each was properly secured before separating the new guides from their partners. Then all the fun began again.

Now that they were in opposite roles, they each thought they would better understand what to do. The guides had run the course and knew what kinds of instructions would be helpful. The runners had seen the course and so they had an idea of what was to come. But these were barely advantages, for the same frustrations kicked in once the race was on.

The new guides had to remember to keep their calm and not take their frustration out on their partners. The runners had to put their faith in the guides and their memories, but they soon found that running the course was very different than narrating it. In most cases, they hadn't been trying to remember the course at all, they were so caught up in giving orders.

Having sat in the sun for two hours or so, the mud pit was much more uncomfortable for the second set. It was hard in some places but soft in others. It was also warmer now, which made the course that much harder.

When they reached the cargo net, however, Gabrion noticed something interesting. The runners had watched as the last group struggled on the netting. Now, some of them took charge while they were on the field. Avarra was the first one to reach the net and she made a few strides before the next three joined her. She called out to them in a powerful voice, superseding the calls of the guides. "Listen to me. If you're on this cargo net with me, follow what I say until we're across. Start with your left leg. Ready? Go! Left. Now right. Now left. Right." She was able to get them into a rhythm and it helped to reduce the frantic pulls and tugs of the rope.

Not too many of the guides witnessed the concerted effort as they instructed their teams over one of the balance beams, but a few who did tried to enact that plan to help them all across. Suddenly, they were sporadically working as teams instead of competing solely as individuals.

On the journey back, the one real difference was that one sloped climbing wall. In this direction, they were climbing the ropes straight up without being able to run their feet along the wall until they were near the top. It was difficult labor and several of them fell off and had to rest before trying again.

The run times were better on the way back, but it still took one group almost two hours to finish. Gabrion didn't care. They had all made it through and not a single one of them had given up. It was more than he had expected.

The fighters were more than happy to shed the gear and celebrate completing the course. Gabrion canceled their evening session, saying they had endured enough and deserved a chance to kick back and think about what they learned.

While he ate his own meal, Avarra stepped into the mess hall and asked if she could join him. "It was a harrowing exercise you put us through, sir."

"And you all succeeded," he said, tipping his mug.

"You asked us to think about the lesson from today and some of the men just think you and Urrith are insane, sir. Sorry for saying so."

He grinned. "Continue."

"But I gotta say, sir, I was plucked out of a mine in the southeast. I was stronger than half the men around me, so when the king's guard came looking for volunteers, I got volunteered."

Gabrion frowned. "That doesn't sound much like volunteering."

"It wasn't. Not for me, not for most of us. But for me, I feel like I'm going to be defending my home by keeping Kallisor safe. Some of the rest, they're resentful of being here. They think it's all a waste and they're going to die."

"I won't let you all be fodder."

"Sir, yes, that's sort of where I was going." She squirmed in the seat, trying to find the right words. "Sir, you see, we really did learn something out there. Lots of things; well, some of us, but still. Like, in a battle, you're the guide and we're the ones who can't see, so we need you to get us safely across. But then, we're the ones in the actual heat of it, so sometimes we got to band together too. And, and some of us got totally lost without orders. But I saw you, sir, that first time when some of the men got caught in the net. You didn't let them hang there or get hurt. You slipped over and helped them out. See, I think the most important thing I learned out there was… you're gonna protect us, sir. Keep us safe as you can."

Gabrion's jaw firmed as he saw the light in her eyes glimmering. "Remember, Avarra, all I can do is show you what to do. When it comes to a battle, you're your own best defender and protector."

"Yes, sir!"

"Now go on and have some fun. I'm glad the course today taught you something of value."

She stood and saluted him then spun on her heel before heading out.

Urrith stepped over after she left. "You okay? You're pale all of a sudden."

Gabrion looked at him and shoved the rest of his meal away. "I've had enough of being everyone's protector for today. I'm off to bed."

Urrith watched as the warrior stormed off. "Gabrion?" he whispered, confused.

CHAPTER 34

Dariak's Decision

"THIS IS WHERE we part ways," Lurina said as she tugged the reins and stopped the horse. The creaky wagon came to a halt at their destination.

"Thank you, Lurina. I hope I'm doing the right thing." Dariak hopped off the wagon and retrieved his staff and a pack of provisions Lurina had prepared for him.

"Right or wrong, it's the decision you made, so you have to live with it. Maybe it's wrong for one reason but right for another. Who's to say? Follow your heart and your head and you'll be fine."

He smirked ruefully. "That's part of the problem; my head and heart don't agree on this one. But you're right. Time to see what comes next. Thank you for everything."

"One last thing before you go," she called after him, then threw down a tightly-wrapped bundle. "Your leaf-clothes aren't likely to wash well. You'll need your cloak back. Travel well, Dariak."

He thanked her again and gladly stripped himself of the chafing outfit he had been wearing since he and Randler had come into the forest, and which he had replaced after the fire. He infused a hint of magic to end the binding spell, and the leaves fell away as if it were autumn. As he donned his robe he mused that the forest had no sense of winter about it. The leaves were still a vibrant green, as though they would deny winter's breath to the very last leaf. There truly was a mighty magic in the forest.

He hated to leave it behind him. But he knew he had to. He had to claim the last jade from Pyron. He was at a great disadvantage, for he was without the other jades and without Randler. He had to hope that Astrith could keep Randler in as little pain as possible. Then, once Dariak claimed the healing jade, he could return and treat his beloved.

"Forgive me for leaving you, Randler. I hope you'll understand." He felt around in his pockets for the myriad spell components he had in them when they had entered the forest, and was relieved that they were all in place.

He was venturing off without any pieces of jade to assist him, but he knew he had the skill within himself to defeat Pyron's madness and claim the jade for his quest and for Randler.

Without a single shard, he couldn't hone in on Pyron's location and so he traveled blind as he ventured northwest. There were several settlements west of the forest that the older mage could have gone to for refuge, but a mage felt most comfortable surrounded by his peers. Dariak banked on that notion, especially after all the events that took place in the southern tower. Pyron would want to ensure that other mages would stand against Dariak's quest and so he would travel to the northern tower.

As a young boy, Dariak's mother had taken him to the eclectic dwelling in the north. He hadn't felt comfortable there, and it was partly why his mother had brought him. She wanted him to see what mages could be, as a warning. The mages in the northern tower were seldom sane or friendly. Dariak remembered the nightmares he'd had after his visit there, but his mother comforted him, easing his fears and apologizing for his disquiet. Yet she never said she regretted bringing him, or that she wouldn't have brought him if she had it to do all over again.

He sort of felt that way now with his decision to leave Randler to the forest people. He had to move on and see his decision through, regardless of the consequences. And one day, maybe the bard would understand, as Dariak had come to understand the lesson his mother had for him.

The day was relatively young as he ventured away from the forest. Lurina had cautioned him not to remain close to the wood, for he would no longer be under Astrith's eye and could not be protected. He didn't question it, for the infrequent enemy encounters within the forest had already felt unnatural. He could only imagine the influx of creature contacts if he was truly on his own.

Besides, out in the open, he had a wonderful chance to breathe the crisp, winter air and he could see the landscape and keep himself wary of others. It served him well as the day wore on, for the fields were the home of many feral creatures.

After a time, he stumbled across a pack of leomers. The cat-like hunters had verdant coats of thick hair that carried a scent that masked them. They traveled in a swirling set, crouching low and ever changing positions, their green hair looking more like wind-blown grass than anything. Dariak mistook them for just that.

One leomer hissed and pounced up from the group, and Dariak jumped aside just in time. He rolled on the ground and came to his feet as two more of the creatures bounded over to him to attack. As with the triggans, Dariak had only heard stories of these beasts. He tried to remember anything about them, but the frenzy was on.

Dariak reached into his pockets for the spell components he knew best, pulling for earth and fire powers to have at his disposal. The first thing he did was enact the Shield of Delminor. It was lucky he did, for one of leomers skittered around and leaped at him before he was ready with anything else. The creature hit the invisible wall of force and had its weight magnified so it fell, moaning and crying as it tried to get up.

He reset the spell, using a clump of dirt as the catalyst. He then brought his staff around to swipe at three of the approaching felines. The leomers nimbly jumped over the attack and crashed into Dariak's chest, knocking him down. He threw his weight back and rolled feet over head, hoping to disentangle himself from the leomers.

The beasts would only have stood at Dariak's knee, but their agility and flexibility were astounding. The feral cats twisted and maintained their hold on the mage even as he rolled about this way and that trying to dislodge them. What he couldn't understand was why the Shield of Delminor hadn't stopped them. Thinking fast, he wondered if they were indeed affected but were still clutching him and so only felt heavier than they were.

But they were moving effortlessly, he noted, swinging his arms around and dislodging them at last. Teeth and claws raked his skin as the felines were flung aside, but he didn't dwell on it. If they had poisonous claws, there was nothing he would be able to do anyway.

As the three critters gathered themselves, Dariak spotted five more weaving closer. He wanted to use a larger scale fire spell, but after the incident with the triggans, he was hesitant, so he turned instead to the air. Waving his arms wildly, Dariak called upon the wind and swept the area in front of him with great force, much the way Sharice had battered him in her basement. *"Tevilister conicus rethribur beleagen fross kurrath knarr writhrenar froe!"*

A strong windstorm erupted from Dariak's hands, cascading outward and catching the leomers off guard. The cats mewled as they were tossed on their backs, save the one still fighting the Shield of Delminor. The leomer in the lead had taken the brunt of the spell and was lying on the ground nearly unconscious from the battering wind.

The rest of the pack flipped up and pressed forward to attack. Dariak wasted no time summoning another powerful gust. Perhaps if he could keep knocking them over, they would lose their will to fight. He called the words again, empowering them with his breath and swirling arms. Reaching outward, he sent the gusts toward the leomers, already setting his mind to his next spell while he waited for this one to work its course.

But when the wind crashed into the leomers, they were completely unfazed. The wind washed over them like nothing more than a simple zephyr. They moved on, six of them, escaping the spell completely and pressing their advantage.

Dariak was stunned by what he saw and his mind jumped off his most recent thoughts of his battle with Sharice as he scrambled to call his next spell. He wasn't sure what spell components he would need, but he let his mind do the work for him anyway. *"Shorricus brak wreth fineah!"*

Sparks flared at his fingers, but he couldn't launch them outward at his foes. Instead, he charged ahead and lunged for the nearest leomers, grabbing them where he could and sending the lightning bursting through them. One of the felines howled in agony and collapsed unmoving, while the other one hissed furiously but was more angry than hurt. Dariak acted quickly as the creature screamed at him; he swung his foot and kicked it full in the face, knocking it yards away.

In the seconds he had before the others reached him, Dariak sliced his finger on a fragment of glass and he erected his basic protection spell. The four leomers converged on him and pounced. The first cat crashed into his shield and collapsed, but the other three were unaffected.

He thought he understood it now, but he set up the Shield of Delminor to be sure. He let one of the leomers get close enough to activate the spell, but the creature slipped right through unaffected. It was all the confirmation he needed, but that would only help him not waste energy and time. He still needed to defeat them.

Dariak wiped the sweat off his face and set the hydration into his next defensive spell. He already suspected that one of the leomers would fall to the spell, taking all possible damage from it so that the rest of the pack would be protected. It would leave that leomer out of the fight but it would prevent the mage from reusing that spell against its brethren. And that protection would last throughout the battle, apparently.

Dariak had one more test to run before he was finished, so he dove, avoiding an attack, and grabbed for a few pebbles. He imbued them with power and launched them at the two remaining leomers. Upon impact, the pebbles exploded into countless cutting shards, embedding themselves into the creatures' flanks. But then moments later, the felines shook their bodies from head to toe and the bits of stone fell off them.

Now he knew. The first leomer that had taken the impact of the Shield of Delminor now absorbed all the earth spells, not just the one. It certainly made this much more interesting and dangerous.

He was running out of ideas and energy, so he called for his fire darts to take down one of the two remaining leomers. He then decided to let the last one jump him and he would simply wrestle it until he broke its neck.

The first part of his plan went perfectly. The leomer took the fire dart and fell, while the other one merely stumbled for a moment as the protection was set in place. Then it pounced for Dariak, who crouched and was ready for it. The cat's mouth opened wide, its fangs ready to bite, its claws prepared to gouge out his eyes. Dariak's hands grabbed the beast and he twisted his body, bringing the feline out of the air and crashing it down. His hands struggled to move toward the neck as its hind legs kicked powerfully to dislodge his grip.

Dariak shouted and strained harder, reaching for the neck and then dropping his body weight on it, waiting to hear that fateful snap that would end this struggle at last. But it didn't come. No amount of crushing did anything to hurt the beast, but its claws were doing damage to Dariak.

He was at a loss and he flipped himself over, throwing the animal aside. He rummaged through his pockets and when the leomer pounced again, Dariak raised a dagger up and cut into the beast's flesh, killing it at last.

With the last of the pack downed, a low keening wail echoed over the field. Dariak pushed himself up and watched as the eight bodies writhed in place where they were, then as they continued to wriggle, they slid ever so slowly into the ground, disappearing below the surface until there was no evidence of their passing at all.

Shaken, Dariak hastily gathered himself and jogged away from the site. Clearly, the leomers would one day rise again to beset another adventurer. He couldn't imagine many others would have been able to take them down, especially if throttling them did nothing. Then he remembered the one he had kicked in the head. He had already broken one's neck. Their magic then had prevented him from doing it again.

Or maybe, he considered as he kept moving, that only one could have been subdued by physical means, and that last leomer went down not because it was cut, but because it was cut with metal, one more of the elements. It was a disconcerting thought, because it meant that a team of soldiers had little chance of defending themselves against the leomers unless they had a dozen different types of material to defend themselves with, or if the leomers traveled in much smaller packs elsewhere.

It was hard not to wonder what would have happened if there had been more of the beasts in the scuffle. He was nearly out of elements to use against them. He had only missed shadow, beast, nature, and healing, though he couldn't see how any healing magic could have stopped the leomers. Perhaps he would have had to try to use a dissonant version of healing, like the spell Elgris had used against him a year ago as he had fled Kallisor castle with Gabrion and Kitalla.

Thoughts of healing magic swept through his mind and he realized he had to stop running long enough to seal some of his wounds. He opted to pause for a while to catch his breath.

There was no shelter in this part of the land, so he dropped to the ground and focused on calling to the healing energies. His body ached from every cut and scrape the leomers had given him. There did seem to be a mild toxin, but only enough to make his insides feel itchy. Like Quereth had tried to teach him, he sent the healing through his body, looking for signs of fluctuations which would indicate other damage. It was one of the hardest healing spells he could muster, but only it would allow him to know if the poison was worse than it seemed.

Overall, he was fine. The threat of the leomers was apparently in their ability to protect each other, which would undoubtedly allow them to overwhelm an unprepared traveler. Having subdued them, Dariak felt a grim confidence.

One of his worries along the journey was that he had come to rely solely on the jades for magic and he wasn't exercising his skills enough. Now, traveling without them at all forced him to acknowledge that he was well-versed in many types of magic now. The jades must have been imparting their knowledge to him even when he wasn't aware of it. He had no formal training of air or lightning magic, yet he had summoned strong spells from some glimmer of memory.

He considered the jades and what their purpose was in the land, where they came from, and how they had migrated to these two kingdoms when there were other lands scattered around the world. But he actually knew the answer to that. In all the world, only Hathreneir and Kallisor had ever known magic. It was as if the ancient gods had only played in these lands.

Dariak scoffed at the notion of the ancient gods. Like most of the people, he had shunned them early on, agreeing with the populace that they had no need of gods to run their daily lives. There didn't need to be any kind of divine influence that affected whether someone was born a mage or a warrior. If there had been gods long ago, they had surely moved on to tend to some other world. What gods would have allowed their children to fight each other for so long and still with no end in sight?

It was easier to think some otherworldly being had created this place and all the things in it, even the leomers. It allowed blame to lie elsewhere. It gave a way for people to pass responsibility off to some unseen other force. And if the gods were there, why hadn't they made any efforts to show themselves in many long centuries at the least?

Dariak knew he was exhausted, even entertaining these thoughts. But it did lead him to an important question: Who left the kings in charge? How was their lineage determined? He knew the answer, of course. One was the heir of King Kallisor. The other of Queen Hathreneir. Yet, why should their lines have to hold the power after all this time? Why, when all they ever managed to do was keep the kingdoms at war?

It was going to end, he said to himself. Once the jades were reunited, he would find a way of ending the relentless strife. He would do it without gods and without kings.

He just wasn't sure what he would do it with.

CHAPTER 35

Kitalla's New Best Friend

KITALLA DRAGGED VERNA away from the dungeons of Magehaven and asked one of the mages to escort them to a private room. The acolyte obliged, seeing the fire in both sets of eyes, and after ascending two floors he left them in a large open space.

The chamber was badly damaged, likely from Kitalla's last time here. Burn marks scarred the walls and floor. Blood stained the stone all over. Even tufts of beast fur could be seen.

Verna had made no noise on the way, seething at her circumstances and the random nature in which she had been freed. Now she faced Kitalla, wondering what to make of the leather-shrouded woman.

Kitalla didn't make her wait. "Check your attitude, soldier. You're not leaving this room until I let you."

Verna scowled. "You'll be dead before you know what hit you."

"Good, you've got some spark. Or are you just a yammerer?"

Verna growled like an angry lupino and charged. Hands reaching out to tackle Kitalla, she pounded across the floor. Kitalla was ready for it and sidestepped, letting her fly past.

"Focus, girl."

"You'll pay," Verna promised, turning and reassessing her target. She should have expected her opponent to be trained for battle if she had a past with Ervinor. She stepped toward the thief, who barely registered any form of defense. "Protect yourself!"

Kitalla laughed. "From you? Do your worst."

Verna pounced and, as she expected, Kitalla stepped away, but this time Verna was ready. She landed and turned on her heel, leaping off again in Kitalla's direction. The thief was mildly surprised but reacted quickly by dodging the angry fists that flew toward her. She turned and shoved Verna's back as she went past, sending her sprawling to the floor.

"You're barely even trying," Kitalla accused.

With a shout, Verna sprinted and tucked in low, determined to grab Kitalla around the midsection. Kitalla leaned back, grasping Verna's arms in the process, and dropped to her back, flipping the soldier overhead. Verna landed with an angry thud.

"Do you even have any training? You're dreadful at this. Say, would you like me to close my eyes?"

"Don't mock me!" Verna rushed ahead, stopping just before Kitalla and kicking her leg out. Kitalla hopped over it, but Verna punched at Kitalla's belly while she was in the air. She coughed as she landed and Verna thought she had her. She stepped in to grab Kitalla's hair and wrench her to the ground, but didn't get the chance. Kitalla let her step forward, then she swept her leg out, knocking Verna down.

With another scream, Verna rolled closer to Kitalla and grabbed her arms with all her rage. She pulled and pushed and Kitalla let her wear herself out, taking care only that Verna didn't head-butt her in the process. The woman's legs were thrashing too, but Kitalla took the brunt of their damage stoically.

Winded, Verna finally slowed down and Kitalla used that moment to roll herself on top of Verna and pin the soldier's arms to the floor. "See, now if you had better control, you wouldn't be in this position."

Verna raised her hips sharply, pushing Kitalla up and over, but the thief landed on her feet. She waited while Verna rose up and crouched low for her next attack.

"So what's your story anyway?" Kitalla asked. "Sounds like you messed up."

"I'll rip your eyes out!" Verna charged, avoiding Kitalla's defenses, almost scoring a scratch. But Kitalla allowed that sense of victory to blind the girl and she snapped her wrists up at the last second to deflect the blow, after which she spun Verna around and pulled her close.

Kitalla whispered hotly in her ear. "I'm rather attached to my eyes, thanks."

Verna responded by thrashing around, to no avail. She even stamped her foot onto Kitalla's ankle, but the thief felt no pain. Not until after this was over, she told herself.

After a few moments, Kitalla pushed Verna away, splattering her to the floor again. "It would be a lot easier if you told me what happened."

Verna looked up at Kitalla, who didn't seem the least bit winded. "What are you?"

"I'm trained. Seasoned, some would say."

"Old, you mean," Verna corrected bitingly. Kitalla's jaw dropped at the comment and Verna took her chance. She sprang up, throwing her whole body weight at Kitalla. They crashed and sprawled on the floor.

Kitalla went on the offensive. "I…" She slapped Verna's face. "am…" Her knees came up and pressed into Verna's abdomen. "not…" One arm crossed over Verna's neck, exerting enough pressure to promise death if the woman persisted. "old!"

Verna glared into Kitalla's eyes, slowly putting together what she had said, and then all of a sudden, the soldier burst out laughing. Moments later, Kitalla joined in, freeing her captive and moving a few paces away.

"So you do have a weakness," Verna said, rubbing her bruises. "Who knew it was vanity?"

"A momentary lapse."

"If I ever spar with you again, I'll be sure to bring along a mirror to distract you."

Kitalla pulled a face. "Ugh, I bet you'd set it up to reflect your ugly cheekbones at me and I'd be looking at you twice!"

"You tramp!"

Kitalla raised her voice in mock anger. "So?"

Verna took a breath to retaliate but then laughed again. "I ask again; what are you?"

"The correct thing to ask is who, not what."

"Not dressed like that."

Kitalla checked herself. "There is absolutely nothing wrong with my outfit. Besides, I wasn't the one just let loose from a prison cell."

Verna's face curled into a scowl and the mirth was gone. "Fine, you want to finish this fight, we finish it." She jumped up on her feet and raised her fists.

Kitalla yawned. "Boring."

She held her stance for a minute or two, but dropped her fists when Kitalla didn't move. "Tell me what you are and maybe I'll tell you my story."

Kitalla shook her head. "No respect. You must have hit your head too hard or something. Is that hair naturally red or are you bleeding? No matter. If you must know 'what' I am, then I'm this: I'm the wild card. But I can see in your eyes that you'd like to be that instead."

"You know nothing about me."

Stretching out on the floor to be more comfortable, Kitalla responded, "Well, you sound like you're from Marritosh. You can fight—if you call that fighting—so you're either born to a fighting family or you're a refugee. From what I heard downstairs, you were in charge of one of Ervinor's teams, which means he trusts you, so you must have some kind of leadership skills. That, or he lusts after the backside of an ursalor, considering your looks."

"You've never seen an ursalor, not unless you were born to one."

Kitalla chortled. "I helped take one down, actually, and the mages here employ the cubs at times. You'll see them eventually; you'll probably think they're siblings."

Rage flashed on Verna's face again. "Speak not of siblings!"

"Ahh. Another piece of the Verna puzzle. What happened to your kin?"

"Me, me, why is it always me you ask about? Why aren't you telling me anything about you?"

Kitalla clapped her hands once. "Because you're the one just released from the dungeon. I could have you go back there if you like it better. I guess the men would be willing slaves to your charms down there. Or do you hold out for Ervinor?"

Verna grunted and shook her fists, pacing in circles. "You are infuriating."

"Ah, so now you know what I am. What are you?"

"I'm commander of the Wrens in Ervinor's army."

"I see. Do you really think you still hold such a title after what happened?"

Something in Verna seemed to slip away then and Kitalla noticed it clearly. "Of course."

But the thief knew better. Verna was afraid of losing her position in the army, but whether it was in pursuit of Ervinor or something else, she wasn't sure. "What good are you to a general if you can't follow orders?"

Anger welled inside her again and she shouted, "All he wanted us to do was sit outside on our rears and wait for the mages to ask us to tea. But we have to train. We have to be strong. We can't wait for others to baby us, to lay their weapons down. We have to be ready. I wanted to teach my team not to be afraid, not to let fear be our master, and he questioned my tactics. He told me to stop what I was doing. Then the mages attacked and I defended us. But the general would let us fall to their spells. He'd let us all die so he wouldn't have to kill them."

"And you want to still follow this general?"

Her jaw trembled and she looked at Kitalla. "Yes."

"Why?"

"Have you seen him?"

Kitalla rolled her eyes grandly. "He's prettier than a sandorpion at sunset. Is that a reason to follow someone?"

Verna shook her head. "No, no. Not that. His arm. It's gone, but he fights on like he's got six arms. His body is weak from it, but he tries not to show it. He rose up out of nowhere and defended Marritosh to the end. He got the villagers out before they were all killed. He isn't even from here. He's Kallisorian. But he defended my people from harm. He believed in us and he fought for us, at risk and injury to himself."

Kitalla nodded. "He sees people for who they are, not where they're from or what they've done. I understand the allure."

Verna's eyes squinted, not knowing if Kitalla was serious.

"No, really," the thief said. "It's very attractive to have that brave knight rise up and save us. Better even to fight by his side." Verna showed a slight smirk at Kitalla's approval, though it didn't last long. "However," Kitalla reprimanded, "a commander in an army must obey orders and not think for herself, risking the livelihood of the people who are hers to protect. Train them to defend themselves, yes, but also train them to follow orders. You can't do that if you don't follow them yourself."

Verna sneered. "And do you also obey his command?"

"No. But in some ways, I helped train him. It's why I'm not in his army; he can't order me around. I fight with him as an equal."

The soldier stared at Kitalla for a long time, trying to piece it all together.

"Ask him," Kitalla offered. "He'll tell you. He's open like that when he can be. He's a good friend that I haven't spent nearly enough time with."

"Then you should go talk to him, no?"

"I should indeed, especially for busting me out of my cell."

"Your what?"

Kitalla smiled widely. "I didn't think you'd caught that part of the conversation. Ervinor was down there to get me out of my cell. It's lucky you called out when you did. You'd be rotting in there and Ervinor wouldn't even know you were alive yet."

"You! You!" she stammered, after which she pounced. Kitalla rolled out of the way, laughing heartily.

"It's all true, really," Kitalla said as she dodged Verna's next attack. "Every bit of it." She dropped as Verna swung high, then she leaped away as the soldier's feet kicked low. "Now, now, be reasonable!"

"You had me believing you, but you were just another prisoner." She screamed and darted for Kitalla, who sporadically ran, feinted, or rolled out of the way.

"Prisoner or not, if I'm right, I'm right." She ducked under a punch and then grabbed Verna's hips to slide her away. "This is silly. You can't defeat me, so stop now, soldier, and wise up."

But Verna was angry. She felt like she had been played by some random thief. Though she had been in Marritosh while Kitalla was there, their paths had never crossed. She was a face in a crowd, nothing more. Now this criminal had tugged at her heart and made a fool of her, taunting her to confess whatever this woman wanted her to say. Verna wouldn't have it. She would stop it. She would—

Kitalla chopped her hand at Verna's neck and ended the scuffle. The soldier collapsed, unconscious. Kitalla dusted herself off after making sure Verna was really out. "Well, that could have gone better."

CHAPTER 36

The Tower Falls

ERVINOR SPENT A few days trying to calm everyone about the recent events, including the sudden death of Vinnek, the arrival of Kitalla, and the release of Verna and her team. The last was the hardest to achieve, because she had launched herself and her group into the tower with the intent of slaying the mages within. The young general kept his own temper in check as the Mage Council yelled and sought retribution for things that were unreal. Through it all, Shelloni wore an amused grin at the turmoil.

He struggled to keep the peace within the tower with the different factions inside. The fire mages wanted to bring Verna to justice, but the healers felt she could be cured of her rashness if only they could reclaim the healing jade and send her through a Trial. The rest were torn in their allegiances, some siding with Ervinor's explanation of a misunderstanding, and others wanting to expel the non-mages from their midst.

Frast, Quereth, and Lica did their best to assuage the fears of the mages within the tower, but it wasn't easy, for the three were aligned with Ervinor and so they weren't always trusted. Quereth had the most sway with the other mages for he spoke calmly and with authority, but Lica was brash and Frast was frustrated, and their words were frequently discounted.

Kitalla saw the rifts tearing throughout the tower. The temporary peace was not going to last and she feared an all-out civil war within the structure. Mages erupted into heated arguments over seating arrangements and food choices. It didn't bode well. But Ervinor was in charge of things here, with the Council, so she spent her time trying to whip Verna into a proper commander.

Ervinor woke one morning and his right shoulder ached painfully. He tried to rub away the annoyance but it persisted, as it sometimes did. He opted to run through some exercises to clear his mind and ready himself for the day. He didn't know where he found the strength to push through some days, but he believed in the final outcome and he wanted to have a part in it, so he found the will to go on.

He dressed himself in the special armor Herchig and his wife had crafted for him, always remembering the old man's tales when he fastened the straps in place. He needed his vociferous friend's wisdom right now. The tapestry was coming apart at the seams and he knew he needed to find a way to keep it from unraveling, but there was no unified purpose for the mages. Even their leaders were divided.

Several meetings were set up throughout the day, starting with his least favorite: resources. The refugees from Marritosh, as well as his own fighters, consumed food and water and ale within the tower. The mages were wary of the supplies disappearing without any efforts to replace them. And though Ervinor had encouraged Barcel to see to the task, he was new to his role on the Council, having replaced Vinnek, and he didn't know what to do. The rest of the Council offered little help, for they were doing their best to keep their followers in line.

"If we send mages out here, here, and here, they can forage for herbs and meat," Barcel said once the meeting had commenced, "but whom do we send? It can't be only my mages, can it? That's not how it's been done before."

"Tell me, then, how *was* it done before?" Ervinor asked, trying not to be impatient.

"I don't know, but I don't ever remember Vinnek sending us all out at once."

"Have you spoken to the other Council members?"

"Yes, and Rothra said it's his mages' turn in the training rooms so they can't be assigned elsewhere. Shelloni says that if the fire mages are staying here, her mages must also remain to keep the fire mages in check. In check from what?"

Ervinor nodded. "Indeed. There shouldn't be need for protection here. And it isn't as if Shelloni or any others are sending all their forces." He pounded his fist on the table. "Why must everyone make this so hard? It's gathering food and water. We all need it to survive. Why must this be a contest?"

Barcel hedged. "It'd be easier if everyone contributed."

Ervinor looked up at the mage. "I would gladly send a contingent to join the mages but I've been told not to by the Council. They claim it is a conflict of interest to allow the fighters free rein here. Yet they are unwilling to aid in feeding the people who aren't helping."

Barcel collapsed in a chair. "Then it's a lost cause."

"Nonsense." Ervinor paced about, scratching his head. "Don't give up so soon and don't be bullied by the other members of the Council. I know you're new to the task, but believe in yourself, Barcel. You were already next in line under Vinnek and I'm sure it was no mistake. You're ready for this task. It just came sooner than you expected."

"I don't know."

Ervinor really didn't have it in him to bolster this young man. He had to fight himself not to start shouting, for that would only shut the mage down and prevent any chance of getting through to him. "What if the mages gather the materials and my men work to process it? Then it's not a free ride."

"No, the mages prepare the meat in their own ways. Water spells to keep things moist. Air spells to create vacuums that prevent decay. Ice spells for preservation."

"What of work? Repairs? Anything?"

The mage shrugged his shoulders as if he were lifting the weight of the world. "I don't know enough of the day-to-day things to know what's needed."

"Then I need you to find out so we can resolve this. The others won't agree to a resupply task until this is settled."

"No, they won't."

"Then I need you to act fast and learn what you can so we can resolve this," he repeated, "preferably before nightfall. Go."

Dutifully, but with a beleaguered stride, Barcel left the meeting chamber and held the door open for Ervinor's next attendees.

Shelloni and Rothra walked in, their faces taut. Ervinor could only guess. He smiled, somehow. "Please, have a seat. What's on your mind?"

The two of them started shouting at once until Ervinor intervened and asked Shelloni to voice her concerns first. "My mages have training to do. The fire mages are taking over the training rooms."

"It is our time!" the fire mage seethed.

"Now, now," Ervinor interrupted. "Shelloni, finish."

"Finish what? I'm done. We want our training time. He won't let us. Figure it out."

Ervinor then gestured to Rothra to speak. "It's our time to train. The edict was set years ago that in times of war when the fire mages outnumber other factions, we are to have access to the training rooms when the moon is between its third and fourth quarter for no less than four hours per day and per night. We're at war, the moon's in place, and we will have our training."

"This is preposterous!" Shelloni shouted.

"How so?" Ervinor asked.

"The only reason he claims to have more fire mages than any other faction is because of the fire mages in *your* army who happen to be here."

Ervinor raised an eyebrow. "You're allowing them to train?"

Rothra hesitated. "Well, the training schedule is based on the need for defense within the tower and so—"

"So, no," Ervinor finished. "If you're not allowing them to train, then you've no right to count their number among yours."

"They are fire mages and so they are, by default, under my jurisdiction and protection."

Ervinor stepped closer. "If you cycle them appropriately through training sessions, then I would be inclined to agree, but it doesn't sound like that's your intent."

"Well, I—" He stopped himself and grumbled low. "Fine, we'll open the rooms."

Shelloni laughed. "This is a good day. Thank you, Ervinor." She stood up to leave.

"Not so fast," the general interrupted. "We need to discuss the plans for restocking supplies here."

The conversation continued with shouting and blaming on both sides, but eventually Ervinor was able to work an amenable solution, provided the other Council members agreed. With Shelloni and Rothra supporting the plan, he felt it would work.

Ervinor needed a break before his next session so he stepped out for a walk. He looked at the intricate architecture, hoping to find some kind of inspiration, but he was too consumed in the menial woes of the petty mages to get lost in the beauty he was seeing. His own commanders were of little help in assuaging his concerns, for when he asked them for updates, they had numerous problems to report and few solutions.

Needing a break from the mages, Ervinor traveled down to the first floor to visit with the refugees. Conditions were mediocre at best for the people, which bothered Ervinor. These were Hathren citizens who deserved food and shelter from their own mages. They did not deserve to be held captive on this first floor of the tower with periodic deliveries of food that led to brawls among the strong. He could see the suffering and it irked him. The mages were living above their means and though they had a way of hunting for food, they were bickering instead of working together. Seeing hungry children made things worse.

Perhaps he was in too bad of a mood already, but seeing these people hardened him. He stormed back upstairs to hold his next meeting, his back a bit straighter, his jaw firmly set. He climbed three sets of stairs and walked through a mess hall where the acolytes talked and laughed over their meals. He watched as someone lifted a bowl of stew and poured it over a friend's head, chortling at the expression on her face.

"For this?" Ervinor shouted, his voice cutting through the din. "For this?" he said again when the mages quieted down. "You refuse to work together, refuse to go out and gather provisions, for this? So you can pour soup on each other?" He grabbed a plate of unfinished meat left at a table. "People fight for scraps within your own tower and you leave food behind uneaten? Unwanted? Have you any idea how much of this food could have gone downstairs to feed children?"

"We never asked for them to come here," shouted a voice across the room.

"It's war; you don't get to have everything all nice and happy. What's wrong with helping your fellow man just because he is in need?"

"They oughta go and feed themselves," someone else yelled.

"How?" Ervinor shouted. "They aren't allowed weapons to go fight for themselves, not that they know how to fight. They aren't even allowed to leave this tower without—"

"Excuses!"

Ervinor slammed the plate on the table, shattering the ceramic and splattering the food. "Enough! This ends now. I need volunteers, right now, to bring food downstairs immediately. Whether it's a full plate or the parts you won't eat. Let's go."

A handful of mages stood right up to comply, but others shrieked in outrage. "That's our food! Give that away and we'll have nothing left!"

"It's the right thing to do," retorted one mage.

"It's suicide for us!"

"We can't treat people like this. What if the roles were reversed?"

"We're mages; it will never be reversed, you fool!"

"How dare you!"

Before he could stop it, tensions snapped. Mages leaped across tables to throttle those on the opposing side. Chanting started and Ervinor cried out over it to be heard, but he was too late. His own frustration had fueled this fight. He wouldn't be able to stop it so easily.

The acolytes summoned their very best, which was thankfully not much in the standards of mages. Weak ice darts cracked against tables. Mild fireballs singed without burning. When the spells were not enough, daggers and fists flew. Ervinor stepped in where he could, trying to wedge himself between pairs of fighters to distract them and make them see reason. It wasn't something he could do alone.

The sounds of fighting were heard outside the mess and others ran to the fray after spreading word. Soon, the infighting spread throughout the tower and Ervinor's hopes of ending the struggle collapsed. He needed his fighters' help to stop this.

Rushing from the room, the general sprinted downstairs to one of the meditation chambers where Frast and Quereth had been spending a lot of time. Finding them, he filled them in and they raced above, hoping to figure out a way to neutralize whatever spells were being cast. Ervinor then dropped down another flight of stairs, seeking his soldiers and asking for their help.

"I know they haven't shown us deep courtesy, but we must do what's right and put a stop to this before anyone is seriously hurt. I need your help to get up there and tackle the mages. Stop them from casting spells. No weapons, no punching. I need your restraint, but I need your help."

As one, Ervinor's army dashed up the steps to do his bidding, many of them grimly pleased with the task. They had been allowed their place within the tower, but they had not been openly welcomed, and many mages who crossed their paths eyed them with scorn. But Ervinor trusted his soldiers. They would do as he commanded.

He raced off to find Lica to help corral the others. Instead, he ran into Kitalla and Verna engaged in a sparring session. Both women were winded and tired, but he urged them to help.

Verna was visibly torn at his request. She still blamed him for wanting to leave her in the dungeon, but her time with Kitalla had taught her to respect his leadership. "No killing," she echoed, rushing off to help the rest.

Kitalla paused for a moment, eying the general carefully. "It isn't your fault, Ervinor."

"I didn't say it was."

She grabbed his good shoulder and held him firmly. "I see it in your eyes. That darkness there. Whatever happened, you're not the cause. Things here have been tense, just remember that."

"Kitalla—"

"No, no, general, sir. I'm off to do my part!" She grinned, then playfully jabbed him in the chin before jogging off.

He didn't know where to go or what to do, so he turned and ran back up to the mess hall. He was weary, and by the time he reached the fourth floor, he was winded and needed to rest. He could hear the sounds of battle continuing, so he drew a few quick breaths and rushed forward to assist.

In the mess, his soldiers had done their part. Many of his fighters dodged spells and dagger thrusts, slipping past the mages' defenses and bringing them down without harming them. They pinned the mages' arms and held them tightly. One soldier per mage. Unfortunately, that left Ervinor's team at a disadvantage, for more mages were coming to the aid of their brethren and soon the numbers swelled in their favor.

Ervinor tried to call for a ceasefire, but like Verna's rampage outside the tower, his cries went unheeded. Everything was slipping away from him. He glanced over across the way and saw a few of the Council members arrive, aghast at what they witnessed. He rushed over to talk to them, but they saw the soldiers taking down the mages and so they backed away. Ervinor knew it wasn't a good sign.

"Kitalla!" he called out, seeing her punching a mage in the gut and knocking him out of the fight. "It's going to get ugly in here," he warned. "I don't kn—"

Kitalla watched as Ervinor stumbled and collapsed where he stood. Glancing around, she saw the soldiers fall to the floor or lose their charges. The mages were loose and she had no idea it was because of the safeguard Ervinor had agreed to when the mages admitted them to the tower. The Council members had activated the sleep spell they'd placed upon the fighters.

The mages rose up and kicked and hit the soldiers who had taken them down, defenseless though they were. They forgot their own squabbles long enough to make sure the soldiers were unconscious, then their arguments began anew. Kitalla looked at Ervinor and knew there was little she could do to help him.

Several thoughts raced through her mind, each crazier than the last. It was up to her to solve this insanity, for only she hadn't fallen like the rest. Swiftly, she considered trying to wake Ervinor and the others, but the kicking and beating by the mages hadn't brought the soldiers around. Kidnapping a Council member was farfetched, for their spells would eventually overpower her, even with the jades in her possession. Letting the events play out on their own seemed reckless and dangerous for everyone. One other thought crossed her mind, the craziest of them all, but it was all she had. She darted from the room.

Mages everywhere were in an uproar, some in pure confusion without knowing anything more than trouble had come to their home yet again. Kitalla avoided them all, rushing for the stairs and flying up them, floor after floor. She held on to her flickering inspiration as she went, pushing her tired limbs as if they were fresh and alert. She channeled out the pain she felt, like so many times before.

The upper chambers were mostly void of mages running around trying to hurt one another, for which she was grateful. Those few she came across were startled by her appearance, but she was gone before they could question her presence. Up again and around she went, desperately tapping into her memories.

Poltor had trained her in the art of rapid memorization. He had said it was a vital skill for thieves. They needed to know where things were at a moment's glance. Escape routes had to be mapped instantly without doubt. Yet conviction mattered the most. Poltor had put her through many paces to ensure she learned the lessons well. Those skills had served her in Grenthar's dungeons, and she was determined to apply them now.

Her last visit to the tower had brought her to a few secret rooms, led by Frast, where they eventually located the beast jade. She had been propelled by the fire jade and though it was in her pocket now, she could tell it wasn't offering her any support this time. Nor were the metal and glass jades. This was all her own.

One more flight and she pushed harder, reaching for her destination, not even knowing if her idea would work. But it had to work, for it was the only thing left to stop the madness in this place. The mages had not activated the traps on the upper floors, probably assuming the fighters in the lower levels were unable to get so high up. It didn't matter either way. If there had been traps, she would have devoured them and continued onward.

At last she reached the room she sought. Windows opened to a bright day all around, contrasting the sadness below. In the center of the room was a giant diamond surrounded by a number of benches and chairs, some of which were broken or scorched, some which had recently been brought in to replace others that had been beyond repair.

Now came the hard part.

Kitalla stopped and listened carefully. She couldn't hear the fighting, it was so far below this level. But she knew it was still going on, for the mages were angry and they would rampage until they ran out of energy or until enough people lay dead that they lost their will to fight. She hoped no one was dying, though it seemed unlikely considering all the tension.

She took a deep breath and pushed those thoughts away. The sunlight called to her, so she turned her head and stepped toward the windows to breathe in the fresh midday air. Calmness. Peace. They were the last emotions in her heart right now, but she reached for them anyway.

Then she imagined a great and wondrous scene. Sunlight basked a fertile land with a crimson-golden glow. Grass fluttered merrily in a sensuous breeze. Trees swayed gently, their branches bobbing calmly up and down as if squirrets danced upon them. A mild stream swished back and forth, refreshing.

As she held the image in her mind, she turned around to face the diamond. And then she danced. The steps were deep and graceful and she poured herself into each tenuous motion. Fingers fluttered like falling leaves, caught in a slipstream and twirling in the air. Her feet swayed like gleaming flowers, their dew-strewn petals glistening in the healing sunlight. Her body twisted and bent low, like a tigroar returning sated from a hunt to its litter of cubs, settling down among its kin and purring warmly.

She swept her body across the room and back, arms flying upward and around her torso, caressing herself with love and kindness. Kitalla became the embodiment of peace in her dance, and she spun around softly, lightly, her feet tapping across the floor like delicate raindrops on a warm day. As the droplets fell from her imagined sky, the sunlight beamed through them and cast flourishing rainbows in every direction, drawing all eyes upward at the wondrous display. The strands of her dark hair became rainbows and she dragged her hands through them and shook them playfully, causing the colors in the sky to swirl together.

Forward, backward, side to side. She danced and she danced, pouring her breath into the scene and projecting it out toward the diamond in the room. She knew it was linked to the mage barrier surrounding the tower. She knew that barrier initiated the Trials. Her heart held firmly to the image in her mind, rather than shift toward her heart-wrenching Trial. But her mind remembered that the mages were all connected here. Through the Trials. And she had learned in the few days she had been here that the jades were gone from this place and that the mages were weakened and nervous, for they drew power from this crystal core. This diamond. This heart-stone of the tower.

So she danced to the diamond. She bathed it in every glorious emotion and image she could muster. She laughed aloud, sending its sound outward full of child-like mirth. Dipping low with a twist, she sent her other arm high. Then she rose up, twisted the other way with a forward step and bent low again, reaching her other arm above. Around she went, her body growing weary. Each lunge, each twirl, each created vision drew strength from her.

Dariak had told her that her dance skill was different from the power that mages employed. Where mages drew energies from other sources and channeled them through words, Kitalla's skill came from within. And whether it was a side-effect or an intentional result, Kitalla's skill allowed her to do what no other mage had the power to do: affect the mind.

Sweat raced down her face and body. Her eyes squinted closed against the effort. She didn't have much more to give. The jades were not helping her. She was on her own. But she was used to that. She was strong because in many ways she had always been alone. She didn't fear it. She didn't regret it. It was fact. It was simply part of her.

Three more steps. Four. The vision faded. Sparks flared into her mind as her body fought to remain awake and functioning. She worked those sparks into her scene as magical fire meant to light the sky in celebration. She called to them to bring cheer and awe to all the watching crowd.

She had no way of knowing if anyone was watching, but at last her body grew too weak and she dropped low with one massive sweep of her arms and could not rise again.

CHAPTER 37

Gabrion's Test

NEWS OF THE obstacle course raced through the outpost. Ordren allowed all his subordinates to participate in the training session, feeling it built camaraderie among the troops. Many of the fighters who went through the course tried it again with new partners, determined to complete it faster and faster while learning the habits of their new guides and runners.

Urrith and Gabrion ensured the course stayed fresh by adding and moving obstacles now and then, sometimes between the forward and reverse runs. Injuries occurred at times but nothing major and the healers were able to resolve them swiftly.

After a few runs through the course, Gabrion promoted Avarra to captain, with Ordren's approval. She had proven herself an effective leader in the heat of the moment and he wanted to start giving her some responsibilities, particularly since new arrivals were expected any day now.

"Where do the recruits come from?" Urrith asked one day, but Gabrion knew the answer. He had listened well to the last batch of fighters and most were wrested from their homes if they looked strong enough to swing a sword. He didn't like it, and he knew that if Andron had come to Savvron during wartime, then Gabrion himself would have been forced into battle. He preferred that he'd chosen to stand up and defend his home.

"It doesn't matter," he said to Urrith. "It's up to us to ensure they live and can return home one day."

Urrith heard the grim tone and grabbed Gabrion's shoulder warmly. "We will get them all home once we're done here."

The afternoon was spent in fight training, where Gabrion's impressive swordsmanship was shared with the rest of the troops. As with the obstacle course, veterans and trainees alike attended Gabrion's sessions. It made him feel needed and important, but not vital. And for Gabrion, that was a good thing.

Avarra took her role as captain seriously. She kept her fighters in check and barked at them if they fell behind in their exercises. She had a warmth about her, though. She may not have exactly volunteered to be a soldier but she was willing to do her part for the land and if that meant she needed to crack the whip, then she did. If her compatriots needed a friend, she supported them. All the while, she shouldered their burdens and never showed signs of being bowed by them.

During the afternoon exercises, Gabrion gave her a series of warm-up tasks. They mostly involved stretching and jogging around the walled-in training field. Then each trainee took a sword and buckler and Avarra lined them up in a grid and presented them to Gabrion.

He eyed the fifty men and women carefully from his stance. "Shena, Helris, fix your positions."

"Sir," Shena replied, "I stand at the ready."

"Aye, sir, as do I!" called Helris.

Gabrion shook his head. "You stand with all the rest, sword in right hand, buckler in left."

"Yes sir!" they echoed.

"But you both favor your left hands in combat," he continued. "Thus you should switch arms."

"But sir, formation," Shena called.

Gabrion called them to the front of the pack. "Now turn and face your troop." They did so. "As you can see, your swords are now in the wrong hands. Fix it." Slightly embarrassed, the two fighters moved their swords to their left hands and bucklers to the right.

Gabrion nodded and paced from side to side. "Formation matters because it shows the enemy that we are a united force. It strikes fear into others who may not be trained to work as a unit. But we must not let formalities put us at a disadvantage. If you're stronger with your left hand, then you'll carry your sword there. It's as simple as that. Are there any others who need to adjust their equipment? Do so now."

"Sir!"

After a few others rotated their weapons and shields, Gabrion called again. "It's a benefit and a curse to be armed reverse to your opponent. You can strike in places they're not used to defending. But you're also more vulnerable in other places. I regret I haven't focused on this difference before now. From now on, as we train, we will be Easters and Westers. Easters fight right-handed. Westers, like Helris and Shena, come now and step forward and join us on this side of the line."

Five others left formation and lined up in a pyramid behind Gabrion. He then moved his sword to his left hand. "Today we Westers will hold off your attack. Easters, pace back to the wall. Once you touch the stone, turn and charge. No blood today. If your body is struck by iron, you're out. Go!" The Easters turned and marched toward the rear wall.

Gabrion then turned to face the Westers. "Always use your greatest skills in battle. When the others come, be limber. We're outnumbered roughly five to one. Watch for openings and take them."

"You're fighting left-handed, sir?" Shena asked.

"The practice will do me well."

The first row of fighters touched the back wall and turned to sprint ahead. Only seconds passed before the next wave touched the wall and raced ahead, but it was enough of a delay for each row of six fighters to be met briefly by the Westers.

Ordren looked over the training field as the two factions clashed, and he shook his head in amazement. Gabrion moved around like a phantom, avoiding every sword aimed at him, and he was the only one fighting without a shield. He had said once that a buckler got in his way, and Ordren could see that he was right. The recruits battled hard, making sure their blades were turned so as not to cut into the others. Two Easters went down on the first wave, and Ordren noted something odd. Gabrion never made an actual strike. He parried and he dodged. He even pushed the Easters into his fellows, but he never swung his sword to take a hit. Perhaps it was a training mechanism, but after Kitalla's departure and Gabrion's initial stillness, he wondered if something else was at work.

The scuffle lasted for nearly half an hour, all fifty or so fighters eventually falling until it was Gabrion and one other scrapper. Avarra had been determined to be the last one standing, but she took a blow near the end of the engagement and sat frustrated on the sideline.

Gabrion squared off against Jarraf, who looked both invigorated and nervous being the last. The wiry youth was two years younger than Gabrion and had a hard look in his eyes. His upbringing had clearly been difficult but he hadn't spoken of it. Gabrion could only wonder what ghosts haunted the man.

Jarraf lurched in with his sword and Gabrion sidestepped easily, spinning about and pushing the fighter away. Jarraf turned, raising his shield to block a strike that wasn't coming. He then charged in low and Gabrion jumped to the side, turning and kicking the man's backside and splattering him. It didn't count as a weapon strike so Jarraf stood back up and entered his battle stance again.

Gabrion held himself at the ready, sword still in his left hand. He swiped it through the air in challenge and Jarraf accepted, racing forward and bringing the weapon up toward the right side, but at the last minute, he stepped one foot forward and turned inward, bringing the sword around behind himself and attacking from the left. Had Gabrion held the sword in his right hand, he would have easily parried it. As it was, the attack slipped through and Gabrion had to collapse to avoid being hit. Jarraf sensed a victory and swept his sword around, casting it toward Gabrion, but the warrior rolled to his side and crashed into Jarraf's legs, knocking him over. The fighter lost his balance and as he fell, his own sword swept around and clocked him in the head, ending the bout.

Healers tended to Jarraf and a few others who took more than casual damage, but the rest of the fighters stood and reset the field to try again. Avarra took charge of the next session as Ordren called for Gabrion.

"You've had quite an impact on the fighters," Ordren noted. "They all look up to your skill."

"I'm just trying to help them defend themselves, sir."

"I notice that defense has become your primary strategy."

Gabrion didn't bite. "New recruits are coming soon, sir. I'm hoping these men and women will help bolster the rest as they come and help in their training. Is there something you'd like me to do other than train them, sir?"

Ordren shook his head in annoyance. "Gabrion, listen to me. I remember those days after the fall of the Prisoner's Tower. You were there, a fugitive, but you didn't flee to save yourself. You remained there to help the people who needed it. You risked being captured by me and my men."

"There were more important things to contend with, sir."

Ordren stopped walking and grabbed Gabrion. "Snap out of it, Gabrion! I left Pindington to follow you. I didn't join Dariak's quest for his sake. I came because of you. No more of this 'sir' nonsense, do you hear me? I only hit you with that because you were lost in shadow. But look at you now. The fighters admire you. I've worked hard to keep these men and women strong and well-honed, but you have true inspiration here."

The warrior pulled away. "I have work to do, sir."

"Gabrion!" the commander growled. "I need an ally here. I need a partner in this place. I need you. Won't you stand with me and help me to fortify this outpost?"

The young man stopped and stood there silently for a few moments. He then turned and stared Ordren in the eye. "The Gabrion you met in Pindington is gone."

"You're wrong," the gruff commander said. "He's hurting, but he isn't gone."

"I have work to do, sir."

"Fine. Return to your task, for now. But we'll—" His sentence was drowned out by a deep horn blowing through the keep.

Gabrion lifted his head. "The recruits are early."

But Ordren's face was stern. "No. Hathren troops have broken through. Call to arms!"

Gabrion shuddered. He knew this was an outpost on the edge of the fighting, but all reports had said that the Kallisorian troops that had crossed the border were secure and held back the enemy. This was a relatively safe haven from the actual fighting. He was just holding here, helping where he could, because he couldn't go home and he couldn't rejoin Dariak. His skills tagged him a warrior, but he could no longer fight. Not after everything that had happened.

Ordren saw the hesitation and he shoved Gabrion into action. Propelled forward, Gabrion's instincts kicked in and he charged through the outpost, back to the training field. "To arms! To arms! Hathren troops approach!"

It took a moment for them to respond, for their greeting at the outpost had been a staged assault, led by Gabrion himself. But the look on the warrior's face told them that this was real. "Turn your blades today," he called to them once Avarra had them in line. "We must protect this place and our lives. Take down the enemy."

"Kill them all!" one of the fighters cheered.

"No!" Gabrion shouted. "Turn your blades, I said. Knock them down. Knock them out. Take them down."

"But they're Hathren scum!"

"They are *men* and *women* fighting because they were ordered to. Are you any different?" Gabrion waited for an argument, but it didn't come. "I know the lust is there to slay them all, and they'll likely have orders to kill us, too. But I urge you to take them down but leave them alive. Wrap your waists with rope or leather, bind their hands if you must."

Avarra stepped up to Gabrion and whispered, "Sir, is this wise? Aren't we leaving ourselves open to being defeated? We'll be seen as weak."

"I have given an order, captain."

"Yes, sir, but what of the other fighters?"

"I will spread the word, but they may not comply. Disable the Hathrens, Avarra. Just disable them. Don't kill anyone."

"Sir!" She saluted, then turned to address the troops and help them stock themselves with binding straps wherever they could. Gabrion, meanwhile, ran to find Ordren to ask him to spread the no-kill order.

"Gabrion, that's madness."

"You wanted me as your partner just moments ago, didn't you? This is what I would advise you to do. No killing. No more of it, Ordren. It's the only way for this to stop."

Ordren paced back and forth, nonplussed. Gabrion waited silently on the outside, screaming madly inside. "I'll give the word, but if we lose too many men, I will lift it."

"Thank you," Gabrion acknowledged and ran from the room.

Ordren watched the warrior depart. "We'll play along for now, Gabrion. I hope I'm not going to regret this."

C H A P T E R 38

The Magitorium

DARIAK'S LONELY JOURNEY through the western plains of Hathreneir was only mildly eventful. He passed a few hunters and shared meals with them and battled a handful of feral creatures defending their nests. The landscape was flat with little shade, save random patches of shrubbery. Though he yearned for some form of companionship, he chose to avoid the larger settlements, fearing they would only distract him from his goal.

So he pressed onward for several days, foraging when he could, and dipping into his provisions when he had to. Small brooks wove their way through the land-scape, making the whole area feel like an oversized map with travel routes sketched into it. Eventually, he saw the top of the northern mage tower come into view and he hastened his steps to reach it.

The structure looked much like the Prisoner's Tower in design, just not as tall. It was a whiter stone than the southern mage tower, but it felt sturdier, as if it were meant to stand despite the magic being used within, rather than requiring its powers to hold it upright. The doors were solid oak with brass knockers all over them.

"What's with all the knockers?" he asked himself, wondering which one to pull. He reached but the nearest brass hoop was electrified and he jerked his hand away in pain. "What?" Another knocker seemed oddly warm to the touch, whereas an-other was ice cold. Each of the dozens of handles was imbued with some form of magic and Dariak realized that it must be a test.

He stepped back and considered the door for a time, thinking of the spells he knew already and how they might help him disable the defenses. As he fumbled in his pocket for a pebble, the door creaked open and a wild-eyed mage poked his wrinkled face out.

"Whatcha want?"

"I seek entrance," Dariak replied, wondering why the old man kept looking all around.

"Who's with you?"

"No one. I'm here alone."

The old man pushed the door and shook his head admonishingly at Dariak. "Then why in all the blazes did you go on and hit all the knobs? Have you any idea how much noise that makes?"

"I—well, no."

"Daft foreigner," the man accused. "Well, come on in, you idiot. You're making me keep this door open and if it's open for much longer, the warblebees will escape."

Dariak accepted the invitation and stepped within. "Warblebees?"

"Don't know a lick about your surroundings do you?" the man grumbled, shoving the door closed. "What, did you wander here lost or something? Looking for a free meal and someone to knit you some shoes?"

"Knit some…?"

"Bah, never mind, you. Go that way, let Rmfrmr help you. Go on, Rmfrmr, that's right. Go." He gestured with a gnarled hand and Dariak stepped away, glancing once over his shoulder to see the old codger grabbing for things in the air that, to Dariak, were invisible. Perhaps they were his warblebees.

He had been here once before as a child, but his memories were foggy at best. Everything seemed new to him.

The foyer was small and lined with wood everywhere, which Dariak found interesting. Mages didn't often surround themselves with wood, unless they were nature mages, for too many of the elements could enflame or break it. He walked over to a door on the left side and knocked gently.

"Pardon me, is Rmfrmr here?" he asked.

A middle-aged woman with gray streaks in her hair raised her head from a book she was sniffing. "Sorry?"

"Rmfrmr," he repeated. "Am I supposed to speak with you? Are you Rmfrmr?"

The woman slammed her book down and stood with surprising agility. "I'll kill him!" she screamed, shoving Dariak aside and storming past. No one else was in the alcove so he followed her. She stormed over to the old man who was still catching his invisible insects. "*Jallibrathea krethha norch konnaie!*" she shouted, curling her fingers and blasting the man with a small fireball.

"Whoa!" Dariak jumped in. "Take it easy!"

But the woman did not relent, stamping her feet and pounding her fists into the singed doorman. "I am *not* fat *or* deaf, you goat! Knock it off!"

The man started cackling wildly. "Rmfrmr, Rmfrmr!"

She kicked him and then turned to Dariak at last. "My name is Remfermar," she hissed, "but call me Remmie. This old coot torments me endlessly saying I cannot hear a dratted thing. Always talks funny around me, he does. 'Room for more,' indeed! Just trying to see how much I understand."

"Oh. Well, Remmie, I am Dariak."

"*The* Dariak?" she asked, her voice filling with awe and her face lighting up.

"I—uh—"

Then she broke into laughter, much like the old man's. "Fool newcomer. Come inside and get some food." She pointed at the floor at one of the square tiles that had a few striations. "Beware those tiles, Dabbilack, we don't know what they're made of."

"Dariak," he corrected.

She looked at him. "Eh? You talking to yourself now?"

He opted not to explain. Instead, he took in his surroundings as Remmie guided him through the floor. It was a small-feeling place, but not because it was any smaller in diameter than the southern mage tower. Instead, the entire area had been sectioned off with random walls jutting here and there, leaving a narrow snaking pathway through the center floor. Openings appeared all along the place and Dariak could hear chanting, snoring, yelling, and other noises from within. Along the ceiling was a metal pipe that glowed with a yellow light, illuminating the way. It had apparently been installed before some of the partitions had been erected, for it disappeared frequently behind the jagged walls.

They broke through the area into a larger study with tables and books everywhere. Dariak saw three other mages in the room but none of them was even looking at books. One was curled up on the floor, apparently sleeping. The other two held hands and stared at each other, but he didn't get the sense there was any romance between them. Remmie ignored them and made her way over to a table, where she sat down, picked up whatever book was there and then pressed her nose inside to sniff it.

Dariak waited for a moment. "Remmie?"

"This page; it's very interesting."

"Remmie, you said you were bringing me to get food?"

"I said no such thing," she growled. The woman looked up and eyed him cautiously. "Oh, Dabbilack, it's you. What can I help you with? Do you want to smell this tome?"

"Ah, no thank you. Where can I get some food?"

Remmie shook her head. As she lowered her nose into the book again, she muttered, "The *kitchen.*"

He didn't know whether to laugh or shout so he stepped away and noticed five doors leading away from the study. Peering his head into each one gave him little information about where each one led, except the one that opened to a tiny broom closet. It wasn't even as deep as his forearm, but no less than eight brooms were packed inside. Stepping away, he decided the place was a certainly not suited for a long stay.

He debated using a systematic approach to exploring the doorways, starting on one side and then returning to go through the other doors, but after the little bit he had already witnessed, he figured he might as well go on instinct. Logic didn't seem to have a place here.

He went into the doorway to the right of the broom closet and found himself in another narrow walkway with walls erected haphazardly on either side. The place was rather confining. Unlike the other passage, this one did not open up along the way, but he could still hear voices through the wood and stone. When he came through the other side he found an elderly man sitting in front of a fireplace, his back to Dariak.

"Good day, sir, I am Dariak. I am sorry if I am disturbing you."

"I wondered when you would come here," the ancient man said, his voice barely louder than his rattling breath.

"You... knew I would come?"

"They all come. Some day. They all come here. To see me. To find things they have lost. They all come. Sit down. Join me here."

Dariak did as requested, crouching down beside the gnarled man and gasping when he saw what the elder mage looked like.

"Yes, yes, look upon Xervius." He turned to face Dariak fully.

The old man's face was horribly mangled. His cheeks were caved in as if his face had been smashed by boulders and never repaired. His left eye sat much lower than his right, but as Dariak looked intently, he could see that the man had no eyes. Or rather, the orbs had been replaced with bluish-purple stones, one in each eye socket. The skin was dark in places, light in others, as if he had fallen in a fire and still sported the charred flesh. His nose oozed a constant stream of some yellowish gunk that drizzled into his mouth, which was cracked and misshapen. His lips seemed like they had been dissolved away by a thick acid, with only traces of pink fleshiness remaining. His chin had a massive gash in it as if a sword had cut upward, cleaving the bone.

It took all Dariak's resolve not to wince away in disgust. "Is there… anything I can do to help you? Are you hurt?"

Xervius wheezed a laugh. "I have employed every magic power I have ever known. These marks are but a list of my accomplishments."

"I… see."

"You do not. Nor do I, for that matter. But pretty gems look far better than empty holes gazing into my brain, do you agree? The gems are pretty?"

The bluish-purple jewels glimmered in the firelight. "Y—Yes, they are."

"Good lad. Polite lad. What is your purpose here at the Magitorium?"

"I seek someone."

"I am an old man," Xervius said. "Do not waste my time by hedging your request."

Dariak cleared his throat. "I seek the healing jade. I believe Pyron would have brought it here."

"Pyron," Xervius echoed. "Now there is a name I have not heard in many a year."

Dariak's face fell. "Then he isn't here."

"You give me much credit, lad. It isn't as if I hear everything that transpires within these walls. For what need do you seek the jade? To help a loved one? To stop others from using its magic?"

"To stop what?"

Xervius took a deep, ragged breath and slowly let it out. "If you hide the jade, others cannot use it. If you take the jade, you can use it. But why do you want it?"

"I would unite the jades and stop the war in this land."

Xervius laughed, which was a horribly rattling sound. "You cannot do it."

"But I must."

"You cannot. Not even great Delminor succeeded there."

"You… respect my father?"

"Fool," Xervius accused. "I *am* your father."

"W—what?"

The hollow cackling wracked its way out of the old man. "All mages are Delminor. Every skill we use is thanks to him, whether other mages know it or not."

"Oh." Dariak settled down. "I don't follow, though."

"His teachings, lad. His work was spread throughout the land. All mages tap into energies he taught us about."

"But that's only recent."

"Eh," Xervius hedged. "Delminor revolutionized magic in his time. Only old mages call upon spells like they did before Delminor's time, and that they only do because they are broken. Everything from effective spell components to words of power; Delminor gathered them up and distributed them. All mages alive are Delminor."

"But there are many books before his time that mages use."

"Yes, but who broke the runes and translated them?" Xervius paused for a moment and licked his charred lip with a mangled tongue. "Fine, deny your father's prowess, but I tell you, no mage today uses magic that Delminor didn't have some connection to."

Dariak's brow furrowed and he considered the words for a moment. He knew his father had been a great mage but it seemed outlandish to assign Delminor as the one man to have unlocked all of magic for every mage in the world.

"You ought to know of his connection, being his son."

"It makes no sense that he would be the link to all magic."

Xervius snorted. "It is only one way of viewing things. But consider your purpose here."

"The jade," he said, then inspiration struck. "The jades!"

"Hmm?" the old man prompted.

"He was connected to the jades and *they* tie to all the magic."

"Now you have it." Xervius turned his ghastly face back toward Dariak. "And that means that now all mages are you."

Dariak shook his head. "Many mages stand against me, and my father."

"But you are connected to the magic, through the jades, and thus to other mages. I did not say they will like you, or obey you, or want to be your friend. I only say there is a connection."

"I see."

Xervius grinned. "No, you don't. Not yet. But no matter. Tell me what you plan to do with this jade of yours."

"As I said, I will bring it together with the others and use the power to stop the war."

"And as I said, you cannot. Not even Delminor succeeded there."

Dariak groaned in frustration. "He was bound by the king to work for the kingdom. His research was abused and put to war, despite his intentions. He didn't have a free chance to do what he needed to do to put things right."

"And you do?"

"I have a better shot at it, yes."

"Hmm." Xervius considered for time, slowly licking the ooze that leaked out of his nose. "You may be right, but I do not think you will yet succeed. There is something else."

"What is it?"

"I… don't know. It doesn't feel like it is time yet."

"Time? For what?"

"For me to die."

Dariak's brow furrowed. "Please explain."

"I went through many trials in my day to see the end of many things. And I have seen many things end. But the one thing I have not yet seen is the end of war. So I am still here, waiting. And it does not feel as if it is near. Not yet. I have more time ahead."

"How can you—" he stopped himself, confused. "Who are you?"

"Xervius, as I said. Think of me as a watcher, for I can do little else now."

Dariak looked at the grotesque old man. "How long have you been here?"

"Eight thousand years." Dariak's eyes popped open wide, but then Xervius cackled in his garbled, watery laugh. "You want very much to believe in fantastic things, young Dariak. I am a decade or two older than your father would have been today. Maybe three."

"Is there anything else I can do to stop the wars?"

"Keep believing in yourself and your goal. You may yet get there."

Dariak could tell that the conversation was drawing to a close. "How can I find the healing jade?"

Xervius smiled his broken grin again. "All mages are you. You are all mages."

CHAPTER 39

Kitalla and the Jades

KITALLA PEELED HERSELF off the floor and pushed herself upright. Head to toe, her body ached and felt heavier than it ever had. She looked around and saw that she hadn't moved at all. She was still in the upper chamber with the focus crystal that empowered the Trials. Darkness surrounded her and she hoped it was just because night had fallen.

Her mind reeled with her inspirational dance. Coming up here to channel her abilities through the diamond was a streak of madness and wonder all in one. Nothing had compelled her to do it, as far as she could tell. She simply needed to be there and use her skill to reach out and quell the disturbances below.

She caught her breath. The fighting seemed so distant in her mildly entranced state. She sharpened her ears, trying to discern any sounds within the tower, but she heard nothing. It could mean many things, she knew. Perhaps the fighting had played itself out fully and no one was left. Or, maybe everyone was asleep if her enchantment had worked. More likely, though, was that the events were taking place lower down and they were too far away for her to hear.

None of it mattered though. Her body felt odd. She couldn't rise at all anyway. If they found her, she doubted she could fend them off.

Kitalla reached into her pockets, searching for the three pieces of jade in her possession. Setting them out in front of her, she took her time to contemplate each one.

The metal jade was her deepest companion of the three, for she had claimed it from Grenthar's dungeon. The master thief had challenged her in countless ways, with this sole prize awaiting her. She didn't know back then what the jade would mean to her. It was just some fanciful rock that Dariak had insisted on claiming. They had traveled all the way to Pindington to make progress on his quest of assembling the shards of the Red Jade.

Her body had been broken and mended more times than she cared to recall. But the metal jade seemed to call for her, as if it knew she could rescue it from its prison. It had needed her. Somehow. She had come to think of it as a friend in some ways, silent but ever present. It had risen up and protected her in dire times, such as when the blacksmith's furnace had erupted in Pindington, or when Heria had trapped her and Gabrion. The jade had kept her safe.

Yet coming here to the tower that first time had stripped away all her armor and the jade had not protected her then. From her past. The mages had dredged up deeply buried memories that were bitter enough to recall, never mind relive in any way. Now she dwelled on those days more and more. Her inner strength had always been unique but now she understood that it had started years ago when she had not been able to protect herself from harm.

But that Trial had left her feeling exposed and raw. She moved her gaze away from the metal jade and turned next to the fire jade. Its heat had also called to her. Having left the team and metal jade behind, she went alone to Hathreneir Castle, hoping to reunite with Poltor, but he hadn't wanted her after all they had been through. Events unfolded that led her through the castle, and she even passed by Gabrion's Mira as she sang to her child. And then the fire jade had reached for her from its hiding place, and it bade her to leave through a secret exit.

Kitalla nodded. She understood that part of her impulses were actually guided by the jades themselves. Perhaps she would have found the exit from the king's chamber on her own given time, but inspiration had struck sharply, and it only could have been the influence of the shard. They were more than mere embodiments of their inherent powers. She just didn't know what or why they were speaking to her.

Then she crossed back to Kallisor in search of Gabrion. The lost soul. She needed him more than she liked to admit. Even now, after he stood beside her and let her face the eaglon battle on her own, she knew in her heart that she hadn't truly abandoned him. No, she just wanted to give him something to pursue. A challenge. His own little trial. But to do so, she had to remove his shield so he couldn't hide any longer.

Her eyes swept over to the glass jade. It hadn't offered her any obvious help so far, but it had been near her the longest of the three. The elder of Gerrish had gifted it to Gabrion before their arrival in Pindington. She reached for it and wondered why it seemed so distant from her. Perhaps it was too close to Gabrion and he was distant. Sure they had been intimate with each other, but his heart and mind were elsewhere all the while. She knew that, even during those times when he seemed to melt in her arms. She knew he was far away.

Kitalla lifted the glass jade and turned it over in her hands. It had a faint beige glimmer deep inside it, while the rest was clear as glass. She traced her finger along its gritty surface, idly pressing harder and harder as she went. At last, the sharp edges cut into her skin and she watched dazedly as beads of her ruby blood rolled down the jade. But then she gasped when the blood vanished, absorbed within.

All of a sudden a new sensation swept over her. It was faint, but clear to her now. There was a slight hum from the glass jade, as if it resonated with her, trying to read and understand her. She smiled to herself, recalling the times she had entered a new village and just wandered around, observing the people, talking to only a few of them, getting the temperature of the place. The glass jade was doing the same to her.

She turned her gaze back to the other two and she realized that she had blooded herself on them both too. The metal jade was early on, that very first time she had held it. The fire jade connected to her as she escaped the king's chamber. She remembered the catch of the secret door had cut her. Then the fiery energy had propelled her back to this tower to find and rescue Dariak and the others, giving her inhuman stamina that hadn't made any sense to her back then. Not that she had really questioned it.

And now she could feel the connection to the glass jade. A new warmth washed over her, for now she was less alone than before. These silent companions would all be vigilant. They would all protect her.

Not long ago, she would have spurned the idea, hating herself for taking any form of comfort in it. But she knew she couldn't do this on her own. Dariak's quest, crazy as it was, was something the mage needed to be present for. She wouldn't be a general, helping to keep the men in line, but she would be on the field holding off the attackers until Dariak's work was done. She would be integral to his success. But she wouldn't be able to do it alone, and suddenly that was acceptable. She didn't need to shoulder the burden alone anymore.

Her hands slid down to her belly as she remembered her lost child. She hadn't known back then how alone she was. Joral may have been a nobleman with a far-reaching lineage, but he was a sheltered lad. When things went sour and they needed to be strong, he did what he could, but he wasn't strong enough. He hadn't lived long enough to be able to seek revenge for what had been done. But Kitalla had. Then and there, even as the baby lay dead inside of her. Even as her body was weak, wanting to die. She rose up. She found a way.

So she had only counted on herself since then. Discovering her dance skill at that time helped her to focus on something, and it also allowed her access to food and shelter she may have had to beg for otherwise. Mind control was not a skill for the mages, but she could manipulate people. A few moves, a powerful image, and she could make unsuspecting people see anything she wanted them to.

It wasn't a skill she ever should have had. It was something that came to her only when her life had hit its lowest point. When everything else had been stripped away, one last ray of strength rose up in her.

The jades hummed in tandem and she took them into her hands, letting her mind wander freely, letting the jades speak to her, if they really could. She had never listened to them like this, but she had also had never been so drained yet conscious. Pouring her essence into the dance to try to shut down the chaos of the tower had truly left her exhausted. Yet it also had invigorated her by allowing her to open herself up to the jades as they sang their unheard song for her.

Kitalla considered her dance skill again. Its uniqueness. Its power over others. Its source. The jades wafted energy through her and she drifted along the waves, her mind swaying and reaching.

And she didn't know how she knew, but she knew it with definite certainty. The dance skill, that single power, had been given to her by someone so incredibly special, she had never thought of it before. And moments ago, cutting her finger on the glass jade, watching it absorb her life force and connecting her to its power, made her realize the truth of it.

It was her unborn child. Somehow, that tiny growing baby boy had the skill. And when the mayor had pierced his body inside of her, the baby's blood had mingled with her own and she became connected to it. She absorbed her child's gift into her own essence. She knew it was true. The dance power had not been there before. It had not come from her or her family line. It had come from Joral.

Joral, a nobleman. A man with ties to the royal families of long ago. A man with no great cunning or tenacity. A man not singularly brave, but who was willing to flee in order to live.

Kitalla's thoughts whirled out of control and she recalled the songs Randler had sung. She remembered the things his mother, Sharice, had told them when Dariak had won the lightning jade. And now, as she sat heavily on the floor of Magehaven communing with the three jades, she knew undeniably that Joral was descended of the Forgotten Tribe. And their baby would have been the heir, but because he had been punctured inside of her, the lineage passed on to her. She had taken it in.

And so, in essence, Kitalla was now the heir to the Forgotten Tribe, linked by blood to the original King Kallisor and Queen Hathreneir.

What she didn't know, however, was how that otherwise connected her to the jades. Or why she suddenly felt a great sense of unease.

CHAPTER 40

The Wary Raven

ERVINOR GROANED AND rolled around on the floor of the mess hall, his mind disoriented and foggy. His body ached and he recalled that chaos had come upon him once again in Magehaven. He silenced his moans and cracked his eyes open enough to peer around.

Not a single person stood inside the room. There were bodies littering the floor across the mess hall, but no one seemed to be alive. He wanted nothing more than to count himself among the oblivious, but someone had to try to right the wrongs that had happened here, whether these men and women were dead or just unconscious.

He remembered Verna's original charge into the tower and the assumption he had made when he saw the bodies sprawled on the ground. But she hadn't killed any of them; they had been ensorcelled. Ervinor pushed himself up, feeling a deep grogginess peeling itself away from within, and he realized that magic had brought these people down. Perhaps there were no casualties.

One tired arm pressed against the floor and worked to help raise Ervinor to his feet. He swayed eerily back and forth before his equilibrium kicked in properly. He hated feeling this way, but it would never get better, not unless the mages could find a way to give him a new arm.

He dragged himself over to the nearest body and was sad to see a pool of blood beneath the corpse. His hopes had failed him again, but he didn't resign himself to despair. He moved to investigate the next man, who had apparently taken down the first and suffered an attack himself.

"You're not all dead," he muttered to himself, pressing on to the next body. It was one of his soldiers, a Sparrow, and she was breathing very gently. "I knew it." He tried rousing her, but she would not awaken.

"Sleeping." He nodded to himself, remembering. "The defensive sleep spell knocked us out, didn't it? But then, why didn't the mages finish us off?"

Training his eye on the positions of the bodies, he could see that his soldiers had collapsed in the same manner he had. The mages had moved away from them and, from the blasts marring their clothes and the furniture in the room, had continued their feud unabated.

Yet now the mages were also senseless. He wondered why. Surely the masters had not sent their own kind to sleep. Considering the tensions in the tower, it would have led to worse problems, for the masters would not likely have agreed to knock their own factions out and then be betrayed by the rest. It had to be something else.

Movement caught his attention across the way, and Ervinor hobbled over, still trying to shake off the magical slumber from his muscles. He was relieved to see it was not a mage waking up. He wasn't ready for that. But was he ready for Verna either?

"What happened?" she asked as her eyes fluttered open. Her voice was thick and her words were hard to distinguish but Ervinor managed. "Who are— oh. Ervinor, sir, what's the situation?"

"Verna, can you rise? Do some stretches and limber up." She nodded and did her best to comply while Ervinor elaborated. "Everyone has been knocked unconscious by some magical means, I'd wager. As far as I know, you and I are the first ones up. But I have no idea how widespread this is."

She rubbed her face and then followed suit with her arms and legs. A few deep yawns kept her from responding but she finally found her voice. "What are your orders?"

He looked at her sternly for a moment, seeing a strange war within her that had nothing to do with the weariness. "Are you ready for my orders or should we discuss what happened in the dungeon and before?"

Verna stood upright. "I'm still angry that you would choose to leave me down there after finding out I was alive. I don't agree with the way you handled that and some part of me feels I owe Shelloni for letting me out then and there. But, I choose to follow you, Ervinor, if you'll have me."

The general tried to read her eyes. "I don't mind that you question me, Verna. In fact, it's better to have some opposition once in a while so I don't become complacent. But I need to know you won't fly off the handle again. I need to know that if you challenge my decision, you will do so calmly and rationally, and not within earshot of the entire army. I need your point of view, but in the proper place. Can you do that?"

"You wish me to speak my mind?"

"Yes."

"I didn't expect that," she said. "I didn't think I could disagree with you and still be in your army."

Ervinor's voice was stern but not harsh. "Disagreeing and disobeying are different things. If you are to serve in my army, you need to know and understand the difference."

"Aye, sir!"

"Very well, then. Verna, I need you to reconstitute the Wrens and bring them back into the fold. We have work to do here, and it sounds like there's about to be a lot more of it than I'm ready for alone."

She immediately understood what he meant, for bodies throughout the room started fighting back against the slumber. One by one, men and women awoke and battled through the fog to awaken fully.

As they awoke, Ervinor noted one important fact, and it gave him a moment's peace. Only his fighters were waking up at the time, so he would be able to position them effectively to keep the mages from continuing their own scuffles. He just wasn't certain what that best method would be.

He surveyed the damage in the room and he made a decision he would have preferred not making. He called Verna over to issue new orders and she agreed with the necessity, after which she set off to coordinate the plan. Frast and Quereth joined the effort, albeit grudgingly.

Little by little, the soldiers under Ervinor's command gathered the mages together from nearby locations and bodily dragged them into the mess hall. There, they bound and gagged each of them, setting them against the back wall and each other. Ervinor only made exceptions for the Mage Council, whom he propped up on one of the benches and left unfettered.

When the work was done, he gathered his forces together and called out to them. "My friends, I thank you for your help. But I caution you that our work is not done. We must wait for the spell to wear off so that the mages are conscious. I will address them, and once I have spoken, we will release them."

The fighters murmured in confusion, not happy about the prospect of freeing the people who were subjugating them and causing most of the issues in the tower itself.

Frast found Lica wandering in a lower area and brought her up to Ervinor, who laid out his intentions. She argued at first, but then she too acquiesced to his logic. Each of Ervinor's commanders guided their troops to positions within and around the mess hall, determined to protect the calm when the mages awoke.

It took some time for the mages to stir. Ervinor noted that the masters were the last to awaken from their slumber, and soon the room was full of bound mages wriggling in their seats upon the floor, trying to escape their predicament.

"Hold still," Ervinor called out. "Hold still. You are only bound temporarily. I will release you soon if you remain calm." His words had the reverse effect of scaring them and causing many to moan or rock in panic. The army stepped in and made their authority known by standing over them and speaking sternly for them to stop and wait patiently. Soon, order was restored.

At last the masters awoke around the room, as did the members of the Mage Council. Shelloni shrieked her outrage first upon seeing the other mages gagged in front of her. Likewise, the rest of the Council rose up and started screaming at Ervinor.

The young general bore the insults and threats stoically, waiting until they had vented their frustrations at this treatment and he could finally be heard. Quereth, Lica, and Frast remained close to Ervinor, listening intently for spell words mingled in among the venomous words, but the Council members were simply outraged and not looking for more fighting in the tower.

"Peace," Ervinor said at last, beseeching the Council members for compliance. "Please hear me and then we will end this stalemate."

Grumbling, the other mages settled down. Shelloni eyed Ervinor angrily. "This will not end well, young man. You have created enemies with us here today."

"Be that as it may, you have little choice but to listen to what I have to say." He raised his voice so it would carry through the chamber. "Hear me, patrons of the tower. Events here have unfolded in a desperate manner. Tensions have escalated to a boiling point and now they have erupted.

"I know things have been difficult for everyone. Having me here with my troops has also been a major burden. But the problems were not only our fault. This very day, your own anger was turned against each other, and mages battled mages in an effort to vent your frustrations." He looked to Shelloni, who scowled at the assessment.

"In my time here," Ervinor continued, "I have striven to find a way to balance the differences between the factions, while also fortifying my own strength so that we can all weather the coming storm. And there is a storm. There is war. Eventually, many of us will be dragged into it, but this time I'm hoping for a new outcome. For a true end.

"But I realize now that most of you aren't ready for the war to be over. You need it to continue because you are used to it. The fighting here showed me that. The treatment of the refugees supported that. I regret to say that I find it completely unacceptable for the work we are setting out to do."

He looked at the Council members, some of whom looked bored with this recitation, which wasn't altogether different than the speech he had used to convince them to help him with his plans in the first place. But the mages stayed quiet, hoping this nonsense would be over soon.

"I have come to a decision. We are leaving."

The large chamber hummed with gasps of disbelief, mostly among Ervinor's people. They turned their eyes away from the fettered mages and faced their general, wondering at his plan.

Ervinor waited for the room to be calm, glancing briefly at the masters who eyed him suspiciously. "We are leaving," he repeated. "In three days' time, we will leave your tower so that you may continue whatever work you see fit to do. I ask a few things of you before then, however. First, I beg of you to care for your refugees. Feed them, clothe them, bring them into your fold, or take it upon yourselves to escort them safely to a new haven. They are your people and they deserve to be protected by you all."

Shelloni narrowed her eyes. "What next, then?"

"Second, I plan to leave this place to find my own haven where my forces can train as we wait for Dariak's return. We will then continue under his leadership to make our effort to end the warring. My second request is for your assistance."

The Mage Council raged at this request, shouting that he had no right to ask for their help after everything that had transpired in the tower since Dariak had first returned. They banged their fists on the table and the gagged mages bobbed their heads in agreement.

Ervinor let the anger play itself out once again, waiting to finish his request. "I request your assistance," he echoed. "Let me explain. I need advice on where to go. My mages could use spell components and spell books that would assist us, if you have anything you can spare. We could use some provisions or suggestions on the best places to forage for them. And most of all, we need volunteers. If the Council allows their charges to make their own decisions, then I would ask each person here to decide whether they would join my quest, freely, willingly. If you believe in the cause I have explained, then I could use your help. But I will not have your elders decide for you this time. And I won't abide petty squabbling. I will only accept you if you agree to follow me as a member of my army, willing to tolerate the others around you, willing to take orders from me, and willing to devote yourself to my cause.

"I will not force anyone to come. Even those of you who have sworn yourselves to this task already; I offer you a chance to be relieved of your duty. Whether you remain here, if the Council allows it, or return to your home, or what have you, I ask only that you be true to your heart's desire."

He then turned to the Council members, whose faces were unreadable. "I beg your patience for those three more days and I encourage you to squash any further rebellions within your tower while we are here."

Shelloni barked a laugh. "If you're ready to leave, why not go now or in the morning? Why three days?"

"I wish to give a little time for each man, each woman to decide for themselves without rushing to an answer. Also, I'm exhausted and need a respite before taking to the road. I will step down from my recent duties and return full sway to your able hands, so that I may gather myself for the journey ahead." He allowed the weariness to show on his face. It was no farce. "So I ask the Council this one last question: Will you allow us to remain here in absolute peace for three days and then allow any willing patrons to join me on my way?"

The Council members turned and consulted each other heatedly before reaching an agreement, which Shelloni delivered. "We will agree to your terms, but only if you take the refugees away with you."

"I feared you would say that," he said. "You can't even care for your own people. I will agree to take them as long as they are portioned appropriate amounts of food and water over the next three days."

Another brief conference occurred and then Shelloni nodded. "Very well, Ervinor, we have an accord."

"Very well." He turned to his commanders. "Anyone who wishes to volunteer should speak with Frast, Quereth, Verna, or Lica. And I ask you all to spread word of this to anyone else who is not here. Now, release the mages, then let us retire to start gathering our belongings."

As the mages were unbound, they looked around more carefully at the Council members for guidance, but they seemed to have truly agreed to Ervinor's terms. Angry expressions turned to frowns and sulking, but soon the mess hall cleared out and only Ervinor was left with a handful of others.

Shelloni was among them. "You really believe in this fool's quest, don't you?"

"Yes," he answered with conviction. "It won't be easy, and I have no idea how we will accomplish it, but I do believe in it. And I realize that we can no longer stay here, for a good many reasons. It's better we move on and leave you here to tend to your needs. Thank you for accepting my offer today. We'll be gone soon."

"Indeed," she muttered, staring at him oddly for a few long seconds before turning and walking away.

CHAPTER 41

The Breakthrough

HATHREN FORCES BROKE across the field and raced toward the outpost. Gabrion and his troops were at the ready, set with instructions not to kill the enemy. The men and women were nervous about defending themselves while protecting the lives of their foes. But they saw the fire in Gabrion's eyes and they believed they could win without losing a single drop of blood.

Ordren's men were less confident. They balked at the orders at first, but their commander set his captains to keep the men in line. If the battle turned sour, Ordren himself would blow a horn to open the field to proper fighting. For now, he was willing to allow Gabrion his game.

"There will be mages," Gabrion cautioned, letting his voice ring out to his fighters. "The three of us will deal with them." Urrith and Avarra stood tall as his captains, eager to prove themselves. "We will be hard-pressed not to kill anyone. But we will prevail. I lead you to this battle because we must defend our lives, but we don't need to take their lives to succeed. We will be victorious! We will be victorious! We will be victorious!"

With the troops cheering excitedly, Gabrion raised his sword overhead, turned, and charged. Under orders, his battalion marched behind him, screaming and waving their weapons as they went.

The world slipped into slow motion for Gabrion as he pressed his feet into the ground, carrying himself one step closer to a fight he did not want to have. His eyes swept the forces in front of him, counting quickly and seeing that they were over-matched three to one, and he knew that once their mages entered the fray, it would be madness. His heart thundered nervously as if this was his first battle.

But in that first battle, back in Savvron, he was defending his home. He was a novice then with no practical battle experience until that very day. Many of these fighters were the same. He remembered the moment when everything changed. The rogue who was battling his friend Bryn simply twirled as if in a dance and with a fatal cut of her dagger, Bryn had fallen. Gabrion hadn't seen an alternative then. He simply paid the favor back by cutting her down.

He had killed that day, and in every battle since then, he had killed again and again. So many lives were lost to his hand. So much blood spilled. So much knowledge and training lost. Families torn asunder. So many futures erased.

He knew most of the fighters behind him faced their first fight, too. He wanted their definition of battle to be different than his own, to set a new tone. To that end, he needed to be as elusive as the wind, despite the odds, and he needed to keep his troops in line.

It would cost him some energy, but he bent his head low and ran a little faster, pulling further away from his team. Urrith and Avarra did not follow suit, and the rest of the fighters kept their own pace, which was what Gabrion wanted.

"No more death!" Gabrion shrieked as he approached the Hathrens. "Lay down your weapons. No more death!"

Mocking laughter echoed from ahead and Gabrion knew he had been heard and that the commander had estimated Gabrion's chances of survival as poor. He would prove them wrong.

Ten swordsmen raced in and Gabrion drew what air he could, bringing his sword about to meet them. He let the first man strike, and as he dodged, two others lanced in. He spun to the side and swept the flat of his blade across their backs, knocking them to the ground. "No more death!" he cried, spinning about and blocking the next attack. Parry after parry, he struck only with the flat of his blade each time, knocking the soldiers down but not killing them.

Moments later, the rest of Gabrion's forces swept in and the battle was on in earnest. Urrith drove his team toward the left flank and Avarra took to the right. Swords and shields were raised in defense and it took every bit of restraint to keep from stabbing and thrusting at the enemy.

The Hathren attack was merciless, however. If they noticed the tactics of the Kallisorians, they paid no heed. Their swords and axes swung dangerously through the air, seeking the heads of the defenders, determined to bring a swift victory and to take the outpost as their own.

The mages held back until the first wave was complete, then sheets of rain and ice littered the battlefield. The Hathrens were cloaked against the attacks, even sporting small spikes on the bottoms of their boots to keep from slipping on the icy patches.

Gabrion threaded through the field of fighters and made his way toward the mages. Always the first target of an assault, the mages were ready for him, working in tandem to maintain defense and offense. The warrior noted that there were six mages spraying the field with magic. Urrith and Avarra would have to each take two.

Gabrion charged in, swinging his sword left and right to make his way between the fighters, taking care not to slice them directly. Swords fell, shields broke, but no blood littered his blade. He, however, took some minor gashes for all his trouble. But he knocked down or pushed away his attackers, keeping his eyes on the mages, hoping his captains would do the same.

"No more death!" he kept calling, hoping someone would hear him and understand; hoping someone would see his actions and realize that his words were true. He pushed his way through the fighters and approached the mages in front of him.

"No more death!"

"Just one more for you," one of the mages snarled as her companion turned gnarled hands his way. He judged the direction of her spell from the angle of her arms and threw himself to the side, then rolled to his feet. He repeated the move as the mages swapped roles. He had no idea what spells they were sending, but he assumed they were of ice and water like the rest.

At last he found a moment where the mages' timing slipped. He jumped forward and tackled the nearest spellcaster, then he grabbed the robes of the other and pulled her down as well. After a few quick punches, they were out cold.

He couldn't rest, for some of the fighters had broken formation and were coming for him. There wasn't time to bind the mages' hands or gag them, so he rolled to the side and sprinted off, seeing that Urrith was about to take down his target mages, but that Avarra was behind, stuck in the larger fray.

"No more death!" he chanted as he ran over to her, kicking out and disarming two fighters as he went. "No more death!"

He targeted the mages but glanced over to see what was taking Avarra so long. She defended as best she could against three attackers. The rest of his troop did the same, and though he could see some casualties, his fighters obeyed the command he had laid out for them.

His eyes swept back to Avarra as she dodged to the left and then parried to the right. She looked tired but a fire in her eye told Gabrion that she would keep pressing on, ready to triumph. He was about to turn away when a fourth fighter ran up from behind and swung his sword.

"No!" Gabrion screamed, hurling himself toward them. "No more death! No!"

But Avarra was hit badly and she lost her sword. She swung her buckler around to clobber the four fighters surrounding her, but Gabrion could see she wasn't going to be able to hold them off. He reached them, pulling two soldiers away and throwing them down. Avarra deflected a third attack, but then another sword cut through her defenses and the wound bit deeply into her neck. Her gurgling scream rattled through Gabrion.

"Mother!" he wailed. "No! Mother!"

The sword in Gabrion's hand turned and flew forward into Avarra's killer, hacking the life away. The sword then whipped around and slew the next foe. A wild rage consumed him. His eyes glazed with fury and he snarled like an angry tigroar.

The tide of the battle changed suddenly, but he didn't know it. All he knew was that his home was in jeopardy and without him, people—his family—were dying. His left arm swept down and absconded with a second sword, after which he bellowed in a painful rage that shook the air.

Enemy fighters turned to him and raced to their deaths. One after another, Gabrion's swords flashed through the air in a blinding fury, cutting down any who drew close. He pressed himself forward to the commander, laying waste with every step. The clatter of swords and bone echoed around him, but his eyes were set. He ignored the mages, who were trying to rally a concerted spell to take down the madman, but Gabrion's fighters overwhelmed them.

Swords whipping madly, Gabrion stalked closer to the commander, bedecked in thick iron armor and helmet. He had a host of armored soldiers guarding him and they stood at the ready, watching the haunted warrior approach without any misstep along the way, no matter who threw themselves into his path. He simply cut them down with a deadly accuracy that unnerved anyone who watched.

Ten paces away from the commander's guards, Gabrion's frenzy came to an abrupt end. He crossed his swords over his chest and he screamed until his face was beet red. "I said no more death. But you would not listen. If you want to die, then come for me. If you wish to live, then lay down your swords. Sit in the dirt and live. Or lie upon it in your blood, dead."

He growled with each breath as he waited for an answer. The rest of the field continued its battle and Gabrion honed his ears for any fighters approaching him from behind.

The commander saw the insanity in the warrior's eyes and the obvious talent. He hesitated for a moment, then drew his horn from his hip and blew out three staccato bursts. "I cannot defeat you today," the commander spat. "Do your worst."

"Throw your weapons down," the warrior hissed. "This fight is over."

"Do it," the commander said and his guards obeyed. Their swords were tossed and they stepped away.

"Why wouldn't you listen?" Gabrion demanded. "Why did you fight?" His voice was heavy, aching with pain and rage. "Why is everyone so quick to throw their lives away? Isn't there some other way?"

The commander stepped forward and removed his helmet, throwing it down and raising his chin. "Slash my throat, Kallisorian scum, but don't waste my time with nonsense."

Gabrion could see that the man would not be reasonable, so with a hearty lunge, he punched him in the face, splattering him to the ground. "I didn't want anyone to die here today."

He turned around and saw that everyone was staring. Some of his fighters were hurt or dead, but the entire Hathren force lived, save the two dozen or so he had slain in his berserker rage.

"We could have killed you all," he called out, stepping away from the commander who clutched his face in pain. "We could have all fought to the death, and then where would we be? Dead, or alive just to die in a fight tomorrow." He looked around and found where Avarra lay dead. "No more death," he implored. "No more."

He knelt beside his captain's body and shook his head. "Did she deserve to die here? Has anyone deserved this kind of death? Did my mother, who was protecting children when the town was invaded? Did she deserve to die? Do any of you? Anyone?"

He rose up and walked away, the whole contingent of fighters from both sides stepping back to give him a wide berth. The Hathrens had not seen such ferocity in a fighter in some time and the Kallisorians were horrified by the killing he had done, particularly after his own decrees not to harm anyone.

He paced back to the outpost, leaving the two sets of troops intermingled on the battlefield in a bewildered state. They eventually disentangled and regrouped, obeying their leaders by maintaining the cessation of the battle. The Hathrens kept a short distance away but set camp, either to plot the next foray or to wait to hear what else the crazy warrior would say when he returned; they had no doubt he would return.

The Kallisorians trudged back to the outpost, heavy-hearted, carrying their dead. Six bodies were laid to rest that night and though Gabrion wanted to be there as the ceremonies were conducted, he couldn't.

Instead he sat in his room, head in his hands, rocking back and forth trying to make sense of what he had done. No one else was ever supposed to die because of him. He hadn't intended the deaths in Jortun; he could almost blame those casualties on the confusion of the glass jade, which had slain Mira because she had wholly broken his heart. No, he wasn't ever supposed to lift a sword in anger again. It had to stop. His blind rage facing Mira should have been the end of his killing forever. Yet now once more he had given himself over to bloodlust. Once more, he had killed to gain an advantage.

Never again.

Never.

CHAPTER 42

Discoveries

DARIAK SPENT SOME time trying to navigate the random rooms of the Magitorium. Each floor was a strange venue in many ways. He did come to learn that each level was somewhat themed. The wooden walls of the bottom floor did not extend above. The second floor was mostly stone and offered places for travelers to sleep. The third floor, interestingly, was a giant maze of ice.

He stepped onto the floor, pulling his robes more tightly around himself. The walls were thick with translucent ice. He could see movement and odd shapes through the barriers, but nothing specific. As he walked through the maze, it felt to him like he was being chased by specters at every turn.

One wall of ice slid open and a hobbled man waddled out from within. He was covered head to toe in thick furs and he shivered terribly. "Sir, can you help me?"

Dariak shrugged. "I've only just arrived and I'm trying to find my way. You look cold. Do you need warmth?"

The man turned his head upward and scowled. "Mind your tongue, neophyte. Warmth is for the ones who don't know their inner strength. You curl yourselves up around fire to heat your hearts from the inside because your heart can't do it for you. Bah! Leave me be."

"You said you needed help."

The man took another look at Dariak, then shook his head. "Not from the likes of one who is chilled by the ice."

"But you're trembling and wrapped in several layers," Dariak argued. "Are you not battling the cold?"

The man gritted his teeth and flashed his hands out at Dariak, too fast for him to react. In seconds, his whole body was trapped within a huge block of ice. "I'm an old man, but it doesn't mean I succumb to the ice like a young one such as yourself. So feel the ice now. Learn what it means to be cold." He turned around, apparently forgetting why he had come out of his room, and returned to his solitude.

Dariak shivered within the block of ice, his skin numbing instantly and then stinging from the cold. He couldn't think of any spells in his little prison, nor could he move at all to free himself. He needed a blast of heat to melt enough of the ice away so he could escape. But after about a minute, the spell wore off and the ice vaporized, leaving him shaking on the ground.

He looked ahead and couldn't determine which way would lead him through the icy chamber. Rather than face the low temperatures any longer, he turned around and returned to the stairs, jogging up them to restore a sense of warmth.

The next floor was an odd sort of workroom. It was enormous, with a giant furnace in the center and stalls erected around the perimeter, with workstations scattered everywhere. He immediately pushed himself toward the furnace to melt away the cold that lingered in his bones.

"G'day," smiled a chipper old lady sitting on a stool by the fire. Her hands wove in and out repeatedly and Dariak could sense the energies coming from them, apparently keeping the furnace burning.

"Hello. I was wondering if you could help me."

"No, s'ry. Busy day, t'day. Gotta keep the fire 'ot t'day. Move on, move on." He tried to interject another question, but she ushered him on while her fingers continued working their spells.

Irritated, Dariak stepped away from the central furnace, seeking other mages in the area who might be able to offer some guidance. As he walked, he saw that the workstations were similar to those found at a blacksmith's shop, but with some differences. Anvils and bellows and buckets of cold water were everywhere, but also numerous bins of spell components. He inspected a dagger on a bench with intricate lines carved into the blade. They looked more like fractures to him as he inspected it, but his musings were interrupted by the proprietor.

"No touch, no touch," the man said. He sported a thick gray beard and heavily wrinkled skin, but Dariak sensed that he wasn't actually very old at all. "Dangerous, that, if you're not careful."

"I don't doubt you; this dagger looks like it will break on the first use."

The man cackled. "Little you know, lad." He hefted the dagger and wielded it normally, then he struck his bench with the tip of the blade. Small blue sparks of lightning erupted from the strike. He noted Dariak's reaction and gleamed. "Aye, indeed. Infused a flicker of lightning magic into that blade. Only good for a few strikes before the magic's used up, but it might work to paralyze a foe."

Dariak took the dagger to look at it more carefully. "Amazing. I've never heard of such a thing. Infusing weapons with magic?"

"Aye," the man smiled. "It's what we all do here. Vallinar is my name and daggers are my specialty. Staffs over there, shields, and so on 'round the room. Trouble is, it isn't very stable work and the magics never last that long."

"But, why would you need to make these?"

Vallinar laughed. "Why not? Who wants to cast spells all the time? Besides, what if you're in need of defending from some brigands and the one fighter with you can't use a lick of magic and you need it to take them all down? It's where these come in handy. If we can ever figure out the right balance."

"Amazing," Dariak repeated.

"Eh, not so much, really. Think of antimagic armor that Delminor made years ago. He found a way to create channels in the fabric by lacing it with special metals that draw the energies down into the ground. So in a sense, he already had the idea of locking magic away inside of things."

Hearing his father's name spoken reverently again felt good. He had feared all mages had turned their backs on him. It figured, though, that he would have to come to the most remote host of mages to find them. "I wonder if you could help me."

"Nah, no time. See, it's only a few hours a day I can even do this, and you're already interrupting me plenty."

"It will only be a moment. Has anyone here seen Pyron?"

"Never heard of him. But I can't speak for anyone else. Now, unless you want to help me with this next part, move along."

Dariak hesitated, for a part of him truly wanted to witness the next steps and to learn about the magic being employed here. Perhaps once his business with the jades was complete, he could return. He handed the enchanted dagger back to the smith and walked on.

Many of the stations were empty of workers, and he realized that it was by design. He counted a good forty workshops around the perimeter of the massive chamber, but only every fourth one was occupied at present. Vallinar had said he only had a few hours to get work done, and Dariak surmised that they had to work in shifts because of the instability of the magics they were using. Yet they didn't seem to share their workspaces, save the central furnace that supplied heat to the various forges around the room.

A few stations over, Dariak saw a table of staffs. He reached his hand out to one that was artfully entwined with metal strips of various colors. The top was crested with a ribbon of iron upon which perched a figurine of a massive eaglon.

"Staff of Fireballs," whispered the worker. She smiled toothily and winked lavishly at him. "Want to buy it? Just twelve thousand pieces of copper."

"Twelve thousand!"

"It's only a one-time fee, and you may get several uses out of it."

"May? It's not guaranteed?"

She twittered with laughter. "Nothing can ever be guaranteed, my friend. Why, even with the best defenses, you may never get to use them if someone sneaks up behind you and strikes when you're least aware."

Dariak couldn't help but look over his shoulder to ensure no one actually was doing just that. "I see," he said. "I'm only looking right now. But I'm curious; how do you keep the staff from exploding on its own?"

The woman's smile faltered slightly. "Well, the metal here is meant to draw away errant energies, but things happen." She glanced over to the next workstation where char stains marked the floor. "Regardless, it's a bargain for your defense. In fact, I'll make it eleven thousand."

Dariak smiled politely. "Do you sell many of these?"

"You would be the first to own one. As a special offer, I'll sell it for ten thousand, five hundred."

"Thank you, but as great as this staff is, I really just need information on a mage named Pyron."

She frowned. "You don't have two coins to rub together, do you?"

"Well, no," he admitted.

"Stop wasting my time then. Go on, shoo!"

"What about Pyron?"

"Shoo! Or I'll show you how this staff works! Shoo!"

Frustrated, Dariak wandered off to find someone else who might speak to him. As he walked through the room, he was amazed by the different types of equipment he saw. Half the chamber was devoted to weapons, like the daggers and staffs he had seen. The rest showcased enchanted armor.

"Bracelets of Delminor!" called out a mage close to Dariak's age. He was a good looking fellow with stark blond hair and wild green eyes. He pointed to a set of gold bracelets.

"Indeed? What do they do?"

"Why, they triple the wearer's weight once they're both snapped in place!"

Dariak laughed. "Why would I want to be three times heavier?"

The mage's face crinkled in consternation. "Well, I have no idea, but they work. At least for a little while."

"That seems to be a common theme here. The enchantments wear off quickly."

"Indeed, they do, Master…?"

"Dariak."

"Tyrrus," the mage greeted him. "You say Dariak. Are you *the* Dariak?"

He rolled his eyes, remembering Remmie's welcome. "Not this again."

"Son of Delminor himself?"

"Oh, well, yes."

The mage's eyes opened wider and he dropped to his knees in homage. "Oh, great son of Delminor, it is with utmost pleasure that I meet you. To hear your words, to breathe the same air, I honor you!"

Embarrassed, Dariak cleared his throat, "Thanks, but you can get up, Tyrrus."

"I would humbly offer these bracelets to you as a gift for your presence here, but we are forbidden to release them from this chamber."

"Forbidden?" He thought back to the mage moments ago trying to sell him the fireball staff, shaking his head.

"Indeed. Not until we prove the safety of these enchantments can we part with them. Oh, but I do wish I could give you something in return for your visit."

Dariak saw his chance. "Perhaps you have heard of a mage called Pyron? I am searching for him."

"Isn't he the Council Leader in the southern tower? What would be his business here, O Great Dariak?"

"There is no need for titles with me, Tyrrus. Please."

"Oh, he speaks to me on common ground! Why thank you, Dariak the Wise!"

With a sigh, Dariak ignored the moniker and answered the man's question. "Pyron was indeed the Council Leader as you say, but he has since fled and I thought he would come here. He has something I need and I must convince him to give it to me."

"You are new to this tower, then, I take it?"

"Yes."

"Then remember that you may not use magic here against another mage. If you do, we are required to band together to take you down. And we would not want to, but we would be compelled to."

"Compelled? Is there some kind of magic binding you to the task?" He thought of the mage who had imprisoned him in ice but decided not to mention it.

"In a sense," Tyrrus acknowledged. "Anyone who doesn't comply is expelled. And for many of us, this is our only home and only here can we pursue what we would pursue, much like your esteemed father had his time to experiment."

"My father's lab was not here," Dariak hedged.

"No, no, not for long, but he had a place to be. A place to work. A place to craft his spells and learn new secrets to share. Oh, how I wish I could give you these bracelets, but they would throw me out just the same. I can't risk it."

Dariak shook his head. "Nor would I want you to. Besides, they would only be useful to me right now if I could snap them onto Pyron's wrists to pin him down."

"Ah!" Tyrrus' face lit with excitement. "Indeed! That can be their purpose! Ah, now I can sell them!"

He couldn't help himself. "To whom? They can't leave the room."

Tyrrus grinned. "Among ourselves, of course. It's how we barter for spell components here. New treasures, to be used for as long as they can. They're sort of like toys, you see."

"That makes sense," he said as if it did make sense to him. As he considered it, though, it reminded him of his three-month stint in the Prisoner's Tower, where he was more than happy performing all sorts of complex spells just to earn enough food to get him through to his next set of spells. Perhaps these experiments in enchanting were just as alluring. He wondered what sort of objects he would make.

"You know," Tyrrus interrupted his thoughts. "Usually the important mages go up to the eighth floor. It's above us workers here. It's where they philosophize. They sit and talk and sit and talk. It's boring, if you ask me."

"Indeed. Thanks, though; that might be helpful." He patted Tyrrus on the shoulder in gratitude. "Say, have you tried reversing the weight spell? Make a belt or something that reduces your weight? That might be useful."

Tyrrus' jaw dropped open wide. "Or a haversack! Think of all the provisions you could carry and how light the pack would be! Oh, you are indeed Delminor's son! I have work to do! Thank you! Thank you!" He immediately scurried off, muttering to himself, grabbing for random things from all around him. Dariak couldn't see how the objects he gathered would work together, but he knew he had to keep moving on or else he might end up staying around to find out, and then he might not want to leave.

Dariak headed back for the main stairs and ascended to the eighth floor. Here, the whole place was covered in marble. He could feel energy resonating through the floor to keep it from crushing the floors underneath. The gray-white marble shone with an inner light that kept the room aglow. Cushioned benches were scattered around the area in clusters, designed as conversation nooks throughout the chamber. Tyrrus was right; this was a place for pure communication. There were no trinkets or books of any kind. Just pots of tea and water, apparently, and trays of sweets that wouldn't rot if left out for hours.

There were four sets of conversations taking place in the chamber at that time. Three women were in deep discussion about the best combinations of ingredients for water spells, while a pair of males debated the best ways to clean clothes with magic.

"No, whisk the air up and around and through to make the tunic flutter in the air. Then lash it with water and soap."

"If you do that, you'll spray water everywhere; what's wrong with you? No, put it in a basin and agitate the water by wringing it around and about."

"Fine, but then batter it with air to dry them. If you use fire, you'll burn them."

"A good point, very well."

Dariak bit his lip to keep from chuckling, and he dared not interrupt. There was an ominous sense in this room that these conversations were vitally important to the people engaged in them. If they were at all like the workers on the fourth floor, then he suspected they would be angered by intrusions, rather than welcoming.

A pack of six old mages was huddled around a marble table, each with fingers on the slab. One of them spoke and walked his fingers ahead three steps, after which another mage groaned and pulled her hand from the area completely. She then called something out and side-stepped her other hand across the table, causing a third mage to be displaced to some other location on the surface.

Intrigued, Dariak walked over. "What are you doing?"

They ignored him, at first, making a few more moves until one of the mages was booted from the table entirely. "Ack," she growled. "Nature always folds first." She looked up at Dariak. "You have never witnessed the Balance of Essence before?"

"No."

"It's simple. We each represent a force of energy, like fire, water, and so on. Each is imbued with a set of skills and we take positions on the table and go through the steps until there is one winner, which is usually fire or lightning."

"It's just a blank surface. How do you know where you can move to?"

She smiled pityingly. "Poor thing. We read the energies in the game and don't need a game board, if you will."

Dariak looked again and concentrated. This whole tower was laden with magical energies and the ones they used were slight in comparison, which was why he hadn't noticed. "Ah," he nodded once he saw the various lines of force extending from each hand. The mage representing fire and water made a move that put water in jeopardy but allowed fire to dominate a section of the field. Earth walked in and subdued the water, after which lightning overpowered shadow.

He looked at the mage who had turned her attention back to the game. "Does it always go the same way?"

"No," she crooned as if talking to a child. "You see, there are many ways one can shift and sway the energies, but some are inherently more destructive than others."

Dariak looked again at the energies. "What of healing energy? Where is it represented?"

The mage glanced at him. "You're not blind then. No, we can't use healing energy in this, for it throws off the whole game."

"But why?"

She narrowed her eyes. "We have books upstairs that would better explain this. Who are you anyway?"

"I am Dariak, son of Delminor."

She raised an eyebrow. "Many have claimed to be Delminor's son, seeking favors."

"Nonetheless, I am he."

"Then we should be wary of you, stranger, for your ways may not be compatible with ours."

Dariak eyed her carefully. "Why would you be wary around me? Who told you to be wary?"

She waved a finger at him. "You will not get information out of me, young Dariak. Know that we were warned against your intrusion and I will not speak to you further."

"But—"

"No." She then turned her focus back to the game and refused to answer him.

Annoyed as he was, he walked away from the group feeling a little closer to his goal. Pyron must be here, if these mages were cautioned against him. He walked over to the last group in the room, but their debate about the benefits of tree bark versus tree root would not be disrupted by his questions in the least. He tried adding his input, but it only served to prompt more questions among the group with angrier, heated responses.

Resigned to continue his search alone, he ventured up to the next floor, which housed one of the tower's kitchens. He opted to pause for a snack and gather his thoughts. The Balance of Essence game seemed important and it reminded him of Randler, who had often spoken of the balance between the jades.

Thinking of Randler made his heart heavy. He had abandoned him in the forest, unaware of his fate. He hoped Astrith knew some form of nature magic that would allow him to mend the bard somehow so that he would be able to restore his legs. No one should have to suffer such an injury.

He also needed Randler's objectivity right now. He was too mired in his mission to separate the details and organize them well. Randler was particularly good at that. It was a necessary skill of a bard, to look beyond the details to reach the hidden truth, and then build up a fanciful tale around the seeds of knowledge so stories would be shared without losing their meaning.

Most of Randler's repertoire revolved around the Forgotten Tribe and the distant connections to the original king and queen of these lands. Dariak felt it was more than just a mild obsession with the bard. The tales felt important, connected to his quest in some way. But he had no way of judging how.

Dariak made his way to another floor and found one of three main libraries. The books here were musty and old and the whole floor carried their scent. He remembered the library in the southern tower, though he hadn't spent much time there in his recent visits. He wondered if these shelves would hold similar texts to those down south. Despite his need to find Pyron, he needed a break from talking to mages who didn't want to be helpful.

Looking for a pattern among the shelves was like trying to sort out sand crystals. The books were scattered everywhere and examining the titles didn't help at all. One shelf housed books on herbs, fire magic, swords, and the history of a town in Hathreneir, among other random things. Another shelf had tomes of ancient magic, taming feral creatures, methods for purifying water, and so on. He groaned, realizing he would need to ask for help.

"Get away from my shelf, thief!" called a voice nearby. A blue-robed mage staggered over, scars marring his body from head to toe. The robe itself was too short for him and knobby legs and arms peeked out from the cloth.

"Your shelf?"

"Grr, if you want my books, you have to use the Exchange like everyone else. You can't just waltz in here and start browsing around."

"The Exchange?"

The old man squinted. "Over there, that big counter marked 'Exchange.' Now get going!" He swatted his hands at Dariak and then inventoried the items on the shelf to ensure none of the books had been removed.

Dariak made his way to the designated counter and saw two huge tomes. A bored-looking man sat at a bench, thumbing through a book upside-down. "Excuse me, can you help?"

"What book do you need?"

"I'm not sure. I was hoping to look around."

The man glanced up at Dariak and scratched his head. "That's what that book there is for," he said, pointing to the larger tome on Dariak's left. "Find the one you want, then write your request in the book there." He gestured to the other book. "When it's available, it'll be on your shelf."

"On my shelf?"

"Eh? Don't you have a shelf here? Well, that's another matter." He bent down low and retrieved a ledger. "Let's see here…" He thumbed through the pages until he found what he was looking for. "Well, Grezzish died some weeks ago so his shelf is free now. Tell me your name and I'll assign it to you. Floor three, aisle nine, sixth from the bottom."

"I'm not here for a shelf. I just wanted to browse."

"You from the southern tower? Ah, figures. No, we don't have time for that sort of thing. It's the lot of we librarians to keep everything organized. Can't have people touching the stacks themselves; we'd never find anything. So, your name?"

"But what if someone wants a book and it isn't with the person who is supposed to have it? How do you find it then?"

The man pouted. "If it isn't on their shelf then it's in their room and they're using it. What an odd question. Your name?"

He hesitated for a moment and then asked, "What if I said my name was Pyron?"

"Then I'd say you've been wasting my time with these questions. Why, are you testing me to make sure Horru trained me right?" He flipped through the ledger. "Here, Pyron of Magehaven: Floor two, aisle seven, top shelf. Why bother me with questions if you already have a shelf here?"

Dariak cleared his throat. "Sorry." The man rolled his eyes and went back to his reading as two other mages walked over to the counter to write in some book requests. Dariak stepped away, keeping his eyes lowered, and took the stairs up to the second floor of the library, which was the eleventh floor of the tower. He found the aisle markers and worked his way toward Pyron's shelf, surprised the mage would even have one here. He wondered if Pyron had come to the tower before or if his book selection would be more recent.

He reached the designated space and climbed a small ladder to reach the top shelf, curious about Pyron's reading interests. Knowing the tomes on his reading list might provide some key to getting through to the old mage. Four steps up the ladder and he could see the shelf.

But it was void of books.

Disappointed, Dariak climbed back down and sat on the floor, resting his head in his hands. Nothing was working out for him today. After a few minutes, he decided to wend his way down to the sleeping quarters on the second floor and get some rest, hoping a fresh start would give him better ideas.

"That's him," said the librarian's voice nearby. "He's the one that gave the false name."

Dariak looked up to an angry set of mages.

"You!" hissed one of them.

It was Pyron.

CHAPTER 43

Stories in the Library

ERVINOR FOUND KITALLA after his discussion with the mages and informed her of his decision to leave the tower. She said little but agreed that it was the right move to make. They only needed to determine where to go from here, and Ervinor frowned before walking away.

Kitalla's mind swam with thoughts, mostly about her revelation concerning her connection to the Forgotten Tribe. Queasiness remained with her now, and she had no idea why. The jades in her pockets resonated in a spiraling pattern, and she wondered idly if they could be causing the discomfort somehow.

Though she knew the truth of the matter, she still sought out the library to find some kind of proof. When she had infiltrated Hathreneir Castle before taking the guise of Jareesa, she had spent some time in the library where tall, lanky Mearan had shown her a text detailing the royal lineage. She chuckled to herself as she recalled the odd manner Mearan had of pronouncing things to sound smarter, oblivious to the absurdity of how it really sounded.

She knew the mages' loyalties were torn, but that was no different now than before except it was more widely known instead of whispered secretly. It took a few tries before she found a mage in the library who was willing to help her find what she needed.

"The Forgotten Tribe? That's a fairy story," Bertan scoffed. "But we have some bardic collections of the tale. What else? Royal lineage, right." He eyed her carefully. "You don't actually believe—"

"Regardless of what I believe or what I'm looking for, isn't this a library? Can't you just show me where the books are without all the speculation and criticism?"

He wasn't ready for such a sharp retort and he stammered in reply before guiding her to the books she requested. The anthology, *Lines of Royalty*, was close by and he handed her the hefty tome and whisked off to the next section. She followed dutifully, determined to get this part over with.

"Here you are," the mage said, gesturing to the aisle of books.

"Which one do I need?"

"All of them, if you're really going to try to make sense of anything."

She gaped. "*All* of them? There isn't a summary somewhere?"

The mage snorted. "Well these two shelves are composed of 'summaries' if you can call them that. They're more editorials by mages who have done the research and scoffed at what they've found. These here," he said pointing to a set of eight red spines, "are less opinionated but also less detailed. The rest of those books are tales by bards gathered through the ages. But who knows as to the accuracy of them."

"Aren't bards known for their accuracy in story-telling?"

"Yes, sure, when they're young. But they travel when they're young. They don't tend to write them down until they can't travel anymore. And by then, the mind starts slipping. But these here," he pointed a colorful set of books, "were drawn by one of the queens many decades ago. She would sketch the events as she understood them, often during the bard's song. If you can interpret pictures well, some say this is a strong source. But if you need text, I say start with the compendiums and then refer to the old texts for clarification." He looked at the defeated look on her face and felt truly sorry. "Good luck. I would help you if I could, but I have other things I have to attend to."

"Thank you for your time." She let herself sink to the floor with the lineage in hand. She flipped it open from the back, assuming it would be organized chronologically. Even still, it took scanning thirty or so pages before she found what she was looking for.

Jurshi (daughter), Joral (son), Jellira (daughter), Jannar (daughter)

It was Joral and his sisters. Linked to their names, she saw two upward-branching lines, one for his father and the other for his mother. Each spiderwebbed out to their own siblings and children, as well as their parents, and so on. She noted absently that Joral's siblings each had at least one child but his own name simply ended. She never had the chance to officially marry him and so her name was not even with his.

This volume was not as neatly kept as the one at Hathreneir Castle, and it took longer for her to work her way through the endless lines of history. More than once she missed a page and had to backtrack to find her place and then continue again. Each generation spanned roughly thirty to fifty pages, some more detailed than the rest.

Some time later, she flipped up and up and up again, eventually reaching the place she knew she would reach. She had to; it was the royal lineage. Kallisor and Hathreneir were at the start of the book, each with their own splinters of children, only two extending from their mutual line. Joral's line traced back to that line. The mutual tie between the king and the queen. He was not just descended from one or the other. He was indeed of the Forgotten Tribe, though clearly his bloodline had been heavily diluted through the ages. Kitalla touched her belly, knowing that no matter how thin that regal blood was, it was still strong enough to carry down so many generations later.

She ignored the footnotes claiming discrepancies and speculations in the timeline. She knew it was true and this tome simply added further validation for what was in her heart. She flipped the book back to Joral's name and caressed the parchment with her finger.

"What have you given me?" she whispered. "What does it mean?"

Kitalla looked again at the names of Joral's sisters and traced the few descending lines of their children, only three of whom would be of an age to marry yet. She had never met them and Joral rarely spoke about them, preferring to consider himself an only child just to spite them. She wondered, though, if they all carried a latent ability like Joral had. At least, he had never said anything of being able to channel magic through dance like she now could.

As she considered it, she realized that it was a silly thought, for none of the Kallisorian nobles would openly practice magic in any form, and any of them who possessed magical skill probably denied it for fear of losing status and wealth. She also remembered how charming Joral was, and perhaps in some way he did use the affectations of magic to sway people, even if he didn't know he was doing it. It would make a sort of sense for nobility to foster the ability to affect the minds of others. It would allow for them to make better deals when bartering and enforce stricter treaties and sway alliances in their favor.

But, then, did all nobles have the inherent skill? What singled Joral out among his entire line and among his siblings? Was it a trick of fate like why some children had different colored hair than their parents? Kitalla groaned. She was getting nowhere. She closed *Lines of Royalty* and stood up to explore the wall of the Forgotten Tribe.

"Randler, I could really use you with me right now," she muttered. "How am I supposed to sort through all this in less than two days?" She considered taking down one of the drawing books Bertan had pointed out, but a collection of songs drew her attention first. She pulled a black-bound tome from the shelf and set it safely on the floor before opening it.

With battered eye
With weakened limb
No one ever stood to rise again.
With aching soul
With failing goal
No more hope remained for them.
Reach now outward, friends, and look inside
For there the secrets of hope reside.
Look not to others but to yourselves.
Look not to fairies, dwarves, or elves.
Quell your sorrow, anguish, woe.
Only then find your path to go.
The way of the Forgotten Tribe.

Kitalla winced, then flipped to another random page in the song book.

Hacking, bloody, restless revenge
the King avenged his powerless son.
He raged across the field, so light, so free
for he needed to slay his Queen.

He crossed the plains and razed the trees
leaving boulders broken to dust in his wake.
He pushed onward ever, never tiring at all
for he needed to slay his Queen.

He met her on the watery shores as she
ripped fish from the mouth of the sea.
He scorned her as she stood there
for he needed to slay his Queen.

With curling fingers, whispered words,
shards of ice pierced through the air.
Unnatural forces were at work
and he needed to slay his Queen.

Kitalla frowned and turned the pages over again, hoping her third try would be more informative and succinct.

You cannot reap the land in pain.
Kill, kill the King!
You cannot plant without the rain.
Kill, kill the King!

However hard you try to doubt,
You cannot leave the mages out.
Kill, kill the King!

You cannot fight for all your life.
Kill, kill the King!
You cannot raise swords on your wife.
Kill, kill the King!

Lay down your weapons, let us speak
Else you won't live, for you are weak.
Kill, kill the King!

Kitalla slammed the book shut and shoved it away, wondering if she should have started with the picture books after all. But if interpreting poems and songs was going to be tricky, surely deciphering some sketches would be just as challenging, if not more so. She sat still for a few moments and then pushed herself to reach for one of the illustrated tomes.

The pages were thicker than the other books, perhaps because of the different parchment required for painting. Leaflets of a thin waxy paper separated the individual pages to preserve the illustrations within. Kitalla opened the book and set it on the ground again, leaning over to read the inscription.

The Lady Cathrateir
Sketches for Mhunforia

The Images depicted within are Sketches of the Noble Bard Mhunforia's Tales of the Forgotten Tribe. Though some claim these Tales to be for children, they Live within Me and thus I draw them. Scoff not at My interpretations of the Tales, for if that is your Intent, place down this Compilation and seek elsewhere.

Kitalla grinned. "I think I like her." She turned to the next page, which showed the bard's name and the date of his recitation. The following page depicted the first image.

Though the tome was perhaps two hundred years old, the paint had not faded at all. Rich green grass swept up a knoll in the deep of a starry night. Dark trees rose in the distance, and Kitalla had the sense from the picture that it had rained hours earlier. A young girl laughed as she sprinted up one side of the hill, a yellow and blue dress flowing around her with glorious ribbons in her hair. On the other side of the knoll was a stern boy, determinedly climbing up as if to conquer the grassy mound.

Kitalla had no idea what to make of it at first, but as she flipped over to the next page, she saw that the scene continued there. Suddenly she felt a little more at ease, for she would receive a series of images for each tale, rather than a single drawing. Perhaps she could indeed glean more from this work than from the songs or histories.

The second page showed the boy and girl reaching the top of the hill and crashing into each other. A bolt of lightning flared in the sky overhead, and the shadows of the children extended down the hill, elongating their forms and slightly altering them. As Kitalla looked, she realized that the shadows represented each child as an adult, and when she examined them again, she could see the outline of a crown upon each shadow's head.

The story continued and the children rolled down the hill, covered in mud. Kitalla flipped back to the first page for a moment, wondering how she knew it had rained and that the grass was wet. Something glimmered in the paint; perhaps it was that. The muddy children rose up and, rather than yell at each other, they laughed heartily, holding hands and skipping off into the distance. There the tale ended.

It all seemed so innocent. A chance meeting, the potential for disaster, an unlikely union. She turned to the next tale and started interpreting the pictures.

"Kitalla," called a voice nearby.

She jumped, for she hadn't heard anyone approach, she was so engrossed in the images. She glanced up. "Frast."

"Ervinor has been looking for you."

"I am a bit busy, actually."

He glimpsed the books nearby. "Reading up on the Forgotten Tribe?"

"I think it's important."

"So does Randler. But, Kitalla, there really isn't time for this right now. We need you down below."

She nodded absently. "Frast, you have the beast jade still, don't you?"

He furrowed his brows. "Yes, and we have kept that secret so the mages don't try to reclaim it."

"Smart," she approved. "Are you 'connected' to it?"

"What do you mean?"

"It is... a *part* of you?"

"Kitalla, what—"

"Just answer me."

He thought about it for a moment. "No, not really. I mean, I can call to it and it responds in some ways, but I can't do anything with it the way Dariak does. Even Randler has better skill with his shadow jade than I do with this."

She grinned slyly. "Randler again."

Frast's face turned red. "Why do you ask? About the jade," he added hurriedly.

"No, no, what's this about you and Randler?"

"I have to get back to Ervinor."

"No, no, no," she teased. "I can tell you really want to talk about this."

He hesitated for a moment, then gushed. "Well, I think he's wonderful. The way he stands for what he believes in but supports his friends too. He's a voice of reason when everyone gets caught up in chaos. He keeps Dariak from abusing magic. He keeps Gabrion calm. He even helps you, and you can already do anything."

She tipped her head. "Why thank you."

"And his eyes. They're gorgeous. Full of knowledge and wonder. He sees the world differently than most of us. It's almost like he makes a record of everything and locks it away until he needs it, and then he just summons it up and shares it when we need it the most. And the way he plays his lute. His fingers glide so gently over the strings. Did you ever watch him? He sways with the music, ever so slightly. You have to really look for it. He's... well, like you asked me about the jade, it's like that with him and the music. He's connected to it. It's part of him somehow. He *feels* it and he shares that connection with us when we listen." He was going to continue, but Kitalla was biting her lip and her cheeks were twitching.

She laughed. "You've got it bad."

Frast blushed again. "Well... He's downright perfect in so many ways."

"Does he know how you feel?"

"Sort of. When we went to free Dariak from here. He sort of knows."

"It sounds like it didn't go well."

Frast's face dropped and he fidgeted with his fingers. "He's committed to Dariak. And even that makes me want him more."

She raised an eyebrow. "Because you can't have him?"

"No! Because it was just the two of us and he—he remained true."

"What did you do, pin him down and try to have your way with him?"

"What! No!" He squirmed, and Kitalla loved every moment of it. "We were buried under the sand. It was just—we were—it was tight quarters, is all. Anything could have happened, but it didn't. I think... I think that night I lost it and went crazy about him."

"But as you said, he is committed to someone else."

Frast's voice went heavy. "Yeah."

Kitalla waited a moment and saw the anguish on the mage's face. "Look, you'll find some—"

"Don't say it, Kitalla. I have to hear it from Quereth all the time. 'Plenty of sandorpions in the desert, Frast.' 'Keep looking. Don't give up.' And, 'Don't hold on to what you can't have.' Ugh." He punched his fist into his hand. "I wish I could, just once, have things my way. No reasons why it can't be my way."

"You've been hurt before," she surmised.

"Several times. But this time it's different. Except that I can't even *be* with him. I want it, Kitalla, more than anything. I want him. I wish there was a way I could have him. I wish there was a way he would want me just as much."

"You can't control how people feel."

"Well, *you* can, but only for a short while."

Kitalla's eyes opened wide. "You're not suggesting…?"

He stared at her for a moment and then his jaw dropped open. "I would never! No, Kitalla, I don't want you to influence him with your dance moves. No way. I just… I just want him to want me for me, regardless of anything else."

At last, Kitalla stood up and she wrapped her arms around the tormented mage. "Listen, Frast," she said, pulling back so she could look into his eyes. "You can't change how you feel, but you have to come to terms with the situation. You have to find a way to move on from it."

"I know that. Up here," he said, tapping his brow. "But the rest of me won't listen. I swear, Kitalla, next time I see him, I may just tackle him and kiss him before he can stop me."

She laughed. "I doubt you'd get the chance. He's rather nimble."

"I know!" He lit up. "Have you ever watched the way he moves? So graceful. Like every muscle flows like water. One step into the next, like the notes of his music, ever graceful, ever flowing."

Kitalla laughed. "Oh dear. We need to find you someone here you can roll around with to burn off some of your… romanticism."

"Funny," he said dourly. "I've tried to find someone else, but my heart's not into—What is it?"

Kitalla's face was furrowed and she glanced downward. "I don't know why, but the jades are rattling like crazy."

Frast reached into his own pocket and nodded. "Even the beast jade. Come on, Ervinor asked me to get you anyway. Let's go."

"Sure." She sighed, glancing at the book of drawings on the floor. "Then again, maybe the jades are just feeding off your lust for the bard."

"Kitalla!"

CHAPTER 44

Captain of the Ravens

ERVINOR SAT IN a meeting room alone with a cup of hot tea. He wanted something much stronger, but he knew he couldn't afford to be addled in any way. He thought announcing their imminent departure would ease the tensions in the tower, but he was wrong. Now he was faced with numerous additional complaints from all sides and he couldn't even push them away.

One of the refugees from Marritosh, Zasha, came to him demanding to know where they would be taken and why they had no say in the matter. Ervinor explained as calmly as he could that they could choose a nearby destination and he would get them there safely, but they were no longer welcome in the tower. She didn't care to hear it, insisting the mages should allow them to stay.

"Then ask them," he said wearily. "Go up to the Council and ask them."

She fumed indignantly. "But it was you who razed our home! You who dragged us to this terrible place! You're the one who deals with these mages!"

Ervinor stood tall and spoke succinctly. "The mages razed your home. We fought them off. The king sent troops. We tried to hold them off. Herchig and the others decided to evacuate you. Not me. If you would like to take it up with him, then go back to Marritosh and rifle through the ashes until you find him."

Horrified, her face screwed up.

He maintained his level tone. "We've overstayed our welcome here. You may try to remain, but I can't protect you if you do. Regardless, I leave in two days. You are dismissed."

Verna stepped in from her post and escorted Zasha out, adding more words on the way. "We all know what's happened, and it's a tragedy the mages won't protect us, but Ervinor has the right of it. We survive if we follow him. I urge you to rally together and be ready to follow." She waited for Zasha to exit before closing the door and turning to Ervinor. "You struck a chord in her, calling on Herchig. She'll fall in line."

"I hate to use my friends in any way, but I had nothing else to say to her."

Verna saluted sharply. "Herchig would understand and he would be grateful he could be of assistance to you."

The general smiled tiredly. "Thank you, Verna. Dare I ask who's next?"

"Forgive me, sir, but I took the liberty of sending away Shelloni. She wished to rant at you about tying up and gagging the mages yesterday."

Ervinor rubbed his face with his hand. "Again? Doesn't she ever get tired of trying to tear me apart?"

"I think not, sir."

"Thank you for sending her away. I need less petty nonsense and more time to get ready to leave here."

"Sir, if I may. Didn't you tell the mages they were going to have to deal with these matters on their own so that you *could* prepare to get away?"

He nodded. "I did, but they keep sending everyone to me, as if I wasn't clear yesterday. 'I'm leaving, anyone who wants to come, pack up and follow.'"

"Except the refugees, but yes," she added.

He sighed. "Of course. Verna, have any of the mages come forward yet with the advice I asked for?"

She grinned. "I believe Quereth, Lica, and Frast have news on that front. You have an hour until then, sir."

"Good. Then can you fetch Carrus for me?"

"You don't want a break, sir?"

"I do. That's why I need him."

Verna saluted again and left to find the sturdy warrior who had single-handedly kept Ervinor safe during the siege on Marritosh. He pictured the burly man, hoping his wounds had been tended between then and now, and hoping he was up to the next challenge.

The door opened and Carrus entered the room, shirtless, his body covered in sweat. He was heaving deeply. "Sir!" He saluted, standing tall.

"Be at ease, Carrus. Sparring?"

"Yes sir."

"Close the door and come forward." Ervinor stood up from his seat and walked around and sat on his desk so he would be closer to eye level with the soldier. Instead, he was eye-level with the man's powerful chest and it made him feel uncomfortable. Ervinor had never striven to be as muscular as this man was but even if he wanted it now, it would be a great challenge to achieve it with only one arm. He thought he would always be lopsided now.

"Sir?" Carrus asked, noting the scrutiny.

"Just lamenting in my head. Sorry." He stood up and tried not to pace. "I never properly thanked you for your help back in Marritosh."

"We're a team, sir, and I was at your side to keep you safe."

"Yes, and you did an exceptional job of it. I wanted to thank you." He held out a hand and Carrus accepted it.

"I am honored, sir."

"Carrus, I have something uncomfortable I need to say to you. I have no idea how you will take it, for I don't really know you very well yet. But I need to say a few things that may seem odd before I can say what I must say."

Carrus blushed. "Sir? I am honored, sir, but I rather fancy the ladies, sir."

Ervinor burst out in laughter. "No, it's not that." He chuckled again. "I prefer the ladies myself. No, this has to do with your role in the army."

Carrus' blush deepened. "M—my apologies, sir, I did not mean to suggest—"

Ervinor dismissed it. "It's fine."

"The way you were looking at me, sir, when I came in—I just thought—"

Ervinor shrugged. "I admire your strength, Carrus, and I don't think my body will ever reach that peak. That is all."

"I see, sir. Sorry, sir."

"Carrus, relax." Ervinor gestured for him to sit but he preferred to stand. It made things a little more challenging. "I need you to be able to talk to me openly."

"Sir?"

Now Ervinor felt awkward, wondering if this was a mistake. "Listen, I need your help once again, but I need to know, first, if you're willing to do it before you accept."

"I will do anything you require, sir."

"No. Listen first." He gave up and started pacing. "I don't have the stamina any more to run at top speed. I can't make these decisions for everyone without it taking energy out of me. I can't balance my position as well as I could before.

"You're a good soldier. Great, in fact. You take charge in battle and you protect your comrades when they need you. You follow orders when they're given but you think for yourself as well. You're twelve years my senior but you accept my leadership."

"Thank you, sir. I accept your leadership because you lead us well."

"I do what feels right. But I know I can't keep this up for long, young as I am. And it's here that I need your help." He turned and gazed Carrus in the eye. "I will not assign this task to you, but I will ask you to think about it and then either accept or deny it. I need someone to take over as captain of the Ravens."

Carrus stood a little straighter. "Sir, I am grateful and honored that you think of me for this task."

"I'm not resigning from the army, but I can't command the Ravens and lead the army while also dealing with the troubles of the refugees who will be traveling with us. I need to know that I can rest the Ravens in capable hands in a time of need. The Ravens would still be most closely assigned to me, but I need a captain who can coordinate the details."

The warrior fidgeted in place. "Sir, I've never yearned for a position among the leaders. I'm a fighter at best. I'm a comrade to the men at my side, not one to issue orders."

Ervinor tried to hide his disappointment. "I understand."

But the man wasn't finished. "Yet you have need of me, sir, and though I haven't aspired to the role, you seek me out to fill it. You've confided in me a great need. Some of us have seen that you're struggling, but you push ever on and it invigorates us. I will rise to the challenge for your sake, general. I'll do as you require because we need you and if this helps you, then I will do it."

"Carrus, I am so glad." He stepped forward and gripped the man's shoulder. "I do need you and I thank you for accepting."

"If I may, sir? You carry yourself as if you're my age, not as someone with half my years. We don't see you as young at all. Not even Herchig saw you as such. I have no idea where your strength and wisdom come from, but I'm glad to be at your side."

Ervinor grinned weakly. "I forget my age sometimes. Something about the war ages us all, I think, and we find our places quickly, whether it's among the leaders or among the fallen. You're not forty years old yet, but by the time I reach your age, I'll have spent more than a third of my life with one arm not two. When I consider it that way, it's hard for me to be strong. So I do remember Herchig, and I try to keep him in my heart as a guide and mentor. Maybe one day I'll even start rambling like him."

"I plan to be there to hear your tales and help you embellish them, sir."

Ervinor's smile was wide. "I look forward to it. Now, Carrus, go freshen up and return swiftly, for I have a captain's meeting coming at the top of the hour and you should be introduced officially."

The big man saluted and stepped from the room, and Ervinor sank into his chair with a deep sigh of relief. He wasn't entirely sure if Carrus would be the best captain but he trusted him the most and he needed that more than anything.

It wasn't long before the five captains arrived. Ervinor explained Carrus' promotion and they spent a few minutes congratulating him before taking their seats to get to the heart of the meeting.

"We leave in two days," Ervinor started. "Our first priority is to determine our destination."

Frast spoke first. "We have a few mages who've made some divergent suggestions."

"Indeed," Quereth chimed in. "We've been told to head to the far west, far north, into the southern ocean, and back to Kallisor."

Lica laughed. "Perfect and helpful."

Ervinor frowned. "Those options all seem distant."

"Plus we have the refugees to worry about," Verna said. "They won't do well on a long trek."

Lica groaned. "We should just return them to Marritosh and have them rebuild it."

Verna stood up angrily but then forced herself to sit without speaking. Ervinor noted the action and approved of her restraint. "Not very compassionate, Lica," he admonished. "That was their home and it burned before their very eyes. There can't be much left of it to salvage. Not material-wise; not in their hearts either."

Lica turned to Verna. "I'm sorry. That was heartless of me."

The captain of the Wrens nodded curtly and focused her eyes on Ervinor for stability.

Ervinor took the reins and went through the options. "To the south are larger beasts to deal with, which would be dangerous to the refugees until we pass through the marsh lands. The west puts us closer to Dariak and Randler but further from the war itself. If we return to Kallisor, it'll weaken our presence here. I don't think many of the Hathrens joining our fight will necessarily stay with us, just as Ordren refused to come to Hathreneir. If we headed east, but not as far as the border, we end up passing too close to Marritosh, and I'm not looking to torment the refugees with that."

"Then it's north," Quereth summarized. "But where exactly?"

Silence fell and Ervinor swept his gaze to his newest captain. "Carrus, what are your thoughts?"

"Sir?"

"What's your opinion on where to take the refugees?"

"Wherever you think is best, sir."

Lica placed a hand on Carrus' knee. "Dear, he is asking for us to help him decide where that best place is. Do tell us what you're thinking."

"Sir, I would rather not say."

Ervinor stood and paced. "Carrus, I know you've only just come into your position, but I need your feedback. I need you not to keep secrets from me. It is here I need you to be strong and proud and not to be the obedient soldier."

Carrus cleared his throat. "Yes, sir, I only regret to say it for what happened before." Ervinor knew what was coming, but he insisted Carrus say it aloud. The warrior squirmed, but eventually caved in. "They need to be brought to the castle, sir."

Ervinor shuddered and his right shoulder started to ache.

"We can't!" Quereth said.

"Would they even take them in?" Frast wondered.

Lica shook her head. "I think it's the only place close by, if these stupid mages won't keep them."

Verna nodded. "It's the best place for them."

Ervinor dropped heavily into his seat. "I know. I don't want to face it, but I know. Going back there… It's the hardest thing I've had to think about." He massaged his damaged shoulder intensely, trying to keep the trepidation from his voice. "Frast, can you go find Kitalla and bring her here? I need her input on this."

Without word, Frast scurried from the room. Lica was already chanting healing spells in Ervinor's direction. "Thank you, but it's mostly in my head."

"I will take them," Carrus announced suddenly.

"I'm sorry?" Ervinor asked.

"Bring the army nearby, but not too close. Then I'll lead the refugees to the castle proper and leave them there. We'll return to you and then move on to a safer location."

"That's a decent plan," Quereth said.

Lica snarled. "But if they open fire on you, then you're goners without enough fighters to get away or to protect the refugees. Perhaps I should take the Eagles with him and watch his back."

"Too many variables," Ervinor decided. "If the king sends out a host of fighters, then even two contingents of our forces will be too few. And if we send the Nightingales as well, then we're spreading our forces too thin. We aren't a large enough battalion to fight back whatever troops the king is hoarding at his castle while keeping the rest of us away, and we can't sacrifice any one group to bring the refugees in." He tilted his head toward Carrus. "But I'm glad you suggested it, because I need those ideas."

Quereth squinted at Ervinor. "You're saying we all go or none of us do."

"Yes."

Carrus perked up again, determined to prove to Ervinor that he chose wisely in selecting him as captain. "Then I'll take the Ravens in first with the refugees and the rest of you will follow right behind in case anything goes wrong."

"You mean 'when' it goes wrong, dear," Lica corrected sourly. "But it's a good idea. Still, I think two of us together is better though. I will go with Carrus."

Quereth sighed. "By standard procedure, it would be the Nightingales to go in with the Ravens."

"Why is that?" Carrus asked.

The old mage smiled softly. "Because we would be further north from the other teams, so the Nightingales should be in the mix."

Ervinor eyed the mage with a grin. "You figured that out, did you?"

"Nightingales, North. Eagles, East. Yes," Quereth agreed. "Smart planning, on your part."

"Then are we agreed?" Ervinor asked, looking at each of the captains.

"We just need Frast, but yes," Lica acknowledged. "And I don't see why he would object."

"Nor I," Quereth chimed in.

A knock at the door interrupted them and Ervinor called for the messenger to enter. "You must come now, general!"

Ervinor leaped to his feet, the others close behind. They followed the messenger down the hallway and into the larger room, where he veritably sprinted for the stairs and thundered down them swiftly. The others kept close. They reached the bottom floor only moments later, and Ervinor feared another riot among the refugees. Instead it was something else altogether.

A group of eight men and women greeted them, heavily clad in vines of ivy as if it were armor. Between them was a stretcher with a moaning body upon it. Ervinor stepped forward and recognized the injured man immediately.

"Randler!" He gestured to the eight forest people. "Come inside and tell me everything."

CHAPTER 45

Uneasy Truce

"This is madness, Gabrion!"

The warrior's face was a mask of stone as he sat in Ordren's war room. The commander paced back and forth, stamping his feet and swinging his arms violently as he spoke. But Gabrion didn't care about Ordren's anger. He only needed to endure it for a few moments longer.

At last the door opened and three Hathren soldiers appeared, followed by their commander. He saw the agitation on Ordren's face and the aplomb on Gabrion's, after which his back straightened and he stalked inside even more cautiously.

"Commander Ruhk of the Royal Army of Hathreneir," introduced one of his subordinates as the commander stepped forward and angled his head in tense greeting.

"Commander Ordren of Kallisor. You have met Gabrion already."

Ruhk glanced around the chamber. "No guards? Just the two of you? Or do you have mages on call nearby, Kallisorian scum?"

Gabrion spoke softly. "I don't need guards."

Ruhk's lip twitched. "Well I will not do without mine, so don't even ask."

Gabrion poured a glass of wine into a goblet. He took a sip to show it wasn't poisoned and then set the goblet in front of him. "A drink, Commander Ruhk?"

"You will not lure me into a false sense of security, scum. I came only as a courtesy."

"Indeed," Ordren said, but Gabrion silenced him.

Ruhk took the goblet Gabrion had poured and sipped from it. "You drink this swill? It's no wonder my king wishes to decimate your land. You can't even make proper wine."

"The fighting must end," Gabrion said. "Our kings have run our lands dry and they will lead us to ruin. It is we who must stand tall and put an end to this."

Ruhk set the goblet down and stepped back. "You're traitors?" He looked from one to the other, aghast. "Of Kallisor," he echoed Ordren's greeting. "Not of the king's army. What madness is this?"

Gabrion replied, "There can be no more death, Ruhk. Not in this manner, at any rate. The kings play us like pawns in a game and if it continues, there will be no people left for them to play with."

"Blasphemer! Our king guides us toward prosperity by taking down lowlifes like you."

"And my king thinks he does the same," Gabrion acknowledged. "As do the people who fight for him. And so they all line up and then they die."

"It is necessary to wipe out evil by any means."

"Evil," Gabrion repeated. "We're evil?"

"All men from Kallisor are evil."

"Nonsense!" Ordren said. "We're no more evil than any one of you!"

"I agree," Gabrion added. "But I don't think you are evil at all, Ruhk. In fact, I believe there are a very few people in the land who could really be called 'evil.' Instead, we're all just stupid, because we let ourselves be led by men who cower in their castles."

"Traitorous scum," Ruhk snarled. "You dare belittle my king? When I step from these walls, I will bring my forces in and they will tear you asunder. We will show you how to defile a man."

Gabrion stood up at last. "You will indeed gather your fighters and you will bring them in. But there will be no fighting. There will be no killing."

"You're mad!"

Gabrion stepped around the desk and Ruhk's guards tensed in response, ready to defend their commander. "Yes, perhaps I am. I've killed too many people not to be. I have erased the lives of hundreds of fighters. You see, I have been training the men and women here how to fight and how to defend themselves. But in our battle yesterday, I bade them not to strike. So they did not. I assume your casualties were low? The only men who died fell before my own blades. I killed them because you wouldn't listen. You needed to see that we're not weak or helpless here. We could have decimated you. But we *chose* not to. We value life here and we would welcome you inside to experience it for yourselves."

Ruhk backed away. "I don't understand. What is your purpose?"

"To show you that we are the same. So you can see that we fight because you attack. We fight because a king says so. Yet if we had a choice, we would not fight."

"How do I know this is not some ruse to lure us in so that you can slay us?"

"As I already said, we could have taken you out yesterday if we had chosen to do so. Our purpose is to end the war, not prolong it. Come and learn from us."

Ruhk eyed Gabrion oddly. "You truly are insane, warrior."

"Tell your men to come in, to partake in our wares, but to do so as if my men are just men, not enemies. Tell them to come in and learn from each other. Think of it as a scouting mission if you must. So long as none of my people are hurt, then you will be free to go yourselves, unharmed, with any information you can take with you."

The commander's eyes narrowed sharply. "How will I know your men will obey such a decree?"

"I believe their performance yesterday is proof enough."

Ruhk couldn't argue. "The heat of battle is an easy place for one to lose their head, but your forces kept theirs. Having a host of Hathrens here, though, may prove more challenging."

"We have to be strong, Ruhk. We have to show them that we're just people and that we don't need to die in order to prove ourselves."

Ruhk looked at Ordren, whose face was unflinching. "You will abide these rules?"

"It was Gabrion who brought me here," he said.

It wasn't the affirmation Ruhk was looking for. He scowled and spun on his heel. "Expect us by nightfall."

After he stormed out, Ordren calmly closed the door and then turned to face Gabrion. "I am at a loss."

"How so?"

"I have no idea how I came to follow someone so ridiculously idealistic." His face curled into a snarl. "It was one thing to amass our own forces to put a stop to the war, but this? Having a camping party with the Hathrens? You've lost your mind, and you're going to get us killed. I have tolerated your eccentricities up to this point, but you've gone too far. When they return, we will finish them off and I demand your obedience."

Gabrion stepped toward Ordren until they were nearly nose to nose. "You will do no such thing. The killing stops, Ordren. You joined me in Pindington because you believed in that cause. You believed that the war needed to end. Yet now you would throw it away because you're scared?"

"I am not!"

"You're terrified," Gabrion corrected. "But you know something? So am I. They outnumber us threefold. Yet it's the only way to gain their trust. It won't be easy having them here. It won't be simple. But that's the whole point. The kings have done what's simple, rather than face what's hard. When have the kings ever met to discuss the lands, their needs, their desires? Never. They sit in their castles, sending messengers, and they assume they understand the world around them. No more, Ordren. No more. We'll make them see, and it has to start here. Now."

"You're going to regret this. Fights will break out. Some of the king's own men are here. They'll balk at this. They'll see it as rebellion and they'll send word back to Kallisor and then we're finished for good."

Gabrion set his jaw and locked his gaze with Ordren's. "Then we have to hurry and make this work."

Silence hung in the air as Ordren tried to craft a new argument, but he was unable to. "You're serious about this."

"I need your help, Ordren. I need you to help keep these men in line. And if fights break out, I need your help to quell them. I need you to be willing to stand with the Hathrens if necessary and take the side of justice, not vengeance. I can't do this without your support. I need you to believe again."

Ordren slid away from Gabrion. "You're a fanatic. But you really seem to believe this has a chance."

"It won't be easy."

"We have preparations to make, sir." Ordren stood upright and snapped a hearty salute to Gabrion, after which he left the room.

Gabrion released a deep breath and sat at his desk for a few minutes, arguing with himself over the wisdom of this plan. Yet he knew deep in his gut that peace had to start somewhere. He hated that it had required him to demonstrate his prowess on the field. After all, how could killing others bring peace? But perhaps fear of his skill would be enough to temper the others, so they could give this a chance. It was far-fetched and he was worried, but he couldn't let that show. He had failed in so many things, but in this, he would not fail.

Hoisting himself up and donning his most confident aura, Gabrion stepped out of the war room to spread the word to the rest of the outpost, ready for resistance, which he met in droves.

C H A P T E R 46

The Healing Jade

DARIAK LOOKED UP at the angry mages and he struggled to keep himself from crying out in shock. "Pyron, at last," he said as calmly as he could muster. "I have been looking for you."

"No doubt," the old man snarled. He turned to the mages who were with him. "Grab him and bring him to my quarters."

"But he needs to face the Board for his crime," said the librarian.

"After I speak with him." When the man hesitated, Pyron continued, "It was me he impersonated. Shouldn't I have a chance to confront him? You may be there, of course."

The mage was torn but he finally acquiesced and they guided Dariak out of the library and up to Pyron's chambers on the fourteenth floor. Dariak's mind raced, wondering what would happen to him now. The last time he had faced Pyron, the mage had encased him in antimagic bindings. This time, he had no jades to protect himself with. And though Tyrrus had warned him that mages could not use spells against each other in the Magitorium, he doubted Pyron would need to abide by those rules.

Clearly, Pyron was in good standing in this tower. He lived in an enormous suite with its own privy and miniature kitchen. The bedroom was sectioned off and he had a separate reading room, which was where they brought Dariak. All that was missing was a private laboratory where he could practice incantations, but in a tower full of such rooms, it was unnecessary. Dariak accepted a cushioned chair, but the librarian and his two guard mages opted to stand.

Pyron took another seat. "So, Dariak, have you come to tear down this tower, too?"

The black-haired mage shook his head. "Don't be ridiculous."

Pyron scoffed. "Ridiculous? Were you not at the destruction of the Prisoner's Tower in Pindington? Did you not wreak havoc in my own tower?"

"You've known me all my life, Pyron. You mentored me when I came to the tower as a teenager. But now you've shunned me. What happened?"

The old mage's voice was tight. "You know very well."

"The accident that killed Kerrish," Dariak muttered. "I tried to explain that, but you wouldn't listen."

"Who in his right mind would ever sacrifice his own life for a meager cause? To stand in your way? No." Pyron scowled. "I knew Kerrish. He had too much ambition to die so he could hurt you."

"Then you didn't know him well enough. You didn't know he hated me for being different, for being interested in his son. You don't know how he loathed me for letting his son see that he wasn't alone in his feelings." Dariak fought the urge to stand and stalk around the room in anger. "What father would ever want this for his son? Not to know the love of a woman, to bear children and carry on his line? Kerrish couldn't handle it and he often raged against me, even as a lad. And when he realized that his son was like me, you can't imagine what he did."

Pyron's jaw tensed. "You are twisting history."

"No, I am revealing it, Pyron. Kerrish was a powerful mage, but a terrible man. He tortured Kesh. Humiliated him. I heard bits of it and even those were horrific."

"This is far from the point. You brought death and destruction to the tower, Dariak, and you must pay for that crime."

"This is entirely the point, Pyron. Kerrish was your friend, though you disagreed with him on the Council. Did he ever tell you about the escapade between Kesh and Lorianna? How he stood in the room, leering over the two of them, coercing his son to bed her? Watching them, spells at the ready if they refused?"

"You lie!" Pyron shouted, standing up, his fingers hardening to stone.

"You will never know, will you? It's my word against your convenient memories. No one ever knew why Kesh killed himself, though, did they? Well, perhaps his father knew."

"So you had a motive for murdering him that day," Pyron decided.

"Don't be a blind fool! Look at me, Pyron! Don't you know me?"

They stared at each other for a while, then Dariak sighed. "I can see you don't. You think I changed. You think I would have murdered him in cold blood to satisfy some old vengeance. You truly believe I would slay him so I could claim my right to the jades and sway the Council. But your logic is broken."

"No, Dariak, your mind is filled with lavish ideas of changing the world and you sought power that was beyond your scope. Even your father was wary of the jades and he sought them only to learn more about them, not to unite them."

"But he did unite them."

"He had little choice. But you would wander in, claim them all, and bring them together to unleash some unknown force upon the land, to what end? To stop the fighting? Dear boy, don't you think it will only increase the fighting? Don't you see that it will only bring others to tear you down instead? The enemy will be different, but the result will be the same. War will continue, regardless. But instead, you will kill the lands we are trying to protect, by using all that power."

Dariak listened carefully and let the words sink in. "You sound like Randler, who wanted to steal the jades away and throw them into the sea where they could not be found."

"No!" Pyron snapped. "They must not be destroyed."

Dariak laughed mirthlessly. "You fear their power but you also fear their loss. You're a mess."

"There is more to learn from them, but only if we proceed cautiously. I will not condone handing the jades over to you, Dariak. I will not allow it. You will destroy us all."

Dariak stood and walked over to lean against the wall. "I would not have killed Kerrish in secret. I wanted his crime to be known. I wanted you all to know his darkness so you would judge him and punish him. All my life, I've been met with looks of scorn and disgust. But it's those who persecute people like me who are the true villains. I'm just a man. I don't hurt anyone by being different. I wanted him to face his crimes before you all, but my quest didn't allow for it. I needed to gather the jades and bring an end to the larger threat, the one that will ruin us all.

"And then there was you, Pyron. You, who helped to raise and train me. But when my need was great and when the accusations flew toward me, you collapsed under the weight of your peers. You showed your weakness to me and you refused to hear my words, to hear my truth. Even now, you writhe around trying to evade me. It breaks my heart, because I always looked up to you as a father. Because my father is *dead*. Yet you were there to guide me in his place. I only want what my father wanted. To find peace in this world. To bring us together as one people, not as warring enemies.

"Even in your own tower, under your own guidance, you couldn't stop the fighting. Mages are angry with other mages because they excel in different elements. It's absurd and you don't even see it. You accept it as normal and move on with the day, complaining of all the things you need to tend to. But I intend to change it, Pyron. I *will* change it. People will be judged on their actions, not on what they are or where they were born. It's what I'm fighting for. It's what my friends are fighting for. And despite his personal wish for the end of magic, it's also what Randler is fighting for."

Pyron's face was inscrutable. "You love that bard yet he would end magic if he could."

"Magic was used against him. I understand why he feels that way. But he accepts me and he knows that I am close to magic. He's my grounding force and he keeps me sane. He'll ensure that your greatest fears do not come to pass. He'll keep me from destroying our world."

"You speak like a lovesick child."

"Does that mean I'm wrong?"

"Bah!" Pyron threw himself back into his chair. "I'm too old for this romantic nonsense. You can't change the way people act by showing greater force, Dariak. Your plan is flawed."

"It doesn't matter."

"How can it not matter?"

"Plans change all the time." Dariak walked over to his chair and pushed himself into it, though all he really wanted to do was crack Pyron and the other mages over the head, claim the healing jade, and rush back to Randler. "I have no desire to take the healing jade by force, but I will if I must."

"And bring the whole Magitorium down on your head?" Pyron chortled. "That's why I came here. These mages will unite when it comes to it. You cannot harm me."

"I can challenge you to a duel, can't I? We can go outside this tower and have it out, mage to mage. And when I win, I will forgive you for denying me my birthright and I'll go on to change this world."

Pyron pulled the healing jade from his pocket and held it in his hand. "I am impervious with this, you realize. How do you intend to take it from me? You cannot cut me. You cannot burn me. Will your other shards help you in this?"

"They are not with me," he said. "I am here alone. Just me. If you will not give the jade to me willingly, then I will defeat you for it."

Pyron laughed heartily. "You don't have your precious jades with you? How do you hope to overpower me without them?"

"Why, are you afraid I will win? Is that why you won't accept my challenge?"

Pyron's face lost all its mirth. "You are a rambunctious upstart, Dariak, and your arrogance irritates me. But I did help to train you as a mage, so I know the foundations of your skill and I will not allow you to best me."

"Then we battle?"

"We battle."

C H A P T E R 47

To Walk Among Friends

KITALLA AND FRAST sprinted down the stairs, following the pulsations of their jades to the first floor of the tower, ignoring Ervinor's meeting on the third floor. They scrambled past bewildered mages who instinctively flung up defensive spells just in case. They reached the bottom floor and watched as Ervinor and a host of others marched from the room to an antechamber. Kitalla raced ahead, Frast on her heels.

They burst into the room as Randler's writhing body was set upon a table inside. Frast's knees weakened at the sight of the injured bard. "What happened?" he whispered.

A thick cloth was pulled away, revealing Randler's crushed legs. They winced at the sight. One of the forest people turned to Ervinor. "Your man was traveling with his companion through our wood. In short, a tree fell upon this one and crushed him. Astrith worked what magic he could but he could only stop his body from rotting. He has not the skill needed to mend this, so we brought him here to the mages."

Another member of the vine-cloaked foresters spoke next. "Astrith did fashion these for him, if you are able to mend the greater damage. They should help to facilitate his recovery." She handed Lica a set of crutches that could lock together about Randler's waist and support him, as well as the staff Dariak had crafted for him in the woods.

A third member spoke next. "There is little else we can tell you, but Astrith was insistent that you receive these." He handed Ervinor a sack and bowed his head.

Ervinor handed the package to Quereth to inspect and the old mage gasped. "It's the other jades!"

Panic streaked down Ervinor's spine. "What happened to Dariak?"

"From what we know, he continued his quest for the last of those pieces. From what we know, he is fine."

Frast stepped forward, shocked. "He left Randler with you, in this state, so he could go after the jade?"

"It would seem so. Now if there is nothing else?"

"You're leaving?" Lica asked. "You only just arrived."

"This… structure. It is unnatural and we will not endure it. No, we must return home." Ervinor tried to encourage them to stay, but they were adamant and somewhat nervous. They had nothing else to impart to these people, thus they took their leave so they could tend to Randler.

Frast struggled at the sight of the bard. Randler's skin was clammy and pale and he randomly twitched in pain. Frast wanted nothing more than to grab the man and pull him close, telling him it would be all right, somehow, some way.

Kitalla watched the frustration on the mage's face, so she set her hand on his shoulder and whispered softly. "Talk to him, Frast. Let him know we're here and we'll do what we can to help."

He thanked her for the permission, for it allowed him to take Randler's hand in his own and to bend low, crooning in a soft, comforting voice. No one was fooled by the farce but they had other concerns.

Ervinor's face was taut as he looked at the damage to the legs. "How can he recover from this?"

Kitalla kept her voice low. "He may not. But if the mages can come together, there may be a chance."

He turned to her. "You're saying they could save both of his legs when they could nothing for my arm?"

She sharpened her tone. "Your arm was cut clean off. This is different." Without waiting, she turned to Quereth. "Get them."

He didn't need any clarification. After handing the sack of jades to Ervinor, he flew from the room.

Lica gave the chamber a cursory search. "We need to make him more comfortable and we will truly need a lot of skill for this to work."

"Will they help?" Carrus asked.

"How can they not?"

Verna grunted. "These mages are selfish."

"No," Ervinor whispered, looking down at the sack in his hands. "They will help."

Shelloni was the first to arrive, which was no surprise to Ervinor. She seemed to hover nearby wherever he went. "Now you're asking favors?"

"We're desperate, Shelloni. Look at him and tell me you won't lend a hand. What will it cost you, some energy? Some spell components?"

"Yes. But why should I? Let the mages who support you do this work."

Lica stormed over. "This is serious. Get over yourself and do the right thing for once. We need every mage here who can work a healing spell and that's the end of it. Summon the legions and return here quickly. The longer we wait, the less likely he will recover."

"Of all the nerve!" Shelloni shrieked.

"She's right," Rothra said from the doorway. "I have no love for these fools, but how can we turn our backs on this?"

"Think of the drain on our resources," she argued. "Are your fire mages going to replenish them? This isn't worth our effort."

Kitalla grabbed her and spun her around. "Yes, it is, you insignificant turd." She withdrew the glass jade from her pocket and thrust it into the woman's hand. "It's only a loan, however."

Shelloni looked down at her hand and gasped when she realized what it was. "Y—you have the jades?"

Ervinor held up the sack in his hands. "Nearly all of them. So use them to the best of your ability to heal him. Then you can commune with them until we depart in two days." He saw the hunger light in her eyes. "I suggest you fix him fast, as it will give you more time with the jades for yourselves."

Kitalla walked over to Rothra and handed him the fire jade. "Don't get too used to it," she warned. "You've seen me angry."

They had never spoken, but Kitalla had fought against Rothra on one of her excursions in the tower, and he knew she was not to be trifled with. He nodded slowly. "I will return it."

"Yes, you will. Now don't you two have preparations to make?"

Lica chimed in, "Frast, Quereth, and I will also be part of this."

"No doubt," Shelloni muttered. "And surely Ervinor will set up a contingent of bodyguards to ensure we do our best and don't try to keep the jades for ourselves."

"Should I?" the general asked. "Or maybe we won't leave until I have these all back in my possession. And I know how badly you want us gone."

Kitalla tapped her lip. "True, Ervinor, but maybe their lust for the jades will be stronger. I'm going to go limber up, just in case." She strode from the room, feigning a leap at Rothra, who shrieked and took an involuntary step back.

"Come," Shelloni muttered foully under her breath. "Surely Quereth has rousted the others by now. Let's coordinate this quickly." She turned back to Ervinor. "We will need those, please." He handed her the sack of jades.

"Lica, Carrus, Verna, keep an eye on those shards," Ervinor requested, after which they left the chamber.

Only Frast was left, but from the look on the mage's face, he wasn't going to leave any time soon. Ervinor stepped over and clapped the man's shoulder. "Frast."

"Don't say it, Ervinor."

"He is Dariak's man."

"Don't say it," he breathed.

Ervinor cleared his throat. "Frast, will you be assisting the procedure?"

"Yes. I wouldn't be anywhere else."

"Then perhaps you should join the others to hear the plan."

He shook his head slowly. "I can't leave him, Ervinor." The general did not respond, so Frast turned to face him. "He isn't mine. I know that. But for now, here, today, it's all I have. Just let me be with him right now. It's all I have."

"You're setting yourself up for a lot of pain later."

"I don't care," he whispered. "Please, go and do whatever you need to do before the others return. Let me be with him."

"I have nowhere else to be."

Frast raised his voice in a painful wail. "Won't you just get out of here? For ten minutes? Please?"

Grudgingly, Ervinor turned and left the room. As he pulled the door closed, he saw that Frast had leaned closer to Randler, almost as if to kiss him. He hoped the mage wasn't going to do anything foolish, but he worried that staying might be even worse.

Kitalla was waiting for him in the main chamber. "I thought you were off to warm up," he commented when he saw her.

"Just making a point." She smiled, then looked over Ervinor's shoulder. "Frast is still in there, isn't he?"

"Yes. He's nearly insane with grief."

She frowned. "It's only going to get worse."

"That's what I told him."

Kitalla shrugged. "Listen, Ervinor. I can't be nearby when they do this spell."

"Why is that?"

"For one reason, I've been through major healings like that; it's how I know it's possible for them to succeed. For another, like you, it's too close to home, if you know what I mean." She nodded toward his missing arm.

He grumbled then nodded.

"But also, I need to be the backup in case the mages don't return the jades."

"You're going to take them all down yourself?" he mused.

But she was serious. "How do you think they fell asleep last time?"

He gasped. "That was you? How? I just thought their sleep spell backfired or something."

"So did they, apparently. But it was me. And I need to be ready so I can do it again if I have to, though I'm hoping I won't. I'm telling you this because I'll be going into hiding until it's time for you to leave. You won't be able to find me."

"Then how will you know if they have the jades if I can't get word to you?"

"I'll know." She smirked mysteriously. "Be careful, Ervinor. Once they have time to work with those shards, they may be reluctant to hand them over, even if it means allowing you to stay here. It's imperative, though, that you gather them back swiftly and leave."

"What if Randler isn't ready to be moved by then?"

She patted him on the shoulder. "Leave Frast here with him. I'm sure he'll take good care of the man."

Ervinor groaned. "Just to make it that much worse."

"Worst case scenario, is all. But two days. Get out of here with the jades. All of them."

He leaned in. "Even the one still in your pocket?"

Kitalla grinned. "See? You're learning. This one will join you once you're out of here, and I will carry it to you," she finished with a wink.

CHAPTER 48

Healing Music

RANDLER WAS CAREFULLY moved to one of the larger training chambers on the second floor. The walls were protected against errant magic which, in this case, was more to keep outside energies from interrupting them. The bard was placed on the floor, Frast ever at his side. Shelloni regarded him with scorn.

Over three dozen mages were in the room, as well as a host of soldiers, at Ervinor's insistence. He didn't want any of the tower's people to think he wasn't watching. The mages were spread around in symmetrical positions, with the strongest healers standing nearest to Randler. Eight masters surrounded them, each clutching a jade securely in hand. The rest of the mages stood nearly at the perimeter in small groups, each poised behind one of the shard-bearers. Behind them all, spread evenly along the walls, was Ervinor's crew.

The masters communed with their jades and Rothra raised his head. "Something's wrong. The energies aren't balanced."

"Indeed," Shelloni agreed, turning an angry eye to Frast. "You have a shard on you, don't you? Given the severity of this task, wouldn't it have seemed more appropriate for us to know this beforehand? Come on, which is it?"

"The beast jade," he said simply, ignoring the fury on her face as it dawned on her that he must have had the jade with him since his arrival and no one had suspected.

"Fine," she hissed. "Go stand there between Devrin and Lica. That should accommodate the balance."

"No. I'm staying here."

"Nonsense!" He didn't respond. "Fine then! Give your shard to Morguth."

"No."

Ervinor stepped in. "Frast, this isn't helping."

But Frast had a plan in mind. "Shift yourselves around to balance the forces if you need to, but I'm not leaving his side. Besides, with me here, you can channel the energies through me. Through the beast jade."

Rothra could see that Frast would not be convinced to change his mind, so instead he called for three of the mages to shift position. "You're a fool, Frast. Courageous, but a fool."

"Why courageous?" Ervinor couldn't help but ask.

Shelloni smiled toothily. "Every aspect of the spell will pass through him and into the bard. And every resurgence of the magic will come back through him as well. In essence, he will feel every part of it."

"Frast!"

"No, Ervinor. It's Randler's best chance. The magic has to be focused. I will be the conduit."

Shelloni blew out her breath. "Well, it will certainly help. But if you die, it's no fault of ours."

"I understand."

"Frast…" But, like Rothra, Ervinor could see the man's commitment to the plan, so he stepped back against the wall and braced himself.

Shelloni looked across the room at Ervinor. "Because he is a bard, we have decided to use an older ritual to try to appease his suffering. Witness genius in the making."

It took everything Ervinor had not to roll his eyes.

Rothra held aloft the fire jade and called aloud, "The fire of life burns in us all, giving us power to grow strong and tall."

Devrin raised the air jade. "With pulsing breath, both in and out, the gift to sing, cry, scream, and shout."

Old Pollineena called to the lightning jade. "The spark of life, of light, of hope; we cannot understand your scope."

Shelloni intoned, "Water flows within our veins, blood to our feet, blood to our brains."

Vatrus was next. "Shadows in the light conceal. Draw away the pain we feel."

Quereth hoisted the earth jade high. "Your bones, your skin, all from the earth, loaned to you upon your birth."

Yndros called, "Invisible glass, which we cannot see; guide us now where we cannot be."

Lica clutched the nature jade tightly. "From forces of this world unknown, we beg our brother, be resewn."

And though the scripted phrases were complete, one other jade needed to be aligned to the process. Frast could sense it and so he called to the beast jade. "Burning deep with feral might, be strong now; survive this plight."

The six healers surrounding Randler's body linked hands, encircling Frast and the bard. They began their chanting as one unit. "*Brethos teschnus retrifar kaie k'nor beon spentirricus laie.*" With a step to the left, the circle pivoted and called the next verse. "*Reprefar mentillius corvuthe kaie.*" The healers stepped again, this time raising their joined hands upward, and moving closer to Randler so they could twist around without breaking their link. "*Recticos berlimmiean frethnor murscht.*" They untwisted as they bowed low, stepping back again. "*Channethor rethribos noctro kaie.*" Then the process repeated.

As Ervinor watched the dance, he felt enthralled by the precision. Each mage knew his or her part in this routine, but bringing it together as one felt powerful. Chanting sounded to his left and he turned his head to look. The mages behind Rothra now did their own dance, each step ending with their hands reaching for the master. After four repetitions, they stopped, and the next group to their left began, sending waves of energy toward Lica.

Once the eight groups of empowerers finished a circuit, the masters all turned left so that when they stretched their right arms out to the side, their jades pointed to Randler. The masters cast their spells in pairs. Fire and lightning. Earth and shadow. Air and glass. Water and nature. The mages holding the pairs of jades stood opposite each other in the circle.

Impressive as it was so far, Ervinor suddenly realized that it was only the preliminary parts of the spell. For, as the last pair of masters ended their incantations, Randler and Frast both howled in agony. The healers repeated their dance, drawing energy from the masters behind them, who in turn pulled energy from the empowerers. The next circuit of empowerments happened, not singularly like before, but in the same pairs as the masters, and so the circuit swept around much faster.

As Ervinor watched and listened, the chanting worked its way through a series of crescendos and falls, with the outer ring of mages acting like the chorus of a song, ever repeating and supporting the rest of the melody. The masters carried key parts of the tune, but it was the healers in the center who sang with the great unified voice, carrying the heart of the song. But all the while, the odd music was punctuated by the horrific cries of the man being healed and the conduit who channeled the energy.

The tempo increased and when the healers twisted around, they broke their holds, stepping back, clapping, then rejoining the circle. The rhythm was powerful and Ervinor wondered if all magic spells held these components or if it was only during major incantations like this. Perhaps this ritual existed this way because, as Shelloni had said, it was an ancient one. It reminded him of his one-time fascination with magic. How could something so beautiful be shunned as dark and evil?

Randler's cries pierced the room with a rending shriek, but the mages did not break their stride. Shelloni had chosen her supporters well, for they were properly trained to remain focused. Only Frast showed signs of wear, but he clutched the beast jade in his hand, unable to chant with anyone considering his pain. He rocked back and forth to try to allow the energies to flow more swiftly through him, but it was the release of Randler's suffering that made it unbearable. He leaned forward, tears streaming from his eyes. "Hold on, Randler. Hold on. Please."

The bard cried out again, as if each burst of noise expunged some pain. Frast felt the same release, albeit only barely. He wondered then if he could try to help in a better way, rather than allowing the fire to burn through him both in and out. Perhaps he could find a way to provide an outlet, without disturbing the fluxing energies in the room.

The beast jade vibrated in his hand and he let his mind escape into it for a time. Within, he sensed a willingness to help. Maybe it was because its brethren were in the room working in unison, but he didn't care why. Frast reached within, imploring the jade to help save Randler. He felt a tug against his will and he accepted the call. Clutching the shard tightly, the surface sheared into his skin and drew in his blood. The beast jade pulled his consciousness within and then the pain grew worse.

The next surge of energy swept through Randler, tugging on the broken scraps within his legs, reminding them where they were supposed to be, and trying to drag them into place. It was the source of the pain, and though the bard was mostly unconscious, he cried out each time the pieces moved inside of him.

But Frast didn't want him to suffer anymore. Kind, gentle Randler. Beautiful Randler. Intelligent, talented, wonderful Randler. He couldn't scream anymore, for it would ruin his throat and his silky voice would struggle to caress the words the way they needed. He asked the beast jade to save Randler, to ease his suffering, regardless of the cost.

And so the next bellow erupted solely from Frast. It was an inhuman cry, almost beastlike in nature. Whether it was tigroar or ursalor, he did not know, but the raging fury that scorched him from within felt like true and ultimate bliss, for his ears did not echo with Randler's shouts. It was only his own voice. He could endure it, if only to save beloved Randler. He begged the jade to continue. To keep Randler safe and whole.

Ervinor was unnerved by the sounds emanating from the mage. It sounded like a beast was trying to claw its way out from within him. Yet when he saw that Randler's agony seemed lessened, he understood what Frast had done. He wondered if the bard would even realize it and if Frast would ever know.

The mages caught on to the change of energy in the room, now feeling the pulsating of the beast jade that hadn't been there before in earnest. The masters altered their spells with new keywords, while calling louder or softer to balance the screams. The healers in the center hadn't stopped moving from their very first step, and they showed signs of strain. But each was devoted to this task and none even paused to wipe sweat from a brow. Stepping, twirling, bowing, rising, they maintained the rhythmic flow and Ervinor wondered if it was somehow related to the everyday life functions of breathing lungs and a beating heart. His chest pounded in anticipation as the mages drew close, then swept away.

He turned his attention back to the empowerers along the perimeter. They showed greater signs of weariness, though they cast fewer spells than the rest. Yet Ervinor likened it to the coals of a furnace that needed to burn the brightest and shed the most power so that food could cook or so metal could be bent. Without their strength, none of the rest could be, and so those mages must have been pouring themselves into the casting.

And then, the drain became too much and one of the mages fell. Immediately, the others in that group showed added strain, but they pushed on, unbalanced. He didn't know what propelled him, but Ervinor ran over and pulled the fallen mage out of the way, then took her place. He had been watching them the whole time and their routine remained the same with every passing. He mimicked their movements, not knowing if it could even help since he was unable to draw upon the energies himself.

Yet when the next round came, he matched the steps and the gestures the best he could with one arm. Spinning, lunging, reaching toward Quereth. It seemed to help, somehow, but he couldn't explain it.

After the next set he broke from the group briefly and he caught the eyes of his nearest soldier and waved his hand in the air, then he jumped back in line as the next dance started. The soldier was hesitant, but he understood, as did the rest. They watched and watched, and when they memorized the steps, Ervinor's fighters joined the empowerers around the room, adding to their efficacy.

Frast's cries still tore through the chamber, and Ervinor thought he saw blood seeping from his lips. Perhaps he had bitten his tongue, but he couldn't dwell on it. The dances were coming faster and faster as the rhythm continued to increase. The mages pressed on, even the masters who still held their arms aloft, jades aimed toward Randler's legs.

Soon the tempo was so great that the empowerers went through the motions at once. They danced, they danced, they repeated the steps. Pressing on, faster and faster until soon it was too much and the mages started to fall. Around the room, the mages tripped or collapsed, drained of their energy. Ervinor wouldn't be one of them. He kept pushing and pushing, though a nagging thought burned in his mind. He had no idea how this process would affect him or how long it would take to recover. The mages would have their way with him, keeping the jades because he couldn't stop them. They might kill him or lock him away.

But he pushed it aside, the strain causing flashes of light to sparkle in his mind's eye. It didn't matter, as long as the spell worked. As long as Randler could be healed.

Then the depths argued with him again, making it harder to push through the quickening paces. Was it fair to give himself away to heal the bard, when his own arm had been lost? Shouldn't the bard also have to learn to adjust to life without his limbs?

But did he wish his fate on anyone else? He conceded that he didn't, but it still didn't justify this mindless push to give all he had to help this spell to completion. He groaned, squeezing his eyes tight against the errant thoughts, hating himself for wanting to quit just to preserve himself. No, he had energy left, he had to go on. He had to keep moving. Had to—

At last his body quit and he collapsed. He opened his eyes, seeing only a few empowerers on their feet. Most of his soldiers had already fallen. The masters continued their chanting, but two were on their knees. Only the healers in the center maintained their poise, but that was the purpose of the outer rings, he realized. The healers were the ones doing all the real work. He was just a horse pulling a royal stagecoach. A slave pushing a grindstone.

A general guiding an army.

He struggled against the exhaustion, wanting to be alert when the spell was finished. He heard a clattering sound and saw that Shelloni had collapsed, the jade spilling from her hand. And Quereth. One by one, they fell away and the chanting grew dimmer and dimmer. Frast's bellows were only weaker because there was little strength in his voice, but even lying on the ground, even with Frast huddled over Randler, Ervinor could see the raging agony.

And before he fell to darkness completely, Ervinor strained his eyes and he thought he could see that Randler was no longer half flat. Perhaps the spell was working after all.

The brief glimmer of hope cast away the last dregs of determination that kept him conscious.

CHAPTER 49

Building Trust

TRUE TO HIS WORD, Ruhk guided his troops to the outpost as the sun fell low in the sky. Gabrion was ready. His forces were on the sparring field, clustered close together so the larger contingent of fighters had room to join them. Ruhk had his fighters line up save the ten trusted soldiers Gabrion had requested he hold aside. Ruhk and Gabrion joined Ordren on the wall overlooking the men and women.

"Welcome, Hathren fighters," Gabrion hailed. "I know not what your commander has told you of this experiment, but I will describe it to you now so there are no misunderstandings. My name is Gabrion and I am from Savvron, a small town on the southwestern border of Kallisor." He waited while Ruhk's men muttered their hatred of anything to do with Kallisor.

Then he continued. "I was dragged into this war because I was able to fight. I wanted to defend my home, my family. So I learned to wield a sword, as you saw yesterday." He waited for them to think of the carnage he had wrought. "But my goal is not war. It never was. I brought myself to your lands because I intended to save someone dear to me who was taken away. I failed in that mission."

Gabrion cleared his throat. "Yet all along, I traveled with a mage from your lands and I agreed with his goal. To unite our lands as one and to put an end to the needless fighting."

Cries of outrage echoed up from the populace. Ruhk bellowed aloud angrily, "Silence!"

When the crowd settled, Gabrion proceeded. "I ask you here today to put your pasts away while you are here. Forget your pride. Forget your allegiances outside these walls. Spend the next few days learning about each other. Learn that we are all men and women with dreams and families. Leave your thoughts of war elsewhere and discover each other."

"To what end?" called a voice from below.

"To see that we are the same and that killing ourselves is pointless. It's a waste of life and it needs to end."

"How can we trust you?"

"I have invited you into my home," Gabrion said, spreading his arms out wide. "I offer you to partake in what we have here. But I have some ground rules and these apply to Kallisorians and Hathrens alike. They are as follows: No one is to harm another person here. No fistfights. No knife-fights. There will be no subterfuge within these walls."

He waited again for the noise to lessen. "I realize I'm asking much of you. So I will offer you this. If you need to burn off your anger, you may do so, as follows. You may officially challenge each other to one-on-one duels, which must be delivered and accepted properly in front of an official. You will then come to this field and here you will battle. But I challenge you not to kill each other here, only come to work out your frustrations."

"What's the point of that?"

Gabrion laughed. "If you want to hone your skills then you must learn better control, and to do that, you must learn when to strike and when not to. In this outpost, you will focus on when not to strike, to fight without killing, as I had intended yesterday until a demonstration was deemed necessary."

Grumbling echoed from below and he felt Ruhk tense up beside him. Ordren remained stiff and silent the entire time, staring mostly at the back of Gabrion's head, his face unreadable. The optimistic warrior pressed on. "I have asked Commander Ruhk to select ten champions. I have also selected ten. They will wander through the outpost in pairs, one Hathren and one Kallisorian, each with red armbands. They are the officials who will keep the peace. They will reprimand you if needed, regardless of whom you ally yourself with. So remember that I demand there is no brawling here. Official bouts only. Aside from that, you are to mingle and learn about each other."

"I have nothing to say to a Kallisorian!"

Ruhk took a step forward and shouted, "You will obey! I have agreed to this little challenge and you will obey my command. If you are unable to follow my orders, surrender yourselves to the dungeon at once!" His anger rang through the training ground and his troops all lowered their heads. He apparently was serious and they knew it. "By the end of this evening, I expect every one of you to learn the names of three enem—ahem," he stopped himself. "Forgive me. I expect every one of you to learn the names of three people whom you have not served with before. Learn the names of their hometowns, their families, and find out why they joined the war."

Gabrion didn't care for the last part, but it was something they all could answer. "If anyone is uncertain of the requirements, remain here. Else, head inside. There will be no duels until tomorrow, if at all. And I would prefer not to see any. You are to remain in the common areas until the horn is sounded."

"One last thing," Ruhk barked out, and Gabrion had no idea what was coming. "No ale tonight for anyone. No mead, no wine. Nothing that will alter your senses or make you wag your tongue too loosely. Perhaps tomorrow, but tonight we all remain dry." The disappointment was palpable.

Gabrion looked over the assembly and waited for them to quiet down. "Dismissed!"

The twenty officials had already been briefed and paired off, each swearing fealty to this mission in front of Gabrion, Ordren, and Ruhk. They were stationed throughout the outpost to keep an eye on the large host and to help ensure the crowds remained in control.

Gabrion turned to Ruhk. "Thank you. Excellent call about the mead."

Ruhk clasped Gabrion's arm. "I'm uncertain about this exercise, and I still think you're crazy, but my men can use a few nights without fear of attack. That, more than anything, is my motivation for agreeing to this task."

"I can accept that. And I hope that by the time you depart, we do so on the same side."

Ruhk tensed, but then he realized that Gabrion hadn't suggested his defection to the Kallisorian army. "We shall see, Gabrion. Ordren." He nodded his head and went below.

Ordren let out a breath. "They are fearful now of retribution, but that won't last, Gabrion. I'm warning you; people will die during this experiment of yours."

"You know, Ordren, I'm getting tired of your pessimism. If I wasn't here trying to bring the two sides together, then most of them would have died on the battlefield yesterday. So before you call this a failure, let's at least try to make it work."

The commander's voice went low. "I wouldn't let most men talk to me like that, Gabrion."

The warrior considered his response carefully. "Should we go find an official and schedule a duel for first thing tomorrow?"

Ordren looked at him, perplexed, then realized he was joking. "All right, Gabrion. Let's get down there."

He grabbed Ordren's shoulder before stepping away. "I'm serious, Ordren. I need you to find a way to believe in this, if only for a few days. Please."

The older man pouted but then pulled away to join the masses downstairs. Gabrion peered over the wall and saw about two dozen people milling about the training area. Wondering if they had questions, he climbed down the ladder that accessed the field and approached them.

"Good evening, all," he said. "I am Gabrion."

"We heard," one woman sneered. "Are you the one who cooked this whole thing up?"

"I am."

"Get him!" she shouted, pouncing at once. Gabrion grabbed her wrist and fell backwards, pulling her with him and flipping her overhead. As she landed with a thud, Gabrion continued his roll and rose up on his feet. He took a punch to the gut from one fighter but he kicked out at another, knocking him down. Gabrion pushed aside his nearest attacker, who barreled into another, disorienting her. Gabrion righted himself and grabbed for the next flying fist, twisting the arm around and snagging the assailant tightly.

"Enough!" he bellowed. "This ends now!" He shoved the fighter down, watching as the others held their battle stances. "If you have a quarrel with me, then schedule a duel."

The woman who spoke first rose up and spat on the ground. "Forget it. I'm out of here. Who's with me?" She stormed away, determined to flee the outpost.

She did not expect her commander to intercept her. Ruhk appeared and grabbed her by the throat, shoving her to the ground like a sack of grain. "You're pathetic and small-minded, Gerta. Rallied your best friends here, too, did you? Can you not follow orders?"

"You traitor!" she cursed. "Wait until the king hears about this. He'll have your head. All of you. He'll have your heads. Every last one of you."

Ruhk whistled and seven of his soldiers rushed over from nearby. "Take Gerta and her friends down to the dungeon at once." He looked up at Gabrion. "If that is fine with you."

The warrior nodded, signaling to Rotchie and Krethos, the nearest officials. "Rotchie knows the way." They escorted the pack to the dungeons.

Ruhk turned back to Gabrion. "You do fight well, warrior. It's tempting to challenge you to a duel just for the sport of it."

"I get the feeling that my schedule may be booked rather quickly."

"Indeed!" Ruhk chortled, slapping Gabrion on the back. "Very well then, we'll wait. Perhaps when you're weary I'll have a chance of besting you. Should we go in now and set an example?"

The commander was right. They needed to be present in the common areas. They walked inside together into a crowded room, one of many now. Mostly, Ruhk's men stayed distant from Gabrion's. The warriors nodded to each other and crossed paths to greet their would-be foes. Gabrion stepped toward a pack of four fighters who were talking to each other while glancing over at the Kallisorians.

"And they stand funny, too," one was saying.

"Probably smell funny."

Gabrion inserted himself. "After a long day, sure, but who doesn't? Hello, I am Gabrion of Savvron."

The men stammered, their faces lighting red, wondering how long he had been listening. "I am Gressep of Kreathe."

"Morques of Kreathe."

"Frethe of Rossbur."

"Herrin of Marritosh."

"Nice to meet you all," Gabrion said as warmly as he could. "May I ask… were you poking fun at anyone in particular or everyone in general?"

They stood erect and offered a salute. "Sir!" they said in unison.

"No, no, I'm not angry. I'm sure some of my men are doing the same thing. Remember, your challenge tonight is to cross the lines and meet each other. Come with me." Grudgingly, they followed him over to three of his fighters across the way who were similarly huddled together by themselves. "Shenna, Lorrni, Friya," he introduced them. "Please meet Gressep, Morques, Frethe, and Herrin."

The four men were shocked that he had remembered their names in the noisy room, but they were more intrigued with the fighters Gabrion had introduced them to, for they were some of the better-looking women in the outpost. Once the hesitant flirting began, Gabrion excused himself and meandered away.

Some of the men and women took it upon themselves to bridge the gap at the behest of their commanders, but it didn't always work out for the best. Feelings were easily trampled, and more than once the officials had to step in to quell some arguments that could have readily escalated into brawls. All in all, however, when Ruhk and Gabrion left the common rooms, they had high hopes.

A horn sounded, signaling the end of the required mingling session. Numerous parties remained in heated discussions, some about battle tactics or favorite recipes, but most scampered back to the people they knew and trusted the best, glad the first ordeal was over.

Gabrion smiled. "Ruhk, I wanted to talk to you about tomorrow. See, we have this obstacle course…"

CHAPTER 50

The Duel of the Mages

IN THE NORTHWESTERN tower, the mages were torn between anticipation and concern. They held firmly to the tenet of non-violence among their numbers and within their walls. Sure, spells sometimes went awry, particularly because many new spells were explored by the people here, but the damage was rarely intentional. They respected each other's work and were often more intrigued by the results and how they could benefit from them than to try to squash or steal ideas.

Some of the mages vehemently opposed the duel between Dariak and Pyron, fearing that such a contest would upset the delicate balance the mages had established over the years. It also could open a crack in the security of the Magitorium. Perhaps allowing one violent act, even freely agreed upon by both participants, would open the door to other such acts. Also, a number of the mages within the tower had skewed lines of morality as it was and seeing mages casting spells at each other might create too much temptation.

There was no Council, however. The rules were established by the people themselves and they agreed to follow them because they had functioned well for countless years. At times, the mages needed to allow for exceptions to their rules, and in some cases, like establishing the central workspace for enchanting items, the benefits were obvious, if dangerous. This duel, though, was a cause for greater concern.

Dariak found himself hounded by worried mages once the duel was announced. He had to endure a day's worth of incessant prattling—some of it in his favor—and it severely interfered with his preparations. There were no actual shops within the tower where he could purchase any particular spell components. But even if there were, he had no money with which to purchase them. So, though it forced him to surround himself with the people and to remind them of his purpose, Dariak had to socialize with mages throughout the tower to barter for the things he needed most.

The bartering itself was mostly harmless and it reminded him of the run-around tasks he had completed back in Kaison to raise the funds needed to pay for the services Elgris and his healers had provided in the sanctuary. Likewise, he ran from one mage on the ice floor who could properly store slices of tigroar meat, which was needed by a fire mage on the sixth floor who had firegnat venom, desiccated tree ashes, and snap-crack peppers. Dariak had never heard of the peppers before, but a nature mage had requested them for her midday soup, for added flavor. She had also requested the tree ashes, claiming that only a fire mage had the skill to fully burn down a tree and leave no moisture behind, which was important to some concoction she was working on. The firegnat venom was a reluctant choice, considering what had happened against Kerrish in Magehaven, which had propelled Pyron to oppose Dariak completely, but he needed the potency of the venom.

Obtaining the glass shards had been challenging, for the mage who possessed them had insisted that Dariak recap highlights from his journey for the man's amusement. The caveat was that Dariak had not been allowed to speak and the mage seemed to know some key details and corrected Dariak when his performances didn't match.

As Dariak scurried from one floor to another carrying out errands and retrieving a slowly growing supply of spell components, he heard many whispers from the people he passed. Some talked of their own concerns, but his ears sharpened when he heard talk of the duel. The mages seemed split in all areas. Some believed the duel would generate a new branch of exploration into magic, whereas others felt it would bring about the downfall of the tower. The mages were also divided about who they thought would win. Pyron was vastly experienced and a true master in his own right, but Dariak was creative, energetic, and the son of Delminor.

The day was exhausting and once he had finished his preparations, he ate some food and went to get some rest. During the night, arguments erupted all around and they centered on the whisperings of the day.

"Can you please take your debate elsewhere?" he asked wearily, having to step out of the sleeping chamber to find the two middle-aged mages who screamed at each other. "I have a busy day tomorrow and need my rest."

"I told you to keep it down!" said the younger of the two. "You've upset him. Now go on."

The older mage raged angrily, her eyes flaring. "This is a terrible idea and if my shouting ruins the duel and forces it to be canceled because he can't lift his head, then so be it. Step aside, Nastren, and let me speak my mind."

"You will leave him be," Nastren said, clenching his fists and stepping in front of Dariak protectively.

Dariak tapped the young man on the shoulder. "Nastren, is it? Thank you for defending me, but it's fine. Let me hear her words."

The middle-aged woman straightened her spine and gave Nastren a scornful gaze. "So much for your defenses, little one," she said, before turning to Dariak. "You can't go on with this duel."

He had endured this all day and so he asked in a bored tone, "Why not?"

"You will die and if you do then we will lose one of the greatest resources the mages have ever known. You must not throw your life away to this foolish pursuit, Dariak. You must cancel the duel, and if I need to detain you here tonight, then I will crush you against my bosom and hold you here. You won't sleep this evening and you won't rise tomorrow for your fight. We need you here, don't you understand? You can't perish."

Dariak was surprised by the impassioned speech. "Thank you for your kind words," he said, somewhat hesitantly, wondering if she literally meant to crush him against her bosom or if she was merely speaking from the heart. "I don't intend to die tomorrow, however."

Nastren made a supportive bark of a sound. "Ha! See that, Me'arra, he'll be fine. He won't need your company tonight. He'll be fine without you, so head on off to your forge."

Me'arra fumed and her voice grew even louder. "You can't send me away just so you can stay with him yourself." With a growl, she turned to Dariak. "So who will it be? Him or me?"

Nastren perked up for a moment. "Or both!"

"Whoa, whoa!" Dariak said, lifting his hands up and taking a step back. "This is what you're fighting over? Really?"

"We're not the only ones." Nastren grinned. "But we won the right to come down here to spend time with you. The others all lost."

"L—lost how?"

Me'arra grumbled. "Is this even important? Arm-wrestling, some. Puzzles and riddles, others."

"Yep." Nastren nodded playfully. "We were the best among them all."

"Listen, both of you, get out of here now and leave me be. I'm going to turn around and go get some sleep. Actual sleep. I don't have time for company."

"But we got all this way!" Me'arra complained.

"No," he answered. "I'll be setting up a defensive perimeter around my area now, so neither of you, or anyone else for that matter, should disturb me. So move on."

"Spoilsport," Nastren lamented. "After the duel, then."

Me'arra punched him on the arm. "Idiot, he won't be alive."

But the two mages walked away, bantering the whole while, and he found himself oddly amused. "I don't think I will be vacationing in this place for much longer," he muttered, turning back to his bed and setting up a triggered fireball spell with some of the firegnat serum he had earned that day before lying down to sleep.

The morning came upon him moments later, or so it felt. His eyes popped open, ready for the day. He indulged himself in a hot bath, one of the best luxuries in a tower full of mages wanting to practice their talents. He could have pulled the water himself and added the heat, but he needed to rest his skills, so he left the spellcasting to the mages who wanted to support him. Some nature mages even wafted in flowery perfumes, adding a delicately delightful aroma.

Dariak spent the morning as quietly as possible, taking some food and eating it off in the corner by himself, nodding pensively to anyone who tried to strike up a conversation, but keeping his mouth loaded with rolls and fruit so as to have an excuse not to speak without seeming entirely rude. Then, as midday approached, he gathered himself and walked down to the bottom floor where he left the Magitorium.

The field in front of the tower had been altered overnight, much to Dariak's surprise. Earth and nature mages had erected sets of tiered benches reaching outward in two long groups that faced each other on either side of the battle area. The grass itself was coated with a layer of water to fend off fire spells. Additionally, a pool of water rested at opposite ends for Dariak and Pyron to draw upon if necessary. Impromptu banners fluttered in the air, suspended by magic. One banner was deep-set blue with a black trim and various indiscriminate figures and nonsensical words emblazoned across them. The other banner was white and gold with majestic mountains and a glaring sun.

Already, dozens of mages were seated in the benches, allying themselves with either the blue or white banner. Dariak noted the cheers of praise from the one and the looks of scorn from the other. He faced his supporters on the blue side and bowed, which caused the mages to erupt in wild applause. He crossed the field toward the opposite side, bewildered at the turnout for this duel.

According to the rules they had established together, neither mage was allowed to walk into the fight with any defensive spells preset. Thus, Dariak stood his ground, debating which spells to enact first once his adversary arrived. They agreed not to use any weapons directly against each other, opting to make this more of a contest of wills than physical agility. The duel would end either when one conceded or died. The winner would claim the healing jade for his own.

The sun reached its zenith, thereby reducing any advantage either would gain by the sun being in his foe's eyes. All that remained was for Pyron to join him.

The doors of the Magitorium opened wide and thirty or so mages filed out, taking their respective places in the stands. Pyron then stepped from the tower, today enwrapped in a white robe with gold trim that matched his banner clearly. White shoes covered his feet, though by the time he took his place on the field, the effort to provide white shoes was essentially lost to mud. Pyron opened his arms wide and dropped an outer cloak behind him, which one other mage at his back caught and hoisted up reverently overhead before whisking it away. Pyron's supporters had apparently worked throughout the night to ensure he looked as regal as possible.

Dariak didn't care for the posturing. He had a stronger claim to the healing jade than Pyron did and the mages here should have intervened and persuaded the master mage to hand it over without this display. Yet despite all the mages who loved Delminor for his contributions, they dared not rise against each other. Pyron's own tower could learn from them.

Xervius staggered out onto the field, his mangled body supported by two younger mages and some magic that Dariak could sense even from his position. The ancient mage raised his gnarled hands and he intoned a spell similar to one Sharice had used to distract Dariak in his fight for the lightning jade. Xervius used the wind to carry his voice to the mages in attendance.

"Welcome, friends, to the battlefield of Master Pyron of Magehaven and Dariak, the son of Delminor. These two cannot resolve their claim over the healing jade, and so this duel will determine its owner. Both have a valid claim and so they will battle evenly."

Dariak bit his tongue, for the claim was not in fact equal. But that was irrelevant. He needed to focus on the coming fight.

"As members of this tower, we have a strict policy not to harm one another, and by allowing this duel, we put that policy into question. I urge you to remember that neither of these men resides in our tower and once this battle is over, we will resume our respect for one another and we will not engage in these duels again. I am not your leader, but I insist this is so. The spells of these two casters may fly into the stands, and so you may wish to protect yourselves, but you must not interfere with the duel itself. Let it come to its own end."

Xervius waited as most of the mages enacted protection spells, though some opted not to, perhaps to explore the effects of being hit by certain spells, or out of arrogance that they would simply not be harmed. Once he was confident that the people were protected, Xervius continued. "Dariak issued the challenge, and so I ask of you, Dariak: Have you any last words before we begin?"

Dariak raised his chin. "I ask that Pyron abide my right and hand over the healing jade so that no one need be hurt here today. It is mine by right and I would have it for I have need of it. What say you?"

Pyron waited for Xervius to give him the chance to speak, then answered, "You poor fool, trying to abandon the very duel you initiated. No, you will not claim this jade from me today. For all mages and all of Hathreneir, it must not fall into your hands."

Dariak was not permitted to speak unless Xervius allowed him to, but the sightless old man did not give him the option. Instead, the slashed and wounded arms rose into the air and he finished the introduction, "Once I have taken my seat, this duel commences. Fight well!" His aides helped him to the benches on Pyron's side where he turned and sat down, refusing to cover himself in any protection spells, despite the protests of his helpers.

Dariak and Pyron stepped toward the center of the field, each setting up defensive measures. Already the field was loaded with magical energies and it would make reading each other much more challenging, but Dariak did not care. He would find a way of breaking through Pyron's defenses and defeating him.

Dariak dropped, punching his fist downward, calling, "*Dorrifus frithos catshalla.*" His hand sank into the dirt, which rumbled briefly and erupted underneath Pyron's feet, where the earth blasted upward to knock him over.

But Pyron was ready for the spell and he avoided its effect by stepping off the mound as it formed under him. The dirt rained harmlessly in the air, but he applied his own magic and sent the particles flying to Dariak.

The black-haired mage swept his arms in wide circles, deflecting the projectiles and casting them aside. At least he knew now that Pyron was still nimble. He swept his arms upward and around his head, twisting and bending his fingers as he went. Then, bringing them down, he cried out, "*Territisior frezhia hortess kaie.*" Reaching outward, the wet ground in front of him turned to ice, stretching forward until it also froze the area around Pyron.

The old mage grumbled and launched a small fireball into the icy ground, but as he did so, Dariak grabbed a ball of muddy earth and threw it hard, adding wind behind it to increase the impact. Once it was airborne, he summoned the Shield of Delminor, projecting it outward, as he had only learned to do recently, adding massive weight to the mud. Pyron was splattered from head to toe and his robes lost their glimmering luster. The old mage fell immediately to his knees.

Dariak took another step closer, dipping his finger into the firegnat serum, preparing to incinerate Pyron with it. But the old man was not injured or beleaguered in the least. He was, in fact, an earth mage and he disabled the weighted effects Dariak had sent his way, but merely allowed himself to fall as a ruse.

Pyron rose, his arms swinging wildly in the air, his voice calling loudly, *"Rethritos brienan torrifors nieh, k'tanaos loprilor brenitan errvitros!"* Walls of stone sprang up around Dariak, surrounding him. The stone pressed inward, trapping his arms and preventing him from empowering a spell to escape. *"Lindridos freth kaie!"* An invisible wall of force encased the outside of the stone column. *"Barrenoshis frethnibar lorrenticus!"* Then the stone exploded into thousands of pieces. The invisible wall kept the debris inside, which therefore caused the entire force of the spell to crush Dariak.

The young mage screamed as countless stone shards eradicated his defensive shields and then impacted him from head to toe. He fell, writhing in pain, blood seeping from wounds everywhere. He tugged on the healing energies, eager for some relief, but Pyron was not finished yet.

The old man stomped closer, bringing out a vial of reptigon serum and uncorking it, pouring some of its contents into a ball of mud he scooped up from the ground. The vitreous serum immediately began eating through the grass and dirt. Pyron lobbed it over to Dariak, who still rolled on the ground in pain, oblivious to the new disaster heading his way. Pyron waited until the toxic sphere hovered over Dariak, then clapped his hands together, screaming a word of power that shattered it, spraying poison all over Dariak's wounded body.

The toxin immediately found its way into his bloodstream through the cuts and scrapes, adding a new layer of agony. He cried out louder and tried to roll away from the area, knowing more toxin must be on the grass nearby, but he needed to get away from Pyron for a few moments so he could pull on the healing energies.

However, Pyron would not let him. The mage's hands rose into the air, and as he started chanting, Dariak knew what the man planned to do. Aching terribly, his body twitching against the poison, Dariak scrabbled for the energies inside of him. The firegnat venom was still on his finger and he used it to empower his spell, clutching a fistful of dirt as well. He tossed the dirt overhead and Pyron watched it briefly, but Dariak then launched his other hand forward and released a massive fireball.

Pyron was caught off guard and he flew backward from the impact of the fire. His robes burned and he called immediately for help from the healing jade to prevent any damage to his body. His skill with water magic was decent, but he hurried over to the pool of water at the edge of the field to help douse the flames, all while keeping the healing energies flowing. He glanced back to Dariak, sitting on the ground, his body slashed and oozing, but otherwise still. He doubted Dariak was finished and wondered what the upstart was planning next.

Dariak first wrenched his boots off his feet, tossing them aside, then pulled a small dagger from his robes. Weapons were not allowed in and of themselves, but he could use it as a spell component. His body already hurt terribly, and so this spell would do little else to him. He called for the key phrases he needed, then he pushed himself upright, staggering in the process. This was the spell he had used in Savvron, killing Gabrion's protector in the process, which then prompted the young warrior to join this journey, albeit not the way he had intended. Dariak pushed his essence into the dagger and swept his hands apart, releasing the energy, which cut himself as it left him. Spell-daggers lanced through the air, impaling Pyron and marring his scorched robes further, now with blood.

The old mage cried out in surprise but he did not hesitate to draw upon the healing jade. When the spell-daggers winked out of existence, no wounds were left in the man's skin. Only the robes showed any signs of damage. Pyron laughed aloud. "You cannot harm me!"

Dariak reached back toward his water pool and called for it to rise into the air. Winds came next, spraying the water across the field toward Pyron. Dariak then drained the water drops of all heat, turning them to sharp icy darts, which crashed into the older mage. He knew he wasn't being efficient dragging the spell across the entire expanse of the field, but he needed to keep the master on the defensive.

Dariak watched as the ice darts impacted Pyron, cutting the old man's skin. Each pelt that formed was instantly erased and Dariak knew the mage was utilizing the healing jade fully. Even across the field, he could see the contempt in Pyron's eyes.

Dariak's bare feet remained firmly lodged into the soil, but his hands worked frantically. He reached into his cloak and found a piece of cactus one of the nature mages had given him during his bartering. No one else had wanted it, so he figured he would put it to use now. He called a random spell aloud to draw Pyron's attention and he could see the mage winding his arms up defensively, but because Dariak hadn't infused the spell with any intent or related component, nothing happened. Instead, Dariak used the moment's distraction to lather the rest of the firegnat venom onto the piece of cactus. Finally, he rattled off the spells he needed for this to work.

First, he threw the cactus in the air toward Pyron, who immediately countered by lobbing a wad of dirt in the air to weigh it down. But Dariak anticipated that and projected an inverted instance of the Shield of Delminor so that the added weight would have no effect. The projectile continued its path unabated, and Pyron already started drawing on the healing jade in anticipation.

Dariak hadn't used the spell too often, for it was draining, and he hadn't used it on a plant since he was a teen, but he enacted the engorgement spell on the flying cactus, drawing upon the powers of nature for support. The cactus doubled in size, then tripled. He fell to his knees, imploring the plant to grow larger still. And once it had quadrupled in size, Dariak activated the firegnat venom.

Each spindle on the cactus was infused with the venom and each needle erupted into a massive blaze. The explosion shook the air and knocked over the spectators sitting closest to where Pyron stood. He shrieked in pain despite the healing jade, calling eagerly for its help, his anger rising.

As Dariak knelt in the muddy grass, he reached into the dirt again and again with his mind. He had removed his shoes to facilitate a connection, and as Pyron maintained the healing forces during the prolonged firestorm, Dariak pulled and pulled from within the earth. He didn't know exactly what he was looking for, but he knew the answer was there. Xervius had given him the key.

As the fire flickered in the air and dissipated, Pyron was doubled over on the ground, coughing to clear his lungs. The healing jade helped him with that as well, though perhaps more dominion over air would have been better.

Dariak stared across the field and targeted Pyron as his body shook and slowly rose. The old man turned around, saw the younger man's posture, and decided that Dariak was weakening. Pyron reached into his robe and pulled out a stone. Taking inspiration from Dariak's own spells, he coated it with firegnat serum and dropped down, plunging the stone deep into the earth, sending it over to Dariak, ready to explode underneath the son of Delminor.

But Dariak didn't care about the incoming spell. Instead, he found the thread of hope he was looking for, grasping it mentally and drawing it within.

Pyron's heated stone swam underground toward him, and as it broke the surface and erupted like a miniature volcano, Dariak simply rose up and bore the pain.

Dariak watched as Pyron fumbled around for another set of rocks, presumably to rain down upon Dariak and pelt him into submission. But when the fiery geyser ended and Pyron glanced across the way, he was startled to see Dariak standing up. Strong.

Uninjured.

Baffled, Pyron hurried his steps and threw the stones upward, cracking them midair and forcing them to batter against Dariak's face and torso. But Dariak endured them as if they were nothing more than bits of dust.

Dariak stalked forward, dragging his bare feet in the dirt, seeing genuine panic on Pyron's face. He summoned his basic fire dart spell and launched flames toward the old man, but there was no effect. Pyron could still heal away any damage instantly.

Xervius had reminded him that he was connected to all magic, and so Dariak had reached through the earth to contact the healing jade. Drawing some of its power had kept Pyron's last attack from harming him, but Pyron could still heal. Tapping into the jade was not enough. He needed to channel Randler's knowledge of dissonance and draw the healing away from the jade entirely.

He didn't know if it was possible, even if he had the other jades to assist him. But he needed this shard if there was any hope of saving Randler. He needed to win.

Dariak dropped to his hands and knees, digging his fingers into the moist soil. Pyron gasped across the way and Dariak wondered if the old man thought he had collapsed in defeat.

If he had, he reconsidered quickly, as chanting filled the air. *"Rethritos brienan torrifors nieh, k'tanaos loprilor brenitan errvitros!"*

Dariak felt a second stone column rise around him, pressing inward on all sides to confine him. Previously, Pyron had encased the column with a force field before shattering the stone, but this time was different. Connected now to the healing jade, Dariak felt its energy tugged toward Pyron for protection when the stone exploded.

Acting fast, Dariak cleared his mind of the battlefield and the cheering audience. He ignored the swelling energies of the stone column and he focused entirely upon the healing jade. There were no spells to use against the shard. All Dariak had was his experience with the other jades and his will to succeed.

His father's lifeblood had been absorbed into all the jades and Dariak focused on the beating of his own heart and the pulsing of the healing power across the field. It thundered under Pyron's pleas to swirl around him. The old man was a master but he did not work with the resonance of the jade. He treated its power like a subordinate and Dariak saw his chance to intervene.

Extending a tendril of his magic power through the soil, Dariak called to the healing jade and shared with it his need. He let his thoughts sway with the power of the jade, allowing himself to get swept into its embrace. The power swirled around Pyron, and Dariak felt himself carried along. Once, twice. Then he flipped himself upside down mentally and started a new wave of energy counter to that of the healing jade. His essence undulated in perfect contradiction to the healing the jade was trying to provide.

Pyron shouted, *"Barrenoshis frethnibar lorrenticus!"* The stone around Dariak's body shattered once more. The debris pelted into him, but this time it also erupted into the audience and into Pyron himself.

The old man's scream snapped Dariak's essence back to his body and he watched as Pyron ripped the healing jade from his pocket and implored it to heal him.

But though Dariak's thoughts had returned to his body, his weaving energy had surrounded the jade fully and the only healing that left the jade went through that connection and into Dariak. None of it escaped to heal Pyron.

Dariak crawled across the field, keeping his body in contact with the soil and, by proxy, with the conduit he had established with the healing jade.

Panic welled on Pyron's face and he sputtered a few random spells, but each one pelted Dariak to no effect.

The slithering mage locked his eyes on the old master, drawing closer and selecting among his weaker spells. He flung a pebble with one of his forward crawls and empowered it to rocket through the short distance between them.

Pyron was blasted off his feet. He landed hard on the wet ground and though he loudly implored the healing jade to assist him, he realized that he held no providence over it any longer.

Bleeding and bruised, Pyron held the jade outward and, with a trembling lip, spat, "I yield."

C HAPTER 51

Exodus

K ITALLA MADE HER way through the tower for what she hoped would be the last time. There wasn't much of a chance to prepare for the coming journey, but she needed to gather a few key items.

Her first stop was the library, where she returned to the section dealing with the Forgotten Tribe. The elegantly drawn illustration books by Lady Cathrateir were simply too big for her to secret away. There also wasn't time for her to sit and try to absorb all the information.

Instead she pulled down the last book and flipped through the various tales the bard Mhunforia had shared with the imaginative queen. Certain images reminded her of tales Randler had sung along their journey, but she found one that looked unique. She dropped herself to the floor and flipped through it.

The diagrams were vastly different than the others she had seen, even in this same tome. The lines were harsh and direct and she had trouble discerning any people or events in what she saw. It was almost as if the Lady had had a fever and drew random visions instead of the tale, but Kitalla recognized a few brush strokes that appeared like a signature in the other paintings and she guessed that this tale was just different.

Having concluded as much, she flipped back to the beginning of the story and tried to make sense of it. The first image started with a deep blue field with gold and silver stars glittering brightly, all mingled together. The next image showed two falling stars, and Kitalla assumed they were Lady Hathreneir and King Kallisor.

The third drawing showed the fallen gold star glowing with eerie light, while the silver star looked sharp and pointed. Then the two clashed and the fourth image was a strange mess of colors. Kitalla had the sense of an explosion from the two coming together, with pieces raining down on either side, but only two of the streaks of rain were silver-gold. The true heirs.

From there, the images were made of skewed lines swaying across and around, looking more like balls of yarn, knotted and seen up close. She couldn't trace the patterns at all, try as she might. An orange line swept up beneath a green loop, but the orange did not emerge where it should have, instead appearing in the lower right part of the page. Kitalla turned the book around, wondering if it was inserted improperly, but it still made no sense.

The next three sets of drawings followed the same vein, though it seemed as if fewer and fewer threads were woven together. Then on the last page, Kitalla was taken aback because it was a deep blue field with a faint outline of the land, but it was hardly discernible. No lights lit the sky and no colors marked the edges. She feared what it portended.

She considered taking the book with her while she hid in the tower until Ervinor's departure, but even if she did, she realized that she wouldn't have time to go through it any more thoroughly. With a heavy sigh, she returned the book to its location upon the shelf and trolled around the tower looking for supplies.

It only took her an hour to gather the things she needed to camp out comfortably. She could have done the job in much less time, but she had no need to rush. The mages and Ervinor were busy trying to mend Randler and she had a while before they were expected to finish.

Kitalla made her way quietly up through the tower until she found a small chamber not too far from the empowerment room that hosted the giant diamond. While she sat there, she stocked her leather gear with the daggers she had procured, then she meditated. It wasn't something she did often, but if she planned to bring the tower to stillness again, she needed to be ready.

* * *

Lica and Quereth sat with Frast and Randler. The bard was asleep, his body mostly healed. He was weak, however, and the newly formed legs had no strength in them. He would have to build them up to a point where he could walk on them again. The mages examined the special crutches Astrith had supplied for Randler, awed at the magic they felt within them. They were made of vines and wood and were intuitively supple yet sturdy, as if the magic within them sensed the needs of the wearer and adjusted accordingly. They weren't strong enough to support Randler alone, but they would certainly facilitate his recovery.

"Shall we?" Quereth asked after they set the crutches aside.

Frast smiled warmly. "Thanks, you two. It means a lot." His voice was raw and quiet and they could barely understand him. No amount of healing made it any better. Each word was hard to force out and he winced when he spoke, sometimes coughing up blood when he tried. They understood him because they listened well and they also had known him for some time and anticipated his words.

"We do this just as much for him, you realize," Quereth retorted.

But Lica waved the older mage to silence. "Don't listen to him, Frast. We can see how important this is to you. But the mages assured us that he'll be able to heal on his own, so you needn't worry."

Frast shook his head. "I want him to be better."

The three mages linked hands with each other and created a circle with Randler, and then Quereth and Lica started chanting. Frast listened to the cadence, regretting that he couldn't join. His terrible screams during Randler's healing had shredded his vocal cords, but he didn't lament the loss of his voice; he had asked the beast jade to channel anything through him to spare Randler the same fate. He wondered if his own voice would ever recover, but since the healers hadn't been able to give him any relief, he wasn't hopeful.

Frast still had the beast jade in his pocket and it continued to supply Frast's wish. So as Quereth and Lica swept healing energies through the bard, all aches and pains were channeled into Frast and he moaned in reaction, sometimes wincing so hard he broke the healing circle.

After one such moment, Quereth lowered his hands and he looked at Frast with concern. "I don't know if I can continue to do this to you."

"Please."

"You're like a son to me, Frast. Seeing you take on his pain and knowing that I'm part of the reason for it… it's very difficult. I don't know that I can do this for much longer."

Lica looked at the gray-haired mage. "You've been saying that a lot lately."

"And yet I keep pressing on, yes. But forgive me if I don't have your youth, Lica."

She blushed, and it was something Frast had never seen before. Lica was a hard, middle-aged woman, whose children had shown magic skills at an early age and were executed. In grief she went on a rampage, but Quereth had found her and subdued her, introducing her to the Underground, where she could unleash some of her fury amongst her peers. Hardened, but anxious to do something useful, she had made her way to Pindington, trying to help the people where she could, keeping as much distance as possible from the Kallisorian king. Her sarcasm was sometimes deep and cutting, but it was her way of dealing with difficult situations. Frast had never seen her wilt under a compliment before. It was almost unnerving to think she could react to flattery.

Lica turned to Frast, oblivious to his musings. "One more round, then, Frast, but then that's it until we're on the road." They had enacted these healing circles nearly every hour since Randler's initial treatment, once the three of them had the strength for it, breaking the routine only to sleep. Their goal was to make the bard travel-ready by nightfall, but it didn't look promising.

"No, three more times," Frast gurgled painfully. "Right up until we leave. Please."

"You will have to do this without me, I'm afraid." Quereth stretched and stood up. "It seems I'm more exhausted than I thought. I'm sorry, Frast. I can't go another round right now."

The younger mage was dejected, but Lica remained and performed the spell until Frast's eyes rolled in his head and he looked ready to pass out. She then disengaged from him and kissed him on the forehead.

"He's a lucky man to have you watching over him, Frast. But I hope—"

"Don't," he begged.

She looked at him pityingly and then nodded. "I'll try to come back later for more, but I'm also wearing out from this and we've got a journey ahead of us tonight."

He tried not to appear sad and failed miserably. Lica patted him affectionately on the head and left the room, seeking Ervinor.

The young general was down in the common area trying to organize the refugees into a semblance of order. He urged the acting leaders of the people to do their best to keep the citizens in line until they reached their destination, and to spread the word that he would strive to protect them along the way, so long as they kept their squabbles to a minimum. He assigned Carrus and Verna as the key liaisons for the refugees and then left to tend to other business.

Lica caught up to him as he ascended the stairs. He saw the expression on her face. "What is it?"

She ignored the abruptness considering everything he had going on. "Too much, Ervinor. Randler insists he can be moved with us, and some of the mages are making a litter for him. Yet I think it's a bad decision to bring him along. He needs to be able to rest and heal, not be dragged across the desert where any number of feral creatures will attack."

"I already discussed this with the Council and they refuse to allow him to stay. They threatened to kill him if we leave him behind. Frast too."

"After all the work they did to restore his legs?"

He nodded. "Indeed. As Shelloni explained it, it isn't the result of the spell that mattered but the process of enacting it. They don't have a lot of reason for coming together to cast such spells, I guess."

Lica breathed an annoyed laugh. "We should give them lots of reasons. Maybe it would teach them to work as one set of mages instead of ten."

"I agree with you, except the part about us giving them the reasons." Ervinor grinned tiredly. "Could you imagine that? A group of rebels from Kallisor fix all the in-fighting within Magehaven of Hathreneir. Good for us!"

Lica chortled. "Not so crazy an idea, you know, considering what our real mission is."

"Good point. So, what's the other thing on your mind?"

"It's nothing," she lied, deciding not to burden him.

He didn't pursue and that told her much. "Are your Eagles ready to fly?" he asked instead.

"Every last one of them, including the fifteen new recruits." She sighed loudly, tinged with exasperation. "I have so many new names to learn. It's irritating."

Ervinor shot her a glance and then snorted. "Yes, you're terribly burdened, aren't you?" He smiled. "I guess I shouldn't ask you to take this meeting with Shelloni then?"

Her eyes went wide. "I would love to! Problem is we might end up with some dead mages instead of the jades back."

"Hmm." He pretended to consider. "That might be worth trying."

With a laugh, she clapped him on the back and went off to check in with her group. Ervinor continued through the tower, climbing more stairs until he reached the Council chamber. The mages were already assembled and stared at him with disdain as if he had kept them waiting for hours.

"We're nearly ready to be off," Ervinor announced without pretense. He was finished coaching his words around them. "I'll take the jades back now."

Shelloni stood up and walked over to him. "I think we'll just give you this one." She pressed a silvery crystal into his hand and Ervinor struggled not to cringe.

It was Kitalla's metal jade.

Shelloni grinned smugly as she spoke. "See, in the time we had to commune with the shards, we realized there was another one in the tower that we hadn't noticed before. Do you know where it was?"

"No," he replied honestly. Kitalla had hidden herself well for two days and he had made no attempts to locate her.

"Imagine," Shelloni continued, an edge coming to her voice now. "Up near the focus room. Just the jade. And hasn't your dear friend Kitalla gone missing? She is admittedly and frustratingly elusive. But we pieced it all together."

Ervinor withheld a frown and kept silent.

"It seems she can use this to send us to sleep, did you know that?" She then pointed upward in revelation. "Oh wait, of course you did. How else did you manage to knock out the mages but not yourselves? I'm surprised at her control over that jade. She isn't even a mage."

He lifted his left shoulder in a shrug. "You should bring her in here and ask her."

She smiled viciously. "Clever boy. I'm sure she's fine. But she won't have the chance to use that jade on us again. We blocked the upper floors and she won't be able to leave them. Meanwhile, a team of mages is hunting for her."

He sounded tired. "Then why give this to me if you don't want her to have it?"

"So you can take it out of this tower!" she yelled. "Then we will send her out after."

"Let me go to her."

"To make sure she's okay?" Shelloni mocked. "No. Pyron did that for Dariak and it cost us. I won't make the same mistake."

"You'll just make other mistakes that are even more costly," he said. "Give me the rest of the jades, Shelloni. It was our agreement."

"You were to leave this place by nightfall, not leave behind a sneak assassin who would knock us out when we are least suspecting, leaving the door wide open for you to storm back in and be rid of us all. We will not succumb to your subterfuge."

Ervinor shook his head and leaned to the side to peer at the other mages sitting behind Shelloni at the Council table. "Do you all hear this? What's with the conspiracies? Return the jades to me and we'll leave peacefully and at once."

"But you did not give us time with that jade," Shelloni stepped into Ervinor's view. "So let's trade that gem for the others."

The young general shook his head. "You had access to eight of the shards. Don't be greedy. Hand them over or we are not leaving."

"You have no leverage with us."

Ervinor looked around at the members of the Council, but only two seemed uncomfortable with these events. Ervinor shook his head slowly and focused back on Shelloni. "You said you don't want to make the same mistakes that Pyron made, yet here you are, refusing to hand over the jades though they were promised to me. It sounds like an echo of what was done to Dariak on his first arrival here, and you know how that turned out."

Shelloni's eyes opened wide with rage. "You dare threaten us."

"I—" But then he wasn't sure what he was going to say. Instead, it looked like Shelloni's head started to shrink to an impossible size. Her hands expanded but her torso collapsed. Everything about her became distorted.

"What is this?" the mage screamed. "Rothra!"

Yet he faced the same struggles, his vision warping and twisting about until nothing made any sense. "Help me! Everything's all… inside-out!"

"What madness is this?" Shelloni demanded, trying to grab Ervinor but failing. Her shifting, twisted body stumbled and collapsed.

Ervinor knew what was happening. Kitalla was trapped in the upper chambers and she was using her dance skill to influence them all, yet again. He knew she hadn't exaggerated about setting the mages all to sleep, but he was still amazed by it.

His own vision started to clear immediately and he saw the members of the Council writhing around, reaching and grabbing for things around them and missing or crashing painfully into them instead. But no one was actually mangled, Ervinor realized. They only seemed to be, to an alarming extreme.

There wasn't time to ponder things. He went around to the different mages until he reclaimed the entire set of jades, finding that the glass jade was missing. He debated tying the mages up and leaving them, but he knew that would only add to the problem, so he turned and ran from the room after ensuring the shards were tucked away tightly into his pockets.

Frantically taking the stairs, Ervinor crashed into Carrus who was coming up the other way. "Sir!"

"Carrus, find Lica or some other mage and get upstairs to the focus room. Kitalla is there now. You have to grab her and get her down here. Hurry!"

Carrus and Ervinor sprinted off in different directions, each taking care not to step on the fallen mages littered everywhere. Ervinor's fighters had also succumbed to the eye-twisting visions. He shook one of them and brought her out of the trance. "Waken the others!" He tried not to think about how Kitalla managed to remove the effects from himself and Carrus while keeping the others entranced. Instead, he scrambled to get his soldiers in line.

"It's a little earlier than expected, but we must move out immediately. Spread the word." The fighters abandoned what they were doing before the trance and returned to their battalions, grabbing their supplies and making their way for the lower levels.

The refugees on the first floor were difficult to herd but Verna managed to get them in line after punching out a few who refused to follow orders. They came to understand the severity of the situation and her Wrens all but pushed them out of the tower.

"Sparrows!" Ervinor called. "Find your captain on the second floor and assist with Randler. We leave now! Go!"

"Nightingales, with me!" Quereth shouted over the growing din. Clearly word had reached him and he swept in, taking charge of his battalion and nodding to a grateful Ervinor as he fled.

"Eagles and Ravens, evacuate at once. Assemble outside, beyond the mage barrier." Ervinor's voice rang out and the soldiers obeyed, scrambling to find comrades and escape.

Ervinor stood around, not sure where he should go. As general, he knew he should be out with the rest of the assembling army. But as friend, he was torn between supporting Frast and finding Kitalla with Lica and Carrus.

Frast's Sparrows took one option away as they assembled into a mobile litter and carried Randler gently down the stairs toward the exit. Frast groaned with every jostling step and soon they hoisted him up too and bore him out of the tower.

Ervinor decided that if powerful Carrus and talented Lica were unable to free Kitalla from the upper floors, then there would be little he could do to help, so he grudgingly turned and followed his soldiers outside.

What could have been mass hysteria with the premature departure was instead an organized march. Verna was at the lead with her group and the refugees. Quereth's team slowly circumvented them to take the northern quadrant, while the Ravens and Eagles fanned out to flank the refugees to keep them safe. The Sparrows were at the back of the pack, but they weren't in any sort of defensive posture, merely trying to keep Frast and Randler from further harm. It wasn't exactly as planned but it was so close that Ervinor just watched in awe for a moment, then had to remind himself to continue.

As they hurried away, he glanced back and thought he saw flashes of light at different parts of the tower, slowly working their way down to the bottom. Not long later, Carrus arrived with Kitalla slung over his shoulder and Lica wheezing fearfully behind him.

"Keep moving," Lica huffed when she caught up to Ervinor. "They're after us!"

C H A P T E R 52

Defensive Measures

"PRESS ONWARD!" ERVINOR shouted, looking over his shoulder and seeing dozens of mages emerging from Magehaven. "We can only stay out of range if we keep moving!"

Ervinor's army had swelled to nearly five hundred, though only roughly two-thirds of them were committed to him and his cause. The rest were refugees being escorted away from the mages. Nighttime descended as they dashed from the tower hours ahead of schedule.

They needed to reach a safe haven. Ervinor could think of no other place for them than the castle. It was a hard decision for him to make, but it was in the best interest of the people, and his mission all along was to help others.

If only the mages had been trustworthy. It was infuriating dealing with them and his patience had worn thin. He could see glittering lights as the mages marched behind his army and he had no idea how he would respond when they caught up.

And he knew they would reach them. His own fighters could push on for a while, but the refugees would set the pace on this march. The citizens were already unhappy about their departure from the tower; they had little reason to push themselves for Ervinor's safety.

Groaning in frustration, Ervinor jogged ahead, finding Carrus plodding along with the Ravens, still carrying Kitalla. "What happened?"

Carrus breathed heavily. "She was dancing in front of some large crystal. She didn't seem to hear us when we got there. I grabbed her and we left. She's been out since."

"Don't wear yourself out, Carrus. I need you. Get some others to transport her." The man nodded and Ervinor jogged off again.

Cries of pain echoed through the air, mingled with wails of sorrow. Ervinor made his way over to Frast, his body jostled about on the shoulders of five men. "Frast, what can we do?"

He could not answer. Randler was nearby, carried in similar fashion, but the bard made no sound. His face winced, however, and Ervinor realized that he was hurting as well, but Frast verbalized the pain for both of them.

"Frast, this has to stop!" But the mage was incoherent and merely sobbed and moaned some more.

Then all at once the men and women came to a halt and the darkening sky flickered with brilliant blasts of colored light. "They can't have reached us so soon," Ervinor muttered, looking for spellfire racing through the air to trace back to its source, but he didn't see any. Instead, the flashes originated in the north, and were not being launched overhead. Racing to the front he saw the reason why.

Quereth and the Nightingales were engaged in combat, while locking the refugees behind them to keep the feral creatures away. An errant fireball lit the sky, revealing a host of shadowcrows. Lightning flared out next, catching a pair of the creatures and ending their flights, but many more remained.

Ervinor surveyed the ground and he saw movement along the horizon. "Sandorpions too?"

"At night?" one of the refugees called, terrified. "They're day creatures. What are they doing out at night?"

Carrus arrived with a few of his soldiers, swords in hand. "Where do you need us?"

Ervinor smiled inwardly but kept a stern expression on his face. "Let the mages deal primarily with the fliers. Fill the gaps and support where necessary. I need to find Lica."

The Eagles were in position at the eastern edge of the army, and Ervinor appreciated that everyone had kept to the plans despite the rushed exodus. Lica was winded after fleeing the tower with Carrus and Kitalla, but an angry fire lit her eyes. Ervinor ran to her. "Lica, I need you."

"Can't go now, sir," she retorted, pointing to her side. "Rodia and eaglons are heading in and we need to prepare."

"We can't fight them. Get someone to manage the defenses but come with me. Now."

She hesitated for a moment but saw the determination in his eyes. She gave orders to Throssha and then followed the general. He led her back to the source of the cries and moans. Once she saw where he pointed, she understood what needed to be done.

"There isn't time to waste. You know the mages are coming up from the south. I have to lead them in defense. Can you take care of this?"

"Go."

And he did. On his way, he swung by to see Verna, instructing her to hold the western line and to let her mages have free rein over slaying any beasts that came too close, but to keep near the army. "No one is to run off from the main force." She saluted and Ervinor left her to her duty, walking to the host of Sparrows, who otherwise would have been under Frast's command. "The mages come from the south," he told them. "They're angry and will most likely try to kill any of us they can. The rest of the forces are busy with feral creatures coming from every direction. It's up to us to keep these mages at bay."

The Sparrows prepared themselves, dropping their provisions and withdrawing their weapons or spell components. Defensive spells were set up where possible and Ervinor stepped before them all, facing the pursuing mages from the south. Ervinor touched one of his pockets, feeling two pieces of jade tucked safely inside. He wanted to verify that he had them all but didn't want to make it look to the others as if he was searching for something or nervous, so he trusted that the other shards were with him. They couldn't help him, he knew, for he had no way to call on their powers. He simply wanted to know they were with him.

He reached up over his head and pulled the sword from its scabbard. One of the Sparrows, Lorreq, approached and used her nature-based healing skills to add a second layer of protection over the antimagic armor Herchig and his wife had crafted for him.

"You thief!" screamed a raging voice across the field.

"It's unwise to criticize yourself in front of others, Shelloni!" Ervinor said.

The woman swung her hands in the air and freezing water rained down upon them. Ervinor's mages fought back with bursts of heat. While it didn't stop the water, at least it didn't bite as badly.

Three mages caught up to Shelloni and they worked in tandem to augment her spell. Rain and thick chunks of hail pattered down. The fighters who had shields raised them overhead to block the pelting bits of ice, but it exposed their bellies to a barrage of poison-tipped thorns.

Ervinor held back, dodging where he could, and removing the barbs where they struck. The mage casting them was too far away and the thorns were only dangerous on exposed skin, for they lacked the momentum to penetrate even basic armor. He didn't want to kill any of the mages if he didn't have to, but as the rage on Shelloni's face was illuminated by a bolt of lightning, Ervinor knew that someone in this fight would have to fall. As he realized this, other mages caught up to Shelloni and started unleashing their own spells.

"Charge!" Ervinor shouted, leaning forward and sprinting headlong to clear the distance between himself and Shelloni. She seemed surprised by the move, for she stopped casting whatever spell she was crafting and rummaged frantically through her pockets. Moments later, the wet sand turned into a giant sheet of ice and Ervinor's feet flew out from underneath him and he slid precariously forward with several of his fighters.

The sky was almost completely dark now, except for the flashes of spellfire. Ervinor pushed himself upward, using his sword for leverage, and strained to see where Shelloni was. He need not have worried, for the angry mage was solely targeting him for her spells. She strafed him with a flurry of ice darts, then wound her hands around to explode the ice into cutting debris that bit into his skin.

Ervinor blocked out the pain as best he could, bringing his sword to bear while struggling to remain upright on the ice. Two long water snakes reached out from the mage's hands and whipped back and forth, striking him and biting into his flesh, numbing him with frigid fangs. Shelloni laughed maniacally as she swept her whips around again and again, crashing them into the young general one blow after the next.

There was nothing he could do to fight them off. His sword was useless and the defensive spell that Lorreq placed on him had already been consumed as it tried to heal the minor cuts from the ice darts. His antimagic armor kept the snake bites from hurting much, but when the cold whips struck his face, he cried out in agony.

He reached into his pocket, fumbling for one of the jades for help. He didn't know how to summon its power, but he needed help and he was too weak to keep getting up on his feet and pressing forward. The fire jade came to his hand and he blocked out Shelloni, begging for help. The orange jade lit with a tiny glow, but nothing stronger than usual. He clutched the shard to his chest, hoping it would hear the terror in his heart and protect him, but there was no response. Instead, the sharp edge of the jade cut off one of the loops that Herchig had sewn into the tunic.

The water snakes paused their attack only long enough for Shelloni to reenact the spell. She enjoyed watching the young man writhing on the icy ground with no help coming to him, while his troops were busy dealing with the rest of the mages. Ervinor used the brief respite to shove the jade back into its pocket and reach for the poison darts in the tunic. He threw a fistful of them at Shelloni and they struck her protective barrier and broke it down, but the darts did not strike her directly. She laughed at the failed attempt.

Ervinor couldn't glance around or call for help, for the icy whips flogged him again. He grabbed his sword and flung it toward the mage, but she lashed out with one of the snakes and deflected it safely away. Each strike hit harder and Ervinor understood that the magic armor was losing its strength. Soon it wouldn't be able to channel away the magic attacks and he would succumb to the brutal beating.

Only one thought remained to him then. The jade had cut one of the loops and the thick cord that ran along the seams of the tunic was loose. He grabbed for it and tugged with all his might. The cord snapped upward from one loop to another, shredding the tunic in pieces and exposing his body to attack. But with a flourish of his arm, the whip that Herchig had hidden along the seams came free.

Shelloni was confused by Ervinor's decision to disrobe in front of her, but she delighted in the loss of his armor, taking a few steps forward to strike him even harder. His skin glistened with blood after each bite of her water snakes.

Ervinor clung to his desire to live, raising his whip in his hand and snapping it toward the mage. The green rope flashed out and cracked against Shelloni's ankles. The whip did more than startle her, however. Immediately, her own icy snakes vanished and she cried out in dismay, scrambling immediately to bring forth yet another set. Ervinor pulled his whip back and struck again. This time it wrapped around her calves, and Ervinor rolled onto his side to tug the cord, bringing the woman down.

Shelloni screamed as she fell, grabbing for spell components and bellowing magic into the night sky. However, her spells didn't work. Ervinor's whip was stuck on her legs, so he flipped onto his knees and crawled closer, keeping a tight grip on the emerald cord as he went. Shelloni saw his approach and tried to scramble away, but Ervinor tugged the whip and kept her from rising.

He reached her at last and he saw the terror in her eyes. "Don't kill me," she begged. "Don't kill me!"

"Why shouldn't I?" he asked rhetorically, curling his hand into a fist, still clutching his corded whip. Furiously, he punched her in the face, breaking her nose and knocking her out cold. Ervinor disentangled his whip and stood up, lashing the cord outward to the mages on either side of him, each of whom was engaged in battles with the Sparrows. As with Shelloni, Ervinor's whip stole away their magic, leaving them defenseless.

The half-naked general staggered in the darkness to strike at the other attacking mages, ending their spellcasting and bringing about their defeat. The few mages still upright saw the turn of events and either threw their hands up in surrender or ran back for the tower.

"Take your comrades with you and go home," Ervinor demanded, his body bleeding. He felt he would swoon but he held his ground until the mages did as ordered. They dragged Shelloni away by her shoulders and Ervinor found it morbidly amusing that she would undoubtedly burn with a rash on her backside.

Lorreq survived the onslaught and made her way over to Ervinor, using what spells she could to heal his wounds. "These need a lot of tending, sir."

"I need the rest of my tunic, Lorreq. Where is it?"

She was perplexed by his concern for the shredded shirt, but she followed behind him, keeping the healing energies flowing.

Ervinor lifted the three main flaps of fabric that had been his tunic. The cord should not have torn the tunic apart, but he had pulled so hard on it that the loops caught and ripped the seams instead. It didn't matter, he told himself solemnly. He would repair it somehow.

Glancing around, he could see that his team had defended themselves well, but that three had died. The fighters tended to the injured and the dead and he did not interrupt them.

The rest of the army was still busy and Ervinor wanted nothing to do with them at the moment. Despite the healing Lorreq was sending him, he was battered and exhausted. However, he knew he wouldn't be able to rest until the creature situation was under control as well. "Can you please keep doing that and come with me?" he asked Lorreq as she swept her hands through the air and sent healing into him.

Ervinor did not consult with the captains whose teams fended off the attacks. Instead he headed for Lica, whose task was far more important. The woman was drenched in sweat, her lips trembling from repeated spells she cast into Frast. He was clearly fighting against her intrusion and she did everything she could to convince him to stop.

"Lica, step back," Ervinor said sadly. "I hate to do this, Frast, but there is no other way." He handed the pieces of tunic to Lorreq, keeping only the green whip in hand. With help, he wrapped the cord around Frast's waist. It took only seconds for the spell linking Frast to Randler to be canceled. At once, the bard cried out in pain.

Frast gasped. "No! No! Don't let him suffer! No!"

Ervinor reached deep into Frast's pocket and pulled out the beast jade, which pulsed hotly. "Lica, do something," he pleaded, handing it over.

While she closed her eyes to commune with the jade, Ervinor removed the antimagic cord from Frast's body then retrieved the pieces of his tunic and set them on top of Frast. The mage was terrorized at being disconnected from Randler and he wept for the damage that would come to Randler's voice if the bard kept screaming as he was now doing.

"Frast, listen to me," Ervinor said. "The beast jade is drawing the creatures in to us. We need it to send them away. Here, these are the other jades. Which one will help you?"

Frast fumbled around with the tunic, reaching into the various pockets and trying to discern the jades from their textures. "The shadow jade; give it to Randler," he managed to say. He then withdrew the air jade and sliced his finger on it, making an instant connection to the shard. He called to it, imploring the jade to obey him in his time of need. As with the beast jade, which channeled the feral screams from Randler through him, now the air jade channeled direct sound. Soon, Randler's cries lessened and Frast's began anew.

"I hate to hear you suffer, friend, but I know why you do it," Ervinor said. He took the rest of the jades and turned to Lica, who was now casting a series of complicated spells.

Soon the chaos around him came to a sharp stillness. Ervinor bade Lica to keep charge of the beast jade for now so that they would remain unharmed by the feral creatures. He hadn't counted on using the jades along the way, but that was typical among non-mages. He had planned the nighttime journey because there were fewer threats than during the day, but if Lica could maintain a protective shield around the camp and therefore keep the creatures at bay, then it made no sense to him to push through the darkness.

"Set up camp!" he called. Lorreq remained with him until she ran out of strength and needed to retire. He thanked her for the help and then sought out Carrus and the Ravens. His tent was already erected, for which he was grateful. He asked for a few supplies from one of the soldiers, crawled into this tent, and dropped to the dirt, setting the tunic pieces on the ground. Tired as he was, he had one more thing he needed to do before he could sleep.

Taking needle and thread, he set about repairing Herchig's tunic.

CHAPTER 53

Error in Judgment

THE FIRST NIGHT in the outpost with the mingled Hathren and Kallisorian troops was partly a disaster. Though the initial meet-and-greet had seemed successful, once the people went to sleep, the hardest grudges surfaced. Gabrion was rousted out of the bed by a pair of officials, whose panic was obvious.

"Murder!" cried Ruhk's man, Ventch. "You have to come, sir."

Gabrion threw on a tunic and followed Ventch and Lucson down the steps and through to the sleeping quarters where Ruhk and his guards held three men against the wall. To the side, four fighters were slain, two of whom were naked. "What is this?"

Ruhk turned away from his soldiers. "Gabrion, I don't know where to begin. These men murdered your fighters in their sleep. I would kill them myself but I believe you should have the right to administer their judgment."

The warrior stared at the four corpses for a while longer, trying to recognize them despite the mutilations. Three of them were among his more recent trainees. Easy victims. The fourth was one of their own. Stone-faced, Gabrion turned to the three murderers. "Speak."

"About what?" one of the spat.

"Who are you and why have you done this?"

"You're all Kallisorian scum!" shouted the blond soldier. "Even this… traitor." He spat at Ruhk.

The Hathren commander pressed forward and leaned his arm into the man's throat, stopping only because Gabrion intervened. "Don't kill him."

"You would let these men go free, Gabrion?" Ruhk asked. "Are you that idealistic? That foolish?"

"I will abide by the rules I set here for this experiment." He then eyed the three soldiers and pierced them with his gaze. They each winced with the anger they saw. "My name is Gabrion and I am from the town of Savvron. You have killed three of my warriors. I would know who you are."

"Three?" Ruhk interrupted. "Four are dead."

Gabrion nodded. "Yes. One is your man, Frethe."

In his fury, the commander hadn't noticed the identity of the naked man. He pressed his arm into the blond man's throat. "Explain!"

The prisoner coughed and then responded. "He went off with them last night. Sympathizer. Traitor. He deserved it."

Gabrion thought Ruhk was about to snap, so he interjected, "Your names. Now."

Ruhk coerced the blond soldier to speak first. "Hrall of Marritosh."

The brown-haired man to his left whimpered, "Ornicus of Jorgens."

The smallest of the three pouted and met Gabrion's eyes. "Peth."

"From where to do you hail, Peth?" Gabrion demanded.

"I was born in Warringer."

Gabrion's eyes lit wide. "That's—You're Kallisorian!" Ruhk was just as shocked as Gabrion.

"I am," he answered, raising his chin defiantly.

"Why would you do this?"

"You think I care anything for you weak Kallisorian scum?" He spat on the floor. "No, my mother got drunk in a tavern, then she bore me, and sold me off for money. I was bounced around as a slave all my childhood until I made my escape to Hathreneir. They took me in and I vowed revenge on you cowards."

Ruhk shook his head. "I had no idea, you little liar, passing yourself off as one of us." He spoke over his shoulder, "I will defer to your judgment since we are your guests."

Gabrion responded by turning to Ventch and Lucson. "Officials," he summoned, "I call for a duel, first thing come daylight."

"You're insane," Ruhk hissed.

Gabrion ignored him. "Unlike the other duels in this place, it will be a fight to the death." He turned to the prisoners. "Do you accept, or should we carry out your judgment here and now? Your commander looks anxious to be your executioner."

The three men agreed to duel, deciding that the chance to fight back was better than cold execution. They were brought down to the dungeon and held in a cell next to Gerta and her team, whom Ruhk had imprisoned the day before.

Silently, Gabrion stormed off and sought out Ordren to update him on the events of the morning. The outpost commander was furious that he was not included in the discussion with the prisoners and he cautioned Gabrion that he would not tolerate such insolence for much longer. Gabrion didn't care how angry Ordren was. He knew that bringing the two factions together would not be easy, despite how he tried to carry himself. His greater surprise was that only four people had died through the night, but he hoped for that to be the last insidious act within these walls. He explained as much to Ordren, but the older man was unconvinced.

A few hours later, Gabrion walked to the outer training yard, with nearly the entire contingent of fighters gathered to witness the event. Most of the fighters were disgusted by the murder that had taken place, though some lamented that they hadn't been part of the killings themselves. Gabrion ignored the taunts from both sides and stood before Ordren at the far end of the area. The three prisoners were held at the wall.

Gabrion turned to the audience. "A heinous crime was committed last night within these walls. Four fighters were murdered in their sleep, three Kallisorian and one Hathren." The gathering gasped, having thought all the victims were from Kallisor. Gabrion announced their names, "Prendis of Gerrish, Friya and Shenna of Pindington, and Frethe of Rossbur. The Kallisorians were not committed soldiers in the king's war, but farmers and millers taken from their homes because the king had need. Their first fights took place here, just days ago as part of training. They had never killed a man. Yet they died, defenseless, in their sleep because of these three cowards who would not face them in a proper duel. The Hathren died for befriending one of my fighters. In terms of war, these three men butchered babies last night."

The crowd roared in an awful cacophony. The Hathrens felt the description was harsh, but the Kallisorians raged against them.

"Hold!" Gabrion shouted, and it was testament to the respect his men felt for him that they quieted down quickly. Ruhk's men followed suit soon after.

Gabrion scanned the gathering. "I decreed when you arrived that no violence was to occur within these walls except in an official duel. Though four innocent soldiers lay dead this morning, I will adhere to my own rules. These three were not summarily punished for the crime which they openly admit. Instead, I challenged them to a duel this morning." Everyone knew that part already, hence their attendance, but Gabrion was enforcing an official tone.

"However, because of the circumstances surrounding these events, I have made two alterations to the rules for this bout—and this bout only—unless any more of you are foolish enough to cast aside your humanity within these walls." At this, the crowd fell eerily silent, wondering if perhaps the prisoners would not be allowed weapons, or maybe they would be blindfolded and Gabrion would cut them down piece by piece, or worse.

"I don't wish any more people to die. Yet I can't let the murders of innocent men and women go unpunished. Therefore, this will be a fight to the death." The people were surprised, but not completely, considering the circumstances. Then Gabrion announced the other alteration and there was a universal gasp of shock through the crowd, following by whispered murmurings. "If I face any of these men single-handedly, it would be an unfair bout. Therefore, I will fight them all at once."

Ordren gasped. "What! Gabrion, this is madness. No, I won't allow it."

Gabrion turned around and responded quietly so no one else would hear. "Don't interfere, Ordren. After all, if I succeed, then such crimes should end here. If I fail, then you don't have to deal with my nonsense any longer and you can stop placating me. You won't have to pretend you believe in me anymore."

The three prisoners looked almost cheerful at the announcement and they immediately started whispering battle strategies to one another. Gabrion ignored them.

"I will ask Commanders Ordren and Ruhk to officiate this battle. No one from the crowd may interfere, not on my behalf, and not on theirs." He then turned and bowed his head to Ruhk and Ordren and stepped to the side to select a sword for himself. The prisoners were brought to another weapon rack to choose as well.

Ordren hesitated in bewilderment over Gabrion's plan so Ruhk spoke first. "I present the challenger in this duel: Gabrion of Savvron, defender of the murdered soldiers." The Kallisorian troops cheered in response, as did many Hathrens, Gabrion noticed. Apparently, they were as horrified by the act as everyone else.

Ruhk waited for the crowd to quiet down before announcing the challengers. "Defending their cowardly lives," he spat, his contempt palpable, "are Hrall of Marritosh, Ornicus of Jorgens, and Peth of Warringer." The last announcement was met with shock once again. The Hathrens were stunned that a Kallisorian had been in their midst for years, though some denied the possibility outright as a ruse. The Kallisorians were aghast that any man from their land could be battling against them so coldly. The fighters looked around the gathering, wondering if anyone else was hiding such a secret.

At last, Ruhk initiated the bout with the blast on his horn and all eyes turned to the combatants. Gabrion stood tall and strong, eying the three prisoners, whose hunger for freedom made them look dangerous.

Blond Hrall was the hothead of the group and he leaped in first with a double-handed blow, twisting his body while cutting down and across, determined to rip open Gabrion's chest on the first strike. The nimble warrior hopped backward to avoid the attack and then swung his own sword into the man's exposed back, splattering him immediately to the ground.

Ornicus and Peth coordinated better than that, coming in together and separating so Gabrion would be flanked. Ornicus thrust high and immediately swept low, getting Gabrion to focus on him while smaller Peth dipped in and cut from the side. Gabrion pivoted and missed both sets of attacks, but the two men pressed in again rapidly. Ornicus brought his sword around, keeping his buckler up and blocking a strike, while Peth spun, aiming to get Gabrion from behind.

The warrior jumped into the air, right over Peth's low swing, taking a small cut on his arm from Ornicus. Gabrion responded by dragging his sword downward and crashing it into Peth's weapon, creating a terrible jarring sensation for the little man, almost causing him to drop the blade. Gabrion stepped into the swing and back-turned to his left, sharply cutting his sword across and biting into Ornicus' buckler, cracking it in half. The man staggered back and threw the damaged shield away, bringing both hands to his blade and stepping in with renewed vigor.

Peth shook his hand to free himself of the jarring sensation, but by the time he had his sword ready, Gabrion was on him full force. The tall warrior cut downward, then across to the left, up again, down to the right, and each time the scrapper parried the attacks, but the jarring grew worse and worse and Peth backed up with each crash of Gabrion's mighty sword until he stumbled and fell on his backside.

Before Gabrion could finish him, he sensed someone nearby, so he pivoted and brought his sword sharply about. Hrall had recovered from his first misstep and now blocked Gabrion's attack, swinging as wildly as Gabrion had against Peth. But Gabrion was ready for it. He set his back leg into the dirt and matched each swing, whether high or low, deep or wide, and Hrall's face turned from a mask of rage to one of panic. He started to give ground, backing away, his offensive strikes becoming defensive as Gabrion roared and took control.

Ornicus ran in to distract Gabrion from the right, but the warrior made wider cuts with the blade, blocking the brown-haired fighter while still pressing Hrall back. Peth, meanwhile, stood again, grabbed his sword, and charged.

Gabrion waited for it, having baited the small man. As he heard the footsteps rushing up behind him, he parried twice more and then Hrall stepped in with another deep swing of his sword, while Peth rushed in from behind, and Ornicus cut down and across. All three swords reached for Gabrion from different heights, and the warrior collapsed intentionally.

Gabrion swiped his blade in a giant circle across the dirt. Hrall's powerful sword caught Peth in the skull, killing him instantly, while the little man's own attack dug into Hrall's side. Ornicus tried to pull his blade, but he had put too much force behind it, and as Hrall staggered forward, both from the attack Gabrion made on his ankles and the side wound inflicted by Peth, Ornicus' sword kept falling and it hacked viciously into Hrall's back.

Gabrion rolled to his left to avoid the bodies falling on top of him. He pounced onto his feet and turned to defend himself, but there was no need. Hrall and Peth lay dead on the field and Ornicus was on his knees, retching after killing his friend. Gabrion walked over to the remaining prisoner, standing tall and essentially unharmed.

The brown-haired man looked up at Gabrion, tears streaming from his eyes. "What have I done?" he asked, turning and staring at his sword sticking out of Hrall's back. "What have I done?"

Turning away, Gabrion called to Ruhk. "This duel is over. Take him to the dungeon for now."

Ordren walked over to Gabrion. "But what of retribution for his crime? You can't mean to let him live."

"I can, Ordren. Look at him. He killed someone he cared deeply for. He'll never get over that. It's a worse punishment than death." He met the man's eyes with intense clarity. "I would know."

He handed his sword to Ordren and stepped away from the dueling area. The crowd cleared a wide path for him. At first, he intended to walk away, to return to his room and while away the day and debate the merits of this experiment. But he looked at the faces of the men and women on either side of the field. Their expressions were a wild mix of emotions and he realized that he could not desert them now.

"If you wish to die, then line up and I will slay you. Or," he corrected, gesturing back to the two corpses, "I may cause you to kill each other instead. But know this, every one of you: I cherish your life and I will not take it lightly. Yet if you take the life of another human being while you're under my watch, then your life will be the payment. I don't care if you're Kallisorian or Hathren. Let your actions determine who you are now. If you need to battle, summon the officials and establish a duel.

"For the rest of you, who wish to give life a chance, I urge you to meet at the northern gate in two hours' time. Don't come if you can't set aside your hatred, your loathing, and your discrimination. Don't come if you are small-minded and stupid. This world has no use for you if you can't open your hearts and your eyes. If you think I am wrong, then challenge me and I will teach you properly.

"I would rather we remain civilized here and take a few days to learn about each other, as I've already said. But if your prejudice is too strong and you can't abide a sense of honor and civility, then band together and hide in your quarters and don't surface until I open the gates. I have no use for such as you.

"To all the rest, who feel as I do that the crime committed last night was unforgiveable and disgusting, who wish to open yourselves up to even the possibility of a better tomorrow, then I say again, meet me in two hours at the northern gate."

As he left the area, he heard whispers among the otherwise silent crowd and he pretended not to.

"He didn't even strike a fatal blow to any of them, but he clearly could have at any time. He really believes in this doesn't he?"

"He may have let Ornicus live, but did you hear him? He's heading to the dungeon. Probably kill him in his sleep just to be fair."

"I guess some Kallisorians can really fight. Did you see the way he moved about? Maybe we should go, you know, find out more."

"That man is trying to change the world and I'm not sure if I can handle that or if I like it. But I'm curious. I never thought we could get along with each other. Is it even possible?"

"Hey, Nersha, let's go talk to the Hathrens over there. That's what Gabrion wants, right?"

Return to the Forest

THE MAGITORIUM BUZZED with excitement. Mages recapped the battle between Pyron and Dariak with new and wild embellishments that beckoned for even more fanciful tales. Though Dariak had never actually sprouted wings and taken to the sky, Pyron bowed his head low as if he had. The old man was aghast that Dariak had defeated him and he spent the next couple of days keeping quiet and trying to figure out where he had erred.

Dariak, on the other hand, was exhausted and spent a good portion of the time simply eating and resting, walking around for some circulation but little else. The mages who approached him left with unanswered questions, as Dariak was not in the mood to talk. He kept the healing jade with him at all times, tucked into an inner pocket in case someone struck up an impromptu challenge.

Some of the fears of the mages were realized as more calls for duels were made. Many would-be challengers had been injured during the actual battle, and they regaled their friends with tales of the power they felt from the various explosions, wondering if the duel itself was the cause of the augmented energies, or if it was just the two mages who had taken the field. Xervius did his best to assert to the rest that the duels were forbidden within the walls and undesired outside of them. Considering his vast dealings with the magical forces, his word was enough to quell any actual fighting.

When he finally had the strength, Dariak made his way up the tower to visit with Pyron. They had crossed paths a few times since the bout, but had yet to speak. The old man was not pleased to see him, preferring to let Dariak quietly vanish from existence instead. Yet Dariak pushed his way in and Pyron surrendered to him, again.

"You're sulking," Dariak accused, trying for a jovial tone. "It doesn't suit you."

"If you came here to bother me, you have already achieved that goal and you may leave."

The seriousness cut through him, so Dariak opted for a more direct approach. "I don't understand you, Pyron. When I was growing up, you looked like a man who could do no wrong. You trained me, you guided me, but now you're... lost."

Pyron stared, wearing an expression that told Dariak to finish and vacate.

Dariak held his gaze for a few seconds before shaking his head and turning away. "Fine, then. Stay and wallow here. It's such a waste."

"How did you do it?" Pyron asked as Dariak moved for the door. "How could you possibly strip me of the jade's power?"

"I am connected to them all, Pyron. As I always said, the jades are rightly mine."

"Bah! Nonsense. That doesn't explain why it would stop working for me while I clutched it in my very hands."

Dariak shrugged. "There are positive uses for energy and negative. It's something I learned from Randler on the journey. So when I reached the healing jade and brought its power unto me, I also sent back an inverse version of it to prevent it from working for you. Dissonance," he explained, then a thought occurred to him. "I've experienced it before, actually. Elgris, in Kaison, used a major sort of anti-healing spell against me. You could sort of say that that's what I sent back to you, but with the healing jade in your hand, as you said, that anti-energy wouldn't be able to kill you."

"Anti-energy," Pyron marveled. "I don't know if you're mad or inspired."

"It's the same as drawing heat out of water to make it freeze. It's opposite to the use of adding heat, isn't it?"

Pyron frowned. "It has never been discussed that way. It was always just moving the heat from the water to the air. It was never described as generating an anti-fire spell." He swallowed hard. "You… did something similar when you violated the Trials to save your friend, didn't you?"

"Violated," Dariak echoed sourly. "I don't know why I came up here to talk to you."

"To gloat, of course."

Dariak firmed his jaw and stared at the old mage. "I thought maybe you would see to reason, to understand that I was meant to have these jades. I thought maybe you would get your head out of the sand and look at the world around you, to see that change is coming. I thought perhaps you could be part of that change. But instead, you're just an insecure, poor old man, cowering behind lies and fear. It's no wonder your tower is falling to a civil war and no wonder you ran away. It was convenient having me and this jade as an excuse, but that's all we were, an excuse. You would have run off anyway."

"I'm finished with you," Pyron snarled, reaching for his door to slam it shut.

"I agree with you on that," Dariak said softly. "Be well, Pyron. May we never cross paths again." With that, Dariak strode away from the chamber and took to the stairs, his head reeling and his heart pumping. He truly had thought in some way that he could have reached his old mentor, but too much damage had been done. Apparently, there were some things that even the jade couldn't heal.

He wandered around the Magitorium for a while, searching his thoughts for any supplies he would need before venturing back to Randler in the forest. Along the way, he was stopped by various mages who wanted to learn more about the spells he had used and whether or not he had poisoned or otherwise sabotaged Pyron to win. Dariak shoved his way past them, seeking his one other ally in this whole place.

Yet Xervius would not speak with him. The wretched mage was still recovering after being blasted by Pyron's final stone spell and he refused to allow Dariak to use the healing jade on him. His aides met Dariak outside and ushered him along, saying the old man would meditate for the next days or weeks and that he could return then.

Dejected, the son of Delminor decided that it was time to leave the Magitorium. He was weary and could have used another couple days' worth of rest, but Randler was in much greater need and he had already tarried for too long. With a sigh, he returned to his borrowed chamber and gathered his things, ready to depart at once.

"Oh good, you're here!" greeted a familiar voice. Dariak walked into his room and saw Nastren lounging on a chair. "Surely you've got time for some company now."

Dariak grumbled and shook his head. "I appreciate the attention, but I was about to get out of here. If you'll excuse me."

The mage pouted. "But I wanted to hear all about it, from your side. You did the impossible, Dariak. You should revel a little."

Dariak smiled politely. "Thank you for offering your ear, but I don't really need to discuss the duel."

"Oh. Well perhaps I could tag along a while—"

"No, thank you," Dariak interjected kindly. "I wouldn't be able to give you the attention you deserve."

"Well…" Nastren hedged. "I guess not."

Dariak walked over and wrapped his arms around Nastren. "Thank you," he whispered in the man's ear. "I appreciate you offering to be a friend, but I have others to get back to, imminently."

He smiled. "Oh, before you go," he called out suddenly. Nastren leaped off the chair and scooted from the room, returning moments later with a small haversack. "Take this with you."

"What's in here?" he asked, opening it to inspect the contents.

"Something I've been working on for a while. Healing potions. Nature and healing fused together into a leaf of honeywort, steeped in hot aloe juice, and scented with cinnamon to be a little more palpable."

Dariak raised his eyebrow. "Does it really work?"

Nastren shrugged carelessly. "It's like the weapons and things, you know. It works, a little. Just a little, but it's the first batch that hasn't evaporated after a day. I know you've got the healing jade now to keep you safe, but I thought it could help maybe."

"Thank you," he decided not to argue, setting the satchel with his things.

Nastren understood that his welcome had expired. He gripped Dariak's shoulders and held him steadily. "Safe travels, Dariak. I hope we meet again. Soon."

After the young man's departure, Dariak grabbed some food and wound his way out of the Magitorium, grateful to leave its wild interior—and the doorman's reported warblebees—and enter the fresh clear air of the cool winter day.

He knew he needed to commune with the jade to target the rest of the shards for the fastest path back to Randler, but he needed to put some distance between himself and the tower first. Too many mages were eager to learn about his spells, and he suspected they might follow him outside if he lingered for too long.

After about two hours, he finally settled himself down on the chilly grass and withdrew the healing jade. It pulsed with a misty white color and its surface felt enticingly soft. Placing it in his hand, he let his mind wander, feeling the energies within. He knew the other jades were far from him now, deep within the forest, but he reached anyway. The healing jade would want to reunite with its brethren, so he sat there in silence for some time, letting the energies float around and through him, stretching ever outward.

At last he felt a tug and he looked up to see where the jade had guided his hand. He was not surprised by its eastward orientation, but it was aimed further south than he suspected. It didn't matter, so long as he could bring the shard to Randler and heal the massive damage that was done to his legs. He hoped Astrith had found a way of starting the mending process in the meantime so that Randler would not lose them altogether.

Before he rose up to continue his journey, he tapped into the shard one more time, seeking its protection. He didn't need it to prevent him from being attacked or to fight off beasts if he came across them. Instead, he knew he was going to push himself hard now, and he urged the jade to give him the stamina to make haste. He felt a cushion of sorts waddle over his body and he accepted it as affirmation. Dariak stood at last and drew a few deep breaths. Then he ran.

The mage was no athlete, despite the time he had spent on the road. He was trim and he could maintain a firm walking pace, but running had never been his forte. Always after a few minutes, his lungs would feel like they weren't drawing any more air and his legs turned rubbery, threatening to drop him on his face. If the ground was hard enough, even his shins would start lancing him with searing pain that made him want to be carried to his destination.

Not so with the healing jade, however. All the aches and pains were removed from him as soon as they entered. His breathing was heavy from the exertion, but he felt the cleansing air with each gulp of breath. His lungs heaved in time with his pace, six steps on an inhale, six on an exhale. Step after step, his feet devoured the landscape and carried him swiftly across it. He could not run any faster than he had before, but he was able to maintain it easily and that boon allowed him to make his way to the forest in record time.

He wondered idly if it was how a horse felt as it ran. He hadn't ridden them that often, but they seemed to relish a good run, even with riders on their backs. Dariak laughed as he pictured himself in the form of a horse, galloping across the field and focusing only on the road ahead.

He knew there were feral creatures in the area but he ignored them, pressing ever onward. If they attacked him outright, he would respond forcefully, yet even the lupinoes he spotted kept their distance from a running man who felt no fatigue. They stalked him for a time, but he never wavered in his gait and eventually the beasts decided he was not worth the effort to track.

As night fell, he set himself on the ground and napped, setting only the most rudimentary defensive spells around himself while trusting the healing jade to protect him from harm if necessary. He knew it was a risk but his success in channeling the shard's energy during his bout with Pyron led him to believe in the deeper connection with the magic that Xervius has spoken of. That, and his previous experience with the jades was evidence enough of their ability to protect him.

Dariak awoke to a frigid dawn encrusted with dew and he summoned his fire darts to warm himself. He popped open one of the potions Nastren had given him, mostly out of curiosity, and he sniffed the liquid inside. It was a foul scent, and the added cinnamon did little to mask it. The mage had claimed they were healing potions, and though he didn't need healing, he did need a drink. He was also curious about the effects of this potion and whether he could sense any of the magical properties within it. There were no dangers around him so he pressed his lips to the flask and took a few sips.

The viscous liquid coated his throat like tacky syrup and he choked on it as it took its time getting down his throat. He grabbed his water flask and tried to wash the pasty liquid out but it was of no use. He cleared his throat numerous times, trying to free himself of the thickness, never mind its horrendous flavor. Leave it to a nature mage to make a drink that tasted like mud and bark, he thought, gagging.

At last the potion was out of his throat and he felt it ooze its way down his insides until it reached his belly. There, his stomach rumbled angrily at the intrusion. Dariak tried to feel for the energies stored within the potion, but his body was so uncomfortable that he couldn't concentrate well enough. He thought he might vomit up the few sips he had taken, but then he feared that the goo would take its time getting back out, so he fought the urge to heave.

The discomfort in his stomach passed and he could feel the potion work its way to other parts of his body, but only because he could suddenly sense the imbued magic. It really worked. The healing potion was making its way through him, seeking wounds to fix as it went. The essence of healing was unmistakable and before he lost himself in the awe of it, he turned his attention down to the jade to ensure that it wasn't causing the sensation.

The shard was cool and resting. Dariak smiled, for Nastren truly had enchanted a broth with magical ability. It was yet another advancement for magic that could alter the world in the years to come. Potions like this would give mages another place to exercise their talents and would help to bridge the gap with the commoners who feared the mages, for they could simply purchase the treatment and administer it at will without a mage looming over them casting spells.

Clearly the process needed more refinement, he admitted as he started belching. Yet he sensed that if he had had any wounds, they would have mended, if only a little. Coupling that with the enchanted weapons and armor, Dariak knew that he needed to complete his quest all the more quickly. If flaming swords and icy shields were equipped to basic soldiers and they went off to war, the damage would increase hundredfold. The warring had to stop before the enchantments were perfected and could be used. He needed to press on.

Dariak took a few bites of bread first, however, trying to clear out the lingering halitosis. Then he was on his feet again, supported by the healing jade and its unwavering strength. He ran as fast as he could, marveling in the pace once again. By nightfall, he reached the edge of the forest.

Before he entered the line of trees, he communed with the healing jade again to check his destination. It still suggested he veer further south, so as he crossed into the woods he jogged onward until he found a path, then ventured slightly to the right. It wasn't long before he was greeted by other forest folk.

"Halt stranger," called a tall youth clad in thick vines about his waist. "You must claim your business in this place."

"I see the trials to get in from the west are not as intense as travel from the east," he noted, remembering the series of fights he and Randler had endured upon entry. "I am Dariak and—"

"You must come, Dariak. Astrith has bade us look for you. This way, and hurry."

Panic welled inside of Dariak, for the curt command could only mean that Randler was in danger. The guide left the trail, leaping through random trees and branches like they were an open field. Dariak pushed onward, still channeling the jade for support, pressing to keep up with the lanky young man.

His first trek through the forest had taken several days, but then Lurina and her troupe purposely misled him through the woods to better understand his motives. Now his guide led him through in a fraction of the time. They stopped to eat and to take a few hours of sleep that night, but by the next midday they reached Astrith's village.

The elder greeted Dariak solemnly, with head bowed low and his voice heavy. "Welcome to the forest once again, Dariak."

"Where is Randler?" he cut through the pleasantries.

"I regret that I couldn't do much for your friend but sustain him."

"I have the healing jade. Let me see him and I'll do the rest."

Astrith's eyes opened wide. "I had not thought you would acquire it with such alacrity. Your friend is not here, I am afraid."

Dariak struggled to maintain his composure. "Where is he, Astrith?"

"I sent him to the mages in the south. It seemed to me that they would have the best chance of repairing him."

Dariak paled. "You sent him to the tower? He will be in danger, Astrith. When? How long? How?"

Astrith drew a deep breath and folded his fingers slowly into his lap. "You are racing too fast, Dariak, and you must stop for a moment."

But Dariak would not be calm. "You led me on a fool's chase through this forest and in the process, Randler was seriously hurt. I have the means to save him, but you've sent him off to the mages who wanted me dead. To the same tower that Randler himself infiltrated to rescue me. They aren't going to take lightly to his return, not even in his condition, and you want me to be calm?"

"You must be calm or I will speak to you no further."

Dariak paced away from the wizened man. "What good will it do for me to linger here and wait for you to reveal anything to me? I have the healing jade. I can target the others. I'll go and find him myself. I don't need your help."

"I suppose you could," Astrith said, his voice growing louder. "But if you would count me as an ally then you will stop your prattling and heed my words. Thus, I require you to sit and be still."

"Time is short, Astrith."

"Time is irrelevant, Dariak, for if you are meant to reach him then nature will see that it is so. It is the way of nature to unfold events in their due course."

"What, like fate or destiny?" he scoffed. "Nature is a great and awesome power, I will grant you that, but it is not the foreseer of such things."

"Are you so sure?"

Dariak growled. "How can you ask me to delay my mission? Perhaps I should ask for how long you wish for me to sit."

"That would be a prudent question, indeed," Astrith commended. "Two moons would suffice."

"Impossible! How can you ask me to rest my haunches here for two more days while Randler is out there in danger? He needs me. It cannot wait."

"And yet, when his injuries were fresh and his life was in its most critical state, you left him to my care."

Dariak stopped pacing. "I couldn't help him without the jade. It would have made things worse had I stayed."

"Perhaps, but I suppose you will not know now." Astrith stood up from the tree trunk upon which he sat and then walked over to Dariak. "I can assure you that his injuries are well enough tended that even without your precious jade he can recover."

"But how—?"

"Nature is connected in many ways, young mage. Nuances in the earth and on the wind. They speak to me when I have the will to listen. For my failure to heal your friend, I was intent on his recovery and I assure you that efforts were made to restore him. He is not in danger at this time, else I would not delay you. Yet you are here and so I will assert my will upon you rather than let you flutter away with only the chance of your return."

Dariak tensed. "What are you asking, Astrith?"

"You have a great task ahead of you, Dariak, but you are not centered. If you do not have a center, then how can others come to rely upon you in the times ahead? I require time to show you the center so that it moves with you and allows you to do what you must. It will allow me to assist you in your time of greatest need, which is yet to come. However, if you will be rash, then go on and run to your friend and perhaps you will muddle through without me. I would think, however, that you would benefit from all allies at this time. Still, the choice is yours to make."

Dariak closed his eyes and took several deep breaths, digesting Astrith's words. "Are you certain that Randler is all right?"

"Yes."

"Don't make me regret this, Astrith. What is it you need me to do?"

Astrith smiled broadly. "First, you must cleanse yourself of the mages and your journey."

He rolled his eyes. "Another bath? Fine. Lead the way."

Midnight Camp

KITALLA AWOKE TO a deep, starry sky and blinked in confusion. She hadn't expected to be outdoors after performing her dance routine in Magehaven's crystal chamber. They weren't moving and the camp was very quiet, but she noticed that she was with the right people. There were few tents and she was surprised she wasn't inside one of them, yet as she came to more fully, she understood that her need hadn't been great enough.

Besides, she was lying on a thick tarp next to Carrus, the big lug. She surmised by his proximity that he had been the one to rescue her from the tower after whatever had happened, and considering her unconsciousness, he was clearly continuing to protect her even if it meant having to sleep in the cold nighttime air.

She ached with the chill, but Kitalla wasn't one to complain about such things. Instead, she pushed herself upright, feeling around for her daggers and for one particular piece of jade. With a smirk, she pulled the glass shard from her pocket. Its gritty surface felt reassuring to her, for it meant that she hadn't lost her touch as a thief.

Indeed, she had set a minor trap for Shelloni and her followers, camping out in an upper room near the empowerment chamber. Leaving her metal jade with a crumpled blanket gave Shelloni a burst of confidence and excitement, thinking she had bested Kitalla. Yet, Kitalla had also stolen a hooded mage robe and the arrogant water mage hadn't noticed the intruder among her contingent of followers. The master kept her hand clutched on part of her robe, and it signaled to Kitalla the location of the glass jade. It was easy enough to pat Shelloni on the back in congratulations while simultaneously reaching into the robe to withdraw the shard that was in her possession.

After the mages left the area, Kitalla had circled back around and sought her connection with the glass jade, trying to read the energies of the other jades around her. She felt them moving about the tower and convening in one chamber, but they did not draw together too sharply, which Kitalla interpreted as resistance to handing the shards over to Ervinor. Thus she gathered her things, walked into the diamond chamber and once more brought the mages crashing down.

The effort had been difficult, even more so since she tried to keep awake the people she knew best, such as Ervinor and his captains. She had no idea if she was at all successful, but since the army was out under the night sky and the glass jade hummed merrily in her hand, she assumed that it went according to plan. Pleased with herself, Kitalla stood and wandered around the encampment.

A cursory glance showed her that she was resting with the Ravens, who had split into several smaller groups and surrounded the refugees. Amidst the gathering were the few tents in use, and she figured Ervinor and Randler would be housed in them, as well as some of the elderly or children who had fled from Marritosh's destruction.

Around the perimeter were the other four battalions, yet Kitalla was puzzled that none of them was on full alert. Less than half of the Eagles, Nightingales, Sparrows, and Wrens were on watch. Of the captains, only Verna and Quereth made rounds through the camp. She hurried over to Verna to find out why.

Verna responded by nodding to one of the tents. "Not to worry about the creatures. Lica has it under control for now. And we turned away the mages. I don't think they'll be after us any time soon."

"Frast? Randler? Ervinor? Are they all fine? Did we lose anyone?"

"Quereth has a better mind for how many we lost in the escape, but the others are here. Are they fine? Well, it depends on your definition." She shrugged. "Watch is on for another hour, though, so I have to continue my rounds."

Kitalla didn't argue with her or try to get any more information. It was heartening to see the woman taking a more official role as captain and so Kitalla moved on. Quereth looked haggard and she hated to bother him, but she had questions.

"Ah, Kitalla, you're awake at last," he greeted her warmly. "Walk with me a bit."

"I just saw Verna, but she seemed preoccupied. What have I missed?"

Quereth smiled sagely. "Verna has been nervous since our general ordered the lesser watch, but I think he's right. Lica should be able to keep the beasts away for now."

"She said the same. She also said the mages wouldn't be coming for us?"

"Indeed. They awoke sooner than you perhaps anticipated. We had a head start, thanks to you, but they trailed us and attacked. We defended and now we are here, a day later. Yes, you were out cold and we dared not wake you unless we needed to. Fortunately, we could let you rest until your body was ready. That skill of yours is becoming potent, I should say."

Kitalla shrugged and shook her head. "I think it was more the focusing crystal in that room up there. It's connected to the whole barrier surrounding the tower. I will say, though, that it's draining pouring out the energy like that."

"As Dariak described it once, you create the energy from your own will," Quereth said. "You don't manipulate the forces around you to channel them."

"Yeah, he said it was different than how you mages do things. I'm still unsure of a number of aspects of it." She breathed a sigh through her teeth. "What's the news on Randler?"

"Oh, so you don't know. He is over there." He pointed in the bard's general direction. "He has been out of it since he was brought back to us."

Kitalla rubbed her right arm. "It'll take some time. Maybe I should go see him."

"Very good then. I will continue here."

The thief tipped her head and made her way through the sleeping encampment, peering into each of the six tents, confirming her suspicions about the occupants. Most were indeed elderly or orphaned children with a few guardians. Ervinor was sound asleep in his tent, which was surrounded by four guards, so she didn't disturb him. In another tent she found Randler and Frast as well as Lica with a host of seven mages huddled in a corner.

"Cozy," she said, stepping inside and walking up to Randler. The bard looked withered and tired. Beside him was Frast, his head turned to the side, in deep sleep. She tried to ignore the line of drool escaping his lip.

Lica rocked back and forth in the corner with the other mages, who seemed to be chanting in a low cadence with her.

"Empowerers," Randler whispered to her.

"You're awake then?" she breathed.

"No need to use such hushed tones, Kitalla. I have no choice, for Frast has been stealing my voice. As for the rest of them here, no one will even hear us." He lifted his head, trying to sit up and Kitalla reached forward to help him.

"How are you?"

"It hurts immensely. I understand Frast has been channeling the brunt of the pain through himself so I won't have to endure it, but in doing so he has also been keeping me sedated and unable to speak. It's almost a relief that he fell asleep, except now I feel the agony. I tell you, Kitalla, it is great."

"In a way, I had it easier. When my arm was crushed in Grenthar's dungeon, the healers were on site. They already knew my physiology completely and were able to put the arm back together swiftly. Plus, I was delirious through most of it. It still aches all the time, though."

Randler touched her arm. "I can't imagine any part of that being easy." He held her gaze, denying her rebuke. "I've been unable to learn much about what's been happening. Where is Dariak?"

Kitalla's brow furrowed. "From what I understand, he went on to find Pyron and the healing jade. You were brought to Astrith who sent you here when he couldn't fix you."

Sadness welled in Randler's eyes. "He abandoned me for the jade."

"I don't think it was quite like that," she hedged.

"Always the jades for him, Kitalla. They have always been his utmost priority."

Kitalla didn't know what to say, for it was a difficult point to argue. "I'm sure he felt the healing jade, of all things, was a priority so that he *could* help you. You know that's his weakest field of magic."

"Perhaps," he said, unconvinced. "Yet the mages here came together, didn't they? It hurts, but I can feel my legs again. I know they work. They're weak and in a lot of pain. I have to convince Frast to stop putting me under so I can start learning to deal with this."

"I'll talk to him." She looked over to Lica, who was still rocking and chanting. "What's the deal there?"

"Bear with me, for I'm making a number of assumptions, but I think she has the beast jade now and she must be using it to keep us safe. Yet she needs the others there to give her the strength to work the spell."

Kitalla smiled. "You can tell that, being in a coma and all?"

But Randler couldn't return her grin. "I felt the energies of the beast jade tearing through me while they were healing me. It was like being bitten by thousands of firegnats and reptigons. And when I would try to cry out with the fury of it all, the sound came out of Frast instead. I know that each magic force in the world has its providence, but many of them overlap in unique ways. I would guess that the roaring of the creatures in the world connects the beast jade to such sounds. I felt the pain pulled out of me, and seeing Frast like this when he's passed out is clue enough as to where the energy has been going. Yesterday, though, the beasts were ripped away from me and I was filled with these great gusts of wind. I think he switched jades."

With a nod, Kitalla stared deeply at Randler. "I know you're not happy about all the magic you've endured in your life, Randler, but I think it's given you a keen insight on the matter. Dariak would agree, I'm sure."

Randler frowned. "Dariak. Yes, we did have a few debates on the subject, always trying to flesh out new meanings."

"Resonance and dissonance."

"You've been listening."

"It's hard not to on this quest for the jades. Even with the other things going on, there's always the jades."

His whispered voice was solemn. "Indeed. I know Dariak needs me in his own way, but what's to become of me when this is all over?"

She laughed. "You're ridiculous. You have to then go around the world and tell people—in song—that the wars are over, one town at a time. You're going to be so busy on your quest and Dariak will be following you along the way."

He grinned despite himself. "So it will be the reverse of what we've been doing. The jades are gone and now he'll follow us. Amusing."

"One can hope."

They sat in silence for a few minutes and Randler tried to massage his legs, but the stabs of pain made him wince, which in turn nearly woke Frast from his slumber. The bard wasn't ready to be shoved back into darkness. "Oh yes," he said suddenly. "Frast had the presence of mind to return the shadow jade to me."

"That's... useful."

"Actually, it is. It's been with me longer than any of you, Dariak included. Having it nearby helps me feel calmer. Funny, though. Many bards sing of comforting sunlight, not solace in shadow."

"I don't know, Randler. I think everyone finds their own comfort where they do. For me it was in stealing trinkets from the lords and ladies and pawning them off for food and clothing. It made me feel like they were contributing to the welfare of Poltor and his group, of all of us. I know we weren't altruistic with what we did, but other peasants could have followed suit." She looked down at her hands. "Even just yesterday, I guess it was, when I lifted the glass jade off Shelloni, I felt powerful. Skilled. Worthy."

"Kitalla, you're certainly more than worthy."

She smiled. "Thank you. Still, it felt different. With everything else we're trying to do here, gathering people together and stopping wars, I feel ridiculous that an act of petty theft gave me any comfort at all. Sort of… felt good that I haven't lost my touch."

The bard nodded slowly. "We hold on to the things we do well. They're part of us, even if they're not commonly accepted or desired by others. I guess it's like when I went into the tower to free Dariak. Like the time I stole the jades from Halrone. Both goals were important to me and needed stealth that's out of my league, but achieving them felt wonderful."

Kitalla sighed wistfully. "Yes, I forget about your evil days as a dastardly thief. You should talk about those times more, I think. Sing bawdy tales of wresting the riches from the kings and so on."

He chuckled softly. "I'm not proud of those days, but they are a part of me, aren't they? Perhaps I should."

The phrase "part of me" sent shivers down Kitalla's spine and she shuddered. "Speaking of tales," she started, hoping it wasn't too far off topic to ask about, "what's with your fascination of the Forgotten Tribe?"

"There is a lot of morality that can be pulled from the tales. Often the Kallisorian side of the saga relates to the brutality of the king, but he was just a man who feared the potential of what magic could do. He fought against it to protect the people around him, but at the cost of his whole family. On the other hand, Hathreneir tried to enlighten the people to the wisdom of sorcery and how it could be used for the greater good. Yet there are tales of how she also abused the power."

"You haven't sung of those."

"Not around mages, no. Not even as cautionary tales because the mages tend to be touchy when they're told not to use their skills. One tavern I played in was nearly razed by an angry set of mages who screamed at me, asking how it would feel if people told me I couldn't use my natural talents. What if the music was inside of me but I wasn't allowed to share it? It made me think, but it didn't change my mind on the whole magic thing. I side a little more with Kallisor on that one."

"Is there… an ending to the tale?"

Randler's brow furrowed. "To the tale of the Forgotten Tribe? Well, not precisely."

"I saw this picture book in the tower, penned by Lady Cathrateir."

The bard gasped. "I don't suppose you brought that out of the tower? I would have loved to have seen that if I knew it was there."

Kitalla did her best to describe the tale that was depicted within, with the ribbons of color spreading out in all directions, with each page turning to fewer and fewer hues until only a darkened sky remained. Randler listened intently with his eyes closed, picturing each scene as she described it.

"No," he said at last. "I had not heard that one. It sounds like the end of things from the way you describe it."

Kitalla groaned. "I was hoping you weren't going to say that."

"All the lights from Hathreneir and Kallisor wending together and then vanishing, leaving the world in darkness… It's too bad I can't look at the book directly, but I know you, Kitalla. If you describe it that way, then I'm sure it's accurate. You're too keen on details for it not to be. I'll have to think about it and try to tie it in with the other parts of the tale."

"All right," she said. "Let me know if you come up with anything."

He eyed her for a time. "It isn't like you to put stock in such things. What's going on?"

"Now who's being keen?" she deflected with a grin. "I may have to wake up Frast before you start asking too many questions."

He chuckled and allowed the conversation to change. They spent the next couple of hours reminiscing about parts of the journey and speculating on what was yet to come. All the while, Randler watched Kitalla closely, trying to discern whatever it was that she was keeping secret.

CHAPTER 56

Northward

AT THE APPROACH of dawn, Ervinor's army awoke and packed their things for the continued trek to the north. The castle itself was not far away and they could reach it by tomorrow if they pushed hard, but Ervinor was reluctant to press the refugees onward.

At least, that was the excuse he kept using for not keeping a faster pace, or rather, one of several excuses. Kitalla was awake now, so she was no longer a burden to be tended to, but Randler was still unable to carry himself. Lica was also immobilized during her communion with the beast jade. Plus, Ervinor tried to hold training sessions throughout the day to better enlist the new mages who had joined the cause at the tower.

What he didn't want to admit was that his fear was growing. The king had no reason to hold back his forces when the army arrived. Ervinor didn't want to be sucked into yet another useless battle where perhaps he would lose another limb. Or worse, his life.

He fidgeted with his tunic. He had mended it to the best of his ability but it sat differently on him now and rubbed against his shoulder wound a bit more than it had before. He wasn't actually sure if that was the case or if it only seemed that way, but it didn't matter. Tugging and twisting the fabric kept his mind occupied as they marched through the desert.

Ervinor and his captains had put a stop to several bouts among the refugees. The discontented citizens were shuffled about like cattle, ready to be dropped off at the king's doorstep, not even knowing if he would take them in. Only a handful of them took to their situation well, seeking a way into Ervinor's army if the king refused them. Though he would have preferred having their allegiance outright, he accepted their offers. Still, in his heart, he hoped their king would reach out to protect them. Else, why be a king?

During an afternoon halt, Ervinor checked on Randler, who tried to walk with the special crutches Astrith had sent with him. Frast hovered nearby, which made Randler more nervous than comforted, but at least Kitalla had gotten through to the mage. Sure, the pain was evident on Randler's face and his groans were disheartening, but he wasn't crying out too often and the intuitive crutches did a portion of the work for him. He knew Randler couldn't get more than a couple of steps without needing a break at first, but he was upright and essentially on his own.

Lica, however, was wearing out and she confessed that she didn't know how much longer she could keep the beasts away. "We have to get there fast, Ervinor, or we're going to have them upon us."

"Can no one else use the jade?"

She whispered quietly. "If too many mages use the jades directly, they may do what Shelloni and the rest attempted to do. We can't risk the temptation. Even the ones who seem committed to this quest may turn from us. No, not after all we went through to get them back."

He consented to her logic and assured her that he would try to make haste. Afterwards, he made his rounds to visit with the captains. Quereth made no complaints, but he was clearly exhausted already. Verna looked charged up and ready for a battle. Carrus was split overseeing the Ravens and Frast's Sparrows, while Throssha maintained control over the Eagles in Lica's absence. Everything seemed to be moving along well enough until a call came from the south.

Ervinor raced through the ranks to find Carrus, whose whistle had called above the din of the people. He intercepted the messenger and ran to Carrus' side. "Where?" It was a needless question.

To the south, the sandy desert shifted and shimmered wildly. Distant shapes waggled in the sunlight. "For how long?"

"Not long," Carrus grunted.

He couldn't believe the mages were striving to overtake them again. The shimmer visions suggested they were using magic to catch up with the army and the only plus to that was that the mages casting those spells would be weary. But anyone else they were transporting could lob spells at will into Ervinor's forces. "Carrus, can I leave this to you?"

"We will hold them off, sir." He called, "Sparrows, prepare for battle!"

"Take the Ravens, too. Don't argue. I don't want any of you to fall." He then ran off to rouse the other battalions. "Move out!" he shouted, repeating his cry until others took the chant and the soldiers and refugees broke camp.

He hated to split the troops again, but his priority was the safety of the refugees. The Wrens, Eagles, and Nightingales adjusted their positions to enshroud the commoners along the journey, filling the gaps left by the Ravens and Sparrows. Ervinor hurried to the head of the Nightingales, leading them at a rapid pace and pressing to reach the castle swiftly. The massive structure was already on the horizon and it loomed ever closer.

Yet as they made their way across the land, Ervinor spied more movement ahead. At first he thought it was just a gathering of feral creatures, wondering if Lica's spell had faltered, but as they moved closer, he saw they were soldiers. The king's.

"To arms!" he called. "Prepare yourselves!" This was no time for a fight with the refugees mixed among his number. But he couldn't send them ahead on their own either, for the soldiers might simply strike them down. He debated briefly about cutting west or east, but if he did, he knew they couldn't outrun the king's men and with the mages coming up from the south, it would only get worse.

Quereth pushed his way up to Ervinor's side. "A few of the mages are banding together to erect a protective wall ahead of us. It won't last long and they aren't sure if they can maintain it while we're on the march, but we've been practicing the spell itself when we can."

"That's great news, Quereth, thank you. Maybe it'll give us enough time to explain the situation and hand the refugees over. Take whatever resources you need." He then gathered the nearest twenty fighters and aligned them in a defensive row to stand behind the barrier for when it fell. The men and women grimly took their weapons in hand and stepped in line.

With the recent volunteers from the tower, Ervinor had over a hundred fighters at his disposal, even with his forces split to the south. Their experience on the battlefield, however, was a key factor that worried him. Only the mages who had traveled with him across the lands had been in battle situations, as far as he knew. Some of the newcomers might know their first taste of fear. Suddenly Verna's scare tactics seemed a worthy training strategy for new recruits.

A horn bellowed across the desert and distant shouting could be heard. They were too far away to engage in a charge, Ervinor decided, but he couldn't take a chance and stand his forces down. Instead, he marched onward, bringing them ever closer to the fighters.

As they approached, Ervinor saw there was a host of forty soldiers hacking away at a pack of sand rodia. When Lica's protective spell drew near, the rodia scattered and fled, squealing madly. The fighters were confused by the sudden departure and only then even noticed the approaching army. They scurried into fighting positions and lifted their weapons in anticipation.

Ervinor jogged ahead and held his hand up high. "Hold!" he called out. "Hold your weapons steady!"

The commander of the troop hesitantly stepped forward to greet young Ervinor, looking over the man's shoulder as if to assess the amount of time he had to determine whether the one-armed man was friend or foe. The commander gave an official Hathren salute, but Ervinor did not know the proper response. "State your business!"

Ervinor assessed the troop in front of him and had the impression that they were relatively new to the king's employ. The men were younger than other fighters he had faced here and the fact that their approach had gone mostly unnoticed was a definite indication. "I am Ervinor and I am guiding a host of refugees from Marritosh to the king for protection. I seek no quarrel with you or your men."

The commander's tone was sharp. "Marritosh defected from the kingdom months ago. There are no refugees the king would wish to see."

"They are innocent people. You cannot turn them away."

The commander looked again at the approaching forces and then faced his own men. "Kill them!"

Ervinor's eyes opened wide as he drew his blade and brought it into position. The commander charged him directly, seeing him as an easy target, but Ervinor proved him wrong. Ervinor swung his sword bitterly, intercepting an incoming strike and pushing the commander back a pace. He then pulled away and immediately lunged, swinging the sword wide and bashing into the commander's right side. With a wild bellow, the burly man retaliated with a fist to Ervinor's face and he couldn't avoid the strike.

Meanwhile, the rest of the king's fighters raced toward the Nightingales, weapons swinging in the air, ready to pounce. When they were but five paces away from the fighters, however, each soldier crashed into an invisible wall of force and collapsed. Most of them shook it off quickly and scrambled to their feet, but Ervinor's fighters were already upon them.

"W—What?" the commander gasped, seeing his whole line of fighters simply drop. He missed his strike and Ervinor spun about and clobbered him in the back, knocking him down.

"I said, we mean you no harm. Call off your attack." Ervinor pressed his foot against the man's neck to drive home his point.

"Traitors, the lot of you," the man growled under Ervinor's shoe. He wriggled about and muttered madly under his breath. Ervinor should have been more alert, but he thought he had the commander beaten. He wasn't expecting the man to cast a spell.

Steel darts erupted from all over the man's body, lancing outward with minimal force, but enough to pierce Ervinor in a few places. The general leaped back and reached to remove the darts, but they disintegrated when the spell was finished. The commander rose, grabbing his sword and laughing menacingly.

The rest of the king's soldiers had similar defenses. Each one was a mage in his or her own right and spells started to fly. Quereth's team was recovering from the barrier spell and they were unable to deflect the new projectiles. Other mages tried their best to come to their defense, but some were too far away to help as they protected the refugees.

The commander ushered a stream of spells as Ervinor leaped in to stab the man. His strongest spells were metallic in nature, and when Ervinor's blade penetrated the man's skin, little damage was effected. In fact, Ervinor's sword warped with each strike. The commander laughed again and swept in with his own blade.

Two of the king's soldiers had been taken down by the Nightingales, but the others were pressing strong. Verna screamed madly and rushed in with a crazed look in her eyes. She wove around and through various enemies, refusing to settle for just one. She cut one mage-warrior high in the face, and then brought her sword down low, slicing into the thigh of another. Spinning again, she pushed on and jabbed her sword into a third soldier, then launched herself into a fourth to ground him before he could hit Quereth with a spell. After two hard punches to the soldier's face, Verna scrambled up and continued her fury.

As the commander attacked Ervinor, a new spell caused tiny bits of metal to fragment off the sword and pelt Ervinor's body. Though it meant the commander's sword slowly decreased in size, the repeated damage wore away at Ervinor's stamina. He flinched and jerked away, unable to mount an effective assault. He hated to do it again so soon, but he sheathed his sword and reached for the antimagic whip he had reattached to the tunic. The long cord came away more easily this time and he wound it in the air and lashed out at the commander.

More of the king's soldiers fell and the others started to panic. Fireballs erupted wildly into the fray, sometimes blasting into comrades as well as foes. Ervinor's fighters, however, maintained their composure overall and the mages pressed in where they could to quell the magic.

With the whip enwrapped around the commander, his spells faltered. He understood what was happening so he reached for the cord and wrenched it away. Ervinor recoiled and snapped his wrist again, sending the whip back to the commander. The big man roared in outrage and he swept his sword down, snapping the cord in half. He threw down the part that entwined him and readied his weapon for a vicious strike.

Quereth and the other mages pressed forward to subdue the soldiers, helping their fighters to push back the attackers. The soldiers did not relent, even as they were pressed into the desert sand. They thrashed about, knocking down their assailants, trying to turn the tide in their favor. Ervinor's standing orders were not to kill unless absolutely necessary, but the fighters and mages started to wonder if the soldiers needed to be cut down permanently.

Meanwhile the commander continued slashing his sword violently at Ervinor, who was hard-pressed to hold off each attack. His body ached from the shrapnel the man had launched into him, and now he had lost the antimagic whip Herchig had crafted for him. He didn't know which pain was worse, but he was determined to take down this man and make him pay.

One of Ervinor's fighters lost his patience trying to subdue the king's soldiers and he swiped his blade fatally into his adversary. The woman's blood splattered outward and as it struck his skin, he screamed in agony.

Quereth hurried over and gasped. "It's poisoned. Their blood is poisoned. Knock them down but do not cut them." He looked up at Ervinor's bout and saw how hard-pressed the general was. There was work to do, but he needed to help Ervinor.

The commander stomped closer, spitting as he called more words of power to his aid. Spittle struck the sand and sizzled, releasing acrid smoke that made Ervinor's nose wrinkle. The general pulled back, bringing his sword up to defend the endless attacks coming his way. As the burly man pressed on, his chanting grew louder and louder and soon his blade took on a reddish hue. Ervinor parried the next attack, but the commander held the position this time, pressing into his foe. The glowing blade radiated with searing heat that cut into Ervinor's blade, melting it slowly. In moments, the commander would break through.

Ervinor struggled to pull away, but the commander kicked out and knocked him down, then dropped on top of Ervinor and cackled wildly as he pressed the sword lower and lower. There was nothing Ervinor could to do stop him.

Ice darts flew out then and crashed into the commander's back. Quereth was there, his arms already swinging around to launch a second barrage. He had to control the projectiles, though, taking care not to cut into the man's flash in case his blood was also tainted. The ice battered the man repeatedly on the back and head until he lost his grip and Ervinor was able to shove him aside.

Rolling away, Ervinor regained his footing and ran ahead, sword swiping down. Quereth saw the attack coming as the commander struggled to right himself and he wasn't sure what to do. "No!" the mage shouted, calling up a protective shield and placing it over the commander to prevent Ervinor from cutting into him.

The commander laughed wildly at the turn of events and he rose up, ready to strike the confused general down. Quereth prepared a powerful fireball spell and ran in, shoving Ervinor aside and launching the incendiary into the belly of the burly commander. The fireball exploded as the commander's sword impaled Quereth. Both men fell, dead.

Ervinor cried out in horror as the explosion blasted him away and knocked him over. He scrambled back to Quereth, but even the best healers couldn't restore a life that was already gone. The commander's midsection was obliterated, his oozing blood splattering to the sand and releasing more acrid smoke that made Ervinor turn and retch.

The rest of the king's soldiers continued their struggle, using their own acidic blood as a weapon now. The mages and fighters pulled away, not sure how to deal with this threat. Verna continued her attacks, but she was wearing out.

Then magefire erupted from the south. Fire and ice floated through the sky, landing in the fray. "The south has been breached!" Verna screamed. "Prepare! Prepare!"

Ervinor pushed himself up and grabbed his sword. Not only would they be fighting these magic-infused soldiers, now the mages of the southern tower were coming. He didn't want to fight anymore, but he wasn't about to throw his life away after Quereth's sacrifice. He pushed on and swept his sword around, then looked upward and sprinted out of the line of fire.

"Eagle mages, hold them back!" he shouted over the noise. More spells flew in and clattered all about. "We can do this, everyone. Hold formation and attack."

"Belay that!" Carrus bellowed, charging in, his body drenched in sweat. "Ervinor, stand down."

Carrus had never disobeyed him and so the general conceded to his captain, calling for his forces to stop fighting. The king's soldiers took the news with delight, cheering loudly and renewing their attacks, hoisting their comrades back on their feet to slaughter these easy victims.

But the ceasefire only applied to the forces under Ervinor's command. Additional spells erupted and Carrus issued orders for the fighters to clear a space around the infused soldiers. The spells sailed through the air and crashed into the enemies. Ervinor was baffled and he dropped his weapon, watching as the spells came faster and faster, beating down on the mage-warriors and obliterating them.

Soon the stench of charred flesh filled the air and Ervinor tensed when he saw a host of mages come forth. He recognized them, especially the leader who stepped forward and bowed his head in greeting.

"Rothra of the Mage Council, master of the fire mages of Magehaven, at your command, General Ervinor."

C H A P T E R 57

The Summons

THE TRAGIC EVENTS at the outpost added to the tensions the men and women already felt while housed with their sworn enemies. Gabrion's show of skill that morning was cause for concern among the Hathrens in particular, for they did not know if all the Kallisorian warriors were as skilled as Gabrion or if he was the only one. After seeing his moves during his three-on-one duel, no other duels were called.

It was all well for Gabrion. He didn't want anyone to die anymore. People should be allowed to be different and just live. He thought back to when he met Dariak, that terrible day in Savvron. His townspeople had died, but Dariak hadn't killed any of them, except Andron. Yes, he had been cocksure and determined, but he had only used minor spells to fend off the rest and to make it look like he was fighting in earnest.

He missed his travel companion, Gabrion realized suddenly. The mage had caused the warrior to leave his home and venture out into the world. They had faced many obstacles together, but they had been apart for so long now, Gabrion felt empty. He wondered if Dariak had acquired all the jades and was waiting for the right moment to use them.

Or Randler, strumming his lute and crooning softly, soothing their woes like no one else could. The bard could always refresh their minds and ease their pains even when healing magic failed. He had a knack for choosing songs that fit the situation well, to either invigorate the fighters or quell nightmares. Perhaps if Randler had been here, there wouldn't have been any fighting at all.

He thought of Ervinor, the young general leading the army in his absence. Even Herchig had said that Ervinor had an old soul and deep wisdom. Everyone around Gabrion seemed blessed with something special. He wondered if they were all placed there by design or perhaps they were drawn together in a manner similar to the jades themselves, vibrating when in proximity to their mates.

And of course, there was Kitalla. He felt shame for his actions with her in Jortun. They were acts of solace and need and he regretted indulging himself with her, even though she appeared to have enjoyed it. He wished he could go back and handle things differently, instead of feeling like he was carrying around a stain on his personality.

She had taken the glass jade from him, and it must be in Dariak's hands by now, he assumed. He turned toward the western sky and frowned, feeling disconnected and aching deep within. He had wanted to save Mira and then to save the world. He wanted to believe in Dariak's envisioned future where war was a rarity and people could live freely from day to day. Yet he was now so far removed from all that.

Instead he was here, standing between the two great armies with troops approaching the outpost periodically. He knew there were other places further north and south where the soldiers could cross in either direction. Sure, the border guardians may help keep the Kallisorians at bay, but Dariak had said the burned-out mages who served as the guardians feared large groups and that their protection would be limited anyway.

And here at this central outpost along the western Kallisorian border, Gabrion had brought in the enemy and begged them to meet as men, not soldiers. Ruhk had only agreed, he knew, because he feared Gabrion's ability and thought the warrior would kill him otherwise. But his attitude had shifted to one of hope, and he was unsure why. Perhaps all people wanted the warring to end and this one glimpse of a new future was all that was needed.

Gabrion turned north and looked down at the field below, smiling despite his darkened thoughts. Before him stretched the obstacle course and forty men and women were running it presently. Unlike some of the previous runs, where half were blindfolded and half were deaf, Urrith had suggested something different and Gabrion thought it was a great idea.

Hathrens were paired off with Kallisorians. They were not impaired in any way except one. The pair was lashed together. Inner hands and legs were tied together, making them funny-looking three-legged monsters staggering about the course. They stumbled wildly up the ramps and clutched the ropes to swing over pits or to slide safely from the walls. Some arguments erupted, of course, but Gabrion felt the banter would have happened even if members of the same faction were secured together. One after another, the pairs muscled their way through, most celebrating the victory at the end of the course.

Urrith ran among the course to maintain the flow. His Hathren partner, Yuvia, was a great assistant. She took cues well from him and did her best to keep her own comrades in line. They were one of the pairs of officials whose sole purpose was to maintain peace in the outpost during this exercise. Gabrion smiled down at Urrith, pleased with how well he rose to his task. The man was a year younger than Gabrion and he would make a great commander one day.

Ruhk stepped up beside Gabrion and clapped him on the shoulder, laughing. "This course of yours is entertaining. Look at Heiva and Morsh over there. She looks like she wants to bite his ear off if he doesn't keep up with her."

"It's a sign of affection," Gabrion chortled. "I wouldn't be surprised if they dine together tonight."

"I'm not certain how long this peace can last between us," Ruhk said suddenly. "Yet it does feel nice not to be constantly looking over my shoulder."

"Why can't it last?"

Ruhk shrugged. "We have been taught all our lives to fear and loathe each other. Surely you understand that a couple days playing together can't simply change that? It's just a matter of time before the old walls are rebuilt and people remember they're facing off against each other on the battlefield. It's a pity, really."

Gabrion's jaw firmed. "Maybe we can turn the tide, if we hold on to this. I realize it's idealistic and naïve. But who's to say that it can't last? Why don't we try to hope for the best, to keep the peace?"

Ruhk bellowed with laughter. "That's what I like about you, young Gabrion. Always full of light and hope."

His voice went low. "I think we've seen enough darkness in our lives."

"That may be," Ruhk acceded. "Yet the heart of man is hard to change."

"What of you? If we meet on the field weeks from now, what then?"

Ruhk smiled widely. "If I see you, I run. Simple as that. No way I can defeat you, friend."

"You wouldn't join me?"

Ruhk's face hardened. "Gabrion, I have family back home and they are in the heart of Hathreneir. How can I abandon them to join your cause fully? How do I take on the mask of traitor and leave them to face judgment for my crime? Could you do the same?"

"I have done the same, I'm afraid. Yet I believe in the new future where we're united as one great people. It won't be easy, as you said, but don't you see that we're just people here? There's no reason we can't work together every day."

Ruhk slapped Gabrion on the back. "You speak like that and you make me feel like it could happen. United," he echoed. Then he grinned and drew in a big breath, his eyes growing wide. "That's it, Gabrion. You're missing a name for your little band of misfits. You can't be Kallisorian or Hathren, can you? It will keep you divided. You need a name. You should be: The United."

Gabrion's brows shot up. "You would give us a name?"

"Someone ought to, and if you win, then I can always tell my children's children that I was the one who named the rebellion."

"I don't like it when you phrase it like that."

"Nonetheless, it's a rebellion, isn't it?"

Gabrion was quiet for a few moments. "I suppose it is. Fighting back against the wrongs. Moving away from the way things have been for so long. Changing the minds of the people around us."

"Don't forget banding together and turning against the kings. That's an important part of what you're doing. I don't envy your decision. You're going to be very alone in this."

Gabrion turned to the commander. "Not if you stand with me. Not if you give the future a chance."

"It doesn't seem possible, I'm afraid. I respect what you're doing, but I don't see how you can change how people are. I have too much at stake to simply throw my lot in with you."

The warrior sighed. "I see. What of your soldiers?"

"I will do this for you, Gabrion: I will allow them to choose for themselves and I won't retaliate against them. But they will need to understand that if we face each other in war, then we will fight as we must."

Gabrion punched his fists together in frustration. "You wouldn't stay your swords for us?"

"How could we? It would mark us as traitors just as surely as if we turned and fought openly against other Hathrens."

Disappointment weighed on Gabrion and he didn't know what to say in response. He knew it would be hard to change the minds of others, but he thought he had been getting through to Ruhk. The commander had been so agreeable to the challenges Gabrion had set forth. Perhaps he was only curious and never had any intention of opening his mind to possibility.

The runners completed the obstacle course and Urrith and Yuvia reset the challenges for the next set of participants. Ruhk gave Gabrion a feeble smile of reassurance and turned away, heading off to some other part of the outpost. A few moments later, Gabrion went off as well.

He wandered around, seeing that in many cases, the Hathrens remained with their own and so did the Kallisorians. Some groups did mingle, but overall they remained segregated. He struggled to keep his head and hopes high as he made his way to the war room where Ordren waited for him to report in.

The Kallisorian commander was at his desk, writing fiercely. "Gabrion, sit," he said, nodding toward a chair. He continued his fevered scribbling and Gabrion abided in silence until he was finished.

"Is everything well?" Gabrion asked when Ordren finally set the quill down.

"No. No, it isn't. Word has come from the king. He summons you to the castle and I'm to ensure you get there immediately."

Gabrion stood. "Preposterous!"

"Nonetheless, it's true. Word of your arrival spread, as news does. He is unhappy with the recent events at his outpost and the king would like a word with you."

"I won't go."

"I was afraid you would say that. I will have to restrain you and send you along with a contingent of soldiers to keep you in line." He whistled and the doors burst open with six Kallisorian soldiers who had been at the outpost with Ordren since his first arrival there.

"I met our beloved king once in service to the throne. I brought Dariak to him as an invader, turning him over so justice could be dealt. Did I ever tell you this story?"

Ordren's tone was exasperated. "You've brought this on yourself, Gabrion."

"The king refused to hear my words," Gabrion cut in. "He twisted what I said and marked me as a traitor and threw me into the dungeon with Dariak."

Ordren rose from his seat and shouted back. "Well you've given plenty of evidence that you're in cahoots with the mage, haven't you? You're turning the men against the will of the throne and that, too, brands you as traitor. I say the king had the right of you."

"No, this was before my journey really began, back when I hated Dariak and had never fought in a real battle. I was as blind and novice as they come. The king couldn't even tell that I was just some farm boy trying to do the right thing by turning over an evil mage. But he wouldn't listen. He bade me to kill Dariak in cold blood, but I couldn't do that. It was wrong. And for it, I was sentenced to death."

Ordren shook his head. "This is all irrelevant. You're to go to the king and speak with him of the events taking place here. Use your silver tongue and maybe he'll send you back home."

"If you send me to him, he'll remember me, and I'll be slain. I won't return to the castle just to be slaughtered."

"Well, you won't stay here!" Ordren yelled. "Guards, take him."

The six soldiers, swords drawn, stepped forward. However, they did not strike. "Gabrion, sir, won't you listen to reason?" one of the asked. "Come away with us, sir."

"I will defend myself if you try to take me."

"Sir," another spoke up, "you said you wanted no fighting within these walls during the presence of the Hathrens."

Gabrion turned toward Ordren. "Using my rules against me?"

The commander pressed his lips together. "If you break your own rules, then why should anyone else follow them? What's most important to you, Gabrion? The 'peace' you have here or your freedom?" He looked at the guards. "Take him to the dungeon until the convoy gets here."

"Sir!" The guards stepped forward and Gabrion grudgingly followed. They led him down the stairs and into the basement where he had come to be alone on his first day here. But the cells were not empty this time. The angry members of Ruhk's team, who had attacked Gabrion after his introductory speech, were still detained.

"Well look who it is!" Gerta snarled. "Looks like a turn of events is at hand, isn't it?" Her laughter echoed in the stony chamber.

A single cell was opened and Gabrion walked calmly inside. He turned to the guards ushering him within. "I won't be returning to the king. I'll bide my time here for now."

"Orders are orders," the man replied.

"Ordren would keep us divided and won't open his mind to peace. You need to think for yourselves. All of you."

"We cannot release you."

Gabrion nodded his head slowly. "I understand, Ravik. You may go now." Confused, the soldiers locked the cell and left the dungeon.

Gerta was still cackling at Gabrion's predicament. "Not so popular now, are you? Where are all your ideals? You're just a stupid fool, aren't you?"

But Gabrion wasn't listening. Instead, he looked around his cell, trying to remember his first day here. Falling to his knees, he ran his hands along the floor but there was nothing. It was simply flat stone and a layer of dirt and sand. He glanced over to Gerta's cell and furrowed his brow.

"You may be good in a fight," she taunted, "but look at you now, on your hands and knees like a sick puppy. You're a whole lot of nothing!"

"Check the floor over there," he called to her. "Is it flat or is there something carved into it?"

Gerta stopped ranting long enough to listen. "What are you rambling on about?"

"The floor. Check the floor. There should be a shape carved into it."

Perplexed, Gerta stepped away from the bars and ushered her group to move aside and check. She bent low and felt along the stone. "Some strange sort of triangle, yes. We've been ogling it for days now," she said mockingly. "We thought of cutting more of these into the stonework to spruce up this place a bit. Why are you wasting my time?"

Gabrion kept himself calm though he wanted little more than to sink down and ignore the raving woman. "Run your fingers in again. There should be part of it that's deeper than the rest."

Gerta's hands were too small so she had one of the others come over. He reached into the deeper groove Gabrion had cut and gasped in pain. "What is that?" the man cried out.

"A trap!" Gerta squealed. "Oh, you will pay for this, you little—"

"Enough!" Gabrion shouted. "It's clear you don't have half a brain in your miserable, childish head, so shut your mouth and listen. It's what you're best suited for, isn't it, soldier?"

She was taken aback by the abrupt tone. "How dare you!"

"Gerta, listen to him," the man with her said. "Gabrion, what do you want me to do?"

"What's your name?"

"Lorquel."

"Thank you, Lorquel. Have your men keep that woman quiet, then." Gerta balked at the comment but three soldiers moved over and restrained her, clamping her mouth with large hands. Some of the others in the group were agitated by the action, but Lorquel barked at them to stop.

"What next?"

"Reach back into that crevice. That sharp object you found… remove it."

Lorquel pouted at the thought of reaching blindly into the stone again, but he heeded the calm words of the warrior. Taking more care this time so as not to cut himself again, he reached in and his fingertips brushed a sharp bottom layer. He shifted his hand back and forth but he couldn't feel anything move and he said as much.

"You have to," Gabrion said. "I know I cut into that stone and left jagged edges in there. But it's just thinner bits of stone. You have to be able to break something off. Keep working at it."

Lorquel tried again, grunting as he cut himself numerous times. Then there was a click sound and he rose up triumphantly with a sharp piece of rock between his bloody fingers. "I have it!"

"That's your escape key. Pick the lock and get yourselves out of here."

Lorquel handed the sharp stone to one of the others who was more suited to lockpicking, then turned to Gabrion. "Why?"

"Kallisorian troops are on their way to pick me up. You won't want to be here when they arrive. I told you when you came here that I wanted no killing, and I meant that. So free yourselves and get out of here. I don't recommend you linger about trying to rouse your comrades as you go. You're better off fleeing."

"Got it!" the rogue cackled as the prison bars swept open.

Gerta yanked herself away from the others and stalked over to Gabrion, spitting on him through the bars. "Rot away, boy warrior."

"Two guards on the stairs leading up, four more by the exit," Gabrion warned them.

Lorquel stepped over to Gabrion's cell. "We should get you out, too."

"No. I'll be fine. Go. Flee this place. And don't leave that piece of stone behind. Discard it somewhere away from here. I don't want it around."

"But how did you know it would be there?"

"The Path of Pain," he muttered, shaking his head. "Lorquel, take care of yourself. If we meet on the battlefield, I pray we refrain from harming each other. Now go!"

Hesitating in indecision, the soldier bounced in place for a moment, then bolted from the room, leaving Gabrion alone in the dungeon.

"It can't be what the elder of Gerrish meant," Gabrion said aloud to himself. "But if it helps, then so be it."

The sunlight shone through the small upper window and slowly traced its way across the floor. Gabrion sat in silence, wondering when the others would notice that Gerta's troop had knocked out the guards on their way out and escaped. Meanwhile, he sank back and tried to clear his thoughts and rest his body for the events that were surely to come.

From the Ashes

DARIAK SAT IN a tree hut meditating, as demanded by Astrith. The leader of the forest tribe had given him a series of chants to repeat, saying that he needed to utter them until he was summoned. Because he had agreed to remain with Astrith, he felt obligated to comply.

Thus, Dariak was poised on the floor, his legs folded underneath him with his ankles crossed. His hands were overlapped at the wrists, resting against his torso, with his fingers curling upward, but his thumbs pointing outward in front of him. Astrith had him practice the pose several times before sending him off to this meditation chamber, insisting that he keep his back straight and his fingers and thumbs perfectly in place. Since Dariak was a mage, he understood the importance of proper gestures and rituals, though the words he spoke had no bearing in magic at all. They simply washed over him and made him feel a sense of calm.

The leafy door of the hut was pulled open and Yehyona entered, once again wearing nothing at all. Dariak stood up and followed the woman as she guided him on a circuitous path through the forest village. The area was dark, lit only by thousands of blazebugs that winked with their myriad colors as they fluttered about. As Yehyona went, she swayed left and right with the nighttime air, dipping her hands low, or twisting about like a leaf caught in a zephyr. She moved with such grace, Dariak couldn't help swaying along with her.

None of the other villagers were in sight and Dariak found their absence unnerving. Yehyona led him silently toward the south, toward the communal pool. Here, she cupped her hands into the water and doused her skin in its beauty. Before Dariak could do the same, she leaped into the air and continued onward, spinning and stepping with an easy yet random gait.

At the shallow edge of the pool where the water gathered into a tighter stream, carrying off impurities, Yehyona sprinted and pounced over the waterway, giggling delightfully as she did so. Dariak was mesmerized by her fluidity. His guide pressed onward, stopping at times and listening, it seemed. Yet once the wind fluttered again, she continued her erratic procession.

Dariak felt as if he were following a lone leaf through a journey in the woods, resting here and there, but ultimately flying toward some unknown destination where it would seed the soil and bring new life to the land. He felt silly for thinking it, but he couldn't shake the sensation.

Yehyona turned northward and now led Dariak back toward the village proper. Though they could have saved time by heading north from the meditation hut, there was a definite purpose to this trek. The wintery air was cold as the season came on stronger each day; bringing him down by the pond made him realize how chilly the temperature had become. Yet now as they worked their way back toward the village, Dariak could feel a welcome sense of warmth ahead.

The blazebugs lit their way, flashing blue or green or yellow or white, and Dariak admired their concerted effort to illuminate their path. The insects never usually congregated in such massive packs, but Astrith had providence over this forest and even these creatures obeyed his whim. Though as Yehyona brought him forward, he noticed that the blazebugs were not to be the only source of light for the evening.

Dariak's attention was first drawn upward to the canopy of trees. During his travels in the forest, the branches and leaves were fully intertwined, blocking all sense of the sky above except random rays of sunlight that managed to burst through in the daytime. Tonight, however, the tree limbs had parted, opening a wide copse to the sky overhead. A wild white moon shone brightly, its light tickling the leaves and aiding the blazebugs in their purpose.

As they drew nearer, villagers became noticeable along the edges of the path. They, too, were in their most natural state, but their backs were turned and their arms were upraised, with a high crooning song echoing softly from their lips. It sounded like a chorus of nymphs singing to the trees and, in some regards, he realized he wasn't too far off the mark. He closed his eyes and read the energies in the area, sensing that these villagers were the ones tugging on the tall trees and keeping their upper branches clear of the center.

Dariak opened his eyes again, surprised that he had missed something wild and obvious. Yehyona still danced her way ahead, but now he could only see her writhing silhouette, for ahead of them was a gigantic, roaring inferno. A deep trench of water surrounded the blaze, and outside of that was another host of villagers baring themselves to the elements, adding their voices softly to the song that echoed in the background.

Yehyona finally bowed low and settled herself on the dirt, the leaf coming to its final rest. Before her stood Astrith, his body cloaked in a thick robe of leaves and twigs. Dariak glanced around and only he and Astrith covered their bodies in any way. He wondered at the significance of it.

Astrith swept his hands to the side and Yehyona fluttered promptly away, leaving the forest elder bearing down on Dariak in the moon- and firelight. He gestured for Dariak to settle himself on the ground and assume his meditative position, after which Astrith raised his hands up high and with a powerful, resonant voice he added to the song that echoed around them.

Here we reach, ever now, into life and death.
The forest, strong; branches wide; leaves carry breath.
Bare your soul to ancient ways, powers that rule this land.
I beseech you, hear me, connect us all; from heart to hand.

Five dancers appeared and moved in unison, their arms swaying like branches, their feet flowing like flowers. They stepped to the right, bending low, sweeping their arms around and then up high and wide, tracing the sun as it raced through the sky. They then fluttered down, seemingly at random, but Dariak could feel the intentional differences in their movements. Energy flowed through them and connected them and they moved together perfectly, like fingers strumming on a tabletop, each one in a different position, yet working together to create a single staccato rhythm.

Another set of dancers joined the first, while Astrith sang of the bounty of the earth, honoring the life it shared with its inhabitants, and seeking a balance to all there was. Now ten dancers moved together and the bonfire took on a swirling cone-like shape. The men reached high as the women swept low; they pivoted together and then pounced to the right and then left, turning and reaching again. The movements were fast, fast, then slow and graceful. Fast, fast, then slow. Dariak was captivated by it all.

Singing rang out all around him, but he couldn't distinguish the words, not even from Astrith standing right ahead of him. He knew that he was still using his normal tongue, but suddenly the words were incomprehensible. A shred of panic welled up inside of him, and the song increased in volume to refocus and calm him.

Dariak remained on the ground with his legs folded and his hands cradled against his torso. The firelight flickered behind Astrith, its brilliance continuing to swirl about, reaching up higher and higher into the sky, piercing the tops of the trees as if it would touch the moon itself and bring its power down to them. The image felt oddly comforting and Dariak smiled, taking in a great breath of air. As he exhaled, he spoke the meditation phrase Astrith had given him to practice. He hadn't intended to say anything, but his mouth opened and he added his voice to the soulful song that rang throughout the forest.

The brilliant blaze of the fire overpowered his eyes until it was all he could see. Astrith vanished from sight, as did the tireless dancers and the powerful trees themselves. In moments, it was just Dariak and the towering flame. Yet though the fire was enormous and clearly beyond his control to subdue if something went wrong, he did not fear it. There was comfort in the energy of the flames.

With his hands still poised intently against his chest, he felt a strange force press against him, as if someone had thrust a melon against his hands and tried to push it into his heart. He strained his back to remain upright and he continued chanting the words of the meditation without realizing he was doing it. Something else compelled him now. He was a cog caught up in a greater mechanism. Alone, he was insignificant and meaningless, though he also felt he had the power within him to effect change in the world around him. He didn't know how he could be useless and useful at the same time, but the sensation remained with him, coddling him, and filling him with a sense of calm.

Dariak realized his eyes were open and that he wasn't blinking. The fiery blaze now danced and swayed as if it were one of the dancers strutting around the camp and singing. Sparks crackled in time with the musical voices surrounding him, and then ashes rained down from above.

At first he thought it was snow, for the bits of fluff felt cool and soft. Yet the ashes were pulled from the fire and launched into the air, where they then drifted down, cooling along the way until their remains touched Dariak's face. Each one felt like a piece of something he had long forgotten and he yearned to know more, to feel more. Absentmindedly, he pulled off his tunic and cloak, then returned to his meditative pose, now feeling the magical caresses along his entire body. Each ash struck his skin like molten joy, erupting feelings in him that he thought were impossible.

As the euphoria swept over him the fire continued its own dance, releasing more and more ash into the air. And once Dariak's skin was covered, he felt a sense of complete contentment and peace. A life fulfilled and happy. A bliss that every man, woman, and child deserved to know.

He pushed his eyes closed to relish the sensation more completely and as he did so, the echoing song pressed into his mind, sweeping around with such passion his very soul was moved. Tears streaked from his eyes and he smiled without knowing why.

As his body saturated in the energies of the forest, his mind focused and started to make sense of various things around him. No, he corrected, not around him, but in him and through him. He felt the energies of the earth rising and falling through him, magics both new and old. Memories flashed in his mind's eye of spells he knew as a teen and the new enchantments that were being attempted in the Magitorium. The shape of the world pulsed with vibrant colors and he became dizzy, on the verge of passing out.

Dariak opened his eyes, not wanting to swoon and miss any part of this experience. The fire continued its swirling, sputtering dance, and then a dark shape emerged in front of him. It was human in appearance but he couldn't tell who it was, nor could he remember any names anyway, he was so entranced. The figure spoke, though the words only echoed in sporadic parts of his mind. He needed to concentrate on each word and then piece them together into some semblance of coherence. It was as if random members of the village called out one after another to complete each phrase.

"Power of the jades. Ages long ago. Forces of the world around. Unite as one. Complete the task as no one could before. The pieces gathered are not all. Incomplete and yet nearly so. A way exists. A single thread of a tapestry unraveled. Begin anew, balance restored. A life lost in vain to pave the way for you to forge ahead. A gift to you that you may succeed. Assemble them. Recreate the Red Jade. Seek your goal as only you can. Your destiny awaits. Dariak."

Hearing his name shocked him and he jerked upright and lost the connection to the energies around him. He blinked several times to restore his vision and he strained to focus on the setting. The fire was small, like a regular campfire. Moonlight still rained down from above, but slowly the trees leaned back into place, their leaves and branches intermingling. The dancers huddled on the ground, uniformly curled inward and facing the fire. As he scanned the area, Dariak saw that the villagers by the trees slowly lowered their arms and stepped away, the canopy of protection restored.

Astrith walked over to Dariak, now sitting naked in the cold nighttime air. "The energies of the world are all connected," the old man said softly. "They remember things that have come to pass and they sense the path of things to come. Now those energies have passed through you and imparted some wisdom for your journey ahead."

Dariak tried to make sense of what he was saying but the man's language still seemed foreign and it took a few moments for him to decipher the words. "I was connected to energies of the past?"

"Yes. A rare honor, but deemed necessary for you. Have you gleaned any meaning from them?"

Dariak looked up and tried to remember. He paraphrased one part of it, "A life given in vain to forge my path ahead." He swallowed hard, thinking of the human shape he had seen and the warmth of the energies passing through him, the sense of familiarity that was with him. "Was that... Delminor? Was that my father?"

Astrith touched Dariak's shoulder gently. "I cannot interpret any of it for you, Dariak. Though, it is possible that traces of your father were mixed with the energies. He was, after all, a man of this world. Beyond that, he was a great mage who often manipulated the energies here. And more than that, he united with the jades and died by them."

"Was it... really him?" he breathed.

"Not precisely, Dariak," Astrith said. "If you felt him, you may simply have created him in your mind from what you remember of him. One way or another, however, the words in essence must be true. What remains for you now is to commune with those words and discern their meaning." Astrith stood and signaled to the other villagers, who all rose and returned to their huts. The forest elder lingered for only a moment more before leaving Dariak to his thoughts.

As the mage sat there, contemplating the words he had heard from the ashes, he closed his eyes to block out the campfire. The inner warmth and contentment were still with him. He drew a deep breath and exhaled slowly. "Father..."

CHAPTER 59

Mourning

ERVINOR'S ARMY WAS in disarray. Too many people were hurt, scared, or dead and he had no idea how to handle it all. His first order of business was to push the fighters a little further north so they were not resting in the poisoned sand pit where the mage-warriors had fallen. Their altered blood released a stench worse than the burned flesh of the men who had died from spellfire.

Rothra was affronted that Ervinor did not greet him with a warm and friendly welcome, but Carrus interceded as liaison until the general was in a better mood for a meeting. Instead, Ervinor kept his distance from the newcomers as he tried to make sense of the loss of his friend and captain, Quereth.

Lica was a mess over the mage's death, and she could no longer maintain the defenses of the beast jade, nor could she instruct another mage in its use. Thus, Verna took charge of setting up defenses against the feral creatures that would come to them, though Rothra suggested that the beasts would stay away while the poisoned sand continued to reek.

Quereth was only one of seven casualties from the battle and Ervinor had to outwardly maintain a balanced amount of grief for all of them, though he just wanted to drop his duties and mourn for the man who had given his life to protect him. Ervinor knew what had happened and he hated it. Quereth had bemoaned the journey since their arrival in Marritosh and though he could have left the quest at any time, once Ervinor had intervened on the mage's behalf in the Hathren castle, the old mage felt obligated to remain. And now his journey was over, repaying the debt owed to the young general.

It didn't make it any easier for Ervinor to accept.

Kitalla saw the pain in the man's eyes and she stepped over to him, placing her hand on his good shoulder. "Mourn him, Ervinor. I'll take care of the rest." He started to argue, but she silenced him. "No, just mourn him for now."

She turned to the nearest fighters and called out orders. "Prepare to burn our dead, but set aside a separate pyre for the captain of the Nightingales." They saluted and did her bidding, and she patted Ervinor on the back before stepping away.

Kitalla's next task was to meet with Rothra and ascertain his purpose for coming. He had touted his allegiance to Ervinor, but she doubted his sincerity. She meandered through the army until she located the huffy mage.

"Rothra," she greeted with a light, amused tone. "How wonderful to see you."

He eyed her suspiciously. "Somehow, I doubt you mean it."

"Funny. I was going to say the same to you. You've really abandoned your precious tower to join a group of traitors on their way to confront your king?"

"I'm sure it looks dubious from your point of view, but we have our reasons."

Kitalla sat down right beside him and put on her most interested face. "Let's hear those reasons."

"I don't suppose I could just tell you that it's our business?"

Kitalla gave him a wide smile. "No." She eyed him for a moment as he gathered his words but she interrupted him before he could speak. "Oh, don't get me wrong, Rothra. We're grateful you were able to come here to our aid at a time of need. It's just bothersome after all the nonsense going on in your tower that suddenly you've run out from the Council to wander the lands with us. And also convenient that you were able to intercept us at such a dire time."

Rothra's face lit red with outrage and his tone was biting. "Do you accuse me of sending those men to meet you just so I could ingratiate myself upon you?"

"I couldn't have made the accusation any better myself," she said. "And I'm not accusing you; just noting the odd coincidence."

He opened his mouth a few times to reply but couldn't find the right words. At last, he answered, "I was appalled at Shelloni's deceit when it was time to return the jades to Ervinor. He had offered them to us and we were to return them, but she told us to hold them back until she was certain of his intent."

"Fascinating," she said, her tone belying her statement.

"I—" Rothra grunted in annoyance. "Fine, I agreed with her at first. Not to return them all, anyway. To just keep one for the tower so we could continue our work. But I did not expect her ruse of capturing you in the upper levels. I merely thought we were going to assert ourselves over Ervinor. Taking you prisoner was not something I would have agreed to for this purpose."

"Well, she didn't actually know where I was." Kitalla grinned. "But I'm glad her lie upset you. It says you might be human after all."

"Watch your tongue."

Kitalla's voice sharpened. "Me? You mages agreed to borrow and then return the jades, but now you're confessing a plan to keep one of them. But I won't kill you for it. Not now. We need you fire mages to light the funeral pyres." She kept a straight face but her eyes glimmered with a hint of mirth.

He didn't know what to make of her. "Funeral pyres? That's enough to let us live? As if you could even get through our defenses."

"Now, now," she said calmly, "I'm not here to argue, but to find out why you've joined us. All I understand so far is that you're mad at Shelloni. That still doesn't explain why you followed us, unless you're still planning on bringing a jade or two back to the tower."

Rothra narrowed his eyes. "You're astute, Kitalla. That would be a grand success for us here; however, it's not our purpose. The mages who came with me are concerned for the welfare of the refugees and we have come to ensure they reach the king safely. With an escort from Magehaven, you're less likely to face disaster."

"You were a little late for that. Nice sentiment, though."

"You're impossible to talk to," Rothra grumbled. "Where is Ervinor and why won't he see me?"

"He lost a dear friend, so you will have to wait, especially since most of the time in the tower, you made his life miserable. You and Shelloni, in particular. Such petty bickering all the time that you turned to him to sort out your nonsense. And then when he needed your support, you threw him out." She shrugged. "I can't imagine why he would make you wait."

Rothra considered the words and then his shoulders sank down. "I suppose you're right, though I hate to admit it."

"Great," Kitalla said cheerfully. "So tell me, then: How am I supposed to convince Ervinor to trust you long enough to escort us to the castle? And beyond that, how long after we reach the castle will it be before you turn around and shoot fireballs in our faces? I'm rather partial to my nose in particular, so I'd like to know."

"Charming and disarming," he commented. "It is no wonder he travels with you. To answer your question, we will not attack until the king himself orders us to."

"Rothie, you can do better than that."

"Rothra," he corrected angrily.

Kitalla rolled her eyes. "If you want me to take you seriously, then be reasonable."

"What would you have me say? I cannot disobey the king."

Firming her jaw, Kitalla pierced him with a look. "You're going to try to convince me now that you, as a member of the Mage Council, can't at all sway the king or cause him to hold his attack for even a moment. You're that impotent?"

The mage stammered for a moment. "I think I need to stop speaking with you now, if you will excuse me."

"Not so fast," she warned. "If you and your mages travel with us even for the day and a half it will take to reach the castle, then you had better behave as part of this group. You will protect us until we withdraw. I assure you that Ervinor has no desire to attack the king or the castle or the people. He only wishes to deposit the refugees and be on his way. You will see that it's done safely and that we are able to depart without incident. And if you cannot commit yourself to such a plan, then pack your things now and return home, for we don't need you."

He almost visibly withered under her gaze. "You needed us in that battle."

"We would have defeated them eventually, though with more casualties, I'm sure. You did us one service, and we are grateful. But I'm telling you that you need to pledge yourself to us up until our departure from the castle, which—as I said— will be immediately following the safe release of the refugees into the king's custody. And this pledge cannot be like any others you've made to us before, with caveats or ulterior motives. Commit or flee."

His focus turned inward as he contemplated her words. "May I discuss your conditions with the others?"

"Be my guest, but you only have an hour. If you aren't going to stay, then I don't want you here to mourn our dead."

Kitalla stood up and wandered off, looking for Frast and Randler. They sat together in one of the tents, Randler with a lute in hand. He strummed a deep, sad melody, clearly striving to put words together to work with the tune.

"Frast, a moment," Kitalla summoned.

The mage was distraught but he left Randler to his work and followed Kitalla outside. His voice was hollow and his throat was raw. "Yes?"

"I know you're suffering, but I need to know a few things."

"I'll try," he breathed, "but it hurts for me to talk."

"First, are you still channeling the pain away from Randler?"

"Only when he sleeps now."

"You have to stop. I thought we had settled this. No, don't say it," she interjected. "I understand why you're doing it, but pain is a natural part of healing and he needs to heal quickly, now more than ever. Besides, look at the damage it's doing to you."

"I don't care if I lose my voice if it allows him to continue singing."

She placed her hand on his shoulder. "If you hurt your voice any further, you'll lose the ability to use your magic, won't you?"

He nodded. "I already have, actually. Can't put enough power into a single word, never mind a spell. But it's worth it to me."

"Giving up your livelihood for a man who doesn't return your affections? It doesn't sound fair."

But Frast smiled. "It doesn't have to make sense to you. I just know I've done something good for the world by helping him."

She withheld rolling her eyes in exasperation and moved on to her next question. "Do you know anything about those mage-warriors that attacked?"

"Yes," he whispered. "Dariak mentioned the border guardians."

"Mages who lost control of the powers and became consumed by magic," she explained. "But aren't they set along the border and kept under wraps by the rest of the mages?"

He nodded. "Yes, and so they are. But these mages were ones who either only came close to exceeding their limits or who refused to submit as guardians. They're basically retrained and repurposed to act as suicide fighters."

"Suicide fighters?" Kitalla echoed.

"Yes, well, once they activate the poison in their bodies, they don't live for long. It can't be undone. It's how the mages control them, actually, poisoning them but then keeping the toxins dormant. However, the fighters themselves can also unlock the poison, making their own bodies into weapons."

Kitalla shook her head. "Sometimes, I really don't understand you mages. So willing to hurt yourselves just to make things happen."

Frast shrugged. "We do it for love, of one thing or another."

"Hmm," she crooned. "Now I just have to figure out what Rothra's intentions are and whether or not we can trust him long enough to get these refugees to safety. Any way to read him?"

"Maybe the fire jade can help somehow, but I don't know. Kitalla, I'm sorry, but my throat is giving out right now."

"Go back to Randler, then," she said kindly. "Help him find the words he needs."

Later, Rothra gave his commitment to Kitalla, then gathered the fire mages for the funeral pyres. The following hours passed too quickly for her liking. The night drifted in, bathing them in darkness, save the sporadic torches lit throughout the camp. At the northern end, the funeral pyres were established. The six dead fighters were in a row in front of a larger pyre reserved for Quereth. Most of the mages in the army gathered around the pyres, each prepared to add his or her skills to the proceedings.

Ervinor stepped from his tent first, without a tunic, emphasizing the shoulder wound he had received protecting Quereth. He bared it now in homage to the mage, not to show what he had given to save Quereth's life in that previous battle. Instead, it served as a reminder of Quereth's devotion and heart, that he sacrificed himself to protect Ervinor in kind rather than vacate from the army and seek a quieter and more peaceful end to his days.

Not everyone had seen the damaged shoulder and they cringed from the sight of it, hating the reminder of the horrors of war. But Ervinor kept his head high and ignored the flinches of his fighters.

Lica and a few other mages shuffled outward next, Quereth's closest friends. Lica could barely see where she was going, her eyes were so flooded with tears. She may have mocked or teased the old mage when she had the opportunity to do so, but she loved him as dearly as she had ever loved anyone. Now his deep wisdom and heavy voice would no longer ground her when she was in her most irrational moods. He would only live on in her memory, and it left her feeling as maimed as Ervinor.

Friends and close comrades of the fallen fighters stepped forward to huddle closest to the pyres. Sobs echoed through the cool night air.

Kitalla and Frast escorted Randler to the front, where they surreptitiously supported him with the help of his special crutches. He insisted on standing for his performance tonight, regardless of the pain lancing through him now. He took his lute from Kitalla and strummed several bars of a deep fugue.

The lives around us, we have lost.
The reasons are not found.
None can ever fathom the cost.
As we lose our friends to the ground.

Learra, warm of heart and soul.
Bryarr, tender, wise, and sweet.
Polsha, determined to meet her goal.
Jerva, we only recently did meet.
Hethic, a Marritosh fighter of ol'.
Throssha, a stand-in captain in deed.

And at the general's side
was a man whose courage and pride
rose high up into the wind
and did not ever rescind.

For Quereth, the wizened advisor
gave his life in a fire,
protecting the general from harm,
for that was Quereth's dear charm.

We gather now as we commit
the bodies of our fallen
from their lives, now forfeit
to the fires' brightest calling.

We gather now as we commit
the bodies of our fallen
from their lives, now forfeit
to the fires' brightest calling.

The final verse was a standard funeral chant and was echoed by the gathering, repeated again and again as the mages swept their arms up high and ignited each of the seven pyres. Air magic kept the stench of death from wafting over the crowd too strongly, while water mages tended to any ashes fluttering the wrong way.

Rothra and his fire mages tended the blazes for the two hours hence, ensuring the heat raged powerfully into the darkened sky. When all the fuel had been consumed and only ash and scorched sand remained behind, the earth mages drew the remnants into the sand and cleansed the surface by bringing forth a fresh new top layer.

Some of the mourners remained on vigil throughout the night, Ervinor and Lica among them.

CHAPTER 60

Unnatural Walls

KITALLA TOOK TEMPORARY charge of the army as Ervinor slept after mourning through the dark hours. She commanded Carrus and Verna to flank the east and west of their forces, while she took charge of the northern edge. The Nightingales were now without their captain and though some of the fighters within the group could potentially have taken command, Kitalla thought was it best if she stepped in for now.

The Wrens and Eagles did not appreciate being ousted from their usual posts, but Lica and Frast were in no condition to lead their forces. Instead, Kitalla bade them to mingle with the refugees and help to keep the people upright and on the move.

And indeed, she did move them, even with the general sound asleep. Kitalla enlisted Rothra's help in bringing the mages together to create a sort of rolling caravan that transported the people who were immobile after the night's emotional ceremony. He had argued at first, claiming that his mages couldn't perform such a task, as they specialized in fire magic, but Kitalla reminded him that they had followed across the sand at a magical rate and so must have some form of secondary skills available to them. Grudgingly, he obliged her request.

As the afternoon approached, Ervinor awoke from his slumber and he was shocked to find they were en route to the castle.

"We couldn't stay there," she said. "If the king's men didn't return on time, he would send more, and probably a larger set of them, to find out what happened. At least now we'll be on the advance and we can intercept them before they expect us."

"I'm not arguing. It's a good plan."

"Are you awake now or just checking on the situation?"

He saw the exhaustion on her face. She still hadn't fully recovered from her actions inside Magehaven. "I'm fine. Go get some rest." She saluted him officially and went off to the magical caravan.

Ervinor made his way around the camp, assessing the mood among the people. His fighters were grim with their recent loss, but determination pushed them ever forward. The refugees, however, were growing anxious.

"Back in line, peasant," growled one of the Eagles. "We've almost got you to your king and not one of you has died, so stop your griping."

"Yarra, what is this about?" Ervinor intervened.

"Sorry sir, this rabble is unhappy that we haven't stopped yet today."

"Rabble?" Ervinor echoed. His tone sharpened significantly. "I believe these people were uprooted from their homes and sent off into the wild. Perhaps you would appreciate their trials more if I had stranded you at Magehaven and left you in the hands of the people who kicked us out."

Yarra cringed at the seething anger. "Sir! Sorry, sir!"

"Your apology goes to this man, Yarra." He turned to the middle-aged man and asked, "What is your name, good sir?"

"Hallis," he replied. "But don't think scolding one of your lackeys in front of me is going to make me feel any better! Bring us to a halt and let us make camp for a night or two."

Ervinor shook his head. "I am afraid we can't, Hallis. The longer we tarry here in the desert, the less likely we'll safely reach the castle."

"Who asked you to bring us there?"

Ervinor stared at the man sternly. "If you don't agree with the destination, you're free to venture off on your own."

"You're as bad as the rest of them," the man spat. "What if we rallied against you? Then you would take us where we want to go."

"And where is that?" Ervinor asked, genuinely curious. None of the refugees had spoken up thus far about a destination. Even in the tower when Ervinor had asked for such input, no one had stepped forward.

Hallis glared at Ervinor. "You think you're so smart. My son is older than you, by the looks of you. What gives you the right to bully us into submission?"

"I don't follow," Ervinor said. "I only asked where you would like to go."

"I can read your intent clear on your face, like all the rest. You want me to tell you where we should go so you can drop us off at the castle and then take off and destroy the place we want to go to."

Ervinor blew out a sigh. "I'm not sure how I can help you, then, Hallis. You don't want us to take you to the castle but you don't want to tell us where else to go. If that's the case, then we continue with my original plan. Good day."

He walked off after giving Hallis a chance to suggest an alternative, but the man only wanted to complain. Ervinor overheard similar conversations as he made his way to the head of the pack, and he realized that they needed to press onward to the castle before fighting erupted. Kitalla had been wise to get them moving for more reasons than the one she had given.

The trek was not an easy one, especially since Lica was unable to link with the beast jade. The distraught army was attacked numerous times as they went, but Ervinor's fighters were determined not to lose any more people here in Hathreneir, and they fought bravely, taking down the creatures that assailed them.

By the end of the next day, the castle was within reach. The walls loomed ever closer and Ervinor cringed with anticipation. The king hadn't sent any further warriors to intercept them and it gave him cause for alarm, though not everyone agreed.

"He doesn't see your forces as a threat, is all," Rothra tried to explain. "You may have taken down a small band of mage-warriors, but they die off anyway."

"Perhaps his eye is too far focused to the east," Carrus offered, seeing the distress on Ervinor's face.

"No," the general decided. "The king has his defenses ready. Why send them out to us to die one group at a time, when he can hoard them all here and face us with insurmountable numbers?"

"I agree," Kitalla chimed in. "Though on the flip side, when I was here earlier, their numbers were not as great as we would suspect."

Ervinor looked at her cautiously. "But after your stay, the fire jade went missing. I'm sure he tapped the villages for more reinforcements. They probably hadn't arrived yet by the time Gabrion and I came here."

"Perhaps." Kitalla forced a smile, trying not to consider what other changes Gabrion's visit may have effected. Killing the queen surely would not be taken lightly. "However, it seems the point is moot right now." She pointed over Ervinor's shoulder.

A group of forty fighters and ten mages escorted a page on horseback, garbed in lush green silks. He rode forth to greet Ervinor, a scowl marring his face. "I bid you greeting from his most royal highness of Hathreneir, the great desert king. I hail as Brellar. To whom do I speak?"

"I am Ervinor, general of this army. I do not approach your gate as an enemy."

Brellar interrupted whatever else the general was about to say. "You don't think we would welcome such as you into our ranks as Hathren soldiers, do you?" He laughed and fifty voices behind him echoed the mirthless sound.

"I merely bring to you refugees from your land who need your liege's protection and a new home. Marritosh was lost and these men, women, and children are homeless without you."

Brellar's eyes narrowed fiercely. "Marritosh burned some time ago and we lost a battalion to its destruction. What has taken so long to bring such 'refugees' to us?"

"We sought solace at Magehaven, for it was closer to the town. However, the mages expelled us."

"It is true," Rothra interjected, stepping forward and pulling back his cowl. "I have taken flight from the tower for the sole purpose of escorting these people safely to the king."

Brellar turned a curious gaze toward the mage but his tension did not ease, nor did he dismount his horse in greeting. "How can I judge your words, mage, when you have neglected the usual lines of communication?"

Rothra bowed his head. "It was necessary to maintain my silence while with these folks, else they think my goal was to betray them. They speak truly, however. The refugees need their king."

"Betray," Brellar barked. "You ignore the tenets of our land and secretly bring these forces to our door and you are concerned that your actions would have shown them your betrayal. Mark me now, mage, that you have in fact proven your loyalty to them over the king and you will be dealt with accordingly."

"What!" Rothra shouted. "This is preposterous. I have the right to travel these lands with whatever company I choose to keep, without impunity, and without judgment from the likes of you. You will admit me and Ervinor to the king and we will discuss this matter with him."

Brellar shook his head. "In times of war, I have the authority to challenge your admission, and I exercise that right. Turn away from here or take up your weapons and defend yourselves."

Ervinor growled. "We have no wish to fight you."

"That will make our task easier," Brellar sneered. Then, raising his hand over his head, he yelled, "Charge!"

Much to Ervinor's dismay, Brellar's troops responded immediately, raising swords and calling spells at once. Brellar had to be more than a simple page to have such authority, but whatever the reason, it wouldn't matter, if the king's forces won.

Ervinor signaled his fighters to defend themselves, but to keep to his goal of trying not to maim or kill the foes. Rothra, however, was only a visitor to Ervinor's group and his anger at being snubbed enraged him.

Calling to his comrades from the tower, the fire mage stepped into a patterned gait that only years of practice could have prepared him for. He dipped low and twisted around, bringing his arms spiraling upward, all the while clicking out the words of a complex spell from twitching lips. As his fingers fluttered with each motion, he struck into his pockets and withdrew spell components with such grace, Kitalla thought it looked as if he were cleverly pickpocketing himself. Before the first clash of swords, Rothra's initial spell erupted and it was swiftly augmented when the rest of his mages matched his practiced steps.

A wall of fire flared up between the combatants, first only two feet high, but then rocketing upward into the burgeoning night. The fire flashed angrily, streaking outward, threatening the king's men as they approached.

Brellar called a halt, but Ervinor couldn't tell more than that. He spun around to face Rothra. "Kill no one," he warned. "Remember our purpose here."

As the moments ticked by and Rothra's mages continued their augmentations, the fire wall spread further and further out to the sides, creating a blockade that neither faction could cross. Dashing to run around the wall became unfeasible as the length continued to expand.

"Keep on alert," Ervinor cautioned. "We have no idea what defenses they will have against this display of force."

Rothra shot him a belittling glance but he could not respond without canceling his spell. His intricate steps were difficult to follow, and he almost looked like a drunken man caught in a fireplace, anxious to be free even as the alcohol ignited within him. The writhing of Rothra's body was reflected in the dance of the flames themselves.

Kitalla whistled at the growing fire. "This is bad."

"I know," Ervinor said. "Now the king will summon all of his forces to take us down. We may not stand much of a chance."

Rothra grunted in pain and his chanting grew louder in response. Ervinor only glanced at the mage for a moment before realizing that the king's mages were retaliating. He eyed the fire wall and looked for weaknesses in its coloration.

Kitalla also tensed and drew her daggers, her eyes scanning intently. "There!" she called.

She didn't wait. Head low, Kitalla raced ahead, aiming toward a blackened oval that was forming in the wall. She could see the fighters on the other side and she knew they would break through at any moment. She pounced through the gap and threw herself immediately to the ground, rolling aside just in case.

Ervinor screamed for her to stop but she went anyway. The opening wasn't wide enough for more than one person at a time and though he knew his place was with his army, he was also the man in charge of diplomacy. He needed to be there, thus he sprinted and threw himself into the growing hole.

Kitalla was on her feet, her daggers flashing wildly from left to right. Six swordsmen pursued her carelessly, and they continuously clanked into each other as they all tried to strike at once. Kitalla leaped and spun in the air, kicking her feet out and catching one soldier in the head, stunning him. As she landed, three swords swept toward her, but they interrupted each other, rather than cut into her.

Ervinor was less lucky. He drew his sword from its scabbard and he faced off against his own group of six fighters, but they were much better coordinated in their efforts. Two lashed in with attacks, then as they stepped away two others poked their swords in, and so on, working as a fluctuating set of pairs, continuously striving to exhaust their foe and then subdue him.

But Ervinor wasn't about to die here. His goal was to deliver the refugees safely. These people would not fault him for his intended actions, and they certainly would not bring him down. He alternately jumped and dropped to avoid the repeated sword cuts, unable to bring his own weapon about to strike back. Yet he did not surrender himself to their mercy, for it was clear that mercy was not an option. Kicking out at the many feet did little, for the soldiers simply shifted their weight and the next pair was ready to strike.

Kitalla knocked down four of her attackers and they were swiftly replaced by others. Yet as they drew near her, their actions became muddled and ineffective. Kitalla kept moving and shifting her body, evading attacks with each successive step. Sliding down low, reaching up high, she moved gracefully as if there was no threat to her well-being. She saw Ervinor out of the corner of her eye and because he was too far off to help directly, she started to shift her way toward him.

Three other fighters jumped through the gap in the fire wall and they took on other soldiers, but they struggled to hold their position. The king's soldiers saw the lesser skill in the newcomers and they strained to push them into the fire itself.

As Ervinor continued his frantic motions to avoid the incessant sword-thrusts, he dropped his weapon and, when he could, grabbed for the poison darts that remained in his tunic. He didn't have many left from the original batch Herchig had given him, but he needed their protection now if he was going to survive this. Clutching the darts in his hand, he squatted low and then leaped high. With a spin, he tossed the darts, catching two of the soldiers in the face and sending them screaming away from the fight. For a few moments, Ervinor's situation improved.

Kitalla, meanwhile, still worked her way over to him, but now eight soldiers tended to her, thinking they would be more successful than the bungling idiots who had already fallen to her skill. But even with eight fighters attacking her, she kept herself moving fluidly and the soldiers reached out to hit her as if they had no actual idea where she was.

Verna burst through the fire wall, the opening for which widened as the king's mages continued their concerted efforts to bring it down. The Marritosh native helped free the other two fighters who were losing their fight against the soldiers, and once she evened the odds by taking down three of the king's men, she scoured the area and set herself a specific target. Brellar.

The page-commander had removed himself to the line of mages, calling out orders to the rest of the troop. He demanded the fire wall be brought down before its energy was blasted into his soldiers, which would undoubtedly slay them on impact. He only had rudimentary training in sensing the energies; he was no mage, yet he could sense the enormous strength being poured into the wall. And though he looked at the indomitable Kitalla bringing down man after man, Brellar required his mages to break the wall ahead of anything else.

And because the mages were so focused on the wall, Verna was able to slip past them, swinging two swords around and facing off against Brellar directly. The man snarled and pulled out a poison-tipped flail and his shield, though he remained aloft on his horse.

Verna screamed in anger and raced ahead, swishing her swords with each step. Her inhuman cry startled the horse and it whinnied and backed away, but Brellar tugged the reins and kept the beast planted. Verna drew close, sweeping the swords, reaching high to bite into Brellar's body, but the man tugged the horse and it sidestepped out of the way. He then brought his flail down, nearly grazing her arm.

She didn't flinch away from the attack. Instead, Verna lunged closer to the man, driving her sword up and cutting his arm. He was too late to pull away. He dropped the flail and wailed in agony. The horse panicked with the sound and it reared up and snapped its jaws at Verna, who barely avoided being trampled. As the horse thrashed about, Brellar was thrown off, after which the beast ran off to safety.

Verna stalked the man as he writhed in the dirt, his shield forgotten. She crossed her swords and stuck them into the ground at his neck, pinning him precariously.

Kitalla continued her elusive dance, finally reaching Ervinor, who had taken a few shallow wounds. The soldiers became befuddled at Kitalla's approach, their rhythms disrupted and falling askew. Ervinor tried to stand, but there were too many people thrashing about for him to get a strong purchase. Feet clamped down on his ribs, his arm, his legs, and once Kitalla realized he was screaming, she immediately stopped what she was doing.

It took a few seconds for the soldiers to shake off their befuddlement, but by the time they did, a large gap had formed in the fire wall and the Nightingales poured through to put an end to the scuffle.

The king's mages were caught in their spellcasting as they tried to crush the fire spell that parted the two forces, yet as Ervinor's army seeped through the opening, many of the fighters remembered their training; always take out the mages first.

Minutes later, the entire battle site was brought to a screeching halt, and not a single person had perished.

Ervinor's mages sent healing energies through him, giving him the strength he needed to face Brellar for one further exchange. The general approached Verna as she stood guard over her prisoner, her swords still pinning him by his neck.

"Let him up," Ervinor ordered.

"This will not endear you to the king," Brellar scowled. "He will hear and believe my version of events here."

"Very well then." Ervinor said, realizing that the man was bathed in hatred. "Let us bring you back to your beloved king." He called aloud to his forces. "Bind them and bring them with us."

"May we gag them?" Verna asked.

"Only if they speak ill or utter any spells. Gather them up and let's move out."

It took some time to imprison the king's troop, but once the task was done, they continued their march. The refugees were more nervous now, for the spokesman of the king had tried to kill them, turning them away at the mere mention of who they were. Ervinor could not calm them himself, but Randler drew out his lute and strummed away a melody, singing of hope and better days to come.

Night fell in earnest and the fire mages enacted basic spells to light the sky. The castle drew ever nearer, and as they reached the outskirts, Ervinor could see that the defenses had been tightened since his previous visit. Guards were in place along the roads and no villagers roamed the area without escort.

"I am Ervinor," he shouted as soon he felt he was near enough to be heard. "I bring refugees to place in the care of your king. I also return a host of your fighters. I beg audience with the king."

"You arrive at a late hour, Ervinor," responded the nearest guardsman. "The king does not meet with vagrants in the dark of night."

"What would you have me do then?"

The guard considered for a moment. "If you overtook our fighters and have them in your midst, then they are yours to tend to in the interim. As are the supposed refugees. The king will see no visitors until late morning."

"Preposterous!" Rothra barked, storming ahead. "Look upon me and know that you cannot deny me entrance to the castle proper."

The guard examined the mage and his back straightened in alarm. "Master Rothra, whatever are you doing with these people?"

"Ervinor may be young, but he commands this army and he already informed you of its purpose here tonight. Awaken the king if you must, but be off with you immediately."

The guard was torn, but he held to his orders. "I'm sorry, great mage. But if I allow you inside at this hour, there will be repercussions that I can't endure. No, sir, I'm regretful, but I can't permit even you, great sir."

The mage drew in a rattling breath of anger and Ervinor intervened this time before Rothra summoned another wild spell. Ervinor saluted the guard. "We shall concede to your will, good sir. Mind you, we will necessarily set up defenses in the event that the night is not peaceful."

The guard turned his head fearfully away from Rothra, who shook with rage. "You will not need defense from us, so long as you remain beyond the wall."

Ervinor nodded. "Nonetheless, we need to ensure our safety." He turned around and gave the signal to make camp for the night.

Kitalla managed to calm Rothra down and head off to sleep in case they needed a sudden miracle. She bolstered his ego for the sole purpose of convincing him, and it worked, as she suspected it would.

"You're even more exhausted now after that scuffle than you were this morning," Ervinor noted.

Kitalla shrugged. "We're all tired."

"You used your dance skill again in that battle to bewilder the fighters."

She gleamed. "I even pulled some of the energy from the metal jade into the mix. It made it easier to ensnare them with their swords and stuff."

"Kitalla," he started, then fell silent.

"Hmm?"

He shook his head, unable to find the words he wanted to say. "Have Carrus and Verna set up a perimeter, then you and I need to get some sleep. I'll need you as fresh tomorrow as possible."

With a quick salute she ran off to carry out his command. He then made his way back toward his tent, which a few of the fighters had already gotten together. Yet before he went inside, he detoured to visit Randler and Frast.

The bard was in terrible pain from the long journey and Frast was huddled nearby, offering what healing herbs and tonics he could, since Randler had refused to allow him to channel away the pain with the jades.

"I may have need of your silken tongue, friend," the general said by way of greeting.

Randler smiled warmly through his aches. "There is little I can say that you cannot say already, but if you need me, then I am yours to command."

"Thank you." Ervinor looked at Frast. "I know you're busy helping Randler here, but I need you back in charge of the Sparrows."

"There's little I can do," the mage struggled to say with his broken voice. "I can't even give orders any longer. I'm sorry, Ervinor. I can't."

The straggled voice reminded Ervinor of just how badly the mage's throat had been damaged and he realized the truth of the words. He nodded slowly, frowning. "I am sorry, Frast. You're right. I will have to replace you, I'm afraid."

An awkward silence followed before Ervinor turned away and left them. He also needed to consult with Lica to bring her back from her despair over Quereth's death. But as he considered it, he realized that he couldn't handle one more loss tonight. In case she would tell him that she could no longer lead either, he avoided the conversation instead and returned to his tent. Somehow, in some way, sitting at the door of the Hathren castle town, with a host of refugees and prisoners under his watch, with an unknown number of soldiers waiting to greet them come morning, and a persuasive conversation with the king looming ahead of him, Ervinor managed to fall asleep.

Ousted From the Outpost

GABRION PACED AROUND his cell, hoping his requests to speak with Ordren would be heard, but after a day and a half of asking, the commander had not come down. No other visitors had arrived either, save Ordren's most trusted soldiers, who only brought down food and emptied his chamber pot.

Overhead, there was constant noise and Gabrion worried about what it portended. Had the Kallisorian and Hathren soldiers been fighting against each other? Had the Hathrens been expelled? No one would give him any indication of what took place in the world above and the silence was aggravating.

As he wandered around his cell, he heard a commotion by the door. Closing his eyes, he focused his thoughts on trying to catch the snippets of conversation carrying through the air, but it wasn't enough for him to piece together. Then the talking turned to shouting.

"You will allow me to enter immediately or you risk all-out war right here and now in your beloved outpost." It was Ruhk's voice.

Apparently his threat held little weight, for Ruhk's next words rose up high. "Very well then. But tell Gabrion that Hathren forces are on the way. It seems Gerta and the rest alerted nearby patrols. Ah, it dratted well was your fault, you pathetic lot of fools. How else would they have escaped the dungeon?"

There was a pause in the conversation as the guards responded directly to Ruhk but below Gabrion's earshot. Then the commander bellowed, "Fine, fine, I will go, but mark my words; I will return in two hours hence and I *will* speak to Gabrion one way or another, so be ready for me."

The booming voice died down and Gabrion sat down to think about Ruhk's words. If they were true, then a battalion was on its way, and it seemed as if Ordren might not be preparing for the attack well enough. However, if Hathrens were indeed coming, then why wouldn't Ordren immediately expel Ruhk's forces? After all, additional Hathrens would only add to Ordren's troubles.

Yet it was the end of Ruhk's shouting that affected Gabrion the most. He doubted the man had shouted his warning for the guards directly. Instead, he thought the commander was trying to alert Gabrion himself of some plan.

There wasn't anything he could do in the interim, so Gabrion set himself to a series of limbering stretches, in case his hunch was right. Halfway through his routine, he stopped and shook his head, thinking about the exercises he was doing. They were familiar and not because he had been doing them for months. He considered his surroundings and the crunches and jumps he performed, and then it struck him. Gabrion was following the ritual warm-up exercises from his days in the Prisoner's Tower where the strongest men had labored to supply the tower with various needs, including cycled water and boulder-powered lifts.

He hadn't thought of his incarceration in a while. It seemed so long ago, it could have happened to some stranger and he had only pictured the events in his mind while listening to one of Randler's songs. Those days had been grueling, but his body had gained a good deal of muscle mass that he later transformed into fighting prowess. Coupled with his natural skill, he was a veritable killing machine when he wanted to be.

The irony struck him that he now sat in a cell because he had been trying to stop the killing. Ruhk had become a temporary ally in the experiment, but he had made it clear that it was only for the moment. Yet, when the two hours passed by and another commotion sounded by the door, Gabrion started to wonder.

The dungeon door burst open and Ruhk stomped inside with three fighters, two of whom were Gabrion's. The burly commander handed a key ring to one of them, unwilling to fumble with the lock on Gabrion's cell himself.

"You look better out of there, lad, so let's go," Ruhk said.

"I intended to wait until I would speak with the king of what we were accomplishing here."

Ruhk barked a laugh. "You won't have a chance, I'm afraid."

"Because Gerta alerted another group from your army and they're on their way."

Ruhk nodded grimly. "Indeed, but there is another problem for me. You see, this little experiment of yours branded us as traitors through and through. They're coming to kill all of us now."

"I'm sorry." And he truly was.

"No, Gabrion, I'm not. You see, I've been thinking about it." He tilted his head and tapped his temple philosophically. "My king is ready to kill all of us and turn us out as traitors because you and I broke bread for a few days. Your king, and his followers like Ordren, are just as mull-headed. You missed a bit of fun, actually. We've taken over this place."

Gabrion's eyes shot up and he paled. "What!"

"Now, now, no one was killed. But Ordren and his lot are now stuck in his little war room. A good twenty of them or so. Somehow they had it in their heads that they would get the rest of the Kallisorians here to rise up against my fighters and push us out, while Gerta's reinforcements came and destroyed us, as if we couldn't fight for ourselves, but whatever. Solid enough plan, though, I will admit. But something happened that your buddy wasn't expecting."

"I can't imagine."

"Can't you?" Ruhk grinned, and he clapped Gabrion's shoulder strongly. "Your troops and mine banded together in the end, you see. No one was happy to hear you were sent down here. Well, most weren't happy, anyway. Still, the rest of your men, like Urrith and your other officials, came to me asking if we could find a way to work through our differences after all. Well, you know I wasn't about to turn my back on my king—family back home and everything—but the message from Gerta was clear. It even had the royal seal. We're already traitors.

"Well, none of my boys are going to side with the Kallisorians, and only a few of them would rather face execution, but the rest of us decided to follow you and your new way of things. At least for now," he finished flippantly. "Oh, and pretty much anyone who isn't locked up agreed, too."

"I—I don't know what to say."

Ruhk took a sword from one of the fighters and handed it over to Gabrion. "Say you'll lead us properly now."

As Gabrion looked at the man, he realized that he was serious. He had just committed himself to Gabrion's cause. He reached out and accepted the sword. "We have work to do then. Let's go speak with Ordren."

"I figured that would be your first order of business." And off they went.

As they worked their way through the outpost and up to Ordren's office, the others cheered at seeing Gabrion released from his prison. He raised his hand in greeting, awed that they rallied behind him so willingly. He only hoped it would last.

The door to Ordren's study swung open, a host of guards ready in case the commander or his followers attempted to escape. But they were huddled around the room, clearly defeated.

Gabrion stepped up to Ordren, shaking his head. "I'm disappointed in you."

"Shut your mouth, little child," Ordren spat. "Your stupid rebellion won't last long and you know it. It will only be a matter of time before the king sends another group to this place and then what? You'll warp their minds too? Maybe soon you can all bake cakes together and sew dollies for little girls."

Gabrion frowned and turned to Ruhk. "I hate to do this, but there isn't much choice in my mind. Find me one fighter for each of these men. Be sure they are devoted to the cause."

"What are you going to do with me, Gabrion?" Ordren wondered, fear lining his eyes now.

The warrior turned his deep brown eyes and bore into Ordren's soul. "I am sending you and your soldiers to the king with an escort strong enough to ensure that you won't try anything. While you're with the king, fill him in on everything that has happened here. And tell him that he needs to open his mind to my way of thinking, because if he doesn't then there won't be much room left for him in his own land."

"Traitorous bastard!"

Gabrion debated whether he should remind Ordren that he himself had deserted the king half a year ago when he fled Pindington and joined Gabrion in the first place, but seeing the blind anger in the man's eyes, he decided against it. "I'm making you a messenger, Ordren. Though, if you prefer," he said, his voice growing cold, "you could just challenge me to a duel."

The commander's face went white but he said nothing else.

When the volunteers arrived, Gabrion shook each hand and thanked them for their service to him. Urrith took charge of the group, saluting Gabrion.

"I'm proud to have you leading them, Urrith." Gabrion gave his instructions, to guide Ordren for two days to the east and then to set them onward to the rest of the way to the king. Urrith's men were then to return to the outpost for further instructions.

The captain saluted again. "I'll ensure that we live up to your ideals, Gabrion. We'll return in four days' time." With that, Urrith and his team each took a prisoner and left.

Ruhk whistled low once they were gone. "But the thing I don't understand is how you're sure Ordren won't turn around once they're set free and try to kill Urrith and the rest."

"He knows he won't be able to," Gabrion explained. "These men have been training with me since I arrived here, but Ordren hasn't been. He would likely be the easiest target of them all. And being close enough to the king, he would be better off reaching his majesty and securing reinforcements first. There is also a chance that his original discontent will resurface and he may run off on his own. Either way, survival will rule him at that point. Now Ruhk, we need to find another twenty or so who would remain here in the outpost for Urrith's return."

"What? You make it sound as if we are leaving."

Gabrion nodded. "We will meet this battalion on the field and quell them there. I won't have them enter this place and disturb the truce we've established here."

Ruhk's jaw dropped. "I don't know what to make of you, but if you're serious, then we need to move out immediately. It won't be long before they would be able to reach us here."

At the top of the hour, Gabrion, Ruhk and nearly two hundred fighters stormed from the outpost, making haste to the west. The winter air was biting, but it prompted them to jog to keep warm, thus adding to their progress. They camped only once before coming to the Hathren forces in the freezing desert evening.

"Halt, invaders!" cried the Hathren commander. She had long, rich hair flowing beneath a jewel-encrusted leather helm. Her body was covered in iron armor, with other gems fused at key locations.

"Ishalie," Ruhk returned. "How well it is to see you."

The woman snarled. "Don't speak to me on such friendly terms, scum. You deserted the king to fraternize with these vermin."

"I admit I was curious about Gabrion's proposal, and you would do well to listen to his words, for if you do not, then you will be sorely defeated this night."

Ishalie barked a laugh. "You may think you outnumber us, man to man, but you would be mistaken. Mages!" At once her four mages chanted their spells, calling to the beasts of the desert, summoning them to their aid. Sandorpions, eaglons, shadowcrows, and sand rodia all answered the call, appearing from nearby nests set up for the purpose.

"Stop!" Gabrion shouted. "There will be no killing today!"

"Speak for yourself, soldier boy," the Hathren commander snarled. "Attack! *Attack!*"

Gabrion brought up his sword and ignored the nearest threats, charging only for the Hathren commander. If he could overwhelm her, perhaps she would surrender the same way Ruhk had done. Reaching her was difficult, for the beasts that joined her battalion brought the numbers well above two hundred and her soldiers were well accustomed to fighting alongside the feral creatures.

Ruhk sprinted off to deal with the mages, his sword cutting down three eaglons as he went. He wondered belatedly if Gabrion's no-kill rule applied to the desert creatures, but he had to let the thought go as two sandorpions slithered in front of him, raising their tails to strike him down. Ruhk weaved to the side and avoided their strikes, stepping into a soldier's range of attack. He turned to parry, but he missed and took a gash in his arm. Yelling, Ruhk spun around and dropped, crashing the flat of his blade into his attacker's knees, bringing him down. He then swept his sword up and thrust into the underbelly of one of the sandorpions as it pounced on him, trying to gouge out his eyes with its front pincers. The beast squealed and thrashed as Ruhk propelled it on top of the man who had cut his arm. He then pushed himself up to fend off the other sandorpion's attack.

Gabrion's charge took a similar pattern, as he kicked up one sand rodia and grabbed it with his left hand, then hurled it into the face of an oncoming swordsman. He then twisted and dodged an eaglon attack, kicking his foot up and catching the bird in the abdomen and knocking it from the sky. Two soldiers approached him, swords at the ready. Gabrion taunted them each in turn with his sword, trying to get them to let their defenses down. At last one pounced and Gabrion batted the man's sword aside, then grabbed his wrist and hurled him into the other attacker, felling them both. He didn't wait to knock them out, but pressed on to subdue Ishalie.

The Hathren commander shouted as Gabrion approached her. She had a wild look in her eyes as she pulled out a sword and dagger, ready to take down the young warrior. She entered a hunter's crouch and stepped cautiously side to side, her lips moving frantically.

Gabrion wasn't fooled. He leaped immediately to interrupt whatever spell she was trying to cast. His sword swept in and she deflected it with the dagger, returning the strike with her other arm. Gabrion dropped, kicking his legs out, but she jumped over his attempted sweep and brought her sword around again, her lips continuing their chanting.

One of the garnets on her headdress flared to life as she completed her spell and a wild flame extended down her sword arm, resting on the blade. It flared with each swipe of her sword, sending stinging waves of heat in Gabrion's direction. He swatted the sword away, but she kept a firm grip, cackling now that she felt she had an advantage.

Ruhk scurried away from another set of creatures and approached one of the beast mages. He offered an easy surrender, but the mage scoffed at him for the attempt, so he lunged at her and punched her into submission. The next mage stopped his chanting and retaliated by calling up a flurry of ice darts, striking Ruhk as he battered the first mage. While the icy projectiles cut into his skin, Ruhk grew furious and he jumped up and sprinted to the mage and tackled him as well, pummeling him until his chanting stopped.

Without the guidance of their masters, some of the beasts became bewildered and attacked any fighter nearby, regardless of which side they were on. The ensuing chaos helped Gabrion's troop to overcome their foes more easily.

Ishalie, however, proved to be an able foe for the young warrior. She had enacted a second spell which allowed her to move more quickly than before. A second gem on her helmet was aglow as the spell held. Gabrion kept his sword and body moving rapidly, dodging wildly, and blindly anticipating more moves than he cared to imagine. He acted on instinct, but the fiery sword helped him trace her movements, for the blazing blade left visual traces in the darkening sky and his body responded accordingly.

Some of Gabrion's fighters took care of the other two mages and Ruhk was free to assist his new leader. He sprang toward the flaming sword despite the wracking pain from his wounds. Gabrion was tiring, but he continued to pounce nimbly, poking his sword here and there, trying to score a minor wound that would at least slow the woman down, yet he had no idea if he was successful. Ishalie continued chanting spells but Gabrion couldn't see any actual effects from them, and he wondered if she was using the magic to heal any damage he was causing.

The fiery sword swept in from one side and as Gabrion parried it, Ishalie brought in the dagger, cutting into the warrior's side and dropping him to the ground. He immediately rolled away then regained his feet, clutching his wound. Gasping for breath, Gabrion hoisted up his sword, narrowing his eyes to track the movements of the roving fire sword.

Then all at once the flaming weapon fluttered upward and then landed in the sand. Ishalie screamed, after which the air filled with sounds of punching. Gabrion squinted in the growing darkness to see Ruhk's body pinning the woman down, his fist crushing the fight out of her until at last she stopped struggling.

The rest of Gabrion's battalion fought admirably. They fully employed their dodging skills, sweeping low and out of the way as their attackers lunged for them, and then striking back to render them unconscious. During the entire scuffle, two of Gabrion's fighters took fatal wounds, but no one else died. Even many of the feral creatures survived, most fleeing once the enchantments of the mages were gone.

Gabrion only had three mages in his entourage and they rushed over to him to treat his wounds first. After repairing the worst of the damage, they tended to Ruhk, and then spread out among the rest to assist where they could. Gabrion was not used to having dedicated healers who barely fought in the actual battle, yet he was grateful for their support once the fighting was finished.

"What will we do with them?" Ruhk asked, looking over Ishalie as she lay on the sand, her face showing signs of the beating she had taken.

"We'll have to—" Gabrion stopped, his attention snared by something in the distance. "Ruhk," he pointed to the west. Far off, a wild fire burned into the night sky.

"That must be near the castle," Ruhk estimated.

"It must be Dariak," Gabrion decided. "Listen, Ruhk, we're all tired, but we need to press onward and reach that incendiary."

"I don't know if everyone will be able to. Besides, what of her and the rest?"

Gabrion sighed heavily. "I just—I have to go there."

Ruhk clapped him on the shoulder. "Then go. Take whomever can travel with you. The rest of us will tidy up here and then we will follow."

Gabrion looked around the battlefield and nodded slowly. "You all did well tonight. And you, Ruhk, especially did well. I could see the anger and hurt in your eyes, but you kept true to me, and for that I am grateful."

Ruhk playfully nudged Gabrion in the chest. "Knock it off, you're going to make me blush."

CHAPTER 62

Dariak's Return

THE FOREST AIR was refreshing and crisp, full of life and wonder. Dariak opened his deep blue eyes and marveled in the vibrancy all around him. The leaves, the cot, the air; they felt alive and within reach. He stretched upward and created a gentle breeze by wafting his hand left and right, and he rejoiced in the sensation of the air brushing against his skin. As he lay there, he ran his fingers up and down his body, as if he were feeling his flesh for the first time. Something inside him had changed.

He rose and stepped from his chamber, staggering out into the evening air. Astrith sat on a log nearby, gazing into a gentle flame. The elder greeted the mage softly. "You have awoken."

"I think…" Dariak started, then tried again. "I think it's the first time I've ever been truly awake."

"The feeling will pass," Astrith said sadly, "unless you remain here and devote yourself to our ways." He lifted his gaze from the fire. "I see you have neglected to clothe yourself this evening. Was that intentional or an oversight?"

Dariak looked down and chortled. "I didn't even notice."

"Then you are ready for your next challenge, Dariak, for you have shed a trace of your vanity. You've opened yourself up to a wider purpose. You have touched the heavens and the trees and the earth, and you have seen that you are but a glimmer of the world around you. And in that, there is no need to be self-conscious."

Dariak crouched down and nodded slowly. "I still don't fathom all that I experienced last night, but I agree that I see more now than I did before."

"It too will pass. Yet perhaps you are different enough to hold on for a while longer than most." He smiled slowly. "Your quest, however, must continue, for you have fires in your heart that need tending. People are depending on you and have been fighting for you, and it is time you rejoined them."

The mage looked down at the ground. "I know. Though I don't understand what I'll do when I reach them."

"You will do as your heart demands, and whatever that means for the rest of us… Well, we will simply have to wait and wonder."

"Astrith… About the energies last night…"

But the old man shook his head. "No, Dariak, there is nothing else I can tell you besides that which I have already said. Linger here if you will, but I fear you will miss your rendezvous if you do. I think your place is instead with the people you have drawn around you. You would do well to go to them. They will have missed your presence and they will need you in the days to come."

Dariak knew he was welcome to stay if he so chose, but Astrith was right; he needed to go. He returned to his bed and donned his cloak, ensuring he had the healing jade, then set off, following its vibrations as they led him to the east.

Dariak's mind raced as he let the forest fade away behind him. There was such life and vividness in the wood. He couldn't imagine leaving it behind and becoming as disconnected as he had been before. Yet he knew in some way that even feeling this way made him part of the larger whole. His ideals were no longer the simple yearnings of a younger man, but they were calls of the greater energies that needed him to facilitate their message to others. It was he who could bring peace to the land in a way no other could. He was connected to all the energies, not just those of nature. And unlike his beloved father, he was not bound to the king's will and desire. He could act as he saw fit.

Yet he still needed to reach his friends. More than that, he needed to find and heal Randler, whose unnecessary suffering had gone on for entirely too long. With the healing jade, he could mend the bard's agony and, once he united the jades and brought peace, he could settle down with the man and they could find a better life altogether.

Dariak breathed in the nighttime air and turned himself to the east, aching to reach his destination with haste. On foot, he would need perhaps three days to make the journey, if he accounted for the occasional intrusions of the desert beasts who would invariably meet him along the way. Or perhaps they would now sense his deeper connection to the whole while it was still new and fresh; maybe the creatures would step aside and let him reach his goal without impedance.

The mage grinned, knowing it was a ridiculous thought. However, the idea that followed it was less absurd and he set himself to the task immediately. His recent lessons in the Magitorium and the forest had shown him that he possessed a deep connection to the energies in the world around him. Why not call on them now? Why not ask them for help in his time of desire? Though he knew it was desire, not need, he opted to call anyway.

Dariak stretched his mind outward and reached far and wide. His feet bathed in the dirt underneath him. His lungs drew in the fragrant air. The essence of nature filled his very soul, and he knew that these powers would work well together. He pushed his foot forward, sweeping his arms through the air, then stepped with his other foot, pulling ahead with his hands. The ground beneath him melted into a glimmering pool and the air tensed like a lifeline, tugging him forward. Meanwhile the essence of nature kept the forces in balance, allowing him to essentially ski across the sandy earth as if he were cascading down a steep mountain.

Pull after pull, he went, drawing the energies through himself without any spell components or the necessary jades. He simply used his connection to the energies to facilitate the process, and as he made his way, he relished in the ease of it all.

Every breath was crisp and fresh; every step carried him yards ahead. The landscape rushed by him as if he were an eaglon diving across the desert.

After a few hours of travel, he saw a deep fire light the eastern sky. The brilliant blaze swept up into the air, swirling about, and falling away again. Dariak focused his thoughts on his haste, hoping to propel himself to the source of those temporary flames, for the healing jade confirmed that the other jades awaited him there. At last he would unite them and have the strength he needed to stop the war.

But he needed to get there first, and so he urged the energies to pulsate within him faster and faster, drawing him ever closer as the land whizzed by. Yet though he was connected to the energies of the world, he still required strength to maintain them. His desire to reach his friends could not overpower the growing fatigue that gathered within him. The energies faltered as the hours pressed on, yet he did not relent. He urged himself to reach them, to reach his friends, to find Randler.

Dariak filled his mind with thoughts of the bard, aching for leaving him behind in the forest, but grateful that he had claimed the healing jade at last. He knew there would be more to mend than just Randler's legs, but it couldn't be helped. The quest for the world was greater than any one of them. His heart beat with the truth of it, as it must have also done for his father. For Delminor to give his life to try to assuage the fighting, he must have known deep within himself that his life was merely one necessary spark of hope. It was a spark that Dariak intended to turn into a blaze.

The night fell away as the sun peered over the horizon and Dariak neared his destination. Silhouettes of soldiers moved about and he targeted them, reaching out blindly to be recognized before he was attacked errantly. He had been gone from the group for so long, he half-wondered if anyone would know him at all.

The need to keep the energies circulating around him waned and then faded completely. Dariak fell to his knees and huddled there to catch his breath. He rose and strode toward the warriors without any further rest. It was time at last to rejoin his comrades.

Dariak was exhausted from his frantic journey through the night, but the dawn light met him with no hope of rest, for a violent battle was underway.

He had no sense of who was fighting yet, only that the healing jade called for him to press into the center of the scuffle. Warriors swung their swords aloft as mages swept their arms around, casting spells. Dariak felt the energies pulsating all around him, and he realized that these mages were only deflecting incoming projectiles. They were not attacking.

He called his own protections about himself as he plunged into the fray, seeking the center where he knew his friends and allies were engaged in the scuffle. His presence was barely noticed among the others for he slipped in from behind and not from the front lines.

Swords and maces flew toward him but he dodged low, seeking only to escape unhindered. Other fighters came in to defend against the attack and Dariak used the diversion to slip away. He had little stamina left to subdue the enemy forces seeping through. And in some ways, he wasn't completely certain who his allies were, for Ervinor may have launched this assault for some reason, and the king's army might be the defenders. He doubted it, but he didn't want to find himself mistaken later.

Pushing through the crowd, Dariak stumbled across a pack of terrified villagers, cowering together and refusing to do more than scream and cry. They were surrounded by numerous fighters, both attacking and defending, but the people themselves only wept and prayed for the fight to end.

Angrily, Dariak shouted above the din, "Get on your feet and defend yourselves. Take up shields and hold off your attackers. If you lie there, you leave your life in others' hands. Be brave and rise up now. Cast aside your fears and defend yourselves. Rise up! Rise up! I care not how old you are. Grab a shield and defend yourselves." Only a few responded to him, but they returned to their huddled positions once they saw that none of the others stood with them. Frustrated, Dariak moved on.

Soon, though, he made his way toward the heated battlefront and at last he saw faces he knew well. Ervinor and Kitalla shouted commands while swinging their own blades around, holding back the king's men. From this vantage, it was clear to him what was happening. They were at the castle and the king defended his land, but Ervinor and his forces held off the attack.

The young warrior dipped and wove about, smacking his foes with the flat of his blade. Even with his life on the line, he did his best only to subjugate his enemies, not kill them.

Kitalla was also a blur of movement as she flashed about on the field. She cut low, nicking one man's trousers, then she spun about and punched another in the face. The thief pounced next, grabbing the wrists of another fighter and shaking the sword from the man's hands. He tried to bite her, but she smashed his skull with her own, knocking him out. She shook off her own pain and launched herself toward the next assailant, each time avoiding attack and either parrying with a sword or punching with her fist.

Mages ran along the ranks, fistfuls of herbs trailing behind them as they projected healing spells into the defenders. Dariak was highly impressed with their efficiency as well as their abundance. Ervinor had clearly enlisted the help of other mages along the way.

He didn't see Randler or Gabrion, but they could be anywhere. The ringing of steel and iron echoed incessantly through the air, and the grating sounds hurt Dariak's ears, especially after his recent respite in the forest. He wanted more connection to nature and less to the cold hard metal. But he knew if he stood idle for much longer, then steel would make its way into this life, irreparably.

The healing jade throbbed in his pocket and he knew suddenly that would be as impervious to attack as Pyron had been. That calmed his thoughts long enough to allow him to focus. He knelt slowly, reaching out for the other jades nearby. He could sense them calling out for their lost brethren. Kitalla clearly had the metal jade. Near her or with her was the fire jade. The beast and nature jades were somewhere behind him, and so forth. He let their locations call to him and he stretched his fingertips out as if he could caress each one.

Mentally, Dariak pulled the jades across and down, over and through, weaving their energies into a larger whole. Some of the elements shied away from the attempt and he didn't have time to enforce them. Beast, nature, water, and earth accepted his call with the least resistance, and so he grasped their energies and swept them together, drawing up power from the healing jade as he did so, for it helped to maintain his strength for the duration.

"*Noss, shoni nofferus. Derripethicar kryie malliyon greth,*" he chanted, not knowing where the words were coming from. "*Jassikorruth bwaranalus norch k'wai prosthrafar bretchigon kyrecshio.*"

The energies compelled him to dig his hand into the sand and sweep a great arc into its surface. As he did so, great cries of terror erupted before him. He couldn't look up, for more words rushed to his mind and he spat them out, his eyes turning up to the morning sky as a flock of eaglons dashed across his vision, answering his unknowing call. The violent birds screeched in unison, creating a piercing shriek that rent the air. The cry continued for several moments, and all around him, Dariak could tell that people were falling to their knees, clutching their skulls in pain.

He dragged his fingers through the sand again, creating a deeper trench. This time he was less surprised by the frightened cries in the distance, for he understood now that the small trench before him was becoming a much larger ditch ahead.

The scream of the eaglons ended and the avian beasts swept low, their poisonous talons outstretched but not quite aimed to strike. Powerful wings swept down and up, keeping the birds aloft over the battlefield.

Tremors rumbled in the ground near Dariak and so he dragged his fingers again into the sand, widening the trench until he reached every sensation of trouble around himself. Soon there were deep patches everywhere with bewildered cries echoing in the distance, until at last the noises faded slowly away.

He felt the energies withdraw, including that of the healing jade. He had taxed himself entirely too much and his body couldn't sustain the effort any longer. Bereft of the magical energies, Dariak's body reacted to the turmoil he had endured since leaving the forest. Blisters formed on his feet and hands. His muscles raged with exhaustion, and with the loss of the healing jade's assistance, he fell over, his body shaking with wrenching spasms.

CHAPTER 63

Battle Dancer

KITALLA'S MORNING WAS not off to a good start. The dawn sun lit the eastern sky and showed her an army awaiting the break of day. They had turned back the king's men during the night, but the Hathrens had not acquiesced to the show of force. Instead, they rose against it.

Into the desert, hundreds of fighters and mages met the rebels, swords poised for battle. They had assembled through the night and Ervinor had not awoken her in preparation, opting to give her a little more time to rest. Kitalla hated such surprises.

Tightening her leathers briskly, she strode from the tent she shared with Verna, pushing her way past the refugees and striving to reach Ervinor's side. She could hear his voice calling out as she approached, but whatever words he used, they were ineffective. As she reached him, the king's army erupted into battle.

Kitalla had chosen two short swords for herself this morning, and she brandished them with fury. With a feral cry, she lunged ahead, pushing past Ervinor and crashing into the front line of men. Her swords rang out in a piercing song as they clattered against her foes, alerting everyone around her that she was a threat not to be taken lightly.

It was difficult for her to defend herself without killing the others, but she managed. Summoning a battle tune Randler had recently composed, Kitalla fell into the rhythm and let her body do its work without interruption.

Two swordsmen rushed her from the left and she bent low under their blades, letting them run past her into other defenders. With a grin, she swept her blades up fast and clipped another soldier as he approached. She pounced into the air and kicked him in the chest, then landed with a turn, bringing her swords down and striking another foe. It was a simple twist of her blade that kept her swords from cutting into these foolish men. They were not going to subdue her, but neither would she kill them.

Early in her quest, Kitalla would have slain the soldiers without a second thought. Too much had happened since her thieving days. Too many past pains had resurfaced and too many new scars had scratched her heart. She did not want to be surrounded by death any longer. She wasn't sure when she had truly changed, but

Kitalla knew that she was no longer just supporting Dariak's cause; she yearned for it, too.

Arrows whizzed by and one grazed Kitalla's arm as her mind drifted, causing her to drop one of her short swords. She grumbled in annoyance, more at herself than at the archer, and she retaliated by seeking out the attacker and taking him down. The fire in her eyes terrified the young man and he backed away as she approached, his fingers shaking under her glare. She thought he might faint and save her the trouble of knocking him out.

Once the archer was down, Kitalla faced another set of foes she would rather have avoided: Mages. A team of fifteen mages had joined the soldiers and worked their magic now that the fight was on. Over half of them focused on healing the wounded, and Kitalla ignored them. Instead, she turned toward the offensive spellcasters, determined to reduce their influence before it turned the tide.

The two air mages were the easiest for her to stop. They swept their arms around with blinding speed, sending waves of cutting wind at her. When the bursts of air proved ineffective, they mingled sand with the attack, trying to blind her. Yet Kitalla simply stalked through the sand and wind as if it were a calm, spring day. Panicked, the mages tried to slow her down by thickening the air and weighing her down, but such a spell of wind was barely as effective as Dariak's Shield of Delminor, and Kitalla was able to easily push through the effects.

If the air mages had any inkling that Kitalla possessed the metal jade, and that its power diffused the air, they would have fled. Instead, they combined their skills to summon a greater windstorm, determined to lift her body up high and drop her crashing to the ground. For all their effort, though, the metal jade mocked them and left her untouched. Kitalla rushed in and smashed their heads together, dropping them to the sand.

Seeing the plight of their allies, three other mages scattered off, avoiding the strange woman who was impervious to their spells. They sought other quarry, but Kitalla was not ready to let them go so easily. With a smirk, she chased after a lightning mage, determined to stop him before he could release paralyzing blasts of energy into the fray.

As she went, swordsmen intercepted her and she worked her own magic with every step. She grabbed the wrist of one man, twisting harshly until it popped and he fell down, screaming in pain. Kitalla then avoided a woman with a mace long enough to sweep the legs from another soldier, after which she spun around and brought down the mace-wielder. The woman did not fall easily, though, and she kicked out at Kitalla, stunning the thief's left hand and causing her to drop one of her swords. Kitalla bashed her fist into the woman's face, even as the soldier brought her mace down upon Kitalla's back. The damage was minimal, so Kitalla groaned through it and pressed on.

She continued her pursuit of the escaping lightning mage, but Rothra joined the fight. Fire erupted from the mage's hands, striking the ground and causing the lightning mage to jump around avoiding the fire. If circumstances were different, Kitalla would have laughed at the spectacle.

After defending herself for nearly an hour, Kitalla finally caught a brief rest as the attackers squared off against other defenders. She looked around but she could not see the faces of her friends. Each was off in his or her own section, fighting strongly, or so she hoped.

Thirty seconds seemed to be all the rest she would get, for three swordsmen broke through the line and sought to take her down. She hoisted up her sword, then dropped quickly as arrows and spells flew through the air. The soldiers ignored the projectiles and ran all the faster. Unlike many of the others, these men carried shields on their arms, and though Kitalla knew she could take them on a regular day, she felt she needed to change things up.

Tossing her sword, Kitalla channeled a sultry song of Randler's, one he had sung at camp to make the others blush. The tune followed the tale of a young couple, madly in love, on their first night passionately engaged in that love. The song itself never specifically stated what happened that night, and the words left it open to interpretation. The couple may just have gone for a walk in a garden, holding hands, and kissing. Or, with a slightly skewed and open mind, the careful descriptions hinted at a vivid and raunchy affair. Kitalla held the risqué images in her mind as she stepped about and brought her arms up her body. With a shifting of her hips, the three men were instantly entranced and, moments later, their shields were down and their swords were up, reaching into the sky as if to bring down the light of the sun upon her. Kitalla swept closer to them and then used the momentum of her dance to crack them in the head each in turn.

A battle, however, was no place to dance for long. So she spun and dove for her sword, then ran off and hacked her way back toward Ervinor. As she went, she shouted encouragement to her allies, sometimes supporting them with her sword, other times commanding them to tighten their focus.

Just when her day was on an upswing, the ground fell out from under her, literally. A wide trench split the ground, drawing her and many others within. She first suspected that it was the doing of the king's mages, but the soldiers were just as baffled by the collapse. Kitalla called for help as she scrambled to climb the sloped and sandy edges where there was no purchase. Moments later, the trench widened further and more people screamed as they slipped within.

The trenches swallowed members of both sides of the battle and the entrapped combatants debated the wisdom of taking down their foes versus focusing on escape. Kitalla called orders for them to climb out to higher ground, but it was too difficult as the sand flowed with every attempt. "Come together!" she called out, summoning her fighters to her side. Likewise, the king's soldiers drew together, though they were unsure about Kitalla's intentions.

With nearly twenty fighters at hand, Kitalla turned her back on the Hathrens and called out orders to her comrades, instructing them to create a human pyramid so they could breach the top of the trench and effect an escape. The three burliest men dropped to their hands and knees, where two more climbed on their backs and took a similar position. Kitalla then helped two others climb up to a third tier, but this pair remained standing, carefully setting their feet on the more-protected areas of the men's backs. They were high enough, and so Kitalla helped another fighter scramble up the tower and try to reach the edge.

But a deep, piercing cry shook them and the human tower collapsed in a painful heap on the ground. Kitalla looked up to a row of eaglons hovering overhead holding a wild and powerful screech. Everyone in the trench grabbed their ears and ached for the horrible cry to stop. When the sound died down, they were surprised by the completeness of it.

Kitalla thought perhaps the eaglon cry had destroyed her ears, for all that echoed was silence. People were moving and clearly moaning in pain, but she could hear nothing. There was no clashing of swords overhead and no eruptions of spells. The eaglons hovered, ready to strike, and Kitalla was extra cautious after having been struck when she had dragged Gabrion away from Jortun. Yet the birds did nothing as they hung there in the sky.

She deliberated briefly but then decided to try escaping the trench again. She called commands to the people around her, but they too were deaf. Looking around, the Hathrens also struggled under the odd silence of the area. It didn't matter to Kitalla. She proceeded to give orders by tapping people on the shoulders or arms or legs and pointing where they should go. It was tricky at first, but she kept her frustrations in check and managed to recreate the human pyramid. After that, she was able to help a number of fighters climb up out of the trench.

Nearby, the Hathrens mimicked her actions for no other reason than it was working. They also pulling themselves from the sandy crevice and Kitalla shook her head and laughed. She peered at the eaglons now and then, wondering when they were going to abandon their odd positions and leave them be. She didn't need to wait long for her answer.

The eaglons opened their mouths once more, but only briefly. This time they emitted no sound and they flew off, apparently agitated over being held there for so long. The silence remained for several moments more, but then noise returned slowly. Kitalla felt as if she were at the bottom of a lake, locked away from the world, and she was swimming upward getting closer and closer to the surface and the world around her. Then at last she would burst through and hear the world again, and so she did. The fighting had apparently continued unabated overhead. She needed to escape this trench.

The extra fighters had escaped and claimed some rope, which they threw down for the others. Now the members of the pyramid ascended one at a time. Kitalla clapped her hands to encourage their haste. But they were not quite fast enough.

Just as the spell holding the eaglons in place had faded and the silencing shroud had waned, so too did the walls of the trench collapse. Like a giant wave of sand, the walls fell inward, swallowing everyone still within.

Kitalla saw the sand rushing in and immediately starting running in place, kicking her knees up high. "Hurry!" she cried out to the others. "Follow my lead. You Hathrens, too. Before you're lost. Hurry."

The sand flooded them and Kitalla's quick jogging pace allowed her to hop upon the inrushing material. It wasn't easy and her feet kept getting caught, but she managed to keep herself going while the trenches refilled. Some of the others were not as nimble, however, and she watched as the fluid ground prevented them from keeping their footing. She wanted to help them, but there was little she could do without getting trapped herself.

"Keep moving!" she bellowed. "Keep—"

The battle overhead was still engaged and some fighter had apparently lost his shield. The equipment fell through the air and it clocked Kitalla on the head, knocking her immediately unconscious. Her body fell limp and the sand swept up and buried her.

CHAPTER 64

Ervinor's Sacrifice

THE BATTLE RAGED on for hours and though the combatants grew weary, they pressed on for glory. The king's men strove to eliminate the heathens at their doorstep, whereas all Ervinor wanted was to drop off the Marritosh refugees and be away.

The general had pushed himself hard through the morning scuffle and during the unexpected sandy trenches that swallowed dozens and dozens of fighters. The bizarre eaglon pattern went unnoticed until their piercing cry and the ensuing silence, but Ervinor sensed that the two events were not connected; the eaglons hadn't deafened anyone. Instead, something had changed in the air. Every breath was hard to take, as if the air itself had stopped moving. Only the rush of adrenaline kept them pushing through it, for if they stopped, they would have died at the hands of the king's soldiers.

Then the enchantments ended and everything returned to normal, though many fighters had been trapped in the sand when the trenches refilled and Ervinor shouted for his nearest captain. "Lica! Get them out of there."

The woman was still distraught after Quereth's death, but she did her duty well, gathering her Eagles and setting them to the task of digging up the trenches for survivors. Other fighters helped to defend them as they worked, but even some of the Hathrens abandoned the fight, trying to rescue their friends. Mages were employed to move whole clumps of sand, but the only clue as to where to dig were patches of emptied, untrampled sand, and those did not last for long.

The field fell into disarray. Ervinor scoured the area, looking for Verna and Carrus so he could relay orders to pull back and regroup. Likewise, the Hathren commander corralled his troops so they could relaunch their attack.

Instead he found Rothra. "Ervinor, this is madness!" the fire mage screamed. "I'm fighting against my own people at your behest."

"*You* followed *me*. This is not the time for complaints. We're struggling and we need to regroup. Get the word out to fall back and withdraw toward the refugees. They're why you came, after all, isn't it? Go to them now."

"And you?"

"Fall back," Ervinor repeated. "Spread the word."

Rothra scoffed at the command. Ervinor thought he would deny the orders, but instead the mage surprised him. He clapped his hands together and then blew into the hole where his thumbs met. Flapping his fingers as he blew, he created a loud flute-like note that sounded wholly unnatural in some ways. It drew the attention of everyone nearby. "Withdraw! This way!" he bellowed, then he blew into his hands again.

"That's a neat trick," Ervinor complimented.

"I'll teach it to you some time. No magic needed," the mage grinned smugly.

"Thanks, but it looks like it requires two hands."

"I— Sorry, I—"

But Ervinor shrugged it off. "Get the rest to the refugees. Go." The mage ran off and did as commanded, finding others to help him as he went. Ervinor meanwhile returned to the center of the camp on his own, trying to think of a new plan of defense against the attackers. They were at the doorstep of the castle and he had no idea if the king had a hundred soldiers within or ten thousand. He needed a way to get a message to the king without losing any more of his meager army.

A horn sounded across the way and chills ran down Ervinor's spine, but when he watched the resulting activity, his fear turned to relief. The Hathren commander had called for a retreat. Ervinor understood well enough that it was a temporary cease to strategize, but he didn't care. Any moment of rest was welcome indeed.

With a jog, Ervinor made his way to the refugees at the center of his army. Many wounded fighters gathered together and the mages united as healers to do their work in force. In teams of three, the mages combined their spells and swept healing energies over several fighters at a time. Some wounds were irreparable, but they managed to reduce the suffering.

A team of mages approached Ervinor and he greeted them warmly. "You're doing well. Continue your work." He nodded his head in salute and stepped away.

"Sir!" they called. "We're here to do just that." One of them pointed at Ervinor's torso and arm. He had been cut in numerous places and his clothes were covered in his own blood. In the heat of the fight, he hadn't even noticed. Immediately, the mages went to work, drawing the energies up and about and around, filling the young general with a great sense of ease and calm and completeness.

Refreshed, Ervinor hurried away to his tent where Randler and Frast awaited. He hoped the bard might have some ideas of how to send word to the king directly. Yet when he opened the tent, he saw something he was not expecting. It was Dariak.

The mage was asleep and no amount of prodding woke him. "Randler, how?"

"I don't know," the bard said. "Someone found him out there, surrounded by some hand-made grooves in the sand."

Realization struck. "The trenches! At least that explains that. He must have just returned and tried helping us out. Randler, we need him to awaken. Now. Only he can break through this mess and reach the king in any kind of meaningful way."

"I'm trying, Ervinor, but there's nothing I can do."

Ervinor wouldn't accept that. "Play your lute, sing a song, kiss him, for all I care. He *has* to awaken." He knelt over the mage and shook him roughly, calling his name, but Dariak didn't flinch. "What of the jades?"

Shrugging, Randler pulled out the shadow jade, holding it in his hand firmly. He closed his eyes and concentrated on the inner darkness of the crystal, calling to its power to try to remove the darkness from Dariak. He grasped the power as strongly as he could and pulled sharply.

Standing nearby, Frast felt the energies being drawn into Randler and he tensed protectively. "No," he breathed, reaching out to take the shard away. "Randler, you can't."

Ervinor could barely hear the damaged mage. "What is it?"

Frast struggled to get his throat to work, but he forced out the words, "He's trying to take Dariak's swoon unto himself."

"What? How?" Ervinor asked reflexively. "Randler, no, don't hurt yourself."

The bard ignored them both and he pulled harder, watching as the shadow inside the jade spread more fully within the shard, until there was nothing to see but a solid blackness. He then pulled one more time and the shadow fled the gem and entered Randler, drawing him into the darkness itself. Frast caught him as he collapsed.

But it worked. Dariak roused from his slumber, looking around, confused.

"Dariak!" Ervinor said. "It's been so long. You've finally returned."

"What? Is the fight over then?" he asked, sitting upright and grabbing his head.

"Just a break, I'm afraid, and we need your help to make it last."

Dariak peered around. "Randler! Is he hurt?"

"Yes," Frast hissed sourly, eying Dariak with scorn. "But he's asleep now."

"What happened to your voice?"

"Dariak, there's no time," Ervinor interrupted. "Randler is fine. We need your help out here with the rest." When the mage hesitated, Ervinor grabbed his arm and implored, "If we lose this battle, then he dies. Come. I need your assistance."

Grudgingly, Dariak acquiesced. At least he knew Randler was here and alive. They stepped away and entered Ervinor's tent. "What is the situation?"

Ervinor updated him about the refugees and the king's refusal to accept them, and the following battle that had started with their arrival the night before and had reignited through most of the day. "I don't know how to make them stop long enough to listen."

"It may be that only a show of greater force will work at a time like this, though I hate to admit it."

"That was my fear as well, mostly because we don't have that greater show of force."

Dariak turned grimly to Ervinor. "With the jades, we will have it." He pulled the healing jade from his pocket. "We have them all now, Ervinor. Now is the time to bring this to an end."

Ervinor drew a deep breath. "You succeeded."

The mage tried not to relish in the joy on Ervinor's face, but he couldn't help himself. "It's true. We can do this now. Where is everyone else? I need the rest of the jades, too."

Ervinor introduced Dariak to Carrus and Verna, whom he had only barely met in Marritosh. "These are two of my captains."

Verna scoffed. "This is the mage who's going to change the world? Are you sure?"

Dariak met her challenge with his own. "Ervinor trusts you to lead men into battle? You'd be better off slicing apples."

Verna's face curled in fury but Carrus intercepted. "I do believe he's teasing, Verna."

Dariak grinned. "A wise man. I meant no offense, as I'm sure you meant none toward me."

It took visible effort for Verna to keep herself in check. "No, sir."

Ervinor stood tall. "Carrus, Verna, I need you to find Lica and Kitalla and send them back here with their jades." The captains ran off to do his bidding.

"You've grown," Dariak said.

He shrugged. "I supposed I've had to. We've been through a lot since you left." Suddenly he felt overwrought with emotion as if he could now lay down his burdens and let Dariak take them from him. He wanted to let himself cry in relief and misery to be free of the stress and the constant balancing of the personalities around him. Seeing Dariak, in some ways, felt like he had returned home and the fighting was over.

Dariak could see the sudden change in Ervinor's expression and the redness forming around his eyes. "Hold it together a little longer, my friend. We aren't done yet."

Ervinor crushed his knuckle between his eyes, taking deep breaths. "I know," he whispered. "I know." He paused for a moment, not willing to look up at the mage. "We lost Quereth the other day."

"No!"

"Saved my life."

Dariak could feel the man's guilt over the loss. "Yours is a life worth saving, Ervinor. I'm sure he did what he thought was best."

Ervinor wanted to argue and shout his true feelings on the matter, but he knew the words were meaningless. They wouldn't come to him anyway.

Verna burst back in, huffing madly. "Come quickly."

Frantically, they made their way to the front lines where Lica was waving her arms wildly about, chipping away at the thick layers of sand. Four other mages assisted the best they could, but the stronger earth mages were engaged elsewhere, trying to free the trapped fighters.

Lica's eyes went wide when she saw Dariak but she did not greet him other than to say, "Something is preventing me from getting any deeper, and I'm certain people are down there."

"Down there?" Dariak asked, but then he understood that his actions upon arriving in the camp had caused this. "You're certain?"

"Yes. But I don't have the strength."

Dariak glanced around. "Where is the earth jade?"

"Back with Frast," Ervinor answered.

The ground rumbled as if it were going to collapse further. "No time." The son of Delminor dropped to his knees and reached into the sand. Closing his eyes, he listened for vibrations of energy from below, seeking the men and women trapped underneath as well as the source that prevented Lica from helping them.

His thoughts met abruptly with a solid wall. Startled, he had to settle himself before probing it again. There was no stone or wood, only metal. "Kitalla," he muttered. Dariak pulled one hand up and placed it on the healing jade in his pocket, then sent his mind outward again, seeking the metal jade's cooperation. Instead, he was struck with the words of a strange spell and though part of him wanted to deny them, he chose instead to speak them.

"*Hacckanorrishon writthen shie contorrious rechtibar.*" Wind or earth magic would have been his first calls for this situation, but it was the metal jade that spoke through him. The sand coagulated like molten iron and separated into individual pools, which then cooled and returned to sand, now piled in oddly random places. Yet where the sand had moved away, bits of hair poked through.

"Dig!" Ervinor called and everyone responded. Fingers swept the sand away, revealing a dozen men and women strangely huddled together around Kitalla. Among the men and women were Hathren soldiers and though they were grateful for the rescue, they were terrified by what would happen to them next. Perhaps these fiends would throw them back in the pit and let the sand fall and suffocate them. They need not have worried.

Kitalla dusted herself off and threw her arms around Dariak in greeting. "You're back!" Then she shoved him over. "Took you long enough." Without delay, she spun around to the Hathren soldiers. "Go back home, all of you. Today's fight is over. Your lives were spared. Be grateful for it and save yourselves from whatever other nonsense is to come."

"We would be traitors to desert our king in this time of need," one shouted.

Ervinor stepped in. "We came here only to deliver your people to your king, but his reaction was to tear us down and to deny your own citizens. Perhaps he doesn't believe our claim. I challenge you then to come and meet the people of Marritosh and take back to your king word of what you see."

The soldiers were skeptical. "You'll kill us once you take us into your camp."

"Not after I just saved your lives," Kitalla promised. "I'll come with you if that helps."

The Hathrens looked at her, uncertain. "You have strange power to draw us together like that under the sand. And stranger power to conceal us within a metal box. I have no desire to be accompanied by you, despite my gratitude for my life."

"I am the general of this army," Ervinor said. "I'll give you a sword and you'll come with me to see the refugees."

Verna gasped. "A sword? Ervinor!"

"We came here for one purpose, didn't we?" He nodded sharply and Verna turned her sword over and handed it to one of the soldiers. "Come and we'll view the refugees together."

It was an odd and tenuous procession. Ervinor allowed the soldier, Piori, to keep the sword pressed to his back along the way. Kitalla and Dariak joined them, ready to stop any of the Hathrens from killing Ervinor or anyone else. Verna and Lica ran off to help free others trapped in the sand.

The refugees were a huddled mess by this time, and they whimpered when the group arrived to greet them. Ervinor introduced the group as a whole and Piori eyed him suspiciously. "How can we trust they're not secret warriors that you intend to plant within the castle?"

"Look at them," Ervinor said sadly. "They're broken and defeated and sad. Few among them could even hold a sword, much less fight with one. Speak with them if you would. Determine who they truly are and bring that news back to your king. I only wish these people to be cared for, and your king should be the one to answer that call."

Piori stepped away and did as Ervinor suggested while the others waited. He spoke to nearly a dozen of them, but he could barely make out anything intelligible from them, they were so upset with the fighting. One upstart lad, however, told Piori news that disturbed him greatly.

"You have prisoners here," Piori hissed. "You say you're here for one purpose, but you keep the king's men prisoner? Are these people then prisoners, too?"

Ervinor had forgotten about the soldiers they had taken in their previous battle. "We needed to hold them until we could return them to the king as well. We neither harmed them nor killed them."

"I've seen enough!" Piori yelled angrily. "Release me back to my king."

"You have to listen—"

"You've taken hostages, Ervinor. I see that now. You would beg the king's ear to drop off refugees, but once your foot was in the door, you would hoist up the prisoners you have and beg for something else. You disgust me."

"It isn't that at all. You're not listening."

But the man shut down and pushed away from them. "What then? Kill me? Imprison me too?"

The general frowned. "I promised you would not be harmed. You are free to go."

"Ervinor!" Kitalla interjected. "He will skew the tale he tells the king. Taking prisoners and preserving life is better than slaughtering everyone you see who is different from you. But he'll spout poison to the king and we won't find a home for these people. You're giving up a chance here to turn this battle around and to save their lives."

Piori stared at Ervinor, awaiting his response, but the general had already decided. "I made a promise. And we have fought hard to defend ourselves without killing. Once the king sees that, we'll make progress with the refugees." He waved some fighters over to escort the Hathrens back to their camp. Not long later, a horn sounded and the fighting commenced once again.

Ervinor sighed deeply. "Here we go."

Gabrion's Charge

GABRION AND HIS volunteers trudged through the sand, trying to reach the location of the blaze in the previous night's sky. The place was deceivingly further than the warrior had thought, and reaching it was wearing on his nerves.

He felt alone on the journey despite the forty-odd fighters with him. Though he had built a few basic friendships with some of them, they were still mostly strangers. His heart yearned to see Dariak and the others, though part of him was nervous about reuniting with Kitalla.

The Hathren king's troops had been through this part of the land in detail over the past months and so the number of feral creatures was at a minimum. They scuffled with some beasts here and there, but they traveled mostly unhindered.

It was mid-afternoon before they reached their destination, and Gabrion was surprised that a battle raged in full force. Their arrival came as a surprise and the king's men first thought they were reinforcements gathering together to help them. But Gabrion recognized a few of the fighters from Marritosh and he knew then which side was his to join. He drew his sword and rushed in, clobbering three of the king's men before they realized that the newcomers were not allies. Gabrion's team reacted swiftly to his actions and they also sought out the Hathren attackers and took them down, keeping to their vows not to kill unless absolutely necessary. It certainly added a depth to the challenge of fighting off three hundred or so men.

The defenders rallied behind Gabrion's arrival and fought with renewed vigor, unsure of why these new troops were on their side but not caring much either. Swords and maces rattled about, crashing into weapons and shields. The king's fighters were mostly clad in iron armor, which thankfully slowed them down but made them harder to defeat. Gabrion channeled his innate skill and moved like a leaf fluttering in a windstorm, but he attacked like a battering ram tearing down a castle gate.

Magefire was also present in the skirmish, but both sides had mages who were dealing with the effects. Fireballs were disrupted by ice barriers. Lightning strikes were dampened with magically erected wooden shields. Summoned beasts were struck down by other creatures, or in some cases the animals were warred over for control by two opposing mages and the confusion rendered them inert.

A horn sounded and Gabrion hoped it would be a call for a cessation of the fighting, but there was no such luck. In the distance he could see that more fighters were released from the castle to join the fray. He had no idea how many soldiers the king had housed within his walls, but he knew their meager forces would not hold up against them all. He needed to get into the castle, reach the king, and put a stop to this battle.

To do that, he would need help. He had not yet seen his comrades, but he knew they had to be here. He struck down a few more foes, taking some minor scrapes and bruises in the process, then he headed off toward the center of the fighting. If Kitalla was around, it's where she would be.

Gabrion swept low and moved fast, knowing his goal was more important than simply staving off the attacks of a few men. He was already tired from his long, forced march but it didn't matter. People were going to die here if it didn't stop soon. Nicked and cut, he finally found a sight that invigorated him.

Kitalla moved around the battle at a rapid pace, but he could tell she was exhausted; she didn't have her usual smoothness and finesse with each strike. Instead she smacked into foe after foe and clobbered them messily, her breath heaving, then she found the will to take another step and do it again. Left to her own devices, Gabrion wondered if she would take down the whole of the king's army. He watched for a moment before realizing that she was only knocking out her quarry. She wasn't killing anyone.

Mud flew across the field and splattered the soldiers indiscriminately on either side. The sandy terrain became a gritty slag and the fighters' boots slogged in the muck, reducing their accuracy greatly. Gabrion glanced around and saw Dariak in the distance, his arms waving madly, and he grinned despite the circumstances. The mage was too far off for the moment, but Kitalla was close by. Rushing over, Gabrion swept his sword around, parrying attacks aimed his way. When he reached Kitalla, she almost lopped off his head, but he turned his sword upright and deflected her attack.

She gasped, then spun and struck down a soldier. "Gabrion! Get out of here before you get yourself killed."

"Not likely," the warrior said, stepping in and slicing his blade across and down, intercepting a blow meant for Kitalla. They turned back to back and knocked down five others before a brief respite allowed them to say any more.

Kitalla's face was flushed from the exertion and she panted heavily. Gabrion wondered how long she had at been engaged in this battle and was about to ask when Kitalla groaned and shoved the warrior aside.

"Go home, Gabrion. We've got a real battle going on here. You're a liability to us." She stared at him for a minute and then added, "Or are you going to fight now?"

Gabrion hefted his sword in answer. "I'm sorry for what happened, Kitalla. I never meant to let you come to harm."

"We never meant for a lot of things, Gabrion, but we have to own up to them. I could have died from those eaglons. And you just stood there, dumbstruck. How can I count on you now? Here, with all this? Things are falling apart at the seams, Gabrion. How can I count on you?"

"We need to get word to the king to put an end to this fighting. Even if just long enough to tend to the wounded."

"Gosh, why didn't we think of trying that?" The thief shook her head. "The king is deaf today. The only word reaching the castle is the call for more soldiers."

Lightning flared nearby, reminding them that the battle was still on in earnest. Gabrion turned to join the fray, but Kitalla stopped him. She reached down to a fallen soldier and removed his mace, which she jammed into Gabrion's hand in place of his sword. She took his blade for her own, equipping herself again with two swords. "Maybe you'll fight better with that."

Gabrion had never used a mace before. It was weighted on the wrong end from what he was accustomed to, but after a dozen practice swings, he felt more aware of its unique balance. The two stepped back into the battle, seeking a way to possibly end this skirmish and regroup.

Fire and ice raged about and they dodged the magical attacks, trying to reach the mages responsible for them. Their tired bodies moved because they had to. They battled because if they didn't then they would die, and so would the others here. Yet all either of them wanted was to catch their breaths and greet each other properly.

Sand swept up into the air and pelted downward toward an unsuspecting group of Hathren soldiers. The two of them stepped in to take down the distracted fighters and then they turned their attention to the mage who had set the sand on them in the first place.

"Dariak!" Gabrion called. "It has been too long."

"And such a place to reunite," the mage muttered sourly. He swept his arms around and a ball of sand rose up from his feet and then blasted out toward another host of soldiers. "Have you come to turn the tide?"

Kitalla grumbled. "Not likely. Gabrion isn't at his best these days."

The warrior looked hurt. "I'm here and I'll do my best. You'll see, Kitalla."

Dariak had no idea what had happened between the two, but there was clearly a decent amount of hurt. He knew he had his own pains to face soon when the battle relented long enough for him to talk to Randler.

"Your 'best' used to be good enough, warrior, but today, I wonder. Still," she added quickly, "it's good to see you again."

It was all he was going to get and he knew it. "I didn't come alone. Forty others are with me on the eastern edge of the battle. More should be on their way soon, too."

"It will help, but not enough," Kitalla lamented. She whistled aloud six times and waited as she heard an answering cry not far away. Soon after, Ervinor made his way over to them.

"Gabrion!" the general said. "You have returned to us at last, and none too soon, as you can see."

"Can't we break through to get into the castle to reach the king?"

"Not a chance. We've had the mages banding together to draw the spellfire of the others, but they have more mages than we do. Their defenses are too strong, even for the likes of you all."

"Then it's a hopeless fight," Gabrion murmured.

Kitalla sighed. "I told you to go home."

"I hate to admit it, but I think Gabrion's right." Ervinor pointed west then east. "They have enough soldiers to fight us on all sides if they want to, and I suspect there are more soldiers within the castle itself." He grunted in frustration. "The stupid king. We just wanted to escort his people here to safety. Now we're trying to keep them safe within our ranks while we hold off attacks from without, all as we try to subdue them without killing anyone. But they're fighting full force. I'm about ready to call a retreat."

Dariak let the words sink in and nodded. "No, there is one more thing to try first. Take me to Randler. And get me all the jades."

Gabrion's eyes shot open. "You can't be serious!"

"We have little choice. Now come on."

Ervinor saluted and ran off to spread the word. Some of the mages in their army were using the jades and they needed to relinquish them immediately. It would greatly weaken their defenses, but Ervinor put his trust in Dariak. He instructed Carrus and Verna to pull the troops closer together so they could continue to fend off the attack.

Meanwhile, Kitalla escorted the mage and the warrior to the main tent. Inside, Randler sat on a mound of sand that Lica had drawn up for him earlier. Now she was off in the battle and Randler sat in contemplative silence with Frast.

Dariak's appearance was hard for the bard and he had no idea how to respond. Likewise, Dariak was at a loss, for as he looked upon Randler, he recalled how he had abandoned the man back in the forest. It was hard to meet his gaze. And harder still to look at the man's legs.

"Randler, I—"

"Don't," he cut in. He shook his head, seeming aged beyond his years. "Did you get it?"

Dariak swallowed hard and nodded, pulling the healing jade from his pocket. "It is here. Let me help you—"

But the bard interrupted him again. "I'm in no condition to assist in this battle, Dariak. Use that to help the wounded."

"We're here for another reason," Gabrion said.

The bard hadn't even noticed him. "You've returned to us, too," he said needlessly. He glanced at Kitalla and the others. "We have been assembled again after so long."

Kitalla clapped her hands. "Let's save the group hug for later. We're falling apart out there and we need to act now to put a stop to it."

"Act..." Then Randler's eyes opened wide. "You don't mean—"

Dariak nodded. "It's the only way. And I'm going to need your help. You're the only one who really understands the concepts of resonance and dissonance, Randler."

Frast shook his head and his broken throat choked out the words, "You're going to assemble the jades?"

"We must," Dariak said. "If we don't then we won't last the day."

"More and more troops expel from the castle," Kitalla added. "Just when we make some progress, they bring out a fresh host to push us back. And we're dying out there, too. Even if the few of us charged in with our jades, there would be too many casualties here and the refugees would be unprotected in the interim." She glanced around at the gathering. "I don't know about you all, but my magic skills are rather weak. So I'm heading back out there to do my part until you're ready here." She reached her fingers into a pocket and withdrew the metal jade. "You'll need this, Dariak."

It wasn't the first time she left Dariak with the metal jade before running off on another errand. At least this time she wasn't abandoning the group. She pulled her swords up and turned to Gabrion. "Ready to prove to me that you're really here to help?"

Gabrion hefted the mace and followed her outside. Their hearts weighed heavily but they had a task to do. They rushed ahead to the front lines, pressing through their comrades to give them a much-needed rest, and then they swept into action.

Kitalla screamed aloud as she charged toward a burly fighter wielding a lance. The man moved nimbly and Kitalla missed her first attack completely. She turned and brought her swords around, striking at the iron armor protecting his back. Sparks flew but no damage was done. The lancer laughed at the attempt as he came around to crush the thief.

Gabrion was caught up in a scuffle of his own and he brought the mace through the air, crashing it haphazardly into his foes. He understood easily why a mace was a preferred melee weapon for mages and younger soldiers; its balance allowed for a more powerful strike even if the attacker lacked in physical strength. But it lacked precision, and to keep his vow, Gabrion needed to be precise. Each stroke of the weapon taught him how to better wield it and, as with the other battles on his journey, the more he fought, the better he became.

Likewise, with each stroke the lancer took at Kitalla, the better she understood how to defeat him. He was left-handed and stepped forward with his right foot before each power attack. Kitalla kept her swords swirling around and blocking his advances, but she also stumbled several times, baiting him.

After one such stumble, Kitalla rolled over and launched a fistful of sand at the man's eyes, but his visor protected him. She knew it would, but it was an important part of her strategy. Kitalla sprang to her feet, hoisting one of her swords. She swept it around and cracked its blade into the man's shoulder. He bellowed another laugh as he brought his foot up and then pressed it into the sand to give strength to his next attack. But his foot came down on Kitalla's second sword and the man lost his footing and fell.

The thief capitalized by wrestling the lance out of his hand and then bashing it against his helmet until he fell unconscious. Then it was a matter of reclaiming her swords and pushing on to the next bout.

All the while, Gabrion hammered away with his mace, taking care not to bash anyone too powerfully in the head. He crushed some arms and legs, perhaps some ribs, but each victim was left relatively intact. Their lives would carry on, though they may need a strong dose of healing magic if they would live normally. He pushed himself toward the castle with each strike. He wanted to get inside somehow and plea to the king. But as the battle continued, he could tell that it was a fool's dream.

A horn sounded and the gates of the castle pushed open. Gabrion's heart leaped for an instant but his hopes were immediately dashed as two hundred more soldiers stormed out from the castle.

Gabrion considered his personal vow to stop killing. They were greatly outnumbered and the odds kept turning against them. If he maintained his restraint then he would surely die here. Yet if he allowed himself to open up and slay his foes, then would his journey mean anything anymore? Sure, he had killed many people already on this journey, but it had seemed expected and normal.

But after slaying Mira, everything had changed. Each life had seemed important again, like it had during that first battle in Savvron. His first kill had filled him with revulsion and he hadn't wanted to continue the fight, but Andron had assured him that it was necessary, because he had to protect his home.

And truly, the Hathrens were not holding back their attacks. They did not value their lives any more than did their king. Perhaps he should allow his skills to overpower them all. Perhaps he should allow himself to slay his foes instead of just wounding them.

But always his thoughts came back to Mira and his actions against her. No, he needed to protect her in some way. He needed to preserve the lives around him. He needed to—

As his mind tumbled around, his body worked its magic, striking and parrying foe after foe. He barely saw any of his attackers as he thrust his way through the fighters. By now the fresh soldiers were about to reach them and Gabrion was far from rested. He glanced around for Kitalla and he could see that she too was struggling. They had gotten separated so he pushed his way closer to her.

"I will protect you," he said to himself, his eyes focused on Kitalla. "I will keep you safe." His arm swept around and dislodged a sword from one of the soldiers. Gritting his teeth, he bent low and took the sword in his left hand. He mostly used it as a shield, but then he saw Kitalla fall and he feared for her safety. He couldn't imagine what he would do if he allowed her to be hurt. No, he wouldn't allow it. Vow or not, he would save her from her plight.

Three swordsmen whirled around the battered thief, their blades nipping at her body and slicing her lightly. Each wound was meaningless, but the whole of them added up to excruciating pain. Kitalla rolled around in the sand, which made the pain worse. She lamented giving the metal jade to Dariak, for right now she could use its support.

But the thief wasn't finished yet. The swords came in and she twisted and turned around, not allowing any one strike to harm her fatally. Her legs kicked out when they could but the soldiers were able to avoid her attacks. She needed one of them to falter briefly and then she would tear them all down, but the trio worked in unison without fail. Plus, they had just joined the fight, whereas she had been battling all day.

In a desperate move, Kitalla accepted a deep cut to her left arm so she could reach up and pull the man into the sand. He toppled over her and the other two inadvertently jabbed their swords into him. The cuts were far from fatal but the man wailed in agony. Exhausted, Kitalla couldn't push him off her and his iron-weighted body crushed her underneath.

She gasped for breath, wondering what she could do next to escape. She considered her dance skills, wondering if she could affect these men with mere facial expressions, but even if she could have, she didn't have the mental focus to concentrate on swaying them in any way. Her left arm blazed in agony as sand scraped into the wound.

Then all at once the weight pressing down on her was gone. She glanced up and Gabrion loomed over her, extending a hand to pull her to her feet. He was covered in blood, she noticed, but as she looked at the three soldiers who had bested her, she realized that Gabrion hadn't killed them. The blood from their wounds had marred him when he moved them.

"I guess you're not useless after all," she said.

Without warning he scooped her up in his arms, after which he jogged back toward the rest of their fighters. Carrus saw them coming and he cried in outrage, seeing Kitalla in such a state, and he stormed ahead to clear a path for Gabrion so that Kitalla could be brought to the mages for healing.

After he deposited her to the healers, Gabrion returned to Carrus and saluted him. They hadn't spoken before but they sensed each other and immediately fell into a rhythm, bashing away foe after foe. Both men took hits as they went but neither let the cuts slow them down. It became a friendly rivalry to push ahead of the other and make just one more strike before exhaustion claimed them.

They clobbered dozens of soldiers, leaving the fallen foes to the less-experienced fighters to tend to. They made their way across the field, beating and bashing their weapons into the armor of their enemies, with old battle songs strumming in their heads.

And when Gabrion thought he couldn't take any more surprises for the day, another one greeted him. The ground shook ominously and people fell over from the tremors, they were so strong. He glanced around for the source, wondering if Dariak had already completed his task, but no giant colossus rose up into the sky.

His shifted focus cost him dearly, for a nearby soldier saw the distracted warrior and stepped in, bringing his shield about and bashing Gabrion from behind. Carrus struck back, but it was too late for Gabrion. He was out cold.

CHAPTER 66

The Assembly

DARIAK, RANDLER, AND Frast stood inside the tent as Kitalla and Gabrion ran off to help the fighters. Tension filled the room as they waited for Ervinor to gather the jades for Dariak's purpose.

Frast looked from one to the other, not sure what to say. He knew Dariak's return was inevitable, but he had hoped that by this time, Randler would have seen how wrong Dariak was to leave him and how right Frast had been since then. Yet as he looked at them, he doubted everything.

"You left me," Randler whispered.

"Randler, I—" He saw the intent expression on Frast's face. "Perhaps you could leave us for a minute?"

But the mage would not go. "I've been on your side for a while now, and in your absence, I've done everything I can to assist Randler. I won't leave now."

"What happened to your voice?"

Randler answered for him. "When the mages of the tower healed me, they channeled the energies through the jades. But it wasn't enough. Frast used the beast jade to focus the healing and to siphon away my own suffering. It ruined his throat."

Dariak took the healing jade in his hand and held it aloft. "Let me try to help."

At first Frast stepped away. His damaged voice was a tribute to his love for Randler, but it also prevented him from casting spells and thus his livelihood was gone. After a moment, he nodded and lifted his chin for Dariak to approach.

The son of Delminor closed his eyes and sought communion with the healing jade, searching for the best means of tending to the damage, but no answers came to him. It was as if the energy itself was blocked and immutable. He cast the energies outward anyway, but there was no effect. Frast felt the warmth from the spell, but no healing occurred.

"I feared that," Frast said, crestfallen.

Randler added, "The mages haven't been able to do anything. Every spell falters and his throat gets no better. I thought perhaps that when he had channeled the beast jade in such force, it created such destruction that basic spells couldn't help. But I had hoped that one jade would overpower another."

Dariak tried a few more times, but then he shook his head slowly. "I am sorry."

"One of many tasks you've failed," Frast said.

Randler frowned. "Frast…"

"No, he's right," Dariak said, though he didn't fully understand Frast's anger.

The tent flap opened and Rothra entered grandly, his face a mask of disappointment and his voice dour. "Then it's true. Dariak has returned."

"Rothra? You've joined this fight?"

"A long story," he dismissed, "but when word came that the jades were to be handed back at this moment, Ervinor sent me personally to you so that I could argue why such a maneuver is folly. Dariak, we need these jades for our defenses."

"I understand, but we need to put an end this outright. There is only one way left to us."

But the fire mage did not agree. "You're a bigger fool than your father, Dariak. Call the colossus here and now and you will slay us all. You will stomp about and flare your power and every man and woman will suffer for it. Your father acted only because there was no alternative. You act because you are weak."

"That's enough, Rothra," Dariak snapped. "Perhaps with your deep wisdom, you have an alternative that will end this battle at once?"

Only then did the fire mage's face show signs of weakness. "Pity, no. Even banding together, their mages counter our every move. I don't know whether to wish for your success or your utter failure." He extended the fire jade to Dariak's hand. "I will rally the mages to bolster our defenses and to end our offensive strike. Perhaps at least I can manage that much to keep us alive against this plan of yours." Spinning on his heel, Rothra stormed out.

Soon after, another messenger arrived with other pieces of jade. Dariak cleared a space on the sand and set the jades in a line, shaking his head. "I have no idea how to unite them." He spread his hands over the shards and read their energies, trying to sense some sort of connection. His father had obviously found something else, yet it was beyond Dariak's reach.

Randler nodded at Frast and the two of them handed over the shadow, beast, and earth jades to the growing collection. As with the others, Dariak read their energies, trying to find a pattern so he could unite them correctly. At last, the glass jade arrived, completing the set.

The eleven shards had been scattered across the lands of Hathreneir and Kallisor, each finding its own way. Some, like the water jade, had become trophies. Others, like the glass jade, had been beacons of hope to those who awaited a new day. Dariak gazed into each of the pieces and wondered at their innate powers and how they connected to the world around them. "There must be a pattern."

Randler could sense the energies from the jades with his meager training as a boy, and he used that to identify each one. "Let's line them up the best we can. Some of these have stronger emanations than others. Let's begin by laying them down in that order."

Dariak nodded and started with the earth jade on the far left. Its pulsations were the most grounded of them all. Beside it, he set the glass and nature jades, but then decided that the glass worked better closer to water. Frast contributed, moving the healing jade to the far right side and placing the lightning and air shards nearby. They struggled with the layout of the eleven jades, for the jades resonated with each other as well as within. Setting two side by side caused other sets of vibrations. At first the water jade was relatively tame, but when the glass jade was set next to it, it trembled visibly. Yet when the glass jade was set elsewhere, other jades reacted one way or another. There seemed to be no solution.

"It's not a song from an instrument," Randler muttered. "It's a set of instruments working together. We're going about this all wrong. Let's try something else." Then slowly, he slid them across the sand into a circle, trying to balance the strength of one jade with the weakness of another. He started by setting fire and water to the north and south. East and west received the air and earth jades. "These interfere with each other, so set them apart."

Dariak lifted the lightning jade, clutching it in his fist. "It's like the air itself burning when lightning strikes." He set it to the northeast between the air and fire.

"And metal draws it easily," Randler added, setting the metal jade opposite the lightning jade. "But shadow blocks out the light," he said, biting his lip. Tentatively, he set the shadow jade between the metal and earth shards.

"No," Dariak said. "Not there. It feels wrong." He reversed the metal and shadow jades, so that metal and earth were side by side. "Better."

Frast took the nature and beast jades next and placed them between earth and fire, with the raging beasts closer to the burning flame. Across from them, between air and water, Dariak set the healing and glass jades.

"That's all of them," Randler said needlessly. "What do you feel?"

Dariak closed his eyes and reached out over the circle of jades. "It's like they're talking to each other. Reaching out. Seeking each other. Pulling and pushing all at once. But…"

When he didn't elaborate, Randler asked, "What's wrong?"

"There is something missing." Dariak squeezed his eyes shut and concentrated. He tried moving the shards around to different locations, but doing so upset the balance more than restore it. Eventually, he reset them and focused on the flow of energies from one to another. The strain built up on his face and he worried that he wouldn't be able to reason it out. "It isn't quite right. If only…"

"What?"

"If only I could have gotten to my father's laboratory and his notes. He had to have made a record of this somehow."

"Dariak, how would you even know? He couldn't have combined them before that one moment. There's no way he would have been able to write it down."

Dariak shook his head. "My father never did anything rashly. He would have tested it first. He would have known. He would have written it down."

"Lot of help that does us," Frast rasped. "We need to act."

They were silent for a moment longer and then Dariak nodded slowly. Randler didn't like the look on the mage's face, and he thought he knew why, for he had come to the same conclusion. "Your father used his own life to tie them together, didn't he? The conductor leading the orchestra."

Dariak closed his eyes and turned away from the bard. "He must have. It would explain why the energy took the form of a man. You've seen enough spells to know that energy blasts out randomly. It doesn't hold a shape unless commanded to do so by the caster. When the jades were united, they became a colossus… because he had joined with them. It's the only answer."

"And then, Dariak," Randler said solemnly, "when the spell faltered, he died."

The mage bobbed his head slowly. "When the spell was disrupted, he was no longer protected. The arrows pierced him. He fell and the colossus disappeared as the jades exploded outward. The unification of the jades could not hold because his life expired."

"But perhaps, Dariak, he died because the jades were not meant to come together. Perhaps they tore him apart?"

Dariak's chin sank to his chest. "Your quest, Randler, was once to separate the jades and to keep them from ever uniting. Yet here we are at that precise moment. And here your beliefs surface once again." He looked up at the bard. "Would you stop me now?"

They held their gazes for a time and Frast looked from one to the other, trying to read them. He knew their history and that Randler had stepped from his own quest to join Dariak's, which was directly as odds with his own values. Yet they had both grown close on the journey. Frast didn't know what he wanted to happen. Perhaps uniting the jades was necessary because the king could not deny them and the fighting would have to stop. It was also possible, however, that the show of force would prompt the king to attack more aggressively to bring them down. In the end— for Frast—it came down to Randler. He would support whatever the bard wished.

Dariak drew a deep breath and moved until he was seated inside the ring of jades. He reached his hands out and held his palms over the shards, reading their inherent energies.

Randler gasped. "Dariak, no!"

"I have to. This has to end."

Frast saw the horror on Randler's face and he couldn't understand it. "Randler, this has been his quest all along. To bring the jades together and to end the fighting."

"But not to end like this, here and now."

Dariak lowered his head, unable to move as he heard the tremors shaking Randler's voice.

Frast stood up and gestured to Dariak while talking to Randler. "You two went off to find the healing jade," his throat wracked. "When you were hurt, he abandoned you. He could have come with you, Randler. To the mages, to heal you."

"It is true, Dariak. You did abandon me."

The black-haired mage agreed. "At the time, I didn't think I could help you without the healing jade. I thought I needed it because I'm not strong when it comes to healing. I saw no way of helping you. And…" He swallowed and tried to find the words. "And, I couldn't accept that you were so broken. What if you never recovered from it? I couldn't…"

"Ervinor gets by just fine with his malady," Randler whispered.

"But he isn't the same," Dariak argued, though he hadn't spent any real time with the young general since that injury.

"I would not have left you," Frast interjected, his eyes boring into Randler. "In fact, I haven't left you. I've given you everything, even when you and I alone went to Magehaven to rescue him. And when the healing wasn't working on your legs, I did what was necessary to help."

"Frast, you've been an amazing friend," Randler said.

"But that's all, isn't it?" the mage finished. "Just someone around to rely on. Not someone worth loving."

"What?" Dariak said.

"Frast, no, just listen!"

But the mage was hurt. His ragged voice grew agitated and even raspier. "Dariak plans here to end this fight and save hundreds of lives at the cost of his own. And look at you... the pain in your eyes, knowing you're going to lose him to his quest. To his jades. To his father's shadow. And it's been his quest that has kept you two apart." He choked and grabbed Randler's staff for support, then used it to keep himself upright as he finished his tirade. "When you've needed him most, he left you behind in the care of strangers. Because, as he was just saying, because he couldn't face you. Because he was afraid."

He coughed violently again, blood rising to his lips. His throat raged in agony but they needed to know his pain before Dariak was gone for good. "But I let the jade take over me so I could save you. Just to keep you from harm. Just to—" He stepped away when Randler tried to get up to console him. "No, your choice is clear. Maybe I was being selfish, too, wanting to be loved by you. Wanting to touch you, hold you. Wanting to be the one you turned to."

Frast looked at Dariak, still sitting hunched over within the circle of the jades. "Your quest was to save people, Dariak. But all you've caused is pain. Whether you bring those jades together or not, you'll only cause more pain." He drew a thick breath of air and pushed to finish. "I can't bear to watch this any longer. You two decide what's best. Without me."

Randler and Dariak couldn't meet his gaze as the mage stabbed the staff into the sand and pulled himself toward the exit to leave them. Through his tears, he looked one more time at the bard and the mage, and Frast knew with certainty that he never had a chance of earning Randler's love. Their heads were down in similar fashion, but they both bore the deep responsibility ahead of them now.

He couldn't take it. Frast continued toward the exit. Then he lifted the staff and stepped back, swinging the weapon with all his might, cracking Dariak at the base of the neck and splattering him to the sand.

Randler screamed in outrage. "Frast! What are you—?"

Frast threw the staff aside and grabbed Dariak's cloak, tugging at the mage with a crazed look on his face. Randler struggled to stand on his weakened legs and he merely fell to the sand as he tried to make his way toward the scorned mage. Pain lanced through him as he scrambled to help Dariak.

Frast, meanwhile, grabbed Dariak around the chest, bodily pulling him to the side, and threw him harshly to the ground. He then took Dariak's spot in the center of the jade circle, where he reached around and quickly restored the positions of the jades.

"I may not be able to have your love," he rasped. "But I can do this one last thing for you. Farewell, Randler."

Frast reached out for the beast jade, for he knew it the best of them all, and he beseeched the crystal to heed his call one last time. Light flared from within the shard and it pierced into Frast's body, reading his desperation. The healing jade lit next and then one after another the jades erupted with light, all aimed toward Frast in the center. He thought he had known pain before, but this gave new meaning to the concept. He wondered if it was like being skinned alive and then doused in an acidic poison, all while the removed flesh still sent waves of agony to his brain. Or perhaps that was only the beginning, for the sensations grew worse every moment.

Frast's awareness expanded as the jades infused him with power and he caught a last glimpse of Randler on the ground. The bard gazed up at him with grateful, yet terrible, tears in his eyes, and it was the only expression of love he would ever receive. It didn't matter now, though, for Frast could feel the energies of all the land pulsating through him. The ground trembled dangerously as he pulled the energies in.

Random thoughts whisked through his mind and he wanted to entertain them, but he had to stay focused. He could already sense what Dariak had said; something was missing. It was intangible, but it left him with the sense that he only had a few brief minutes of this state before it would all be over.

The king had to stop the fight.

The raging fury in his body threatened to tear him apart and end his attempt at once, but he needed to do this for Randler. He cared nothing for anyone else. He knew deep inside that he could eradicate everyone and leave only Randler by his side, yet he also understood that doing so would cost him Randler forever, for the bard would never look at him again. He wanted so much to show Dariak the pain he had caused the people around him, but the straining energies reminded him that he did not have time to tarry.

The king had to stop the fight.

Frast focused on the one goal, allowing the beast jade to guide him. He poured his entire spirit into the shard, letting it sculpt his essence into one it knew better. His body rose up like an enormous eaglon with lightning for wings. Flapping downward splattered the area with fiery rain and when he cawed aloud, he could hear the horrified cries of the people below.

Fireballs and ice darts flew up at him from terrified mages, but the power of the jades was unstoppable. He dipped his bird-like head forward, knowing he wasn't a bird, but he wasn't a man either. He was a manifestation of wild energy, powered by the jades whose ancient magic coursed through the land. Frast lost all sense of himself, clinging to his mission.

Reach the castle and stop the king from fighting.

His electrified body lanced forth and raced across the sky and into the facing wall of the castle. Stone erupted outward and vaporized, leaving no debris except a fine dusty rain. The king was just ahead, but already Frast could feel the world slipping away. Each tendril of energy grew weaker as if his fingers and toes were being pulled off and burned to ash. Then his hands. His feet. His arms. He couldn't control it. Piece by piece, the energies pulled him apart.

The pain overwhelmed him and he couldn't think of his mission any longer. He had no joy, no fear. The king was only paces away from him, but he had no awareness left of what his purpose was. There was no Randler to please. There was only—

In a thunderous clap, Frast was gone.

CHAPTER 67

Battle's End

ERVINOR STOOD IN the field, his jaw agape. The ground had shaken and now an enormous bird flew overhead, fire and ice and lightning spraying out in all directions. He could see the Hathren forces turn their attentions immediately skyward, and as the magical creature screamed, their ears ached as if they would burst. He rallied his men for one final push and, raising his sword over his head, he shouted aloud and ran. The others responded well, tearing through the Hathren forces with haste, while they feared for the fate of their king.

The giant creature flew at the castle and disappeared within. Ervinor knew it would only be moments before the castle exploded, and though there was an ear-splitting boom, the walls remained intact, except at the point of entry where hunks of stone broke away and crashed below. Then over the din a bellowing horn with a deep, mournful note echoed over the field. All eyes turned toward the castle and the fighting came to an abrupt end as large white sheets of fabric were draped over the punctured walls in surrender.

Ervinor's army cheered with their victory and it took all the general's fortitude not to collapse with relief. The Hathren soldiers set down their weapons and their mages flooded the area with healing magic, but nothing seemed to happen. Another horn sounded and the Hathren troops pulled away, returning to the castle, though they did so warily, in case the intruders gave chase. But it was not Ervinor's intent to attack them now.

The general rallied his captains and the wounded were brought to the mages for healing. However, their spells would not work, and in the chaos they all assumed it was just exhaustion hindering them. The fighters themselves employed whatever healing skills they possessed, in terms of splints, bandages, and herbs.

Assessing the damage was disheartening. The Hathrens hadn't refrained from killing, but the defenders had fought bravely and less than forty had perished. It was a grim fate to lose anyone, but in the face of the relentless assault, they proved themselves to be veritable champions.

Carrus and Verna joined Lica and the rest as they gathered in the general's tent. Randler was there, his face stricken and his legs crumpled in pain underneath him. Beside him sat Dariak, shoulders low in defeat.

"The king surrendered," Ervinor said. "The Hathren troops are returning to the castle. Dariak, whatever you did—"

"It wasn't me," he said miserably. "It—it was Frast."

Lica gasped. "Where is he?"

"Gone," Randler whispered.

"I don't understand," Lica stammered. "I thought Dariak was going to unite the jades. Did you hand it over to Frast just to save yourself?"

"No," Randler said. "Frast took over. As a gift… to me."

Kitalla stepped forward and used a quelling look to silence Lica's ensuing protest. "He was brave and he saved us. To Frast!" She raised her hand up high and dared anyone not to honor the salute.

"But why?" Lica wondered, tears streaming from her eyes. "No, never mind," she said as she saw Dariak draw Randler closer. "I understand." She cleared her throat and wavered as she spoke. "We've lost so much."

"Indeed," Verna said, "and we aren't even finished yet."

"Well," Ervinor said, "I am." The others turned to face him. "I believe in your quest, even after all we've lost. But I don't have it in me to lead this army any longer."

"Ervinor," Gabrion started.

"No." He shook his head. "I lost an arm and three close friends already; Frast, Quereth, and Herchig. Never mind all the other people I barely knew who died defending us. I watched over these people because you needed me to as you ventured off to gather the jades. Now that you have them together, it's time for me to move on. Quereth stayed with us out of duty, though his heart was no longer in the fight. Because he stayed overlong, he's now gone. I wish to honor him by living."

Verna stamped her feet on the ground and those who knew her best prepared themselves for a tirade. Yet she surprised them. "I would not have followed these others into battle, general. I followed only you. You have my word that I will see the refugees from Marritosh placed in safe havens. Rest easy knowing that your task will succeed."

"Ervinor, stay with us long enough to achieve that," Randler said.

But the young man shook his head. "I will not follow Quereth's lead there. No, my time is now."

Carrus cleared his throat, still uncomfortable speaking his mind among his leaders. "There are some who would return to a calmer life as well, general. Perhaps you can travel together for a time."

"Are you among them?" Verna asked.

The burly man smiled. "No. As you said, there is more to do and I aim to be a part of it."

"So, then, what's next?" Lica asked.

Rothra answered. "We seek out the king, if he still lives, and hand over the refugees as intended. After that, I have no idea what the rest of you intend, but my mages and I will return to Magehaven for contemplation."

Ervinor saluted him. "We could not have reached this point without your assistance. Thank you."

"Bah!" the mage spat. "I was merely looking out for the welfare of the Hathren people."

"Perhaps when you return to the tower, you can slap Shelloni around for me?" Kitalla offered.

With a laugh, Rothra tipped his head. "As you wish, my lady." He shifted his gaze around the tent. "What of you then? Take the jades and ravage the world?"

Dariak shook his head. "Not quite. When my father died, the jades were separated and stolen and needed to be found again, which took years. But when Frast united them, something different happened." He unfolded a piece of cloth onto the sandy floor. "He drew in the energy and became an entity, like my father did, but he didn't carry the jades with him. They were left here. Look." He held out the fire jade for Rothra to inspect.

"Why, it's… empty." The startled mage handed the shard back to Dariak.

"Nearly, yes. I can barely sense them now."

"What does that mean?" Kitalla asked.

"It means that, for now, we're on our own. So we'll have to be extra careful. The jades won't be able to protect us until we can find a way of restoring them."

Lica cleared her throat. "What if we stopped here? Let this moment be the end of it? Surely the king will listen to reason now. You won't need a second show of force, will you? He'll see that he can't resist and he'll have to listen. Don't you think?"

Randler smiled up at her. "I wish it could be so easy, but the blood of war has burned this land for ages. It will take more than one defeat to stem the tide."

"Then we'll be ready," Kitalla declared, pounding her fist into her hand.

EPILOGUE

The Pieces Assembled

MERIAD CLOSED THE giant tome and watched her grandson sink back in his bed. The air was cold and ominously quiet, but she waited until he was ready to speak before pressing him.

"So much," he said at last.

The old woman nodded. "Indeed. And still the tale is not yet ended. Some tasks yet await these adventurers."

"I thought Dariak was going to die there. I don't know why Frast did what he did."

"His love for Randler was strong."

"But Randler didn't love him back."

"Love doesn't work like that. Not always. You see, Frast gave himself so that Randler could be with his true love. If Dariak had died, Randler would be inconsolable. He may never have recovered from it, even with Frast's help. Now, though, Randler has a chance to work through it."

The boy sighed. "I think Frast was right. Randler should have gone with him instead. Dariak isn't good for him. The jades are more important to him."

Meriad laughed. "Just you wait until your heart is swayed by some pretty girl or boy and then we can discuss this again."

"Gran-mama!"

She ruffled his hair and sat back. "There are still things happening there. Their journey isn't over yet."

"Well, it is for Ervinor."

"Yes, indeed. And what do you think about that?"

He considered for a time and then shrugged. "At first I thought he was being a coward, bowing out like that. But he's really been through a lot. I think it's okay for him to want to stop."

"I see. Then you don't feel he should have pressed onward to fight for Dariak's quest until his very end?"

"No," the boy answered after a moment. "If I were him, I would have wanted to stop a long time ago. I mean, he was kind of young and he was running the army."

"Yes, but he was a young man with a strong heart and the others saw that. They followed his ideals, much as they followed him. And it was easy for them all to claim they were following Gabrion or Dariak and that Ervinor was just filling in for a time."

"He was a real hero."

Meriad smiled. "Even though he was a Kallisorian?"

She caught him off-guard. The Hathren youth contemplated and then nodded. "Yes, even though he was from Kallisor."

Beaming, Meriad ruffled his hair again, much to his chagrin. "It warms me to hear you say that, for it means you're opening your mind and your heart to other possibilities than to those forced upon you by others."

He fixed his hair and cleared his throat. "What happened to Gabrion's friend Urrith from the outpost? And Ruhk?"

"Ah, yes, you listened well. You know where they are now, don't you?"

"Ruhk is near Gabrion, so I guess he would find them soon. And Urrith… wasn't he escorting Ordren through Kallisor?"

"Certainly."

"Did he? Was he able to arrange a truce?"

"Urrith's orders were only to take Ordren's group further into Kallisor," Meriad corrected warmly. "However, in terms of your question, think of what Randler said at the end."

He pursed his lips then nodded. "It would take more than one show of force to change their minds because the fighting has gone on for so long. I see." He tilted his head and eyed her curiously. "Does that mean that real peace can't ever happen?"

Meriad considered her words carefully before answering. "We have had peace for a time, have we not? Who's to say how long it will last?"

"I hope it's forever."

"That would be nice, dear. It certainly would."

The Forgotten Tribe

The Excited Child

THE WINTER ENDED prematurely and Meriad was grateful. As a child, she used to love the winters, though her hometown hadn't seen much snow. The air had seemed crisper and cleaner in winter. But as she whiffed the wonderful scents of early spring, she remembered why this was her favorite season.

As she had done for years, the old woman arrived at a stony keep to visit with her grandson, who anxiously awaited her arrivals. She tutored him in many things, but her recent visits had focused on one task, the telling of the story of the Red Jade.

The story itself was written in a careful script with a few drawings for emphasis and it was bound in a thick leather that had seen better days. The tale was nearing its conclusion and she believed that this trip would at last reveal to her grandson the end. She would miss the excitement in his eyes when it was over, for she knew few other sagas that were as entertaining to a youth.

She was greeted warmly by the boy and escorted as usual to his room. He had grown some since her last visit and he was clearly taking well to his training. She didn't even feel the need to ask about it, but he updated her anyway and kept talking while she supped, as was their routine.

"And I've been thinking a lot about the story," he segued. "About all the things that have happened. Like there's Dariak from Hathreneir, who finally got all eleven pieces of jade, but now they're empty. And his boyfriend Randler from Kallisor who was badly hurt and Dariak abandoned him, but Randler still loves him. Of how Frast couldn't get between them, even after all the things he did for Randler.

"It just made me realize that maybe my situation here isn't so bad."

Meriad looked up from her soup, stunned, but he waved his hands and continued.

"You've also got Kitalla, who was attacked and lost her baby when she was younger, and then she became a thief to support herself. She only joined the quest to get stronger, but now she's fighting for a better future. She has this amazing skill that can influence other people while she's dancing, and that's a skill no one else has. She concluded that the skill came from her baby. And then she came to the realization that her lost baby was one of the Forgotten Tribe."

"And who are they?" Meriad prompted.

"Descendants from the original King Kallisor and Lady Hathreneir. There are few from that line left as far as anyone knows. Randler sings of them all the time. And there was an eerie book in the Hathren mage tower that Kitalla saw which had parts of the tale shown in pictures. The last one Kitalla saw showed everything going dark." He shuddered.

"Who else have we learned about?"

"There's Gabrion, of course. He's a warrior from the village of Savvron and he joined Dariak's quest accidentally. He quested after his sweetheart, who was kidnapped, and then when he met her…" His voice grew quiet and he shook his head, unable to finish the sentence. "He was lost for a while but he came back to the group and is fighting again."

"But not killing," Meriad noted.

"Right. In fact, none of them are anymore if they can help it."

Meriad set her food aside and asked, "And where did we leave off?"

"Dariak's army won a huge battle outside Castle Hathreneir. The jades were assembled and massive damage was done to the castle. Ervinor, who was leading Dariak's army in his absence, left the fighting, and I don't blame him. He lost a lot of things, including his arm. So now it's Dariak, Randler, Kitalla, and Gabrion together again. They also have Lica, who's a mage from Kallisor. Also Carrus and Verna are captains in the army. Carrus is a big burly guy who joined up in Kallisor but didn't stand out as a fighter or leader until their time in Hathreneir. And Verna is from Marritosh, which burned to the ground, and she's a bit unstable, but Kitalla helped set her right."

"So now?"

"Now the jades are empty, the castle is ruined—I think—and Dariak still has to figure out how to bring the jades together properly to stop the Kallisorian king from keeping the war going. And he doesn't want it to end like the War of the Colossus from twenty years earlier where so many people died, including the kings and his own father. No, Dariak just wants peace."

Meriad nodded slowly. "And so—?"

"Oh!" he interrupted. "I forgot. There's Ruhk, a commander from Hathreneir who sort of teamed up with Gabrion and was coming to help him fight. And then Urrith, whom Gabrion trained, who is taking one of the Kallisor king's old commanders, Ordren, back to his homeland."

"Very good."

"Oh, Gran-mama?"

"Yes, dear?"

"Will we learn anything more about Randler's mother? Or Gabrion's father? Or that thief, Poltor, who trained Kitalla? Or are their stories done?"

Meriad smiled. "I could tell you, but I would think it would be more interesting if we found out along the way…" With that she opened the tome and took some time thumbing through the pages until she reached the next chapter. "Do you have any predictions?"

He thought for a moment and bit his lip. "Just one."

"Oh?"

"I think... I won't want this story to end." He grinned and hunkered down in his bed, waiting for her to continue the saga.

She winked. "Some stories never really end, my dear."

CHAPTER 1

Castle Hathreneir

DAWN LIGHT SLIPPED over the horizon, cascading across the desert sand, turning it a deep crimson. Amidst the blood-hued land, the walls of Castle Hathreneir lay in ruins. The cold gray stone rested in heaps of rubble upon the ground, dust wafting through the air, obscuring the view of the once magnificent palace. The main entrance to the castle lay buried and thus it was necessary for visitors to scale a crude set of rope ladders while the mess was cleared away.

It was at this place that Dariak and his friends had gathered. Banding together as one unified force, they had pushed back against the king's fighters and, after a wild call of magical force, they had succeeded. But there had been many casualties.

Dariak's father had once served the old king as advisor and court magician. Delminor had been a prominent mage, whose research into the shards of the Red Jade helped push magical knowledge further ahead than any other single mage had ever achieved. Yet in the War of the Colossus, the mage had given his life to put an end to the fighting by uniting the jades and unintentionally wreaking havoc on the battlefield. And there, he had died.

The jades were carried away by both sides of the war and it took time for Dariak to grow strong enough to pursue them. His quest had brought him to the land of Kallisor, where he made a handful of unlikely friends without whom he could never have reached this point of his journey. The jades were reassembled and once again they were called upon to put an end to the fighting.

It hadn't gone as planned. Dariak, who was connected to all the jades through his father's blood, could have channeled the energy more efficiently, more precisely—at least he believed so. Instead, Frast had knocked him out and substituted himself into the reaction. Summoning the power of the jades had worked, and Frast had become the manifestation of a giant magical eagle, and his flight had decimated the entire front half of Hathreneir Castle. As with Dariak's father, the act had cost Frast his life.

Now Dariak entered the demolished throne room of the Hathren king. There were blood stains everywhere on the polished marble. He knew Frast's attack had killed a number of men and women within the castle, but the man they needed was nowhere to be found.

He had taken this path before, but Dariak stepped to the back of the throne room to a door on the western side. Passing through it led to a number of personal chambers for the king and his family, but as with every other search, the hallways were empty.

Dariak sighed, running his hand through his jet black hair and shaking his head in confusion. There were no signs of other exits, except the one Kitalla had mentioned in the king's bedchamber. Stepping toward the lavishly decorated room, Dariak located the secret catch and slid the door open.

But it was useless because debris was piled up outside the hidden exit. The king could not have had time to run down the hall, open the doorway, and escape before the damage blocked the egress. From all the information Dariak had gathered, the magical avian beast had crashed into the throne room, where the king was in attendance, and then dissipated. By then, all the damage had been done and the king's chancellor, Ieran, had ordered a surrender so they could assess the damage.

The king wasn't the only person of interest who was missing. His son and heir, Perrios, was also gone. Dariak headed toward the nursery and saw signs of a hasty retreat. The infant had been there when the walls came tumbling down, yet he had been swept away, presumably by the king himself.

Two weeks had passed since the major incursion and though a tremendous amount of work was needed, things were starting to settle down. Dariak was the de facto leader now and he found Ieran to be a willing servant. His intuition suggested that the angular man was a bit too servile, but there were too many things to worry about for the moment. His primary goal was the safety of the people.

A chill ran down Dariak's back as he looked around the baby's room. On the floor was a deep blood stain that the king had not been able to remove ever since it had marred the floor. The mage knelt beside the darkened blotch and shook his head sadly.

He had been separated from his friends for a long time but since the battle's conclusion, he had caught up on all the major events. He knew that this blood was Mira's, a simple girl from Savvron. Dariak had joined the party that invaded the village, though he had not known that the purpose was to capture the girl, who had been having secret dalliances with the Hathren king. It was in Savvron that Dariak met his warrior friend, Gabrion, though it had taken some time for them to work toward a common goal. Gabrion's quest had been the pursuit of Mira, but when he found her safe and content in the king's court, complete with betrothal to the king himself and an infant child, Gabrion's quest had come to a bitter and devastating end. The jade in his possession had channeled his pain and this long-dried splotch of blood was all that remained of the woman he had quested after.

With a heavy sigh, Dariak made his way out of the king's personal wing, his mind turning over the other events that needed tending. The people of the castle and its surrounding town were terrified of Dariak's small army. Even the soldiers bowed their heads in Dariak's presence, and it was unnerving. Sure, his forces had proven themselves superior, but he expected more resistance than this.

Ever supportive, Randler encouraged Dariak to remain positive about these events. The refugees that had been escorted from Marritosh were now settling in with their fellows. The few prisoners Ervinor had been forced to take were released to the king's guard as a sign of trust but many resigned from their posts, dishonored at being taken at all.

Dariak considered Ervinor for a moment. The man from Kallisor had given up much in Dariak's name, and after countless battles, the loss of his arm and dear friends, he had left the group, turning the army back over to Dariak.

Too many ideas swept through the mage's mind. He wanted to spend time with Randler and reconnect with the bard. They hadn't had much of a chance for romance along the journey, and the recent events had put a serious strain on their relationship. After Randler's legs were crushed in the northwest forest, Dariak had left him to pursue the final shard of jade, and though Randler said he understood, every time the mage looked at him, he could see the pain and distance he had created.

There was also Kitalla, whose agility and drive were unparalleled, but she too had seen much on their journey and now carried a haunted look in her eyes that made Dariak wonder if she would soon follow Ervinor's example and wander off on her own.

The young warrior, Gabrion, was wounded inside, but his time at the eastern outpost had helped him to grow back into a semblance of himself. Master at swords, he now spent his time shunning the blade and taking up hammer and wood, devoting his strength and stamina to clearing the damage their group had done.

Dariak also had Ruhk to consider. The Hathren commander had defected, in a manner of speaking, and joined Gabrion's team at the outpost. But Dariak wondered if the man's loyalties would remain with his new allegiance or if, being back at the castle, he would try to reclaim his standing with the king and avoid the penalties of treason that would surely place his life and the lives of his family in jeopardy. For all appearances, it seemed as if he had indeed changed to a mindset of resolving the conflicts in the land, but the past two weeks had been so focused on repairs that few schemes surfaced anywhere.

He knew Kitalla would be on alert for danger. She already had ears around the town, listening for whispers of rebellion against them, as well as for news on the whereabouts of the missing king. Yet she too strove to restore the balance in the town in terms of trade agreements and property disputes. It was a task she had volunteered for, determined to use the time to keep active, while collecting information. Dariak hadn't understood her reason for taking on such a role. It seemed far from her expertise, but he didn't argue with anyone volunteering to step up and take on duties.

Likewise, he was grateful that Carrus and Verna, captains in his army, took over training the fighters. Carrus took a hard-pressed approached, pushing the men and women through powerful exercises that honed their bodies in terms of strength and endurance. Short-fused Verna developed battle simulations where she instructed just a few of the fighters to engage in nonstandard formations to throw off the rest of the trainees and force them to adapt as they went.

A unique issue, magic spells were inert after the energies consumed by the jades. Even simple spells faltered uselessly, and though that set the mages on edge, it also kept them from turning their powers against Dariak.

All in all, things seemed almost tame and organized. After the trials he had endured thus far on his journey, the feeling left Dariak awake every night, peering out the window, and asking dozens of questions to the people around him to ensure that they were indeed keeping aware of everything.

He climbed up to the room he had taken for himself, peering in first at Randler, who was already fast asleep. The bard had turned down his offer to share a room for now, saying that he woke up in pain all through the night and it would prevent Dariak from ever clearing his head and getting rest. The mage knew it was just an excuse, but he didn't argue.

Instead, he settled himself in his room and pulled open a pouch that he kept tucked underneath his cloak. Spilling the contents on his mattress, Dariak sifted through the eleven pieces of jade he had traveled through two kingdoms to claim. He could sense the innate abilities of each one even without touching them. They pulsed with his heartbeat, the earth jade more than the rest.

He gently caressed the shards, feeling the odd texture of each one. The glass jade had a gritty surface like a fine coating of sand. The water jade was perpetually damp, though it wouldn't sustain a thirsty man.

Dariak closed his eyes and focused his mind on the jades, wondering what he should do next. Like seeing a man atop a faraway hill, he knew the power was within, but it was so far away that he could not reach it. He wondered how he could restore their strength, for he would need their support to maintain the newfound peace in Hathreneir and also to quell the fighting with Kallisor.

Yet as he sat there communing with the jades, he only felt a cold and unwelcoming silence.

CHAPTER 2

Chancellor Kitalla

"EXCUSE ME, IS someone home? Please open the door," Kitalla said in her most polite tone. Her long dark brown hair was tied in a tail behind her head and her deep brown eyes glinted with authority. Word of her visits had already spread throughout the castle town and the people did all they could to avoid her. In her opinion, it made this game all the more entertaining, and infuriating.

She rapped on the door a second time. "I did just follow you back from the market. I know you're home. Open this door, please."

After some scuffling sounds, the door shook and then moved. An older woman huddled behind the door, which she had barely opened. "Sorry, miss, I didn't hear you."

"Very well," Kitalla uttered sweetly. "You know who I am, I presume, and why I have come?"

"I can't say I do, my lady."

Kitalla had no idea why all the townsfolk insisted on playing this game. Three other conversations that selfsame day had started in precisely the same manner. They didn't seem to realize that wasting her time was a bad idea. "I am Chancellor Kitalla, advisor to the Regent Dariak who has assumed control of this locale after surrender by your glorious king."

"What a charming welcome," the old woman lied.

"As you must know, the recent events have brought turmoil to you and your fellows. There are many families displaced from their homes and in need of housing. I'm here to assign some folks to reside here." She pulled out a scroll and offered it to the woman, who made no effort to reach for it.

"A wonderful obligation," the woman said. "Yet there aren't any spare rooms in my little hovel. I'll keep your needs in mind if my situation changes. Thank you for coming." And with that, she slammed the door.

Kitalla drew a deep breath to steady herself and cracked her knuckles in anticipation. Then with a hearty kick, she blasted down the door, stripping it from its hinges, and smacking the old woman in the face and pummeling her to the ground. Kitalla shook her head; she had even given the fool a few seconds to get out of the way first.

Stepping inside, Kitalla first hoisted the wood door off the woman then contin-ued her one-sided conversation in a loud shout. "Since you clearly cannot hear my words, you force me to speak in this fashion. I did not come to your abode request-ing space. I came to assess how much you will surrender. And because you have been so cooperative, you will enjoy a greater chance to help your kingdom by ex-tending the duration for which your help is required." She cleared her throat and only then pulled the woman to her feet.

"Have you any questions?" Kitalla said softly.

The woman scowled and it was clear she wanted to spit in the chancellor's face, but she controlled herself. It certainly wouldn't do to anger this woman further.

"The tour please," Kitalla requested, lowering her tone now that she had made her point.

Grudgingly, the woman escorted Kitalla through the small house. There were two bedrooms, a kitchen, and an extra workroom, where the woman had a loom and various cloths and threads. After the walkthrough, the woman brought Kitalla to the front door and waited for her to leave.

Kitalla nodded. "A nice house. I would almost want to stay here myself." The woman's face immediately went white with panic, as Kitalla had intended. "But it is a curious little place."

"W—What do you mean?"

"Well, first of all, one of those rooms upstairs was rather empty. I thought you were fully stocked up here on residents."

She fidgeted with her fingers. "I—well, it is my son's room and he keeps it sparse in there."

"Indeed? He wouldn't happen to be off fighting in the east, would he?" The woman bit her lip and looked away, confirming Kitalla's suspicions. "Then he's not going to need this place for some time, I would think. Much obliged. A small family could camp out in there."

Though Kitalla was new to the area and her role was only recently invented, even the old woman knew she could not refute this demand. Anyone who had re-sisted too far met with support from the throne itself, complete with a contingent of soldiers under Ieran's name. No one knew how long this new regime would last but they had to play along with it for now.

The woman visibly folded. "Very well. A small family then. I know times are hard, but my son is all I have left. I didn't want his place disturbed. Forgive me."

Kitalla touched her hand to her heart and nodded as sincerely as she could mus-ter. "I do forgive you, and I do truly understand your pain." Slowly she smiled and the woman wilted even further, fearing what was to come next. "It is a charming house, like I said. But I was wondering…"

The woman swallowed nervously but did not prompt Kitalla to continue.

"I couldn't help but notice a few things. First of all, wherever do you store your food? That kitchen you showed me was functional, but it was barely more than a firepit."

"Food is scarce," was the terse reply.

"That must explain the other bit, then. No privy. Not inside. Not outside. That would certainly explain why you are so irritable." She then turned her gaze sharply on the woman. "Or do you expect me to believe that you go to the tavern to take care of such business?"

Clearly, the woman wanted Kitalla to believe that, but also it was clear that pursuing such a farce would anger the chancellor even more. Without pretense, the woman growled and then led Kitalla to a somewhat hidden door that led to a floor downstairs.

The basement was crowded with all sorts of supplies, from cooking utensils to extra furniture. The entire horde looked as though Kitalla's visit was expected and the woman had hidden everything from blankets to forks. A standard privy was sectioned off in the corner, too.

"Much better," Kitalla announced. "Now, let's walk through the house once more and you can show me all the other little hidey-holes."

"There's noth—"

Kitalla raised an eyebrow and the woman silenced at once. "The outside of your house is bigger than the inside. Even the floor plan down here is larger than what you showed me upstairs. You Hathrens are a crafty lot. So many of these homes have hidden rooms and walkways. It's truly amazing. Chancellor Ieran never alerted me to such designs, but they're commonplace, aren't they?"

At last the homeowner dropped her aloof visage. "Fine, you brat. We may need to follow your demands for a time, but it won't be forever, you realize."

"Oh?" Kitalla asked, her voice lilting with innocence.

The woman saw the threat in Kitalla's eyes and she gulped, wondering if she had overstepped her bounds. "What's the real reason you're here?"

"Finding homes for refugees, as I said."

"Not trying to see if the king is hiding here?"

Kitalla did not react. Instead she waited for the woman to say more or to give something away with her movements, but she didn't.

"You can't find him and you think that by searching our homes for him, you'll squirrel him out. And once you check a place, you pack it with strangers who owe you a debt and keep an eye on it for you. A crafty plan, I will have to say."

"Thank you. I came up with it myself."

The woman sneered. "You won't find the king here. So come and I'll show you every nook and cranny. I hope you're not afraid of spiders."

"Spiders don't bother me. Close-minded people do, however. I have to tell you one thing, though. Maybe you can help."

"I will not help you!"

"No, I suspect you wouldn't. But the sooner we find the king and put him back on the throne, the sooner the Regent and I skip out of town."

"Put him back—" The woman caught herself and hated that Kitalla had triggered a reaction. With a snarl, she added, "As if. You just want to flush him out so you can finish off killing him."

Kitalla laughed. "Yes, because I so enjoy telling people to open up their homes to strangers and ruining their daily routines."

"You certainly look like you're enjoying yourself."

"Gotta make the best of things in any situation," she responded lightly. "Now, you were about to tell me which way the king went."

The woman shook her head. "While you waste your time with all of this non-sense, you'll wake up one day and see that the king has returned and you won't be able to stop him regardless of what wild magic you have at your disposal. You won't be able to kill us all before you die."

"I see. So you admit to being part of an uprising. That does sound rather trai-torous."

"W—What?"

"Come with me then. Your presence is needed in the castle." Then she corrected herself, "In the dungeon, rather. No, you won't need your shawl."

"You can't do this!" the woman shrieked as Kitalla reached out to grab her arm. She bolted away and ran to her kitchen, grabbing a knife and holding it shakily at Kitalla.

The one-time thief stepped in and snapped the knife out the woman's hand so fast, she barely registered Kitalla's movement. "What will it be, then? The king? Or the castle?"

The woman tried to run, but Kitalla stuck her foot out and grounded her. "Don't kill me," the woman cried.

She sighed. "You Hathrens just don't listen. We came here to speak to the king. He sent out soldiers. We tried to hand over refugees of your own land and the king tried to kill them. It was never our intent to attack you or kill you. You don't under-stand it now because you're still hung up on being hateful and angry, but we're here to end the fighting all around. Wouldn't you rather your son come home alive than die in a stupid, needless battle?

"For now, we need to get this place back in shape. That requires people like you making sacrifices for others who are less fortunate. You can expect twenty visitors by tomorrow. You'll make them feel welcome here, and you'll do your very best to accommodate their needs in your own meager little way.

"So few of you Hathrens were even willing to open your homes up to your fellows in need. But what if it was your home that was decimated? What would you have done then? You would have needed the kindness and willingness of others to care for you. The castle can't support you right now and you would be turned aside. What then, you crazy woman?"

Kitalla took a deep breath. "Once everyone is settled in, we'll be putting out work demands on rotating shifts. So it isn't as if all the people assigned to this place will always be in here. They just need a home base until they can fix up a home for themselves. But everyone is pitching in, even you.

"Selfish Hathrens," Kitalla muttered, eying the woman who just stared up at her from the ground. "I hope our way rubs off on you, and I assure you that our way is not a Kallisorian way. No, it is a third way. A new way. It's one that would bring all the people together and build a better world than what we have now.

"So, get off the floor. Stand up and think about a better world. Because king or no king, things are changing. No more tyranny like we've all endured for generations. No more raising children to send them off as fodder for war. No more of people dying because the kings refuse to work together. That's the part we're changing."

The woman looked up at the impassioned speaker and she shook her head. "How?"

"It wasn't our plan to destroy the castle, but since the damage was done, we're using this opportunity to make you all band together. That's my real purpose, if you must know. Diplomacy is not my talent, lady. I'd much rather toss this knife across the room with a dozen others and show you where my skills lie. But this is vitally important. You all have to come to understand that it's time for less selfishness and more openness. And in time it will be easier.

"But for now, let's take a real tour of your house."

With a disgruntled sigh, the woman did as she was commanded, keeping a wary eye on the knife Kitalla kept in hand. After another hour or so, Kitalla was satisfied that no one was hiding.

"Very well, then. I'll be going. Expect visitors." With that, Kitalla tossed the blade, letting it land barely an inch away from the woman's foot. Heaving an unhappy sigh, Kitalla stepped from the house and moved on to the next.

CHAPTER 3

Ieran's Allegiance

PROGRESS IN THE castle town was slow. Many people still needed permanent living arrangements, but few places remained for anyone to go to. Clearing out the rubble from the front of the castle was taking longer than expected, too; for each piece that was pulled away, more stones fell from the rest of the structure. Dariak and the others were at a loss on the best way to proceed.

"It's not looking good among the people, either," Kitalla added. "They're definitely hiding something from us. And I believe they'll rebel against us before long."

"I don't believe that," Ieran said.

"You would benefit from making us believe that, if you're helping them."

The gray-haired chancellor's face erupted into an expression of outrage. "You dare! I have thrown my lot in to help bring these matters to a peaceful resolution during your stay."

"During our stay," Kitalla echoed. "Precisely my point. Once you kick us out, you won't need to comply any longer."

Dariak groaned. "Kitalla, this isn't helping." He looked like he had aged fifteen years in the past three weeks. "Ieran, we need to find the king, explain our purpose here, and then bring the Kallisorian king around. Isn't there any way…?"

The older man shook his head. "I have no knowledge of the king's whereabouts nor how to find him."

Kitalla scoffed. "Convenient."

Gabrion banged his fist on the table. "Kitalla, that's enough!" The young warrior pierced her with his gaze. He was nearly seven years younger than her but he was the only one who could speak to her in such a manner and not incur her anger. "You've been stuck among the people for too long. You're losing sight of what we're here for."

She raised her eyebrow and shook her head. "Oh, Gabrion, calm yourself. I'm merely pointing out that we're strangers here and we can't necessarily trust Ieran. What's the harm in letting him know our suspicions?" She swiveled around to look at the king's advisor. "You know I harbor no ill feelings for you, I would hope, but I can't naïvely accept that you're doing everything to help us. You may say you're on our side and understand our beliefs, but people don't change so quickly."

Ruhk laughed. The Hathren commander drew the attention of everyone at the gathering. "You're right there, I will admit. Though Gabrion here did spin my head around to your line of thinking, it was no easy matter. Indeed, it took a show of force on his part that coerced me to even listen, if I valued my life. And just when we were breaking through the barriers of discrimination, we were attacked. I was ready to pull my men away and battle in the name of great Hathreneir, but the king had heard of our collaborations with traitors, and so we were instantly branded the same. We were all cast off by our king without any chance to speak of our actions. It left us with nowhere to turn, unless we joined Gabrion's team."

Ieran shrugged. "Some say you should have fought anyway and taken the chance of earning your place back in the king's graces."

But Ruhk was unconvinced. "No, sir. Defection is unaccepted here. Even if we had brought down the Kallisorian king, our penalty was known. In that moment, life was the better alternative for us."

"It's the same in Kallisor," Gabrion said. "Dariak and a Hathren team decimated my hometown, but because I brought the mage to the king alive rather than dead, I was seen as a possible collaborator and sentenced to the same death."

"Lucky for me you didn't take him up on his offer for freedom," Dariak said.

"I couldn't have killed you in cold blood. Not even then." He turned back to Ieran. "You've looked out for your people in our time here, as well you should. Yet it's clear that you don't fully support our ideals."

Ieran's back straightened, worried about where this was headed. "Is that so? What else must I do to convince you all of my loyalty?"

Kitalla laughed. "Loyalty? You served your liege for how many years, but now that we're here, you turn immediately to serve us? Where is your loyalty aimed? Your own survival?"

"Kitalla," Randler intervened. The bard sat in a larger chair than the others, for his legs were still damaged and weak, and they were encased in the living crutches the forest leader Astrith had crafted for him, though their effectiveness was greatly reduced at the time being. Randler ran his fingers through his cinnamon-colored hair and let his warm voice soothe them all. "Ieran has shown his loyalty without wavering. He is here for his people and for them alone. Surely he has had some disagreements with his king over his own beliefs. His support of us is no different, for if we continue to fight today, then more of his people will suffer. It is, thus, to his benefit and ours if we work as one."

"Until their king returns," Kitalla appended. "That's my point, Randler. This is a false calm. It isn't the peace we're seeking. I see it in all of my dealings with the people in the town. They're just biding their time, waiting for the resurgence to begin."

Carrus, a warrior of Kallisor who joined Dariak's army before their journey into Hathreneir and who was recently promoted to captain, asked, "What would you have us do, then?"

Kitalla wanted to break the tension by slamming her hand on the table, shouting, "Kill them all!" but she knew that no one would be amused by it. Instead, she turned to Verna. "Your thoughts?"

"Ha!" The woman was a child of Marritosh in the south, a favored supply line for the king's army. Every family had borne children only to lose them to one battle or another. Each child was trained to fight, and when the need arose, they were carted off to war. Verna's father had answered the call that had come for her, leaving her to tend to her siblings, but she hadn't been able to protect them all.

"That's not a helpful answer," Kitalla commented as she waited.

Verna shook her head. "We're spending a lot of time trying to figure out how to keep this place from rising up as a power against us. If we leave, then all the old rules come back into place. If we stay, then we await the day the people revolt. We've enforced rules upon them, packed up their homes with stranded people, and we've assigned them jobs to do to get this place back in order. What we haven't given them is a reason, other than the option of living or dying."

"We haven't threatened to kill anyone," Dariak argued.

"Not explicitly, no. But it's implied. If they don't do as we ask, then we'll retaliate against them. So they submit, for now. It isn't unlike my childhood when the king sent requests for fighters. We complied because we had no choice."

"And then," Gabrion said, "when we arrived and told others of our new way of thinking, of our plan to end the fighting, many men and women joined our ranks."

"Defying the king," Ieran pointed out. "And so when you arrived here at first, we did not admit you."

Kitalla groaned. "They were not the same people. We brought you the people who had never turned from the king in the first place. But you never took the time to listen."

"We're talking in circles now," Ieran said. "What would you have me do, Regent? What duties do you require?"

Dariak looked around the room and wasn't sure what to say, but he thought he understood something that Verna had implied and if he was wrong, it couldn't hurt to try anyway. "Gabrion and Ruhk, Verna and Carrus, go out into the town. Take a team with each of you and get to work building some new homes."

"We already have people doing that," Kitalla said.

"Only by hand. Take teams of mages with you to help with the reconstruction."

"Sir…" Ieran started.

"I know. Magic is still unstable at the moment. But perhaps in concerted teams they can keep the energies intact."

"I'd advise against it. The state of things is tenuous already. Enough mages have damaged the people around them with spells they've used safely for years. You're opening us up to a dangerous situation. I cannot agree to this plan."

"You don't have to," Dariak said sternly. Then to the others, "Take six to eight mages per team and a few others who can help with the heavy lifting."

Ieran stood up. "I must protest. You will endanger countless lives in this endeavor."

"Your counsel has been noted."

Kitalla eyed the chancellor for a minute before adding, "Unless you have a way of stopping us?"

The gray-haired man wilted under her stare and he sat back down, his lips twitching in annoyance. "You will cause the people great harm if you do this."

"Then somehow we'll repay them for their troubles," Gabrion said, rising up and summoning the others to follow him.

Once the four were gone, Ieran glared at Dariak. "Making a show of help will do little to appease the people."

"If you have nothing constructive to say, then keep quiet," Kitalla snapped.

"Sound advice," Randler scolded.

Kitalla glanced appreciatively in his direction, but realized he had aimed the remark at her. Frustrated, she folded her arms across her chest and leaned back so far in her chair she almost tipped it over.

"There is another matter that needs tending," Dariak said to Ieran. "With a few hundred extra people living here now, how long will food and water last?"

"Not long, especially with magic failing." The chancellor lifted his chin as if speaking to a petulant child. "You may have noticed that the castle and town are surrounded by a vast desert and that the royal gardens were destroyed in your attack."

"Ieran, I already had one mentor turn against me. I realize that when I left Hathreneir to gather the jades I lost your support as well."

"On the contrary, Regent, I never had much love for you as a child either." He tried to withhold his contempt but failed. "I worked with you when I was required to, nothing more. Our liege once believed you had the potential to surpass your father and would bring us victory. To that end, I did my best to instruct you."

Dariak nodded. "I see. Then it seems that aside from my mother, I never had much personal support until this past year."

"Yes, your mother. Perhaps you should pay her a visit, then?"

"I intend to, once things are more stable here. Now tell me again: What is the food situation like and how will we persevere through the winter?"

"Through the winter, sir?" Ieran asked hesitantly. "I had not thought you would stay so long."

Kitalla snickered, then waved away the others when they turned to her. In her view, everything was moving according to plan.

Chapter 4

Reconstruction

As requested, Gabrion and the others ventured into the town surrounding the castle with a host of mages and soldiers to help put some of the area back together. Gabrion and Ruhk led one team while Verna and Carrus split off with a second group. Each team was comprised of Hathrens and Kallisorians, and intentionally so, even among their leaders. Perhaps showing the populace how they could work together successfully would have some positive effect.

Because housing was Dariak's primary concern at the moment, they made no attempt to repair the castle. Instead they approached a nearby home that had been decimated by the energy of the jades and set to work. The soldiers dug in and shifted away the largest bits of debris, while Gabrion cajoled the mages into a concerted effort of their own.

Magic required a delicate balance in order to work. Mages drew energies in through the use of spell components, body gestures, and carefully crafted phrases, whose inflections augmented the power of the spells. Typically, a mage's intent was imprinted within the spell so as to cast it upon a target rather than scatter it haphazardly.

Yet since the jades had come together three weeks earlier and erupted in force against the castle, the magical energies were hard to draw in and even harder to control. The mages strained to complete even the easiest of spells, and it set them all at a severe disadvantage.

Unlike Kallisor, Hathreneir allowed mages to work in the open, though not usually in large groups that could threaten the balance in the land. Thus having their powers shackled now made the mages feel utterly frustrated and useless. They wanted to fight back against those whose actions led to this dampening of their powers. Even those who had traveled with Dariak for some time showed anger at this turn of events. Dariak had assured them all that the energies would return to normal at some point. It just needed time. After all, the War of the Colossus twenty years earlier had not left a permanent dead zone in the land, and that had been a greater use of the jades' powers.

Now Gabrion brought eight mages together, talking to them about their inherent skills. "It will take all of you working together to pull this off."

"If we even can." Jerrul frowned. "Imagine trying to fight if you didn't sleep for weeks, had no food or water, and you were reduced to one tenth your size. You wouldn't be very effective, would you?"

"I certainly wouldn't quit until I had tried," Gabrion returned. "Band together, now. You're all earth mages, and I need you to find a common ground to work on. We'll hoist up the walls, if you can use your skills to support them."

"We will try," Jerrul muttered skeptically.

With a nod, Gabrion joined Ruhk and the soldiers as they dragged debris out of the way. They shifted broken furniture and belongings as well as shattered walls and doors. Gabrion worked as hard as anyone else, and no one faulted his orders. He gathered the men together and they dragged the largest segment of intact wall they could find and lifted it into place. Then Gabrion called out to the mages to work their skills.

Six of the mages immediately entered a repeated pace, stepping forward, raising their hands, then pulling back and lowering their arms. Forward and backward they moved, their lips rattling off a deep cadence. As their hands swept up and down, their fingers pulsed and twisted, tugging at the energies all around them. After several minutes, nothing happened, but before Gabrion could ask what they were doing, the other two mages dropped to their knees.

Each mage scooped up a fistful of dirt and brought it up overhead, letting the dust cascade downward over their bodies. They spit into their hands and repeated the process, now with a slightly solidified mud. When spittle no longer sufficed, they reached for canteens and poured larger amounts of water into the dirt and then scooped up the mud and raised it high, letting it splatter themselves messily. To Gabrion, they looked like young children playing in the mud.

The wall grew heavy, even with several men holding it upright. The mages continued their chanting and their motions, and the two mud-bearers stepped forward one small motion at a time. When they reached the wall, the mud was a deep consistency and they spread it along the bottom edge where the wood touched the ground. When all the moist sludge was set in place, the team of mages altered their positions and began a new incantation. To set the mud, they had to convince the dirt to seep into any crevices and cracks and bind them shut. Doing so expelled the water, which pooled in small areas.

After nearly twenty minutes of incessant spellcasting, the mages lowered their arms and closed their mouths, giving Gabrion the signal that they were finished. The wall seemed sturdy, so Gabrion pulled away, but as soon as they released it, Ruhk let out a cry of alarm, and down the wall fell.

"It's no use! I told you!" Jerrul whined. "Even using six of us just to draw enough energy for the rest, we couldn't do much at all. This is hopeless."

Gabrion inspected the damage and shook his head. "The wall is definitely stronger than it was before, but the seal with the ground couldn't hold the weight. Rest up, get what components you need, and return within the hour."

"To what end?"

"Just follow orders, Jerrul, and you'll see." Grumbling, the mages went off.

Ruhk whistled low and shook his head. "What now?"

"Everyone listen up," Gabrion called to the soldiers all around him. "Let's dig through this mess and prop up the walls the best we can."

"Sir, we don't have enough materials to keep them together," one of the soldiers pointed out. "It's like building a house of cards."

"That's right. So let's start by finding the strongest cards we can and set them up first. Come on!"

There was little to salvage in the mess, but Gabrion would not let them stop. They used the frame of a dresser to help keep two partitions somewhat aligned. One soldier held each wall while everyone else dug around for more. In the end, they needed to scavenge materials from two other nearby houses just to get enough to serve as the basis of a single home.

Eventually the mages returned and Gabrion gave them their task. Instead of trying to link the wood to the earth itself for support, he had them bind each partition together, sealing them neatly into a solid box. It took nearly two more hours just to connect the various pieces, but when they were finished, the structure held.

"We still need to try to link it to the ground so it doesn't blow away," Jerrul said. "After that, you need to figure something out for a roof."

"You seem a bit more optimistic," Ruhk noted with a burgeoning belly laugh sounding in his throat. "And here I thought this couldn't be done."

The mage shook his head. "If I had full use of my powers, this would have been a much easier task. But I guess if we do pull hard enough, we can get some things done anyway." He flicked his gaze to Gabrion and referenced his earlier denial. "I suppose even the bite of a firegnat can change the outcome of a fight. Of course, I'm still curious to know who's going to volunteer to live here first. I, for one, am not sure I trust this structure yet."

Gabrion smiled. "One problem at a time. Ruhk, can you continue here for a while? I want to check on the others."

Even though his body was tired, Gabrion pushed himself into a light jog to limber up his legs. Bending and lifting was one thing, but running always felt better to him. Carrus and Verna had taken their team further north, closer to the other inhabitants of the town. When Gabrion arrived, things were not going well.

Verna was screaming at the top of her lungs. "—met such a careless oaf as you! Get on your feet and stand over there and don't you dare say anything else. No! Not a sound."

"What's all this?" Gabrion asked. From appearances, they had been pulling apart the fallen structures and reassembling them in a fashion similar to the one Gabrion was using. The mages were all passed out, as were the soldiers who had been moving the heavy boards around. Carrus was bleeding from numerous cuts and scrapes, and as Gabrion examined the area, he saw that Carrus wasn't alone.

Verna continued raging, her face flushed a deep crimson, and her wild hair flying every which way as her head shook in anger. Her speech escalated in speed and Gabrion could barely even understand her anymore. The target of her ire was a pair of teenagers.

Gabrion tried to intervene but Carrus stepped in and pulled the warrior aside. "Better let her get it out of her system."

"What happened?"

"The short version? We were trying to secure the walls. Those two boys were playing catch. One of them smacked into the mages and disrupted the spell and everything came crashing down. That was after a few other failed attempts and it looked like we were about to make some progress."

"We've had troubles, too, but we'll get there." Gabrion watched as Verna paced back and forth, now shouting about responsibility and attentiveness. "She's really worked up."

Carrus gestured to some of his wounds. "We all got banged up pretty badly. I think Roveena broke her arm too."

"What of the other villagers here?"

Carrus shrugged. "No one offered to help. And when we said their assistance would be welcome, they just backed away and went about their business. Well, mostly, anyway. I hate to say it, but it's like they don't want our help."

Verna finally finished her tirade and she stamped over to Gabrion, forcing herself into a calmer state before greeting him. "We have had some difficulties," she said through clenched teeth.

Gabrion nodded. "It seems as if you should call it for now and use the time to tend to your wounds."

"I tell you, Gabrion, these people are interfering on purpose. First the old woman with her packages slips and falls and it takes three men—three!—to get her back home. Then another woman comes over with a bucket of water, demanding we all take a break and she wouldn't stop pestering us until we did. Two men came in 'to help' but only managed to trip over everyone and everything until I sent them off. Now these boys. I've about had it."

"Report back to the castle. There may be something else going on here." He called to the rest of the team. "Anyone who needs their injuries tended, head back to the castle with Verna. The rest of you, I could use your help."

It was a sign of how angry she was that Verna didn't argue against being sent away. Carrus tried to remain behind, but Gabrion assessed his wounds and insisted he return for treatment. Five others joined Gabrion as he returned to his team.

The four main walls were upright and the mages chanted wildly, tossing bits of mud at the base of the walls. They were spread out, surrounding the structure, but they chanted in unison. The two mages Gabrion had with him watched the cadence and, when the chanting permitted it, joined the casting.

Ruhk walked over to Gabrion, his face a mask of confusion. "It makes no sense. This is the fourth iteration they try, but whatever they do, the mages can't secure the base of the house to the earth underneath."

Concern clouded Gabrion's features. "Verna's group was also having trouble. What of the walls themselves?"

"They seem rather secure. But it would be like camping in a tent without tying it down. One strong gust of wind and swoosh!"

"Very well, then. After this attempt, let's head back inside."

"Really? I thought you would want to try some other things first? Like digging trenches under the walls or something."

"Typically I would, Ruhk, but I have the feeling we're up against something else that we didn't expect. We need to consult with the others about it."

"More foul play?"
Gabrion nodded. "I just hope it isn't coming from within our own ranks."

The Bard Endures

OVER THE NEXT few days, Gabrion and the others made further attempts to build new houses near the castle, but it wasn't easy going. They were able to link the walls together and assemble thatch roofs, but they couldn't make any progress on securing the foundations. Even Ruhk's idea of digging minor trenches for the walls didn't work. The stony ground was completely solid and, even with pickaxes, they were unable to make a dent in it.

Gabrion already had his suspicions and Dariak agreed; some form of magic was making the area impenetrable. But without magic to help them, they had no idea how to delve deeper. Kitalla offered to scout out a new plan of attack, but she insisted they all keep to their usual tasks and not inform Ieran of their secondary goal.

While the majority of the team was off investigating, Randler continued pressing himself through his exercises to strengthen his damaged legs. On their own they ached terribly. Bending his knees, lifting his legs, and putting weight on them all escalated the aches to intense pain. He struggled not to cry out at such times, especially if anyone was nearby. And it seemed as if there was always someone nearby.

Cold air wafted through the window, reminding Randler that they were in the heart of winter. It wasn't at all like the winters he knew in Kallisor. The desert kept the area dry and golden, but even though the sand warmed in the sun and radiated that heat all around, the wind itself was chill. It was the only indication to him that winter was upon them.

He reached down and massaged his left leg, shuddering at the waves of fire that laced up at his touch. Pressing and squeezing, he continued the massage, keeping the blood flowing for the following challenge. He tried to picture his leg as a lute string. It was necessary to tighten the string further and further, almost to the point of breaking, just so it would produce the perfect quality of sound. Perhaps the string itself felt like his leg did now, and each twist of the knob would send shudders through its core.

With one leg ready, he worked on the next, now turning his mind toward repairing a drum. Tugging the fabric was necessary for creating a sharp and deep thud, and the skin there, too, probably felt the strain as it was tightened into place.

With both legs as limber as possible, Randler stretched his fingers—the conductor before the show—and reached toward the oversized bedpost. Setting one foot on the floor and tugging gently, he stepped up and swayed as his body accepted the rush of agony. He had never danced in a fire nor walked upon sharp needles, but he imagined that those sensations were comparable to what he felt now.

Remaining erect was challenge enough, but he wasn't done. Beside the bed was his staff, the same one that Dariak had crafted for him on their journey through Astrith's forest. It was crude in design but it was sturdy. With a solid thunk, he set the staff before him, then he lifted his foot and shuffled it forward a step, transferring his weight from one leg to the other. All the while the symphony of pain swirled through him in massive waves.

With the healing jade and help from the mages, the pain was present, yet manageable. Now that magic had been rendered ineffective, he was all on his own. A few of the mages had prepared herbal remedies, but the tinctures and poultices usually only made him feel aloof or dizzy and did not help where he needed it.

Three more steps passed by as he considered the wild variety of herbs and fruits he had imbibed in various teas. Some were purely delightful in their own right, and he planned one day to create a berry and basil tincture just to unwind.

He stopped making progress as a particularly strong wave of pain swept through him. His vision clouded and he teetered precariously, which flooded him with anxiety. He remembered his first solo performances as a bard and the wild jitters that shook him before he started to play. Breathing deeply always helped him stabilize and he did so now, drawing in careful breaths and releasing them slowly, expelling the sensations of his body with every exhalation.

When his vision stopped flickering, he continued to walk forward, ignoring the pressures building in his head with all the focus this one simple act was taking. He had walked all his life and never had such a chore of it. He looked over his head and glanced back to where he started, disappointed that he could practically hop backwards and land in bed. All that effort and he had barely moved.

Yet he needed to remain positive in light of this. He let the pain wash over him and he felt it swish from side to side, rising up, sinking low, wafting all around. He hummed along as he pictured it, letting the notes drift into and out of himself, drawing together into a new and powerful melody.

And as the notes pulsated in a mix of rhythm and chaos, there came an unexpected crescendo, with all the instruments banging out in a loud, fiery chorus, like a tilted tree finally breaking from its roots and smashing to the ground. And once the violent rush of sound exploded in Randler's ears, it drifted and wafted away slowly, leaving him behind all alone with nothing. Nothing.

Nothing except the press of cold stone against his face and the drizzle of blood from his nose where he had cracked it when he stumbled.

He lay there a while, wondering if the music would start up again or if he would only have silence. He could hear drums starting up in tribe background as pinpricks rattled up and down his legs. The drums were joined by a low, wailing flute, building louder and louder until it overpowered the percussions and drew all of Randler's attention. He held on to the melody, not wanting to let it go, even though it brought with it all the reminders of his suffering. Yet where did most creations come from?

The heart, the soul, and where better to feel them than in the depths of despair where the body was so hurt it couldn't distract him with any other desires? The music was all he had. It was the only companion that had always been by his side.

When the keening wail subsided, Randler summoned more of his mental music by pressing his hands upon the floor and shifting himself upright. Staff in hand, he struggled to reclaim his footing, but his legs were just too weak. He barely made it off the bed earlier; now rising from the floor was a much greater challenge and he couldn't do it on his own.

He knew he should have kept Astrith's crutches on during this endeavor, but he worried that he would grow so accustomed to their support that he would never walk on his own again, and that thought drove him mad with worry. He would never dance again, and what good was a bard who could play music but not revel in it?

Randler slid his body over to the wall, taking the staff with him. After a rest, he tried again, buttressing himself against the wall while climbing up the staff hand over hand. His left leg was stronger than his right so he used it first for support and, though he wavered, he remained upright. Bringing the right leg underneath was easy then, though the reverberations through his body threatened to spill him to the ground once more.

Turning his head to the right, he could see the bed waiting there, taunting him. He felt like a prisoner chained to the dungeon wall with food placed barely beyond his reach. And he was terribly hungry.

He considered pushing off the wall and hoping for the best, but his nose was still bleeding from his first fall and he could only imagine what other damage he would do if he missed the bed, or worse, if he cracked his head against the frame.

While he waited for courage to well within himself, he thought about the jades and the loss of their powers. He wondered how the stories of the Forgotten Tribe tied into that, and how the picture book Kitalla had seen in Magehaven would connect. Randler thought of the music in his mind and he focused on crafting words to bind with the notes.

With a single waft through ancient trees,
the lady did meet her man.
They laughed and danced and joined in song
and so crossed an empty span.
Bound together in an ancient time, when
the trees were but a foot tall.
They came together to create a new land;
they did not hope to fall.

In the past with the errors of pride,
the man was strong and the lady thus died.
In the future where the world is unknown,
too many hopes have already flown.

Two children born to the lady and king;
each of them kept one.
Kallisor, with sword held high,
did try to train his son.
Hathreneir, with magical skills,
did then raise the girl.
But war broke out between these two;
their lives would then unfurl.

In the past with the errors of pride,
the man was strong and the lady thus died.
In the future where the world is unknown,
too many hopes have already flown.

The children of the Forgotten Tribe,
did one day face each other.
Urged by the father then for the sister
to be killed by the brother.
Yet he refused, he ran away, hid himself
from the scorn of his father.
Thus it was the king of Kallisor,
killed his first and truest daughter.

In the past with the errors of pride,
the man was strong and the lady thus died.
In the future where the world is unknown,
too many hopes have already flown.

Estranged from the vicious, warlike man
who had given him life,
the truest son of the king of Kallisor
found for himself a wife.
Though little is known across the land
of the timid boy's adventures,
it could just be that he kept quiet;
freedom from conjecture.

Stephen J. Wolf

In the past with the errors of pride,
the man was strong and the lady thus died.
In the future where the world is unknown,
too many hopes have already flown.

Years pass by and lines intertwine,
descendants now are lost.
We've no true king to lead us now,
and so we pay the cost.
The divided factions, left and right
ever are they at war.
And yet we seek to come together
to finally say, "no more."

In the past with the errors of pride,
the man was strong and the lady thus died.
In the future where the world is unknown,
too many hopes have already flown.

The lines are blurred and all the kings,
though, yes, truly descended,
are only from the single royal lines;
not the one intended.
So now we yearn for a fresh new day
where peace can be at hand.
Where are you, of the Forgotten Tribe?
We need that kind of man.

In the past with the errors of pride,
the man was strong and the lady thus died.
In the future where the world is unknown,
too many hopes have already flown.

And as I ponder the history of events in
this world in which I live,
I realize that we've always had help
from those who would give.
We have had the mages, the soldiers too,
and indeed each single jade.
Yet how will we all come together?
Or will we be lost in shade?

In the past with the errors of pride,
the man was strong and the lady thus died.
In the future where the world is unknown,
too many hopes have already flown.

Randler's body fell again, but this time by design. He allowed himself to slip forward onto the bed, the staff clattering to the floor, its task complete. The bard yanked on the blanket to help roll himself upon the mattress and then he lay there, staring at the ceiling, as the fervent fire within his body welled up and consumed him, burning away the rest of his solemn day.

CHAPTER 6

The Chancellor Sings

TENSIONS IN THE Hathren castle and town mounted as the days passed by. All the people had been placed in homes and given vital work to do to help restore order to the place, but resistance flourished everywhere. Castle guards were summoned regularly to settle minor disputes among the people, but whenever Dariak or his comrades arrived, immediately the troubles vanished. At first it seemed as if the people were just afraid of their new Regent and his friends, but the frequency of the issues should then have decreased, which was quite the opposite of what was happening.

On one particularly busy day, fifteen reports of riots reached the castle and guards were dispatched to each occurrence. Gabrion, Ruhk, Verna, Lica, and Carrus separately attended some of the incursions, and, as before, those squabbles ended instantly. They tried finding other cases of trouble and discovered that the town was quiet. The other guards, however, took hours to return, and none of the group could find them amidst the people. It was a terrible sign.

Ieran, meanwhile, scurried about the castle, his tunic all askew and his face drenched in sweat, as he reported all the disasters to Dariak with utmost urgency. Always, he looked to be at his breaking point and he frequently confessed his confusion about why the fights were incessantly erupting.

"Send another team," Dariak ordered. "Dismissed."

Randler looked at the mage after Ieran left. "I guess it's soon, then."

"If only we knew exactly when, and how to stop it." He sat heavily on a chair. "We still have about twenty of our soldiers here. But only that."

"The part I don't understand is why the men and women committed to our team are also gone for extended periods. You don't think they've turned sides, Dariak?"

"If they have, then we have to get out of here before it's too late." The door opened and Kitalla walked in, her face stone cold. "And I was hoping for good news."

She grabbed a goblet of wine from the side table and drank it down. "So much for peace," she said, pouring herself a second helping. "I don't suppose you've gotten those jades to work yet, have you?"

"Not yet. How bad is it?"

Kitalla threw herself into a chair and kicked her feet up. "We haven't done a very good job of paying attention to the people around us. We send our guards, they come back. But not all of them. Actually, quite a few haven't returned in days. We've been so busy rushing out to help these people that we haven't noticed."

"What are you saying?" Randler asked, leaning forward. "They're being taken?"

She nodded. "And I know where they're being held but I haven't figured out how to get inside." She saw the confused look on their faces and she grinned. "I have my sources." Indeed, her mentor, Poltor, who had trained her as a thief was currently working his own form of magic in the area. Though he had disowned Kitalla after she left his group, she had apparently convinced him to shed some information during their time there. It suggested to Dariak that Poltor feared for Kitalla's life, because if his connection to her was discovered, his livelihood would drastically change.

Randler interpreted, "Then the guards who side with the king return here for their duties, all the while depositing our supporters into some sort of holding cell. Soon we'll have no one left but ourselves."

Kitalla smiled as if he had just given her a diamond the size of his fist. "Without magic on their side, they've had to be crafty. Our own altruism has worked against us because we haven't been watching closely enough for subterfuge, since we've been doing everything we can to rebuild their stupid home. And in that ti—"

The door crashed open and Ieran staggered in, his face bright red, his breath wheezing. "In the southeast quadrant. Two men struck down with swords. Fire to a bakery. We have to hurry!"

"The people can figure this one out themselves," Kitalla said. "Seriously, they have to learn that their actions have consequences. We're not their parents, after all."

Ieran's face burned redder, if that was possible. "But the fire will spread and we have no water magics to quell the flames. People will die. I cannot accept that." None of them seemed concerned so he shouted, "The people turn to you for help. If you don't answer, they will turn against you."

Kitalla groaned, biting a fingernail and inspecting her work. "It seems they already have. Besides, we don't even have anyone left to send."

"There are still men left to send," Ieran insisted. "I will send them myself if you do not."

Kitalla gave an audible gasp. "You would act without the Regent's permission? Worse, against it?"

Dariak waved his hand to calm her. "Ieran, of course we wouldn't even think of letting the people suffer so. Perhaps once you have sent them, you can return here and we can devise a means of ending these outbursts before they continue. Perhaps we'll need to post soldiers throughout the town? Or establish a curfew? Or close all but the necessary shops and locations? Or—"

"Hold! Hold!" Ieran panicked. "The fire must be dealt with first. I will return presently and—"

Dariak looked at him, wondering why he had stopped, but then he understood the reason. Kitalla had risen from her seat, setting her goblet aside and focusing her attention on the king's chancellor. Her eyes lit with a sultry fire and she stepped forward by crossing one leg over another, her hands tracing the lines of her hips with each step. Sliding her fingertips up her body, she reached for the laces on her tunic, untangling the top and tugging at the leather. She turned slowly away, bending over, reaching her hands up to her face, removing the tie in her hair that kept it neatly tucked away. Then with pulsating motions, she swept her head around, fanning her luxurious hair in all directions, her body swaying with the motion.

The lascivious gestures would have even turned Randler's and Dariak's heads if they were not somewhat immune to her dance skills from all the time they had spent together. Ieran didn't stand a chance. His jaw dropped open and he swayed in time with her hips, his eyes nearly bulging out of his head.

"Come on, baby," Kitalla crooned, keeping her rhythmic gyrations going. "It'll be over soon, won't it? I can't stand the waiting any more. When do we get rid of those evil people in the castle, huh, baby?"

"W—W—Well it isn't like the king's birthday when we know it's coming," he drawled. "But wouldn't you rather talk about something more pleasant, milady? You do look ravishing in that dress."

"Oh," Kitalla demurred, "you say that to all the ladies." She turned and bent low again, sweeping her hands around in perfect, repetitive harmony. "But, Ierie, you know I can't give you what you want until I'm not worried any more. I'm just so scared."

Dariak withheld a laugh so as not to interrupt the trance, but he sensed that something was wrong. He looked at Kitalla and realized that she was struggling to maintain the illusion while also holding a conversation. Randler seemed to notice too, for he started humming a sensual tune, punctuated with minor taps on the armrest of his chair. The slight melody helped to focus Kitalla, but she wouldn't hold on for long.

"Honey cakes," Ieran pleaded, "you know I can't tell you. What if you slip and tell the wrong person? Come here, love, let me have you in my arms. I'll comfort you and take all your worries away." He reached out and moved toward her. Kitalla couldn't move away from him, and Dariak suspected that if they touched then the trance would be broken. He needed to help somehow, but even though he could sense the energies projected from Kitalla, he couldn't augment them.

Dariak took on the role of King Prethos and strode forth, barking out, "Chancellor Ieran, what foolishness is this in my own royal bedchamber?"

Ieran stumbled and his jaw quavered as he turned to face Dariak. "Sire, no, I— We didn't—No, sire, you shouldn't be here, not yet. It's safe. Get back underground and wait for our soldiers to secure the castle."

"You dare tell me to wait?" Dariak said in a deepened voice, grateful that Kitalla was able to insinuate unto Ieran the he was the king. "I will not live in squalor any longer."

"Sire, just two more days. Hold out that long. It's almost over, sire, please. Here, have this woma—"

Kitalla dropped the dance and took the remaining step between them, clobbering the older man and felling him to the cracked marble floor. "Not much time," she panted heavily. "Better… get him to the king's bedroom."

Dariak took his arms as Kitalla grabbed his feet. He grinned. "I'm glad that skill doesn't work on me anymore."

"I'm more... surprised that it worked... at all."

They deposited Ieran in the king's chamber, hoping he would think he really had seen the king there. As they walked back, Dariak commented, "I've always said your skill was different than that of us mages. You provide the catalyst for the energy and project it outward whereas we have to draw the energy in from somewhere else first."

"Explains why... I'm so winded then."

Dariak nodded as they rejoined Randler. "Yes, and I've never seen you dance and speak simultaneously before."

"Never tried it before. But having him just gape at me was disconcerting." She took a moment to catch her breath and then turned to Randler. "Thanks for the tune. It helped. Your music usually does."

"Dance is a physical expression of music, so I'm glad it ties well to your skill. It's unfortunate I can't have the same influence on others with the music as you do with the dance."

"Maybe if you try pulling the energies while you play?" Dariak suggested, but Randler gave him a glance that he should know better than to offer such an idea. Randler was not a huge proponent of magic and had faced a fair share of difficult times at the hands of mages, including his mother, who once used her spells to repeatedly punish and heal him.

"I—I can't really be the only one," Kitalla said suddenly. "With a skill like this. Just, no one's seen it, that's all. I can't be the only one." Her eyes glazed over and she sank down.

Randler shrugged. "Maybe you have ancestors from another land where they channel magic differently?" Such stories were unheard of, but it could explain her special talent if it were possible.

Dariak shook his head. "I'm pretty sure my father would have found some information on something like that, somehow. I don't recall anything about magic in other parts of the continent, aside from bigger, crazier monsters in some places. The rest is rural and simple. No magic."

"Unless they hid their skills from others," Randler argued. "Why show a stranger what you can do until after you get to know him? Maybe your father didn't spend enough time trying?"

Dariak didn't know how to react. It was an odd thought anyway, but putting down Delminor in the process was hurtful.

Kitalla didn't catch any of it. She was thoroughly drained from the experience and her thoughts tumbled around. She thought she knew where the skill came from, for she had had a revelation in Magehaven. Years before, she had fallen in love with a young nobleman, Joral, and was pregnant with his child. After a skirmish, the infant was killed while it was still within her body, and after its removal, she had discovered that she had the ability to influence others with her dancing. It had happened all by accident, but it was there, nonetheless. She knew that she was tied to the Forgotten Tribe through that child, through the baby's father, Joral, whose ancestry went all the way back to the original king and queen. The dance skill was a lost talent of the Forgotten Tribe. She knew it in her heart, but she was too exhausted to share it with the others just then. Darkness swept around her and she accepted its call.

CHAPTER 7

Ieran's Task

IERAN HAD NO idea that he had been bewitched. He awoke in the king's chamber with a raging headache and an overturned bottle of wine that Dariak had planted there for effect. He looked around the chamber, embarrassed that he was there, then gathered himself up and went about his duties. He had many things to attend to, including the continued dismantling of Dariak's forces while maintaining his air of concern for the people. The prior king had chosen him well all those years ago, and Ieran enjoyed his current role, though it was certainly taking a toll on him. He rubbed his head gently, scolding himself for his indulgence.

Not that he remembered drinking the wine in the first place. Or coming into the king's chamber at all. But he must have done so after sending troops off to the blazing bakery in the southeast. Yes, a celebratory drink for a successful subterfuge.

But some part of him said no. Some part argued that that wasn't what had happened, but he had no idea. There was the harlot who had come to him in his time of desire and he had wanted to bed her so very badly. Yet she was skittish and wanted to ensure the trouble would be over soon.

And, he realized with a streak of fear running down his spine, he had told her. He remembered it now. He had told her that the uprising would happen in two days. Indeed, that was the plan. The king had been gathering soldiers in the lower dungeons of the castle and Ieran had kept their location and plans secret and silent. But, now, he had slipped.

"Kitalla," he murmured with a snarl. He lifted the spilled wine bottle from the floor and smelled it, trying to discern if it was poisoned somehow. Perhaps some hallucinogenic herb or aphrodisiac, he wasn't sure. But the wine just smelled like wine, not that he was an expert in such things.

Yet now he had to assume that Dariak knew not only of an impending retaliation by the king, but the appointed time. There was no choice; they would have to move it up. Immediately. There was no time to waste. If Dariak had proven one thing about himself throughout his life, it was his resourcefulness. He could not allow this farce to continue any longer.

Ieran made his way quickly to his chamber to check his day-long hourglass. It was a tall cylinder with markings to denote the approximate hours. There was also a central release in the device so he could reset the clock as needed. He went there now and saw that some time remained. He had only been out for a few hours, which was much better than he had expected. Glancing out the window, he saw that evening was upon them. Perhaps a siege in darkness would be the best strategy.

With a grin, Ieran disrobed and then donned a basic guard's uniform, which he always did when he wanted to be undetected. He stepped in front of the hourglass and reached behind the device to activate a catch in the stone. With a soft grinding sound, the wall slid forward and opened into a narrow, dark passageway.

He had discovered the passage as a child when his father was a servant under the previous king. Ieran had always been craftier than his old man, and finding the hidden dungeon had been a boon that helped him earn his position. He had found the secret door in the king's chamber as well, though he hadn't had permission to be there when his made his discovery. Instead, he kept the information to himself until he needed it, and the king was ever grateful for the knowledge.

Ieran smiled as he stepped into the path, having taken it so many times that he could navigate it in the utter darkness that remained when he pulled the door closed. Thirty-eight steps spiraled downward, then a plateau for five steps and another set of twenty-three steps. Eighteen paces ahead, he put his hand up at chest height until he touched a damp wall. It took some feeling around for the specific brick he needed, but then he pushed open the wall and stepped into the lower dungeons.

The area was perpetually dark, but some illumination always filtered down to this level, either from the sun, moon, or torches in the castle above. The cavern itself was essentially sealed off from the outside, but the creators had lined key walls with a highly reflective metal that brought light in through a crafty series of channels along one edge of the border. High above, the tiny crevices that existed between the castle ground and its supporting walls went undetected.

Ieran counted a hearty three hundred paces before coming to the end of the corridor where he turned left and placed his hand on a wooden panel. Pressing the wood, he signaled his presence. It was quieter than a pre-arranged knocking pattern, for simply moving the wood was signal enough. The design of the area would have enticed a would-be thief to turn to the right instead, down another corridor that led to other rooms. Those rooms were intentionally set up to distract looters, not that any such fiends had discovered these tunnels in over fifty years.

With the wood panel displaced, Ieran waited a few moments for the sentry to notice. Once the wall swept inward, Ieran nodded and entered the chamber to bring news to the king.

The first thing Ieran noticed as he entered was that the quarters were much more cramped than on his last visit, as the number of people taking refuge here had doubled. Many of them he recognized as the king's own guard who had been working above for three weeks to coordinate this counterstrike. All of Dariak's men who had joined the guards to quell the riots in town were here, too, bound and gagged and unable to do more than whimper and moan. Among them was a balding man who kept his eyes squinted and averted so no one would see the intelligence in them.

Ieran grinned at the results of his hard work keeping Dariak busy and sending all the warriors off to stop the staged incursions. Smug, his step took on an extra bounce as he pushed his way through the crowded area and found the king at the back of the chamber.

"Your visit is unexpected, Chancellor," the king said by way of greeting. "What tidings do you bring?"

Ieran bowed his head and tried to maintain his feeling of pride despite the admission he was about to make. "It seems our foes suspected my true intentions. They drugged me late this morning and in my stupor I let slip that we had plans two days hence, though I offered no more information than that."

The king's lip curled into a snarl. "Tell me, Ieran. If you were drugged, then how can you be certain of how much you divulged?"

"I assure you, sire, it is all I offered." He certainly wasn't going to explain the nature of his drugged state to the king. Lusting after a wench and telling her any news would anger the king greatly and likely bring about his own death, despite all the value he brought to his liege. He would rather not invent some counter story either, unless pressed, hoping the king would let him remain vague.

"We will have to act sooner than planned," King Prethos concluded. "If Dariak knows when to expect us, he may have defenses in place, though I cannot imagine how he would be able to fend us all off." He smiled despite the circumstances, looking around at the soldiers in the chamber who had come to his side at his call.

A baby gurgled nearby and the king bent down and shook his son's impromptu crib. "Easy, child. Soon we will return to the light above. Soon you will have your revenge on your mother's murderer."

After the baby settled back to sleep, the king looked over his shoulder at Ieran. "We will not be able to set the stage as intended. We will have to open the third wall."

Ieran frowned. "It will expose this place after all these years, sire. Surely—"

The king's eyes flared with anger. "If not for your carelessness, it would not be necessary, Chancellor. Besides, the secret of these tunnels is lost. Look how many there are here now. It is not just the few who were trusted to know. It is all of my guard and Dariak's as well, and word will leak regardless. We might as well use the last defenses of this place to earn back my throne."

"Yes, sire. It will take an hour or two to make the arrangements."

"Press for the hour," the king said. "I grow impatient with the waiting. I would see the night sky this eve. And I would see the end of Dariak and his cronies." His voice lowered to an angry hiss, "Especially Gabrion."

Ieran bowed his head and stepped away, speaking to a few soldiers and giving instructions about how to detach the third wall from this portion of the dungeon. He pointed to a few key locations in the stone and bade them to find other patterns in the walls and to remove those bricks all around. Once those supports were removed, he would be able to unlink the outer wall and this partition would fold outward, letting the soldiers spill onto the castle grounds. There were fifty or so such supports that needed tending and Ieran entrusted the task to those closest to the king, giving them a warning before he left. "If you fail to remove even a single one of those sets of bricks, then the wall will not open and the king will not reclaim this day. He will find you to answer for your lack of diligence." The men saluted, confident in their task.

With a final look around, Ieran glanced at the fighters. All the able bodies were on their feet now, limbering up for a fight. Some were stretching and bending. Others were attacking imaginary foes with invisible weapons, pushing their limbs through the motions. Ieran rubbed his hands in anticipation, excitement welling inside himself again. He looked around at the captured fighters one last time, knowing they would be unable to help Dariak when it came to it. His eyes swept over the balding man on his way out and he laughed to himself at the helplessness he saw.

Indeed, it was going to be a good night. Ieran retraced his steps to his room, peering through a peep hole to ensure his chamber was empty before pushing the wall open. "One hour," he muttered to himself. It wouldn't be much time, but it was possible. He needed to get to the remains of the courtyard on the western side and find the locking stones so they could be released. He located two of the king's guards and waved them over.

"You," he said to one of the men, "find the Regent and then come up with some diversion. Argue about wages or complain about the missing soldiers or whatever strikes your fancy. Just keep his eyes on you."

"Yes, sir. For how long, sir?"

"As long as you can, but at least twenty minutes." The man saluted again and went off, after which Ieran turned to the other guard. "Go alert the others. It's tonight, within the hour. Tell them to be ready but not to draw attention until the time is right."

"Yes, sir!"

Still dressed as a guard himself, Ieran stepped off with an official-looking stride and made his way to the western walls as if to take over guard duty. Instead of ascending to the upper wall, however, he ducked into the shadows and made his way to the keystones he needed to release. He found it difficult not to laugh maniacally into the night.

CHAPTER 8

The Ambush

DARIAK AND HIS closest companions sat in the empty dining hall with some scraps of food, while Kitalla slept in a nearby chamber after her recent actions. The news they had gleaned off Ieran rankled in their heads, and they wondered how it would be possible to fend off the king's forces with their diminished army and without magic. No one was optimistic.

Gabrion grumbled. "We've lost so many of our friends to this plan of theirs. Perhaps it's best if we leave this place."

Verna scowled. "Kitalla warned us you'd want to turn and run at the first sign of trouble. No, I say we get crafty and set up some traps."

"In the king's own castle?" Ruhk scoffed. "Not likely to work. There are hidden passages here, but I don't know where. They could sneak in from any number of places and we would have no means of stopping them."

"What if we make a stand here?" Carrus asked. "Or some other defensible room? We'll raid the armory to stock ourselves up and then we pin them in the doorways and knock them down one at a time."

"That's the closest thing we have to a viable plan," Randler said. "Perhaps we should pursue it?"

Dariak shook his head. "It's a good plan, but if anything goes awry, then we're trapped and then we're dead. If only…" He finished with a disappointed sigh, touching one of his pockets.

Randler saw the motion. "The jades are drained. We have to do this on our own."

"We still have nine others of our army here," Verna added. "They're training outside."

"All well and good," Dariak said, "but I'm of little use in a hand-to-hand skirmish."

"I disagree," Gabrion argued. "You've done a great many things with a dagger and some rocks and so on. Dariak, don't lose hope on us now. We need you with us."

"Funny, coming from a guy who won't kill his foe when he's backed into a corner," Verna said. "Is that what's going to happen here, too? You're going to massage them into a slumber and lay them down in a bedroll until it's all over?"

Randler snorted despite his attempts not to. "Verna, clearly Gabrion is going to do his best. Besides, I thought we were all going to defend without killing. It's not our purpose here."

She shrugged her shoulders. "I'll clobber them calmly like all of you, but if it's a choice between my life and theirs, I think this world's better off with me in it than dead." She swiveled her head back to Gabrion. "What of you? Is this place better with you alive or not?"

He glowered at her but didn't know how to respond. His emotions warred within him. How could he justify killing anyone else in this castle when his last visit had prompted him to kill Mira? It was bad enough he had broken his vow already; he needed to be strong and not slip any further.

"Enough," Dariak said wearily. "Carrus, let's begin with your plan and find a defensible room."

"The king's bedchamber?" Randler asked. "Kitalla knows of the hidden exit there."

"As will the king," Ruhk refuted. "No, he may even know how to open it from the outside and then we would be ambushed. What of the forward courtyard?"

"The one lying in shambles after the jade attack?" Verna asked in bewilderment. "Not a very stable place for a fight."

"Of course it isn't and that's the point. If we spend the next couple of days fortifying it, we could hold our own there and if things go bad, we just slide down the rubble to regroup another day."

"Perhaps this room is the best place after all," Dariak said dourly. "Three entrances and we could barricade two of them and force the king's men to enter through the third."

They debated the plan for some time until a guardsman came running into the room in a panic. "Regent Dariak, there you are at last!"

Dariak closed his eyes. "Calm yourself, soldier. What news do you bring?"

"It's Chancellor Ieran," he huffed. "He—" The man coughed and sputtered, reaching for a goblet of water to steady himself. The others waited with anticipation. "The chancellor," he started again. "A villager came up to meet him to give word of a disturbance in the town—"

"How surprising," Verna muttered.

"—but when the chancellor was going to come to you with the news, the villager panicked that he wasn't going to be taken seriously. So he leaped and tackled the chancellor to the ground. They wrangled around a bit on the floor and I was able to jump in and put an end to the bout."

"Very good, soldier," Dariak commended, clearly seeing the man wasn't finished.

"But, sir, you don't understand!"

"Let me guess," Dariak interrupted. "Chancellor Ieran was hurt and needs my help."

The man stammered for a moment and then shook his head. "Well, no, sir. I offered to get him help, but he said that the need of the people was of greater concern. He sent me to fetch you so that you may dispatch assistance."

"Very well, soldier. Go on and do what you can to help."

It wasn't the response he had expected. "But—but..."

"Surely you are capable of the task?"

"Sir, I—no, sir, I cannot. You see I—well, that is, I—" He stopped and cleared his throat. "Well the truth is, sir, that with all the other men away, I've been on this shift for two days with hardly a break at all. I don't have it in me to tend to this matter on my own, sir."

Dariak scratched his chin. "Yes, that is quite the conundrum."

"S—sir?"

"You're too tired to do the job because we're short-handed, but sending others out at this time would leave us with even fewer hands, and therefore you would have to endure yet a longer duration at your post. However could I resolve such a paradox?"

The soldier wilted under the mage's glare. "I can tend the wall a while longer, sir, but I wouldn't do well at venturing into the town."

"No, soldier, you are clearly too exhausted to continue work this evening. Carrus, on your way to the privy, would you kindly escort this poor fellow to a bedchamber for some rest?" He turned to the soldier who made odd sounds of denial. "Now, now, don't argue. You clearly aren't up to your duties and so you're of no use to me. You need to rest and be fresh. Off to bed with you now. If you don't comply with these orders, I can force you."

Swallowing hard, the man allowed himself to be ushered from the room by the burliest companion among them. Carrus tended to his duty well, understanding that the man was to be locked in a cell and that his attendance to the 'privy' meant the armory.

Once they were gone, Randler shook his head. "We don't have much time, do we?" Immediately the team set about the frantic task of barricading the room. The dining tables were upended and propped against the doorways, blocking two entrances completely and the third halfway. They slid the chairs across the floor and used them to buttress the tables, but it was clear they wouldn't hold for long. Even when they dragged over the sideboards for added support, the defenses were flimsy.

Carrus returned quickly with an armload of weapons. Randler took a bow and a quiver of arrows, then hobbled across the chamber, utilizing his special crutches for the task, waving off help as the others prepared. Verna grabbed a sword, then swapped it for another that was less balanced, preferring the way the slightly off-center weapon felt as she swung it. Gabrion debated the better sword, but took up a mace instead. Carrus equipped himself with a war hammer and handed over some daggers to Dariak, while Ruhk grabbed a pair of short swords. The leftover weapons were hidden around the room in various locations in case they needed them. Hopefully in the heat of the fight, none of the king's men would notice that the carpet was lumpy in places.

By the time their meager preparations were complete, the sun had gone from the sky and only the wall sconces glimmered with hope. They looked around and realized that something terribly important was wrong. They hadn't woken Kitalla.

Verna sprinted toward the half-open entryway, ready to find the thief, but a resounding crash shook the floors and knocked down one of the barricades. Ruhk and Gabrion hastily reassembled the barrier, shoving extra chairs against it, even knowing the futility.

Shouts echoed soon after and a low thunder groaned, drawing louder and closer to their location. They wouldn't be hard to find. The seconds pounded by like an eternity as they awaited the onrush of doom. Verna and Carrus stood near the center of the room, poised to lead the defense. Ruhk and Gabrion each bolstered a barricaded door, as Randler and Dariak moved toward the back.

The cries grew louder as the forces drew near. Gabrion felt an attack against the upended table. "It begins!" he called needlessly. Only moments later, the first fighter rushed around to the central entrance, clambering over the barrier and meeting Carrus and Verna's opening strikes.

The duo swept in and disarmed the man quickly, bashing against his head and knocking him out cold. Verna then hastily shoved the body up against the table for added support, which put the unfortunate soul in jeopardy of being trampled. There was no time for a debate, for a host of other fighters leaped through the opening and pressed their attack.

Verna brought her sword around, blocking a blow, then kicked her foot into the soldier's gut, but it didn't stop him. She turned and swept her arms toward him, cracking the flat of her blade into his shoulder. He was only stunned for a moment and Verna used that instant to spin back around and wallop him in the neck, dropping him.

Carrus dealt with his foes with more brute force, allowing his muscles to mow down the enemy. Each strike of his hammer battered the soldiers, rendering them inert at least long enough for him to take down someone else.

Between Carrus and Verna, arrows flew. Their tips were deadened with small scraps of Randler's tunic, but the projectiles stung terribly as they hit. Randler nocked his arrows quickly and fired when his comrades were not in the way. He wished he had enough mobility to get himself into position instead, but he made do.

It took all of their resolve for Gabrion and Ruhk to leave the first wave to the others. Increased battering sounded against the barricades and it wouldn't be long before the tables collapsed and the king's men seeped through and surrounded them. They had to remain at their posts, but they were worried about the others.

Verna took a few cuts as three men surrounded her. She released a feral cry as she spun wildly around, swiping her blade out at random. She dipped low, then jumped high, remaining agile and erratic, but the soldiers would get further attacks past her defenses soon. Thus Dariak sprinted across the room and tackled the man nearest him, though he hadn't judged his actions well and they toppled into Verna and knocked her down. Randler fired two quick shots and stunned the other two fighters.

The table near Gabrion cracked at last and a host of ten fighters burst through, overwhelming the warrior. He grabbed a chair in one hand and swung it around to get himself some space, then he threw it at one of his assailants and turned his body around, bringing down the mace and crushing the basic iron armor of the soldier in front of him. Pivoting back the other way, he leaped toward another soldier and knocked her down by pummeling her legs. He leaned forward from that attack and when his hands hit the floor he kicked his legs up and back, sending two others sprawling. He righted himself quickly and continued his frantic defenses, trying to stop the tide before they were all overwhelmed.

Dariak and Verna disentangled and entered the fray again, this time a bit more cautiously. Verna sported a number of wounds now, as did Dariak, but they ignored the pain and pressed onward. The half-barricade had broken apart and the king's men entered unchecked. Moments later, the sound of splintering wood racked the hall again and Ruhk's barrier collapsed. They had hoped that leaving one entrance partly open would entice them to concentrate their efforts there, but clearly the king knew better than to allow the enemy to control his attack.

Ruhk cut high and low with his swords, sending sparks flying as he parried various strikes. Five men pressed him back and he couldn't hold them all off. Two split away and turned for Randler, but the bard struck them down with his arrows. His attacks were highly effective, but his quiver was already nearly empty.

Slowly, the team was pressed closer and closer to the back of the room where Randler was poised. Each faced off against half a dozen fighters and there was no way they could overcome the odds; based on the power behind the incoming strikes, there would be no option for surrender, either.

Gabrion took a nasty cut to his arm and he shouted in pain, sweeping his mace frantically and blindly about. Until the wave of pain passed, he couldn't control his actions well, so he hoped for a few lucky hits but mostly to have his foes step back a pace. Then, as his vision cleared, he saw something both marvelous and unnerving.

Over the heads of the foes, he could see Kitalla running down the hallway, daggers in hand, her deft movements shoving aside one soldier after another as she raced toward Gabrion in the dining hall. She cut the men who did not heed her warning and she clobbered the rest with the hilts of her daggers. To Gabrion, she looked like a bolt of lightning striking down an old tree, parting it in the center and leaving it dead and immobile on the ground.

Her running steps met little resistance as she sprinted ahead, but Gabrion was not safe to watch for long. He saw only glimpses of her pace, hope lighting in his heart at her arrival. He kept his own body moving, felling as many men as possible, even though his vision was blurred from the damage he had taken. He risked a glance over his shoulder to see Kitalla's progress and he nearly vomited.

Her mouth was opened in agony. Blood spurted out from various wounds and in a loud, harrowing thud, her body fell lifelessly to the ground.

Terror gripped Gabrion's heart and his body moved of its own volition. He lost himself in what he saw, and he knew he had to reach her, to drag her away from the battle and to heal whatever wounds had been inflicted. But he knew instinctively that she was already dead, that he could do nothing for her.

It was Mira all over again. He hadn't protected her. He had let her die.

Gabrion's mace bashed in the face of one soldier as his left hand caught another by the neck, snapping it and crashing the body to the ground. He roared in wretched pain as he brought his weapon about, decimating anyone within reach. The whole world was falling apart around him and he couldn't control himself any longer. It didn't matter who died anymore. Losing Mira, he had lost his will to fight. Watching Kitalla fall, he lost his will to live, but he wouldn't just hand over his life until he had taken Kitalla's body away and buried her properly. He had to reach her and prevent the soldiers from desecrating her any further than they already had.

As he pressed into the relentless crowd of fighters, he kept watching for signs of her, but she did not rise up to fight. No soldiers near her made any movements that suggested she was attacking from below. She had simply fallen and was gone.

A fleeting thought swept through his head, that she was merely lying in wait, to surprise the enemy and to attack them from behind, but he knew he was being foolish. That wasn't Kitalla's way in a fight. She was brash and forceful and she was omnipresent. Her listless body on the cold stone floor filled Gabrion with a wrenching emptiness and he clung onto it and used its power.

No less than thirty soldiers fell during his advance toward Kitalla. His mace flew about unchecked. He felt as if his enemies collapsed before he even reached them, he was swinging his arms about so rapidly. His body was lacerated in many places, but none of it mattered. He felt nothing, nothing at all as he approached Kitalla. He registered the deep wounds in her sides and the billowing pools of blood that was her life force seeping away. If he could only scoop it up and push it back into her, he could save her. Somehow, maybe. But he knew it was ridiculous.

It was just ridiculous. He touched her neck and it was cold. No pulse. Her eyes were open, staring, but they did not see. Kitalla was truly gone.

The warrior shed all trace of humanity as he tossed his mace aside and picked up a sword. With it, he stalked back to the dining room with a fierce light in his eye, determined to put an end to the fight once and for all.

The rest of the team was in dire straits. Blood splattered everywhere, but they did not give up their defenses. Randler's quiver ran dry and he started swinging his bow around like a sword until a sword became available. He could barely stand, and so he defended himself the best he could from his chair, reaching and hacking madly until one soldier stepped in and upended him. Sprawling on the floor in pain, the bard turned over and flashed the blade around in a crazy panic, knowing he was done for.

Ruhk stepped in and slashed at Randler's attackers, leaving himself open to damage. He took major wounds on his back and legs, but he never slowed down. If this was his time to die, then he would do it defending his new friends and his new way of life. He would die with a dignity that he had never felt before. Sure, he had served the king diligently, but it was always in duty. Now, having sided with Gabrion and his plans for a peaceful future, he felt an inner fire guiding him onward. Defending that hope was a worthy cause. Breath after breath, he kept his swords moving, parrying more than attacking because it was all he could manage to do.

Verna and Carrus ended up back to back, their weapons singing out in an embittered war song. The ringing clashes against their foes established a certain erratic staccato that filled them with a powerful energy that kept them pushing harder to get through this battle. Dariak was already down, though they had no idea if he was unconscious or dead. It didn't matter either way. The king apparently had supplemented his forces with fighters from the town, and the flood kept coming.

They heard an inhuman rage in the room and they turned to see Gabrion thrashing madly about, slashing with a sword and cutting down anyone in his path. So insane was the expression on his face that the king's men fled his assault and did everything they could to get out of his way, tripping errantly over the weapons tucked under the carpet.

Their wonder cost them as they took some blows and nearly lost their weapons in the process. Verna added to Gabrion's wild screams and started thrusting with abandon, no longer caring if she killed her prey or not. The foes needed to be stopped. Carrus, meanwhile, took a nasty gash to his left leg and he could barely stand any longer. After a few more swings, he went down, and though he tried to defend himself from there, he was terribly ineffective.

Verna heard a cheering cry from the hallway. A sound of victory. But she wouldn't have it. Not here, not today. No, she was going to keep them from killing Carrus and herself, whatever the cost. She crouched down and grabbed a second sword, which changed her balance greatly, but she didn't care. Raging, she spun and sliced around and around, taking care not to move too far from Carrus. The cheering in the hallway sounded again, and she fought the urge to succumb to the inevitable defeat. She had felt that feeling before and she had pushed through it. But she had never faced such a relentless horde of soldiers. When the shouts echoed a third time, her will almost escaped her completely.

And as the shouting drew near, she heard panic. At first she thought she was screaming and that Ruhk and Randler were also yelling, though Randler was out of the fight now anyway. No, and it wasn't Gabrion either, although he was tirelessly hacking away at his opposition, his face still locked in a mask of insanity. No, the panic came from elsewhere.

It took her a moment to realize that the fighting was becoming less intense. The king's men were no longer concentrating on her so much. Sure, she was still swinging her swords and ducking and rolling about, but she wasn't up against five men at once, or even three. Their attention was turned. Drawn away.

One last time the cheering sounded and then she realized that she knew that sound. It was a rallying cry. And she had taught it to the men who used it now. She risked a glance toward the door and she almost wept in shock and denial. The king's men were falling. They were all crashing to the ground, and the cause of it was the missing army members.

Verna strained to hold on to consciousness despite the emotions raging through her and despite all the injuries she had endured, including, apparently, a broken wrist. She raised her voice, echoing the rallying cry and the men and women of the army responded in kind as they rushed into the room, spreading out and relieving Ruhk of his burden and Verna of hers. Even Gabrion finally stopped sprinting around the room, his body succumbing to its injuries and dropping him to the floor.

She was the only one left of the companions still fighting. Some part of her was prided by that, that she had endured where everyone else had fallen. She looked again and saw that Ruhk was still awake, but from the looks of him, he would tumble shortly. Verna had never much believed in herself before. All of her bravado and feistiness was a defense against her failings all her life. Yet here she had endured and pulled through.

A balding man stepped up to her, his hands empty of weapons, but Verna sensed something ominous about him, as if he couldn't be trusted. His voice was reedy as he grinned at her. "Lady, set yourself down gently before you collapse and break something. This fight is over and we have taken the king."

She fought against his words. "Taken the king? You're not making sense."

"You're beleaguered and not thinking clearly, milady. Set yourself down before you—ah, too late." He sighed playfully and clapped his hands as if dusting them off. Verna had collapsed in an exhausted heap at his feet. The man looked around and waved over one of the fighters. "She looks important, don't you think? Put her with the others. Everyone else, let's clear up this little party. We do have enough rope, don't we?"

CHAPTER 9

The Regent of Hathreneir

THREE DAYS PASSED as the damage from the battle was sorted out. The companions had taken serious damage and without the benefits of healing magic, they were unable to rise quickly to tend to the situation at hand. Instead, they were all at the mercy of their benefactor.

Dariak fared the best of the team, having taken a bad bump on the head which had rendered him useless in the bout. His body was covered in bruises and a cracked rib or two from being trampled upon, but he was otherwise able to rise and assess the rest of the damage. He walked around to visit his friends, keeping an inventory for when he felt strong enough to face the captured king.

Randler's legs had taken further damage in the battle, and Dariak feared that the bard may never walk properly again because of it. He winced in pain even as he slept and though Dariak closed his eyes and begged the healing jade for any inspiration, the shard was cold and silent.

Carrus and Verna had thrown themselves fully into the fray and their bodies showed it. Their bandages were replaced frequently and it took time before they stopped losing blood. Luckily, some of Dariak's army had skills in healing and they were able to ensure the pair received proper nutrients during their extended recovery time.

And then there was Ruhk, who had intercepted the line of Randler's attackers. The Hathren commander had proven himself to Dariak in this fight. The deep gashes would leave noticeable scars, but he figured Ruhk would be honored by them.

Gabrion suffered the most, though he hadn't received the worst of the physical wounds. He had a tortured look in his eyes and a vacant expression, moaning aloud, calling the names of Mira and Kitalla.

Turning from his friends, Dariak passed his eyes over the host of other casualties, shaking his head and feeling a deep sadness in his heart. They had lost so much and all because the king could not bear to listen. He knew it had to stop and he needed to stop delaying. He just wasn't ready yet.

"That's not a good face for you, friend," greeted the balding man who had freed the imprisoned fighters and had come to their aid. "Come, there is soup and you look like you need a whole cauldron of it."

Dariak followed solemnly, watching the man as he walked. "I admit. I don't get it."

"What's that?"

"Your help." He clapped the man on the back and shook his head. "When Kitalla last came to you, you turned her away. And that was after you left my side. When did you start taking up causes, Poltor?"

The man grinned to himself. "Kitalla was always my cause, once I got to know her. I turned her away because she no longer needed me."

Dariak forced a laugh. "Nonsense. You denied her because she was going to expose you if people saw you together."

The thief grinned. "Very well."

"So why?"

His face scrunched together. "She's like a daughter to me, if you must know. And if I didn't intervene, then her death was certain before any of the fighting began."

Dariak stared at him for a moment, wondering if that was the truth of it, and Poltor understood the penetrating glare. The thief sighed and shrugged. "Fine, Dariak. You know me too well. It's true; I wanted to protect her. But the allure of breaking into the hidden dungeons and turning the king's own plans on his head was enticement enough."

Dariak nodded. "That, I believe. As for Kitalla…"

Poltor shook his head. "Don't ask."

"I want to see—"

"I told you not to ask. The answer is no."

"I don't—"

But Poltor cut him off. "You'd best spend your time thinking of what to say to the king. We can't keep him and his cronies cooped up for long, you realize. You have to find a way to make him stand down. If the people in town rally together, there's nothing more we'll be able to do."

"Thanks for reminding me of my duties," Dariak snarled. "This isn't something I can do alone, however."

"We can wake your friends. They just won't be able to do much good at your side. And I fear if you wait too long, then you're all going to perish."

Dariak noticed the word choice. "You have an escape plan for yourself, then."

Poltor gave a sinister grin. "I didn't spend weeks as a manure peddler so I'd smell better. Of course I have an alternative. I'll tell you a little secret; part of it involves getting as far away from you as I can. You draw too much attention." Then, as if to prove that he was serious, he shoved Dariak back the way they had come, though he kept moving ahead.

Dejected, Dariak headed back to his comrades, his mind a jumble of thoughts. Poltor had given him quick updates on the state of things. Most of Dariak's army had lived through the ordeal, though a dozen had not. The mage shuddered as he listed the names in his head. The king's men were all in the dungeons, guarded by trusted fighters. Poltor had also given Dariak a list of men and women who had defected to the king's side when the circumstances had turned against them, and so his army had diminished even further. He hated seeing people he knew either dead or incarcerated, but he had to be careful whom he trusted.

Absentmindedly, he found himself rubbing the jades in his pocket. Still nothing. He knew inside himself that they would not remain inert forever, but he felt like he had gone both deaf and blind now that his powers were useless. Dariak was connected to magic, but here it was inert, and for his larger scheme he required the power of the shards anyway. He needed to seek out his father's laboratory in the north and discover a means of restoring the jades. Of course, that depended on his father having discovered such a trick, and he had no knowledge if it was so.

Yet how was he supposed to leave this place with all the injured and dead? How could he depart knowing the king would find a means of taking over again? He berated himself for falling so quickly in the bout, but it reminded him that he was a shadow of himself without his magic. What would he even look like as he faced the Hathren king?

Dariak strolled back to the infirmary and drank an herbal tea that one of the healers made for headaches. He sipped it, focusing on the flavor and setting his troubles aside. For once, he wanted someone else to stand up and take care of things, and not just to change the tide of a fight. He wanted to follow someone else for a little bit. Poltor was certainly clever enough, but his motivation for helping waned and soon he would move on whether Dariak held the reins or not.

Gabrion was no longer capable of keeping the army together, though Ruhk had suggested otherwise. They hadn't spoken much overall, but Ruhk had told Dariak of his defection and how only Gabrion's inner spirit had changed him. But Dariak knew it wasn't enough.

When he considered Carrus, he thought the big man could rally others behind him, but he always looked uncertain when he was challenged to speak for himself. He was an amazing fighter and a well-selected captain, but Dariak didn't believe he could lead the army.

Despite himself, he frowned when he thought of Verna. If given the chance, she would not only have twenty-hour training sessions, she would probably whip anyone who complained of feeling tired. She was an able tyrant, he thought to himself, and she meant well, but she was no leader. Not of the whole unit.

No, it fell to him to stay in charge, and he knew it always would until he quit his quest. The jades had been assembled, but their purpose had failed. He had failed. He had allowed Frast to overpower him and channel the energies. Yet as he thought about it, he wasn't even sure if he could have done better if he had pulled the jades together himself. He thought back to aligning the jades, feeling that something was amiss. Frast must have felt it too, and if he had been able to return from his attack on the castle, he may have been able to shed some light on the missing component.

Dariak clenched his fist in frustration. Now he was wallowing in useless wishful thinking. He needed to be more practical. Every jade was in his possession and though they were currently useless, he had to unlock them.

Gabrion stirred, moaning out in pain and drawing the attention of Dariak and the healers. Salves were applied to wounds and water and food were ushered down his throat. Dariak stood at the warrior's side during the ministrations, then he took the younger man's hand in his own and squeezed it tightly.

"Be strong, Gabrion. There is much yet to do."

With a groan, the warrior murmured, "Kitalla."

"She isn't here."

"Kitalla…"

Dariak could see that Gabrion wasn't listening, once again lost in his own anguish as he had been during his Trial at Magehaven. Dariak could picture the blind ogre sitting at the campfire hearing snippets of repeated conversations. He patted Gabrion's hand and set it down, turning away to get some more rest. With an agonized tone, Gabrion whispered one more time.

"Kitalla…"

CHAPTER 10

The Funeral

GABRION'S EYES CREPT open and he looked into the misty light that filtered into the room. Thick gray clouds covered the sky in deep mourning, bringing an unnatural chill to the desert palace. As unholy as it was, it filled Gabrion with a sense of truth. Such clouds belonged here this day.

His body ached from head to toe and he lamented the loss of healing magic. His groaned at himself in scorn, for he had grown up in Kallisor where magic was despised, and the town of Savvron was no exception. Yet his time with Dariak and the others had shown him that not all magic was evil. It could be a force for good.

But it could not bring back the dead.

Pain lanced through him as he remembered all the recent events, including the images he did not want to see. Try as he might, still the sight of Kitalla bleeding out on the floor remained with him as if his eyes would always be stained with the image, blurring everything he would ever do.

Gabrion had gone through many changes on his journey, from timid teenager to powerful warrior. He had also been a killer, of both man and beast. Killing in battle had been normal, acceptable. But here in this accursed castle, he had become a murderer, and that was far worse.

Mira had hurt him profoundly, wounding his very soul. Her abduction from Savvron had been a ruse to bring her to her lover once and for all, when Gabrion never even had a clue that she fancied anyone else. His own advances on her had been reciprocated, he had thought. They had spent a lot of time together, growing closer, but apparently she had only seen him as a diversion to keep herself busy until she was of age for her man. And then, that selfsame man had sent his troops into Kallisor to claim her, and Gabrion's town had succumbed to terrible loss.

He hadn't even thought it when he learned the truth, but Mira had been a traitor, seeking the hand of the Hathren king though living in Kallisor. But Gabrion couldn't ever fathom why the king himself had yearned for some peasant girl, though perhaps the randomness of it, the challenge of it, had been lure enough.

And when the truth was revealed to him, Gabrion's body channeled the glass jade that had been in his possession and he destroyed Mira. He hadn't meant to, but still, his rage and hurt were so complete that he believed deep down that she deserved it. And he despised himself for feeling so.

Kitalla had then sought him out as he hid away in Jortun. They had their dalliances and he had let his guard down, had given her his heart, even though it was still broken. Then he let Kitalla down and not just once. No, he had repeatedly failed her since then: refusing to fight the eaglons, hiding away in the outpost, delaying his return to her side.

And now again he had failed her. Sure, he was hard-pressed in that battle, but when he saw Kitalla approaching from the hall, he hadn't moved himself toward her. No, he continued his own confrontations and awaited her arrival, relieved that she would be able to free him from his situation. He had waited there for her, battling surely, but not protecting her. He had wanted her to come and protect him.

His selfishness had cost her life.

Broken and beaten, Gabrion was a hollow shell and he didn't know why he even drew breath any longer. Pushing himself up, he relished in the pain that ignited through his body, for he deserved it. He squinted as he looked around the chamber and he could see several other wounded fighters still recovering. But everything was gray, colorless. The only vibrancy he saw was the afterimage of Kitalla's dead body echoing over everything before him.

"Gabrion, you're awake, good, good," said Gretcha, the healer who had been trying to revive him. "Don't move so much. Relax."

"When is it?" he breathed.

"When...? Oh, five days after the battle. Be still, let me get you some tea."

"Has it happened yet?" It was hard to force the words out. "The funeral?"

Gretcha nodded and answered too eagerly for Gabrion's taste. "Oh yes, yesterday indeed. It didn't make much sense to delay."

Gabrion coughed and he thought he would vomit. He had missed it. He couldn't even say good-bye to Kitalla properly now. It was done. It—

"Oh wait, no, Gabrion, I'm sorry, no, no, I'm all messed up. There *was* a funeral yesterday but it was for the Hathren soldiers who died." She patted his arm, not realizing how close she was to getting smacked by him. "Tonight is the funeral for our losses."

"All of our losses?"

She looked at him, confused. "Well, yes. Wouldn't really make sense to bury some and keep others for display."

He shoved her away and she crashed to the ground, but he didn't care. Peeling himself from the bed, Gabrion planted his feet on the floor and, with all the determination he could muster, he rose. Gretcha cautioned him about reopening his wounds, but he ignored her, focusing his thoughts on moving his legs and reminding them of their purpose. A cold chill ran through the room and he found it fitting for his thoughts. Pace by pace, he made his way to the door.

He had never been on a boat before, but he had heard tales and it felt to him now like he was on a sea in great turmoil. His body felt all wrong as he moved about, barely able to function. Each step was a challenge and he wondered when he would crash and if he could get himself up without help. His side and arm lit with searing pain and he knew he had disturbed his wounds already, but none of that mattered.

He would endure through the funeral and then he would add himself to the list of casualties, for no more good could come from his life.

He shuffled down a darkened hallway and waved off the help of a fighter who passed him by. He located a small, empty room and there he set himself down in silence and cajoled his limbs to function better. Just for one more task. He massaged his legs, moaning as he pressed against the lacerations, yet he persisted, needing the mobility back.

Gabrion stretched and rubbed his muscles, rising and pacing the room, sitting down only when he thought he would otherwise fall. Eventually, he managed to keep a relatively even step, with a few minor stumbles. Then, continuing to pace, he turned his mind to other matters.

"Kitalla," he began, speaking aloud to help himself focus. "She was a brave and noble fighter, but she would rip your throat out for saying so." He shook his head. "No, that's ridiculous."

He started again. "Kitalla was a woman against whom no one else could compare. Her finesse, her skill, her charm were beyond the... Kitalla was a woman uncontested. She could do anything she ever set her mind to, whether it was fight, or cook, or keep the team together, or steal."

He sat down and rubbed his head. "Why can't I think of what to say?"

Gabrion stood again, reaching for the words, trying to channel Randler's bardic talents. "Kitalla was a thief," he started again. "Not by choice or desire, but because circumstances led her there. Growing up I would hear stories about the terrible people who were thieves, but Kitalla wasn't one of them. Perhaps few of them are as terrible as we imagine. Sure, she fought and she plundered, but not for sport. She did it to survive. What don't any of us do just to survive? We work. We battle. We sometimes kill." His voice cracked.

"Kitalla was not a killer, though many died by her hand. No, she calculated her odds of survival with the keenest sense and then she did what was needed to survive. I didn't understand her at first. I was a naïve little boy in some ways when I met her. And she was so much older—and not just because she was dressed as a hag." He smiled despite himself, thinking of the spirited Kitalla as he had come to know dressed up in such a fashion. "She was ever wise and cunning, but she saved my life even when I had lost everything."

He considered for a moment. "Actually, she saved me more times than I ever realized. I had given up that day when my king had thrown me into the dungeon as Dariak's conspirator, which was as far from the truth as possible. Kitalla effected our escape. She led us through Kaison, even managing to get us into the shops to better equip ourselves for our journey. And then, through all the battles, against guards, lupinoes, bounty hunters... She was always there, just a step ahead of everyone, pressing on and saving us all."

He paused to catch his breath as his body reminded him of its wounds. "Her trials in Grenthar's dungeon were impossible and yet she endured them. I couldn't tell you where she found the strength to succeed, but she did, tearing down Grenthar himself in the process. I think in many ways she still bears those scars." He caught himself and choked. "Bore those scars."

Pacing again, he continued. "She found every way imaginable to get through every obstacle, and the more I learned about her, the more I realized it was all just a part of who she is. Was. She broke in to this very castle and stole the fire jade from the king's own chamber. I have never condoned thievery, but I can't help but marvel at her skill. Flashing her daggers, whipping through a battlefield, you name it. She was a force that couldn't be tamed." He bit his lip, for in the end she had indeed been tamed.

"She rescued me from myself, from my loss. And there it was that I fell in love with her, but I couldn't give her what she deserved. I deserted her when she needed me most. And in the end, it cost the ultimate price. The one price we all have to pay some day. The price that is the last one you pay as you leave this world behind. That price… that I would gladly go back and pay for her if I could."

He wiped tears from his face as he lifted his head. "Your time in this world was too short. The pains you endured were too numerous. I pray you a better existence where you are now. A happier time. Better friends than I've been. Truer joys than you ever had here. If there even is a 'someplace else.'" He lifted his arm up high. "To you, Kitalla. To you."

It took Gabrion some time to calm himself as he wept, his body shuddering in agony. No one ever knew when they were going to die until the very last moments, but he wondered if his wounds would bring him to death's door. He had been severely hurt before, but mages had always been around at some point to quell the worst of the damage and to ensure he would recover. This time, in this magic-dead zone, it was different. And he refused to mount a horse and scuttle off to some other place where magic functioned, not after his failure. Dariak would protest, he knew, but once the ceremony was over, Gabrion would secret himself away and let the world fade at last.

The sky was even darker now and he needed to move or he would miss it. With a great heave, Gabrion pushed himself toward the door, clutching his side as he went. Two fighters tried to help him, but he denied their efforts. "Just tell me where Dariak is."

He made his way to the courtyard, hoping to speak to the mage before the funeral procession began. He wanted it made clear that he had prepared a eulogy for Kitalla and that everyone needed to hear his words. She needed to be remembered in all the best ways possible without lavish embellishments. Leave that to the bards.

His body wanted nothing more than to drop to the ground and be still. Gabrion refused to accept the demands. He staggered onward, seeking the courtyard where Dariak would be, probably with Randler and the others, and a pile of carcasses would lay behind them with a separate, special pyre for Kitalla.

Noises echoed ahead of him and he wished they all were solemn and quiet, honoring the dead as they should. He could make out talking in the guardroom before the courtyard, and he figured Dariak was preparing his final words. He could make it in time, if he just kept moving.

Torches lined the halls and guided Gabrion on ahead, yet still they were lost in the gray mistiness that enveloped Gabrion's eyes. He wondered idly if he would ever see properly again or if the world would always be so drab and sullen. Even if he remained in the shadows forever, he realized, his forever would not likely last the night. He would stand vigil as Kitalla's body burned in the flames, and then he would find his release at last. All that remained was to honor all she had done.

He drew closer to the voices and as he recognized the tones of his friends, he felt weaker and weaker. How could he face them at all after what had happened? Maybe they wouldn't blame him for Kitalla's death even though it was his fault for not seeking her out. If they did not blame him, then they were fools and did not see the truth of things.

Still, the echoes of their voices in the air sent chills down his spine. It was like sneaking up on them in camp as Randler and Kitalla talked about dance moves and Dariak spoke of magical energies, while Gabrion returned from a successful hunt, bringing food for them all. He thought in some way that he would round the corner and see them all sitting around a campfire. He wanted it so badly, he thought he even heard Kitalla laughing in the distance.

Too far a distance, he remembered.

A few more steps and Gabrion reached them at last. They were mostly somber with the upcoming ceremony, and Dariak's arm was wrapped tightly around Randler, their backs to the warrior as he approached them.

"Dariak," Gabrion pushed through his lips. "I wish to say words for Kitalla this evening."

"Gabrion!" the mage turned around to greet him and in that motion, Gabrion's heart leaped into his throat, for he saw a shadow across the room and it looked just like Kitalla. He slammed his eyes shut and turned his attention to the mage.

"Gabrion, are you all right?" Randler asked. "What happened in the infirmary? Gretcha was in quite a state."

"Tonight," the warrior breathed. "You have to let me speak. Of Kitalla. Of all she has done for us. Of all she has been for us."

Dariak's brow creased. "I don't think so, Gabrion. It wouldn't be appropriate."

"How could it not be?"

Tinkling laughter sounded from the shadows across the room and Gabrion glanced over again, hating that sound at such a solemn time. He could see Verna laughing, chatting with someone who was just out of view.

"Gabrion?"

"Kitalla," he said, distraught. "I saw her. I know what happened, Dariak. You can't shield me from it."

"What are you talking about?"

Another voice rose up then, "Yeah, what's this about?"

Gabrion turned to the newcomer, his face creased in confusion. "It can't be! You—you're dead!"

Nonetheless, Kitalla stood there in front of him. "No, Gabrion."

"But I saw you…"

She nodded her head, her face unreadable. "Yes, you saw me, Gabrion. And yes you saw me die. But I did not die."

The warrior clutched his head and Dariak shifted him over to a bench by the wall. "I don't understand."

Kitalla gave a look to the others and they stepped away, but only just. She sat beside Gabrion to explain. "The wall in the courtyard collapsed. It's there the king's men came from. I awoke and followed them to you all. I was at the rear of the pack and when I saw how badly they were attacking and how hard-pressed you were, I had to do something drastic."

Gabrion stared at her. "You ran up the line and cut them down side to side. It was… marvelous, but I didn't go to help you. You—you died."

Kitalla tentatively placed her hand on Gabrion's shoulder. "No. I never struck a single one of them, Gabrion."

He squeezed his head. "I don't understand."

"Magic doesn't work here right now, but my dance skill does." She watched him carefully as she broke the information to him. "I saw you, Gabrion, and I saw how you were fighting, but it was going to cost you and everyone if you didn't fight like a true warrior."

He turned his head toward her, not sure he wanted to hear any more.

"You were holding back." Her eyes flickered back and forth between his. "So I danced."

Gabrion's breathing became labored and he felt like the floor dropped away from him. "What do you mean you danced?"

Kitalla broke eye contact with him as she dredged up the words and told him. "I bewitched you, Gabrion. I made you think I was coming to your aid. I made you see me joining the fray." Then she breathed. "And then I made you see me die."

Coldness ran through Gabrion's body.

"I thought it was the only way to get you to fight. The only way for you to hold off the soldiers until Poltor could free our fighters and bring them to help. The only way—"

"You," Gabrion hissed, cutting in, "made me imagine your death? You made me believe you were gone? Just to make me snap so I would kill?" The cold chills were gone, as was all the pain in his body. He felt nothing any more. His world had been destroyed, but now he felt as if he didn't even exist. "How could you?"

She shook her head. "It was the only thing I could think of."

Gabrion stood slowly, bracing himself against the wall. His body staggered but he refused help from the others.

Kitalla rose up as well, watching him closely.

"You twisted our relationship against me," Gabrion whispered. "You took everything away from me."

"To give you the only chance of survival, yes."

"I lost—" but he was utterly baffled. He recalled all the things tumbling through his mind, all the heartache and self-loathing, but it wasn't all real. She hadn't been able to use her skills against him for a long time, so why now? Or perhaps she had been using them all along. Perhaps he was just a dumb puppet at her beck and call, doing all the things she wanted him to do. Maybe she had entranced him to slaughter Mira so she could have him to herself. Maybe she had guided him to Savvron after their fight with Heria so she could bewitch his father to convince Gabrion that his mother was dead—perhaps then she wasn't. Maybe everything was a lie.

She stood there as his mind fell to pieces and she became a stranger to him. Over and over he kept remembering the agony in his soul at the thought of her death, that he was prepared to follow her this very evening into the abysmal unknown. Her sacrifice... hadn't been a sacrifice at all. It had been staged, all to manipulate him into killing again.

The cloudy grayness of his vision grew deeper and he couldn't see or hear anything anymore, except the one person who had ripped out his heart and then stood there staring at him, feeling justified for doing it. Something in him snapped and his fist lashed out, clocking Kitalla in the face and splattering her to the ground.

He felt his body being restrained and there was a faint echo of shouting that seemed miles and miles away. He saw Kitalla look up at him from the floor, the pain in her eyes having nothing to do with her bruised jaw.

Convincing the Hathren King

THE DAY AFTER the funeral ceremony for the members of Dariak's army, the mage decided he finally needed to deal with the Hathren king, even before trying to repair the damage between his friends. Further delay would only allow the peasants of the castle town more time to organize a revolt, and they barely had the forces they needed to maintain their current prisoners.

Dariak decided to greet the king in the remains of the throne room itself, the symbolic seat of power in the land. It was mostly in disrepair and, to Dariak, that best represented the state of things anyway. It took convincing to get all his friends to gather for the meeting. Some looked at Kitalla oddly, shocked at the actions she had taken in deceiving Gabrion during the battle. Only Verna seemed to truly understand.

Randler stood beside Dariak despite the added injuries he had sustained. He could barely walk again, but once he was upright, it was mostly a matter of discipline to remain so. Ruhk stood on Dariak's other side, a man chosen by this king as his commander, and perhaps a man whose words might be heard, even if only just. Gabrion took a place as far from Kitalla as possible, unwilling to even look in her eyes. Carrus stood with him. Verna and Kitalla flanked the other side of the room.

The team remained silent and fractured and it took all Dariak's resolve to wait without trying to mend the recent wounds to his friends. He doubted Gabrion would ever forgive Kitalla, but her actions had indeed saved them all. Nonetheless, he had other matters to focus his energies on now.

The guards at the rubble-strewn entrance of the hall parted to allow the prisoners inside. There were no doors left to open or to ceremoniously slam shut. Only the booted heels of Dariak's allies clicked into place to let the rest know that there was little chance for escape.

At the head of the procession, Poltor stepped with head held high, feeling more important than he ever had in his life. Not only had he found the king's hidden lair, infiltrated it, and released the hostages within, he also would effect the king's execution if this meeting went badly. His belt was lined with so many daggers they merely looked decorative at first glance. A dangerous pattern, but nothing more. However, each blade was sharp and ready for action.

With an odd salute and bow, Poltor greeted Dariak, then he spun on his heel and faced the king and his chancellor, drawing their attention to his belt in warning. He stepped silently aside and sank into the shadows.

The king looked battered and exhausted. He had taken some damage in the bout and though his wounds had been dressed, he had shunned most of the treatment offered to him, preferring to bear the role of beleaguered captive. Ieran, however, had taken every salve and sedative, and he stood there almost bouncing within his own skin at the situation.

"King Prethos of Hathreneir, I welcome you," Dariak started officially. "As you know, I am Dariak, son of the great mage Delminor. I have ousted you from your throne and taken rule as Regent. However, I wish neither you nor this kingdom harm."

"Spare me," the king said sourly. "Get on with your sentence."

"Then I challenge you to listen, and I don't mean for you to merely let the words hit your ears, but for them to ruminate in your brain and in your heart." He ignored the disgust on the king's visage. "It was never my intention for us to fight."

The king's voice was cold and loathing. "Bringing an army to my doorstep—twice—does not exactly convey those sentiments."

"It was necessary for us to show our strength, lest you turn us away or kill us on the spot. We wished only to be heard."

"Refugees, prisoners, talks of peace… All impossible things."

Dariak shook his head. "Improbable, from your perspective, but not impossible."

"It is the truth," Ruhk stepped forward, drawing the king's sneer. "Sire, I served under your command for years—"

"And deserted in the blink of an eye," the king finished. "You were never among my highest ranked commanders. It is of no surprise to me that you turned traitor to Hathreneir."

"No, sire," Ruhk replied in his most respectful tone. "It is you who is the traitor to the land, for you bleed her dry of every man and child who can lift a sword. You throw them into battle while you remain here sending out soldiers without ever seeing the state of things before you."

"Brazen words from a malcontent."

Dariak tried to stop Ruhk from continuing, but the man had one last thing to say. "Would you raise your own son and train him just to send him to the front lines?"

"It is the right of the king to choose his soldiers," the man said calmly, almost with amusement. "Only one of nobility would understand the situation well enough to make the proper judgments."

"Proper judgments!" Verna barked. Kitalla grabbed for her but she wrenched herself away. "You're a tyrant who tears families apart without concern or care for their hardships. You shred us all down to nothingness just to fatten your belly on your throne."

"Do I know you?" the king asked in a bored tone.

"My father enlisted in your army twice so that I would be able to raise my siblings after our mother perished."

But the man shook his head. "No, it doesn't sound at all familiar." The laughter in his eyes said otherwise. "Come now, what else, what else? You all have complaints and woes. Do share them now."

Kitalla responded by taking a slow, deliberate step forward. Her eyes bore into his and she stepped without any expression on her face, her arms only slightly moving with each tiny step. Her fingers did not twitch, her lips did not curl. She merely approached him until she could feel his breath upon her face. His eyes twitched back and forth, wondering what she was planning, but without a word or comment, she stepped away. The king visibly trembled despite all of his attempts to control himself.

Into the silence, Gabrion whispered. "Where are they?"

The question perplexed everyone in the room and they all turned to him.

He saw only the king, and the king's face now lit a deeper red as he faced his wife's murderer. "Where are they?" Gabrion repeated.

The king kept his voice level. "Of whom do you speak?"

"Mira was here and she came with her parents. They haven't surfaced in any of the searches of the castle or among any of the dead. Where are they?"

"I fail to see how it is of any business to you, murderer of their only daughter."

A dangerous tone filled the warrior's voice. "Where are they?"

The king drew a deep breath and he sighed almost comically. "Killing Mira was not enough? You wish to slaughter them as well?"

Gabrion cleared the space between them in a heartbeat, his hand grabbing the scruff of the king's tunic. "I would pay them my respects and accept their punishment."

"Suicide is too easy so you would let them kill you. Tsk. Tsk. We could put an end to your suffering now if life pains you so, young warrior."

"Not likely," Dariak intervened, "as you're here at our mercy, not the other way around. Tell him what he wants to know."

The king turned to his chancellor. "Where did I banish them to?"

"Banish!" Gabrion shouted.

The king drew strength from Gabrion's outrage. "Their children die so easily in Hathreneir. First their son and then their daughter. What need did I have of them? If they had stayed longer, their ill will may have befallen me next since they had run out of offspring. Tell them, Ieran. It is of no consequence."

"You're certain? These cretins are likely to kill them. Very well, then. They were escorted north to the Undying Stone."

"How do I get there?" Gabrion asked.

"Go north," the king answered, as if speaking to a daft child. His attitude received a shove from Gabrion, who released him and stepped back.

The meeting was not going well in Dariak's view, and Gabrion's odd question had derailed everything he had wanted to say.

Randler also noted the loss of momentum and interjected. "Our lands have been bitter enemies since the early days of Lady Hathreneir and Lord Kallisor."

"Not a history lesson," the king complained. His attempts to taunt the group seemed to be working. He realized, of course, that if things went awry, then he would be the first casualty, but if he could break them down then it would be all worth it in the end.

Randler was not distracted by the interruption. "For centuries we have spent countless lives on defending our lands from each other, but what if it was no longer necessary? For a moment, consider what life would be like if there was peace."

The king scoffed. "There would be no progress, you ignorant fool. We all push our abilities further and further to overcome the worst blows of our enemies. Take the fight away and you remove our reason to push past where we are today. Why, the defenses within this castle wouldn't even exist if we hadn't felt it was necessary generations ago to have additional security. You may have located a hidden passage or two, but you haven't hit upon the heart of things here."

"Because with the right levers pulled, this castle becomes a great, towering stone giant," Kitalla guessed. She plastered an overly broad smile to her face, looking insane in the process. "Or perhaps you're referring to the trapdoors in this room that could either drop you to the lower floor or could collapse this whole half of the room?" His lip twitched and he gave himself away. "We've already secured those defenses, as well as the ones from the floor above, where keystones can be released to drop the ceiling stones upon us." She turned to Verna. "Did I miss anything?"

She nodded readily. "The oil channels. Opening the sluices above to let the wall sconces run together carrying a river of fire to any number of locations. Oh, and the pressure plates with the arrows, not to mention the—"

"Enough!" the king growled. "You're... rather well-informed."

From the shadows, Poltor called out, "Thank you, sire."

Kitalla huffed. "It's too bad we want to try dealing with you alive, because I would have enjoyed testing out the cutting wall on the second floor. Looks painful."

"Even if we haven't discovered every little loophole here," Dariak took over, "we're prepared to stand against you if we have to. But we would rather not have to."

The king rolled his eyes. "Yes, yes, yes, do let's finish this part of our chat."

Dariak decided to cut to the ending. "Make a list of reasonable demands from the Kallisorian king. What resources do you need? What purpose do you have for wanting to invade Kallisor?"

"You mean other than to bed their women?" the king asked purely to anger Gabrion, which worked.

Dariak laughed, trying to deflate the rage on the warrior's face. "Funny. I suppose you were only able to bed Ieran until your little attack on Savvron, then? Surely he knows you *quite* well after all this time."

Ieran was more put off than the king and he shouted, "You disgusting pervert! How dare you even conceive of such a thing!" He thrashed around and the guard at his shoulder had to grab him to make him stop.

The king sighed. "Don't insult Ieran's manhood. It's childish."

"Then be serious yourself," Dariak said. "Make a list of demands from Kallisor and a list of concessions. It's my intention to break down the animosity between our people and unite these kingdoms. To do so, you will both need to do some bartering."

The king enunciated every word. "I do not see the point."

"Hathreneir is my home, as it is also Verna's and Ruhk's. But this land is dying. The desert waste keeps expanding. No one talks about it but it's obvious. If the mages weren't able to draw from the elements around us, then we would be beggars, all of us. But it can't last forever. Another two or three generations? Do you really think it's possible to defeat Kallisor in that much time? We haven't had a decisive victory—or defeat—in centuries. What's another hundred years? You haven't been to Marritosh recently and you have no idea how few people were left to join your forces before it was destroyed. Supplies are just going to dwindle further. And what then? You said it yourself, war pushes us to be more creative and devious and crafty. Every advance you make here is met by the Kallisorians. Every war ultimately ends in a stalemate.

"Isn't it time for there to be a change? Or do you think you're going to go down in history as the king who conquers Kallisor? Write your name in the annals for all the future generations to see? Great King Prethos, defeater of sin, conqueror of evil. It isn't likely to happen. Tell me, sire, how many people can name one king beyond your father? How many of their names are renowned at all? Only the originators; Hathreneir and Kallisor. Perhaps you can name them all, but in the minds of the people, that means little. You're here now because your line traces back to royalty, but you're a happenstance. You're not directly important."

Every statement struck a blow to the king and though he stood resolute, his eyes lowered with every passing phrase. Dariak pressed on.

"What if your name went down as the man who changed the world? What if you became as memorable as Hathreneir herself? Where they fell apart, you drew us all back together. You say we need war to make us excel, but I beg to differ. My father pursued magic for its own sake, but he sold his knowledge to your father to earn the freedom to continue his research. The mages in the Magitorium don't toil there for the benefit of war. They seek to enhance their skills purely for scholarly interest, to see what they can accomplish. Who's to say we can't all be that way? That we can't all achieve our best and push ourselves further just because?

"Who built the mage towers? Was it warmongers? No. The first settlements were not for war either. We've lost our way and we've been lost for a good long time. Prethos, Ender of War. Are you so lacking in creative spirit and drive that you can't find another purpose for our people? That, beyond fighting, there is nothing left? It's time for a new regime, a new system, a new peace."

Dariak shook his head slowly as he continued, "I grew up under the shadow of war but didn't experience it until my quest. I grew up loathing Kallisorians, but I've come to see that their struggles are my own. Isn't it tiresome looking ever over your shoulder waiting for the day you prematurely die because you overlooked an assassin or a stray arrow from the training ground? Are you so afraid the people will rise against you if we don't have a common enemy? Do you doubt your leadership so wholly that you can't change the ways of old into something new?"

The king's face was unreadable. "What would you have me do?"

"Ruhk?" Dariak turned to him to answer for his heart was racing and he had no idea where any of his inspiration came from, but he felt it was leaving him.

The commander snapped to attention and explained the events that transpired in the outpost under Gabrion's eye. "It wasn't easy trying to trust one another, but we did it. Most of us. It isn't an easy thing, sire, but it is possible."

"Why tell me this?" the king asked. "You will kill me after this meeting anyway."

"No," Dariak countered. "Killing you would be no better than all the deaths we've had already. It would only cause the people to rise up in further anger, then even more lives would be lost. It's important that you, as their king, condone this plan."

"If I do not?"

"You don't have a choice," Gabrion answered, again drawing confused looks from everyone. "You will comply for one year, under duress."

"You cannot torture me," the king rebuked. "You can't even kill me, by your own admission. If you try to leave me to this task with guards hovering around me, I will simply kill myself and bring about your destruction. You won't even be able to use your jades because that would require you to obliterate everyone around you and that would be worse than any war. There is no way you can force me to obey this ludicrous plan."

Gabrion turned to Randler for a moment and then focused back on the king. "Your beloved chancellor keeps a detailed record of your comings and goings, no doubt for some future biography. In his notes, he lists only a single heir."

The blood drained from the king's face, and Ieran's. "You wouldn't," he breathed.

"You haven't seen your son recently, have you?" The truth of it was clear. Poltor had separated the infant as a means of keeping the king quiet until this audience, but Gabrion apparently had other plans for the child. "And to ensure you don't give fruit to another heir, you will be castrated."

Even Kitalla gasped.

"Preposterous!" the king sputtered.

Dariak cut in. "Or perhaps we can find another alternative."

"Celibacy?" Verna chimed in. "I'm not sure I would believe it. Even if we surround him only with other men, who's to say some nature mage can't find a way of carrying his seed to some wench?"

The king sank down to his knees, shaking his head. "You are all worse than any tyrants in history."

"Not at all," Gabrion said. "You see, by forcing you to endure the new ideology for a year, you may realize its merit. And if you simply give it a wholehearted try, then your son will be returned to you unharmed. Get yourself killed by any means, and your line ends."

"And if, at the end of the year, it is determined that this… peace… isn't going to work?"

"If you've truly endured and given it a truthful attempt, then your son will still be returned to you."

"And then we both die?"

"No." Gabrion held his gaze until the king realized he meant it. "It only took a number of days for a contingent of fighters from opposing sides to see the allure of setting aside their weapons. With the king's endorsement and adherence, a year will be more than enough to prove our point."

The king raised his head. "But if you are wrong?"

Dariak answered. "If, at that time, my quest has ended in failure, then I would see no point in pursuing it further. I'd find a remote place to live out my life as far from war as possible."

The king stood up, seeing a weakness to their plan. "But what of Kallisor? If we withdraw, we will be invaded."

Dariak rose up fully. "I will stop them. This land will be safe."

"You cannot protect an entire border," the king argued. "You are not making sense."

"I have my allies. I have the jades. Kallisor will be stopped and a peace between you will be negotiated."

"Once we both settle upon an appropriate list of concessions," the king added skeptically.

Dariak nodded. "Like any good agreement."

The king held the mage's eyes for a long, silent time, debating the conditions. "Your concession; you will not castrate me."

"We will consult the healers and mages and see if there is a way to sterilize you temporarily."

"It isn't necessary," Kitalla said. "It takes a good long while to produce a child at any rate. Surely by then it won't matter. Besides, why not just make it another condition? If he mates with a woman or otherwise manages to impregnate someone, we execute his line."

The king's jaw tensed. "What security will I have that my son will be safe in the interim?"

Kitalla smiled. "If he dies, we'll line up all the women we can find and let you mass produce."

Dariak would have laughed if the situation wasn't so tenuous. "Trust will have to begin somewhere. We will trust you to run this kingdom our way for one year, granted with support from the people who got me this far. You will trust us to protect your kingdom and your son."

"Go ahead," Gabrion pressed. "Take your time deciding."

C H A P T E R 12

A New Beginning

IT TOOK SEVERAL days to set the new path for the kingdom of Hathreneir. The king was allowed to spend a short amount of time with his son each day, under careful guard, and it helped to fortify the infant as a bargaining chip. Ieran was irate at the turn of events but even he conceded to the king's decision.

Getting word out to the people was a challenge, but Prethos made a solid show of his support for this new ideology. He spoke of it as if it was his own idea, as if he had sent Dariak out on his quest over a year ago for the sole purpose of discovering the feasibility of peace. The people were confused but because the king persisted in his responses, they eventually acquiesced, though enacting the plan would take time.

Prethos was even astute enough to inform the populace that Kitalla's housing plan had been all part of his strategy, but that he had needed to test the loyalties of a select group of individuals in the kingdom. He expressed his deepest apologies for forcing the rest of his subjects to endure the difficulties and the confusion.

When he was asked about the fighting, including the magical bird that had decimated a good third of the castle, he hesitated for only a moment, but then explained that it was the work of the traitors he had tried to ferret out with his plan. They had infiltrated the higher ranks and had brought about their own destruction. It was a lesson for himself, he had said, that he needed to be even more vigilant in his rule, for no one ever should have been able to insinuate themselves into his ranks in such a manner. He craftily preyed upon the sympathy of his people, and they blamed the infidels and not the king himself.

As the days wore on, his tale never wavered. He instructed the soldiers of the new way of things and he demanded they cast aside their hatred and prejudice or leave his side. No one resigned, mostly because it was perhaps the only job that ensured the safety and wealth of their families. Grudgingly, they accepted his orders.

Messengers were sent out to ride across Hathreneir to bring the decree to all the subjects. Prethos kept Dariak and Kitalla nearby to ensure that his missives were accurate and that there were no alterations or substitutions as the messenger tubes were sealed and the riders were sent on their way. It was all more than Dariak could have ever hoped for. And of course, that made him uneasy.

"And now, Dariak," said the king one afternoon, "it is time for you to fulfill your part of the bargain. I have spread the word of this new peace and collaboration. You must now tend to the safety of Hathreneir. If you do not, then I will need to act; and I assure you, my actions will not coincide with your desires. I would understand if you require a day or two for preparations, but I would be wary if you claimed to need more than that."

Dariak called his captains and friends together and they discussed the events that needed completion.

Gabrion was adamant. "I'm taking the baby north to Mira's parents. I'll bring a few soldiers from our army and his. You all take care of the rest."

"You're awfully bossy these days," Kitalla said.

He glared at her but did not respond.

Dariak frowned. "I was hoping you would come with us to the east to help us stop the skirmishes, but I can see you're set. Fine, the task is yours."

Gabrion stood and nodded his head to the gathering. "I'll make the necessary preparations and be on my way."

"Just like that?" Kitalla hissed. "You coward." He turned away but Kitalla pounced and grabbed him. "I get it; you're angry and hurt. I did a terrible, heartless thing. Fantastic. Now you know who I truly am. That doesn't give you the right to walk out on the rest of the group because you want to go sulk and play nursemaid."

Gabrion's body twitched as he fought to control himself. "You tore away my last bit of hope, and then walked up to me and said it was all a hoax. Maybe you think I'm running away again, but I'm not. This time I'm not doing anything for anyone else. I'm not going into mourning because I killed Mira or lost you. I'm bringing that child away from this place. Away from the fighting." Then his eyes went cold. "You know full well what happens to an infant in battle." He pointedly looked at her abdomen and she took an involuntary step back. "If you think I'm running away this time, you're mistaken."

"How will we rendezvous with you later?" Randler asked, hoping to keep the two of them from coming to blows.

"If I'm meant to find you, then I will." With that, Gabrion gave Kitalla one last, pained look, and then he left.

It took the thief a while to focus on the rest of the conversation or to take her seat again. She stared after him, warring with herself, but ultimately letting him go.

Lica tapped on the table and offered up the next task. "Dariak, if we're going to stop the fighting out east, we will need help. Rothra went back to Magehaven and once the king's missive arrives, he may find that he has the support to help us. Let me go take care of convincing him."

"A good idea," he agreed. Then he turned to Ruhk, "I need you here."

He nodded. "Understood, and expected. In fact, I would have been insulted if you hadn't said that."

"Insulted?"

"I would have thought you doubted my conviction."

Randler chimed in again. "No one doubts you, Ruhk."

Verna snickered. "I don't know, Dariak, what if the king offers to clear his name and restore his position in the Hathren army? He might be the poisoned thorn in the garden."

Ruhk angered with the affront, but Poltor diffused the moment. "Missie, why do you think Dariak's taking *you* away from here?"

Her jaw dropped and she turned to Dariak. "What!"

The older man laughed and slapped the table. "So impetuous, so young. Have you ever thought of being mentored by someone like me?"

Verna returned his gaze and answered, "I suppose it depends on what you'd intend to mentor me in."

He grinned. "I do have many talents…"

"All right, all right," Dariak interrupted. "Actually, Verna, I was going to give you the choice of supporting Ruhk here or heading east with Carrus."

She sank back in her seat and considered her options. "My father is out there fighting somewhere. As much as I want to find him, he would be furious seeing me there. After all, he went to war in my stead. If I showed up, he'd feel it was all for naught. But also, Hathreneir is my home and I would like to have a hand in its new beginning. I would like to remain here."

"With me?" Poltor said toothily.

"As if you're staying," Dariak said. "I would ask you your plans for now, but I'm sure you've got something surreptitious up your sleeve."

"A banana?" Verna muttered, causing a few chuckles around the room.

Poltor tipped his head. "You rightly assume I will not linger for long, nor will I tell you my intentions. And I appreciate your candor about not asking."

"But you're going to stay to hear all of our plans first?" Lica asked.

Poltor smiled. "Naturally."

Kitalla finally pulled herself together and joined the rest. "Where do you want me?"

"I thought perhaps you should go with Carrus," Dariak said.

"I see. Then you're not heading the same way yourself."

"I have to visit my father's laboratory. His research may be able to shed some light on the jades and other aspects of magic that I haven't considered yet."

Kitalla turned to Randler. "And you?"

The bard tilted his head toward the mage. "With Dariak, of course."

"You can barely move," Dariak protested. "You would be better off here until you're better recovered."

Kitalla rolled her eyes and her voice was biting. "Not this again. You're really going to leave him behind *again*? Have you learned nothing from watching me and Gabrion? Or do you *want* to end your relationship with him?"

Dariak was taken aback. "What! No! I just—"

"Spare us the 'I want what's best for him' nonsense," Kitalla said. "Keep him or ditch him. Decide it here and now." Then she turned to the bard. "I'm sorry, Randler. I'm not being very delicate."

He shrugged. "I'm a little curious myself about his answer."

Dariak gasped. "What!"

"What will it be?"

Dariak shook his head. "We'll get horses for the trip. It's going to be—" but he stopped himself from warning about the rough ride. "We'll leave at dawn."

Kitalla clapped her hands together once sharply. "It sounds like everything's all set then. Let's break the news to Prethos and then go have a farewell feast."

The king showed a clear sense of relief that they would be heading out so soon and he accepted Ruhk and Verna as chancellors in his court. Ieran balked at the appointments and it wasn't until Prethos threatened to remove him that he calmed down.

Once the meal was over, the members of Dariak's army and the king's were split into various groups to either journey north with Gabrion, south with Lica, east with Carrus and Kitalla, or to remain behind and continue the efforts to rebuild the castle and to enforce the new philosophy among the people. Kitalla took a majority of Hathren soldiers, hoping to deplete the castle somewhat and reduce the chance of another takeover attempt, and along the way she could teach them the importance of following her orders. Additionally, having them could assist in influencing the rest of the skirmishers.

Gabrion had avoided the meal, instead spending his time completing a special rucksack so that he could securely carry the king's baby on his back. He then allowed the king one last opportunity to visit with Perrios before setting off into the night with a host of ten fighters.

"You'll keep him safe," Prethos demanded.

"You have my word."

"That means little to me, you realize."

"I know. Nonetheless, it's true. This place is in turmoil and a child should not be part of it. Besides," he added with a darkness to his tone, "if you set up some sort of mutiny, then Perrios would be in grave danger, even if you tried to account for his safety."

The king's voice was stern. "I committed to this effort to end your own influence here and to restore my family. If that means I must go without my child for a year, then I will make do. War is the only thing we know, and by the look of your physique, and the death in your eyes, you know it all too well yourself. Whatever happened in that outpost was a fluke and it was among a small number of lonely men and women, all of whom were far from their homes. Your optimism about this peace is going to cause disaster, and it is fitting that you should be the one to set it all in motion."

"You're wrong, but only time will show you that." Gabrion took Perrios from the king and tucked him into the rucksack and then, with the king's help, strapped it onto his back. "Have you any message for Mira's parents when I reach them?"

"Yes," he said, his face curling angrily. "'Don't kill my son.'"

CHAPTER 13

Urrith and Ordren

URRITH SAT IN an alcove inside a dark cave, trying to keep his breathing calm, but he was being hunted and it wasn't easy to be still. A month had passed since Gabrion had sent him from the Kallisorian outpost to escort Ordren and a contingent of the king's supporters back to the monarch. It should have been a two-day journey to bring the men far enough into Kallisor to release them and then a two-day journey back to the border outpost to rejoin the rest of Gabrion's new regime.

Things hadn't gone according to plan, unfortunately. Gabrion had sent Urrith with enough fighters that they evenly matched the Kallisorian supporters, but in the end it wasn't enough. The pack allowed themselves to be led deeper into Kallisor, heading for the castle in Kaison, but after a single day of travel, Ordren showed that he wasn't as helpless as he had made himself seem.

Indeed, the older commander had allowed Gabrion to usher him out of the outpost because he knew he didn't have the support there to reclaim it. The group moved to the east and, though they barely spoke, the soldiers with Ordren knew him well. Some had even come along with him from Pindington and had stayed at the outpost when Gabrion and the others had first ventured into Hathreneir. He didn't need to issue any verbal orders. All he had done was raise an eyebrow, tilt his head, then nod.

It had happened so fast, Urrith still couldn't believe it. The soldiers all turned on their guards, himself included. Urrith was one of only four who had survived the surprise attack and it was a terror the seventeen-year-old wasn't ready to deal with.

Urrith was nimble and flexible, able to bend and dodge more fluidly than some of the best dancers in the land. He had grown up in northern Kallisor, trained since birth to serve his king as a warrior, and he had shown great aptitude. A host of beasts had attacked the town and, even at ten years old, he did more to protect his home than most others. At fourteen, his father had sent him to the king to be further trained, and the king had seen fit to usher the boy off to the outpost to be sent to the front lines. As one of the youngest fighters there, he had always been left off doing chores or sparring with the few people who deigned to entertain him, often to their chagrin.

But young Urrith hadn't seen an actual battle where blood was drawn and people were slain. True, he had seen Gabrion kill a host of Hathrens to make his point to Ruhk, but it was different than the slaughter that Ordren's men had committed. They had turned and slain people they had trained with for some time. People they had dined with and slept beside. There was something dark and unsettling about it, and every time Urrith dwelled on it, he shuddered.

He looked around the dank cave, hoping he wasn't making any noise. It was still light out and Ordren's men hadn't yet given up on finding him.

Urrith had been lurking in the shadows from one place to the next, keeping out of reach of Ordren and his gang. He had scurried off from the first strike, sprinting to a copse of trees and scrambling up the boughs. Ordren and his men hunted down the other three fighters first and slew them before fully pursuing Urrith. By the time Ordren tracked him down, he had moved on to a thicker forest area, heading deeper into Kallisor, even though he wanted instead to return to the outpost and warn Gabrion of what had happened.

Over the weeks, Urrith had stumbled through a river and come across a sleeping pack of lupinoes, who awoke to his presence and gave a chase of their own. He still had his short sword, but he was no match for the beasts, so he had run as fast as he could manage, dodging trees and debris as he found his way into a forest. The lupinoes had kept pace with him and had even managed to rake his body with a few angry claws.

Luckily for Urrith, a group of travelers was passing by and they fended off the lupinoes and tended the best they could to Urrith's wounds. He wanted to stay with them, but it would have meant endangering them, for Ordren was still in pursuit. So he had slipped away in the night when he felt he had the strength to carry on. Eventually, he found this cave and had taken refuge within for a few days since.

Urrith listened carefully, tilting his head to hear better. His thick black-brown hair swept in front of his eyes and he brushed it absently away. There were no footsteps out there now, but he dared not assume he was in the clear. Not yet. Not when the soldiers had been there hours earlier.

His stomach grumbled and not just from hunger. He frowned, knowing that his choice of meal was limited. Scrounging around, Urrith upended a small rock, then another, until he found a few worms, which his picked up, brushed off, and then consumed. They barely kept him fed, but it was all he had until he could effect a proper escape. Not that he knew where he should go next.

Rocks clattered outside the entrance and the blood drained from his face. Urrith glanced around and squinted against the light that barely drifted inside. The shadows cast over various rock formations had daunted him ever since he had come inside here, but he needed to ensure they weren't actually moving. He crouched low, keeping his eyes ahead toward the opening, then he stepped to the nearest bit of stone, keeping his hand on his scabbard so it wouldn't hit anything.

Footsteps sounded at the entrance and Urrith froze. He couldn't make out the muttered words, yet the message was clear. They were about to enter the eerie cave and pursue him. He had hoped that after two days with no sign of him that he would have been left alone. But apparently Ordren had made it clear that he was not to be left alive. After all, the commander had made a point of slaying the others when they had been caught.

Urrith's deep-set eyes trained on the entrance of the cave, and with every passing second he hoped the newcomers would turn and walk away. He knew he was being a foolish boy wishing for such a ridiculous thing, but it didn't stop him from thinking it. Today, it seemed, his luck would run out.

Two soldiers unsheathed their swords and lit a torch as they pressed into the cavern. The flickering light cast even spookier shadows on all the walls, and Urrith shivered despite himself. He could just make out their faces, and they were indeed Ordren's men. Two of them. Just two.

He could fend off two men. He had held his own against Gabrion at the outpost and that had been a challenge against a powerful and greatly skilled opponent. Gabrion had then folded him under his wing and entrusted him with so much… And he had failed in the one task that had mattered most, but Urrith tried to shrug that off.

His mind was wandering too much, he knew. But he couldn't focus. He was too frightened and he hated admitting that to himself. Urrith's options were few and fear prevented him from considering them fully.

He crouched lower still; hopefully they wouldn't see him and they'd leave. Their footsteps moved closer and they spoke to each other in low tones he couldn't hear. Moments ticked by like hours, and Urrith's trepidation only grew. His palms were sweaty and he doubted he could even lift his sword, never mind defend himself with it.

He scolded himself for his terror, taking a silent, deep breath, and pulling his sword ever so slowly out of its sheath. Turning it over in his hand, it caught a glimmer of torchlight and cast a reflection upon the ceiling overhead, giving away his position.

The two soldiers rushed in and brought their swords to bear. One soldier swept the torch at Urrith's face to blind him as the other, taller man leaped in with his sword. Urrith shrieked, falling back and kicking his foot up, catching the torchbearer in the groin. The youth then twisted to the side and reached out with his short sword, deflecting a blow in a shower of sparks. He pounced to his feet before the man could strike again.

The torch lay on the ground, deserted, as the other soldier rose, brandishing his weapon fully now, his face an angry snarl. Urrith jabbed left, causing the tall man to pounce back, then he swept right and nicked the arm of the other assailant. The tall soldier reacted quickly, cutting downward as he stepped in with a lunge, striking Urrith in the shoulder.

Urrith took the hit and allowed his body to drop to minimize the damage of the actual strike. Sparks of searing pain erupted in his body but he knew it would only get worse if he didn't do something about it. He could barely see through his tears but he was used to fighting with his vision impaired. He had adapted to having his hair long sweeping in front of his face because he thought it made him look more interesting and older. Now it allowed him to focus through his blurry sight and still judge the actions of his enemies.

Unfortunately, the sounds of the fighting rang through the cavern like a summons and the other soldiers milling about outside heard the noise and made their way within. He risked a quick glance to the distance and saw the misshapen blobs of three other men approaching, and he doubted they would be the last. Ordren had left eight men behind to search for him.

With a screech, Urrith leaped up and turned away, wiping his eyes quickly and then sprinting to the back of the cave. He hadn't been able to explore it properly without a light and he didn't have a chance to swipe the fallen torch. Instead, he ran blindly into the unexplored section, keeping his sword out ahead of him, tapping it along the wall to guide him.

He was in a panic, with no hope of escaping this nightmare. Not only would his mission be a failure, he would die at it. It certainly wasn't how he thought his life would end. As a young child, his father had told him that dying in battle was a great honor if it was in defense of the kingdom, while dying any other way was a pointless waste of his training. And here, Urrith ran away from his destiny because he had no idea how to defeat eight foes at once—even if his shoulder wasn't badly wounded.

Urrith ran and ran, and he realized he was whimpering aloud in fear, like a scared little baby, he chided, but he couldn't stop; his life was about to end terribly. If only he could have died at Gabrion's side, then it might seem worthwhile, for Urrith believed in Gabrion's vision of the future. He agreed that the war needed to end, even despite his lifelong training and love of swordplay. There would always be beasts to fight, and so even if peace came to their lands, his skills would still be useful. Yet, not if he died here.

He stopped himself from his panicked sprint and turned around in the darkness to catch his breath. Footsteps echoed down the corridor and soon torchlight flickered once again. Urrith reached around to get a sense of how large this pathway was and there was little room to maneuver. He felt the walls closing in on him, pressing against him until it was too hard to breathe. He hated himself for the terror that gripped him. Why couldn't he be braver and stronger, like Gabrion?

The walls continued to close in around him and even the light approaching from afar seemed to lessen, as if it were being pinched out of sight. He blinked his eyes in the utter darkness and realized that something was happening.

It wasn't as if the soldiers were moving away. No, they were just… He wasn't sure what. He reached out to the wall to steady himself, but the rock seemed pliant somehow. It was springy to the touch, then damp, and the next thing he knew, it was a wall of dirt, somehow suspended vertically. Before he could stop himself, he fell through and crashed to the rocky floor.

He heard a guttural voice sputter unknown words and he had the sense that the dirt wall behind him had become solid rock once again. The voice cautioned him to remain silent for a few moments and Urrith didn't argue, willingly lying there trying to make sense of what was going on.

A distant echo sounded on the other side of the restored wall and Urrith realized that the soldiers had run past his location. He looked up to see his benefactor, but it was too dark. A gnarled hand reached down and took Urrith's uninjured arm, guiding him to his feet and then tugging for him to follow. He was so relieved not to be dead, he openly obeyed.

He couldn't see anything, yet his guide apparently could. There were no obstacles but they made several sharp turns this way and that until eventually a dim glow shone in the distance. Urrith slowed down nervously and his guide had to stop and tug on his arm again to get him to proceed. They pressed on until they broke into the evening twilight.

It took a few minutes for Urrith's eyes to adjust to the illumination. As he gazed around, he realized they weren't outside at all. They were in a large stone chamber somewhere and it was lit by a series of blue-burning sconces along the walls.

He gasped. "Magic?"

His guide looked down at him and pulled a cowl from his white-haired head. "Welcome to the Mage Underground, young one."

CHAPTER 14

To Delminor's House They Go

KING PRETHOS ACQUIRED the two best horses in the area for Dariak and Randler, and he had Chancellor Ieran prepare a veritable feast for them to take on the road. He even sampled the wares at random to ensure them that none of it was poisoned. He wanted there to be no delays in their departure, and though it filled Dariak with concern, he had to set it aside. With saddlebags loaded, they set out to the northeast toward Delminor's laboratory, the cold morning their only other companion.

Travel wasn't easy for Randler, but he made no complaints. The special braces that Astrith had made for him held well as he tried to straddle the horse and keep himself aloft. Luckily, the king had also chosen well and the horse was a strong, but tame, beast and Randler had little he needed to do.

Dariak also noted the ease with which his horse rode the sand, simply trotting along as if it knew the destination and had full confidence that they would face no difficulties along the way. The mage only wished that were true, but once they left the immediate area of the castle, it was likely that the desert beasts would swarm around them. If he had his magic, he wouldn't mind as much. As it was, any creature they met would need to be regarded with care. He only hoped they would leave the magic-null area before any encounters.

Randler tried a few times to focus on crafting new songs as they went, hoping the task would occupy him enough so he wouldn't notice the repetitive jostling of the horse underneath him. Each step the beast took was steady and strong, though it still required effort and a press of his legs to keep from sliding off. In the end, it was too much effort to allow him to focus on the things he wanted.

It was unfortunate because so much had happened and he had been so enwrapped in the events, he hadn't had an opportunity to write any new ballads to record those events. Frast alone deserved a dramatic fugue to commemorate his commitment to Randler and his great sacrifice. The combination of the jades into a flying maelstrom of magic was also worth a song and Randler struggled to find the right words and notes to immortalize what happened.

His mother would laugh at him for it. She had never supported his bardic talents, wishing instead that he had followed her example in becoming a secret mage in Vestular. He had no doubts about her ambition. With his help, they could have potentially overrun the whole northern quadrant of Kallisor and challenged the king himself all in an effort to lift the ban on magic in the land. The irony, of course, was that such a show of magical strength would have fortified the ban rather than lift it. Still, Randler suspected his mother would have relished the challenge, for it would have put her life on the line, with his support, and she would have had to summon her inner strength to win. If she won, Sharice would have reveled in the victory. If she lost, then it wouldn't much matter to her corpse anyway.

But he hated magic, when it came down to it. It had only brought pain to his life, in so many ways. Never mind the times its energies had healed his wounds; he would never have needed such help if magic hadn't jeopardized him in the first place. His recent injuries were Dariak's fault, for he had toppled the tree that crushed Randler's legs, leaving him in this tenuous state. Yet even grander than that, Randler's whole original quest had been to find and bury the jades so their powers would fade into antiquity. Instead, he had fallen in love with Dariak and turned his mind around to support the mage's journey, though every bit of progress always set them back somehow.

Even now, they had claimed all the jades, but the shards were completely inert, leaving behind a shroud over the castle and surrounding area that subdued all magic in the process. There was no telling how long the effects would last, nor how far they extended. The people of Hathreneir relied on magic for many things, and they were headed for difficult times without it. Nature, water, air, earth, and healing mages all worked symbiotically to produce crops from the desert sand. Now their skills were useless and Randler didn't envy King Prethos' task of keeping the peace once the people realized the severity of the problem.

Randler shook his head. Part of him was dumbfounded that he felt any sort of pity for the Hathren king, yet at the same time he knew that running a kingdom wasn't an easy or straightforward task. Trying to keep the peace among his closest friends was challenging enough. Dealing with the rampant demands of an entire country had to be daunting.

He suspected that was why royal lineage carried down the way it did, with princes and princesses taking over for their fallen liege. Each generation was raised with the knowledge that they too would run the kingdom and their childhoods were deluged in matters of state and diplomacy. A common man couldn't easily take over the throne with a show of force, for his rule could never last. Difficult decisions were sometimes necessary, and only a respected ruler could withstand the backlash. After all, King Prethos had pillaged his own towns of their young men and women to add to his army and none of those villages had banded together in rebellion.

Perhaps there was some unknown secret among the kings that allowed them to drain the resources of their people in such a way and still retain control. Why didn't the people rebel? Why hadn't they ever?

Randler's horse tromped along and the bouncing reminded him that he was alone with Dariak and the mage hadn't tried to talk to him at all. He wondered if he should break the silence, but he always filled the emptiness. If Dariak wanted to talk, he could start the conversation once in a while. He knew he was just frustrated and in pain, so he let the thought pass.

Instead, he considered his current quest. He was part of a small team rebelling against the kings of two lands and hoping to bring about a new and lasting peace that would forever change the future of those kingdoms. He wracked his memories for other tales of heroes undertaking a similar quest, and couldn't think of any. Each time he thought he had a name of some other Dariak, it slipped away as if he wasn't allowed to remember it.

He knew he felt delirious because his mind carried his thoughts to an odd place. He wondered idly if there were some mental magic that prevented him—and everyone else in both lands—from thinking of heroes who had risen against the injustice of the kings, trying to end the wars. Only Kitalla had ever shown control over the mind in any sort of magical sense, yet perhaps she wasn't the only one with such a power. Maybe, even, no one knew they had the ability and just exuded the subterfuge naturally. Or, better yet, maybe the kings themselves were trained as children to channel the unknown and secret power, and their rule was bent on enslaving all their subjects to serve them in every way imaginable, and only the threat of war kept anyone from discovering the secret and dispelling the power.

Hadn't Gabrion's own Mira forgotten the tragedy of Savvron that occurred when she had been abducted? The warrior had told Kitalla of the bizarre shifting of events in Mira's recollection. Perhaps her marriage to the king had infused her with the mind magic and had warped her memories…

"Randler!"

He heard it, for sure, but Dariak's voice was so far away. He didn't even want to talk to the mage right now. He was onto something big, something unimagined before, something that could help them to change the tide forever.

"Randler!"

He shied away from the resonant tunes of his lover's calls, finding them irrelevant to his thoughts. Too much else to—

"Randler!"

His reverie broke and Randler felt a searing heat burn through his eyes, and it took a few moments to realize that it was only the sun. He wasn't moving, though, and Dariak raced toward him in a panic. Apparently, Randler had fallen from his horse and laid supine upon the sand.

"Randler, what happened? What is it? Are you hurt?"

"It's no wonder you didn't want me on this trip. It was stupid of me to come," he said sourly, though he wasn't sure where his annoyance was really directed, only that it involved Dariak somehow.

Dariak looked hurt at the comment. "Randler…"

"Just get me up."

It took some time to make that happen. Randler's body was weak from the ride and Dariak decided they needed to set up a makeshift camp so they could rest. He went about digging a wide circular trench in the sand to deter sand rodia from bothering them. Tethering the horses wasn't possible, so he linked their reins together and kept them nearby.

"I'm dead weight to you," Randler said once Dariak settled down.

"You're not. Randler, what are you even saying?"

He didn't know what compelled him. Perhaps it was Kitalla's own question before they had left the castle. "Why do you love me, Dariak?"

The mage blinked hard. "I don't understand…"

"What is it about me that you love?"

Dariak stared at him and realized that Randler needed an answer. "Randler… You're amazing," he fished for some place to start. "You're smart, you're kind. You're talented. You—What's this all about?"

"Those aren't reasons to love someone."

Dariak's voice grew annoyed. "What? What do you want me to say? You're gorgeous? You have lovely eyes?"

"You can do better than that." He stared for a moment then squinted slightly. "Can't you?"

Dariak was quiet for a time, too focused on Randler's reasons for this odd line of questioning than finding an acceptable answer. The silence hit the bard too sharply and he lowered his head in sadness.

"I see."

"You're not making any sense, Randler. What's this all about?"

"Ask me."

"What?"

"Ask me what I asked you."

"What you—Why do you love me?"

Randler lifted his head and his russet eyes were wide with shimmering tears that did not fall; they glistened and gave a powerful edge to his words. "I love your determination, Dariak. You never accept defeat, regardless of the challenges placed before you. From fallen comrades to insurmountable battles, you press yourself onward, hard, and you find a means of grasping just one more ounce of inspiration to succeed. You're driven in a way that I've never seen in a man. Gabrion's quest for Mira was but a shadow of your journey, for you forged the path each and every day, and your goal isn't clear-cut or finitely defined. You press on because you believe in something so strongly that your very soul demands it, and you let nothing stop you. I love you because you show me a way to live that's worth living."

Dariak gulped at the recitation, understanding now why Randler considered his answers so weak and pathetic. "Randler…"

"Dariak, time and again, I've been shown the truth of you and I've denied it every time. I don't know that I can anymore. Deny it, that is."

"What are you saying?"

"You're always going to pursue some lofty quest, and I'm just a sidekick along for the ride. I'm here to chronicle your efforts, nothing more." He raised his hand to silence the protest. "Sure we've had our dalliances and they've been adventurous in their own right, but when it comes down to it, your quest will always be more important than me."

"Where is this coming from, Randler?"

"I've spent too much time watching you. You look out for me, it's true, but in the end, I'm more of a liability to your quest."

"You're no burden!"

He waved his arms in a giant circle. "Look at us now. We've stopped because I'm weak and fell from my horse. You'd be riding on if not for this."

His voice took on edge of anger. "Now you're going to wallow for coming with me?"

"No, no, it isn't that. Every step of the way, I've been a distraction from your quest. Even now, as we were riding here, my mind was wandering off on some random tangent and it cost us time on this trek. But that isn't my point either. Your focus is the quest. I'm a bonus."

"Stop this."

"I can be your lover, Dariak. But I'm not your love."

"What are you—?"

Randler shook his head. "I know you don't follow my line of thoughts at times. Like in the woods when I remembered those times as a child and they resonated with me against your feelings for Gabrion. Now, it's something else."

"What else?" the mage asked, his voice emotionless.

"The kings, the wars, the one unknown magic in the land and your compulsion to crash against it all. You've taken on a centuries-old task that no one else has even dreamed of doing. There are no tales of other warriors rising up against the kings like this. It's always about the kings fighting each other and the heroes that win this battle or that. But you, you've broken out of it, like you've awoken from a dream they all cast upon the people. And because you're the only one who's awake, your destiny is far different than any of us who are still sleeping."

"You're... losing me."

"I'm saying that your quest is bigger than your love for me. Your quest has always taken a greater priority in all ways and in all things. I could recount so many events this past year that prove that. And I'm not saying you're wrong to pursue your quest so strongly. I'm pointing out that I understand it now; your first priority is ever to your quest. I'm just an amusement along the way."

"Randler, this is ridiculous."

"No, Dariak. It's the truth and if you sit back and think about it, you'll realize it's true." He stopped and waited.

Dariak looked at him, shaking his head slowly, but he couldn't think of any words to use in argument. As the silence hung in the air, he wondered if the bard was right or if he was just too shocked to think clearly.

"I'll still be by your side," Randler offered after he couldn't wait any longer, his heart aching. He had hoped Dariak would yell and scream and tell him he was wrong. The silence hurt. "We'll still have our laughs. For now, at least. I still believe in your quest and I do love you in an unfathomable way. I just know that I will always take second place... at best."

"I'll prove you wrong, Randler. You'll see."

The bard shook his head. "Don't. It'll only cause you to fail the one thing that matters to you most." Then, only to placate Dariak, he said, "Once the war is done and we have some time, we'll revisit this, and then we'll have time to be together properly."

"I'd rather give up this quest and be with you now."

But they both knew it wasn't true and Randler protected Dariak's pride with his answer. "If you did, my love for you would die. Remember what I told you; it's your dedication that draws me in. So, giving up on your quest would also be giving up on me. You need to stay focused on the quest, Dariak. Anything less, and all of this is for naught."

Dariak took a few steadying breaths, focusing his eyes on Randler. "My quest was never in question until now."

Dariak didn't receive the response he thought he would get. Instead, Randler nodded. "I know. That's my point. Your quest was always the certainty. Always the priority. Always the source of your drive. Always the one thing you had to plan for, to strive for. It's not your fault. It's who you are. It's what brought you to Kallisor in the first place. It's what enticed me to follow you."

"You followed me for the jades," Dariak argued weakly, knowing it was useless. As badly as it hurt, he realized deep down that Randler was right. He cleared his throat a few times, trying to get it to work again. "What now?"

"Same as before," the bard said calmly. "We get to your father's laboratory and research everything he knew about the jades so we can bring about the culmination of your quest."

"And then?"

"I'm sure there will be something new to tend to."

They sat in silence for a while, and when Randler was ready to ride, they pressed onward.

CHAPTER 15

The Mage Underground

URRITH WAS LED through a winding maze of stone corridors buried underneath the soil. His guide escorted him without answering his questions, merely prompting him to keep moving. The youth owed his life to the man and so he obeyed for now, but the lack of answers grated on his nerves.

Flashes of light flared all around the place. Some passages lit red and gold while others glimmered in blue; all the while, robed figures ran this way and that. Urrith could hear the archaic language of the mages echoing in parts of the spidery halls and it made him feel entirely uncomfortable. The villagers of Kallisor and Hathreneir had their own accents and dialects, yet they all spoke the same language. Here, it was as if everyone used the mage tongue to communicate and he felt terribly out of place as if no one would understand him and he would have no idea how to communicate with the rest. It was an odd sensation for the teen, being surrounded by dozens of people while feeling utterly alone. Though as he considered it, he supposed it wasn't too different than his first arrival at the Kallisorian outpost.

A gnarled hand clutched Urrith's shoulder and prompted him to turn left. He did so and smacked into a wall. He pulled back but the mage pressed his body forward, shoving Urrith into the stone. He tried to resist but the rock wall slowly drew him in, like sinking into a mud pit, and expelled him into a chamber on the other side. Urrith took stock of the setting.

Three mages—he assumed they were, anyway—sat upon some large misshapen boulders that seemed like misplaced stony thrones that had melted somehow. A tall bookcase stood in each corner and a thick wooden table rested in the center of the chamber. Three tapestries hung from the walls, each depicting the elements flourishing in one way or another. As he gazed at the orange-tinged weaving on the left, he thought it resembled a fiery sunset with wind blowing sand upon a small settlement, though the more he stared, the more he realized that he was only adding his own interpretation to the image, for it was just a random wash of hues.

"State your name, child."

"I'm no child!" he barked, turning his gaze to an old woman whose body was so entrenched in her boulder that she seemed to be part of it.

"Everyone is a child to me, deary."

"Urrith," he answered after a moment. "Of Wraethen."

"Curious and puzzling," the old woman commented. "If memory serves, Wraethen is north of Pindington, far to the east. You, however, arrived from the border with Hathreneir. Have you an explanation for such a discrepancy?"

He brushed his locks out of his eyes and tilted his head to regard her, but aside from being the oldest person he had even met, he couldn't judge anything else. "I was born in Wraethen. When I had trained enough I went to the king to be a soldier, but was sent to the outpost instead."

One of the male mages snarled. "So you're a sympathizer for the king. Janning, why did you bring him?"

The old man who had escorted Urrith there stepped from behind him to answer. "He was pursued by the hunters and on the verge of being slain. It seemed to me his life would be better dedicated to our cause than to the ground."

"The hunters?" Urrith asked.

"Indeed," the old woman said.

"But it was just Ordren and his cronies. They were at the outpost with Gabrion for a while, and Ordren himself had been there for months before then in support of Gabrion's quest."

"Sadly, no," the matron said. "We are aware of Gabrion's journey, as well as the fact that the warrior actually tags along on Dariak's quest, not the other way around."

Gabrion had essentially told Urrith as much, though he had never met any of the warrior's other companions, unless seeing Kitalla unconscious in the healing chamber counted. "I thought Ordren just changed his mind against Gabrion when he took in the Hathrens. Are you saying that's not the case?"

"The king is aware of more than you know and he would not have allowed his key outpost to be manned by a third party. Ordren was always in the king's employ, though we were uncertain about the details until his settlement into the outpost. You see, young Urrith, a bit over a year ago Gabrion and Dariak escaped execution with the help of their friend Kitalla, and the king does not forgive such a thing. Ordren and a host of others were sent across Kallisor in an effort to capture them.

"At first, the team escaped one scuffle after another, and when they reached Pindington, Ordren used a new tactic. He managed to have his soldiers sequester the three fugitives without getting his hands dirty. But if they could escape under the king's nose, then they certainly would attempt to flee a less-guarded dungeon." She paused for a moment to consider. "Not that the Prisoner's Tower wasn't well-guarded, mind you.

"Ordren bided his time and when the tragic events befell the city, he played the role of malcontent and helped the rest escape the city rather than take them back into custody. He gathered his most devious of soldiers and then they set out with a host of mages who wanted to join Dariak's quest. It was the perfect cover to learn what the mage and his team were up to. And when they crossed into Hathreneir, Ordren orchestrated his departure from Dariak's side, taking up the task of messenger to the king about the goings on."

Urrith scratched his head. "It's such a long duration for such subterfuge."

"Some people are truly dedicated to their work."

"But why didn't he just capture or kill them when he had the chance?"

The old woman shrugged. "I would surmise the king gave new instructions at some point. Perhaps Dariak's quest for the jades became known to the king and he wanted to wait until the pieces were assembled. I suppose that's what I would do if I wore the king's boots."

"So then, who are you and how do you fit into the picture?"

The old woman flashed a tender smile. "My name is Frethia, and we are all members of the Mage Underground, a not-so-secret society of magic users. As for how our interest connects to these events, I believe it should be obvious, even to one as young as you."

He frowned at the dig against his age and considered. "Dariak's quest for the jades. You want them for yourself."

She nodded. "Yes, though perhaps not quite the way you might think."

"Then you don't want to cause a huge upheaval to all the people of Kallisor by thrusting magic in their faces at every turn?" His lip twitched, trying to keep himself from smirking.

She caught his suppressed laughter, and released the energy she instinctively pulled into herself. "Take care with your wit, child, for not all will understand such humor."

"Yes, Frethia."

"Though I will admit that some among our order would love the chance to do just that. Yet that is why we are here; to maintain order among the chaos. The Seven are not all old like the four of us. We take it as our duty to protect the Underground and to ensure none of our members push their luck too far."

Urrith assumed 'the Seven' were some sort of council so he didn't bother asking. "You said your society isn't very secret."

"Indeed. The Kallisorian king is aware of our numbers."

Urrith was genuinely surprised. "He can't be!"

"Well of course he knows, little one. Where else do his healers and mages train? How else does he develop new spells for use against the Hathrens, especially now that the tower in Pindington has fallen? How else does he clothe his soldiers in antimagic garments? He gets all of that knowledge from us."

Urrith staggered over to a boulder and sank onto it. The solid-looking surface conformed to his body until it was perfectly comfortable. His mind raced, however. "But our king despises magic and he sends fighters out to squash mages everywhere. When I was just five, a set of them came to my town to take Seccina away because she was suspected of magic. It was terrible. They killed her father because he didn't hand her over at their demand."

Frethia sighed sadly. "I didn't say the king was merciful or kind or tactful or a dozen other things. I merely said he makes use of our skills. Why, it's possible he rounded up your friend in an effort to recruit her so she would fight in his court when she matured." She saw the confusion on the boy's face and she pitied him. "You grew up in a warrior's town in a land where magic is shunned. Yet healers abound in many settlements, employing the same energies as mages. The king has no quarrel with them, perhaps because he receives a percentage of their earnings.

"But if you think about it, lad, we're always at the mercy of the mages of Hathreneir. What good are swords when the enemy can wave a hand and mutter the words for a fireball? Of course the king has defenses against them. And he maintains the secrecy of it because it is expected."

Urrith's eyes opened wide. "Then Gabrion's plan can work after all. The people on both sides really can come together. We all doubted it before because how would anyone here accept the Hathren mages? But you're all here, aren't you? And you have the support of the king."

"Not precisely," Janning interjected. "He tolerates us as long as we are secluded down here. That's different than acceptance."

Urrith nodded. "I see. So if you're not looking for total domination with the jades, then what are you looking to do with them?"

Frethia's smile was sinister. "Young Urrith, everything we have told you so far is somewhat common knowledge. Our plans for the jades are not, so forgive me for denying your question. We still have the matter of your loyalty to determine."

"I'm loyal to Gabrion," he answered readily. "It's why Ordren wants me dead and why he killed the others."

"Perhaps. It certainly is plausible. Though Ordren fooled a great number of people before and if you hail from Wraethen, then it's possible your family had dealings with Ordren in Pindington and you could very well be a spy working against us."

"I'm not!"

"We will see, young Urrith. For now, join Janning and he will get you to food and a place to sleep. I suggest you indulge yourself while you can, for your time here comes with a cost."

"It seems everything has a cost," he moaned.

"Life is tricky that way."

Janning placed his hand on Urrith's shoulder and pushed him back through the stone wall. The young warrior shook off the odd feeling of being crushed, deciding that he didn't much like magic so far. As Janning took him down another winding path, Urrith considered the times in his life he had encountered magic, and as he did, he realized that he had never really seen it at all. Or, at least he had never seen a blatant use of magic. No spells had been conjured before his eyes or anything. He didn't like the idea that words could hold the power to shape the world around him. The concept made his training feel useless.

The kitchens were quite an experience for Urrith. Mages used their skills to prepare and serve the meals. In many ways, it was a place for them to show their prowess and finesse with certain magics. For instance, it took a team of six mages to brew a pot of tea, and watching them left Urrith's jaw dropped open.

The first mage took a round metal tray and set it on a wood table. He spread his fingers out wide with his middle fingertips touching, but his palms facing his chest. "*Wrash'bnar korrithaur wraffentoen presh!*" As he intoned the words, he slowly lifted his hands upward while curling them together until his thumbs touched. As Urrith watched, the metal tray warped and stretched upward into a crude teapot without a lid.

The next mage waved her hands in a dramatic rhythm, casting, "*Forrithur happsenar drefficant pe'arro.*" Above the makeshift pot a mist coalesced and released a flood of tiny droplets.

Two air mages joined their skills to levitate the filled pot in order to move it over to a metal grating. "*Wesshian corribus etthena kaie.*" Then fire was set below with rapid finger flicks and an incantation of, "*Hekkontar querralan frai,*" from the eldest of the mages working on the tea.

At last, a wispy-haired woman crushed a set of herbs over the pot and let the bits sift into the boiling water. "*Retricorius frethinius kaie broshe.*" Within seconds, the room filled with the lush fragrance of the steaming tea.

Urrith blinked at the ordeal a few times before shaking his head. "That was… really a waste of time and energy, wasn't it?"

Janning smirked. "I suppose it depends on how you view it, little one." Urrith cringed with the new moniker. "It's like when you spar or lift weights to become stronger. To an outsider, it looks ridiculous to perform such tasks for they don't really accomplish much. But they make you stronger, and so you repeat them over and over again. It's much the same here. We don't always use our spells to move through walls and such."

"I'm both curious and baffled by what must be needed to make a stew."

This time Janning laughed. "Beast mages to tame the creatures used for their meat. Sometimes healers withdraw the body's natural healing ability to kill the animal. Sometimes an air or water mage will suffocate or drown the poor thing. Nature mages, like here with the tea, release the most beneficial nutrients and flavors from the vegetables and herbs. And so on."

"And this helps you become better mages."

"Indeed. Now, I assume you're hungry? Shall I have a meal prepared for you?"

Urrith nodded slowly. "As long as I don't have to watch them make it. I think I've had enough magic for one day."

"Oh? You don't support the arts?"

He knew he had said something dangerous and he hoped it wouldn't be held against him. "I never really saw much of magic, so this is all just a bit new for me."

"I see." Janning didn't seem too pleased with Urrith's answer. "Very well, then let us go sit over here so you can idly wait." They shifted over to another section of the kitchen and the mage had the youth sit with his back to the others so all he saw were random flashes of light on the wall. "Once you've eaten, I will take you to sleeping quarters. I'll also ask Vinke to sit outside your chamber, should you need anything."

He was seventeen, but even Urrith understand what that meant. "I won't wander around; I promise. You don't need to post a guard."

Janning smiled sadly. "Yes we do, for we don't yet know where your loyalties lie, in terms of our pursuits. Frethia told you a good deal for a stranger, and you need to think about the repercussions of what she said. If you feel you can support us, then you're welcome to remain under our protection while we discern how you may be the most useful. If, however, you have no wish to help or if, in fact, you intend to bring us harm, then have Vinke escort you from this place to a haven above ground. Then, you will never see us again. Under pain of death."

Urrith stared at the older man. "You would let me leave, knowing I might try to return and take you down?"

Janning grinned. "Good luck finding your way back in. Vinke is a master in earth magic. He won't bring you to some stairwell, you see. No, he would raise a platform and mash you into the earth and deposit you safely up above."

At first it sounded terrible, then Urrith realized he had already experienced the sensation. "Like when you pushed me through the wall."

"Precisely. But on a grander scale, is all." Two plates were put in front of them by one of the kitchen mages and Janning lifted a fork to start eating, but before he took a single bite, he added, "Please keep this in mind, young Urrith. If you choose to stay, it must be because you're willing to support us. If we later learn that you're here under false pretenses, there will be severe penalties. And I do assure you, there are worse things than death."

Urrith gulped, then found a way to mechanically eat his meal.

C H A P T E R 1 6

Carrus' Support

KITALLA AND CARRUS left the Hathren castle with a contingent of sixty fighters, only ten of whom had traveled with them before. The rest were soldiers of Hathreneir who believed in their king more than anything else. They accompanied Kitalla because Prethos required it of them.

She waited until they were safely away from the castle before turning to them and giving warnings and orders. "There are five of you to every one of us, but I requested this on purpose, because none of you stands a chance at defeating me. I thought if you had a lot of allies here, you would cooperate more. So I'll give you a few minutes to sort yourselves out. Five of you to one of my men, not including me or Carrus. Go on, now, don't dawdle."

"Our liege bade us follow and obey you, but this task is ridiculous," one of them complained.

"I'm sorry, I don't know all of your names yet. Are you one of the king's generals? A chancellor? A page? A champion of food? Scrubber of halls? Anything? Ah, I see. You're a grunt. Do what grunts do, and obey."

The man stammered, then shook his head, turning to his companions and splitting up as ordered. Carrus, however, looked at Kitalla with concern. He hadn't known her particularly well, but her behavior seemed unusual.

"Now that that's all settled. I'm going to take a page out of Ervinor's book and, let me tell you, that really means something, because there aren't too many books I've even read, much less model my tactics after." She waggled her fingers in the air and continued. "Now that you're in ten groups, pair up into five groups." She waited while they did so. "Good, now… You," she said, gesturing to one set of fighters, "you're the Nightingales. You stay to the north of us. You," she said, pointing to the next set, "are the Eagles and will stay to the east. Wrens are to the west. Sparrows keep south. The rest of you are Ravens and will secure the center. Datch, Merrlis, Yllina, Paerra, and Ferithor… you're the captains of each group, respectively. You all report to Carrus."

At this point, everyone was confused, for the five captains she had named were loyal to the king and not to her. The ten fighters from Ervinor's army were taken aback and they required every bit of discipline not to say something. Likewise, Carrus adopted an expression as if he had known of this decision beforehand, but it took all of his restraint not to look at her like she was crazy.

"Is there a problem?" Kitalla asked. "I'm quite willing to accept complaints at this time."

"I didn't ask to lead some stupid group," Merrlis whined, his face curled into a snarl. "I'll follow and fight because the king asked me to. That's all. Find another lackey."

Carrus rose to his suddenly appointed role with haste. "You will address *me*, captain. You will not speak to Chancellor Kitalla directly if it involves matters of combat or your task. You will not question the orders of your superiors, *soldier*. Do you have a problem?"

Merrlis looked at the enraged man and shrugged. "Why would you put someone like me in charge? It's stupid."

Kitalla waved her hand toward Carrus, thanking him for whatever he was about to say but dismissing it too. "If you're unhappy with my decision, then let's work this difference out. First, I will not debate the finer points of my decision with you. Second, you will merely obey because it's expected of you. Third, if you can't abide the first two rules, then you may battle with me right now and try to kill me. That's the only way you will be released from your duty, Merrlis. You will have to render me inert."

She really didn't think he was dumb enough to try, but he pulled his swords out and he lunged for her, blades spiraling in the air. With a sigh, Kitalla side-stepped the attack and kicked high, turning her body downward so she could catch him in the back. Merrlis went down in the one hit.

"Would anyone else like to challenge my decision?" She waited while Merrlis regained his footing. "So? Shall we continue our debate or would you like to assume command of the Eagles now?"

"What do you expect from us?" asked Ferithor, a lanky fighter who preferred an ax. "We've never led a battalion before. Tasking us with this is asking us to die."

"Maybe that's the goal," Datch said.

Kitalla waited and the five captains proved to her then that she had a challenging road ahead, for they bickered back and forth for a while before they even let her speak again. "If you don't think you're capable of following my orders, then by all means, return to the castle and tell King Prethos that you couldn't abide his command. I'm sure any consequences for that will be far less than my own. So take this chance now while I offer it, for if you make any effort to desert me on this task, I will not only have your head, but also any other part of your body that you hold most dear. And when I say 'have' it, I'm not sure if I'll want it as a trophy or as lunch."

Everyone cringed at the thought, but she was going for absurd. They all waited in silence, each staring at Kitalla in confusion. She seemed so different to any of the fighters who had ever known her, but they had to admit that none of them knew her quite that well to begin with. Perhaps she actually did nosh on the intestines of men who failed her. They shuddered at the thought.

"Great, then," she said with a clap of her hands, breaking the silence. "Spread out some and take your positions. We march toward the east and toward the fighting.

Just remember, all of you; you're under my command now, so you may not join any battle unless I permit it. Especially if it involves other people. Is that understood? I'm glad. Move out."

The five sets of fighters broke apart and then ventured east, with Kitalla bobbing along as if she were strolling through a park toward a picnic. Carrus stared at her, wondering if he should ask about her antics or play along with them. In the end, he kept true to form and remained silent.

After some time, the desert creatures became aware of them and attacked. Kitalla hopped in excitement and withdrew a short sword she had taken along with her. She preferred fighting with daggers, but when facing sandorpions and eaglons, it was better if the weapon had some reach to it.

"Eagles and Ravens, attack! The rest of you, hold back and keep wary of others." Then, with a strange grin on her face, Kitalla charged ahead, metal flashing in the sunlight like a beacon. Four sandorpions scuttled toward her, tails raised and ready to strike. She didn't care. Kitalla bounded into the air and stepped lightly on one creature, twisting her torso aside as the tail whipped at her. She leaped backwards, flipping onto the next sandorpion and arousing its attack. As the tail lashed toward her, she reached out her left arm and snagged the appendage, then jumped and spun around as if the tail were a pole, landing on the sand behind the beast. The confused creatures swept their tails out again, inadvertently striking each other instead of their intended prey.

It only angered the beasts, but Kitalla was off to her true quarry, the eaglons. The feathered fliers swept rapidly toward her, and Kitalla inadvertently shuddered in recollection of the last time she had been in such a situation. Then, she had depended on Gabrion to assist her, but he was gone now—in more ways than one— and she would not be bested by them again.

Her sword swept upward, whistling in the air. The eaglons swerved aside, cawing aloud and focusing on her. Poisoned talons flexed as their wings pounded angrily. Kitalla felt no threat today, however; if only the eaglons had understood the implications of that, they would have fled for some other battle.

With a twisting leap, Kitalla brought her sword about and down, then up again. The tip of the blade caught the chest of one eaglon, rending it from the sky. Enraged, three more banded together to bring her down, but she merely used their new positioning to her advantage. Kitalla ducked low, cowering under their assault, but once they were close enough, she sprang into the air, throwing sand in their eyes with one hand and swiping across with her sword in the other. Blinded, the eaglons did not see the onset of her fatal blow.

Only three other eaglons remained and she was eager to destroy them before the others could reach her. With a cursory look over her shoulder, it seemed the rest of the fighters were having difficulty with the sandorpions. She could see Merrlis hacking away with a panicked look on his face and there were more cries of panic from the soldiers than from the beasts. Once she was finished, she would turn and offer them a hand. But, first things first.

She knew she couldn't repeat her recent tactics with this final set of beasts, for they wouldn't likely fall for it if they had witnessed the defeat of their comrades. Eaglons weren't nearly as smart as lupinoes, but they were nonetheless intelligent.

They had to be in order to hunt for food or to mate without poisoning themselves with their toxic talons. It was accepted among the bestiaries that eaglons were susceptible to their own venom and that they couldn't prevent the poison from escaping their claws. As she considered this, it gave her an idea.

Turning on the spot, Kitalla pounced for the eaglons she had already felled. With a few well-placed swipes, she cut the talons off the birds and then used a corner of her tunic to lift the severed digits for her next feat. Kitalla had always excelled at throwing daggers and had used her skills to earn meals and lodging when times were bad; although, she had never tossed knives dipped in poison before. Taking one talon from her protected hand, Kitalla held it carefully between her fingers and then snapped it toward the nearest of the three remaining eaglons. As expected, the bird maneuvered aside, but that was its undoing, for Kitalla had sent a second talon after the first. The sharp nail bit into the eaglon's face and the venom did its work moments later.

She was lucky enough to take down a second eaglon with the remaining talons, but the last bird eluded her attacks. Undaunted by the deaths of its flock, the final eaglon shrieked and tucked its wings in tightly, turning its body into a rapidly plunging spear. Kitalla had no time to devise an elaborate defense. She merely dropped and rolled aside. The eaglon barely missed her, then it fanned out its wings and came about swiftly, prepared to fold in again and seek her heart.

Though the creature spun with great haste, it was no match for Kitalla. As soon as the eaglon had swept overhead, she had launched her sword into the air and it sailed effortlessly toward its goal, slashing one wing off the unsuspecting bird and bringing it crashing to the desert.

An awkward pain rose from within her as she looked around. It was an awful feeling and she checked her skin for wounds, but she found none. The wrenching agony made no sense, but it knocked her to her knees and caused her to double up in pain, anxiously trying to escape its clutches. There was no specific source of the anguish. It was simply there, paralyzing her.

Then out of nowhere, Gabrion stepped toward her and he knelt beside her and stroked the hair out of her eyes. "Are you all right?" he asked.

She looked up toward him, and then she grabbed him, pulling him in and wrapping herself around his massive torso, pressing her lips to his and drawing away his breath. He held her firmly and returned her kisses, his strong hand stroking her hair and trying to calm her down. She wilted in his arms and cried against his powerful chest. He quietly held her there, keeping her cheek against his heartbeat to instill her with peace.

"What happened to us, Gabrion?"

"Shh," his chest rumbled in response. "It's all okay now."

"Where did it all go wrong?"

He held her as she wept amidst the fallen eaglons, his warmth seeping into her soul. "Be still," he whispered.

She pulled away and tried to look at him through teary eyes. "But Gab—"

Yet as she looked at him, she realized that it wasn't Gabrion at all. It was Carrus. Her thoughts tumbled madly for a moment but as she saw the look in his eyes, she understood the truth. He didn't see her as weak, nor was he taking advantage of her pain; he was merely being for her what she needed. He didn't take his eyes away from her as she stared at him and he didn't pull his lips away when she pressed hers against his a second time. They remained there, locked together until she was able to rise up on her own.

"Carrus."

"No need," he said. "The battle is over. We should move on."

"I don't know what came over me."

He looked at her and shook his head. "Yes, you do, Kitalla. Don't lie to yourself."

She made a face. "I saved his life. And he hates me for it."

"He may come around," Carrus said, though he didn't sound convincing. "But we don't have time for it now."

She firmed her jaw. "You're right, of course. Usually it's Gabrion going off on some rant like this. I'm supposed to be the one who's all business."

"You're hurt. Dealing with that will take some time."

"As you said, we don't have time for it now." She punched her fist into her hand. "I'm just so… frustrated and angry. And hurt," she confessed with a whisper.

He looked at her for a moment and then he placed his hand on her shoulder. "Then use me."

"What?"

"Use me as if I were Gabrion. Just so you can get through this."

Kitalla's eyes opened wide. "You don't realize what you're offering."

"I'm beyond scorn and jealousy. Even if I weren't, we need you to be sharp and to be yourself. If that means a bit of… unconventional medicine, then so be it."

"Well, just be certain. I can be exuberant."

"Don't worry. I don't bruise easily."

Before she could respond, Merrlis approached, his eyes lowered somewhat. "Forgive my intrusion, but will we be off soon?"

"Yes," Kitalla answered curtly, annoyed at the interruption. She noticed his averted gaze. "What is it?"

"Perhaps another soldier would be a better leader for the Eagles? I barely did anything at all."

She examined him intensely and then shook her head. "No, I chose you and you will rise up to the challenge."

Carrus looked ready to argue but then he clamped his mouth shut and waited.

"But there are others who would rather have my position," Merrlis said. "All I'm going to do is get someone killed."

"With an attitude like that, you're certain to make it happen," she said. "Or are you looking for a second round with me?"

Merrlis gestured at the dead eaglons strewn upon the sand. "You did all that single-handedly. I wouldn't stand a chance at defeating you."

"Precisely, and now that you know how good I am, then you have cause to trust that I know what I'm doing by putting the lot of you in charge. We will not have this conversation again, Merrlis. Lead the Eagles well or go back home. Decide now."

He pouted. "Both options will lead to my death."

"Not if you lead well. Back in line, soldier. We move out momentarily."

When the troops were on the move again, Carrus went around to each pack and offered some constructive advice to each captain. Along the way, he also assuaged the discontent of his original fighters, ensuring them that Kitalla had it all worked out, though he kept to himself that he doubted the truth of that. When his rounds were complete he found Kitalla and walked with her.

"Are you trying to get them all to rebel?"

She rolled her eyes. "Even you don't get it."

"Then enlighten me."

"Gladly… after we take care of those sand rodia." She whistled aloud and called for the Sparrows to lead the assault against the new menace.

Carrus watched Kitalla as she pulled out two daggers and joined the Sparrows. To no one in particular, he muttered, "I think she summoned them just so she wouldn't have to answer my question."

CHAPTER 17

Entrance to the Laboratory

IT TOOK DARIAK and Randler nearly two weeks to reach the village where Dariak grew up. A few families milled around, tending to the land and keeping the place in working order while the mage was away. Their horses were taken to the barn for washing and feeding, while Dariak cautiously escorted the bard to the main house. On foot, Randler struggled even with the magic crutches. He accepted Dariak's support without word.

"Master Dariak, you have returned at long last!" an older woman greeted. "Come inside, dear. There is some soup brewing if you are hungry. It will be ready in no time."

"Thank you, Keela. We could use a meal. We'll await in the sitting room." He took Randler away from the entrance to a large wooden room with a massive sofa and three well-padded chairs. The walls were lined with bookcases and windows. A hand-woven carpet covered the floor, its colors somewhat faded, but the pattern was just as intriguing as he remembered. He used to spend time as a child tracing the patterns, wondering if they were representations of great magic spells that would unlock the keys to the world.

Randler hunkered down into a chair with side arms to better prop himself up. Keela brought in some tea and set it on a table next to the injured bard, after which she poured the first cups and then bowed herself out of the room.

"I had no idea you grew up with servants," Randler noted.

"Don't start."

"It's an observation, not a criticism." He gestured to the books on the wall. "That's a lot of reading material. Will we find what we're looking for here?"

Dariak shook his head. "These are the common histories and fantasy tales that anyone can own. My father prided himself in having full collections of things."

"Like the jades."

Dariak nodded solemnly.

"Then the rest of the books?"

"So now it's all business, then?" the mage asked in annoyance.

Randler furrowed his eyebrow and sipped his tea. "I guess you don't want to talk."

"What's the use? Every time we talk, one of us gets hurt."

"Look, just because I pointed out the importance of your quest—"

"Not now, Randler. Please, I beg you."

They stared at each other in silence for a time, then Randler couldn't take it anymore. "Does your mother still live here?"

Dariak swirled his teacup a few times before taking a lengthy draft and nodding. "Yes."

"Should we go see her, then?"

"There will be time for that."

Dariak had never spoken ill of her, so Randler was confused by the response. "Surely you two get along better than I do with my mother."

Keela entered then with the promised soup and a tray of small sandwiches. She turned her eyes from Dariak to Randler, sensing the tension in the room, and instead of lingering to serve them, she set the tray down and left.

"Let's eat," Dariak suggested, taking one of the bowls of soup and two sandwiches. He noshed quietly, hoping Randler wouldn't keep asking questions. The bard took the hint and kept silent, though he struggled to reach the food from his seat and he moaned slightly with each motion. He ignored Dariak's offered assistance and managed on his own.

Once they were sated, Dariak stood up and stretched. "Come."

"Yes, sir," Randler muttered under his breath, pushing his body to stand. He squeezed his crutches, afraid he would topple over any moment. If only he hadn't fallen off the horse, he would be able to move about much more freely. Dariak seemed impatient with all the delays and it only made Randler feel worse.

They stepped from the room and walked down the main hall. Wonderful smells wafted from the kitchen and Randler's spirits rose despite the rest of his mood. They pushed on down the hall and Dariak escorted Randler into a dark room at the end.

It took a moment for Randler's eyes to adjust to the darkness and, as he gazed around, he noted that the walls were all draped in thick tapestries. Even the windows were covered, effectively blocking out the sunlight. A large rug spanned the floor, and Randler glanced at the ceiling, surprised that it was bare. He thought for sure there would be another tapestry on it.

The furniture was sparse. One dresser stood against the far wall. A small table rested nearby, and next to that was a child-sized bed. In it was a woman with deep gray hair, mangled as if it hadn't been washed in years.

"Hello, Mother," Dariak whispered, approaching her. He knelt beside the bed and took her hand in his. Her skin was leathery and cold. "How do you fare today?"

Essalia was not nearly as old as she appeared to be, yet her body was terribly frail. Her breath came in rattling gasps and her eyes held such dimness that she barely seemed alive. "The weather makes she."

Randler's brows creased in confusion but he didn't say anything.

Essalia blinked slowly and then moaned softly. "When the three forests sank up to the sand, it said nothing of the red joy in your pride. Even under the wisest bush, they sing anger into the ancient wind."

Dariak listened intently as if anything she uttered made sense, though Randler was baffled. Clearly, the woman had lost her mind, and Dariak was just there to be by her side. Essalia continued to ramble and Randler watched as her son held her hand in silence, speaking only to prompt her to continue. Feeling like he was intruding upon them, Randler held his breath and then quietly tore himself away.

Step by step, Randler made his way to the kitchen, seeking out Keela for some form of company. The woman tended to a roast chicken and several side dishes and she offered Randler a taste of each one.

"This is absolutely delicious."

"You're too kind, sir," she demurred.

"It's Randler, if you please. These truly are marvelous. Your talents would thrive in a bustling city."

"Oh, such a place isn't for someone like me, sir—Randler," she corrected. "I like the quieter life, myself. I'm quite content here, actually, and I'm not wanting for anything."

"I understand. I'm not trying to suggest anything to the contrary."

She smiled softly and added some spices to the soup. "Is there anything else you would like, sir? Something I could help you with?"

He considered asking about Dariak's mother but then he decided against it. "I'm just giving Dariak some time, is all. Perhaps I could lend you a hand while I wait?"

Keela delighted in the company as Randler chopped vegetables with great finesse, banging down the knife in time with various songs he sang as he worked. He even helped to wash the used cookware, though she protested at first, saying he need not lower himself to such tasks.

"You can make it up to me with a particularly delicious dessert." He winked, feeling more cheerful than he had in weeks—maybe even months, he conceded.

Eventually, all the cooking was finished and they chatted about nonsensical gossip. Randler didn't learn anything of value, though he didn't mind. It was comforting to talk without anything of importance weighing down the conversation.

Dariak appeared at the doorway after a while. "Randler, let's go."

With a bow, Randler kissed Keela's hand. "Thank you, my lady, for the company." She practically wilted with the attention, after which she fanned herself with her apron.

They left the house and walked over to a small shack that Randler hadn't noticed, tucked beside the barn. The wood was very old and the door creaked loudly as Dariak opened it. "The laboratory is through here."

"It seems an easy way to access such a place," Randler noted, trying to sound conversational.

Dariak said nothing, instead pulling the door shut once Randler was inside. An unlit torch hung on the wall and light seeped in through the slats of the roof. The only other detail Randler saw was a trapdoor in the floor. "Stand on that," Dariak said.

Randler opened his mouth to comment about Dariak's terse commands, then he shrugged and obeyed. Dariak stepped beside him, nearly shoving him out of the way accidentally. Then the mage bent down and knocked his fist on various pieces of wood around their feet. *"Fethrikkar b'joulicht."* He stood back up and put his arm around Randler to steady him. "Don't move."

The trapdoor rattled and sank downward into a wooden shaft. Dirt rained in through some gaps where the wood wasn't fused securely, but Dariak didn't react to it.

After a time, the motion stopped and Dariak pushed open one wall of wood. Light filtered in through the channel they had traveled from above, though it was barely enough to see by. Dariak stepped forward and Randler did his best to keep up.

"This part will be difficult in your condition," Dariak said.

"Should I wait here then?" He tried keeping the edge out of his voice, but failed.

"No. Unless you'd rather not come." He then pointed to a series of rounded stones on the floor. They spanned the length of a large hallway. "You can only step on the stones and only in a certain pattern. If you miss, you'll be stuck in a tar-like muck until I can get you out. For the most part, you should be fine. But you'll have to jump here and there."

The prospect of jumping didn't sound like a good idea with the pain in his legs, but he was determined to continue for this part of the journey so he nodded and Dariak went ahead first, cautioning Randler not to follow until he signaled that it was safe. The mage stepped on each of the first four stones, then he skipped one. He took the two next steps, then he made two larger leaps, landing on the third stone ahead each time. He took one final step and then reached a platform on the other side.

Randler braced himself, counting aloud as he took his first steps across the stones. "One. One. One. One," he started. "Now two." He hopped over the next stone, landing precariously on the second slab. Pain lanced up his legs and he winced as he looked at the next stone ahead of him. He reached his foot forward and took the next two steps. "One. One," he huffed. Now came the tricky part. Dariak had taken two leaps at this point, and Randler's legs already ached badly. He glanced over his shoulder seeing that he had as many steps ahead of him as behind.

He took his time judging the first jump. He had to clear two stones and land on the third. He thought he could manage it, though the landing might be hard. It didn't matter. He had to push himself onward. He took a deep breath and argued with himself not to close his eyes. "Three." He leaped.

The stone crashed up into his legs as he landed and he thought his crutches would snap with the impact, it hurt so much. He wobbled forward and almost fell onto the next stone, which would have pinned him in the murky trap, if Dariak's warning was true. The ground looked perfectly solid, so it was easy to think there was no actual trap, but Delminor had been a powerful and crafty mage. Of course he wouldn't have made a trap obvious.

It took a few minutes before Randler could push himself onto his feet again. Dariak watched from ahead with concern, but he made no effort to help. Randler wondered in part if offering assistance would set off the trap or if Dariak was being difficult, then he scolded himself for his thoughts.

Randler stared at the next stones, turning his emotions toward attacking them instead of Dariak. "Three, then one. And then that's it," he murmured. His legs shuddered and he almost lost his balance without even trying to move. He took a steadying breath and then decided he needed to just be rash. He bent his knees and pounced. He knew he wouldn't recover well after the landing, so he didn't really try to. Instead, as his feet impacted the third stone, he leaned forward and hopped again, forcing his body onto the following step and then bounding off that to the platform with Dariak. He crumpled into a heap and clutched his legs, wailing in pain.

Dariak knelt beside him and tried to offer comfort, but words were useless. Randler's writhing made his heart ache and he wished he could do something. Magic was dead, though, and—

As he considered magic, Dariak realized that they were far away from the castle and the energies might actually respond. He closed his eyes and reached into his robe for some herbs, which he crushed in his hand. *"Menicodi reppretharricon kaie."* His hands hovered over Randler's legs and he felt the energies coalesce in the air and penetrate downward into the bard. The spell worked. Dariak repeated the incantation several times until Randler was able to sit up on his own.

"Thanks."

"I had forgotten magic might work again here. It's a bit weak, though."

"Still helpful."

They waited a few minutes more and then continued. Dariak assured him there weren't many more obstacles to pass and that he could disarm them himself. Randler followed quietly behind the mage, paying little attention to the rock walls that passed by and not caring much about the luminescent moss that kept the place lit.

At a dead end, Dariak pressed on a series of bricks in what looked like a random order. As he clicked the fifteenth one, a snapping sound echoed and the rock to their left slid open. Inside was a small square chamber with four torches that Dariak lit and a small pool in the center. Randler also noted four pedestals at the opposite side of the room. Dariak wasted no time. He took one of the torches from the wall and set it upon a pedestal. Next he scooped up a handful of dirt from the floor and set it upon a second pedestal. Randler guessed that water and air were next, and when Dariak confirmed his suspicions by dripping water on one pedestal and blowing on the last one, a crack appeared in the back wall, revealing the final door to the laboratory.

Dariak entered first and Randler could hear him chanting his fire dart spell, after which the chamber erupted with light. As he passed through the doorway, Randler noted a hearty musty smell and some other scent he couldn't quite place. He grabbed the wall for support as he glanced around the chamber.

It wasn't what he expected for a laboratory, not really. In fact, with all the bookcases and chairs, it looked a lot like the sitting room in Dariak's house. "It's going to take a lot to work through all these books."

Dariak gave a short laugh and stepped up to one of the bookcases. He yanked on a shelf and the entire bookcase slid forward on casters and pivoted, revealing another bookcase behind it. Reveling in the look on Randler's face, he shifted aside a few other bookcases in the same manner. "My father owned a copy of every book he could ever find, and sometimes had copies made of books he liked. You could almost say this is the library of both our kingdoms. He even developed the magic that purifies the air so the books don't wither much over time. That's that funky smell you might have noticed." He pointed to one of the alcoves he opened with the second row of bookcases. "There are more bookcases behind those too. This room goes on a while."

Randler's jaw dropped. "I can't believe it. It's… overwhelming."

Nonchalantly, Dariak shrugged. "Wait until we get to the spell books."

"Okay, I need to sit."

"Not yet, if you can wait. It's more comfortable inside." Dariak led the bard through the stacks of books, sliding specific bookcases aside, stepping through, and then pulling them back into place. Randler noticed that some of the walkways between the rows of books were closed off, making this room more like a maze than a library. Eventually, they came through to a wide open chamber with a grassy hill and a small pond.

Randler gasped. "You're kidding me."

"If you can't spend your time outdoors, bring the outdoors to you."

Randler staggered forward and bent over to feel the grass and to drag his hands through the water. "It's real."

"So are they," he said, pointing to a small row of bushes on the other side of the hill. In the bushes was a nest with a few small swallomers sleeping soundly. "My father employed magic of all kinds down here."

"But how is it still… running?"

Dariak laughed. "He created a delicate balance in this particular room. It sustains itself like it's its own ecosystem. It's missing insects and some other things, but there's enough here to sustain the life you see."

"Astounding." He turned slowly around and it didn't feel at all as if they were underground. "Dariak, if I sang of this place, no one would ever believe me."

After the initial shock wore off, Dariak pointed around the chamber. "This room we're in is the garden area. Over there is the fortified magic room, where it's possible to cast spells without any of the energy escaping. There's a bedroom. That's a kitchen. That's the exercise room, though my father rarely used it. That's his study. And *that* is our destination; the real library."

"The real library?" Randler echoed. "What were all those other books we saw?"

"They were real, too, but nothing of consequence to us. This is where the important things are. Come along and then we'll sit for a while." They made their way around the small hill and went through the room toward the northeast section. Inside, as Randler expected, were more bookcases, fully loaded with massive tomes. He shook his head in pure amazement.

"This is absurd. How are we ever going to get through it all?"

Dariak pointed to the three bookcases on the left wall. "Those are directories."

Randler rubbed his eyes and Dariak walked him further into the room until they reached an open section with chairs and tables. Randler settled into a lounge chair and stretched his legs out so he could massage them. "It's going to take us forever down here, Dariak."

He shrugged. "It won't be as bad as you think once we get started. But Keela should be ready with dinner if you're hungry."

He grinned. "I'm famished. Wait, are you going to head all the way back upstairs, then?"

Dariak shook his head. "Of course not. There is a mechanism in the kitchen here that matches with the kitchen upstairs. It's sort of like the lift we used to get down here in the first place. It's too small for a person to fit, but it's perfect for getting food—and messages—up and down."

Dariak left to tend to dinner and Randler turned his head, marveling at the endless amount of information stored down here. His mind hurt just thinking about it. At the same point, the bard hungered for all the stories in those books, and he wondered how many he could read and turn into worthy ballads for others to enjoy. It seemed like an interesting challenge, but even more so would be the task of crafting songs for the most important tales. They would each need to be unique, unless their content overlapped and he could intermingle the melodies properly. He would also have to consider various instruments and tempos to evoke the proper moods.

Randler nodded. Dariak may have his quest here, but now the bard had one of his own. Grinning, he tapped his fingers randomly on the lounge chair, building himself a library of beats.

CHAPTER 18

Lica of the Mages

LICA'S JOURNEY TO Magehaven was tricky, for the soldiers who attended her were not particularly skilled. Two died to sand rodia, which made her angry for their incompetence. She was not an old woman, but she was certainly old enough to be protected by younger men, and when she had to break out her daggers and leap into the vermin, sympathy left her.

"Move out," she barked, pulling her hair back into a tight bun after the battle. She pointed to the unfortunate youths who had died. "And leave them to the scavengers. Such nonsense, all of you. You didn't see the sandorpions or the swallomers or the rodia. What good are you?"

She stomped through the sand, the eight other fighters trailing behind her, heads hung low. They didn't even argue with her, and that concerned her, too. They truly had no fight in them whatsoever. As the afternoon hit high, she called a stop so they could eat. "Eska, the waterskins. Ijul, the rations. Let's not tarry for long, though. We should try to reach the tower by morning."

The two men she had named looked at each other and shrugged their shoulders.

"What is it?" Lica asked.

"We don't have no rations," Eska said, scratching his chin.

"Or no waterskins," Ijul added.

"Where are—?" But she stopped herself, because she had a feeling she knew what they were going to say, and when Eska spoke, her suspicions were confirmed.

"Think Mettli and Awrish had 'em. Prob'ly why the sand rodia went after 'em first and got 'em killed."

Lica squeezed her eyes shut and strained to remain calm. They were still relatively near the castle after a day and a half on the journey and she could tell the magical energies were still stunted. It was probably a good thing too, because she was in quite a rage and would likely have flared a fireball at them right then. In a tersely controlled tone, she asked the group, "Does anyone have rations or water?"

"Not a bite or a drop, ma'am," chimed Feruth.

Lica pressed her hands to her temples. "Do you mean to tell me that none of you, who've lived in this desert region all your lives, carry small pouches of supplies upon your person for emergencies?"

998

"I ain't got no person, lady," Ijul said, affronted. "We don't own people here in Hathreneir."

The words to numerous spells came to mind, but she held back. "I would say that it's pretty clear that you don't intend to help me on my way."

"We done what the king told us," Eska argued.

"And what, pray tell, was that? Sabotage my trip?"

"Now listen!" Feruth shouted. "It were you that told us to leave the others."

She spoke through her teeth, "That didn't mean to leave the supplies with them!"

"Well, how's we to know? You didn't say."

She puffed in anger. "Very well then. Listen to these words and obey them well. Go back to your fallen comrades. Drag them back to the castle. Then speak to your king and have him reassign you elsewhere."

"What o' you?" Eska asked. "You come back wit' us?"

She forced a smile. "No, I'm off to Magehaven."

"Bu' the king, he says, we gotta get you there us'selves," Ijul interjected.

"And you will tell his royal—" she strained and struggled to force out the word, "highness, that I decided you needed to tend to your wounded. If you need to tell him that I snuck off while you were sleeping, then so be it! Just be gone!"

"You sure?"

"Never been more sure in my life."

Eska nodded slowly and then called out to the others. "All right, men, you heard her. Gather your belongings and let's high-tail it back to the castle."

Ijul saluted. "Aye, sir, we'll make it back with haste."

Lica noted the instant change in dialect and understood the farce at once. It didn't matter anyway. She made a few rude gestures when they turned away and then she pushed herself into a fast shuffle across the sand, wondering if the two men who died earlier had even been hurt at all.

She was too old for such a journey, but she kept telling herself she would be safer with the mages than amongst the king's men. It made her worry about Ruhk and Verna, who would be tending to the affairs of state in the early days of Dariak's call for peace, but they were young and would handle themselves, she was sure.

A pack of reptigons slithered across the sand and Lica wondered if the creatures would attack. Without magic, she was terrible in a fight, but perhaps her mood sent off some foul aroma, for the beasts not only didn't attack, they scampered away. Lica immediately scanned the horizon for a deeper threat, but there was none.

Thirsty, the mage reached into her robe and withdrew a waterskin, sipping just a little bit. Of course the others had them too, she huffed, but then she pushed the thought aside. The soldiers weren't worth her time to think about, though it did raise questions about the intent of the king. Had he sent them along to sabotage her on purpose? Or had the men decided to do that on their own so they could return to their liege? As she considered, she decided they had rebelled on their own, for the king needed to make the appearance of cooperation, at least in the beginning.

Lica's musings were interrupted by movement along the surface of the sand. She slowed her gait and watched as the sand shifted and shimmered like a mirage. Some type of creature made its way along the surface, but she didn't recognize it.

Instinctively, she pulled a pebble out of her pocket and cast a protective enchantment from it, not caring if magic was defunct. The stone warmed, just barely, signifying that she had least a modicum of protection from projectiles, but she wondered if tossed sand would even be deflected by the shield for long.

Moving quickly, the mage hurried ahead, keeping her eyes on the shifting surface as she went. Perhaps an injured creature was writhing around, but the movements were too precise for that to be the case. The bungling soldiers might have been able to tell her what approached, but then again, they probably would have told her they didn't see anything.

She shifted along for a few measures before the creature made itself known. With a low rumble, the surface parted and a head the size of Lica's midsection rose out of the sand, followed by numerous beige segments that writhed about, bringing it toward her. When the entire creature was above ground, Lica could see that it had a second head as its rear, as if it were an earthworm that had accidentally sprouted a second mouth after its end had been severed.

The large worm scurried along the sand, seeking out Lica as she tried to avoid it. She was, of course, at a severe disadvantage, and the beast came upon her swiftly. A round maw opened wide, with sharp teeth threatening to wrap around her face and gnaw it off. She didn't have time to cast a spell—if it would even work—so she reacted by turning toward the annelidium, as the Hathrens called them, and grabbing it around its flank.

The move caught the creature by surprise, and if it had been a one-headed worm, the stratagem might have worked. Instead, the annelidium bent up its rear head and snapped its jaws toward her. With a yelp, Lica released the worm and dropped to the sand. She debated against using her dagger, for fear that cutting it would prompt it to sprout more heads.

"I will not be worm food," she hissed, reaching into her pockets and grabbing various spell components. She first tried a fireball, but the meager flame sputtered as soon as the words left her lips. She knew magic wouldn't help her now, but she was a mage and mages were supposed to be smart enough to not be eaten by giant worms.

As she fumbled, the annelidium slithered around and repositioned itself, rolling its body away from Lica and then wrapping both heads back toward her, making it look like a demented and oversized horseshoe. The snapping maws irked her, for they clacked shut in a strange rhythm as if they were singing before supper. The heads waggled in the air, gyrating in counterpoint with the motions bringing the entire body closer and closer to its prey. Lica took a final deep breath as the annelidium pounced for her.

One mouth opened wide to consume her and she did not resist. Instead, Lica brought her left hand straight up over her head and let it sink into the beast's throat first. The teeth scraped the side of her face as the head descended. She had the sensation of being knocked over, and then she realized that the other head of the worm would want to eat, too. The annelidium apparently feasted by stunning its prey and then devouring it from both ends.

Even as the warm, gooey saliva drenched her, Lica grinned in defiance, telling the beast mentally that it wasn't wise to burn a candle from both ends. The teeth sank into her skin and she panicked a little, but just as with the inept soldiers, she kept her cool. The teeth didn't cut too deeply on their own, but they worked with the gyrating body to pull her deeper inside.

Her upraised arm was drawn within and it felt tingly as an inner acid started working on her flesh. It was then she opened her fist and dropped a mix of powerful herbs, including wolfsbane, one of the most potent poisons that grew in Kallisor. As she waited for the poison to take effect, the burning along her hand grew worse and because her whole body now felt wet, she assumed that the two heads had probably come together over their meal and she was completely within the annelidium.

There was very little air and the dark stink made her want to retch. She thought about reaching for her dagger now, but she doubted she would have the strength to cut through the beast's hide, nor to struggle through whatever small opening she would manage to make. She reminded herself again that cutting the worm would probably cause it to regenerate anyway, so she jockeyed her thoughts back to her initial plan, wondering if was going to work.

The acid made her hand feel as if it were on fire and she tried to recoil it, but the walls of the annelidium pressed in tightly now as the creature tried to consume its meal. She could barely move and thrashing about did nothing for her predicament. The only thought that circulated through her mind was that she really was going to die because a worm had decided to eat her.

A sharp tug pulled at her midsection and she yelped in pain. Lica realized that this was probably where the worm ripped its meal in half. The wrenching pull yanked again and she bid farewell to her legs, sad they were about to be removed. She wondered absently if they would make their way around the insides of the annelidium until her feet reached her partially-digested hand. She hadn't touched her toes in years; this certainly wasn't the way she thought she would do so again.

The whole creature lurched then, repeatedly. Lica's body was battered inside the fleshy segments and the gripping teeth pulled harder and harder. She knew her spine was ready to snap from the tugging and thrashing, but then the beast slapped to the ground one more time and was silent.

She waited a moment, wondering if it had lost interest in her for some reason, though she understood slowly what had happened. None of the thrashing was due to normal digestion. The wolfsbane had been consumed and the creature had violently died. Lica wished the beast had vomited first.

Instead, with a wounded hand and little air, she had to wriggle out of the massive worm covered in its saliva, which served the auspicious job of coating her in sand once she escaped. Gasping for air, Lica struggled to pull her legs out of the second mouth, but she felt it was prudent to do so before even attempting to do anything for her damaged arm.

Covered in gooey sand, Lica turned to look at her hand and she winced when she did so. The skin was blistered and peeling back, and she understood that only some strong healing magic would ever be able to repair it. The damage was worse than if she had fallen into a roaring campfire; herbs wouldn't be enough. It was all she had, though, so she used some of her limited drinking water to cleanse the wound, and then she wrapped it in cracked aloe leaves. She decided to be grateful that at least it wasn't her dominant hand that was hurt.

Exhausted and aching, Lica pushed on. As the night crept in, her skin darkened with innumerable bruises from the bashing within the annelidium. Without Magehaven, she wouldn't have much in the way of shelter. Even if she could manage to dig herself a deep enough trench to bury herself within, clearly that wasn't an option for her.

As she plodded along into the night, she felt an odd sensation tingling along her skin. She had never really noticed it before, but once she understood what it was, she knew she had always felt it. Without delay, Lica drew out another leaf of aloe, biting on the stem to release some of the soothing sap. *"Mendillius faroniq kaie preshino."* She sent healing energy down and through her arm, gasping as the skin tried to mend itself. She spent a few minutes recasting the spell until the throbbing stopped.

The cold night air wafted over her as she rested upon the sand, far enough from the castle now that her magic had returned. She cherished the tingling sensation that ran along her body and she wondered how she could ever have forgotten it. Perhaps she had spent too many years hiding her skills among the villagers throughout Kallisor and so had pushed this feeling away. Or maybe her time in the Mage Underground had left her so angry and jaded that she wasn't as well-tuned to the energies as she should be. Perhaps those were reasons she had never been more than a gruff woman with a good heart who never felt accomplished.

Lica frowned at the frustration in her soul. She needed to rest, but she wasn't sure she should try to sleep out in the open like this. She estimated another four hours of solid travel before she would reach the tower and though her body protested, she opted to push onward.

Aside from a flock of shadowcrows who squawked at her and flew on, Lica thankfully met no other feral beasts on her trek. She was prepared with spells, though, and perhaps they sensed her renewed connection to the energies and thus kept away. She didn't care why they left her alone. It only mattered that she keep moving forward one foot and then another until the tower's invisible barrier pressed against her skin.

Lica's previous visits to Magehaven had not been restful and she didn't expect this visit to be any better. However, the bedraggled woman had to put her faith in the humanity of the mages. She crossed the threshold of the barrier and then let her strength give way, dropping to the sand in much the same way the annelidium had collapsed as it died. She even twitched and writhed about to avoid pressing her wounds into the sand, and then she went still.

CHAPTER 19

The Warrior and the Babe

GABRION'S JOURNEY TO the north took place as a forced march with a host of twenty of the king's best soldiers and the woman who had tended the child since his birth. Alosia was a trusted servant of the king and had served his family for decades, taking the role from her mother before her. She frowned upon this journey at all, but was grateful to be assigned to the party.

"I'll hold him for a while," she offered.

Gabrion shook his head again. She had asked nearly every twenty minutes to take the baby into her arms, relenting only when they stopped to eat and she was allowed to spend some time with the infant. The rest of the time, Perrios was propped in the carrier Gabrion had crafted and the little tyke bobbed up and down on the warrior's back as their horses carried them across the northern stretch of desert.

They encountered creatures periodically. Sometimes the archers in the group merely shot down enough of them that the rest turned and fled. Other times they pressed the horses into a run and escaped conflict. The few times they engaged in battle, the soldiers dealt with the creatures, keeping Gabrion far from the fighting so as not to endanger the baby. The guards worked as a truly united team, with four men on point at all times, and they rotated regularly. Each man performed every job in the group, including digging the trenches for their relief breaks or setting up the camp defenses.

There were two mages among the group and once they reached the edge of the dead zone, they flexed their skills and enhanced the party's protections with spells. Gabrion could sense the resonating vibrations that swept around them. The pattern was mesmerizing and dizzying all at once, but he didn't tell the mages that he could sense the energies. He remembered early on in his journey when Dariak had first cast the glass protection charm about him and he noted the tingling sensation; Dariak had been surprised that he could feel it. Perhaps it was uncommon for an ordinary person to feel the energies, thus keeping quiet about it seemed prudent under the circumstances.

Alosia brought her horse beside Gabrion's and she examined him with concern. "You look exhausted, Gabrion. And your thoughts are far from here. I could take Perrios off your hands for an hour."

He groaned. "The boy is no burden to me."

She lifted her nose. "Perhaps not. But if you fall over out of exhaustion and kill the child, then this trek means little. As would your little uprising. And your life."

Gabrion turned and smiled at her. "You're a happy little lady, aren't you?" She pulled a face and he continued. "You sound all full of concern for young Perrios, but what you really want is for me to falter so you can end this whole ordeal."

Her lip twitched but she said nothing.

"The part I don't understand is why it matters to you. After all, you're still doing the same job and you'll be looked after as before. Certainly that coffer on your horse isn't just for show nor full of useless baubles. The only difference is that I'm in charge of the baby instead of the king. Your life won't change much, so why be raw about it?"

"This... excursion was forced upon us and you have, in essence, kidnapped this child to serve your own purposes. Who's to say what your plans truly are? As if your stated goals aren't bad enough: fraternization and peace with Kallisorians."

"Well, you're 'fraternizing' with one now," he pointed out.

"Sniping and fraternizing are different things. Still, the king ordered us to obey and so we shall."

"Until you find a way to overcome my plan, that is."

She narrowed her eyes. "We do not take the orders of our king lightly. Unlike you, heathen, who abandoned your own liege for some fool's errand. You may intend to build up some new world, but how can it stand for long when you didn't stand by your own king? You rebelled and you left your land. You say you want peace, yet you've slaughtered dozens of Hathrens. You're no role model for us to follow. Who's to say you won't set us up and then leave us to our own devices too?"

He felt like he was being baited and all he wanted was to knock her from her saddle. Perhaps she was willing to take a few hits if it showed he was ill-suited to watching the child. In response to her tirade, he clenched his jaw and focused on the path ahead, keeping still until she let her horse fall back a few paces.

Two days later they arrived in the town of Jorgens, where they stocked up on supplies and rested the horses for a day. They took residence in the mayor's manor overnight, which made Gabrion feel uncomfortable, for the place swarmed with servants tending to his every need. Alosia continued her attempts to wrest Perrios from Gabrion's watch but the warrior denied her at every opportunity. He wondered idly if she would take the baby and flee back to the castle if she had her way, or if perhaps she meant what she had said about obeying the king's orders to follow Gabrion.

The team ventured out the next morning, and as they did so, the desert faded to green land at last. Gabrion had started thinking that all of Hathreneir was a wasteland, but the trees and plains that opened before him reminded him otherwise. The new environment brought other feral creatures to their party, but the soldiers still scurried off and took care of every threat as if they were protecting the king himself.

Gabrion admired their tenacity and wondered if the rest of the king's men were all as well-trained.

He knew they weren't, per se, because he had battled them when the king had tried to take back his castle. Though he wasn't exactly himself during that bout. He gritted his teeth, remembering Kitalla's horrible ruse and all the pain it had caused him. Angrily, he shoved the thoughts aside.

The horses plodded along on the fertile soil for four more days until they reached an imposing brick wall. It extended far to the west and the east and it was twice as tall as Gabrion. At first, he thought he was looking at the side of a mountain, for all the stone, but this structure was manmade. They all dismounted and Gabrion walked up to the wall to look at the mortar between the huge stones. He was admittedly impressed. Many major constructs were crafted by mages because they could shift the land easily and erect amazing structures, like Magehaven itself. Yet this wall had been crafted by hand. Each piece was imperfect, yet securely placed.

"Welcome to the Undying Stone," announced a page who had opened the main gate for them. It had slid silently open and Gabrion hadn't even noticed. "Lodgings will be ready for you shortly in the earl's abode. You may bide your time at the Rusty Inn Tavern, around town, or, if your need is great, then you may seek out the earl immediately. Ah, yes sir. This way, then."

Five stable boys were summoned to tend to the horses as Gabrion and the others were escorted through a winding cobblestone street. The young warrior tried not to look agog at all the stonework, but it was literally everywhere. Each house, shop, bench, wall sconce, flower box, route sign, and pathway was made of stone. Every structure had been handcrafted and, in many places, repaired numerous times over the long years. Many of the rocks had been dyed various colors to reduce the drab gray tones that otherwise would have permeated the small city, but the colors themselves were muted and calm.

It was too much for Gabrion to take in all at once so he focused on the soldier walking in front of him and marched until they finally reached the earl's estate. The structure was, of course, another stone house, but its size was magnificent. If he hadn't been to two castles on his journey, he would have easily mistaken this place for one, and not without reason. The three-story building had battlements and parapets like any good castle, and there was even a five-story tower off on the western end. Unlike the painted stones throughout the city, the estate showed its gray proudly.

A horn echoed in the air to announce their arrival, the sound of which startled the baby, who woke up and cried in earnest. Gabrion instinctively bounced as he walked, creating a gentle rocking sensation as he went, all the while speaking in crooning tones over his shoulder until Perrios calmed down. Even Alosia seemed impressed that the baby silenced so quickly.

Once they were inside the estate, all but three soldiers disbanded. Gabrion, followed closely by the nursemaid, was brought to a sitting room with a lavish marble fireplace and veritable thrones carved of stone. They were padded well, though he still had Perrios on his back so he couldn't sit down. Alosia poured herself a drink from a sidebar and stretched out in one of the oversized chairs.

"I'll help you get that pack off so you can sit down," she offered.

"I will say, you're persistent."

"Just trying to help," she said, though her sneer said otherwise.

He had no idea how long they would be stuck in the room together with the three soldiers, who had taken up strategic posts around the perimeter of the room. Gabrion tried talking to them, but they refused to answer him, so he turned to Alosia. "What do you know about this place?"

"Just the basics." She sipped her drink again. "The Undying Stone was an old fort at first. It was built centuries and centuries ago—millennia, if you're silly enough to believe that version. There were no mages back then because it was in the time of the gods." She choked back a laugh at the notion of gods overseeing their land. "There were wild animals everywhere and the people needed a place to be, and the 'gods' inspired them to create the fort of stone. Little by little, the people here added to the fort until it was a village, then a town, and now a bustling little city. Of course, magic became known in the land at some point in time, yet it was decided that this place would always be crafted by hand, in honor of those who first settled in."

"Very noble."

"Sentimental babble, if you ask me."

Gabrion shook his head. "Nothing seems to please you. Don't you even see the importance of their decision to add to this place with their own sweat and blood? They could have taken the easy way out and just called up their mages to shape the stone overnight, but no, they built it. They worked at it. It grew because they made it so. It may have taken longer and been harder to do, but they *earned* the protection this place affords, and they became stronger for it. And adhering to their traditions—"

"Stop there, sword boy," Alosia interjected. "Don't speak of traditions to me. You don't follow them yourself, so hush."

He couldn't argue that point. "Still, they're strong because of what they've built here."

She looked at the expression on his face as he tried to work out what he wanted to say next, though she understood well enough. "Oh I see. You're saying that our kingdoms will also be as strong as this once we build a new future with our own hands. You're so… clever." Her tone belied her compliment.

"Stone and mortar are two very different things," he said. "One is solid through and through and you can stack a pile of them up one on top of another. But they fall apart after a while. They settle over time and things fall between the cracks, quite literally. Mortar, on the other hand, is a pliable, malleable substance. On its own, it's little more than putty and you can't build a home out of it."

"You're a craftsman now?"

"A home made just out of stone will leak and eventually it'll tumble down and crush you. A house of mortar won't even stand. No, they're very different. They each have their own uses. Yet it's when you put the two together that they can make a place like this. Elegant, strong," he fished for a word and found one from the name of the place, "undying. It'll be the same with our two kingdoms."

"Not a craftsman, then. A philosopher. A foolish one, but a philosopher nevertheless."

Gabrion shook his head. "You're so blind, you won't even listen."

"Blindness is a fault of the eyes," Alosia mocked. "Deafness is that of the ears. Blindness doesn't make anyone unable to hear."

Gabrion grunted in frustration. "Listen to yourself. You're so close-minded, nothing can get in. Not even a thought of something new. I'm not even asking you to accept the idea; just to think about it."

She swirled her drink. "I'm sorry, were you saying something important?"

He shook his head. "You wonder why I won't let you take Perrios for any bit of time. I'll tell you. He's the future of this land. He has to grow up with an open mind. He can't be like you. One day he'll need to make important decisions for the good of the people and he'll need to be free to consider all the options available to him, not just the ones that have been laid in front of him. If you weren't such a narrow thinker, then I'd have no qualms entrusting him to your hands. As it is, I won't let you touch him ever again."

Alosia stood up, enraged. "How dare you!"

Her cry awoke the baby again and when Alosia strode forward to tend to him, Gabrion shoved her away with one hand. "Open your mind. Consider a different view. Only then will I let you hold him." He then bounced in place and hummed with his head cocked to the side. It took longer to settle the child, but he nodded off again.

Soon, though, Perrios would need to eat and then be changed, and it was with great relief that the page entered the room to escort them to their living quarters. A crib had been set up in one chamber and Gabrion insisted that Alosia be escorted to a different room, even though they had intended for her to stay with the baby.

When the arrangements were settled, Gabrion spent a while tending to Perrios' needs. The child was restless, yet he slept well after all the time being jostled around on the journey. Gabrion sank into a chair beside the crib, and as he watched the cherubic face twitch periodically, his own eyelids grew heavy. He reached for the words of a song to help him stay awake for a little while longer to watch the peaceful sight of the infant nestled in his crib. He didn't even realize what he was singing, just that he knew it from his heart.

Sleep my beloved for night has come to us.
Close your dear eyes and turn your thoughts inside.
Dream now, for there you will see the light and the hopes of your tender heart.
You will be at peace as you drift through clouds of wonder and harmony.

Rest now, my child.
You will be strong.
Rest now, my child.
One day you will shine.

Stephen J. Wolf

No one can harm you while I am here by your side.
No shadows can fall here for I am your light.
Your dreams will guide you to your morrow and you will be safe with each step you take.
You will achieve all that you wish and all of your desires will be filled.

CHAPTER 20

In Support of Dariak's Mission

KITALLA LED THE troops across the desert toward the front lines of the war. They met various beasts and she delegated each fight to the dominion of one of her five battalions. As they went, the soldiers grew more confident in their skills and they slowly came around to Kitalla's decisions, though she still acted erratically at times. During the trek, she took advantage of Carrus' offer on numerous occasions and always, after, she was both calmer and wilder, as if her conscience burned with conflict.

"We'll be upon the war soon," Carrus said one morning. "Perhaps even today. Are we ready?"

She stroked his chin. "All I have left now is making Dariak's peace a reality. If that means we have to work a few sudden miracles, then that's what we'll do. So in short, yes, I'm ready. And if I'm ready, then we're all ready."

"I'm expecting trouble. Once these men meet up with their own kind, they may turn away from what you've done."

Kitalla laughed. "Do you really think Merrlis, who could barely tie his bootstrap two weeks ago, will cower and submit to the others now that he has been so successful leading his Eagles?"

"That's why you picked the runts to take over, isn't it? Build them up so they owe you fealty. Rather crafty."

"I can't take credit for the plan," she admitted. "I stole it from Poltor. After all… it worked on me."

He touched her arm delicately. "You were never a runt."

She smiled sadly and pulled her arm away. "Listen, Carrus," she said, her voice serious, "you've been a great support to me these past weeks."

"Shush. I'm only saying you've never been a runt. Don't get all sentimental now." He kept his tone between sarcasm and honesty and she didn't know how to read it. "It's early yet and I doubt the Sparrows have food ready. We have some time."

She eyed him narrowly, then, with a sharp twist, she shoved him back down and pounced upon him, a chuckle echoing quietly in her throat.

As the morning wore on, Kitalla led the group toward a haze in the east. From afar it appeared to be campfires lit, even in the daytime, which meant that shadowcrows were probably plaguing the area. Kitalla moved to the Eagles where she guided Merrlis onward. He obeyed her advice and offered suggestions of his own, which Kitalla accepted and told him to initiate. She then moved off to the Nightingales and gave instructions there that would fortify the gaps that Merrlis had inadvertently proposed in his plans. As she had come to expect, Datch sought to prove himself with adaptations of his own, and though they left the western flank exposed, Kitalla agreed enthusiastically.

Since Yllina of the Wrens was the meekest of the bunch, Kitalla first spoke to Paerra of the Sparrows and received his recommendations. As with the rest, Kitalla listened intently and then asked about the plan for the archers in the group, prompting the captain to consider actually using them in the event of a battle, and then she moved on to Yllina to lay out orders to cover the final weaknesses in the scattered plans.

Kitalla had realized early on that the five captains had little skill defending themselves or their groups, and they were unable to compromise coherently with each other over strategy, so she devised this technique of having them covering each other without even realizing it. Each one felt as if their words were heard and obeyed, and none realized they were being craftily manipulated.

Kitalla's final task was to consult with Ferithor of the Ravens, and since he was enamored with Carrus, he never questioned anything he was asked to do, so long as Carrus was there when she delivered the news. Then, with all the plans set, Kitalla gave the final order to move out.

It took about three hours for them to reach the camp of Hathren soldiers. The commander greeted them skeptically. "Weapons at the ready!" he said to his men. "I am Commander Mzark of the Hathren army. Declare yourselves."

"I am Kitalla and we come from Castle Hathreneir and from your king."

Mzark raised an eyebrow. "'Your' king, you say? Is he not 'our' king?"

"I did not misspeak," she said confidently, though in fact she hadn't meant to phrase it that way. It set things on a tenuous opening that she had hoped to avoid. "You're likely aware of the events that have transpired at the castle and messengers advised you of the king's political situation."

Mzark sneered. "Indeed. Though the decree came on royal parchment, the messenger did not seem convinced of its… authenticity."

Kitalla rolled her eyes in exaggerated fashion, and along the way she spied the locations of six archers, three mages, and a handful of soldiers peering out from behind various tents. Kitalla knew their approach could not be concealed, but the defenses in place set her hackles high. She hoped her captains were ready. To Mzark, she said, "It is sincere."

The commander propped his foot up on a rucksack in the sand and he set his thumbs on his belt, his belly overhanging in jolly fashion. "Were that so, the chancellor would have sent a proper emissary with your forces."

Kitalla grinned. "Oh! Then worry not, for I am one of King Prethos' chancellors. I orchestrated the lodgings after the castle was destroyed." She focused her eyes on the man and tried to convince him to stand down.

"Destroyed… no doubt by you and your fellows here."

"No, wait!" Merrlis shouted suddenly. "Wait, wait!" He ran forward, waving his arms. "It's true what she says, the ki—" And he fell dead to the ground, an arrow sticking out of his throat.

Kitalla wasted no time giving the signal for her forces to enact their battle plan. She took the reins of the Eagles, issuing Merrlis' flawed orders, knowing the other four groups would compensate for the weaknesses. The swordsmen rushed forward through the camp, barely hacking at any of the Hathren soldiers as they went. Their destination was the far edge, where the element of surprise would allow them to take the soldiers posted there. Kitalla ran with them for part of the way, stopping only to ensure the other groups were getting into position.

The Sparrows flew in toward the right, sweeping around and hunting down the Hathren fighters at their posts. Meanwhile their archers tracked the projectiles in the sky to determine their sources, then launched their own missiles in retaliation. Kitalla nodded; things were working out as planned. The Nightingales swept the northern edge of the camp, fanning out and knocking down tents, as part of Datch's plan, whooping as they went. This, of course, left them more exposed to incoming projectiles, but Kitalla had compensated by sending two of the Ravens' mages to assist. Soon, spells fluttered into the air and the fight was on in full.

Kitalla withdrew her daggers, her only goal to hunt down the commander and subdue him. All of her team was under orders not to kill any of these people, and they had been more than grateful at the demand, for these soldiers were their kin and this battle was only a misunderstanding.

Carrus' battle cries echoed over the field as he swept his war hammer about, deflecting one attack after another. He brandished a shield on his left arm, using it to bash his opponents to the ground once their weapons were pushed aside. He plowed his way through six fighters easily, taking only minor cuts in the process.

Despite herself, Kitalla admired his skill and she pulled back against a tent to watch him. He wasn't nearly as graceful in battle as Gabrion, but Carrus thundered with an immense power that told his foes they had no chance against him. He was a quiet man most of the time, but here on the battlefield, he howled like a tigroar as he pushed through.

Lightning exploded nearby and Kitalla scolded herself for letting her mind wander at a time like this. Hathren mages targeted her, their arms flailing in practiced unison as they combined their electric spells into a more powerful bolt. Kitalla watched carefully, flicking her eyes to the side to ensure she could escape, and when the mages opened their hands and the lightning flew, she dodged and rolled in the sand. The mages were quick, and they sent a shower of blinding sparks toward her, making it difficult to see anything at all, as if the sun was flitting down through millions of pieces of broken glass. Kitalla squinted against the effect and charged forward.

They hadn't expected her to rise so quickly or to push into their spell, and one of the mages panicked and ran off to a safer spot. The other growled in defiance and brought his arms up high, then swept them out to his sides and down. He shouted archaic words and the sand in front of Kitalla solidified into sharp spikes.

The first steps caught Kitalla unaware as her foot was pierced and she lost her balance. She couldn't afford to fall, for she would be skewered. Whirling her arms around, she managed to keep upright, but her other foot was stabbed in the process. The mage worked another spell as Kitalla staggered across the spiked sand and took the only chance she had. With a quick flick of her wrist, she snapped one of her daggers forward, followed moments later by a second one. She then immediately pulled on the energies within her, projecting the image of an eaglon flying at the chanting mage. Her hands fluttered like wings as her legs strained to hold her position.

The mage launched a small lightning blast at the nearest eaglon and the dagger exploded with a blinding flash. The second dagger went unseen and it struck the mage in the shoulder, knocking him down. Despite her pain, Kitalla smiled. It was becoming easier and easier to throw images at unsuspecting victims.

"Get that fire out!" Mzark bellowed, and Kitalla saw that the tents in the north were all ablaze. Apparently the Raven mages had gotten a bit overzealous in their efforts to keep the Nightingales safe. Kitalla had to wait for the spike trap spell to dissipate before she could go their aid, though she was surprised that the spell hadn't ended when the mage went down.

Then she remembered the second mage who had scampered off, and as she turned her eyes, she saw that he was still sweeping his hands in front of himself and then poking them upward into the air, mimicking the very spikes themselves. He was clearly an accomplished earth mage since he was able to hold such sharp stakes together from a distance, especially as they were made of sand.

The spike field was too wide in all directions for her to escape and as she tried to move, the field shifted with her, with new spikes forming as she stepped. Her feet bled, reminding her that she was injured and trapped. Leaping away was clearly not an option, for she would land upon the stakes whichever way she pounced. The mage was too far away for a dagger throw, but perhaps not too far for her special skill.

Kitalla imagined that she was in three places at once and then she focused her thoughts on the mage. She needed to move the energies through her body to give power to the conjuration, and each step she took injured her foot in another spot, making it increasingly difficult to concentrate on the image. But if the mage kept the trap intact, then an archer would easily be able to take her down, so she didn't have a choice. Kitalla jumped forward a few paces, and blades lanced into her feet and calves as she landed. It was a necessary move, for the mage needed to believe that she was no longer in the same place she had started.

The imagery seemingly took hold, for the mage's head turned erratically from left to right, tracking his prey. The spike field grew less dense as he tried to spread it over a larger area, and Kitalla found a soft patch of sand to stand on, though she was hardly idle. To keep the image active, she had to continuously channel the energies from within herself, so she needed to keep moving. Slowly, she took careful steps ahead, making the extra images of herself move in different directions to throw off the mage. When she was close enough, she slipped a dagger out of her boot and waited until the energies called for her arms to move upward, then released her weapon. It wasn't a well-thrown dagger, for if she had stopped to aim it, the illusion would have ended immediately. Instead, the knife lobbed through the air and the hilt cracked against the man's head, disrupting the spell. Kitalla shouted with each painful step as she ran to the mage and tackled him, rendering him inert.

Carrus, meanwhile, plowed through the field, leaving both sides of the battle in awe. He made his way toward Mzark, who seemed to welcome the challenge. The oversized commander pulled out a halberd and wielded it with two hands. The massive weapon flew through the air and came crashing toward its target. Carrus barely avoided it and, with little effort, Mzark swept it back into the air and brought it down again. The commander looked like a chubby child swinging a sheaf of wheat.

Carrus kept his eyes alert for an opening, hoping the man would tire quickly from the exertion, but he didn't even look winded after a dozen powerful strikes. Off to the side, a mage chanted frantically, aiming it at the commander, and Carrus realized that she was providing healing magic to the leader so that he would not tire. Unless someone took out the healer, their duel would be a draw.

But Carrus wasn't content with a stalemate, nor would he rely on another to subdue the mage. Instead, he raised his sonorous voice into the air and charged. The halberd swept in like lightning and Carrus blocked with his shield. The concussive force cracked off a large portion of the shield and sent jarring pain up the warrior's arm. He did not relent, even as Mzark stepped back and brought the halberd around again. Carrus recovered from the first strike and rushed in, charging angrily. In came the halberd and down went Carrus, catching the weapon in his left arm and dragging it to the sand with his weight.

Mzark jerked forward with the sudden move and yanked on his weapon to reclaim it, but Carrus had thrown his whole body on top of the halberd. Awkwardly lying over it, he turned on his side and swept outward with his war hammer. Mzark leaped away, releasing his grip on the halberd, which gave Carrus a moment to stand. As the commander reached for his fallen weapon, Carrus lunged and used the momentum to throw his war hammer into the commander's side, crushing bone. The heavyset fellow collapsed.

Carrus wasted no time. He hurried to the commander's side and reclaimed his weapon. The mage still sent healing energies and already the internal wound started to heal and, as the pain lessened, Mzark's face eased up, meaning he would rise up in a few moments and continue fighting.

Turning on the spot, Carrus whipped around and launched his war hammer again, this time aiming for the support mage. The unexpected attack caught her off guard and she crumpled when the the hammer struck her in the abdomen. Carrus swept back around and mashed his fist into Mzark's face, rendering him unconscious.

Soon after, the Hathren troops lost the will to fight. Kitalla's legs were tended to and then she and Carrus brought order back to the camp. The Hathrens were corralled in the center with Kitalla's forces surrounding them on all sides. Only three people had died during the scuffle, and all of them had been Kitalla's. She took the losses out on Mzark by punching him hard in the gut three times.

"What now?" Mzark grumbled when he could talk again.

"We trade," Kitalla said, hovering over him with a threat in her eyes. "A host of us will return to the castle and there, you will confirm the—what was the word you used?—authenticity of the decree. And while you're there, you'll reform your ways for the designated year or spend it in the dungeon."

"I'd rather die."

She leaned in close. "I could make that happen." The expression on her face was all he needed to believe her. "Good. You'll leave us thirty of your men. The rest of you will return to the castle with fifteen of my men. And I assure you, it's in your best interest not to turn against them, for if you show up at the castle with prisoners, or without them at all, there will be consequences. On the other hand, if you arrive with them all intact, you will find the king most welcoming."

"How can I even trust what you say? If I kill your men and return to the king, I will be a hero for ridding the land of men who have turned against him."

She shrugged. "If the messenger lied about the decree, then perhaps. If it isn't a lie, then think about the repercussions. Yet if you prefer, or if you think you can't behave, then I could send you back there as prisoners. I'm sure there's enough un-burned rope here to secure you."

Mzark growled.

"Good," Kitalla said. "Now, when you return, let his royal majesty know that a host of Kallisorians will be following you a couple days hence."

"What!"

"Yes, that's our next destination. We will subdue them as we have done you, and then we'll send them to the castle to be folded into the new peace. And little by little, my team and I will funnel away the fighters on the front line until everyone is trying to eke out a living in your castle. Any questions?"

Mzark blinked innumerable times, trying to make sense of her declaration. "You intend to populate the castle with Kallisorians?"

She nodded. "And Hathrens. And you'll see that the king will support that."

"Impossible."

"Well, if I'm wrong, then you get to be the advance guard warning the king about the arrival of the 'enemy.' I suggest you pack light so you can get there all the faster." With that, she turned and walked away, seeking out Datch, who had already agreed to lead the refugees back to the castle.

Mzark's face twitched, and he looked more distressed trying to figure out what had happened than he had after all the damage he took from Carrus.

CHAPTER 21

Volumes of Lore

RANDLER AND DARIAK spent countless hours and days poring through the books in Delminor's library. The sheer amount of information was unfathomable and it said much about Delminor's attention to detail and desire to learn. The library itself was housed along sprawling corridors and though there were reference cards and books, Randler often found himself scratching his head, wondering where he should turn next.

It was easier for Dariak, having spent time there before, and he checked in with Randler periodically, but often he was quiet, flipping through endless pages of text. His father had conducted innumerable experiments relating to the shards of the Red Jade and, even with the indexes, there was a lot of ground to cover.

"Randler!" he called out one tiresome day. "Come here; you have to read this."

The bard struggled on his weakened legs to reach Dariak, who had tried multiple times to use healing magic to repair the damage. Though Dariak had learned of connecting to the magical energies in an intimate way, healing magic still escaped him when he needed it most. Only in his battle against Pyron had he shown mastery over the power. Now he could only manage to keep Randler from hurting; the strength in the man's legs was another matter entirely.

When Randler finally reached him, he fell into a chair and took a moment to catch his breath, though he could see the odd expression on Dariak's face and it made him curious. "What have you found?"

Dariak handed over a burned leather tome that was frayed around the edges. It seemed to have fallen into a fire at some point and was hastily rescued. "It's an interesting bit of history relating to Hathreneir, Kallisor, and the jades." With the book on Randler's lap, Dariak flipped open to a particular section that was scrawled in the heavy hand of Delminor.

It is said that history is written by the victor, and whosoever it is that wins then sheds himself in a heroic light, battling back the forces of evil that had thought—however foolishly—to try to vanquish him. In our lands, this is a strange paradox, for both kingdoms have taken turns thwarting the efforts of the other, and always with disastrous results. Upon reading our histories, we all speak of the evil 'others' across the border, but no one ever quite claims victory. I find this perplexing, for it suggests that neither side ever feels as if it has truly won.

Randler looked up from the book. "He makes an interesting point."

"Yes. And in the last war, there was an effort to break that stalemate, if you recall."

Randler nodded. "The kings decided to bring about one last hurrah and whoever won that fight would tip the tide and claim victory over both sides."

"And they were stopped one more time," Dariak added. "In part, this time, by my father."

"Do you think he intended to restore that balance?" Randler asked hesitantly.

His voice was solemn. "I don't know. Perhaps a journal entry will reveal his intentions, but I haven't gotten that far yet. Either way, he gave his life to make an impact; I just wish it had done more than pause the fighting. Anyway, keep reading."

Eons ago—if you will allow me to be melodramatic for I cannot currently recall the exact span—there were mages working in Kallisor to help fertilize the land. Now, if you know anything of the history of Kallisor, then you know that magic is grossly discouraged, and the king would have such mages slain for their efforts. However, it had been a difficult crop year and Hathren forces geared up for battle, assured of a victory in the time of hunger. Thus the king himself had decreed the help of those mages, for magic has always been accepted by the Kallisorian king when it has suited him—and if you are a Kallisorian reading this, do not be blinded by fealty; read the histories.

Randler laughed. "He has quite a sense of humor."

Dariak grinned. "That was an order. He wasn't joking."

Well, those nature mages worked with the earth and water mages and they did their best to bring food forth from the land. Now, there is some speculation as to why, but something went very wrong. Energies swept up in wild torrents and the land became plagued with a famine that lasted for a long year and a half. Hathrens took advantage of their weakened foe, but their spells went awry as well, and the warriors of Kallisor were able to stave off the enemy in yet another stalemate.

One theory among the lesser informed is that the Hathrens had infiltrated the Kallisorian ranks and boobytrapped the efforts to fertilize the land. This is nonsense, and originates from the minds of small thinkers who cannot see beyond their own hatred. I am not saying that such tactics have never been employed, but it is foolish to think the Kallisorian king, who protests the use of magic, would have allowed any strange mage to work magic in his land. He would, of course, have used the mages he keeps on staff for such emergencies. The likelihood of infiltration there is minimal, for it would be a lifetime commitment for a rather small chance of retaliation. Again, that is not unheard of, but improbable, and when compared against my findings it becomes irrelevant, too.

Randler let out a low whistle. "Famine happens. It's crazy to think it had anything to do with magic."

"I think initially it was a natural famine, but then it was made worse by the magic. But he isn't finished yet."

Randler rubbed his chin and turned back to the entry.

Another theory suggests that the reason for the banning of magic in Kallisor stems from the errant energies of such events. This is more plausible but it does not account for the king's willingness to allow those mages to perform their tasks. In any regard, it is only when one cross-references other major happenings that the truth emerges. Bear with me.

After the unexplained famine in Kallisor, there was a severe drought in Hathreneir. In an effort to keep the populace from dying of dehydration—or, in some unwelcomed and 'traitorous' plea of asking Kallisorians for help—the mages banded together and drew water from every source they could reach their magics into. This pulled water from plants, grass, animals, the humid air, and so on. No source of water was safe from the efforts of the mages. The magnitude of their work had a drastically negative effect upon the land. The once-fertile fields of Hathreneir died. It started around the castle where the topology changed. The dirt and grass became dead things and over time their decay withered them down to sand. In truth, it is more complicated than that, but understanding the basics is enough for now. The point is that Hathreneir was weakened and Kallisor attacked. Lo and behold, the attack was repelled, and not because of greater power, but because the climate was changing and the Kallisorians were ill-prepared for it and they could not endure the changes.

"That's... amazing," Randler said. "I've listened to the major histories and that tale wasn't among them. The desert simply began to appear and no one had ever hinted at a reason why."

Dariak shrugged. "Surely, the Hathren mages wouldn't want it known that their skills had caused it. That would make magic seem even more dangerous than ever before, and maybe the ban in Kallisor would become even more absolute."

"And worse," Randler surmised, "magic could have been curtailed here too if the people knew of it and panicked." He considered for a moment. "But the Hathren king would have known about it, wouldn't he? How else would that information eventually get to Delminor? The truth would have to be out there."

"Yeah, so?"

"Well, wouldn't the king have tried to ban the magic himself then? I mean, the mages had turned his castle lands to a barren landscape. Even if you love the mages, I would think some restrictions would be put in place to prevent such a thing from happening again."

"That's a good point," Dariak conceded. "But read on and that may explain why."

So here is where the connections come to be: in neither case, from famine to drought, could a team of mages actually draw enough magical power to effect such major alterations to the land. It is an impossible feat. Even a set of a hundred spellcasters working in unison could not draw the power necessary to change the climate of a section of land. If you believe it is possible, then you must not understand the scope of magic or the interconnectedness of the various forms of energy in our world. You may, then, wish to confer with other texts better suited to your level of knowledge and return here when you can properly understand.

Dariak interrupted. "He's actually not being condescending there."

"I can't imagine how not."

With a shrug, Dariak replied, "I guess I just knew him and he was really trying to say that it was impossible to grasp the idea without knowing the rest first."

"Like trying to build a house from the top down."

"Exactly."

There were other catalysts in those events. I draw your attention to them now, because I have come to realize that the shards of the Red Jade have a deeper connection to our world than anyone has yet guessed. What mage would have the gumption to believe he can reseed a famished land? Only one with the support of the nature jade, and perhaps the earth jade. But something went wrong when he tried to tap into the powers. I believe he had used quite a good measure of the nature jade's ability and the jade needed replenishment before it could continue to serve. However, the jades are seemingly indestructible and infinitely powered. Where else would such an object refill its lost energy but to draw it from the earth itself? You see, I believe the dire famine in Kallisor was a result of the nature jade withdrawing its support from the land, rather than offering its skills. Why would that happen? I could discuss it at length—and perhaps I shall in a future tome— but for now, suffice it to say that the nature jade took the energy it needed for some desperate reason.

The drought in Hathreneir is similar, and was most likely the cooperative efforts of the earth and water jades. It would stand to reason that the nature jade was still in Kallisor, possibly being examined and probed to try to release its hold over the famine, the effects of which lasted a good ten years or so, by some accounts. The mages in Hathreneir would have heard about the efforts of the nature mages and they would have—true to form— wanted to improve upon the attempt and thus succeed where others had failed. However, in using the two jades in unison, the mages created a similar depletion of the energies in their own land, and the effects were devastatingly worse. Even today, the desert continues to expand and grow. I wonder if I, or my colleagues, will find a means of ending the ever-stretching death and halt the sandy wasteland from reaching the entire borders of the land. So far, no one has succeeded.

"Unchecked, it will likely spread to Kallisor, too, won't it?"

"Yes," Dariak said. "And at some point, no amount of physical labor or magical spell will be able to sustain life here. It's been a difficult adjustment over the years as the desert has expanded. But if you notice, even with the sun overhead, it has never been blisteringly hot like you would expect from a real desert. Hot, for certain, but not deadly."

"You're saying that it's a magical sort of desert then? That some kind of spell is permeating through the land and altering it?"

"My father said it, yes, in that 'other tome' he referenced."

"Then..." Randler stopped and then looked up at Dariak. "Wait, Dariak, is that why he was gathering the jades?"

"He had many reasons, but yes, that is one of them. He wanted to understand why the jades were draining the land and perhaps bringing them together would be the key. That's another discussion, though. There's more here for now."

Randler set his questions aside and continued reading.

Perhaps you disagree with my assessment that the jades are responsible for the avid destruction. You are welcome to disagree, but then go find proof to the contrary. Until then, I will maintain my assertions, for I have amassed information regarding countless events throughout the history of our lands where wild moments altered the very fabric of our reality. One further case in point, the feral creatures. Old tales never speak of them, unless they have been translated by some foolish bard seeking to craft wild tales without a thread of truth. I'm all for embellishment, but it ought to remain within the realm of reality. I digress.

The old stories speak of eagles and dogs and wolves and snakes. We have them too, but they are non-threatening when compared to their feral counterparts. Not to say a snake bite couldn't kill, mind you. However, the mere cry of a tigroar can deafen a man. Lupinoes have the cunning of the greatest philosophers and hunters. Eaglons have poisonous talons that kill upon contact. These are not natural creatures and they did not exist if you look back into the histories. No, they all came about around the same generation and I would bet my laboratory that some mages were experimenting with a shard of jade and they knew nothing about it. Today, we know there is a beast jade, and I am certain that those mages caused the shard to alter the very nature of some of our creatures. Now they are an added threat to our safety and they, too, help to maintain the stalemate between Kallisor and Hathreneir.

I would continue here, but it would take me from the point I am striving for. The jades are inherently connected to our land. We must proceed carefully when exploring their abilities, for the results can be catastrophic. I would like the opportunity to work with other pieces than the ones I currently have. I think it may be time to step from my books for a while and seek out these historical treasures—or terrors, I'm not sure. But to anyone reading this, the message is clear; do not use the jades rashly, for the consequences will be dire and long-lasting. Educate yourself first and then explore with caution.

The volume ended there and Randler slowly closed the cover. "I almost want to focus on his interpretations of the histories rather than read the histories myself."

Dariak beamed with the compliment. "The funny thing is, my father would snap at you for that, saying he isn't infallible and that you can't even trust his work. He always wanted people to think for themselves. But from my point of view, thanks. That means a lot."

C H A P T E R 22

To Protect the Child

SLEEPING IN THE Undying Stone was challenging for Gabrion, and not for lack of comfort. His room was furnished with soft, padded bedding, luxurious pillows and any number of blankets of various style. He could choose to sleep as if in a cloud or upon the cold stone floor, assuming he rolled the plush carpet aside.

His insomnia came, instead, from his concern over Perrios. The baby had endured the journey and had held his own, but he had barely eaten anything all day and he slept fitfully. Alosia repeatedly knocked on Gabrion's door when the baby cried, offering to help but not offering any suggestions. Gabrion was resolute that she would not touch him until she widened her narrow mind.

Their arrival to the keep was at a rather inopportune time for the earl, who was currently dealing with a number of local issues and bounced from one task to another. Earl Thedris introduced himself briefly, asked if they needed anything, but scooted away before he really listened. Instead, one of the pages took their requests and tended to their needs.

"I do apologize." Brannis bowed. "There was a bout of rain a few days ago that overflowed the lake up north and the water spilling all over the land was disastrous. The earl is striving to balance compensation to all of his substituents, while also appropriating supplies from one zone to another."

"We're here from the king himself," Gabrion said. "Surely that has some priority."

"Indeed it does, which is why you are here and not at the tavern. Listen, I do realize that this is a terrible inconvenience for you, but there is nothing I can do right now other than see to your needs."

Gabrion's eyes narrowed in suspicion. "It doesn't feel right."

"Nonetheless…"

"Fine then. I'll deal with you instead of the earl. I suppose it doesn't matter either way. I've brought young Perrios here to be with his grandparents. I would like to see them."

Brannis nodded and wrung his hands nervously. "They have a hamlet on the western edge of the lake and currently their home is flooded. It's why your request wasn't met when you arrived yesterday. The earl moved up their meeting to discuss their losses and needs so they would be able to meet with you later today without having that on their minds. I do hope that is satisfactory."

"Take me to their hamlet and I'll see them there."

"I can't." Brannis said. "Only work crews are permitted in that area at the moment."

"Then I will work. Give me tools and I will assist."

Brannis looked pointedly at the baby, who waggled around in his crib. "Should I summon Lady Alosia to tend to the child then?"

Frustration lit Gabrion's face a deep red. "You seem determined to thwart my efforts at every turn."

"I regret you see it that way. If you could just keep calm for a few hours, then I'll come for you when everyone is ready." With that, he bowed and left.

There wasn't anything else Gabrion could do without violating the restrictions that had been placed upon them as visitors. He was allowed to stroll the front sections of the fort, including the rock garden he had no interest in seeing, and that was roughly it. Instead, he took some time to limber up and work through a series of exercises to help hone and sharpen his muscles.

Complications with bartering delayed the meeting for two days. Gabrion seriously considered breaking the restrictions and seeking out Mira's parents now, but he remembered his purpose and forced himself to stay in control. Rampaging through the keep would jeopardize his stance as Perrios' protector and as the bringer of a new peace between the kingdoms. He realized belatedly that he was probably being tested for just that.

He spoke occasionally to Alosia, trying to sway her to his way of thinking, but he always regretted it. She seemed as immutable as the ubiquitous stone in which he dwelled.

To while away the hours, Gabrion talked to Perrios. It pained him to speak of the child's mother, but he felt he owed it to both of them, so he spoke of Mira as a child and of the great times they had had running through Savvron, playing together and with their friends. He also spoke of the times when Mira stayed with him as her parents ventured into Hathreneir to visit the her brother's grave.

He wondered now at the truth of Kyrell's death. He had been told that Kyrell and a few friends had snuck into Hathreneir on a dare and that Kyrell had been caught and slain. Now he wasn't so sure. Perhaps it was possible Kyrell was called away on assignment and was no longer allowed into Kallisor, and Mira hadn't been allowed to visit with her parents because she might have told someone of their true task.

Shivers ran down Gabrion's spine, for he hated considering that Mira and her family were spies for the Hathrens. The king had basically suggested such, and considering where Mira had found herself—namely, wed to the king—even Gabrion couldn't deny it.

He dwelled on the unfairness of it all. He had loved Mira with all his heart and had quite literally travelled across the lands just to find her. Now he tended to her son, and the child should have been his, not the enemy king's. Gabrion shook his head. He had to stop thinking of Prethos as the enemy if Dariak's quest was to succeed. Yet it was hard thinking that Mira's family had lived in Savvron all those years as spies for Hathreneir. He wondered when Mira had been told about their allegiance and how she had taken the news.

Mira had always been full of light, however, and even if she had shown signs of sorrow or conflict, Gabrion knew he wouldn't have even noticed. No, he was too intent on protecting her and making her laugh to ever consider that she was not on his side.

"But she had a wondrous laugh," Gabrion crooned to the young child. "The birds would sing along with her and the sun overcame any clouds in the sky. You have her magic within you, little Perrios, and I know you're a beacon of light for the future of us all. You'll be a way of bringing us together in ways no one else could. Because, you're like your mother and people will love you just for being who you are."

The swaddled baby wriggled around and made a few cooing noises as he listened to the tone of Gabrion's voice. "Yes, little one, soak in all the knowledge you can and don't be blinded by the people around you. Some will tell you that Kallisorians like me are evil. I'm not. Though," his voice quieted for a moment, "I've done some horrific things.

"But you'll be better than that. You'll rise up above us all and you'll be the one factor no one ever counted on. You'll live in a world where war is history and progress is the future. We don't have to fight each other to make progress in the world, regardless of what your father and king says. War is only one means to progress. But it isn't the only way."

He lifted the child from his crib and paced around his sunlit room, rambling on. "Mira and I used to talk about all the things that don't exist but should someday. They sound silly now, but what if? And I don't mean with magic and stuff, but with… I don't know what to call it. Take a wagon for example. It needs a beast of burden to pull it, but that taxes the poor creature and some task masters don't know when to let their beasts rest. What if there was a way for the wagon to move on its own?

"We tried to make one, you know, your mother and I. It was a small thing and we used water inside some little casks. No, we didn't fill them up all the way, just less than halfway actually. Mira sat on top of the plank and used a branch we found to steer it—well, that was the plan anyway. See, the cart only worked going downhill. I had to rock it back and forth to get the water moving in a rhythm, and then it took over and rolled away down the hill. The stick did little to help control where it was going, and Mira ended up falling off.

"Now don't be upset, she wasn't hurt much at all. We were kids, anyway, and at that age, sometimes getting hurt just makes a thing more interesting. We really felt like we were onto something. I'm a little older now, so I understand that the cart would have gone down the hill even without the water in the wheels, but that's not really the point, is it?"

He wiped Perrios' chin. "We just wanted to make something new, something that wasn't going to hurt anyone. It would help people, if it had worked. And that's why we have to stop the war. We can put our heads together and come up with ways of dealing with the feral creatures all across the land or figuring out better ways to grow crops, to make better houses, and so on.

"And if I'm going to go there, then I have to jump in with both feet, don't I? We have to give the mages some freedom. Let them use their skills to help us all. But I'm Kallisorian and that's a tough thing to accept. Of course, the truth is I've already benefited from the magic of others. I never would have escaped Kallisor without Dariak's protection spells, and wouldn't have recovered from Heria's tortures without healing magic."

He sat on the edge of his bed, cradling Perrios in his arms. "But magic can be bad, too, so we have to find a way of keeping things in balance. How do we let the mages use their powers without letting them take over the land? But I have to admit, little one, that the mages here in Hathreneir don't quite have the run of things, do they? I wonder why that is."

Gabrion's door creaked open and Alosia stepped inside, an odd look on her face. "You left it open," she gestured needlessly. "I was listening. You're an odd one, thinking all these things."

Rather than argue with her at her intrusion and for eavesdropping, he implored, "Tell me why the mages don't run things here, Alosia. They have the means, don't they? Why aren't they the leaders?"

She looked at him, confused. "I never asked."

He rolled his eyes. "You really just take the world as it's presented, don't you? You never think about anything other than where you're going to eat or sleep."

She nodded her chin toward Perrios. "That's not entirely true. But your speculations are ridiculous."

"I don't think so. The mages have the ability to do whatever they like with their minds and the energies in the world. In Kallisor, mages are often put to death for using their skills, so they hide and work their magic in secret. Yet here, they have places they can work freely and yet they haven't risen up against the king. You've never thought about why?"

"There has never been a reason to. I suppose you have an idea, though?"

"It could be a few things," Gabrion said. "There may be some force working against the mages that only they know about, or some secret agreement with the king. But I don't think that's it."

Alosia laughed. "Maybe they're just happy tucked away in their towers and keep to themselves."

"Well, yes, actually."

Alosia's face curled incredulously. "I was being facetious."

"Think about it, though. Most people stay where they are because they're happy to be there or they can't move for one reason or another. Feral creatures have habitats through the lands and they rarely venture outside of them because they have all they need, plus it's dangerous for them to venture out. Perhaps it's the same for the mages. Maybe they really are content to work with the energies and don't need to conquer everything in order to make a point."

"I can't listen to any more of this drivel."

"Why not? Is it bothering you? Does it make an eerie sort of sense?"

"No," she sneered. "I'm just looking to get out of here before you turn this 'revelation' into another lesson about how our kingdoms have to come together as one and stop fighting."

"Come on," he said sourly. "How could I even make such a claim after that?"

She didn't realize he had baited her. "By saying that if we remove the two power centers and let people get on with their daily lives, they would find a sort of inner happiness, like the mages and the monsters. Then they too could be chipper people and get through the day without the fighting on the horizon. They would focus on other things and have families and—" She heard what she was saying and then she coughed and glared at Gabrion. "I hate you." With that, she stormed out.

Gabrion bounced Perrios gently on his knee. "Maybe that was progress after all."

CHAPTER 23

The Castle in Disarray

NEARLY TWENTY DAYS had passed since Verna and Ruhk were left in the Hathren castle to mind the king and the new regime. In that time, a few groups of fighters had arrived from the east, sent by Kitalla and Carrus after whatever magic she worked to subdue them, and each of the meetings with the king had been the same. First there was distrust at the new order, then came outrage when they were assigned lodgings with mixed company of both kingdoms. A few fights broke out here and there, and after a brief adjustment period, usually a day or so, they were put to work.

King Prethos kept himself to the background when he could, but Verna and Ruhk made frequent demands of his time to show his support of the peace they tried to instill upon the people. Dutifully, he donned his ceremonial robes and spoke with authority, always sounding as if these changes had all been of his making. His sour attitude behind closed doors, however, belied his acceptance.

Verna kept a watchful eye on Ieran, who always seemed to be around at the mention of trouble among the people. He seemed almost eager to know which citizens would rise against the new regime and more than once she had spotted the chancellor seeking out such malcontents after their complaints had been lodged.

Verna had cozied up to one of the disgruntled peasants before he was taken under Ieran's wing, and so Verna knew who was involved in the unknown future uprising. She decided it was time to give Ieran something else to do that would keep him a bit more occupied.

The whining chancellor arrived at her call and he bowed his gray head low. "You needed me, Chancellor Verna?"

"Indeed, Ieran, I do. I'm afraid that the last two shipments of food are poisoned. We can't eat the food and we certainly can't serve it to His Majesty. I need you to gather a fresh batch of vegetables and meats before the day is out or it's going be a rather long night."

His face wilted. "Surely this is something your men can tend to?"

She looked honestly regretful. "No, it isn't. When Mzark arrived a few days ago, it was hard enough turning him around to the new way of things. Now that Lurrish of Kallisor is here with his men, it's even worse. I've got every man loyal to us on point, ready for brawls at any moment."

He rubbed his hands together absently. "So your little scheme isn't working then?"

"Oh, it is. The new troops are still working to clear the stone away from the front of the castle so we can rebuild it properly, and they're surely tired for all their effort. Yet silly men sometimes try to rise up against the truth anyway."

Ieran's lip twitched despite himself. "Then Ruhk?"

"His people are spread thin through the town, getting the people to work together. You know that. Sorry, Ieran, this task has to fall to you. Our numbers have increased, surely, but clearly I can count on someone like you to ensure the food coming in is safe for consumption."

"Eh," he hedged. "There isn't really any way I can... Well, you see, it's..." But he couldn't come up with a good excuse.

"It'll take you a few hours at most, unless you really have some difficulties. But we're all hungry at the end of the day, so it'd be best if you can return before then. Or," she added with a slight grin, "you're more than welcome to personally sample the poisoned foods to see which samples are safe for us to eat. I can even provide you with a bucket."

He snarled. "Very well, Verna. I will leave at once."

There was, of course, nothing wrong with the food, but she needed him out of the castle so she could rifle through his ledgers and seek the largest groups of malcontents. She had to stamp out the insurgents before they really did band together.

Unfortunately for her, Verna found herself summoned to the king moments later. The timing was too perfect to be a coincidence; she assumed Ieran had run to him after their meeting. Prethos thwarted her plans at ransacking Ieran's room, demanding updates about security in the castle and the safety of the town. He also required a sudden inspection of her new guards who would be responsible for fortifying the castle should they be attacked, and so though Verna had gotten rid of Ieran for the afternoon, she was unable to make use of the time.

Out in the town, Ruhk was exhausted and frustrated and he found it particularly difficult to keep himself in check. He was a full-blooded warrior at heart, as had been three generations of his family on all sides. Being diplomatic was vastly difficult, especially when people were argumentative for no reason at all.

Magic was still essentially dead near the castle and the mages had all been assigned tasks with shops to tend to inventory and such. Most of them were accepted willingly, but some shopkeepers tried to do without them.

"I won't have some outsider in my shop fingering all my things."

"I'm only here to assist and I have knowledge of your craft so I can help better than most."

"Knowledge of my craft, bah! You're just looking to make off with my things, swine."

"Once the null field lifts and I can ply my craft again, I would have no need of your things."

"Aye, you say that now, but what if the—whatever you called it—never lifts? Then you'll be needing all my things and you'll never leave."

"That's nonsense. If it doesn't lift then I'll move on to a place where it doesn't exist."

"Then go there now!"

Ruhk clapped his hands together loudly. "Are you two quite finished here?"

The mage shrugged. "I've only tried to do what I was assigned to do. Perhaps there is other work for me to tend to?"

"No," Ruhk said stiffly. After all the hours it had taken matching up the new residents with the old, he wasn't about to allow exceptions. That would only create more problems once word got out.

"It's my shop and you can't say who's able to work here."

"I can, actually, by decree of the king. We all make sacrifices in this time of crisis and you will accept this offered help without further complaint."

The portly man's face lit a deep red, his anger rising. "Get out of my shop, the lot of you!" He stamped his foot and raised his fists in warning.

"I wouldn't recommend that," Ruhk warned, but the man had lost himself in anger. He ran forward, pummeling Ruhk's chest furiously. The commander took a few careful steps away from the shop door and out into the bustling street. The shopkeeper pursued, blinded by the injustice of it all, his arms flailing about. Ruhk called several warnings for him to stop, but he didn't.

Ruhk took the brunt of the man's anger, hoping he would wear out quickly and submit, but instead, the continued hits empowered him to swing again and again. Bruised, but not hurt in any major way, Ruhk took most of the punishment, blocked a few hits aimed at his face or other less protected areas, and when he could see that the man was out of control, he grabbed the battering wrists and spun on the spot, bringing the man close with his arms behind his back. Ruhk then tugged hard on the arms with a slight twist, causing the shopkeeper to scream out in agony.

"Well, it seems to me you won't be able to use your arms until they heal, so it looks like you're going to need some help after all. Any questions?"

"You're a… bloody tyrant, you are."

Ruhk turned to the mage. "Your first order of business is to tend to his arms. Make him a pair of slings and then good luck."

Without word, the mage complied and though the shopkeeper tried to shrug away from the help, he simply couldn't.

The villagers nearby responded to Ruhk's behavior with mixed reactions. Some accepted that he had given the man every chance to back down and accept the new order of things, but others felt the tactics were barbaric. At least he was a full-blooded Hathren walking around the area, for if he had been Kallisorian, he might not have been able to carry himself back to the castle if all the shady looks were any indication.

As he made his way through the day, he kept turning his thoughts to Gabrion and how he must have felt in the outpost bringing together two warring factions under one roof. There hadn't even been any official decree of peace then; he had just insisted upon it and made it happen. And sure, a few people had died there, but it wasn't easy to change people who didn't want to be changed. He realized that would always be a problem, and this plan of uniting the kingdoms would need some real policing if it was going to last long enough to take effect.

Ruhk checked in with his team throughout the town and then headed back to the castle to reconvene with Verna. The two of them felt the heavy burden of keeping everything together, but in the end, it was better than having to do it all alone.

"Then his royal highness chewed my ear off on the uniforms," Verna griped over a salad. "I never even got close to Ieran's room."

"No matter." Ruhk sipped a glass of wine. "I think we have to focus on the people around us and make sure they see eye to eye with our goals and then hope they rise up to protect us if the time calls for it."

"Hope?" she echoed. "My life hasn't done well on hope."

"Maybe not, but I think we need to have a bit of it for this to work, don't you? Besides, we're not entirely alone in this. At some point, the others will return and that will make our jobs a lot easier."

Verna snorted in denial. "More likely, Kitalla will send half of Kallisor into the castle and we'll be up to our eyebrows in unhappy people."

"We already have that honor, Verna."

"Mzark brought a lot of anger all by himself," she said. "And hacking away at the stone has done little to calm him down. I think it's time we institute another of Kitalla's witticisms."

"Oh?"

She nodded with a grin, sipping her wine and then swirling it just to watch it spin. "Let's make him captain of the royal guard."

"You can't be serious!" Ruhk shook his head and then laughed. "Never mind. You're crazier than she is, after all. And you know what? I think you may even make it work."

Verna tipped her glass toward him. "Most of the guards here are loyal to us, so it should be hard for him to change them overnight. Maybe in a week's time, but he'll have others to train, I think. Besides, it's not like I'm handing them over to him and going on vacation."

"He'll be distrustful and he'll test you."

"And we will all make mistakes," she agreed. "But you know… Ervinor put his faith in me when he had no need to. There were plenty of others who could have captained the Wrens, and even after I made a mess of things, he kept me in that role and he challenged me to be better than I was."

"Mzark isn't on some quest for redemption, Verna," Ruhk said carefully. "He's going to put his energy into usurping us and trying to get us out of here."

She grinned. "Yep. And I doubt he'll be all quiet and stealthy as he goes about it."

"And that'll put Ieran on edge that he'll be found out—" Then he understood. "Oh! Ha! Verna, you're a genius."

She sipped her wine again. "Well, Ruhk, I thought you'd never notice."

CHAPTER 24

An Oversight

SHE KNEW IT was bound to happen. Still, she had hoped it would have been for something menial, like burning dinner or failing to strap her leggings on tight. Instead, it happened at a time where too many forces needed to be held in place and not falter. Yet, that's when it happened.

Kitalla misjudged the situation.

She and Carrus had visited almost a dozen encampments as they neared the border between the kingdoms. At each stop along the way, they battled for a time, thankfully battling some less than others, and then Kitalla issued new orders. The Hathren camps had the word of their king to adhere to and not all were as skeptical as Mzark had been. Others, though, had needed some serious convincing. Kitalla's troop always fought without killing, even when they took losses. She was adamant about this and her will forced them all to obey.

The Kallisorian camps were harder to convince, but her heritage, with Carrus' support, brought over similar submissions among the captains. Though they were reluctant to venture off to Castle Hathreneir, most complied with Kitalla's numerous urgings. One small battalion purely joined Kitalla's forces to see her actions up front, while another faction denied her orders and retreated to Kallisor.

With each confrontation, Kitalla shifted her troops around. She had come from the castle with sixty or so fighters, and though she continued to travel with a similar number, their faces had mostly changed. Each group sent to the castle was escorted by people Kitalla had empowered with the task. Her original five captains were all gone now, only Merrlis having fallen in battle. The rest had each led the defeated forces to the Hathren king for the next phase of peace. Each time, Kitalla had kept some of the new fighters to bolster her troop, sometimes Hathren, sometimes Kallisorian.

In each case, she also appointed a new captain for the Eagles, Sparrows, and so on. Their rule did not last for long because eventually they were asked to escort a group of their own to the king. Soon, Kitalla barely recognized anyone aside from Carrus. She had spread the loyalty too thin.

The morning erupted with arguments cresting over the sand, and Kitalla sprang awake to put out the verbal fire. Kallisorians and Hathrens were enraged over the preparation of breakfast. Kitalla swept in and stopped the nonsensical debate, giving a third recipe for them to follow. It didn't resolve the matter, but instead turned them all against her, though they held off their demonstration of their united anger until later.

Carrus was also up and heading off a sparring bout in the Nightingales. The friendly contest had turned nasty and clubs flailed through the air furiously, cracking bones and raising terrible welts. The burly warrior threw himself in the tussle and separated the combatants, noticing only then that they were all Hathrens from different battalions and, for whatever reason, had lost control. The Kallisorians in the group were taking bets on the sidelines and were furious with Carrus for interrupting.

From there the tensions spiraled out of control until all sixty fighters battled each other, and Kitalla and Carrus were pressed together in the center trying to regain control. There was entirely too much commotion for Kitalla to even try using her dance skill to calm the troubled fighters. Instead, she grabbed her daggers for defense and channeled one of Randler's best rhythms to guide her steps. The drum beat built slowly and she moved her arms in time with the music. She brought her arms out to the side and deflected an incoming sword throw, raising her leg up and clobbering another attacker. Finishing her spin, she lowered her leg and kicked up the other one, cracking a third fighter in the head and felling him.

One down, at least fifty-five more to go, she thought, wondering if along the way Carrus might also take a swipe at her just for fun. A spear came flying toward her and she dropped one dagger as she leaned aside and grabbed the wooden pole, wrenching the weapon away from its owner. She quickly reversed the direction of the strike and jabbed the man in the gut with the butt of the spear. Kitalla then hoisted the spear and shoved it into the sand, marking her location. She reclaimed her dagger and howled to draw all attention her way.

This rout felt personal and she needed to tend to it personally. Carrus was blocking with his shield and parrying with his war hammer, but Kitalla decided not to count on him. He had been a worthy companion so far, but her failure to recognize the gaps in her leadership with this group may have been due to her dalliances with him. Or not, she didn't know. But it didn't matter. She had to end this scuffle herself and if Carrus supported her, then all the better.

Four more challengers arose to Kitalla's call and they raced ahead, swords in front to impale her. Two of them maintained their charge as the other two swept their swords upward when they drew close. Kitalla pounced into the air to avoid the swords. She didn't expect the elevated strikes, but she was prepared to meet them anyway. Her arms swept down and out and she deflected the attacks easily, her legs bent up high, kicking her assailants' chests, stunning them. The two men knelt to the sand as the other two halted their charge and turned around. Carrus clobbered them both with the hilt of his hammer, then returned to his fight.

Kitalla sprang up and punched the other two swordsmen to unconsciousness. Instinctively, she dropped to the ground, just as a pair of arrows flew overhead. She looked to her right and saw a team of archers readying their bows for another try. Clearly, everyone was fighting for themselves, clinging in small groups of the people they knew, for those arrows could have struck anyone. Annoyed, Kitalla spun about and let her daggers fly. One archer took a hit to the shoulder, while another tried to deflect the attack with her bow, but she missed and the knife caught her hand.

The third archer launched an arrow as Kitalla turned about and pulled more daggers from her boot. She wasn't fast enough to avoid the full attack, but the graze to her side was minimal. Two swordsmen entered the fray and she paused to deal with them, keeping an eye alert for another arrow.

These two fighters were better trained than most of the other scrappers she had traveled with. Her twists and kicks were met with brutal counterattacks and her arms shuddered with their intensity. Agility was her greatest ally as she faced them, for they worked well together, filling in the gaps in each attack and defending against her strikes. Kitalla was hard-pressed to maintain her footing, for if she fell, she didn't know if the sand would provide a solid enough surface for her to spring away.

One sword swept downward and smacked into the sand beside her, causing her to step over it, but it put her in line with the other sword, which came in low. She turned and held her daggers out before her, catching the incoming sword with a jarring crash. Her arms folded in sharply against her chest and numbed from the impact. She couldn't hesitate, though, for already the sand behind her shifted as the first sword was drawn again. Kitalla pushed her feet hard against the ground and she tucked her head into her chest, entering a forward flip. The sword against her chest was wrenched away, cutting into her leather tunic and drawing blood. And as her feet were in the air for that one moment, an arrow pierced her left foot. She landed heavily on it and screamed.

She knew there was no time to tend to the foot, but she couldn't do anything with the arrow in it. Collapsing to the ground for a mere three seconds, Kitalla wrenched the arrow out and blindly threw it toward the nearest swordsman, catching him off-guard long enough to delay his fatal strike. Kitalla rolled aside and hopped up on her right foot, unable to see through the tears in her eyes.

Seeing her weakened state, the two swordsmen rushed in, and they were not the only ones. Kitalla ignored the new threats coming closer and focused her energy on finishing off the experienced swordsmen. She bent her knee and pounced for the nearest blur of movement, sweeping her arms in front of her to push away a possible sword. Her body crashed into his and toppled him to the ground. She scrabbled for his face with one hand and then swept in the hilt of her dagger with the other, knocking him out. She then quickly rolled over, assuming correctly that the next soldier was on the move. Kitalla hit the sand as the fighter's sword struck the downed swordsman, cutting through his chestplate and killing him.

Kitalla wiped her eyes quickly and blinked against the pain in her foot. The swordsman withdrew his grisly blade from the corpse and hacked at Kitalla. Reflexively, she lifted her foot to block him but she misjudged the distance and the sword bit into her toes. She screamed again, reaching blindly for the dead fighter's fallen sword. With a mighty yowl, she swung the weapon about, and it cut into her assailant's chest, batting him lifelessly aside, blood splattering her like warm rain.

Pain and rage overwhelmed her and she automatically stood even though she just wanted to lie there. She snatched two swords from the fallen fighters, setting her daggers aside, and a fire burned in her eyes that only fools would ignore. Sadly for them, she was surrounded by fools.

The swords became whirling death as she stalked one aggressor after the next, cutting them down without a care. She limped fiercely and that drew attention, but she deflected attacks with one arm and struck for blood with the other. Soon the area was littered with dead or severely wounded fighters. She could barely even see for she was splattered in the blood of her foes and the tears that ran unchecked down her face.

She heard her name echo in the distance and she turned about, cutting an arrow out of the sky. She didn't hesitate; with a series of painful hops, she hurried over to the frantic archer as he fired off four more arrows, all badly aimed or deflected. Her name sounded again as she brought the swords down to lop off the man's head, and the power in the tone distracted her long enough for the archer to pull away and drop his weapon.

Kitalla felt her body thrown face-down to the ground. She flailed about, batting away her attacker, but she hurt too much to win this match. Her swords were ripped from her hands and tossed out of reach and then powerful legs came up and pressed into her back, making it hard to breathe. All she could tell was that no effort was made to kill her, and when she couldn't struggle any more, she went limp.

Carrus held her there for a few extra minutes until he was sure she was calm. Fearing retaliation, he leaped off her and sprang away rather than let her up slowly. The move saved him a severe beating, for Kitalla came up fighting. She threw sand in the air and whirled her feet around to knock down her attacker, but he was safely out of range.

"It's over now, Kitalla," he said when he thought she would listen. "Kitalla. You need… help."

"Leave me alone!" she raged, clutching her injured foot. "I can do this, don't you understand? If I can only make them *listen* to me. And if they won't listen, then I will *make* them listen. How many are left? We can *do* this Carrus. I'm not letting anyone take anything else from me, do you hear? They *will* listen!"

"Shh," he crooned.

"I will *not!*" she screamed. "All my life I've had everything taken from me and I will not let this task be one of those things. I will secure this peace even if it only lasts a short while. Even if it means I die in the process. Say what you will, Carrus, but I will not give up this quest, even if you think I'm crazy for it. I don't care! It wasn't my quest at first. I just went along to get stronger so I could defeat anyone who came my way. But somewhere, somehow, I found that I *need* this peace. I need to feel calmness and serenity.

"I know I botched this assignment up but it was working up until today. It *is* possible, Carrus, I'm telling you. If we just keep trying harder then we will make it." She rocked back and forth, not realizing how hard she was clutching her foot. "Nothing is going to stop me. Not soldiers, not stupidity, not some silly king, and certainly not you. So don't try to tell me to cool off and go home. Don't tell me I can't do this. Just leave me alone if that's what you think."

He waited for her to catch her breath between sobs. He tried to speak but she started her tirade over and over until he reached in and clamped her mouth shut with his hand, taking the half-hearted beating she gave him with her fists. "Hush now," he said. "I said you need help, and I meant bandages for your wounds. Nothing more than that."

It took her time to digest what he said and then she felt foolish for her outburst. He didn't seem to care, though. He just waited until she was ready for him to start dressing her wounds, stoic and quiet. The survivors of the onslaught, and there were not many, tended their own wounds and so Carrus and Kitalla had plenty of time to take care of the damage.

As Carrus peeled the torn and bloody boot from Kitalla's leg, she wailed in agony. In the course of the battle, some of the leather had fused to her wound and Carrus had to use one of her daggers to cut the rest of it away. The arrow wound through her foot was terrible enough, but the swordsman's last attack had cut deeply.

"Kitalla," he said hesitantly. "You've lost two toes."

She didn't seem to hear him, she was writhing so much. Carrus looked around quickly, but of the three mages they had acquired during the trek, all were dead. She needed more healing than he could offer with herbs and rags. They would have to head back to the castle immediately and hope that magic was effective there again. He knew Kitalla would be angry either way and it was possible that bringing her back that way wouldn't get her to the help she needed, but he also knew that the damage was too great to risk losing her foot. Ervinor had survived without an arm, but Carrus doubted Kitalla would do well without a foot.

He summoned the other survivors to his side and explained the situation brusquely. "Gather your things; we're bringing her back to the castle now. If you can't comply, run off somewhere else. We move out in three minutes."

And so they did.

C H A P T E R 25

The Impact of Magic

URRITH RUBBED HIS eyes and looked around the dark stone chamber, wondering why he was still kept against his will in this dismal place. He had spoken to several mages about trying to leave the Underground, but he apparently hadn't demonstrated his loyalty well enough. Someone clearly suspected he was aligned with Ordren, who had been hunting for Urrith over the past few weeks.

"They're trying to kill me, not rescue me," he insisted every time he was questioned. "What can I do to prove it to you?" But no one had answered him.

There were no physical pathways out of the area; each mage had to open his or her own portal out of the Underground, and those without the inherent skill to do so relied on an elder mage to grant passage. He understood the need for such precautions, but it didn't help that he couldn't leave and return to Gabrion with an update on Ordren's allegiance.

And so, with nothing else to do with his time, Urrith submerged himself in mage culture the best he could. He had no affinity for using magic and couldn't even feel the pull of energies around him, which the other mages described as a constant tingling sensation at the recesses of their senses. The constant yammering of spells still made him uneasy, but not as much as the endless parade of fireballs and lightning blasts summoned all around him.

He hadn't seen Janning in days, and he wondered if the old mage had been reprimanded for bringing Urrith here in the first place. The other elders hadn't seemed entirely pleased with his arrival, but they could have just as easily brought him back to the surface and left him for dead. Perhaps they had been afraid that he could inform Ordren of the location of this part of the Underground. Still, without a mage to open a path, there was little a regular man could do.

And, Urrith noted, the king already had communications with the mages, so Ordren hardly needed to infiltrate their home anyway. Or maybe the king only knew of one place to consult with mages and wanted instead to control the entire area. He didn't particularly care; he just wanted to be released.

For a while now, Urrith had allowed other mages to work spells in his presence so he could learn more about magic and so they would start to trust him more as they came to know him better. He talked with them when he could, but they always seemed more focused on working their spells than actually getting to know him.

The thought reminded him why he was lying there in the large stone chamber, far from the bed they had offered him. He had agreed to allow a team of mages to construct a virtual mattress for him composed mostly of air and dust. It didn't seem very safe to him to float in the air for any reason, yet the mages were thrilled when he accepted their request.

"We... can't have another mage lie in the cloud because... he would tug on the energies out of habit. We've tried. So we need someone like you who's blind to magic."

It had made a certain sort of sense to him at the time, though once the casting had begun he understood better. The air mages had little control over what happened and creating a pocket of air strong enough to support a man was a difficult feat and, even with six mages casting in unison, they hadn't been able to support him; he had crashed with a thud. Earth and healing mages had stepped in quickly, leaving him on a contoured stone bed with none of the pounding pain he would have felt from the impact. Regardless, he rubbed his head in memory.

"You're awake," one of the air mages said, his tone nervous. "Erm, about the experiment..."

He waved his hand. "Never mind that. If you don't keep trying new things then you'll never get stronger."

"We think we need more mages to empower the spell. Air is hard enough to control as it is and using it to buttress a body takes a whole lot of effort. Much more than a plate or a pot of water."

He was afraid to ask but did so anyway. "Will the rest of you be trying again later today then?"

"Nah," Jatta answered. "They have other things to do and I need to iron out a few other aspects of the spell first."

"Like what?"

"You wouldn't understand."

Urrith wasn't insulted by the comment, for it was likely true. "Try me."

Jatta spent the better part of an hour breaking down components of the levitation spell in the simplest form he could, laying down various spell components as he did so to help Urrith keep track. "This calls the air, and this helps us maintain it for a time. The hard part is making air blow while also containing it."

"Can you have it blow in a circle?"

"Thought of that. The first time we tried it, the potato sack spun all around and launched spuds in every direction." He chuckled at the memory and then sobered. "No, to lift a person up, we have to make the air flow upward with enough force to lift and support but not enough to make the person fly away, or suffocate. Not yet at least," he added almost in a whisper as if that was a secret.

"So your goal isn't to make comfortable bedding, then?"

The color drained from Jatta's face and he cleared his throat a few times before pointing back at the items. "The snail shell here catches the energy in a spiral and in a sense slows the spell down..."

They continued talking for a while and Jatta barely heard any of the comments or questions that Urrith made along the way. Like most of the mages he had encountered so far, Jatta was self-absorbed and secretive. He surmised that Jatta's goal was to eventually develop a spell that would allow an air mage to fly with a good amount of control over his flight path. As of now, objects could be propelled somewhat haphazardly and some minor control over the flight path was possible. Cushioning a landing posed a challenge, and that was with a team of mages working together.

"Keep at it," Urrith said some time later. "All new things take time, and this seems pretty complex, but I'm sure you'll get there. Want to grab some food?"

Jatta passed on a meal as he sat with his spell components and shifted back into trying to find a better way to balance and control the energies.

Happy to be relieved of duty, Urrith wandered off and tried to find some food, which in itself could be a challenge for there were no set dining hours here. Instead, he had to find a handful of mages willing to ply their craft to making a meal, as on his first day. Once, he had tried to visit the kitchen and prepare himself a snack but was quickly ousted from the storage area and sent on his way. Opting not to risk angering another group, he searched for two hours before he could find enough hungry mages who wanted to cook something.

Sated, Urrith returned to his room for a nap. However, Janning was waiting for him. "You have been summoned."

Resignedly, the youth bobbed his head and followed the old man through a series of random corridors until they emerged in a place Urrith did not suspect. They were outside. He blinked against the late afternoon sunlight and looked to his guide for answers, but the old man had deposited him and then returned to his crevice in the stone wall.

Urrith glanced around, wondering in which part of Kallisor he had been dumped, but it didn't look familiar. He suspected he was further north than where he had entered the Mage Underground and that didn't bode well for him. He was unarmed, alone, and more feral creatures were known to traverse the northern lands where fewer settlements were around to keep the creatures at bay.

Though he was grateful to have been expelled from his entrapment, he did wish the mages could have at least given him a sword. With a shrug he stepped away from the rock and surveyed the area.

The fields were hilly and a faded green, with a chill wind skirting through the blades of grass. The sun beamed down, keeping the area bearable on the late winter day, though he could tell that nighttime would bring a terrible chill and his leather jerkin would hardly protect him. Shelter was his top priority, and with any luck he could fashion a weapon along the way, not only for defense but to capture food as well.

The horizon held few clues for him to identify his location. The castle wasn't close by, and based on the hilliness of the area, his first guess was accurate; he was further north. He didn't know any of the northern settlements except by stories some of the soldiers had shared at the outpost, but he couldn't remember any specifics.

Urrith opted to head further west and then north. If Ordren was patrolling the area at all, then it should help keep himself out of the search radius. Ultimately, Urrith wanted to head back toward Hathreneir to find Gabrion. He didn't want to return home or go to any place within Kallisor at the moment. His homeland felt foreign and unwelcoming. He also worried that Ordren and his crew would rise over any given hill and slay him, or perhaps the mages would change their minds about releasing him and draw him back within their fold.

He was fed and rested, so Urrith was able to maintain a light jog as he went, keeping his eyes and ears alert for anything out of the ordinary. The sun sank low and he continued heading somewhat toward it, hoping that anyone following him would have a harder time seeing him as he went. When his legs tired, he stopped and stretched, then continued at a walk, all the while grabbing a few stones and pocketing them. So far they were his only means of defense, but a well-thrown rock was a worthy weapon.

As the sun dipped lower and lower, the chill deepened and Urrith hastened his pace to keep himself warm. The hillside was void of trees and he had no means of making a fire. He wasn't sure how he was supposed to survive the night, much less make it back to Gabrion. He consoled himself, thinking of the tale he would tell one day and all of the embellishments that he could add to it, hoping he wouldn't jinx himself for thinking it could be worse.

A short time later, he heard the welcome trickling of a stream and quickened his steps to reach it before the sun was completely gone. The water was ice cold, yet refreshing after his lengthy trek. He scavenged the area for a few water herbs and munched on them for a modicum of sustenance. Because of the oncoming cold and his lack of shelter, he knew he needed to keep moving through the night. In the distance he could see a cluster of small fires and, from their numbers and proximity to each other, he realized they belonged to a town. It sparked a bit of hope in him, so he hopped up and continued his trek.

He was only seventeen and though he had some worries chasing after him he was able to set them aside and focus on the path ahead. Thoughts of pastries and hot cider made his stomach growl, though instead of begrudging the hunger, he kept reminding himself how great that first meal would taste, and perhaps he would be able to convince the bar patron to pass him a mead to warm him up, too.

Urrith's preoccupation with his journey kept him from noticing a distinct thundering in the area. If he had caught it, he would have examined the darkened sky and seen that there was no lightning to accompany the rumbling sounds. Oblivious to the danger, Urrith didn't bother trying to conceal himself until it was too late. He hoped it was a pack of lupinoes that would see him as unworthy of their time, but six horses crested the nearest hill, torches beaming from the two riders flanking Ordren.

"Cautious for so long and then you go and run a trail so obvious a child could follow it," the general reprimanded. "You didn't even try walking through the stream to cover your tracks. We held back, waiting for an ambush, but there was none. You really were just out for a careless stroll. How is it, then, that you eluded me for so long?"

It was all Urrith could do to hold himself together. He was cold and hungry, and he knew how this would end. He glanced around but there weren't even any trees he could hide behind. He considered flinging the stones he had been gathering, but he felt foolish for even thinking they would help. He was pitted against six of the king's greatest trackers. By the time he clobbered one man, the other five would be on him and there would be no guarantee he could hit a single one of them.

Ordren stared down at the teen with a malicious grin on his face. "I couldn't stop Gabrion's little show back at the outpost without risking my life. I was shocked it even worked at all. I thought that little murder scene would be the end of it, but he somehow kept it together even then. It hadn't even taken much to convince those men to mount the attack. Just a few whispered words in their ears when no one was paying much attention."

"It's people like you who ruin our chances at peace," Urrith spat.

Ordren laughed. "Ah, he has some fight in him yet! Be wary, fellows, he may make fools of us all before the night is through." The air filled with the mocking laughter of the king's men.

"It doesn't matter if you tear me down, Ordren. Gabrion's plan will succeed and you'll be ousted from yet another home. How many would that be for you? Four?"

"You're a fool to try to taunt me. Your death is in my hands. It can be quick and painful, or just painful." He jerked his head slightly and the five other men walked their horses around Urrith, surrounding him at last.

"It doesn't matter, Ordren. The more time you waste on me, the less time you have to try to stop Gabrion from his mission. And even if you strike me down, it won't do anything more than make me one more casualty to the senseless war. It won't even mean anything."

Ordren dismounted and pulled his sword from its sheath. "So your version of begging for a quick death is to say that your life is meaningless? Pathetic."

"That's not pathetic; it's the truth. My death won't change the world. You're after the wrong 'villain.' You fooled me, Ordren, when I trained under you. I thought you were a hero to be honored and adored. Yet when Gabrion entered that outpost, I saw the truth immediately. You're no hero. You never were. I don't even know why you bother fighting. You'll never be remembered in the histories. No bards will ever sing of your deeds. You'd only ever be a footnote: a fool who tried to stop the great peace that is due to come to this land. You might be a lesson to children growing up of how not to be. Of how great men are not made. Of how morons thrash around in the night killing anyone they can because it's the only thing they have any control over. Because they can't change the world around them any other way. You're the one who's meaningless." He wanted to continue because Ordren seemed enthralled by the tirade, but he ran out of things to say.

The general's face was set in a cold stone and he nodded his head once to his soldiers and they dismounted as one. "Brace him. Hold out his arm." To Urrith, he growled. "I will be the man whose story is told to remind children of their place. One limb at a time, little boy. Count them as I cut them off and while you scream your platitudes to the empty night." He stepped forward and grabbed Urrith's face. "Take a good look at me before you die and learn the truth about the world. Power wins."

Urrith tensed and squeezed his eyes shut as Ordren flexed his fingers and prepared his sword. One of the soldiers dug his fingers against Urrith's face, forcing his eyes open. Clearly, Ordren wanted him to know the exact moment of impact. The youth tried thrashing about but he was held fast. Indeed, the last thing he would see was Ordren, a vicious expression on his face, stepping one foot at a time, sword raising up, then crashing down.

And then there was an eruption of fiery agony. Urrith screamed at the top of his lungs, the pain racing through his body. It flashed so brightly in his eyes that the sky illuminated for just a moment and then went dark again. Massive heat remained at his left shoulder where Ordren's blade had struck. As horrible as it was, he had expected it to be even worse. His body collapsed and it surprised him that his captors had released him. Perhaps they didn't want his blood all over themselves.

The pain subsided quickly and Urrith raised his arms to wipe his face. And it took a moment for him to realize he still had two arms and all six of the king's men were flattened on the ground, the torches flickering wildly in the night.

Dumbfounded, he merely stood there, not knowing what had happened. He gaped at the fallen men, turning slowly and trying to get himself to move. He had to grab a horse and sprint away, but his body wouldn't comply. Perhaps, he thought for a moment, he was actually dead, gazing down at them and seeing it wrong.

Several yards away there was a sound and Urrith turned to face it. Three people hurried toward him. "Move it, you fool, get over here!" Confused, Urrith obeyed.

One of the people was Janning. Another was a healing mage, and the third was a nature mage, who had opened her conduit to the Underground from a nearby hill.

"What happened?" Urrith asked, stunned.

He was ushered inside and Janning answered brusquely. "All those spells you've been volunteering for haven't been at all what you've thought. We were weighing you down with protection spells and once we had the right combination, we sent you out to confront Ordren."

Urrith made sense of it quickly. "You sent me out as bait?"

Janning made no pretense. "Yes."

"What if they had killed me?"

"Then it would have meant our spells had failed."

"Comforting," Urrith said sourly, his body trembling from delayed terror.

Janning shrugged. "Well, take comfort in this, then. We no longer doubt your allegiance in relation to Ordren. We welcome you now openly."

It took all he had not to vomit.

CHAPTER 26

The Ends of Kings

DARIAK AND RANDLER could barely stand to look at another book. They had pored over countless volumes, and though they learned much, their eyes begged for something else to focus on.

Randler set his book aside and rubbed his temples. "I'm done for today. Your father is quite the crafter of words, but he does carry on sometimes."

Dariak gave a half-hearted laugh. "For a solitary man, he certainly did have a lot to say to others. He was great with giving advice to whomever he came across. It was often helpful, but still. He always had something to say."

"Dariak… How do you even know how he was? Weren't you only about two years old when he died?"

The mage nodded. "I have some odd flashes of him, even from then. But it was all from Mother. And these texts. More than anything, they taught me who he was. Don't you agree?"

Randler considered for a moment. "I certainly can't argue. These tomes have a personality all their own. It makes me sort of jealous, to be honest. Will my own works show my voice?"

Dariak placed a placating hand on the bard's shoulder. "Of course they will, and not just your songs and words, but also your music. Your soul lives in what you create."

Randler smiled for a moment and he tried to push away the trouble they'd had so he could enjoy the moment. But in his heart, he knew that was a setup for added disappointment. "So, where are we now?"

Dariak frowned. "Still a couple cases left to go, I'm afraid to say, but I'm winding down to the last few records he has about the jades. This," he said, hoisting up the green leather tome in his hands, "is one of the last recordings he made specific to the jades. Most of the others are spell-related, from what I could see."

Randler nodded. "Is there any reason you didn't start from the recent stuff?"

Dariak raised an eyebrow. "You know why as well as I do."

Indeed he did, for Delminor frequently referenced his older writings as he went on, and without that foundation, his later notes were impossible to follow without cross-referencing. "Right. He hated repeating himself."

"I do think this book will give me most of what I'm looking for about bringing the jades together as one. He's discussing the various powers and how they can be paired off in twos and threes. It's only a matter of time before he reaches the whole set."

"It's a shame you can't skip to the back to see if he gets there."

"Yeah, well, his most prized books have an added feature that you may not have come across with the histories."

"Oh? Did he encode them?"

"In a sense. Here."

Randler took the book and flipped open to the first page and at the bottom it said, "Progress onward to page 13." He ignored it and turned to page two, but the sentence he was reading didn't make sense. He then flipped to page thirteen and saw that the words had continued there after all. Two pages later he saw another note to skip ahead a dozen sheets and continue there.

"Incredible."

"Infuriating," Dariak corrected.

"That explains all the flipping you've been doing back there. I thought you were just having a hard time of things."

"The last six volumes or so were written this way, and it's been all I could do not to tear the books apart. Still, though, it was a good way to discourage some errant mage from stealing all his secrets easily. He even crafted a few spellbooks this way, so that if you didn't pay attention to the page order, you'd end up with unexpected results, or none at all."

Randler touched Dariak's hand tentatively. "He was a brilliant man, and you're definitely his son. You'll find the answers you're looking for."

Dariak considered the new estrangement between them and it took all of his resolve not to grab Randler's hand and hold it. He stared at the delicate strength in the bard's hand and slowly he turned his eyes away. "How are your histories?"

"Happily, I haven't learned a whole lot of new things, in terms of major events. It means the stories I've heard are actually true after all and I can continue sharing them." He stretched a knot out of his back and his shoulders cracked in the process. "One thing, though, that I did find interesting. He had two whole volumes where he spoke of a number of other royal lines, all of which have died out for one reason or another. The only line that continued was the Hathreneir-Kallisor line. After them, no other nobles really exist."

"Interesting," Dariak hummed.

Randler shot him a glance. "You mean 'boring' don't you? I think it's important. I can't quite figure out why, though. And Delminor spent some time recalling how they all died. I found it rather odd. Was he always so macabre?"

Dariak's brows furrowed. "No. How did they die?"

"He only followed the elder sons, noting that in many cases, the lines intermingled and so he had some overlaps. Anyway, one of them died in a huge fire; apparently the people revolted back then and they took torches to his home. Another one fell in battle, and your father focused on the type of sword that was used to kill the heir. He said it was a finely-honed iron blade, longer than a man's arm and unadorned except for the warm blood."

Dariak shook his head. "That doesn't sound like my father's work."

Randler shrugged. "I'm summarizing. I know where the book is if you doubt it, but it was his voice in the words. If you prefer, I could do my best to summon his dialect."

"No, thank you. Knowing you, you'd catch the cadence exactly and that would be unnerving. How did the other lines die out?"

"Some were unremarkable in their ways, though tragic. One line ended when the heir, a boy of six at the time, fell in a pond and drowned. Another had a reputation for climbing the northern mountains and while he was there a storm blew in and he was struck down by lightning. Apparently, he would climb alone at times and it took the kingdom a few weeks to find his remains. They hadn't been certain how he had died except for the odd scorch marks on his skin. They ruled out fire because he didn't look like he had been engulfed in flame, just blasted with it and dropped.

"At first, I wondered why they didn't suspect a mage of foul play, but Delminor tackled that as if he thought I was going to ask. The reports said he was protected against magic—but your father argued that spells were much too weak back then anyway—and that one blast would not have gotten through unless it was some other natural force."

"My father did like to be thorough when he wrote," Dariak said needlessly.

"I'll say. Hold on a second." Randler raised a finger and closed his eyes, bobbing his head for a moment until he recited:

Flying on a horse
Speeding like a bird
Couldn't take a breath
Couldn't speak a word.

"Sorry, one of the heirs died because he was born with weak lungs and he always had trouble breathing. He would have these fits where he couldn't take in any air and he would gasp and gasp until he could calm himself down. Well, his advisors stepped in and smothered him, preventing him from going out and being active. They wanted to ensure he had an heir of his own first, but he rebelled and he escaped one afternoon on horseback. In the excitement, he had one of his breathing attacks and he suffocated from it."

"That's awful." Dariak's lip then twitched into an odd grin. "Was that verse in the book or are you crafting a song about these heirs?"

"The latter," he admitted. "It's an interesting collection of stories that are all uniquely linked together. Delminor singled them out because they were royalty, but when I was reading through it, I felt like the stories were more important than just that."

Dariak agreed. "There must be a reason he focused on them for two volumes. What else was there?"

"A rockslide," Randler answered succinctly. "Another climber had a bad accident there. Someone else, younger, was mired in quicksand and wasn't able to free himself. There was also a king that liked to hunt, but he was eviscerated by his prey. Delminor was unfortunately descriptive there." He shuddered involuntarily. The bard pursed his lips, thinking of the other stories that were mentioned in Delminor's books. "There was one that seemed very unlikely to me."

"Oh?"

"One young boy was terrified of the dark. He had to have torches lit at all times otherwise he would panic, even if the moon was bright that night. The healers said they couldn't calm him down with any kind of remedy. They just needed to keep a light on. As the years went by, he dealt with the fear more and more, but he was still frightened by it. One day, he was on the road with an escort and they were ambushed by bandits. The kid was taken captive and held prisoner. Apparently, they kept him locked away in a dark cell underground with no light at all. He inexplicably died, and Delminor insisted he died of fright."

"Being in a cell is certainly scary enough without an added fear compounding it."

"True, but being so afraid that your body just… dies?"

Dariak shrugged. "Think about some of the scuffles we've been in. The heart beats fast and you run out of breath. Maybe he worked himself up into a real frenzy and his body couldn't cope."

"That's about what your father said."

"I guess he and I think alike sometimes. What else?"

"Well, the last two stories were very dramatic and I had no idea what was going to happen while I read them. It's been a while since another person's tale caught me by such surprise. In the first, the prince was minding his own business, getting to know the ropes of leadership, sparring in the yard with the knights to keep in shape, heading out on hunts for sport, and so on. He was extremely outgoing and active and got himself into dozens of predicaments, but always escaped them in the end.

"He heard word that a bandit raid had ended with the kidnapping of some village girl and he was so outraged that he went and battled the brigands and brought her back. There was a celebration in the castle for his bravery, but the bandits were furious. They launched an assault on the palace and threw flasks of oil through the feast hall windows, followed by lit torches. The entire place lit ablaze and everyone scampered for safety.

"The prince helped to usher everyone from the hall and saw that even with the help of the guards, his father hadn't yet left. Perhaps it was some noble stance, that the king wouldn't leave until his people were safe, but he remained behind. The prince ran to him then and they fled together. But before they made it out, the ceiling collapsed and killed the king. The planks cracked the prince on the head and he was trapped in the fire."

Dariak let out a low whistle. "Terrible way to go."

"But he didn't die!" Randler announced. "That's just it; he was nearly dead a hundred times it seemed. No, he lived through the ordeal with massive burns all over his skin. At the time, the mages couldn't heal, so he was tended by traditional herbalists. They created this brew to help fortify his body as he healed, while they treated his burns with aloe and some other salves. His luck ran out then, though, for someone had miscategorized the herbs, and when they made a whole batch of his healing drink, they added aloe to the mix. He started having all of these stomach pains and digestive issues and he eventually died from it."

Dariak cringed. "I spoke too soon. *That* was a terrible was to die."

"It wasn't uncommon for herbalists to get a mixture wrong," Randler explained. "Still, though, they were slow on fixing the concoction."

"Which could have been intentional," Dariak noted.

"True."

"And the last one? How did he die?"

"It was another wild tale, actually, where the king was utterly hated by the people and they rose up against him and rampaged all over the place. Delminor went into such detail, mostly describing the ways the king could have died but didn't. A sword thrust missed its mark, a lupino was killed by a stray arrow before it could sink its teeth into his neck, even fireballs from the mages swerved away by some air pockets that just seemed to keep him safe."

"Another lucky soul," Dariak said oddly, his mind elsewhere. "He didn't... get strangled by a vine or knocked down by a tree, by any chance?"

Randler gave him an incredulous look. "Well, yes, actually. In a sense anyway. The people won the revolt and they captured the king and set him to hang. They tied him to the tallest tree near the castle and when they went to release the stool he was standing on, the branch broke from the tree and smashed his head in." He stared at Dariak for a moment. "You heard that before?"

"No. It had to be something of nature."

"It did? I don't follow."

"Trace it back. One died by fire, another drowned in water, another because he couldn't get air."

"The iron sword—metal. The hunter from a beast attack. The quicksand."

Dariak nodded. "Lightning on top of the mountain. That wild fear of the dark. Even the aloe; a healing force that was never meant to be taken internally, and it was probably compounded with a handful of other herbs with other side effects that they didn't know of back then."

"The landslide," Randler finished. "Yes, so that was the death by earth."

"Were there any other stories?"

The bard shook his head. "No, but Delminor commented at the end about an unfortunate death that would likely occur to the descendent of Kallisor and Hathreneir, and he wondered in what form it would take."

"Did he... speculate?"

"No. Why?"

"Something you mentioned with the one who died by the aloe. You said that the mages couldn't use healing magic then. It didn't come about until after that death."

Randler's eyes popped open wide. "You think their deaths opened up new channels for magic based on how they died?"

Dariak shrugged. "Possibly. And those deaths could have been the moments when those jades came into being; no one quite knows when. Or how. It seems too convenient for there not to be a connection, else why would my father have only documented those deaths? There were plenty of other royal children in the mix. It's possible for it to be a..."—he fished for a word—"'gift' passed along to the firstborn male. It would take some extra digging to discover if all those heirs were the first male."

Randler's voice lowered to almost a whisper. "What if there is one heir left?"

"There's no way of knowing."

But the bard believed otherwise. "I've been following the tale for too long to ignore it now, Dariak. I know most people believe it to be a farce, but there is something in there."

"You mean the Forgotten Tribe. The lost true line of Lady Hathreneir and King Kallisor."

Randler nodded vigorously. "The firstborn son ran off and vanished into obscurity. Yet I know there are lineages that trace those ancestries back. Didn't Kitalla say Magehaven had something along those lines?"

"So does the library at Castle Hathreneir," Dariak agreed. "How are we supposed to find some unknown potential heir from a line centuries old? Even if the line is traced in the lineage to current day, what are we supposed to do upon finding that person? Kill him to end the line? And then what?"

"I have no idea. But maybe…"

Dariak raised an eyebrow in question.

"Well, if all the other jades came about at the end of a royal line and we only have one royal line left—"

"The two kings would argue that point," Dariak cut in.

Randler waved it off. "Their lines are not from the firstborn son of Hathreneir or Kallisor. But Dariak… think about it… What if the reason the land is always in turmoil and we're always at war is because there is some other magical force in the world that's trapped and can't get free? What if freeing that energy bursts like a blister and lets all the pressure out? What if that's the missing piece, Dariak?"

"It's a crazy notion."

"That doesn't mean it isn't a possibility."

Dariak sat back in his seat as he considered Randler's words. "So you're suggesting now that we hunt down this last heir and slay him to see if that creates a new magic force in the world and stops the war?"

Randler frowned. "It does sound insane when you phrase it that way. But essentially, yes."

Dariak rubbed his eyes. "I don't know. I'm a little confused to hear you even wanting to discover a new branch of magic. Wasn't it you who wanted all magic to end?"

"Dariak…"

The mage waved his hand dismissively. "I need to read a little more about my father's attempts to fuse the jades together. I can't imagine that the answer lies in murder."

Randler swallowed hard. "I don't mean to sound callous. It's just one stray thought, you realize. It's also possible that it's far from the mark, and we just have to find the proper way to unite the jades to release their energy back into the world. Maybe that's the reason for the mess here; they might be trapped against their will."

The mage's head sank low and he sighed. "I think that's what my father was leading up to. Unite the jades to release their powers back unto the land. He talks a lot about the imbalance of power here and there and that storing up energy in one place for too long invariably leads to destruction. And then, he tried to use his own life to unleash that power and send it back to the world around him. But it didn't work, did it? His life just… ended, and the shards of jade were dropped back to the ground."

"Dariak…"

"I'm not saying he died in vain. Not necessarily. But if releasing the energy of the jades isn't the key, then maybe… murder is."

"Dariak!"

The mage rubbed his eyes again. "I'm being crass, calling it that. But if we strip away the rest, isn't that what we're saying?"

"It's speculation, regardless."

"The irony is delicious, like the War of the Colossus, where the kings wanted to end the wars by staging a huge battle. And here we're talking about ushering in peace by killing a man."

Randler frowned. "It's… It's not the same thing."

"How isn't it?"

But Randler couldn't think of anything.

CHAPTER 27

Magical Malcontent

LICA STORMED THROUGH Magehaven in a fury. Her wounds from the annelidium had been treated and she felt fine, but the mages refused to let her go. The Council of Mages denied her demands for an audience and it was all she could do not to lash out at the acolytes.

The first floor of the tower was locked against her entrance. She had tried over the course of four days to break through the doors, but she was unsuccessful. Her earthen spells had no effect on the wood, indicating that larger forces kept the structure in place. She couldn't properly sense the energies in the wood to try to tear them apart, for the entire tower was rampant with mages casting spells and she was unaccustomed to the influx of all that feedback.

She thought her previous stay had been stressful; however, she likened this visit to imprisonment without even knowing her crime or sentence. The massive fonts of energies on every floor irked her in ways they hadn't before. She wondered what was wrong with her now.

"Stop casting those rock pellets and get over here," she demanded of a young acolyte who struggled with his magic. He looked at her in confusion, but the irate expression on her face warned him not to disobey. He trundled over and asked what she wanted. "I *want* to speak with someone on the Council, Rothra in particular."

"There's nothing I can do about that, matron."

"Don't you 'matron' me, you fool!" Lica scolded. "I know you can't help with what I want, so I thought I would help you instead, if you can handle advice from one such as me."

"But the masters said I was to learn it on my own."

"Ha!" she barked. "I would bet they were trying to be rid of you for as long as possible so they could go back to their tea!"

"W—Why are you shouting, Miss Lica?"

"Miss?" She laughed. "Poor thing, that's been a long time since I've been a miss. 'Lica' will suffice, Gennry. Now, tell me about that rock spell you're working on."

Sheepishly, Gennry set a small line of stones in front of him. He told Lica the words of power and the pebbles all shuddered and then flicked out randomly, pelting ahead without control. "I want to be able to shoot them like from a slingshot."

1047

"So use a slingshot," she said dourly, then sighed. "Your hands are all wrong. See, look, by crimping your forefinger, you're blocking the energy from the stones. Keep them straight while you work the energy into the rocks. After that, then bend them to keep the energy within you. When you're ready to send them flying, then flick those fingers."

"That's all I'm doing wrong?"

She gave a motherly smile. "No, dear, but you're only launching those pebbles an arm's length away, and that's not very useful, is it? At that distance, you'd be better off learning to coat your hands in stones and punching your foe. Come now, try again, and once you've got the distance you're looking for, you can work on other aspects of the spell to build control over how you're aiming, which pebbles you're flinging first, and then you can learn to fling larger objects."

"That's... wow, thank you!" He beamed as he scooped up his stones and scampered away.

Lica looked up at the ceiling and lamented, "There, I did someone a favor, now where's mine in return?"

The training floors were closest to the main entrance to the tower but the constantly misfired spells were tiresome to deflect and the buzzing of energy was downright irritating, which explained why most of the acolytes on the floor trained alone. Only a few elder mages spent any time there, and usually only if they wanted a seat on the Council, to prove their skill above others.

In some ways, Lica wanted to grab a handful of mages and enter one of the old sparring chambers where the Trials had been conducted before the advent of the jades. She doubted she could control her ire well enough against a younger mage and she feared her skills were too unpracticed to survive against someone stronger.

Mostly, though, she was just frustrated with her situation and her mind was racing. Up the stairs she went, making note of the scorch marks from her companions' previous visits and escapes from this place. She wondered when her time would come to bust through the gates and leave this place behind; then she shook her head, knowing she wouldn't be able to do it on her own anyway.

A few more days passed, which Lica spent in the library. She looked through the histories and sought a handful of earth-magic books to brush up on her skills, though she opted only to commit them to memory, rather than head to the training grounds to practice them. For Randler's sake, she also scoured the shelves for information on the Forgotten Tribe, and for Dariak she hunted down tales about the Red Jade. Her heart wasn't into any of it and she found nothing she thought was noteworthy. She did find the paintings by Lady Cathrateir that Kitalla had glimpsed through, and she considered stealing them just for spite.

As the days wafted by, Lica's rage boiled within her ever more powerfully than each day before, like a mountain ready to explode into a fiery volcano. She kept herself out of trouble, watching for signs of weakness from the mages around her, not that she really knew which mages to watch. What amazed her the most was that the entire Mage Council, enshrouded in their representative colors, was never to be seen. Their meeting chamber was locked with innumerable enchantments and there was growing talk among the novices that perhaps the masters were all dead inside.

Lica scoffed at the notion but couldn't entirely dismiss it either. The tower remained locked and she couldn't escape without a major ruckus. Banging on the Council doors did nothing. Yelling at mages and knocking down bookcases in the library had no repercussions.

And so, the volcano erupted.

Lica stormed up to the mage chamber with a staff she had absconded with from a darkened room. She emptied her pockets of all her spell components, littering the floor in the process. Then she sat down and used a large rock to cast an impenetrable wall around herself, lest she be disrupted. It was a new spell for her, but it worked on the same principles as other protection spells. She bashed the rock against her knuckle until she scored a drop of blood to link her essence to the stone, ensuring the spell would hold longer. It was buttressed against the wall and the chamber door, but it didn't shield her from them, as she needed to reach them with the energies. Then she really began her work.

"Kathkarothakur brendishan roque porro kroschkator." She swept her hand through the pile of dirt and coated her hand in its silkiness. *"Ormadushinor thrakkishar."* Cracking a set of twigs into thirds, she laid them in a grid pattern to represent the powers that sealed the chamber door. Her fingers worked quickly and when she paused between spells, she cracked her knuckles and rubbed the soreness from them.

"Jrakoulich frei k'nnarsh." Lica took a small hammer and crushed a pebble after several tries, then used the rock dust to smother her hands in a second layer of earth. *"Mortshican fruthristra kaie wroque."* With a chisel to hack off a small chunk of the wall surrounding the door, she completed the spell by hammering the fragment into dust and coating her hands with a third layer.

"Brakka forius, krathrotsh fruthia. Kaie." With a shout, she brought her hands over her head and used them like a sledgehammer to smash the twig grate at her feet. In response, the door to the Council chamber exploded in a rain of debris, pelting Lica excruciatingly, bouncing off the inside of her protective field and raising welts everywhere on her body.

As the dust settled, Lica pulled her aching body from the floor and pushed her way into the darkened room, squinting to see anything of importance. She had only been to the chamber once as an audience member in support of Dariak's claim to the jades, but she remembered there were windows along the right wall. She staggered in the darkness and found a shutter, then unceremoniously ripped it from its holdings with her earth-infused fists. She had forgotten the spell would still be in effect for a while but it didn't matter. The mages needed something productive to do.

When her eyes adjusted to the light, Lica took stock of the room and was dismayed. The Council members had indeed been fighting with each other, and not just with words. Scorch marks marred the ceiling and walls, a pungent odor from some poison made her nose twinge, and the floor was littered with six bodies. As she bent to examine them she noticed the cloying scent in the air and she covered her mouth and nose to mask it as best she could.

She hadn't met all of the Council mages but she could tell that these casualties were all members. Even in death, their faces held an arrogance that signaled their position. She dug through the bodies, trying to identify any of them, but she found neither Rothra nor Shelloni in the carnage. Either they had been obliterated completely or had escaped, if they had been present at all.

Lica scrounged around looking for... she didn't know what. Perhaps one of them had a key she could use to open the doors downstairs, though now that she had broken the seal on the Council door, she realized she could probably do so again to leave the tower. It would leave these mages in turmoil without their leaders, but they hadn't been particularly kind or hospitable to her anyway.

Lica bent over one mage and rifled through his cloak, seeking ingredients she could use to escape the tower without having to forage among the lower levels for them. As she did so, a mild thunder echoed in the distance and before she knew what was happening, fifteen mages ran into the room, staffs and knives at the ready.

At the head of the pack was Shelloni, a mad look in her eye. Her usually well-kempt hair was wildly askew and her robe was burned and torn in many places. "Grab her before she causes any more damage!"

Lica saw the trap for what it was and she didn't even bother to plead her innocence, though she didn't submit, either. Her empowered fists charged forth and cracked one mage in the chest, knocking the wind out of him and sending him sprawling to the ground, where two others stumbled over him. She then bent lower and scooped up a handful of dust. "*Brobbaforius!*" she sputtered, throwing the specks into the air, where they hovered. It was another defensive spell she had read about in the library, and when Shelloni's group unleashed their spells upon her, the dust absorbed the majority of the energies, and Lica was hit with only minor damage.

Shelloni screamed and spun her arms in a wide circles. Lica recognized the motions and focused her attention on the vibrations underfoot. Sure enough, rock spikes lifted from the floor with each upward thrust of Shelloni's arms. Lica retaliated by grabbing one of the spikes and hacking at its base with her enchanted hands, after which she lobbed it across the way. It was meant as a show of power, not as an attack, but then she changed her mind and called a spell forth to shatter the stone as it reached the other mages. They were blasted with bits of stone and they shrieked.

Lica raised up a defensive wall to stop the mages from advancing physically, even though it meant she was relatively trapped in the chamber. If she didn't defeat the lot of them, then she wasn't likely to leave anyway. Her pockets were void of materials except those she had scavenged off the fallen Council members, and she had no idea what to do with salamander scales, but she was desperate.

While Shelloni and the other mages chiseled their way through the earthen defenses, Lica chanted wildly, pulling pieces of rock, stone, and the salamander scales together. Her fists crushed everything into a fine powder, and then she pulled the dust together into numerous rocks, filled with raging energy. She felt drained from all the spellcasting but she pushed on with her next effort.

The earth wall crumbled enough so the other mages could reach in and cast their spells, and Lica used the same technique she had shown to Gennry days before. One by one, she flicked her enchanted pebbles at her foes, blasting them in the face or chest as they reached the opening in the wall. Each mage screamed and stopped attacking.

Lica could hear Shelloni muttering on the other side of the wall and instead of waiting, Lica rushed up to the gap and flung one of the stones at the Council mage, amazed to see the rock crash into the woman's face and then explode in a miniature inferno. Shelloni shrieked and collapsed.

She hadn't expected such a result, but Lica didn't particularly care about the damage to Shelloni and her cronies. They had baited her into the Council chamber and clearly had intended to lay the blame upon her for all the deaths that had occurred. Shelloni would then have risen up and taken leadership of the tower, and after everything she knew of Shelloni, she decided she could never let that happen. Still seething, Lica stuffed one of her remaining firestones, as she decided to call them, into Shelloni's mouth and then she coaxed the unconscious mage to swallow it. She didn't stick around for the gruesome explosion.

Lica hurried away from the area, anxious to use her rock hands and firestones to bust through the tower doors and be free of this place forever. A voice called to her and she ignored it, lowering her head and taking to the stairs.

As a middle-aged and somewhat stocky woman, all the excitement took its toll on Lica. Four steps down, she tripped and tumbled down the stairs, breaking her arm and a foot in the process. She tried to stand but her body gave way and she crumpled, furious with herself. Other mages approached her cautiously, fearing a wave of vicious spells for all the words sputtering from her mouth, but had they listened carefully, they would have realized that it was only a string of profanities.

"Lica! Are you hurt?" called the voice that followed her from the floor above. "Metris, Fluva, start the healing magics at once."

To her surprise, Lica was not bound in any way and as her anger sated, she looked at and saw a battered Rothra on his knees, trying to help her to sit up. "What in the name of creation is going on here?" she demanded.

"In short, it's a coup," he said. "Are you able to stand yet? Oh Fluva, do hurry."

Lica gasped. "A coup? Whatever do you mean? Most of this place looks normal."

Rothra recapped quickly. "Since my return, things have been tenuous. Once the declaration from the king arrived that we would be working in full cooperation with the Kallisorians, everything fell apart. The Council went to deliberate on the merits and validity of the decree and everyone was split on what to do. Shelloni had already decided and that's when the fighting began."

"Shelloni should be dead," Lica informed him, "but send someone to check just in case."

"Aphris, go and make certain."

The healing spells worked well and Lica found the pains were gone and she was able to stand on her foot, even though she could still feel that it was broken. The healing magic sealed the damage even as Rothra hoisted her up. "There is another matter that had us divided even before the king's missive."

"You mages here are always divided. It makes no difference to me. Whoever is willing to accompany me back to support Dariak's quest should come and let everyone else remain here in this accursed tower. I really don't care about the rest of it, Rothra."

He forced a smile on his face. "You may be interested in this one piece, anyway."

"No," she insisted. "Get me my volunteers and send me on my way. I don't even want to know where you've been since I got here or why the sky is blue."

"You will need to rest—"

Lica's face lit red and she punched Rothra in the chest. Luckily for him, her rock fist spell had dissipated. "I will not tarry here any longer as your prisoner, regardless of the pretense!" she screamed. "Get me what I need and send me on my way!"

"Fine. You will be on your way this very afternoon. Though I would suggest—"

"Watch yourself, mage."

Now Rothra's patience met its end. "You *will* listen to me, woman. For just a moment. Now be silent!" Lica frowned, thinking of a few spells in case she needed them. But Rothra calmed himself quickly and finished his thought, "As I was saying, I would suggest you take a short detour to the east."

"Whatever for?"

"Stop by Marritosh on your way."

"To what, pay my respects? It was destroyed, Rothra."

Rothra grinned despite himself. "I know. But if you go there you may find a handful of mages willing to add to your complement from here."

Her curiosity won out. "Why are there mages there?"

Rothra practically beamed. "Marritosh is being rebuilt. By Ervinor."

Lica gasped. "Truly?"

"He came by here after the jade incident at the castle and he requested help to rebuild the town—at least some parts of it—before he headed home for good."

Lica found herself smiling. "I think you might be right. I may need to take a slight detour."

CHAPTER 28

Deception

THE DAYS LANGUISHED by for Gabrion as he awaited his meeting with the earl of Undying Stone. From one catastrophe to another, Gabrion's audience had been postponed. He had no idea how many of the delays were real, but the night they were raided certainly brought him to attention.

Alarms sounded late and Brannis, the earl's page, burst into Gabrion's room, which woke the baby in a panic. "We have been invaded. We think they're after the child! Hurry!"

Eyes popping awake, Gabrion grabbed a sword in one hand and Perrios in the other. He hurried after the page, shouts echoing all around the keep. Barefoot and barechested, Gabrion honed his attention to his surroundings, prepared to protect the child at any cost. He knew the king's soldiers would be strong defenders, and because the whole purpose of the fort was to withstand invasion, he knew there was little risk of their success, but it wasn't worth lowering his guard.

The two of them skulked through the halls, and guards sprinted this way and that. They kept out of sight, with Brannis in the lead. He whispered instructions to Gabrion and to a few other guards they passed along the way. Clanging metal rang through the air and it took all Gabrion's efforts to keep Perrios from crying. He tucked the sword under his right arm and reached over with his fingers to play with the child that was cradled on his left arm. If only he'd had time to grab the special bassinet he had crafted.

Arrows flew through the air and thunked against the stone walls. Gabrion ducked, trying to ferret out the location of the archers from the angle of the arrows. He pointed them out to Brannis and they were able to better avoid them. Other soldiers scrambled in, swords and maces swinging madly. Soon, the clamor was too much and the baby screamed in fear.

"Over there, and hurry!" shouted a deep, booming voice.

"They're onto us," Brannis shrieked. "Come!" He lowered his head and whisked through the stone halls, turning left, dodging right, taking the third hall and then ducking into a second passageway. Gabrion kept on his heels, looking for pursuit while keeping the baby secure.

"Where are we headed, Brannis?"

"To the secret caverns below the keep, of course. It's the most defensible place there is here and it's the only way to keep Perrios safe. That's our only priority, while everyone else fights off the brigands."

"Who are they?"

"Not now, Gabrion. Come on!" Brannis sprinted ahead and they took a flight of stairs down at rapid pace. They darted across a wide hallway, shouts echoing all around them, including the child's. Brannis turned sharply right into a pantry and, hands trembling, he fumbled with the shelves of a bookcase. Before Gabrion could ask what he was doing, one of the shelves pushed slightly inward then sank down and a secret door opened.

Brannis reached for a torch on the wall and an arrow sliced into his hand. He yelped and grabbed the torch with his other hand, then plummeted into the darkened corridor. Gabrion followed and pushed the door shut behind them.

"Let me see your hand," Gabrion offered.

"Not yet; we have to get away from this entrance in case they know of it."

"Is that likely?"

"Likely enough to be a concern. Move!"

They sprinted down a long corridor that had numerous alcoves on either side. Gabrion couldn't see much, but it felt as if some of the alcoves were actually passageways that Brannis ignored. After several minutes of hurried running, Brannis slowed and then inspected the stone as he went. When he found what he was looking for, he turned left and guided Gabrion further in. Perrios had begun to settle down by then, from the rocking sensation of being swaddled against Gabrion's chest as he ran or from the sense of pure strength emanating from his protector.

They descended another set of stairs and now the sounds of fighting were entirely gone. Their footsteps echoed loudly on the stone, though Brannis told Gabrion not to worry about the noise, for no one would hear it from above. The torchlight flickered in the dank air so they reduced their pace to keep from blowing it out entirely.

"They know you're here with the heir," Brannis explained. "They want to bring him back to the king, even though the king's wish was to keep him here, safe from any possible skirmishes. They aren't listening to the king's missives and Earl Thedris is being hunted as if he's a traitor. He's down here. As are the child's grandparents."

"When did all this happen?"

"They went into hiding soon after your arrival. The earl has visited with them daily to ensure their well-being, though he was underground when the bandits broke through the gate and he had to lock himself in for fear of being discovered. I hadn't expected him to be gone for so long and when I went to tend to him before bed, he wasn't there. Then everything went wrong and I ran to you."

"Why didn't you tell us any of this beforehand?" Gabrion growled. "We could have made better preparations."

"We didn't know who was responsible for arranging the ambush, so we told no one."

"Fools."

"Be as angry as you want later. Right now, focus on that." Brannis pointed ahead to a large door. "Give me a minute to open it." He struggled to remove the bolts with his damaged hand while also holding the torch, but he managed it. He held it open for Gabrion.

The warrior took a step forward and then hesitated. "Wait."

"We don't have time, Gabrion. They're bound to find us. We have to get inside."

"Why was this door bolted from the outside?"

Brannis paused briefly. "It's the second entrance to the hideout. The other one opens from inside. This opens from without. It's a precaution."

The stillness ringing in Gabrion's ears lessened and Brannis fidgeted, looking around. "Gabrion, you have to hurry. They're coming. Those noises off in the distance, they're on the next floor up and it won't take them long to find this level. Please hurry."

"It's all very convenient," Gabrion said. "How am I to know you're not the one trying to steal this child?"

"I'm not!" He looked terribly distressed but was otherwise unreadable. "I don't want him to die, Gabrion. Please believe me."

The echoing sounds in the distance grew louder. From within the opened doorway, a single set of footprints approached. Moments later, Earl Thedris appeared. "What is taking so long? We must be quick."

Brannis sighed in exasperation. "He doubts me, milord, and won't enter the haven."

The earl nodded sagaciously. "He is wise to doubt you in a time of confusion. But as you can see, young protector, this is where the child will be safe. Don't tarry." He held Gabrion's gaze for a moment and then returned inside. Brannis held the door, veritably bouncing in anticipation.

Gabrion considered the options and decided he had to go in with the earl. The king had sent him here directly to keep Perrios under the earl's protection. It had to be safer than trying to fend off a host of rebels with a baby in one hand, a sword in the other, dressed only in his undergarments.

Brannis followed the warrior inside and pulled the door closed, spinning a wheel that locked the door securely. One other torch was lit and the earl had returned to sit within its luminance, some papers scattered around, as well as a small bundle of straw.

"Where are the others?" Gabrion asked. "Mira's parents?"

"Sleeping," Thedris said calmly. "Over there by that wall." He pointed to a dark area that Gabrion couldn't verify, though he did hear some erratic breathing as if they were having nightmares.

"You should have told me what was going on. I could have helped."

"You have helped plenty, young warrior. Now, set the baby here." He pointed to the straw bed. "Brannis, why don't you help him with his sword?"

"I'm fine," Gabrion argued. "Besides, your man is hurt. You should concern yourself with him."

"The child," Thedris said, his tone odd. "Place him on the bed."

Chills ran down Gabrion's spine at the strange command. Swiftly, Gabrion released the sword from under his right arm and snapped his hand down to catch the hilt. "What's really going on here?"

Thedris waved his hands to the darkness and six guards stepped silently forward. "This child will be returned to his majesty and the farce will end immediately."

"What!" Brannis shrieked.

"Kill him," the earl declared but Gabrion parried the sudden blow from the nearest guard. The resulting crash made Perrios cry. "See what you've done? Now lower your weapon and place him on the bed." His eye flashed to the side and Gabrion understood the glance well enough. A guard had been summoned to step in and take the child.

"You can't have him."

"And, what, you will fight off me and my men while holding that tot in your hands? Don't you realize that in this darkness, you're likely to miss?"

"And if he dies, then your hope dies too."

"Not so. You see, if he dies, then it falls upon your head, not mine. If you fail, then your mission fails." He glanced to the darkness again and the soldier jumped in to attack.

Gabrion spun and blocked the blow but he was not expecting Thedris to lunge for him. Or rather, to lunge for Perrios. The earl grabbed Gabrion's left arm and then brought a jeweled dagger over, holding the blade over the baby's crying face.

"What now?" Thedris crooned. "Kick me out of the way and you risk me dropping this knife."

Gabrion's eyes bore into the earl's and he realized the truth of it. He released his grip on the baby while another soldier stepped forward and snatched the sword out of Gabrion's other hand.

"Good. Now, Brannis, take this child away while we finish off this unfortunate guardian."

At first the page seemed reluctant but Gabrion gave a subtle nod and so he complied. With the baby in hand, Brannis shrank into the shadows and the earl gave a malicious laugh.

"You poor fool," the earl chided. "Coming here, thinking you—"

Gabrion had lowered his hands to his sides while keeping his face a mask of rage. As the earl gloated, Gabrion used the last weapon he had. He pulled on his undergarments and ripped them right off his body, snapping the fabric like a whip and lashing Thedris in the face, shocking him silent. The other guards rushed in quickly, which the naked warrior expected, and he swirled the garment around, interfering with their strikes in the darkened room.

Gabrion snapped the rag at one guard while jumping and kicking toward another, who dodged the blow. A sword swept in and Gabrion barely ducked in time. He pulled his rag again and lashed it out anew, befuddling one man after another. He managed to flick it fast enough that they had a hard time judging where he was trying to strike, until he was able to bash his fist into one face and then knee another in the groin.

Thedris could see where this was going, so he grabbed the torch and turned to head for Brannis, determined to escape. Gabrion dove into a roll and bounded onto his feet, running hard to tackle the earl. The torch went flying and Gabrion was lost in darkness. He felt the man struggling underneath him, trying to do some damage, even raking his nails into Gabrion's skin. Thedris also made enough noise so his guards could find him and intervene on his behalf. Gabrion heard the approaching help and so he rolled over, hoisting Thedris up and then pushing him into the darkness with his legs. The earl crashed into his own guards as they came running.

Gabrion hopped onto his feet and recovered the fallen torch, after which he ran for Brannis. "We have to get out of here."

"But the others," Brannis whispered. "The grandparents."

"They're really here?"

"They were, earlier at least."

Gabrion muttered under his breath. He couldn't leave them at the mad earl's mercy, but he wasn't sure he could defeat the fighters in the dark either. He still clutched his undergarments and so he turned and headed back to the muffled rumblings of the men still trying to get up. He stomped and kicked as he approached in case any of them had disentangled themselves in the process. Doing so, he inadvertently sliced his foot on a fallen knife. He picked up the jeweled instrument and then swept the torch around in front, trying to see the tangle of men.

They weren't too far away now, he knew, and they could see exactly where he was. A slight scraping sound echoed and Gabrion tensed, waiting for a sudden sword strike. It came in the form of a hurled blade, and the only warning he had was the grunt of the man who had tossed it. Guessing at its trajectory, Gabrion leaned away and spun his rag around to deflect the attack. The blade struck the cloth and clattered.

But the attack also gave away their exact position, so Gabrion bolted and stumbled toward them, four of whom were unconscious from smacking the stone floor. That left three others that he knew of and an unknown number of fighters who had been in the room waiting in the dark.

Gabrion realized that the darkness was his biggest foe and any of the other men, the earl included, could be sneaking past him to reach Brannis and Perrios. And so he pulled away toward the baby and he worked at ripping his undergarment into pieces as he went, lighting the strips with the torch and dropping them on the ground. The pieces weighed little enough that movement would scatter them.

He set a rough perimeter as he drew closer to Brannis and then he tuned his ears to the darkness. The leather-soled guards made no sound, nor did the silk-booted earl. Then, all at once, several pieces of the burning cloth fluttered and Gabrion caught glimpses of oncoming feet. He tensed in anticipation, which was made worse by random muttering from Brannis. Gabrion wondered if he was trying to soothe the upset child, but then the room erupted in a flash of light that lasted just a few seconds.

It was unexpected, but Gabrion saw the locations of his targets, though they had recoiled from the flash. He pounced and lashed out with the jeweled dagger, cutting into their arms, seeking only to disable them. He also bent and swiped a sword, holding it ready in front of him.

Brannis cast the light spell again, this time for longer, and Gabrion used the precious seconds to cut off the earl's belt and used it to bind his hands. He then visited the rest of the soldiers and bashed them to unconsciousness.

With a final blast of light, he saw two huddled forms in the far corner. Gabrion limped over to them, his foot trailing blood with every painful step. He removed their gags, but it was clear that the man was dead.

"Can you walk?"

"I—I—think so," the old woman stammered. "Oh, but Yorrish! My dear Yorrish! No!" She dissolved into a fit of tears.

"We can't stay for him. I'm sorry. We leave, or we die. Come on." He took her hand and led her across the room to where Brannis had moved. The page fumbled with the door lock he had set when they had entered. Nerves were getting the best of him, and Gabrion feared he would drop Perrios in the process. Trying not to, but doing so anyway, Gabrion essentially dragged the old woman faster with each step.

Brannis opened the door and they stepped into the elongated hallway, but other torches approached with rapidity. The page looked at Gabrion. "What do we do?"

"What about the other door you mentioned inside?"

"I'd never find it in time. Not with all them in there and them out here and the pressure and—"

"Okay, okay, calm down. Here, give me the child." He took Perrios as Brannis massaged his wounded hand while trying not to drop his torch.

"You've got a fight coming," the old woman declared. "Give me the baby while you defend us."

Gabrion didn't see another option. "Brannis, seal that door, and then stay with her." He handed over the jeweled dagger, keeping one torch and a sword for himself.

The incoming fighters hurried their steps when they noticed the torchlight. The thundering echoes of a dozen footfalls filled the area, keeping Perrios terrified. Among the fighters, Gabrion noticed, was Alosia.

The nursemaid observed Gabrion's nakedness with more than a passing glance and then she spat on the ground. "Hand that child over, now, you depraved scoundrel."

"I've already explained when you would be allowed to touch him again."

"You won't get away with running off with him. You'll only make things worse, whatever you were planning."

Gabrion's brows furrowed. "I was keeping him safe from the bandits."

"Likely story," she sneered. "The only bandits tonight were the ones more loyal to the earl than to the king. And since you're down here right now..."

Gabrion lowered his sword. "You weren't trying to take him back to the king?"

Alosia snarled. "I thought I had explained it to you well enough that I intend to obey my king."

They stared at each other angrily until at last Gabrion decided she was telling the truth. He didn't know why he believed her, or Brannis for that matter, but he did. "The earl and six of his fighters are in the room behind us, all wounded but alive. And there is a dead man in the back corner." Four soldiers went off to secure the room.

Alosia's eyes kept wandering as Gabrion stood naked in the flickering torchlight. "How do you even explain this?"

"Rousted from bed in a panic," he answered brusquely. "How about handing over a cloak or something."

"No," she grinned lasciviously. "I think this should be your new outfit."

Chills ran down Gabrion's spine, for her comment reminded him vaguely of Kitalla. "Does anyone have anything they can spare so I can cover up?" One of the fighters offered a long tunic and Gabrion accepted it gratefully.

At last he turned to Brannis, Perrios, and the old woman. "Are you all okay?"

Brannis nodded, cradling Perrios. "Yes. We should get going now, I think."

Gabrion leaned down. "Meriad, are you injured? Come on; we need to get above."

The woman's face was lined with tears. "But Yorrish!"

"We'll bring him with us. Come on. Let's get out of here."

CHAPTER 29

The Last Book

WITH ACHING EYES and tired fingers, Dariak put down the last of his father's diaries. A deep sorrow rested on his face, and he didn't know what to do next. The mage stretched and paced around the library, his thoughts awhirl.

Randler slept, a book open on his chest. The tome rose and fell softly with each gentle breath, and Dariak's heart ached with the turn their relationship had taken. He loved the bard as much he had ever loved another person, yet clearly it wasn't enough. What he didn't understand was whether Randler's demands were normal or excessive. Was Dariak's love overshadowed by his quest as the bard thought? When he considered it, he agreed, much to his dismay.

In the end, it might not matter anyway, he thought, turning back to where he had set the book down. It hadn't had a pleasant ending at all and for the first time, he wished his father had been wrong. Yet all the evidence pointed to the same thing: to unite the jades, someone would have to die.

The weight in his chest grew heavier, for he understood the cost and he would pay it when the time came. But would the others continue his mission if he was gone? Sure, they had done so in the past, but his quest was still ongoing and he hadn't yet achieved his goal. Without him to remind them of the focus, would they pursue it, or would they return to more mundane tasks?

Dariak tried to imagine what death was like. A morbid thought, to be sure, but necessary. Would he drift up to the skies like some people believed, so he could oversee how things progressed with the land, at least for a little while? Or would he just be snuffed out like a flame with no connection at all? Perhaps it was why the ancients believed in gods, for it gave them a sense of higher purpose to their struggles and it gave them a place to go to when they died.

He didn't know what he believed, but as a mage, it seemed likely to him that the energies that made up his life would dissipate back into the world, where other mages would learn to draw on them and craft them into new spells. Perhaps that was where inspiration came from: a set of flowing energies passing to a new person and opening a fresh path of ideas to pursue. Or that energy floated around, giving the entire populace a stronger base of knowledge to build from that allowed them to aspire to greater heights. He pictured it like a group of men trying to construct a mountain.

In their lifetime, one group wouldn't be able to make it very high, but after generations of adding to the foundation, it could tower over the land.

He knelt down and took Randler's hand, slowly stroking the soft skin. He delighted in the sensation of the warmth mingled with the tiny hairs that started from the wrist and wound their way up his arm. Dariak smiled, cherishing the stolen sensation while Randler slept.

After a time, the bard's tender eyes opened and he examined the sadness on his lover's face. "Bad news?"

Dariak stifled an answer, holding that hand whose caresses had possessed a magic of their own. He let the memory fill him and drag him forward. Randler did not shy away, tossing the book to the floor and welcoming Dariak's advances. They moved slowly, experiencing each other as if for the first time, touching here, kissing there. Then they drew upon their knowledge of each other and dissolved into ecstasy.

Relaxed and content, Randler stared at the sharp lines in Dariak's face. His jaw was taut and his throat pulsed as if he had something he wanted to say but didn't know how. Randler understood the feeling, for the knot in his throat was the same. He wondered in some way if he had misjudged Dariak's dedication to their relationship, but that nagging inner voice reminded him that this calm would only be temporary.

"Your father's library should be immortalized," Randler said softly, unable to speak directly of what was on his mind.

"For now, it will have to remain here, until the mages in general can forgive the flaws of my father and honor him again. If they ever can."

"Some things take time. I believe that when some more time has passed, they will again revere him."

"You really think it's possible for people to forget that Delminor was the mage who failed the last time? That they'll forget it was his magic that doomed the fighting to continue and allowed our king to perish?"

Randler wasn't sure how to take the questions, for Dariak's tone was off. "I do believe that, yes. Mages will continue to advance. Many will wonder where past inspiration came from and when they check the histories, they'll find your father's name and they'll honor him."

The mage nodded absently. "Everyone has his day, I suppose."

"As you will have yours," Randler said. "Dariak, I know you well enough. What is it?"

"Nothing."

Randler took Dariak's face in his hand and forced him to meet his gaze. "Tell me."

Defeated, Dariak exhaled and explained softly. "The jades are manifestations of the elements, which we know. They link powerfully with the world around us and normal everyday things connect to the jades. Many years ago, the jades were kept away from each other, each in an area that best suited the shard. The lands all thrived and people were happy with the day-to-day routines. Sure, there were fights and disagreements—people are people—but there wasn't constant war or the ever-growing desert or the feral beasts, and so on."

Randler nodded. "The histories all say the same thing, neglecting the jades. Then some mages came to power in what's now known as Kallisor and they rampaged until the people rose up and ousted them. It's where the original King Kallisor grew up and he despised magic ever since."

"Those mages had found the first pieces of jade and channeled their energies, but they couldn't control them at the time. It's like what happened at the Prisoner's Tower in Pindington with the lightning jade. The mages were inexperienced with the element and dealing directly with the jades, and it destroyed the whole place."

"And would have destroyed us, too," Randler recalled with a shudder. "If not for your quick thinking."

Dariak's lips twitched upward with the compliment, though his mood was too somber. "My father discussed the findings of other mages, using the jades, combining their powers, and so on. Then he sought the jades out and gathered them all together so he could explore their effects himself. At first, he didn't make any groundbreaking discoveries, until he had four pieces."

"What was so special about the four?"

"The elements themselves didn't matter, he later found, but the more jades he brought together for a single task, the harder it was to contain them. He described it as dropping rocks into a well, but each time you drop a stone, all the stones double in size. Put the first stone in, it's the size of one stone. Add a second one, and it's like you have four instead. Add a third, and you've got the equivalence of ten rocks, and so on."

"And four stones is like tossing twenty-two into the well," Randler said, "and by then the stones are getting too big to throw in and the well is pretty full."

"Yes, and at some point, the well itself breaks because it can't hold them all."

Randler swallowed deeply. "So when Frast channeled all the jades through himself with the one intent of uniting the jades, that's why he exploded into the fiery falcon."

"Essentially."

"So what does that mean? Can the jades not be brought together?"

Dariak wrung his hands together, and the motion made Randler nervous. "My father had some postulations. He believed the human spirit could be strong enough to channel all the jades properly and unite them, but we've both seen that he's wrong there. He died and so did Frast. He also wondered at your thought, whether the jades weren't meant to be combined into one, however he had found numerous texts, though ancient, that said the shards all originated from the one Red Jade."

"There aren't many stories about the Red Jade directly."

Dariak shrugged. "There is a reason for it. Do you ever read tons of stories about the sky? Or trees? Air? No, because they're just there, part of the world. And the Red Jade was once just something that existed. It was hinted that it was a conduit to the old gods or a relic of some powerful magician who had gathered all of magic into one place for all the world to enjoy—or, in another version, that same wizard had locked the magic away so others couldn't abuse it."

"What did Delminor think the truth was?"

"He wasn't sure, and he said it didn't matter. He only gleaned the fact that the Red Jade did exist and that it was the key to restoring balance to the land."

"But wait," Randler said, scratching his head. "I read about the shards, how the other lines of royalty all ended and a shard came into being. But if the Red Jade was first and then was broken down, how is that possible?"

"The Red Jade was first," Dariak said confidently. "It was split and shared among the royal families of the time, before these lands took on their current names. My father wasn't certain, but he postulated that the jades were passed down to the first male heir. But it wasn't like a family goblet kept in a chest. It was as if the jade itself had become part of each king, and passed internally to his heir. Those deaths you read about were the ends of the other royal lines, for the seed of the true heir carrying the jade had not been passed on. So upon his death, each shard manifested itself."

Randler added, "And each royal family would have lived in a different part of the land, keeping their powers from each other and balancing them across the kingdoms."

"There's some speculation here, but yes. While the jades were living within the kings, there was relative peace and magic was weaker. As they died and the shards came to physical being, the imbalances started."

"And your father realized the powers were not meant to exist as separate shards. So he started bringing them together."

Dariak nodded. "Recreating the Red Jade would either allow magic to flourish or it would reduce its effects to where it was before. He would restore the balance of magic and therein stop the war. Even if that meant sealing magic away from the world, he was willing to do it. The problem, though..."

"All those oversized rocks in the well," Randler finished.

"Yes. With eleven jades, imagine the amount of force needed to keep them together. He tried many different ways to achieve it, but the most he could ever contain on his own was eight."

"That's impressive in itself."

Dariak smiled slightly. "True. He even employed other mages to help with the barriers needed to channel the energies into one location, but despite with the extra support, he never surpassed eight. He believed the complexities of the magic needed the complexities of the mind to maintain them."

"I see," Randler said softly. "So he included himself in the mix to bring them together."

"And it burned him out. As it burned Frast. As it will burn me."

Randler held Dariak's hand tightly. "It doesn't have to, Dariak. We can find another way."

"There isn't one, and my father even said so. Without restoring the Red Jade, magic will always be imbalanced and the world will forever experience turmoil. I don't have a choice, Randler. I have to unite them and recreate the Red Jade. It was always my goal before, but I hadn't thought it would be so impossible. Or so final. Frast may not have realized what he was channeling. My father had suspected but couldn't have been prepared either. I'm more experienced with the jades. I've been connected to them my whole life through the blood bond. I can succeed where the others could not."

"Yet you expect it to kill you."

"My father believed that to hand yourself over to the jades was to release yourself from this existence and to take on a new sense of being within the Red Jade, ever policing the energies, ever guiding and protecting the balance."

"Thus the power of the mind," Randler concluded. "You would have to rule it with some creativity, some logic, and with a keen sense of negotiation between the forces. Dariak, it would be worse than conducting an orchestra with a thousand different instruments simultaneously playing all different songs and trying to have it sound pleasant to a single audience."

"That about sums it up," Dariak agreed. "And because I know that going in, I know I can do this."

"It's crazy, Dariak, don't you see? There must be something else."

"Just one thing: I give up this quest. We find resting places for all the jades and hope they remember their old tasks of protecting the land."

Randler painted a smile on his face. "Then we could build a house somewhere, have a little garden out back. We'll have friends over for some wild laughs and bawdy songs."

"We'll cook grand feasts," Dariak added, "and seasonally rearrange all the furniture for fun. You'll bring in money from your songs and your desserts. I'll be the hunky man around the house, fixing things, tinkering with small projects, and making toys."

Randler burst out laughing. "Making toys? And why do you get to stay at home while I'm making all the money?"

"I'll need time to learn some skills other than magic," he said honestly.

"Well," Randler drawled, "I can think of one skill you've mastered and could rake in tons of gold with, but I would be too jealous to allow you to do it."

It was Dariak's turn to laugh. "Making toys it is, then."

The mirth dissipated quickly and Randler pulled Dariak closer to him. "I don't want to lose you, even if it means saving the land. Hopefully, we can find another way."

"Let's not dwell on it for now. We have all the information we came for, so we should head back to the others. I'd rather like to get out of here." A smirk then grew on his face. "But before we go, what do you say we make sure you're right about those skills I've mastered?"

"Again? So soon?" Randler teased. "You'd better impress me."

"Oh," Dariak crooned. "I intend to."

CHAPTER 30

Standing Before the Seven

URRITH SAT SILENTLY in the room provided for him by the mages. It was more comfortable than the previous stony room they had given him, but it was still just as much a prison to him as before. He wanted to leave the Mage Underground more than anything, but the Seven had to convene and decide his fate; he was merely waiting for them to gather and deliberate.

"Bide your time," Frethia had cautioned him after his ordeal in the outer world. "All things have a time and a reason."

The upset youth hadn't been able to bite his tongue. "And my purpose as bait has been useful to you, but what has it done for me?"

The old woman had narrowed her eyes coldly and walked silently away.

Several days had passed since then, though the lad refused to even count them anymore. He woke up, ate food, and found little things to keep himself busy, like cutting twigs into uniform sizes for one mage or labeling herbs for another. At first, Urrith had tried avoiding all the mages and their hobbies, though boredom was worse than interacting with them, and exercising for long felt terribly out of place here.

Janning appeared while Urrith lay on his bed staring at the ceiling, contemplating his future. The older mage said nothing other than, "It's time." Urrith didn't bother arguing or asking for any other information. Most of his dealings with the mages so far had been locked in secrecy or lies anyway.

When he had met the first few members of the Seven, they had convened in a dank, stone room with oddly shaped thrones. This time, Urrith's jaw dropped at the elegance of the entire setting.

A long gathering hall had been blockaded around three edges and massive wooden tables had been brought in, presumably by earth and nature mages who had drawn the trees in through the rocky ceiling and then molded them into their desired form. It still seemed a waste of energy to Urrith, but he reminded himself of Janning's comparison to sparring and he sighed, taking in the rest of the setting.

The walls were draped with a series of tapestries, though as he looked more closely, Urrith noticed that they were the work of the nature mages, who had drawn vines and flowers and herbs together into intricate patterns that not only visually flattered the space, but added a deliciously welcome fragrance to the room. Along the wall, stone sconces stood out with variously hued flames dancing within.

Seven lavish chairs were aligned in an arc at the far end of the hallway, and in each seat, except Janning's, was a mage whose eyes glittered with knowledge, even from across the room. Along the wide table sat a large host of mages, all members of the Underground, gathered here for the discussion of Urrith's plight. He didn't care to have such an audience.

Janning guided Urrith toward the Seven and a slight breeze wafted pointedly through the chamber. At first Urrith was irked by it, for it was persistent, then he grew accustomed to the constant fluttering of the wind and he was able to ignore it. Its purpose became clear when Janning announced their presence, for the mage's voice echoed on the breeze and carried to all the others present in the hall.

"To the Seven, I present young Urrith, traveler of the lands who has come here seeking asylum within our domain." Janning bowed his head and then took his seat among his peers, facing Urrith as judge.

"I did not come here intentionally," Urrith said. "You make it seem like I knocked on your door but I didn't."

Janning's voice took on a sharp edge. "Without our help, you would have perished at the hands of Ordren."

"Twice," Urrith agreed, his annoyance at the mages poking through. He had told himself to remain calm and to behave himself, but too much had happened and he was impatient to be on his way. "You saved me when I was first hunted by Ordren, and then again when you threw me out into the world as bait."

The Seven muttered amongst themselves in disapproval. Frethia leaned forward and gave a gesture of caution with her hand. "We could have left you there or tossed you out without our protections. In addition, you have not been treated unfairly here."

"Except that I haven't been allowed to leave," he argued despite himself. "I've been a prisoner and a tool this whole time."

"Silence your complaints," Janning warned, but another of the Seven intervened.

"No, let him share his feelings," said a middle-aged woman near the end of the arc of chairs. Her curly brown hair had random streaks of gray throughout, making her appear to have been caught in a snowstorm on her way in. Her dark eyes held what Urrith thought was a bit of insanity. "I remember my boy at his age; if he doesn't talk about how he feels, then he will surely explode."

"It isn't necessary to make fun of me," Urrith said.

"Isn't it though?" the woman taunted. "Children like you think you're older than you are and yet beg the protection of their elders as if they're newly out of the crib. Which are you? Older or younger? Do you need us to coddle you or be direct?"

Urrith gritted his teeth and decided to channel as much aplomb as he could. "Fine. I'm here before you to learn what you're going to do with me. Am I free to go?"

"Well, listen to him!" the mage quipped.

Janning groaned. "Enough, Sharice, let's get to this."

"Where do you intend to go, young Urrith?" asked Frethia once things were quiet.

"I would return to Gabrion and his comrades. They're currently in Hathreneir and I wasn't meant to be separated from them for so long."

"Gabrion?" Sharice asked. "I recognize that name."

"You know him?"

"I met him briefly. He was traveling with others."

Urrith nodded. "Yes, though I haven't met them myself. He told me a little about them. Dariak, Kitalla, Randler, Lica, Frast, Quereth, Ervinor, and a bunch more."

"And what is it they're doing in Hathreneir?"

"This isn't relevant, Sharice," interrupted the haggard mage to her left.

"I beg to differ, Connello. Shouldn't we know this boy's purpose in returning to these adventurers?"

Another of the Seven, Beyana, cleared her throat with a watery grumble. "I believe you know their quest better than the rest of us, don't you dear?"

Sharice shrugged. "I know what they told me."

The mages bantered back and forth and Urrith waited until the conversation returned to him. He tackled the posed question as succinctly as he could. "Gabrion hopes to bring peace to the land by having people learn to work together. He managed to get the western outpost to accept Hathrens and Kallisorians and they worked and lived together for a time. If the Hathren king hadn't sent troops to end the truce, then we'd all still be there now."

"Idyllic as ever," Sharice accused, "though it sounds as if he has truly adopted the heart of Dariak's quest. But I wonder, little one, how many mages were among you?"

"Just the healers, really," he said. "I suppose a few joined when Ruhk and his team ventured into the outpost, but they kept their powers to themselves for all I could tell."

"Some 'peace' Dariak is creating," muttered one of the other Seven.

Urrith heard the remark and was affronted by it. "Hold your tongue," he demanded angrily. "The mages were welcomed just like everyone else and no one pressured them to keep quiet; they did it on their own."

"Temper, temper," Sharice admonished.

"No, you listen to me for a minute. I grew up in Wraethen, which is probably as far from mage-friendly Hathreneir as you can get. I had no experience with magic for my whole life. Not really. I saw some things here and there, but I stayed away from it because it frightened me. I became a soldier and joined the king's side to protect the land."

"We don't need your life history."

"That's enough, Sharice," Frethia warned. To Urrith she added, "Please continue."

"I fought for the army and I trained under Ordren for a while. I should have realized he was solely dedicated to the crown. I didn't see through him when he followed Gabrion and the others out of Pindington. I went because it was where he went. But then I met Gabrion. He was different than Ordren. I learned about

Gabrion's heart and what he yearned for. It was in working together in the outpost that I saw Gabrion for who he was."

"An aloof, brainless swordsman?" Sharice inserted.

"He was a true hero, rising up against the injustices and the prejudices—something you clearly can't do, making all your snide remarks from your comfy chair." Urrith grimaced but didn't let himself get too sidetracked. "No, he told us to put aside our hatred long enough to see what the other side was like and so we did. And we found out that, sure, we have our own traditions and habits, but deep down we all want the same basic things out of life."

"Kittens and puppies?"

Janning shouted, "Sharice, that is enough out of you!"

"I don't care," Urrith said. "She's probably scared she might learn something."

Sharice gasped. "You do have fight in you, little one. Please, do go on."

Urrith tried not to roll his eyes, but failed. "Anyway, we discovered we could work together and the reasons we hated each other seemed artificial. It wasn't easy and there were complications, and if Gabrion wasn't such a talented swordsman, he never would have been able to make his point."

Frethia's brows furrowed. "How so?"

"Basically, anyone who violated the peace had to face him in challenge, and he couldn't be bested by anyone. Once they saw him in combat, they all obeyed the decree and did their best to make it work." He looked around at the Seven. "I don't know enough about you to really know, but I would guess it's like how you're all sitting up there. You were probably chosen to represent the rest of the mages or"—he looked at Sharice—"you earned your seat through other means."

"You're not suggesting I did anything... untoward?" she asked.

"No," he said truthfully, "but I would bet you bullied your way in." She opened her mouth to object but he quickly added, "And you probably have so much skill with magic that no one could get you off this council, and they probably wouldn't want to."

Sharice's mouth closed and she tilted her head to the side. "Well, congratulations. I don't know what to say to that."

Janning barked a laugh. "The kid's got you pegged, at least."

Sharice shot him a glance. "You're lucky we're not allowed to hurl spells at each other here."

Urrith jumped at the opportunity. "See that? You made an agreement to work together and to not raise your skills against each other. That's all Gabrion did at the outpost. And once we had those rules in place, things started to work. Mostly."

"Some trouble is to be expected when you're dealing with a lifetime of prejudice and learned personality traits," Frethia said.

Urrith nodded. "Yes. Then the Hathren king sent more fighters to take over the outpost because he'd heard of the defection of Ruhk and his soldiers. Ordren also tried to pull away from the new collective. In the end, Gabrion had me escort Ordren through Kallisor while he went to stop the oncoming soldiers. That's how we were separated."

"Then I found you at Ordren's mercy and brought you here," Janning concluded. "You have since proven the truth of your adversarial relationship with Ordren and it's now time for us to decide what to do with you."

"Not yet," Urrith said, surprising everyone, including himself.

"Oh?" asked Connello from his perch. "I thought you wanted out of here?"

"I do, but you have to understand something first. I told you already that I was never around magic much when I was younger. Yet since being here, I've been inundated with it. You mages do everything here with magic. It's overwhelming for someone like me."

"There, there," Sharice crooned sarcastically.

"But you've all watched me, or had me watched at any rate. How have I reacted to this?"

The Seven were quiet and it was Janning who spoke first. "You've shown your discomfort on numerous occasions, but you've ultimately made an effort to learn more and to accept the way of things here."

"I've even allowed you to practice your spells on me. I don't even care right now that you were just setting me up to test my loyalty. What I'm saying is that I believe in what Gabrion showed me. And even though you all made me uneasy, I've tried my best to accept you and all of this." He glanced at each of them in turn. "I may just be a kid to you, but I want the world to be more peaceful. I don't want anyone to feel like they're less than normal because they're different. I can accept mages living up in the world with everyone else. I can accept Hathrens in my hometown. As long as everyone tries to make an honest go of it and try to get the peace to last, then I'm all for it."

Frethia drew Urrith's gaze and held it. "It's true we were dishonest and unfair with you, lad, and you have my apology for that. It's clear we've underestimated you. I can see where our dealings with you could have as easily turned you away from us and away from mages, and you would be certainly justified shunning us."

"We don't know if he means all of this or is just saying it for our benefit," Connello said.

"No," Sharice refuted. "He reminds me too much of my son in this. His words are true for him, just as Randler always spoke from his heart."

Urrith's eyes opened wide. "Randler is your son?"

"Yes. He and I don't see eye to eye on things, either," she added with a grin. "He turned from magic early on and it could just as well be because I am such a— how did you put it?—a bully. Yet even though we bullied you, you're looking past that and seeing us as a group of people who, in the end, want to be at peace and not persecuted for our skills."

The other members of the Seven stared at Sharice with incredulous expressions on their faces. She noted the perplexed stares and rolled her eyes in response. "All right, that's enough, all of you. I've had a lot to reflect on since Randler's visit."

Connello couldn't resist. "You mean since his partner defeated you and claimed that jade you were hoarding."

Sharice kept her temper in check, though the exertion of doing so showed on her face. "Nonetheless, it seems that times are ripe for a change."

Perrsa, who had remained silent thus far squirmed in her seat. "You must realize the implications of what you're saying. Our domain here has been essentially untouched by the king for decades because we've kept our hands clean and eyes averted. If we decide at this time to make a stand, we risk losing everything we've gained, while earning the scorn of all the people and being hunted down as in the olden days."

"A worthy objection," Frethia said. "It is true. We must consider the balance of things to come versus those to be lost." She turned to Sharice. "Do you think this Dariak has the ability to truly complete his quest with the jades?"

She considered for a moment. "He is resourceful, certainly, and had an affinity to the jades that I've not seen in anyone else. Will he succeed? It's impossible to say, for the jades themselves are strange artifacts and they may object to his quest and prevent it from completion. However…"

"Get on with it," Connello implored.

Sharice cleared her throat. "My tenure among the Seven has been productive for us all, yet I still have some hunger left in me for greater things. I know not how the rest of you feel, but as wonderfully decorated as this hall is today, I think I might prefer the chance the convene under the stars and meet without fear of persecution." She hesitated then growled and banged her fist in her hand.

"What is it?" Frethia asked.

"That dratted Dariak and his little speeches. He teased me with such ramblings and I denied him out of spite. Yet he was right in the end. I do want to be free, not tucked away under the stone or locked in a mage tower in Hathreneir." She looked around at her peers. "I believe it's time for the Seven to vote on whether we lend our support to Dariak's quest or remain here for another generation."

Urrith couldn't help himself. "What about me?"

Frethia raised a wrinkled eyebrow and shot a glance at the youth. "Clearly you have inspired us, little one. Surely you would like to witness at least some of the fruits of your labors?"

Dejected, Urrith frowned. "Then you're not letting me leave."

Janning cleared his throat. "If you wish to depart, you may do so and I will escort you myself at once to the surface with a mage or two to support your journey to the nearest town. Or, give us a little more time to decide our fate first. We may decide not to intervene at this time. We may throw our lot in completely. Or, more likely, we will be torn on the matter and need to work through a contingency." He glanced around at the entire assembly. "It seems a number of us are curious about the possibilities of a newer future, but curiosity will not necessarily translate into action. We'll need some time to deliberate. You don't need to remain here if you don't wish to. So I will leave your present fate up to you, young Urrith."

He considered for a moment and then nodded his head resolutely. "I wish to return to Gabrion as swiftly as possible."

"Very well then," Janning accepted, rising in his seat to begin at once.

Urrith grinned and cut him off. "Swiftly," he repeated. "So don't take too long deliberating amongst yourselves before we go."

Sharice laughed and shot him an approving smile before the Seven adjourned.

CHAPTER 31

The Gathering

VERNA AND RUHK had their hands full keeping everyone in line at Castle Hathreneir, but several recent events made their days less difficult. The dead zone for magic was dissipating and mages were able to ply their craft more and more each day. This helped the new chancellors in many ways, for they were able to give the mages greater duties that better fit their stations, which quelled their fears that they would be marginalized in the new ideology. Earth mages helped with the reconstruction of the castle. Nature mages assisted with the food supply, and healers worked almost nonstop patching up various wounds. Mages with other alignments were also gainfully employed throughout the castle and town, and soon everyone felt useful again.

What made Verna even happier was the return of Carrus and Kitalla, though she had wished their arrival had been under better circumstances. Kitalla was irate with Carrus for abandoning their quest on the front lines, even if it would have meant losing her foot to the damage she had received in the impromptu skirmish, but he stood by his decision and had no qualms about telling her so. Healers went to work on Kitalla's wounds and within a few days she was able to walk around with only a mild limp and an accompanying wince of pain, which the healers insisted would eventually go away.

Matters improved even more when Randler and Dariak arrived some days later from their research. The only members of their crew they were missing were Lica, Gabrion, and Urrith. The debate the team engaged in now was whether to wait for them or to venture forth soon.

Prethos and Ieran sat with the group as they contemplated the next course of action. "You have ventured through the lands to acquire the jades," the king said, "and now you have them, as well as your father's words on combining them. It seems this is the time to make your mission known to all."

Dariak stared intently. "You mean for me to go into Kallisor and confront the king."

"I can't say what your best course of action would be, young Dariak. I believe this task is of your design."

"But you should go soon," Ieran chimed in. Everyone looked at him suspiciously; he whimpered and cast his gaze fervently around, scrambling for a reason.

"The longer you wait, the more people will die at the front lines. Not all of the battalions were stopped by your comrades. Wouldn't it be better to act quickly?"

Kitalla grumbled at the reminder of her failure. "He almost has a point, Dariak."

"Almost?" Ieran echoed.

"Yes. You're leaving out the part where you want us gone so you can stop play-acting your new role here."

"How dare you!"

"Enough!" Prethos ordered. "Keep this conversation focused on the matters at hand."

"I beg to differ," Kitalla said despite the warning look Dariak gave her. "Once we're gone, who's to say you're going to keep doing things the way we've dictated? I suppose some of us could remain here to ensure it."

"No," Ruhk chimed in before the king could respond. "We've set things in motion and it's been enough time for the people to adjust to it all. I'm sure His Highness will maintain things in our absence."

"I appreciate your vote of confidence," the king said sincerely. "You do, of course, still have your insurance in effect, if you still worry that I might not keep to my word with you."

Verna spoke next. "I would agree with Ruhk on this."

Kitalla looked like she wanted to argue and Randler had seen that expression enough times to know that she was about to voice her objection, even if just for the record. He opted to supersede her comment. "It wouldn't make sense for things to revert back to the old way here just yet anyway. Dariak has all the shards and we know how to bring them together to form the Red Jade. Once he has done so and the fighting is ended, he would come back here to reset the current situation anyway. It would only lead to some possible casualties and the king losing his throne."

"These threats are not necessary," Prethos assured them. "I made this agreement. For one year."

"And two months have already passed," Ieran pointed out.

"Have you counted the hours too?" Kitalla sniped.

Dariak raised his voice. "Please! Enough already." He knew Kitalla was upset with her failed attempt out in the field and over the loss of two of her toes, but he didn't have patience for the sarcasm now. "I've drawn up a list of materials we will need for the journey to the border. I think it seems fitting that we return to the outpost where Gabrion conducted his experiment and use that as our focal point."

"A good choice," Ruhk said. "It's already a strong symbol of our success."

"What items do you require?" Prethos asked. He took the offered parchment from Dariak and perused it. "Some of these items will take time to procure."

Verna struggled not to smirk as she offered a suggestion. "Perhaps Chancellor Ieran would be able to work on getting those things while we make our preparations?"

Ieran scoffed at the notion. "There are pages for this sort of thing. Surely I'm better suited at your side, my liege?"

Prethos turned his gaze between the two of them.

"Look at it this way," Verna added. "The sooner you get it all done, the sooner we get out of here. Who else would work so hard?"

"She makes a good point," the king said, a hint of a smile on his face.

"Preposterous!" Ieran shouted. "I'm not an errand boy!"

"You are today," the king said. "I agree; you have yearned for their departure daily. You would make the shortest work of this task."

"But—"

The king raised his voice. "I have decided. You will make this your utmost priority and you will complete it without delay."

Ieran took the parchment and examined the items listed there. "These things are absurd! Thirty-six eaglon eyes? The tongue of a tigroar? Eighteen petals each from a hundred and fifty-two roses? Whatever do you need these for?"

"I require them for my quest," Dariak said simply. "Surely you have the large tents and other provisions closer at hand?"

"We do," the king said. They waited in silence for a moment while Ieran contemplated the other obscure items on the list. Prethos turned to his chancellor and cleared his throat. When the man met his gaze, the king reminded him, "I told you to begin without delay."

"W—Wh—? Now?"

"Now."

For a moment, Ieran seemed as if he was going to argue with his liege, but then he thought better of it, bowing his head sharply and vacating the room. As the door closed behind him, he let out an odd noise of frustration that tempted the others to laugh.

"Thank you, Your Majesty," Dariak said.

"Your father served my father well in his time," Prethos said. "I was too young to understand much of it, but I was instructed by the histories and my chancellors. Your father never wanted much from war, but his wild imagination was applied to battle schemes anyway. I don't know if your actions will seem any different to the historians, but I am curious. I have witnessed strange behaviors among my people these past weeks and you make me wonder about the future you envision."

Kitalla narrowed her eyes. "That's a fine sentiment if it's true. But, if I may ask without seeming too skeptical, is that your only reason for your support here?"

"Kitalla…" Carrus cautioned.

But Prethos raised his hand. "It's all right. What would you have me say, Kitalla? Do you want me to confess that I'm hoping Dariak obliterates Kallisor completely so that, when the year has passed and I have my son returned to me, I can take both lands under my rule and do as I see fit?"

Her jaw dropped open. "Yes, something like that."

The others were stunned by the near-admission but Prethos laughed heartily. "Schemes abound, as all of you know, and there is no way for me to prove to you that I mean what I tell you. My goal is the happiness of my people. I have always thought that happiness required the downfall of Kallisor so that we could allocate their resources to the people here who are struggling. Peace between our kingdoms is hard to come by when even messengers go missing between our castles."

"Killed on both sides of the border," Kitalla noted.

"Yes. I will admit that I am obeying your demands under duress, but that does not mean that I can't see the truth of what is happening around me."

Ruhk and Verna exchanged glances, wondering if the king was alluding to the secret host of rebels Ieran was gathering under his wing, but they kept quiet.

"Dariak, son of Delminor," the king said officially, "now that you have returned and command the unified power of the jades; if you so decree, then I will return the regency of this kingdom over to you until you depart upon the next leg of your quest."

Dariak bowed his head. "A generous offer. However, it would be best for you to maintain your status and for the rules to be kept consistent. The people have had enough change already."

"In that case, perhaps you all would like to retire for the night?"

The group disbanded and went to the quarters assigned to them. Kitalla avoided Carrus' room, since she was still upset he had brought her back to the castle with so much other work to do out in the field. She wondered how long she would hold her grudge, and she suspected it wouldn't be for too long; he was too entertaining a diversion for her to remain angry.

Verna and Ruhk checked in with their respective captains before reconvening in her chamber to discuss the assignments they intended to leave when the group departed. They debated about whom to leave in charge as captain once they uprooted Mzark from his post by taking him with them on the journey.

"He'll be furious," Ruhk warned.

"I don't know that we can leave him here, though," Verna said. "No one would remain behind to keep him in check, and we can't demote him before going without causing a ruckus."

"I don't know. Taking the captain of the guards on the journey may also cause some problems." They debated back and forth a while until the hour grew late and they drifted off to sleep.

Meanwhile Dariak and Randler sat together discussing some of the minutiae they had learned from Delminor's library. Randler wanted to ask about Essalia's condition, but Dariak didn't want to talk about his mother at all. They had barely said good-bye to her, not that she was likely to notice. Randler wondered what spells had gone awry to put her in such a state.

The thought made him wonder about something the king had said earlier. "It was interesting that Prethos spoke of history books and chancellors educating him as he grew up."

Dariak yawned. "It's how many kings learn their place."

"True, but he didn't mention his mother at all."

"Ah," the mage muttered. "The story is, she died of illness months after giving birth to him." They sat silently for a time. "I know why you bring that up in particular. You want to know what happened to my mother, don't you?"

"I'm curious, yes," he said.

"She… believed in my father's work," he explained softly. "Pyron was my chief magical tutor, but my mother did her best to train me, too. We even visited the Magitorium together when I was young, though she brought me there in a cautionary capacity, of what not to become. It was a trying experience for me." He cleared his throat. "At some point, I left to train at Magehaven. Years later, we got into an argument and it prompted her to return to the Magitorium. There, for my sake, she ripped into the energies. They burned her out."

"I'm sorry…"

"She did it for love, but of course her goal wasn't to fry her mind. She was escorted back by some of the other mages who explained what happened to our servant. She was able to tell me the story herself, but other events led her to greater damage, and that put her in her present state." He shrugged sadly. "I didn't know what to do, and Pyron counseled me to follow my heart. At the time, my heart told me to gather the jades and save the world, then maybe I could spend some time trying to help her."

"You've never talked about her before."

"It's hard to know what to say. Some people believe I've abandoned her, but I haven't. Well," he added with a deep sadness, "I suppose you best understand her situation. You're in a similar place, aren't you? My quest first. Everyone else comes after."

"Dariak…"

"Maybe it's a failing of my father's line," he said. "He was just as focused on his magic, even when it was being ripped away from him for war. In the end, he was never able to be there for the rest of us, the way he always had promised. It'll be the same for me, you realize."

Randler shook his head. "It doesn't have to be."

"I told you everything my father's notes said about the Red Jade. It's very likely that uniting them will do to me what they did to him and to Frast. I won't be able to live up to any other promises then."

"We don't even know if they can be joined right now. They're still"—he dropped his voice to a whisper in case anyone was eavesdropping—"empty."

"That will only affect *when* I bring them together, not *if*. When it comes down to it, Randler, you know I'm speaking the truth. You're the one who pointed that out to me in the first place."

The bard was lost for words, so he took Dariak's hand and kissed it tenderly.

C H A P T E R 32

The Grandmother

"LEAVE ME TO grieve, Gabrion," the old woman had asked after the chaos that had brought about her husband's death. "We'll speak of other matters later."

It was another delay for his task and Gabrion was torn between frustration and understanding. The woman had lost Yorrish, whom she loved dearly, and now it meant that her entire immediate family had perished in some form or other.

Still, they were Hathren spies and there was an anger in Gabrion's heart that wanted to barge into the woman's chamber and have his words with her. He didn't know how he tolerated the prolonged mourning period, but he spent it with Perrios.

The baby had taken a couple days to settle down from the panic in the keep. The whole place was in turmoil after the earl's attempt to steal the child. Brannis did his best to take over the earl's duties while they awaited judgment from the king. A trusted messenger had been sent, though it would be some days before an answer would return.

When he could, Gabrion stood with Brannis in the earl's audience room, and there he helped the page build a stronger sense of confidence with his new de facto post as earl. It wasn't easy deciding the fate of others around him, and he anxiously awaited the word of the king.

"You won't always be able to rely on others to make your decisions for you," Gabrion warned him, rocking Perrios in a crib off to the side of the audience hall. "I wouldn't be surprised if Prethos turns over the Undying Stone to you."

Wide-eyed, Brannis gasped. "You don't think he would, do you?"

"Truth be told, I would be more surprised if he didn't offer it to you." The warrior stepped over to the page and clapped his shoulder warmly. "You proved your fealty clearly, as far as I can see. The earl would have taken Perrios away without your help. You preserved the king's desire and have held to those original orders."

Brannis let out a low sigh. "I suppose, but I've only ever acted as a messenger. I'm not fit for leading this place."

"I'm sure you've been involved in a fair share of decisions, too. But except for random events, what real decisions would you need to make here? This fort is relatively self-sufficient and highly defensible. Keep your people fed and the rest should fall into place."

"You make it sound so easy."

Gabrion shrugged. "I'm sure there's more to it, but I believe you're capable. So, if the offer comes, I hope you would accept."

"Your belief in me means something. Thank you."

Gabrion then played the role of Brannis' page as he opened the doors to the hall and admitted the few petitioners of the morning, announcing each in proper fashion. Mostly, they were people who had been inadvertently caught in the recent subterfuge and wanted compensation for their troubles. In some cases, the petitioners sounded like collaborators of the earl's, but Brannis did a fair job of balancing the food allotments over the next few weeks. The rest of the visitors made offerings for Brannis' continued support of their ways, and by the end of the session, the page felt he actually could handle this task.

Alosia arrived with food as the afternoon set in and Brannis and Gabrion settled at the table to eat while the nursemaid tended to the baby's cleanliness. Her effort to protect Perrios in the underground caverns had earned her some time each day with the child. She never tried to take him out of Gabrion's sight, though that was never something they had discussed. He wondered idly if perhaps she finally believed that he did want what was best for Perrios, or perhaps she believed that only Gabrion had the ability to truly protect the heir. Regardless, it was one less thing for Gabrion to worry about.

After quarantining herself for over a fortnight, Meriad finally emerged from her room in the keep, dressed all in black, clearly weakened from her grief. She hadn't eaten much of the food that had been left for her each day, and in some ways she looked ready to join her husband at any time.

One of the guards summoned Gabrion and he gathered up Perrios and met with Meriad in the rock garden. He hadn't yet visited the site, for it seemed odd to have a garden of rocks within an entirely stone keep. He hadn't expected the lush amounts of sculpted life within the garden.

True, all of the specimens were stone, but they were intricately carved into vines and flowers with delicately painted hues that glimmered in the sunlight and gave the impression that they were waving in a gentle breeze. Several paths sprawled outward, each a different color, guiding him to unique sections within the maze-like area. The garden was bathed in sunlight yet the paints showed no signs of fading, and Gabrion realized it was because artisans constantly renewed the space to keep it fresh and alive.

The sapphire-hued path led toward the northeastern edge of the garden to a shadowed nook with huge arching stone trees protecting a beautifully ornamented bench underneath. Carved birds were perched upon a faux fountain that boasted a glimmering azure coating inside to give the impression of clear, sparkling water on a bright blue day.

In contrast, Meriad sat upon the shadowed bench, her body hunched over, her very presence sapping the joyous, calm mood of this corner of the garden. Gabrion took a seat beside her and waited for her to speak, bobbing Perrios in his arms.

"I don't even know what to say to you, young Gabrion," the woman started. Her voice rankled as if she were twenty years older than her nearly sixty winters. "It's like you're ten people all rolled into one and I don't know to whom I speak."

"Similarly, I don't know what to say to you. However, there are some things that need to be said."

"Yes."

"Why were you a spy for Hathreneir?"

Her voice went sour. "That's why you've persisted in speaking to me? I would have thought there would be some other reason."

"There is. But I need to understand why you were in my village when you held no allegiance to us. I need to know who you are before I can give you my sincere condolences. If I offered them now, they would be false, for you're not the woman I knew in Savvron."

She lifted her head and peered at him with tired eyes. "You don't sound like a lovesick child anymore. Might that be because you murdered my dear, sweet Mira?"

"It was…"—he wanted to say 'an accident' but he couldn't, for in some way that was a lie—"…unfortunate."

The woman barked a foul laugh. "Unfortunate that you showed up and cut the life out of her defenseless body." She pulled her shawl tighter around herself. "I don't know why I agreed to speak with you."

"You agreed, I would guess, because I am Perrios' keeper now. And he is your last tie to Mira."

"As well as yours," she pointed out. "Is that why you kidnapped him from the king?"

"That's only one side to the story and you know it. The king sent his best men with me to protect the child while the others take care of things at the castle. There was too much turmoil there and it was no place for him to be."

"Such a thoughtful guardian," Meriad sneered. "And why here, of all places?"

"Because you're here and you're his family."

"What if I… don't want to have anything to do with him?" she hedged.

"Then you wouldn't have cared to meet with me."

She frowned, for he was right. "Oh, very well, Gabrion. But the only way I'll be able to talk to you is if I pretend you're some stranger and not the boy who ruined everything."

He let the remark go. "Fine."

"You wanted to know why I enlisted our family as spies? It's simple. Farming isn't easy in Hathreneir and the land in Kallisor is much more fertile. Also, working secretly for the king had its perks, such as the marriage lottery, which was how Mira came to be selected in the first place. Well," she amended, "after she auditioned well for the role of queen."

"Auditioned?"

"Don't be an idiot. Do you really think the king would just marry some addle-minded peasant who wasn't a pleasure to look at, demure when she needed to be, sultry when it was required? Once Mira was old enough to understand the situation we were in, we brought her to the best advisors we could in order to train her up right. And when the inspections were made of potential brides over the course of the years, Mira always proved herself a fit choice."

Gabrion's face scrunched in confusion. "For how long—?"

"Mira met the king some five years ago and they had their… adventures together."

"But she and I were so close."

"No, you were a foolish child madly in love because she practiced her wiles on you and kept you blinded to who she really was." She seemed to enjoy the anguish on Gabrion's face. "Though as time went on, she began to waver, so it was important to seal her fate."

"I don't follow."

She sighed mockingly. "I didn't think you would. You were always a boy of action who followed his heart and never saw the world outside of himself. It was becoming clear that Prethos was infatuated with Mira, but he risked losing her to you if he waited too long. So Yorrish and I," she choked on her husband's name and took a moment to gather herself. "We went to Prethos and warned him."

"I can't believe that would have worked. He had the pick of all the women in the land."

Meriad rolled her eyes; Gabrion wasn't as gullible as he seemed. "Fine. We informed him that Andron was in the village and that he was training fools like you to rise up against Hathreneir. It would only be a matter of time before dear, impressionable Mira was caught up in the enthusiasm and followed one of the young, muscled warriors instead of the distant king." She shook her head. "That wasn't enough to convince him, so we offered a proposal."

"Savvron in exchange for Mira," Gabrion surmised.

She seemed impressed. "Yes. He had already chosen Mira but hesitated because she was younger than he wanted; however, knowing the specifics of the village, the best targets, the best defenders, the best way to neutralize the town without the blame coming back to the Hathren throne…" Her voice trailed off and she shook her head.

"That isn't how it played out. In fact, it led to the resurgence of the fighting."

"Mostly because of you, dear boy, and your mage friend who tagged along but wasn't aligned to the plan. You were supposed to die that day, along with all the warriors-in-training. And enough homes were meant to burn that the people of Savvron would all have been crippled and unable to reach the king."

"You're barbaric."

She shrugged. "I had to protect my family, and getting Mira away from you was essential to that."

"You had friends there!" he accused. "You sentenced them to die."

"A spy never really has friends, Gabrion. The people who know I'm a spy don't trust me. And the people who don't know, I can't confide in. You're right, though. It was barbaric. I was willing to sacrifice the whole of Savvron just to get my daughter wed to the king and bring my family home to Hathreneir, not as beggars but as royalty. I was greedy and it cost much."

"And Mira…"

"She knew."

Perrios made a gurgling sound and drew Gabrion's attention. He had been tightening his grip inadvertently and the poor child didn't understand the added pressure.

With a deep breath, Gabrion loosened his hold and shifted the baby, trying to keep his thoughts together.

"You're saying Mira knew that Savvron was going to be destroyed?"

Meriad nodded. "Attacked, at least. She may not have understood all the implications of the plan, just that the day was coming when she would be leaving Kallisor altogether, and there would be some casualties along the way."

"So when I met her in the castle and she denied the truth of what happened in Savvron…"

"She was lying to you," Meriad said bluntly. "I said earlier that she had trained to be the king's wife and to do that, she had to show utmost support for him in all things. It didn't matter if your feelings were hurt in the process. She had everything she ever wanted and Prethos loved her dearly. After all the things I had done in my life, she was finally happy."

"I should believe your remorse?" he scoffed.

"Whatever the reason, every effort I made to improve my family's life brought disaster." Tears glimmered in her eyes though she strained to fight them. "I wed Yorrish because he was a carpenter and my family were farmers. At first, I didn't love him at all; his livelihood would better sustain a family than mine. My family disowned me because I walked away from their trade.

"Our son was trained to fight and I pushed him to enlist with the royal guard. He trained nonstop at my behest and he hated me for it. By the time Mira was born, Kyrell was a squad leader, but he was sloppy and it didn't look like he would be promoted further."

Meriad wiped her face and continued. "His best moment was overhearing the king's chancellor talking about ways to infiltrate Kallisor; it was how we learned of the benefits of espionage, so we signed up and moved to Savvron. Mira wasn't even a year old. Because of his connection to the royal guard, Kyrell was our key messenger. Those 'stunts' he did sneaking into Hathreneir were all missions. One went awry when his friends realized what he was up to and he perished."

Gabrion stared at her for a while. "And then you essentially sold Mira to make things better but that didn't work out either because of Dariak, who failed to kill us like some other mage would have. And the ironic part: I quested to find Mira and rescue her. Her death was never part of my plan. Even now, knowing that she was aware of those things and was an enemy to my home, I don't even hate her for it; she didn't really have a choice, did she?"

"No, not really," Meriad admitted. "We only fought about it once and she threatened to leave us and stay with your family and never speak to us again. I told her to go right ahead and that we would leave for Hathreneir the very next day and she would never know our fate. Obviously, she didn't follow through with her threat, and her decision to stay cemented her resolve to our cause."

"For all the time we had, I never really knew her," he said.

"No, but now you do. And you know who I am now, too."

"Some pieces are still missing. Why are you here? And why had the earl kidnapped you?"

Meriad stretched her back briefly and readjusted her shawl. "After Mira's death, we were banished from the castle. We were sent here because they had need of carpenters and farmers, and though our age prohibited us from actually doing those things ourselves, we were able to teach others how to make things grow. We've had to work for our food again and after a year of luxury and freedom, it has been a difficult time." She saw the blank look on Gabrion's face. "Not that you pity me, I can see."

"Just go on."

"No matter. We worked hard to earn the good graces of Earl Thedris while we've been here and he's seen fit to take our counsel on certain matters. We did, after all, serve the king well for years, even if the results were always disastrous in the end, personally speaking."

Gabrion's eyes opened wide. "Certain matters," he echoed. "You're the ones who suggested he kidnap the child and return him to the king."

Her head lowered sadly. "I merely wanted to wrest him away from you, Gabrion. You killed Mira. What was I to expect of you here? To kill us? To slay the child in front of us? I had no idea. The earl misunderstood what I was saying, however, and once things were underway, he took us underground and trapped us there to ensure we wouldn't reveal his plan."

Meriad pulled her shawl tight and the tears in her eyes quavered and fell at last. "I wanted to take the baby from you so you wouldn't harm him. I didn't intend for the entire keep to erupt into a civil war, divided between loyalty to the king and loyalty to the earl. And true to form, Gabrion, my half-conceived notion fell apart and cost me dearly yet again. Yorrish was too frail to withstand the cold dungeon and he died two days before you even found us. And there I was, tied to him, feeling his body grow ever colder, silent and stiff and haunting me."

She dissolved into a flurry of tears and despite everything, Gabrion felt sorry for her. "I don't know what to say to you, Meriad."

When her tears were done, she wiped her face on a corner of her shawl and she took a few more minutes to pull herself together before turning to the young warrior. "That baby is all I have left of my family." She turned her wrinkled face down to see the boy, who had fallen asleep some time ago. "Yet I dare not touch him, for I'm a cursed woman. Everything I do shatters around me. Protect him, Gabrion, by keeping him away from me." Her hands trembled as they rested in her lap.

"Life is full of pain," he said. "Great pain, in some cases. You've had a tough life. I don't condone the choices you've made, but many people would make similar choices and not face the consequences you've had to face."

"I don't want any more pain. I am finished with it," she whispered.

"No," he argued, and he didn't know why at first but he kept picturing a triangle. "You caused terrible anguish to so many others. You can't give up now and free yourself from this life."

"What would you have me do? Rot in a dungeon for the rest of my days? Face punishment from the king? Tell me, Gabrion, what would satisfy you?"

"You persevered all your life, trying to eke out the best possible situation by taking every shortcut you could think of. In the process, you dealt out pain to others and you received a great deal in return. Now, you have to complete your mission with a lesson in patience."

The keywords trigged his memory; it was the advice of the Elder of Gerrish and the triangle he had shown Gabrion long, long ago. It was the same triangle that had caught Gabrion's obsession when he was in his darkest places, but now it suddenly made sense to him. He hadn't been patient himself before; he had thought time alone was patience, but it wasn't. Patience had a greater quality to it than simply waiting in silence for events to unfold. Patience meant controlling oneself while pushing ahead against the trials of life. It wasn't the same as perseverance, where the path was carved by the individual. No, patience was being a stone in a river with the water passing all around; it wasn't the fish swimming upstream.

Suddenly he felt oddly out of place, sitting here with an infant in his arms when the kingdoms were at war. He was a warrior, meant to rise up against the fighting and stand solid in protest. He was meant to be the beacon that others could flock to, who would join his side and abandon the needless bloodshed because they knew in their hearts it was right. He wouldn't have to convince them if he only showed them the way. Soon the one rock would become many and the river would be dammed, unable to flow, and the tide of war would come to an end.

He didn't need to wield his sword against an enemy. He needed to rise up and stand above the rest to show them what to do. It all seemed so simple now.

His mind flashed to his efforts at the outpost and the success he had found there. He hadn't been in a mode of perseverance there. He had been a vehicle of patience, of calming the throngs of fighters and making them experience the given moment, and most of them had joined his idealism.

Gabrion looked down at Perrios and then turned his gaze to Meriad, wondering for how long he had been silent. Meriad's expression showed no signs of impatience while she awaited her sentence.

"You will teach him a better way," Gabrion said. "You're right, though. I won't allow you to raise him as your own, but you will be instrumental in his upbringing."

Her voice rattled with curiosity. "How?"

"You will tell him our story. All of it. He will learn both sides of things, unlike any of us have ever heard before. He will know your treachery and your pain, as he will know mine. He'll learn to see the truth of things because a new world is coming where the wars will no longer be between our peoples. We'll need a king who can rise above prejudice and tradition and who can carve a new and bright future."

She gaped at him. "But Gabrion, how? Everything I touch…"

"You will not raise him," he reiterated. "You will guide him. You will be honest with him in all things, even those things that are hurtful. He must know and understand reality, not the imagined biases we all carry around. He will accept everyone in all things, so long as their intentions are pure. And for those who seek to cause harm, he will know them for who they are and he will persecute them appropriately."

"How do you expect me to impart all of that upon him?"

"Just tell our story and he should be able to see it himself. And where he missteps, you can be there to set him right again."

She looked bewildered. "And this would satisfy all the wrongs I have done, in your eyes?"

"I killed his mother. Whether my anger made it happen or it was an accident, I will never know. But perhaps he'll see both sides of it and judge me accordingly. Yet, he needs the chance to reach a point where he's informed enough to make such judgments and can make them fairly and wisely." He stroked Perrios' tiny hand. "He may condemn me for what I've done or he may honor my other deeds. Or both. Aren't we all complex in the end? No one is just good or evil, are we? We all do and think and feel things that others could take well or poorly." He thought then of Kitalla's last use of her dance skill to bewitch him, making him errantly believe she was dead and the anguish it had caused him, and he wondered if he could forgive her for it now.

"How will I know the whole story, Gabrion? I know my part in it, and some of yours, but in truth, I know very little."

"We all have parts to tell," he said. "And among my friends is a bard who will set the facts down for others to experience and decide for themselves if we were heroes or villains. For now, Alosia will care for Perrios and you will watch from afar, until you better know the tale of our journey."

"And if I cannot?"

"You will, Meriad, for it is your duty now."

She cleared her throat. "If the child is to remain here, then I can't be here myself. I'm a cursed woman and I will not bring that destruction down upon him. He is the last vestige of my family and I will step away." She saw the argument foment on Gabrion's lips and she interjected, "But I will visit periodically to keep an eye on him and to guide him, as you say. I think the journey to and fro would be suitable penance for what I have done while keeping me clear from interfering too much in his life."

Gabrion considered the idea and then agreed. "It would be for the best, Meriad. Teach him well and let him make his own decisions on the difficult matters."

"And what of you, young warrior?"

"I have someplace else to be right now. I ran from my responsibilities and it's time I return to them."

"I see." She looked down at Perrios. "He has many of his mother's features. But I will admit, I hope he comes to learn the wisdom of his protector." She turned her gaze pointedly at Gabrion. "You should take him away now and make arrangements for his future."

Gabrion stood and examined Meriad one last time before he stepped away. She seemed already stronger than when he had arrived, and he believed at last that everything was falling into place, despite the chaos it had taken to get there.

CHAPTER 33

The Wrath of Prethos

CHANCELLOR IERAN GRUDGINGLY worked toward completing the supply list for Dariak, though no one could understand why the mage needed the obscure materials he requested. Every mage Ieran spoke to shrugged and each herbalist scratched his head in confusion. The process irritated him and his patience ran thin.

All he wanted was for Dariak and his cronies to leave the castle and for things to return to normal. However, with each passing day, the king seemed more resolute with maintaining the current state of things. Not everyone was as happy with the new order as they made it appear. Citizens complained constantly, their words coming to Ieran by secret messengers. Numerous shopkeepers were infuriated with the forced labor given to them to manage. Many people wanted life to return to the way it was before the castle had been attacked. Even news from the Undying Stone had told him of the earl's failed attempt at wresting the heir away from Gabrion.

Though Ieran sent pages around to do most of Dariak's grunt work, he took it upon himself to meet with key figures in the castle town. Wendall hosted gatherings among merchant sympathizers and old Frolla organized the townspeople directly. Ieran kept communications with them open at all times, knowing he would need their support when it came to fixing things.

Among the castle guards, Ieran had a number of key allies as well. They were stationed both at the castle and around town, keeping a vigilant eye on the daily happenings and watching for a time when they should act. Tensions mounted when Verna and Ruhk strutted around unexpectedly and it was difficult for some to keep their hidden plans secret.

All the conspirators were bound by the one concept that their king was now merely a puppet and he needed to reclaim his former glory.

Skulking around the castle and town came naturally to Ieran, who had always engaged in secret affairs with various women and kept tabs on mercenaries visiting the area, in case their sights were set on taking down the king. His father had trained him well to use the hidden passages scattered throughout the castle so he could come and go as he pleased even when others thought he was napping or off to get a snack.

On one such trip, Ieran paid a visit to Mzark, recently appointed captain of the guard and both an ally and a nuisance for the chancellor. They gathered at the back of the mess hall in a storage room with a concealed door which allowed Ieran to enter and exit without being seen. For all anyone would know, Mzark had gone into the room looking for napkins.

"Any news?" Ieran asked in a whisper.

"The usual," Mzark growled. "The six of them keep popping up at random places and it's infuriating. How does his majesty permit this indecency?"

"Shh," Ieran cautioned. "Mind your tone. He's biding his time until they depart. When this nonsense began, we expected them to leave members of their group here permanently and our plans to deal with them were sketchy at best. They have too many supporters to their cause and we can't afford to lose any more of our people right now."

"I don't see why our king has rolled belly-up like a docile dog."

Ieran ground his teeth. He always seemed to forgot that Mzark was single-minded and short-sighted. "His majesty is merely playing along to the utmost capacity because by the look of things now, they will depart as a group and none of them will remain to enforce their rules."

"That won't stop them from coming back and reinstating them."

Footsteps outside the storage room prompted Ieran to duck into the hidden recess while Mzark rummaged through various supplies as if he were looking for something. When the visitor departed, Ieran did his best to set Mzark straight. "We have to maintain an air of agreement while the six of them are here. You know young Perrios is tucked away as ransom for our cooperation. If any of them knows what we intend to do when they leave, then they won't go. We'll be stuck in this situation for who knows how long."

Mzark pounded his fist into his hand. "It aways comes back to them, doesn't it. How can six little people change the way things are done for a whole kingdom? It's absurd."

"Once they're gone, it will all be fine."

"Gone…" Mzark echoed, a glazed look coming over him.

Ieran saw the hunger there and it made him nervous. "We have to bide our time, Mzark. Don't do anything rash."

"No." Mzark smiled toothily, unnerving Ieran even further. "Nothing rash. What of you now?"

"I will tend to the king and update him on the progress of my… scavenger hunt."

"Bring him food, while you're at it," Mzark suggested. "It'll give you an excuse to bend his ear a while longer and keep him from hearing the poison of the others."

"A good thought." Ieran was surprised. "And what of you?"

"Patrol," Mzark said brusquely. More footsteps approached the storeroom and Ieran gave one last warning glance before disappearing into the alcove.

Mzark turned and saw one of his companions pacing. "Barrith, come." The foot soldier approached and stood erect, awaiting orders. Mzark smirked at the instant response and decided that Ieran's plan was flawed. The longer they waited, the harder it would be to return to the way things were meant to be. He twisted the chancellor's words around and said in a deep rumble, "Ieran says that the six need to be 'gone' and then we'll all be fine."

"When sir?"

"Gather our allies and let's make this happen immediately. The longer we wait, the more likely word will get out and then it's all for nothing. I'll need you to meet at the second floor armory in an hour." Barrith saluted and stepped away as if reporting for duty on the wall.

Rubbing his hands together, Mzark laughed to himself. While Ieran was running around shopping for obscure nonsense, the captain had been setting plans against the six companions. All he had needed was Ieran's support, but it was clear the chancellor was willing to bide his time. He strode purposefully through key hallways and signaled his fellows with specific hand gestures. At the top of the hour, he met Barrith at the armory.

"Everyone is in position," the soldier reported. "The companions are in their usual place. All we need is Ieran's go-ahead."

"He has given it, and so we shall begin immediately."

"But… he isn't here."

Annoyed, Mzark struggled to keep his voice level. "He's tending to the king himself to ensure his majesty isn't caught in the fray. That'll give us a few more men we can use to subdue the others. I assure you that he backs our plan."

"Very good, sir. Word has also been sent beyond the walls to bolster our efforts if required. We need only light the western torches, sir."

"I know the signal, Barrith; I designed it. Hopefully they won't be needed. Now, let's go."

Sternly, Mzark stalked down the hallway, Barrith at his side. Their weapons were sheathed at the moment, but that was only to allay suspicions among the rest of the guard. They ascended the stairs to the fourth floor where Dariak and his companions convened each night after their meal.

With a hearty shove, the wooden doorway crashed inward, catching the six companions off guard within. Mzark charged in, unleashing his halberd and bringing it about to crash into Carrus, who had taken him down in the desert.

The burly warrior sprang out of the way and brandished his war hammer in defense. Mzark's rage welled up and he battered with terrible speed, and it was all Carrus could do not to take a direct hit. It was similar to what Carrus had faced upon their first meeting, but this time the wild captain didn't have the support of a healing mage to keep his body moving and vibrant. Carrus bided his time defensively while Mzark lashed out.

The rest of the team was overwhelmed by twenty other fighters who charged into the room, and from the sounds outside the doorway, more were on the way. Kitalla tossed three daggers out, striking wounds to a pair of attackers, then she pulled forth two more to use in melee. Dariak was unprepared for a rout and he scrambled to pull on the weakened energies in order to shoot a few fiery blasts at the guards rushing him. Randler had a knife and he hobbled to Dariak's defense, weaving in and out of sword strikes, hoping for a lucky hit or help from the others.

Verna and Ruhk were the least surprised by this insurgence and they sprang to action immediately. Swords flying, they cut down a handful of fighters quickly, taking care not to wound them mortally, which wasn't easy in the enclosed chamber.

More fighters arrived and Kitalla took a quick survey of the room. Fifteen enemies were fresh and well-coordinated. Randler and Dariak were barely staving off their foes. Ruhk and Verna, though seemingly enjoying themselves, were battling wildly and were bound to tire quickly. Carrus was hard-pressed to hold off Mzark's advances and the two other swordsmen who joined the fray. She debated where her skills would best be suited and then decided to change things up entirely.

With a brutal kick to one man's face, Kitalla cleared space for herself, emptying her daggers onto the floor in front of her and drawing as much energy from within as possible. She emptied her mind of the scuffle taking place around her and turned her thoughts to a desert landscape with deep pits of quicksand creating sinkholes everywhere. She felt the energy burn within her and her body called for her to dance to the scenario she created.

Bringing her arms up high, Kitalla wilted slowly, twisting her body down to the ground, sinking ever into the floor. She grabbed one dagger and flourished upward, summoning vile plant-like monsters rising up from the centers of the pits, snapping their jaws at Mzark and his crew. With a flick of her wrist, she launched the dagger outward, mimicking the biting snap of the plants, delighting in the sounds of confusion from the fighters around her. She pirouetted and fluttered downward again, envisioning a bright sun burning overhead, blinding them. Another dagger flew and struck an unsuspecting soldier.

Soon the fighters turned their attentions to the summoned beasts, wondering what mage had been able to overcome the weakened magic in the area to create such an effect. Some remembered Dariak and turned toward him in earnest, but Verna and Ruhk intercepted, keeping him safe.

"Barrith!" Mzark howled over the chaos. "Get those signals lit!"

"Yes, sir!" the man responded, dropping to his knees and crawling to the door and escaping.

Kitalla continued to dance and move about, keeping her position hidden by placing a chasm beneath her own feet so no one would be tempted to come close. The sands grabbed for the guards' feet while the snapping plants mounted their own attack. She lost herself in the vividness of the setting, bringing forth spitting cactuses and angry eaglons to add further complications, and all the while her body moved fluidly and swept the energies into the room with such power, no foe could resist them.

She didn't know how she was able to maintain it for so long, but she didn't care. It felt glorious to create the imagery and bring it effectively to life within the minds of those who would have slain her friends. She may have lost two toes out in the field when the battalion dissolved into chaos, but here she was the master over everyone.

To prove it, she deepened the power of the pits and drew them slowly together. She could see the fighters struggling against the sand traps that weren't really there, coming closer and trying to help each other escape to safety. Up and down her body went, turning from sand trap to writhing plant, and when her daggers were exhausted, she raised her voice, adding an eerie wail to the scene. The men looked around in terror, wondering what foul beast would rise up from the ground to devour them. Some tried to flee, but Kitalla hid the doorway and guided them toward the wall, where they crashed painfully.

She laughed at the sight and wondered what else she could do with this power. Her arms reached forward and as she twisted downward she spiraled her arms, pulling them closer and calling for the sensation of a wild gust of air. Two men fell to the devouring sand, where they screamed in panic to be saved. Even Mzark was affected as he squinted against the blowing sand and sun, and Carrus was able to finally subdue him outright. Knocked to the ground, Mzark lost his halberd, and Kitalla was quick to envision the weapon getting sucked into the sand and lost.

The others hurried around the room and ended the struggle, while Kitalla masked their movements by blurring their forms completely, for if the attackers had seen them walking over the quicksand, they may have realized the truth of it. Instead, she disguised each of them and when their hands struck at the guards, the men all curled into terrified balls, ready to submit to the horrible creature that had been summoned.

Kitalla cackled when it was all over but she didn't stop the illusions. Instead, she brought the sun down from the sky and turned it into a blood-red fireball, with tendrils of flames lashing out at each attacker and causing them to scream in pain. Her companions called for her to stop but she couldn't hear them, for she was lost in the conjuring.

Dariak was the only one who could stop her, and he did so by channeling the energies she released and reforming them into other spells that wouldn't harm anyone in the room. He used her fireball to turn the ceiling into a brilliant glow and the sand and wind brought in the cold night air from the hallway. He pulled on the energies powerfully, trying to drain her so she would stop, because it didn't seem as if she could stop herself.

Randler assisted by adding song to the room, first with a fast tempo, and then reducing its pace little by little. He sang of the Forgotten Tribe, and how their numbers had dwindled over the years until they were merely a legend passed along to future generations. His tempo decreased until he sounded as if he were singing a funeral dirge, casting a sad requiem over the final end of the Forgotten Tribe when one day their line would have to run out.

Dariak fell to his knees, drawing the energies away, and then it all vanished and Kitalla's illusions collapsed when her body gave out and she fell to the floor. The captured fighters gasped when the room reverted instantly to its original state, and they wondered how they ever could have been fooled into thinking they had been fighting out upon the sand in the midday sun.

Heavy footfalls echoed in the hallway and Verna took charge of the oncoming fight, but there was no need, for it was the king and a handful of his guards. Among them was Ieran, his body limp, carried by one of the soldiers.

"Is everyone all right?" Prethos asked.

"We are relatively unhurt," Ruhk answered, his arms and face covered in small cuts. "How have you fared, my liege?"

"Ieran was at my side when this little coup went into place," he said, turning to the guard who carried the chancellor. "Wake him."

Bruised and beaten, Ieran was a mess. He whimpered pitifully, begging for forgiveness, saying it wasn't his fault at all, but Prethos wouldn't hear his pleas. The prisoners were all propped up against the wall as Prethos checked each of the companions, wondering what had happened to Kitalla.

"You could say she was injured in the fight," Randler started, "but in fact, she was the reason it ended without any real bloodshed. She'll be fine."

"You are withholding something," Prethos accused.

Dariak filled him in. "Kitalla has a special skill to create illusions and she used it to confuse them all, but something went wrong and she couldn't stop herself until she fainted."

Ieran gasped. "Illusions? Sire, you see? They have been duping you all this time."

"Silence him if he speaks out of turn again," Prethos warned. He turned to Dariak. "Kitalla has not been here much and could not have 'bewitched' me. My thoughts are my own. As are yours," he said, facing Ieran and Mzark. "Explain yourselves, and be wary."

"My liege," Mzark began, "you have been fooled by these people. They wish the ultimate destruction of everything we hold dear. They needed to be stopped."

"And you, Ieran?"

"I—I don't know what he's talking about."

Prethos gave a mirthless laugh. "You're a fool. You think I didn't know you have been plotting against the coming year? You didn't think I knew about the guards you have all throughout the town? You think you're the only ones with allies in high places who can tell you secrets? Don't you know I have thrived on the information I have gathered through secret sources? I don't only send spies to Kallisor, you realize. I have them here as well. How else would I fully understand the nature of the people around me? Each with his own agenda and each with a mind to be foolish when it suits him."

Mzark growled at the comment. "None of the men I work with support your current status as a puppet, your majesty. Release us and let us destroy these villains and return this kingdom to its former glory. Sire, if you don't, the entire kingdom will rise against you and tear you down. Even now, the townspeople are rallying to our aid."

"Oh?" Prethos wondered. "Because Barrith went and lit the fires on the western wall?"

Mzark winced. "Er."

"Barrith!" the king called, and in came the guard.

"Yes, sire, I am here."

"You see, Mzark, Barrith is a childhood friend and he has told me every part of your schemes since the beginning."

Ieran hissed and turned an eye toward Mzark, "I warned you not to flap your tongue."

"Ah," Prethos said, "at last you admit to your role in this, Ieran."

"I—No, wait! That isn't what I meant."

"Enough of the nonsense now. Poor Ieran, all this time, hating every decision I have recently made. You don't even realize how much my loathing for you has grown in these past few weeks."

"Sire?"

"You skewed the information from the front lines when Dariak and his comrades had come to speak with me. I believed your information that they were seeking to destroy the castle, and so I agreed to send the fighters out to stop them. They assembled the jades and decimated the castle and I was forced to retreat while you handled events up here. My own attempt to reclaim this place failed, for they were a nobler force working for a greater good. I was unhappy at first to lose my power to them, but in the weeks that have passed, I have seen the wisdom of their ways. It isn't perfect, and it's too idealistic to become full reality, but with a strong governing hand, it can happen."

He stepped forward and focused on Ieran. "Yet as my eyes were opened more and more each day, you dug your heels in to ending the peace without even giving it a chance. What did you have to lose, Ieran? You still would have been my chancellor and I would have always needed your services. Yet you plotted against me and tonight is the culmination of your treachery."

Ieran's jaw dropped. "Treachery? I didn't call for this coup. It was Mzark all along. He gathered them all together and put this into effect."

"Actually," Barrith said, "if I may interrupt for a moment, your conversation in the storage room with Mzark was overheard. It is true that Mzark acted tonight before you were ready, but you were going to wait until the six companions were gone, probably so you'd have an easier time of taking over."

The emotions warring on Ieran's face were telling. He didn't know who he was most angry at: Barrith for eavesdropping, Mzark for not securing the mess hall before their chat, the king for siding with the companions, or the companions themselves for coming to their land in the first place. "You're all... fools," he spat. "You're going to bring this land to ruin. Your father would rise up from his grave if he heard you bedding yourself with them! His spirit will curse this place, just you watch. Hathreneir will be no more! The long line of kings ends here, now that you sit upon the throne, you misguided idiot. Once everything was restored here, we would have rescued your son, but you were too weak-kneed to even consider it. You let him be taken away by some deranged moron and trusted that his well-being is being met. You don't even know the chaos that has befallen him."

Prethos raised his chin and his voice was stern. "You would be surprised what I know, Ieran. I heard of the attempt by Thedris to take my son back to me, and I know that order has been restored by Gabrion and Brannis."

"Y—You... How could you know that?"

"As I said to you before. I have my sources. I did not send a reply because I have been waiting for you to tell me the news that you received from the official messenger. But perhaps you have been too busy to notify me?"

Ieran hissed, "Yes, that blasted list of nonsense supplies; that's why I forgot to inform you immediately."

"That blasted list of supplies," Prethos informed him, "was my way of keeping you busy and watching what moves you were making. Dariak has been ready to depart for days and had no need of those things."

Ieran paled. "What!"

"I was warned of your loyalties, Ieran. I tested them. And you failed."

"It was… a ruse?"

Verna gave a rough laugh. "And so was promoting your friend over there to captain of the guard."

"What?" Mzark barked.

Prethos nodded. "I thought she was insane to suggest it, but it certainly was enough to nudge you further along your traitorous path, wasn't it, Ieran? And you, Mzark, were never one of my best commanders: Why else would you be camped out on the front lines at an undeveloped stage of this war? You were among the most expendable and so you were sent out there on your own long ago. I keep my best men nearby until we are ready to fully proceed."

Mzark took the words like a blow to the chest. He realized the truth of them and all his bluster faded away.

Prethos stood ramrod straight and adopted his most regal tone. "Chancellor Ieran and Captain Mzark of the Royal Guard, I hereby charge you with treason against the crown of Hathreneir. Have you any words in your defense?"

Mzark couldn't find anything to say, but Ieran snarled. "Mark me, Prethos. Follow this path and you'll bring ruin to us all. There's time still to correct your errors. I can help you. I have tremendous support for the old ways. Let's rebuild this kingdom into the grand force it was in your father's day."

Prethos waited but Ieran could see the words fell uselessly away and he stopped talking.

"By decree of His Royal Majesty, King Prethos of Hathreneir," the king announced officially, "Chancellor Ieran and Captain Mzark knowingly admit their involvement in a plot against the king and will therefore face immediate punishment for their crimes." He reached his hand out and Barrith offered him a sword.

Dariak took a step forward. "Is this necessary?"

"We strive to build a peaceful society, but to ensure that, there are times where punishment must be administered for heinous crimes. These two cannot be contained in a prison cell. They will not reform. And so, I decree that they will be executed."

"Others may rise up in their defense. You may be creating martyrs," Dariak warned.

"I will deal with them as I must, if I must. Just as I will deal with these two now. I will not tolerate treason." He stepped forward and pressed the sword through Ieran's heart, followed by Mzark's. As their bodies slumped to the ground, the rest of the fighters who had followed them squirmed uncomfortably, fearing they would be next.

Prethos had other ideas for them, however. "The rest of you will endure a period of servitude to the kingdom. When and if I decide you have earned your redemption, you will be released and free to go about your lives. I assure you, however, for rising up against me, that your future will not be easily won. If you attempt to free yourself before my decree, then you will be slain. If you find this unacceptable for your actions here tonight, speak now and I will administer your punishment more acutely." He pointedly looked at the bodies of Ieran and Mzark. Cowed, the fighters remained silent.

"And so, Dariak," Prethos turned at last, lowering his tone, "I may not be the most reputable or beloved king to grace this castle, but I will obey your edicts for the time allotted. If you are successful in convincing my counterpart in Kallisor within that time, then perhaps the future you envision will be possible."

"Together, we will make it so."

"Together, then."

CHAPTER 34

The Outpost Revisited

DARIAK AND THE others didn't remain at Castle Hathreneir for long. Once Kitalla was on her feet again, they borrowed the king's best horses and headed east. The beasts of burden were expert sand runners and were able to maintain sprints for relatively long periods of time. Prethos had also given them a family secret before leaving, a special blend of herbs and grasses that, when burned, staved off most of the feral predators. The drawback was the terrible scent, and Kitalla almost preferred facing off against sandorpions and eaglons.

As they drew further from the castle, Dariak felt an improved connection to the energies. The dead zone was weakening, but it still had its effects closer to the castle. He flexed his skills and summoned a few random spells for practice's sake. Likewise, Verna, Kitalla, Ruhk, and Carrus took shifts sparring with each other while Randler accompanied their bouts with some rapid music.

In ten days, they left the desert behind them, reaching the border between the two kingdoms where the outpost stood upon the horizon.

As they gazed upon their destination, Ruhk brought up his horse in consternation. "This is madness!"

In the three months since his last visit to the outpost, the white-washed walls had been splattered with a dark, dingy mud color. Red and gold flags hung from the battlements and no less than twenty warriors could be seen patrolling the narrow ledges across the top. A huge fence had also been erected around the place, superseding the original stone wall that had marked the boundary before. Ruhk surmised that the wild obstacle course that Gabrion and Urrith had created was dismantled to house the added forces that milled about.

"It looks like we'll have to take this place," Kitalla commented, flexing her fingers in anticipation.

"Should we wait for the reinforcements from Prethos?" Randler asked.

"No," Dariak decided. "They won't be here for several days and if they arrive, I don't want this to become a major war zone."

"Perhaps we can knock on the door and ask nicely to have the place handed over to us?" Verna offered sarcastically.

Kitalla grinned. "Good thinking. How about you and I strip down to our unders and sidle up to the men in there and work our way through to the captain? It's been a while since I've had such fun."

Carrus gave her a glance, then realized she meant playing the part of some form of group subterfuge. "They wouldn't stand a chance against you."

Verna started untying her tunic. "Sounds good to me." She saw the shocked expression on Ruhk's face and burst into laughter.

"Someone's coming, anyway," Dariak said. From behind the fence, they could see a man atop a horse hoisting the banner of the kingdom of Kallisor.

"With all those guards, it's a wonder they didn't greet us out on the sand," Ruhk growled.

Carrus grumbled, placing his hand on his war hammer, looking around suspiciously.

An opening appeared in the fence as the captain rode through, flanked by ten fighters, all in iron armor with shields and swords at the ready. "I am Gevvin of the one true kingdom of Kallisor. State your purpose for coming to this outpost of the Great King Kallion of Kallisor."

"The one true kingdom?" Verna whispered to Kitalla, who shrugged.

Dariak stepped forward. "I am Dariak, son of Delminor, and I have come to this outpost to put an end to the war."

The captain laughed. "Your name is known to us. Were you not held prisoner in our King's dungeon some time ago? Were you not slated for public execution? Were you not deemed a traitor to the land of Kallisor?"

"It's all true," Dariak said lightly. "However, your king's decision was mistaken. I merely want to end the war and find a way for both kingdoms to work together as one united force."

"Ah. You're among the oddities who occupied this outpost before. I assure you that your ways are flawed and you will not retake this place."

"It's not our intention to fight," Dariak said. "But if it is necessary, then we will defend ourselves."

"Then defend!" Gevvin shouted. "Take them out! Attack!"

Immediately, the team was surrounded, for five pairs of fighters were hidden beneath dark brown tarps. They jumped up in ambush, pressing the six companions tightly together while the captain's entourage raced ahead.

Kitalla wasted no time channeling her dance skill. She knew deep down that they could overcome this fight by hand, but the power of her skill had been overwhelmingly successful and she wondered how long it would last. Her initial reason for joining Dariak's quest had been for augmented power, and now it seemed she had acquired it. There was no point in keeping her skill at bay when it could make this skirmish all the easier.

The rest of the team, however, launched into action. Randler fired off his bow at the enemy, seeking to distract the fighters and to cause minimal damage to their limbs while knocking them out of the fight. Many of the arrows thudded against the iron armor, but if he could aim it just right, he knew he could strike a few good hits anyway.

Dariak's arms and body waved around as he called to the earth below their feet. He drew on his inherent connection to the energies and worked to loosen the soil underneath the hooves of the captain's horse. Gevvin may have remained at a safe distance to guide the battle, but Dariak hoped to unseat him anyway.

Carrus, Ruhk, and Verna became blurs of activity, their weapons flashing in the daylight. Splitting up, they surrounded the other three companions and parried the incoming fighters. Sparks flew as weapons crashed together and soon the air was filled with the sounds of battle.

Above the din of shouts and stabs, the captain's horse let out a terrified cry. Dariak's spell had pinned the beast and it strained to be free. Bucking wildly, the horse threw Gevvin to the ground, where he hit with a resounding clang of armor. Carrus kicked off two of his attackers and ran to capture the captain, hoping it would put a quick end to the bout.

Kitalla moved with increasing speed, sweat pouring down her face. Dariak could feel the energies exuding from her, but it appeared as if they had no effect. Kitalla groaned in frustration, wondering why her skill was suddenly so useless. With a disappointed sigh, she dropped the attempt and caught her breath quickly, taking up her daggers and filling in the defenses where Carrus had left them to pursue the captain.

Kitalla charged ahead, screaming wildly, her arms rising up high and then cutting low. Her blades struck the chestplate of the fighter before her. The soldier brought his shield about to bash her away but Kitalla pivoted and brought the daggers around the other way and upward, cutting into the armpit and scoring a nasty blow. The man wailed in agony and Kitalla threw him to the dirt, leaping onward to her next foe.

Verna saw Kitalla in action and smirked inwardly. She always had such finesse to her attacks, but Verna did not. Instead, she barreled her way into her opponent, smacking the fighter with frantic sword strikes and keeping him on the defensive. Back and back he stepped, trying to bring his sword or shield into place so he could turn the attack around. But Verna did not relent. She pounded fiercely, delighted in the growing panic in the man's eyes as she battered his armor, crushing it in places and making it harder for him to breathe.

Ruhk used grand swings of his sword to keep the enemy moving. Facing off against two fighters, he swept wide, twisting sharply and cutting back with great agility. The two fighters were unable to step through his attacks, for they were slowed by the weight of their armor and lacked the easy strides Ruhk was able to make. Ruhk himself used to wear the heavier trappings, but his short time with the companions had shown him the benefits of dressing more for speed.

Though he was bruised from his fall, Gevvin rose quickly and met Carrus' attack. The left-handed captain stood up and deflected the first strike with a gauntlet, then turned and punched the warrior in response. Carrus dodged the blow and turned quickly, bringing his war hammer crashing into the captain's side. The iron armor accepted the blow but Gevvin moaned in pain. The captain retaliated by bringing his sword in, which Carrus ducked underneath and grabbed. He shook fiercely, trying to get the captain to release the weapon.

Gevvin reacted by pouncing forward, knocking Carrus over and trapping him on the ground. The edge of the captain's shield dug painfully into Carrus' shoulder and he struggled to flip the man off himself. After several tries, he managed to free his left arm and reach for the captain's helm, hoping to pry it off and then punch the man in the face to subdue him. Gevvin released his sword to push away the groping hands and Carrus grabbed hold of the unarmed fist and rotated the other way. Gevvin flopped off the warrior and onto the dirt, scrambling to rise up before he was slain.

Carrus was faster, however, and he claimed his war hammer and Gevvin's sword, aiming them at vital organs and threatening to end him, though the captain didn't know he was bluffing. "Call off the fight," Carrus commanded.

Gevvin coughed and nodded, reaching up to loosen his helmet. Along the way, his fingers slipped under his breastplate and unearthed a hidden dagger, which he threw at Carrus, catching him in the throat. The burly warrior gurgled as he collapsed.

Dariak saw him fall and he ended his earth spells, running forward with healing energies. Without the support of his allies, he became the prime target, for Kallisorians were trained to take down mages at all costs. Three swords flashed through the air, hunting Dariak down. Kitalla launched a dagger and caught one man in the nape, right under his helmet, killing him. The other two escaped her throws and sprinted.

He didn't care what the cost would be for himself; Dariak couldn't let Carrus die for his cause. The warrior hadn't slain the captain because of the call for peace, and now his life lay in the balance. Dariak's cloak hindered him slightly as he went, but he didn't care. He ignored the incoming strikes and dropped to his knees, pressing his hands to Carrus' throat and calling frantically for the healing energies.

It was Verna who saved Dariak's life, for she abandoned her foes and charged after the mage. With a wild battle cry, she lunged through the air, tackling one of the swordsmen. She then flung her weapon at the other man, and the impact to his helmet knocked him down.

Only the captain remained a threat to Dariak, and Verna scrambled to her feet to intercede. Her toes dug frantically into the ground, propelling her ever onward, trying to reach the visionary whose quest would change the world. The captain pursued his immediate threat, however, ignoring the feral shrieks from the oncoming scrapper. Even Randler's arrows did not deter him. His sword cut downward, preparing to sever the mage's head clean off.

Dariak's arms rose up and around and then rested again on Carrus' neck, energies pouring from bloody fingers as the mage tried to infuse the man with healing. It was the energy he understood the least, but in moments of desperation he had felt some success. He pulled again, hearing all the chaos around him and knowing his end was nigh, but he didn't care. If he couldn't save one of his closest companions and supporters, what good was his quest anyway? He also knew that he didn't have the time to erect any personal protections, for Carrus' wound was too great.

Gevvin's sword struck Dariak's neck and the blade bit into his skin with a fiery agony. The mage felt his body pressed to the ground as the metal cut in. His head crashed into Carrus' and he lost his focus on the healing spell completely.

Gevvin stood over Dariak triumphantly and prepared to lift his weapon to strike again. This time, Randler's arrows were shot with fatal purpose and the captain's face exploded in blood. Kitalla, Verna, and Ruhk focused their attention on the remaining battlers, while Randler painfully hurried to Dariak's side, tears streaming from his eyes.

"No, Dariak, no!" the bard shouted, tugging on the mage's body. The blade was wedged into the back of Dariak's neck and he madly wrenched the weapon out and cradled Dariak's head in his lap. "No, you can't die, Dariak!" His tears blinded him as he rocked the mage back and forth.

More fighters arrived from the outpost though they stopped at the sight of their captain dead on the soil. They drew their weapons and took defensive stances as Kitalla turned toward them, a crazed look on her face. She snarled wildly, her daggers poised to kill. Ruhk and Verna joined her soon after, once they had subdued the others.

Dariak's healing spell hadn't been enough, especially after it was interrupted. Carrus let out a final, gurgling gasp.

Randler continued to cradle Dariak, trying to hold the wound to keep him from bleeding out. He knew the damage to the neck would be fatal anyway, but he didn't care. "You have to stay with me, Dariak."

Moaning, the mage whimpered. "Stop… shaking me."

"Dariak!" Randler wiped his tears and tried to focus but he couldn't see. He felt Dariak moving around, reaching for the wound and sighing.

"The jades," he whispered, barely able to speak.

Kitalla faced off against the new fighters. "Who else would like to perish today?" she called. "I am not in a pleasant mood." She jabbed her dagger at one man, who jumped. "You?" Then she targeted another man, eliciting that same startlement. "You? Weapons down or face our wrath!"

"Oh, the stars!" one of the men stammered. "He's alive!" His finger wavered, pointing toward Dariak.

The mage sat up, grabbing the back of his neck. He was oblivious to all but Randler. "The jades," he said again. "Weak, but trying." He winced in pain as the healing jade sent tiny wafts of energy toward Dariak's wound, repairing the damage. He could feel the other jades trembling as if they were giving their minute strength to the healing jade.

"Be still," Randler crooned. "Everything's going to be all right."

"Mage trickery!" one of the fighters shouted. "We should kill them now!"

Kitalla launched a dagger and it caught the man in the small of his neck, killing him instantly. "Who's next?" she hissed. "Stand down!"

Uncertain of what to do, the fighters looked again at their fallen captain and the twenty other soldiers who had been downed during the ambush. Coupled with the rising of the mage, who should have died for all accounts of the strike he had taken, the fighters realized they had two choices; surrender or perish. Almost in unison, their swords were tossed to the ground.

"Verna, check on Carrus," Kitalla ordered and the woman obeyed at once.

Ruhk stood with Kitalla, keeping a wary eye on the eight men standing before them. "He's dead," Verna called with a strangled knot in her throat. "Carrus is dead."

"No," Kitalla growled, an intense pain lighting inside her. "No, he can't be."

Ruhk turned to her, "Kitalla?"

"No!" she screamed, rushing forward and throwing her daggers at the soldiers who had surrendered. Two fell dead instantly as she withdrew more knives from their buckles. Two others fell before any of them realized they were being executed.

The four remaining soldiers dodged the incoming attacks and reclaimed their weapons to fight against the distraught thief. She battled solely on instinct, and that was fatally dangerous to them. Her body slipped between their defenses, reacting to subtle twists of their arms and bends of their hips. Kitalla raged and grabbed one man by his helmet, bringing his head down and her knee up, bashing his noseplate in.

A sword slashed across her back and she yelped, spinning around and lunging for the assailant. She knocked him to the ground and yanked his helmet off, then used it to bash his skull. Her wild eyes rose up and watched as a sword cut downward. She reached out with her left hand and took a deep gash in her palm, while pulling her right arm around to take the blade itself and wrench it from the fighter. Screaming, she swept the blade around and clobbered the soldier with the hilt, then smacked him again and again until he fell to the ground.

The final fighter had his hands over his head and he cried in terror, seeking refuge from the insane woman. He sought out Ruhk's protection, falling to his knees in supplication and when Kitalla pursued the man, Ruhk intervened, blocking her strike and then grabbing her around the waist and tackling her. Verna hurried over and it took the two of them to restrain Kitalla.

Dariak recovered well enough to stand, thanks to the healing jade, but there was nothing he could do for Carrus. His life was already gone, and he stared at the man, his heart aching. He glanced over at Ruhk and Verna who used all their strength to keep Kitalla still. "Let her go," he said.

Kitalla's eyes were wild. She shoved her comrades away and hurried over to Carrus, where she crashed to the ground in horror. Great wracking sobs shook her and her voice pierced through the air in agony. "Not you too! No, no, no, it can't be! No!" She lifted his torso and pressed it against herself, rocking back and forth. The scene made the others feel terribly uncomfortable, intruding on an intensely private moment.

Perhaps it was his discomfort or maybe it was practicality, but Ruhk cleared his throat and muttered to Dariak, "We have to secure the rest of the outpost, and soon. If they reorganize in there…"

Verna touched the man's shoulder. "Let's go then. We can handle it." With a determined look in their eyes, they lifted their swords and ventured through the fence, declaring the outpost captured and demanding the surrender of the other inhabitants. Those who had seen the fighting surrendered immediately and insisted their comrades do the same.

Randler plucked the string of his bow in a slow rhythm, watching Kitalla as she continued to squeeze Carrus to her breast, as if she could resurrect him by her will alone. With a mild, tender voice, Randler lifted himself in song.

A warrior of the strongest heart, who lived a life so brave.

He stood up tall with his companions and risked his soul each day.
With blazing sword! With shining eyes!
Carrus is a man to cherish in our hearts.

He came to us from a land distant, a place now he cannot see.
Yet we will honor his every action, from the smallest to greatest deed.
With mighty arms! With sharpest mind!
Carrus is a man to cherish in our hearts.

An able fighter, was this man, and he rose up as a leader.
Though the odds were stacked up high against us, never did he teeter.
With powerful strikes! With sonorous voice!
Carrus is a man to cherish in our hearts.

His final grace in defense of a friend, saving us all this day.
He took on the captain and turned the tide, and that's how he shall stay.
With deepest friends! With eternal grace!
Carrus is a man to cherish in our hearts.

He and Dariak wiped tears from their eyes, then the mage set some protection spells around Kitalla. There was no moving her, and she was entitled to her grief. They left her there, with her memories of Carrus and all the comfort and support he had given her when she otherwise would have fallen to pieces.

Her whimpering cries continued for hours.

CHAPTER 35

Looking Ahead

RUHK AND VERNA stood side by side, swords poised for battle. They had infiltrated the outpost, demanding its surrender, and though most of the men and women acquiesced, they doubted the sly looks of more than a few.

"You watched what happened with the advance guard and your attempted ambush," Verna reminded them. "We have the power to overcome all of you, if you choose to resist."

"Which we don't recommend," Ruhk added. "Put your weapons down and rest assured that we won't harm you if you comply."

"How are we to know?" called a voice from the crowd.

"Guys, it's all of us against the few of them," shouted another.

"No," argued a third. "What they did to Gevvin, did you see that?"

"Plus they have a mage. And he came back from the dead."

The panic welled with each passing statement and Ruhk tightened his grip on his sword. "Silence!" he bellowed, making more than one soldier jump in surprise. "If we were here to kill you, we wouldn't be standing here speaking to you in this manner."

"You're just afraid you can't take us all," called a younger woman from the rear.

Verna snarled. "Do you want to test your little theory, honey?" She ignored the warning from Ruhk as she spun her sword around, ready to sprint forward and hack away at the people in front of her. "If anyone wants to fight, then let's go. I just lost a dear friend out there and I assure you that I wouldn't mind cutting a bunch of you down as payment. Come on, then!" she screamed, her voice breaking madly. "Who's first?"

Thirty pairs of eyes flickered back and forth, wondering who would take the challenge. Verna taunted them again, but the crazed look on her face held them all at bay. It took one fighter to throw down his spear, and the rest followed suit.

"Get yourselves inside to the mess hall," Ruhk commanded. "We'll explain our presence there." The fighters filed out and Ruhk stepped up to Verna, who hadn't relaxed her stance at all. "It's going to be fine, Verna. Some of them are good fighters, but most are new recruits if you look at them."

She stood transfixed for a few moments and then took a shuddering sigh and focused her breath. "It dawned on me when I said it that Carrus is really dead. I did actually want to hurt them."

"I know," he whispered. "Keep that insane glint in your eye, though. It seems to be working."

Verna turned that gaze on him and he hopped away from her, wondering if she might strike him for the comment. "Let's get this part over with," she said.

The entire outpost gathered in the mess hall, including those who hadn't been heading toward the field. Forty-three nervous Kallisorians looked up as Verna and Ruhk strode through the doors. Ruhk walked with a calm surety, even stepping over a loose plank in the floor that he remembered from his last visit there. It was a subtle action, but it made the gathering even more uncomfortable, for clearly he knew his way around.

Ruhk began by explaining their purpose in coming to the outpost and the changes that had recently taken place back at Castle Hathreneir. The announcements were met with much rebuke, but he kept calm and explained the events more thoroughly. Not long later, Dariak and Randler entered through the doors behind him. Ruhk turned the speech over to Randler.

"Be at ease," the bard said, raising his hands in supplication. "Our purpose is one of peace and you will have a choice this night. You may adopt our philosophy and join us as we defend this place, or you may head to Castle Kallisor and deliver a message to our king."

"What message?" cried a non-believer.

Dariak took a step forward and answered. "You will tell him that King Prethos of Hathreneir will be in attendance here, in this outpost, a fortnight hence."

The room echoed with a shocked gasp. "You can't be serious! This is our outpost. It's inside Kallisor. If he comes here, he'll be killed."

Dariak waited for the people to quiet down. "You're wrong. We're here to secure this place for him. We'll make the necessary preparations so that no one will die here."

An angry voice rose from afar. "We shoulda killed 'em when we hadda chance!"

"The only way," Dariak continued, unperturbed, "that King Prethos will remain here and not venture further into Kallisor, is for your king to come here himself."

The outrage continued. "It's a trap. You'll pin him here and slay him when he arrives. What assurance do we have for his safety?"

The mage waited. "I will give you one assurance. If the king does not arrive here within the month, then we will enter Kallisor outright and storm up to his gate to speak with him there."

Shouts echoed angrily around the room and Dariak brought his hands together, calling the words to his fire dart spell. He flicked his fingers and released the pinpricks of light across the room, reminding them all who was in charge now. Moments later, an uneasy silence lingered.

Ruhk clapped his hands together once sharply, causing everyone to jump in their seats again. "Anyone who would join our cause, remain here. Everyone else, you have an hour to gather your belongings and flee this place. And I remind you, you're to summon your king to join us here, and if he has the mind to bring you along, then you'll see that we are honest in what we say."

All but five Kallisorians rose up from the benches and retired to their barracks to gather their things. As the sun began its descent toward night, the fighters marched away from the outpost, making haste to warn their king of the danger they left behind.

The five who remained were all healers who employed magic to aid their craft when they could. "We honor the tenets of our king," Elliera explained to Dariak, "but we would prefer this peace you offer to bring." She bowed her head. "If your words ring true, then we will be allies for you. If we find deception among you, then I promise that we can use the energies to prevent healing as well."

"Then I'm glad to welcome you all to our efforts."

A few hours later, the outpost was essentially empty. Ruhk and Verna searched for stragglers who might be hiding to ambush the group, but they found no one. Randler and three of the healers prepared food, while the other healers made arrangements for Carrus' burial.

Dariak sat alone in the war room, the jades splayed out on the table before him. In turn, he moved them around, communing with their weakened essences and feeling how the energies shifted when he placed them next to different elements. Sitting there with the jades reminded him of Frast's sacrifice months ago, and now Carrus was also gone. Quereth had fallen, Ervinor had lost an arm, and countless others were dead because of his quest.

Dariak lifted the nature and beast jades, feeling a strong connection between them. He thought of Astrith in the western forest, wondering if he could return to the wizened man for guidance once this leg of his journey was complete. The idea of sinking himself into the swaying natural energies of the world appealed to him and he wished there were a way he could lose himself in them now.

It was a useless notion, of course, for King Kallion would march with haste upon the outpost and then the final events needed to come together. Yet, a deep fear caught in the mage's throat as he considered it. Was he inadvertantly recreating the War of the Colossus? The armies of both kingdoms would arrive at the outpost and the kings would face off against each other. He would unite the jades, giving his life in the process, but would the outcome be any different than what his father had done some two decades earlier?

That moment had cost the land much and Dariak didn't know if the twenty years of relative peace were worth another such price. He set the jades on the table and lowered his head, trying to focus on the energies again and setting his doubts aside.

A while later, the door opened and Kitalla slipped inside, her face puffy and her hair ragged. Dariak had never seen her so defeated, even after the trials she had endured in Pindington and Magehaven. He didn't know what to say to her, so he waited as she stepped up to the table and threw her body into one of the chairs.

"Tell me what happened," she said, her voice raw.

"Which part?" he asked, though he suspected what she meant.

"Why didn't the dance work? Why did Carrus die?"

He nodded slightly. "I've considered it carefully. I'm not certain if I'm correct yet, but I believe it's true. But I don't know if you want the answer."

Her eyes narrowed and her lip curled into a snarl. "Don't toy with me, Dariak."

"It comes down to the energies," he explained, gesturing to the shards in front of him.

"They were drained at Hathreneir."

"Yes, and a dead magic zone was the result of their spent power. Your dance skill flourished all of a sudden. It was stronger than it ever had been."

"True."

"It was the only energy still flowing," Dariak continued. "That special skill of yours. It isn't the same kind of magic as the spells I know."

"You've told me this before. Your magic comes from channeling the energies from without, through spell components and words and gestures, and then the result is created."

"Correct."

"Whereas, with me, it's all from me. I generate it. I get that... So?"

He stroked his finger on the earth jade, feeling the fine layer of dirt that was perpetually present there. "So there were no other energies around, thus your skill seemed magnified by comparison."

Kitalla considered. "You're saying it's like a torch in daylight and the same torch at night. It only appears to be brighter when the rest of the world is dark, even though it isn't brighter at all?"

"It's like that, yes. But, staring at a torch in daylight doesn't hurt your eyes the same way because the area is flooded with light and your eye protects you against it. When you see that same fire in the darkness, it's jarring on the senses and over-whelming. Your skill overwhelmed everyone because all the other energies around them were dampened, so yours stood out more."

"Interesting. But it *felt* different, Dariak. When I envisioned each time, it was so vivid and alluring, and that's not the same as it used to be."

He shrugged. "You've also been using the skill more and you've become more proficient at it. I believe you've also tried to incorporate some of the energy-drawing skills I've shown you. It would all add up."

"Until today."

Dariak's eyes fell away and landed on the jades in front of him. "The jades have started to awaken."

She stared at the mage, thinking. "You're telling me that because they've begun to awaken, my dance skill isn't going to work anymore?"

Dariak shook his head. "No. Actually, it's sort of the opposite in a way. Kitalla, when you started that routine out there, the energy radiated off you like always. However, it didn't go where you intended it to go." He looked pointedly at the jades again.

She followed his glance. "You're saying they absorbed it?"

Dariak nodded. "Remember that bout against Mzark before we left? You lost control of the skill and energy kept pouring out of you wildly. You couldn't stop yourself. I think the jades were trying to reach out to you, but they were unsuccessful then."

"And so this time, they took that energy inside and started to heal."

He dipped his head. "Essentially. It was the healing jade that kept me alive with that blade in my neck. But it wasn't strong enough to save Carrus as well. It seemed to realize that, and it stopped protecting him and focused all its power on me. It's the only way I survived."

Kitalla closed her eyes, digesting his words carefully. "You're saying that my dance skill ended up saving your life because the healing jade absorbed the energy."

"Yes," he said, seeing anger boiling in her eyes.

"Yet, if the jades hadn't been draining me at all, then the illusions would have allowed us to take over this place without losing Carrus in the process." Her fists clenched and she saw the truth in Dariak's face. Furious, she grabbed the nearest jade from the table and smashed it to the floor.

Dariak waited as she vented her anger, throwing the unbreakable jades around senselessly, her chest heaving from the exertion. Eventually, she crouched down to the ground and clutched her head in sorrow.

"Easy now," he said softly.

"My dance skill could have saved us. Instead, it went to the jades, but they weren't strong enough to save us. Not all of us." She sniffled, then pounded her fists on the ground. "No more of this!" she shouted. "I won't stand for this anymore!"

"What do you mean?"

She shoved him aside and darted around the room, gathering up the jades and slamming them on the table. "I won't lose anyone else." Dariak approached her but she spun around and shoved him to the stone floor. She then faced the jades and danced.

At first her steps were forcibly calm, and she struggled to maintain an easy pace. Her arms lilted up and around, while her hips twisted softly to the side. In her mind, she battled the rage in her heart, forcing the calmness to permeate her body. Two steps to the left, three to the right, bowing low, bringing her arms high, she continued to dance pouring out images of serene landscapes and fluttering butterflies, with mild clouds wafting ever so slightly across the sky.

"Kitalla, stop!" Dariak called uselessly as he rubbed his side and peeled himself off the floor. Hobbling up to his feet, he made his way over to her, feeling the energy gushing from within her. He reached out to grab her and was thrown again to the ground by her strong hands.

Kitalla's legs kicked up and back, then she spun, her movements gaining speed. Sweat beaded on her brow but she didn't care. The jades had stolen her chance to protect Carrus. What did her pain matter anymore?

From the ground, Dariak reached into his pockets and pulled forth a short twig. He muttered the words of a protection spell and managed to find his footing again. He charged forward, tackling Kitalla and digging the edge of the twig into her skin, cutting her mildly. Angrily, she pushed him away and he banged his head on the wall, losing himself to furious sparks running across his vision. It didn't matter, however, for he had enacted his spell.

The protection magic redirected the energy exuding from Kitalla. It turned the errant forces back around and away from the jades that were thirstily drinking them. Even across the way, Dariak could sense the flow of Kitalla's strength absorbing into the shards and reigniting them. But now he had intervened and disrupted the energy, and Kitalla lost her focus and took a misstep, twisting her mangled foot and stumbling.

"No!" she howled. "You can't do this, Dariak! Leave me be! Let me empower them and then go, go finish your quest and leave me out of it."

He dragged his body across the floor and took her in his arms, despite her protests. "I will not let you throw your life away to this quest. Kitalla, you can't do this. It isn't what anyone wants. It isn't what Carrus would want. Like all of us, he fought for what he believed in."

"But he's dead."

"We'll all be dead someday. But think about how you want to die, Kitalla. Is this the real you? Weeping and weak? Throwing your life away? To magic, of all things?" He turned her around and bore into her eyes. "Is this really what you want?"

"I've lost everyone, Dariak. My father, mother, Joral, Gabrion, Carrus, my unborn child. Everyone. Poltor has dismissed me, even crazy Heria is gone. We'll finish this quest, perhaps, but then what? What's left for me, Dariak? I wither away? Do I become like old Klerra in Gabrion's hometown, rambling and telling stupid stories?"

"You don't have to," he said. "You can start anew. Find a new purpose."

"Nonsense!"

He shoved her hard. "And what do you think I'm going to do? All my life, I've been on this quest, from the moment my father died when I was just two years old. Everything has been about this coming moment. What do you think I'm going to do when it's done?"

Her chin sank low and then she shook her head sadly. "It's not quite the same thing, Dariak."

"How not?"

She lifted her gaze and he saw an intense pain in her eyes that was even worse than what he had seen so far. "Your father united the jades, and he died. Frast united them. He died." Her voice was level and calm and irksome. "How will your attempt end differently?"

Chills ran down his spine, for he knew she was right. He couldn't answer.

"I thought so," she muttered after a time. "Someone else I will lose." She cleared her throat. "So don't lecture me about starting over. Agreed?"

He swallowed hard. "Agreed."

Kitalla stared at him for a moment, her mind racing, wondering if she should talk to him about her unborn child and her connection to the Forgotten Tribe. But Dariak would ask a hundred questions and she couldn't deal with it then. Instead, she grasped his hand briefly, squeezing it supportively, then letting go.

"Come on," she said, rising up and pulling him to his feet. "There has to be some mead or wine here, don't you think?"

He threw his arm around her and sighed. "There'd better be."

CHAPTER 36

Reconstruction of Marritosh

LICA APPROACHED THE desolate town of Marritosh, which had burned to the ground at old Herchig's command so the companions could escape the wrath of the Hathren king's forces. Not all of the villagers had managed to escape the fires, Herchig included, and the entire area reeked of death and decay.

She had approached from the southwestern edge of the dead town, having come from Magehaven. Roughly two dozen mages had joined her quest once the chaos had settled there and Rothra had assumed proper control of the tower. These mages were at her command and they had already shown her some loyalty by stepping from their home and following her, and also in protecting her from the feral creatures on the way.

She still wasn't accustomed to having so many mages around her. Her time in Kallisor's Underground had been enlightening, but only in some places did the mages practice their skills openly. She had been part of the eastern sect, which kept relatively quiet, practicing only on a forced schedule, so that no wild flux of energy would ever be noticed by the people above the land.

Yet the mages from the tower employed their skills constantly, and she found it difficult at times to accept without cautioning them to still their efforts. Along the way, though, she plied her craft more and more, delighting in the freedom.

Lica knew it was silly. Most of her journey with Dariak had taken place in Hathreneir and she had been allowed her magic at all times. She chuckled; she wasn't making any sense.

The mages passed by the broken buildings as they made their way through the ruins to the northern edge of the village. It was where Herchig's home had been, and she understood Ervinor enough to realize he would start there. As they approached, she could feel a powerful pull of energies, and it caused her to feel dizzy. Staggering slightly, she called for her group to press onward.

Lica had seen the Hathren mages combine their efforts to great spells, including the one that had repaired Randler's legs. What she saw before her made those other efforts seem meager by comparison and part of her wanted to abandon her current task and join them.

Six earth mages stood in a circle around a small hut, their footfalls striking the ground heavily in a unified dance. Their arms struck upward, then downward, and they repeated those motions without losing their stride, their voices rumbling in a hearty cadence. Air and water mages worked with other earth mages, crafting bricks from the fallen stones. Each stone was crushed and then mixed into an amalgam that was refashioned into new bricks, which fire mages blasted and cured. Nature mages drew impurities out of the soil used to buttress the bricks, and they also strengthened the ropes needed to hoist the blocks higher and higher.

Even working together in this fashion, the mages had only succeeded in restoring three of the old structures, though those were stronger now than ever before. The huts of wood were gone, now being replaced with the fortified stone. Lica felt the power of the six earth mages along the circumference and she sensed that their efforts were necessary to keep the energies contained within their circle as the others worked. They acted as a virtual wall, turning the energies aside and back to the others within so they could continuously draw upon them.

There was no sign of them stopping and Lica was unsure what to do. She could sense a similar longing among the mages with her and she nodded her head, giving them leeway to join the mass casting. The working mages welcomed the help without question and with the doubled number of mages, the pace increased.

Lica marveled for a time, then broke herself away, walking around the circle and seeking out Ervinor, who wasn't hard to find.

It hadn't been terribly long since they had last met, but Ervinor's face lit up when he saw her, and he ran forward, throwing his arm around her in welcome. His clothes were firmly wrapped around his body and he was marred with dirt and scrapes, all drenched in sweat. "Lica, whatever are you doing here?"

She smiled. "Well, in a sense, I came to see you. No one expected you to remain in Hathreneir."

He shrugged. "I have an obligation here."

She nodded. "I understand. Herchig's sacrifice won't ever be forgotten."

"That's the goal," he admitted. "In fact, we have one metal mage here who's been helping me create plaques to post around the completed buildings, detailing the efforts of those who have fallen. I want this whole town to come back to life, but never to forget the trials it endured."

"You've made some great progress already."

"It's much slower than it should be, honestly. The mages are fantastic, but they're not physical laborers. It takes much longer to create these buildings without sweat and muscle. But I'm not complaining; they're all taking this project on with such personal pride and effort, it's like Herchig is here guiding us all. We're just doing what needs to be done, plain and simple."

"It's an admirable task." Then she grinned. "I'll be honest, there's a part of me that wants to throw myself into the mix and help."

"You'd be a huge asset!"

Lica laughed. "You just want me to help with the cooking."

He winked. "That too. But really, you've got great finesse with earth magic, and you'd really help the rest of them come together. Before we arranged the mages around the periphery, the whole land would shake and knock over anything we set up. Trying to secure it all before the walls toppled was impractical, but Crenya had the idea of the energy barrier and since then it's been a huge success. But it costs us those mages to maintain it."

"It seems to me those earth mages would be better suited to creating bricks than maintaining the wall."

"I agree, but we tried. No one else was able to stabilize the ground well enough for the buildings to stand. But you're here now, Lica. You can help us."

She hated to deny him. "I'm sorry, Ervinor. I'm still on Dariak's quest, you realize. I was gathering mages so we could help support him."

The young man's face twitched. "I figured as much, and I do still support him. More than you may realize, actually. But Marritosh is my priority right now."

"I won't ask you to give up any of your mages," Lica assured.

His face reflected his relief. "Thank you."

"And," she added, a small grin coming to her face as she considered, "I think we can even spare a few days to give you some help for now."

Ervinor's face erupted with joy. "Lica! That would be terrific. I know exactly the project you can help me with."

"Oh?" she asked, puzzled. "Shouldn't we continue the work you're already doing out there?"

He took her hand and pulled her inside Herchig's restored house. Lica's eyes widened at the detail he had put in to recreating the structure. She hadn't spent much time there, but the old man's wall of swords and his random trophy shelves were all in place. Clearly, that one metal mage at his disposal had done more than engrave some iron planks with history.

Ervinor led her through the house and out into the back yard, which again boasted a tall fence to protect them within. Despite the ruinous state of the town, Ervinor had insisted upon the wall, for it reminded him of the countless hours he had spent with the rambling old man. The wall itself was already elaborately decorated with sheets of iron, detailing a number of anecdotes Herchig had shared with Ervinor, and on some of them, the young general had added his own interpretations and explanations of how the advice had helped him on his journey.

"It's incredible, Ervinor."

"This is just the beginning. At first, I was keeping a journal while we were traveling. Nothing grand or anything; some comments here and there about what we were doing. Once I lost my arm, I couldn't write any of it down anymore, and I was afraid it was all going to be lost. Then, talking to Herchig, I realized how important it was to record these stories, so I learned to write again with my left hand. It hasn't been easy and I was keeping it secret around the others because it seemed silly."

"No one would have thought that," she said. "Randler in particular."

He shrugged. "Maybe. Anyway, Siella has been helping me transfer my notes onto these plaques, and we've been working together to create more and more of them. Soon, I want the whole tale recorded."

Lica chuckled. "You'll run out of wall space before too long. A lot has happened, even before you and I joined the quest."

He grinned, his eyes dancing. "I know."

"What is it you're not telling me?"

He guided her over to a table in the corner of the yard. Upon its surface rested a wood-carved structure that she had dismissed as a pile of scrap wood blocks. Looking more closely, she gasped.

"Is that why you're rebuilding this place from magic-fortified stone?"

He smiled broadly. "It definitely is. I'm rebuilding this town, Lica, but I'm making it more than it was."

"King Prethos won't be too happy about your plans."

Ervinor laughed. "He can still have his castle."

Lica shook her head and let out a low whistle, examining the wood structure again. "If I'm judging the scale right, that's going to be enormous."

He nodded. "I told you, I'm still supporting Dariak's quest. We have to get the basic structures in place here first so we can start building upward. This place," he said, gesturing around, "will be part of the ground floor. Visitors will be able to come and pay their respects and learn about the struggles we've all endured trying to secure a true peace. And these plaques will be spread throughout. You're right that this wall won't hold all of them. But once this project is finished, there will be plenty of space."

Lica clapped his shoulder. "Some people would say when you lost your arm, part of your mind went with it. But not me, dear friend. I think this is one immense and worthwhile project."

"So you'll help?"

Lica gazed at the model again and scratched her head. "It's going to be difficult to get the entire foundation to be secure. You've got the right idea of it, building up these smaller structures soundly, preparing to add more on top of them. But for it to all come together and not topple over, we have to do this part first…"

CHAPTER 37

Empowering the Jades

THE DAYS FOLLOWING their arrival at the outpost were immensely busy. There were only ten of them, trying to set up defenses against the upcoming approaches of both kings and their forces, while also taking care of day-to-day concerns. The food stores were stocked well enough for the group of them, which alleviated the need to venture out hunting, but cooking and cleaning took time of their own.

"Let's go again," Kitalla said.

Dariak looked up from the floor, the eleven jades spread around him in a wide circle. Each day, he had communed with the shards, hoping to find a means of uniting them without sacrificing his own life, but they were silent. He wondered idly how his father ever learned anything from them.

"I'm ready for another session," Kitalla prodded, as Dariak sat there immobile.

At last he looked up and frowned. "Are you sure?"

"You need them."

She was right, of course, but he hated to admit it. While they waited for the kings to arrive, Kitalla and Dariak worked intently, trying to restore the energy of the jades. Several times a day, Kitalla used her dance skills to produce the life-giving energy the jades thrived upon. Little by little, the shards' strengths were restored and Dariak could now channel them for small tasks. Yet the drain on Kitalla was starting to show. Her movements were not as graceful and her sleep was ragged, leaving deep marks under her eyes.

She didn't wait for him to answer, not that she had asked him permission in the first place. The thief started by drawing her hands together in front of her chest, then sliding them up over her head. As she separated her arms out to the sides in a delicate arc, she twirled her wrists about, fluttering like leaves. Dipping from the waist and swaying to her left, her arms swept upward gently as her right leg kicked out. She bounced into the air and landed softly, bending low with her back upright, her hands still spinning in the air.

Sitting in the center of the jade circle, Dariak felt the energies rise up from Kitalla's body and fill the air. The delicacy of her dance enticed him to lower his defenses against its effect so he could witness the scene she projected from her mind, for it seemed a truly graceful place. Around him, the jades pulsated hungrily, reaching for the floating energy.

Dariak focused, tracing the lines of force from the jades, ever wondering what drew them to Kitalla as she leaped and danced about. He had never fully understood the depth of her skill and he regretted that their journey hadn't allowed him the time that was necessary to do so. When he perished, his curiosity would have to fall to some other mage who could perhaps help Kitalla learn the true nature of her power and thus complete her reason for joining his quest in the first place.

His mind was wandering, he realized, and he drew a few careful breaths, steadying his thoughts and bringing himself back to the present. Kitalla's movements were powerful but carefully controlled. She rose up onto her toes, stretching her arms outward as she bent sideways, one leg rising in counterbalance. With a subtle bend and flick of her knee, her body turned ever so slightly. The tiny hops were barely noticeable as she pivoted around, holding her other limbs tight.

Dariak likened her stance to one of the massive trees in Astrith's forest to the west of Castle Hathreneir. The trunks were immensely powerful yet they wafted ever so gently in the breeze. He needed that strength for himself now, as events drew closer to him. He didn't know how he would be able to keep the two kings from warring when they arrived, but he had to find a way.

The group had striven to set up safe traps for the Kallisorian forces, including some covered trenches designed to slow them down. Dariak had used the water jade to gather moisture into large vats that could be emptied into the outpost or outside of it if fires raged errantly. The process had also encouraged him to tap into the earth jade to create sluices in the stone walls that would bring the water where it would be needed most. Each sluice had a control rigged up near the vats and anyone could open them to let the water flow. Though his own connection to magic allowed him to draw upon the energies more directly, his immediate goal was to remind the jades of their prowess.

Kitalla moaned suddenly, and Dariak shook himself alert again. The tall tree was wilting; Kitalla's moves were no longer strong and sure. The jades had pulled too much from her and she hadn't been able to stop the dance. Her body bounded about now, still generating the energies, but whatever peaceful landscape she had been envisioning was now likely ravaged with broken chasms and fire raining from the sky.

Dariak remained calm, drawing in a deep, steadying breath. As he exhaled, he pushed his arms out in front of him and swept them in complete circles, as if wiping dust off a long-forgotten table. He breathed again and repeated the gesture, focusing his thoughts upon the jades that surrounded him. At first they ignored him, but his continuous sweeps distracted them and they turned their efforts toward the mild energy cyclone he made as he sat there.

With the influence of the jades distracted, Kitalla was able to disengage from the dance, letting her body sink to the floor, where she rolled around, trying to restore feeling in her limbs. Her chest heaved erratically as she fought to reclaim her breath.

Eventually the jades settled down and returned to their quiet states, each gently radiating a tiny sliver of its essence.

"That was close," Kitalla huffed, pushing herself up from the floor. "What happened?"

"Kitalla, I'm sorry—"

"Never mind that," she interjected. "Just tell me what happened."

"I couldn't keep my mind focused."

She frowned. "I see. So what does that mean? Are the jades getting too strong?"

He shrugged. "It could be connected to their increasing strength. But more than that, I think it's got something to do with your skill itself. It's as if your power is interfering with me directly."

Kitalla's brows furrowed. "But you haven't been affected by my skill for ages now."

"I know. I don't know what it means."

She sighed. "I do. It means I can't help the jades anymore without risking them draining me completely."

Dariak nodded. "I agree. Next time, I may not be able to intervene."

Kitalla glanced down. "Dariak, what's up with the jades?"

He turned and noticed it too. They weren't sitting calmly by like he'd thought. Each jade pulsated gently and with each burst the shard trembled slightly and made a soft humming noise against the floor. The earth and nature jades flickered brighter than the rest, with intermittent flashes from the water jade.

"It's like the illusion," Kitalla said. "I was a giant forest, waving in the breeze with a river swirling through it. Look at them, Dariak."

He made his way over to the nature jade and it was hot to the touch. "It's as if they're still seeing the illusion and empowering it." He closed his eyes and focused his senses on reading the energies in the room. "Yes, those three in particular are resonating still. The others are periodically supporting them with energy."

Kitalla closed her eyes and tried to see the energy flows herself, but she wasn't as skilled as the mage at reading the patterns other than the ones she channeled, particularly when she was exhausted. "What does it mean?"

"It's almost like they're talking," he said slowly, feeling the vibrations in the air. "If I could only..." His eyes glazed over and his hand reached out as his voice faded away.

Kitalla reached out and grabbing him. "Dariak, don't! They'll pull you in. You have to resist it."

He blinked his eyes tightly a few times and shook his head. "Thank you. I—I wonder if my father felt something like that when he called all the jades together. All I wanted was to give myself over to them. And they would respond to me because I'm connected to them all. They would carry out my goals because they have the power to do so."

Kitalla caught the haunted look in Dariak's eyes. "It was an illusion, designed to make you forget yourself so they could use your energy to restore themselves."

"You sound certain."

She nodded. "It's what they make me feel too. Can you stop them?"

Dariak closed his eyes and traced the lines of energy passing between the shards. He stretched his hands out and swept them in a path perpendicular to the energy, deflecting them outward and upward, away from the other jades. He hummed to keep himself focused on the task, but it took numerous tries to break the link between them.

A sharp pounding immediately rang in the distance. The door burst open and Verna splattered to the floor in surprise. "Are you all right?" she gasped, regaining her feet.

"Yes, why?" Kitalla asked.

"There was all this greenish light coming from the room but the door wouldn't open. I've been banging on it for a while now trying to get your attention."

"We didn't hear anything," Dariak confessed.

Kitalla frowned. "We may need to take a break from the jades for a few days."

"You may be right."

Verna looked from one to the other, her face curling in frustration. "Don't you even care why I came?"

Dariak gasped. "Oh! I thought it was because you saw the light."

"No. Prethos is here, or will be by morning. And…" She let her voice drift off, her eyes sinking low.

"And?" Kitalla prompted.

"It looks like he isn't alone."

C H A P T E R 38

Gabrion's Return

THREE HUNDRED AND fifty fighters arrived at the outpost, each bearing the crest of King Prethos of Hathreneir. In addition, there were over a hundred mages, whose robes also bore the king's insignia. At the head of the procession were the king himself and Gabrion.

The companions met the arrivals with mixed emotions. Randler found a battle horn and used it to toot a triumphant tune. Ruhk and Verna stood erect, eying the newcomers, wondering if everyone would behave themselves. The Kallisorian healers tucked themselves away in their sanctuary, determined to let Dariak introduce them at a later time.

As nervous as the healers were, the moment was even more intense for Dariak and Kitalla. For the mage, it signaled that his quest was nearly over. For the thief, it meant meeting Gabrion again, and she had no idea how to look him in the eye after the time she had spent in Carrus' arms. Though part of her felt it was of no concern of his, she couldn't shake the feeling that she had betrayed him, again.

Gabrion dismounted from his horse and approached Dariak, throwing his arms around the mage in a deep embrace. "I have been so lost, my friend."

Dariak returned the gesture and held the warrior tightly. "You have been found once more."

Kitalla stepped over, determined to put an end to her angst. "You seem to be one baby short since the last time we met."

Gabrion accepted the taunt and gave her a sad smile. "He's safe for now, but it won't last if we don't put an end to the fighting. I was wrong to leave you all. We have work to do here."

Kitalla blinked uncertainly. "Gabrion…"

"It's all okay, Kitalla," he said, taking her hand and squeezing it gently. "I know now what you did to me was for the best. We wouldn't have survived that attack otherwise."

Prethos strode up. "Surely this is not the time for such things. I believe matters are more pressing."

"It's true," Verna said. "You're here now, but we're bound to be very busy very soon."

"Lupinoes?" Kitalla asked hopefully.

"No," Verna answered seriously, her face a mask of stone. "A host of fighters comes from the southeast."

Chills ran down Dariak's spine and he absent-mindedly shoved his hands into his robes and felt around for the jades. Time was slipping away from him.

Ruhk saluted his king. "Sire! We can show you to the command center of the outpost."

"No," Prethos said, raising curious glances from the companions. "I am here in support of your quest, Dariak. You have my compliance with your rules. If I were to enter this structure, it would be an unforgivable act in the mind of Kallion. I will remain here with my warriors and take whatever action you deem necessary to your cause."

"But sire—" Ruhk argued.

"Thank you," Dariak cut in. "Your dedication is inspired, my liege."

Prethos turned to Gabrion. "Your friend here has ensured me that my son is safe in the Undying Stone. He also reminded me that we have a duty to our futures, not just to ourselves. I am hopeful, Dariak, that your plan succeeds here this day. After the things I have seen among my people, I believe it is time for a true change in matters."

"What if it means you lose your title of king?" Kitalla asked.

"Ever the prickly one, aren't you?" Prethos returned with the hint of a smile. "Nonetheless, if your efforts here succeed, then I will do what is necessary to maintain the peace throughout Hathreneir. If that means abdicating my throne, then I will. Having my son taken from me, though harsh, was what I needed to realize how important he is to me. The events that have played out at the Undying Stone and in my own castle have made me understand that my land is not as safe as I had thought. My son's future matters more than anything. Show us all a new way, Dariak and friends, and I will follow."

Prethos saluted the companions and returned to his fighters, calling out orders to set up camp and basic defenses. With the Kallisorian forces not far away, he wanted his place on the field secured. A few tents were hoisted quickly in preparation for casualties and to dole out supplies. The fighters noshed on small snacks and drinks, though some skipped the food and turned to limbering up for battle.

Along the journey to the outpost, Gabrion had spoken at length to the king about their adventures and the lessons he had learned along the way. Prethos, in turn, had given Gabrion free rein over the fighters, allowing him to deliver marching orders and instructions for battle. Everyone understood that they were not to kill the Kallisorians if at all possible. The mages were ready with their healing spells and defensive walls. The fighters were armored well and protected with shields. They all knew it was likely that the Kallisorians would strive their best to slay them, but Gabrion had challenged them to be ever stronger by overpowering their foe without any fatalities.

Randler tried to get Dariak to eat something, but the imminent arrival of the kings had sent him into a panic. The black-haired mage muttered randomly, pacing about the outpost. He fidgeted with the jades, pulling out one after another, asking them random questions and hoping that his urgent pleas would be met with answers.

Unable to console the man, Randler left him alone, seeking the others and trying to keep himself calm. "Is everything ready?"

Gabrion tilted his head once sharply. "The Hathren forces will not strike except to defend themselves. The mages are prepared to heal any wounds they can and to deflect any spells that may come our way."

"Spells," Randler echoed. "Do you really think Kallion will bring mages?"

"His father did in the War of the Colossus. It isn't unlikely to happen again."

Ruhk cleared his throat. "As long as the Hathrens are truly on our side now, then it gives us a chance."

Verna shrugged. "Maybe. It's still two factions vying for power."

"Better than three," Kitalla interjected, agitated with the conversation.

"Still, it feels a lot like the histories are mocking us," Verna said. "Like we're all here to try to change things but the books are going to laugh at us saying, 'oh look, they did it all again.' How is it even possible we've got both kings meeting here now?"

Randler shrugged. "There are certainly cycles through history. But they don't all end the same way. This is our chance to write a new chapter."

"What happens if they fight?" Ruhk asked.

"Our forces will defend," Gabrion said.

"And if Kallisor persists?"

"Then Dariak unites the jades," Randler whispered.

Kitalla met his gaze and the two of them realized they each knew the implications of that. They swallowed hard and Kitalla added, "Let's try to keep things calm so the fighting doesn't even happen."

"It's a shame Carrus couldn't be here with us at this moment," Gabrion said solemnly.

They all tilted their heads down. "I wonder what he would say?" Ruhk muttered.

Kitalla forced a laugh. "He probably wouldn't say much of anything. He'd just wait for it all to happen and then he'd step in and get things done." She risked a glance at Gabrion.

They had only spoken briefly after entering the outpost, but enough had been said. The warrior saluted. "Carrus fought with all his heart, as I did until my grave error in the Hathren castle when Mira fell at my hands. Since then, I've been lost and confused about everything. Protecting Perrios reminded me of why I took on this journey in the first place. I have regrets," he admitted. "Some very deep regrets. But I don't intend to keep looking back now. We have work to do and it'll begin before we even know what's happening. I want you all to know that I'm back with you for a reason. I'm here to fight. I won't let you down."

"Gabrion…"

A horn sounded in the distance; the Kallisorian troops announced themselves. Dariak hurried downstairs to the others and the companions reached together, joining hands in the center of where they stood. They met each other's eyes and confirmed their resolve.

"Let's make history," Kitalla said, exuding more confidence than she felt inside.

CHAPTER 39

King Kallion

DARIAK, RANDLER, KITALLA, Gabrion, Verna, and Ruhk all stepped from the outpost into the midday sun. The sky was a vibrant blue and the few clouds wafting overhead floated without any concern for the events unfolding below them. The brisk winter air was stifled by the sun beaming down. It had been a mild winter, but the chills the team felt had nothing to do with the temperature.

Each companion had their favored weapons available but not at the ready. Randler's bow and arrows were slung across his back, while his legs were buttressed by Astrith's magical crutches. Kitalla was ready with a plethora of daggers tucked into the various folds of her leathers. On his back, Gabrion had strapped a special spiked mace, a gift from King Prethos upon his arrival to the castle. Ruhk and Verna both had blades on their hips, his slightly longer than hers. They held themselves with such poise, they seemed more ready for a grand ceremony than a potentially fatal battle.

Dariak stepped forward, his pockets brimming with spell components. Under his cloak and around his waist was the belt Randler had fashioned for him long ago after the bard joined the journey. In each pocket was one of the jades, tucked away but ready for use if needed. The shards were arranged around Dariak's hips in the same configuration they had devised when Frast had brought the jades together. The mage could feel the energies passing from one shard to another, both around him and through him. His stomach was queasy from it, but he needed to keep them close in case everything fell apart.

With the mage in front, the companions stepped forward to meet the king and his envoy of thirty soldiers. The rest of the Kallisorian forces waited in their lines for their king's commands. There were so many of them, Dariak couldn't even see to the back of the battalion.

The king had dressed well for the occasion. His body was covered from head to toe in vibrant silks and velvets, with all the stitching laden with gems. He glimmered in the sunlight, sparkling like a giant rainbow, ready to blind them all and then decimate them. His dark hair was coifed royally upon his head, with long strands of gray hanging from the sides of his head and ending with more gemstones. As his horse moved underneath him, he rattled like a bag of marbles.

A red-and-gold-bedecked page stepped forth with a scroll and began reciting, "Hail King Kallion of Kallisor, son of the late King Kallibron, son of the late King Kalliforth, son of—"

"Enough," barked the king. "These fools know who I am."

Two knights stepped over to help their liege from his horse. The king was not particularly tall, but he nonetheless had a commanding presence, even with all the distracting gemstones tinkling along his trousers, armor, robe, and cape.

"I am Dariak, son of Delminor—"

"I don't precisely care," Kallion interrupted. "I have come because my lands are threatened by heathens. I heeded your warning and I have arrived with the means of removing you. If you cherish your head, then depart my land forever, all of you. If you wish to stain this land with your blood, then remain. It is no more difficult than that."

"You cannot defeat us," Dariak said, to which the king laughed.

"Why? Because you have Hathren forces waiting to defend you? Because you can use magic? It will not help you, I can assure you."

Dariak straightened his spine. "There is no need for war any longer."

"So you say," the king spat. "Yet have you seen the state of pitiable Hathreneir? Soon the entire kingdom will be a desolate wasteland. It's no wonder they have violated the border and come here at your whim. We will not allow them to steal our land from us, nor will we allow you to help them."

Gabrion stepped forward, his face creased in anger. "You are as one-sided and deaf as you were a year ago. It's a wonder a man like you can run a kingdom."

Kallion laughed. "Perhaps you think I have forgotten the treachery you and your companion brought to my home, but I have not. You may have escaped the hunters, but it seems I need not have wasted my time searching at all, as here you are, all together." He turned to one of the knights. "Forgive me for sending you on such a useless errand. If I had only known."

The knight took off his helmet and the companions gasped, for it was Ordren. "I accept your forgiveness, my liege. The efforts were not a waste, however."

"Ordren?" Gabrion asked. "I don't understand."

"Of course you don't. You only see what's in front of you, little one."

Dariak tapped his chin. "That's why you remained at the outpost, then. I see now. You were always a spy for the king."

"Defender of my homeland, you mean. Today is the day my oath is fulfilled. I will bring about your downfall and end your madness."

"Now, now," Kallion intervened. "I did offer them the chance to waddle off freely, didn't I?"

"He isn't going to listen," Kitalla whispered needlessly to Dariak.

"You cannot defeat us," Dariak declared. "Even if you were to strike us down, others will follow and you will be overwhelmed in the end."

Kallion's voice echoed with mocking laughter. "Do you hear this?" he asked of the envoy around him. "He already suggests he will fall today."

"No," Dariak corrected. "I'm pointing out the fact that your time is over whether you like it or not. And if we fall today, we know our work is not in vain. We know that our future will come to pass regardless of your close-mindedness. What assurances do you have? Whether you survive this day or not, your time is at an end."

"You speak nonsense," Kallion said.

"Yet you fear it as truth, else you would not have come with such haste."

"I warn you one last time," the king barked. "Retreat to Hathreneir or perish."

Dariak mumbled to himself then let out a sharp, piercing whistle. Immediately, the sound of rushing water could be heard. Dariak swept his hands from his sides upward and out toward the Kallisorian king. *"Wrethribos tedalor trinvarious."*

Before the Kallisorians could react, a huge wave of water burst forth and sprayed the envoy. Dariak's whistle had alerted the healers to open the vats and his magic had guided the water from there. It wasn't how he had wanted this meeting to go, but he needed the king to see that he was serious.

"Your spells will do nothing to me!" the king screamed. He was completely dry, and so was a three-yard radius around him. Dariak had suspected that the gemstones were not for show, and now he knew how far the king's protections extended.

"No harm was intended," Dariak said. "I'm merely pointing out that your attitude stinks and is in need of a cleansing."

Kallion clenched his fists and brought them over his head, after which he slammed them down at his sides, the signal for his forces to launch an attack. Ordren whooped, raising his sword over his head and leading the strike, while the Kallisorian king stood still, letting the rest of his forces fight for him.

Dariak went immediately to work, drawing upon the powers he knew best. He scooped a fistful of dirt from the ground and muttered a quick incantation, *"Frethios brokka tur!"* Dropping to the ground, he pounded his fist into the soil. Ahead of him, Ordren's charging soldiers stumbled as the ground fell out from under them, depositing them into trenches that had been set up earlier.

Soon the sky was littered with arrows. The companions dodged the ones they could, but Dariak had covered his friends with Shields of Delminor and as the projectiles impacted, they fell heavily to the ground, leaving only minor gaps in their protection. Randler fired his own bow in return, but his target was the king himself in his glittering garb. He doubted he could even hurt the man at this distance, but if he could unnerve the king, it might help to demoralize the rest of his forces.

Gabrion released a loud whistle, though a different pitch than Dariak's and not fortified with magic, then he and Kitalla headed toward the northern flank, while Ruhk and Verna took the southern edge. They didn't stray too far from each other, but they did need their space. Soon the air rang with the sounds of furious battle.

The Kallisorian contingent was better armored than the companions, and thus it took several strikes from Verna before her first foe went down. She smashed her sword against the man's chestplate, then pushed him back with a kick. As he swept in with a blow, she parried with a sweeping strike, then spun and brought the sword up against the man's side. She heard him grunt with pain so she turned and struck his other side. She kicked out again and he stumbled, cracking his head on the ground. Though his helmet saved him, he needed time to right himself, and by then Verna was on to the next man.

Ruhk hacked away at the soldiers like he was cutting down trees. He knew he wasn't supposed to kill anyone if he could help it, but he had to employ his strength up front to keep from being overwhelmed. Once the fighters were scattered about more, he would show more finesse, but for now he just wanted to survive the first wave.

Gabrion and Kitalla hadn't battled together properly for many months. Too much had happened, but they quickly found their rhythm again. They remained back to back as fighters swarmed around them. Kitalla kicked out with her feet, disorienting the fighters, then she followed up by slashing with her daggers or by tossing them. Gabrion pivoted around her agile body, sweeping his mace in wide arcs, pummeling the staggering soldiers once Kitalla had dealt the first blow. He took down his fair share of fighters on his own, too, but some part of him delighted in the teamwork more.

All the while, Dariak cast one spell after another, tapping the jades for inspiration. He managed to turn a few nearby bushes into foot traps, pinning fighters in place with agonized cries of pain. The wet dirt became a muddy slag that prevented anyone from crossing it with haste. The unfortunate Kallisorians caught in the muck wailed in dismay, struggling to free themselves, while their comrades scattered and went around the mess.

As the companions dealt with the king's envoy, the rest of the king's troops marched forward to join the fray. But they were not alone, for Gabrion's whistle had alerted Prethos, who brought the Hathrens forward as well. Despite having over four hundred and fifty fighters and mages on their side, the Hathrens were outnumbered by Kallisorians at least three to one. The odds would have been better if the Hathrens weren't under orders not to kill and the mages hadn't been told not to use offensive magic. Still, they stepped up to the challenge and the battle raged on.

Dariak called upon the earth to shake the ground under various packs of men and women, trying to destabilize them and keep them from fighting well. Sweat poured down his face as he called one spell after the next, exhausting his supply of spell components with each attempt to break the spirit of the enemy. As he worked, his mind drifted toward the jades and he struggled not to call on them for more than simple inspiration, for once he tapped them for energy, he knew he would have to draw upon them all.

"Dariak!" Randler shouted, hurrying over. "Look out!" His legs were much stronger than they had been, but the bard was still not fully healed from the damage he had taken in the forest. Reaching Dariak was a trying task and he shouted in pain as his legs protested, but he didn't care. He grabbed Dariak around the waist and dragged him down.

"What?" Dariak gasped, flipping over and seeing Randler curled up in pain on the ground. Moments later a huge boulder smashed into the dirt where Dariak had been standing and shook the ground ominously.

"I'm fine, Dariak," the bard cried, answering an unasked question, the tears on his face declaring him a liar. "Get up and go."

It was hard to tear himself from the bard, but one of the Hathren mages hurried over and immediately set to wrapping Randler in healing energies. When it wasn't enough to quell the pain, she called over two others for help.

Meanwhile, the companions and the Hathrens kept glancing up at the sky, which made their melee attacks noticeably less effective. There was no rhythm to it, but now and again, another huge boulder plummeted to the ground, sometimes killing unsuspecting fighters in the process. Dariak blasted the fourth such boulder with magic, trying to deflect its course, to no avail. It was too heavy for air to affect it and applying earth magic only drew it toward him faster. His spells were harder to cast with this new threat, but he couldn't tell from where the boulders originated. He launched a few mild fireballs into the Kallisorian crowd and when he thought a new boulder would be coming, he focused his sights on the horizon.

There, in the distance, over the heads of the soldiers, a giant arm rose momentarily into the sky and a boulder was released. "Incoming!" Dariak screamed, trying to anticipate the trajectory. With a heart-rending crash, the stone blasted into the side of the outpost, ripping down a huge portion of the wall.

The catapult was too far away for them to do anything about right now. The companions pressed forward through the battle, seeking the king or the massive catapult in the process. The boulders were not all aimed toward the same target, for some of the enormous stones shook the ground nearby while others impacted the outpost or elsewhere. They didn't know if it meant there were multiple weapons or if it was simply too difficult to control.

"No! No!" shouted one of the Hathren mages as a boulder fell from the sky and crushed no less than a dozen people. He hurried over, trying to help, but in the wild panic he left himself defenseless and was cut down by the enemy.

Little by little, things started to fall apart and Dariak's heart raced ever faster. He would have to decide soon if it was necessary to unite the jades to end the fighting, yet he didn't know how much control he would have once he did so. He frantically called out to any feral creatures in the area, tapping the beast jade for help. Few creatures arrived, but their presence gave him hope; at least the energies were responding.

Ruhk and Verna struggled against the seemingly endless tide of fighters, but they did their best to stay together. Between combatants, Verna gasped, "You know… we have to… get that contraption!"

"I agree," Ruhk huffed, hacking furiously with his sword. They made it their mission to approach the huge catapult and to end its rain of death. With an angry charge, they slashed their swords wildly in front of themselves, racing ahead and startling the soldiers in their way. They made some progress toward their goal, but were stopped eventually and they had to spend time defending themselves.

Kitalla and Gabrion came to a similar conclusion concerning the king. If they could pin him down, they might be able to call off the battle. Or perhaps the man was callous enough to not care if he was captured, so long as the fight was won. Regardless, they pressed their way toward the intermittent sparkling light that signaled the king's location.

The two of them were weary, but the need for their skills kept them moving. Kitalla had been drained by the jades a day earlier, while Gabrion had been on the march. To them, it didn't matter. Each step toward the king was another chance for them to complete this quest and to end the war for good.

"Down!" Kitalla shouted, sweeping Gabrion's legs out from under him as a launched spear came flying in from the side. She leaned out of its way and responded by throwing her dagger forward while Gabrion bounded back onto his feet and defended Kitalla from an assailant approaching her from behind. Undaunted, they stepped their way through the battlefield, pushing further back and toward the hiding king.

Dariak brought his arms up wide, cupping his hands over his head, drawing the light of the sun through his fingers and into the crowd, blinding a number of fighters in the process. He hadn't used many light spells but he always found their effects intriguing. Some of the armored fighters even pulled their helmets off because the light had brought in too much heat and made it hard to function.

As the mage reached for another spell idea, he saw Prethos out of the corner of his eye. The Hathren king was covered in blood, mostly his own, but he fought hard, swinging a flail overhead and using it to deflect the attacks of others. He took a sword strike to the arm, yet he didn't waver. He noticed Dariak watching him and he tipped his head in honor and pressed ahead, cracking the flail into one soldier's head and then deflecting another's attack. Dariak called for healers to assist the king, then returned to his spell.

Randler, meanwhile, was essentially out of the fight. His sprint to save Dariak had aggravated his weakened legs and he was in too much pain to stand on his own, even with the help of the magic crutches. The mages had tended him the best they could, but he needed prolonged healing for the type of damage he had sustained, so they had dragged him to the other side of one of the fallen boulders where he could keep tabs on the battle and still use his bow if needed. He felt useless in such a crucial time, so he turned his thoughts toward the jades, hoping to puzzle out some unknown solution to them so that Dariak wouldn't have to die when he united them.

The catapult kept launching its missiles into the foray and the massive boulders were wildly destructive. The fighters who barely avoided them shook their heads, wondering how they even managed to load the stone into a weapon in the first place. There was no time to consider the idea, for each fighter was hard-pressed to maintain his stance and to keep fighting.

The companions were all marked with wounds, some superficial, some deep and dangerous. The Hathren mages trailed behind them, sending healing energy to keep them fighting, but one by one the mages were slain by the Kallisorians who were trained to always obliterate the magic-users as a top priority. It wasn't long before the Hathren team was essentially without the benefit of magic at all.

Randler's attempts to puzzle out the jades was fruitless with everything happening around him. He turned his thoughts instead on holding his bow and trying to take down a few Kallisorian soldiers. The fighting was far enough away from him now that he was in little danger, but not so far that a well-placed shot wouldn't reach someone. He aimed, prepared to launch, but then a boulder entered the sky.

He watched its trajectory and roughly estimated where it was headed. He followed the path down with his finger and he saw, even from his post, that the man underneath it had no time to escape. Two hands rose up as if to catch the stone and with a heart-wrenching thud that shook the ground, the man was gone, cloak and all.

Randler's cry burned his throat wretchedly. *"Dariak!"*

CHAPTER 40

The Catapult and the Mages

OBLIVIOUS TO THE fate of their friend, Ruhk and Verna huffed and wheezed and fought their way toward the catapult. Its effects were devastating and they had to put an end to it, regardless of the cost. Verna had taken several deep cuts to her legs and left arm. She also had a gash on her cheek that stung fiercely from all the sweat running down her face.

Ruhk wasn't much better off. His arm felt broken and his side had been badly pierced by a spear. Wincing from the pain, he kept his sword flailing about, no longer caring what kind of damage he did to others. If they didn't stop the catapult, then too many allies would perish and there would be no stopping the Kallisorians from then invading Hathreneir and taking over both kingdoms. And despite Kallion's claims that Hathreneir was a useless wasteland, Ruhk didn't believe for an instant that the king had no desires for the land.

Strike, parry, step, step, strike. Ruhk kept a rhythm going, only altering the direction of his hits. He needed the pattern to keep him focused after the overextended rout. His sword arm grew heavy, but if he paused for a rest he would die. Some part of his old hatred welled inside of him and he used its power to keep moving.

As Verna's strength waned, she loaded each attack with the names of her family. Her siblings and her mother were honored for many hits, and her heart ached for her father because he was out on the battlefield somewhere, but she didn't know where. He was likely in northern Hathreneir fighting off minor skirmishes, or perhaps he had met his doom already. She drew on his sacrifice to save her from this insane fighting, wishing she could have stayed home for his sake and honored his wish. Instead, she promised she would meet him again, even if that meant reuniting in the afterlife. Not that she believed in one.

As they hacked their way ahead, the catapult drew ever nearer. They were relieved to notice that only one such contraption was in use, but when they saw how it was operated, their hearts sank.

Two giant ursalors were strapped together with a massive chain that fed through a large metal loop. As the beasts were enticed to walk forward, which led them away from the battle itself, the arm of the catapult was lowered and secured in place. A large cart of giant stones was nearby and a stone sluice had allowed the boulders to be rolled down from the cart and onto the catapult arm for launch. The ramp, however, had cracked and fallen to pieces. Ruhk and Verna were not entirely surprised when a team of mages chanted wildly and swept the next boulder into the air and settled it haphazardly on the catapult. They lacked precision with such a large projectile and its mass caused the catapult to teeter to one side or other, leading to the erratic flight paths.

With a snap of the launching pin, the arm swung up, catching on a horizontal bar and sending the boulder sailing through the air. The mages then worked to stabilize the catapult while the ursalor handlers encouraged the beasts back into place so they could rearm the weapon.

Ruhk and Verna were unsure at first where they should focus their attacks, but if the mages turned their skills against them, they would be at a disadvantage. Despite the massive beasts that could run amok and crush them, they set their sights on the five mages and raced ahead.

Other soldiers in the area tried to stop them, but they barreled through and brushed them aside, seeking their quarry. The mages continued their casting, hoisting one boulder magically into the air, oblivious to the oncoming charge. Verna raised her sword, ready to strike one mage down, but Ruhk pounced and shoved her aside, taking an arrow in his shoulder. With a scream of pain, he wrenched the arrow from his flesh and gripped his sword. Verna recovered from the tumble and tucked her head low, racing across the distance to the mages. The boulder hovered in the air, drawing closer to the catapult, when one of the mages saw her coming.

With a gasp of shock, the mage lost concentration and the spell manipulating the boulder faltered immediately. The massive stone dropped and rolled, crushing three of the Kallisorian soldiers. Verna continued her pursuit, but the air mage recovered quickly and turned her skills against her. With a furious gust of wind, she smacked Verna in the face. It was like running into a wall and Verna fell to the ground, stunned.

Ruhk could barely see through the pain in his body, but he charged for the mages. He saw Verna tumble aside and reached his hands out before him in case a similar spell was erected. He plowed against the agony as he reached the mages, barreling into one and knocking her down. Another mage pulled upon the energies of the earth and kicked a pile of dirt at Ruhk. Each bit of muck hardened to stone and pelted him. He didn't care. The catapult had to be stopped, whatever the cost. He swung his sword like a huge fan, deflecting many of the incoming pebbles, after which he tried to reach the mage directly.

By now, all five mages had turned their attention on the two assailants, bringing minor spells around to deflect them and to keep them detained until the other soldiers could sweep in to defeat them. Verna jumped repeatedly, trying to avoid snapping mouths that appeared in the soil under her. Ruhk struggled against a whirlwind that carried innumerable pellets of earth. He could barely hear against the tumult of the wind, and he feared he might crash into Verna at any moment.

The onrush of soldiers filled them with panic, and the spells of the mages were overwhelming them. Verna refused to perish under such conditions and as she bounced around avoiding the moving traps, she set her sights on the nearest mage and then launched her sword. The blade flipped end over end as it went and the mage had to stop her spell to deflect the projectile. It gave Verna a chance to rush ahead and, with a wild scream, she tackled another mage who aimed his spells toward Ruhk. The mage hit the ground with a thud and Verna punched him unconscious.

The projectiles swirling around Ruhk lessened somewhat, though the wind continued unabated. He leaned his body forward and let it push ahead blindly. He crashed into the side of the catapult and scored a gash on his left arm. The pebbles thudded into the machine and soon were gone. All he had left was the wind to contend with. Using the catapult as a guide, Ruhk held his other hand over his eyes, trying to make out shapes in the distance. There was too much motion for him to concentrate on, but he knew roughly where the mages were and so he pushed himself away from the weapon and charged, his sword swinging chaotically.

He felt the blade bite into one foe on the right, then another on the left. He didn't stop to spar, moving on and keeping the blade in motion, hacking toward one shifting blob, then another. His sword strokes were inefficient and sporadic, but the wild nature of the attack made it hard for anyone to defend against him.

Verna grabbed some random spell components from the man she had knocked down and she turned toward the next mage. Without thinking of the consequences, she cracked the waterbeetles in half and flung them into the next spell the mage was casting. The unintended spell component was drawn into the invocation and the rush of air that followed was laden with a thick slime that splattered everywhere. Verna heard the curses from the mage as he tried to shake the mess off his robe so he could grab for other components, but she didn't give him a chance. The sucking sound of her feet was an ominous warning for the fate coming to him and the mage panicked, trying to grab anything from his pockets before she reached him. And even though he did manage to wrangle a mess of leaves from one pocket, he didn't have time to enact any sort of spell. As with the previous mage, Verna hammered against him until her fists punctured his defensive spells, allowing her to knock him out.

Ruhk felt the bite of several other blades nipping at his skin and he wondered if the entire battlefield would soon be covered in his blood. His mind raced, thinking of the family he had left behind so he could serve the king, wondering what stories would ever reach them about his adventures. He doubted his wife would understand why he defected to Gabrion's quest, nor why he now gave his life to take down a catapult, when he could have sent others ahead to accomplish the task instead. He thought of the raging fight they would have if he could somehow return, knowing she loved him dearly and was merely looking out for his wellbeing. But he wouldn't get to have that argument if the soldiers continued to pummel him.

Thinking of his two small children, Ruhk roared and spun with the whirlwind that continued to disorient him and slow him down. He whipped the sword up and down as he did so, feeling resistance here and there as he connected with the combatants seeking to take him down. He turned faster and faster, propelled by the wind itself, and soon he spun with such speed, he had no sense of where he was or what was happening. His vision filled with a plethora of sparks from his sword smashing against iron armor and other weapons, but the attacks did not relent. One sword reached into the whirlwind and cut a long gash across Ruhk's midsection.

As he reached his arm down to grab for the wound, his spinning increased, and he realized suddenly that his feet were off the ground, turning wildly with the maelstrom. Centripetal force made it difficult to hold his blade any longer, and he tried to grab it with two hands, but he couldn't bring them together and the sword flew away. He vaguely heard a scream in the distance as a response.

The two remaining mages altered their tactics, turning their spells inward, defending themselves against intrusion. The earth mage grabbed dirt and mashed it against her skin, then called for it to coat her completely, essentially covering her in stone. Her movements became sluggish, and because of that, she couldn't cast spells effectively, but the density of the outer armor was such that Verna couldn't even dent it with her sword. The warrior turned instead to the last mage.

The young man's eyes were wild with fear as he pulled wind around himself in wild torrents. Some blades of air lashed out at Verna, while others deflected her strikes away from him. He couldn't control them directly, having empowered them to protect him at all costs. The wind whirled around and battered against Verna, causing her to squint and lose her aim. She lunged for him, but the gusts of air deflected her and splattered her to the ground. With a growl, she stood and charged the mage, weaving uncontrollably left and right as the magic pushed her around.

She threw her sword again, regretting it instantly as the wind snagged it and reflected it back at her. Dodging low, Verna reached up and grabbed the sword, blade first, cutting her hand in the process. She reversed the blade, taking the hilt again, and risked a glance at the stone-covered mage who was biding her time. Grateful for that reprieve, Verna focused on the air mage and tried again. Leap after leap, she missed the man by mere inches. Each time he seemed to be elsewhere, but she knew she was the one who was being deflected. She grabbed her sword again and pounced. But as she felt her body being pushed away, she curled in tightly, bringing the sword around as quickly as she could. The blade hacked into the mage's robe, and he fell to the ground with a blood-curdling cry.

The earth mage wailed in horror, dropping her stony armor and rushing to the air mage's side. Tears filled her eyes as she saw blood welling up quickly from his wound. Weeping, she threw her arms around him and waited for Verna to finish them off.

Instead, the mad warrior crouched down and, through gasping breaths, asked, "Do you know any healing magic?"

The woman wailed. "What good will that do, when you'll just cut us down moments later?"

"I won't," Verna promised. "No one is supposed to die today. Go on. Heal him."

Without waiting, Verna turned around and saw Ruhk stumbling about, his body covered in blood. She rushed to his aid, striking down the three soldiers who pursued him. "I'm here! I'm here!" she shouted, catching him as he fell over, retching from the frantic spinning.

Exhausted, Ruhk wiped his mouth and turned to Verna, "It's been a good ride."

"Don't you talk like that! There's more for us to do."

He shook his head, his chest heaving. "I can barely feel anything. I'm done."

Verna smacked him. "Ruhk! Don't you quit on me now. Rest a moment, sure, but you're not finished here today. Do you hear me?"

Ruhk tried to smile but his pain was terrible. Blood leaked from numerous wounds, and Verna realized there wasn't anything she could do for him now. Except win. She gently touched her hand to his face, closing her eyes and wishing she could do something else.

"Stand back," said a terse voice behind her. Verna turned around and saw the earth mage with herbs and dirt in her hands. "He's going to scream, but it might save him. Shall I?"

"Yes."

The mage went immediately to work as Verna turned her gaze around the site. The air mage she had cut lay on his back, breathing slowly. Twenty or so soldiers were unconscious or dead—she wasn't sure which—as were the other three mages. The ursalor handlers were nowhere to be seen, and Verna wondered if they had met their fate already or if they had fled.

As predicted, Ruhk howled in raging agony as the earth mage worked her magic. She patted leaves and dirt onto his major wounds and cast a quick healing spell that sealed the lacerations abruptly. His body twitched and would have thrashed about if the mage hadn't first pinned him to the ground with her spells. He screamed again and again, eventually passing out.

"A life for a life," the mage said, looking up at Verna.

"Get your man out of here," the warrior said. "This battle wasn't meant to happen. Unless there's a way to get the fighting to stop, things will get worse before they're better. So, get him out of here and get to safety."

"I don't understand what foe leaves her enemy alive to rise up another day, bu—"

"I'm no enemy," Verna said sharply. "We wanted only to speak with your king, not this. But we had to be ready in case... of this."

"What of him?" she asked, pointing to Ruhk.

Verna shook her head, her face a mask of confusion. "I don't know."

"Are you really here to stop the fighting? It's what we were told. The ruse you're fighting under is to bring peace."

"It's no ruse."

They held their gazes for a time and then the mage nodded slowly. "Maybe you're right; I don't know. But you look like you've got fight left in you. What are you going to do?"

Verna glanced over her shoulder at the two ursalors that stomped their feet, trying to break the harness linking them together. "It looks like things are going to get interesting soon."

"You can't protect him and take them on at the same time."

"I know." Her voice cracked as she added, "I'm sure he will forgive me."

The mage stared intently again. "I'll take him with me. With us."

"You will? Why?"

A tiny smirk flickered onto her face for a moment. "To see if you're telling me the truth about why you're all here. Come find us when it's all over. Head for Warringer."

"Thank you," she breathed, a sense of relief washing over her. "I'm Verna."

"Illuria." The ursalors cried out in rage, smashing into each other as they tried to shatter the restraints. "Here, Verna." She set a leaf in Verna's hand and cast a minor healing spell, the effects of which numbed some of the pain in her body. "That'll help your wounds not bleed so fast."

"Thank you. You'd better go before those two break free."

"Good luck to you."

"And you." Verna touched her hand to Ruhk's face one last time before she found her sword and stepped away.

CHAPTER 41

Ordren's Strike

GABRION AND KITALLA continued to battle as one unit. They moved so fast and with such precise countermoves, they looked like one being with four arms and legs expertly navigating the battlefield and tearing down any opposition. Fatigue was irrelevant to them as they lashed out with mace and daggers, their bodies pirouetting about and cutting through the Kallisorian forces.

They were easily identified as a threat, and the soldiers homed in on them, trying to stop them. But it was like trying to hold back a stampede. Gabrion's smashes with the mace stunned one man after the next, while Kitalla clobbered their iron helmets with the hilts of her daggers or crushed their chests with her foot. Each strike was filled with the power their adventures had built within them and the soldiers fell one after another.

Ordren saw the efforts of the companions and growled. He ordered fifty foot soldiers to surround them and to press inward, determined to drown them out with numbers. As they went, the captain hefted his sword and continued searching for his prey.

Kitalla noticed the increased numbers immediately and she warned Gabrion of the change.

"Got it," he said between strikes. He dug his heels in the ground and bent his legs, swinging the mace around in challenge. Kitalla took a few steps away from him, pulling extra daggers from her pockets and arranging three knives in each hand, making her fists look like large metal talons.

With a unified shout, ten soldiers flooded in first, surrounding the duo. One man snapped a whip at Kitalla's feet, trying to snag her ankle but missing. She retaliated with a spin-kick that knocked him backwards. Two swords came cutting in and she dropped to the ground to avoid them, pushing herself up instantly and flashing her arms out to the side, her blades thudding against the chestplates. Another swordsman rushed her as her body was wide open, but Kitalla jumped and kicked the sword with one foot and the man's face with the other.

Gabrion's mace became a whirl of activity as he thundered against the oncoming torrent of fighters. His swings were so powerful that when he sideswiped one soldier, the soldier invariably crashed into the man beside him. The momentum of the weapon allowed Gabrion to pivot sharply and snap the mace back the other way, tracing a möbius path in the dirt. The shaft of the mace Prethos had given him was noticeably thicker than others he had used, but no one would have noticed his discomfort, his attacks were so effective. Periodically, he altered his stance so no one would deduce his rhythm and take advantage of it.

Six soldiers down, then seven, and Kitalla called to her favorite battle rhythm and pushed her body to the beat. She used her de facto claws to rake against the leather straps binding armor together, or to sever the ties of scabbards and other paraphernalia. A few soldiers tripped over their fallen items and added to the confusion. She glanced around and saw Gabrion's sweeping strides, grinning at the power in every strike.

Over his head, she saw more soldiers approaching. It seemed the Kallisorian king was worried about the two of them in particular, and she was both delighted and annoyed. The Hathren fighters did their best to assist them and they were able to intervene with a number of the attackers. The air was loaded with the cacophony of war.

"We have to move!" she cried.

Gabrion glanced around and understood. He whistled back to her, gesturing with one hand, then he smacked down three more soldiers as she finished her quarry. Gabrion then took the mace in two hands, one at the head and the other at the base. Kitalla charged toward him, leaping as she approached. Her feet tapped the overly thick handle of the mace as Gabrion hoisted up with all his might. Kitalla flew through the air, flipping as she went, pulling out of her roll as she reached the ground. Surprised, the soldiers in the area were unprepared for her initial strikes and four more went down quickly.

After tossing Kitalla, Gabrion spun with the king's mace in front of him and charged forth, bashing out to the sides and around, stunning one foe after another until he reached her and the growing pile of unconscious bodies at her feet.

They were both marked with numerous superficial wounds, but they didn't care. The king wasn't too far away now and they had to press through and bring this rout to an end. With a piercing whistle, Gabrion called for help from his Hathren allies, so he and Kitalla could focus on their goal. With a wild cry, Kitalla raced onward, her arms flashing out to the sides and her body occasionally bouncing into the air to kick out or avoid a blow. Gabrion rushed along with her, and soon they cleared a path to the king while the Hathrens took over against the lesser soldiers.

"So we meet again," Kallion sneered, his gleaming armor catching rays of sunlight and distracting them. "You don't think you're going to defeat me so easily, do you?"

"Put an end to this," Kitalla said. "That's the only way for it to end well for you."

He growled. "Oh, I'll end it all right. *Desha florious kaie!*" With a clap of his hands, the gemstones lining his body lit with inner light that beamed outward like a shining beacon. The light made it impossible to see him directly and they had to avert their eyes to avoid being blinded.

"Now the king himself uses magic?" Gabrion raged.

"Defensive purposes only, as is my prerogative."

"You had soldiers in Kaison using magic to increase their speed and accuracy, too. If you're going to use magic, why not drop the farce that you're against it and let mages live freely?"

Kallion laughed. "Mages are meant to be kept on a thick leash and used when I deem necessary."

"Then you learned nothing from your father's mistakes," Kitalla scolded, tuning her ears so she could discern when the king had moved or if others were approaching.

"Mistakes? His only error was in not anticipating the Colossus, and who could blame him? Nothing like that had ever existed before. This time, however, I'm ready."

"What makes you think your sparkly dress can stop such power?"

"It will," he said. "Perhaps you recall when the Prisoner's Tower fell in Pindington? You all were there. Ordren told me of the chamber your Dariak had created that protected him against both the power of the lightning jade and the collapse of the tower. My mages have worked since then to fortify my defenses, and you will see that when your companion rises against me, I will remain unharmed."

"Is that all you care about?" Gabrion asked. "Your own safety? What of your people? Are they similarly protected?"

Kallion snarled, revealing his answer. "Enough of this banter, you fools. How do you intend to defeat me when you can't even see where I am?"

Kitalla answered by tossing one of her daggers, which clunked against his chest and broke one of the gemstones. "I'll take my chances."

With a wrangling cry, the king rushed against Gabrion, swiping his sword and catching the warrior's arm as he dodged out of the way. The two companions closed their eyes against the glimmering armor and used their other senses to guide them. Kallion cut in low with one hand, bringing a shield around with the other, striking Kitalla in the chest. She hadn't counted on a shield, but now she knew it was there. She called out to notify Gabrion of it as well.

The warrior explored his enemy blindly by stabbing with the mace and listening for footfalls, which was difficult to do considering all the noise around them. Kallion slipped past Gabrion's defenses and jabbed him in the thigh. Gabrion struck back with a sharp turn of his mace, which smacked into the king and crushed a few more gemstones.

Kitalla waited for a chance to strike, taking a quick peek and regretting it; the light was still too intense to look at. She realized her daggers would only be helpful if she could throw them accurately. Melee was not an option while she couldn't see. She spun around and took stock of the surroundings, noting that no other fighters were in the immediate area. They apparently had moved away from the blinding light, perhaps fearing the magic that was unleashed, or perhaps Kallion had ordered them away under the circumstances.

A heavy strike clobbered Kitalla from behind as Kallion bashed her with his shield. She had only turned away for a moment but he capitalized on it, crushing her against the ground, leaving her gasping for air. Gabrion heard her fall and retaliated with a massive strike that knocked the king aside. He struggled to remain upright but faltered and collapsed like broken glass.

As Kallion righted himself, Gabrion reached Kitalla and helped her to her feet. "I'm fine," she gasped.

They turned and faced the king, his glowing armor showing no signs of fading at all. The tinkling gemstones told them he was on the move again and they raised their defenses, listening carefully and preparing to hold him off.

Kitalla was struck from behind again and she kicked back hard, catching her assailant in the groin as she fell forward.

"Ack!" the man gasped, and she immediately recognized it as Ordren's voice. She kicked her feet up, turning away from the glowing king and focusing her rage on the newcomer.

Through squinted eyes, Kitalla could see the captain's sword swinging in for a strike. She deflected it with her daggers and kicked out. Ordren blocked it with some sort of shield in his other hand, but he laughed and she knew it was no shield after all.

"Careful now," he mocked. "You might hurt him."

The statement caught Gabrion's attention, panic flooding through him, for in that instant he thought Ordren had somehow managed to have baby Perrios in his hands. It was impossible, but the flash of fear gave Gabrion a blast of extra speed. He abandoned the king momentarily and pursued Ordren, seeing that the captain held a gruesome trophy: the head of King Prethos.

"Good luck with your peace now," Ordren mocked, throwing the severed head at the warrior.

"He's mine," Gabrion claimed, and Kitalla nodded, turning back toward the king, his armor shining as brightly as ever.

"I told you your immature plan would never work," Ordren said, firming his grip on his sword. "There's no way we Kallisorians would welcome Hathrens into our kingdom. They've destroyed their land. Let them deal with the consequences of their actions."

Gabrion ignored him, wiping his hands on a dry patch of his tunic, then taking up his mace, giving it a few practice swings. "It's been my recent mission to fight without killing. For the death of King Prethos, I lift that restriction now. Prepare to perish." He growled and rushed in, sweeping the mace around. Ordren took a step back and parried the blow easily, turning and slicing through the air to snap Gabrion's spine, but the warrior was ready; he had already twisted his torso, bringing the mace back defensively. It cost him his balance, but it saved his life.

Rising from the ground, he now faced the blinding light emanating from the Kallisorian king, and Ordren was a mere silhouette against it. Fitting, Gabrion thought, that the captain showed up as a blight of darkness against a field of sparkling light. Ordren let him lie there for a moment, flexing his fingers in anticipation. He needed only to take small steps to close the distance between them and finish off the prone man. One step at a time, he approached.

Gabrion tightened his grip on the mace. Its handle was thicker than most maces and only he knew why. At the end of the handle, the top unscrewed under his hand. He tossed the disc aside and stuck two fingers within, prying out a metal pole. With a scraping sheen, Gabrion removed a sword blade from the inner handle of the top-heavy mace. It didn't have a hilt and the blade was narrower than he was used to, but it didn't matter. Prethos had given it to him from his personal armory; it was only fitting to employ it against his killer. He held the special sword in his right hand, keeping the hollowed mace in his left.

Angry with the change of events, Ordren barreled in, wielding his sword with two hands. Gabrion deflected the strike with his sword, then brought the mace in low, catching the captain in the leg. Ordren wasn't slowed by the hit, shifting around and whipping his blade through the air. Gabrion dodged the attack, using the weight of the mace to keep himself from falling and striking back with a cut of his sword.

Ordren took the hit on his gauntlet, brushing it aside and kicking out with his foot. The steel-tipped boot crushed one of Gabrion's ribs, but he brought the mace down on Ordren's knee with a sickening crack. Hollering in pain, Ordren hopped away and refocused himself, keeping his sword ready for Gabrion's next strike.

They had spun around again and the light was behind Gabrion now. He rushed Ordren but the captain saw him easily and parried without any difficulty. Gabrion decided that the man was wearing some sort of antimagic hood under his helmet that prevented the king's eerie glow from reaching him. It also meant that he had to keep himself between the king and the captain so he could see.

Gabrion cut in quickly with the sword, striking the captain's back. Ordren spun around and the two of them went into a flurry of high-paced attacks, their swords clanging fervently. They held each other's gaze, letting their bodies read the movements of their foe and react accordingly. Ordren stepped to the side, turning Gabrion, but the warrior didn't care. Little by little, Ordren turned them around so that the light beamed out behind him, their swords sparking.

Gabrion didn't need to see anymore. His arms responded to the feel of the sword in such a way that it was more of an extension of himself than a weapon. Being so, he was able to keep the blade moving precisely and rapidly, each hit nicking at Ordren's resolve.

The captain maintained his fury, but he saw the unwavering light in Gabrion's eyes, and the sheer determination in his mission. He doubted himself for just a moment and, with that, his sword missed.

The narrow blade flew over the top of Ordren's weapon and sailed unchecked toward the captain's head. The strike slipped in between the collar of the chestplate and the bottom flange of the helmet. Biting deeply into Ordren's neck, Gabrion claimed his victory. He staggered to the ground to catch his breath as Ordren's body enacted its death throes and left him still upon the soil he had tried so hard to defend.

CHAPTER 42

To Tame the King

AS GABRION TURNED to battle Ordren, Kitalla faced off against King Kallion. She kept her eyes squinted, listening for the tinkling gemstones on his armor. At first she wondered how his light spell had lasted for so long until she heard him recast it under his breath. It gave her some hope, for if she could silence him, the light would fade and she could take him down.

Kallion moved swiftly, despite his accoutrements. He wielded his sword and shield deftly, as all kings of Kallisor were powerful fighters.

Kitalla entered the battle with a handful of her daggers and she began by launching one toward the blur of light. She heard it crash against him and fall with a thud to the ground, but at least she knew exactly where he was.

With a dash, Kitalla charged in, her arms moving quickly to deflect his sword. She felt the clash to her right, so she spun left to avoid the shield, bringing her hands around to smack her daggers into his back. A gemstone got in the way and came dislodged from the cape. Kallion turned briskly, snapping the cape in Kitalla's face as he did so. She took a step back, but pushed in quickly, her eyes closed, swiping her blades up and down and around. She felt a few strikes connect, and delighted in the impromptu grunts of the king, but he responded by blasting her with his shield and knocking her to the ground.

Kitalla spit blood and rose up again, peering briefly through her eyes to discern where the source of the light was. Then she charged. This time, as the tinkling sound of the gemstones grew closer, she jumped into the air, bringing her knees in tightly and then kicking out hard. Caught unawares, Kallion took the blow to his shoulder and fell over. Kitalla landed harshly, but she stomped around, trying to smash his shoulder and render his arm useless. The king howled as her feet came down and she felt his blade smack her legs half-heartedly.

She was apparently crushing his shield arm, for he writhed underneath her but was able to bring his weapon about. He struck again and though she tried to deflect the attack with her foot, it was a difficult task without being able to see, and she slipped. Kallion took advantage of her lost balance and lifted his torso up, spilling her to the ground. Swiftly, he rolled up and brought his sword down upon her. She heard his incoming grunt of exertion and so she rolled aside and avoided the blow.

Kitalla bounded to her feet and tossed another dagger to judge his distance from her. The knife clattered against his shield, but he groaned in the process. Assuming his arm was in pain, she rushed ahead, this time tucking her daggers away first. Kallion held his shield in front, bracing himself behind it, and Kitalla smacked fully into the iron with a thud. She then wrapped her arms around it and jumped, twisting her body to the side as if entering into a cartwheel. The motion twisted the shield fiercely and Kallion screamed in response, throwing his body to the side to alleviate the strain.

Disentangling herself and stepping back to catch her breath, Kitalla heard the king moan as he removed the shield and tossed it aside. With a smirk, Kitalla pulled out her daggers and raced in again. Kallion deflected her attack with his sword, but her goal was his wounded arm. She gripped the forearm and pressed her fingers into the grooves where the shield had been strapped. Kallion dropped his sword and pried her away with his hand, throwing her to the dirt and then reclaiming his weapon.

As he looked at her, he could see that she tiring. Her body was also marred with cuts and scrapes and her graceful steps became more erratic. He grinned to himself, deciding that he was on the verge of victory.

The king laughed as Kitalla struggled. "You're done for. I will break your spirit and then I will have my way with you."

Kitalla's face tightened with the declaration, but the vile king wasn't finished with his threat.

"You'll beg for death but I won't grant it to you. No, I'll lock you in my dungeon and I'll take you any time I desire."

Kitalla's face burned red as flashes of the mayor of Wroque flitted into her vision. Her heart pounded and drowned out the other sounds of battle.

"Oh, you tremble before my prowess, I see," the king sneered. "Give yourself over now and I won't cut off your hands first."

Her supply of daggers was low, but it didn't matter. She channeled her rage into her special skill, deciding that the jades were far enough away that they wouldn't interfere. She slammed one foot into the soil, then the next, letting her anger fuel the images she projected toward the braggart.

At first the king continued his taunts, preparing himself to defend against her attacks. He wondered why she didn't pounce ahead, thinking maybe the light worked better than he had hoped. Then, as he looked around, he noticed the sounds of battle were dying out. Little by little, his soldiers faded away into nameless heaps upon the battlefield. Deep clouds rolled through the sky, filling the air with ominous blasts of lightning. With all the iron armor strewn about the battlefield, the lightning reached forth with fury.

Kallion saw Kitalla approach him slowly, a raging fire burning in her eyes as she stretched her arms and neck, ready to sink her weapons into him. She came directly for him, unfazed by the lit gemstones, and so he called to the light spell again. "*Desha florious kaie!*"

Lightning erupted all around, its brilliance matching his own. One bolt blasted the ground mere yards away and he smelled the odd scent of the seared air, but worse, he covered his eyes from the light.

Kitalla leaped in then with a yell. Her daggers hacked away at the gemstones covering his armor. The illusion fell away and the king shouted in anger, bringing his sword about, but Kitalla was too close and she slipped under his arm, cutting more and more until his cape fell to the ground.

"It won't help!" he shouted, turning and kicking out. With the illusion gone, he could see again, and though Kitalla was blinded by the brilliance of his gemstones, she was so close to him that it didn't matter.

Kitalla kept on alert as Kallion rampaged about, trying to free himself. She deflected one blow after another, taking only a few light hits in the process. She pressed her hands against the top of his thigh, pinching fiercely and causing the muscle to spasm. Kallion's hands came down and she took a shot to the head and pulled away for a moment.

The tinkling sound was less than before and she knew she was succeeding at her plan. The man grunted, so Kitalla stepped back in and grabbed his arm, twisting it behind him painfully. He yelped in agony, then tried to free himself by stomping on her foot. Having recently lost a few toes, the pain was great, but Kitalla tugged harder on his arm, wondering how much more she could pull on it before it cracked.

The king leaned to the side and Kitalla responded by twisting his arm further. There was little else she could do without releasing him and she wasn't surprised when he tried snapping his head back to crack her skull. Prepared for it, she used his momentum against him and yanked further on his arm. The king wailed in agony and made a final desperate attempt, flipping his sword overhead and into Kitalla.

She screamed in pain and released her grip, clutching a deep wound in her shoulder. Her right arm twitched in uncontrollable spasms and she felt blood rushing from the gash. Focusing her thoughts through the pain, Kitalla approached the king and resorted to furious kicks. She bashed him in the gut, then struck him on the side of his head, forcing him to yank off his helmet before another blow would crush his face. He staggered backward as she pursued him, her legs smashing him one blast at a time.

She could barely see anymore and the wound was leaking blood too fast. She didn't have any way to staunch the flow and Gabrion was still busy with his match. Her time was coming fast but the king still moved about. She screamed as she charged and pounced on him, mashing his face into the dirt and pounding him until he fell unconscious. The light spell faded and he could no longer reinstate it.

Kitalla tried to examine the wound, but it was too close to her neck to see. She reached with her left hand, shrieking in agony as she touched the gouge. Dizziness swept over her and she felt utterly helpless. The blue sky overhead lost its hue and became the dreary gray she had envisioned for Kallion. The lightning strikes were like the blasts of pain that shot through her body as she sank to the ground. She first fell to her knees, gasping, trying to cling to something of importance that could keep her alert. Then she weakened further and fell to her side. Writhing around, she kept telling herself that she wasn't done yet. She had to hold on a while longer. They hadn't won yet.

Gabrion saw her fall and he remembered the sensation he'd had at the castle when she had caused him to imagine it. This was worse, for in his heart it was entirely too real. He rose from Ordren's corpse and sprinted to her, reaching down and calling her name.

"Gemmetodariak," she gasped in a rattled voice.

Gabrion didn't argue, for the mage had the healing jade. He looked around and didn't know where he was, so he hefted Kitalla up in his arms and hurried to the last place he remembered seeing his black-haired friend. Kitalla's breathing was ragged; he didn't have much time.

CHAPTER 43

The Mage's Plight

DARIAK WAS ONE of the few mages left on the field; all the healers had been attacked as primary targets and most had perished or fled the battle. He pulled one set of spell components from his pockets after another. The terrible boulders rained down intermittently and the whole scene felt like a sad, lost cause.

King Prethos was covered in scrapes but he fought with all his heart. Dariak admired the way he deftly cut through the defenses of the Kallisorian fighters and subdued them without killing them, keeping to his word.

Then Ordren appeared and Prethos was hard-pressed to defend himself. The king used a small amount of magic for a protection spell and a water spell that muddied the area. Dariak turned his energies on protecting the Hathren king, sending his fire darts at Ordren to distract him, but they had seemingly no effect.

Instead, Dariak called to the powers of the earth and he dug a quick chasm with his hands. It had worked better in the sand outside Castle Hathreneir; however, Ordren stumbled and missed his attack, allowing Prethos to strike instead. Dariak straightened his back, reaching for the nature powers, coercing the grass to become sharp blades to pierce through Ordren's boots. His arms swept up like sharp spikes and as he glanced skyward, he realized he had forgotten something.

The incoming boulder was too close for him to do anything about. His vision filled with the incoming stone and quick images of his life snapped before his eyes, one of them Ordren sweeping his sword clean through Prethos' neck and killing him. And then the boulder smashed Dariak into the ground and all he saw was darkness.

His body ached from the impact and he didn't know how he was breathing. More than that, he didn't know how he was alive. He lay there for a few minutes wondering if he was really there, or maybe it was one of those moments where the soul refused to believe he was dead so it lingered in his body. But he felt pain. He felt himself breathing, and surely a soul wouldn't. There was a searing heat around his waist and at first he thought his body must have been severed in half.

Then he remembered the jades. In times of crisis the jades had protected the companions. Here, they had again, though no single jade had the power to help him alone. He felt for the energies pulsating through him and he sensed the earth, air, nature, and healing jades working in unison to keep him safe.

He tried to move his hands and found it difficult. Pushing his thoughts to the earth and nature jades, he implored them to help, but they were weakened after the exertion. He sent his thoughts along to the beast and lightning jades, wondering if they could share their powers with the others so he could escape this stony prison and return to the battlefield. He allowed the energies to flow through his body and into the other jades, and little by little he was able to claw his way to the surface, not unlike a man buried alive.

He emerged from the topsoil and saw a stricken Randler crouched nearby at the boulder. The bard had made his way to Dariak's side and waited there, fearing the worst, unable to do anything else. They hugged briefly and Randler strained to pull himself together.

"How long was I out?" It was a needless question as the sky was dark overhead.

"Prethos is dead. Ordren too. Kallion was down but he's already rallying his troops for another strike tomorrow. Our forces regrouped over here in the interim." His face was pale. "Dariak, it's Kitalla. You have to come."

They hurried to the nearest tent where Kitalla lay on a blanket, a frantic herbalist scrambing to cover her wound. "It's too deep!" the woman said, sweat streaming down her face.

Dariak leaned over and examined the damage, wincing at the depth of the cut. Gabrion held Kitalla's hand tightly, not willing to let her go. Dariak reached for the exhausted healing jade and set it on her shoulder. Closing his eyes, he tapped the jade for its power, calling to the other shards for their assistance as well.

As he worked, Randler asked Gabrion, "Where are Ruhk and Verna?"

"No idea," the warrior said absently. "They went after the catapult."

"They must have had success," Randler said, "because the boulders have stopped. But they didn't return with the call for retreat."

Kitalla moaned and pushed her eyes open. "Save the jades, Dariak."

"Not at the expense of you." He focused his thoughts inward and called for the other jades to respond. In particular, the metal and fire jades reacted, sending cold and heat through Dariak's body and into the healing jade. A warm white light emanated from the shard and the wound in Kitalla's shoulder started to seal itself.

When metal and fire were drained, Dariak drew upon the rest. Water, shadow, and glass were next, each offering what power they could. The shards all went cold and dim, though they were not as still as they had been after Frast had united them. Nonetheless, Dariak could draw no more energy from them.

Kitalla's face creased in pain and the wound was still not fully closed. The herbalist resumed her work, trying to alleviate the agony, but it would take the work of magical healers to succeed quickly.

"That was foolish," Kitalla said.

"Keeping you alive?" Dariak asked. "You're probably right."

"Wasting the jades on me," she corrected. "Kallion will rise again and you'll need them to stop him."

"No," he argued. "You're a bigger threat."

Kitalla coughed quietly and then drew a few deep breaths to steady herself while the herbalist continued her work. "You know, it's strange."

"What's that?"

She spoke slowly, gasping here and there. "I'm lying here in all this pain, having come so close to death, and all I'm thinking about is that stupid book."

"Which one?" Randler asked.

"That one you wanted."

"The drawings by Lady Cathrateir?"

"The same. That one set of drawings that confused me. You remember?"

Randler nodded and explained. "You said the sky was full of light and then all the lights slowly went out and then there was darkness. But it wasn't very clear what was meant by it."

"The silver and gold skeins… Then the colored light, with the silver and gold still lingering around. The other colors fading away and then yes, there was darkness." She turned her gaze to Dariak. "I think… I think those colors are the jades."

Gabrion stroked her head. "You're delirious."

"No." She fought against the pain and exhaustion as they swelled upon her. They could see she was struggling to speak and they begged her to rest. "No," she repeated. "The jades. They're the colored light."

"All right," Dariak said, trying to make sense of her tired ramblings. "What about them?"

Her breathing was labored and she struggled to push the words out. "They faded away, one by one. Your jades. Now. Faded away."

"It could… be connected," Dariak said, his concern for her clouding his thoughts.

Kitalla took a few breaths, her voice fading to a whisper. "The silver and gold. Randler. The Forgotten Tribe."

"Yes," he said. "Those tales were of the Forgotten Tribe, and those threads represented Lady Hathreneir and King Kallisor."

"They drew… in… the colors," she breathed. "Then, darkness."

"Yes, but so?"

"The Forgot—" she started, then she passed out.

The team lingered for a short time, keeping silent vigil and then they left Kitalla to rest. They convened in the tent set aside for Prethos and there the king's commanders bowed their heads to the companions in homage.

"Our king was lost this day," one said. "It was his wish that we turn to your leadership should anything happen to him on the field."

"Thank you," Gabrion said. "For now, secure the perimeter and keep a watch for Kallisorian forces. We don't want to be surprised in the night."

"Yes, sir." With that, the commanders left.

Randler sank into a small chair, rubbing his aching legs. "I don't understand. What was Kitalla going on about?"

Dariak dropped to the ground. "I have no idea. There's been something going on with her for a while now. I haven't been able to put my finger on it."

Randler's brow creased in concern. "It'll come to you, I'm sure. Listen, we've been inundated with all the lore from your father's library and now we're in the heart of the war."

"My father's library," Dariak echoed. His mind ached, knowing something was barely out of reach, but he couldn't bridge the distance.

Instead, he methodically pulled the jades from their pockets and set them down. "Now I'm back to where we were at the castle. The jades are almost completely empty and I can't hear them anymore. There's no way I'll be able to unite them tomorrow if I need to."

"Do you think the fighting will continue for long?" Gabrion asked. "We both lost people."

"And we weren't supposed to lose anyone," Dariak said. "Yet from what I've seen, I think Kallion will push until there's nothing left, one way or the other." He rubbed the sides of his head. "How many fighters do we have remaining?"

Gabrion groaned. "From the original count, about two hundred swords and three mages."

Dariak swallowed. "We lost more than half of our forces."

"And they did not," Randler said. "Because we're keeping them alive."

"We'll be slaughtered tomorrow." Dariak closed his eyes, reaching his hands over the jades, wondering what he should do. Uniting the jades at full strength was sure to kill him. How would bringing them together in this condition affect him? He assumed they would have to draw more energy from him in the process and that would burn him all the faster. The weight of it sat heavily upon him.

Gabrion saw the sour expression on Dariak's face and pity on Randler's. He understood the implications of the jades, but the sadness was too disheartening, so he stood up and stretched. "I'm exhausted," he announced, a silly grin working its way to his face.

"I don't think I'll get any sleep tonight," Dariak said.

"You know," Gabrion added, "so I thought I'd… you know…" He pulled off his tunic and tossed it to the floor. "…get ready for bed." With that, he dropped his breeches and stretched again, showing off his entire body to the other two.

Despite his sorrow, Dariak belted out a laugh, recalling a time long, long ago when he had propped himself up on a cot to watch Gabrion's unintended nightly show, and the conversation they had had about it. Their friendship had grown after that, and though they had been through many tragic events, they still clung together. Dariak walked over and wrapped his arms around the big warrior, who returned the embrace with all sincerity.

Gabrion dressed himself again and the three spent the night trying to decipher Kitalla's ramblings, but when they made no progress, their chat turned to happier times along their journey.

"You as the bumbling merchant in Warringer, when Kitalla threw all those daggers at you," Dariak said.

Gabrion added, "Kitalla, completely duping me, dressed in rags and pretending to be a lost soul on the road."

"Randler, giving us songs along the way, honoring those who've left us or urging us on toward our goals."

The bard smiled. "Dinner with my lovely mother."

Dariak laughed. "And the smell of burned hair."

"You did overpower her, didn't you?"

He sobered for a moment. "Thanks to the jades. They've been there for us all along the way."

"And they'll help us see this through, too," Gabrion said. "We're ready to change this land and to bring the people together. We've all had our hardships and our trials along the way. It's time now."

Dariak looked at the two of them intently. "Will you three stay together once we're done here?"

"Dariak…" Randler started.

"No, Randler, there's no point denying it. When I bring the jades together, I'm going to die." A knot tightened in his stomach as he said the words aloud. "We all know it."

"Don't give up like that," Gabrion said.

"I'm not. It isn't as if I *want* to give up my life to save this land. Yet, in some way, I know it's the cost of my quest and all the experiences I've had. If my sacrifice truly saves us, then I'm ready."

"I'm with you, Dariak, until the very end," Randler said.

Gabrion gave a sharp nod. "As am I, regardless of what happens."

"You have to be there for Perrios," Dariak reminded him. "He'll need your guidance, especially now that his father is gone."

"And his mother," Gabrion pointed out. "I may not be the best role model for the boy." He looked at Randler. "But I told his grandmother that you would be recording our tale at length and that she should share it with him when he's able to understand it."

Randler shivered. "It feels like we're all saying good-bye. I don't like it."

"Should I disrobe again?" Gabrion asked.

Dariak grinned. "Yes. In fact, when we head out tomorrow, let's all show up naked."

Gabrion laughed. "That'll scare the wits out of them."

They joked around a while longer until a page tapped on the tent flap and tensions mounted instantly. The young man bowed his way inside and stammered, "S—sorry to interrupt, but—"

Gabrion's voice took an edge of authority. "Speak. Have we been infiltrated?"

He shook. "In a m—manner of speaking. There is someone here to speak with you."

"Show him in," Gabrion commanded.

Dariak quickly tucked the jades away and the three companions shifted around and stood together. The tent flap opened and Dariak's jaw fell to the floor. A dark-skinned old man walked inside and took stock of the surroundings. He nodded to each of them and then took a seat.

"Astrith! What are you doing here?" Dariak asked.

The keeper of the forest cleared his throat and took a sip from a water flask he kept on his hip. "I told you, Dariak, that we are connected to the energies of this land. We felt the deep sadness that occurred when your friend gave his life as he brought the jades together. It was more painful than when your father ripped a hole through the energies. I know your intention and I'm aware that the pain will come again."

"So you wanted to be here for it?"

"No, but the others of the forest fear the effects the jades will have when they are brought together."

"You... came to stop me?" Dariak hedged.

"No," Astrith said. "There are some in our coven who believe we can make the process unnecessary if we assist the tumult here. There are others yet who feel we have the power to block the effects of the jades from further ravaging our land."

"From here?" Randler asked.

"Indeed. Much like a pile of stones may deflect a river. Setting up defenses here could redirect the energy elsewhere."

"You don't sound convinced," Gabrion said.

"I've not met you, young warrior, but you read me correctly. You see, when the jades have been united, they have stolen great energy from the land. The ever-spreading desert is but one effect. The warmer winters we have recently had is another. Greater varieties of feral creatures, and so forth. I wonder what dangers we face with the jades up for two unifications so close together. I don't believe we can redirect where the energies go, nor from where they are drained, but it is my custom to listen well to the words of my people. Thus, we are here."

"How many?" Gabrion asked.

"Fifteen, if you count me among the number."

"Oh."

"The rest have remained in the forest to maintain it."

"We're grateful for any help," Dariak said. "What can we expect from your people?"

"You can't," Astrith answered mysteriously. "Do what you feel you must. Forget we are even here. That will allow us to do whatever we can do, disconnected from the rest. That is our condition."

"We can try to stay out of your way," Gabrion said.

"It will not be necessary." He reached his hands out for Randler, placing his fingers on the supports he had sent for the bard. "This should help," he muttered, as the vines and twigs shifted slightly and formed better to Randler's body.

The old man pushed himself upright. "Now, if you will excuse me, I will go see if I can add any support to your injured friend before turning in for the night."

"How do you know of Kitalla?" Gabrion asked.

"You called upon the jades to heal her, did you not? They worked in unison to try to repair the damage, yes? We sensed that as well. We also know that it's not the first time you united the jades attempting to heal her."

Randler's eyes opened wide. "You could feel that all the way from Pindington?"

Astrith tipped his head. "Yes. And if you recall, once the jades had been used symbiotically, soon after, there was massive destruction."

Dariak's brow furrowed. "The lightning jade went haywire and brought down the Prisoner's Tower."

"Indeed. It would not be much of a stretch to think that one may have caused the other."

A strange sensation fluttered in Dariak's chest. "You're implying that all those people died in Pindington because I used the jades to heal Kitalla, which set off a… chain reaction in the lightning jade? You're saying it's my fault?"

"Not yours, per se. The jades themselves upset the balance. Think of your father."

"Then when I unite them, I may not just kill myself in the process. Many others could die along with me."

Astrith offered a slight shrug. "Maybe not at once, but over the years to come, I would suspect some parts of life would be out of balance once again, causing hardships. Now then, warrior, show me to your friend." Gabrion led the old man out, leaving Dariak and Randler alone.

The mage grabbed his head and tugged in frustration. "What am I to do?"

Randler shook his head. "I don't know, Dariak. I just don't know."

CHAPTER 44

Verna's Reprieve

THE NIGHT HAD a bitter chill, the only reminder that it was winter. Verna had watched as Illuria used her magic to transport her lover and Ruhk away from the battle site by making the earth shift and roll. It wasn't the smoothest ride, but the injured men were secreted away. Verna vowed to find Ruhk again and to apologize for sending him away like this, but she couldn't let him die. She knew he had a family somewhere in Hathreneir, but that didn't affect her feelings for him.

Once they were gone, she was essentially alone with the two ursalors that banged against each other, trying to break apart the harness that bound them to the catapult. The enormous bear-like beasts roared with fury and Verna knew she had to subdue them somehow. If they escaped, they could rampage through the battle-field, and though that might put an end to the fighting, many people would likely die. If they fled and pursued Illuria and killed Ruhk in the process, Verna didn't know how she would live with herself.

She hadn't rested for more than a few minutes before making her attempt against the ursalors. Three thick chains remained for them to break through before they were free, and their thrashing made it obvious that time was running out. Verna scoured the area quickly, claiming four swords in addition to her own, strapping them to her back with strips of tunic she ripped from a fallen soldier.

Trekking closer to the enraged monsters, Verna kept hopping away in fear, for the bodies were easily fifteen feet long and six feet wide. If they could be tamed, a whole family could travel on one's back and the powerful legs wouldn't even register the added weight.

"For Ruhk," she muttered to herself, running ahead and trying to keep from screaming. With a mighty leap, she grabbed onto one back leg, her fingers ripping at the ursalor's fur. The beast let out an annoyed shout and briefly turned its head toward her, but the collar around its neck tugged on the chain and prevented it from reaching her.

Grateful for her luck, Verna pulled one hand and foot up at a time, careful not to rip the fur out of the beast's hide. Her goal was to gain purchase on its back and then use the sword to pierce its skull or spine. Valid plan, she mocked herself, except that the creature started stomping its feet.

Verna clutched harder, trying to remain attached to the hide, but the violent shaking was too much and she hit the ground hard, rolling away quickly as the heavy foot continued to stomp. The metal chains rattled and she wasn't sure if she heard it moaning or if it was her imagination.

Dusting herself off, Verna watched again for the ursalor to calm down while its partner took turns rampaging. She wondered how the handlers had even kept them in check at all, and she figured they must have been mages with providence over beasts. No one else could possibly tame these things.

Making a second attempt, Verna scrambled up the hind leg as quickly as the thrashing would allow. She pulled out a few unfortunate clumps of hair and lost her grip, plummeting back to the ground and angering the ursalor even further. Frustrated and aching, she looked around for something she could use for leverage.

The ursalor handlers apparently employed whips to help control the beasts, and when they had fled they left the whips behind. She did her best to tie the four of them end to end, making a rope she could toss over one of the creatures. She knew just from looking at it that it wasn't nearly long enough.

She then saw a few daggers on the ground. She hated to do it, but at the same time, she *was* trying to kill them, so she tied a dagger to one end of the whip-rope and headed back to the beasts again.

She leaped and climbed as high as she could, and when she felt her grip failing her, Verna stabbed the dagger into the ursalor's flank, the whip hanging free. The beast howled in pain and it rose up on its hind legs, dumping Verna once again to the ground. Stomping around, the ursalor crashed into its companion, which angrily retaliated and the two started fighting in earnest.

The chains of the catapult shook terribly and threatened to break at any moment, but worse than that, the undulations dragged the catapult closer and closer. Verna stood, inching away from the ursalors, and was almost clocked in the head by the massive weapon they were dragging. The beasts wrangled for a few minutes before deciding they couldn't kill each other and returning to their attempts to break free, presumably so they could turn back on each other for the kill.

Verna grumbled, wondering if she should climb on top of the catapult and try to leap over onto the ursalor's back from there, but as she watched, the catapult was wrenched erratically, and unlike the furry handholds of the ursalors, there was nothing for her to hold onto upon the catapult.

She looked at the dagger with the whips flailing about. She had stabbed it in deeply, for it remained in the beast's haunch. She considered a few other options, then decided that the whip was the best bet. She hurried forward one more time and climbed the tied whips hand over hand, causing the dagger to dig further into the creature.

This time, Verna kept climbing as the ursalor rampaged in pain. She moved little by little, hugging the warm body with all her might. Yet, before she moved too far away, she grabbed the dagger and yanked it from the ursalor's flank, causing another spasm. She clung to the beast, ripping out tufts of fur here and there and moving her hands and feet to other areas, keeping a grip.

Eventually the ursalor calmed down and the other beast tugged on the chains. Verna crested the backside of her beast as a sickening crack sounded and one of the chains snapped apart. Immediately, her ursalor rose up on its feet and yowled with a throaty roar, its whole body shaking in the process. She felt her grip slipping away and so she jabbed the dagger into its lower back, then grabbed the whips for support.

The thrashing was worse this time, for the broken chain allowed more room for movement. Verna lost her grip on the ursalor and swung wildly from the whips, slamming into the monster's side with a hefty thud. She merely held on tightly as the creature jounced and, when she could, she scaled up to the top.

Breathing heavily, Verna lay flat across the beast's back, digging her knees and arms in for support. The two creatures continued heaving around, with the catapult slowly following behind them. After catching her breath, which wasn't easy because the ursalors also smelled terribly, Verna skulked forward, trying to get in the vicinity of its head.

Unfortunately, she hadn't accounted for the motion of the ursalor's shoulder blades and as the creature stood on its feet again, its arms batting wildly at the two remaining chains, she started to lose her grip again. She didn't want to fall from ten feet up, so Verna squeezed with one hand, then reached over her shoulder with the other, removing one of the five swords. Holding it awkwardly as the beast dropped back down, she plunged the blade into its flesh.

Blood splattered from the wound and the ursalor's cry was even worse than before. At first, the beast lashed out at the other ursalor, then it threw itself to the ground, rolling onto its back to kill whatever was clinging there. Verna barely leaped away in time. She rolled repeatedly in the dirt and then shook off her pain as she heard another massive crack. Only one chain to go.

Now both beasts were screaming and jumping wildly, and the catapult was yanked along, crashing into one then the other. This angered them and they raged all the harder. Verna couldn't believe the power they had, and they were only now truly showing their strength. The final chain snapped and the two ursalors turned their attacks on the catapult that had been battering them. The massive weapon, able to launch huge boulders, was dismantled in minutes, with huge chunks of fortified wood scattered left and right like she might toss a twig.

The smell of blood from the battle made them wrinkle their noses, and she knew what would come next. She had to prevent it. The dagger with the attached whips was still lodged in the one ursalor's flank, so she hurried and scampered up. The creature howled, feeling her presence now, and it turned its head to try to snap at her.

Verna took one of her other swords and jabbed it hard into the ursalor's spine. As expected, it came to its feet and then flipped onto its back, trying to kill her. But it didn't succeed because the other ursalor misunderstood the challenge and it attacked in full.

Powerful claws raked viciously as the two beasts rose up on their hind legs and wrangled. Verna was too high to jump away safely, so she kept shifting her grip, keeping as firm a hold as possible, alternating as needed between the two swords and the dagger she had implanted in its hide.

The ursalor strikes were devastating, and only another ursalor could withstand them. Verna's beast slashed at the other's face, ripping out an eye and causing a retaliatory strike that sent Verna flying, despite all of her attempts to hold on. She felt a deep snap as she landed and she knew some of her bones had broken.

The two beasts battled it out for some time until one released a low, braying howl, after which it turned and scampered away, clearly defeated. The other ursalor, still sporting the swords and dagger, stayed behind, standing and declaring in no uncertain terms that it was furious and everyone was going to die.

Verna couldn't use her left leg or arm. She also realized some of her ribs had cracked as well. The ursalor heard her groaning, or perhaps it just smelled her, as she was covered in its odious blood. With another roar of challenge, the ursalor stomped, edging closer to her, baring its many teeth. Verna swallowed hard, pulling another sword from her back and holding it before her with her right hand. If it was going eat her, she was at least determined to cause some damage on the way down.

The ground shook with each step the beast took and it reared one last time.

Verna forced her eyes open as all fifteen feet of ursalor shook in the air, ready to pounce. She rolled up onto her good leg, then managed to stand. The beast charged. Verna threw herself to the side, barely escaping the stampede. The ursalor came to a halt and turned slowly around. In agony, Verna pushed herself up and the beast approached again, this time bringing its head down to roar in her face. Verna threw the sword and nicked the corner of its eye, causing it to howl in rage.

She didn't know what propelled her, nor how she was able to overcome her pain to do so, but Verna hobbled quickly over to the ursalor and grabbed the hanging whips that still dangled from its flank. With her one good hand and leg, she pushed and shoved and earned her way back up on top. The ursalor dropped to its four paws and looked around for her, but couldn't understand where she had gone.

Verna tucked the end of the bottom whip between her teeth, hoping she could clench her jaw tightly enough so as not to scream as she dragged herself across the monster's back. She had two swords left at her disposal and she was determined to use them. She winced as she climbed, her whole left side arguing with every motion. She grabbed onto one of the two swords she had already planted in the beast's hide and it was then the ursalor knew where she was.

First, it turned its head around to bite her and, remembering its next move would be to flip onto its back, Verna struck preemptively, driving one more sword into its spine. The ursalor cried out and as it thrashed around.

Verna knew she was finished. She didn't have the strength to hold on. As the ursalor rose up on its legs, Verna screamed, feeling her body plummet downward. With her mouth open, the whip was released and fell with her, and though she scrambled for a handhold among the beast's fur, she failed. But the whip got tangled around her arm in the process, snapping tightly, and effectively securing her to the beast.

Verna's broken body smacked against the side of the animal, the tug of which added to the creature's pain. She had overwhelmed it, though, much as the beast had injured its companion, and with a deep keening wail, the ursalor lumbered off, away from the battlefield.

With Verna still hanging off its side.

She was in such agony, she couldn't even feel any more. She would have passed out, but the constant jogging of the monster kept her from unconsciousness. Her mind flared with harrowed pleas for it to end. No more thrashing. No more of this unfathomable agony.

The sky darkened as the beast trounced onward, but then it brightened again, and Verna knew she was dying. Red, then blue, then white flashes erupted all around. She didn't understand it and she didn't care to even try. Some eternity passed by for her and she felt the whole world fall away, until her body smacked hard once more as it impacted the ground.

She heard words she didn't understand and light flickered wildly everywhere. Nothing made sense to her. Why couldn't she just die already and stop suffering so?

"It's going to be a long road, but you'll recover," someone said.

Verna shook her head. "Don't lie."

Laughter tinkled in her ears. "After all that, she still has life in her yet. Urrith, get her something to eat. Soup, maybe. Or just water."

"Already on it, Sharice."

Verna tried to open her eyes. "What…?"

"There now," Sharice crooned softly. "The Kallisorian Mage Underground is here, at your service."

"I don't—"

"Shush, now, and try to sleep. Your fight is done. But the rest of us have a war to stop."

CHAPTER 45

The Red Jade

THE MORNING SKY was dark and ominous. Thick clouds had rolled in through the night, effectively blotting out the sun and any sense of hope. Dariak gazed up at the darkness, his body exhausted and his mind weary. The night had passed too quickly and he hadn't felt any inspiration regarding the jades.

Randler stood quietly beside him, wincing occasionally as spasms shook his legs. They hadn't spoken in a few hours, and they were both afraid to break the silence, for they feared the thoughts passing through the other's mind.

The encampment stirred and Dariak tensed in response. There hadn't been any signs of subterfuge overnight; no rogues pouring poison into their food or anything. It was, perhaps, the one detail that made this battle feel different for Dariak, signaling that it wasn't just a recreation of the War of the Colossus.

"I wonder what they'll call it?" he asked aloud, his voice breaking. Randler looked at him quizzically. "When the fight is over and they record it."

"You won't have to wonder. You'll be around for it."

Dariak gestured to the horizon. "They're awakening. The battle will recommence soon. Gather the others."

Gabrion arrived with Kitalla, whose body had been greatly healed by Astrith and his followers. She was sore and stiff, but ready for the day. Gabrion had taken up a sword this morning, determined not to fail Kitalla on the field.

"Just the four of us?" Dariak asked.

"Ruhk and Verna never returned," Randler said.

"We've got four mages and a hundred or so men ready for the day," Gabrion added. "We lost some to injury overnight and others lost the will to battle after Prethos was slain."

Kitalla sighed. "And they still have about a thousand. Plus their king."

"Astrith is around, but he refused to commit to any command."

Dariak shook his head. "Don't count on them. Astrith has something else in mind, I believe. Perhaps he just wants to bear witness here. But anyway. Randler?"

The bard nodded and raised his voice before the final battle.

Days long ahead when this tale spreads, we see the light yet to come.
We will stand strong, for we belong in this land from start to the end.
Their forces are large yet we are brave, and we shall rise up to win.

Swords held high, we will defend until the end.
Spells to bind, for us to heal and then to mend.
Joined in kind, the future is in our hands.
War will die, may the Red Jade free our lands.

"The Forgotten Tribe," Kitalla muttered, touching her hand to her belly.

"They come," Gabrion announced needlessly, seeing motion up ahead. "Dariak?"

But the mage shook his head, fear creeping up his spine, so Gabrion turned around and walked toward their forces, raising his voice as loud as he could.

"We fight, this day, in defense of honor. We seek a means of ending the turmoil forced upon our lands by the traditional blindness of the kings. Though Prethos has fallen, his eyes had opened at last and he urged us to bring about a new world where war is not a constant. He joined our cause of freeing the people of this land from giving their children to battle, only to lose them before too long. We rise up today and defend the belief that a better world is possible, that we can, if we work together, bring that new lifestyle forward. Today we honor each other and we respect all life. Raise your swords in defense today and use those blades to block your foes. They will see the truth of our actions and a new way will come to pass. For honor!" The troops all cheered in response, raising their weapons in the heavy air.

Kallion's forces approached and the king sat upon his horse, his armor damaged but still loaded with glittering, energy-deflecting gemstones. Confidence exuded from his poise and the hundreds of fighters behind him. He only needed to take down the last few mages and then the rest would be easy enough, for the fighters in his rebalanced envoy were of the highest skill in his land.

"There is time for you to call off this folly," the king shouted.

Dariak's jaw tensed and he shook his head, but he couldn't speak. Randler saw the hesitation and he stepped up to respond. "You speak of folly, though you stand before the son of Delminor, the great mage who summoned the Colossus in the last war. You face us with the belief that your defenses can withhold against the power of the jades, but you'll find yourself to be wrong. Call off your men and let's talk this through and find a resolution that wi—"

"Attack!" Kallion shouted impatiently, having heard enough. The air filled with the sound of thunder as all the king's fighters ran forth, swords flashing left to right.

The companions gave each other one final look and nod. The four of them had been together on this journey since the beginning and today, they knew, it would come to an end. Sword, dagger, bow, and magic, the four turned to face the enemy and let the battle commence.

Kitalla and Gabrion rushed in first, and the hundred fighters on their side followed enthusiastically. The thief bobbed up and down as she deflected one attack after another, her goal to slip through them all and reach the king once more. The combatants, however, pressed together too tightly, and her tactics failed. With a grown, she hunkered down and set to battling directly.

Gabrion had no plan in mind except to keep Kitalla safe, thus he followed her and did his best to fill in any defensive gaps that arose because of her recent injuries. He reached in with his sword and smacked a soldier's arm aside, then whipped around and belted the man in the face with his fist. Kitalla slipped aside and tripped one fighter, bringing her dagger's hilt down on the back of his neck.

To win the day, every person on their team needed to best at least seven others, but everyone was weary and Kitalla knew that most of the Hathrens would struggle to defeat even two. The rest would fall to the four companions.

Randler's bow sang with precision as he launched a host of arrows into the fray. The iron armor of the Kallisorians still deflected the majority of the attacks, but repeated hits made it difficult for the fighters to advance accurately. He continued filling the air with projectiles.

Meanwhile, Dariak worked his magic to cut rifts in the ground and slow them down even further. He felt the urge to drop the soil down and then fold the fighters into the land, but that would surely kill them. With every spell he set loose, the urge to kill grew stronger as desperation set in. His fire darts blasted forward, burning holes in the iron breastplates and filling the air with screams.

Kallion enjoyed the scene as the fighting raged about. His foes would easily be overwhelmed this day, but he decided to ensure their fate. He lifted his horn and blew it fiercely. Moments later, an echoed blast sounded in the distance.

Another battalion hiding off beyond the plain jogged heartily into the battle, and they were not alone. The group arrived with a host of feral creatures that had been trained to fight alongside them and to viciously cut down their foes. The clanging of armor and shouts of pain were soon augmented by the howls of lupinoes and tigroars, among others.

Dariak's eyes widened and he let his current spell fizzle out, reaching into his robes and fumbling for the jades. They pulsed as he touched them and he closed his eyes, relying on Randler to defend him. He heard the bard draw his mace and strike back at an oncoming opponent. Dariak couldn't help. He needed to unite the jades.

The mage drew a deep and slow breath of air, reaching his essence downward into the shards arranged around his waist. He felt their energies respond in anticipation, their tendrils of power hungering for this moment. He called to the earth jade to initiate the joining, then next to nature, and around the circle until he had tapped them all. And he brought his hands down and grabbed the unseen forces together, yanking them upward and gathering them into his mind, where he organized them into a whirling mass of light.

His body tingled as the process started and he filled with terror, knowing his life would be torn from him, but determined to go ahead with it nonetheless. His ideals needed to live, even if he could not, and so he reached further and drew upon the jades with passion, pouring their strengths into him and preparing himself to reach out and stop the battle.

And as he raised his hand upward, prepared to strike, he felt a ripping sensation in his mind, like parchment shearing in two. Crying out, he opened his eyes, feeling around for the cause, but there was none. Randler had defeated the foe and held off another attacker. The Hathrens tangled with fighters and beasts alike. Gabrion's sword rose up and down, and he could even see Kitalla leaping and bounding about, her hands and legs flicking into the air as she battled.

He turned his thoughts inward and he realized what had gone wrong. The jades were too drained from healing Kitalla and they didn't have the strength to unite, even with his essence as the binding force. He lowered his hands and turned around in panic, for he had no chance now of putting an end to the fighting. They had come all this way and it was just going to end. Likely, Kallion would claim the jades as his own and he would take over the entire land and no one would be able to stop him.

He wanted his anguish to end, but he saw an odd motion out of the corner of his eye and curiosity won out over despair. He turned and saw Astrith and the forest folk hurrying toward the trees off the northern end of the plain. Dariak dashed after them; perhaps Astrith could help him bring the jades together after all. At the very least, Dariak would coerce them to join the fight instead of hiding in the treetops.

Sudden anger propelled him, wondering why Astrith had even come to this place at all if they were only going to cower. The fifteen forest folk reached the trees and they ran around behind them, escaping from view. Dariak doubled his pace.

As he reached the line of trees, he shouted Astrith's name in fury, challenging them all to come and defend the land. What he didn't know was that Astrith and his fellows intended to do just that. The forest folk stood with their bodies pressed against the trees, eyes closed and looking asleep, for all Dariak could tell. Yet as he stood there, he felt a welling up of natural energy. He felt for the nature jade, but when he focused his thoughts, he realized it came from the others.

The bodies of the forest folk slowly absorbed into the trunks of the trees, the massive boughs shaking in response overhead. Dariak watched in amazement as the bark melted somewhat and from the inside of the tree stepped tall, very treelike beings. His last encounter with such creatures had been a disaster but as he looked at them now, he finally understood. The forest people had donned the garb of the trees and had shaped their essences into those of triggans. He tried not to think of the ones he had defeated in the forest.

The fifteen gangly figures stepped away from the trees and lumbered forward into the battle. The Kallisorians panicked, turning their swords upon them, but the blades were no match for the thick bark. The triggans stomped ahead and ignored them, turning their efforts on subduing the beasts that rampaged about. Sweeping branches struck into rodia, scattering them. Root-like feet stomped and kicked into lupinoes, sending shrieks of dismay into the air. The lupinoes pulled back and re-grouped, dodging Hathren blows in the process, then they coordinated an attack and focused upon one triggan at a time.

Kitalla snickered as she thrashed about the battlefield on the back of a tigroar. The unfortunate beast had come for her and she had flipped onto its back after bashing it in the face. Since then, she had guided the poor creature by tugging on its thick fur. There was no shortage of men to bite, else the tigroar would have turned its focus upon its rider. They took down a dozen fighters until one Kallisorian real-ized the only way to end its stampede was to kill the beast. With a blow from behind, the young fighter stabbed into the tigroar, causing it to rear up and throw Kitalla. He then put the tigroar out of its misery.

Dariak hurried back to Randler's side. The bard fought wildly, his arms swiping through the air and bringing his mace about. He moved as if his legs had never been crushed back in the forest, and only Astrith knew why, for upon his arrival, he had added extra enchantments to the living vines, giving them supple strength that conformed best to Randler's body.

Whatever the reason, Dariak was vastly impressed with Randler as his cinnamon-hued hair whipped about with one strike after the next. Dariak reached into his pockets and resumed his spell-casting, hoping his mind would solve the jade issue while he worked.

The battle continued and the Hathren forces were failing. Gabrion counted ten comrades fallen already, and they couldn't afford to lose any more. He shouted in rage and scoured for a second sword. Grabbing one, he whirled the blades about, striking one foe after the next. Kitalla was out of his sight and so he turned his efforts toward her original goal, who sat high upon his horse, lance in hand, striking down at one enemy or another but keeping ultimately out of the main fighting.

Fire exploded in the distance and Dariak gasped in horror. They were already overwhelmed with men and beasts. They couldn't handle anything more. Thunder echoed in the air and Dariak looked up at the thick clouds, wondering if lightning would strike them all at random.

The sounds of fire and lightning continued and shouts of panic followed soon after. Dariak glanced around for the rest of his companions, hoping they were aware of the new threat, but aside from Randler he had no way of notifying them. The bard finished his scuffle and turned a weary eye to Dariak. His skin was sliced in numerous places, sweat and blood oozing everywhere.

Dariak cast a few healing spells on him and jumped when a massive bolt of lightning seared through the air and blasted to the ground, striking almost as harshly as the boulders had the day before. Another bolt shot down soon after and the screams of pain and panic erupted more wildly. Gabrion and Kitalla pulled back and made their way toward the others.

Yet as he finished healing Randler's larger gashes, Dariak noticed something odd. The lightning took down Kallisorians. Each strike was centered on a pack of fighters that waited for an opening to attack. The smell of charred flesh filled the air and added to the scent of ozone.

Kitalla arrived and called aloud, "Dariak, it's working! Keep at it."

Cackling laughter answered as a team of mages pushed through the combatants and appeared before them. "That's not Dariak's doing!" a familiar voice chortled.

Randler gasped. "Mother!"

Sharice laughed again, turning around and raising her arms up high, wiggling her fingers and then blasting them forward. Lightning emanated from her hands and lashed out at a team of Kallisorians, scattering them to the ground.

Urrith trotted up behind her and his eyes went wide when he saw Gabrion. He rushed over and threw his arms around the big warrior. "You're alive!"

"It seems like you completed your task," Gabrion said.

"About Ordren…"

"He's dead," Gabrion finished.

"Where are your mages?" Sharice demanded, cutting off further conversation. "You're being slaughtered out here."

"Most are gone," Dariak said. "And we're trying not to kill anyone, so keep that in mind."

"Preposterous!" she balked, then gestured to Urrith. "This little upstart wasn't exaggerating?"

"Not at all. Too many have died already."

She scoffed. "Fine, whatever. Let's get back to work then."

Eight mages turned their attentions back on the fighting, the tenor of their spells altered so as not to fatally harm anyone. Sharice delighted in her lightning blasts, though she reduced the amount of energy she drew for each one. Teaming up with Janning, the two lashed into pairs of fighters at a time.

Fire and water spells littered the field, creating a hazy steam that added to the oppressive dankness of the sky. Another mage, Dresh, beckoned to darkness, casting blinding shadow clouds around whole sections of the battlefield, adding to the sheer chaos.

Above it all, Kallion watched from his horse, growling. A set of ice darts headed for him but the spell dissipated long before it could reach him. Angry at the turn of events, he decided it was time to even the odds. He lifted the horn to his lips once again and blew out a staccato tone.

More spells filled the air and the entire field overflowed with rampant energy. The added spells were not from Sharice and her pack, but from mages loyal to Kallion. The deliberations in the Mage Underground had split the mages in three. Those honoring the quest for peace had joined Sharice. Another sect had hurried to the king, offering their services so they could subdue the others. The final set of mages had remained underground, unwilling to reveal themselves or to involve themselves in such affairs.

The dark sky flickered with spellfire. Dariak couldn't even keep track of everything. He knew only that every advantage on his side was soon squandered by the Kallisorian king. With the jades depleted, he still wasn't sure what would happen next.

Randler took a sword slash to his arm and yelped in pain, smashing back sharply and accidentally killing the assailant. Dariak filled Randler with healing energy, after which the bard returned to the fray.

Kitalla turned her attentions to the lupinoes, which were still focusing their efforts on taking down the triggans. Three of the treelike beings had fallen and a fourth looked ready to keel over. Kitalla hurried over and intercepted one lupino's attack, knocking the beast out of the air. The other creatures ignored her at first, focusing on their woodland prey, but when Kitalla slew one of the others, they reevaluated their target.

Six lupinoes turned as one, red eyes burning with anger. Kitalla growled at them, daring them to even try to harm her. She pulled out two extra daggers, ready to throw them when needed.

A triggan stepped in, swatting a lupino in its flank, causing it to howl angrily. Kitalla wasted no time. She rushed forward and pounced into the air, aiming for the back of one of the wolfish beasts. The creature saw her coming and it opened its jaw wide, flashing long, pallid teeth. Kitalla fed it one of her daggers, kicking its head as she came down.

Two others leaped for her as she landed, and she barely escaped by rolling aside. The two beasts crashed into each other with a sickening crack. Kitalla drew knives up into their gullets, ending them. The remaining lupinoes pulled back, debating their next move. A triggan grabbed one, lifting it up high overhead and hurling it into the fighting nearby, where the creature intercepted an errant fireball spell and fell dead.

It was enough for the remaining lupinoes. They lowered themselves down on their haunches and scampered away.

A hearty scream echoed nearby and Kitalla rushed over. Sharice lay on the ground, parts of her body covered in metal plates, the smell of burning hair unmistakable.

"Stupid metal mage," she hissed furiously, pushing off Kitalla's offers for help.

Kitalla saw burn marks on the metal pieces covering random parts of Sharice's robes and she realized one of the mages had set them there, and then Sharice's own lightning blasts had backfired. She was more stunned than damaged, and once the woman was on her feet again, Kitalla ran off to find Gabrion.

Randler slowed down as the fighting continued. He took more damage with each new fighter that appeared and Dariak was of little help to protect him. The mage had cast eighteen different sets of the Shield of Delminor on the bard and within moments, the spell was depleted from the incessant attacks. Exhaustion was going to be their biggest downfall.

Kallion's forces continued to fight hard, but they were so numerous, they were able to pause between bouts and catch bits of rest. Over a hundred of them had been taken out of the fight either with deep injuries or unconsciousness and only about twenty had been slain, and mostly from Sharice's entrance. Yet they still outnumbered the Hathrens five to one. As Kallion assessed the situation, he grinned to himself, for they were sure to hold their ground.

Dariak separated himself from the fighting, turning his thoughts back to the jades. He closed his eyes and concentrated, reaching out and feeling their essences. He had hoped with all the rampant spellfire raging through the air, the jades would draw that power in and be restored. Yet as he examined them, they hadn't acted at all. He punched his fists together in annoyance and tried to coerce the shards to draw upon the energies, but they refused to obey.

A pained cry drew his attention and he watched as a triggan toppled over, then struggled to rise again. Even the magic of the forest wasn't strong enough for the sheer willpower of the Kallisorian king. The top of the tree-creature shook, shedding leaves as it did so. The fallen pieces littered the ground and burned like acid to anyone who stepped upon them. The triggan then made its way to Dariak and fell to its knees.

As he watched, the woody being softened, losing its bark exterior to flesh. It shrank in height, the mass condensing to the proper proportions of man. When the transformation was complete, Astrith lay in an exhausted heap, naked and wounded. "There is little else I can do."

"I feel the same," Dariak said. "I can keep casting the same spells to delay the inevitable, but I'm running out of time. And now the jades won't even respond."

"It is still your wish to unite them? The land may not thank you for it."

"What choice do I have? We can't even pull away from this battle now. Kallion is too convinced of his victory. If we flee, he'll hunt us down and slay us; I'm sure of it."

The old man nodded. "I do agree with that assessment." He gauged Dariak's face carefully and then he sighed. "There is but one last act I can do for you then, but once it is completed, I will depart for home."

"You're already injured. I'll figure something else out."

Astrith actually smiled. "Thank you for that, young Dariak. May the battle turn out in your favor."

With that, the old man pressed his fingers together as he closed his eyes. Dariak thought he heard chanting but the man's lips did not move at all. Then Astrith sank down, lying in the dirt, and slowly, slightly, his body became one with the soil. The change was so subtle and natural that Dariak didn't notice until too late. All at once, Astrith's body was gone, the only reminder a slight patch of dirt.

Dariak reached for the soil and patted it gently, barely believing that the old man was gone. The dirt was warm to the touch and he thought in some way he could feel a heartbeat, but whether it was Astrith's or the pounding of the battle, he had no idea.

With a heavy heart, the mage stood up, feeling for the jades and pulling them out of their holsters one at a time, pressing the shard to his forehead as if it would allow him to see through its inner eye. He felt the mild outer coating of each one—

> the tingle of the lightning jade
> the roar of the beast jade
> the dampness of the water jade
> the heat of the fire jade
> the smoothness of the metal jade
> the fragrance of the nature jade
> the refreshing hum of the healing jade
> the gritty dirt of the earth jade
> the gentle breeze of the air jade
> the cold darkness of the shadow jade
> the jagged edges of the glass jade

—yet none of the jades spoke to him. He brought them together in pairs, hoping to elicit some response, knowing he really didn't have any time for this. But if he didn't unite them, then all was lost. He had to keep trying.

A strange sound echoed to the west and it reminded him of a dying animal, howling its last defiance to the air. He turned, wondering what new foe was appearing and he had to rub his eyes. For standing just yards away was Lica, a host of mages, and Ervinor. They rushed forward and gathered at Dariak's feet.

"Ervinor!" Dariak smiled, throwing his arms around him. "Lica. How is this possible?"

"Astrith," Lica explained. "Remember when we first went into Hathreneir and we were taken in by that odd border guardian and brought far into the land? Well, Astrith commanded it to bring us here."

Ervinor shrugged. "It wasn't any less disconcerting the second time."

"But how?" Dariak asked.

Lica patted him on the shoulder. "The border guardians are mages who went wrong and lost their minds to the energy. Your friend was so well tuned to the energy of the land, he was able to give the poor fellow a sense of order in exchange for passage. As for how the thing was able to save us travel time, I'll have to leave that for Astrith to explain. All I could guess was we went through the ground and it shifted along with us and somehow that was faster." She shrugged.

"I'm glad you're all here. We're not doing well."

"We… not entirely here to help," Ervinor hedged. "We have orders of our own." With that he lifted his left arm and whipped it overhead in a giant circle. At once, the fifty mages scattered, spreading out evenly to encircle the entire battlefield, where they started chanting in unison.

The appearance of the extra mages set Kallion on alert, and he yanked out his horn and belted out a new set of notes. His forces responded at once. So far, many of his men had been battling for a few minutes, then rotating out. Now, they all entered the fray simultaneously, fully armed and without mercy.

"I'm not really here to fight," Ervinor said, "but let's get me a sword so I can defend myself."

Lica saw Randler nearby, throwing his body into every attack, barely able to parry anything thrown at him. "Randler!" she shouted, running toward him and projecting healing energies in his direction. He reacted at once, his posture straightening and his attacks holding more firmly. He blocked his attacker and then swept out the man's legs, grounding him. Leaping over another sword strike, Randler landed on the man's belly and winded him.

"Lica, what are you doing here?"

"Sort of here to help," she said offhandedly. "Come on. Dariak needs you now." They dashed off to help him with the jades.

Meanwhile, in the midst of the battlefield, Gabrion and Kitalla hammered away at the enemy. Their clothes were gashed and their skin was covered in more blood than sweat. The wounds Kitalla had taken the previous day were aggravated by several attacks she had failed to block and her movements were slowing down.

Beside her, Gabrion was gasping, his arms aching from swinging both swords without rest. His goal of reaching the king was fading away as impossible, for every time he made progress, the king pulled his horse further back and ten more fighters took his place. "Why isn't Dariak uniting the jades?" he shouted as a blade cut into his shoulder.

Kitalla dodged low and struck her dagger out in a feint, distracting her opponent so she could kick at his shins and startle him. She then leaned forward and pushed him over, letting him fall as the next attacker leaped in, nearly chopping off her ear. Her body ached and she wished the healing she had received could have been even stronger than it had been; though without it she wouldn't have been on the field at all. The thought of her healing session flittered through her mind as she heard Gabrion's question, and then she understood.

"The jades are drained." She handled the next two combatants by grabbing their gauntlets and smashing upward into their faces. "Gabrion, come on!" She nodded her head sharply and the warrior instantly obeyed.

They pressed their way through the fighting crowd, helping the other Hathren soldiers as they went. The poor fighters were exhausted but they kept their weapons and shields moving well, holding back as many Kallisorians as possible. Along the way, they spotted Urrith, Sharice, and Janning, each using their skills to defend the people around them. They caught sight of Kitalla and Gabrion and opted to follow.

Because it looked like a retreat, the Kallisorians did not pursue them in earnest, and so they were able to make their way back to Dariak without wasting too much time.

The mage was crumpled on the ground, his face a mask of anguish as he clutched the various jades in his hands, trying desperately to draw them together. He appeared badly injured, though he had very few actual wounds. Everyone gathered around him, hating to leave the fighting to the others. They kept glancing over their shoulders, ready to return to the fray at a moment's notice.

At the edge of their hearing, the sound of chanting echoed. The fifty mages from Marritosh had their hands raised before them, their legs spread wide as if they were straddling an ursalor. With synchronized thumps, one mage, then the next, and so on, stomped the ground, swirling their hands around in a wide circle. The dark gray sky overhead wavered as they did so, and even Gabrion could sense the energies rising up all around them.

"What are they doing?" Urrith asked.

"A magical barrier," Lica explained. "To keep this fight contained. It's what we were charged to do. It's almost fully erect and when it is, nothing will be able to pass through until they stop chanting."

"Almost like the barrier around Magehaven," Randler said.

"Yes. It should contain any damage from the jades."

Gabrion bent down and touched Dariak's shoulder. "Friend, we need you now to bring them all together and put an end to this. We won't last much longer."

The mage turned his face upward. "I'm trying." He brought the beast and nature jades together, making a clinking sound in the process. "They aren't talking to each other at all."

Kitalla stared at Dariak for a time, knowing what she needed to do. Only her skill had helped to empower the jades, but she also realized that with everything happening all around them, she would be caught in the thrall of the dance and the jades would drain her completely. She kept quiet as her comrades spoke, struggling to clear her mind, picturing some serene landscape for her dance. If it was to be her last performance, she wanted it to be peaceful.

Oblivious to Kitalla's inner turmoil, the others called out numerous suggestions for Dariak to try and he commented on the ones he had attempted and then performed the ones he hadn't. Yet even with the jades in an evenly spaced circle, nothing happened.

The fighting nearby erupted in spellfire and the team turned around to a triplet of mages guiding three others forward. They welcomed the newcomers with surprise as the mages turned back around to stave off the attacks of the Kallisorians.

It was Verna, Ruhk, and their new friend Illuria. They all had seen better days. Verna dropped to the ground, her body still badly damaged from the ursalor fight, and Illuria waved her arms around, sending healing energy into her. "I told you you weren't ready for this."

Lica added her own spells to Verna and to Ruhk. "Whatever happened to you two?"

"Ursalors," Verna muttered. "Dariak. The Red Jade."

He pounded his fist on the ground. "I'm trying!"

Their arrival provided the cover Kitalla needed. She let her thoughts turn inward and she closed her eyes, seeing a vibrant seascape rushing out in front of her. She stepped across the surface of the water, a flowing white dress catching in the breeze. And as she hovered upon the water's surface, her body shifted around, stirring the water and spraying into the air with delicate grace.

"Kitalla, no!" Dariak yelled, feeling the energy emanating from her. The jades all hummed hungrily and reached for her. He held the shards tightly, sending his mind into them, intervening in their attempt to draw energy from her.

But the draw was so powerful that the shards themselves slid across the surface of the soil and inched closer and closer to the thief, whose body echoed the dancing visions in her mind. Gabrion grabbed Kitalla, trying to stifle her movements, but she overpowered him and didn't slow at all. Stunned, he stepped away, shaking his head, not understanding what was happening. The companions stared at Kitalla and then all at once they were swept into the illusion with her.

She danced upon the water, and in the air the rest of them floated on pearly clouds. Kitalla delighted at their arrival, laughing merrily and creating a soft tinkling sensation in their minds. "You've come."

"Kitalla, you have to stop the dance!" Dariak warned.

"You can't unite the jades while they sleep," she said gently, her voice echoing softly.

"Then we'll flee here and try again another time."

She smiled, her body glowing. "This is the time, Dariak, and we both know it. The jades are calling to me and I see them coming. I cannot stop now." She turned around, her body hovering ever so lightly.

"Kitalla!" Gabrion called.

"Forgive me." Her body shifted and she reached her hands out wide. "Sharice, still so powerful. Urrith, ever brave. Ervinor, boasting of honor. Janning, faithful to peace. Lica, clinging to hope. Verna, brash and strong. Ruhk, ever devoted. Illuria, I sense your desire to heal others. Gabrion, my beloved. Dariak, wise and cunning. Randler, keeper of the secrets of the Forgotten Tribe."

"Kitalla?" the Dariak asked.

"I understand it now," her voice echoed more loudly. "The truth of it. My child, who died unnamed, unborn, was Joral's son and he was the last link of the Forgotten Tribe."

"What!" Randler said.

Kitalla's ethereal voice explained, "The jades, Dariak, respond to me because I am connected to them in a way even you are not."

"Kitalla, stop this!" Dariak shouted. The cloud wiggled underneath him as he reached for her, but this was her illusion and she controlled it fully.

"With my essence, I empower the jades. With my will, I fulfill the destiny of the Forgotten Tribe."

"Kitalla, no!" Verna screamed. Glimmers of colored light flickered on the water, rising up into the air.

"The light of the jades have all gone dark, and only the silver-gold glow remains," she uttered, describing the painting in Lady Cathrateir's book. "And soon the last heir will vanish and all the errant lights will be gone."

"That will leave us in darkness," Randler said.

"Not darkness. I understand it now, for the jades know the truth. Not darkness, Randler; peace."

They all watched Kitalla as a gleaming golden dagger appeared in her hand. No one could stop her as she placed the blade against her belly, pressing the tip in deeply and cutting a large circle. They heard her scream outside the illusion, but they were all entranced and could not help her. The pinpricks of colored light all gathered around her and started to spin wildly. She cut away her stomach and revealed a strange emptiness, not the gore they thought they would see. The dagger vanished and Kitalla reached inside the void, her hands disappearing into her belly, and there she tugged and strained and pulled.

And when her hands came free, a new shard emerged. She held the jade out before her and Dariak could hear faint whispers emanating from it, even from his perch upon the cloud. The myriad colors of light spun rapidly and the whole scene filled with the dizzying effect.

Kitalla called out to Dariak. "Take each a shard. Hurry." Her voice faded until they could only hear the echoes. "Before I die. Unite them. Hurry."

At once, the illusion faded and the battlefield opened before them. Kitalla lay in a pool of her own blood, her life escaping rapidly. She clutched the twelfth jade in her twitching hand, her eyes glazed, and her lips trembling as she bled upon the land.

Gabrion and Lica ran to her aid, but Dariak, his heart in his throat, stopped them. He swept the shards up from the ground and shoved them indelicately into the hands of the others. To Gabrion he gave the glass jade; Sharice took the lightning. Ervinor claimed the metal shard, while Urrith grasped the water. Lica held the nature jade, and Janning accepted the beast jade. Illuria, confused at what was happening, allowed the healing jade to be pressed into her hand. Dariak tossed the fire jade to Verna and the air jade to Ruhk. Randler hefted the shadow jade, leaving Dariak with the earth jade that had started his adventure so long ago.

Kitalla's dance had sated the jades with energy and each companion could feel the trembling essences within. They hoisted the shards into the air and Dariak closed his eyes, calling to them to come together. He felt the swirling energies and their desire to unite. Yet now there was an influence affecting them in the form of Kitalla's new shard, which Dariak identified as the mind jade.

A pang erupted in his heart, for he suddenly recalled the words of his father who had said the jades could only be controlled and balanced properly with the unlimited power of the mind. And Kitalla's unborn child had been the key all along. It explained her dance skill and its ability to influence the minds of others. It also accounted for the unique way in which she channeled energy. Dariak had often noted how the power emanated from within her, unlike the magic cast by other mages. She had, in essence, always behaved like a jade herself.

The twelve energies swirled lavishly together and each companion held tightly onto their shard, resisting the urge to release it. The magic drew them together anyway and they could not refuse the call. Twelve jades reached together, all centering upon the mind jade.

When Randler and Dariak had arranged the eleven jades before Frast united them, they had constructed a circle of power with them. But it was not the proper arrangement for the jades after all. As the shards drew their hosts together, they pushed and pulled each other into the proper configuration.

On top, air, fire, and lightning spun in a triangle, while on the bottom their opposites of earth, water, and shadow balanced them. Around the center, five jades hovered in a circle between the other six. Nature, beast, metal, glass, and healing shards spun in a direction to counter the other six. And in the very center of the sphere of jades was the newly formed mind jade, its tendrils of power reaching out and guiding all the others.

With the jades assembled, their hands were cast off the shards and the magic drew the pieces together. Each shard emanated its natural hue as they met in the center, surrounding and protecting the mind jade, much like a skull protecting a brain. A wild humming echoed into the air and light flashed outward violently with a deep gust of wind. The jades spun rapidly, rotating about a pivoting axis, turning faster and faster until all anyone could see was a richly glowing sphere, as wide across as a man, with a crimson center radiating from within.

It was then Kitalla's body failed her and she breathed her final breath.

Dariak reached out, compelled to take the artifact in his hand. The energy singed him, but he didn't care. The essence of the Red Jade coursed through him, reading his purpose this day and he understood now why the jades had always protected them. Each shard had been borne of a human life and each wanted to keep the balance in the world. It was his goal to restore that balance and so he allowed the Red Jade to use his body to effect the changes that were needed.

Dariak released the red orb and it floated up over his head, shining like a bloody sun in the gray sky. He raised his hands into the air and he called for the fighting to end. The power of the mind jade reached outward on the wind. Rain fell from the clouds overhead, sending a deep calm over the field. The violently flung spellfire from the mages all changed in essence, the anger and rage fizzling away. Every aspect of the world around them filled with Dariak's mission of peace and acceptance. He willed it upon them all and they were powerless to disobey.

The Red Jade lifted Dariak from the ground, carrying him over the battlefield, drawing upon his waning strength to spread his message to those below.

At once, the fighting came to an abrupt end. All fighters dropped their weapons, taking the sensation into their being and looking at their foes anew. Even the feral creatures halted their strikes, hunkering down and blinking their eyes against the strangeness.

Dariak filled with overwhelming joy, feeling how each combatant changed, sensing their shift in thoughts, opening up to new possibilities. He smiled widely and the Red Jade reached outward to spread Dariak's power across the entire land. He understood Kitalla's certainty now. The jades honestly wanted to restore the balance that had been disturbed centuries ago.

But the mages surrounding the battlefield were still casting their barrier spell. Astrith had not anticipated the mind jade or the restoration of the balance of magic that would occur when the jades were united. Thus the spell was contained within the area, bouncing back and reverberating with the Red Jade itself. Dariak felt the twelve pieces inside the sphere tremble with the effort of reaching beyond the barrier, and he begged them to rest.

They did not understand, for it was his will to spread the peace across the entire land. It was his desire to rid the land of all turmoil, but now he beckoned for it to remain here alone. He felt the confusion of the mind jade as it attempted to reconcile the conflict. Dariak was exhausted, but he focused himself on calming the Red Jade, imploring it to ease back before the reflected energies built up too great a resonance, which would likely shatter the newly assembled sphere. He drew upon Randler's knowledge and showed the magic that if it continued to exude its strength, then it would bring about its own undoing, and that in turn would destroy everything he and the jades had ever worked for.

The effort to contain the power of the Red Jade seared through Dariak's mind and he screamed in agony, feeling his body burn as the extra energies coursed through him repeatedly until they wore out. The world darkened for the mage, the great son of Delminor, but unlike his father, he knew in his heart that he had succeeded in his quest.

He allowed himself to laugh mentally as the Red Jade absorbed the last of his essence, ending its outpouring of magic and thus keeping itself from breaking apart.

With the spell completed, the glowing red sphere plummeted from the sky, crashing into the ground, unscathed. Beside it fell Dariak's lifeless body, his face frozen with a grim smile.

CHAPTER 46

To Start Anew

THE LIGHT OF the Red Jade diminished, its task complete, but the effects remained. Everyone upon the battlefield stared abashed at the damage they had caused, wondering what they could ever do to repair it.

All save one.

King Kallion hopped off his horse, screaming at his troops and demanding they lift up their swords and end the fight. His gem-studded armor had indeed been strong enough to deflect the power of even the Red Jade, and only his bloodlust and rage remained. He grabbed a sword and smacked it against random fighters, trying to incite them to defend themselves. Though they did not accept the hits full-on, they did not retaliate against them either.

Furious, Kallion shoved his way through the daft men and women, making his way toward the site of the fallen artifact. He reached it, first bending over and spitting on Dariak's corpse. "And so you fell," he mocked. He reached down and took the Red Jade in his hands. It was as wide across as his chest and it hummed with veritable energy, as the shards inside the sphere were endlessly spinning. He grinned to himself, for the Red Jade would be more than a delectable war trophy; it would give him the power he would need to take Hathreneir too.

He felt the Red Jade tremble in response to his malicious thoughts and he laughed at the impotent reaction. "You will serve me well."

"You are wrong," said a voice, and Kallion turned around to see the companions gathered around. Gabrion had a sword at the ready. "Hand it over."

Kallion rubbed the surface of the sphere, wondering how to channel the magnificent power he felt inside. He knew a little magic but not enough to spontaneously read the orb. "This is mine."

Gabrion shook his head. "No, it belongs to the land, not any person. Hand it over or I will take it from you."

Kallion laughed and he turned to run, but Gabrion charged too. He leaped through the air and tackled the man, the gemstones cutting him. Kallion thrashed about, but his grip on the massive Red Jade faltered and it slipped from his grasp. He turned over and bashed Gabrion in the face. The warrior took the beating and then wrestled the man to stillness.

"Well, go on," the king taunted. "Finish me!"

"No more killing today," Gabrion said.

"You have to kill me or else your little game ends here and now."

Verna stepped forward. "I don't think so." She gestured to the hundreds of Kallisorian fighters who stood nearby. "Your allies are not quite on your side anymore."

"What would you do with me?" Kallion asked.

Ruhk staggered over. "You are no longer a king."

Kallion adopted an expression of horror, then acceptance. "It seems I have no choice. You clearly have won this war."

Gabrion released the man and they rose to their feet as Illuria fetched the Red Jade. As they glanced at her, Kallion grabbed Gabrion's sword and slashed Ruhk with it, then turned it around and stabbed Gabrion.

"No!" Randler shouted as the warriors fell to their knees. Illuria dropped the Red Jade and immediately joined Lica in sending healing energies to the wounded men.

Ervinor and Janning stepped in next and clobbered the king, using the flat of a blade and an outstretched foot. Kallion lay on the ground, hands outstretched toward the Red Jade. Ervinor and Janning then proceeded to remove the antimagic armor from the man so the mages could work to restrain him better.

"What should we do with him?" Lica asked.

"Leave him alive," Gabrion said. "We have all made our mistakes and we all have much to atone for. Maybe some time in his own dungeon will clear his mind until he's ready to join the new way of things."

"We'll take care of it," Sharice said, summoning Janning and Illuria with her gaze. "You have other things to attend to now."

The next few hours were spent clearing the battlefield and mourning their losses. The Marritosh mages lowered the magical barrier and the remaining triggans reverted to their human forms. Kallisorians and Hathrens joined together to bury the dead and to bandage their wounds.

Kitalla and Dariak were lifted by their friends and encased in specially designed coffins that the earth and nature mages crafted with their skills. Kitalla's gutted stomach was covered over and her body was dressed in a clean set of riding leathers. Dariak's cloak was repaired and arranged officially around his body. Sealed from air, their bodies were preserved in order to survive the trek to their final resting places. A third box was constructed to hold the Red Jade.

"If it's all the same to you, I would bring them to Marritosh," Ervinor said.

"But it's burned," Gabrion said.

"Not all of it, and not for long." Ervinor then explained his plans for reconstructing the town and the work they had already accomplished, with Lica's help. "It will be the new center of the land, with a palace and everything, and we can even host the Red Jade there, now that it exists."

"What about the mages of the tower?" Verna asked.

"Rothra is in charge of them now," Lica explained. "And he will ensure the Red Jade remains protected."

Ervinor turned to the bard. "What do you think, Randler?"

"I..." He shook his head, his face puffy and strewn with tears. "I can't believe he's gone."

"Randler..."

"Take them. He would want that."

"And you, Gabrion?"

"Keep Kitalla with him," the warrior said. His face was a mask of pain and he needed to grieve, but he had lost himself enough times in grief upon the journey, and so he held together for now, keeping the agony alive but subdued. When time permitted, he would weep for Kitalla, and he knew it would be worse than his grief over Mira. He clamped his jaw and he set the thoughts aside.

"What will everyone do now?" Urrith asked hesitantly, glancing at the others.

Ruhk cleared his throat. "I must return to my family, but then I'll return to Castle Hathreneir to keep order there."

Verna blew out a sigh. "I intend to search for my father. He's either out there along the border in a battalion or he's perished, but I will find him and bring him home to Marritosh."

Ervinor clasped her shoulder. "A home will be waiting for you."

"Thank you, though I don't know how much use it will get for a while."

"Why is that?"

"We're the only ones who know this fight is truly over," she said. "We need to spread the word out there. It isn't going to be easy and it's going to take a lot of effort to convince people. I won't be able to rest until the sacrifice of our friends is known and understood by all."

"You're right," Randler said. "We need to tell our tale."

"What of you, then?" Ervinor asked.

"I'm coming with you to entomb Dariak and Kitalla of course." He paused and swallowed hard. "But then I will resume my role as bard and travel the land, spreading the tale—and now the resolution—of the Forgotten Tribe."

"C—Can I come with you?" Urrith asked.

Randler considered for a moment, not quite ready to accept a traveling companion, but the hopeful look in the youth's eyes was irresistible. "I will need a protector."

"Speaking of which," Verna started, turning to Gabrion. "What of you?"

"I will visit the Undying Stone to ensure Perrios is safe and well-protected. Then I need to distance myself from all of this for a while."

"Where will you go?" Ruhk asked.

"I may venture to the south."

This shocked the group, for the south was known to be a vast and dangerous place with massive creatures and violent storms.

Ervinor looked at him with concern. "You would abandon this land you've fought so hard for?"

"No," he said. "Our lands are heading for a time of peace and prosperity. I don't want the south to interfere with that. Just for a while, I may explore a bit."

Lica frowned. "I don't like it, Gabrion, but do what you have to do. Just be safe." She glanced around and then leaned in conspiratorially. "What do you think Sharice and the others are going to do?"

Randler wiped his eyes and considered his mother. "She'll bring the Mage Underground to the surface. Kallisor will no longer shun magic, if I know her. After all the spells she cast in this battle, she won't go back into hiding easily."

"Times are really going to change, then," Urrith said.

"Some people won't change easily," Verna said, gesturing over her shoulder to where Kallion was sequestered by the others. "But if we hold true to our ideals, then others will follow."

"That's why Kallion needs to live," Gabrion said. "He'll be the most resistant of anyone alive. Yet if one day even he can see the benefits of focusing on life instead of war, then we really will head into a brighter future."

The field slowly cleared of people until the companions were all that remained. Randler brought out his lute and he strummed for a while, trying to steady his voice so he could sing properly. Despite his attempts, he wavered but no one cared, for they all experienced heartfelt emotions that night.

Days long ago, when this tale unfolds, we see the pain of the lost.
They were friends, companions to the end.
Their destinies intertwined.
Raising their hands to the woes of the world, they reached out to shine.

Dagger held high, it is where she showed her strength.
Spells to bind, with his passion at his side.
Joined in kind, they rose up at any length.
Then they died, for they simply would not hide.

She was a woman with strength in her heart, and with that she always fought.
Turmoil existed throughout her life,
Yet she ever rose up to stand.
An unborn child of noble heritage, she kept the secret inside.

Dagger held high, she always could defend.
Spells to bind, with the dance skill so unique.
Joined in kind, she made us all her friends.
Then she died, giving us strength at her peak.

He was a man whose quest was long, for he followed his father's shadow.
He journeyed on from land to land,
Seeking power no one could fathom.
Then he gathered friends and jades alike, bringing them together in the end.

Head held high, even facing his own demise.
Jades to bind, even though they all were drained.
Joined in kind, we followed his wizened eyes.
Then he died, and so just the Red Jade remained.

The Path Revealed

MERIAD CLOSED THE giant tome and stared at her grandson as he wept heartily in his bed. His little body shook as the events of the story unfolded and she wondered if it had all been too much for him.

She looked around the room, and it felt oddly different now that the boy knew the truth of things. This was where Gabrion had taken him as an infant, leaving him in Brannis' care after Earl Thedris' failed abduction. Brannis had raised the boy as his own, permitting Meriad's visits as per Gabrion's instructions. And though Brannis was open-minded and welcoming of the peace between the lands, some of the people who met with Perrios tried reminding him of the old days, planting seeds for when he learned of the death of his father at Kallisorian hands.

She had struggled to keep him free from prejudice, and it had been a hard penance for her betrayals in her life. Each time he had spoken of Kallisor with some scorn, but in her recent visits, his anger had subsided, as she had hoped it would.

Perrios wiped his eyes and stared at his grandmother. "You did some pretty awful things, Gran-mama."

"I did."

"But I still love you."

She smiled kindly.

"I used to think everything was so easy," he said. "When you told me that Gabrion killed mama, I thought I would hate him forever. But now, I don't know. I'm not even sure what I think of her, not that I ever knew her."

Meriad's face curled into a frown. "Don't speak ill of your mother, child, for it wasn't entirely her fault that she did what she did."

"I know. You put her up to it." He could see the pain on her face and he felt bad for it. "I'm sorry. It's just a lot to make sense of."

"I understand, Perrios."

"So this story… it's all true?"

Meriad nodded. "Yes, Randler spent the five years after the Red Jade was assembled getting it all written down. It's also carved throughout the halls of Marritosh Palace. He created this copy for me so that I could impart it to you."

"Marritosh Palace," he echoed in awe. "I hope to see it someday."

"You will. For it is your birthright to govern from there."

"What?"

"Yes," she said nervously, wondering if this was the time to tell him, but realizing that there was no point in delaying. "You are the last descendent of royalty, Perrios. The companions agreed that you had the right to lead the people."

His jaw dropped. "Me?"

She smiled. "Yes."

"But... I don't understand."

She placed a placating hand on his knee. "The simplest way I can explain it is this: Gabrion realized that I had changed. He also witnessed your father's acceptance of the concepts of peace. So, they decided that you had it in you to be a fair and open ruler. But you needed to understand the unbiased history of the land before you could ever know of your destiny. You need to be able to recognize that people are people and you must treat them as such, without prejudice."

"Oh," he breathed. "They really believe that much in me?"

"So do I, little one."

"I—I'll do my best, Gran-mama, but I don't even know the first thing about what to do."

She laughed gently. "You won't be alone. Ervinor has been acting as Regent in your absence and he will serve as your advisor when you're ready."

His eyes went wide. "I actually get to meet him?"

"Indeed. You may even see Randler, too; he's still traveling around singing the tales."

"What about Gabrion?"

Meriad shrugged. "I don't know. When everything ended ten years ago, he came here with instructions for your care and then he went off on his own. No one has heard from him since."

"Maybe he had some troubles in the south?" Perrios guessed.

"Maybe one day we will learn."

"Gran-mama, there's something about the Red Jade I don't understand."

"I'll try my best to answer."

"Well, when Delminor united it during the War of the Colossus, everyone called it the Red Jade even though it was incomplete. It only had eleven jades because the twelfth one hadn't been made yet."

"Go on."

"But after Kitalla... died... and there was the extra jade, and they were united, it was still red. Wouldn't it have been a different color or something?"

Meriad's smile grew wide. "You're a wise young man, my Perrios, and you think clearly and well. But remember, that twelfth jade was the mind jade. When Delminor united the shards, they were combined with the essence from his mind, so it was still that blood-red color, but they hadn't joined into that perfect sphere because his mind was not really a part of them."

"I see. So, does that mean that mages can use mind magic now?"

"They are learning," she said. "They don't have the individual jade, however, so the mages must learn to read the magic from the energies in the land itself, so it's taking a lot longer than some of the other magics. But I'm sure it'll be just as common a magic as fire or water."

"Wow. How will I defend against it?"

"That's where Magehaven will help you, dear. And there's the Magitorium, too; they've been experimenting with things for years."

Perrios sat quietly for a moment and he felt his eyes tearing up again. "I can't believe that Kitalla did that to herself."

Meriad bit her lip. "It's possible the power of the jades overwhelmed her, but Randler believes she knew the actual truth at that point. There was a jade missing and its essence was inside of her. She gave her life so balance could be restored to the land. And you know? It has been happening. The desert is receding, and the feral creatures are less dangerous. Weather has been returning to normal, too. The Red Jade truly is as it was meant to be now."

He frowned. "And it burned out Dariak's life, too."

"That, too, was his choice. If not for that barrier, he could have allowed its energies to reach out across the land. But he had united the shards the way they were intended to be and he must have known that if it broke apart, then it would have been hard for anyone to put back together. Look at the War of the Colossus; eleven shards and it took twenty years for Dariak to find them all again."

Perrios rubbed his eyes. "And now the Red Jade had been together for ten years."

"Yes. And the goal is to keep it that way."

"Gran-mama?"

"Yes?"

"Now that I know the whole story, can we go to Marritosh? And, I'd kind of like to see Kallisor. And go to Savvron to see if Gabrion ever went back there. And have they been able to repair all the damage in Pindington? Have the mages been accepted by everyone yet?"

He drew a breath to ask more questions but Meriad waved him to stop, laughing as she did so. "One step at a time, young Perrios."

He realized he was being over-exuberant, so he calmed himself down. "Okay, okay. But do you think we can?"

"You're about old enough for travel, I would think. And I wonder how you'll be when you meet Kallisorians now."

He made a face and she couldn't read it. "I don't get that either."

"What's that?"

"Well, if the wars ended and everyone is being ruled out of Marritosh, why do we still call them Hathreneir and Kallisor?"

"That's an excellent question," she said. "I suppose it's just habit. Plus it gives us an idea where things are, but I hadn't even considered that."

"If I'm going to be the king of both lands one day, do you think I might be able to name it or something? And get rid of the two names?"

She was stunned again. "It's a rather interesting thought. Whatever would you call it?"

He pursed his lips and considered for a moment. "I'm not sure, but I kind of like"—he paused, trying to make sure he would pronounce it correctly—"Kitariak."

Any worries she may have had about his heart or prejudices all melted away. He wouldn't claim the land under his name, but rather honor those who had perished trying to save it. The single word told her much and a great weight lifted from her. She had fulfilled her penance, she knew suddenly, and her grandson would learn and grow into a wise, fair, and beloved ruler.

She smiled, her grateful eyes glimmering. "I think that sounds lovely."

Acknowledgements

I AM SATURATED with emotion. I'm ecstatic that the tale is complete. I'm devastated by some of the events that took place. In this process, I feel that I am Randler, just reporting upon events that occurred, having only minor influences over the actual moments that took place within. The characters live inside me and they told me their story. As Gabrion desired, I hope I have been honest in my recollection.

I've said before that this process is not one I've completed in isolation. This has always been the effort of a team of adventurers and I am ever grateful to all those who have seen fit to share my journey.

I must take an extended moment to thank my younger sister, Kim. She has always been my soul-twin and we have ever supported each other in our lives. In our darkest hours, we were there and pulled each other through the chaos. In many of my stories, there is a character based upon her. In this saga, that was Kitalla. Imagine this story without Kitalla, and that would be my life without Kim. Like my sister, Kitalla has a feisty side and a determination that is unparalleled. Several trials that Kitalla faced during her journey were reflections of what Kim has endured in her life. When I think of it all, I can barely fathom where she finds the determination to keep pushing on. And if you think Kitalla's drive was far-fetched, then you don't know a soul like my sister's.

To my sister Lisa, Bob, and the kids, thank you so much for all the love and support. You don't even know what it means to me to have you on my side all the time. Verna was feisty and wanted to protect her family, and Lisa, that's always been you. Thank you.

To my brother John and his wife Lisa, I appreciate your support too, and I'm grateful to have you as family.

As always, I must lend my thanks to Jared Reed, whose music and friendship were true inspirations in this tale. We talked of the magical jades long before they existed in Kallisor and Hathrenier. Their powers were unknown to us both, but we explored them and over time they exploded onto the page. Jared's music always inspires me and I delight in hearing it. It is my hope that he and I can collaborate to bring that music to all of you, so you can hear the melodies of The Forgotten Tribe, of Mira's Song, and Kitalla's ever-important battle dances.

Though Randler was initially intended to represent Jared's influence in my life, he soon shifted focus and became my dear Kevin. The bard is ever supportive of Dariak and even when they misunderstand each other, their love shines through. Though several aspects of their relationship have no connection to our own, the underlying power of their love is what echoes for me.

My best friend, Lois, exists in Lica. Lois is an amazing and compassionate friend and she faces every day like it's a new adventure. And though Lica was sassier, her strong spirit is Lois through and through. She faced trials and still saw the greater good ahead of her and pursued it. When Lica didn't know what to do, I thought of Lois, and the way opened clearly. Always will I esteem Lois, and may we have endless adventures together.

During the crafting of this tale we lost Kevin's beloved mom to cancer. I didn't know how to deal with it and I struggled terribly. The loss of Gabrion's mother was a sad echoing shadow of the turmoil we all experienced and one day I hope to do proper justice to the wonderful woman Liz was, and is in our hearts.

To my dad-in-law, John, in many ways Rothra resembles you. He was a fiery mage, featured moreso in book three, but despite his own trials, he rose up to do what was right and he supported the others, took control over the errant mage tower, and guided Lica to her friends. Thank you for being there for me and for Kevin.

I wish to also thank Rochelle Deans for the amazing attention she gave to this series, helping to ensure consistency throughout and pointing out places where the story was unclear or untrue. I can't thank you enough for all your assistance in helping me to bring about the best story I could.

There are a few people who took this journey with me, reading the tale before it reached your hands. To my beta-readers, I can't explain how important your feedback was to this story. Jared, you kept me motivated every single day. Joseph, your critical eye challenged me and when you shared your thoughts and feelings, I knew I had captured the essence of what I wanted to share with the world. Taylor, your enthusiasm has inspired me to continue onward, and I have grown so much from your feedback. Thank you for your attention to detail and for the deep analyses you've given me. With all your support, I am stronger.

I realized at one point that I had not thanked Merlin, Monty, or Shadow at all, and so in book three, I pitted Dariak against a pack of leomers, cat-like creatures that protected each other against all forms of attack. Thanks, my kitties, for the love and warmth you've shared, and for taking care of each other too. It really means a lot!

Thank you, too, to all my friends for the support you've shown me, especially as I've striven to improve this tale and share it with the world. To Joseph and Christina, Larry and Jeremy, Jenny and Harvey, Lois, Jared, Chris, and everyone I'm forgetting… You enrich me in ways I can't even explain. Thank you all for being a part of my life and for sharing your life with me in return.

To my students, too, I thank you so much. I can't name you here, but I wish I could. I am inspired by you every day and I hope I, in turn, light a lamp in your world and give you some insight by which to grow. You influence me. You support me. And I support you too. I hope your own journeys in life are successful, happy, and that you enjoy life to the fullest.

Stephen J. Wolf

To my readers, thank you for investing in this world and for all your support and feedback. Your reviews and comments mean so much to me and I'm ever grateful.

To dad, you're my Delminor. As a kid, I always wanted to follow in your footsteps and to make you proud. You faced many trials in your life and often your hands were tied but you always did your best. Like Delminor, you pushed on anyway and you will always be part of my story.

Mom… You were my first fan. And you've always been an inspiration to me. Thank you for always being on my side, for always fighting to ensure I had what I needed to get by, for always protecting me when I needed it. In some ways, you're Essalia, Dariak's mom who educated him as a child, protecting him even at cost to herself. In other ways you're Sharice, Randler's mom who taught him to be strong and to fight for what he believed in. Thank you for helping me to be the man I am today. I miss you daily and hope you're watching from the great beyond.

Thank you everyone. I love you all.

ABOUT THE AUTHOR

STEPHEN J. WOLF is a science teacher with a PhD in science education and a penchant for fantasy books, movies, and video games. Growing up, he loved learning how things worked. When he saw Mr. Wizard's World for the first time, he knew then that science was his place to be. From learning about how fireworks light up with different colors to understanding the mechanics of an acid-base reaction, chemistry and physics became his passion.

Stephen started writing in eighth grade when his English teacher challenged the class to craft three different scenes. One scene focused on a person, a second highlighted a location, and the third detailed an object. In the moment of the quick-fire writing prompts, Stephen linked all three tasks together and created his first short story. The following year he crafted his first novella, then expanded it to a trilogy, growing as a writer along the way.

With some short stories used in his classes, Wolf communicates a love of reading to his students through creative connections between science and magic. His short story, *A Shocking Journey*, teaches the fundamentals of electricity and magnetism, as experienced by a middle school class, through a series of "magical" experiences that allow the students to visualize the concepts.

Wolf also learned to code in JavaScript and brought coding classes to his school. He has since written two coding books.

Stephen lives in New York with his husband, Kevin, and their cats, Merlin and Monty. You can visit him at *StephenJWolf.com* and explore the world of Red Jade and find his other works at *Red-Jade.com*.

***Coding for Kids:
Learn JavaScript:
Build the
Room Adventure Game***
red-jade.com/cfk1

Learn JavaScript while creating an adaptable text adventure game that challenges the player to locate items in a house and to escape by finding pieces of a passcode.

***Coding for Kids:
Learn JavaScript:
Build Mini Apps***
red-jade.com/cfk2

Learn JavaScript while creating fifteen different apps, including Tic-Tac-Toe, 23 Pennies, Hangman, Treasure Quest, and Battles in Kallisor.

***Of Ages Past
A Poetry Collection***
red-jade.com/ofagespast

Read 94 poems about love, friendship, loneliness, fun, science, and betrayal.

***Garinor's Adventure
A Choose-the-Fate Novel***
red-jade.com/garinor

Garinor is taken from his home but things go awry from the start. He needs your help to guide him through the kingdom and toward his destiny.

Did you enjoy the story?

Please consider leaving a review!

tinyurl.com/redjadeomnibus

Be sure to check out

Red-Jade.com

For maps, character sketches, and more.